SOMETHING
Like
POSSIBLE

Also by Miel Moreland

It goes Like this

SOMETHING *Like* POSSIBLE

Miel Moreland

Feiwel and Friends

New York

A FEIWEL AND FRIENDS BOOK

An imprint of Macmillan Publishing Group, LLC

120 Broadway, New York, NY 10271 • fiercereads.com

Our books may be purchased in bulk for promotional, educational, or business use. Please
contact your local bookseller or the Macmillan Corporate and Premium Sales Department
at (800) 221-7945 ext. 5442 or by email at MacmillanSpecialMarkets@macmillan.com.

Library of Congress Cataloging-in-Publication Data is available.

First edition, 2023

Book design by Julia Bianchi

Feiwel and Friends logo designed by Filomena Tuosto

Printed in the United States of America

ISBN 978-1-250-84581-8 (hardcover)

1 3 5 7 9 10 8 6 4 2

To Madison, and to all those who see themselves in her

Some of the thematic material in *Something Like Possible* includes non-graphic depictions of sexual assault and self-harm, as well as bullying, homophobia, biphobia, and nonconsensual outing. Please read with care.

CHAPTER ONE

Thirty-Two Days Until Election Day

On the worst day of my life, my girlfriend breaks up with me.

Then she fires me as her campaign manager.

And then I rear-end Mr. Braun's red Chevy Malibu while trying to exit the West Plymouth Charter High School parking lot.

"It's okay," my driving teacher, Ali, says immediately, her leg tense on the instructor brake, like if she pushes down hard enough, she can rewind five seconds, to before my bumper hit his and I'm staring at the end of my career, for the *second* time today. Ruined before I even get my driver's license.

I keep my own foot pressed on the brake and let my head hit the steering wheel. I want to unbuckle my seat belt and flop away, except I'm in the dang driver's seat and, in theory, I'm supposed to be driving.

Craaap.

"Madison, take a deep breath," Ali says.

The only reason I have not actually melted into a puddle of humiliation where a fifteen-year-old girl used to be is because school let out an hour ago, so the parking lot is empty except for a handful of teachers' cars. That, and the Chevy's alarm didn't even go off.

"When you took this job, did you have to sign a confidentiality agreement?" I ask.

It's essential to identify and lead with your priorities.

"Let's focus on backing up a little, okay? Why don't you try putting the car into reverse," says Ali. "Don't forget to check your mirrors."

I put my hand on the automatic gearshift. I check the mirrors. I back up about two feet, then jolt to a stop.

"Can we get back to the confidentiality issue?" I ask.

"Please put the car in park, and then turn it off," says Ali.

I obey before twisting to face her properly across the console.

"Let's talk about what just happened," she says.

"Do I need a lawyer present?"

Ali presses her faded-red lips together, but not like she's irritated. More like she's trying not to laugh at me. Which is rude. This is serious business.

"You don't need a lawyer. I'm a driving instructor, not a cop. You misjudged the distance and ended up denting someone's bumper. It happens to everyone at some point."

"You didn't stop me," I point out. "You could be held liable."

Deflection is a tried-and-tested strategy.

Ali keeps talking, but I'm only half listening. How could I have been so *thoughtless*? Nobody wants someone who has already proven to be a careless driver steering their ship.

Jade didn't want you even before, I think, and then I push the sour feeling way down beneath the tires I didn't stop in time.

I look out the window at the soccer fields covered with heavy

March snow. By next week, the parking lot will be flooded with the runoff. Today, though, there's no slippery excuse.

"Madison," Ali says, loud, like it's not the first time she's said my name. "We need to leave this person a note, and then you need to call your guardian. We'll reschedule the lesson."

"I can't do that," I say. "We have to do the lesson."

Between the class president campaign and my babysitting job, I have a seriously limited amount of time for these official driving lessons, which are a pain to schedule. Every teen in the west metro is vying for the same after-school hours. And I need to make *one* step forward today, instead of free-falling backward, hitting every rung on what seemed like steady ladders.

"It's policy: We don't continue the lesson after an accident."

"It's just a little dent." I lean forward to peer through the windshield at the other car, familiar to me after spending every other Monday last semester on the Associated Student Body elections task force. Mr. Braun, the advisor, always had us walk into the lot as a group. He'd put his stuff in his car before returning to talk with those of us waiting for our parents in the descending dusk.

"It's policy, and I think if we started driving, you'd find you're too shaken up to focus."

"I have excellent focus," I say.

"Sure," says Ali. She pushes a pen and a pad of paper at me.

I don't get further than printing *Mr. Braun* right below the driving school's logo before there's a knock on the window. I jump, the pad and pen falling into the wheel well. Mr. Braun is bending down, looking between me and his car. The sandwich I ate for lunch somehow turns to lead in my stomach. Next to me, Ali unbuckles her seat belt and opens the door.

Go time, I tell myself. If there is a way to salvage this, I have to find it in the next three seconds.

Because "this" doesn't only mean my dignity. Mr. Braun is the one who first told me about the Youth Politics Boot Camp back in October, after watching me unofficially take control of the ASB elections task force. YPBC is the elite summer program of all my election-night-map-inspired dreams. Its curriculum alternates on an every-other-year cycle, and during even summers, like this one, it functions as a training ground for those of us who want to be organizers, staffers, public policy analysts, communications directors . . . campaign managers.

Immediately after I learned about it, attending YPBC this summer became an essential early part of The Plan, which was supposed to begin with running Jade's victorious bid for junior class president and end with heading a successful campaign to elect the second female president of the United States by the time I'm forty. Mr. Braun submitted his recommendation letter just two weeks ago. This accident is the worst kind of embarrassing, like I betrayed the trust he had in me. The fierce desire that normally burns through me whenever I think about the possibility of YPBC turns acidic.

By the time I manage to open the car door, Ali is shaking Mr. Braun's hand, blushing. I hope it's because she's embarrassed she let me hit his car, and not because of the easy smile, Hollywood hair, and slacks-and-dress-shirt combo that made the girls in my freshman civics class swoon. I swear there was a competition for who could get the most personal information out of him during project work days, but he always laughed off the blatant fishing. Once I was involved in the task force, it became obvious he reserved the best anecdotes for ASB kids.

"Little bit of trouble getting out of the lot, Madison?" Mr. Braun says, raising one hand as if to shade his eyes, even though the sun's afternoon glare is neatly diffused by wispy gray clouds.

"I'm really sorry," I blurt. I meant for my explanation to be worthy of a national party convention speech. The reality is . . . not that.

"Would you believe, this is not the first time a student has crashed into my car?" He smiles, affable, at Ali, so they can share a grown-up look about how irresponsible we all are.

"I wouldn't say I *crashed*." I dart around him so I can examine the damaged bumper.

It's dented and the red paint's scraped to Iowa and back, but it's not like it's a total loss or anything.

"Let me give you my card," says Ali, and ducks back into the car.

I square my shoulders. "I've never been in an accident before."

The garbage barrels my parents bring to the church parking lot for our practice sessions don't count. Their whole raison d'être is to be knocked down. Accidents sound . . . expensive. And expenses beyond college tuition are not in The Plan. Or the budget.

"Don't worry about it. Insurance will take care of it," says Mr. Braun. He squints down at the bumper. "It doesn't look like a hard fix."

"Yes, but—I mean, of course it's not. I hope." I swallow and start over. "Is this going to affect the ASB election?"

Since I was on the elections task force, I know there's no official definition of a campaign manager, so I can't exactly be barred from participating. But I can't stand to bring up the possibility that Mr. Braun could rescind his YPBC recommendation. Even though I don't have a candidate at the moment, that's a solvable problem in a way losing his respect is not.

It probably says something about me that I'm much more worried about student government elections than what my parents are going to think. They won't come out and say it, but they've been expecting me to take out the mailbox for the past three months, ever since I got my permit.

Mr. Braun's face scrunches together. "The ASB . . . teachers don't get a vote."

"I know it's more complicated than that," I say.

He shakes his head, smiling again. "I promise you, one student, one vote. There are no conspiracies to be found here."

But inside my head is a furious list of all the ways he could sabotage my candidate. Once I *have* a candidate again, now that Jade has fired me.

CHAPTER TWO

Thirty-Two Days Until Election Day

Chelsea picks me up in the 2005 Toyota Camry our grandfather left her. Sure, she was only fifteen when he died, but her parents took care of it for her, and now my parents take care of Chelsea. When they first asked me over winter break how I would feel about Chelsea living with us until the start of next school year, I was thrilled. Chelsea has always been my favorite cousin, the one I followed around at Thanksgiving as a little kid. Still do, honestly.

The reason for the extended visit turned out to be a lot less fun than a sudden desire to usher me through my sophomore year of high school. Chelsea's university had decided not to expel the boy who'd assaulted her. Nowhere in Wisconsin, including her parents' house in Oshkosh, felt far enough away. She's transferring to the University of Iowa in the fall, but for now she's taking classes at a community college in Minneapolis and working part-time as a social media assistant.

"Wanna talk about it?" Chelsea asks as I finally make it out of the school parking lot. She's confident enough in spring's inevitability to have traded her familiar winter coat for a vintage aviator jacket thrown over a pop-punk tour T-shirt.

"I'll have to repeat it in an hour anyway," I say.

"Be that way," she says, but I can tell without looking that she's smiling. "Anything to say that you aren't planning on repeating?"

I try not to share any real secrets with Chelsea, not because I don't trust her, but because I don't want her to feel guilty about keeping anything from my parents. Since she's not really my sister, it doesn't seem like a fair position to put her in, not after everything.

Besides, I don't have any real secrets.

I came out to my parents as bi last June, and their hugs were happy and without hesitation. They took pictures of me and Jade before homecoming in the fall. There was a cold snap that weekend, the way there often is in Minnesota as September drops into October, with an avalanche of leaves and a periodic dusting of snow. In my favorite picture, a candid, Jade has a green shawl tucked around her shoulders, the ends trailing behind her as she walks down our two front steps. I'm already standing on the little path to the driveway, my hand extended, the sleeve of my gray blazer just so. Both of us with green corsages on our wrists.

We look—well, we look fifteen, really fifteen, still baby-faced compared to the seniors and definitely to Chelsea and the actresses who play sophomores on TV. We don't *quite* look like a political power couple. But it would have made for a nice photo insert, the glossy center of a much-anticipated memoir. *High school sweethearts, homecoming sophomore year. Photo taken by Madison's parents*, the caption would read.

The only other important thing about me isn't a secret either. I've been tracking exit poll results by precinct since I was eight, and the party-line breakdown of registered Minnesotan voters by county since I was nine. Maybe at first it was simply because my parents watched the news a lot, and I had a good memory for statistics, and I liked the way it made the adults around me think I was clever and precocious. It might have stayed that way, something I cultivated because I was good at it, if it weren't for Rockford Lake.

When I was ten, city councilwoman Talia Rue knocked on our door. Except she wasn't a city councilwoman then. She was an accountant, a single mom of two young kids, and she was equally single-handedly starting a campaign to clean up Rockford Lake, which was too toxic to swim or fish in. I tried to show off—listing the results of recent local tax levies—and she asked if I would want to testify at the next town hall. I was hesitant until she told me I could come to a pre-meeting strategy session with the other witnesses. I'd never been in a room full of people who were all interested in the same thing I was. I hadn't realized those people existed in my town, instead of far away in DC or on TV.

Although the supply-room strategy session had felt cozy, the official meeting space for the town hall was too cold. There was a constant thrum of background noise, shuffling papers and late arrivals, that eventually would become soothing, but just then only amplified my nerves.

Yet almost as soon as the first witness took the mic, it hit me, like lightning, or Cupid's arrow, or campaign ads the week before an election. Because—

Oh.

It turned out that all those numbers I was memorizing really *meant* something. Not simply in a literal, methodological sense—it ran deeper than that. Those numbers were hopes. Plans. The twisted past and the twisting branches of the futures at play. It felt like something had come unlocked within me—or maybe that something about the world had become unlocked, and Talia was ushering me through the door. Everything looked different. Everything looked possible.

There's ice covering Rockford Lake right now, but Amrita and I have gone swimming in its clear waters for three summers. My eighth-grade science class did a field trip to the natural filtration pond created at one end. Every time I pass by its new playground, I think about the postcards I hand-addressed with my wobbly cursive. There's something that exists for my community, something that's *better*, because I found out that the one thing superior to indulgent praise is actual results.

And the project moved a lot faster once Talia Rue was on the city council.

I want to do it again—first at my school, and then everywhere else. But between Jade and Mr. Braun, that dream seems at risk in a way it's never been before.

I turn away from Chelsea to stare out the window. We pass a park that was surely someone else's intro to town halls, years ago. "I'm a shitty driver—way worse than I thought, which is just *great*—and it was a shitty day."

"Awww," Chelsea says. "Even before the driving lesson?"

I nod.

"That sucks. I'm sorry. But hey, we're almost home. Worst is over, right?"

Wrong. So wrong.

Because an hour later, I'm explaining to my parents how I got into an accident. Without leaving the freaking parking lot.

"You'll need to write Mr. Braun an apology note," my mom says.

My face flames. I feel like I'm about six years old again.

"I will. It's—" I push my fork around my mostly untouched pasta. "He's also the faculty advisor for the Associated Student Body."

"And that means he doesn't deserve a formal apology for you hitting his car?" Dad says.

"No." To my horror, I choke on the word, my throat swelling shut against an explanation I'm too humiliated to articulate. "But he hates me now. So he won't help me."

Even though Mr. Braun said not to worry about it, even though he was joking with my instructor—wouldn't you hate someone who'd been so careless with your things? Who'd had access to power—even the low horsepower of a lesson vehicle—they clearly didn't know how to handle, and let their own plans crash over yours? Especially when he's gone out of his way, more than once, to help me. Mr. Braun is everyone's favorite teacher: the preppy girls'; the sports guys', who give him high fives and fist bumps as he passes through the cafeteria; *and* the theater kids', because he grants them automatic extensions on assignments during tech week. I'm already outside of so much at school. I don't want to be the one student he resents, even if he's too professional to say it.

"I imagine everyone's emotions were running a little high. Write the apology note; give it some time," says Mom.

Class president intent petitions are due on Friday.

There is no time, I think.

Note to self: No more unforced errors. Be vigilant near deadlines.

Of course, if I have it my way, as soon as I graduate from college, my life will be nothing but deadlines: one FEC deadline to the next, one debate to the next, one election to the next, each cycle spinning directly into the following. All morning, my body was thrumming, heady with the excitement of it. For all of four hours, I felt like the happiest, luckiest girl in the world. I had a candidate, a plan, and an imminent deadline. Years of waiting and watching others, now behind me. And then, of course, lunch happened, and with it, the one-two punch of dumping and firing.

"We'll talk about the money later this week, once Mr. Braun has submitted his insurance claim," says Dad.

And then there's that.

"Yeah," I say, quiet.

"There's no shame in waiting, if that's what ultimately seems best. Not everyone gets their license right away at sixteen. It's better to be safe." Mom smiles at me, but I just look down.

Car accidents are for careless people, not for people in honors and AP classes, people with *plans*. But like so much else today, I guess I'm wrong about this too.

After dinner, I should get through some homework, but I haven't let myself check Instagram all night. It's time. I need to know how subtle—or not—Jade is being about our breakup.

Our breakup.

The words still don't seem real, and my fingers tremble as I unlock my phone. As I suspected, Jade changed her profile picture. Instead of us clutching each other while wearing sparkly dresses on New Year's, it's now just her, shades down in what I know is the passenger seat of her brother's car. Her Story feels like an actual slap: fifteen seconds of Jade lip-synching to Ariana Grande's "break up with your girlfriend, i'm bored."

Were you bored? I think, blinking back tears.

I wasn't.

It's true that her douchey debate friends were beginning to feel like genuine annoyances rather than a cutely forgivable quirk, but I was dating Jade, not her friends. I knew where we fit into each other's lives. Running her campaign had always been part of The Plan, after all, even before I'd heard of YPBC, even before we started dating. Her, the shining debate star candidate. Me, the hyperfocused campaign manager. Win-win. She'd loved it, hadn't she, those last, lingering weeks before we got together in August, when we sat together in her backyard and sketched her ASB takeover? Her eyes sparked stars as she watched me plot her win.

We met last year in my spring elective, Debate 1, when we were assigned to each other as class partners. By February, I was fantasizing about winning debate tournaments together, and then her heart. As it turned out, I didn't even really like debate—the formal tournament kind, that is. I didn't like how you had to be prepared to argue either side, and I *really* didn't like the emphasis on shoving out three hundred words (or more) per minute. In my opinion, some points are best heard when you let them breathe. Breathing, I came to understand, is not the point of high school debate.

Still, I spent that whole semester, and then the summer after, waiting breathlessly on Jade's every look, until August, when she asked if she could kiss me, and I could only nod.

The breakup was completely unexpected. You're supposed to see *signs* in your partner when they're about to dump you, right? Someone doesn't suddenly start voting conservative if they were reliably progressive before. You can track the money, the gradually changing op-eds, the think-tank meetings. But Jade and I still ate lunch at the same table and still partnered for in-class exercises in Marketing—and still planned her class president campaign together.

I wasn't off her schedule, until I was. When she pulled me aside at lunch today, leading me to the back staircase no one uses, not even for make-out sessions, all she said was that it wasn't working. That I'd changed. Her words were fast, detached, rehearsed. I couldn't get a word in to protest that I'm the last person anyone can accuse of changing. The one thing about my fifteen-year-old life that my nine-year-old self would find surprising is *Jade*.

Her parting shot was to accuse me of only caring about my YPBC application, and she flounced away before I could reply that asking her to read my personal statement *once* shouldn't count against me. I didn't realize your class president campaign manager wanting to go to YPBC was a breakup-worthy offense. If anyone changed, it's Jade, who had seemed enthusiastic about YPBC when I first showed her their website in the fall, and then distinctly less so as I started working on my application.

I close Instagram without checking to see if she deleted any of the captions from the pictures I took of her, the ones where she would write things like "📷 my most patient gf." I can't even decide what would be worse: seeing those pictures still up, ones where she's laughing or smirking or pouting at me but I'm neatly extracted, or seeing the photos gone altogether, because she'd rather scrub out happiness wholesale if it was at all attached to *us*.

I press the backs of my hands against my cheeks and my eyes. I try exactly one deep yoga breath. Then I give up and reach for my phone again. It's time—past time—to get some best-friend perspective on this.

Me

So . . . Jade dumped me

And fired me

Typing the words is somehow more final than hearing them, but Amrita's immediate response does more to settle my heartbeat than a half-assed yoga breath ever could.

Amrita

I'm so sorry

I saw her story

I didn't want to message you about it first

Why didn't you say something in class?!

I flop onto the braided rug that covers most of what little floor space there is in my bedroom. Amrita and I have fifth-period English together, directly after lunch.

Me

In shock

Didn't want to talk about it where anyone could overhear

Amrita

<3 <3 <3

Me

Will you check snap for me?

I don't have Snapchat, but Amrita does. She uses it with some kids she met at an art camp a few summers ago, although I think more for sharing photos of found art in nature than in-progress sketches.

Amrita

She put a pic of her w/ D3 on her snap story

D3 is what Amrita and I call Jade's debate friends, these three guys whose last names all start with D. I'm not exactly going to miss sharing a lunch table with them. I *am* going to miss Jade knocking her knee into mine as we brainstorm campaign color schemes.

Amrita

And also . . .

The three dots appear, disappear, reappear. I sit up so fast, I'm dizzy.

Me

Also what???

Amrita

Something about how she's ready to meet cute girls, kissy face

It's like I've belly flopped onto a row of upturned pushpins. *Wasn't I cute enough?* I think.

Maybe Jade didn't like the A WOMAN'S PLACE IS IN THE HOUSE (AND SENATE) T-shirt I wore today. Maybe she's never liked it, or the button-downs I get on clearance at Kohl's. They're always telling us to dress for the job we want. I imagine presenting a slideshow of my selfies from last March, last August, this February. *See?* I'd say, righteous in a way I was too shocked to be in the stairwell. *This is who I've always been. Take it or leave it.* I already had my answer, though. Jade saw who I was, and she decided to leave me.

Amrita

You okay?

Me

Just a lot to think about

Instead of thinking about any of it—like how long she's been ready to dump me if she's already looking for the next girl—I head back to Instagram, where my profile pic is the two of us holding posters at a rally against gun violence. I change it to a solo shot instead, one Amrita took of me. I'm tempted to leave up the rest of our pictures, refuse to contribute to my own erasure, but the anger that I've been pushing aside all day—in favor of class and the mortifying accident and dinner with my family—burns through me.

You want to get rid of me? *Really* get rid of me?

Fine.

And I go through them all.

Valentine's Day, with flowers for her and chocolates for me. That snow day in January, when we convinced her brother to drive us to French Park for sledding, and we didn't even care that we had to share the hill with all the elementary school kids. More than a dozen of us on random days, nothing special except that we were together and happy.

At least, that's what I thought.

I don't stop at the picture of us from September, our first posted kiss, #official. I keep going. Summer at the community pool, selfies

I took while hoping she would like or comment. Last spring, debate practice sessions during lunch, our perfect academic-allies-to-lovers meet-cute.

Gone, gone, gone.

There's a knock on my door as the first sob escapes me.

"Sweetheart?" Mom says, rushing in. She kneels down and wraps me in her arms. "Oh, honey, don't stress so much about the accident, okay? We're just glad you weren't hurt."

I shake my head, sniffing and crying. "It's Jade," I manage.

"Did something happen? Is she all right?"

"She's *great*, apparently." My voice is trying to be hard, but it's undercut by all the tears.

"Oh?"

"She fired me. During lunch. And d-dumped me."

"Baby, I'm sorry." Mom squeezes me tighter, kissing the top of my head. "I'm so sorry. Do you want to tell me what happened? What she said?"

I shake my head, my throat too clogged to speak.

"You're a great friend, and I know you were an attentive girlfriend. It's her loss." She runs a hand up and down my back. "Can I help at all? Can I get you anything?"

I lean away so I can cough and wipe my face. "No. It's okay. I should . . . I'm okay."

"You know you best." Mom gives my shoulders a last squeeze, then levers herself off the floor.

I wait until the door shuts with a click before forcing myself back to my desk. From where I sit, the situation is bleak. A new ex, a new profile pic, and a pile of textbooks.

Homework, right. Because no jumbled feelings about a high school girlfriend—however pretty, however previously perfect—are going to get me into the U with a full-ride scholarship, or Georgetown with dream-enabling financial aid. It's true that David Plouffe didn't finish his BA until 2010—after Obama's first, no-drama victory—but I don't think you can pull off that kind of thing anymore, especially not as a girl.

And then I remember, as suddenly as if Bernie Sanders himself were shouting in my ear. Because the thing besides my transcript that was going to get me into all those schools, with all that money? YPBC.

And the thing besides my transcript that was going to get me into YPBC?

Managing Jade's campaign for junior class president.

Winning.

Now I need a plan B.

CHAPTER THREE

Weeks ago, when everything was still going according to The Plan, I submitted Jade's campaign blueprint for my Youth Politics Boot Camp application. If I'm not managing her campaign anymore, I'll have to withdraw. YPBC is very strict: You have to be *leading* some kind of project, not simply showing up at a political group's volunteering events every weekend (which I already do).

I blow my nose and try to focus on compartmentalizing. The dumping I can handle . . . later, with Amrita and chocolate and probably a cathartic movie where the ex is subjected to a scathing monologue about what they're missing out on. But the looming logistical mountain of the YPBC application is an immediate five-alarm fire. Just thinking about the firing makes me feel about two inches tall. Because if someone who's known me for over a year, someone who's watched me cry when I talk about the first person I ever registered to vote and swoon over spreadsheets and plan, plan, plan—if Jade wants to fire me, when I *know* she also really wants to win this election—then maybe I'm not as good as I thought I was.

> Reality check: Was Jade just indulging me the whole time?

> But I'm not actually any good and now that she doesn't want to date me, she doesn't have to pretend?

Amrita

> Your message could not be received because of the following errors: factual untruths; hyperbolic self-deprecation; misplaced doubt.

> Please try again.

I roll my eyes even as I grin.

Before Amrita showed up in third grade, I'd never had a best friend. I guess it's not that long to wait, in the scheme of life, but you don't need to have a nascent data obsession to figure out that no one's eyes go straight to yours when it's time to pick class partners. I was the kid who was always nagging everyone else to follow the rules of whatever the playground game was, the one adults were constantly reminding that "life isn't fair." Like that was an excuse. Like adults don't *shape* whole parts of your life when you're little. Like there's no point in trying, and even identifying unfairness is a waste of time.

But when I prepared to stage a one-person sit-in of the art room because we'd spent six straight weeks studying male European painters as our "History Hop" each class period, Amrita sat down next to me.

"My mom already emailed a suggested artist list. A better one," she said. "Ms. Seymour said I can read an art book if I want instead. But I don't think that's fair."

"It's not," I agreed quickly.

"Do you want to look at my book with me anyway? I've already read it a lot, so you can tell me when to turn the page."

When I nodded, Amrita revealed a thick book with glossy pages, the kind I now know mostly sits on people's coffee tables unread. The book fell open to a spread about two-thirds of the way through, clearly a much-beloved page. I don't remember the exact painting Amrita showed me that day, but I do remember the artist, Amrita Sher-Gil, and my new best friend's determination to follow in the footsteps of her namesake—sooner rather than later.

With everyone else, we're pressured to smooth down our too-intense edges and our too-focused wants. When it's just us, we can just be . . . us, without explanation or apology.

Me

You're right

It's not me, it's her

Firing me the week intent petitions are due was beyond petty

I lift my chin. I'd much rather focus on how wrong Jade was to fire me than on the fact that she broke up with me. I don't handle power-lessness well, but I can definitely match someone else's petty. Sweet, sweet ex revenge. Elle Woods owning the LSAT. *What, like it's hard?*

I text Amrita again.

Me

Done being sad. Ready for revenge

It takes Amrita a few minutes to reply this time, so I pull together a playlist, lots of Halsey, a little Lizzo.

Amrita

I can do ice cream with a rom-com this weekend if you need it

Amrita's lack of bloodthirstiness is honestly her worst quality. She's the most placidly ambitious person I've ever met. For her, revenge is just another form of ridiculous high school drama, which is an irrelevant distraction on her way to a solo exhibit at the Metropolitan Museum of Art.

Me

Remember how Jade fired me not even 12 hours ago? With a breakup as a bad news bonus?

When I *need* to manage a campaign?!

Amrita

I know! I'm sorry

She sends a sad cat GIF.

Me

I need a sidekick

Amrita

No one has ever needed a sidekick less than you

Me

I'll cancel your Blizzard debt

Clean slate on all ice cream purchases . . .

Amrita

Tempting, but no

Me

I'll let you do another hand plaster!

Amrita

You were going to do that anyway

The problem with only having each other is that neither of us has any bargaining chips. I'll have to make my own revenge.

"Here's the situation," I say, spinning around in my chair to face the room.

It's this weird habit I have, probably from all my years as an only child with working parents. I don't like quiet. I do like hosting strategy sessions.

Usually, there's no conference table audience to be had, so I make one up. I used to spend whole chunks of time before Mom or Dad came home this way, lecturing an invisible 2032 candidate on their faux pas, explaining to a phantom reporter why the makeup test policy at my middle school was unfair. By this past fall, I was already known by sight to both the city council (beyond Talia, of course) and our state representatives. If there's a town hall and I have a ride, I'm there. Even on nights when I don't speak, there's something invigorating about sitting in a room with a dozen or so people who care like I do, that drive for change burning inside our chests. When I do plan to ask a question or make a statement, I always test my messaging on my pillows first.

"Jade fired me." My voice doesn't wobble this time. "So I'm down a candidate. Down a win."

I like the sound of that. Not *being* down a win, but the rhythm of it. I'll keep it.

What do you do when something's missing? When you need it to get where you're going?

You replace it.

I don't need a girlfriend.

I do need a candidate.

And I really, really could use a win.

I push my biology textbook aside in favor of my Life Notebook. My Life Notebook is where everything goes that's not strictly related to a class. My planning notes for the Gender-Sexuality Alliance lobbying trip at the state capitol last month. Pending legislation I want to research.

The junior class president race.

I know what I need to do, but work—even the best kind of work—is best with my best friend.

Me

No rom-com, no sidekicking . . . but all this could be yours!

I send Amrita a picture of my bed—blanket smoothed—and clear floor. Then I send her another of my open Life Notebook, the class president pages pressed flat against my desk. She doesn't exactly need the advance notice that the campaign will be my focus, but since it's a school night, her parents like confirmation there's an intention to do something other than, well, rom-coms and romantic revenge plots.

Amrita

You're slow tonight

I started packing up five minutes ago

She sends a photo of her peach backpack, an expensive set of colored pencils peeking through the open front pocket. Her parents usually buy her new ones before she truly runs out, and the leftovers become my version of the Baby-Sitters Club Kid Kits. The neighbor kids from my regular babysitting gig have strict screen-time limits, so I'm happy for any novelty that will get us through those after-school hours.

While I wait for Amrita, I settle into the junior class president race. I already have an initial list of known candidates, but before I start my selection, I head back online to check for unexpected entrants. To supplement my social media deep dive, I also message a handful of almost friends I have in other friend groups. *Have you heard if so-and-so is running?* I ask, filling in the name they're most likely to know. Most of the time, even if the answer is no, they'll follow up with who they *do* know is running. And every time the conversation drifts to Jade, I pull us back, stomach tense and blinking hard.

Sammy wants to focus on scibowl, but Zack asked me to sign his intent petition today.

No idea, sorry . . . I just heard about the breakup w/ Jade and I wanted to say that rly sucks, u were so perfect! :(

I WISH Clarisse would run!! You already know about Carter, right?

I do already know about Carter. At six foot one and as the star of our otherwise mediocre baseball team, he's hard to miss.

Reese decided not to do it, too scared of the speech. Anais told me that Annie might be considering tho . . .

Annie I sort of know from civics last year, so I message her directly to follow the rumor.

Every reply reminds me of how much I want to run an ASB campaign, instead of begging my political volunteering group to let me throw something together for them last minute. This is *my* school.

Following the candidate leads makes me feel like I'm a detective, piecing together all the clues that make up the greatest case yet—the campaign. Except I'll get to introduce evidence and influence the outcome. The more candidates I place on my mental map, the more confident I feel. Jade can do what she wants: I know how to do this.

When I feel certain of the final candidate list, I print off their yearbook pictures and stick them to my whiteboard with silver US Capitol magnets. Their blandest selves stare back at me in black and white.

"Hey, Sunny," Amrita says, tapping on the doorframe and walking right in.

It's an old nickname, from way back in elementary school when I started complaining about being called "Maddie" and Amrita decided best-friend privileges meant she should have a nickname for me that no one else did. In nine-year-old logic, turning the unused "-son" at the end of my name into "sunny" was pretty clever. Now Amrita says it'll keep me honest. I can't fall into political cynicism and corner cutting with a nickname like *Sunny*.

"Hiii. Do you need newspaper? I saw the pencils and didn't prep for charcoal or paint."

"Maybe I'm here so you can help me with algebra," Amrita says, shaking her head and settling on the rug.

"Uh-huh. Test's not until next week. Pencils or paint?"

"Pencils."

Amrita pulls out her sketchbook and writes the date in tiny print in the bottom corner. Her thick hair is creation ready, semi-subdued in a messy topknot. She pushes up the sleeves of her salmon-colored arts camp sweatshirt while dissecting me with narrowed eyes.

"Can you unfold a little?" she says.

I'm sitting in my desk chair with both knees bent, feet curled against the edge of the seat. "Don't you want to draw people *authentically*?"

"I will title it *Portrait of a Young Bisexual* so nobody gets confused. Just give me a bit more to work with."

I shift, so one leg is bent under me and the other is crossed on top. Asymmetry is more interesting to look at, and gives Amrita different shadows to sketch.

"Okay." She waves her non-drawing hand briefly at me before repositioning it on the sketch pad, steadying the pages. "Talk. What's your plan?"

"Eight running," I say. I gesture to my photo-covered whiteboard.

Even just looking at it sends tingles up my spine. One of them is going to be the next junior class president. If I have it my way, it'll be the person I decide to help tonight. Maybe that's a little arrogant, to think that I can play queenmaker, but it feels good. Honestly, after the day I've had, I need to feel like my choices—the ones I make with my full attention, in a part of my life I'm actually good at—matter. My campaign core can't be changed by ex-girlfriends or car accidents.

"The class reps?" Amrita guesses.

I shake my head. Neither of the sophomore reps is throwing their hat in, which would normally surprise me—five out of the last eight junior and senior class presidents were ASB reps first—but one of ours is moving to Ohio in June, and the other is tired of skipping her ballroom dance practices to deal with bylaws.

"Who's the not-even-if-it-got-you-into-Georgetown?" Amrita glances between my left foot (socked) and her page.

"Kevin Corvi."

Kevin once spent most of the field trip bus ride to Mixed Blood Theatre calling me a dyke. Amrita was home sick that day, so I had to sit there alone the whole way into the city, waiting for someone other than me to tell him to shut up. One of his friends tried, an early "Hey, dude, never mind that bitch, did you hear about Courtney Olson," but it didn't work. Maybe Kevin's changed in the last fourteen months. I'm not interested in trying to find out, up close and personal. I flip his photo on the whiteboard so he's just a white rectangle instead of someone I still avoid in the hallways.

"Not even for RISD," Amrita agrees. "Next option?"

"Carter McLaughlin."

"Is that baseball Carter or hacker Carter?"

"Baseball Carter."

"Sad for you, good for election integrity." Amrita erases a line of my leg.

"Yeah, I can't spend the next month talking about pep rallies and nothing else." Pep rallies are fine if you're into that sort of thing—except as far as I can tell from Carter's public Insta, that's his *only* thing. I'll admit that our mascot, the West Plymouth Blue Jay, is kind of cute, but how many times does someone really need to post "Go Jays"? Maybe once. I flip his picture too. Next . . . "Zack Cohen."

Amrita bites her lip, *not* out of concentration, I know, but because of lingering embarrassment over multi-year middle-school crush she had on Zack, a lovable (apparently) but disorganized theater kid. I give her a moment to decide on something to say. "How hard do you want to work? When you're writing this in your memoir, what's your story?"

"My story is . . . a great person needed a boost to become a viable candidate. Who then became the *winning* candidate."

"So hard, but not *Zack* hard."

"The election schedule doesn't have enough time for me to get that kind of messy into shape." I'm almost regretful: It *would* be quite the feat, a true testament to my prowess . . . and yet. "It's too risky. If it came down to Carter and Zack, I'd obviously vote for Zack, but as a campaign partner? Pass."

The magnets snap satisfyingly against the board as I reattach his photo, facedown. Three down, none of them even close to a good match for me.

"Chin up," Amrita says.

She doesn't mean metaphorically. I readjust.

"So, the girls," I say. "Annie Delaney. Strong candidate, except that she comes with Brooklyn. Which means Brooklyn's parents' credit card, which is tempting for campaign T-shirt purposes, but . . ." I shake myself out of visions of a two-thousand-dollar campaign budget. Annie doesn't do anything without her bestie, and even if Annie *technically* accepted my offer, I'd have to fight Brooklyn the whole way. My candidate should put me first. Or, you know, my ideas.

"You need more decision-making power than Brooklyn will give you." Amrita pauses to clean her pink-framed glasses on her shirt.

"Like, a *lot* more." I sigh even as I flip her picture around. "Riley Wu."

There's a moment of silence from both of us: mine, respectful; hers, skeptical. Riley has enough charisma to win the Iowa caucus without breaking a sweat, and that's more valuable in a class

32

president race than any credit card. The flip side of that charisma coin, though, is . . .

"Do I get a no-drama-queen veto in this process?" Amrita asks. She makes a long, smooth stroke down the page, my right arm whispering into view.

". . . Yes."

Riley's last breakup somehow managed to derail the sophomore class retreat, thanks to the number of people she charmed into acting as go-betweens. As one of the few fully uninvolved, it was a semi-welcome distraction from all the bonding that definitely wasn't going to happen between me and my classmates anyway. But a campaign doesn't have room for those kinds of disruptions, so I turn her picture around.

With Riley and Annie out, that leaves three.

First: Marisa Perez, who moved from Brooklyn Center to the apartment complex at the end of my street two years ago. Our dads work together at a supportive housing agency, so I met her before we started at West Plymouth. Marisa is a rising Model UN star—she always cites her grandma, who emigrated from Mexico as a teenager in the '70s, as inspiration for joining—plus this year she's in AP Spanish while taking Chinese as her elective. In terms of determining the most academically ambitious candidate, it's not even a competition.

Second: Victoria Ferrand, a theater techie who's also involved in every club with a volunteering angle. We sat at the same table in ninth-grade English, allies by default in a class full of people who never did the reading. In our poetry unit, we each had to pick a Minnesotan poet, deceased or contemporary, and present on their life and one of their poems. Victoria memorized the poem she chose, even though that wasn't a requirement.

And Jade, obviously.

But Jade is no longer a contender for my rose. I should have flipped her picture first, but as I do it now, it's with a single, painful what-could-have-been heartbeat.

Looking at the final two, my excitement builds. The real choices at last.

One of you is going to win, I think.

"Marisa or Victoria," I tell Amrita. I don't even say Jade's name. "I need to look more into their socials—how close are you?"

"Now's good."

I turn back to my computer, and Amrita and I work in silence for a while.

Victoria's Insta is private, but I guess I requested to add her last year, probably after the poetry unit. She uses a lot of rainbow filters and stickers—not the straight-up pride ones, though, only the cutesy ones. I've never seen her at GSA before, but this is kind of a *lot* of rainbow for a straight girl. Maybe she's not out to everyone who follows her? I like the idea of helping a potentially queer girl. I still want sapphic rep on ASB, after all, I just don't want to be represented by *Jade*.

I keep scrolling Victoria's page, and—*of course*. Victoria is the current ASB parliamentarian, which basically means she has to keep track of all the procedural rules. It's reserved for a sophomore each year, and you have to be nominated by two teachers to even get on the ballot. Almost no one cares about the parliamentarian race, mostly because it's understood that it's real work. *Almost* no one, because I cared about it back then, since it matters who knows

34

the rules enough to manipulate them (or not), and I care about it now, since her position means Victoria has something no other candidate can claim: ASB experience. Incumbency is worth a thousand gold stars in my book.

But the junior class president race calls for a different kind of campaign than the one she used to win the parliamentarian position. I scroll back to the top of Victoria's Instagram. Not a single post about her intent petition, even though I know she's running. On a hunch, I check her friends' accounts too: again, nothing. I'm not surprised. Most of Victoria's friends seem kind of boring—making the same posters for the community service club, event after event; plodding away on tech crew with little chance of being promoted to crew head. Not enough imagination to realize they have a thousand-star candidate and fill the (social media) sky with her praises.

Marisa's latest post, meanwhile, is a nicely formatted infographic about improving the school's environmental policies, complete with image descriptions in English and Spanish. Further sleuthing reveals at least a quarter of the people who liked the post also shared it to their own Stories. I knew before tonight that Marisa was a great classmate—and this post proves she's already a viable candidate. But for my YPBC application project, I need to be needed.

"Victoria needs me," I say.

"Jade did too. Does this one deserve you?"

I'm not ready to think more about Jade tonight, but I let the sweet underpinnings of Amrita's no-nonsense question shore up my shaken confidence. I open Victoria's profile again and map out my decision one last time. Victoria: poetry past, parliamentarian present . . . presidential future.

"I think so."

"Good." Amrita initials the sketch and tosses me the pencil.

I slip off my chair and put my initials next to hers, right below the arch of my graphite foot. Then I stand up and flip over Marisa's picture so Victoria's face is the only one I see. She's looking at the camera with a closed-mouth smile, and her usual curls are straightened.

Are you ready to be junior class president? I ask her grayscale eyes.

I grab my phone and, grinning, open a DM with Victoria.

The Plan is back on track.

CHAPTER FOUR

Thirty-One Days Until Election Day

@WestPlymouthPress: ASB election season starts this week! Check out these highlights from past years' most creative campaigns

First period doesn't start until 8:20, but there's a zero period for school breakfast and ACT prep classes that I plan to use as my campaign time. I have a smoothie at home and beg a ride from my dad so I can meet Victoria in the cafeteria when it opens.

I hate to let Jade think she has any impact on me, but I admit I chose my outfit carefully today. What screams *I'm cute* and *you didn't deserve me* and *it's totally fine that you're ruining my life* but also *job interview*? One day, fifteen years from now, there will be candidates jockeying to have me on their staff. For now, I have to pay my dues and make my case.

I decided on a blue long-sleeved dress, structured at the waist in a way that makes me forget I'm ever self-conscious about my belly and hips. Black leggings lined with fleece, in deference to the forecasted high of thirty-four degrees. For good measure, I added my

Jays Jigsaw charm necklace, a plain silver chain with the tail feather piece that was handed out at the student gallery opening.

When the jigsaw was originally created by a handful of senior guys as a woodshop project, it didn't include more than two non-sports events. This year, the "civic engagement" events the ASB candidates will host throughout next week have been assigned their own pieces. If I wanted to complete my jigsaw and thus obtain bragging rights to West Plymouth's most hyped tradition (which I don't), I'd have to show up to all the sophomore candidates' events. All thanks to Amrita, of course.

Since she was the one to design the mascot puzzle this year—the first underclassman to be asked in the quasi-official tradition's seven-year history, and the first artist to design the pieces to be easily converted to charms for necklaces or earrings—it feels like I'm wearing a little echo of her support to this all-important campaign meeting. And if wearing a single-charm JJs necklace makes people think I'm remotely interested in attending thirty school events so I can cart an ever-jinglier backpack around and then take a triumphant picture of the completed metal Blue Jay at the end of the year . . . maybe that wouldn't be so bad during campaign season.

When I enter the cafeteria, I scan the tables for Victoria's brown curls. Someone taps my shoulder, and I jump, preparing a smile as I spin.

It's Marisa, though, still bundled in a puffy purple coat.

"Oh! Hi," I say.

"Hey," she says. "I saw your dad in the lot just now."

"Yeah, I convinced him to drive me today—sorry, I should've offered you a ride." My voice scratches with guilt. For all my talk about Rockford Lake . . . my neighborliness could use some work.

"Want to join me? Or are you waiting for someone?" Marisa asks. She glances back toward the entrance, and her long dark hair bounces from its high ponytail.

Does she know? My hands start to sweat.

I suddenly feel awful about my process last night too.

I have nothing against her, I remind myself. *I prefer candidates with experience, that's all.*

Except . . . that's its own problem, isn't it? Crap. Everything about this was easier when I didn't have to evaluate the candidates *or* my selection criteria. It's too late to reconsider now: I already made my pitch to Victoria.

"Waiting for someone," I manage to say.

"See you later, then." She smiles and moves past me toward the food line.

"Bye!" I call after her, but I'm already distracted by a sneaker squeak behind me.

"Am I your second meeting?"

Victoria.

Her eyebrows are raised, her arms crossed over her folded-up gray peacoat.

"No!" I clear my throat. "Marisa and I are neighbors."

"Did you make this offer to her first?"

"No . . ."

Why is she being so combative about this from the get-go? Maybe she just wants to know she's my number one. Which she is.

As of ten hours ago.

"Are you getting something to eat?"

I shake my head.

We sit down at an empty table near a window. Victoria settles her coat on a second stool and smooths the wrists of her black-and-white-striped sweater. She's wearing a Jays Jigsaw necklace, too, although hers has more charms than mine, separated from each other by round beads of West Plymouth blue.

At this point in the year, the hard-core JJs completionists—which is a majority of the student body—show off a curated collection of the most recent event charms, or the charms for events they know a lot of students missed and so will never acquire. Victoria's necklace features the eye from the fall play, a talon that I'm pretty sure was for boys' soccer, and part of the wing from homecoming. I don't know what other pieces Victoria may have collected, but I like that she's kept her necklace as a place to display the charms for events she personally cares about.

I only have one charm left, since I gave my homecoming wing piece to Jade after she lost hers over Thanksgiving break. It felt good to be generous with my girlfriend, this girl who had snuggled close to me on a harvest hayride and who could make me laugh with a single lifted eyebrow during ridiculous assembly announcements. Now it's irritating on principle, but still one less physical representation of our broken relationship for me to banish.

"Sorry I couldn't really talk last night," Victoria says. "I was kind of in the middle of something, and also super tired."

"No worries," I say, even though I'd been antsy, unable to fall asleep for hours.

Why couldn't she say yes right away? What if she says no?

"So you want to . . ." She trails off, waiting for me to fill in the blanks.

"Manage your campaign," I say promptly.

"For junior class president."

"That is what you're running for, right?"

"Yeah, but—I want to be clear that this is ASB. Aren't you already working on, I don't know, real campaigns?"

I try not to preen, but I can't help the giddy, golden rush that bubbles up my spine and escapes in a grin.

"Barely, since it's winter. I do voter outreach letters most weekends."

"Still, that's so cool."

I'm caught on her eyes—warm brown and undiluted by the overhead fluorescent lighting.

"Thanks," I remember to say. "But I'm looking to do more. And unless I'm mistaken, you're in need of a campaign manager."

I know most other candidates don't have an *official* campaign manager, just a loose cohort of friends, but I'm serious about this, so I need someone who can, if not match my intensity, not dismiss it. Plus, for my YPBC application, I need to be the acknowledged lead.

"A single woman in possession of an intent petition must be in want?" Her voice is teasing.

"Something like that," I say. "Look. I've been volunteering for campaigns for a few years now. I'm in Graphic Design 2 *and* Intro to Marketing this semester. My Global Issues Problem Solving team was a finalist at state last year, and I'm active in the GSA events committee."

I had to drop Global Issues Problem Solving this year because the after-school meetings interfered with my babysitting schedule. Getting into YPBC will help to show colleges that I'm still serious about my political goals. Of course, getting into YPBC now requires Victoria.

Victoria cocks her head. "Do you have a résumé?"

Obviously. I open my Life Notebook and pull out a copy from its insert folder.

"I didn't—" Victoria's eyes are wide as she scans the page. She looks back up at me. "I was kidding."

"I don't kid about politics."

"I thought I got that, but I'm *really* getting that now," she says.

I hope it's a compliment. It'd better be, if we're going to work together.

"Do you want to win?" I ask.

"Of course I do."

"Why?"

"Because . . ." She straightens her shoulders. "Because I think I'm the best person for the job. I'm on ASB now, and I know how to get things done. I'm in a lot of different clubs, so I'm accessible to a significant part of our class. I want to get us that catwalk for the theater, *and* an active allyship workshop for teachers and students. And create more separation between the main board and the Student Judiciary Council. And—" She catches herself, blushing. "I care about making our community better, and not in only superficial ways."

"Well, I want to make you junior class president."

"Why?" She parries my question back at me.

I think again about my whiteboard rose ceremony.

"Because none of the other candidates has experience on ASB. Because you have real ideas. And . . ." I stop myself.

Because I think the real reason I chose Victoria over Marisa is less about ASB experience or being needed, and more about that day we went on the field trip to Mixed Blood Theatre. I don't know where Victoria was sitting on the ride there. I don't remember anyone else, just Kevin and his friend and the blurry, looming silence of all the people who pretended it wasn't happening. On the drive back, though, Victoria sat with me, her face firm in a way that told me she knew what had gone down. She didn't ask about it. She didn't make me relive the humiliation by showing me pity. We talked about the play and our poetry projects.

"And?" Victoria asks.

"I think you pay attention. And when you see something, you don't look away."

My gaze drops down to my Life Notebook. It's not even eight o'clock. Not too early for The Plan, but definitely too early for personal stuff like this.

"And I need a campaign manager?" she says, her tone soft.

"You do. You're reasonably well known and liked, but—no offense—some of the other candidates are more popular. You need an actual strategy. And none of your friends are capable."

Victoria laughs. "No punches pulled."

"If we're going to do this, we have to be honest with each other," I say.

"It's not like I disagree with anything you said." Victoria glances around the room, which has slowly filled with our classmates. "If we're being honest . . ." She lifts her chin.

I nod.

"Isn't Jade Weaver running?" Her cheeks are pink.

All the golden sparkles drop back into my stomach and coalesce into something heavy and sticky.

"Yes."

"Why aren't you *her* campaign manager?"

"She . . ." For half a second, I consider lying. Pretending that *I* was the one who decided it was too fraught for us to continue our campaign partnership after our romantic breakup. But the last-minute change is so obviously not my style, and I did literally just request honesty. "She decided she needed space, given the breakup."

I could respect that need. Probably. If she announced it a few weeks ago. If she seemed the least bit apologetic when she informed me I would have to find someone else to "write my YPBC essay for me." As if there was a single word in my application that came from her.

"So I *am* your second choice." Immediately, Victoria flinches. "Oh my god. I can't believe I just said that. I mean, I'm sorry."

I toss my head. "Anyway, now I'm free to choose the real best candidate."

Victoria nods slowly, biting her lip. "What if you get back together?"

"That's not going to happen. I didn't exactly spend last night crying into a bowl of ice cream." It's technically true: There was no ice cream involved in my literally-on-the-floor sobfest. Already, the memory of those tears has hardened in my chest, and I know I wouldn't go back if she offered. "I spent last night figuring out who the other candidates are. I'm here with you, and as you said a minute ago, I don't kid about this stuff. When I'm in, I'm in. And I want to be in with you."

I can see the moment she decides, her brow smoothing out, a subtle dimple emerging in one cheek.

"Madison, will you be my campaign manager?"

"It would be an honor," I say.

We shake on it.

CHAPTER FIVE

Thirty-One Days Until Election Day

There's no time left to talk strategy before first period, but it turns out we're both in C lunch today, so we plan to meet up then. It's not like I'm invited to sit with Jade and D3 anymore, and I have a sixth sense for days Amrita will opt for a stool in the studio rather than one in the cafeteria.

In first-period Spanish, a lot more heads turn toward me than usual. Lauren, a girl I often see with Victoria in the sophomore lounge, offers a sympathetic grimace, but most people look away as soon as they realize I'm looking back, like breakups are contagious. Welcome to my first full day at school this year not being somebody's girlfriend. And not just *somebody's* girlfriend: Jade's. Stunning blue eyes. A laugh so charming, you couldn't help but back her up, even when she was wrong. An uncanny ability to be assigned to whoever she wanted for group projects. When you were in a group with Jade, you preened: You knew you'd been chosen. You knew there was value in being her choice.

And here I was, on the outs.

There's a social cachet to dating someone. You're envied,

accepted into that club of people who got someone else to like them back. I realize that's messed up. But it was nice while I had it. While Jade was giving that to me.

Maybe, I think, *I should be in a relationship where I feel like we're giving that to each other.*

Or, more realistically, stay single and focused on Victoria's campaign.

In the extended passing time between second and third period, Mr. Braun waves me into his classroom.

"Hey, Maddie," he says.

I try not to frown. Chelsea's the only one still allowed to call me that. I'm not a little girl anymore. Maddie is pigtails and a gap-toothed smile, refrigerator drawings and not knowing what Medicare is.

Madison is the heart of a battleground state.

Madison is important. Madison is to be taken seriously.

"Hi, Mr. Braun," I say.

"I wanted to check in with you, after yesterday. See how you're doing. Learning how to drive can be scary." He smiles sympathetically.

I nod, even though I don't really want to. Driving, which millions of people do successfully every day, shouldn't scare me. Responsible, recommendation-letter-worthy kids don't dent their teachers' cars.

"So don't even think about it," Mr. Braun says, even though *he* was the one to bring it up. "We'll let the insurance companies take care of everything, and we'll focus on our work here."

It's exactly what I want. It's almost . . . too easy?

Note to self: Take the win.

Except I would never tell that to a candidate. In politics, favors are never simply favors. Favors come with expectations.

He's a teacher. Not everyone is playing your game, I think.

I smile. "That sounds great. Thank you for being so understanding."

I'm not going to get a better opening than this, so I pull out the apology card from inside my Life Notebook.

"What's this?" he says as I hand it to him.

"Saying sorry."

"You didn't have to; I know you didn't mean to," he says.

He claps me on the shoulder, his thumb a brief pressure against my collarbone.

"It's the right thing to do," I say.

I don't mention that my parents were the ones to suggest it.

Mr. Braun waves this aside. "How's the campaign? Are you ready to win?" He bounces on his toes a bit, like a little boy.

I guess he's not all that much older than us. Not much older than Chelsea, anyway. He's only in his third year here, and he came straight from his teaching master's. Last year in civics, everyone else liked him because he never took off more than one letter grade for late assignments, no matter when they were turned in. I liked that we got to design our own final projects. He's an easy enough grader that I could have gotten an A with half the work, but he's the kind of teacher you step up your game for anyway, because he knows what you're capable of and expects you to meet it. My APUSH teacher this year just wants us all to pass the exam.

"You know I'm not running, right? I'm managing someone else's campaign."

"C'mon, ambitious girl like you? There's plenty of time to collect intent signatures. I'm sure your friend won't mind." Mr. Braun crosses his arms, playful-stern.

I bite the inside of my cheek to stop myself from too obviously *glowing*. He sees my ambition, and he names it like it's my due. Even though he's a few degrees off from the desired trajectory of my dreams.

"No, I'm sure. I'd rather win behind the scenes," I say.

It's the strategy and logistics that make my heart race. And there's something delicious about the idea of being virtually unknown to most, but vitally important to those on the inside.

"If you're *sure*," he says. "Let me know if you want to run any ideas by me—for yourself or someone else."

"Is that fair? Since you're the advisor?"

"I don't get a vote! I'm always happy to help students."

"Well, thanks," I say.

I'm not going to ask an adult for help on *my* first campaign . . . but if the offer of advice remains past our election day, that would be amazing. Mr. Braun is the type to walk into Target for cereal and walk out with three new best friends. Politics runs on connections, and I could use some mentorship there.

"You should get to class," Mr. Braun says, glancing at the clock over the door. "Stop in anytime."

I'd rather stay, because next up is what *used* to be the high point of my day: the one class I share with Jade.

Marketing doesn't have assigned seats, so when I walk in, I'm surprised to see Jade sitting in her usual spot. *Why would she do that, if she's so set on avoiding me?* I resist glaring, barely, as I walk across the room. She fired *and* dumped me. Does that really mean she gets to keep our classroom spot? We should have talked about it, clearly. Where is the TikTok advice channel about teen dating prenups?

I end up sitting behind Peyton, top scorer on the girls' hockey team and current junior class president. Maybe a seat change isn't such a bad idea after all.

Ms. Melamed starts to pair people up to work on an in-class assignment. I stare at the back of Peyton's head—and her Jays Jigsaw earrings, from boys' and girls' hockey—fingers crossed. *This* is the kind of insider info I'm here for.

"And you three, in the back," Ms. Melamed says, pointing straight at me.

Peyton turns around. Her white-blond hair is cropped short, and the effect is soft and fluffy above a nose that has absolutely been broken. "Hi."

"Hey." I keep my expression normal, not like I'm hoping we speed through the assignment so I can grill her about her winning campaign. Which she won as an out lesbian. I mean, damn.

"Hi," says another voice behind me.

I half turn.

It's Victoria's best friend, Louis, pronounced Louie, since he's Haitian American and the French were colonialist assholes. He's wearing a Captain America T-shirt and an expectant look.

"Oh, hi! I forgot you were in this class." I wince. "Um, sorry."

"I'm offended," he says, speaking across me to Peyton. "I am extremely unforgettable."

"You are, absolutely. I didn't mean, like, *always*, I meant, like, today. Since I've been talking with Victoria," I say.

"Mm-hmm," he says. He rubs a hand over his buzz cut. "Okay."

"For real—your presentation on comics marketing? That was incredible."

"I'll allow it." He winks.

We're still wrangling over the wording of our final answer when the bell rings. Peyton immediately concedes to Louis's suggestion, and her bag is already packed by the time I cross the last *t*.

"Hey, wait—can I talk to you about ASB sometime?" I ask.

Peyton almost trips over my unzipped backpack. "What?"

"Campaigning tactics? Because I—"

"Um—look, I have to get all the way to physics, so . . ." She glances at the clock.

"Some other day!" I agree. I get that when you're asking someone for a favor, you do it on their schedule. Which usually isn't when they're supposed to be learning about force equations on the other side of the building.

Louis watches Peyton rush out, then turns to me with a grin. "You should sit with us at lunch."

"Already planned," I say.

"Well, well, well," he says. "See you then."

By the time I glance toward the door, Jade's already gone.

51

I find Victoria and Louis easily, both sitting on the same side of a table near the windows. I'm not sure where the rest of their usual crew is; maybe they have a different lunch. I don't look around at my old table, the one where I know Jade must already be holding court with D3. There's a tug on my gut, a regretful rope pulling me toward last week, when I knew what political jokes would make her laugh. I sit across from Victoria and dig into my container of pasta salad.

"Madison has my conditional approval," Louis is saying. He takes an authoritative bite of sweet potato.

Victoria rolls her eyes and looks at me. "You already had *mine*. Unconditionally." Her cheeks flush, but that might just be the cafeteria lighting.

I pull out my Life Notebook. "If we could get down to business, then?"

Folded between two pages are calendars of the next three months, which I printed at the end of graphic design in fourth period.

"Whoa. When did you have time to do this?" She seems genuinely shocked that I, her actual campaign manager, have come prepared to a meeting. A smile breaks through her surprise as she starts to scan the calendars.

She's so easily pleased. She really needs to raise her standards.

Just wait, I think. I'm going to blow this girl's mind.

"We had work time, and I already finished the project," I say, and smooth down the pages.

"Walk us through it," says Louis.

I jab my finger on today. March 22.

"We're starting a little late, but we'll catch up soon. As in, today. Intent petitions are due Friday."

"We know this," says Louis.

"Let her talk," says Victoria.

"You need verified signatures from people in our grade. How many are you at now?"

"The forms were only available starting yesterday," says Victoria.

I raise my eyebrows.

"Seven," says Louis. We wince simultaneously. "She thinks it's presumptive to ask people who weren't early arrivals to her birthday party."

Behind Louis, I can see Riley's table, so overflowing that one of her friends is sitting on another's lap, and someone else is perched on the table itself, their tray balanced on their knees. I can only hope her organizational skills are in inverse proportion to her popularity.

"Okay, so let's get it done by lunch tomorrow, at the very latest. Sooner, if we can," I say.

"Why, though? We have so much time. I mean—you know I know people, right?" says Victoria. "I have a real shot at this."

"I know," I say. "And if you didn't, I would get you one. But the point is, while everyone else is procrastinating on those last two signatures, turning in the form, and all the rest, you're going to be first in line. Maybe second."

"Why second?" says Louis.

"Because I gave Jade all this advice last week," I admit. Last month, honestly, but then again last week, when we were making our final preparations for the early days of the campaign. The

53

thought of that afternoon—the way I gave her my best smile and brightest plans—leaves a bitter taste in my mouth.

Louis grimaces.

"She might ignore it now. But she was already halfway done when she fired me." I stab at my pasta.

"Rude," says Louis.

"Basically. Anyway, poster spots and speech slots go based on intent petition turn-in time. This should all be in your candidate packet."

"I didn't get a chance to read all of it last night—I'm sorry," says Victoria.

"Well, that's fine. I've had the packet memorized since September," I say.

"Oh, from the task force!" says Victoria. She clears her throat. "I mean, I saw your name on the report."

I feel off-balance, and not because of the backless circles the cafeteria has instead of chairs. Jade didn't even remember I was on the task force most of the time, so I'm flattered that Victoria can reference it all these months later. I forget that my classmates are downstream of all my efforts to get my teachers to notice me. I don't really connect with anyone but Amrita here, and that's fine by both of us, but it would still be nice to have some sort of proof that everything that makes me way too much . . . is actually benefiting this community I'm floating through.

"Was your conclusion that it's kind of a shitty system?" says Louis. "Because right now with the whole intent petition order thing, you're rewarding the people who know the most other people, or are extroverts, or know on the first day that they want to run."

"*Agreed.*" I point at Louis. The task force wasn't allowed to change the rules, but our recommendations are now "under consideration," hopefully to be implemented by the *next* round of elections. Welcome to government. "You should have been on the committee—maybe it wouldn't have taken so long to convince everybody else." I switch my focus to Victoria. "And *you* can motion to change that once you're class president. For now, I know the rules, and we're going to use them to win."

"Good. Um, what's next?" Victoria asks.

"The weekend. You can't officially campaign until next week, because the faculty advisors review the intent petitions and make sure everyone is eligible."

"That sounds like a hidden trap," says Louis.

It's not *hidden*—the rules are clear and publicly available—but I take his point.

I look at Victoria. "Any skeletons in your closet I should know about?"

"Just me," she says.

Louis laughs.

"What?" I say, looking between them.

"I'm gay," she says.

I think back to all the Instagram rainbows.

"Not out?"

She shrugs. "To friends, yeah. It's not going to be in my speech or anything."

"No problem," I say, then grin. "Since Peyton's the current junior class president, it's *obviously* a position reserved for gay girls. Out or not."

"*Yes!*" says Louis. We high-five across the table.

We spend the rest of lunch talking about the campaign materials we'll need to develop: posters, buttons, and I'm definitely pushing for some baked goods on Election Day itself. Democracy should be delicious.

Thirty Days Until Election Day

On Wednesday, Victoria and I spend zero hour asking people to sign her intent petition. Victoria does most of the talking, and not just because she's the candidate: In my excitement, I tried explaining her platform *way* too fast to the first person we saw. I can't keep the grin off my face. When the warning bell rings for first period, Victoria has nine signatures more than she needs.

"We did it!" she says, throwing her arms around me.

"You know a lot of people," I say.

"Come with me to turn it in, during break?" Her voice is shy, but she's smiling like a spring-bright sun.

Part of me is tempted to sprint it over to the office now, but I don't want to risk us being late to class.

Instead, we meet up outside the office between first period and assembly. Victoria does a little happy wriggle, right in the hallway.

"This is so exciting!" she says. "It's, like . . . real now."

"Almost." I push open the office door and wave her through.

"Good morning, girls," says Ms. Morin, looking up from her desk. "What can I do for you?"

Victoria glances at me, then turns the force of her smile on Ms.

Morin. "I'm here to drop off my intent petition. For junior class president."

"How exciting," Ms. Morin says, holding out her hand.

Victoria opens a folder and passes her the petition. I've had a weird fear that between zero hour and now, the signatures would have slipped off the page, but they're all there, in blue and green and black and one—Louis—in bright red.

"Please, can you tell us our position? What number we are?" I ask.

First, I think. *Please.*

Plenty of people are already willing to write Victoria off, I know. Not flashy enough. Not popular enough. But you can't ignore first place.

"I think I can do that," says Ms. Morin, opening a filing drawer and slipping the petition inside. "Let's see . . . There was one yesterday afternoon, and then another before you this morning. So, you're third."

Third.

Not good.

I can't look at Victoria.

"Who?" I ask. "I mean, sorry, can you tell us who, please?"

She can.

Marisa came in second, early this morning.

And first, as I predicted, as I dreaded, is Jade.

CHAPTER SIX

Thirty Days Until Election Day

Part of me is smug that Jade is still following my advice, even though she fired me. And dumped me. Part of me is appalled. What right does she have to use *my* suggestion? She's trying to have her cake and eat it too. A week ago, she was sending me heart emojis, and now I'm not good enough to greet in class—just good enough to have my campaign plans exploited. A wildfire of hurt rushes through my chest, kindled by every way Jade's wronged me.

As for Marisa . . . I definitely underestimated her. Standing under the office's buzzing lights, I'm tempted to resent Victoria for existing. Like she tricked me into volunteering for her when another candidate—a capable, clever candidate—might also have wanted me.

If I'd asked Marisa, and if she'd accepted, I could be second.

Maybe even first.

But it's not Victoria's fault. It's not her fault that in our shared English class last year, she performed a poem that kept time with my heartbeat, whose ending lines rattled around in my brain all spring, making me feel that I knew her, even when I didn't. Or maybe that she knew me. It's not Victoria's fault that Kevin's running, and I was reminded of that day on the bus. I was the one who couldn't stay objective.

After the office door shuts behind us, we don't go far. We hover in front of a poster reminding students to check the lost and found before spring break, and I wonder if a winning campaign can be dug up from between sweatshirts and scarves.

"Madison?" says Victoria, her tone uncertain, right as the bell rings.

I make my voice brisk, like I've still got everything under control. "We'll talk at lunch, yeah?"

She straightens. "Definitely. See you then. Thanks for your help."

It doesn't sound sarcastic, and how she can sound genuine when I've only done a mediocre job is another mystery I'm left with as a crowd of students separates us and I'm carried in their wake to assembly.

Because of our school's weird schedule, I don't have Marketing today, so I don't see Victoria *or* Louis until lunch. I'm finalizing my strategy—I mean putting my morning textbooks away—when one of Jade's D3 bumps into me, his shoulder pushing me against my locker.

"Oh, sorry," he says, but carelessly, his lips pulled into a smirk. "Didn't see you."

"What the heck?" I say.

"Just thinking about how I wasted, like, six months of lunches listening to you talk about winning, and it turns out you can't compete. You should've stuck with Jade." He turns away and keeps walking. His Jays Jigsaw pieces—ten of them—dangle from a braided leather cord the guys have decided is masculine enough to allow them to attach their collections to their backpacks.

"*She* dumped *me*," I say, a beat too late and a notch too loud. It's not the kind of sentence you want to say to someone's back. From any angle, it looks pathetic.

I slam my locker closed and march down to the cafeteria.

"What's up with you?" Louis says as soon as I sit.

"Huh?" I busy myself with pulling out my Life Notebook and my lunch.

"You walked in with this whole . . ." He makes a hand gesture. "Vibe. Like you're a little pissed."

"But righteous about it," adds Victoria, scrutinizing me from across the table.

"Not important," I say.

"We like to keep our campaign manager happy," says Louis. He readjusts the lettuce on his cafeteria chicken sandwich.

"Uh, thanks?" I say.

He's got it all backward. I'm supposed to be the one keeping *them* happy. Like when Jade was assigned her third choice for debate team topics in September, and nothing I said to comfort her seemed to help, until I offered to make a bibliography on the apparently impossible subject. I know my role here, and unlike some people, I keep my commitments. That means owning up to my mistakes.

"I need to apologize to you." I look straight at Victoria.

"Wait, what?" she says, her hand freezing halfway toward her bowl of questionable school soup.

"I told you we could get second, and it was okay to wait until sometime today to turn in the intent petition." Damage control is only for outsiders, so I make sure to maintain eye contact when I say, "I was wrong, and I'm sorry."

"Aren't we third?" says Louis. He says it like it's *fine*, which it isn't.

"*Yes*," I say. "We should have been more aggressive at lunch yesterday, instead of planning. And I definitely should have stopped us once we hit the requirement, so we could've beaten Marisa this morning."

"I had fun this morning," says Victoria.

"I did too," I admit. "But I should have made us stop anyway. The order is too important."

"You're not the only one making decisions here. I could have stopped us too. And I didn't," she says.

"I'm really sorry." This time, I choke on the words. Not because I don't mean them, but because I mean them *so* much, from deep in my bones where everything I've done and wanted—beginning with the Rockford Lake campaign—has built me up, and now the mediocrity of this simplest, earliest campaign moment might crumble it all.

"Not to be that guy, but you can calm down," says Louis.

I ignore him, waiting on Victoria's next judgment.

"Stop apologizing. Because you don't need to. You're doing me a favor, and I'd probably be last without your help."

It's not really a favor—more of an exchange—and Victoria knows it, since I explained about the YPBC application requirement in between signatures this morning.

She glances at my Life Notebook. "In practical terms, what does this mean? What do we lose out on?"

I take a deep breath. This, I can handle.

"It depends on how strategic Jade and Marisa will be about their speech slots. Third is . . . all right because no matter what, you won't be trapped deep in the middle. If one of them takes the last slot, we'll put you first or second. First isn't always great, but most people will still be paying attention through the second. You want my best guess here?"

"Always," says Victoria.

"Jade picks first, Marisa picks closer. She'd rather take her chances on the audience getting their second wind because they know she's last than on Jade nailing her speech and no one caring who comes right after."

"I'm not intimidated by Jade," says Victoria, her voice low.

"I mean, good, because unfortunately Jade's not stupid enough to waste her first-choice slot on a center position," I say.

"You wouldn't have dated her otherwise," says Victoria.

"Smarts aren't everything." Louis is literally wearing a T-shirt with a sketch of Shuri in her lab across the chest, but okay.

"So I'll plan to have an amazing speech that will land no matter what. Got it," says Victoria, and again I'm surprised by the sincere determination in her voice.

More than surprised. Compelled, just like on Monday night when I was remembering her poetry performance. I'm starting to think there's way more to Victoria than even I gave her credit for, and I want to see it all. And share these awesome depths with the voters, of course.

I breathe easier as I fall back into my familiar planning rhythm. "For the posters, we'll presumably have lost out on the key water fountains, but there should still be space near the main stairwells.

And I'm thinking we'll want whatever's left in the language and arts wings, for sure."

"A lot of the actors will go with Zack by default," says Louis. "They stick together."

"I'm the one with a plan for catwalk funding," Victoria reminds us.

I point a carrot at her. "Exactly. And because of ranked voting, as long as enough of them put her first *or* second, overall she'll come out ahead of Zack."

"As long as she doesn't slip into third again, right?" says a sickly voice behind me.

I whip around.

Jade.

"What are you doing here?" I ask.

Jade doesn't even *have* this lunch on Wednesdays.

"Finished my test early. Thought I'd stop by. I knew third place would be bugging you," she says.

My stomach drops so fast, it's basically a speeding violation, and shame pulls my eyes toward the sticky linoleum. *Is she trying to make me look bad in front of my new candidate?* When we were together, Jade was never mean. She let me rant about group project partners without time limits and always dug out her heating pad if we were having a movie night while I was on my period. But this . . . this is mean.

I force my gaze from the floor back up to Jade. Her goldenrod hair falls smoothly over one shoulder: polished and posed. Even though she was theoretically talking to me, her eyes keep skipping across the table to Victoria, and there's a twist to her lips that's more hurt than vengeful. My shame coils into anger. She has zero right to be jealous. She dumped me, and now I get to move on whenever I want to.

63

There's a harsh beat of silence, one I should fill with a retort, but the shock lingers enough to blur any potential comebacks.

"I think you should go," Louis says, steadily looking between us.

Jade ignores him. Now that I'm listening for it, the quivering undercurrent in her voice is easy to pick up. "Turns out you need me way more than I need you."

"Actually, what I'm hearing is that Madison's advice to you was so solid, it landed you in first place," says Victoria. "I think you're only here because it's hitting you that you don't have Madison anymore. This is the one card you got to play early, and now you've got nothing."

"There's—how many days until the election?" Louis asks, glancing at me.

"Thirty," I manage.

"Thirty days to go. Victoria doesn't need a flashy start to finish on top," he says.

"We'll see, won't we?" says Jade.

"We will," says Victoria, her tone firm.

"Bye, Madison." Jade wiggles her fingers and saunters off.

I look at Victoria. Her lips are pressed together, her brown eyes serious.

"I'm sorry," I say. "I never—I never would have guessed she would do that. I'm not here to bring personal crap into this. That's not what I'm about."

"I know," says Victoria. Something about her voice is a little off, kind of distant.

"You said that was her one card, and—" I stumble as the conversation plays through my mind again, the way Victoria and Louis defended me. "And thank you for saying all that, but I don't know that it is. I can't predict, or promise, that there isn't going to be more weird drama from her." I look down at my food. I know what I have to say next, even though every part of me is screaming against it. "Which means letting me help might make things more difficult for you. So if you want me to stop, I understand."

"You are *not* quitting because you have a petty ex," says Louis. "No thank you, none of that."

"Victoria, I want to win this for you, but now—"

"We're going to win this together," she says. Her eyes refocus on me. "Okay? Louis is right. A technically middle speech slot, some mediocre poster spots—whatever. If that's all it takes to make me lose, maybe I don't deserve to win."

"You deserve to win," I say.

"And Jade just proved she doesn't. That sounds like a problem you can help me with." Victoria's gaze is fierce. "Are you still in?"

"Yeah. I'm in." Because of course I am. I'm still wired and shaky from Jade's jealous taunting, but my throat clears and my stomach stops roiling.

"Is it wrong to say I'm glad she broke up with you?" Louis says, almost sly.

"Louis!" Victoria is, for some reason, blushing.

"It's okay," I assure her.

"Do you want to . . . talk about it?" Victoria asks. "Not the logistical election piece, I mean. Like the bit where she's your ex and is more bitter than you thought."

"God, no. We've got way more important things to talk about than my ex." I take another deep breath and flip to a new page in my Life Notebook. "Intent petition was, well . . . that's done with now. Let's talk slogans."

By the time I head to English, my mind is full of Victoria's words, not Jade's. It's a good trade. But my heart is still twisted up with the possibility that I've lost us the campaign almost before we've had a chance to start.

CHAPTER SEVEN

Thirty Days Until Election Day

"**J**ade needs to leave Victoria alone," I say to Amrita as soon as we're huddled together at our usual table in English.

It's still a few minutes before the official start of the period, aka prime time to fill her in on the lunch drama she skipped in favor of the art studio.

"What happened?" Amrita sets her copy of *The Great Gatsby* next to her already open laptop.

Our teacher gives us an in-class work day for each essay, and I love her for it. Especially today.

"Jade got all up in my face about Victoria's intent petition order," I begin, but before I can explain the rest, Eric, one of our school's many mediocre baseball players, interrupts from the next table.

"You're talking about the class president campaign, right?"

I eye him hesitantly. After the *moment* in the lunchroom, I'm not feeling too friendly. "Yeah."

"What do you mean, petition order?"

So I tell him: speeches, the posters, et-campaign-cetera.

"And Victoria's *done* already?" he blurts, when I've barely finished talking.

"Yeah," I say again.

"Damn," Eric says, but to his phone, not me. "She's on ASB now, isn't she? Her picture's on that board. She's the one to beat."

I can't tell if we're on the same page about *wanting* her to win or not. Before I can launch into our campaign spiel, Eric turns away, clearly done with me, and gets caught up talking about spring training with some other guys.

"So, what about Jade?" Amrita reminds me why I mentioned intent petitions in the first place.

I repeat what happened in the lunchroom—all of it. It feels like one of those mad-scientist game apps, only instead of mixing molecules, it's sadness and betrayal, anger and guilt. Still with plenty of explosive potential left.

Amrita frowns. "I mean, that was really aimed at you, not Victoria."

"It had to do with the campaign."

"The campaign was the excuse to be rude to *you*. You're the one Jade needs to leave alone."

I realize now that the retelling made clear what living it hadn't: In my head, it was all about Victoria, but Jade never spoke to her at all. Hearing Amrita draw this same conclusion—that it was personal, not professional—makes it hurt more. I don't want to look at it like that, maybe because my instinct is for this to be about Jade's fierce competitive spirit, and nothing to do with the *us* she doesn't want anymore. I click to open my essay draft with more force than my trackpad deserves.

Amrita adjusts her glasses. "If you want to look objectively at how she's feeling—which you don't have to—it seems that she's a little hurt that you moved on to someone else so quickly."

Sometimes I hate that Amrita's dad is a psychologist. She always wants to be so *reasonable* about other people's feelings.

"I haven't *moved on*! Not like *that*." The last thing I want to do is cry in class, so I don't think about the knife-twisting ache when Spotify starts our song despite my breakup playlist instructions, or when I see Jade's ponytail swishing during passing time and have to remind myself she's no longer seeking me out for a quick smile, an assured touch. "But I *had* to go for someone else's campaign."

"I know that, and you know that. Your ex-girlfriend apparently didn't."

That's . . . weird, right? Campaigns are my *thing*. Shouldn't Jade know me well enough to predict I'd jump to someone else's? I never pretended to be anyone I wasn't, and now she's somehow shocked I've . . . kept going the way I always would have.

At the front of the class, Ms. Glen clears her throat. "I've released comments on your outlines in Canvas. You should review those now, and I'll come around to answer individual questions."

Amrita taps my hand. "Hey. I know you're sad Victoria's not first, but third is totally workable. Don't take Jade too seriously. You know you're going to come out on top."

And there it is, the best part of Amrita's calmness: Because while I'm a mess of wanting, so desperate that anxiety sometimes undercuts my confidence, she just *trusts*. She talks about my plans like they're a foregone conclusion—and not like some font of false cheer, the kind of friend whose overhyped enthusiasm makes you think they don't *really* believe in you. Amrita's so good at what she does, I believe her when she tells me I'm going to make it.

Everything feels real when she says it in that steady voice, a place where all my dreams are something like possible.

"Ladies," says Ms. Glen at my shoulder. "Less talking, more writing."

"Sorry," I say.

I almost add that we were discussing our essays, but I'm not sure what Ms. Glen already overheard. Sometimes teachers know a lot more than they let on.

Amrita ducks her head. "What are you writing about, anyway?"

"Driving," I say.

What else?

It's a relief when I'm finally able to escape to my room after family dinner, which itself was a relief after a few hours of mediating elementary school siblings' protracted arguments about *Paw Patrol* characters. Despite my intentions during my candidate rose ceremony two nights ago, today has decidedly *not* been a win. Not a good omen for my second day as Victoria's campaign manager—but there's time left to start salvaging it.

I pull up my modified campaign plan, the one I'll have to submit to YPBC with an explanation soon. It's . . . missing something. A campaign that would work for Jade isn't going to work for Victoria, especially not when Jade continues to use my original plans. It needs something more, something special and sparkling. I don't just want to win. I want to *amaze*.

Within reason. West Plymouth isn't like those schools you

see on TV shows, where the whole student body turns the class president election into some *Scandal* zone of sabotage. When it comes to elections, that is. The *play nicely, children* announcements we get at the start of each semester usually include a reference to Jays Jigsaw, because more than one collection has been stolen or destroyed throughout the years, often by disgruntled exes.

At least I can be certain my singular remaining charm makes *this* a nonissue between me and Jade—although based on her lunchtime behavior, if she could make it a thing, she would. It's like as soon as she figured out I was going to help Victoria, Jade wanted to make sure I couldn't forget about her.

I shove away all my lingering annoyance at Jade and push myself to fall under the heady spell of planning. For *Victoria*, this time. It isn't as hard as I expected. Every bullet point of the plan, every note on the calendar, seems to send a spark dancing across my fingertips. Even in its unfinished form, the new plan's enough to make me feel like I could take down hypocritical House members and walk away whistling.

I open my Life Notebook and turn to my empty-bed audience. "Here's the situation. We've got the third-pick spot, which means Victoria will probably be right after Jade for speeches . . . which is fine, because—because . . ."

I sit up straight.

Because Victoria won our school's Poetry Out Loud competition this fall and went on to perform in the state competition. When Victoria said she wasn't intimidated by Jade, it wasn't bravado. To a slam poet, a debater is just a fast-talking warm-up act.

It's Victoria who's the headliner.

71

CHAPTER EIGHT

Thirty Days Until Election Day

I haven't seen Victoria's state Poetry Out Loud performance, so I head to YouTube, fingers already tingling, like a campaign spider-sense. I find it easily on the contest host's channel and settle in. Her endings are crisper, her volume adjustments that much tighter, from her performance in our school's auditorium right before Thanksgiving break. Clearly, she practiced.

I watch it again, and again. My heart races when Victoria speaks fast, her voice up and up, calling us with her—and then slows when she slows, drawing us closer in a different way entirely. I can picture her giving the campaign speech already, inviting and electrifying.

Note to self: *This.*

It's four weeks until speeches, though, so I need to find a way to grab on to this power and inject it into the campaign early. It can be good to have something bold up your sleeve for the speech, the best kind of October surprise (or in this case, April). But some qualities are too valuable to hold back for that long.

Even though I know peeking at the comments is almost never a good idea, I can't help myself. I want to know if everyone else is seeing what I'm seeing, the brilliance and the passion. Near the bottom, one of the earliest comments catches my eye.

Congratulations again on an awesome performance, @victoriaspeaks. It was so great to meet you at the competition!

There's only one thing that could mean, right? But I'm always going to fact-check my sources.

Me

> How did I not know about your youtube channel??

> You have to tell me this stuff, campaign rules ;)

I pound out another page of my *Gatsby* essay before she replies.

Victoria

> Um . . . how did you find that?

I tell her immediately. I make sure to add that I loved her state performance. She seems a little uncertain, so I wait for her to reply before watching any of the videos on her channel.

Maybe she doesn't want you poking around, I think.

I'm almost done with a biology chapter when my phone vibrates.

Victoria

> Some of it's pretty old, but I keep it up to show . . . growth? Kinda weird

My fingers race across the screen.

Me

No, that's really cool

With anyone else, I would probably tell them to take down lower-quality early attempts. Victoria's decision doesn't make me feel like she's naive or childish, though. It makes me think she has integrity. Or *honesty*, like we promised each other at our first breakfast meeting. I add it to my ever-growing mental list of unexpectedly impressive things about Victoria Ferrand.

Victoria

Well anyway, you can watch them if you want to, although idk why you would

I frown at my phone. Victoria's not usually this insecure. Plus, she got to *state*. It's not like she flunked out in the classroom competition. Her channel of poetry videos is no doubt better than many twentysomething guys' open-mic endeavors, at least if Chelsea's stories are anything to go by.

I pick up my phone again.

Me

Thanks :)

I hesitate, then send a few more.

Me

I still remember how amazing you were last year in English

I think about that poem all the time

And the way you said it

I cross my fingers for another fast response, and for once, luck shows up.

Victoria

There's a long minute where the three dots appear, disappear, and reappear on my screen, but ultimately all she sends is *thanks*. Even though "thanks" is basically a conversation ender, I don't want to be done talking to Victoria. There's this itch in my fingers to just say one more thing, and I can't ignore it.

Me

You're welcome!

Gonna watch some for sure :D

See you tomorrow!

Miracle of miracles, Victoria responds right away.

Victoria

Haha, if you really want to!

Good night :)

Right when I've started watching her very first video, Chelsea sticks her head in my room. "I need a break—you're taking one too?"

"Sort of. Want to watch slam poetry with me?"

"Hell yeah."

We settle on my bed, my laptop balanced between my left knee and her right.

"Who's this? She's cute," Chelsea says.

The video is paused ten seconds in. Victoria's in a purple dress, her mouth caught in a half-open smile.

"My *candidate*," I say.

"Cute candidate." Chelsea pokes my side. I try to squirm away, but it only destabilizes the laptop.

"No commentary, please."

When we start watching Victoria's videos, we don't stop until we've watched them all.

Twenty-Nine Days Until Election Day

@WestPlymouthPress: Class president intent petitions aren't due until Friday, but these three candidates have already raced ahead of the rest . . .

It's kind of incredible what a good seating arrangement will do for my mood, because Marketing has quickly rebounded as my favorite class again. Combined with Victoria's poetry performances whirling through my head, it's almost easy to ignore Jade sitting in our old spot. If I've changed—new candidate, new seat—it's only because she's made me.

"Hey," I say to Peyton as soon as she's dropped into the desk in front of mine.

She half turns around, one eyebrow quirked.

"Hey there," she says.

I don't even care if she thinks of me as some pesky-but-endearing baby queer. In fact, that seems like a great outcome. Adopt me, O Girl Who Wins. Teach me your victorious ways.

"How's ASB going this year?" I ask.

"It's fine," she says. Her smile is bemused, but there's something a little guarded in her eyes.

I straighten my shoulders and prepare my pitch (again). "So would—"

"Aww, look who decided to join us!" interrupts Louis, slipping behind me.

He's wearing a deep red satin button-down, for no discernible reason that I can think of. If his regular *school* wardrobe spans from Marvel to night out, I'm really curious about what he holds back. Or maybe that's his secret: He doesn't hold anything back.

"It's clearly the superior corner," I agree. I don't let myself look over toward Jade.

"I was going to come get you if you *didn't* sit here, just so you know," he says. His voice is light and casual, but there's a faint hint of protectiveness that makes my shoulders relax. I didn't even realize how much I'd physically tensed up when I walked into class.

At the board, Ms. Melamed starts talking. I've been vibrating on an idea high for almost twelve hours, though, so I turn back toward Louis.

"By the way," I whisper, "I had the most brilliant idea."

"Oh?" he says. "Does it have to do with our favorite girl?"

"Obviously."

"Do I get to hear about it?" he asks.

"At lunch," I say, smirking.

"So now you're inviting yourself to lunch, I see. Getting pretty comfortable pretty quick." His tone is teasing, but I check his expression, just to make sure he's not being playful to cover up actual irritation. He catches me looking and rolls his eyes. "We'd love to have you. I can come with an embossed invitation next time if you need it."

"Is it okay if Amrita sits with us too?"

"Oh my god, yes. You and Victoria can talk campaign stuff or Kristen Stewart or whatever—I *need* to talk with Amrita about that still life series she did, with all the big needles and fabric."

"Louis? Madison?" Ms. Melamed calls. "We're starting now."

Instead of explaining, I write IT'S AMAZING in big letters near the corner of my notebook, angled so Louis can read it. It's good to build up a healthy sense of anticipation. You want people waiting on your next move.

"Louis tells me you have an idea," Victoria says as soon as I'm sitting across from her in the cafeteria.

I like that: Straight to the point. Gay to the point?

Today, her curls are tucked away in a bun, but there's this loose ringlet on one side that's extremely cute. I wonder if she knows it's cute, if she left it down on purpose when it fell, instead of redoing the bun altogether or attacking it with a bobby pin.

"You know Peeta's survival strategy for part of *The Hunger Games*?"

"Okay, that is *not* what I expected you to say," Louis says.

"Excuse you, Captain America," I retort.

Next to me, Amrita laughs before taking another bite.

Victoria clears her throat. "I assume you mean the part where he used his frosting skills to camouflage himself."

"Thank you, *Victoria*," I say, with another pointed look at Louis. "Basically: Play to your strengths. And we are going to do exactly that, and it is going to be *spectacular*. You're going to go viral."

Victoria's eyebrows shoot up. "Um, did you actually go to my YouTube channel last night? Because if so, you saw those view counts. 'Going viral' is not a strength of mine."

"It would help if you gave people the link," says Louis, twiddling his thumbs and gazing up at the ceiling.

Amrita and I share a look. I had to say this to her a lot in eighth grade, the year she got *really* serious about her art—serious in the kind of way even an intense nine-year-old doesn't realize exists—and then really shy. I don't have to remind her to share her links anymore.

"Anyway," says Victoria, staring straight at me, clearly in a rebuke of Louis.

"Right, I should have been clearer. Going viral could be the side effect of us playing to your strengths."

"Which are . . ." Victoria prompts.

Not letting homophobes completely ruin my day. Being kind, even when it must have been scary.

But for the purposes of this conversation: poetry.

I hold up one finger. "Connecting in this low-key way, so a million people know and like you without quite realizing how you did it. It's absolutely going to help our ground game." A second finger. "Knowing the freaking rules of how ASB works, so you can plausibly say you'll be able to get stuff done that no one else will." Third finger. "Spoken word, holy crap, how and why have you been hiding that?!"

Victoria blushes. "It's nothing."

I round on Louis. "It is *not* nothing, tell her."

"I've tried," he says. "Maybe you'll have more luck."

"This kind of self-deprecation has no place on the campaign trail," I tell her.

"This . . . isn't on the campaign trail," she says. "It's just me."

"And that's where my brilliant idea comes in." I take a bite of the pear I cubed this morning, savoring the tang and their twin looks of anticipation. Amrita doesn't know my idea either, but she's amused rather than anticipatory. "We'll do the usual, of course. *V for Victoria* posters. Buttons and a couple of T-shirts if we can—we can talk budget later. But. If you really want people talking about you—and you do—you need to reach them via social media. And you're going to do that through spoken word."

"Um, what?" says Victoria.

It's not exactly the enthusiastic response I was looking for.

"Sorry, I mean—can you . . . explain more?" Victoria says. "I don't think I'm exactly getting what you mean. Spoken word isn't all that cool. It's not, like, a basketball . . . throw . . ."

"The term you're looking for is half-court shot," says Louis. "But good try."

I seize back control of the conversation. "You're right, it's not traditionally cool. And, sure, they're probably not going to show up at state next year or follow your YouTube channel. But they will watch and share TikToks of mini pieces where you introduce yourself, sketch out a couple of plans, act like a winner. And then they'll vote."

"I think what Madison's getting at is that our classmates overall have proven they're willing to accept a contained amount of weird *if* it's done really well," says Amrita.

She would know: Kids who have never invited her to a birthday party leave genuine, gushing comments on her Insta art posts all the time. Some of them even talked to her at the student gallery opening in December, after they were done posing with their friends' artwork. It helped, of course, that Amrita was the one who designed the JJs puzzle pieces they were all quick to claim at the start of the event.

"And you can do this really well," I say. I hold out my fist toward Amrita, and she taps it with her own without looking away from Victoria.

We never tag-teamed to convince D3 of anything, mutually agreeing they were always going to be a lost cause, and it feels *good* to be us, teaming up and having each other's backs, with people I genuinely like.

"It's not . . . too weird? Too nerdy? I don't want people to laugh at it," says Victoria, sounding apologetic.

"Louis? What do you think?" I ask without missing a beat.

"I love it. I think it gives you a little personality other than 'girl who knows the rules.' The people who are going to think it's too nerdy were never going to rank you first anyway." He turns to me. "I assume we were never really going after them."

I shake my head. "I think Carter will have most of them locked down. If you look at the numbers, we don't need first rank from them. Middling, yeah, that would be helpful—but maybe you can film one at a hockey game or something."

"Pandering. I can do that." Finally, Victoria smiles.

I snap my fingers. "*Yes.* Thank you. And if the first one doesn't go over well, we'll stop and try something new, I promise."

"No need for promises. I trust you," she says. "I'm in."

CHAPTER NINE

Twenty-Nine Days Until Election Day

Mrs. Charleson walks in right as Trevor pushes Lacy down the single step that separates the kitchen from the sunken living room. Untimely parent arrivals are the universal curse of babysitters everywhere. Sunken living rooms, too, to be honest. It pretty effectively reminds me that while at noon I'm a persuasive campaign manager, for three hours *after* school, I'm a regular fifteen-year-old pretending to be calm in the face of snack meltdowns and sibling rivalry.

After Trevor apologizes, Mrs. Charleson stops me before I can head toward the mudroom. "Madison, do you have a minute? I'd like to chat about this summer."

"Yes, of course!" I take the tall chair next to hers at the breakfast bar. If I had known we were going to have a future-employment talk tonight, I would have risked wearing a nicer sweater.

In the brief pause while Mrs. Charleson sips her iced coffee, I imagine a slew of ways to accept.

"Can you remind me when you're getting your license?"

"June," I say, practically before she's finished her question. "I'm sixteen in June."

She nods. "That's right. That's what I thought. You know Todd and I love having you here with the kids after school—the kids love you too."

I nod, excitement unfurling my smile wider.

"We're starting to plan their summer activities, though, and unfortunately we need someone who will be able to drive them both."

My smile freezes, stiff as the ice that's still on the lakes, and just as brittle. I support new teen driver laws in theory, for public safety . . . but right now, they're a huge personal inconvenience.

"I hope you understand it's not because we don't trust you overall—it's a timing thing. But we wanted to let you know so you can make other plans, if you were holding some time for us this summer." Mrs. Charleson's expression is open, her eyes warm and genuine.

But I feel like I've crashed through the ice, and now the wintry water is filling the cab while I'm too in shock to make a move. It's true we never formally talked about the summer before . . . but they'd said a few little things, and I'd said a few little things, and it seemed possible. Their last after-school sitter worked for them over the summer—but I guess she must have been older.

"I understand." I nod and swallow hard. "Definitely, yeah. Activities, that's important."

"I knew you would understand. And we really do love you," she says.

We exchange a few rounds of compliments before I can escape.

It's a short walk home, but long enough that I can admit I was counting on something truly unspoken, and I shouldn't have. That's never a stable foundation for a plan . . . but it was part of

The Plan anyway. What other job can I get as a new sixteen-year-old that will let me take two weeks off for YPBC right in the middle of the summer? My parents have had enough conversations with me about college debt to know that not working isn't an option.

"New plan," I tell the curb, wet from that afternoon's snowmelt, but I don't get any further than that before I'm home.

"How were the kiddos?" Mom asks when I walk through the door.

"Same as usual," I say.

"Good, good," Mom says. She bends to check on whatever's in the oven. "Put your stuff down, but don't start anything, all right? Dinner will be ready soon."

I head down the hall, my head full of everything I had to push aside while babysitting: campaign plans; my upcoming math test. Jade.

I drop my backpack near my desk and swipe through the notifications that accumulated while I worked. Louis requesting to follow me on Instagram. A daily news roundup. Two emails from local political groups about upcoming events and trainings. Missing these trainings so I can finish my homework is probably how other people feel about missing parties when they're grounded. Everybody they like and want to like them is there, *in it*, together, and they're stuck watching the Insta Stories.

After dinner, Dad waves away Chelsea's offer to help with the dishes. Turning to me, he says, "I know you've got homework, but stick around for a minute. We heard from the insurance company earlier tonight."

I slump back into my chair.

Crap.

Even though I knew it was coming eventually, I wasn't expecting it to happen so fast. This sucks. Sucks in a way that's worse than a B minus on an assignment. I can recover from one B minus. At the end of the semester, on my transcript, no one has to know. This is real, in a grown-up way that catches me off guard.

"Bumpers are more expensive to fix than you'd think," Dad says.

I nod, staring down at the table. "I'm really sorry."

"We know it was an accident—that's why they're called accidents. We know that you're a careful, thoughtful young lady," says Mom.

Parents always say "young lady" when they want to have a big talk with you.

"We're asking you to be more diligent about making time to practice with us, if you're serious about getting your license," Dad says.

"I am. I will," I say, my cheeks burning.

Mom takes a deep breath. "I know you're not going to like this, but it's part of being in this family, and part of accepting the responsibility of driving. You'll need to cover the cost of the extra lesson, which is ninety-five dollars."

"Okay," I say, my voice small.

Ninety-five dollars is more than Georgetown's application fee, but not by much.

"Our insurance deductible is five hundred dollars," Mom continues. My jaw drops. She holds up a hand. "We're not asking you to pay all of it. You work hard, and you're responsible with your money. But we'd like for you to pay half."

Three hundred and forty-five dollars for two seconds of not paying attention. I draw a shaky breath as I nod.

I try to say "Okay," but I can't seem to speak. A tear drips down my nose, then another.

It's not so much about the money, which I have in savings. I *know* I'm only a sophomore, and I have time to make up the application fees or textbooks that three hundred and forty-five dollars represented.

It's about being the kind of kid who messes up that way at all. That's not me. I don't want that to be me. It's not supposed to be me. I got a perfect score on the permit test. I don't have the radio on when I'm behind the wheel, much less my phone in hand. Learning to drive is supposed to *help* me be a more useful campaign volunteer, not siphon off my college fund and make it harder for me to be respected by my most relevant teacher.

"Oh, baby," says Mom. "Come here. Let's have a hug."

I practically crawl onto her lap, Dad standing up to embrace us both.

"We're so proud of you," he says nonsensically. "All the time."

"These are just growing pains," says Mom. "We love you so much."

Note to self: Keep that.

CHAPTER TEN

Twenty-Eight Days Until Election Day

On Friday, I rush to Marketing. I have unfinished business with Peyton. When I get to the door, however, Jade is waving goodbye to someone. Amrita.

I stop short.

"Hi," I say, my gaze fixed on Amrita to signal that this is by no means a general greeting.

"Hey, Madison," she says.

"I'm surprised you're still talking to Amrita. I thought you were too busy ditching her for any queer girl who will glance your way." Jade's lip curls.

For a second, my mind's a spinning wheel of confusion. Then the words filter through, and my heart rate kicks up to "someone shared a sexist meme on our class Discord" levels. Nobody gets to question my commitment to my best friend. Definitely not someone I just met last year, who is the only one in this situation who's ditched anybody. Honestly, why is Jade pretending to care? She and Amrita never developed a friendship that existed beyond their connections to me.

"I . . ."

I don't even know what to *say* to that. It's so obviously untrue. And that's really what Jade wants to talk about after her whole dramatic scene in the lunchroom yesterday? This makes two fully unprompted confrontations in a row. Three if you count the breakup itself. The confusion isn't so much insult to injury as infection, ruining any chance for a clean recovery.

Jade looks me up and down, clearly finding something lacking in my dark jeans and WE PERSIST shirt. "Who's it gonna be? You've been getting pretty cozy with Peyton in Marketing. And the whole school can see you all over Victoria at lunch."

My cheeks flame. Victoria and I haven't even done a fist bump since we shook hands on Tuesday. Except, I guess, for our victory hug when we turned in the intent petition Wednesday morning. That *so* does not count.

"Jade—" Amrita starts.

"Or is it Marisa?"

"Marisa's queer?" That's news to me.

"Oh," says Jade. At least she looks sorry.

"You can't just out people!" I hiss, glancing around the hallway.

No one's paying attention to us, but you shouldn't carelessly throw around someone's sexuality like that. Belatedly, I realize that beyond her friends, Victoria isn't out-out either, but there's being closeted to everyone and being closeted to cishets, and it seems like she's more in the second category.

"Not cool," says Amrita.

Instead of acknowledging Amrita—which is almost funny, given that ignoring Amrita is exactly what she accused me of doing—Jade blurts, "I didn't think you were *that* kind of bi girl."

What. The. Heck.

This whole conversation has been a ladder of crossed line after crossed line, the kinds of lines I assumed were so obvious, we never had to discuss them. You don't out people. My bisexuality doesn't mean I'm promiscuous—and that's before getting into the specific shaming of *that* label. The unexpected breakup would seem like less of a betrayal if the aftermath didn't feel like Jade's tossing rocks at the window she closed.

"You need to stop," says Amrita.

"Why are you being like this?" I finally ask. It's a genuine question, though I can't mask the hurt in my voice. "You don't even want me anymore. So, like, what's any of this to you?"

"It's interesting to see how fast you move on." Jade purses her lips.

"Again, you broke up with me. And you're the one who made that cute-girls Snapchat post!"

"So you saw that."

"Like a dozen people weren't texting me about it on Monday night," I say quickly, before Amrita can confess to being the go-between.

"And how many of them wanted us to get back together?" Jade says.

I do a legit double take. "Um, it doesn't matter, because *we* don't want to be together. You don't even want to be friends. And if you've changed your mind about *that*, well . . . maybe you shouldn't have been a jerk this whole week. So." I cross my arms. "Not that it's any of your business, but I'm not dating anyone. Or chasing anyone, or whatever you think is happening. I can be friends with queer girls without wanting to kiss them."

"Well, this sounds fun," says Louis, stepping out of the general throng and toward our huddle by the door.

"Not really," I say, with a hard look at Jade. "Some people don't understand intra-community solidarity. Or boundaries. Or breakups."

"Better than not understanding *relationships*," says Jade. Somehow, it lacks the venom I think she intended.

"What?" I say.

I spent months trying to show Jade what an amazing girlfriend I would be, and then several more months . . . doing the same, except with kissing and coordinated outfits to school dances. Anything it seemed like she wanted, I tried to give to her. I'm not bothered by having one best friend and one reciprocated crush in fifteen years, but because those numbers are so preciously, precariously small, I hate to disappoint either. Hated, in the case of Jade.

How could I have misunderstood trying to make her happy? How could she not have told me if I was messing up? How could she look at my goddamn *relentlessness*—for her, for campaigns— and tell me I'm the one who changed?

"You heard me."

"We're blocking the door," Louis points out.

Jade flounces inside.

I stay frozen in the hallway, hurt filling up my lungs like water and pushing out all the air. I'm not a perfect person. I'm not the nicest person. But what did I ever do as her girlfriend to deserve this?

Amrita pulls me in for a hug, and I squeeze back, not ready for words.

After the bell rings, I don't look at Jade as I take my now-usual seat on the other side of the room. I keep my eyes focused on where I'm headed, where I'm at. The whiteboard in front of me has nothing to do with Jade.

"You okay?" Louis asks.

I can feel the tears welling in my eyes now that the heat of the moment has been left behind in the hallway. I shrug and shake my head, blinking rapidly. I will *not* cry in front of Jade.

"Tell me about it later?" Louis says. "If you want."

I clear my throat. "Irrelevant-exes drama."

"That sounded like some not-irrelevant stuff to me," he says.

"Maybe."

Peyton walks in with a few other juniors and glances between us as she sits down.

"You both look pretty serious for a Friday morning," she says.

"It's nothing," I say.

I don't want to be *that* younger queer kid, with constant interpersonal drama . . . but now that Peyton's here, I refocus on the kind of sophomore I do want to be. I take a few deep breaths, clearing my lungs and leaving nothing but air to ask for all the things I still want.

"Hey," I say, tapping Peyton on the shoulder. I push away every lingering thought of the way Jade made me feel in the hallway: off-balance, somehow both small and like I was demanding too much space. "Can we meet up sometime to talk about your ASB campaign and stuff? Next week?"

Especially with my wild card spoken word idea, I want to make sure the rest of it follows a tried-and-true path to victory. I didn't have this in with Peyton when I was making Jade's plans, and I don't want to waste it. For Victoria, of course, and for the sake of catwalks, but also for me.

Peyton hesitates.

"Please?" I add. I almost say it'll be painless, but let's be real, I have a lot of questions.

I can see the moment she decides to say yes, her mouth shifting into an almost smile. "Sure, of course. When are you thinking?"

Peyton agreed to meet with me after school on Monday, so my steps are upbeat as Amrita and I walk into GSA. I'm a little smug to see that Jade's not here. Biphobia and outing people are not exactly GSA-sanctioned behaviors. That little bit of smugness drains away when I remember there's no post-breakup poll of who was right and who was wrong; there's only the ongoing question of who gets hurt by the fallout.

I wonder if D3 are egging her on, because I like to think I wouldn't have dated someone who went around outing other people, or who disrespected my identity. Amrita wouldn't have stood for it, if I'd known and tried to brush it aside. If D3 are behind her recent behavior, was I negating their influence while we were dating? Or was she always talking about people like this when I wasn't around, and it's only now that I'm seeing it? The uncertainty somersaults in my gut. I thought I knew Jade well.

The idea that I might *never* know if she's always been like this makes me stumble against a table. I look up, scanning the room again, determined to focus on the awesome community in this space rather than my jealous ex. Louis has a different lunch today, but—with a jolt—I realize Victoria's here. She catches my eye and gives us a little wave. There's a pair of empty seats between her and this senior I know, Savannah, so Amrita and I pick our way across the room, saying hi to the regular crew as we pass.

"Hey," I say. "Uh, welcome? Is that patronizing?"

Victoria laughs a little. "No, you're good. And . . . thanks. I've wanted to come for a while, actually."

"I'm glad you came," I say, smiling back. Then I drop my voice. "It's not . . . because of the campaign or me or anything, right? Like, you know you don't—"

"I know I don't have to. I've . . . kind of been waiting for a sign. And it seemed like a good moment," says Victoria.

I relax back into the chair. I'm happier than ever Jade isn't here today. Victoria should get to enjoy GSA without that kind of energy.

And you don't want her scrutinizing every time you look at Victoria, a small part of me whispers.

Which is a natural thing to do when you're having a conversation with someone. Including someone whose sharp eyeliner is in contrast with their soft sweater.

"Hello, my lovelies!" calls our faculty advisor, Ms. Zhao. "Welcome, everyone. Some of you I haven't seen before, some of you spend *way* too much time in my classroom"—scattered laughs ripple across the room—"but I'm glad all of you are here. We have a heavy topic for today, so please be gentle with yourself. I'm going to turn the floor over to Xander first. They'll give us an overview, and then we'll get started on group discussion."

"Is this how it normally is?" Victoria whispers as Xander opens a PowerPoint on the classroom computer.

"It depends," I say, pulling out my lunch. "Sometimes we're preparing for an event, like Day of Silence."

"Or your trip to the capitol," she says.

I'm surprised she remembered. "Yeah, exactly."

"Sometimes we have guest speakers—other LGBTQ adults Ms. Zhao knows come in and talk to us about their lives," adds Amrita.

The PowerPoint Xander projects onto the SMART Board is titled H IS FOR HARASSMENT: LGBTQ+ BULLYING IN SCHOOLS.

I put down my sandwich. I'm not so hungry anymore.

Xander opens the presentation with the statistics, which suck, frankly. Bullying was the first serious conversation my parents had with me about my identity after I came out to them, and even though my most hurtful experience with homophobia happened before I was even really out, their instincts were unfortunately right. Xander's selected studies confirm what we shared anecdotally with our legislators at the capitol visit earlier this winter: It's usually not great for anyone, but it's way worse for trans students and queer students of color. As Xander shares their own field trip harassment story—from their private middle school, which didn't even have a GSA—it's clear they didn't have a Victoria on the way home. When they finish, confidently sitting on Savannah's lap rather than trying to find a nonexistent empty seat for the discussion, Ms. Zhao doesn't even say anything about PDA.

I never told my parents about the day on the bus with Kevin, because what's one bad day? And what's one bad day that ends well? Thanks to the girl next to me now, listening raptly and barely glancing at her food as she nods along to Ms. Zhao's ground rules for the discussion.

It's not that I think I owe Victoria for that day. I know I don't. It's still proof that she's the kind of person I want beside me during GSA. And proof that . . . what I told Victoria on Tuesday in the cafeteria is true. She's a better candidate than Jade, and a better person. By next fall, I might not care whether I've gotten revenge on Jade or not. But Victoria is always going to be the kind of person I want as my junior class president.

As kids start to filter out of the room, Victoria lingers, her hip propped against the table.

"Are you, uh, doing anything this weekend?" she asks. "Both of you."

She pulls the ends of her oatmeal-colored sweater down over her thumbs. All she needs is a fuzzy blanket and mug of hot chocolate to complete the portrait of winter coziness.

"I'll be in Chicago," says Amrita. "Speaking of which—I need to pick something up from the studio before English. See you in a minute!"

I watch Amrita leave, a little confused. Amrita's flying out tonight for a fancy young artist master class and portfolio review weekend extravaganza. All the art she's bringing has been at home and packed for days.

"Madison?" Victoria says.

"Oh, yeah. I'm doing some letter writing, voter registration stuff tomorrow afternoon. Did you want to meet up to go over the campaign videos?" I glance at her as I pack away my lunch containers.

"Oh! Um, if you want—although. I think I need some time to work on drafts by myself first?"

"Yeah, of course. Let me know if you need to bounce policy specifics off someone, or want to talk about the rest of it," I say.

I hope she does. The ideas she's been mentioning at lunch sound amazing, stuff that would have a real impact on everybody here. As a campaign manager, I need Victoria to win regardless of her platform—but as a voter, and as someone who's going to be at this school for the next two years, I really do want our teachers to participate in active allyship training.

"The rest of . . . ?"

"The campaign? Poster design, strategy . . ." I start ticking off on my fingers.

"Right! Right. I was more thinking—" She pushes a curl behind her ear. "One of my friends is having a party on Saturday. Do you want to come?"

Since it's the end of the quarter, the assignment load is daunting. But, as I've been so recently reminded, this week started with my ex-girlfriend firing me and went downhill from there. I deserve a party.

"Are they okay with you inviting me?"

"Yeah, I asked her earlier," says Victoria.

I imagine it as a campaign meme: *Victoria doesn't bring uninvited guests to invite-only gatherings.*

"Then sure, why not? Whose party is it?"

"Lauren's."

"Cool." I know Lauren a little from some shared classes last year and first-period Spanish this year.

"I can give you a ride," she adds. Her cheeks pink—maybe her car is embarrassing? As long as it's not going to literally fall apart under us, a ride's a ride in my book.

"That'd be great, thanks."

We walk toward the door together.

"It's not anything big." Victoria rushes through the words. "It's not even really a party. Just, like, a lot of us hanging out. And they've agreed to help with campaign stuff, so this will be a good chance for you to get to know them."

Victoria is inviting me to a *networking* party. With people who are already primed to like me. She knows exactly what I need.

"Campaign networking, truly the way to this girl's heart." I wink.

Victoria beams at me. "That's what I thought."

When the last bell rings, I take my time getting my coat from my locker. Chelsea's picking me up, and she's running a little late. Since it's Friday, the hallways empty fast, people scattering for the weekend and relative freedom. When I spot Marisa on my way to the sophomore lounge, I call her name.

"Hey," she says, turning. "What's up?"

I nod toward an oddly shaped nook off the hallway, the result of an imperfect building expansion. We duck into it, and when I'm confident no one is nearby, I say, "I thought you should know—Jade outed you today. To me and Amrita. I don't *think* anybody else heard, but I can't guarantee that."

Marisa lets out a sharp breath. "Well. Not exactly what I'd hope from another queer girl, but okay, then." She shakes her head, and the movement flings one of her two fishtail braids over her shoulder. "Thanks for telling me. I ran into her at the queer YA holiday display at the library over winter break, and . . . thought it seemed like a good moment to try coming out to someone other than my three straight best friends. A safe moment. *Fuck*."

"Yeah. I'm really sorry . . ."

"It's not your fault. And you're not—"

"I'm not going to tell anyone. Amrita either."

"Okay, okay. Okay." She repeats the word, like she's psyching herself up to have to reface the world knowing that someone she once trusted would spill such a secret, even though Amrita and I are the last people who would use it against her or spread it further. "I'm gonna—go. But thanks again."

"Yeah, of course. Let me know if you ever want to talk about it? And congrats on the second-place intent petition, by the way."

Marisa gives me a tight smile before heading back toward the lounge, where Mr. Braun is doing some group hug/jump/chant with the robotics team. I linger, wanting to give her a head start, and by the time I move toward the doors again, Mr. Braun breaks away from the robotics huddle, jogging toward me.

"How's it going, Maddie?" he asks.

"Pretty good," I say.

I hope I'm allowed to say that, given that I hit his car this week.

"Good, good," he says, and steers us toward his classroom. "Step inside a moment, will you? Or I suppose you've got places to be, people to see . . ."

"I have time," I say, although my palms begin to sweat.

If it's about the accident, I'd rather know now than stress about it all weekend. And I'd definitely rather have that conversation in the privacy of his classroom, not where any random person could walk by and know my shame.

With the door safely shut behind me, I shrug off my backpack and set it in an empty chair.

"Feeling good about the campaign? I noticed you got Victoria's intent petition in," Mr. Braun says.

"I think we did a great job of getting people to sign quickly," I say.

Something about his words makes me feel uneasy. I like that Mr. Braun values my involvement, but I don't want to minimize the work that Victoria and Louis put in, especially before I burst onto their scene.

Mr. Braun raises his eyebrows at me. "C'mon, you can be honest here. Third? Something tells me if you had done things your way, she would have gotten a higher position."

Part of me preens: We didn't talk strategy, and he still knows me well enough to see it's not the outcome I planned for. But I hesitate. I don't want to make him think Victoria isn't responsible.

He already knows Victoria is responsible. He's the advisor, after all, I remind myself. *He's just trying to support you.* Especially after the car accident, I want to embrace any proof he thinks I'm deserving.

"Next time," I say, with a little smile.

"But I took a peek—you were nine over. The others did bare minimum, you know?"

It's an upside-down way of calling me an overachiever, so I let my smile stretch. And yet . . . intent petitions are a first-past-the-post endeavor: Bare minimum is all that matters, and your strategy should reflect that. Marisa and Jade met the threshold and turned in the petitions immediately.

"It'll be a good campaign. It's no fun to win without real

competitors." I imagine Mr. Braun holding a mic, taking notes. I keep my voice peppy, but the tendril of unease unfurls one insistent bud.

"You know, I could see . . . Extra signatures don't usually happen this early. Sometimes on the ones that get turned in at the end of the submission period, because candidates have been carrying them around forever, they aren't tracking the numbers, that sort of thing. But obviously that wasn't the case here. I could ask Principal Anders if maybe we could bend the rules a little for you girls. A poster slot or something." Mr. Braun watches me carefully.

It's . . . nice of him. Part of me is so, so tempted.

He's offering me a way to partially repair the damage I caused by not just making us late to first period on Wednesday. By not stopping us, because Victoria so obviously loved talking to everyone who came into the cafeteria and I didn't want to cut short her enjoyment. By giving good advice to Jade first.

I shake my head. "I couldn't. I want to win fair."

Mr. Braun laughs. "You turned in a form with nine extra signatures! I'm not stuffing a ballot box here. This would be official. *Fair.*"

Victoria should be here, I think.

It's her call, isn't it? Except as campaign manager, I have to be able to make some of these calls on my own. I have to know what she would want. I have to do the right thing, for her and the campaign. And Victoria cares about honesty and fairness.

"Thank you for the offer—I really appreciate it. But I can't accept, since nobody else knew extra signatures could help them," I say. The little bud of unease curls back into itself. I stand straighter, confident that I've made the right choice.

Mr. Braun puts his hands on my arms and squeezes briefly. "You're a principled girl, Maddie."

"Thank you," I repeat. *That's* a great descriptor, maybe one he can include in a college recommendation letter.

"And you're sure you don't want to run yourself? I think we could work something out. I have a feeling you would find a way to win," he says.

The intent petitions are due to the office in thirty minutes, so this would definitely require breaking the campaign rules I pored over during my time on the committee.

I snort. "Hard pass, but it's nice that you think that! I'm more interested in the campaign process than the actual governing."

Mr. Braun smiles, shaking his head. "All right, but I would be remiss in my role if I didn't at least mention it."

"I'm good," I say.

"There is another reason I wanted to catch you today, when there weren't other students around," Mr. Braun says.

"Okay?" My phone buzzes in my pocket, probably Chelsea.

"A related reason, I suppose," he amends. "Regarding Victoria."

I frown. Is she . . . not doing well in her ASB position or something?

"Nothing bad!" he assures me. "I noticed the two of you walking out of GSA this afternoon. Students can sometimes find it hard to talk to teachers, but I wanted to let you know that, if she needs a resource, I'm here. My classroom is a safe space."

My brain stalls, then spins out in a thousand directions at once. Over everything is an airport announcer: VICTORIA IS NOT OUT. VICTORIA IS NOT OUT. PROCEED WITH CAUTION.

"Oh, she's not—no. I mean, that's really nice of you, but"—I don't let myself pause or flinch or break eye contact—"she was there to support me, since we're friends now."

"I'm glad you have such supportive friends. Sometimes even our friends don't fully understand us, or have too much going on themselves to support us. That's always hard to watch, when my students are going through that."

I imagine Mr. Braun and the young physics teacher, Ms. Tate, having lingering dinner dates, their eyebrows mirrors of perfect sympathy as they discuss how! much! they! care! about all of us. They'll trade off winning Teacher of the Year awards and always thank their students.

"Yeah. Victoria's really chill," I say, shifting my weight from one foot to the other.

It's time to exit this unexpected press conference.

I hold up my buzzing phone. "My ride is here, so I have to go, but—thanks."

"Of course, don't let me keep you," Mr. Braun says, opening the door for me. "Have a great weekend."

"You too, Mr. Braun!"

Nobody got outed, *and* I impressed him with my campaign work. All in all, a successful conversation.

"What kept you?" Chelsea asks after I've tossed my backpack onto the Midwestern-winter car clutter behind us. "New hot girl in your life?"

I angle a look at her from the passenger seat.

"Too soon." She winces. "Sorry."

"The ASB faculty advisor wanted to talk to me. Mr. Braun? The one whose car I hit?" I hate to say it, but it's necessary context.

"Is he mad?" she asks, glancing worriedly as we pull onto the street.

"No, just campaign stuff. He said I should run."

"It's good to have teachers who push you to be ambitious," says Chelsea.

She turns toward church and its empty lot.

I thunk my head back against the headrest. "I'm so ambitious, *being* junior class president would be a step *down*."

"If you say so."

We're quiet until she parks.

"Need a minute? Or are you ready?" Chelsea asks. She shuts off the car and tosses the keys between her hands. "No cars to hit here, unless you go waaaaay over there and hit the secretary's. Or is that the pastor's?"

I groan. "Do not even joke about that."

"Hey, I haven't been driving with you before."

My parents didn't think Chelsea was experienced enough to coach me, but now they're trying to mix it up. Maybe I'll finally be able to *get it* if they change who's teaching.

We swap positions. I need a minute to adjust the seat and the mirrors, since Chelsea has about five inches on me. I take a deep breath as I turn the key, my foot resting on the brake.

This is fine. This is *so* fine. I had thirty hours under my belt before the first lesson—you need five—and I never *actually* got into an accident during any of those. I wish I'd started driving right away last summer, when I turned fifteen, but my parents were waiting for

Dad's raise to kick in before they added me to the insurance policy and let me get my permit.

"You're not going to make it to DC if you won't step on the gas," Chelsea says, more wry than chiding.

I roll my eyes and hit it.

Too hard.

We jolt forward, the car careening across the lot. I resist the urge to stomp on the brakes and only ease up a little on the accelerator. Yellow lines fly under us. The trees bordering the parking lot are a blur in my peripheral vision. I check the odometer: fifteen miles an hour. Before the accident, I could get up to forty before I felt that too-fast wooziness. We come to the end of the lot, and I turn left, intending to circle.

"Whoa," says Chelsea.

"What?"

I slam the car to a stop, then turn to face her.

"Put it in park if you're not going to look at the road," she says, sounding like the driving instructor from my ill-fated official lesson.

I comply.

"So, a couple of things. One, you need to be *way more gentle* with those pedals. The car is going to take you places! Have some respect! I mean, can you tell when you're pressing down too fast?" She sounds curious, concerned, so I'm less ashamed than I otherwise might be.

"Yeah, I can tell," I say, glancing at my knees. "It's just hard. When I'm going, I want to go, and then when I want to stop, I want to STOP, you know?"

Like with Jade and the way she's dragging out the breakup drama. For me, when it's over, it's *over*.

Chelsea shakes her head. "You're going to get into an accident if you do that—a real accident. You should be paying enough attention to what's in front of you to have time to slow down gradually. And if you stop suddenly like that, the car behind you *isn't* going to have that time."

I nod. "What's thing two?"

"You need to slow down before you turn. You can't take curves like that—this isn't NASCAR, you're not a trained stunt driver."

"It wasn't *that* bad," I say, laughing.

Chelsea raises her eyebrows. "Okay, I am exaggerating, but *only a little*."

She waits for my nod.

I put the car back in drive.

We keep going.

CHAPTER ELEVEN

Twenty-Seven Days Until Election Day

Dad drives me to volunteering on Saturday afternoon, since we have to go on a county road to get there and I'm not ready for four lanes of traffic at forty miles per hour. Like I do basically whenever I get into the car, I send a silent wish for June. I can't rely on my parents for rides to every canvassing event. By the time school's out and pre-midterms primary season really heats up, I need to be ready, driver's license in hand. I'll go anywhere they ask of me, as long as I can go somewhere. As long as I can be *part* of this— something that matters, one conversation with one voter linking to the next, until you have an unbreakable red-rover chain that means your community elects someone who will protect your access to health care, no matter your health history. To birth control. To hormones.

When I was younger, all I could do was watch and hope everyone else had my back, and the backs of the people I cared about, and the backs of people I didn't know but nonetheless deserved justice or safety or basic representation. Every time they did—every time the news showed fifty or fifty thousand people marching together, or fifty-one senators committed to, at the very least, doing no new harm—I felt *filled* with it. Overwhelmed at the existence of this kind of community, this kind of care. This big, active commitment to each other.

I don't have to just watch anymore. I can *do*. I want to be present in that big feeling.

I know everybody's way into it is different. Not everyone can march. Not everyone can show up at public testimony hearings. And not everyone can manage calendars and memorize the numbers for all the precincts required to get a politician in a position where they can make the necessary vote. I can, though, which is why I spend my Saturday afternoons at the community center instead of debate tournaments.

"Mom will pick you up at four," Dad says as he pulls into the drop-off lane in front of the low gray building. "Tell Connie we say hi."

"Will do!"

Connie is the lead organizer for the Saturday events, and the one who takes most of the younger volunteers under her wing. None of the other kids from my school show up, and I don't see my political-group people anywhere but here. I almost like that—it's mine, and I don't have to think about the stuff I say following me into APUSH—but it's also kind of isolating. Compartmentalized.

In my personal statement for YPBC, I wrote about community. But right now, all my communities are separate: the Rockford Lake campaign alum who still testify at town halls on parks and the environment; this voter outreach group; the quartet of us who make up Victoria's main campaign team. They don't know each other, and other than Amrita, they don't really know what I'm doing when I'm not with them. Sometimes I feel like I wrote this whole essay about community while having limbs in so many separate spaces, I'm not over the threshold in any of them.

When I push open the door, Trish, one of the college fellows and usually one of the few Black people in the room, is sitting at a table just inside.

"Hey, Madison," she says.

"Hi!" I sign in on the laptop and drop my voice to a whisper. "Have you heard back from any internships yet?"

"Not yet . . ."

Trish puts a finger to her lips as Connie heads toward us.

"Hey, sweetie, how are you?" says Connie.

"Hey, Connie," I say.

When I first started coming, the constant use of "sweetie" threw me off. Like, *excuse me*? But she's a sixtysomething widow who runs the meetings with a velvet fist—once she's done prying into your personal life—and she uses the nicknames for *everyone*, from the grunge midtwenties guys all the way up to eighty-one-year-old Marta, who was involved in civil rights organizing here sixty years ago.

At five minutes past two, Connie calls the meeting to order, and then immediately turns to Trish to present on the day's goal. With her clipboard and dark gray ILHAN FOR CONGRESS T-shirt, Trish is exactly who I want to be in five years.

We're writing letters to people in blue-leaning demographic groups in our sister district, a suburban one in Wisconsin that narrowly went red in the last election. Normally when it comes to campaign work, I like everyone to think I'm twenty-five, not fifteen. But sometimes in these letters, I play up my age for emotional effect. No guilt about this guilt-tripping.

I'm only fifteen, so I can't vote yet, but the decisions our politi-cians will make in the next three years still affect me, I write. *I can't vote with my school in mind, or to make sure I have clean water when I'm fifty—but you can. Your vote counts while I count down the days until mine will too.*

As I address my envelopes, I think about Victoria. What would she write if she were next to me? What would I write to our class-mates if these letters were meant to convince them to rank her first, a few weeks from now? Something like: *Because we deserve a class president who cares about more things than cheering on the basketball team. Victoria cares that nobody's hissing slurs at you in the locker room before the opening buzzer.*

When I pause to stretch and pick up another set of names, Trish does too.

"When are you going to bring your girlfriend to one of these? We'd love to have her," she says.

I flinch. Maybe keeping this group separate from everything else isn't as depressing as it seemed on the way in. The personal is the political, sure, but the specifics of my adolescent private life? Ugh. Rookie mistake. Another unforced error.

"We broke up, actually," I say, hiding behind that plural pro-noun. I sit down again and start copying an address with precise pen strokes.

Having to tell people we broke up, over and over again—it's excruciating. Kind of like coming out, except this time, instead of sharing something I'm happy about and hoping others will be happy about, too, I have to tell people who *were* happy for me about a sad, crappy thing.

"Aww, that sucks," says Trish. She leans in. "I won't tell Connie

until you're ready. Maybe just wait until you have a new partner? She doesn't have to know."

"It's fine," I say, and reach for the stamp roll.

But maybe it would be nice to bring someone with me one
of these Saturdays. Other than a family member, of course. Not
even a girlfriend, necessarily.

Someone like Victoria.

CHAPTER TWELVE

Twenty-Seven Days Until Election Day

Up until now, Victoria's campaign team has been tiny. Tonight, it needs to expand. Still, I know for everyone *else* it's a casual hangout, so I eschew my campaign wardrobe for black skinny jeans and a long-sleeved indigo T-shirt. I run into Chelsea outside the bathroom, where I left my straightener on the toilet seat to cool down.

"Looking cute for anyone in particular?" she says.

I roll my eyes, even as I blush.

"I almost never have time to straighten my hair for school," I say, deliberately avoiding her gaze.

"Mm-hmm. All right, well, have fun. Don't break any more hearts."

"Jade broke up with *me*," I grumble.

"I said what I said." Chelsea winks and disappears from the doorway before I can complain.

Amrita

Social selfie swap go

She's dressed up for one of the master class events, in a pale orange dress with a beaded bodice. Her curly hair is held back by a few silver pins, and she's swapped her pink glasses for contacts. I immediately send her five fire emojis before replying with a selfie of my own.

Me

I'll buy you a Blizzard for every pretentious boy you can successfully ditch before two minutes but no earlier than twenty seconds

Amrita

DONE

Blizzard every time you convince someone to use a spreadsheet for non-campaign purposes

Me

That is way harder than yours!!

Amrita

I'm still paying off Blizzard debt from your elections committee

Let me have this

My phone says 7:58 when I hear a car pull into the driveway. Moments later, the doorbell rings. Of *course* Victoria rings the bell. I'm stuck on the hall bench, one boot on, one boot off, so Dad waggles his eyebrows at me as he heads to the door.

"Hello, come in," he says, and steps back to give her room.

"Hey," I say, jerking my chin at her while my hands are otherwise occupied.

Victoria's cheeks are pink, her round chin tucked into a fluffy orange infinity scarf. She and Dad trade nice-to-meet-yous until my right boot finally cooperates and I snatch my coat from the hall closet.

"Gloves? Scarf? Hat?" Dad prompts.

"*Dad*," I say. "We're literally walking to the car, that's it."

But I swoop up my hat and a scarf from the bench, practically juggling them.

"It's a very reliable car," says Victoria. Her tone is sincere, not sarcastic.

It's kind of adorable.

Endearing, I mean.

"All right, clearly you girls don't need me anymore. Drive safe. Home by eleven." Dad points between me and Victoria.

"We'll be here," she promises.

I can't *wait* to have my own license. It's not like my curfew will change, but at least other people won't have to hear about it.

We walk out to the car. It started to snow sometime between when I got back from the community center and now, a gentle dusting, like the sky's not really committed to it yet. A few snowflakes drift into Victoria's curls.

"Sorry about that," I say, the obligatory I-have-parents apology.

Victoria waves it away as she starts the car. I keep quiet while she backs up, one hand resting on my seat as she looks over her shoulder.

"If your dad had wanted me to drive him around the block to prove that I'm a safe driver, I would have done it," she says.

"Oh my god. *No.* Do not even put that kind of thought into the universe." I settle deep into the seat.

Victoria darts a glance at me, lightning quick, as we turn out of my neighborhood.

"I'm just saying. I would have. I don't want to be accused of derailing the early career of the next Mindy Myers due to faulty driving."

I'm glad I'm sitting down, because my insides sort of collapse into a smudge of swoon.

Mindy freaking Myers. Most people don't know she exists, but over the last few decades, she's quietly become one of the most powerful women in politics. I can't even speak. How does Victoria know I want *exactly that*? I mean, yeah, plenty of people know I want to be a campaign manager for the next Elizabeth Warren, but that's a title.

Victoria gave me a name.

"You okay there?" Victoria asks.

"I had her picture taped to the inside of my locker last year," I say, still kind of in a daze.

"I know," says Victoria. She clears her throat, carefully checking the rearview mirror as she slows to a stop.

"What?"

"I pay attention. I can google like anybody else."

It's just that nobody else *does*.

"Well." I shimmy my shoulders beneath my coat, trying to clear my head. "I can't guarantee Mindy Myers levels of campaign ability here. But I'll do my best."

"I've never doubted that," she says.

The light changes.

Her acceleration is textbook perfect.

CHAPTER THIRTEEN

Twenty-Seven Days Until Election Day

When we get to Lauren's, it's Louis who opens the front door.

"Look who decided to show up!" he calls, half to us, half to the room behind him. He's wearing a bright green T-shirt, the shade of which is frankly optimistic for a Minnesotan March.

You do you, I think.

"Hey, Louis," says Victoria.

"Do you . . . live here?" I ask him.

The driveway was covered in a fine sheen of snow, and I wipe my boots on the mat.

"Just taking over door duties. Lauren's dealing with a spill," he answers. "Shoes off."

Behind Louis, Lauren and a girl I recognize from ninth-grade Spanish are kneeling on the tiled kitchen floor, wet paper towels in hand. When Louis clears his throat to announce us, Lauren jumps up, throwing her wad of paper towels into an open-faced trash can. She's a short white girl with braces and a million freckles. She pushes a piece of hair out of her face with the back of her hand.

"Your timing is terrible, but hey. Glad you could make it."

"C'mon, everyone else is downstairs," says the other girl. Her Spanish-class name was Catalina, but I'm completely blanking on her real name.

The basement is finished with a tan carpet, two mismatched couches, and a leather love seat. Every surface, floor included, is currently occupied by a half dozen of Lauren's friends.

Who are Victoria's friends.

Who hopefully will become my allies, as campaign volunteers.

No pressure.

The greetings are split. About half of them are focused on Victoria, welcoming the rightful guest. Half of them turn to me, some overly cheerful, some a little suspicious. It's not like I'm *un*friendly with any of the people in this basement, but I get it. At first glance, *what am I doing here?*

"We're deciding what show to watch," someone says, while I hover beside Victoria.

"Did you veto the game option?" Not-Catalina asks.

"*I* refuse to sit through another Betrayal," says Louis.

"Oh, c'mon," says Devin, a stout Black boy who writes for the school newspaper and ran one of the spotlights for the fall play. He slumps further into his seat on the nearest couch.

The paper, *West Plymouth Press*, publishes every two weeks, with sporadic online content in between. They're going to do a short feature on the junior and senior class president candidates after spring break. I mean, it hasn't been officially announced yet, but they always do something the week of the election. My guess is that Devin will have to recuse himself. As Amrita would say: sad for me, good for election integrity.

"'C'mon' what?" says Louis. He flops down on the floor.

Victoria sits next to him, tucking her legs beneath her, and I copy her immediately.

"You loved being the betrayer, getting to screw up all of our plans—"

"And win," Louis says, more to me than to Devin.

I smile at them both, trying to seem amicable. Trying to seem like it's not hard to show up after they've all been friends for two or five or however many years, and I share none of their history. Everything has to be explained to me, even the little things that you don't think really matter, like who won the last game of Betrayal.

Amrita's the only person I have that inexplicable-to-outsiders kind of friendship with. I wish she was here, even though I'm thrilled she was accepted to the workshop in Chicago. We could show off our mastery of the Bollywood choreography in *Bride and Prejudice*. I don't know what Louis and Devin got up to when they were younger, but it can't have been as fun as that.

"*But*," Louis continues, now looking around at everyone, "it took forever to get to the betrayer stage. And I do not have that kind of patience tonight."

"Do you ever?" Not-Catalina teases.

The girls on the other couch have clearly given up on the conversation, ignoring our half of the room to have their own. On the love seat, two people whose names I actually know—Joan and Kyle—are holding hands, his legs swung over her lap as they both watch something on her phone. I look away.

"Marvel movies, to be fair," says Victoria.

"You cannot put Betrayal and Marvel movies on the same

spectrum! They are not part of the same plane. You agree with me, right, Madison?" Louis leans backward, looking across at me from Victoria's other side. She twists to watch me.

"Don't drag me into this. Whatever this was—clearly an issue of your own making," I say. My legs are getting stiff already, so I stretch them out in front of me and wriggle my toes to show off my RBG socks.

While Louis and Devin continue their board game standoff, Victoria nods at my feet.

"Why am I not at all surprised?" she says, her voice low.

"I'm extremely predictable." I frown. "I mean, consistent. I won't run a predictable campaign. Not a *bad* unpredictable campaign—"

"I got you," says Victoria. Her eyes crinkle at the corners when she smiles, her curls tumbling over one shoulder, half shielding her face as she tips her head toward me and away from Louis's assertions that card games are infinitely superior. "Mine are so boring in comparison. Or not even in comparison. Just boring."

"What?" I say. Somehow, I've already lost the thread of our conversation.

She shifts, bringing her knees up to her chest, and points her toes against the carpet. Plain white cotton, with a little stripe of purple across the toes and around the top of the ankles.

We both stare at her toes.

I have no idea what's going on here.

Belatedly, I remember: "I like the purple, though. That's nice."

"Like your shirt. Kind of," says Victoria, her eyes darting to my shirt, then her socks, then back to my face. "Yours is a nicer color. Not sock purple."

"Thanks. Sock purple is valid too," I say.

Louis collapses on the floor in front of us, either in victory or defeat, I'm not sure.

"You're astonishing. Both of you," he says. "We are in the prime of our youth, the next . . . two and a half hours ahead of us . . . and you end up at socks. Sock *colors*. You need supervision."

"We do not," says Victoria, weirdly firm.

Somehow around us, there's been a compromise on *Spider-Man: Into the Spider-Verse*. People shift toward the big screen on the wall, Lauren wielding the remote.

"But no Marvel in our Disney marathon over break, okay?" says Not-Catalina.

"The corporate takeover of the film industry is not my fault," says Louis. "The monopoly of media—"

"Can we please start the movie?" says one of the Couch Girls.

"I'm just *saying*," says Louis, but stops himself, like that's the complete thought, and the rest of us can fill in the blank.

Which, yeah, I think we can.

Lauren swings around the remote so it's pointing at the couple in the love seat. "Before we start—Love Seat Rules."

"I was waiting for someone to call us out," Kyle grumbles. He slips out of the chair and pulls Joan up behind him.

"Love Seat Rules?" I whisper to Victoria.

"No couples in the love seat during movies. If they wanted to make out, they should have stayed home," she says.

"Who wants it?" Lauren glances around the handful of us on the floor.

"Victoria and Madison should take it," Louis says, with a smirk that passes me by and lands straight on Victoria.

Victoria flicks him on the arm.

"You and Victoria should," I try.

"Politeness gets you nowhere. You should know that," says Louis, and then, hypocritically, "I insist."

Politeness can get you a *lot* of places. You just have to know when to drop it if it's not working anymore. I look to Victoria. Her friends, her campaign, her rules.

"If you want?" she says.

Louis groans. "I hate you so much right now. I need you to know that."

At this point, I basically just want the attention off us, so I stand, dodging Kyle and Joan's new cuddly carpet position on my way to the love seat, Victoria right behind me.

"But seriously, about the spring break marathon," says Not-Catalina.

I sit down, my butt sinking into the supple leather. I keep my eyes on RBG as Victoria settles next to me. As love seats go . . . I mean, it's not like a single chair or anything. It's not like she's on top of me. But she's not *not* on top of me either. Her thigh is warm against my own. She shifts, and her knee knocks into mine.

"Sorry," she whispers.

I flick her a smile, tuning back into the main conversation.

"Save the *Little Mermaid* for when I'm home from Florida," Joan says, her tone patient despite the clear vibe of Person Repeating Herself. Based on her waterfall of auburn hair, I have an educated guess for her go-to Halloween costume.

"People who are going to actual Disney don't get a say," Louis calls, semi-distracted now by his growing nest of throw pillows, courtesy of Devin.

"Yes, you do." Kyle kisses her cheek.

"It's okay. You don't have to," says Joan.

This is why none of them could run Victoria's campaign. It's a slightly unfair judgment on Louis—since we're in Marketing together, I know he doesn't share everybody else's issues with creativity or decisiveness—but I *also* know he's totally uninterested in the organizational aspects of the electoral process.

"I still have dibs on *Moana* at my house on Monday, right?" says Not-Catalina.

"You guys need a spreadsheet," I say.

"Uh . . . it's a movie marathon. Like, non-superhero Disney films," says Lauren, throwing a glance at Louis.

"Right . . . and it sounds complicated. Who can watch what when and where. That's a job for a spreadsheet if I've ever heard one." I'm not even going to get *one* Blizzard out of this crew tonight, I can already tell.

"This is for fun," says Kyle, speaking slowly, like I might not get it otherwise.

"Yeah, I get that," I say. I leave off the *so?* but I'm feeling it. Hard.

Amrita would let me make a spreadsheet. If we don't start the movie in the next minute, I am definitely escaping to the bathroom to text her about the ridiculous non-spreadsheet people Victoria has been surrounding herself with. Never mind the terms of our deal: If you're going to have this many friends, you need to convert them to the wonders of Excel. How will you get anything done otherwise?

"It'd take the fun out of it, if we were going through some spreadsheet like we're in school," says Joan, apparently picking up on my unvoiced *so*.

I nod like I understand, even though I don't. And even though I know all these people are already solid Victoria voters and nothing

I could say about spreadsheets could change that, I still want them to like me. It's better to have allies than unnecessary enemies. I'm trying to cut down on my unforced error rate, after all.

"Wait," I say, the full conversation catching up to me. "This is all over spring break?"

A few of them exchange uncomfortable glances.

"No, sorry," I add quickly. "I'm not inviting myself or anything—"

"Oh, you could come, you—" Lauren begins politely, and oh my god, these people have to stop just letting anyone walk into their group bonding time. Private events are private events! It's okay to have a firm guest list!

"No, *no*, I only meant—for the campaign," I say, looking at Victoria.

"Isn't the election, like, forever away?" says Not-Catalina.

"Twenty-seven days," I say.

Resounding silence.

"So . . . forever," says Joan.

If I were both five years old and standing up, I would stomp my foot. Twenty-seven days is nothing in election time. We have so much work ahead to get Victoria's message out, and we're not even allowed to do certain things, like put up posters, until *after* spring break. You don't throw away built-in prep time like that.

"You all want to help, right?" I say, amping up the brightness in my voice by a factor of ten. "Victoria for junior class president?"

"Well, of course we're going to vote for her. We're her friends," says Kyle.

Like maybe I don't understand what it is to have friends. Like maybe I am not very, very aware that they're her friends, and I'm here because my girlfriend broke up with me.

"I'm going to make the posters over spring break so we can put them up as soon as we're allowed," says Victoria. "And I know Madison's working during the day."

For some of my classmates, spring break means Hawaii or at least endless sleep, but I'll be babysitting. I don't mind too much: The money will refill the hole the car accident left in my savings account.

"Me too," says Louis. "Hy-Vee, ten to four, that's the place to be."

"We could color them during the movie one night," says Lauren.

"Yeah, that'd be fun!" Joan leans to give Victoria a high five.

I have to admit, I'm a little antsy about the idea of letting them "color" without supervision. Specifically *my* supervision. But I'm also not going to spend my days watching Disney movies with actual children only to spend my evenings doing the same thing, this time for free, with people who don't really want me there.

Well. A week is a long time for *me* to figure out how to play this.

"We're not going to finish if we don't start now," Devin points out.

We start the film.

Victoria shifts, until she's whispering right into my ear. "You can make as many spreadsheets as you want for the campaign. I won't mind. I'll help."

I smile at her, and though she ostensibly turns back toward the screen, we're closer than ever. I'm trying to focus on the dialogue, the visuals, but honestly, most of my concentration is taken up by Victoria. Her curls tickling my left cheek.

I think about Joan and Kyle, curled in together.

Me and Jade, not so long ago at all.

Me and Jade, yesterday in the hallway.

I don't want to think about what she'd say if she were here now, watching us in the love seat, Victoria's head slipping onto my shoulder as the movie progresses.

Screw you, I think.

I don't want Jade in my head anymore. She has no right to it. Definitely no right to comment on how tempted I am, as Miles falls through the sky, to wrap my arm around Victoria and dare anyone to make us move.

Twenty minutes or so before the movie ends, my phone starts buzzing in my pocket. Victoria scoots over, trying to give me space to dig it out.

"Sorry," I whisper as my hand brushes against her thigh.

By the time I manage to extract my phone, the call's gone to voice mail.

Dad. I'm about to listen to it when he calls again.

"Sorry," I repeat, practically tripping over Victoria, and then Kyle and Joan, until I can duck behind the couches and creep toward the staircase. "Dad?"

"Hey, Madison," he says. "Have you been watching the weather?"

I open the door to the main level and step into the kitchen, squinting against the light as I head toward the window near the sink. Snow is swirling across the yard in white waves that make it difficult to see the next house. "Window check says . . . it's really coming down."

I slip into the dark living room so I can see the road. At least four or five inches have fallen since Victoria picked me up. The cars are all covered in thick blankets. Though the snowbanks lining the driveway were still high from this winter's previous snow, there's a fresh coating now, tumbling down toward the pavement, blurring the boundaries.

"I'm coming to pick you up," Dad says.

"What? No." I pull my phone away from my ear for half a second. "It's only ten."

"The roads are getting worse. I thought this system would go north of us, but whatever bit of it we've got is obviously enough."

"The movie will be over soon . . ."

"I don't want Victoria driving you home, not in this," he says.

Honestly.

Let me be a normal kid with parents who aren't glued to their weather alert apps. Let me get stuck in a snowbank with a girl like anybody else. It's basically my God-given right as a Midwestern teenager.

Dad doesn't wait for me to argue. "I'm putting on my boots now. Be ready to go when I get there—the plows haven't been by, but it shouldn't take too long."

"I know." I peer close to the window again.

There's a tap on my shoulder, and I whirl around.

"Everything okay?" Victoria mouths, her eyebrows creased in concern.

"It's fine," I say, flushing.

She doesn't move.

"Are you with someone? Is Victoria there?" Dad asks in my ear.

"Yeah."

We lock eyes, and it's like I'm talking with her instead.

"Have her call her parents. I'll drive her home too."

"I'll ask her. Drive safe."

I slip my phone into my back pocket. For a moment, Victoria and I just stand there, each trying to read the other's face.

"Did we scare you off?" she asks, but with more gentleness than joking in her voice. "Too much Disney, not enough data."

"Too much snow," I say, tilting my head toward the window. "Dad's coming to get me."

Victoria frowns. "I can drive you home, right now. You should've said—I should've been paying attention, I'm sorry."

"I wasn't paying attention either," I say.

"Yeah, but you're not the one driving."

"He wants to drive you home, too, actually." I relay all of his teen-driver-on-slippery-roads-no-plows-no-salt fears.

Footfalls on the stairs. I take a step back from Victoria on some weird instinct. Louis and Lauren emerge.

"Just checking that things are okay?" Lauren says. She flips a switch, flooding the room with light.

"We had to see what was keeping you two up here," says Louis.

I don't think I'm imagining the suggestive lilt to his voice, but when I look to Victoria—to tacitly check if she heard it, too, to let her know *I* know he's got the wrong idea of why she followed me—she's looking down at her striped toes.

I go through the whole explanation again. It's harder, somehow, in the light. With an audience. It's like Dad is undermining my authority here. If I'm so childish that I must be picked up (early!) on a Saturday night, then surely I don't have to be listened to about anything else, like posters.

"I didn't even think of the forecast," says Lauren. "Is it really that bad?"

"It's not good," says Victoria. She moves closer to me again, facing away from Lauren so she can watch the snow fall, and fall, and fall.

That's part of what makes snow dangerous. It doesn't always come with wind. You don't hear it, like the rain, like a tornado siren. It quietly builds up, until you're slipping in it and you can't see the road in front of you.

"How are you getting home?" I ask Louis.

"Well, normally Victoria would drive me, but since she's busy tonight—" Louis holds up a hand to cut off my apology. "I live near Devin and Joan. Devin's mom will get us all later."

"Speaking of." Victoria waves her phone in her hand. "I'm going to call mine." She steps into the kitchen.

"Seriously, though, Madison," Lauren says, snapping my attention back to her. "You're more than welcome to come to anything over break. We'll be at my house on the first Saturday."

"And are the campaign posters welcome too?" Louis asks.

"Definitely. We want Victoria to win," says Lauren. "And we don't want her ditching this marathon for stuff she can just as easily do while watching *Mulan*."

Campaigns are all about multitasking, but usually the tasks are all *within* the campaign.

"Original or live action?" I ask, despite myself.

"I think we're flipping a coin for that one?" Lauren says, glancing at Louis.

"Fun," I say. My internal five-year-old is throwing a tantrum right now. They leave movies up to *chance* like this? Especially when one of the options is a total mess of a film? That's no way to get things done.

Victoria reemerges.

"Well?" says Louis. "Are you going home with Madison?"

Victoria ignores him, turning to me instead. "We did the whole, 'is he sure, we can pick you up' thing, and I went ahead and assumed he is sure and she shouldn't pick me up."

"Perfect," I say.

"Never Have I Ever, to kill the time?" Louis says as Lauren returns downstairs.

"I'm going to kill *you*," says Victoria.

Which thankfully puts an end to that suggestion, because I kind of don't want Louis poking into what Jade and I got up to. And I'm pretty sure that's what his goal was. We didn't actually get up to anything beyond kisses that I would be *moderately* embarrassed about if my parents had witnessed them. I didn't even want us to be getting up to anything other than that.

Part of me was still a little surprised to have had my first girlfriend at fifteen. I didn't think I was the kind of girl to have a girlfriend so young. Before college. Before being a twentysomething in a coastal city. Even when I figured myself out, some part of me expected a boy to come first. Statistically, that seemed more likely.

But there I was.

There Jade was.

With me.

"Earth to Madison," says Louis. "Or are you getting lost in some memories you'd rather not—"

"Don't be mean," Victoria snaps.

"Nothing special," I say.

Louis, for some reason, looks smug.

When a familiar SUV pauses in front of the already-full driveway a few minutes later, Victoria and I scurry for our boots.

"Hat," she warns me, catching mine when it falls out of my coat pocket.

Louis hugs Victoria before spinning her back toward me. "Be safe! But not too safe! Just safe enough!"

Victoria shuts the door behind us. My cheeks are instantly damp from snow, my breath glittering in front of me. I shuffle down the front steps, wishing I had real snow boots on. The ones I'm wearing are waterproofed, but they're not built for warmth. Or traction.

"Careful, there's a—" Victoria tries to say, but it's too late.

The height of the snow had tricked me, making me think there was another step when there wasn't, and then I'm tripping through the air, Victoria grabbing me with one hand, toppling both of us into the snowbank. Victoria basically lands on my back, knocking the wind out of me.

"Oh my god," she says. It's muffled, because her face is mashed against my shoulder. She scrambles backward, but there's no way to get leverage, except . . . by pushing me deeper into the snow. I inhale some, coughing. "I am"—she must manage to stand, because I can no longer feel her body, pressing into mine—"so sorry, I was trying—here, can you, here—"

She takes my hand, helping me turn in the snow, pulling me so I can stand back upright. The front of my coat is caked in wet, heavy snow. My hat is half-pulled over one eye, my eyelashes clotted with snowflakes.

"Here," Victoria says again. "Here."

The moment is in glistening slow motion. She ungloves one

hand, pushing my hat back up, brushing snow from my cheek. Her touch is light and warm.

"Sorry," she says.

"It's okay. Just snow."

"But, cold," she says, like maybe she's not up for forming full sentences right now.

A honk startles us both, and we tip back into a messy hug, breaking the moment with laughter.

"Coming!" I call. It sounds unusually loud against the hushed stillness of the street.

When we reach the car, I open the driver's-side back door for Victoria, then circle around to the front.

"You girls all right?" Dad says. "That was quite a tumble."

"We're fine. I tripped," I say.

Dad pulls away, the tires squelching a little as they find their grip. I fiddle with the heat and turn one of the vents so it blows right in my face.

Victoria's phone rings, a jazzy tune, not the usual preset. "Excuse me . . . Hi, Mom?"

I twist in my seat to watch her. In case she needs something. A pen. A friendly face.

"Is that . . . ? Okay, but what about if we came around—yeah, you're right . . . Well, I don't know . . . No, he's driving . . . I'll ask." She sets the phone against her shoulder. "Mr. Sewall? There's an accident blocking the road to my house. There is a back way, but the hill is super steep, and it's probably not safe to drive right now. But it's only a half mile, so if you drop me off at the top—"

"There's no need for you to be out walking in this," Dad says as we stop at the end of Lauren's street. "Come home with us for a bit."

Victoria's eyes slide to mine. I nod.

She consults with her mom again. Dad gives me a quick thumbs-up. After a few more moments of idling at the stop sign, Victoria hangs up.

"My mom thinks it'll be clear in a couple of hours, if you wouldn't mind? Until then?"

"We'd be happy to," Dad says. "You didn't get to meet Madison's mom or cousin earlier."

"*Dad*," I say.

His face is the picture of innocence.

I give the lighthearted, no-disclosure version of Chelsea's story, but then we drift into silence, the quiet inside the car mirroring the quiet outside. We watch the snug houses, the pristine lawns. This kind of snow is meant for hikes, for angels, for being young and safe and home. It's quiet and still and beautiful and you don't want to be driving in it.

I keep glancing back at Victoria in the mirror. Only a week ago, I was Jade's girlfriend. I was planning our win, that double-edged triumph, my girl and my politics rising together, and now, out of all the other girls who could be in the back seat, it's Victoria.

When we get home, there's a literal flurry of introductions, Mom and Chelsea careful to stay a few feet away as we stomp our boots on the mat and brush off our coats.

"What happened to your shirt? Your back's all wet," Mom says, spinning me and pursing her lips. "And Victoria's socks are soaked." She gives me a look like it's my fault.

Ten minutes later, Victoria's next to me on the living room couch, mug of hot chocolate in hand. Chelsea's ancient, mostly deaf cat, Joey, winds between our ankles. Victoria looks like a Christmas catalog model, all pink cheeks and curls. A Christmas

133

catalog model who is also wearing my fuzzy Sally Ride socks. Something twists in my stomach at the sight, but I'm not sure what exactly.

"Madison has been telling us about your campaign." Mom leans against the double-wide doorway into the kitchen. "Are you interested in pursuing politics?"

"Oh," says Victoria, glancing sideways at me. "Not—not really, not anything big, like Madison. School board, maybe? But I think it's good experience for other things."

"School boards sometimes get more done than senators, for better or for worse," says Mom. "And leadership experience is something you can take with you everywhere."

"I'll be one of those nightmare HOA presidents," Victoria says.

I wonder if she lives in a neighborhood with a homeowner's association.

"No, you won't. Or maybe, like, the good kind of nightmare," I say.

"Are you calling me a daydream?" Her voice is teasing.

"Maybe." The word slips out, her eyes widen, and we both seem stuck in the moment, like the word is snow beneath the tires and the brakes just locked up.

Maybe?

"A daydream—of a candidate," I manage after another second. I wrap my hands tighter around my mug and remind myself that the heat in my belly is entirely cocoa induced. *Entirely.*

CHAPTER FOURTEEN

Twenty-Five Days Until Election Day

I didn't let myself text Victoria at all on Sunday, even though I was dying to. But I know I can be *a bit much* sometimes. I've been called "a lot" . . . a lot. It stung when I was younger—now I roll my eyes. I'm too much? You're not enough. Still, Victoria said that she needed space to work on her campaign poems, so I'll hide my election-induced clinginess for a day.

On Monday, I head directly to Victoria's locker before first period. She's already there, hanging up her coat, and she flicks a smile at me as I approach. Even though it's the kind of small Monday-morning smile that leaves her dimples hidden, my heartbeat picks up a little.

"Hey." I lean against the locker next to hers.

"Hi." She puts her math textbook away before turning to face me. "Busy day yesterday?"

I shrug. "Homework, as always."

And confirming with Amrita that she's more than made up for her election committee debt, and now I owe *her* three Blizzards.

Victoria looks at the scuffed linoleum beneath our dripping boots.

"Did you get a lot done on the campaign poems?" I ask.

She takes a deep breath, and her shoulders resettle, looser. "Yeah, I did actually."

"That's great! You want to go over some of it at lunch? When do you think you'll be ready to film?"

"I need to do some more edits on my own first. But they'll be set for filming next week, I promise." She holds out her pinkie, and I latch my finger with hers.

By lunch, I'm ready to keep dissecting the campaign plan. Louis, though, puts a hand up before I can manage more than a sentence.

"Has anything changed in the last twenty-four hours?" he asks.

"No."

"Are the eligibility emails going out now?"

"You *know* that's not until after last period."

"Cool. It'll be your turn again when there's something to do, but my auntie's neighbor decided yesterday was a good day to start drama, so it's my turn now."

I open my mouth to retort—you never know what strategies you're missing out on because you didn't take the time to think through all the angles—but I glance at Victoria first. There's a nervous slip of her smile when she meets my eyes.

Okay, then.

Note to self: Take a hint.

When Louis is done with his rant—throwing me and Amrita a bone of context here and there—and Victoria has asked the relevant follow-up questions, the conversation lulls. I wait for someone else to jump in, but no one does. Like we're all comfortable . . . being here, eating lunch.

I'm startled when I realize Amrita and I used to have those silences, before Jade arrived. Once Jade was there, I couldn't shut up. I never wanted her to be bored.

I glance across the lunchroom to where Jade's sitting now. D3 are all leaning toward her phone, where she's scrolling through—something. I look back down at my food, until I can feel the weight of someone else's gaze. I think it's going to be Amrita, but it's Louis.

I tilt my head, questioning, but it's clear he's *waiting* on me. And that there are wrong moves. I pick at a sticker on my water bottle and clear my throat.

"So, Victoria. How was your weekend, other than campaign stuff?"

Victoria starts talking about a volunteering event she went to with Joan yesterday afternoon—I get the sense Joan needed a ride and wanted the company—and partway through her description, I let my eyes drift toward Louis.

Louis's nod tells me his conditional approval is, maybe, one step closer to permanent status.

"Any minute now," Victoria says. We're sitting close together on a bench in the sophomore lounge, and her knee knocks into mine.

I touch her arm, even though it's her leg that's bouncing.

Immediately, I pull my hand back. I don't *think* we're casually touchy friends yet, are we? Do I want us to be? Though this bench has nothing on the love seat we shared over the weekend at Lauren's movie night.

"You know you're eligible," I say. My tone is calm, pretending that I'm not just as eager to get confirmation of her official candidacy.

"I *know*."

Louis, sitting on a table in front of us, smirks.

I'm almost at the point of asking her to forward the email once it comes—I still have to meet with Peyton today—when Victoria squeaks and shoves her phone toward me.

On her screen is an email from Mr. Braun:

Dear Victoria,

As faculty advisor to West Plymouth's Associated Student Body, I am pleased to confirm your eligibility to run for JUNIOR CLASS PRESIDENT. Now that your candidacy has been confirmed, please use this link to claim your poster spots and candidate speech slot.

Based on your intent petition order, your election link will be live on TUESDAY, MARCH 29 at 4:30 p.m. Your link will be active for half an hour, so be sure to sign up during this time.

For your civic engagement event, you have been assigned to the West Metro Teen Dance Showcase, this TUESDAY, MARCH 29. You may choose one classmate to accompany you to your assigned event. Please reply to this email with your selected partner by last period tomorrow. As ambassadors from the host school, you and your partner are expected to conduct yourselves with the utmost professionalism. Ticket proceeds from all candidate events will go to our local food bank. The candidate whose event raises the most money will be given two additional poster spots.

You may begin placing campaign posters on WEDNESDAY, APRIL 13. Speeches will be held on WEDNESDAY, APRIL 20, in advance of the election on FRIDAY, APRIL 22.

As a reminder, the full campaign rules are attached here, as well as the instructions for your civic engagement assignment.

Congratulations again!

Warmly,
Stan Braun

Immediately, my brain is off and running about all the things we weren't allowed to do before. It doesn't feel like a chore list—it feels like a small series of victories, or at least all these touch points where we get a chance to invite our classmates into the vision Victoria has for the community.

"Okay, so social media posts right away." I point at both of them. "I have to go show Peyton the plans, but I'll message you later tonight with updates."

I stand up and shrug my backpack over my shoulders. Victoria and Louis are having some best-friend-mind-meld conversation based purely on eyebrow movements, so I wave and start to head for the media center. After two steps, Victoria calls me back.

"Wait, Madison. Will you come with me on Tuesday?" she says.

I turn around and look between her and Louis. "Are you sure? Don't you want to go?"

"Oh, I'm coming to the showcase, obviously. We have a group-chat pact, since you need the turnout, right? But I would *not* like to spend an hour selling tickets to dance moms and then another hour telling people they're not allowed to enter the auditorium in the middle of a number," he says.

"Way to sell it." Victoria rolls her eyes.

"Madison, I think you should go instead." Louis's face is very grave, for no reason I can think of.

"Yeah, I'm in. Of course," I say.

Louis shakes his head in mock sympathy. "Victoria should have signed up to do one of the park cleanup events. I hear they're getting catered food."

"Depriving me of campaign perks, got it," I say, teasing.

"I sent in my availability before you joined! Stick with me and you'll see." Victoria winks, and I laugh.

Something about the moment feels different from Amrita and me teasing each other about spreadsheets and suboptimal conversation partners this weekend. It's a nice rhythm to fall back into, one that I realize I've missed since my breakup with Jade. Actually . . . something that'd been missing for a while even before that. *Huh.* It doesn't hurt that Victoria's so pretty, with her curls loose today, a few caught under her Peter Pan collar.

My phone vibrates in my pocket, and I'm shaken out of the moment. It's a text from Peyton, wondering where I am. I'm officially tardy for my first meeting with our outside consultant. Yikes. Plus, I can't stay too late today, since Chelsea and I agreed we'd go driving again before it gets dark.

"Peyton?" Victoria asks.

"Yeah, I gotta go. We'll talk later!" I rush off before we can discuss any more campaign perks.

In the media center, Peyton waves away my apology and leads us to a reserved spot near the windows. Since we both know the whole point of this is to talk about the election, I'm not shy about spreading materials all over the table: calendars, poster sketches, three scenarios of preferences that will let us leverage ranked-choice voting to victory.

As Peyton's eyes scan over everything, she lets out a low whistle. "Damn."

"It's basically academic. What I need to know is if it's going to work in practice."

Peyton focuses on the calendar first, all my notes about when to post videos and when to have a first speech draft ready. My stomach clenches as I await her judgment.

"You know you could run the most textbook-perfect campaign and lose anyway, right? Like . . . this is high school. Nobody's constitutional rights are on the ballot." She traces the *V* in one of my *V for Victoria* sketches.

"I'm not stupid."

Peyton rolls her eyes. "I just want you to know that even if literally no other campaign is putting this much effort into exactly what time of day they should post on each social media account, it might not matter. Realistically."

"I'm still going to run it this way. The right way, the real way," I say.

"I gotta tell you, my girlfriend ran my campaign last year, and she was *not* this serious about it," says Peyton.

I'm distracted by the mention of her girlfriend. It's not that I think I can map all the juniors' romantic relationships, but I try to keep up on the queer ones.

"Do I know her?" I ask.

"Callie? Probably not. She went here last year, but her family moved way out over the summer, so she's at Wayzata now. It was too long of a commute."

"That sucks," I offer.

Peyton shrugs, and her voice is even when she says, "It's fine."

"What about this year?"

"Hm?"

"Are you managing your own campaign this year?"

"Oh. No, I'm not running again." She flips over one of my calendars, but it's blank on the back. "Anyway—you're *not* the one running, so really, what's it to you?"

"I mean, this is what I want to do with my life."

It's amazing to me that she doesn't know this already. That *everyone* doesn't know this as soon as they meet me, like it's in a little floating bubble above my head.

Peyton raises her eyebrows. "Elect junior class presidents?"

I raise mine right back. "Run campaigns. And yeah, of course, I'm going to be pounding the pavement this summer and fall before midterms. Cog in the great Democratic machine, I get it." I lean in. "I don't have to pay dues here. I just get to *do it*. It's mine. Exactly how I want it—I mean, as long as Victoria agrees, of course."

"Of course," says Peyton, not hiding her laugh at all.

"Plus . . ."

"Here we go."

"There's this Youth Politics Boot Camp I applied to. I need to run a project for my application to even be considered. And it'd be great to show up with a win already in hand."

Peyton fiddles with the stretched-out ends of her long-sleeved T-shirt. "You really want this."

"I really do."

I've wanted this so badly, for so long. Yes, it's a chance to feel like I'm doing something good for this school that doesn't know what to make of me. It's also a chance to prove to *myself* that after reading all these memoirs and volunteering all these hours, my little-kid stats quirk can actually translate into something real when *I'm* the one in charge. That I can actually do the thing I've been promising myself I'm good at.

"And Victoria really wants it?"

"Victoria was running before I showed up. I'm just here to get the job done," I say.

"She's, um . . . she's had a good experience on ASB this year?"

"Yeah?"

She hasn't said otherwise. I assume she wouldn't be running if she hated it.

"That's good," says Peyton, her voice neutral.

"You didn't?"

"I'm looking to do other stuff my senior year," she says. "We can ignore that. You want to win, I'm all about queer girls winning, so let's talk about these posters."

It's not quite the best forty-five minutes of my life, but it ranks pretty far up there.

Just think, I tell myself as we start writing all over my notes. *This can be your whole life. If you win this first.*

CHAPTER FIFTEEN

Twenty-Four Days Until Election Day

@WestPlymouthPress: Receipts are in from Night 1 of ASB candidates' civic engagement fundraisers! Were you there? Reply with a pic of your Jays Jigsaw piece!

At my locker on Tuesday morning, I'm slower to spin my lock than usual, mentally calculating and recalculating the number of tickets we need to sell tonight. It's more soothing than any meditation app.

Of course I turn around at exactly the wrong moment. Amrita and Jade are paused at the bulletin board behind me. Jade is carrying a bouquet of pink roses. When she catches my gaze, she tilts her head before walking away.

Amrita immediately crosses toward me, her mouth pinched. "Do I want to know?"

"To be clear, I was waiting for *you*. She just showed up."

"Obviously. So . . . ?"

"It's not another girl," Amrita says.

As far as I'm aware, Jade is still a lesbian, so I wait in silence until

Amrita explains. I honestly wouldn't care if the flowers *were* from a girl, I realize. Watching Jade flirt with someone else might feel weird at first, but I wouldn't be jealous.

Amrita pulls out her ponytail and begins to twist her hair into a bun. "I'm not even sure why she was telling me, but they're from her parents, since she's been so down."

Meanwhile, I have a car insurance bill from *my* parents. I can either scream or laugh, and since the hallways are filling with kids working their way to first period, I choose to laugh. "She was literally singing about this online. That is like the antithesis of being 'down.'"

And then she made a point of seeking out *my* best friend, right in front of *my* locker? Psychoanalyze *that*.

"Yeeaah," Amrita says, dragging the word out. "I wonder . . . this is only speculation. It's not like we're having heart-to-hearts. But you're kind of a lot to lose, you get that, right? Even though she was the one to instigate the breakup."

"What?"

"I mean . . . so her feelings changed, obviously, but you were so *present* for a full year with her. Texting and praising her selfies and drilling her on debate stuff. Any time she talked about a goal she had, you were there for her, ten thousand percent." Amrita shifts her art history textbook into her other hand.

"Power couple," I say, more wry than wistful.

A small frown appears on Amrita's face. "She didn't do as much of that for you, you know. And every time you were anxious about something—you still came to me."

"That's not—" I start to say, and then stop.

Because when I got a B on the Spanish midterm in the fall, I didn't even tell Jade. I panic-texted Amrita for half an hour about how my GPA was going to be ruined. For a whole week before the next test, Amrita helped me study during zero hour, even though she takes French. With Jade, I was all confidence about getting into YPBC. With Amrita, I confessed my biggest fear: that I was nothing more than a naive, presumptuous Midwestern girl whose application would be the first in the rejection pile.

It's not like I believe some rule that when you're dating someone, your best friend always comes second, in time or secrets or support. But maybe . . . The idea unfurls slowly, like a headline across a news chyron, making me wait for every word: Maybe my girlfriend should have made me feel like it was safe to not always be the very best version of myself. I should have been confident enough in us to share when I wasn't confident in myself.

It's possible that Jade is an excellent debater, an unfortunately solid class president candidate, and a less-than-stellar (ex-)girlfriend. Why did it take me so long to see this?

"You're my best friend. I've known you way longer." I technically don't ask a question, but there's a thread of hesitancy in my voice.

"I'm not complaining. I'm just saying, from an outsider's perspective . . . I think she's realizing what it means to not have you in her corner anymore. And you might want to think about the kind of girl who would be in *yours*." At this, her lips tug up again into a small smile. Like she has someone in mind.

"Thanks for agreeing to come," Victoria says when I hop into her passenger seat that night. "I've been worried all day you would cancel."

"Wait, what? I said I would come."

Victoria shrugs. "Sometimes people have to cancel, and then you have to figure it out. That's all."

"Um, I guess? But it's for the campaign, of course I'm coming!" I snuggle deeper into my coat.

"More Madison for me." Her voice relaxes. "So, my dear campaign manager, because I know you were babysitting until, like, half an hour ago, I am very happy to—for once—have news to give *you*. Good news." She grins, dimples out in full force.

My heart stutters a little. Not just because she apparently has good news about the campaign, but because of how happy she seems to be sharing something with *me*. How happy she's telling me she is to be in that position. It's nice when people want to make you happy.

I realize I want to give that *back* to her. I want her eyes shining, even in the inconsistent glow of the streetlights, because of something I could share with her. I haven't brought her as much good news as I'd like.

"Are you ready?" she says. "I'm not sure you're ready for this."

I twist in the seat so I'm fully facing her. "I'm so ready."

"You totally called the speech order. Jade took first—Marisa picked the closer—so I'm second."

Even though with third pick, Victoria couldn't have gotten a *bad* position, it's a relief to have it confirmed. There hasn't been some last-minute exception that left her stuck in the middle, and the bit of brain space devoted to this empty check box on my campaign list can now move on to something that could actually go wrong.

"Second's great. Second's amazing. People will still be paying attention—and I've seen your YouTube now. You've got this," I say.

Jade can keep her flowers; I have someone who can get us the allyship training that Jade herself has proven we all need, no matter our identities.

"I've got this," Victoria agrees. She checks her mirrors before making a left turn. "It's like . . . even more real now. I'm going to give a speech! Second! I feel like this calls for celebratory hot chocolate."

Yes, I want to say, *absolutely, right now*.

Except if we don't show at the assigned volunteering event, Victoria will be disqualified.

"As amazing as that sounds . . . we have to go to the showcase," I say.

"I know. I was just saying the *feeling* of it. Rain check? Friday?"

Thanks to a weird quirk of the teacher development day schedule, Friday is the first day of break. And Victoria wants to spend part of it getting hot chocolate with me.

"Or are you babysitting?" she says.

"No, Friday's good."

"We're on, then. And one more opportunity for good news, coming right up at seven p.m.! The speech order is set now, so it's like—"

"One thing down, however many to go."

"Exactly." Victoria pauses. "I feel like that's how heist movies start."

"I'm not stealing you this election, sorry."

"Well, I don't know if I can drive you places anymore, then." Victoria glances at me, her lips quirked in half a smile, as if to make sure I know she's teasing. "For real, half these candidates should be begging you to steal the election for me. You know all they'd do next year is complain about how boring the meetings are and then take credit for someone else's prom theme idea."

It's the most judgmental Victoria has ever sounded, and I have to bite down on my grin.

"*Are* they boring, the meetings?" The election task force wasn't, but I never sat in on a regular meeting.

"Objectively? Maybe . . . half the time. But I'm telling you, some of the stuff that happens in ASB meetings is *wild*. Like, reality show material. The personality clashes! Bylaws interpretation! *Budgets.*"

"Zack definitely shouldn't win, then. No need to add 'drama kid' to that."

"Probably not," she agrees.

"And subjectively, are the meetings boring?"

Victoria flashes me an appreciative look. "Subjectively, for me, they're almost never boring. Because I'm boring like that," she says, with this weird bravado in her voice.

"They don't always win, but my favorite candidates are the ones who are really good at the actual work," I say.

"I thought the plan was to win."

"That's always the plan. And we will." We have to. "I'm just saying."

"That I'm your favorite?" Her voice is playful, with a hint of shyness, the verbal equivalent of glancing up through her lashes.

"That's not *news*," I say.

"Just checking," she says, and I can hear the smile in her voice even as I stare out the window. Which turns out to be good, because she misses a turn.

"Uh, you—" I say right as she says, "Oh, crap."

She turns down the next side street to loop around. "I literally drive to school every single day. Wow, okay." Her tone isn't teasing anymore, just embarrassed. "I can drive and talk at the same time. Usually."

"I know," I say, remembering the *Into the Spider-Verse* movie night, which is kind of a mistake, because then I'm thinking about curling into her in the love seat, and lending her my socks, and the way I called her a daydream *in front of my whole family*.

A minute later, we're neatly parked by the auditorium entrance. It's two hours to showtime, and an hour until doors open for the audience. Victoria and I have to set up the ticket table and not get in the way of anyone holding a final rehearsal in the lobby.

We dance across the half-flooded parking lot to the auditorium's glass double doors. When I try to pull one open for Victoria, though, it's locked. I try the other one: also locked. I know they're meant to keep the audience *out* until we're set up, but we need to get *in* first. On the other side of the glass, the lobby is empty. All the dancers must be in the greenroom already. My heart starts to race.

"We could try the side entrance, by the gym?" I suggest.

Victoria wrinkles her nose. "That path is all mud right now. I've got this." She pulls out her phone, selecting a contact and holding it to her ear before I can see who. "Hey, Jules. Ballroom is performing at the showcase, right? Sorry to interrupt your preshow—I'll apologize to your coach after—but I'm front of house tonight and locked out. Can you let us in? . . . Madison." Victoria smiles at me, answering some question. "Thank you!"

A minute later, Juliana pushes open the doors for us. She's wearing tall golden heels and an asymmetrical red dress with a slit up one thigh. "Civic engagement?"

"You know how it is," says Victoria.

"Thanks for letting us in," I add.

"No problem. Okay, I'm out!" She rushes down the hallway back toward the greenroom.

"Break a leg," Victoria cheers.

Juliana waves and disappears around a corner.

"Good thinking, calling her," I say.

"I know people," Victoria says, so seriously it's clear she's teasing me. "That's why I'm your candidate, remember?"

I do.

A door at the far end of the lobby opens, and Eric, a guy in my English class, appears briefly before disappearing back into the theater. I didn't think he was involved in dance, but maybe that was more stereotyped assumption than fact.

"Okay . . . table, cashbox, tickets, and Jays Jigsaw pieces," I say.

Victoria nods to a wooden table propped against one wall, the legs folded in. "Cashbox with everything will be in the booth."

I leave her to it and head for the table. I grab one set of legs, pulling on the smooth wood to straighten it. The leg falls off completely in my hands. The release of tension knocks me back, and I land on the tile floor just in time for the rest of the table to crash onto my knee.

"Ow, *ow*."

I push the table off me, and the other set of legs clatters onto the tile. For a minute, I can only stare at the pieces. I put together *plans*, not furniture.

When Victoria rushes down from the booth, she almost trips over me. Her face is white, and she does a double take as she realizes I'm on the floor.

"Oh god—I didn't—are you okay? I'm sorry, are you hurt?"

"No, it's, I'm fine," I say, although I'm sure to have some nasty bruises tomorrow. That's not my main concern right now. "Is there another table in the greenroom?"

"I—I don't know, but—" She sits down next to me and spins the cashbox in my direction.

The cash is there.

The jigsaw pieces are not.

CHAPTER SIXTEEN

Twenty-Four Days Until Election Day

This can't be happening.

I grab each set of bills from the cashbox: ones, fives, tens. I riffle through the red tickets. No metal wings hiding beneath. No metal puzzle pieces hiding between. The whole reason anybody from the sophomore class—*everybody* from the sophomore class—would come tonight, pay for a ticket, and give us a shot at those extra poster spots . . . has vanished.

Think.

"Okay . . . do you know the stage manager tonight? Can you text them, make sure the pieces made it into the cashbox?"

"On it," says Victoria, and pulls out her phone again.

There's probably a simple explanation for this. The stage manager forgot the JJs are still in their bag backstage, and in three minutes we'll laugh about this. We have three minutes, right?

I check my phone. We have fifty.

"She says the pieces were there when she left the box."

"When was that?"

"Like, fifteen minutes ago. She went to deal with some props thing backstage." Victoria's tone is tense, and I scramble to think.

"Who else was up there? It's just us and the dancers and the crew, right?"

"I don't know."

That's my cue to start coming up with solutions.

"Let's check the booth again. Maybe the pieces were never actually in the cashbox. Maybe they were in a bag that fell . . . somewhere."

We head into the sound booth, my knee protesting with every stair. The JJs pieces are nowhere to be found, and with every crossed-out possibility—under the Skittles wrappers, between the soundboard and the wall, by a cramped bookshelf filled with lighting manuals and old scripts—I can feel the panic creeping back in. Am I destined to ruin every campaign milestone Victoria needs to nail? I need to fix this, *fast*.

Proclaiming defeat, we retreat to the lobby bench built into the wall near the sound booth door. The broken table on the floor only serves to remind me how quickly this "easy" assignment has fallen apart.

"I mean, do we really need the pieces now? We'll write down sophomores' names when they pay for their tickets, and we can hand them out . . . tomorrow, or whenever we find them," I say.

Victoria frowns at her phone, lit up with a new series of messages. "Um . . . I don't think that's an option."

She shows me her screen: Louis has sent her someone's Insta Story, a creator-mode sentence that reads, *Heard from a friend at the auditorium that there won't be Jays Jigsaw pieces at the showcase!*

Next Story: *Might crash the freshman event tonight instead, who's with me?!*

The *West Plymouth Press* Insta account is tagged in both.

My head jerks up, like I'm going to find the source right in front of us, but the lobby is as empty as it was a minute ago.

"Who sent that?"

Victoria navigates to the right profile. "No idea. There's no name in the handle or bio. And they only have two posts, both from today." She angles her phone toward me. "Twenty followers, but their post about some baseball thing got forty-six likes."

"Bet you every single dollar we raise—no, every single dollar Riley raised last night—that whoever made that account is behind this somehow."

"As in . . . they're not just lost?"

"The cash and the tickets are where they're supposed to be. The pieces aren't, and *this brand-new account* knows about that? That's not a coincidence. That's sabotage."

Victoria looks down. "If people think they can't get JJs here . . . they're not going to come."

I'm tempted to comfort her—put my hand on hers, something—but it wouldn't *solve* this. "Yeah. So first thing we need to do is call it out as a false rumor."

"But we *don't* have them. It's true."

"It won't be true in forty-five minutes. Fix the rumor, then the problem," I say.

Victoria makes a quick post on Insta, which I share before writing my own clarifying tweet. I tag the *West Plymouth Press* account for good measure.

Technically, we're lying. And technically, in a real campaign, I wouldn't approve of this strategy. But someone *took* our pieces, the incentive for non-dance kids to come and buy tickets—and vault Victoria to the top of the fundraising list.

Victoria puts down her phone. "Okay, so . . . the rumor's dealt with."

Which means it's time to fix the real problem.

"Good, um, give me a minute to think."

Victoria shoots me a weird look. "And I'll sit here staring into space while you do that?"

"I know it might not seem like it so far, but I'm actually good at fixing stuff." My tone is spiky with defensiveness, and I glance at the broken table. "Well. Not literal fixing like *that*. General problem-solving."

"We're a team, right? A campaign *team*."

"Yeah . . ."

"So that means I do my share of problem-solving. And, uh, I *am* good at fixing stuff. Literally." Victoria smiles, not enough to provoke her dimples, but still a smile.

"Literally?"

"Literally. Someone loosened the screws on the table, that's all. So here's my plan: I go to the woodshop, get the screwdriver, fix the table. You keep brainstorming some JJs solutions," she says.

"You won't be able to get in—that whole wing gets closed off after-hours."

"I've got the access code, and I can get the master room key from the stage manager." Victoria smirks. "Techie perks."

"Sounds like you don't need me at all," I try to joke.

Someone else might have rolled their eyes, but Victoria's expression turns gentle. "Back in five."

"Hurry."

Victoria dashes off down the hall.

I look out at the empty lobby. So quietly I'm barely making noise at all, I start, "Here's the situation. Jays Jigsaw pieces are made in big batches at the start of the year. The pieces meant for all of tonight's events were fully distributed, so we need to . . ."

We need to find a way to make more. Victoria might know the stage crew, the dancers, and current ASB members, but I know the designer.

"Sunny?" says Amrita when she answers the FaceTime call. "Aren't you setting up for the showcase?"

"Trying to. Do you have a secret stash of night-two wing pieces?"

She shakes her head, her curls bouncing out of frame.

"Okay, great, cool . . . Um, any way to make at least three hundred in the next forty-five minutes? Because ours were stolen, someone leaked it, and we need proof we've got them ASAP or people won't show."

"I'm on my way." She stands up, keeping her phone in one hand as she starts digging around her desk for something. "Can we even get into the shop?"

"Victoria's on it. What can we do to set up?"

"I'm going to text you a high-res photo of the full design. You'll need to make a stencil from that, and find some quick-dry metal paint. West Plymouth blue." Amrita practically flies down the stairs toward her garage. "Driving now!"

Ten seconds later, design received and lobby door wedged open with a table leg, I run after Victoria, the locked cashbox in my arms. I smile when I realize she did for me what I've just done for Amrita: propped open the door into the main part of the school so I don't have to wait for her to let me in. As I turn the corner toward the shop, Victoria almost crashes into me, darting aside at the last second while clutching an electric screwdriver and two pairs of safety goggles.

"Back to the shop," I say, panting. "Amrita's coming."

"Amrita?"

"She's this year's creator, remember? She's going to help us make more."

Victoria doesn't turn. "But . . . it's not her campaign."

"If you and I are a team, then Amrita and I are definitely a team," I say.

She hesitates as if Amrita isn't already on her way. "It's a lot to ask, last minute . . ."

"You show up for the people who matter, right? I've done the same for her."

Victoria unlocks the shop doors again.

As I explain the basics of Amrita's solution, Victoria pulls out the supplies: small, thin sheets of metal "stock" that make up the puzzle pieces; cardstock and a pencil for the stencil; the right paint. I settle on a stool with one of the metal squares, Amrita's design pulled up on my phone. Thank *god* she decided to go with a minimalist approach. I've barely finished the stencil—determining the scale factor from the photo to the cardstock is trickier than anticipated—when Amrita power-walks into the shop.

"We're not going to have enough by doors-open," she says. She doesn't pause for breath, heading straight for the hydraulic press. "But we will have enough by the end of the night. You just need some now so they know you're good for it, right?"

Amrita pulls out the two "sets" from her bag, the top-bottom pairs that will attach to the press and shape the original metal

159

squares into the puzzle pieces. She fits the set parts into the press, then takes the first piece of raw metal from Victoria's stack.

"Order of operations: two sets, hand sand, then paint. Normally I'd stick them into a vibratory tumbler to deal with the sharp edges, but the shop doesn't have one and it takes a few hours anyway. Madison?" Amrita says, waving one hand without looking away from the machine.

Planning time. My turn.

We don't know exactly what happened earlier, and we aren't sure what's going to happen in half an hour, but for a brief period of time, my plan runs like clockwork: Amrita makes the pieces; Victoria sands; I paint. Once a few pieces are dried, I post photos from all of our social media accounts, JJs strategically arranged in the cashbox so it doesn't look like we're posting from the shop. At five minutes to doors-open, Victoria and I rush back to the lobby with the shaped puzzle pieces—sanded, painted, or otherwise. My knee hurts with each step, but we don't have time to slow down.

"How long?" Victoria asks, skidding to a stop in front of the disassembled table. Her cheeks are flushed, and several curls have escaped her once-tidy braid.

"Three minutes."

A few people have already started to gather outside, since Amrita unpropped the lobby door when she came in.

"Easy. You hold, I'll screw." She kneels down by the table, and I wince as I join her on the floor.

Victoria makes a sharp, sympathetic noise. "Probably shouldn't have been running all over the school."

"It's just a bruise."

"Still—I'm taking the screwdriver back on my own."

I don't argue with her. She hands me the spare set of safety glasses. I'm sure I look ridiculous, but she looks cute. Her movements are assured as she arranges the first set of table legs against the upside-down top. Once they're positioned how she wants, I hold the legs steady. I should be watching the electric screwdriver exclusively, but of course I'm distracted by her hands, and from there it's only another second before my eyes are helplessly drawn up the sure line of her arms, and then to the focus in her eyes. It's a good look on her. A *really* good look on her. I force my gaze down again.

A few screws later, we switch to the other side. When it's done, my eyes meet hers over the still-turtled table, our faces mirror images of relief.

An alarm goes off on my phone, startling us out of the moment.

"Time?"

"One minute," I say.

Victoria offers me a hand up, which I take. Together, we flip the table over, then carry it across the lobby so it's situated between the outside doors and the auditorium. Too late, we realize there aren't any chairs for us, but we need to start letting in the audience *now*.

"I'll get the doors," Victoria says.

"Wait."

I reach out and pluck her safety glasses off. My thumb brushes her cheek, soft and warm beneath my skin.

"Oh, right." She blushes.

I fold both pairs next to the cashbox on the table. Two dozen completed JJs shine from a Ziploc bag. It's not nearly enough—I hope—but at least the early arrivals can post that some exist. We'll have the rest waiting when the showcase is over.

Victoria glances over her shoulder to the waiting attendees. Her smile smooths into something welcoming but neutral. She walks backward toward the entrance, still looking at me. "And then after this, we can figure out what happened."

It's an hour of pure chaos. At first, Victoria sands while I make change and distribute tickets, and then we swap so I can finish painting. Right before showtime, Amrita emerges with the remaining pieces. I hate having to finish them in the open, where everyone can see there obviously *was* an issue with the pieces, but since the shape is right and the metal legit, only a few people complain once we run out.

"Just bring your ticket to the table after the show. We'll be here, we'll have enough," Victoria says for what feels like the hundredth time.

I hope it's the hundredth time. More people, more money for the fundraiser, more chance of leading the pack and solidifying Victoria's status as a front-runner. I recognize a dozen art kids from Amrita's school exhibits, some fellow ASB committee alums, and the leads of the fall play. Louis rushes in with Lauren and Devin, but the rest of the movie night crew doesn't show.

Even though there's more work to do, it's a relief to wave the last audience member inside and close the auditorium doors behind them. At least, I think it's the last person, until Mr. Braun emerges from the hallway. I tense, and my fingers grip the edge of the table hard. What is he going to think of our less-than-perfect showing? Will this be something else he believes I could've done better without Victoria? Which I couldn't have. Theaters are her turf, and it's her keys that got us into the shop and her screwdriver that means I have a table to grip in the first place.

"Very nice job, girls," he says as he walks toward us. He hands me a five-dollar bill, which I put in the cashbox while Victoria passes him a ticket.

"Thanks," I say.

Mr. Braun looks down at the pile of half-finished JJs, then back at us. "This is . . . unusual."

I wince. Two minutes ago, I was proud of what we'd accomplished, and now shame at the thrown-together offerings threatens to stifle the sweetness of that victory. I've read a hundred times that campaign managers have to be able to think on their feet, but I worry that Mr. Braun will see the pieces and dismiss them as unprofessional.

"We had to improvise," says Victoria. "But Amrita's the original designer, you know, so. It's all legit."

Mr. Braun lifts up one of the pieces for closer inspection. "For an improvisation, it looks good."

Phew. I'll absolutely take that.

"Madison came through with the last-minute stencil." Victoria smiles at me.

"A stencil must have been a breeze compared to your usual

marketing work. I've seen your recent logo design on the display board. For an LGBTQ youth center, I believe? Very well done."

I relax enough to smile again. The logo was for a graphic design project, now showcased on the wall outside the lab as part of my teacher's rotating display of the best work. My parents try to be supportive, but they don't really get my drive, and especially not the specificity of my dream. Mr. Braun's praise helps me feel that I can actually make this happen. Like I've got that something special it takes to break out of Midwestern obscurity and land feetfirst in all the rooms where it happens.

I thank him again before he slips inside the auditorium. Now that the lobby is truly empty except for us, we pull the table back toward the bench and sit down.

"You should go in and watch," I tell Amrita.

"I can help finish these," she says.

"You've already done *way* more than I could have asked for. We've got this," says Victoria. She glances at me. "You could go watch, too, if you wanted."

"What? No, I'm your official partner for this, right?"

"Yeah, but . . . I feel like I've asked too much of you already tonight," she says.

"I *want* to be too much. I mean, I could have done without these specifics, but . . ."

Amrita waves a five-dollar bill in front of us. "One ticket, please."

I roll my eyes as I hand her the ticket. "Don't forget to come back at the end to collect your JJs piece."

"So thoughtful, thanks for the reminder." Amrita winks and heads inside.

"She . . . one hundred percent saved my ass tonight," says

164

Victoria. She pushes a smooth piece toward me, and I arrange the stencil.

"She does that sometimes. Luckily we've agreed that full-on ass saving doesn't count for Blizzard debt purposes." Although if it did, I might still be coasting on the time I spent six hours helping Amrita redo a hanging installation after construction vibrated the ceiling enough to knock everything out of place.

"Blizzard debt?"

It's my first time explaining our system to anyone else, and I'm afraid Victoria will think it's ridiculous, this ever-evolving series of bets whenever one of us has to face off, solo, against the ridiculous, illogical, and frequently discriminatory world, with Dairy Queen as the reward for survival and/or triumph. But when Victoria laughs, she seems delighted, not disdainful.

Finishing the Jays Jigsaw pieces takes the whole first half of the showcase. When the last one is finally drying, I roll out my neck and shoulders. As the stress ebbs out of my limbs, the satisfaction remains. With Jade, I took pride in being the one to offer solutions, who could unveil a solved problem like a magician in front of an appreciative audience. It feels good to have built this one (literally) with Victoria.

After a few minutes of shared exhausted silence, I pull out my phone. The anonymous account who originally posted about the missing JJs is now locked. Out of habit, I check my email next. When I see a new message from the YPBC admissions officer, my stomach clenches.

"Madison?" Victoria says.

Already done scanning the brief email, I sink back against the wall, still worn out but also still satisfied. "The new plans for your campaign were accepted by the boot camp for my application. So now . . . let's win while I wait to hear back."

"Deal. Can I just say again how *cool* it is that you're applying? It's—super impressive. You're going to be amazing." Victoria hesitates, then asks, "Is that what your babysitting money is for? The boot camp? Feel free to tell me it's none of my business."

"No, or not really—they have financial aid. I had to turn in those forms with my original application. But I've heard that some years they don't cover the flights, so yeah, definitely not looking to lose my job," I say.

I'm not ashamed to shop sales or have a small house. It's not like I don't have everything I need and enough of what I want, and I honestly don't mind babysitting. Little kids love it when you know obscure facts about your niche areas of interest, and I admit there's kind of a rush when they explain something back to you that you first explained to *them*. Especially when it's something like how boys can like pink or girls can play with trucks—or power tools.

"You're going to run so many great campaigns, I know it. Thanks for letting me be your first," says Victoria.

"It's a mutual letting for sure. You could have said no."

"I was not going to say no to you! In fact, I wish I'd asked you." I'm startled by this. "Yeah?"

"Yeah. I want to win, you want to make someone win . . ."

I shift on the bench, the words like lemon in an unnoticed scrape, even though I know I should be pleased by them. That's exactly what I want, right? Except there's part of me that wishes her answer had more to do with, well, *me*.

After a beat, I reply, "The perfect campaign match."

Victoria looks down. "Yeah."

We should be talking about what happened to the original Jays Jigsaw pieces—at the very least, planning who among the dance and tech crew kids to ask once the night is over—but I kind of don't want to talk about it right now, not while Victoria looks hesitant and closed off.

"Did you ever dance?" I nod toward the auditorium, where we can hear an Irish step dancing team's lively music.

"Ballet for two years, like everybody else. I wasn't *that* into it, and my mom really wasn't into getting me ready to go at eight a.m. on Saturday mornings." She shakes her head, rueful. "You?"

"Not officially."

"Ooh." Victoria leans in a little. "What does that mean?"

"A few summers ago, Amrita and I binge-watched all the reality dance competitions. Or maybe not every single one, but a *lot*."

"That's sounds fun! But also like watching, not dancing." Victoria raises her eyebrows.

"There *might* have been some attempts at replication," I say, looking at the ceiling.

"Mm-hmm." Victoria sounds triumphant, even in just two syllables. "Do you remember any? We're at a dance showcase—you should show me."

"Oh my god, no."

"*Something*. One tiny little move. I won't judge. If you want."

"Well . . ." There's a giddy, reckless rush up my spine. Not because I'm secretly a good dancer, but because I want to surprise her. And I'm pretty sure she'll be surprised if I agree. "Okay. One thing."

Victoria's jaw drops, and she claps once before glancing guiltily toward the auditorium.

"But I'll need some help." I stand up and offer her my hands.

She takes them without question. Her palms are a little damp, but mine are too. I adjust our grip so I'm in the lead—one hand firmly on her back—and then, praying my arms don't give out on me now, dip her. When I pull her up again a second later, her eyes are wide and her dimples deep as she gives a small laugh. She adjusts our positions again so she can lift her arm and spin me underneath the bridge of our hands.

"Pity there's no inaugural ball for class presidents," I say. My voice comes out breathless. My hand is still in hers.

"Sounds like something I can motion to change," she says in a whisper, not looking away.

The door to the auditorium creaks open, and we drop hands.

"Bathroom?" the man says.

"Down the hall, on the left," Victoria answers. Her voice sounds totally normal.

I clear my throat and sit back on the bench. Victoria joins me. I look at the cashbox instead of how close her thigh is to mine.

Victoria starts to message the techies she knows are working the show tonight, to ask if any of them saw something suspicious. *Technically*, they're not supposed to check their phones during a show, but they're treating the showcase a lot more casually than they did the spring musical. When I was envisioning the campaign strategy as a crime map, the night I chose a new candidate, I definitely wasn't thinking about *actual* theft.

"It's gonna be fine," Victoria says. "It's *already* fine."

"I know. I just wish we could stop doing damage control," I say.

I'm starting to understand why infrastructure week never happens. You can so easily spend the whole time cleaning up the last mess.

Twenty-Three Days Until Election Day

Louis and Victoria find me near the end of break, their faces grim.

"That bad?" I say as we form a huddle in a corner.

"The baseball team did it. As a 'prank,' to help Carter, table included," Louis says. "Though from the sound of it, he definitely helped plan the whole thing. He knew what was going down."

"How do you know?" I ask.

I'm glad it wasn't one of Victoria's crew friends by accident, but it also doesn't feel good to have been the victims of sabotage. Actually, I'm pretty damn angry. Our school isn't supposed to be *like this*. We're supposed to have a totally normal campaign, with a moderate amount of social media shade at worst. Why is this election the one people decided to really care about? And why is it my candidate getting caught in the crosshairs? The unfairness of it all burns through me.

It's bad enough to witness my ex systematically implement all the plans I made for her. Bad enough to watch Kevin, whose homophobic bullying almost certainly didn't start or stop with me, glide through the sophomore lounge, wheedling first one group, then another, into promises to attend his civic engagement event tonight. Now a full conspiracy too?

"There was an all-season sports meeting during zero today. I heard them bragging about it. A few of their girlfriends were performing in the showcase, and I guess they told the girls they wanted to come in early for luck or whatever," says Louis.

"Ugh. Could they have been *less* supportive and not shown up at all?" I say.

Too bad I was too busy making change, handing out tickets, and painting these ridiculous JJs (sorry, Amrita) to pay attention to who looked shocked that we had JJs to distribute at all.

But then the memory hits me like an AOC clapback.

"Wait. Eric was there—we saw him, in the lobby, right when we went to get the cashbox—"

"I bet he was checking up on us, like, that we were about to find out—and the door was supposed to be open. He probably locked us out too," Victoria says. Disgust leaches into her every syllable.

"Bet you one JJs piece he was the one to leak on Insta," says Louis.

I groan. "I do not want to hear about JJs for at least a week, please."

Louis nods solemnly.

"So, now what?" Victoria's eyes meet mine.

"You're the candidate. That has to be up to you. You'd be totally within your rights to tell someone—Mr. Braun, probably, since he's the advisor."

"But what do you think?" she asks.

I tip my head from side to side. I'm about to speak when the bell rings.

"Lunch, yes?" Victoria says, pointing between us.

How am I supposed to focus in my next class, knowing that another candidate directed his teammates to ruin our civic engagement assignment? Maybe I won't. It's another hour to think about what options we have to deal with Carter's sabotage.

Victoria polls us when we sit down to lunch.

"Louis?"

"Don't tell. They're assholes, but they're varsity baseball assholes. I don't think it's going to help," he says.

"Amrita?"

"I agree with Louis. It wasn't okay, but you're going to create more drama if you tell Mr. Braun about it. You came out on top—at least, you had pieces to hand out, and you could even still win the extra poster spots. Don't let this distract you from the campaign." Amrita turns to me, her eyebrows raised, because she already knows I'm about to disagree with her.

"I . . . have some experience with being told I'm too sensitive and take things too seriously. So I say this with the full understanding that if you did tell, there'd probably be a backlash. Because somehow the 'prank' won't be seen as taking the campaign too far, but telling will."

Victoria makes a face, but nods.

"But I actually think you should report them. Like Amrita said, we pulled it off." Nearly without a hitch, although, as predicted, my knee is currently more purple than Ohio. "But what if we hadn't? What if you hadn't happened to know the access code? What if you didn't know you could get the master key from the stage manager?"

"What if you didn't know to call Amrita, and what if Amrita hadn't been available?" Victoria adds.

"There wouldn't have been any puzzle pieces, and it wouldn't have been our fault. But our fundraiser would have tanked, and our credibility been seriously damaged. They didn't *know* we'd be able to find solutions in time. Why should they get to avoid consequences just because we're a great team?" When I say the word *team*, I look meaningfully at Victoria, who smiles back.

She's quiet for another moment, and then lets out a deep breath. "I don't know."

"You don't have to make up your mind right away," says Louis. "Though deciding before we go on spring break would probably be a good idea."

"Yeah, agreed," says Victoria. "Okay, let's . . . talk about something else. I want to think about this a little more. I'll tell you my decision once I've made it—tomorrow morning at the latest."

When I come home from babysitting that night, there's a new email from Mr. Braun, sent to the entire sophomore class.

Carter's out.

CHAPTER SEVENTEEN

Twenty-Two Days Until Election Day

@WestPlymouthPress: Junior class president candidates Annie Delaney and Riley Wu tied for voters' top rank in exclusive WPP snap poll

"It wasn't me."

We all say it at once during zero hour on Thursday morning: me, Victoria, Louis, and Amrita. We spent last night messaging each other between studying for the last tests of the quarter (me, Victoria), fending off younger sisters' bad nail polish combinations (Louis), and endless edits on the background section for the group biology project from hell (Amrita), but it feels like the kind of thing you say in person when you can.

Most of the other candidates messaged Victoria after the email went out. Marisa texted me, a kind enough gesture that I almost wished ASB had a co-president option. *Impressive af to pull that off. Always knew Carter was a dick. Braun seems to have this under control but lmk if you need anything to keep this thing fair.*

Thanks, I wrote back. *Think we're ok. Back at you if anyone gets ideas from Carter and tries it on you.*

In addition to the sophomore-wide announcement, Mr. Braun sent Victoria a separate email to check in. He was like that last year in civics, too, proactively emailing if a student was out sick, without waiting for them to ask what they'd missed. I think every teacher should show that kind of care and attention. This time, I just don't know how he knew to be concerned in the first place.

We stand in frustrated silence near the cafeteria entrance until Victoria shoos us toward our usual table. I'm still walking gingerly after the broken table incident.

"You okay?" she asks. "I should have gotten some ice for your knee when I put the screwdriver away."

"It's fine. And I enjoyed what we did then. During the show," I blurt.

Amrita glances between us, a curious slant to her eyebrows, but before anyone can comment, Zack walks up to the table, his steps hesitant. Whatever grace he gained from the spring musical has vanished, and his gangly arms drift awkwardly at his sides.

"Um, hi," he says.

"Hi," says Victoria.

"Can I join you for a sec? I think . . ." He trails off. At Victoria's nod, he takes a seat next to Louis. "So, if you were curious, which you probably are—I'm how Mr. Braun found out. About Carter, and the team, and the JJs thing."

"How did *you* know about it?" Amrita asks, echoing my thoughts exactly.

Zack grimaces. "I have first period with a lot of the baseball guys, so I was walking with them after the athlete meeting on Wednesday—I run track—and they were talking about it."

Clearly they weren't too worried about facing actual consequences, if they kept discussing it even with another candidate—and as a theater kid, Victoria's most natural ally—nearby. Yesterday's anger unfurls itself again, rooting itself deeper in my gut at the new evidence of blatant impunity.

"So, what, you went and told Mr. Braun?" Victoria asks.

Zack shakes his head. "No, I wasn't gonna, I figured—Louis was there, too, right? So I assumed you would know, and you'd do something, or not, or whatever. I guess I should have checked that you knew."

"Uh, yeah, that would be a good thing to do in the future, the next time you overhear something like this," says Victoria.

"If you didn't go to him . . ." I start.

"Right. Mr. Braun kept me back after class yesterday afternoon. Said he'd been hearing some rumors, knew I was friendly with some of the baseball team . . . I tried to be vague and stuff, because, I don't know, it felt weird, kind of like tattling," says Zack.

"Tattling is a concept for elementary school kids who need to learn to mind their own business. It doesn't apply to sabotage," Amrita says in a firm tone.

Zack ducks his head. "Right," he says again. "Well. He kept asking, just sounding really worried." Zack glances at Victoria. "He was saying how—he wants it to be a fair campaign, and that means he has to be protective of the candidates and the process. So then I told him."

"Thanks for letting me know," says Victoria. She smooths the tension from her face, like a real politician. "And, um . . . I look forward to hearing your speech."

"Don't remind me," he says as he stands up. "Have a good break!"

"You too," says Louis.

I run my thumb against the edge of the table, considering. My backless cafeteria stool seems even more unsuited than usual for providing stability. I don't love Mr. Braun's process to . . . protect the process, because telling him about the sabotage was supposed to be a choice. But now that we know the *how*, I can't help but feel a smug kind of relief. *Carter's disqualified!* One asshole down.

My eyes meet Victoria's, and she gives a small nod. Without planning it, the four of us release a collective sigh, exhaling the stress and confusion of the last two days.

"Our first campaign mystery solved." Amrita raises her hand in an imaginary toast.

"We need a reality show," says Louis, on board with lightening the mood.

Victoria's smile goes sly. "Only if it's dance."

Mr. Braun stops me in the hall during break. He pushes open his classroom door and ushers me inside with one hand on my shoulder, his face grave.

"How are you doing, Maddie?" he asks. "The new JJs at the showcase—it makes sense now. I know that's not how you would've liked it to go."

"Yeah." It feels weird to talk to him about it, since no one *decided* to tell him, but I guess there's no point in pretending he doesn't know. "It worked out okay, in the end. I'm proud of that. I'm glad we figured out . . . what happened."

"My concern is that no one came forward on their own to notify me or another teacher." Mr. Braun holds up both hands. "I know, I know, you all like to handle things yourselves, and normally I don't want to stand in the way of that. You can learn a lot from peer-to-peer conflict resolution." His expression slips back into his usual smile.

"We were going to. I think," I say. "We just needed a little more time."

"I see, I see. I jumped the gun."

I nod.

"It's very important that we have a strong, open school culture. That means taking action quickly so situations don't spiral. But I hope you don't take it as an indication that I don't trust you," he says.

"Oh. No." I'm proud that he's walking me through his decisions. It's as if I'm a peer, not just a girl who didn't speak up fast enough.

"Good, good." He holds out one hand, and when I extend my own, he places his other hand on top of mine for an earnest handshake. The odd grip throws me off enough that I forget to shake back, but I can hopefully correct the weak impression with a do-over when we accept congratulations for Victoria's win. "I know you have class now, but I'd like for you and Victoria to stop by at the end of lunch, all right? Nothing bad, I promise."

It feels bad, though, when we're walking toward Mr. Braun's classroom and run directly into Carter, coming from the other direction. He glares at us, his face instantly red.

"You didn't have to make it a big fucking deal," he grits out. "It was a joke."

"It wasn't funny." I keep my voice steady, but my stomach is clenched. My classmates' annoyance with me comes out as eye rolls, heavy sighs, and letting me do all the work in group projects. I'm not used to this kind of confrontation.

Carter's attention snaps to me alone. I'm aware of every single inch he has on me—ten—and every single inch between us in the hallway—no more than double that. "You were the one who told, weren't you? You can never shut the hell up."

"Stop," says Victoria, at the same time that I say, "Does it matter?"

"I have to miss the season opener." He crosses his arms.

Disappointment rushes through me. One game? That's it? For trying to mess up an *election*?

"Oh, good," Mr. Braun says from over my shoulder. The three of us pivot as one. "You're all here."

The shock steals any breath for objections. This is *intentional*? Victoria and I exchange uneasy glances as we follow him inside. Carter positions himself closest to Mr. Braun, his glare transformed into a faux-serious expression.

"Now, I understand this is a complicated situation. No one's happy, least of all me," Mr. Braun begins.

My jaw clenches. As far as I'm concerned, there's nothing complicated here. Carter and his team sabotaged us and got caught. End of story.

"But we're all in this school together, and we need to find a path to move forward."

I wonder if the principal or guidance counselor decided they simply didn't want to deal with this "situation," because otherwise, I'm not sure why a club advisor is mediating this himself.

"You're good kids. It's easy to get *way* over your head sometimes—what starts as a joke suddenly gets really serious, really fast." Mr. Braun makes eye contact with each of us.

"Yeah," says Carter. His face is still pink, but less blotchy than it was in the hallway.

"So I've asked Carter to make an apology, on behalf of himself and the team, as a gesture of reconciliation. When we walk out of this room, it's all in the past."

I sneak a look at Victoria. Her eyebrows are furrowed, and when she catches my gaze, she gives a tiny shake of her head. This isn't something she agreed to in advance.

"Sorry. Yeah, it just—like, spiraled, you know? My guys were looking out for me, that's all. But too far," Carter adds, nodding at Mr. Braun.

"Thank you," says Mr. Braun. He slings an arm around Carter's shoulders. "I look forward to watching you beat your home-run record this season, okay? See you on the field."

Carter nods. "Thanks for letting me explain."

Without even looking at us again, Carter leaves.

I'm too stunned to speak. Next to me, Victoria clears her throat, but that's as far as she gets before Mr. Braun starts talking again.

"Everyone makes mistakes. I knew I could trust the two of you to be mature and understanding."

I let the praise smooth down my confusion and anger, like

sandpaper rubbing away all the rough edges. I know it's bad to be vindictive. I know I should seek justice over retribution.

Reconciliation, Mr. Braun said.

Be mature. Look at this like an adult. Like a *good* adult. Carter's out of the race, and that's what matters. What do I care about how many baseball games he plays? There will be no election victory party for him.

"Now, you girls go out there and win," Mr. Braun says. He clasps me on the shoulder before pulling open the door. "Prove me right."

"Okay," I say, but I keep my eyes fixed on Victoria.

We already agreed we'd win this for each other.

CHAPTER EIGHTEEN

Twenty-One Days Until Election Day

I sleep in on Friday, late enough that the house has been empty for hours by the time I make my way into the kitchen. I swipe through notifications while I wait for my toast.

Victoria

We're still on for hot cocoa today, yes?

In the stress and chaos of the service assignment sabotage, we never finalized our plans.

Me

Yes!!!

I want to take back the exclamation points—at least two of them—but it's too late. I quickly send another text to mitigate this weird enthusiasm.

Only if you can pick me up though :/

I don't mean to make you keep driving me places!
Cocoa's on me

Victoria

I'm the one who suggested this in the first place! I don't mind picking you up

I hesitate before replying with a heart emoji. Amrita and I throw around heart emojis constantly. Anyway, it feels right.

Victoria sends one back.

I'm watching for her out the window, shoes on, so Victoria barely has time to park before I slip into the passenger seat, taking care to shut the car door gently. Her curly hair is in a thick French braid, the end falling cheerfully over her orange scarf.

"Hey," she says.

"Hi. Thanks for picking me up, Madam Class President-to-Be."

She blushes, then twists to check behind us as she backs out of the driveway. "Let's take the afternoon off."

My instinct is to counter with *let's get some positive momentum going*, but you don't want your candidate to burn out too early in the race, so I agree. And . . . I have fun with Victoria even when we're not talking about the campaign. I wouldn't mind more of that.

"Caribou okay?"

"Sounds good."

"Suburban choices, I know," she says with a small groan, as if I'd complained. "Emily Singh—do you know her? She's a senior, led prop crew for the fall play—was telling me about this really cute, queer-friendly place on East Lake Street. She takes her first dates there, and she asks them on a second if they like the aesthetic."

That's a long drive for a first date, I think, but all I say is, "I know her. She came to GSA's advocacy day at the capitol."

"She's a tea person, though, so I don't have any info on the quality of their hot chocolate."

"Mm."

I'm caught on the mental image of Emily and her rotating cast of first-date girls. Her bringing them to a place she loves and seeing whether they like it too.

"Maybe—" Victoria cuts herself off.

"Maybe?"

"Nothing," she says quickly. "Got myself confused for a second."

I clear my throat. "So when Emily was telling you this . . ."

Victoria glances at me as we wait at a stoplight. "Yeah?"

"Should I be teasing you right now? Was that a hint? Did you miss her trying to ask you out?" I'm not sure when Emily told Victoria about this place—backstage in the fall? Yesterday? The thought itches, though I can't seem to pin down the source.

"*Oh*. No. She's really straightforward about that stuff," says Victoria.

"Smashing stereotypes."

She laughs, but it's not as loose as her usual. "Something like that."

I keep my eyes carefully on the strip mall sign ahead. "Do you, um . . . wish she had . . . said something straightforward to you?"

"No! Oh my god. I don't have a crush on her."

"I just want to know if I'm dealing with a broken heart!" Why else bring her up?

Victoria shakes her head, rolling her eyes, but she's smiling at me. "My heart's pretty good these days."

At Caribou, she insists on paying for my hot chocolate. "I invited you," she says, shielding the counter from me and handing her debit card to the cashier with a pointed look.

"Next time, it's on me, then," I say.

"Sure, next time," she says, airy.

We tuck ourselves into a corner table, under a chalkboard covered half in snowflake sketches, half in tulip ones. Welcome to April in Minnesota: It could go either way.

Victoria traces the rim of her mug, her eyes focused on the foam swirl inside. "I guess I've been wondering—I mean, it's none of my business and I know we haven't really talked much before the last couple of weeks—but how's *your* heart?"

"My heart?"

She flinches. "Yeah. With, um. I mean, considering. The breakup and . . . all that."

Some inexplicable laugh of *relief* bursts through me. She means

Jade. Of course. "I mean, if you get me started on her, I'll be mad by the end." My eyes trace down Victoria's braid, tucked over one sweatered shoulder. "I don't want to be mad right now. I'm, let's say, *irritated* by how she's treated me since, and that I didn't get any warning. But I'm not, like . . . sad about the *fact* of it anymore, if that makes sense?" Victoria looks unsure. "I'm over her. Maybe I'd be dwelling if I still thought she was the coolest person in the room, maybe my heart would feel broken if—" I stop.

"If?" She looks at me, exactly the way she did when we sat across the cafeteria table that very first morning. Soft brown eyes. Dimples on display.

I think: Victoria has always been the kindest person in the room.

I think: There's no one who could walk through the door and make me look away.

I think: I want to give her good news, and sometimes I want that good news to be *me*.

I think: *Oh*.

I push my smile wider, fluttering a hand as if that can mask the fluttering of my heart. "If I weren't so busy with the campaign. There's a lot more to—to like in life than just her."

Victoria raises her mug, and after a second, I raise mine to match.

"To no broken hearts on our campaign," she says.

"No broken hearts," I echo.

Note to self: No broken hearts.

No broken hearts, I think on Saturday afternoon as I address letters to potential voters.

I can't have another crush, not when my last one imploded so spectacularly. I can't afford to lose this campaign too. I can't afford to lose, period.

It was one thing when I was trying to impress Victoria for campaign reasons . . . or at least, when I thought that's all I was doing. Dancing with her at the showcase? Cuddling with her during Lauren's movie night? There's no platonic, professional explanation for any of it. With Jade, at least, I would have stayed on topic. But Victoria? With her curls and her cocoa? A recipe for lost focus if there ever was one.

It's only her dimples, I tell myself, sealing an envelope with care.

It's only the way her poetry makes me feel like I can win. Not win the campaign specifically. Just *win*.

Only with Victoria, there's no "only." There's just everything.

My one saving grace might be that I hate to let people down. A toast—even one made with Caribou cocoa—is more than a wish sometimes. I'll make it a mandate: My heart needs to calm down. At least until the election is over.

No broken hearts, I remind myself again on Saturday night, while I sit in the Charlesons' living room, the kids asleep upstairs. I sketch poster designs in my Life Notebook and don't send any of them to Victoria. She's probably at Lauren's, watching *Frozen II*. I'll send her the ideas once they're ready to be worthy. Which has to be soon, so her group can have their questionable coloring nights.

I perk up when I remember it'll at least save on printing costs. I do *not* think about the way Victoria's eyes brighten whenever I surprise her with something good.

Nineteen Days Until Election Day

"Should your heart be broken after every breakup? And how long should it take to get over?" I ask Chelsea on Sunday. We're out driving again, this time eschewing the church parking lot for a winding neighborhood near the post office. I'm feeling okay at fifteen miles per hour today.

"I don't think 'should' really matters." She nods with approval as I stop oh-so-gently, oh-so-completely at an intersection. "It's just however long it *does*. Even if that person was an asshole to you after, it's totally normal to have that betrayal all mixed up with everything else you're feeling. Maddie, I know you like to be on top of everything, but a few weeks is nothing in the scheme of heartbreak, okay?"

My acceleration is less gentle, but not on purpose. A silver SUV approaches from behind, and I nudge us up to twenty. "What if it's . . . the opposite. What if it wasn't *heartbreak* but a heart fracture? A sprain? A bruise. Even with all the other stuff. Is everything supposed to be heart*break*?"

"Don't forget to keep checking your mirrors. And no, not everything has to be heartbreak. But you were with Jade for a long time, so you should let yourself—"

"So 'should' does matter? Because I kind of . . . really don't care anymore. Does that make me a bad person?"

"*Oh.* No." Out of the corner of my eye, I can see Chelsea turn toward me. "But I'd be very sure it's just a bruise before involving anybody else, you know?"

No broken hearts.

For now, the only broken heart is Amrita's, still in mourning after her bio project partners cornered her into giving up her free Friday for an all-day planning session. It especially stings because her family is spending the rest of spring break in the Wisconsin Dells.

"If you're going to be a teacher with an obsession with assigning groups, that's fine. But you have to think about the dynamics. It's about *balance.*" Amrita gestures, like she's painting the air. Her face is shadowed in the hotel room's poor lighting.

"Three pre-premed kids . . ."

"And me." Amrita turns away from the camera to shoo her little sister out of the room.

I prop my phone against my knees and lean back into my pillows. "It's going to be fine."

"I thought they were going to legitimately murder me when I said I wasn't working on it this week. They'll burn out before they finish residency if they don't learn to take advantage of school-mandated breaks." She says it in the knowing, world-weary voice of someone whose dad has a PsyD.

"For sure."

That was my justification, after all, for the non-working cocoa meetup with Victoria on Friday. I *should* probably regret going, but I can't make myself even pretend to. At least I know now, instead of fumbling through the next few weeks of the campaign without understanding why I want to linger in every hug.

"What's that look?" Amrita says suddenly, leaning into the camera to better analyze my expression.

"What look?"

"A look like you weren't thinking about my bio partners."

No broken hearts. If I don't say it—if I don't name her and this crush and that cocoa out loud—it's not real, right?

"Jade," I say instead.

Amrita raises her eyebrows. "Really?"

"I—it's not weird to be thinking about her! She fired me! And dumped me, not even two weeks ago. I *cried*." A bruise still leaves a mark.

"More than you cry every time your favorite candidates lose their primaries?"

"That's different. That's grieving for a whole future."

"Hm. Because I remember when Jade was going to be a consistent background character in your memoir."

"I'm still running a campaign—" I stop short at Amrita's smug expression.

"You always say 'fired' first."

"I really did like her." The words come out quiet but defensive. It's not like Jade was just a means to an anecdotal end.

Her tone softens. "I know. But maybe . . . less this winter than you did before?"

Later that night, my mind keeps circling Amrita's final observation. It's true that my lips stopped tingling with the same election-night sparkle as when Jade and I kissed in the fall, but I thought that was simply being comfortable with your partner. A stable rhythm with someone whose path is synced to yours.

I stand up, pacing back and forth.

It didn't feel like a bruise that first night, on my bedroom floor. But the more I talk about it with Chelsea and Amrita—and the more I plan for Victoria's success—the clearer it seems that the heartbreak of that day was the loss of the campaign, not Jade. If the two hadn't been twisted together, I would have noticed sooner. Jade wasn't right about YPBC, but maybe she was right that I'd changed, even if neither of us could articulate how.

And Victoria? I think. My stomach lurches like I've missed a step.

I pivot and settle into my desk chair. I keep my back straight.

"Here's the thing," I tell my room. "In Catherine Shaw's comprehensive text, *The Campaign Manager*, one of her ten commandments is not getting involved with the candidate." My bed slumbers on, unmoved. "And much to my chagrin, we—no, I—have already broken that rule for this election once. So I have no excuse for letting it happen again." I frown. "No, for *choosing* for it to happen again."

I already had my heart bruised by one candidate in the last month. Already let my crushes and my plans get way too tangled up. If I let myself finish falling for Victoria—her smiles, the way she likes my socks and spreadsheets—I'll not only compromise my integrity as a campaign manager. Victoria would never go for someone as awkward as I am . . . so, contrary to Chelsea's warning in the car, I know it's not Victoria's heart that is at risk here. It's solely mine. And Victoria is exactly the kind of sweet who could shatter me into pieces. Two hundred and seventy of them, probably, or maybe even five hundred and thirty-eight. It'd take a long time to recover from that kind of damage.

No broken hearts means not letting Victoria break *mine.* Which means choosing to not give her the chance.

"We're professionals here," I say, pointing at the rug. "The personal is the political, but not like this." I scan my room, making eye contact with the bookshelf, the pillows, the closed blinds over my window. "No broken hearts."

CHAPTER NINETEEN

Eighteen Days Until Election Day

@WestPlymouthPress: Final results are in! The top fundraisers: Shawn Guse (sr. class president), Annie Delaney (jr. class president), and Jacob Levine (soph. rep).

It's hard to focus on babysitting when Victoria keeps sending me fifteen-second clips of her policy platform, in spoken word format. Especially when they're good enough to distract me from losing out on the fundraiser poster spots. I compromise: Lacy makes herself at home in my lap, Trevor half-toppled on my shoulder, while I play the videos for them.

"This doesn't rhyme enough," Lacy complains at the end of the catwalk-funding one.

Dutifully, I text Victoria. Our demographic is sixteen-year-olds, not six-year-olds, but considering that I've made Lacy part of my two-person focus group, I owe it to her to pass on the feedback.

"I liked the one where she was really fast," says Trevor. "That was funny."

He means her Student Judiciary Council video. If Lacy could have followed it, she probably would have liked it too: judicial, acquittal, dismissal . . .

"Thanks! I'll let her know," I say.

Me

Sorry for the limited feedback rn, working til 5

But overall I think they're awesome!

Good bones

Victoria

Thanks! :)

Can you meet up tonight to go over them some more?

I know the schedule is for me to post the first next Monday

I try not to swoon over her campaign calendar reference. This is clearly why I *have* to get into YPBC this summer. Once I'm surrounded by fifty other kids who have also Google Calendar–ed the crap out of class president campaigns, I can't get all squishy about *all* of them. Lacy and Trevor are now busy with Legos, so I bite my lip and text her back.

Me

For sure, where/when?

Isn't it Disney marathon week?

Victoria

I'll go later when they start Moana

It'd be fun if you came

My immediate response is a mental row of exclamation marks, doing joyous cartwheels from my brain all the way to my fingers, which are already poised to reply YES. Cue the balloon drop: *Victoria wants me there.*

Then I hesitate. Because as much as I really want more time with Victoria—maybe even in a love seat again, since no one knows about my crush and so isn't going to call us out for violating the movie night rule—I shouldn't. The Plan demands that I focus on the *campaign*, not her cuteness.

Me

Thanks for the invite but I have to pass

Chelsea and I agreed to do some long night-driving sessions while school's out

As soon as Mrs. Charleson returns, I practically sprint home, splashing through the puddles. I'm thankful that nobody else is around yet to see me do the world's fastest tidying of the kitchen counters. When Victoria rings the doorbell, my stomach squeezes tight, like all its atoms want to be closer together, better to guard against the swoopy feelings that now ripple through me anytime she's near.

"Hey," she says, and my stomach flips upside down in surrender.

I lead her down the hall to my bedroom, then carefully leave the door ajar. It's like keeping a pressure valve open; maybe all my feelings can escape out of it, instead of building and building inside this small room as we sit next to each other on the rug.

"So. The videos . . ." She pulls her laptop from her backpack. "Are you *sure* I should do it this way?"

"If you were running for public office, definitely not."

A class president campaign doesn't follow the rules of even the most local of elections . . . but maybe this is the true definition of "most local." And if the saying *all politics is local* is true, then it can start here, with me and Victoria and TikToks and the hope that every like or comment or share is that one more link of connection that's going to lead to allyship workshops and real separation between ASB and the Student Judiciary Council (finally). I want elections to not be another thing where I'm trying to drag everyone else along with me—because I've tried that, and it doesn't work. I want Victoria's campaign to remind them of what they're already excited about, so voting for her is just the natural next step of where they were already headed.

"But . . ." Victoria prompts.

"But since that is *not* the case . . . like Louis said, this is going to be your fun thing that will make you stand out in the right way. And enough of the artsy-popular kids will think it's cool for them to rank you second."

Like in a lot of real elections that use the ranked-choice system, it's not solely about whoever has the lowest number—in which case, if the top votes were split enough, someone consistently ranked third could emerge victorious. At West Plymouth, you *also* have to get at least 50.1 percent of the first- and second-choice ranked votes combined. If no candidate manages that, the top two head to a runoff election at the beginning of May.

The ranked-choice process is our saving grace, since in the typical American system, Victoria would never win outright. Carter (before he was disqualified), Annie, or Riley would probably come out ahead. My strategy hinges on swooping up as many of the second-choice votes as possible. The consensus candidate. The one you trust to do the job after you've given your obligatory first-choice vote to your best friend.

Victoria tucks a stray curl behind her ear. "I want to be elected, of course, but I always thought that the campaign part would be boring." Her eyes catch mine. "I'm glad it's not."

"No?"

"Not at all." She blushes, dimples appearing.

I clear my throat. "Good, okay. I think the first one we should work on is your intro poem. The middle bit kind of sags. Can you bring up the text?"

We don't get around to finishing and filming all of her pieces, but when her intro video drops next Monday, it'll be my bedroom wall in the background.

Seventeen Days Until Election Day

After babysitting on Tuesday, I'm watching Amrita's latest vacation Reel—her posing at the edge of an indoor wave pool—when Victoria and Louis arrive. Louis carries the button maker, while Victoria clutches the small cardboard box of supplies.

We spread out across the living room floor. Louis is wearing a homemade T-shirt with the Wakanda Forever symbol inked on the front. We decided last week we didn't have the budget to print T-shirts. It still rankles to know a couple of the other candidates are buying them, but you campaign with the candidate—and the budget—you've got, right? And we're about to have two hundred buttons.

I try not to think about the fact that the vast majority of US Congress seats are won by whichever campaign spends the most money. *Peyton* didn't spend more than twenty dollars to win last year—way less than two of her opponents—and that's what really matters.

"Where'd you get the button maker from?" I ask. I'd thought about asking Ms. Zhao if we could borrow the GSA one, but Louis said he had access to a newer model.

"My boyfriend," he says. "If we win, I'll tell George we owe it all to him."

"When," I correct, then add, "I didn't know you were dating anyone!"

The only George I know is Georgiana Chablis-Khouri, a Lebanese American girl Amrita partners with in French. *That* George is definitely dating Mark Swanson, the hockey star in my math class. I'm not sure I've ever seen Louis hang out with anyone but Victoria. And the other techies, like Devin.

"He goes to Cooper." Louis ducks his head. "It's kind of new. Well, since January."

"That's awesome. I'm jealous," I say, without thinking.

Victoria, bent over one of the button boxes, jerks up. Louis *hms* and pulls out a pack of the Mylar covers I'd tasked him with buying on the way over.

I straighten my blue cardigan. "I don't know why I said that! I'm happy for you . . . I'll be happier if we get started on these buttons."

We don't have a fancy circle cutter, so we set up assembly-line style. Victoria and I cut out the paper logos I printed when I took the kids to the Rockford Road Library this morning. Louis, meanwhile, mans the press, arranging the button pieces, the logo, and the Mylar before gripping the red handle and pushing one way, then the other, to combine all the elements.

He hands the first completed button to Victoria, who squeals and passes it to me.

I shake my head. "You have to make sure the logo and the button back are both straight, otherwise it's going to hang weirdly."

"It's fine!" Victoria jumps in. "It doesn't really matter. I'm just happy to have help."

"It *does* matter, because these buttons represent you, and you're a thoughtful candidate," I say.

"That can be our test one. Good catch." Louis adjusts the next set of pieces in the press.

This time, the button comes out perfectly aligned.

I cut another sliver of white off my *V for Victoria* logo. The background is a deep purple, because we weren't *actually* going to use a red-white-blue color scheme. Victoria pushes up the sleeves of her cable-knit cream sweater as she reaches for a new logo sheet. This one says *V* in a bright yellow that's supposed to be gold, shining above a catwalk that stretches horizontally along the bottom. I designed it specifically for the theater crowd. I'm confident Zack, our main competition for the theater kids, isn't going to get himself together in time for swag.

It feels so good to have the buttons finally in front of us, the physical manifestation of all those plans and strategies. Each of them serves as some little proof that I know what I'm doing, that I'm *good* at this. There was a reason we made that choice last week, or the week before—and here it is now, and I'm remembering how we got there and agreeing with myself.

The button piles begin to spread in the center of our triangle. I printed pages for five logos in total: two general ones, and three for more specific audiences. I designed a sixth, with a pink *V* at the center of a waving rainbow flag, but that one was just for me. My hands start to cramp a little from the scissors.

"Louis, switch with Madison?" Victoria says. She's not looking at him, though: She's looking at my fingers.

"What?" we both say.

"Repetitive stress injuries are no joke." Her voice is mock firm, but her smile is gentle.

Louis shows me the order to put the button components in before we shuffle. The press is harder to work than I imagined, but it's satisfying too. I push my weight into it—and then, from all these cheap, scattered pieces, emerges something I'd be proud to wear. Proud to represent.

Louis keeps telling me about George. "He's not really out, so I can't talk about him at school. Just in case."

I nod. Since West Plymouth is a charter school, we pull kids who would otherwise go to half a dozen of the regular west metro high schools. Someone sitting near us in Marketing could easily be George's neighbor. "Still, that sucks."

"What, you think I'm the type of guy who wants to brag about his cute boyfriend loudly in the cafeteria?" Louis raises his eyebrows.

"I mean . . ."

He laughs. "And I do! But safety first. And even if it's like, there are a thousand Georges I *could* be dating, this makes him feel more comfortable. That's more important. If anybody's going to out him to his family, accidentally or on purpose—it's not going to be me. I'm never going to make him play some fucked-up calculus of whether prom is worth more than his college fund."

Jade and I never talked about deep stuff like this, identity and out-ness, even though one of the reasons I came out to my parents last June was the huge crush I had on her. I mean, I was pretty sure they would be fine with it.

I'd spent so much of that freshman fall looking back at middle school and thinking, *Wait . . . WAIT . . . you were not a simple, platonic admirer of Leisha's science fair project . . . and her ballet performance in the talent show . . . WAIT.* The spring semester brought Debate 1 and Jade. I wasn't ready, and then I was. And now . . . I'm wondering if I might be ready for a relationship where we *do* talk about more than debate strategy. If I might even *want* that kind of relationship.

Not right this second, of course. Not in the middle of the campaign.

"Even some queer movies mess this up," I say, corralling my thoughts back to Louis and George: the *actual* relationship at hand. "Like, 'if you won't come out to the entire school, you clearly don't love me enough'? That's crappy. George is obviously out to you, and you're able to tell your—friends." I stumble over the word, but Louis is nodding along. "Maybe it's not for everyone, and if you need to be able to go to prom with your boyfriend, that's fine, you just need a new one. But I guess." I stop again. Talking to my bedroom is *so* much easier. "I support you, that's what I'm saying. You and George. Very quietly."

Louis props his chin in his hands. "Could you do it, do you think? You've had an out-out relationship before."

"*Louis*," says Victoria. "That's personal."

"No, it's fine. What he said about George was pretty personal," I say. I fiddle with the handle of the button press, thinking.

My thoughts lead me straight back to Victoria. Who is out to her friends, but not to the school, maybe not even to her parents. Whose real laugh is brighter than sun reflecting off snow, and whose dimples I am dying to kiss.

All at once, I get it, and my eyes snap to Louis's. He smirks.

Holy crap.

I'm almost certain Victoria is oblivious—she's busy putting all the catwalk buttons in a Ziploc bag, hair falling down across her face—but Louis has 100 percent caught me out. Maybe I'm being way more obvious than I thought. Maybe Louis even figured it out before I did. This is not a campaign meeting. This is not even a friendly hangout. This is a straight-up vetting, and I'm in the hot seat.

"I think when you have a relationship with a new person . . . that's a new relationship. And maybe you learned some stuff you want to keep for sure, and some stuff you definitely don't." I keep my gaze fixed on Louis. "But I'm pretty sure there . . . would be . . . a whole range of things that are open to negotiation. Because you're with a different person, with different needs."

"We're not talking about some random 'you.' We're talking about *you*," says Louis. He rounds off a *V for Victoria* circle perfectly.

I swallow. I make another button.

"Oh, that goes in here," says Victoria, holding out the baggie. Our hands brush as I let the button fall, a dull clink against its fellows.

"I couldn't do anything totally secret. I'd want to be able to tell . . ." Well, to tell Amrita, who I haven't told yet about my crush on Victoria. A new revelation knocks into me: Victoria didn't bat an eye when I asked her if we could finish the campaign plan right away so I could use it for YPBC. She's excited for me to hear back. Amrita would probably *approve*. "A couple of people. And my parents. I'm out to them, so I guess I wouldn't feel right not telling them, once we were really together."

Louis nods, once, a small movement that I imagine Victoria will miss as she straightens her pile of scraps and we start talking about the latest failings of Disney+.

When the buttons are done, I begin to clean up, but Louis stops me.

"We need backstage photos!" he says, phone already in hand.

"Ooh, yes! Let's get people excited about the buttons before we can hand them out next week." I rearrange the scraps into a more photogenic pile.

"Are they called backstage photos when it's not theater? And we're in a living room?" Victoria asks.

"I can get behind 'living photos.' *Viva Victoria*?" I say.

The pun isn't that good, but Victoria smirks anyway.

"Hold that," says Louis.

He directs us on a mini photo shoot, first shots of Victoria working the press, then her pinning all five logos onto his backpack, right next to his handful of JJs pieces.

"Wait, hang on." I lean forward, adjusting some of Victoria's curls so they don't hide her face. She freezes, the catwalk button only half-pinned to the fabric. "Sorry, um." I sit back, tucking my hands beneath my legs, my face hot.

"You're *all* good," says Louis.

"Thanks," says Victoria. Her voice is soft.

"And now let's do some with both of you! The candidate and the manager. Pick a button to model, Madison."

I pluck a purple *V for Victoria* button from the floor, but my fingers are shaky.

"Here," says Victoria. "Let me."

I hold my breath as she attaches the button to my cardigan. She keeps one hand against my shoulder, holding me steady. She's *so* close. Her eyelashes brush her cheeks as she looks down, and I imagine my own fingers tracing, whisper soft, over her skin.

"Great!" says Louis. It's more of a chirp, really. "We'll do some standing poses in a minute."

I'm too scared to glare at Louis, in case Victoria notices, but as it turns out, she's doing it for me. Still, she tucks her legs beneath her, her body a handbreadth from mine.

"Now get close! Relax a little . . ." Louis squints at the screen, his voice glittering. "Don't forget that you like each other."

CHAPTER TWENTY

Sixteen Days Until Election Day

My Amrita-less spring break evenings are split between driving practice with Chelsea, analysis of likely voting trends by extracurricular participation, and dodging my parents' invitations to play Scrabble, so in the end, Victoria only has to ask once to convince me to come to a Disney movie night to supervise the poster making.

"Joan should have let you host tonight," I say as I slip into her car. The back seat is covered in posters, in the approved 18x24 size, and a totally rational part of me is terrified we'll drop them on the way in. Mud smears. It's not a good look.

Plus, Joan was the most skeptical of Victoria's friends, back at the snowy movie night before spring break. She's not exactly my biggest fan, and I'm sure she's annoyed that it's *her* night we're crashing with campaign work.

Victoria readjusts the rearview mirror. "I'm not hosting any of them."

"Oh," I say.

I don't know why that's surprising to me. She has almost as many friends as nights of spring break. Maybe I just wanted to see where she lived. That's how friendship works, right? *I'll show you mine, you show me yours.* With houses. Bedrooms. *Wait.*

Note to self: YOU'RE NOT DOING THIS.

Except the early evening light is creating golden streaks across her hair, and her fingers are so steady on the wheel. My own hands, folded in my lap, suddenly feel awkward.

"Madison?" she prompts, like she asked me a question I'd completely missed while debating what to do with my body.

"Sorry, what?"

She throws me an indulgent grin. "Thinking about button distribution?"

"Ha. What were you saying?"

"Just asking how babysitting was."

"Uh . . . fine," I say, because it's somehow a nine-hour blank spot in my memory. "What'd you do today?"

"I finished another video. The parliamentarian to president one?"

"Awesome!" I perk up, relieved to be back on familiar ground. "Can I see it?"

"Yeah, of course."

I take her phone out of a cup holder, and she gives me the lock code so I can navigate to her videos.

Thirty seconds later, I'm in love.

I mean. *Not*—it's a very well-made video, that's all.

"It's *so* good," I say after I've watched it twice. "And those moving boxes in the background of the middle section? Really sets the scene for, like, moving up."

The boxes of Christmas decorations in our laundry room are *still* labeled things like LINENS and KITCHEN (MISCELLANEOUS)

205

even though we moved the summer before fifth grade. Seeing that Victoria's family keeps their old boxes, too, is like realizing that everyone else also has a bag under the kitchen sink filled with other plastic bags. The small spark of recognition that in these everyday ways, we stumble on the same solutions for the same minor problems. Or maybe I'm reading way too much into the boxes, and I'm giddy because when it comes to Victoria, I'm a magpie, and every new fact is shiny and glittering: a major problem to which I have yet to find an ordinary solution.

"Oh, yeah. Thanks," she says.

At Joan's house, we set up in the living room, spread out across a rug while the posters lie flat on the hardwood floor. It's not the full contingent from the *Spider-Verse* movie night, but we still have more people than posters. Victoria and I double up, as do Louis and Lauren next to us.

"This is so exciting," Lauren says, smoothing her sleek hair into a ponytail as we arrange the markers behind us. "Like you're a real candidate."

I focus on distributing poster designs and bite my tongue. Who's to say Victoria isn't real? She has to give a real speech and persuade real people to give her a high ranking. ASB has real budgetary control over real money.

"But more fun," says Joan. She pretends to smear glitter glue on Kyle's cheeks, which is worrying, because there shouldn't even *be* glitter glue in this room tonight. "This is like homecoming posters!"

Homecoming posters don't require careful analysis of what messages to push that will pull in Victoria's base while not activating less-interested groups to bump her down their rankings.

Homecoming posters don't have to strategize around which spots will be available to best target each demographic, after Jade and Marisa have taken their picks.

But it's totally the same thing.

Victoria taps the back of my hand, then lets her fingers settle around my wrist. Her nails are newly painted, and the purple matches the buttons we made earlier in the week.

"The designs look amazing. I know you took that seriously," she says, her voice low. "Thank you."

I nod. Words won't come, not when my attention is so wholly taken up by her earnest brown eyes and her soft touch.

"So, movie time, right?" says Katrina (formerly known as Not-Catalina). She's on her stomach, and she jerks her head sharply to move her long bangs out of her face.

To my horror, this prompts a full five-minute discussion about whether to start with *Pocahontas* or *Inside Out*. I focus on outlining the design in pencil on our poster. Victoria holds the ruler steady as I sketch, shifting to the next line before I can even ask. In the end, it's Victoria, too, who corrals them into agreement on *Inside Out*.

Victoria's knee settles against mine as we begin to fill in the poster. Does she know? I mean, obviously she *knows*, she must be able to feel the mirror image of this gentle pressure—but does she care? Does she care *that way*? The way that I do, the way that I shouldn't, and my fingers are trembling almost too hard to hold the marker.

"Wait," she whispers. "Like this?"

She passes a different marker toward me, her fingers slipping along the back of my hand, and she mimes the shadow effect she wants for the letters.

"Okay," I say.

When she sits back on her heels, her shoulder bumps mine. Suddenly, it's too much. I drop the marker on the rug—cap on, of course—and scoot backward. I just need . . . space. New hands. New heart. Water?

As I edge toward the kitchen, I catch sight of Joan's poster.

"Um, what?" I say.

"Hmm?" She twists around. There's definitely glitter glue caught in her reddish hair and smudged across one sharp cheekbone, and I definitely don't care.

"Did you, uh . . ." I try to find a way to word this politely. "Have a question about the design?"

"Oh! No, the design's great," she says, smiling. "The catwalk and everything. I just thought it could use a little something . . . *more*."

More looks like an absolute mess of glitter around the edges, and random words like YAY! and CATWALK! in round cursive, interrupting the clean, professional look of the original design. Thank god I didn't give her one of the posters that highlights Victoria's more serious plans.

Joan turns back toward the TV, glitter pen in hand. I look at Kyle's poster, which he's barely started. With creeping horror, I realize he's probably *saving* it for her.

I crouch behind Joan so I'm not looming. "It's, um, we're trying to make them all have a unified look, you know? So if you can follow the design . . . as much as possible . . . that would be helpful."

"Uh, okay." When Joan turns around this time, she's not smiling.

"And Victoria and I are pretty far along on ours. So how about you and Kyle really . . . go for this one, and we'll finish his?"

When he hears his name, Kyle turns too. "It's whatever. Let her have it, baby."

"Sure," says Joan, her tone flat. "It's yours."

"Thanks!" I make my voice extra cheery. "Then you guys can just watch the movie!"

Joan raises her eyebrows, obviously meaning, she *was* watching the movie before I came over and pretended not to criticize her poster making. I wouldn't have to criticize if she could follow instructions. It's not like I was requiring anything difficult of her. I set Kyle's poster to the side and head into the kitchen. I'm still looking for the cups when Victoria follows me in.

"Okay?" she whispers. Her eyebrows are scrunched together, but in confusion, not annoyance.

"I just don't get why they don't *get* it." My low voice matches hers.

"It's fine," she says.

"Don't you want the posters to match, though? To look good?"

She trails her hand along the edge of the counter, not meeting my eyes. "Yeah. Of course I do. But they offered to help, so . . ."

"It's not real help if it creates more work later. You can have standards for volunteers, you know."

"But for friends?" Victoria shakes her head. Before I can answer, she places a hand on my arm, steadying herself as she leans toward me. "Don't worry. I've got two extras at home, if it's really a mess."

"You're the best," I say.

Victoria grins. "According to you."

I press a hand to my chest, mock offended. "And isn't that enough?"

"Oh, it is," she says.

And what am I supposed to do with that? *Not* fall in love?

CHAPTER TWENTY-ONE

On Thursday night, Victoria and I FaceTime as she finishes editing another video. Her hair is loose, and she keeps pushing it back, her purple fingernails disappearing into the curls. She's not even in the same room as me, and still my heartbeat speeds up when she smiles.

"So you know how we talked about filming at a game?" she says.

"Yeah?"

"Well, the hockey season finished, like, a month ago."

Annoying. What is the point of living in Minnesota if high school hockey doesn't extend through April?

"I should have checked on that earlier, sorry. Okay, so, new plan . . ."

"Well, that's the thing. We don't need a new plan, necessarily, because the women's professional hockey league—the PHF—is doing an exhibition game tomorrow night. Minnesota v. Boston. My dad got tickets through work, but he's busy, so . . . do you want to go? With me?"

Oh my god.

Is this a date?

It's not a date. It's the two of us, following through on a plan we made weeks ago. Making sure corporate perks don't go to waste. Totally normal and platonic and not worthy of the way my heart is pounding like I've actually just played a hockey game, instead of received an invitation to one. And yet, all those rapid heartbeats sound like *date date date date date*. She likes me enough to ask *me*. That's a golden, sparkling *something* that makes me want to spin around the room.

No broken hearts, I think.

Mentally, I crash back down. Campaign focus. Friendship. Those come first.

"That sounds fun." I clear my throat and add, "And perfect for the video, of course."

"Of course." Victoria looks away from her phone, probably back toward her editing.

"Are celebrity endorsements allowed?"

She laughs. "I don't think we get to meet them!"

"Meet them! *They* should be meeting *you*."

Victoria shakes her head, curls bouncing and dimples deep as she smiles. "Meeting *you*, maybe. So when you're in college you can make them do a real endorsement."

"Hey. This is real," I say.

"You know what I mean."

"Nope." I cross my arms.

"Okay, how about, when you're working on a campaign with a . . . larger scope."

"That, I'll take."

As soon as we hang up, I rush to the basement, looking for

Chelsea. I need to strike the optimal balance between warm and cute tomorrow, and she's the only person in the house who's been to a hockey game as a teenager in the last decade. It's basically a campaign event. You always need to match the occasion.

Fourteen Days Until Election Day

It's not an exaggeration to say I typically spend half the time we're in Victoria's car looking at her hands, so I notice the Band-Aid right away.

"Poster paper cut?" I ask.

"Huh? Oh, no." She rubs against the Band-Aid with her thumb. "We're . . . I'm moving, actually."

"Oh, wow."

She's never brought it up, not even when we're with her other friends. It's kind of a big deal, isn't it? There's a small twist in my stomach, sad that she didn't share this with me.

The background of her parliamentarian to president video rushes in front of my eyes, superimposing on the slow-moving snowscape beyond the car. The twist in my gut doubles and tightens. Those boxes weren't saved and repurposed from some prior move: They were for *this* one. I even commented on them—and she still hadn't told me.

You only want to talk about the campaign, anyway, I remind myself. *No broken hearts.*

I think back to what Amrita said last week, about how Jade and I were all goals and no gentleness, all victory and no vulnerability. In some ways, a lot of my conversations with Victoria have mirrored that . . . but I have this instinctive feeling I could cry in front of her without her complaining to Louis or Lauren later. And I want to be that kind of friend for Victoria—or I would, if comforting her about non-campaign worries didn't seem like a fast track to me needing the exact kind of comfort she wouldn't be able to offer.

I clear my throat. "Moving to where?"

"Still around here."

"Do you like the new place?"

"It's fine." She sighs. "Can we talk about something else? It feels like my whole life is just, moving, moving, moving right now, and it's boring!"

The word stings. "Sorry—I didn't . . ."

"No, not . . ." Victoria glances at me. "You're not boring. My mom is boring, and my dad, and all these relatives who have come over to help, and it's boxes *everywhere* . . ."

"You need a break. I got it," I say. "So . . . hockey, huh."

Victoria laughs, and the sound untwists my stomach and seems to carry me on a cloud all the way downtown.

The arena is noisy, packed even though we're twenty minutes early. There aren't a lot of people wearing Minnesota Whitecaps gear, more clusters of families with matching Minnesota Wild hats. We wait in the concessions line behind two guys in Golden Gophers jerseys loudly talking about their last stats exam, and I convince Victoria to let me pay for our hot dogs.

The seats are good, I think: about fifteen rows up, closer to one net but not so on the end that we won't be able to see what's happening around the other.

"To hockey," I say, tipping my water bottle toward Victoria.

"To women," she says, and winks.

"To winning."

"Cheers!"

As the game starts, I quickly realize that I . . . know nothing about hockey. I thought it was one of those things I'd picked up by breathing Minnesotan air for almost sixteen years, but that was obviously optimistic.

Note to self: Don't advertise yourself as knowing how to connect with Midwestern voters until you know what "icing" means, *not* in the context of *The Great British Baking Show*.

I don't even know how many players are supposed to be on the ice at a time until Victoria starts explaining it all to me (six for each team, including the goalie).

"Goalies are sacrosanct. Do not mess with the other team's goalie, do not—GO, GO, GO!" Victoria's suddenly standing up, jumping and shouting as one of the Whitecaps breaks away, cutting around the Boston Pride defenders and speeding across the ice.

As she slams her stick against the puck, aiming for the goal, I jump up, too, the shout pulled from me by the energy of the crowd, and it's—a clang against a side post, and then neatly into the glove of Boston's goalie.

We groan with almost everyone else—it's clearly a home crowd—but when Victoria turns to me, she's grinning, almost panting, cheeks flushed and eyes bright. "So that's hockey."

I'm in.

Victoria points at the scoreboard, high above the center of the ice, which has more electronic squares for stats than I'd expect. "Even if the score says it's nil-nil, you can usually tell who's dominating by the number of shots on goal."

"More chances to get through," I say.

"Yeah, exactly."

"It's like voter contact. Campaigns do all this research into how many phone calls or door knocks it takes to get someone registered, or actually to the polls. Even before voting starts, the campaign that's talked to a non-hostile voter three times—or to three times as many non-hostile voters once—probably has an advantage."

"Yes!"

There are more breaks in the game than the three periods would suggest. Every few minutes, when there's been a natural stop in play, people come out to shovel away the ice chips that have accumulated by the nets.

Since there's no action to distract us, I venture to say, "You're *really* into this. Like, a lot. How did I not know this?"

Victoria shrugs. "None of my friends are into sports—not counting Louis and soccer—so I don't really talk about it. It's not that interesting if you're not a fan, and . . . I don't know. It's like, if you're into sports, then you must be stupid—"

"You're not stupid," I say.

"—and then on the other side of it, well, I'm a lesbian, so *obviously* I'm into hockey, and so people I'm out to would . . . dismiss it. Like, oh, you're *that* girl. Of course."

"That sucks. Lesbians are cool, and you, specifically, are cool, and we're only fourteen minutes into this game but I'm pretty sure hockey is *also* cool."

"Careful. If you say stuff like that, I'm going to take it as permission to talk to you about the history of the Premier Hockey Federation. And rant about pay inequality."

"Bring it *on*," I say. "I want it."

The whistle blows.

Victoria hesitates, still watching me instead of the game. "I don't want to bore you."

I meet her gaze. "I'm not bored."

The first period ends tied at 0–0, with Minnesota just edging out Boston in shots on goal. During intermission, we stay in our seats to watch the Zambonis glide over the scarred ice, leaving smooth, glistening swaths in their wakes.

In the second period, Boston scores early, answered a few minutes later by two goals from the same Minnesota player.

"Oh my god, you need a hat trick," Victoria screams, jumping as the player taps padded fists with her teammates.

"What?" I shout.

"Three goals by one person! It's a big deal," she says once we've sat down again. "You deserve it, since it's your first game."

Victoria deserves it. Just for . . . being Victoria. A hockey fan who wants to share that jumping-up-and-down, puck-against-the-boards, sticks-caught-together joy.

On the ice below, Boston Pride settles into a rhythm. The arena is hushed. The only sound is that of the puck being caught by each subsequent stick. Pass. Pass. Pass. The puck connects with a clean, sharp snap each time, and the clarity of it takes my breath away. It's all the smoothness of sinking into a bath, without any of the sleepiness. Maybe it's like watching precinct numbers roll in during a landslide victory: yes, and yes, and yes. When they score, a shot high into the corner of the net, I'm not even mad.

Victoria isn't either. "That was *so* pretty."

We film a few clips of the game here and there, and during one of the net-clearing breaks, I turn the camera on Victoria. We decided there would be too much background noise in the arena for her to really perform here, but we can splice the clips together and use voice-over. I don't know if I can get the true jocks to rank Victoria second, but I'm not giving up on them.

The third period is brutal, the movements more aggressive and the passing sloppier than before. I film an (unsuccessful) break-away and post it to Instagram.

"They want to win in regulation," Victoria says. "And they're tired."

I think about the runoff election that might be in our future and nod.

Minnesota gets a penalty, and then, fifteen seconds later, another. Victoria's hand shoots out and grabs mine.

"No, no, no, no, *no*," she says.

I'm too distracted by the feeling of her hand in mine. It's cool and soft, and her grip tells me she's not planning to let go. I squeeze back. I know she doesn't mean it the way I want her to; I know I'm the only available port in the storm of hockey stress. But it doesn't stop me from trying to memorize this perfect pressure, and pretending that she reached for me in the way I don't let myself reach for her.

"What?"

"Five on three!" she groans.

In hockey, you don't take your penalties sequentially. Which means Minnesota now has three players (not counting the goalie) to Boston's five. The remaining three hover in front of their net, while Boston seems to pass the puck endlessly between them, searching for an opening.

"Stall, stall, stall," Victoria commands in a whisper.

When the buzzer sounds to signal the end of the first penalty, Victoria jumps up, pulling me with her. Minnesota seems to take heart from the crowd's screams, and there's a messy scramble toward Boston's goal.

"Let's! Go! Short-handed goal! GO!"

I'm screaming, too, not really words, just inarticulate wishes.

And it's—a miss.

"*So* close," she says. Our hands fall apart.

"Aww, there's still time left," I say.

When we sit, I hesitate for a second. My heart is beating so loud, I'm convinced that if the crowd were a single decibel quieter, Victoria would be able to hear it. Then I wrap my arm around her shoulders. I'm hoping it comes off in a teasing-comfort kind of way. Victoria keeps her eyes on the game, but she settles into me, her head against my shoulder, and I let out a deep breath.

This is okay. Hockey's not real life, right? This is a separate world, and in this world, you're supposed to scream. You're supposed to care loudly and frequently. Victoria and I can touch, a little, and the adrenaline from the game drowns out every last reminder of *no broken hearts*.

Because Victoria feels *so* good next to me. And she's so pretty. And in the last two hours she's convinced me that hockey might be worth falling in love with. Even when you miss.

Two minutes to go.

Game still tied.

Victoria shifts, leaning forward again. When my arm falls away from her back, she laces our fingers together. Between the game in front of me and the girl at my side, I'm barely breathing.

One minute.

And then—Minnesota pulls their goalie. Another player, a normal one, comes on the ice instead.

"What? What!" I scream.

We're on our feet.

"Empty net!" Victoria is bouncing up and down, shouting to be heard above the roar of the crowd. "It's *so* risky, but if you wait long enough—if you need to get ahead—"

Pass. Pass.

Boston intercepts the puck, and my heart is in my throat as they dodge Minnesota players on their quest toward that unguarded net, but—*there*. Minnesota gets control, and there's no one open to receive a pass, but that's okay, she's twisting past the Boston defense, and it's her and the ice and the puck and the goalie and two seconds and one shot—

"Victoria!" I scream, and she wraps her arms around me, and her lips are pressed against mine when the final buzzer sounds.

"Madison," she says, or I think she does, because around us, the crowd is still cheering, waving hats and clapping.

I'm breathless, from the game, the too-short kiss, and a wild kind of hope.

"Yeah?" I'm sure she can't hear me either.

Instead, we watch each other. I don't know exactly what my face looks like right now, but I can guess from watching hers: the lingering smile on her lips, the crease of confusion on her forehead, her eyebrows slanting toward vulnerability.

"Ummm . . ." A sudden, scarlet flush overtakes her cheeks. "Let's get hot chocolate?"

"Okay."

I want to reach for her hand again, but the stairs that will take us out of the arena are overflowing, and it's all I can do to not lose my balance or Victoria in the crowd. We're quiet as we walk to the car, letting the noise of everyone else's postgame analysis fill the silence of the night.

My brain is anything but silent. Hand-holding during a power play is basically like hand-holding during a scary movie: more to do with what's in front of you than who's beside you. It's easily written off. But that kiss? You don't write off kisses. At least, I don't, and I don't think Victoria does either.

What did it mean? What are we doing? What do I *want*? In so many other parts of my life, I know the answers exactly. I want my driver's license and admission to YPBC. I want to win this ASB election and become a campaign manager.

I want Victoria. I want more hand-holding, in hallways and at next year's homecoming. Or just at home, if that's all she's comfortable with. I want kisses where we linger in the moment, instead of being hurried away by a crowd. I also want this election to finish smoothly, cleanly, despite its rocky start and every pothole along the way. I want to keep that promise: No broken hearts.

I'm so lost in my head, when I buckle my seat belt, I swear it's the only thing keeping me tethered.

"Caribou okay?" Victoria asks, and there's a twist to her lips, almost a smirk, like she's sharing an inside joke with herself.

"Yeah," I say, on autopilot, until I catch up with what I've agreed to. I feel like an actual lightbulb has lit up above my head. "*Wait. Was that—was that a date? Last week?*"

Oh my god. Have I been so focused on not dating Victoria that I didn't realize I was . . . already being dated? Part of me thrills at the idea, all fizzy delight. The other part of me is trying to shove *all these unplanned feelings* where they belong: behind a "possibly, later" wall. This other part of me is failing.

"It wasn't a date, but I wanted it to be," Victoria says. I can't quite make out her dimples in the dark car, but I swear they're there.

I'm in total awe of how honest she is. She wanted it to be a real date. She wanted *me*. Wants me, even. I've never had champagne, but I imagine a bottle uncorking now, the force of the spray ripping down the flimsy barrier of my final objections. I feel light-headed. It was one thing to push away my crush when it was theoretical. But now I know how her hand folds into mine, the way our lips can fit together, that when she looks at me, she sees all of me— the dreams and the fears and the plans and the mistakes—and she doesn't look away. Because she doesn't want to.

"Oh," I say. I take a deep breath and mirror her own honesty back. "What if . . . this could be one. A real one."

I'm not certain about our future, but I am certain about tonight.

"Okay," she says. Her smile slips into something soft and satisfied, and as we stop under a streetlight, I lean across the console and touch my thumb to her cheek.

We talk about the hockey game until we're tucked into a corner table. The feeling of unreality from the arena rushes back, except this time, I'm on the other side of it. In her car, I could be anyone, and we could go anywhere. Here, we're at a chain coffee shop, the kind that, a dozen miles west, any of our classmates could be at right now. There's no blackboard at this location, no tulips or snowflakes to examine when I can't quite meet Victoria's eyes. All of a sudden, I'm reminded what a bad idea this is. She's my candidate. A new friend. And I've already made one girl dump me out of the blue this year. I'm not looking to make that a habit.

"Hey. Stop," she says. She reaches across the table, tapping a purple fingernail against my ceramic mug.

"What?" I didn't think I was doing anything.

"You're talking yourself out of this, when you were—well, it seemed like you were—pretty happy at the game, and in the car."

"Well . . ." I keep looking at the table. "It's complicated, isn't it?"

"I wasn't gonna tell you, because—I like hanging out with you, and I didn't want to scare you off, but . . . you're smart, and cute, and you care *so much*. And I really like you. A lot."

Jade and I hadn't exactly said those things. Or at least, she didn't say those things to me, not the very first night we kissed. We just kissed again. It was nice. What I wanted.

I swallow.

"Sorry, am I—? You don't have to like me back. It's okay if it was, like, heat of the moment, and now I'm turning it into . . . Louis told me I should be more confident with you, but, um, maybe I'm too much."

The words send a shock through me, because *Victoria* isn't too much. I'm the one who's too much. I shake myself upright, straightening my shoulders.

Victoria frowns. "You're going to give me a campaign speech, aren't you." It's not a question.

"It's not professional," I manage, because although even *I* know it's a weak excuse, it's the only one I've got left to protect me.

"*We're* not professional!" She holds up a hand. "It's *real*, we're agreed on that. But I'm not actually your boss. I'm just a girl." There's a slight blush on her cheeks, and something in the cadence of her words starts to sound familiar. "In front of another girl. Asking . . ."

"Asking for what?" My voice comes out a whisper.

"A chance. Or whatever you'll give me."

"I think you're going to break my heart," I blurt.

"What?"

"I think—because Louis is right, you know." I nod, my head bobbing. I keep my eyes on the edge of the table, so I can pretend it's the edge of my desk and all I'm doing is talking to my empty bedroom. "I have this . . . apparently obvious crush on you. I can't really say when it started, exactly. But I do." I take a breath, and then another. Victoria doesn't interrupt me. "And . . . Jade didn't break my heart. But it sucked and it was sudden, and I have this feeling that—that I could end up in way deeper with you, and then in a month, or two months, you'll decide I'm not your type after all."

"I hear you, but—hey."

There's a gentle pull in her voice, and I finally look up. It's dim in here, but it does nothing to obscure the determination in her eyes.

"Consider this. Consider that . . . I don't break your heart. Ever. Consider that . . . it's not in my plan. The thing that's in my calendar is making you laugh and holding your hand. If you made a candidate binder on me, the detailed kind that goes into my personal

223

background, there would be a page about my type and your picture would be there. Because I *can* tell you when I first started liking you."

I'm barely breathing. I want to listen to her forever. No one has ever, ever said anything like this to me. I'm considering. I'm considering *so hard*. My heart keeps skipping, and my mind races back through our history, trying to string the pieces together. When could she have started? Maybe our two-move dance at the showcase? Or even the night of the snowed-out movie?

"Last March. Whatever the day was before our poetry presentations. You were talking with somebody else at our table about—I'm not sure anymore, I think a show? And you turned to ask me what I thought, and it was like . . . suddenly I wished I was the smartest, prettiest person in the room. That was it."

"That was a *year* ago."

That's . . . not possible, is it?

She shrugs.

"And I wasn't even . . . I didn't even do anything?" I swear I'm not fishing, but this is so wildly beyond the range of expected answers, I'm clinging to the confusion. As long as I'm uncertain, fact gathering and analyzing, I don't have to think about the waterfall of emotions, and whether I want to risk the rocks at the bottom. "I thought it would be, I don't know. My actual presentation, at least."

Victoria shakes her head. "You didn't have to do anything. That's what I'm saying. An ordinary day, but I could never look at you the same way again."

"You never said anything."

"You were already hard-core flirting with Jade every lunch. I wasn't going to get in the way of that. I really . . ." She leans toward me. "You have to know, I wasn't wishing for you two to break up. I

224

wasn't waiting on it. I'd never want for you to get hurt. It was this, this thing that I felt and that I knew I was going to carry with me for a while because you're amazing, and I was okay with that."

"So . . ." It's not the start of a real thought, just a noise to fill the space while I try to rearrange the past thirteen months. I know you don't have to date someone simply because they liked you for a long time. But let's be honest: When you like them back, knowing about all that time feels good. Like you're someone worth waiting for.

"So I'm not going to break your heart. If you like me, like you say you do . . . take a risk with me."

And because it's Victoria, with her curls and her unexpected confidence, her dimples and deep feelings about catwalks, I say yes.

CHAPTER TWENTY-TWO

Thirteen Days Until Election Day

The last days of spring break are a blur. Victoria and I text frequently, but it's not as much as either of us would like. I'm still babysitting, and there are long stretches of time when Victoria is away from her phone, busy with moving. We agreed that we could each tell our best friends, along with our families when we're ready. I plan to tell mine soon . . . once I've had a chance to talk with Amrita. I know FaceTime will *not* do justice to Amrita's reaction, so I'm holding out until she gets back from Wisconsin.

To distract myself, and because I promised my parents, Chelsea and I go driving more. I can turn into a parking spot reliably now, but backing in often results in overturned barrels, since Chelsea's car doesn't have any of the cameras or sensors that are now standard.

At volunteering on Saturday, Connie greets me with a hug and asks after Jade. I squirm, remembering that I didn't tell her about the breakup.

"I'm kind of seeing someone new, actually," I say, stepping back.

Connie narrows her eyes, hands on her hips. "This is good news?"

"Yes! She's—yes." My face heats up, and I wave at Trish to give me an excuse to duck toward the sign-in table.

"What's this I hear about you and someone new?" she asks in a low voice. Her box braids are up in a twist today, and she's wearing a light blue Stacey Abrams shirt.

I pretend to focus on the laptop. "Could be."

"Could be that you took my advice to not tell Connie until there was someone new?"

"Could be," I repeat. My face breaks into a grin. I'm dying to tell Trish about our respective roles in the campaign, but I want the go-ahead from Victoria first.

"Aww, look at you so happy. Good for you. Bring her sometime, okay?" Trish pushes the laptop toward the new arrivals entering behind me.

"I'll ask her," I say, and I mean it.

A few minutes later, while Trish introduces the day's goal, I think more about her instruction to bring Victoria along. Hockey game aside, Victoria only ever sees me at school, or with her friends. These are *my* people. Or almost my people. I'm trying. I'll get there. And it might be nice to have Victoria with me as I do.

★ ★ ★

Twelve Days Until Election Day

"You're lucky I love you," Amrita announces as I open the front door for her.

"Of course, but why today?"

"Because I just spent four hours in a car with my whole family, and then immediately got *back* in the car to hear your too-big-for-FaceTime news."

She raises her eyebrows, even as she pulls me into a hug. It feels good—grounding. Girls and campaigns may come and go, but Amrita and I are always there for each other.

I tug her into my room, where we settle on the bed. She smooths her skirt over her knees, settling in to wait me out. As if I can wait a single second longer.

"So . . . what I wanted to tell you . . . well, you know that Victoria and I have been hanging out, over break?" My cheeks heat.

Amrita bites her lip, obviously trying hard not to laugh. "Mm-hmm? Anything to add?"

"We're—dating? As of Friday." My voice is high-pitched, and I'm a little embarrassed, but I'm also just *happy*.

"Who confessed first?" Amrita pushes up her glasses, like I'm a very slow research participant and she's an extremely patient scientist.

"You're not surprised?"

"Oh my god. Victoria had the most obvious crush since . . ." She shakes her head. "No, I'm sorry, there's no comparison. She had the most obvious crush. Besides, I watched you and Jade for the better part of a *year*. You think I don't know what you look like when you like someone and they like you back?"

"I didn't even know until spring break!" I hesitate. "It's not too soon after Jade?"

"You're over her."

"I know."

"So, no. You've kept that poor girl waiting long enough."

"Oh my *god*." I bury my face in my hands for a full five seconds before I can regroup. "We're not telling people yet, okay? Other than you and Louis. Because it's only been a few days, and you know she's not fully out."

"Got it." She starts to finger-trace shapes on my duvet, and then adds, "Friday? That means . . . the hockey game? I'm going to tease you about that *forever*."

I might be okay with that.

CHAPTER TWENTY-THREE

Eleven Days Until Election Day

@WestPlymouthPress: Welcome back!!! This week, our newsroom is preparing to profile your ASB candidates. From their allyship advocacy to party-planning tips, we want it all.

Victoria, Louis, and I meet up at my locker before first period. According to our Instagram comments, people *love* the button designs. Today is their grand debut IRL. We pin buttons on each other's shirts, then a bunch more on our backpacks. We'll take them off as people ask for their own.

I was worried that things might feel different with Victoria—in a weird way, or a bad way, or an I'm-not-ready way—now that we're at school again, with linoleum flooring instead of bedroom rugs. Like we'd have to fade back into being our real-world selves, who don't kiss at hockey games. But sitting next to her at lunch, I'm reminded that I fell for her right here. If there are shades of realness, then my feelings are *more* real here, and this is even more right.

Louis is telling us about Annie's attempts to co-opt their APUSH class into a candidate town hall, starring her, when Victoria squeaks, shoving her phone toward me.

"Look at the views!"

It's her intro video, posted ten minutes ago *not* on her YouTube channel but her week-old TikTok. Already, there are thirty views and seven comments. It's not even a blink in the grand scheme of TikTok, but Victoria doesn't need the adulation of millions: She needs a hundred West Plymouth sophomores to like her better than six others. We spend the rest of lunch huddled over our phones, watching the likes climb on TikTok and where it's cross-posted on each of our Instas.

"So . . . that's a yes on posting the rest this week? Or do you want some more time to think about whether this was a good idea?" I say.

Victoria laughs. "Definitely a yes. And—I could drive you home again, if you want."

"Yeah, thanks." I touch my hand to her arm, *casually*. We haven't been alone all day, and ten minutes in her car sounds like heaven. "I don't work tonight, so you could stay for a bit? Watch these video reactions come in . . ." *Kiss again?*

Victoria shakes her head. "Can't. I wish, though."

"Just don't forget to engage with your voters!"

"I don't think I could forget *anything* about this campaign." She looks at her phone again and shimmies a little, like a happy shiver's running through her.

The comments sections are walls of heart-eyes and raised-hands emojis. I can't wait for her to post the first policy video. If it's not fire emojis all the way down, I'll be shocked.

Ten Days Until Election Day

I feel like I'm riding a high, brought on solely by early campaign adrenaline and the rush of watching Victoria's first two videos—her intro on Monday, her parliamentarian to president on Tuesday—spread through the sophomores. Victoria tells me that someone complimented her in almost every class—and yes, she remembered to ask if they wanted a button. I'm jittery with pride.

Of course, we're not the only ones starting the work early (or, you know, on time). Annie and her cohort show up on Tuesday in campaign T-shirts, as I suspected. Jade created a custom Instagram filter (my idea originally). Marisa's Snapchat story urges people to rank her first, in English, Spanish, and Mandarin.

"How many more videos do you have prepared?" Louis asks at lunch.

"Two. They're a lot of work, because of the spoken word part." Victoria makes a face, and I know why: Some of the other candidates have been putting out a *lot* more social media content, but nothing with the It factor of Victoria's pieces.

"Okay, what if . . . duets! Oh my god. I'm totally going to do a duet with yours," says Louis.

"Doing what?" I ask.

"I don't know, does it matter? Cooking? Sit-ups?"

"Thirst trap," says Victoria.

"And?" Louis looks at me. "More engagement, more votes."

"Sold. Can the rest of your friends do them too? Let's make it a thing," I say.

Louis pulls out his phone. I'm pretty sure he's just messaging George, but hey, if George wants to brainstorm thirst-trap campaign duets with him, I support it.

Actually . . . I grab my phone, too, and start looking through her other friends' accounts. Maybe our social media strategy can be more than asking them to share Victoria's official posts (as amazing as they are).

Which is how I end up chasing down Lauren and Katrina after school, weaving through the crowded parking lot toward Lauren's green Highlander.

"Hey, Madison," says Lauren.

"Hi," I pant.

"Is something wrong with the campaign?" says Katrina. Her voice is the wary pitch of someone who thinks they're about to be scolded.

Yikes.

"Nothing is wrong with the campaign. Everything is right with the campaign. You two are *very right* for the campaign. I was watching your videos during lunch, and, wow. Lauren, you were on makeup crew for the musical, right?"

She nods.

"Your *Midsummer* tutorial is incredible. And, Katrina, I know this will shock you"—I let myself smile—"but if it's more complicated than mascara, Amrita does it for me, mostly because it's overwhelming and I don't know how to evaluate any of it like I do voting history . . . but I watched your eyeliner tutorial, and it was so clear and detailed, I feel like I could actually do it."

"Cat-eye would look great on you," says Katrina.

"Thank you! And . . . Victoria's policies would look great on *you*."

They exchange confused glances.

"Look, your content is *solid*. Do you think you could do a couple for Victoria? Like a . . . highlighter tutorial that also *highlights* some of her policy proposals." Half a lunch period is obviously not enough for me to know anything about makeup, but I don't need to know the details: I need to know just enough to recognize Katrina and Lauren are good, and let them loose, if they're willing.

"I've been planning for a *Wicked* look soon—I could definitely use that to talk about why we need the catwalk," says Lauren.

"Yes! That's perfect."

Louis messaged me last night that Victoria's lock on the sophomore theater kids may not be *quite* as secure as I thought. Since Victoria is parliamentarian this year and will undoubtedly be named a crew head next year, there's some grumbling that Zack deserves the president position, like we're in preschool and it's his turn on the swings. It's time for a reminder that while Zack may be fun at the cast party, Victoria is going to deliver the catwalk.

Katrina snaps her fingers. "I haven't done any of these in a while, but I used to be *really* good at the lip sync feature . . . I could do my weekend getting-ready to one of her poems. Parliamentarian to president, maybe?"

"Oh my god, yes. Exactly. You get where I'm going with this."

"This is going to be fun—I've got a million ideas already." Lauren beams at me. "Do you want to see them first?"

I hesitate, then shake my head. "No, you know what these should be like better than I do."

Victoria pulls up alongside us and rolls her window down. "Did you find a cooler ride?"

"Yeah, but you can have her back." Katrina opens Victoria's passenger door for me. "See you tomorrow!"

"Making friends?" Victoria asks, amused, as she turns out of the lot.

Allies is on the tip of my tongue, but I stop myself. Katrina would probably teach me how to do a cat-eye herself if I asked.

"Something like that." I lean back into the seat. "They're going to do some makeup Duets and other stuff with your TikToks."

"You asked them to do that? Those are a lot of work."

"I know."

"Okay, well . . . I don't want you to be disappointed if they don't get them done," she says.

The thought honestly hadn't occurred to me, but then I remember half of them, including Katrina, didn't even come to the dance showcase. "They're your friends, and this is the kind of thing they like to do anyway. But if it makes you feel better, you can ask them."

Victoria slows down to allow another car to enter the lane. "Devin says *WPP* is going to feature one of my videos on their channels."

Privately, I decide that if Victoria won't follow up with Katrina and Lauren, I'll do it myself.

When I tell my family that Victoria and I are dating, their reactions are embarrassingly similar to Amrita's: supportive but unsurprised. I only manage to divert the conversation from their *too*-delighted questions by making Chelsea give my parents an update on my driving progress.

After dinner, I allow myself fifteen minutes of leaving comments on the Google Doc where Victoria has been outlining her speech. I have twice the number of pages to read for English as usual, but speeches are in just over a week, and Victoria needs time to practice with a finished version. I'm about to close the doc when my phone lights up with a new message.

Amrita

Snapchat oppo research update: Jade & John are going to put up posters during zero tomorrow

John is one of Jade's debate friends, one of the guys I shared a restaurant table with before winter formal but who now doesn't even make eye contact.

Amrita

I'm assuming that's when you & V are going

Victoria and I *are* planning to put up the posters before school tomorrow. If it were anyone else, I'd say it's a big building and we likely won't see them at all. But since it's Jade, she'll probably go out of her way to be smug about her spot by the science wing water fountain.

Me

Thanks. Ughhhhh

Right before bed, I message Victoria.

Me

Zero hour poster party!!!

Meet you in the cafeteria :)

I wait a couple of minutes to see if she'll respond, but I'm too tired to wait for long. When I fall asleep, my message is still unread.

★ ★ ★

Nine Days Until Election Day

"Thanks for helping me carry these. And for the ride," says Marisa.

We each hold one side of her trash-bag-protected posters as we walk into school.

"I couldn't let you take these on the bus when my dad was going to drive me anyway."

"Well . . . I *am* the competition." She looks at me slyly. "Or don't you think so?"

"Uh, you definitely are, but . . ."

We navigate down the ramp leading from the main-floor lounges into the cafeteria. There's a tense moment when a corner pokes through the plastic and catches on Marisa's brightly patterned over-sized sweater, but we quickly untangle them without damage to the poster or the knit.

"What I'm hearing is that I can count on you to rank me second."

"Yeah, I'm a sure thing for second."

I probably *shouldn't*. Marisa, after all, has a real shot at winning, and the strategic thing to do is rank our top competitors last. But I can't stomach ranking her lower when she's the only other person I could see doing a great job as junior class president, especially given that I almost offered to run her campaign instead of Victoria's. It's a weird mind trip, ending up in the cafeteria with Marisa and her posters even after choosing Victoria.

Once we set the posters on a table near the entrance, I message Victoria that I'm here. She still hasn't seen my messages from last night.

"While you're waiting, would you mind helping me?" Marisa asks. She nods toward the north wall of the cafeteria, where all the sophomore candidates have a poster spot.

"Yeah, of course." I slip my phone into my pocket and carry the tape Marisa retrieves from her backpack.

We put tape rolls along the back of the poster, and then Marisa holds it close to the wall while I try to judge the angle.

"Did you switch sides over break?" Jade asks from behind me.

I jump, and Marisa almost drops the poster.

"Hey, Jade." I sigh.

"You're so outgoing these days," she says, smiling.

I don't copy her. I don't even know what to say. Haven't we *had* this conversation already? Isn't she bored?

"No Victoria, I see . . . Did she dump you too? They say third time's the charm," Jade adds, nodding at Marisa.

Marisa puts the poster on the nearest table and crosses her arms. "Madison's a friend, and she agreed to help me for a minute. It's not really any of your business."

"I don't get your problem," I say. "I *wanted* to be doing all this with you, but you dumped me. This is . . . obviously what was going to happen."

"Right, right . . . Because you need someone for your application. Two campaigns, even? 'Cause you're not nearly as good as you think you are? And now you have to put quantity over quality." Jade throws a disdainful glance at Marisa's poster, even though it's facedown and she can't see a thing.

Marisa's poster is great, by the way.

"Marisa and Victoria are both amazing candidates. They'd do a lot of good for the school. I'm happy to be helping." I don't bother to get into the fact that I'm helping Marisa to hang this one poster while I wait for Victoria. It's the kind of detail I'm sure will be lost on Jade.

"And if she does need the campaign for her application, so what? It's not like the campaign has to only benefit the candidate," says Marisa.

My heart swells so fast, it's almost painful. Marisa doesn't even *know* about YPBC, but here she is, backing my right to try for it.

"I don't think that's how these things are *supposed* to work," Jade snaps. She's flushed now, hands on her hips. "How do you think I felt, when all of a sudden we 'had' to do this or that for *you*!"

That's how she felt? Not excited for me, not proud of me, not eager to help, the way I'd been with her debate tournaments and her campaign?

"*My* campaign was just about you leaving, because you think you're so much fucking better than everybody else! And you're not, Madison. I'm the one who's going to win. I'm the one who's going to leave. You were supposed to help me with that, but you had to go and make it about you."

By the end of her rant, my jaw is basically on the scuffed cafeteria floor. "I asked for us to talk about campaign stuff *one week* early. I asked you to read a draft because . . . you were my girlfriend, and I thought that's what we were all about. I thought it was both of us, *together*. But you . . ." I try to think about how Amrita might frame it, if she were here. "You just wanted me lifting you up, didn't you? It's not about me leaving or whatever . . . you don't like the idea that I followed you around for ages and I still might get this prestigious opportunity you didn't even apply for. It's not about me thinking I'm better—it's about *you* thinking of YPBC as . . . beyond you, and you couldn't handle that, apparently." I rock back on my heels. "Wow. *Wow*."

"That's not—you're incapable of—you were supposed to—"

"No, I get it. Thanks for breaking up with me, by the way. I really appreciate that." Now I smile.

Jade's cheeks are flushed, and I'm surprised to notice she's blinking back tears. Obviously I messed up *her* plan. But how was I supposed to know I was meant to beg her to take me back? I guess we had a pattern where I tried to give her everything she only implied she wanted, but I wasn't raised to ignore someone's no. She said it wasn't working. She said she wanted us to be over, and I believed her. I know how to distinguish between what's romantic in an almost-breakup song and what's okay in real life. I don't want to be with someone who makes me question that difference.

"What*ever*. Enjoy losing," Jade says.

John enters the cafeteria, and Jade flounces off.

Marisa and I stand together in shocked silence. I am no longer composed of molecules: I am pure awkward.

"Well . . . uh." I smooth my palms on my jeans. "Sorry about that? And thanks." To escape the moment, I check my phone. Nothing from Victoria. Where is she? We've got six posters to put up before first period.

"Has Jade been treating you like that since the breakup? Because that's not okay," says Marisa.

"Yeah, it's . . . weirdly eye-opening? Kind of embarrassing, though. When she's dragging you or Victoria into it."

I haven't forgotten that Jade outed Marisa to me and Amrita before spring break.

Marisa's eyes narrow. "I know you were really into her . . . the puppy-love power-couple thing. But I always thought you could do better."

I feel myself start to blush, and I briefly cover my face with my hands as Marisa's eyes light up.

"Oh my god," she says. "You *are* doing better! Can I know who?"

"No, sorry. It's super new. Please don't say anything," I say. Victoria came out to Marisa during a recently asssigned APUSH partner project on Stonewall—so it's the newness, not the queerness, that holds me back.

"I won't," Marisa promises. "So . . . the poster?"

By the time we have her poster level and secure, a handful of other candidates, plus the usual breakfast crew, have filtered into the cafeteria. But no Victoria.

Marisa frowns as she watches me check my phone again. "She's probably driving."

"I know, it's just. You know."

"I do, yeah. Juliana is going to help me hang the rest upstairs, but I'll see you later?"

I nod. Marisa heads out, posters in hand, and I sit at the empty table. And wait.

And Victoria doesn't come.

CHAPTER TWENTY-FOUR

Nine Days Until Election Day

I wait in the cafeteria until the very last second, so I'm almost late to class. As I rush through the halls, I wince every time I pass another candidate's poster. Victoria's should be there. We had a plan.

The mid-morning break is more of the same. I run between Victoria's locker and mine, unable to find her. Every poster feels like those old portraits in a horror movie mansion, following me. Taunting me.

I resign myself to having to put them up during lunch. I wanted lunch for reviewing parts of her speech with Louis, but apparently that's going to have to wait. Peyton didn't get her posters up until after school the first day they were allowed last year, so at least we'll still be a few hours ahead of the incumbent—but knowing this is a comfort so small, it's basically nonexistent.

On the way to the cafeteria, after what must be the slowest morning of all time, I have to dodge a rowdy huddle, gathered around—is that one of Kevin's posters? I cut into the group so I can see it fully. The poster is roughly divided into three sections, labeled FUN, FOOD, and FREE SPACE below his scrawled KEVIN CORVI FOR JUNIOR CLASS PRESIDENT header. A Sharpie dangles from a string attached to each section, and people are . . . oh god . . . writing suggestions and underlining, starring, and circling their favorites. It's shockingly democratic. It's *engaging*.

It's just because he has no plans of his own, so he needs to steal everyone else's, I think.

Obviously, if *I'd* thought of it for Victoria, it would be "listening to the people" and "openness to others' ideas." Kevin definitely does not have an openness to others' ideas. Or I guess he's plenty open to petitioning for the return of chocolate milk at lunch. It's others' varied identities he can't stand.

A minute later, I'm in theory eating chicken salad, but all I can taste is bitterness and humiliation. My container is halfway empty by the time Victoria slips onto the stool next to me in the cafeteria.

"Ugh, Ms. Glen kept us so late," she says. She tears open a mustard packet and starts to prep her hamburger.

I take a final second to mentally rip up Kevin's poster before refocusing on the ones I actually want to see on the school walls. "Okay, well, eat quickly. Or maybe Louis and I can do the posters ourselves? Did you put them in Mr. Braun's room?"

Victoria drops her bun. It lands facedown, smearing mustard on her tray. "The posters. Oh, crap."

"What?" I say. "If you left them in your locker, it's . . . it's fine, we can borrow some civics textbooks to flatten them out before we put them up."

"Madison . . ." She looks at the ceiling, then at me. "I don't have the posters."

"What?" I say again. All the blood rushes to my head, leaving me dizzy.

"They're—I forgot them. I'm so sorry. I messed up. I'll bring them tomorrow, I promise." If her voice holds apology or resignation or anything else, I can't hear it above my own dismay.

"We were supposed to put them up today. Everybody else is."

As we speak, Kevin and two of his friends are taping another poster to the north wall. It's messily done—way worse than even the poster Joan mangled with her smiley-face enthusiasm—but it's there.

"Well, mine will be here tomorrow."

"That's not good enough," I say. Louis raises his eyebrows, but I keep my focus on Victoria. "I should have taken the posters myself. We needed them *today*. Otherwise we look sloppy."

Jade's accusations from this morning are still ringing in my ears. This *is* a quality campaign, and we *are* going to win. I'm exactly as good as I think I am, *and* I'm not just using Victoria for my application. I want her platform to be enacted; she wants me to get into YPBC.

"I'm *sorry*," Victoria says. She doesn't sound sorry, though. She sounds annoyed. "What am I supposed to do, skip class so I can get them? You don't have to come tomorrow morning if you don't want to."

"What? No. I'll be there." I modulate my tone. "Would you at least text the next time you're running late or there's an issue or whatever? I was waiting for you here the whole time."

Victoria's face drops, her eyebrows sagging. Her dimples are nowhere in sight. "I'm sorry about that. I feel really bad that you were waiting on me." She touches my wrist for a breath of a moment. "That's not how I want to make you feel."

"I just don't . . ." My voice sounds small, even to my own ears. "I don't get why you couldn't text. Or find me during break."

"I had to talk to a teacher. I'm here now."

It's almost enough. I don't want to be clingy. I also don't want to be an afterthought. I wait for her to give some explanation for this morning, but she doesn't say anything.

"So . . . what happened? Why were you late?"

"I misjudged traffic, that's all," she says, stiff on her circle next to me. *Traffic?*

"Isn't your new house still super close to school?"

Something about this whole situation is weird. Victoria may not be the best texter, but she's never late. She doesn't forget things either—not about the campaign, and definitely not about me.

"Can we not do this right now?" Her tone is brittle. "Let's just, can we talk about the speech?"

I try to catch Louis's gaze, but he's busy with his phone.

"Sure," I say. I pull out my Life Notebook and push down my concern about the posters. "Let's talk about your speech."

I'm surprised to find Victoria waiting for me outside my last class. We walk quietly together to my locker, then hers. I tick off the names of the candidates to myself as we pass by the posters. Marisa, Jade, Kevin. Annie, Riley, Zack. Victoria is the only one missing. Frustration builds in my chest.

Mr. Braun stands by a side exit off the main lobby, which the athletes use to get to their away-game buses. When he spots us, he gives a final high five to a baseball player and crosses the hallway.

"Victoria, you're not dropping out, are you?" he says.

Victoria's cheeks turn a deep red. "No. We're, um. I'm putting the posters up tomorrow."

"Just wanted to check in. Let me know if you need a hand!"

"Yo, Mr. Braun, think fast!"

A Frisbee whizzes right above my head, and Mr. Braun catches it easily. On the other side of the lobby, a junior or senior guy I don't know claps his raised hands, signaling for the return.

Mr. Braun looks around the lingering students, making direct eye contact with most of us. "Frisbees are for outside, right? You all heard me say that?"

There's an anticipatory laugh, and Mr. Braun throws the Frisbee back.

Victoria and I head into the parking lot. The air is heavy, still wet after a brief rain shower that morning. The humidity makes even the weak sun feel stifling. My mind is boiling over with how impotent I feel. I should have insisted on being the one to take the posters home after the movie night at Joan's. Victoria should have brought them today. She should have checked her phone. Her whole brand is literally being *the responsible one* and now—

"Can you be done being mad at me about this?" she says. She unlocks the car.

"I'm working on it." I get in and buckle my seat belt.

"Things have been a little complicated recently," she says.

"If you're not fully moved in yet, you could have left the posters with me. I wouldn't have minded."

"Okay, but it's *my* campaign. I wanted to be the one with the posters." She backs out of the parking spot and gets in line for the exit.

That's fair—and I know it's fair—but it's so hard to be reasonable when all those empty poster spots feel like failure. *My* failure, because even though it's Victoria's name on the ballot, I'm the one managing the calendar. And everyone at school knows it.

"Fine. That's fine, *if* you bring them. If you can't—"

"My parents are getting a divorce," she blurts.

"I—oh."

I feel like I've missed a step, like I did after that *Spider-Verse* movie night, except instead of landing in snow, it's a mix of shame and sympathy.

"My mom moved to a town house around here. My dad moved to Medina over spring break. I was at my dad's last night, and 55 was really backed up this morning. I accidentally left the posters at my mom's. I keep forgetting stuff," she says. "At break today—I was in the guidance counselor's office, making an appointment."

"I'm really sorry about your parents," I say.

She doesn't look at me, even though we're still stopped in line. "I've never been great about checking my phone, but I know I've been worse than usual for the last couple of months, because they're always arguing and I'm always caught up in it. Even after they decided to divorce. It's like, whose stuff is whose, what's the custody arrangement." Her voice breaks.

"I'm so, so sorry." I hesitate, then ask, "Why didn't you tell me?"

Victoria throws me a look, her eyes filled with tears. "Because I wanted you to *like* me. I wanted to be the cool, put-together girl.

You didn't want a mess. And I wanted a part of my life that *wasn't* a mess. That was just . . ."

"Well-organized campaign calendars," I say.

"Yeah." She chokes out a wet giggle. "Clearly that's working well."

"Excuse you, it *is*. Your posters are amazing, and everyone will notice them more when we put them up tomorrow. The buttons are *everywhere*." I reach over and wrap one of my fingers around a wayward curl. "If you want me to be the part of your life that isn't messy, I'll try to be that. But you don't need to hide any of this from me. I want to be someone you trust. I won't think any less of you for having . . . a real life, not a movie one. Because I *do* like you. A lot, remember?"

The line in front of us finally clears, and Victoria turns onto the main road.

"You might have to remind me," she says.

Once we're stopped in my driveway, I think about kissing her before I rush off to babysitting. Instead, when I lean over the console, I hug her hard, for as long as I dare.

After my babysitting shift, I message her a string of flower emojis. She sends me an equal number of hearts in return, but she steers our text conversation to comparing poster adhesive options, and she doesn't bring up the divorce the next morning either. Instead, as we meticulously tape each poster's edges to prevent curling, she asks if it's too late to become a GSA regular.

"Too late?" I say. "It's only too late when there's one meeting left our senior year."

When Victoria asks a question, she's invested in the answer, so I'm not surprised when she walks into Ms. Zhao's room for the GSA lunch on Friday, mere seconds after me. Amrita slips in behind Savannah and a few other seniors a minute later, and I move my backpack so she can pull a chair to the end of our table.

Ms. Zhao sits on her desk and claps her hands for attention. "Happy Friday, everybody! We're going to take the week off from anything formal so we can decompress from spring break with our families and build ourselves up before Day of Silence at the end of the month."

Day of Silence is one of my favorite GSA events, a day each year when queer students, educators, and our allies don't talk during school hours to spread awareness about bullying. Traditionally, the national Day of Silence is the second Friday in April, when West Plymouth is on spring break, so we always choose our own day to observe it.

A few stragglers push through the door, trying not to drop their trays as they navigate around chairs and backpacks. When I glance toward them, I do a double take. First, there's Jade, who, for once, ignores me completely to take a seat near the windows. Then there's Lauren, who relaxes when she spots us.

"Room for me?" she asks.

We rearrange our trays so she can sit across from Victoria.

"Victoria mentioned she was coming, and I didn't think I could take another lunch of Joan and Kyle, you know?" Her eyes widen. "And of course I'm an ally."

"We support the use of GSA lunch as an escape from annoying displays of heterosexuality," I assure her in my most solemn tone.

"Especially if you do Day of Silence with us," Amrita says.

For Day of Silence last year, Amrita and I both got early rides, and we spent zero hour in the language wing bathroom. Amrita did my makeup: bi flags on each cheek, rainbow eye shadow. She even braided a purple ribbon in my hair.

"Sure," says Lauren. She opens a container of apple slices. "Tell me when, I'll be there."

The shyest dimple emerges in Victoria's cheek, and I wish I could lean over and kiss it.

CHAPTER TWENTY-FIVE

Six Days Until Election Day

@WestPlymouthPress: Class president candidates' social media game, RANKED (Spoiler: Victoria Ferrand is our #1)

The last weekend before the election, I barely sleep. Rest is not a priority when I need to compare the social media reach of each candidate. Riley's post engagement on Insta is nauseatingly high, and I obsess over her Twitter mentions (because there *so* dang many) until Lauren and Katrina both upload the TikTok makeup videos we brainstormed in the parking lot. Katrina has a bunch of followers from Wayzata, and the comments are gratifyingly full of people joking they'll have to transfer this week so they can vote for Victoria.

I leave notes on Victoria's speech draft at 2:00 a.m., and then again at 5:30, before the sun is even up. Victoria, meanwhile, makes an effort to keep her phone closer. *Go back to sleep*, she sends at nine on Sunday, but it's followed by a row of hearts in rainbow order. *You've got this!!!* in the afternoon, in response to my Story about another driving lesson with Chelsea. That evening, when I'm finishing my math homework, she sends me a selfie as she hangs up posters in her new room at her mom's place.

Me

Not that I don't appreciate the cute (because cute!!) but you know I didn't mean you have to be on all the time right?

Just that there's communication about plans

Victoria

I know but I wanted you to see the cute :)

And I miss not seeing you this weekend

I send her a GIF of Kristen Bell blowing kisses. Then I FaceTime her, because I have a tingling sense that I'm not the only person she misses this weekend. We talk for an hour about her dad, and I try to focus on showing Victoria that I'm here rather than judging him for the ways he's not.

My stress levels aren't helped by the knowledge that YPBC decisions will be sent soon, probably by the end of the week. It's like all the campaign gods conspired to give me the maximum number of things to worry about at once. At least with the campaign, there's work to be done still. There's time to act and to make a difference in the results. With YPBC, all I can do is wait and hope.

Amrita

I know you're vvv busy rn but

Can you look over my apush intro?

My bio group is sending me ALL CAPS MESSAGES and it's ruining my ability to think about the 70s

Normally, we don't really *ask* each other, just send the attached files with messages like HELP and WHAT'S A SENTENCE. My stomach sinks. Amrita knows better than anybody how long and how deeply I've wanted to be a campaign manager, but having that kind of goal was always something that brought us together—a matched set of ambitions—not something that relegated our friendship to second place.

Me

Of course!!!

Never too busy for apush

Or you <3

Amrita sends a sun emoji, the file, and a long message screaming about how *weird* Nixon was, beyond the straight-up bigotry and corruption.

I trust you but am also a little nervous about what's in this essay if that's your preface??

But I open it anyway, because when your best friend asks you to edit her essay on a Sunday night, you say yes.

★ ★ ★

Four Days Until Election Day

On Monday morning, the *West Plymouth Press* releases their profiles of the junior and senior class president candidates. I devour the profiles during break, my eyes skipping from paragraph to paragraph. I want to know everything all at once. Victoria is presented as thoughtful and dedicated, but she managed to include a joke about the parliamentarian position, so I don't think she'll come across as too uptight—the perennial curse of female candidates, even in high school.

Our campaign team debrief during lunch is interrupted by the general commotion when Zack winds his way through the cafeteria, wearing an Audrey II costume that must be left over from last year's *Little Shop* performance and inexplicably singing *Hamilton*'s "The Election of 1800." As far as I'm aware, neither carnivorous plants nor federalism features on Zack's platform, but from the phones angled in his direction, I guess the point is simply *buzz*. Even Zack's not disorganized enough to forget that in a ranked-choice voting system, a recent, general positive memory might be enough to boost you on an apathetic voter's ballot. Ugh.

Soon after Zack's exit, I get a text from Mrs. Charleson that Lacy's come down with the flu. I don't normally work Mondays anyway, but now I'm off the hook for Tuesday and probably Wednesday too. I feel bad for Lacy . . . but since I debated asking for Tuesday night off anyway, I can't lie that her timing is impeccable.

"Speech prep at my house tomorrow after school," I tell Louis and Victoria. "Yes? Yes."

"Yes," Victoria agrees.

Our eyes meet, and we both grin. Even though I'm stressed about everything that's left to do—I'm loving every minute.

I love it a *little* less on my walk to English, when I notice at least a fifth of the sophomore lockers have professionally branded ELECT ANNIE magnets on them. To cut down on paper waste, the administration disallowed locker-sized campaign posters years ago . . . but they ruled that magnets were like buttons and could be distributed and displayed on lockers with people's consent. It's a cool idea, if you've got the cash. Name recognition wins elections, and those bright magnets are now seared into my brain.

But there are still the speeches on Wednesday, equal time in front of the same audience. *Victoria has the words*, I tell myself.

At this point, she *must* have the words.

Three Days Until Election Day

On Tuesday afternoon, we set up in my living room again, with me and Louis on the couch, Victoria standing in front of the TV with a printed copy of her speech.

"My time has finally come," Louis says. He rolls out his neck and stretches his arms.

"What do you mean?" I ask, taking out my own copy of the speech so I can follow along.

My phone is open to the stopwatch app—Victoria gets three minutes—and my Life Notebook balances on my knees. Victoria tucks her speech under one arm as she types something on her phone.

"Because I'm the drama kid here." Louis does jazz hands.

"Didn't you do lights with Devin?" I'm pretty sure I would have noticed if he were in the fall play.

"Yeah, because the cast was tiny and the director stuffed it with seniors. Next year, I'll be onstage."

"I'm sure both of you will be really helpful," says Victoria, finally looking up. "Should I do it section by section to start?"

Victoria doesn't get more than three sentences in, however, before Louis interrupts, his eyes on his phone rather than her. "Katrina wants to know if you're coming tonight."

I freeze. Coming to *what*?

Victoria glances between us. "I mean, that depends on how long this takes. I promised Dad I'd eat dinner with him . . ."

"I hope he's not an early eater," I try to joke.

"We've definitely had our share of nine p.m. pizzas," Victoria says.

"So I can tell Katrina yes?" Louis holds up his phone.

Victoria taps emerald fingernails against the pages in her hands. "I don't know."

"Let's keep going!" I say.

We get through the whole speech twice. We switch the order of two sections in the middle, and Victoria's delivery becomes more confident. When we pause to rework a few sentences near the conclusion, Louis is distracted again, typing rapidly on his phone.

"Now Joan is getting into it. She says that you—"

"Are busy trying to prepare for a speech in front of our entire grade?" I say.

Victoria picks up her phone from where she'd left it on the floor, no doubt so she can see whatever time-wasting thing is happening in their group chat. I don't care that I'm not in it. I care that we're not doing what we agreed to do—what we *need* to do.

"Is it life or death? It is it genuinely a one-time thing that will never, in any form, be repeated? Because if it's not, we need to move on. *Your* speech is a one-time thing that will never, in any form, be repeated. You get one shot to talk to every voter, and it's tomorrow at nine thirty."

"I know that," says Victoria.

"So tell *them* that. It's one night."

"They're . . . You know, Katrina thinks it's fine to stop now that I've run it a couple of times."

My eyebrows are basically at airplane cruising altitude. "You realize that you haven't *actually* practiced in front of an audience before now, right? I don't know how long this is going to take. We're still finding stuff to fix."

Louis keeps his eyes focused on Victoria's blue-striped socks.

"I want to practice, obviously," says Victoria. "I don't want to sound ridiculous tomorrow in front of everyone. But Katrina wants me to come over . . ."

The sentence snaps the last of my patience, and I suck in a sharp breath. "Here's what I don't get. It's not just that you won't demand high standards from them, when you're literally trying to become class president and they all agree they want you elected. It's that they apparently won't let you have high standards for *yourself*, on something that really matters to you. You show up for them endlessly, which is one of the things I admire about you, because it makes you a good friend and it'll make you an amazing class president. And now? Katrina and Joan and all of them, they need to let you show up for yourself." I don't raise my voice, and I'm surprised to realize my hands are steady. "Demand more of people. If they won't show up for you, not really, at least demand you have the space to keep your own commitments."

Victoria is paler than I've ever seen her. "Sometimes people don't show up, even when you ask them to. Even when they promised. Sometimes you take what you can get."

"Well, *take this*. Take this time. Did you tell them earlier you'd go to Katrina's?"

She shakes her head.

"Okay. Good. So there's no problem. If they still don't get it, tell them that I guarantee Jade is not off doing whatever tonight. And she's directly ahead of you, so you need to be so—so on *fire* that nobody remembers a word of what she said, or cares about what anybody else has to say after you. You've got to do better than her, so we have to focus." There's enough earnest energy in my voice to fuel a hybrid to Capitol Hill.

259

"Just Jade?" Victoria says.

"What?" The question throws me off my cadence.

"I only have to do better than Jade tomorrow?"

"I mean, ideally you would do better than everybody. But Jade's a debater, which means she is *seriously preparing* for this, and she'll be right before you, so she's your immediate comparison. Plus, she's—"

"Your ex." Victoria's voice is flat.

"Your competition," I say.

"Who is also your ex," says Louis.

"And? We all knew that going into this. So we know she's a jealous jerk in addition to not being the best candidate for the job." I flip to the next page of the speech. "We're way off track, and I'm sorry for leading us there. Back to the conclusion?"

"Um, no," says Victoria.

I look up, startled. "What? What's wrong?"

"What's *wrong* is that after all this . . . it's really about Jade," she says.

I glance around the room, pausing pointedly to look from my note-covered speech copy to her. "No?"

"Then why mention she's *jealous*?"

Louis stands up quickly. "I'm going to . . . bathroom?"

I nod down the hall, then turn back to Victoria. "I mentioned it because she *is* jealous. Don't you ever just want to beat people because you're better than they are? As a person?"

Victoria shifts her weight. "I guess I'm wondering if you're actually in this for me. Or if you're here because you want revenge on Jade."

My jaw drops. "Okay, first of all, I'm here because you're great, and I want you to win. I think it's only *human* for me to *also* want revenge on Jade."

"Well, then it's only human for me to want you to be in this only for me," says Victoria. She pauses. "And I mean . . . *all* of this."

"All—what?" I'm startled enough that my voice softens, but I'm impatient. And so confused by how quickly this spiraled. This was supposed to be a . . . nothing conversation. Appease her disorganized friends with the knowledge that Victoria needs *one* more night of speech prep, move on, done.

Victoria lifts her chin. "Like, us."

My stomach flips, and I'm aware in a way I rarely am that it's literally full of acid. Any moment now, I'm going to throw up. "*No.* I like you so, so much. Swear to god, that's nothing to do with Jade." I stand up, but Victoria steps back. "Hot chocolate, and hockey, and all that time in your car—that's all you. That's all I want."

Victoria swallows hard. This close, I can see tears in her eyes.

"I think we should go," Louis says, suddenly behind me.

"No, no, we should—we should talk about this. And then—"

"Practice my speech?" Victoria dabs under her eyes with the back of her thumb. "Louis is right. I think we're done for now."

"What does that . . . what does that mean?" I'm stock-still as they head toward the door.

Victoria pulls her keys out of her backpack. "It means I'll see you tomorrow. Don't text me tonight."

"Please—" I try, but I don't know what's supposed to come after.

"Bye, Madison," says Louis. He shuts the door behind them, and all I'm left with is the empty space where two minutes ago, everything was fine—no, where everything was *perfect.*

I stumble to the window and watch Victoria's car reverse out of the driveway. Bewilderment and panic blur my vision, and I miss the moment her car disappears down the street. Will they be back, ever? I thought I was getting a second chance to crack the code: the girl I'm dating, the campaign position I want, and (new and improved!) a best-friend-in-law who supports both our relationship and our shared goals. But maybe I'm not smart enough or *wanted* enough to pull it off. Maybe it should have stayed a daydream, because now I'm stuck with the lingering nightmare.

I start to cry. The tears practically choke me, and I don't bother wiping them away. They fall fast, dripping down my cheeks and chin, wetting the collar of my shirt. I fumble for my phone. It takes three tries to unlock, and my fingers are shaking too badly to text.

"Amrita," I manage as soon as she picks up. "Amrita, I really need you right now."

Then I collapse onto the couch.

CHAPTER TWENTY-SIX

Three Days Until Election Day

In the half hour it takes for Amrita to get her parents' permission to skip dinner and drive over, I dry my tears. I blow my nose. I wash my face and hands. None of it matters when my best friend is standing in my doorway. I start sobbing again, and she pulls me into her. She's short and slight, and my head tucks awkwardly over her shoulder, but her arms are tight around my waist.

"Okay, okay," she murmurs. "Let me take my shoes off."

We crawl into my bed, her sitting up in the corner, my head on a pillow by her thigh. She rubs my shoulder. My limbs are jittery with the urge to do something, to fix it all. A few more tears drip onto my duvet.

"What happened?" she asks.

"I don't even *know*." I turn my face into the pillow.

"I need a little more than that . . ."

"We were . . ." I sniff. "We were practicing for her speech, right? Me, Victoria, and Louis. Some of her friends wanted them to come over for—I don't *know* what, but not anything important, and somehow it . . . spiraled. Like, I thought it was a level-two disagreement, and we'd move on after a minute, but suddenly it was level five and she was saying how I just wanted to make Jade jealous."

"Hmm." Amrita pets my hair. "Do you not want that?"

I huff. "I *do*, and maybe that was a bigger part of everything the first night, but can't it be both? Can't I want Jade to lose *and* Victoria to win?"

"What do you want more?"

"Victoria," I say, without hesitation. "I would have forgotten about Jade two weeks ago if she didn't keep getting in my face."

"So Victoria got mad because she thinks you want revenge? I hate to say it, but that would be in character for you," Amrita says.

"She think it's the *only* reason. And I swear, I swear." I sit up so I can look her in the eye. "I really believe in her. When I was working with Jade on her campaign, it was . . . She wanted to run, and I wanted to manage a campaign, and it fell together."

"Before it fell apart."

I roll my eyes. "That. But I chose Victoria. I want her to win . . ." An almost smile pulls at my lips. I swear I've read this somewhere. Maybe lots of somewheres. It feels good to apply the words to me—to Victoria, to us. "On purpose."

"I believe you. But she didn't?"

The end of our fight comes rushing back to me. It's harder now to keep looking at Amrita. "It's not just about the campaign. She thinks that about—" I squeeze my hands together. "About *us* too."

"Oh my god."

"She told me not to text her," I whisper.

Amrita wraps her arms around me. I start to cry, *again*.

"Do I at least say sorry? Or?"

"No, no. She said not to. You have to listen to her. You can talk to her tomorrow. Sometimes we're not good at explaining ourselves in the heat of the moment."

I nod. "Yeah, but . . . what if she's hanging out with Joan right now? Joan doesn't like me. What if Joan convinces her to dump me? What if—is this *already* a breakup? And I just didn't get it?"

"I should have vetted her," Amrita says, and sits back against the wall.

"You vetted Jade, and look how that turned out." I wince. "I didn't mean that."

"I thought she was going to be your slightly selfish, surface-level first girlfriend. Lots of people have those. I did *not* see the post-breakup stuff happening—but you're only really crying now."

I press my palms to my cheeks. They come away wet. "I cried that first night."

"Not like this. Not for Jade."

"Not like this." I sigh. "Can we watch that rom-com now?"

"We can watch the twenty best episodes of *The Lizzie Bennet Diaries*?" Amrita offers.

I tug the blanket over our knees and tip my head onto Amrita's shoulder. "I'm sorry for keeping you from your sculpture research tonight."

"Shush. Important things are happening."

Near the end of the series, there's a line that tugs on something in my brain. I pause the episode and back it up a few seconds.

"What?" Amrita says. "It's a super-famous moment."

"I think . . ." I bite my lip. "The night we got together, when we were talking after the hockey game, I mentioned that I wasn't sure when I started liking her. I mean, differently from a friend. And she mentioned that she *did* know."

I take a picture of the screen, subtitles on, and post it to Instagram. Victoria probably won't see it tonight, and maybe, if I'm really unlucky, not ever. But I think out of everyone, she might appreciate the idea that *I was in the middle before I knew that I'd begun.*

CHAPTER TWENTY-SEVEN

Two Days Until Election Day

I check my phone right away on Wednesday morning. There's nothing from Victoria. Louis, though, sent a heart emoji in response to my Insta Story, so I guess he doesn't hate me. Does that mean Victoria doesn't either, or is Louis more on my side than I realized yesterday? I don't want there to *be* sides. I want it to be the two of us. One team.

Marisa

I'm heading over for zero—want a ride?

Me

Yes please!

I don't know if Victoria is planning to arrive early today, but on the off chance that she is, and that she'll want to talk, I have to be there. As I get dressed, I try to pretend that the prospect of sitting alone in the cafeteria is a normal opportunity for reflection. Like I won't be frantically wondering if Victoria is going to formally dump me. It's just like Jade to find a way to ruin this. Or maybe it's just like me.

Marisa's grandma drives us to school. When we pull up to the main entrance, I thank her and hop out. She and Marisa have a quiet conversation in Spanish; the only word I catch is "orgullosa": proud.

"Are you ready?" I ask when Marisa joins me on the sidewalk. I take a moment to admire her outfit: an ombré sunset shirtdress paired with purple flats. There are *pockets*.

She takes a shaky breath. "Yes and no? One second I'm *so* ready, I can't believe we have to sit through first period before assembly. And the next . . . like maybe I need another week to work on my speech? Or a month. A year."

"I'm sure you're going to be amazing. Your presentation on urban parks last year in civics was so good!"

"I can't believe you remember that," she says, and opens the door.

"See, proof that it was really good. Plus . . ." I stop near the ramp leading down to the cafeteria. I'm not sure where she's headed.

"Plus civics is kind of your thing," says Marisa.

"That. Five years from now, I'm going to be texting you like, *Can you send me your bibliography? I've got a city council candidate who needs a policy position.* I'll make sure you get a consulting fee."

Marisa laughs, running a hand through her brown hair, loose and curled for the occasion. "I'm holding you to that consulting fee."

"You should," I say.

Before this campaign, I wouldn't have made any kind of reference to knowing her post–high school. We partnered a few times in civics last year, but mostly our acquaintanceship consisted of occasional shared rides from after-school events and one afternoon each summer at the company picnic thrown by our dads' boss. Marisa has her own friend group, and I don't think we're about to start spilling our deepest secrets, but it feels good to think that I might make a connection that lasts, without the long, ambitious backstory I have with Amrita.

Marisa sighs. "Okay. I'm going to find an empty classroom and try not to throw up . . ."

"If it helps, a few years from now, no matter what, I'll probably be the only one who remembers what happens," I say.

"I wouldn't be too sure about that," she says, smirking.

"Well, good luck."

"Thanks. Tell the same to Victoria."

I nod. I check my phone again. Still no message—but she's seen my Insta Story. That's something, maybe? That she bothered to look. Maybe Darcy can convince her where I couldn't. I keep my hand on the wall and my eyes on my sneakers as I make my way into the cafeteria. My heart is in my throat, and I need something to steady me.

When I look up, Victoria is there. I hold my breath until she speaks.

"Hi," she says. There are circles under her eyes that I know are mirrored on my own face.

"Hi."

"Madison, I—" She stops as a group of senior lacrosse boys push past us. She nods toward our table. We're silent until we sit down, her on one side, me on the other. I watch her chipped green fingernails hover over the table. "Madison . . . I'm sorry."

Victoria sets her hands on the table, palms up. I reach across and grab them.

"For?" I ask. I hope she's not about to say, *For needing to break up with you, immediately.*

"For being ridiculous about Jade last night. I know, I *know* I'm not just some revenge plot of yours." She ducks her head. Her thumbs rub against my knuckles. "I had to convince you to give us a shot. And then it turns out I wasn't the one who could separate it all. I guess I'm . . . kind of insecure about this. And stressed about the speech. And I saw an opening to be frustrated and I took it out on you, and that wasn't fair. So I'm sorry."

"So . . . this isn't a breakup?"

"Oh my god." She lets go of my hands to cover her face. "No, no."

"I promise, Jade is . . . she's not *in* this. It's you and me. I don't mean to make you insecure. I sincerely, only meant to comment on basic campaign stuff," I say.

"I know," says Victoria. "And *because* I know that—if I'm feeling jealous, that's on me to manage, not you. You're not throwing Jade in my face."

"I really want you to win," I say.

"Yes, me too. It's . . . Can I say something you don't want to hear?"

"I think you need to." Even though Victoria said this isn't a breakup, my gut clenches.

"I like that you want—the world, basically. You make everything feel so big and so possible at the same time, and I *love* that." Across from me, she tenses, but she doesn't stop talking. "I like that you're

270

the kind of person with high expectations, but I think that only works if everyone is coming in with the same level of high expectations. Like, it's mutually agreed that's the standard we're aiming for. My friends didn't agree to that, and you're not going to be able to change them in the next two days. They *have* shown up for me—" When my eyebrows rise without my permission, Victoria smiles the tiniest of smiles. "Okay, not always, or not perfectly, you're right about that. But here's my compromise: The first time you ask someone to show up in a new way, for a new thing, they might not get it right, because they don't know how." She sighs. "I want to win, and I want to keep them happy, and I want *you* to be happy. I don't know if all of those things can happen at the same time."

I know she's at least *somewhat* right. It's true that this isn't YPBC, where we're all committed to the community of political insiders in the same way, where I imagine we'll all push each other to be near professionals. The problem isn't my standards; some of it is the context. I won't always get to pick the people around me, and I certainly don't get to now.

"I'm sorry. I'll try to be more . . . mindful. I don't want you mad at me because I've alienated your friends," I say. If I wanted to play it safe, that's where I'd stop. I don't. "I still don't think I was completely wrong on that. You should expect—you should *trust*—that the people who say they care about you are going to back you up, whatever that means in the particular situation. When people make a commitment to you, they should keep it, and you're totally justified in being upset if they don't."

"Yeah . . . I told them that too. Well, I reminded them that *I'm* serious about this, so they should chill a bit about everything else." Victoria bites her lip, and I notice tears gathering in her eyes. "It's just really, really hard for me right now to think about showing up, and commitment, and expectations, when—"

"Oh no," I say. "I'm sorry. I didn't mean to get into—"

Her parents' divorce. Their arguments. The missed dinners and poetry performances.

"I mean, you were right, it's just—"

We stumble out of our seats at the same time, reaching for each other, and our hug is long and tight. When we finally let go, Victoria smiles. No dimples, but it's a start.

"Let's go win," she says.

"And then you remind me why I actually like you. I ship it," says Louis, appearing behind her with Amrita at his side.

"Thanks for the vote of confidence." I roll my eyes at him.

"Speaking of votes . . ." Amrita says. "We have some time before first period. If you wanted to practice."

"She was a mess after we left your house. We did nothing," Louis tells me.

"I practiced later. Put my mom on Zoom after my dad went to bed and everything. I wish I'd had your notes, though," says Victoria.

Amrita starts walking backward, headed toward the ramp. "So let's go!"

Victoria waits as I grab my backpack. Louis and Amrita walk a little bit ahead, scouting empty, unlocked classrooms. Victoria glances at me, with just a hint of dimple peeking through. "In the middle before you began?"

I think back to our Caribou date after the hockey game, when she was so sure of us, and when I told her I didn't know exactly when my crush had started. Apparently it's more of a universal experience than I thought.

"Hot chocolate confessions are always true. I thought . . . I could remind you of that."

"Thank you," she says.

We follow the others into Ms. Tate's physics room. I give Victoria a quick nudge toward the front and direct Louis and Amrita to sit in the farthest two desk columns to best simulate an audience. I sit in the center. Victoria checks the order of her notecards.

I take out my Life Notebook. My blue pen hovers over the copy of her speech. "Now. Win me over."

Candidates are supposed to sit in the first row of bleachers in the gym, so the whole time Mr. Braun is introducing the concept of the junior class president race, for those who somehow haven't noticed until now, I'm staring at Victoria's curly half ponytail. Louis and Amrita sit on either side of me. Victoria's other friends fill out the rest of the row and spill over onto the row behind us. If I faint from anticipation, I'll land somewhere between Joan's Vans and Devin's Jordans.

"And now for our first candidate . . . Jade Weaver!"

Jade is exactly as good as I feared. I take notes in my Life Notebook to keep myself focused on the content and not my nerves, and make sure to clap at the end. To my relief, Jade's looking at a totally different row. I hope that means speech prep rebalanced her priorities too.

"Next up, Victoria Ferrand!" Mr. Braun says.

"Good luck!" I say, while Louis whistles.

Victoria takes her place on the gym floor. For a moment, she simply looks out over our assembled class, to center herself like we practiced. She seems confident and relaxed, poised enough to barely glance at her notecards. I, on the other hand, am a steel wool ball of anxiety. I grip Amrita's and Louis's hands tightly.

"When you elected me as parliamentarian last year—and thanks again for that—I wasn't thinking about it as a stepping-stone to junior class president. In fact, as I've recently been informed, *no* parliamentarian in the last seven years has gone on to be elected class president. But what I've learned over the past school year from sitting in on ASB meetings, checking our school's procedures and our budgets, is more important than a piece of trivia that you, too, could know if one of your friends spent a lunch period searching through old yearbooks." There's a smattering of laughter, and Amrita pinches me with her free hand. "And when I wasn't in ASB meetings, I was backstage, checking the prop table. I was recruiting volunteers for our reading buddies program. I was cheering on our soccer teams as they made it to semifinals—for the sixth year in a row, by the way."

A few cheers erupt, dispersed throughout the audience.

She continues, and somehow, I relax with every paragraph. She's a natural. For these three minutes, all I have to do is watch her shine.

Victoria takes a deep breath, and I know she's gearing up for the grand finale. "I am not the lead of the spring musical, and I am not the lacrosse captain. But I know how hard that cast and that team are working, and I understand what they need from the school to make those experiences worth remembering. When I saw our theater crew struggling to place the lights for the fall play and they told me they needed a catwalk—I thought about my ASB meetings and realized, I know how to make that happen. I know how to get that done. When I witnessed for myself the problems that happen when the main board is tied too closely to the Student Judiciary Council, I thought, this is fixable. I know how to get that done. If you've ever been camping, you know there's a saying: Leave it cleaner than you found it. We can leave the SJC fairer. We can leave our stages safer. Last spring, you trusted me to observe. Today, I'm asking you to let me act. If you trust me to represent your interests—and the interests of the *entire* class—please rank me first on Friday's ballot. Thank you."

I cheer like it's the Democratic National Convention and Victoria just received her 1,991st delegate. Louis whistles again, and Amrita claps so hard her elbows jostle me. Victoria sits back down, beaming.

"You were *so* amazing," I say.

Marisa, Louis, and Amrita all whisper their congratulations as Riley situates herself on the gym floor.

As I suspected from the beginning, Riley is all charm and little substance. Unfortunately, that's often all people *want* in a class president, but it does draw a sharp contrast against Victoria's competence-driven speech. Kevin is next, and he, too, favors the flashy aspects, promising to attend at least one match, game, or event for each sports team, like next year's Jays Jigsaw won't practically guarantee that already. Zack does not sing his speech (fortunately for the campaign, unfortunately for my entertainment levels), and he rambles off-topic. Annie's speech is polished, but she spends a full thirty seconds individually thanking friends for their efforts.

Finally, it's Marisa's turn.

"Good luck!" Victoria and I say at the same time.

Marisa takes a deep breath, smiles at us, finds some of her friends in the next set of bleachers, and walks to the front. She's not holding any notecards.

Her speech starts out following a similar pattern to Victoria's and Annie's: leadership successes she's had as part of Model UN, two proposals for how the school can be more environmentally friendly.

"I don't really get nervous for presentations anymore," Marisa says. "I know who I am and what I have to say. But I have to confess, earlier this morning, I was getting nervous for this one." I smile, and her eyes meet mine for a brief moment before continuing to scan the audience. "I want you to know that if elected, I'm going to bring my full self to the position of junior class president. There's something to be said for being first, but there's also something—incredible—about getting to follow in someone else's footsteps. Maybe this is cliché, or too dramatic, but if I'm going to lead our spirit week and serve as the chair of the prom committee, I think we can agree a little drama is essential."

And then Marisa comes out.

CHAPTER TWENTY-EIGHT

Two Days Until Election

The audience gives Marisa a standing ovation. There are tears in my eyes as I wait for her friends to stop hugging her and let her return to the candidates' row.

"That was incredible," Victoria says once Marisa is back in our cluster.

"You're amazing." I'm a little awestruck, I admit.

"Mic drop," says Louis. "I love drama. And you, you absolute badass."

Marisa swings her arms. "Oh my god, I'm trembling! That's why I couldn't have notecards—I knew you'd see them shaking in my hands and be like, why can't she be still?"

"Thank you, Marisa, for that brave and inspiring speech," says Mr. Braun. "And thank you to all the candidates today for sharing your vision for the next year. As a reminder, you'll vote during first period on Friday, so don't be late."

After he dismisses us, Victoria and I linger.

"I think we just lost . . . and I'm not sure I care," says Victoria.

"I can't believe I'm about to say it, but—I was thinking the same thing. Both parts." I'm carefree in a way I know I wouldn't be if any other candidate had that moment. The twin triumphs of Victoria's and Marisa's speeches leave me grinning. In a way, I feel like there's already been a victory here. What can Election Day offer that this morning hasn't?

We start to walk toward the exit.

"Do you care that I . . . didn't do that?" Her voice is hesitant.

The gym is empty, so I take her hand, just for a second. "No, of course not. If you don't want to be out, that's the end of the discussion. There's *no* discussion."

Victoria bites her lip, stalling.

"Hey. Do you *want* to be—?"

She shakes her head.

"Okay, then. That's all that matters."

For the rest of the day, the hallways are filled with talk of no one but Marisa.

Amrita and I almost collide as I head out of last-period biology.

"Did you leave something?" I ask.

"No." Amrita drops her backpack on a chair. "It's the *bonus* meeting for the bio project, to redo our poster for the third time. We're going to get an A already. This is literally for the extra credit."

"Oh my god." It hits me faster than a misapplied "cancel culture!" defense. "You're their Joan."

"What?"

"You don't care about this. I mean, you're at the meetings, but you would rather be doing anything else and it's a huge waste of your time." Part of me is shocked I'm comparing Amrita to Joan, of all people, but the revelation rings true.

"One hundred and five percent on this project is not going to be the difference between them getting into Johns Hopkins or not. My portfolio, on the other hand, is everything."

"You're right. And you're stuck with them, and they're stuck with you." My conversation with Victoria this morning seems to echo forward. "Be a Lauren. They want the extra-credit design points, right? You can give that to them."

Amrita hesitates. "What if I can't think of anything good?"

"When have you not?"

"Sunny."

"If you can't think of anything good, or your fingers freeze up and your drawings are too shaky—they'll still see that you tried in good faith," I say.

"They care about the points." Her voice is wry.

"Yeah, and I care about this election. But I'll feel a lot better about losing to Marisa knowing that Victoria's friends showed *up* with the social media stuff." I'll admit it: They didn't half-ass the videos like the posters or the speech prep.

"So I'm minimizing resentment even if I can't get us to an A plus."

"Well. When you put it like *that*, it sounds bad."

Amrita pulls out her pencils with one hand and shoos me toward the door with the other.

The building empties fast in the spring, since even people waiting for rides will sit outside to enjoy the sun. I spot Carter heading for the locker rooms and take a different staircase to ensure we won't run into each other. I wave to Marisa as she comes out of Mr. Braun's room, but she doesn't see me. I pick up my pace. I need to meet Trevor and Lacy as they get off their bus, so I definitely can't miss mine.

One Day Until Election Day

On Thursday morning, I'm so jittery, I stand up while eating breakfast, shifting my weight like I'm holding a baby instead of toast. Victoria's Insta Story is a clip of her singing along to "One Day More" from *Les Mis*.

In a normal campaign, I'd spend the day shepherding Victoria to final events, or canvassing, or phone banking, or all three. Anything and everything to convince people to get to the polls. Our voting is mandatory—you're marked as absent second period if you don't vote during first period—so there's a huge chunk of my election knowledge I file away under "not this time."

For the first minute I'm back at school, though, I hesitate to campaign at all. It feels disloyal to Marisa. When I spot one of her posters, the feeling lessens. I know she wants to win fairly, with Victoria competing just as hard as she did yesterday. Plus, wouldn't it be great if the final two were Marisa and Victoria? A win-win for queer kids . . . and the whole grade, of course.

During break, I run into Marisa as she walks out of the office. Her light brown skin looks unusually pale.

"Hey. You okay?" I ask.

She startles when she sees me. "Um, Madison. Hi." She looks at the closed office door, then back at me.

I wait while she fiddles with the hem of her blue-and-white checkerboard dress.

"So the thing is." Marisa stops abruptly. I'm startled as tears gather in the corners of her eyes.

I step closer to try to shield her from everyone else walking by. "What happened?"

She bunches the dress fabric together, her hands in fists. "I'm glad that I ran into you, actually. So you can tell—Victoria, and anyone else. I'm dropping out."

I gasp. "What? No—your speech was amazing. You'd be an amazing class president. Did someone . . . say something? I thought your family was—"

Marisa holds up one hand to cut me off. "My family's known for a while. They love me and want me to be happy. It's not anything to do with . . . or I mean . . ." She shakes her head. "It's not what you're thinking. But I'm going to . . . I can't do it anymore."

None of the campaign memoirs I've read prepared me for this. I don't know what to say. We're a quiet island against the fast-talking flow of the hallway.

"I'll tell you why later. I just can't right now. But I'll find you— after the weekend."

"That's after the election," I say.

"I'm already out." Her lips twist. "I mean, I've already dropped out. It's done." She summons a smile. "But I'm rooting for Victoria. We can still make a tradition, quietly."

"I would have helped. Whatever it was," I say.

"You're a good friend. And I'm sorry, I'm *so*—I can't be a good friend back and tell you why right now. I *should*—but—" The bell rings. Marisa adjusts her backpack straps. "Anyway, I'll make a post about it later, but if you see Victoria first, feel free to let her know."

When I tell Victoria at lunch, there's none of the vindication I felt when we learned Carter was disqualified, none of the excitement that we had one less competitor. It's just a deep sense that exactly the wrong person dropped out—and I have no idea why.

CHAPTER TWENTY-NINE

Election Day

"**H**appy Election Day!" My parents burst into my room one minute before my alarm goes off, throwing blue streamers and blowing into New Year's Eve noisemakers.

"Oh my god," I groan.

"I'm making pancakes, so hurry up and get dressed," says Dad.

I chose my Election Day outfit last night: a purple dress with white flowers. It's a little too summery for Minnesota spring, but it's the right mood. Besides, I don't own a suit yet. If I get into YPBC, I'll need one for the visit day we do on Capitol Hill. For now, a dress that will make Victoria smile is perfect.

"Good morning, Ms. Campaign Manager," says Chelsea as soon as I enter the kitchen.

I feel like it's my birthday, the whole family gathered and smiling and making pancakes on a weekday. Dad even arranges the chocolate chips in a V shape.

"How are you celebrating tonight?" Chelsea asks. She hands Dad a bowl of blueberries. When I'm in college, I'm not giving up my chocolate chips.

"We *might* get some food after school—the campaign team, I mean—but we haven't really thought about details yet. We've got to get through the election first."

"Text us as soon as you know," says Mom.

I'm too nervous to eat more than one pancake, but Dad promises to freeze the leftovers so I can have "victory pancakes" tomorrow morning.

"No Marisa?" he asks as I slide into the front seat. He's driving me in for zero hour, so we can have a final campaign huddle and remind the rest of the early-bird sophomores that Victoria should be their top pick.

"No. I texted her last night, but . . ." I shrug.

I get the feeling she doesn't want to talk to me until she's ready to tell me why she dropped out.

Victoria's waiting for me on the sidewalk at school, and I forget to be confused about Marisa.

"Good luck today!" Dad shouts from my rolled-down window.

Victoria waves at him before linking her arm with mine.

We snag a bench near the main hub of sophomore lockers. Louis joins us, then Amrita, then Lauren and Devin. We spend zero hour saying hi to everyone as they switch out textbooks. If they stop to chat, one of us offers them a button.

"I love this," Mr. Braun says as he passes by on the way to his classroom a few minutes before the bell rings. "Great job, everyone! It's going to be an exciting morning."

Even Riley pauses after putting away her jacket. "You've run an awesome campaign—it's been fun! If it goes to a runoff, I hope it's the two of us." She grins, and it's the kind of cool-girl smile that pulls you in instead of pushes you away.

When the first bell sounds, we stand in a tight huddle, all holding hands.

"We meet at the office at break," Victoria says. "And no matter what, seriously—*seriously, Madison*—no matter what, thanks for the button making and poster coloring and speech edits and everything."

"V for Victoria," I say.

Lauren and I head to Spanish together.

"I hope you keep hanging out with us once the election is over," she says.

"I . . . think I will," I say.

"Buenos días, buenos días . . ." Señora Escobar hurries us into our seats. "Okay, class, for the next five minutes, we are in English. Enjoy it, it won't last." She directs us to the election page in our student portals. "Please take this seriously. This is an opportunity to practice civic participation. Your ballot is secret: You can lie to your best friend at lunch. I give you full permission. Vote for who you think will do the best job. Double-check your rank order before you submit."

"There's something wrong with the ballot. Where's Marisa?" someone asks.

"Marisa is no longer running for class president," says Señora Escobar.

A flurry of whispers follows.

"Did she just want to come out? Stay in for the speech and then—"

"*No*," I say. "That wasn't it at all."

I don't know what the real reason is, but I know it wasn't that. I might be the only person in the room who knows there's *something*—so it's my job to defend her when she's not here to set the record straight in her own words.

"Quiet, please. Focus on voting for the candidates listed." Señora Escobar realigns the map of South America that's held to the whiteboard with Colombia-shaped magnets.

Right away, I rank Victoria first and Kevin last. It's not the most strategic choice—I don't think Kevin is our top competitor—but part of me feels like I'll die if he ends up as junior class president. It might be more publicly humiliating, but I'd rather have Jade. I hold a small, internal moment of silence before I mark my second-choice candidate. Marisa should be in that spot.

"When you're done, please put your devices away so we can get started," says Señora Escobar.

I straighten my *V for Victoria* button, review my rank order one final time, and hit VOTE.

Waiting through second-period math is nothing short of excruciating. How can I care about quadratic equations when right now, Mr. Braun and Ms. Morin are huddled in the front office, making sure that legitimately absent students can vote, checking totals and percentages? At least on a traditional election night, I get to watch the votes come in live after the polls close, precinct after precinct, 1 percent reporting all the way through to that projected victory checkmark.

I run a thousand scenarios in my head—ranking flukes and matchups I've already gone over late at night when I can't sleep, or on the bus to school with my campaign playlist muffling the morning chatter of everyone else on my route.

I can't even see the clock from the seat I chose today, closest to the door. My heartbeat is quick and terrified: What if we lose? What if *I* have lost Victoria the election? What seemed inconsequential on Wednesday, when we thought Marisa might win, is back to being essential. Fundamental. Foundational. What if after all this, Peyton's right, and it doesn't matter in high school how close you can get to a professional plan? What if it turns out I'm *bad* at the one thing I want to do? The thing I've been so, so loud about wanting?

When the bell rings and we're dismissed, I'm the first out of my seat. I don't even pause to pack away my stuff: I jam my pencil into my ponytail, clutch my notebook to my chest, and rush down the hall to the office. There are already a couple of juniors clustered near the bulletin board, but I squeeze around them, so close to the board my nose is practically touching the results page. I scan past the ninth-grade results, searching for—

JUNIOR CLASS PRESIDENT
Candidates for Runoff Election (May 2)
Annie Delaney
Victoria Ferrand

I hoped for this—I planned for this—but nothing prepares me for how good it feels, down to every individual atom in my body, to see her name on the list.

Someone pushes me away from the board, and I fall straight into Victoria.

"Well?" she says. Her arms are still on my shoulders, steadying me.

My grin gives away the answer before my words. "Yes! I mean, runoff, but—*yes*!"

"Oh my GOD!" She pulls me in for a real hug.

"A week and a half. We can do this. We can absolutely do this— you're going to be junior class president—oh my god—"

"Give her one break time to celebrate," says Louis, but he's laughing, and his hug lifts me off the ground.

Feet firmly planted once more, I step back so Victoria can receive congratulations from the rest of the group now gathered in the hallway. When I glimpse the top of Jade's head, bobbing toward the bulletin board, I duck into the office to avoid her.

"Maddie, just the girl I wanted to see," says Mr. Braun. He's half leaning on Ms. Morin's desk, writing a hall pass. I can hear Ms. Morin in the connected storage area, taking down boxes.

"Hi, Mr. Braun," I say.

"Congratulations, of course. I'm not surprised," he says.

"Victoria gave such a good speech."

"She did, she did . . . say, would you have a few minutes after school to check in? Some campaign things, since I know you're so interested in the process of how it all works."

"Oh, sure." That's definitely worth a delayed celebration.

"Great. Well, I won't keep you. I'll see you this afternoon," says Mr. Braun.

When I step back into the hallway, Amrita is grinning. She spins me around, and I don't see Jade at all.

After school, I hurry to Mr. Braun's room. Victoria's friends want to go to DQ to celebrate. Victoria promised to wait for me, and I don't want her to be too late to her own party.

"Maddie, come in," Mr. Braun says when I open the door and glance around the classroom, checking to see if I'm interrupting any of his seventh-period students.

I let the door close behind me and leave my backpack on a table. The room is empty except for us.

"Congratulations again. What a campaign!" he says.

"Thanks. It was a lot of fun." I pause as I remember I'm talking to a teacher. "We all worked really hard on it, and I'm glad Victoria's experience connected with the voters."

Mr. Braun smiles, and there's a shade of indulgence that slips away as his expression turns more serious. "There were some twists too. You're friendly with Marisa, aren't you?"

I shrug. "Yeah."

"I'm concerned about her abrupt departure from the race. It's very important to me that we have a process that encourages a diverse set of candidates to run," he says.

Without Marisa, Riley was the only student of color in the race—and we were back to having only one out queer candidate among the final six. Now it's down to two white girls.

"I don't know why she dropped out," I say.

Given how shaken up Marisa looked when I ran into her by the office, I'm pretty sure that's what I would tell Mr. Braun even if I *did* know.

"Teachers see a lot more than most students give us credit for," he says.

I'm not sure what he's expecting as a response, so I give a half smile and wait for him to make his point. I think back to what Zack said, about how Mr. Braun chivied him into confirming the baseball team's sabotage. This time, whatever he knows, or thinks he knows, *I* don't.

"You still haven't heard back from that camp, have you?"

"No. Tomorrow, I think."

"Good, good . . ." he says. "I noticed that you were driving a lot of the organization behind Victoria's campaign."

"Oh, yeah. I mean, I want to be a campaign manager, so it was nice of Victoria to let me help like this," I say. Between my YPBC application and every other conversation we've had during the campaign, he knows this already.

Mr. Braun shakes his head. The indulgent smile is back, and it makes my skin crawl. "Maddie, *you* should be running for ASB. It's too late for this cycle, of course, but it's never too early to prepare. You don't need to force yourself to stay in the background. I know you want to elect senators, presidents—but you can *be* a senator."

For a moment, I'm flush with pride. Even though it's not specifically the future I want, it feels pretty awesome to have my civics teacher tell me I could climb that high in government. His confidence in me extends to the *US Senate . . .*

But apparently not the White House. *Huh.*

I'm quiet for another beat, and I'm sure he thinks I'm flustered by the compliment, but instead I'm thinking, hard, about whether it's a real compliment at all. All our conversations from the past month or so twist a little in my memories, and it hits me, like a dark-money-funded dark-horse election upset, that he was never interested in helping me, or Victoria, at all. At least, not the way I thought he was. He constantly pushed me toward ASB, something I always said I didn't want to do. Again and again, I told him what I wanted, and again and again, he told me to want something else. Like I'm a child who doesn't know what's good for her, and he knows me better than I know myself.

I clear my throat. "Probably there are other girls who could use the encouragement. But I don't want to be a politician. Being out there like that—it doesn't interest me. I *am* interested in managing campaigns."

"I want you to go as far as you can go," says Mr. Braun. He sighs. "So, you want to be the person who gets somebody there. You don't want anybody to get *you* there."

I can get myself there, I think. It's only that the destination isn't what Mr. Braun has in mind.

"Maybe," I say. "Something to think about after the runoff."

I want this conversation to be over, so I can eat a hot fudge sundae and maybe share some fries with Victoria.

"Of course! Watching Victoria could inspire you," he says.

"Maybe," I say again.

"All right, I'm sure you want to start your weekend. No hard feelings, okay? If you don't disagree sometimes, you're not learning. I always want to push the best."

Before I can say anything—like *goodbye*—Mr. Braun wraps me in a hug. It's . . . too tight, honestly. My chest brushes against his, and I can feel my face burn. He probably doesn't even realize it. I try to take a half step away, but his hands are firm, and he rubs one palm down my back. I freeze. There is something like an echo of a thought, not a thought itself, that I am supposed to do something. That there is something to be done.

Confusion rushes through my body, first under his palm and then spreading out. I latch on to that confusion, a lighthouse if not a lifeboat. I feel like I've swallowed my own tongue, and all I can manage is a cough. Mr. Braun steps back, and his hands sweep along my hips as he breaks the hug.

He smiles, bland this time. "Have a nice weekend, Maddie."

I nod, grab my backpack from the table, and practically run out of the building.

CHAPTER THIRTY

Election Day

I don't even know why I'm running. I just couldn't be inside—in that emptying building, with Mr. Braun's blank smile—for a single second longer. Like, okay, Madison, the friendliest teacher at school gave you a hug, so what?

*Your dad doesn't hug you like—*STOP.

*Louis doesn't hug you like—*STOP.

"Madison?" Victoria is standing on the sidewalk outside the main entrance, waiting for me, as planned. "You didn't need to rush! It's fine."

"What?" I don't stop moving, and she matches my fast pace across the parking lot.

"For DQ? Everybody else left literally a minute ago. You're not late or anything."

Right. Right. Of course. DQ. Celebration. ASB election. Mr. Braun, the faculty advisor.

"You're really pale. Are you okay?" she asks.

"Yeah, god . . ." I force a laugh and push nonexistent hair away from my face. "Um, I don't know. Let's go! Let's celebrate!"

Victoria teases me when my fingers are shaking so badly, I can barely buckle my seat belt.

"I have no idea . . . Wow, major adrenaline crash," I say. I keep half laughing to disguise the trembling in my voice.

What. The. Heck.

"I think I know what you need—ice cream!" says Victoria.

"Oh, absolutely."

I joke with her on autopilot for the quick drive to DQ, and with every reply, I push the moment in Mr. Braun's room further and further away. It was one weird moment. Five seconds, maximum. Maybe ten? Time felt—weird.

It's fine, I tell myself. *It's nothing. You got what you want. Time to celebrate.*

At DQ, I'm for once grateful for Victoria's gaggle of friends, who debate toppings and make random low-ball guesses of how many baskets of fries we'll need for the table. Amrita's not here yet, but I'm almost glad of that too. It all feels distant, and I'm not sure I could even manage an eye roll. Instead, I nod and smile so I seem engaged. I don't know why I'm *not* engaged.

"And you! I couldn't have done it without you!" Victoria says, and throws her arms around my shoulders.

I flinch, and she steps back immediately, her eyebrows furrowed.

"Madison? Are you okay?" she says again.

"I . . . Bathroom. Excuse me. Sorry." I slip between Devin and Louis and head for the restrooms.

They're single-stall, and I lock the door fast. I press my back against the door. The handle digs into my spine.

It's just the adrenaline from the campaign, I tell myself. *Victoria's right: Get some sugar. You'll feel better.*

When I close my eyes, the feeling of his hands on my hips pushes through the darkness.

"It's nothing," I say. I pivot so I can face the mirror. "You're tired. You're stressed. You're overreacting."

I mean, seriously, I am. Other teachers have definitely hugged me before . . . I think? Nothing specific comes to mind, but I'm sure they have. I splash water on my face and redo my ponytail. When I get back to the group, I reach for Victoria first.

"Better?" she says.

"Yes!" I'm relieved when I start to grin. "Did they get enough fries? There wasn't a spreadsheet—I don't know if I can trust this."

"We'll get more if we run out, promise."

Amrita arrives, and I buy her a Blizzard. I flip through the ice cream cake book while we wait. When our part of the order is up, we follow Victoria to the three tables Lauren pushed together.

"Speech! Speech!" Louis calls once we're all sitting down.

Victoria rolls her eyes. "Weren't you there on Wednesday?"

"Allow me," I say. I lift my sundae cup. "Or at least—a toast. To Victoria, our next junior class president."

"Hopefully," Victoria adds.

A while later, beneath the overlapping laughter of three or four different conversations, Victoria says, "I forgot to ask—what did Mr. Braun need?"

"Oh. Nothing," I say. "Just, you know. Nothing."

"Okay. Annie and I got an email from him about the runoff process. I'll forward it to you," she says.

"Yeah, great. Please."

When we run out of fries, I'm first out of my seat to get us more.

My family is wide grins and open arms when I get home. I pretend they want high fives instead. I linger on the threshold of the kitchen until everyone else is sitting down.

"Tell us all about her opponent. And the runoff, that's next week?" Dad says.

"No, the Monday after. So we have two weekends before then. The runoff stuff is in the main candidate packet, but Victoria said she got another email about it, so I don't know if anything's changed. I haven't read the email yet." I turn over some peas with my spoon and excuse myself from dinner as soon as I can. After a couple of hours with Victoria's friends, I need space.

"Are you feeling okay? You didn't eat very much," Mom says.

"I had, like, a million fries at DQ," I say.

"Okay, honey. I'll put the rest in the fridge if you want it later." She reaches out, as if to squeeze my hand, but I pass her the Tupperware instead.

When I'm back in my room, I find myself standing in the middle of the rug. Not checking my email. Not scribbling runoff plans in my Life Notebook now that we know Victoria's opponent. Maybe I need a break. Not a whole night off, but an hour or two. A couple of episodes. I grab some comfy clothes from my dresser, but when I start to pull the joggers on beneath my purple dress, suddenly it's not my hands on my hips, it's his, and every instant the worst infinity—

I stumble backward, tripping on the stretchy pants bunched around my ankles. The fabric is clean and soft against my skin. Too clean, given that I've been—at school all day.

I take a shower. I keep the water as hot as I can stand.

When I'm curled up in bed, laptop in front of me and phone at my side, I put on an episode of *Madam Secretary*. The show ran too late on Sunday nights for me as a kid, but my dad would record the episodes and we'd watch them together on Mondays. My mom liked to joke that other dads watched Monday Night Football; my dad watched a fictional woman run the State Department with me.

After two episodes, my laptop starts to overheat, so I close it and grab my phone. My fingers navigate automatically to my email.

Right below an email from Victoria (*FW: Runoff Election Instructions*) is one from Joy Dolat, director of the Youth Politics Boot Camp. I open it so quickly, I don't even take in the subject line.

Dear Madison,

Congratulations, and welcome to the Youth Politics Boot Camp! Your acceptance to this highly competitive program marks you as an emerging activist, organizer, policy shaper, and change maker. We are thrilled to invite you to join us in DC this July for a summer like no other. Please see below for some important information on confirming your enrollment.

Our program runs from Sunday, July 10, to Saturday, July 23. This is an immersive experience, and we expect all students to remain with the group for the entire duration of the program. Please confirm your enrollment by submitting your enrollment forms and non-refundable deposit of $500 by Tuesday, May 31. The total cost of the boot camp is $2,650, which covers tuition, accommodations in a Georgetown residence hall, all meals, and activities. Travel costs are not included. We are unfortunately unable to offer financial aid this summer. However, a generous donor will fund a select number of merit scholarships. Please see this special FAQ page for details on how to apply. Applications for this full-funding opportunity are due on Friday, May 13.

Attached to this email you will find the enrollment forms, instructions on submitting your deposit, and a tentative program schedule. Please don't hesitate to reach out with any questions you may have.

Congratulations again. We can't wait to learn with you in July!

Warmly,
Joy Dolat

Oh my god.

I'm in.

Elation crashes through me, the wave of joy and relief shoving me out of bed. One of my blankets falls to the floor behind me as I sprint into the living room. My parents are on the couch, watching the local news.

"I heard back from YPBC! I'm in!"

"Oh my goodness! Today is truly your day," Mom says, and her voice is all pride.

"Congratulations—we knew you could do it. Show us the email!" Dad makes a space between them, and I sink onto the couch.

I read it again, my finger scrolling slowly. Every phrase sends me to a new high. The director writes as an emissary from another world—with immersive experiences and Georgetown residence halls—and she's saying I'm good enough to enter. When I get to the paragraph about the cost, I stop.

Dad clears his throat. "This is a wonderful opportunity, but we can't—we're able to help you with college, but this is . . ."

"I know," I say quickly.

"And I want you to think very carefully before you use your own savings for this. It's your money, but college is . . ."

"I know," I say again. "College is the most important thing. I won't . . ." I swallow. "I'm going to apply for the scholarship."

Mom ruffles my hair. "That sounds like a good plan."

My eyes catch again on the word *merit*. I think about the email Victoria forwarded from Mr. Braun.

More than ever, I need her to win.

CHAPTER THIRTY-ONE

Nine Days Until Runoff Election

Before volunteering on Saturday, I copy the body of the runoff instructions email into a new document. I leave off Mr. Braun's signature at the bottom. I need to focus on putting together a winning runoff campaign in nine days. It doesn't matter *why* looking at Mr. Braun's name feels like a distraction, only that it is. I can't let anything distract me from the election. YPBC's wealthy donor won't want to support a campaign manager whose candidate came second. My scholarship application needs a full-fledged victory.

Besides, in the light of morning, what I decided in the DQ bathroom feels more certain. The moment in the classroom—I'm misremembering it, that's all. Or I misremembered it at the time. Is that a thing? I'm not going to turn it into something it wasn't, in retrospect.

But I don't tell this to my bedroom audience. I just start filling in the shared campaign Google Calendar. I make a new tab on the election spreadsheet and label it RUNOFF. It's good that I've been preparing for this for a few years already. I don't even have to think.

I take another shower before Dad drives me to volunteering.

"Hey, Trish," I say. "My class president candidate made it to runoffs, in May."

"You go!" Trish says, and offers me a fist bump.

I take a seat as close as I can get to the check-in table. There's a nagging sensation in my stomach, itchy and hollow at the same time, that pushes fumbling words into my throat and back down, again and again. It's *nothing*—so it's *nothing*—so I can ask, right? There's nowhere better to ask than here, this place that doesn't brush against any other part of my life.

When there's a lull between sign-ins, I corral the words into coherence, speaking lightly as if to minimize their touch on my tongue. "Have you ever had . . . like a creepy vibe from someone? They didn't do anything wrong, there's just something . . . off about how they talk to you, and you're not super comfortable with them?"

"For sure." Trish turns away from her tablet to give me a concerned look. "Weird neighbor? Guy who sits behind you in math?"

I shrug.

"Look, listen to your instincts. We've all got 'em. They're telling you something."

"It's not . . . unfair?"

"I'm not saying you do a big call-out post from a bad vibe. But it's not unfair to decide you don't want to be alone with someone, or DM them anymore."

"Okay," I say, and another small wave of relief laps at my toes and cools my anxieties.

I relax into my seat. I can decline additional career chats with Mr. Braun without the choice implying anything at all.

Eight Days Until Runoff Election

The sky is overcast when Chelsea hands me the keys on Sunday afternoon.

"You're getting better," she says as I check the mirrors approximately a hundred times before I back out of the driveway with care.

"Slowly." The words are a grumble.

"Sure, but all that slow adds up."

As if agreeing with her, our street falls away beneath the tires. Five miles per hour. Ten.

"By June?"

I need to be ready for the driving test by then. My birthday is circled in The Plan's calendar, not for anticipatory cake reasons, but for this.

"Maybe by June. We'll work on the other two parking approaches today. You'll need those for the test," says Chelsea.

I take the back way out of the neighborhood so I can turn right instead of left at the uncontrolled intersection onto the busier street. My hands are tight on eight and four.

Breathe, I tell myself as I spin the wheel.

Look ahead. Left mirror. Ahead. Rearview mirror. Ahead. The odometer drifts down, three miles below the speed limit, then five. I push a little, nudge it up.

Chelsea's quiet, which normally I appreciate, because I'm not so good at driving that I can make small talk and still stay between the lines. But today, there's a tight spot in my rib cage that has nothing to do with the road in front of me, and I'm worried that if she doesn't fill the silence, I will.

I don't even know with what.

There's nothing there, I remind myself.

I breathe. I check my mirrors. I switch lanes to get around a stalled vehicle, hazard lights muted in the gray day.

"Did Mom tell you that I got into YPBC?" I say.

"She did! I'm super excited for you. You're going to take over DC this summer," says Chelsea.

Ahead of me, the light turns red, and I focus on a smooth stop instead of replying.

"Have you told your teacher yet? The one who wrote you the rec letter?" she asks.

The tight spot in my chest becomes denser. I grip the steering wheel so hard, my fingers start to hurt.

"No." My voice cracks. I clear my throat. "No."

The light turns green, and for the first time in a while, I shove my foot onto the pedal. The car leaps forward.

"Easy," says Chelsea, like under all this steel, there's still a horse.

"You ever—" I cut myself off.

I miss the first turn into the church lot, but that's okay. There's another entrance around the corner.

"I ever . . . ? You can ask me when we're parked," she says.

But I don't stop.

Because if I don't start now, while we're moving, I might not, ever. While I can't really look at her. While both of us have something else to focus on, something that might really hurt us if I'm careless. My heartbeat seems so much louder in my ears than the engine. Only one is under my control.

"Do you ever think about the way teacher/student relationships end up as throwaway jokes in shows? And not even ones that are aimed at adults, but the YA stuff. *Never Have I Ever*, season two."

It's not really what I want to ask. But it's like the test polls exploratory committees pay for in advance of a formal campaign. *Would you vote for a generic governor with a previously undisclosed chronic illness?*

Have you laughed at a joke that isn't funny?

"*Booksmart*," Chelsea offers after a beat, and her voice is slow, a one-mile-per-hour kind of word.

"Yeah."

I try to swallow, but my throat is dry. I don't turn at the second entrance. The silence builds between us, thicker and heavier than any election playbook, tackier than gum stuck to town-hall folding chairs.

"Is there a reason you're thinking about that kind of thing?"

I'm quiet, even though I know it's all the answer she needs.

"You were kind of off on Friday—did one of your friends tell you something during that election party?"

I shake my head.

When she speaks next, her voice is low and deadly serious. "Whatever happened, it wasn't your fault."

I slam on the brakes.

"Nothing happened!" I press the back of one hand to my mouth, steadying myself.

"Okay—I want to . . . be here in this moment with you. I want to hear you. But I really need us to get out of the road. Can you do that?"

When I resettle my hands on the steering wheel, I find that I can.

The road is empty, so I do a five-point version of a three-point turn and head back toward the church. This time, I pull into the lot. I park on the very edge, nowhere close to the cars that linger after Sunday services. When I turn off the car, I keep the keys clutched in my hands.

Chelsea doesn't ask any more questions. She just sits with me. Waits.

I don't know where to start. I don't know how to, but I guess I already have, in a way. And I want to keep going. I *need* to, because I need someone to tell me if it's all in my head, and to do that, I need to get it out of my head first. The knot in my chest seems to explode outward, like shrapnel, cutting into my lungs and making every breath an effort.

I'm scared Chelsea will disagree with what I've decided: that it was a meaningless moment, another normal thing I'm overthinking. Deep down, in the soft parts still hiding, I'm even more scared she'll agree.

"I . . . You know Mr. Braun?"

"The ASB advisor. The one whose car you hit."

"Yeah."

I grip the keys even tighter, the metal pressing hard into my sweaty palms. A shard of sunlight pierces through the clouds. If I were driving, I'd pull down the visor, but I'm not, so I blink and I breathe and I talk.

"He asked me to come to his classroom after school on Friday. Said he wanted to talk to me about . . . campaign stuff, I think? I don't remember exactly. We had . . . I guess kind of an argument about me not wanting to be a candidate. And then he was like, no hard feelings. And . . . hugged me." I wrap my arms around myself. My elbows hit the steering wheel, but I don't care.

"Okay," says Chelsea. Her voice reminds me of the way people in YouTube videos talk to small wild animals. "Was there something about the hug that . . . confused you?"

I nod, rocking a little in the seat. "He." I drop the keys into my lap, lift my hands, and freeze. "Oh my god. I'm sorry, I'll . . . I shouldn't be having this conversation with you."

Chelsea doesn't hesitate. "I want you to, as much as you feel comfortable." She unbuckles her seat belt so she can more easily face me. "I appreciate your concern—thank you—but this is fine. I'll let you know if it's ever not."

I look out at the lilac bushes separating us from the road and start again. "He put his arms around me." As I talk, I can feel the echoes of his hands. I feel how my own arms were pushed against my sides on Friday. "He put a hand on my back." I spread one palm, holding it in front of me. "We were . . . really close. I couldn't step back. And." I shake my head. "He put his hands on my hips, at the end. Just for a second. But. That—happened."

"That wasn't a hug."

"I don't know. Maybe he doesn't know how to hug people when they're shorter—"

"That's not an excuse when he's a teacher," she says. "Has he ever done anything like this before?"

"No, this was the first . . ." But I trail off. I think back to all the times I've talked to him during the campaign. When I gave him my apology letter. When we talked about the intent petition and the sabotage and . . . I gag. "Fuck. He's *always* touching me. Like—on my shoulders, nothing like—like on Friday, but basically every time, there's something." By my last words, my voice is muddy with tears.

I finally look at Chelsea. Her face is pale. "That's not normal, right? Even if it's not wrong, it's not normal."

"It's not." She lets out a heavy breath. "Am I the first person you've told?"

I nod, and then I freeze again. "Please, you can't tell my parents."

Chelsea bites her lip. "I have to—or you have to—this is too big, Maddie—"

"Don't," I interrupt, squeezing my eyes shut against the unexpected force of my old nickname. "Not . . . not Maddie. Please. He . . ."

"Okay," she says, her tone so, so soft. "Thank you, Madison." She clears her throat. "I think your parents should know. This is too big a secret."

I knew it.

Stupid.

But I'm not surprised, so maybe this is the answer I wanted all along. Maybe I wanted Chelsea to back me into this corner. Maybe I wanted someone to tell me, *No, you have to talk.*

"It's not—he didn't even touch my skin on Friday. Nothing under my clothes. He didn't rape me." I can't look at her when I say the word.

"It's still not okay. You know that, right?" She waits until I nod. It's the first time I really believe it.

And . . . fuck.

Because I really believe it.

"He's your teacher. What he did is wrong, full stop."

"You told me I could tell you anything."

Her face falls. "I know. I *know*. And if this were—if this were

307

anything else—if you were coming out to me, and you hadn't already come out to your parents. Or if Amrita was pregnant, or just . . . Confidentiality, all the way. But for this—I won't tell them, but please, please, tell them yourself."

I knead my fingers against my thighs.

"You know they won't be mad at you, right? You didn't do anything wrong. It's not your fault," she repeats.

"I went to his classroom alone. I shut the door so we could talk about campaign stuff." My throat is scratchy. "If I didn't—if I didn't *want* all this, the campaign, everything, it wouldn't have happened."

"No," says Chelsea. "Can I hold your hand right now? Is that okay?"

I nod before stretching my hand across the console. She presses her hand around mine, firm and mostly steady.

She meets my gaze straight on. "You didn't deserve this. Nothing you could do as a student could justify this. Your ambition is not an excuse. It's a big, bright, wonderful part of you, and it might get you into trouble sometimes, for other stuff, but never this. Please don't ever think that."

I look away and shrug. I'm not sure I believe that. And I'm *really* not sure I want to tell my parents.

"Can I . . . I don't think I can tell them today. Can I wait? Just a little?"

"I'm not blackmailing you. There's no deadline. But I really want you to tell them." Chelsea pauses for a moment before adding, "Are you going to be okay, being back at school tomorrow? If you tell them tonight . . ."

I shake my head. "Then what? They tell the school and I'm the girl who made a big deal because she didn't like a hug? And they tell him not to hug students anymore, and it's awkward when I see him in the hall and—" I pull my hand back. Chelsea lets go immediately.

When I hit his car last month, I was worried about Mr. Braun pulling his YPBC nomination. Now I'm accepted into YPBC . . . but I need Victoria to win the election, and no matter what he said the day of the accident about teachers not having an influence on the outcome, I don't know that I'm willing to risk that. Not when he offered to bend the intent petition rules if I decided to run myself. Not when I'm a week away from having my best shot at the scholarship, something that will make YPBC possible. Not when YPBC is the way to turn a dreamy yellow brick road into an actual ladder.

"I want to drive, and finish my homework, and work on the campaign. That's all I want to do for the rest of the day."

"Okay. I'm here for you. Whatever you need. Whenever you need it. And I'm—I'm so, so sorry. This never should have happened."

I nod. I put the key in the ignition. I pretend I can bury every memory of Mr. Braun deep down, beneath the cracked asphalt.

For the rest of the afternoon, I work on back-in parking. The kind that the driver's ed instructor tells girls to use at night, in dangerous areas, so it's easier to leave.

CHAPTER THIRTY-TWO

Seven Days Until Runoff Election

I take the bus on Monday, and instead of lingering in the hallways, I go straight to first period.

"It's a good thing Victoria doesn't have to write another speech! That took so much time," says Lauren, leaning toward me as I sit down.

"En español," says Señora Escobar.

I snap the lead of my mechanical pencil a dozen times while taking notes, trying to use force to compensate for the way my hands keep shaking. I normally volunteer in class, but today I'm quiet, except when we're told to talk to the person next to us. I don't want to be noticed.

At break, I turn away from the hallway that would take me toward Amrita's and Victoria's lockers. I'll have to face them soon, but I can't yet. I need a little longer lost among people who won't notice that I'm two shades too pale, my eyes on the ground instead of counting campaign buttons. It feels like anyone who really looks at me must *know*, and I don't want anyone else to know.

Whatever sense of isolation I imagined at school last week or last year seems laughable now. Today, that separation isn't just one aspect of my day, mostly forgotten and easily set aside. The fact of this difference, this secret, this shame-that-shouldn't-be feels like the *only* real thing. And it's a repellent force field that can't be breached, no matter how many backpacks jostle me as I head for a bathroom to hide in.

I stop abruptly when I realize the break crowd has been herding me toward Mr. Braun's classroom. I spin on my heel—and almost collide with Marisa.

"Hey," she says.

"Hi." I move to step around her, but she turns to stay with me.

"Did you get my text?"

I haven't checked my phone since I turned my alarm off this morning. "No. Sorry."

"I just—um, if we could talk . . ."

I glance around the crowded hallways. What felt like comforting anonymity a moment ago now feels claustrophobic. My heart rate picks up, and I clutch the straps of my backpack. "I don't—I need to—later?"

"Yeah, of course, not now. Look, about before—"

I don't have a chance to ask what "before" she's talking about, because at that moment, Mr. Braun's braying laugh cuts through all the chatter.

I flinch. Marisa freezes.

When our eyes meet, it's like looking into a mirror. There's a ping-pong moment, where I look at her, and she looks at me, and we register that deep-down fear, and we see that the other has recognized it.

"Let's go," she says.

The bell rings before we can take more than a few steps.

"Can we talk tonight?" she asks.

I nod, nausea already curling in my stomach, the noise of everyone else's conversations too loud in my ears. I don't want to know. I already know.

Marisa disappears into the stairwell. I duck my head and walk to Marketing alone.

Somehow, I beat both Peyton and Louis to class. By myself in our back corner, I take a few deep breaths. There's the smooth surface of the desk beneath my fingers. The smell of whiteboard eraser spray. I'm here. All I have to do is *be here*. Everything else can wait.

Peyton knocks on my desk as I'm pulling out my stuff, drawing my attention. "I hear congratulations are in order."

My eyebrows squish together in confusion. She already congratulated me on Victoria's win last week. "Thanks again for all your advice. It definitely helped us put together the campaign . . ."

Louis smirks.

"Oh, that." Peyton looks uncomfortable for a moment, but then she smiles. "No, I meant. You know."

"No?"

"Victoria said I could tell her about . . . certain hockey-related developments. For the tradition, you know," says Louis.

"*Oh!*" I turn back to Peyton. "I can't say you helped with that, but thanks. It's pretty great."

We're halfway through class before it hits me: Peyton is junior class president this year. Peyton has been on ASB with Mr. Braun. Peyton *didn't run again*. My heartbeat speeds up, and it has nothing to do with our teacher's warning to start our final projects soon. What if Peyton . . . knows something? We're not close friends, and she might really just want to free up her senior year for hockey and her Wayzata girlfriend. But if there's the slightest of chances—I need to know. Especially after my encounter with Marisa during break.

At the end of class, I reach out to tap her on the shoulder, but she's already turning toward me.

"Listen," she says. "Are you going to be around after school?"

"Yeah. I was actually hoping, um, to talk to you."

"I'll meet you in the side courtyard? With the benches. Just wanted to check in about something you said earlier. If I can pull the older queer card," Peyton says.

She probably wants to talk to me about my new relationship with Victoria. Dating someone who's semi-closeted? Or, oh my god, maybe safe sex? *Victoria* and I haven't even talked about sex yet. We've barely been alone since our hot chocolate date.

"See you then," I say.

Lauren and Devin join us for lunch, now that their special tech seminar is over. As much as I've enjoyed our close-knit campaign quartet, today it's nice to have the extra voices, filling in the space I don't feel up to taking.

"You're quiet," says Victoria. "Busy thinking about the campaign?"

"We've got a good plan. Annie can make all the new T-shirts she wants." I put the rest of my sandwich away long before the end of lunch. Even confirming our Runoff Election Day roles—cupcakes are on me, while Amrita is in charge of paper products—can't make me hungry.

I'm used to paying attention in class while running campaign scenarios in another part of my brain, like one of those automatic background programs on computers. That afternoon, even when I try to put every bit of concentration into *The Grapes of Wrath*, my mind keeps skipping: Mr. Braun, smiling at me, his hands at his sides; Chelsea's ghost-white face in the car; whatever words I would find to ask Peyton at the end of the day.

After my last class, I rush out of the building. I used to like being at school when the hallways were mostly empty, the lounges quiet. All that space and silence felt like freedom and possibility. Now the idea makes me feel surveilled, without anywhere to hide.

I spot Peyton right away in the courtyard, perched on a bench with a clear view to the door. I hurry over and lean my backpack against one of the bench legs.

"Hi," I say. I copy her pose: legs crossed at the knee, hands resting on top.

"Hi," she says. Her eyes cut to the door, then back to me. "You go first."

"Oh, no. You go." My heart starts to pound, and I'm glad we're sitting down, even if the bench is a little damp.

I can't believe I'm about to ask her—that.

Am I about to?

I have to, though. I have to know. And if her answer's yes . . .

"My thing is kind of weird and uncomfortable, and we might— get distracted, or you might not want to keep talking with me right away, after," says Peyton. "So you should go first."

"Okay." I nod and stare down at my boots, kicking against a clump of mud on the pavement.

I wait a beat. And then, against my will, another. It's weird now, isn't it? I can't pretend nonchalance if I can't even *say* it.

"Madison?" she prompts.

I startle, even though she's been here all along.

"What's the—I was just wondering why you're not running for senior class president," I say. Every word feels like lead, dropping heavy from my tongue.

"I told you," she says, maybe confused and maybe something closer to wary. "It's the kind of thing that's interesting to do once, but I don't really want to do it again. I want to focus on other things next year. College applications, you know."

"Senior class president is a different role from junior," I say.

I'm watching for a shrug out of the corner of my eye, but Peyton is still.

"I'm just not interested in doing it again. That happens some-times," she says. She tugs down the ribbed cuffs of her West Plymouth Hockey long-sleeved T-shirt.

Right.

Right, I tell myself. So this is probably all in my head, and I should shut up now.

"Why are you asking?" Her voice is cautious. Almost gentle.

"I was . . . I was wondering if maybe Mr. Braun had anything to do with that decision." Before I can finish the words, her hand is gripping mine. Firm, but not crushing.

"Did he touch you," she says, her words so low they seem to scrape the ground. She lets go of my hand and curls her fingers around the edge of the bench. Her knuckles are white.

My heart stops, then shrivels.

If she knows to ask that question . . .

I glance around the courtyard. There's no one near us. I'm on the verge of tears again. The words punch out of me. "I don't know—yes. I think so. I don't know."

"Shit. That's—shit. I'm sorry. I'm so, so sorry," says Peyton.

"So . . ." My heart is in my throat, and it feels too big for my body.

"Yes. In the same . . . probably in the same *I don't know* way that you're thinking. But that's a yes. That's why I'm not running again."

Even though I braced myself for it, it's horrible to hear that *yes*.

Then something about her phrasing niggles at me, and my eyes widen.

Marisa. The moment in the hallway this morning was enough to make me think something must have happened, enough to make me think I had to ask Peyton. But now I connect it to the way Marisa dropped out of the campaign the day after coming out in her speech. I can guess at the why, the what—and the when.

"There's, um—there's another girl in my grade, kind of involved with ASB—" I don't want to out her to Peyton without her consent, especially when it's still only a hunch, an unexpected moment of horrible recognition. "I don't know for sure yet, but . . ."

"You should talk to her," says Peyton. She uncurls her fingers from the bench and sits on her hands instead. "This is why I wanted to talk to you today. To warn you, and your—Victoria—about him. I think . . . I don't know, but I think . . . based on some of the stuff he's said to me . . . he might target queer girls. I'm so sorry. I never should have agreed to help you."

"What? No," I say.

"I should have told you to drop the whole thing. You're out, and working on this campaign gave him so many excuses to talk to you. I *knew* that."

"It's not your fault. It's his," I say.

Peyton grimaces. "It's nice of you to say that."

"I'm not that nice. I'm just really honest." I uncross my legs. With both feet on the ground, I feel steadier. And angrier. "Also . . . all of us opting out? Dropping out? That's not a good solution."

"It's safe," says Peyton.

I look over the courtyard, the budding trees. I imagine the bench is my desk chair. "I want more than safe, if safety means we don't get it at all. We deserve more than that."

"I mean . . . okay. So what's the plan?"

Peyton drives me home. On the way, I call Marisa.

"Madison? Hi?" she says.

"Hi. You said I should call, and . . . not to be pushy or anything, but I'm with Peyton right now—the current junior class president—and we'd like to talk with you. For a couple of minutes, if you have the time and, um, are in a place where you'd be okay—anyway, we're driving back to my house from school." I bite my lip to stop the monologue.

There's a pause. Then Marisa says, "Pick me up on your way."

Chelsea's home when we troop through the front door.

"More campaign recruits?" she asks after she introduces herself.

"Um . . . not exactly," I say.

Chelsea looks between us, taking in Peyton's crossed arms and Marisa's trembling hands. "Okay. Well, I'll be in the basement if you need anything. I'm always—I'm always happy to help. Joey too."

Before Chelsea moved in with us, she used to meet with a therapist regularly. She's still on her parents' insurance, though, and it doesn't cover out-of-state mental health treatment. She got Joey from a shelter instead. Joey is obviously not a replacement for real therapy, but her community college doesn't have a counseling center. You make the best choices you can until you have better ones available.

The three of us sit on my bedroom rug.

"She knows, your cousin?" Peyton says.

"Yeah, I told her yesterday. She's the only one I've told. Other than you, and . . ." I turn to Marisa.

"This is the worst club I've ever been in," she says, and starts to cry.

"You're safe here," I say.

"It wasn't your fault," says Peyton. Catching my eye, she adds, "My girlfriend had to tell me that a lot."

"Have you told anyone else?" I ask.

Peyton shakes her head. "I'm on the fucking hockey team. This shouldn't . . . I should have . . . but I was so confused. It felt so close to nothing. Like if I pushed back—I'd be the 'crazy' one. The angry lesbian."

"What did . . . Can I ask what happened? With you two?" Marisa asks.

Peyton goes first. It's like my story, but more of it. Longer touches on her waist on the way out of ASB meetings. More hugs where her chest—bigger than mine—was right against his breastbone. Once, a hand on her back, thumb brushing just above her ass.

Nothing in the last two or three months, after she told him she wasn't running so she could focus more on hockey next year. She's hoping to be made co-captain. When the sleeve of her shirt rides up, I can see a row of thin cuts on her arm, some faded, some newly scabbed. I told her not to feel guilty for agreeing to help us, but now I feel guilty for even asking. She shouldn't have had to think about him for one more second.

It's not your fault, I try to tell myself, but isn't it? If I weren't so goddamn set on proving to myself, my classmates, my parents, that I'm good enough to do this—

"I hate him," says Marisa. Her arms are around her knees. I put the tissue box in the center of our miserable triangle.

"It still feels—like nothing. Like nothing that *matters*," I start.

"It matters," says Peyton.

I describe the incident on Friday, and the little touches along the way. I'm glad I told Chelsea first, because without her, I'm not sure I would have the strength to tell it today. I'm not sure I would have the belief in myself. I don't know that it feels *easier* now, but I don't have to search for the words anymore. I can describe what happened without thinking about it quite so hard, without having to fully be back in the moment.

Marisa cries through her story. After her campaign speech, he invited her to his classroom after school. He said it was to check in at the end of the day, once she'd had a chance to gauge the reactions of our classmates and think about the kind of support she might need from the ASB faculty advisor. When she tells it—it's still, technically, almost in the same category of plausible deniability that Peyton and I are wading through. But it's worse. And it's clearer.

I don't have to decide whether Mr. Braun *meant* that hug to

319

feel so wrong. Because when you build my story off Peyton's, and Marisa's off mine, there's a pattern. The very worst kind of tradition.

"I don't understand . . . I don't understand, why with me . . ." Marisa fumbles for another tissue.

"It's not your fault," says Peyton.

"We believe you," I say.

"You're the only people I've told. I don't want to cause any trouble for my parents. I don't want my family to worry," says Marisa.

"I think we need to talk to some other girls. Victoria, for one. I don't think Mr. Braun knows she's gay, but . . . he asked me about her once." I shudder. If I hadn't lied—if I hadn't lied convincingly—maybe Victoria would already be sitting on this rug with us, tearful and dimple-less. "I need to check with her."

"And Jade," says Marisa. "I can ask her, since . . ."

Oh god. Pre-speeches, my ex was the only out queer candidate.

"I should do it," I say. I don't think Jade and Marisa have ever shared a class—plus, Jade outed her to me and Amrita, an act that isn't negated just because Marisa's fully out now. This question has to come from me. I turn to Peyton. "Who else?"

When Peyton starts listing names, I grab my Life Notebook. As I reach for a pen, though, I hesitate. I can't make a physical list of queer girls, some semi-closeted, with a connection to ASB. Not in the notebook I carry with me everywhere at school. I rip out a page and use initials. Between the regular student reps, class presidents, unelected ad hoc committees, and SJC members, Peyton can think of one other current member and two from last year who seem to fit the pattern. I add two more names, girls I know from GSA who were involved in ninth-grade committees, and Marisa adds three.

"That list doesn't leave this room," Marisa says. "Because collectively we outed four people, if you count Victoria."

I nod. "And . . . we don't have any seniors on the list. It's his third year here. Not everyone's involved in GSA every year."

"And the really closeted kids won't even go to that," says Peyton.

But they might trust the friendliest young teacher in school.

Marisa snaps her fingers and points at me. "During Victoria's speech, she mentioned knowing when the last time a parliamentarian was elected class president. That was you, right? Her friend who looked at the yearbooks."

I see what she's thinking immediately. "Yeah, that was me. I can go through the last two years again tomorrow. Make a list of everyone who was involved."

"Pay attention to anybody who didn't do it two years in a row. Our sample size is tiny. It could be he's gone after straight girls, and we don't know it," says Peyton.

"Or his targets changed," adds Marisa.

I nod and sit back on my heels. The row of initials, neat in blue ink, stares back at me. Marisa and Peyton look at the page too.

It's Peyton who asks, "And then what?"

That's the question, isn't it? Not the million-dollar one, but the years-of-invasive-questions one, the hope-you-don't-have-a-public-home-address one. The runoff-election-next-week one. For all Mr. Braun's talk about how smart I am, how far I'll go—what can he really think of me, if he'd do what he did, confident that I won't say anything? That whatever willpower he praised wouldn't be turned against him? Did he think me too innocent to notice?

Can I afford for him to know I'm not?

I still need Victoria to win the election. I still need the YPBC scholarship. Maybe this is why he picked me: After the car accident, he already knew I'd do anything. I could be trusted to keep quiet if I thought standing up for myself would jeopardize The Plan. I wouldn't be a senator. I'd just secretly be a survivor.

Mr. Braun denied that he even *could* affect the election, but why should I trust his own promise of integrity? Everything he's said is in question, because everything he's said has been about his disgusting goals, not mine, even when he pretended otherwise. Especially when he pretended otherwise. If what happened on Friday was the explosion itself, here is the nuclear fallout. Here is the toxic waste that I might decide I need to swallow, so he can't steal this election and YPBC from me too.

"I don't think I trust the school. It's our word against his. They'll say . . . You know. That we had crushes on him and then got hysterical," says Marisa.

Mr. Braun, so boyish and beloved. All those giggles in civics, when girls pretended to be more grown-up than we were.

"Let's just start with talking to people first. We don't know . . . we don't know what there is, until then. We don't need to think more than one step ahead." It's the opposite of how I've lived until now, but I know it's what Marisa needs to hear. It's also the simple truth: Without knowing more, how will we know what needs to be done? Or what *can* be done?

"Okay. As soon as we can," says Peyton. She takes my pen and makes circles next to the names of the people she knows.

"Also . . . I know neither of you have told your parents. But I told Chelsea I would tell mine," I say.

Marisa tenses. "Your parents are going to flip."

"Probably," I admit. "I won't tell them your names—if you leave

322

soon, they won't even know you were here—but I think I have to tell them that there's a trend. And . . . Chelsea's here because her school dragged its feet on her Title IX investigation and then decided it wasn't enough to make him leave. Which it was, by the way. So if we, if I, tell them that we don't trust the school's process, they might let it go."

As I speak, I realize how much I don't want to go through what Chelsea did. I don't want any of us to—especially not Marisa, who is probably the only one whose story they'll have to even pretend to care about. I don't want my name leaked online, this one moment following me around forever. I have my memories for that already. I don't want to be the girl at school who's making it up for attention—who's ruining the career of everyone's favorite teacher. For nothing.

"I'll tell my parents too," says Peyton. "This is bigger than me. Madison . . . I'm so sorry. Again. But thank you for being brave, and for telling me."

"And for bringing the three of us together. I feel a lot less alone. A lot less like I'm overreacting," says Marisa.

"I hope this stays a really, really small club," I say.

But as we sit on my bedroom floor, I can't help but feel that my hope is just a fantasy.

Even more than I want to block out what happened in the classroom, I want to block out the memory of disclosing to my parents after dinner. My voice cracking when I said I needed to tell them something. I'd looked them in the eye when I came out to them last June, but tonight, I could only look between the floor and Chelsea.

We moved into the living room. Chelsea stayed, at my request.

When I couldn't start, my mom said, "You don't have to frame it or spin it. Just tell us what happened, honey."

I wish every bit of shame and doubt would live in Mr. Braun's head instead of mine. I wish he had to live through the humiliation of telling his father that someone had noticed his changing body. Had touched it. Had smiled after.

When my words finally sketched enough of what had happened to be clear, my mom's breath hitched, like she was choking down a scream. My dad shook his head, over and over again. I processed their reactions as if through a fog, from another room, my body doing its best to detach itself from the memory I had stumblingly shared.

My parents told me they loved me.

They told me it wasn't my fault.

It was everything I needed to hear and yet somehow it wasn't enough. It couldn't be enough. Because if it wasn't my fault, then someone was at fault. And in our house, faults always had to be addressed.

I was the only other person in that classroom. Any process that could lead to consequences, I will have to initiate. It is a terrible thing to know, before I've ever uttered the word *report*, that the odds aren't on my side. The fear of some future in which, beyond the walls of this house, I am not believed, twists seamlessly into the fear that follows what has already happened. One on top of the other, the sum monstrously bigger than its parts.

I wish Mr. Braun had to rehearse how he was going to move through the halls to avoid us all. I wish he had to think about the best way to tell his crush she might be in danger, if she hadn't already been targeted.

I spend the night on the couch in the basement, with Chelsea on her bed a few feet away. Joey watches us both from her perch on a bookshelf.

Mostly, I wish Mr. Braun doesn't sleep.

Because I don't.

CHAPTER THIRTY-THREE

Six Days Until Runoff Election

Zero hour is the only uninterrupted time available for me to talk to Victoria, so Dad drives me and Marisa to school early. It's weird to think that the last time we carpooled to school together was the day of the election. After Marisa's assault, and before mine.

I cringe away from the word. It's too dramatic. Too real. Too much.

"If you need *anything* today, call one of us," Dad says as we pull into the parking lot. "Even just to say hi. You too, Marisa. High school's a tough time, and neighbors have to look out for each other."

"Thanks, Mr. Sewall." Marisa gets out of the car, but I linger, one hand on the door.

"I will come get you at any time. There is nothing too big or too small to ask, okay? I love you," Dad says.

"I love you too."

Marisa and I escort each other to our lockers, and then she walks me to the media center, where I'm meeting Victoria. I grab a seat in the small group study room. There's a window looking into the main space, and I can see Marisa at a table right outside.

When Victoria arrives, she glances at the empty table in the study room. I know what she's not seeing: no Life Notebook, no printed calendar, no laptop open to a spreadsheet of delegated tasks. I motion for her to shut the door.

"This is different," she says, sitting next to me. "Are we worried about spies now? I don't think Annie's quite that deep."

"It's not about the campaign. Or . . . not directly. Something happened on Friday, and it turns out . . ." I stop before I get too far ahead of myself. And again, I tell the story of what happened on Friday—the slope I didn't realize Mr. Braun was herding me down—and that I'm not the only one.

"Oh my god. *Madison.*" Her eyes are blurry with tears. "I'm so sorry. That's—on Friday, oh my god. When we got ice cream— that's why you were so upset. And I was just . . ."

"I was still . . . in shock. And confused. I didn't tell anyone until Sunday," I say.

"Thank you for trusting me." Her hands flutter above the table. "Can I touch you? Is that okay? Can I hug you?"

I nod. "I would actually really, really like a good hug right now."

The seats in the study room are wide, so Victoria scoots onto mine. I wrap my arms around her and let my head fall onto her shoulder. I'm pretty sure I get snot on her pink balloon-sleeve top.

"What can I do? How can I help?" She rubs the back of my neck with the gentlest of touches.

"I don't know," I say. "The other girls and I made a list, of people we thought he might have . . . so I wanted to check—has he—did you?"

Victoria shakes her head. Her loose curls catch on the zipper of my International Wolf Center sweatshirt.

"I don't think I've been alone with him, ever. The past month or so . . ." She shrugs. "I've always been with you."

I slump further into her, relieved. "Yeah. Okay, that's good. I have to . . . I'm not going to be at lunch. I need to talk to some other girls. Including Jade, by the way."

"Okay. Can I bring you something to eat?"

"I packed food. Thanks, though." Hopefully my stomach would be settled enough to eat it.

Victoria traces her thumb up and down the ridge of my knuckles. "I'll drive you home."

"I—yeah, thank you. That'd be nice." I look down at our thighs, pressed close on the chair, her black jeggings against my blue jeans, loose from having been worn all weekend and not washed. "It's weird, but—and I know it makes *no* sense—and neither of these things were honestly a huge deal—but I guess I've been thinking about . . . what happened on the bus, last winter. Like, I don't care about it anymore, I haven't thought about it in forever, but for some reason when I took the bus in yesterday morning . . . I was just nervous the whole time."

It's not totally true that I haven't thought about the bus incident in forever. Somehow, it keeps coming back, and even though I trust Victoria—even though she was with me that day, when no one else was—this morning, I can't bring myself to admit it. There's a little voice in my head telling me that it's embarrassing that it happened, that it's even *more* embarrassing that I haven't already forgotten about it. Sticks and stones, right? But that day still has the power to hurt, and I've already been confessing so much of that.

"I think it makes a lot of sense," says Victoria. She bites her lip. "I want to support you however I can, but I also think—I'm scared I'm not going to say the right thing. Have you thought about talking to one of the school counselors?"

"I don't really want to be alone in a room with an adult here."

"Oh. Yeah," she says.

I nudge her and summon a smile. "You can go back to the other chair now."

She goes.

"So . . . I don't know what's going to happen here. I don't know if there will be more people. I don't know if any of us are going to tell the school, and if we did, I don't know what the outcome would be or how long it would take." I cough and clear my throat. "You should . . . Do you want to drop out of the race? If you stay in, you could be at risk too."

For all of my hesitancy about reporting before the election (or ever)—for all of my certainty that Mr. Braun could tank my YPBC hopes if he wanted to—those feelings are about *my* personal calculations. I can choose what sacrifices I will make for myself. I can't let Victoria think I'd sacrifice her too.

Victoria's eyes widen. "Oh god. That's . . . I hadn't even gotten that far yet."

"I know. It's a lot to take in."

"I think—" She stops. In a way, I'm grateful for the pause. I don't want her to rush. When she meets my gaze, her eyes are more serious than I've ever seen them. "I don't want to drop out. I mean, I want to *win* this. All of my reasons for running are still there. I'll just have to be . . . on my guard."

"I'll obviously let you know if we decide to report him," I say.

Talking with Victoria makes me painfully aware, in a way I wasn't in my bedroom last night, that every day we don't report is another day Victoria, or Jade, or any other student who catches his eye is in danger. And I'm angry that Victoria has to decide whether that risk is acceptable so she can stay in this race she deserves to win.

"Thank you." She reaches out, and when I turn my palm up, she laces her fingers again with mine.

"So . . . for the campaign, we should probably proceed as normal?"

"Probably, yeah—but are you sure you want to talk about this now?" she says.

I look at the clock. We have a while before first period.

"You should go over the list of social media endorsements. There's some more yearbook research I need to do—not for the campaign."

"Which years do you need?"

It's a simple question, the start of a simple offer, but for some reason it knocks me sideways. I've been falling in love with Victoria for a few weeks, and today I feel the full truth of it, not just in my heart, but in my bones.

I find Jade at lunch, and this time, it's me who pulls her into the dusty stairwell, the one that no one uses except for bad news. We haven't spoken since Marketing on Friday, right after the election results were posted. Her congratulations were tinged with regret, not sarcasm. It wasn't as awkward as I feared, but I have even lower expectations for this conversation.

"What's going on?" she says. Before I can start, she plows forward on her own. "Look, I know I've been an asshole. I was mad that you bounced straight to somebody else. You didn't fight for me, and you fight for everything you really care about. And then I was *more* mad when I saw Victoria didn't care you were using her campaign for YPBC, because . . ."

"Because it made you look like a jerk," I say. Before Friday, this reflection would have mattered to me. Now it feels distant. Some other, younger girl had meaningless drama with her ex. "That's not why I want to talk to you."

"But while we're here, for the record, I'm sorry. It kind of hit me when I was working on my speech and you weren't with me, you know . . . being you. At the end—of our relationship, I mean—it felt like you didn't care, and you used to care a *lot*. I wanted you to care again, even if that was just . . . you being mad at me." Jade doesn't say it like we're in a debate, fast and forceful. Her words are stilted and slow, and I know they're genuine.

I don't have room for the emotions they attempt to call up, but I press the moment into my memory. I'll come back to it at some point, when I might appreciate hearing this acknowledgment from the first girl who really had my heart. Today, her apology can't find a space to grow among the wasteland of Mr. Braun's actions.

"Um, thanks. I kinda need us to be okay, because I have to share something private with you, and I need you to promise to keep it a secret," I say. "And then I need to ask you a question, and I promise I will keep your answer a secret, unless you agree I can share it with—well, I'll get to that in a second."

Jade tilts her head, her eyes darting over my face like she can read the explanation across my cheeks. "Is this . . . an STD thing?"

Her reaction reminds me of my own guess when Peyton first asked to talk to me after school yesterday. Was that only yesterday? I feel like I've lived a year since then, and a decade since the election.

"It's not an STD thing. It's a sexual assault thing."

When I tell her, Jade's mouth drops, her eyes wide. "Fuck. Mr. Braun? But I thought he liked you—oh. Oh." For a second, I tiptoe along the edge of a knife, waiting for the blade to turn on me with any shred of disbelief. When Jade shakes her head, though, it's with horror. "I'm sorry. I'm so—what the *fuck*."

"There are other girls," I say, my voice quiet. "Other girls involved in ASB, or who were candidates. We're trying to figure out . . ."

Jade shakes her head again. "He hasn't . . . He didn't."

My whole body feels like a sigh released.

"Good, I'm . . . That's good." My voice shakes, and I know I need to leave.

There are so many more conversations ahead of me, and I can't bear to linger in this one any longer. I wish I could slip into the cafeteria, tuck my head onto Victoria's shoulder, and let her voice make me feel like the world is mine again. But I have questions that still need to be asked. When I start to turn away, Jade stops me.

"I really—thank you for telling me. That can't have been easy, so I want you to know that I believe you. If for some reason you need something from the other girls who ran, I can do that," she says.

Jade and I dated for eight months. For the first time, I fully trust that she has my back.

I find Amrita before English, and then I find us a single-stall bathroom with a functioning lock. The tears that pricked my eyes during my conversation with Jade spill out, along with this terrible truth.

"I'm going to fucking kill him," Amrita says.

I needed to hear my family's *it's not your fault*, and Victoria's care, and Jade's support, and it turns out I needed to hear this too. She picks up my rage when I'm tired.

I explain why I missed lunch, my mission to find other ASB girls who might be targets. "Someone said there might be straight girls, too, we just don't . . ." I trail off.

The tiny whisper network at whose center I've found myself is one of cis queer girls. Assault isn't really about sex, though. It's about power.

From the articles I read during graphic design when I was supposed to be doing—something else—I learned that abusers strategically do not harm everyone they know. They need people who will defend their reputations. So *I* need a better plan to figure out which groups at school Mr. Braun might be counting on to delegitimize any claims the queer girls might bring . . . and if any others—with different identities from the one pattern we know of—are like us, isolated by forces so much bigger than Mr. Braun but that he would have no trouble harnessing in his favor.

"I think I need to skip English," I say. I've never skipped a class in my life. I've never even thought about it until this second. But I'm taking a full load of classes this year, so I don't have a free period for independent investigations. And with every person Marisa, Peyton, and I ask today, the more this spreads out of my control, and the less time I have. "Victoria's friends have fifth-period study hall."

"Victoria doesn't," says Amrita.

"I know. But I need to talk to Louis."

I actually go to English first. I let all the exhaustion show on my face. When I ask Ms. Glen to let me go to the nurse's office, I make a low-voiced reference to *that time of the month*.

When she excuses me, I head directly to the media center.

In the media center, I don't find Louis.

Devin finds me. When our eyes meet, I know that he knows, and he knows that I know that he knows.

"Can I talk to you?" I ask.

I went looking for Louis because of his soccer connections, but if Devin's already found out, he might be the better choice for this conversation.

Devin nods. "You okay with the group study room?"

"Yeah."

I follow him into the small space, where he shoos out Lauren and Joan. We sit down on opposites sides of the table, neither of our backs to the window into the media center's main area.

"I'm sorry," he says.

"Yeah," I say again, and I push forward, fast, before we can get caught in the apology. "Listen—you're on the newspaper, you're on tech crew. You know people I don't." That's not a high bar to clear, yet Devin nods seriously. "Obviously, rumors are starting from the people I know to contact. But if there are people I *don't* know to reach out to . . . I don't know what I'm doing. Solidarity is—no one should be alone in this."

"For what it's worth, I haven't heard anything from anyone else. It might just be you girls."

Between us, silent: We also might never know.

"And no one. No one else on *WPP* knows? No one else is asking around and—" Something noxious and slimy seems to erupt in my stomach. "Because you know what he's like, right? No rumor uncollected and unquestioned. How long until someone tells him?" The slime triples in mass. What if he's already heard? My whole body starts to tremble.

"Hey. If anyone else on *WPP* knows, they're not exactly bringing it up in the group chat, all right? I'll let you know if I hear about him asking questions or anything," says Devin.

"Okay. Thank you." My voice comes out a whisper.

All at once, it feels like *not* being believed would be the best thing after all.

CHAPTER THIRTY-FOUR

Four Days Until Runoff Election

There are five of us. Me, Marisa, and Peyton this year. George Chablis-Khouri last year, when she was one of our ninth-grade reps in the spring. Yearbook has editorial meetings during Friday lunch, so she stopped coming to GSA when she was promoted from staff photographer in the fall. Like me, George is bi. And then Savannah, a queer senior who's a semi-regular GSA attendee, when she was on the Student Judiciary Council her sophomore year.

I'm upset there are more of us. I'm surprised the number's not higher. I'd never wish that confused horror on anyone else, but I can't help but feel a guilty kind of relief. Not that someone else was hurt—just that we're not alone. It's not some shared campaign hallucination among the three of us. It's been happening since before I ever stepped foot in this building.

Which makes me wonder if it's going to keep happening after I leave. Savannah's and George's stories are closer to Marisa's, but with timespans like Jade's. At first, Savannah said she wanted to graduate and forget about it—it's already been two years. George leans toward talking to the school, but she says she doesn't want to do it unless three of us agree to report together. As individual stories, it's easy to rewrite them as the accidental enthusiasm of a young teacher. Together, it's a pattern of harassment.

Marisa made us all download Signal, this encrypted video and messaging app, for our group call on Wednesday night. I set my laptop on the floor and made campaign buttons until my hands cramped. Then I kept going. There was a rhythm to it: place the materials in the borrowed button maker, look at the person speaking, press, repeat. We had a lot of voters to win over.

On the first day of sophomore English, Ms. Glen handed us a worksheet of famous first lines. We matched them to their books and authors and then discussed what made them compelling. *Anna Karenina*'s first line didn't make me want to keep reading, but it's stuck with me anyway: *All happy families are alike; each unhappy family is unhappy in its own way.* When I'm trying to eat dinner with my family after babysitting on Thursday, I think about saying today is the worst day yet. But it's not the worst. It was just unhappy in its own way.

I had a blister on my palm from Wednesday's buttons. I'd stayed up long past midnight, trying to catch up on all the homework I didn't do while talking with Peyton, and my parents, and then the whole group of us, and my parents again. It feels like all I've been doing lately is talking.

During zero hour, Victoria and Louis put up the additional posters they made this week, hanging them, per runoff election guidelines, in some of the spots vacated by the eliminated candidates. I spent zero hour huddled with Amrita, formally planning all my between-class routes so I never walk past Mr. Braun's classroom and always have someone with me when I'm going through a lounge or by the staff room. When Amrita asked what else she could do, I requested cute GIFs and funny TikToks. I warned her that I probably wouldn't respond, but I wanted to have something nice in my phone after school.

Once I manage to swallow down both dinner and a depressing Tolstoy reference, I want to crawl into bed and sleep until the school year is over. So I do—at least, I sleep for an hour, long enough to dream Victoria and I are sitting together, Mr. Braun heading toward us down the aisle of an otherwise empty bus. I wake up abruptly. My clothes are damp with sweat.

I change into pajamas and open my laptop. Chrome greets me with my spreadsheet of election tasks, from campaign cupcakes to TikTok trends.

Crap.

I'm supposed to do this "tag a Victoria voter" outreach effort on social media. Looking at Amrita's cat GIFs is one thing. I think I'll actually throw up if I have to message a single classmate tonight about anything other than what's currently taking up my whole brain.

You have to, I tell myself. *Don't think. Just do.*

I grab my phone and open Instagram.

I have to do this. I have to get this done. I can't let Victoria down. I can't let *myself* down, not with a scholarship to YPBC at risk.

Focus. I keep the commandment internal; my pillows don't need to hear it. *You think you won't have bad days on a campaign? You think you'll never get shitty personal news and still have to show up?*

Maybe I'm not cut out for this after all.

Maybe I am too fragile for what I've wanted for so long.

Maybe I'm just not that good. I'm just not that lucky. Most

people don't get the world. Maybe I won't even get another clean lake. Maybe all of that—that sneak peek into community, that impact I can hold on to and jump off of—is in the past. The only chapter for a memoir that won't ever be written.

Amrita sends me a hedgehog GIF, and instead of replying with a heart and moving on, I FaceTime her.

"One sec." She holds a finger to her lips. She fumbles with her AirPods, then says, "Hey, Sunny. What's up?"

"Sorry, I know it's late," I say.

She shakes her head. "It's fine. What can I . . . Do you want to hear about my dad's latest cooking disaster, or . . . ?"

Maybe I'm going nowhere. Maybe this whole thing is just telling me, years before I'd know otherwise, that I was always destined to fail.

But I still want Victoria as junior class president.

"I was actually hoping you could help me with something. For the campaign. Tonight."

"I'm all yours," says Amrita.

I send her the instructions for the Victoria Voter plan. I do my math homework with Instagram open on my phone, watching the tags roll in and thinking about all the conversations I've had this week, so many noes but too many yeses.

And after all this talk . . . tomorrow is Day of Silence.

CHAPTER THIRTY-FIVE

Three Days Until Runoff Election

The language wing bathroom is much more crowded this year. Amrita and George are in charge of makeup. Victoria and Marisa stand guard at the door, turning away anyone who actually needs to pee. Louis leans against the radiator, leading us in chants. He's wearing a T-shirt with what he informs me is a representation of Deadpool's mask, in the colors of the pansexual flag. In a lower voice, he adds that it was a three-month anniversary present from his boyfriend.

When we burst into the hallway in a loud, proud, be-rainbowed clump, we immediately run into the entire girls' varsity hockey team, also headed toward Ms. Zhao's room.

"It's a team effort," Peyton says. She looks at me. "They've got our backs."

I know what she means. There's a lump in my throat, and I smooth down my dark blue skirt as I try to swallow. Peyton straightens the ribbon in my hair, winks at Victoria, then links arms with one of her teammates and keeps moving down the hall.

"I like your shirt, by the way," Victoria says. Her quiet compliment guides me back into the moment.

"*Bi* the way?" I tease. There's a moon in the center, above the words NOT A PHASE. *Not* is in blue, *a* in purple, and *phase* in pink.

At first, when we turn the corner toward Ms. Zhao's classroom, I think there's been a mistake, or at least that the boys' hockey team chose a weird location for a postseason meeting. Then I see George kiss Mark Swanson. She points me out to him, and he does this up-nod thing.

"The guys and I thought George and everybody could use some more bodies today," he says. His voice is almost casual, but there's a hardness beneath it. Not toward me, I can tell, but as a response to conversations I know George has had with him this week. "That cool?"

"Uh, yeah. That's great. Everyone's welcome," I say.

Louis squeezes my arm, and I take a closer look at the group waiting to get inside. Every single hockey player is wearing their team T-shirt. Slowly, we filter into the room. Ms. Zhao has a table set up with, of course, more buttons.

I pull Victoria aside. "I don't know if you'd be comfortable with this—I don't think it'll be taken as saying anything about you—but if you are . . ." I reach into my skirt pockets and show her the dozen V pride flag buttons I made on Tuesday, from the design that I kept to myself.

"Oh my god. They're perfect. I love that," she says. "Can I have one? Just for me?"

"Of course. They're really all for you, in a way."

She pins another on my shirt, and then we work our way through the crowded room, carefully distributing buttons to Louis, George, and Marisa first.

"One minute until the bell!" Ms. Zhao calls. "We'll do lunch together in the courtyard, and remember to come back here at the end of the day for a shout! Look around you and notice how loved you are. Allies, thank you for standing with us. My kids who are not ready to be out—this day is yours too. This community is yours too."

Lauren squeezes in between two seniors to hug Victoria. "Found you!" She has an ally badge pinned to her dress, right next to a purple *V for Victoria* button.

"Thirty seconds! Let's be loud!" calls Ms. Zhao.

We all scream and shout.

"Out of the closets!" Louis yells.

"Into the streets!" a few of us yell back.

"Out of the closets!"

"Into the streets!" The response is louder this time as people catch on.

"Out of the closets!"

"Into the streets!"

"Out of the closets!"

"Into the streets!" This time, it's everyone.

The bell rings. The silence is immediate.

Victoria worried that I would feel stifled by participating today. As I sit in class after class, passing notes during partner work and noticing which periods are quieter than others, I don't feel that way at all. This silence is pointed. This silence is a fucking protest.

When it comes to harassment, silence is isolating. Today, I'm connected to people I've never spoken to. We trade glances and nods; we thumbs-up each other's outfits and button selection. We let ourselves laugh, loud, in the courtyard at lunch. It's a day when I remember how much *bigger* this all is. How many people came before me. How far we have to go, even here at West Plymouth, where I dated a girl openly without (much) fear and where two varsity hockey teams are racing each other in silence at one edge of the courtyard.

I hold back my cheers (but not my applause) when Peyton wins a second race, and I think about all the other words I'm holding back. When the school day's over, what do I want to release, and what do I want to keep inside?

After the end-of-day shout, Marisa and I walk to the media center together, where we're meeting the other three. We all agreed that we're ready to make a decision—to figure out if at least two more of us will join George and report as a collective—and I want to know our plan before the runoff election on Monday. No matter what plan that is.

We gather in the group study room. This time, I lower the blinds. I don't want anyone to wonder what the five of us have to talk about.

"Did everyone see the links to the district's policies?" I ask. If this were something for the campaign, I would have printed the relevant sections and passed them out.

"Yeah, thanks," says George. She's wearing light-wash overalls on top of a green T-shirt. On her silver necklace, a figure skate charm hangs between two JJs pieces.

Marisa drums her fingers against the table. "I don't trust it—those policies. They're not going to give us justice. That's *if* they even believe us. And if he knows we're doing this, and nothing really comes of it . . ."

"I don't know about the whole justice thing, but I'm with Marisa. My mom said I was exaggerating. When I told her this week that it wasn't only me, she told me to move on." Savannah runs a hand through the angled bangs of her pixie cut. "You guys are still going to be here next year. I respect if you need to make a different decision. But I want to be packing for college this summer, messaging my roommate, not answering questions about sophomore year."

"I want to tell someone. He's just going to keep doing this," says George.

"Think about the kinds of questions you'll be asked," says Savannah. She looks at a READ poster over my shoulder rather than any of us. "I had a crush on him, like a . . . whatever, a teacher crush. When he started asking me to stay after . . . I liked it. I felt special. I was lonely, and he *understood* me—it seemed like he did, anyway—and for a while, I thought that was *good*." She shakes her head, a fast, hard movement. "I had just come out, and it hadn't gone super well at home at first. I lost some friends here too. The ones I still had—they teased me about him, you know? Joked about how they wished they were on ASB, because he's so cute. And then the way he touched me became—and I couldn't ignore it anymore—but how the hell was I supposed to explain that to anybody else? When even my mom didn't believe me?" She clenches her fists on the table. "It's not fucking sexy; it's fucking illegal. But I've had sex with three different people of three different genders since, and that's going to *matter* to whoever investigates." Savannah deflates into her chair.

By the time Savannah's done talking, I feel—ripped apart. Shredded to the bone. Like the grief found one more layer of my heart I didn't even realize existed and cut straight through. Rage wells up like blood through the cuts.

Marisa was only hours past coming out when he assaulted her. George had moved to Minnesota right before our ninth-grade year. Although she was elected in the spring, most of us have known our close friends since elementary school. It'd be easy to feel broadly liked, but without the kind of depth needed to trust someone with this. And it'd be even easier for Mr. Braun to *assume* that was the case.

After a few beats of horrified silence, Savannah glances at George. "It's not your job to stop him."

George fiddles with her necklace, moving the charms backward and forward along the chain. "It doesn't matter that it isn't my job. It's . . . notifying the school is going to make me feel better. He wants us to be quiet, and separated, and doubting ourselves." George lifts her chin. "Not anymore."

"I'll back you up. No more of this," says Peyton. She's sitting on her hands, a technique she told us she uses when she has the urge to self-harm. Her dads signed her up for therapy when they first noticed, but since she knew the therapist would have to report Mr. Braun, she pretended it was hockey stress. If we report, she could go back and be honest.

Everyone looks at me.

It all feels so unsteady, so I think about my North Star, even though it too has felt dim and wobbly these past few days. The Plan. Five or fifteen years from now, what choice will I wish I made today? What choice is in the best interests not of my sleep-deprived, frantic, current self, but someone in the thick of real life?

Already, rumors of this are starting to circulate. Maybe not our identities, not widely yet, but soon. Nothing on the internet ever really goes away. And if the school does take us seriously . . . newspapers have been known to release names before, even of minors, by accident. I don't want this to be part of my public history, unless *I* make that decision.

But don't I want to be able to say, *Yes, I said something*? Isn't staying quiet the exact opposite of everything I love about myself and everything I want for my future? I don't think Savannah or Marisa are cowards. I don't resent their choice or their viewpoints. But for me, surviving means speaking up.

Of course, there's the campaign to think about, the one I'd been worried about after denting Mr. Braun's car a month ago, the one I still need to win to have a shot at the YPBC scholarship.

The one I'd convinced Victoria to call "real."

This matters too, I think. *This matters now*. It's not only about how I might feel in five or fifteen years. Who knows, *really knows*, what I'll want then?

This year, I'll have to speak with school authorities. I'll have to face whatever my classmates say online. Or I'll have to walk through these hallways, wondering if Mr. Braun is watching from his doorway.

I look up. "I want to report."

I ask them to wait until after the election, and they agree. It's not like we're ready to storm the principal's office anyway. Even without the campaign, we'd need the weekend to plan and prepare ourselves. We each want to reread the policies and think about what we'll be asked to do. George wants to talk with a counselor on a confidential support line.

"If you need anything behind the scenes, like researching, or a message reminding you that your experiences are real, I'm here for that," says Marisa.

When we start to disperse, I hang back. "Marisa?"

She stops and lets the door close again, so it's just the two of us.

"I could go to Principal Anders right now. To get . . . something started with the administration. You dropped out of the election because of him, and that's not fair. You should have a chance to be on the ballot." There's a lot happening that makes me want to curl up inside myself, to hide. I stand straight when I make my offer.

"And if the school doesn't do anything? If he's the advisor next year?" Marisa shakes her head. "Even if—Madison, that's really nice of you. Seriously, that's . . . It means a lot that you would offer to do that. But to be honest, it feels like a settled question for me already. I'm going to put my time into other spaces next year."

"Are you sure?" I ask. "It doesn't feel right."

"It feels right to me. I promise." Marisa hesitates by the door. "But now you have to win, okay? Gotta do that for us."

I smile, so she doesn't see that this wish feels more like a burden than a balloon. "Yeah. Of course."

I need to talk to Victoria.

The sky outside my bedroom window is dark by the time we can both escape the loving, concerned, slightly overbearing clutches of our respective parents long enough for a private video call.

"Hey. How are you doing?" Victoria is sitting in her bed at her mom's house. There's an old blankie wrapped around her shoulders, the kind that little kids sleep with. I love that she clearly still has hers.

"I don't know, fine, maybe. Listen . . ." I glance down at my Life Notebook, even though there's no page for what I'm about to say. "We're going to go to the school, three of us. Next week sometime. So, we have to get through a few more days, but hopefully . . . well, hopefully you win. And hopefully you don't have to work with him on ASB next year."

"I wish we were together right now," says Victoria. "I wish you were here next to me."

"I wish that too." In the spirit of things, I move from my desk chair to my bed. I prop my phone against the pillows at an angle so I can sit against the wall.

"I think you're really brave. I would never, ever blame you if you decided you couldn't report. But since I'm one of the only other people who knows what happened and what you're doing—thank you. No matter what comes next. Thank you, not just for me, but on behalf of everyone who's going to run for ASB after us. They might not know to thank you, so I'll thank you instead." Then Victoria shrugs as if her voice isn't shaking and her sincerity is a penny instead of an incalculably precious gift.

For a minute, I'm too overwhelmed to speak. Finally, I manage, "We don't know if reporting will do anything."

"It's brave, *no matter what*. I want to stay in the race," she continues. "I want to *win*. And I want to do whatever I can, as junior class president or not, to make sure this kind of thing never happens again."

My heart seems to squeeze, which is strange, because how I

actually feel is expansive—an expansive love for this girl and her particular brand of determination.

"That sounds good to me," I say.

"But . . . if *you* can't do this campaign anymore, I understand. I know you're about to say there's a lot more to do, but I don't want you to be triggered. A lot of the time, before we got together, I fell back on talking about election stuff because I knew that was what you were interested in. I don't ever want you to think that's the only or the most important thing on my mind right now. The most important thing is for you to feel safe and supported, okay?" Victoria waits until I nod.

By the time we say good night, I'm drained, empty despite every flag on display at school, the rainbow ribbon falling out of my hair, and Victoria's gentle reassurances. I curl up on the living room couch. I turn on C-SPAN and fall into an uneasy sleep, lulled by the sounds of a Senate subcommittee hearing on campus safety.

CHAPTER THIRTY-SIX

Two Days Until Runoff Election

For the first time in months, I skip volunteering on Saturday.

I'm still not feeling great about my own possibilities, but Day of Silence reminded me that my school community is brimming. Victoria's still in the race, so I've got a campaign to corral through its final days.

A student-run podcast, which interviewed the runoff candidates from each grade earlier in the week, releases the episode that afternoon. Annie's answers are vague but polished, and annoyingly funny. From Victoria's interview, I pull choice quotes, put together graphics, and send them to the core campaign group for social media dissemination. While I try to keep track of pledged votes, I'm also messaging George and Peyton about our plan to talk to someone in the administration. George's stepmom is a lawyer, and she wants to be there when we first make the report.

Behind all my Chrome tabs for the campaign, sexual harassment policies, and homework is the empty Word document I created for my YPBC scholarship essay. Every time I try to start, I get stuck. What can I tell them about myself that will show how much I want this? Especially now, when I'm not convinced I deserve it? What angle best reflects a good investment? I wrote about my other volunteering experiences in my regular application essay, to which the scholarship committee will also have access. There's nothing left but this campaign.

So many of the campaign moments, though, are tainted by Mr. Braun. His offer to basically ignore the intent petition order, which—thanks to some continued reading—I now realize was part of his manipulative grooming tactics. The campaign speeches, because I know what happened *after* he offered Marisa a safe and supportive space. And then the way his "hug"—so carefully designed to toe the line—overshadowed the day of Victoria's first win. I wanted to be screaming congratulations, and instead I was choking on the mustard gas of his oily smile.

Movies made it seem like I would feel powerful when I decided to report. I don't feel triumphant, though. I feel guilty at the possibility, however distant, that a person could lose their *job* because of what I will soon say. It's still so easy—instinctively, protectively—to push off what happened as something that didn't matter. But every time I start to doubt my decision, I think about it happening again to some future student, and *they* matter. I know, without any effort, that what happened is wrong enough that I want to protect them from it if I can. Even though it's not my job. Even though, in the end, I might not be able to. In case my voice is the one vote that tips this investigation in our favor, I want to speak. Convictions are heavy, just like I've always heard, but this one also feels hollow, empty of the visceral satisfaction, the righteous revenge I swear some speech or song promised me.

I beg my parents to let me work through dinner, and for once, they agree. Chelsea brings me a plate of risotto with tofu. I manage to swallow about half of it while she lies on my rug, highlighting her own textbooks. Joey finds us before too long, clearly exasperated by Chelsea's basement abandonment. She curls up close to the textbook pile, her eyes tracking the movement of Chelsea's hands.

My social media feeds are overwhelmed by people posting from a party Annie's best friend, Brooklyn, is hosting tonight. Annie uploads a video of her throwing campaign T-shirts off a balcony. I watch, numb, as the shirts flutter down to land on a group of people in a hot tub.

I work until late, but I find myself drifting, blinking back into awareness and having no idea what assignment I'm on. I forget what tab I was using for my voter research, forget I even *started* the voter research, and redo half the work before I accidentally click on the original tab again.

This is what you want, I try to remind myself. *This is the rest of your life, and you love it.*

But as I email the podcast creators to ask about relative stats for each candidate's segment, I can't help but think, *I can't wait for this election to be over.*

One Day Until Runoff Election

I don't even want to get out of bed on Sunday, but somehow I manage to put away a load of laundry, check on the campaign's hashtags, and annotate a page I think will be important for tomorrow's heavily hinted reading quiz. Then I find Chelsea. She's in the kitchen, kneading bread. I have a niggling feeling I was supposed to help her, but since she didn't come get me, she must not mind too much.

"Hey, when you're done, let's drive," I say.

Chelsea adds more flour to her hands. "Are you sure? I know you've got a lot on your plate right now."

"We always drive on Sunday afternoons. I don't see why today should be any different." I ignore the headache that's been building behind my eyes for an hour. I need the practice.

"Sure, whatever you want."

I feel a little better when I'm in the car, checking the gas gauge and adjusting the mirrors. Everything is normal. Everything is on track. It's all going according to The Plan.

"Let's drive around here. No highways today," says Chelsea.

I turn right out of our street and along another side road. My stomach clenches when I can see another car approaching in the rearview mirror. I'm not going fast enough.

"You're fine. Be steady," says Chelsea.

After another tense fifty feet, I have an octagonal excuse for my sluggish pace, and I put on my left blinker as I roll to a careful, complete stop. It's my least favorite kind of T-intersection: traffic going both ways perpendicular to me, but uncontrolled. Plus, the closest right-hand lane is blocked off for construction. There's nothing to do but wait until, somewhere up the road, a light turns red.

But the cars keep coming. Every time I see a break, a new car rushes in out of nowhere.

"I can't do this. They won't stop." My voice rises.

"Take a deep breath. See that green van? How about after—"

But the green van speeds past, and then so does the space between it and the next car.

"That's not enough space for me. I need more time," I insist.

I glance back. There are now three cars behind me. Waiting on me.

Ohgodohgodohgod.

"Focus on what's in front of you," says Chelsea.

"I'm focusing."

"Do you want to switch? I'll switch with you."

"No!"

"Okay, that's fine too. You can do this. Be confident. You don't need as much time as you think you do."

"Tell me when."

"You gotta be ready for it."

Behind me, a car honks.

"Ignore, ignore—GO!"

I slam on the accelerator, and we burst forward. I twist the wheel left, press on the brakes with only slightly less force to slow us down, and, finally, we're moving again. My whole body is shaking.

"I hate literally everything about what just happened," I say.

"Let's find a parking lot," says Chelsea.

Luckily, those aren't hard to find here. I park on the edge of a strip mall lot, where I have the whole row to myself. I don't know if I'm between the lines, and I don't care. I turn the car off. I try to speak, but the air catches in my throat. I shiver and try again.

"The car behind me, back there. It was a Chevy Malibu." I clutch the keys in my fist.

"Okay?" says Chelsea.

"Mr. Braun drives a Chevy Malibu. It wasn't him," I add quickly. "Some old man. But I saw the car, and for a second, I thought, it *could* be."

"I understand. That's scary." Chelsea watches me closely, but not with pity. It's just that she sees me, because she's been here too.

"And it . . . He could be anywhere, all the time. And it's— obviously, *obviously* I'm glad that what happened wasn't worse. But it's so close to nothing, it's so . . . easily dismissed, that it feels like it could happen again, any time. Anywhere. In health last semester, they were all, don't drink, or at least watch your drinks, don't walk alone at night, all of that." My voice shakes. "I was at school. It was three o'clock in the afternoon. It was supposed to be something about the campaign."

"I know."

"It just makes me think . . . how many more people like that are out there? People who I might meet? Professors, or supervisors. Where they're half a toe over the line, again and again, so you can't call them on it, but it's not right. It's not right."

"It's not," says Chelsea. "And I'm so, so sorry this is a worry you have. Those people exist. You know it, because you met one. There's a lot of good people, too, I promise. I mean, you know how much I *hate* some of those people at my old college. But one of my professors walked me from her class to my next one every day. I couldn't stay, but there are people I'm glad to have met."

I nod. "I didn't say anything. I didn't . . . like I didn't even realize enough of what was happening to say no. I always thought I would know when to say it. I thought I'd be . . . forceful. Clear."

Not long after she moved in with us, Chelsea told me about the self-defense class she took her first year of college. The whole theory was that by creating muscle memory, if you were attacked, you wouldn't have to think at all. Just react. But she'd known the man who assaulted her, and she froze. She couldn't scream, much less shove.

When I was younger, I wanted to be exactly like Chelsea, from the way she wore her clothes to following her exact footprints across fresh snow at Christmas. This parallel path isn't one either of us chose, and I wish the world had let us contain our shared experiences to things like ill-conceived family recipes. Like learning to drive in our grandpa's old car.

"My therapist taught me this concept of the hot-cold empathy gap. It's basically that our understanding is 'state dependent.' When we're not in it—not cold, not hungry, not angry, not scared—we have a hard time accurately imagining what that feels like and what the impact will be on our actions. So, when we're calmly sitting in health class, it's difficult for us to predict how we'll react when we're confused in the future. And then it can be hard again, after something's happened, when we're calm, or mostly calm, at home, to remember exactly how scared or confused we were at the time." Chelsea shifts, tucking one leg underneath the other. "There have been studies on it, specifically on sexual harassment in job interviews. It totally tracks that you would feel it too. It doesn't make what Mr. Braun did any less wrong just because you couldn't process it immediately."

"Yeah." I trace the bottom of the steering wheel with my thumb. "Can you drive us home?"

Back in my bedroom, I turn off notifications on my phone in a final attempt to focus. Everything feels the way driving did the first weeks after the accident: too fast and out of control. There are so many moving parts to keep track of, and you can never look away from anything for too long.

Every time I think I finish one task, I spot something done wrong, or a note I left myself earlier about a final addition to a multi-step agenda item. I take some Tylenol, but the headache doesn't go away. My head feels foggy, and my thoughts slow enough that they must be traveling to me from many, many light-years away. Maybe from the future, when I'll look back on this and not believe how I truly can't stay focused. The way anxiety closes my throat and I choke on water.

Through it all, I'm sure I'm forgetting something. Guilt wraps itself up and up and up my spine, squeezing at my neck.

Note to self . . .

Note to self . . .

Note to self . . .

CHAPTER THIRTY-SEVEN

Runoff Election Day

It hits me as we cross the pavement between the drop-off zone and school. I honest-to-god fall to the ground. My knees are on fire, but it doesn't matter.

"Oh my god. Crap. Crap. *FUCK!*"

Marisa crouches down next to me. "I'm here, it's okay. What's wrong?"

Before she can finish the question, the words are tumbling out over each other, because everything is wrong, and the simplest part of my plan—the part that's not preparing to report a teacher or memorizing facts for a test about a country that keeps failing to protect students or writing an essay to beg for a chance to change it all—was too much for me, the girl who is too much herself. "I can't believe—I can't *believe*—I was supposed to bake yesterday. I was supposed to make, like, two hundred cupcakes. It's under my name on the campaign schedule, I know it is. And I completely forgot." I'm making a scene, tears now running down my cheeks, and again: It doesn't matter.

Because on this last, most important day of my first campaign,

I couldn't make that final stretch. I couldn't follow my Plan or a recipe. I couldn't keep a promise I'd made, not just to myself but to Victoria, to the campaign team, to everyone who wants her to win—for the trainings and the judicial integrity and the safety guaranteed by the catwalk.

"Okay, all right," Marisa soothes me. "Could your dad pick some up? I know that two hundred is a lot on short notice, but maybe if he can stop at a couple of grocery stores . . ."

I shake my head. "He has to go straight to a site visit today."

And I can't drive, and—screw *everything*. Especially Mr. Braun and his Chevy Malibu.

"Okay. C'mon, let's get inside . . . I have wipes and stuff in my bag . . ."

Marisa ushers me into the school. We stop right inside the entrance, where there's a harsh metal bench for visitors. She makes me sit while she cleans off my scraped knees. The whole time, my body is trembling, my mind playing and replaying every moment yesterday I got caught up in trying to remember what I was meant to do. Every second I wasted and failed.

"Pink or purple?" She holds up the wide bandages, like it matters, like I care, like I can make a decision right now.

"You choose. Please."

"Okay, well, I think your right knee should be pink, and your left knee can get purple. Here, have some water."

I've managed one shaky sip when Victoria and Lauren emerge from the ramp to the cafeteria. I drop the water bottle on the bench, where it hits with a clang. How I am supposed to tell Victoria I messed this up for her? I'm the one who told her to demand things. To expect me to be here and to do what I promised, and do it well.

"Oh my god, Madison, what happened?" Victoria rushes toward me. I flinch away before she can touch me, and she freezes.

"Minor accident, doesn't matter. Marisa got me cleaned up. Listen . . ." But she can't actually listen, because I'm not saying anything: I'm too busy crying.

"It's okay," she says.

"It's not—the cupcakes. I completely forgot about the cupcakes. I'm so sorry. I'll, I don't know. I don't know, and I'm so, so very sorry." I wipe my face on my sweater, even though I haven't stopped crying. Maybe this is just who I am now: a sobbing mess who can't make a cupcake or keep a commitment.

Victoria reaches out a gentle hand. I let her help me from the bench, because if she wants me to go somewhere, it seems the least I can offer. "I want to show you something."

Lauren grabs my backpack, and she and Marisa turn to follow us. Still sniffling, I walk with Victoria down the ramp.

Joan is standing behind the first table in the cafeteria.

A table that is covered in boxes full of cupcakes, each of them perfectly decorated with the words I VOTED in West Plymouth blue.

"Oh my god," I say.

Lauren slides around me to stand next to Joan. "When you stopped responding to messages yesterday, we thought something must be up. And since Joan has two ovens—"

"And Lauren is the best cake decorator I know—" says Joan.

"We thought we'd take care of it for you."

I drop Victoria's hand so I can press both of my own to my face. "Oh my god." I wipe at my cheeks *again* and then meet their gazes. "Thank you. Thank you so, so much."

"I don't live my life by spreadsheet like you do," says Joan. "But I thought one day wouldn't hurt."

"You've done a lot for Victoria, and you're doing . . . a lot right now. We wanted to do this for you." Lauren smiles and shrugs, as if this didn't take her hours—which I'm sure it did—as if this doesn't mean the world to me.

"Thank you for, um, for none of you saying, it's just cupcakes, it doesn't matter," I say.

"Voting always matters," says Lauren. "Here. Come try one. I won't tell—I know you're good for it."

This time, I don't rush into the scrum by the bulletin board. Victoria and I meet in an alcove farther down the hall. Louis is in charge of bringing us the result.

"No matter what . . ." Victoria starts.

"No matter what," I agree. We don't have to say the rest; we know.

"This is so much worse than last time," she says.

"Is it up yet?" Amrita finds us.

I shrug, but behind her shoulder, I see Louis approaching. His face is blank. When he reaches us, he takes Victoria's hand. I hold my breath.

"Madam President."

I scream. Amrita jumps, fists raised. Victoria spins into my arms.

"You did it!" we both say to each other.

Holy crap.

After everything—she actually won.

Victoria Ferrand is the next junior class president.

And I made that happen.

Then I look at the group that's gathered around us: Louis and Amrita, of course, but also Lauren and Devin, Marisa and Peyton.

"It was a team effort," I say. I look back at Victoria. I'm so proud of her—of all of us—my heart is squeezing in that expansive way again, like it's just coiling up so it can prepare to burst with joy.

There are as many congratulations as we can fit into the ten-minute break before third period, all of us talking over each other, everything that contributed to her win on top of all the things she can accomplish now that she's won, an ecstatic overlapping chorus. In all the moments I'm grinning too widely to speak, there's someone else there to yell out the news again: *V for Victoria*. When we start to split off to go to class, I catch Peyton's eye.

"Tomorrow," I mouth.

She nods.

I want today reserved only for celebration.

One Day After Runoff Election

Waiting outside the principal's office is a brand-new experience for me. George's stepmom, the lawyer, went in first, I think to tell Principal Anders that someone will be watching to make sure Title IX policies are carried out swiftly and correctly. George herself is in the single-stall bathroom around the corner, because she kept getting distracted from her breathing exercises by the other students walking past us.

So many people offered to wait with us today. If we'd wanted, the little lobby area outside the upper admin offices could be full. In a way, having our friends and parents not here means I can *almost* pretend this is a normal meeting, like Peyton and I are just petitioning for more GSA funding. And until the office door is shut behind us, I need to hold on to some thread of pretending. Otherwise, I wouldn't be able to sit out here and wait to speak.

"You girls aren't in trouble, are you?"

Mr. Braun.

Peyton goes ramrod stiff in my peripheral vision. I lift my chin and make myself look straight at him. There's a smile on his face, casual, certain of its welcome.

"No. We're not in trouble."

"I didn't think so! I didn't see you yesterday, but congratulations on Victoria's win. I know you'll do great things, Maddie."

Next to us, the door to the principal's office opens. Someone is standing in the doorway—Ms. Chablis-Khouri or Principal Anders—but I don't turn my head yet.

I offer my hand to Peyton. She takes it, and we stand to walk together into the office.

"I am going to do great things," I say. "And my name is Madison."

EPILOGUE

"**A**re we calling this a date?" I ask as I slide into the car.

"You invited me to an activity not at school or your house, so I think so? Let's say yes," says Victoria. "Plus . . . I think it's kind of fitting if our first date when we're already together is with your volunteering group."

"We can do something more traditional later this month. A movie, or ice cream just the two of us," I say.

"When will you hear back about the scholarship?"

"The twentieth."

That's assuming I'm able to submit a decent application. I had to ask off babysitting this past week, partially so I could attend the first of what promises to be many excruciating after-school meetings, and partially so when I wasn't in those meetings, I could cry and cuddle with Chelsea and Joey without falling too far behind.

Health class didn't warn me how much *time* it all takes up. When

I'm huddled with George and Peyton, I'm not studying for exams. I'm not organizing for a compost garden, one of Marisa's campaign ideas that she still wants to implement. I'm doing my homework, barely, and definitely not writing my scholarship essay. I want to be coordinating an official volunteer role with a progressive Senate challenger. Instead, I'm coordinating meetings with the victims' advocate we were assigned.

I think about all the other types of survivorship that are surely happening around me, even when I don't see the struggle. There's a lot of time being stolen. And a lot of people pushed out of places and power they have a claim to.

I don't have quick fixes for any of it, but I know that a schedule of surviving, strategizing, and studying hasn't left much space for the quiet joys that still bloom. Incongruent and unexpected, they deserve time too.

"So on the twenty-first, will you go on a date with me?" says Victoria. "We'll need to celebrate."

"Don't jinx it."

"I'm not jinxing anything. I'm just saying, you're incredible, they'd be fools not to see that, and I want to make sure I'm on the calendar to celebrate with my—" She cuts herself off. Her cheeks are pink.

"With . . . your girlfriend," I say.

Victoria glances at me, grateful and grinning. Her dimples are on full display. I've missed those this week.

When I lead her down the hall of the community center, she laces her fingers with mine.

"Are you sure?" I ask.

"Here's a start," she says.

As soon as Trish sees us, she raises her eyebrows at me. "Look who finally brought a friend."

Now it's my turn to blush. "Victoria, this is Trish, my *favorite* college fellow. Trish, this is Victoria . . . junior class president-elect. And also my girlfriend."

"Don't break her heart while I'm gone this summer," Trish says, and hands Victoria a Sharpie for her name badge.

"Wait, where are you going this summer?" I ask.

Trish smiles wide. "DC, baby. Paid summer internship on the Hill. With my favorite congresswoman."

"Oh my god!"

When I whisper the name in Victoria's ear, she shrieks too.

"All right, all right, go sit down. Victoria, welcome." Her smile turns sly. "And enjoy the interrogation Connie is about to give you."

Luckily, Connie is busy on the other side of the room, so Victoria and I can claim seats in peace.

"I'm really glad you're here," I say.

Victoria takes in the room: our hodgepodge of volunteers, the boxes of blank postcards waiting to be filled out, the lists of voters, and my grin.

"I'm really glad you invited me," she says.

Two hours later, there's ink smeared across my fingertips but a skip in my step as Victoria and I head back to her car. Even if Victoria never comes to another volunteering session with me, there's a connection now between these parts of my life. Communities are made one link at a time.

"Can I come home with you?" she says.

I hesitate.

"Not to hook up! I thought, if you wanted, I could help you with your scholarship essay. Someone taught me a lot about editing last month."

"Oh, someone?" I tease.

Instead of circling around to the passenger seat, I step toward her.

"Just some random girl." Victoria runs a hand down my arm, then threads our fingers together. "She likes spreadsheets, I think? Listens to a lot of Halsey. Has a whole collection of cute feminist socks."

With my other hand, I tuck a few curls behind her ear. I kiss her dimples, and then I kiss her lips.

"Yeah," I say, stepping back. "Come home with me."

My parents only subject us to five minutes of small talk before we escape to my room. Victoria sits on my bed, reading my current draft, while I pace.

"Hmm," she says.

"I *know*." I flop heavily into my desk chair, and suddenly the room shifts in my mind. "Could you . . . I have an idea. Could you type for me?"

"Huh?"

"If I start talking . . . will you write down what I say?"

"Sure." Victoria adjusts the laptop on a pillow, fingers at the ready.

"Okay . . ." I let myself spin in the chair. I still want this, maybe more than ever. And I feel a little more sure that I *can* do this. Not only because Victoria won, but because of *how* she won. And because of all the people I know, and all the people I barely know, who believe us. "Okay. Here's the situation."

Twenty-One Days Until Youth Politics Boot Camp

Victoria and I take one last look at the pile of stuff in her back seat.

"Okay . . ." She shifts into drive and pulls away from the campaign headquarters. "Let's go put up some yard signs."

School has only been out for a week, but already Victoria is sporting the start of a summer tan, thanks to her lifeguarding job at the New Hope Aquatic Park. Other than weekend canvassing, I expect to stay winter-pale for at least the first half of summer: The administrative assistant at George's stepmom's small law practice is out on maternity leave, and she offered me the position. Her admin will be back just in time for me to leave for DC and YPBC. Trish even found a grant to cover my flights. The Plan is still The Plan.

Kind of.

After the runoff election, I took the rest of May off from driving. I know I'll get there, maybe even by the end of summer, but I need a little more time. One day, I'm going to be in the driver's seat. And it's going to feel great.

Just . . . a little bit later than planned.

"Where to first?" says Victoria.

I'm not worried about running into Mr. Braun. He resigned before the end of the school year, I guess in the hope that if he pretended to be gracious about this "misunderstanding," we'd let it go. We're not. I'm not stopping until I've done everything I can to get his teaching license revoked.

"A bunch of houses along Winnetka. Great visibility," I say as I check the blue dots on our volunteering app.

Yard sign setup is a two-person job: one person to drive, and the other to jump out and secure the sign. Victoria and I soon settle into a rhythm. We roll the windows down, blasting our new playlist into the sunny afternoon. No campaign songs or musicals, because our favorite lesbian singer-songwriter has just released her first solo album, and it only seems right that we devote the early days of summer to Eva Bell and *Eponymous*.

Midway through our yard sign list, I get caught up talking with a homeowner who wants to join the campaign's phone-banking team. When I get back in the car, Victoria restarts the song, whose beginning I missed while I was writing down his contact information.

"This is why I love you," I say.

"I love you too," Victoria says, laughing.

It's not the first time we've exchanged *I love yous*. The first time wasn't in her car on a blue-sky afternoon, but on a quiet evening I'm sure I will remember long after my memoir is forgotten. And that's how it should be.

Note to self: Some moments are only meant for us.

ACKNOWLEDGMENTS

Write the notoriously challenging sophomore novel. Write the notoriously challenging sophomore novel about a difficult topic in the midst of a global pandemic and political instability. I am not sure I could have done it for anyone but Madison, who is so close to my heart.

This book was completed with thanks to the following:

My agent, Jessica Errera, who was with me every step of the way. There were many, many steps, and most of them were hard. My editor, Rachel Diebel, who loved Madison from the very beginning and ushered this book to new emotional heights. I'm so grateful history rhymed and placed that hockey scene in your knowledgeable hands.

Additional thanks to all those at the Jane Rotrosen Agency and Feiwel & Friends who brought this story to life, especially: Jean Feiwel, Arik Hardin, and Celeste Cass; Julia Bianchi and Bex Glendining for the amazing design and cover illustration; and my authenticity readers.

Claire, for shining your triple-threat understanding of plot, characterization, and proofreading on this book (over and over). For your relentless faith that I could pull this off. Exhibit A: For everything. Happy birthday.

Brennan, for helping me develop the concept for Jays Jigsaw, and my brother, for the manufacturing logistics. Senior Routt, for encouragement and life advice, including the hot-cold empathy gap. Maria, for early comments and enthusiasm. Jasper Sanchez, for the continued 21der solidarity. The Trifecta, for sharing your wisdom so generously. My therapist, L.

My dad, who watched *The West Wing* with me, and my mom, who took me to my first protest (and then some more after that). My parents, who welcomed me home for several months during that first, long pandemic winter.

The readers, bloggers, librarians, booksellers, and fellow authors who supported my debut. Eva says hi.

RESOURCES

me too

"The 'me too' movement supports survivors of sexual violence and their allies by connecting survivors to resources, offering community organizing resources, pursuing a 'me too' policy platform, and working with researchers to add to the field and chart our way forward. We believe that the movement begins with connecting survivors to resources for healing, justice, action and leadership."

metoomvmt.org

National Sexual Violence Resource Center

"The National Sexual Violence Resource Center (NSVRC) is the leading nonprofit in providing information and tools to prevent and respond to sexual violence. NSVRC translates research and trends into best practices that help individuals, communities and service providers achieve real and lasting change."

nsvrc.org

RAINN

"RAINN (Rape, Abuse & Incest National Network) is the nation's largest anti–sexual violence organization. RAINN created and operates the National Sexual Assault Hotline (800.656. HOPE, online.rainn.org y rainn.org/es) in partnership with more than 1,000 local sexual assault service providers across the country . . . RAINN also carries out programs to prevent sexual violence, help survivors, and ensure that perpetrators are brought to justice."

rainn.org

The Trevor Project

"The Trevor Project is the world's largest suicide prevention and crisis intervention organization for lesbian, gay, bisexual, transgender, queer, and questioning (LGBTQ) young people."

thetrevorproject.org

Thank you for reading this Feiwel & Friends book.

The friends who made

SOMETHING LIKE POSSIBLE

possible are:

Jean Feiwel, Publisher
Liz Szabla, Associate Publisher
Rich Deas, Senior Creative Director
Holly West, Senior Editor
Anna Roberto, Senior Editor
Kat Brzozowski, Senior Editor
Dawn Ryan, Executive Managing Editor
Celeste Cass, Production Manager
Emily Settle, Editor
Rachel Diebel, Editor
Foyinsi Adegbonmire, Associate Editor
Brittany Groves, Assistant Editor
Julia Bianchi, Junior Designer
Arik Hardin, Assistant Managing Editor

Follow us on Facebook or visit us online at **mackids.com**.
Our books are friends for life.

Puritan
BOSTON &
QUAKER
PHILADELPHIA

WITH A NEW INTRODUCTION BY THE AUTHOR

E. Digby Baltzell

TRANSACTION PUBLISHERS
NEW BRUNSWICK (U.S.A.) AND LONDON (U.K.)

New material this edition copyright © 1996 by Transaction Publishers, New Brunswick, New Jersey 08903. Originally published in 1979 by The Free Press.

All rights reserved under International and Pan-American Copyright Conventions. No part of this book may be reproduced or transmitted in any form or by any means, electronic or mechanical, including photocopy, recording, or any information storage and retrieval system, without prior permission in writing from the publisher. All inquiries should be addressed to Transaction Publishers, Rutgers—The State University, New Brunswick, New Jersey 08903.

This book is printed on acid-free paper that meets the American National Standard for Permanence of Paper for Printed Library Materials.

Library of Congress Catalog Number: 95-25467
ISBN: 1-56000-830-X
Printed in the United States of America

Library of Congress Cataloging-in-Publication Data

Baltzell, E. Digby (Edward Digby), 1915–
    Puritan Boston and Quaker Philadelphia / E. Digby Baltzell ; with a new introduction by the author.
        p. cm.
    Includes bibliographical references and index.
    Originally published: New York : Free Press, © 1979.
    ISBN 1-56000-830-X (alk. paper)
    1. Boston (Mass.)—Civilization. 2. Puritans—Massachusetts—Boston—History. 3. Philadelphia (Pa.)—Civilization. 4. Quakers—Pennsylvania—Philadelphia—History. 5. Elite (Social sciences)—Massachusetts—Boston. 6. Elite (Social sciences)—Pennsylvania—Philadelphia. I. Title.
F73.3.B33   1996
974.4'61—dc20   95-25467
                                                                          CIP

In memory of Jane

Introduction to the Transaction Edition

The central theme of this book is that the elitist Puritan ethic firmly established class authority and deference democracy in Boston and Massachusetts and lasted from the colonial period down to the twentieth century; on the other hand, the egalitarian and victim ethic of Quakerism failed to produce class authority, resulting in the defiant democracy that has marked Philadelphia and Pennsylvania ever since. Two important unanticipated consequences flowed from these two antithetical ethics: In the first place, the hierarchical culture of Massachusetts produced great leaders on the local and national scene, while Philadelphia and Pennsylvania have produced hardly any leaders of distinction. This difference was nicely shown by a comparison of fifty First Families of Boston with fifty First Families of Philadelphia; while the Boston families produced 188 individuals with 34,365 lines written about them in the brief biographies in the *Dictionary of American Biography* (*DAB*), the fifty leading families in Philadelphia produced only 146 individuals with 15,842 lines (or less than half) written about them in the *DAB*; twenty-eight (28) Boston Brahmins were memorialized by more than 300 line biographies while only three (3) Proper Philadelphians were of such distinction (see Appendix, table A-4 through A-11). Judge Oliver Wendell Holmes, Jr.'s *DAB* biography was 1,324 lines in length while his exact contemporary,

John G. Johnson, the leading lawyer in Philadelphia at the time, made a large fortune but was memorialized in this American Plutarch with only 96 lines. Benjamin Franklin, who was born and educated in Boston and made his fortune in Philadelphia had a *DAB* biography of 2,545 lines; but he was a universal genius and not a member of either city's upper class. Finally, Boston produced three presidents of the United States while Philadelphia produced none; Boston's most famous Irish Catholic was John F. Kennedy, while the most famous Philadelphia Irish Catholic was Grace Kelly; Louis D. Brandeis was the most famous Boston Jew, while the most famous Philadelphia Jew was Rebecca Gratz, the model for "Rebecca" in Walter Scott's *Ivanhoe*.

The difference in the quality of leadership in Boston and Philadelphia had a great deal to do with the religious and ethnic compositions of the two colonies. While Massachusetts was an extremely homogeneous community from the very beginning, Pennsylvania was the most heterogeneous of the thirteen original colonies; by our first census in 1790, for example, the two leadership states of Virginia and Massachusetts were overwhelmingly English with religious establishments while Pennsylvania was about one-third English in origin, one-third German and one-third Scotch-Irish; of course no establishment was possible. Massachusetts Puritans, moreover, were a quite different type of Englishmen than were the Philadelphia Quakers. The original Puritans who came with the Great Migration to Massachusetts Bay, between 1630 and the outbreak of the English Revolution in 1642, came predominately from the eastern and southeastern counties, the most advanced in their day. The Quakers, on the other hand, came from all over England but mostly from the northern counties of Lancastershire and York, the most rural, Catholic, Royalist, and backward but beautiful part of England. The charismatic founder of Quakerism, George Fox, had his vision of a people called Quakers on top of Pendle Hill in Lancastershire. His most important convert was Mary Fell who became the mother of Quakerism. Mary was the wife of Judge Thomas Fell, master of Swarthmore Hall, which became the strategic center of the early days of the movement. Judge Fell, one of the leading Puritans in the county, never became a Quaker; neither did his son, Thomas Fell, Jr. All his seven daughters followed their mother into the movement, as did their husbands; from the beginning Quakerism seemed to have more of an appeal to women than to men; several of the serving maids at Swarthmore Hall joined the movement, one of them eventually marrying two Quaker governors of Rhode Island.

While Massachusetts Bay was a speaking aristocracy and a silent democracy, Penn's colony was a fine example of a loudly speaking democracy headed by a wealthy but silent plutocracy. Sectarian wrangling from its beginning made the colony almost ungovernable; one-man rule, or bossism, has characterized Pennsylvania politics down through its history. Few immigrants settled in the Bay Colony after 1642, and the colony remained a homogeneous people for some two hundred years until the coming of the Irish Catholics in the 1840s. The aristocratic nature of the colony in those two centuries is suggested by the fact that Robert C. Winthrop (1809–1894), the biggest man in Boston in his day, Speaker of the House, U.S. senator, vestryman of Trinity Church for sixty years, president of the Massachusetts Historical Society for thirty years and so forth, was a descendent of John Winthrop, the first governor and James Bowdoin, the great governor of both the Colony and of the Commonwealth at the time of the nation's founding.

In the Epilogue of this book, I wrote as follows:

> At the close of this analysis of the histories of Puritan Boston and Quaker Philadelphia, it is perhaps appropriate to suggest that although America as a whole has been Puritan and Calvinist throughout most of its history (Ernst Troeltsch wrote, in 1911, that "Calvinism...may be described as 'Americanism'"), it has now moved—especially since the 1960s—far closer to the ideals of Quakerism. And it was the prophet of Concord, Ralph Waldo Emerson, who sowed the seeds of the antinomian individualism of our day....
>
> Tocqueville pondered the meaning of America in the age of Emerson and Hawthorne and, with a cat's eye for the future, warned of the dangers of democratic despotism. Quite unlike Emerson, he saw that both anarchy and despotism proceeded from the same cause: "namely, that *general apathy* which is the consequence of individualism." His French contemporaries were quick to see that Tocqueville had studied democracy in America in order to understand the future of his beloved France. Similarly, I have studied Puritan Boston and Quaker Philadelphia with an eye to understanding the future of our beloved, but now troubled, America. There is thus no more relevant way to close this book than by quoting the last sentence of *Democracy in America*: "The nations of our time cannot prevent the conditions of men from becoming equal, but it depends upon themselves whether the principle of equality is to lead them to freedom or servitude, to knowledge or barbarism, to prosperity or wretchedness."

This book is surely more relevant today than when it was first published in 1979. Since then incivility and barbarism have steadily increased; in our era of victim political correctness, moreover, we seem to be stranded between more or less extreme populist ideologies on both the left and the right.

E. Digby Baltzell
September 1995

Preface

This book was written during the most anarchic and anti-authoritarian decade in our nation's history. I began it in 1968, the year that witnessed the assassinations of Martin Luther King, Jr., and Robert Kennedy, the My Lai and *Pueblo* incidents, the Democratic convention in Chicago, and the student rebellions at Columbia University and elsewhere. As I wrote this preface, the mayor of San Francisco had just been murdered, not long after some 900 members of the San Francisco based People's Temple died in Guyana. Social causation is an extremely complex matter, but perhaps this comparative analysis of class authority in Puritan Boston and Quaker Philadelphia will shed some light on why and how we have come to our present time of troubles.

Knowledge about things is no substitute for an acquaintance with them. Most meaningful knowledge is highly personal, and theories about the meaning of facts are rooted in one's autobiography. More than two decades ago, for example, while visiting friends on the coast of Maine, I drove to Brunswick to look up something in the Bowdoin College library. Upon entering the small library, I was confronted by life-size portraits of Hawthorne, Longfellow, and Franklin Pierce. All three men were friends and members of the class of 1825. No three individuals of comparable stature, I thought as I looked at the fine portraits, had ever graduated from the college at my own university or from any other college in the state of Pennsylvania. Why? I asked myself then as I have done many times since.

I have thought about the differences between Boston Brahmins and Philadelphia Gentlemen all my adult life. I am, of course, more intimately acquainted with the Proper Philadelphian (I now write less than two blocks from where I was born). Yet I have often visited relatives and friends in Boston, which is, in addition, the most written about city in America. The organizing theories underlying this book are the product of three decades of reading, writing, and teaching about authority and leadership at the University of Pennsylvania.

The most popular books about the American upper classes have concentrated on the conspicuously consuming leisure time activities of ladies and gentlemen of privilege. There has also been a conspiratorial school of class analysis whose authors have focused on "unmasking" the privileged classes as made up of mere manipulators of wealth and power for their own advantage. Both schools have been successful in appealing to our natural capacity for envy in normal times and our propensity for conspiratorial theories of history in times of crisis. This book takes a very different approach to class analysis. It is my central theory that class lies at the very core of the authority structure of any society and, moreover, that it is the proper function of an upper class in any healthy society to wield authority not through manipulation, force, or fraud but through the respect it commands throughout society for the accomplishments and leadership qualities of its members over several generations. My task in this book is to compare and contrast two privileged classes in order to show how and why Boston Brahmins produced a long tradition of class authority whereas Proper Philadelphians did not.

In all human societies it has been a major function of religion to motivate men and women and to give meaning to their lives. After some thirty years of observing the subtle differences between Boston Brahmins and Proper Philadelphians, I had come to the intuitive conclusion before beginning this book that these differences largely reflect the very different religious ethics of the founding fathers of each city. Bostonians and Philadelphians were and still are motivated by the hierarchical and authoritarian ethic of Puritanism, on the one hand, and the egalitarian and anti-authoritarian ethic of Quakerism, on the other. Ten years of writing this book confirmed these impressions.

Each reader will have to judge the plausibility of the argument outlined in the pages that follow. But all of us will agree, I should think, that class authority has been turned upside down in the past decade and that the Calvinist-Puritan ethic has very little appeal to modern religious sensibilities. Some will agree that the increasingly classless but elitist characteristics of our society today have something to do with our stasis in leadership and increasing lack of pride in ourselves and in our nation.

Although I have always admired the mind of Puritan Boston, my heart and loyalties are rooted in Quaker Philadelphia. Whereas the very different histories of these two cities show the overwhelming leadership superiority of Boston, I must emphasize here that Philadelphia is still in the midst of a post–World War II renaissance that promises much for the future of the city. There are even signs that Philadelphia's citizens of all classes will eventually become boosters and winners rather than detractors and losers. But this is a tale I hope to tell in the future. In this connection, I should like to thank the John Simon Guggenheim Foundation for granting me a fellowship for the academic year 1978–1979 to begin research on the Philadelphia renaissance. Although I have spent most of the year finishing this book, I trust their generosity will be rewarded eventually with another.

In any sociological and historical analysis there is no substitute for firsthand knowledge of places and their location in history. I should like to thank, then, the Society for Religion in Higher Education for granting me a Danforth Fellowship for the academic year 1967–1968. The fellowship allowed me to travel to the British Isles: I visited the Quaker Galilee in northern England, where in 1652 atop Pendle Hill the simple shepherd George Fox had the vision that marked the founding of the Quaker movement; Swarthmore Hall, the first headquarters of the movement; and meetinghouses in the small villages of Lancashire and York. I drove through Wales, where so many of Philadelphia's First Families have their Old World roots: through St. Asaph, where Benjamin Franklin, on a visit to the bishop of Wales, began writing his autobiography, thence through counties with such familiar Philadelphia names as Denbiegh, Marioneth, Montgomery, and Radnor; through beautiful Snowdonia; and to the mining town of Bryn Mawr. Proper Philadelphians will understand why I made a symbolic purchase in the Cadwalader-Roberts hardware store in Barmouth. From Wales I drove to Buckinghamshire, where I inspected the graves of the Peningtons and the Penns just outside the famous Quaker meetinghouse at Jordans; a mile down the road is the Grange, once the home of the Peningtons and the Quaker headquarters in the second generation.

After visiting the colleges of Emmanuel and Trinity at Cambridge, the nursery of New England Puritanism, I drove through the seventeenth-century Puritan homeland of East Anglia: to the ruins of the Abbey of Bury St. Edmunds, whose lands long ago included the manor of Groton, secured by the Winthrops in Henry VIII's time; and to Norwich, once the nursery of Puritan lawyers. I spent the night at the new University of East Anglia, where the administration building, Earlham Hall, was at one time home to the Gurneys and intellectual headquarters for English Quakers in the nineteenth century. Thus began my search for the historical roots of Puritan Boston and Quaker Philadelphia.

I am indebted to Oscar Handlin, then director of the administrative committee at the Charles Warren Center for Studies in American History at Harvard University, where I was a Fellow during the academic year 1972–1973. My time at the Warren Center allowed me to take a further look at various upper-class institutions in Boston, and I should especially like to thank Alexander Williams for his kind hospitality and guidance. It was also instructive to observe educated Bostonians react so favorably to the presidential candidacy of Senator

George McGovern in that critical, antinomian fall. Every Sunday, I attended First Day services at the Quaker meetinghouse just off Brattle Street in Cambridge.

I should also like to thank friends, colleagues, and students who during these years of writing stimulated my thinking on authority and equality in continually challenging discussions. I am grateful to Mary Dunn, Michelle Osborn, Mary Phillips, Dwight Webb, Perry Ottenberg, Peter Bachrach, Robert Forster, Rowland Frye, Michael Zuckerman, Bruce Kuklick, Richard Farnum, Howard Schneiderman, Frank Furstenberg, Harold Bershady, Morton Keller, Van Harvey, David Riesman, Martin Meyerson, and the late Talcott Parsons for their kind reading of and comments on various parts of the manuscript. I am especially indebted to Jean Toll for reading the entire manuscript and to Holmes Perkins and George Thomas, who read and corrected details in my chapter on architecture; to John McCoubrey, who did the same in art; to George Lee Haskins and James Freedman, in law; and to George Corner, in medicine. Margaret Bacon, of the American Friends Service Committee, and Barbara Curtis, of the Quaker Collection at Haverford College, made invaluable comments on my chapter on the Gurneyite Quakers, as did Dennis Clark and Lawrence Bell, on the Catholics. I thank Joanie Prior, Linda Burke, Rachael Bedard and Carol Brooks Gardner for their help with technical details, and Martha Rosso and Bernard Rosenberg for their deft and judicious proof-reading.

I shall always remember with gratitude my friends Richard Shryock, Frederick Tolles, and Philip Benjamin for their stimulating discussions of the ideas in this book in its early stages; all three died before its completion. And similarly with the late Doris Dembo, whose cheerfulness and aesthetic sense made the drawing up of tables and figures a pleasure rather than a bore.

This long journey would never have come to an end without the help and encouragement of Gladys Topkis of The Free Press; how fortunate I have been to have worked with someone with such an old-fashioned and Puritan-like devotion to the editorial calling; I cannot thank her enough.

Of course, as all of us say, any faults in fact or interpretation, bound to be many in a work of such broad historical scope, are entirely my own.

A Problem Defined

When studied with any degree of thoroughness, the economic problem will be found to run into the political problem, the political problem in turn into the philosophical problem, and the philosophical problem itself to be almost indissolubly bound up at last with the religious problem.

Irving Babbitt

Upon this point a page of history is worth a volume of logic.
Oliver Wendell Holmes, Jr.

The idea of a single American social character, as analyzed by modern sociologists and historians, is hardly applicable to the colonial period. From their very beginning, the thirteen colonies formed a mosaic of Protestant ethics, with small minorities of Catholics and Jews. In the early seventeenth century, this Protestant mosaic was predominantly of the right-wing Calvinist-Puritan variety: New England, except Rhode Island, was Puritan; in the trader-commercial culture of Manhattan, where a dozen or so languages were spoken by the end of the seventeenth century, the upper class was largely Dutch Reformed (Calvinist), as was the patroon aristocracy of the Hudson valley; French Calvinists, or Huguenots, after Louis XIV revoked the Edict of Nantes, came in large numbers to Charleston, South Carolina, and New Rochelle, New York. Even the first settlers of Virginia were essentially in sympathy with the Puritan wing of the Anglican church.

In the latter part of the seventeenth century, the left-wing sects emigrated to the New World and found their most prominent, permanent home in Pennsylvania; the English Quakers came first but there soon followed a host of sectarians from Germany. Left-wing sectarians of all varieties were also welcome in

Rhode Island, the "hiving out" state of antinomian and anarchistic perfectionists of the Williams–Hutchinson–Gorton variety. New Jersey formed an interesting and schizophrenic pattern from the very beginning: West New Jersey (now called, with a certain amount of cultural derision, South Jersey) was largely Quaker, rural, and culturally backward; East New Jersey (now North Jersey) was invaded at an early date by Connecticut Yankees of strong Puritan convictions who settled first in New Ark and Elizabeth Town and then spread throughout the northern part of the state, eventually establishing their educational capital at the College of New Jersey in Princeton (which, as we shall later see, became the first truly cosmopolitan, or colonywide, institution of higher learning in America).

In the South, aristocratic oligarchies eventually dominated the planter cultures of Anglican Virginia and Huguenot Charleston; at the same time left-wing Quakers came to the fore in the pine barrens of North Carolina—to this day, North Carolinians speak of their state as a "valley of humility between two mountains of conceit." Though the secular, aristocratic values of Maryland derived from that colony's being part of the Chesapeake planter culture (as was Virginia), they were reinforced by Catholicism, firmly established in that state under the auspices of the Calverts and the Carrolls of Carrollton. Delaware, referred to as "the lower counties" of Pennsylvania until 1777, when it became a separate state, also shared the values of the Chesapeake culture. Georgia, the last colony to be founded, was the victim not of utopian sectarianism, as was Pennsylvania, but of secular philanthropy and paternalistic planning from London.

The social character of the thirteen original states consistently has reflected their colonial makeup. The antinomian tendencies of colonial Rhode Island, for example, prevailed even in the constitutional period. Thus, the state was so torn by internal strife and economic chaos that it sent no delegates to Philadelphia, nor had it sent representatives to the Continental Congress for some time before the convention met to write the Constitution. No wonder that the "Plantation of the Otherwise-Minded" was often referred to, at that time, as "Rogues Island."

In this book I shall be concerned with a historical analysis of social character in Boston and Philadelphia and especially with how class authority and leadership in the two cities was and still is related to the Puritan and Quaker ethics of their founders.

"The world is only beginning to see," William James once told students at Stanford University, "that the wealth of a nation consists more than anything else in the number of superior men that it harbors." In the recent past, three superior Americans with lofty ambitions for their country and the world, and with great capacities for leadership, died by assassins' hands, at relatively young ages, and at the height of their powers. Could it be true that deep down in their collective unconscious the American people mistrust excellence and fear superiority? At any rate, for well over a century many of our most thoughtful citizens, as well as observant foreign visitors, have called attention to the fact that although we both understand and admire success, we seem far less than eager to devote ourselves to the pursuit of fame and leadership.

A young French nobleman, Alexis de Tocqueville, whose classic *Democracy in America* is concerned largely with the consequences of the very high value Americans placed on the idea of equality, felt this to be the case when he visited the United States during the Jacksonian era.

> I believe that ambitious men in democracies are less engrossed than any other with the interests and judgments of posterity; the present moment alone engages and absorbs them . . . and they care much more for success than for fame. What appears to me most to be dreaded is that in the midst of the small, incessant occupations of private life, ambition should lose its vigor and its greatness."[1]

In 1929, Walter Lippmann similarly described the leadership situation in this country.

> Our rulers today consist of a random collection of successful men and their wives. They are to be found in the inner circles of banks and corporations, in the best clubs, in the dominant cliques of trade unions, among the political churchmen, the higher manipulating bosses, the leading professional Catholics, Baptists, Methodists, Irish, Germans, Jews, and the grand panjandrums of the secret societies. They give orders. They have to be consulted. They can more or less effectively speak for, and lead some part of, the population. But none of them is seated on a certain throne, and all of them are forever concerned as to how they may keep from being toppled off. They do not know how they happen to be where they are, although they often explain what are the secrets of *success*. They have been educated to achieve success, but few of them have been educated to exercise *power*. Nor do they count with any confidence upon retaining their power, nor of handing it on to their sons. They live therefore from day to day, they govern by ear. Their impromptu statements of policy may be obeyed, but nobody seriously regards them as having *authority*.[2]

John W. Gardner, one of our more articulate public figures, has concerned himself for some years now with this problem. In 1961 he wrote a brilliant little book entitled *Excellence: Can We Be Equal and Excellent, Too?* Although he is by no means an elitist and apparently has great sympathy for the egalitarian ideals of America, he reveals a keen understanding of the dangers of carrying any virtue to an extreme.

> Equalitarians holding . . . extreme views have tended to believe that men of great leadership capacities, great energies or greatly superior aptitudes are more trouble to society than they are worth. Lionel Trilling says, ". . . all the instincts or necessities of radical democracy are against the superiorness and arbitrariness which often mark great spirits." Merle Curti reminds us that in the Jacksonian era in this country, equalitarianism reached such heights that trained personnel in the public service were considered unnecessary. "The democratic faith further held that no special group might mediate between the common man and the truth, even though trained competence might make the difference between life and death." Thus, in the West, even licensing of physicians was lax, because not to be lax was apt to be thought undemocratic!

This same impulse may be observed in some of our local political contests, in which voters favor the candidate whose folksy, ungrammatical, thumb-in-suspenders style seems to say that he is not in any respect superior to the average voter, and is perhaps a little inferior. "Friends, red-necks, suckers, and fellow-hicks," was Willie Stark's greeting to the voters.[3]

But perhaps the most perceptive analysis of the leadership problem in America was presented by Gardner in 1965 in his final report to the Carnegie Corporation before entering President Johnson's cabinet (the report was appropriately entitled "The Antileadership Vaccine" when reprinted for larger circulation). After noting that the United States today is a far more *open* and *egalitarian* society than ever before in our history, which he seemed to imply is progress in the right direction, Gardner observed that "in the late eighteenth century we produced out of a small population a truly extraordinary group of leaders—Washington, Adams, Jefferson, Franklin, Madison, Monroe, and others." And then he asked: "Why is it so difficult today, out of a vastly greater population, to produce men of that character?"[4]

One might answer Gardner that the cultural values and the social structure of our Founding Fathers' generation of leaders were far more marked by authority, hierarchy, and class than our own. Is there not at least a historical correlation between the high value we place on *equality* today and our lack of leadership, as against the values of *hierarchy* and inherited authority held in that earlier age, which produced such brilliant leadership? As Charles S. Syndor wrote in his study of Washington's Virginia:

> It is nevertheless certain that the high quality of Virginia's political leadership in the years when the United States was being established was due in large measure to these very things which are now detested. Washington and Jefferson, Madison and Monroe, Mason, Marshall, and Peyton Randolph, were products of the system which sought out and raised to high office men of superior family and social status, of good education, or personal force, of experience in management: they were placed in power by a semi-aristocratic political system.[5]

Another clue to the relationship between hierarchy and leadership is suggested by Gardner's list of Founding Fathers. *All* these men were reared in Massachusetts or Virginia; *none* was reared in the colony of Pennsylvania, though Philadelphia was the largest city in the new nation and contained perhaps the wealthiest, most successful, gayest, and most brilliant elite in the land. Not only had Pennsylvanians little to do with taking the lead in our nation's founding, but the state has produced very few distinguished Americans throughout our history, as the figures in Table A–1 suggest (see Appendix I) . Thus, this list of 400 notable Americans in the *Encyclopedia of American History* (1965) shows that Massachusetts produced twice as many prominent individuals as did Virginia and more than three times as many as did Pennsylvania. As might be expected, moreover, Virginia led in the proportion of men of power and authority (including presidents of the United States); Massachusetts, providing a more balanced group of leaders, excelled in arts and letters; Pennsylvanians were more likely to be men of innovation and change, a large proportion of whom made their careers outside the state. Indeed, the sole president from Pennsylvania, James Buchanan, was one of the weakest in American history.

Why this great difference between Pennsylvania and the two leadership states of Massachusetts and Virginia? Why are wealth, a high standard of living, and success—all characteristic of Philadelphia in the last part of the eighteenth century and of American society as a whole today—not necessarily correlated with leadership? What has all this got to do with the fact that Massachusetts was founded on hierarchical and theocratic values; Virginia, on the Cavalier ideals of aristocracy; and Pennsylvania, on the egalitarian and anti-authoritarian ideals of the Quakers?

Virginia, Pennsylvania and Massachusetts were the three largest states at the nation's founding. The aristocratic values of tidewater Virginia in the great generation of Washington and Jefferson were largely a product of the material conditions of a plantation economy. I shall concentrate here on the commercial cities of Boston and Philadelphia, whose great differences in leadership and authority were far more likely to reflect differences in ideas and values. There are, of course, no simple and direct relationships between ideas and action or between ideas and social structure. All human societies are the product (often unanticipated) of complex webs of interacting factors rather than the simple result of mechanical cause and effect. I am arguing, however, that the religious ideas and convictions of the earliest Bostonians and Philadelphians were of great importance in determining the distinct histories of leadership in the two cities from colonial times to the present. In asserting that convictions do have consequences, I am following the late Perry Miller, who, while a graduate student at the University of Chicago, came under the "baneful spell" of John Winthrop's *Journal*. After some difficulty finding a sympathetic publisher, Miller issued his first book, *Orthodoxy in Massachusetts, 1630–1650*, in 1933. Having been an admirer of H. L. Mencken in his youth and all too aware of the conventional wisdom of the time, Miller cautiously wrote in the foreword:

> I lay myself open to the charge of being so very naive as to believe that the way men think has some influence upon their actions, of not remembering that these ways of thinking have been officially decided by modern psychologists to be generally just so many rationalizations constructed by the subconscious to disguise the pursuit of more tangible ends. . . . But I am prepared . . . to hazard the thesis that whatever may be the case in other centuries, in the sixteenth and seventeenth, certain men of decisive importance took religion seriously; that they often followed spiritual dictates in comparative disregard of ulterior considerations; that those who led the Great Migration to Massachusetts and who founded the colony were predominantly men of this stamp.[6]

Similarly, others in the 1930s were questioning the materialist view that ideas and values are merely dependent variables in history. Thus, one of America's leading theologians, H. Richard Niebuhr, published his book *The Social Sources of Denominationalism* in 1929, the height of the debunking age. Niebuhr, at that time, took a sociological approach to religion and tried to show how the structure of American Protestantism was far more likely to be a reflection of class, racial and regional cleavages than of purely credal differences as between denominations. In 1937, however, his *Kingdom of God in America* reversed the assumptions and methodology of the earlier book and attempted to show how the Protestant Ethic had formed and transformed our social structure down through the years.

Only three years before Miller published his first book, Talcott Parsons, another young scholar, translated for the English-speaking world Max Weber's classic *Protestant Ethic and the Spirit of Capitalism*. Partly in opposition to vulgar materialism, if not to Marx himself, Weber had tried to show that there was an affinity between the rise of capitalism and the climate of opinion in those cultural groups and nations that had adopted the Protestant Ethic. Others have continued in the Weberian tradition by showing how various modern institutions were first dominated by Protestant reformers. For example, in 1938, Robert K. Merton published his doctoral dissertation on the relationship between Puritanism and the rise of science in seventeenth-century England. More recently, Michael Walzer has given us a brilliant study of the relationship between Calvinism and the origins of modern radical politics in the West.

In contrast with Europe, where Protestantism was a revolutionary movement within an ancient and continuing social structure, America gave the members of different denominations and sects an opportunity to put their ideas and ideals into practice in virgin sociological situations.

> There were no settled institutions defending the special privileges of the religiously, politically or economically powerful, and by the same token, there were no social organizations of any kind to provide for orderly procedure in the contact of men with men. Whatever else . . . America came to be, it was also an experiment in constructive Protestantism.[7]

Though by no means comparable in rigor to the laboratory or test-tube situation, which is so crucial for testing insights or hypotheses in the natural sciences, taking two areas of the New World and injecting, as it were, Puritanism into one and Quakerism into the other certainly allows for a more controlled situation than Weber was able to find in Europe. A systematic comparison in historical depth of these two transplanted ethics within Protestantism presents an unusual opportunity to test hypotheses about the influence of ideas and values on both character formation and social structure.

Broadly speaking, hierarchy, authority, and leadership are necessary characteristics of all civilized communities; however, a normative culture that stresses the desirability of hierarchy, class, and authority will instill in its members a far stronger desire and capacity to take the lead in both community building and community reform than a normative culture that emphasizes equality and brotherly love, explicitly *rejecting* the need for hierarchy, class, and authority. As a friend who has lived in both Boston and Philadelphia said to me recently: "The people in Boston all want to be chiefs, while in Philly they are all content to be Indians."

AS THE TWIG IS BENT

Emerson once remarked that institutions are but the shadows of great men. Similarly, I should like to suggest that institutions are largely, but certainly not entirely, the shadows of their founders. Thus, no group of men in our history will ever have an influence on our political institutions comparable to that of the Founding Fathers. Just as our whole post-Christian and secular world today is still living, as a kind of cultural rentier, on the spiritual and moral capital built up in the more religious periods of the Judeo-Christian tradition, so the citizens of modern Massachusetts and Pennsylvania, whether they are professing Jews, Catholics, Presbyterians, Espiscopalians, or just plain agnostics or atheists, are still marked, to greater or lesser degrees, by the original ethics of Puritanism and Quakerism. There is, for instance, a great difference between the Puritan Catholicism of Boston and the much milder Quaker Catholicism of Philadelphia (discussed in some detail in Chapter 19). If immigrants absorb some of the values of the host society, one would predict that the Irish Catholics of Boston would be more driven to leadership and excellence than their countrymen who settled into the milder and more egalitarian culture of Philadelphia. Whereas the first Irish-Catholic mayor of Boston took office in the 1880s, the first Irish-Catholic mayor of Philadelphia came into office in the 1960s. Philadelphia has produced no leaders of the quality of Curley, Fitzgerald, or the Kennedys, nor, incidentally, has it ever had an Irish-Catholic Democratic machine in the classic style of New York, Jersey City, or Chicago. It is indeed symbolic that the most famous Irish-Catholic families of the two cities should have produced in this generation a president and two senators of the United States, on the one hand, and a charming expatriate socialite and sometime actress, on the other.

All this is only to say that man is a product of his history, where nothing is entirely lost and little is entirely new. His creative freedom is real enough, but, as Marx would have put it, patterns of culture are never cut out of whole cloth in any single generation. No one has stated my thesis more graphically than Samuel Eliot Morison.

Most writers have emphasized the institutional and material aspects of New England colonial history. This is natural, since the institutions that the Puritans founded, Church, Commonwealth, Town, College, were so firmly established as to outlast the purposes for which they were intended. Church and College and Commonwealth have been patched and altered again and again, without losing all their original character—much as an old mansion of New York City is cut up into flats and offices, yet retains somewhat of its original dignity. . . . It is not, however, my purpose to describe the old bottles that were ultimately to be filled with new wine, or the source of wealth which paid for the wine. Rather do I seek the flavor of the old wine for which the old bottles were originally blown. For the wine of New England is not a series of successive vintages, each distinct from the other, like the wines of France; it is more like the mother-wine in those great casks of port and sherry that one sees in the *bodegas* of Portugal and Spain, from which a certain amount is drawn off every year, and replaced by an equal volume of the new. Thus the change is gradual, and the mother wine of 1656 still gives bouquet and flavor to what is drawn in 1956.[8]

The "mother-wines" of Puritan Boston and Quaker Philadelphia still give "bouquet and flavor" to the styles of life in these cities. This effect, after more than a century of growth and change, was attested to by Henry Adams in his classic study of *The United States in 1800.* New Englanders, he wrote, were "ambitious beyond reason to excell." He then described the strength of the "Massachusetts Oligarchy."

> Its strength lay in the Congregational Churches and in the cordial union between the clergy, the magistracy, the bench and bar, and respectable society throughout the State. This union created what was unknown beyond New England—an organized social system, capable of acting at command either for offense or defense, and admirably adapted for the uses of the eighteenth century. . . . the New England oligarchy struck its roots deep into the soil, and was supported by the convictions of the people.[9]

Though Adams found that the "Quaker city of an ultra-democratic State startled travellers used to luxury, by its extravagance and display,"[10] he admired the egalitarian values of both city and state.

> The only true democratic community then existing in the eastern States, Pennsylvania was neither picturesque nor troublesome. The State contained no hierarchy like that of New England; no great families like those of New York; no oligarchy like the planters of Virginia and South Carolina. "In Pennsylvania," said Albert Gallatin, "not only do we have neither Livingstons nor Rensselaers, but from the suburbs of Philadelphia to the banks of the Ohio, I do not know a single family that has any extensive influence. An equal distribution of property has rendered every individual independent, and there is among us true and real equality." This was not all. . . . Too thoroughly democratic to fear democracy, and too much nationalized to fear nationality, Pennsylvania became the ideal American State, easy, tolerant and contented. If its soil bred little genius, it bred less treason. With twenty different religious creeds, its practice could not be narrow, and a strong Quaker element made it humane. . . . To politics the Pennsylvanians did not take kindly. Perhaps their democracy was so deep an instinct that they knew not what to do with political power when they gained it; *as though political power were aristocratic in its nature, and democratic power a contradiction in terms.*[11]

Adams, in contrasting the social structures of Massachusetts and Pennsylvania, might have been answering Gardner's question about leadership. In fact, the suspicion that "democratic power is a contradiction in terms" is in the air today as never before in our history. As Gardner noted, we are inadvertently educating our young men and women to mistrust leadership.

> The antileadership vaccine has other more subtle and powerful ingredients. The image of the corporation president, politician, or college president that is current among most intellectuals and professionals today has some decidedly unattractive features. It is said that such men compromise their convictions almost daily,

if not hourly. It is said that they have tasted the corrupting experience of power. . . . Needless to say, the student picks up such attitudes. It is not that the professors propound these views and students learn them. Rather, they are in the air and students absorb them.[12]

Although one must respect Gardner's diagnosis of our modern problem of leadership, apparently he failed to understand that the generation that founded our nation was led by men who believed in the need for class authority and classical republicanism as a protection against the dangers of direct democracy. His proposed cure for our troubles is more and more direct democracy. But the real problem is how to institutionalize the choice of leaders from a class of men of some moral education and traditions of authority (one cannot imagine individuals like George Washington or Franklin Roosevelt, to say nothing of Adlai Stevenson or Averell Harriman in more recent times, even knowing what "laundered money" is, let alone carrying it around in satchels from office to office). In short, Gardner's professed ideals are based on the need for checking the propensity of mediocre and unprincipled men to abuse public trust. A stopgap measure at best, it attacks consequences rather than causes and in the long run is doomed to fail.

In our egalitarian age of mistrust, trustworthy men of great ability are increasingly refusing to run for public office or to serve in positions of authority and leadership in society. "The reproach I address to the principle of equality," wrote Tocqueville, "is that it leads men to a kind of virtuous materialism, which would not corrupt, but enervate the soul, and noiselessly unbend its springs of action."[13] In the rest of this book, I shall try to show how and why the Quaker city of Philadelphia, in contrast to Puritan Boston, has suffered from the virus of virtuous materialism for almost three centuries and how its best men, on the whole, have seldom sought public office or positions of societal authority and leadership outside business.

A BOSTON JURIST AND A PHILADELPHIA LAWYER

Tocqueville pointed out that the members of the legal profession held the same positions of leadership and authority in America as that traditionally held by members of the aristocracies of Europe. I should like to close this chapter with a brief outline of the careers of two prominent American lawyers, Oliver Wendell Holmes, Jr., and John Graver Johnson, born within a month of each other in 1841. Although readers will be more or less familiar with the career of Holmes of Boston, very few (including most current members of the Philadelphia bar) will know much about Johnson's brilliant career; for Holmes was driven by the spur of fame whereas Johnson was satisfied with success. Though both men were skeptics in religion, the contrasting careers of Johnson and Holmes are excellent symbols of the Quaker ethic of privacy and success, on the one hand, and of the Puritan inclination toward public authority, leadership, and fame, on the other. This contrast was dramatically illustrated at their deaths in 1917 and 1935, respectively.

Holmes died within three days of his ninety-fourth birthday, at his home in the nation's capital. The funeral was held at All Souls Unitarian Church, and the service was brief. Among other things the minister noted that "Moses chose from among the people able men, men of truth, hating unjust gains, and set them over the people to judge them at all seasons." And, quoting Holmes, "At the grave of a hero we end, not with sorrow at the inevitable loss, but with the contagion of his courage, and with a kind of desperate joy we go back to the fight."[14] The coffin, draped in the American flag, was taken to Arlington National Cemetery for a hero's burial. Former colleagues on the Supreme Court acted as pallbearers. President Roosevelt stood by the grave and led the nation in mourning. Eight infantrymen raised their rifles and fired one volley for each of the eight wounds Holmes had received in the Civil War.

Eighteen years earlier, in 1917, John Graver Johnson was buried in Germantown, Pennsylvania, not far from where he was born. "His obsequies were private," his biographer wrote. "The hour of the funeral had been fixed at the last minute. There were no pallbearers or representatives from the Philadelphia Club or from the bench or the bar."[15] Johnson's *New York Times* obituary noted: "John G. Johnson, in the opinion of some well-qualified judges, the greatest lawyer in the English-speaking world, . . . fairly basked in obscurity, and sought oblivion as far as the general public was concerned with a high measure of success."[16]

Johnson left his proudest possession, a famous art collection, to the city of Philadelphia. For tax purposes the collection was assessed at $4.4 million but it was worth far more. He also left his home to house the collection, along with $2 million for maintenance expenses, to the city. The value of the remainder of his estate was never made public. Holmes left the bulk of his estate—$250,000, or almost half his lifetime salary as a public servant—to the United States of America.

John Graver Johnson was born on the Graver farm on Germantown Pike in Chestnut Hill, then a community of some 500 souls, originally settled by Palatine Germans under the leadership of Daniel Pastorious, who eventually became a Quaker along with many of his followers. There is no historical record of Johnson's ancestors, though some of them originally may have been Quakers. His father, David Johnson, a blacksmith, married Elizabeth Graver, the strictly reared daughter of a solid but undistinguished family, active in local affairs, including the Baptist church. David died when John was still a child, leaving the family in difficult financial circumstances. Thanks to his mother's backing, however, Johnson went through the local school and graduated from Central High School, the foremost public school for boys in the city.

First in his graduating class at Central, he was offered a job as scrivener and office boy in the law firm of Benjamin Rush, a dilettante who regarded the law simply as the proper profession for a gentleman and retired to England within a year of Johnson's coming to the office. The ambitious office boy found the firm's business uninspiring. As his biographer put it, "the traditions of the Philadelphia bar were noble, but encrusted with the mold of stagnation. The leaders were mostly men of social distinction—and acutely aware of it. . . . Behind this façade, fancy prices made legal victory a luxury and defeat a financial disaster."[17] But perhaps young Johnson did absorb some of the mores of the Philadelphia bar of his day, where money was a prerequisite for entering the very class in which the ignoble mention of money was taboo.

While the Civil War dragged on through many Union defeats, Johnson attended to his own career, ignoring frequent appeals for volunteers. Finally, in the summer of 1863, Lee's advance toward Pennsylvania made the invasion of Philadelphia a definite possibility. In the local panic that ensued, Johnson was recruited and mustered into Battery A, First Pennsylvania Artillery, a unit composed mostly of members of the bar. He saw no active service and, with Lee's defeat, got out of the army as quickly as he got in.

After the war, at the age of twenty-nine, Johnson began to build his reputation and fortune by handling the difficult and complex transfer of some useless swampland in South Philadelphia from private hands to the city and thence to the federal government. The swamps became League Island, a major naval shipyard. His client, the Pennsylvania Company, was one of the more successful trust companies in the city. This highly lucrative transaction was brilliantly handled by the young lawyer, who now became the company's permanent counsel.

Johnson's practice and reputation steadily grew during the postwar business boom enjoyed by both his city and the nation. He took all kinds of cases but specialized in corporate law. Among his major clients were P. A. B. Widener and William L. Elkins, traction kings who eventually founded two of the city's largest fortunes. Widener became more than a client: in their frequent poker games together, Johnson taught him how to buy art (see Chapter 16). Though Johnson's practice boomed, he remained a lone wolf, never having any law partner. With the help of a few assistants, he was making over $100,000 a year by the 1880s. In a city of some 1,500 lawyers, fewer than 100 made more than $5,000 a year, and only three had six-figure incomes. Johnson's earnings came from hard work and excellent judgment, not from high fees. In fact, he enraged some competitors by his often ridiculously low fees. No man of Johnson's ability in that day of national trusts formation could long remain a local lawyer: he was admitted to the Supreme Court and argued his first case in Washington in 1884.

Unlike many of his legal peers, Johnson shied away from social life. At the age of thirty-four he married Ida Powell, a young widow and mother, of impeccable ancestry and social position. They had no children together. Johnson loved his home life and privacy and usually returned home at night even when he was arguing a case in New York or Washington.

After 1884, Johnson was continually arguing cases in the highest courts of the nation. Because of his reputation he was offered a number of positions of public authority. He turned them all down, including two proposed appointments to the Supreme Court (by Presidents Garfield and Cleveland) and the attorney generalship (offered him by McKinley). He never held any office in either the local or the national bar association, and in the last twenty years of his life he refused to be interviewed. In a rare public comment, Johnson's evaluation of the Supreme Court is revealing.

> It is the most honorable position in the United States Service, and one which the most eminent lawyer should feel proud to fill. All who have filled the office, or who now fill it, however, have accepted the appointment at great personal sacrifice. The salary of the office is $10,000 per annum, and it is a well-known fact that a lawyer whose attainments would fit him to fill the position, makes in his practice three to five times this amount.[18]

Oliver Wendell Holmes, Jr., not only had very different ideas about public service but in almost every other respect stood for a virtually antithetical set of values, born of a distinguished family tradition.

The Holmeses originally settled in the Milton area of Boston in the seventeenth century but moved to the frontier town of Woodstock, Connecticut, in the second generation. Four generations later, the Boston family founder, the Reverend Abiel Holmes, went down to the center of Calvinist orthodoxy at Yale and eventually married the daughter of President Ezra Stiles. After traveling through the country and spending seven years as the minister of a colony of New England Calvinists in Georgia, he came north to take the pulpit at the First Congregational Church in Cambridge. His first wife having died, he married Sally Wendell in 1801 and thus became connected with the Wendells, Jacksons, Olivers, Dudleys, Cabots, Eliots, Quincys, Bradstreets, and Phillipses—families that had produced patriotic soldiers, governors, senators, clergymen, judges, and delegates to the Continental Congress in Philadelphia.

On the Holmes side of the family there had always been an abiding passion for education and love of the written word, especially history. In many ways the literary reputation of the family began when Abiel published his *American Annals* in 1805, a book that was received with acclaim in both England and America. The *London Quarterly Review* found it an unusual work "for an American" and praised it highly; the University of Edinburgh awarded the author an honorary degree in absentia.

In the meantime, America was changing more rapidly than ever before. Though he had been a good friend of the Unitarian leader William Ellery Channing, Abiel had come to abhor the rational and cold Unitarianism. He clung to the old Calvinism long after his more sophisticated flock had lost their faith and eventually he even refused to invite visiting clergymen of the new religion to speak to his congregation. Finally, in 1829, after thirty-seven years in the pulpit of the First Church, Holmes was forced to resign.

What one generation fights for the next generation often revolts from. Abiel and Sally Holmes had five children. Although the literary tradition of the family was carried on by their son Oliver Wendell, both he and his son Wendell revolted against the forms of Abiel's religion, while still retaining the Calvinist sense of duty and class authority.

Young Wendell grew up during the literary flowering of New England and knew many of his father's Saturday Club friends. He went to Harvard with the class of 1861. Though only a fair student, he was elected class poet.

Fort Sumter was fired on in April of his senior year. True to family tradition, Holmes joined up by the end of the month. He returned from training camp in June to graduate and read his class poem and by late summer was headed south with the 20th Volunteers, the so-called Harvard Regiment. His *Who's Who* biography noted:

> Served 3 yrs. with 20th Mass. volunteers, lt. to lt. col.; wounded in breast at Ball's Bluff, Oct. 21, 1861; in neck at Antietam Sept. 17, 1862; in feet at Mary's Hill, Fredericksburg, May 3, 1863; aide-de-camp on staff Gen. H. G. Wright until mustered out July 17, 1864, with rank of captain.[19]

Holmes returned from the war and enrolled in Harvard Law School. He always said that he had entered law by accident and merely adapted his chosen profession to his more fundamental intellectual quest. He hated business and disliked practice apart from arguing cases. While practicing law for the first fifteen years out of law school, Holmes also developed his literary interests: in 1868, he contributed his first article to the *American Law Review* and became co-editor in 1870; in 1869, he agreed to help James Thayer edit the twelfth edition of Kent's *Commentaries*. In November 1880, Holmes gave the Lowell Lectures at Harvard, as his father had done almost thirty years earlier. Taking the common law as his subject, he spoke slowly and without notes. At one point he said that "the life of the law has not been logic; it has been experience," foreshadowing his role in revolutionizing American law in the direction of "legal realism" and away from the tradition of "legal idealism," which had held the stage in America since the days of Jefferson. In the meantime he was feverishly at work completing his *Common Law*, recognized today as a masterpiece of legal thought. The *London Spectator* called it "the most original work of legal speculations which has appeared in English since the publication of Sir Henry Maine's *Ancient Law*."[20]

In 1882, when an alumnus endowed a new chair at the law school, the president of Harvard offered Holmes the job. Though Holmes would have preferred the action of the bench to the pure scholarship of the academy, he accepted the offer, with a written proviso to the effect that he could resign should he receive an appointment to the bench. Within a year he was sitting on the Supreme Court of Massachusetts, where he remained for two decades, eventually becoming chief justice.

Soon after Theodore Roosevelt became president, Horace Gray resigned from the Supreme Court, and Senator Lodge suggested to the president that Holmes fill the vacancy. Roosevelt had liked Holmes's positions on several labor cases in Massachusetts and made the appointment. Holmes accepted and went to Washington in 1903. Rather to their surprise, he and his wife immediately took their place "among the inmost circle of Roosevelt familiars, the Cabot Lodges, Henry Adams, Owen Wister, . . . Harvard men, with a like background and like taste."[21]

Meanwhile, J. P. Morgan and James J. Hill had chartered a new company, with assets of over $400 million, in order to unite the great Northern and Northern Pacific railroads. The state of Minnesota had attacked the merger, and *Northern Securities* v. *the United States* came to the Supreme Court in December 1903. The Northern Securities Company had a whole battery of lawyers led by John G. Johnson. The courtroom was filled with diplomats, judges, and lawyers, along with Mrs. Roosevelt, Mrs. Holmes, and many other Washington Society luminaries. In one of the most celebrated cases in American history, Johnson played the leading role for the defense; opposite him on the bench, the new associate justice, the handsomest man on the court, sat and listened. Johnson was brilliant. Reporters and spectators were impressed with his rugged but distinguished appearance, as well as with the style of the foremost railroad lawyer in the land. Though several of the judges interrupted from time to time, Holmes quietly took in every word. "Was bigness itself illegal?" he asked himself.

The decision was not reached until March 1904. The government won, five to four. Holmes wrote the dissenting opinion, to the president's dismay: "I could carve out of a banana a judge with more backbone than that."[22]

These two great American lawyers, who met for the first time in the *Northern Securities* case, differed in the following ways, which, in turn, point to the central thesis of this book.

1. Holmes was born into a family and class of leaders with a tradition of authority. Johnson, of humble origins, rose and married into a class of Philadelphia Gentlemen lawyers, that has always chosen private success rather than public leadership.

2. Holmes was an arrogant and vain man with all the vices of aristocracy. William James once wrote that "the only fellow here I care anything about is Holmes";[23] yet he was bound to add, at a later date, "The more I live in the world, the more the cold-blooded, conscious egotism and conceit of people afflict me. . . . All the noble qualities of Wendell Holmes, for instance, are poisoned by them."[24] In striking contrast to Holmes, Johnson was infinitely democratic and humble. Johnson's office in Philadelphia was always filled with clients, rich and poor, who waited their turn. His democratic style has been nicely summed up in the following anecdote. One day, so legend has it, he spent over an hour with a client, a poor black woman, while John D. Rockefeller's lawyer waited in the outer office; he took $10 in cash from the lady and sent Rockefeller a bill for $5,000.

3. Holmes wrote all his life and he wrote for posterity. And there is a steadily mounting literature about him. He was an intellectual from his toes to his fingertips; the literary tradition was bred into him. Above all else he was a teacher: "Holmes is today for all students of human society the philosopher and seer, the greatest of our age in the domain of jurisprudence, and one of the greatest of the ages," wrote one of his students, Benjamin N. Cardozo.[25] In contrast, Johnson wrote nothing, very much in the tradition of Quaker Philadelphia. A contemporary observed, "Johnson never filled judicial station—he rejected it. He never discussed public questions—he refused to. He never wrote a legal treatise—he would have thought it evidence of vanity."[26]

The fear of vanity, especially the "vanity of the word," which lies at the core of the Quaker ethic, is a problem faced by all scholars working on Philadelphia history. The written record is very incomplete; thus, though Johnson's fame at the local bar produced endless oral anecdotes, there exists only one second-rate biography by an admiring younger member of the bar in his day. And Johnson's brief biography in the *Dictionary of American Biography*, written by an obscure author, is not very informative, whereas Holmes's biography, written by Felix Frankfurter, is one of the longest in that reference.

4. By and large, Boston is an intellectual society; Philadelphia is a more visual one. Johnson's one extralegal and extrafamilial passion was art. He not only built a fine collection in the style of the rich men of his day, he also loved every picture in it. Holmes was far less concerned with the visual side of life, which is after all a trait of the highly intellectual, who may know much about art without loving it.

5. The members of the upper classes in egalitarian societies that lack a clear hierarchy of values recognized by all classes tend to avoid positions of authority and to protect themselves from the masses behind a high wall of wealth. Aristocracies, in contrast to plutocracies, are led by a class whose authority is recognized by all, which lessens the need for the protection of pure wealth. Johnson died a wealthy man; Holmes was only comfortable.

PART I

CLASS AUTHORITY
AND
LEADERSHIP

Privileged and Ruling Classes:
A Theory of Class Authority
and Leadership

When the Lord sent me into the world, he forbade me to put off my hat to any high or low: and I was required to "thee" and "thou" all men and women, without respect to rich or poor, great or small.

George Fox

It is impossible to resist the magistrate without, at the same time, resisting God himself.

John Calvin

The theoretical core of this book is part of a larger body of work, some published previously and more to come. My first book, *Philadelphia Gentlemen: The Making of a National Upper Class* (1958), used the social structure of Philadelphia as an example of how a national, metropolitan upper class was formed in America in the closing decades of the nineteenth century. It was no accident that when *Philadelphia Gentlemen* was first issued in paperback it was called *An American Business Aristocracy.* For although Philadelphia had produced a wealthy and privileged class of gentlemen who were undoubtedly the local leaders in law, business, and banking, the members of this class at the same time seemed to have little political or intellectual authority either in the state of Pennsylvania or in the nation as a whole. "Philadelphia," so I wrote in the opening pages of *Philadelphia Gentlemen,* "provides an excellent example of a business aristocracy which has too often placed the desire for material comfort and security above the duties of political and intellectual leadership."[1] The book thus argued that Philadelphia, from colonial times to 1940, had produced a class of gentlemen engaged primarily in augmenting their wealth and protecting their privileged and charming style of life.

The problems of privilege and authority provided the central theme of my second book. In *The Protestant Establishment: Aristocracy and Caste in America* (1964), I tried to show how the American upper class as a whole, because of ethnic prejudice and a debilitating Anglo-Saxonism, tended to move from an authoritative aristocracy to a privileged caste.

> Essentially this book has been an attempt to analyze the decline of authority in America in the course of the twentieth century. . . . The traditional standards upon which this country was built and governed down through the years are in danger of losing authority largely because the American upper class, whose white Anglo-Saxon, Protestant members may still be deferred to and envied because of their privileged status, is no longer honored in the land.[2]

Status snobbery, *The Protestant Establishment* contended, was gradually replacing class pride in America during the twentieth century, especially since the Second World War. And of course we are all of us today, to a far greater extent than in the early 1960s, when *The Protestant Establishment* was written, suffering from the debilitating and disillusioning effects of an ever increasing decline of class authority.

Building on these two earlier works, then, my central thesis in this volume is that the egalitarian and anti-authoritarian principles of Quakerism produced a confusion in class authority from the very beginning in Philadelphia. At the same time, the hierarchical and authoritarian principles of Puritanism insured in Boston, from its founding to the close of the nineteenth century at least, a tradition of class authority and leadership not only in the local community but throughout the state and the nation as a whole. Whereas Proper Philadelphians always have suffered from status snobbery and a lack of class and local pride, Proper Bostonians typically have shown a great deal of pride in the leadership and authority of their ancestors, whom they have striven to emulate.

CLASS AND AUTHORITY

At the close of the Second World War, two American sociologists, Kingsley Davis and Wilbert Moore, published an article that clearly set forth the so-called functional theory of stratification. As social theory must, the Davis and Moore thesis included some covert value judgments, the most important of which ran counter to the egalitarian ideologies of a good many of their sociological peers. Social stratification, so they wrote, was a necessary and universal feature of all complex societies. Their justification of stratification and hierarchy, and the consequent impossibility of equality, revolved around the fact that societies must reward people differently in terms of wealth and prestige in order that the more important positions in the division of labor be filled by the more capable persons.

An extensive literature criticizing the Davis and Moore thesis has taken its place at the core of stratification theory both in this country and abroad. The most perceptive of these critical articles was written by Włodzimierz

Wesołowski (1962). Drawing from his experiences with the more egalitarian and less affluent lifestyles behind the Iron Curtain, Wesołowski came to the conclusion that although stratification and hierarchy are universal aspects of all complex social organizations, there is *not necessarily* a need for great differentials in material rewards and prestige.

> Among the functional prerequisites of social life, it would be difficult not to take social organization into account. Social life is group life. And group life involves the inner structuralization of the group. This structuralization consists among other things in the emergence of positions of command and subordination (as well as of "intermediate" positions at further stages of development). In such a structure, authority is unevenly distributed. For as soon as the positions of authority are filled, those who occupy the positions have the right (and duty) to give orders, while others have the duty to obey them. . . . In consequence it may be said that if there is any functional necessity for stratification, it is the *necessity of stratification according to the criterion of authority and not according to the criterion of material advantage and prestige.*[3]

It is, then, the contrasting Puritan and Quaker attitudes toward the *institutionalization of authority*, not toward wealth and prestige, that lie at the core of my argument here. I should go even further than Wesołowski and make the following generalization: *where authority is well defined and institutionalized there is far less need for rewarding important leadership positions with wealth and prestige than where egalitarianism has eroded any clearly defined hierarchies of authority.* College presidents today, for instance, are probably better rewarded materially than at any other time in our history, yet capable men are refusing in large numbers to take these key positions of leadership—if my thesis is correct—principally because of the recent erosion of the president's authority on campuses all over America. In the late, antinomian sixties, a student who called the president of an ancient university a "motherfucker" to his face and in front of parents and the student body (and got away with it) was attacking the authority structure of his society much as William Penn did by keeping his hat on in the presence of King Charles II; his target was not the inequitable distribution of wealth or income.

So far I have been talking about authority in general. Before proceeding I should like briefly to discuss Weber's three ideal-typical types of authority: (1) the traditional, (2) the bureaucratic, and (3) the charismatic. In terms of the Christian tradition, for instance, the Catholic church tended toward the bureaucratic in that ultimate authority was vested in a priestly hierarchy. The sects, because of their egalitarian values, tended toward the charismatic.* Congregational Protestantism (especially Puritanism in Massachusetts) tended, inadvertently at least, toward what I would call traditional, or class, authority.

I use the term *class authority* interchangeably with *traditional authority* to suggest that where traditional authority in Weber's sense of the term is strong, class authority tends to reign (and vice versa). Thus, in New England, Congre-

---

*The term *sect*, according to Webster, is derived from *sequi* ("to follow,") not *secare* "to cut," and thus emphasizes a group's response to a leader.

gationalism was strong because it was intimately bound up with class leadership. When New Englanders moved to the West, however, they tended to become Presbyterians in their new communities, which had not had time to develop traditions of class leadership. Presbyterianism, of course, was hierarchically organized in a bureaucratic form of presbyters rather than priests. Virginia was and is also a case in point. From the beginning, Anglicanism in Virginia, though bureaucratic (Episcopal) in theory, was Congregational in fact: rule by gentlemen vestrymen rather than a hierarchy of priests and bishops was traditional (and the upper classes preferred it that way, even though the browbeaten clergy did not). To this day the most fashionable Episcopal seminary, located at Alexandria, Virginia, has tended to emphasize Low Church values, far closer to the Congregationalism of the Puritans than to the High Church values of Charles I and the infamous Bishop Laud. (Perhaps it is no accident that the major High Church seminary in the Episcopal church today is situated in the Midwest rather than along the eastern seaboard.)

Several points should be made in discussing Weber's three types of authority. In the first place, it is more useful to think of the traditional, the bureaucratic, and the charismatic as *aspects of all authority* rather than as mutually exclusive types. Franklin Roosevelt, for instance, spoke from the bureaucratic authority of his position as president, from the traditional authority of his established class position, and certainly from the authority of his own personal charisma. Not to belittle his unique personal qualities, I think it can safely be said that a lot of Roosevelt's charisma derived from his arrogant class charm, which was quite different from the "beer-hall charisma" of Adolf Hitler or the "bayou charisma" of his American contemporary Huey Long. F.D.R.'s administration, moreover, was given a kind of traditional authority and legitimacy in a revolutionary age by Roosevelt's close association with men of established class position such as Francis Biddle, Averell Harriman, John G. Winant, and Henry Stimson. In striking contrast to Roosevelt, former President Nixon, though he spoke from the same bureaucratic position of authority, possessed neither charismatic nor class authority. And as the Watergate affair tragically revealed, he was surrounded by an atomized elite of plutocrats and rootless bureaucrats of no class position or normative standards.

In more general and abstract terms, then, I should like to argue that, by and large in human history, when traditional class authority is strong, the bureaucratic aspects of authority, as well as the petty power struggles of professional politicians, may be held to a minimum. In his famous essay on politics as a vocation, Weber stated the problem well.

> There are two ways of making politics one's vocation: . . . Either politics can be conducted "honorifically" by independent, that is, wealthy men, and especially by *rentiers* . . . or by politicians who live "off" politics and receive income from fees and perquisites for specific services—tips and bribes are only an irregular and formally illegal variant of this category of income.[4]

In the same essay, Weber showed how class authority was a "specifically English institution." "The gentry," he continued, "maintained the possession of all offices of local administration by taking them over without compensation in the interest of their own social power. *The gentry saved England from the bureaucratization which has been the fate of all continental states.*"[5]

The idea of authority, to summarize my argument, is the key to an understanding of stratification and leadership. In our modern world of inevitably large organizations, bureaucratic authority, as Weber feared, is in constant danger of degenerating into an iron cage of conservatism run by maintainance men, rather than leaders. Weber also saw the periodic rise of charismatic leaders as the only means of bureaucratic rejuvenation; but, as we have seen especially in our time, charisma often leads to Caesarism of either the left or the right. I suggest that the institutionalization of class authority and leadership is a countervailing force against the stultifying force of bureaucracy, on the one hand, and the unstable force of charisma, on the other. An excellent example of the difference between class leadership and bureaucratic caution is the way Harvard in 1928 accepted Edward S. Harkness's gift of $13 million for its house plan. Harkness first offered his plan to President Angell of Yale, but after some delay in receiving an answer, he went to President Lowell of Harvard, who immediately accepted both the gift and the plan. Among other reasons for Harvard's response and Yale's delay, according to Yale historian George Pierson, was the fact that "Harvard was an autocracy made acceptable by usage and Brahmin self-confidence. . . . Where Angell was a stranger to Yale and diffident about imposing his views, Lowell was himself a millionaire and to the Harvard manner born."[6] Just as Lowell symbolized class leadership against the dead hand of bureaucracy, so Roosevelt and Churchill symbolized class leadership as against the charisma of the bayou and beer-hall Caesars of their day. And let us not forget that when so many egalitarian liberals were wringing their hands and protecting their flanks, it was the arrogant patrician Dean Acheson son of a Connecticut bishop, with degrees from both Harvard and Yale, who stood up to the charismatic demagogue Senator Joseph P. McCarthy, referring to the authority of an ancient text in doing so.

Authority is the institutionalization, or legitimation, of power. When authority capitulates altogether to the social forces of egalitarianism and anti-institutional anarchy, ambitious men, often of few scruples, rapidly adapt themselves to a world of vicious power struggles while the timid retreat behind the walls of plutocracy and irresponsible privilege. Tocqueville explained how egalitarian democracy is all too prone to this tragic situation.

> Men being no longer attached to one another by any tie of caste, of class, of corporation, of family are only too much inclined to be preoccupied only with their private interests, ever too much drawn to think only of themselves and to retire into a narrow individualism, in which every public virtue is stifled. Despotism far from struggling against this tendency makes it irresistible.[7]

In order to clarify thinking here as well as to provide a sense of theoretical continuity with my earlier work, I should like to place such concepts as privilege, class authority, class pride, snobbery, plutocracy, aristocracy, and democratic elitism within more or less the same model developed in *Philadelphia Gen-*

tlemen and *The Protestant Establishment*. First of all, I should like to emphasize that stratification theory as such should not be concerned with whether elites and upper classes are morally or ethically desirable. There are indeed moral and immoral men, but *all social structures* are more or less unfair and, at best, morally ambiguous.

> The fact is that not only property, but the two institutions of property and social stratification are in the same position of moral ambiguity. Both are necessary instruments of justice and order, and yet both are fruitful of injustice. Both have, no less than government, grown up organically in traditional civilizations in the sense that they are unconscious adaptations to the needs of justice and order. The revolts against both of them by both the radical Christians and the radical secular idealists of the seventeenth and eighteenth centuries tended to be indiscriminate.[8]

If we assume that leadership and authority are necessary aspects of all viable social systems of any size and complexity, the question becomes whether or not the unequal distribution of wealth and power is considered to be *relatively* fair and just by most of the people and thus is or is not able to command authority and provide conditions favorable to leadership. Some years ago, Morris Janowitz stated this problem with great insight and showed how these conditions are not peculiar to modern urban America: "Everywhere community leadership faces a common problem," he wrote after a study with Edward Banfield of decisionmaking in Chicago, "namely, the issue is not the manipulation of the citizenry by a small elite, but rather the inability of elites to create the conditions required for making decisions."[9]

THE ELITE AND THE UPPER CLASS

My model of leadership and authority depends on a clear understanding of the difference between an *elite* and an *upper class*. The elite concept refers to those individuals in any social system who hold the top positions in their chosen careers, occupations, or professions. In a free and democratic society, they make up what Thomas Jefferson called a "natural aristocracy." Throughout our history, most Americans have assumed, along with Jefferson, that the Republic was best served by this kind of meritorious or natural elite. Paradoxically, democrats rather than aristocrats have tended to take the view that the naturally gifted, the genetically "best," or the natural geniuses should be rewarded with elite status. At the same time, there is the democratic faith that the hereditary best are scattered throughout the social structure and not concentrated within any hereditary upper class. Thus, Jefferson was a great admirer of the astronomer David Rittenhouse (1732–1796), of whom he wrote: "In genius he must be first, because he is self-taught."[10] It is appropriate that Jefferson valued Rittenhouse above his near contemporary John Winthrop IV (1714–1779), a secure and hereditary member of the New England upper class, even though, according to Daniel Boorstin, Winthrop was "the most accomplished American astronomer . . . descendant of the first governor of Massachusetts Bay and a long line of New England scholar-leaders . . . a man of broad learning and vast energy . . . generally conceded to be the best that America had yet offered in the Newtonian line."[11]

Jefferson's faith in a natural elite (I use *elite* where he used *aristocracy*) has been borne out by history, as American society has continued to produce, in each generation, such natural aristocrats as Benjamin Franklin, David Rittenhouse, and Alexander Hamilton, through Abraham Lincoln, and down to Harry S. Truman and Hubert Humphrey and Martin Luther King, Jr., in our own generation—men drawn from all classes, races, and religions. However, unless natural aristocrats remain celibate (in the style of the traditional Catholic hierarchy), their families gradually will form a more or less hereditary upper class. Whereas elites are formed anew in each generation and according to contemporary criteria, upper classes are always the product (often unanticipated) of two or more generations. An upper class, then, is a *sociological* and *historical*, rather than a *natural*, aristocracy. It is nothing more or less than *a group of consanguine families* whose ancestors were elite members and family founders one or more generations earlier. Thus, Oliver Wendell Holmes, Jr., and John Winthrop IV were members of the New England upper class; John G. Johnson and David Rittenhouse were natural aristocrats and elite Philadelphians but neither founders nor sons of any upper-class family in the city.

One of the most fascinating and touching friendships in American history was that between Thomas Jefferson and John Adams. Bitter opponents in politics, they began an epistolatory friendship after their active political careers had come to a close and continued it until their deaths on the same day, July 4, 1826, the fiftieth birthday of the nation they helped found. The two men were philosophical opposites: Jefferson represented the Enlightenment and the francophile (or "liberal") tradition in America; Adams stood firmly in the Puritan, Federalist, and anglophilic tradition. Jefferson recognized the need for a natural aristocracy and mistrusted the growth of an upper class in America, as his abolition of primogeniture in Virginia clearly showed. Adams, on the contrary, saw the need for and the positive function of responsible upper-class traditions. Interestingly enough, and in contradiction to any ideology that propounds a class determinism of ideas, both men were themselves connected to the upper classes of their colonies—Jefferson through his Randolph mother and Adams through his Boylston mother and his wife's Quincy connections. Both, of course, were also the greatest of natural aristocrats. They were very different, however, in one important respect: only Adams founded an American First Family.*

As long as America remains an open and democratic society, with the traditional emphasis on social mobility and the rewarding of merit, a natural elite of ability and ambition will come to the fore in every generation. But as Michael Young and other social philosophers, from Walter Lippmann to Hannah Arendt, have cautioned, all virtues, even merit, may be pushed to harmful ex-

---

*By and large in history, it has been men of conservative, rather than liberal, temperaments or proclivities who have been the great family founders—John Winthrop, for instance, but not William Penn.

tremes. Thus, the democratic ideal of pure elitism may lead to a kind of anarchy at the top. For the elite concept is merely a sociological category that includes all persons who have been successful in their chosen fields; it is not a real group with normative standards of conduct or admission. This category is all too prone, moreover, to be composed of individuals motivated by the standards of success and individual self-interest rather than by any class standards of honor or duty. The great American anthropologist Ralph Linton saw this possibility very clearly when he wrote that the decline of our bourgeois culture was in part the result of an excess of democracy and irresponsible elitism.

> The lack of a definite aristocratic culture which provides the members of this ruling group with common ideals and standards of behavior and thus integrates them into a conscious society is perhaps the most distinctive aspect of the modern condition. Exploiters and exploited have existed since the dawn of history, but the only parallel to the modern situation is that of Rome in the days of the late Republic. Here also power came to be vested in the hands of a group of self-made men who had no common standards and no feeling of responsibility to each other or to the state.[12]

A STRATIFICATION MODEL

I have conceptualized the relationship between the upper class and the elite in Figure 2-1. I think it can usefully be said that all societies are elitist; in all social relations some people will take the lead and others will be content to follow. A perfectly operating meritocracy, assuming that all its members in each generation were celibate, would result in a perfectly democratic elite composed entirely of Jefferson's natural aristocrats (box 2). This would be a logical but not an empirical possibility so long as men and women mated and produced children. Even though it has always been the democratic and opportunitarian ideal, moreover, this elite situation would tend to create, in each generation, a lonely crowd of atomized leaders, each pursuing his own self-interest, with no common set of moral standards, class cohesion, or anchor in authority. Now, natural aristocrats, or self-made men, are surely no more or no less moral individually than are leaders drawn from the upper classes; it is their moral milieu, as we shall see in a moment, that is different. Without class authority, in other words, there is a danger that gifted and moral men will be forced into a position where, in order to be successful, they must engage in endless petty power struggles. According to my thesis, this very situation—*too much* rather than too little mobility and democracy—has marked the social structures of Philadelphia and Pennsylvania from their founding days to the present (and may be a major cause of our whole nation's loss of confidence and moral direction today). Throughout this book, I shall refer to this leadership situation as *democratic elitism*.

As a matter of fact rather than of theory, in every ongoing social system there is bound to be a group of families of inherited social position, descendants of natural aristocrats; that is, an upper class (boxes 1 and 3). Whereas an elite is a sociological category or concept, an upper class is a real social grouping. All real social groupings, from a band of Bowery thieves to a band of Boston Brahmins, are generators of normative standards; all upper classes create moral milieus in a sense that elites simply do not; there is a code of honor among thieves and Brahmins that does not exist among people listed in *Who's Who* or Dun and Bradstreet's *Directory of Directors*. An upper class, then, is a translator of talent, power, and accomplishment, over the generations, into a system of traditional moral standards.

Figure 2–1   The Upper Class and the Elite: A Leadership Model

Status and Inherited Wealth
(Families)

	High	Low	
High	Box 1 Class Authority Aristocracy	Box 2 Democratic Elitism	Elite (boxes 1 and 2)
	(Class Pride) Traditional Authority	Bureaucratic Authority	
	Box 3 Privileged Class Plutocracy		
Low	(Class Snobbery) Authority Vacuum		

Power and Accomplishment
(Individuals)

Upper Class
(boxes 1 and 3)

Class Authority:	An upper class, normatively if not quantitatively, dominates an elite (elite centered in box 1).
Democratic Elitism:	Leadership by atomized individuals (elite centered in box 2).
Privileged Class:	An upper class has status and wealth without power and accomplishment or class authority (upper class in box 3).
Aristocracy:	Status and wealth in accord with power and accomplishment (box 1).
Plutocracy:	Status and wealth without power and accomplishment (box 3).

To put it another way, whereas power is existential and intrinsic to all social relationships, authority is the translation of power into normative institutions. In Max Weber's terms, it is the function of bureaucratic office and law to do this *rationally.* I contend that it is the proper function of upper classes to manage this process *traditionally.* There are, however, two kinds of upper classes, those that take the lead and command authority and those that rest on their privileges and do not. The former (conceptualized in box 1), as we have seen, is marked by class authority, aristocratic leadership, and class pride; the latter (box 3) is content to rest on privileges and inherited wealth and is prone to status snobbery rather than aristocratic pride.

Following Tocqueville, whose *Democracy in America* is a classic study of the ideal-typical aspects of aristocratic as against democratic social structures, I should like to make a rather broad generalization: whenever the ideals of equality and democratic individualism (Quakerism) are stressed in a society, ambitious men and natural aristocrats will come to the fore through a series of petty power struggles; they will of necessity have small rather than large ambitions involving power and success rather than great accomplishments and fame; at the same time, individuals in inherited positions will have, of necessity at first and normatively later, retreated from authority and ambition to rest on their pecuniary privileges. As all men from Aristotle on have seen, plutocracy is characteristic of every egalitarian society. Social causation, of course, works both ways, from causation, as it were, to affinity, from cause to effect, and back again. When an upper class has no pride in authority and has come to love privilege alone, new men will seek power only in order to attain privileges and comfort, and when a society is marked by mobility and small ambition, so an upper class will be marked by the same. When, on the contrary, a society is marked by the ideals of hierarchy, class authority, and aristocratic social cohesion (Puritanism), ambitious men, both natural and sociological aristocrats, men of inherited position and those of achieved position, will tend to be driven to accomplishment and fame and be less likely to rest on power or privilege alone.

We can assume that natural talent is and always has been as great in Philadelphia and Pennsylvania as in Boston and Massachusetts. It is the values and the moral milieus that make for the differential distribution of accomplishment and fame. Talent is natural and morally neutral; fame is cultural and normative (see Appendix II).

SOCIAL JUSTICE AND SOCIAL COHESION

Democratic social and political theory is concerned with social justice, a vital aspect of which is the need for allowing the most deserving individuals, regardless of class, race, or ethnic origin, to rise into elite positions of leadership. But social justice must always be somewhat modified and balanced by the need for both social cohesion and continuity of traditional authority, which, at the elite level at least, is the social function of an upper class. This raises two important problems: (1) how does an upper class, inevitably formed by the descendants of elite individuals, assimilate new elite members in each generation into its ranks; and (2) how does an upper class motivate its members to contribute to the leadership and authority of their own generation rather than merely rest content with their inherited wealth and privileges? Our opportunitarian society has done quite well in promoting equal access to unequal privileges; it has done far less well in stressing the inequality of duty, or noblesse oblige, as far as the members of its privileged classes are concerned. It is here that the Puritan and Quaker ethics have had very different consequences in upper-class Boston and Philadelphia.

As we have seen, Thomas Jefferson, in the tradition of the Enlightenment and the French Revolution, was concerned primarily with the first problem, favoring a natural aristocracy, or a pure meritocracy, in a society where all careers were open to talented people without the restraints of any hereditary class distinctions. John Adams, in the British Whig tradition of Edmund Burke, was interested in the second problem, the proper functioning of privileged classes. In this connection, Adams' marginal notes in his copy of Mary Wollstonecraft's book on the French Revolution (an angry reply to Burke's famous *Reflections*) are revealing. Opposite Wollstonecraft's statement that "hereditary distinctions . . . have prevented man from rising to his just point of elevation by his improvable faculties" Adams scrawled: "Hereditary distinctions among the Greeks and Romans, and in all Europe since their times, have been essential to the liberty that has been enjoyed."[13] Adams then added another note even more germane to my argument: "The distinction of property will have more influence than all the rest in commercial countries, if it is not rivalled by some other distinctions."[14] When authority and social cohesion decline, money alone talks.

These two problems are intimately related. Upper-class members who take the lead and exert authority will be far more likely to recognize new men of talent and ability and to encourage their assimilation into the upper class. An authoritative upper class, then, is not antithetical to liberty and leadership but rather a correlative of both. Above all, it provides a coherent and cohesive class for new men to join (often through marriage) and defend in the style of Cicero in his day and Daniel Webster in his.

In this connection, it is interesting that Jefferson once compared the leadership of Boston and Philadelphia in favor of the former. The members of the Philadelphia elite in his day, he said, were like a bunch of cut-flowers, colorful, brilliant, and varied, but rootless and quick to fade. The Boston leaders, in contrast, were more like perennial plants, family progenitors, deeply rooted in the soil of New England.

In closing this chapter, I should like to define several terms that I use throughout the book.

1. *Auslander*: an individual from outside the city or state, often one born abroad. To Philadelphia and Pennsylvania, Benjamin Franklin and Albert Gallatin were auslanders. (A Swiss nobleman of distinguished Calvinist ancestry and a disciple of Rousseau, Gallatin settled in the wilderness of western Penn-

sylvania, where he soon became a political leader, serving in the U.S. Congress before becoming Jefferson's secretary of the treasury.)

2. *Outsider*: an individual who, regardless of whether he is an auslander or a native of the city or state, remains unassimilated into the upper class. As far as Proper Philadelphia was concerned, both Franklin and Gallatin were auslanders as well as outsiders. Though Gallatin, as secretary of the treasury between 1801 and 1814, worked closely with Thomas Willing and other leading Philadelphia bankers, he was never attracted by the city; after serving as minister to both France and Great Britain, he ended his career as president of the National Bank of New York City at a time when Philadelphia was still the financial capital of the nation (he had been offered the presidency of the Second Bank of the United States before Nicholas Biddle). The nineteenth-century scientist Louis Agassiz was an auslander who came to Boston from his native Switzerland as a lecturer at the Lowell Institute. In contrast to Gallatin, Agassiz remained in Boston the rest of his life and after his first wife's death married Elizabeth Cabot Cary, a Brahmin bluestocking who became the first president of Radcliffe College. Finally, John G. Johnson was a native Philadelphian who in spite of his fashionable marriage remained an outsider.

3. *Cut-flower*: an individual of great talent and temporary (one-generational) leadership who leaves no family line of any distinction. He may be an auslander or a native, an outsider or an upper-class member (by either ascription or achievement). John G. Johnson was a native cut-flower; and Franklin, a brilliantly blooming auslander cut-flower. Robert Morris, a leader in Philadelphia's upper class and financier of the Revolution, was likewise a cut-flower, dying in financial disgrace and leaving no Proper Philadelphia family line.* (Morris was also an auslander, born in Liverpool, England.) Much like Morris, Daniel Webster was the darling of Brahmin Boston in its most creative age, yet he was both an auslander (from New Hampshire) and a cut-flower. Louis Agassiz was no cut-flower: his son, Alexander, a professor of geology at Harvard, lived at the heart of Brahmin Boston, especially as the developer of the famous Calumet and Hecla copper mining enterprises.

From colonial times to the present, Philadelphia has been led by a far higher proportion of auslanders, outsiders, and cut-flowers than Boston has been. This has been largely the result of the very different upper classes in the two cities, which I shall discuss in the next chapter. In the rest of the book I attempt to show why and how these differences came to be.

---

*Although Morris produced no Proper Philadelphia family of the name, he did produce distinguished sons who, however, moved elsewhere (see Chapter 18).

Boston Brahmins and Philadelphia Gentlemen: An Empirical Test

Other things being equal, in most relations of life I prefer the man of family. What do I mean by a man of family?

Four or five generations of gentlemen and gentlewomen; among them a member of his Majesty's Council of the Province, a Governor or so, one or two Doctors of Divinity, a member of Congress, not later than the time of long boots with tassels.

Family portraits. The member of the Council, by Smibert. The great merchant-uncle, by Copley, full length, with a globe by him, to show the range of his commercial transactions. . . . A pair of Stuarts. . . .

I go (always, other things being equal) for the man who inherits family traditions and the cumulative humanities of at least four or five generations.

Oliver Wendell Holmes

I inherited the fortune and position for which others strive. What I had, because it was habitual, I did not value, and therefore instead of making exertions to increase it, I forgot that any exertion was necessary. . . . I became self-indulgent, and my taste and mental bias leading me to thought rather than action, thought instead of action became a habit . . . and so I shall go on.

Sidney George Fisher

In our highly mobile and increasingly urban society, the nuclear, or conjugal, family has been the main social unit, especially among the middle classes. The extended, or consanguine, family has tended to be strongest at the very top and bottom levels of society. Throughout most of our history the extended kin group has thrived in the more remote and economically marginal areas of the nation, in the Ozarks, for instance, or in the hills of West Virginia and Tennessee. Among urban blacks, where the conjugal family has been relatively weak, the matriarchal extended family of cousins, aunts, and grandmothers has predominated.

The extended family, or clan, also has been strong at the higher levels of American society, particularly in small cities and towns. Though most sociologists have failed to emphasize this point, the Lynds, in their study of *Middletown in Transition* (1937), showed how the Ball family in the second and third generations was forming the nucleus of an upper class in Muncie, Indiana, in the 1930s. Members of consanguine families have lent a sense of continuity and stability to our increasingly bureaucratized and atomized elite structure; for example, the Mellons of Pittsburgh, the Du Ponts of Delaware, the Roosevelts and Rockefellers of New York, the Tafts of Cincinnati, the Mathers of Cleveland, the Pillsburys of Minneapolis, the Pulitzers and Busches of St. Louis, the Crockers and Hearsts of San Francisco, the Fords of Detroit, the Byrds of Virginia, and especially the Adamses and Kennedys of Boston. A sense of loss pervades America today partly as a result of the Kennedy assassinations, testifying to the public's longing for continuity at the top.

Elite individuals may come from a wide variety of ethnic, racial, and cultural backgrounds, but an upper class, as we have seen, is a more or less endogamous subculture. This subculture, referred to as "Society" up until the Second World War at least, had many characteristics of a gemeinschaft, or tribal society. No wonder Henry Adams felt at home among the natives of Samoa: "They are tremendous aristocrats," he once wrote. "Family is everything."[1] The core of Society, as Adams knew, is a group of extended families whose members have intermarried for several generations. Though there is a national upper-class subculture in America, especially since the rise of nationally patronized boarding schools and universities in the last decades of the nineteenth century, each major city has its own upper-class folkways and mores, similar in form if varying in content. Both Boston and Philadelphia, for instance, have upper classes whose members speak with accents that distinguish them from the rest of their city's population; at the same time, the spoken *r*, which is dropped in Boston and emphasized in Philadelphia, is a mark of regional influence.

Of all the upper classes in major American cities, those in Boston and Philadelphia are probably the most alike. A central core of extended families—the Adamses, Lowells, and Cabots in Boston and the Biddles, Cadwaladers, and Ingersolls in Philadelphia, for example—is surrounded by several hundred other prominent families. These family circles are, in turn, enlarged and given form by a host of upper-class voluntary associations that foster a distinctive style of life. The Somerset and Tavern clubs in Boston are matched by the Philadelphia and Franklin Inn clubs in Philadelphia. For the ladies there is the Chilton in Boston and the Acorn in Philadelphia. Both cities have their private libraries, like the Athenaeum in Boston and the Athenaeum and Library Company in Philadelphia; there are historical and genealogical societies, as well as ancestor-worshiping organizations like the Colonial Dames (not the DAR) and the Sons of the Revolution. Although the Boston Symphony and the Philadelphia Orchestra serve the whole community of music lovers, fashionable women in both cities ritually attend the concerts on Friday afternoons. In both cities there are private day schools, in the city during the nineteenth century and in the suburbs today, where upper-class youths are both educated and introduced to a well-defined system of manners and values; their manners are further refined at weekly dancing classes. Until after the Second World War, most daughters did not go off to college, and the debutante ritual was an important rite of passage in which proper young ladies were introduced to the proper adult world as well as to their eligible peers. All of these socialization processes have fostered a pattern of strict class endogamy, as indicated by such names as Cabot Lodge, Godfrey Cabot Lowell, Peabody Gardner, and A. Lawrence Lowell in Boston, and Cadwalader Biddle, Cadwalader Morris, Wistar Morris, and George Wharton Pepper in Philadelphia. No wonder a recent social critic defined an upper-class WASP as someone whose first name is a last name.

Both Philadelphia and Boston, then, have clearly defined upper classes made up of a group of well-known families of more or less ancient lineage and inherited wealth and position. Around this core are several thousand families of proper associational affiliations and of varying degrees of historical position. There is no way of measuring the size of the upper classes in Boston and Philadelphia with any precision. The number of families included in the *Social Registers* of the two cities is perhaps the best available clue. These sources show that the Philadelphia upper class is about 30 percent larger: in both 1940 and 1970, for example, there were about 3,500 conjugal family units listed in Boston's *Social Register* as against about 5,000 in Philadelphia's.

Yet any one generation of *Social Register* families produces only a few leaders of distinction, illustrious ancestors notwithstanding. The majority of upper-class members, in Boston and Philadelphia as elsewhere, then, are content to rest on their privileges and do not become leaders in government or society as a whole. The American ethos (in contrast to the British) dictates this choice. Thus, though the "blood" is the same, the Astors in America have largely been Society leaders of the Four Hundred while their relatives in England have taken an active part in national life. In both Boston and Philadelphia the majority of gentlemen are content to be good family men and successes in their chosen occupations or professions. They are club-men who are responsible presidents or chairmen of admissions committees in their distinguished clubs; secretaries of school and college boards of trustees, country clubs, vestries, and charitable organizations rather than secretaries of state; genealogists and antiquarians rather than historians; successful members of fashionable law firms rather than judges or statesmen; doctors with lucrative practices rather than contributors to the development of the science of medicine; and so forth. There are, quite naturally in both cities, far more George Apleys than John Adamses. In fact, one has the impression that today the Adamses are becoming more like Apley than their illustrious ancestor. (One difference between the two cities, as we shall see, is that though Proper Philadelphia produces its share of men in the Apley mold, no one has ever seen fit or been fit to write about them.)

My purpose here is not to discuss the size, structure, or style of life of the Boston and Philadelphia upper classes in detail. It is enough to indicate that they exist, and have existed from the nation's beginning, in relatively similar form. However, in their production of men and women who have been willing and able to take the lead and exert their inherited class authority on the society as a whole, Boston and Philadelphia are poles apart.

THE ELITE IN AMERICAN HISTORY

Although the George Apleys are the backbone of any upper-class way of life, the continued existence of an upper class can be justified only if it consistently produces people who take the lead in the nation. The most useful index of the men and women who have been the foremost contributors to American cultural history is the *Dictionary of American Biography* (*DAB*). This American Plutarch, modeled on the British *Dictionary of National Biography* (1885–1900), was published by the American Council of Learned Societies in twenty volumes (1928–1936). The original work contains articles on 13,633 individuals, written by 2,243 contributors selected by the editorial board. Although there was no thought of "estimating greatness on any strict arithmetical scale, or establishing any exact order of eminence," according to the editorial policy, "the space given to any particular person reflects in general the editorial judgment of his importance."[2] The vast majority of articles contain between 500 and 10,000 words, some few falling below this level and those of five men, George Washington (the longest: 16,500), Benjamin Franklin, Abraham Lincoln, Thomas Jefferson, and Woodrow Wilson, running beyond the 10,000-word limit.*

The biographies of the men and women included in the *DAB* are an excellent means of measuring the consequences of the ethics of leadership in the original colonial cultures. Although these individuals came from all over the Union and some from abroad, over half of them were natives of six states: New York, Massachusetts, Pennsylvania, Connecticut, Virginia, and Ohio (see Table A–2).† The hegemony of the Puritan-Yankee culture of New England in the period covered by these twenty volumes was outstanding. Not only was the state of Massachusetts first, in proportion to its size, in contributing to the nation's leadership but the Puritan-Congregationalist culture of Massachusetts Bay spawned the culture of Connecticut, the second most prolific contributor

---

*All tables cited in this chapter are presented in Appendix I.

†The 1820s produced the largest number of individuals listed in the original twenty volumes of the *DAB*. If we take the populations of these six states in 1830 and relate them to the number of individuals in the *DAB*, we find the following proportional refinements of the figures in Table A–2. Massachusetts and Connecticut are clearly preeminent.

State	Number in *DAB*	Population in 1830	Number in *DAB* per 10,000 people
New York	1,876	1,918,608	10
Massachusetts	1,868	610,408	31
Connecticut	784	297,675	26
Pennsylvania	1,255	1,348,233	9
Virginia	726	1,211,405	6
Ohio	475	937,903	5
Total United States	13,633	17,069,453	8

in relation to its population. In the late eighteenth and in the nineteenth century, the Puritan Congregationalist culture spread westward, first into Ohio and then throughout the Northwest Territory. This same culture, moreover, spread soon after the Revolution over the mountains and across the Hudson River into upper New York, as attested by Washington Irving's famous portrait of the Yankee schoolmaster Ichabod Crane and James Fenimore Cooper's obsession with the Yankee invaders of his New York. The leadership culture of Puritan Massachusetts Bay, then, was far more extensive than the colony itself.* (Pennsylvania's weak representation in this elite index will be discussed subsequently. Virginia's relatively poor representation, considering the colony's dominance of the nation's top leadership at its founding, can largely be explained by Virginia's failure to provide wide access to higher education, the major way to elite status in our nineteenth-century democracy.)

SEVENTY-SIX PREEMINENT AMERICANS

The men and women included in the *DAB* represent about eight in 10,000 of their fellow citizens, certainly a small and distinguished elite. Within all elite groups, however, there are always a few people who stand out. In the twentieth volume of the *DAB*, the editors listed seventy-five men and one woman whose biographies ran to more than 5,000 words:†

Charles Francis Adams I	Samuel Langhorne Clemens
Henry Brooks Adams	Stephen Grover Cleveland
John Adams	James Fenimore Cooper
John Quincy Adams	John Singleton Copley
Samuel Adams	Caleb Cushing
Jean Louis Rodolphe Agassiz	Jefferson Davis
Nelson Wilmarth Aldrich	Stephen Arnold Douglas
Benedict Arnold	Mary Morse Baker Eddy
George Bancroft	Jonathan Edwards
Henry Ward Beecher	Charles William Eliot
James Gillespie Blaine	Ralph Waldo Emerson
William Jennings Bryan	Benjamin Franklin
William Cullen Bryant	Abraham Alfonse Albert Gallatin
James Buchanan	Elbridge Gerry
Aaron Burr	Ulysses Simpson Grant
John Caldwell Calhoun	Horace Greeley
Andrew Carnegie	Alexander Hamilton
Salmon Portland Chase	Warren Gamaliel Harding
Henry Clay	William Rainey Harper

---

*The cultural hegemony of the natives of Massachusetts and their descendants in Connecticut, New York, and Ohio can be traced to the original Puritan attitude toward education (discussed in Chapter 14). Note that of the 4,611 *DAB* subjects who were graduates of American colleges, 35 percent were educated in either Massachusetts or Connecticut (Table A–2).

†Benjamin Franklin, Thomas Jefferson, Abraham Lincoln, George Washington, and Woodrow Wilson had more than 10,000 words apiece in their *DAB* biographies. *Dictionary of American Biography*, Vol. XX, pp. xii, xiii.

Nathaniel Hawthorne
John Milton Hay
Patrick Henry
Oliver Wendell Holmes
Washington Irving
Andrew Jackson
Henry James
William James
Thomas Jefferson
Andrew Johnson
John La Farge
Robert Marion La Follette
Benjamin Henry Latrobe
Robert Edward Lee
Abraham Lincoln
James Russell Lowell
James Madison
John Marshall
James Monroe

John Pierpont Morgan
Thomas Paine
Edgar Allan Poe
Theodore Roosevelt
Josiah Royce
Augustus Saint-Gaudens
Winfield Scott
William Henry Seward
Alexander Hamilton Stephens
Joseph Story
Charles Sumner
William Howard Taft
Henry David Thoreau
George Washington
Daniel Webster
James Abbott McNeil Whistler
George Whitefield
Walt Whitman
Woodrow Wilson

These preeminent Americans were born in nineteen states of the Union and abroad, yet natives of Massachusetts and New England as a whole predominated:

New England (thirty-one)

Massachusetts: five Adamses, Bancroft, Bryant, Copley, Cushing, Eliot, Emerson, Gerry, Hawthorne, Holmes, Lowell, Poe, Story, Sumner, Thoreau, Whistler, Franklin

Connecticut: Arnold, Beecher, Edwards, Morgan

New Hampshire: Chase, Eddy, Greeley, Webster

Vermont: Douglas

Rhode Island: Aldrich

Middle Atlantic (twelve)

New York: Irving, H. James, W. James, La Farge, Roosevelt, Seward, Whitman

New Jersey: Burr, Cleveland, Cooper

Pennsylvania: Blaine, Buchanan

South (fourteen)

Virginia: Washington, Jefferson, Madison, Monroe, Lee, Wilson, Clay, Marshall, Henry, Scott

South Carolina: Jackson, Calhoun

North Carolina: Johnson

Georgia:	Stephens
Middle West (ten)	
Ohio:	Grant, Harding, Taft, Harper
Illinois:	Lincoln, Bryan
Indiana:	Hay
Wisconsin:	La Follette
Missouri:	Clemens (Twain)
Kentucky:	Davis
West (one)	
California:	Royce
Abroad (eight)	Agassiz, Carnegie, Gallitan, Hamilton, Latrobe, Paine, Saint-Gaudens, Whitefield

Note that five of the six states that contributed the most individuals to the *DAB* also led in this group: Massachusetts, twenty-one; Virginia, ten; New York, seven; Connecticut, four; and Ohio, four; Pennsylvania is the exception, with only two natives at this high level of distinction. Virginia was below the national average in contributing to the whole *DAB*, but it was second only to Massachusetts in this list and first in such nearly mythological founders of our national institutions as Washington, Jefferson, Madison, and Marshall; certainly Robert E. Lee has been the major romantic hero in our history. Whereas the few truly great men of Virginia reflected the aristocratic values of a landed class, the larger number of distinguished men from Massachusetts reflected the Puritan traditions of educated and patrician leadership.

Of the twenty-one men of Massachusetts, all save Bryant, Whistler, Poe, and Franklin made their careers in and around Boston. Bryant settled in New York; the other three—Poe, a nomadic American; Whistler, an expatriate; and Franklin, a world figure—were truly self-born and self-delighting geniuses.*

The most important fact about the Massachusetts group is that, with the exceptions noted, they were all part of the state's traditional ruling class, centered in Boston. To this group must be added the two James brothers, Josiah Royce, and Daniel Webster. William James spent his entire professional career in Cambridge, and his expatriate brother, Henry, felt that if he had an American home, it also was Cambridge. Royce was brought to Cambridge by William

---

*The style of their genius was never better expressed than in Whistler's witty reply to a fellow native of Lowell who once said, "You know, Mr. Whistler, we were both born at Lowell, and at very much the same time . . . you are 67 and I am 68." Whistler promptly replied, "Very charming. And so you are 68 and were born in Lowell, Massachusetts. Most interesting, no doubt, and as you please! But I shall be born when and where I want, and I do not choose to be born at Lowell and I refuse to be 67" (E. R. and J. Pennell, *The Life of James McNeill Whistler* [Philadelphia: Lippincott, 1925], p. 1).

James. Hawthorne, though fiercely proud of his family and class roots in Salem, stood apart as the major Puritan genius of his or any other time, and Thoreau was always cantankerously doing his own thing out in Concord and on Walden Pond. All of which suggests that Boston was the home of the most influential upper class in American history.

Philadelphia, on the other hand, has never produced a man or woman of such preeminence. Buchanan, though he spent his career in Pennsylvania, had nothing to do with the city, and Blaine made his whole career in Maine.

FIFTY FIRST FAMILIES OF BOSTON AND PHILADELPHIA: PATTERNS OF CLASS LEADERSHIP

Geniuses and natural aristocrats like Franklin, Lincoln, Poe, and Whistler are born into every class in almost every kind of society. Nevertheless, the way native talent is employed relates to the cultural values of a given time or place. And in this book we are interested in how such expression fares among the upper classes, the cultural carriers of traditions of authority and leadership. In order empirically to compare the leadership traditions of Puritan Boston with those of Quaker Philadelphia, I selected for analysis a group of individuals included in the *DAB* who belonged to fifty consanguine families in each city (see Table A–3). So as to lengthen the time span of my analysis, I have used both the original twenty volumes of the *DAB* and the three supplementary volumes published since 1936 (the third supplement, published in 1973, listed distinguished Americans who died between 1941 and 1945).

In selecting the fifty families in each city, I tried to choose families with long and unbroken upper-class affiliations. Forty-seven of the Boston families and forty-five of the Philadelphia families in the sample had members listed in the 1940 *Social Register*, ranging from one or two nuclear families all the way to the Boston Cabot clan, with over thirty families in the *Social Register*, and the Philadelphia Biddles and Morrises, with some fifty each. The families were not necessarily living in their city of origin. For example, there were no Mathers in the Boston *Social Register* but several in Cleveland and New York; Winthrops were in Boston and New York; the roughly fifty members of the Peabody clan were living in Boston primarily but also in New York and Philadelphia; and the sole surviving members of the Philadelphia Shippen family, the Edward Shippens, were listed in the *Social Register* of Washington, D.C.

If *Social Register* listing in 1940 was a useful index of family continuity, inclusion in *Who's Who in America* in 1940 was a good index of continued family prominence. Here differences between the two cities were considerable. Of the fifty Boston families, thirty-five had eighty-three members listed in the 1940 *Who's Who* as against nineteen families with thirty individuals listed from Philadelphia. In this elite index (less distinguished, of course, than the *DAB*), the Boston Cabots and the Philadelphia Biddles took the lead in their respective cities (nine Cabots and six Biddles); in fact, two of the Biddles included in

1940—Francis, attorney general under Franklin Roosevelt, and his artist brother, George—were along with Nicholas, the famous banker (*DAB*), probably the most distinguished Biddles in the history of the clan. As with the *Social Register*, *Who's Who* listed native sons living in cities other than Boston or Philadelphia: the only Cadwalader in *Who's Who* was a Baltimorian; the Winthrops, as mentioned, were New Yorkers as well as Bostonians; the most distinguished member of Boston's Perkins family in 1940 was a New York banker; and the Eliots were living all over, from Boston to Washington to Portland, Oregon. And, of course, the most distinguished native American poet of his generation, Thomas Stearns Eliot, was an Englishman.*

I have limited my sample to families whose name has carried down through history. A conspicuous exception was made in the case of the Philadelphia Lloyds because of their great importance in the early decades of the colony and because, as we shall see, the female descendants of Thomas Lloyd married men who formed the core of the city's first upper class. Some distinguished Bostonians and Philadelphians were not included because they were neither family founders nor upper-class members, for example, Benjamin Franklin, Daniel Webster, and the medical pioneer John Morgan.

The selection of the fifty First Families was complicated for different reasons in each city. In Philadelphia it was difficult to find fifty families who qualified in terms of distinguished leadership. There are, of course, many Philadelphia clans with long-term upper-class affiliations (even more than in Boston); yet either they had no members listed in the *DAB* or, more usually, they traced descent back to a cut-flower of conspicuous wealth but without progeny of local or national importance. Boston had too many families of several distinguished generations, such as the Amorys, Dexters, Tuckermans, Thayers, Lorings, Sedgwicks (not included because most of their prominent men were from Stockbridge), Cushings, Derbys, Crowninshields, Weldses, Wolcotts (though Roger was governor of Massachusetts at the turn of the century, the Wolcotts were originally a Connecticut family), Gardners (only Isabel Stewart Gardner appeared in the *DAB*), Storys (Joseph, Supreme Court justice and law educator, and his son William Wetmore, a sculptor of brilliant talent, were giants, but the next generation ended up in Philadelphia and none was left in Boston by 1940), Sumners (Increase was an early Federalist governor, and Charles, next to Lincoln the most powerful man in the nation at the close of the Civil War, had no descendants in the 1940 *Social Register*), and Searses (only Richard, first U.S. tennis champion, was named in the *DAB*). I excluded two of the most interesting Boston families, the Channings and the Sargents: the Channings (six in the *DAB*, including William Ellery, founder of the "Boston religion") because they were originally a Rhode Island family and the Sargents (ten in the *DAB*, including the artist John Singer and a recent governor) because some of them were also part of the Philadelphia upper class. The point is that

---

*It is curious that the most distinguished Lowell of our generation, the poet Robert Lowell, lived in England at the time of his death, in very much the same style (except for his affluent wife) as T. S. Eliot.

the overwhelming leadership superiority of the fifty Boston families was not an artifact of my selection process; if anything, it was the other way around.

FAMILY AND CLASS LEADERSHIP:
A BARE QUANTITATIVE COMPARISON

Although a quantitative analysis of anything so human and complex as leadership is subject to criticism, my method does serve the canon of objectivity, which is at least a useful point of departure.

To begin with, the Boston families had more of their members included in the *DAB*, 188 as against 146 Philadelphians. The Bostonians were half as likely to have only one member of the family in the *DAB* and three times as likely to have more than five (Table A–4). That the Bostonians tended to produce more leaders per family suggested that the leadership span of the Boston families was longer, and indeed Table A–5 shows that more than three times as many Boston as Philadelphia families produced *DAB* leadership for two centuries or more. Moreover, whereas a majority (58 percent) of the Boston families produced leaders for more than a century, only about a third (32 percent) of the Philadelphia families did so. The difference in two-century families is, of course, partly due to the fact that Boston was founded a half century before Philadelphia; when I took this factor into account, however, the time span of family leadership in Boston was still superior.

If the Bostonians procreated more successfully than the Philadelphians, they also produced a greater proportion of exceptional men. As Table A–6 shows, whereas seven of the Boston families had more than 1,000 lines devoted to the biographies of their members, no Philadelphia family could claim this distinction. The Adamses alone had more lines written about them (4,935) than the six leading Philadelphia families put together (4,669 lines). Even more astonishing evidence is contained in Table A–7, which shows that no Philadelphia First Family in the history of the city produced a man with 400 lines or more though thirteen men from the Boston group of families had over 500 lines each. Never has the "antileadership vaccine" proved more effective in America than in the Quaker City of Brotherly Love.

It is one of my central themes that the antileadership vaccine, at all times and places in American history, as Richard Hofstadter pointed out, has been closely allied with anti-intellectualism. Here lies the great difference between the Puritan and Quaker ethics. As Table A–8 shows, the Boston sample was far more likely to be college educated than the Philadelphia group (81 percent versus 54 percent). Of perhaps more importance, especially as a factor in the creation of class cohesion, 95 percent of the Bostonians educated in the United States went to Harvard* and all of those educated in America to either Har-

---

*Down through the years, one's place in Boston has been defined by one's class at the "Family Seminary," as the Adamses called it. A distinguished newcomer to Boston was once being considered for the presidency of a local bank: "What was his class?" casually asked a board member in the course of the discussion. "He has no class," another replied, "he went to Yale."

vard, Yale, Bowdoin, or Dartmouth, all in New England. (One should also add, as a force for social cohesion, the six who went to Cambridge, the British "nursery of New England Puritanism.")

Not only were Philadelphians far less likely to have gone to college, but pride in their local university, and the class cohesion that might have resulted therefrom, was nowhere near so great as in Boston. A plurality (27 percent) but by no means a majority of Proper Philadelphians attended the University of Pennsylvania. The fact that so many (19 percent) went off to Princeton, Harvard, or Yale, as well as to a variety of other colleges, was a reflection of the more atomized nature of the upper class in the city, in turn a reflection of the religious heterogeneity characteristic of Philadelphia from the very beginning. By and large, in the colonial period and in the early days of the Republic, where one went to college (and whether one went at all) depended on the religious traditions of one's family. In Philadelphia, Quakers tended not to go to college, Episcopalians went to the local university, and those of Calvinist or New England origins attended Princeton, Harvard, or Yale. That education was related to preeminence is illustrated in the case of Philadelphia in Table A-9, which shows that Philadelphians who went to Princeton, Harvard, or Yale were the most distinguished (64 percent with 100 or more *DAB* lines), those who did not go to college at all were the least distinguished (69 percent with under 100 lines), and those who attended the University of Pennsylvania were in between (59 percent with under 100 lines). I shall have much more to say on education in Chapters 9, 14, and 17, especially on Boston's pride in Harvard and Philadelphia's lack of pride in and often disdain toward the local University of Pennsylvania.

The members of the fifty families in Boston and Philadelphia were leaders in their city's business and professional communities. Although Table A-3 lists each individual's occupation, the attempt to summarize the sample by occupation proved rather meaningless because men of this level of distinction, particularly those in Boston, commonly engaged in a variety of pursuits. Men of letters, for instance, often trained as lawyers or clergymen, were at the same time educators or statesmen. Philadelphia's Benjamin Rush was a doctor as well as a prominent statesman and social reformer.

If the statistical evidence is overwhelmingly convincing, a reading of all the biographies of the 188 Bostonians and the 146 Philadelphians included in the sample gives an even stronger subjective impression of the differences between the two groups, one anxiously driven to fame and accomplishment, the other far more relaxed and satisfied with moderate success. One reads, for example, of no Philadelphian whose drive for excellence matched that of George Ticknor. His ample fortune would have allowed him a comfortable life in the law and an early retirement, in the style of so many Philadelphians of comparable inherited wealth. Instead he had visions of a more useful and interesting life. After graduation from college and admission to the bar, he went to Europe in order to study at one of the famed German universities. He set sail in 1815, along with his friend Edward Everett, who had just graduated from Harvard and been allowed two years of study in Europe at full salary in order to prepare himself for Harvard's first chair in Greek, recently endowed by the rich merchant Samuel Eliot. At Göttingen, young Ticknor set himself a rigorous schedule.

> He rose at five, studied Greek until seven-thirty on three days of the week, and until eight-thirty on the other three. At eight on the first three days, he did an hour's German with a teacher. At nine every day there was a lecture on the Gospels. Then a fifteen minute walk home, and German until twelve. After dinner he took a half-hour nap, and then a cup of coffee, and at one-thirty began to read Blumenbach's *Manuel*, in preparation for that professor's three o'clock lecture. Then he took a walk with Everett, and at five read Greek with a teacher. From six to seven he fenced, to take care of his health. And in the evening he read German until ten and went to bed.[3]

This earnest and productive young scholar nevertheless managed to make many friends in his four years abroad, among them Lord Byron, who never suffered scholarly bores kindly. He also met such famous members of European aristocratic, scientific, and literary circles as von Humboldt, Chateaubriand, Humphry Davy, Mme. de Staël, Goethe, Scott, Wordsworth, and Southey. Upon his return to Boston, he married Samuel Eliot's daughter Anna and became a professor at Harvard.

George and Anna Ticknor eventually bought a house on fashionable Park Street, where they held court for many years to fashionable and literary Boston. At the same time Ticknor led a busy life as a Harvard professor, a prominent man of letters in Boston with a reputation and a wide circle of friends abroad, and a local civic reformer: "He was the first to acquire in the universities of Germany the scientific method of humane learning; the first to open to American readers the books of the great cosmopolitan poets and prose-writers —Dante, Montaigne, Goethe, Cervantes, and Molière; the first to prove to the countrymen of these that a stranger from the wild lands over the sea might be a gentleman and a scholar, the peer of their ripest and best."[4]

Drawing on his experiences abroad, Ticknor introduced the concept of the university to America, which awaited the founding of Johns Hopkins and the age of Eliot at Harvard before being implemented. Finally, he founded and worked tirelessly for the Boston Public Library, which thanks to his inspiration, became the largest free circulating library in the world by the turn of the century.

Ticknor also did all the things in Boston that were expected of a man of his position. He was a trustee of the Athenaeum (whose books he wanted to use as the foundation of the public library, against fierce majority opposition) and gave of his time and money to many of the benevolent institutions founded in Boston between 1810 and 1840 by members of his class. He likewise helped out needy young men of talent such as Jared Sparks and Bernard Berenson.

He died in 1871, the year Godkin wrote, perhaps having Ticknor in mind, that Boston was "the one place in America where wealth and the knowledge of how to use it are apt to coincide."[5] And Hawthorne, too, appreciated Ticknor's use of his wealth.

He has a fine house, at the corner of Park and Beacon Streets, perhaps the very best position in Boston. . . . Mr. Ticknor has a great head, and his hair is gray or grayish. You recognized him at once as a man who knows the world, the scholar too, which probably is his more distinctive character, though a little more under the surface. . . . Methinks he must have spent a happy life (as happiness goes among mortals) writing his great three-volumed book . . . not for bread, nor with any uneasy desire for fame, but only with a purpose to achieve something true and enduring.[6]

Happiness, deriving from a sense of achievement and of having done one's duty in exercising authority in community affairs, characterized the biographies of many men in the Boston sample. Although liberal in religion, the nine-teenth-century Boston Brahmin was of an essentially conservative habit of mind. At heart a Federalist all his life, Ticknor held values that were far more similar to those of John Winthrop than is often supposed. And although the pursuit of happiness did not rank high in the hierarchy of Puritan values, the biographies of men like Ticknor and Winthrop give the impression that the happiness of pursuit was far closer to the reality of things than the pursuit of happiness.

In Philadelphia, however, one has the impression from the *DAB* biographies that the city's leading men led lonely lives, often neither supported nor admired by their peers. Owen Wister, one of the more gifted men in the sample, once re-marked on this contrast: "When in Boston any fellow-citizen paints a picture or writes a book, he is approached and fostered for Boston's sake and in Boston's name. We of Philadelphia steer quite wide of this amiable if hasty encourage-ment. We seem to distrust our own power to do anything out of the common; and when a young man tries to, our minds close against him with a civic in-stinct of disparagement. A Boston failure in art surprises Boston; it is success that surprises Philadelphia."[7]

Wister was speaking of a deeply rooted tradition in Philadelphia. As we shall see in Chapter 10, most of the birthright Friends who took the lead in Philadel-phia's Golden Age in the eighteenth century were read out of meeting. This Quaker policy of disownment eventually became a Proper Philadelphia habit, highly visible in the class habit of disparaging exceptional achievement. Ben-jamin Rush was certainly the most distinguished Philadelphian of his or any other time, both in medicine and in civic leadership. One of his close friends since the days of the Revolution and the founding of the republic was Boston's John Adams. Though far apart on many civic and political issues, they were both spurred on by a love of fame. Adams and Rush regularly corresponded be-tween 1805 and Rush's unexpected death in 1813. Rush often envied his Bos-ton friend's roots in the upper-class community of New England. In the last year of his life he wrote of his loneliness in Philadelphia.

February 8, 1813

My Dear Sir,

. . . You do me great injustice in supposing I possess a single Pennsylvania or anti-New England prejudice. I know my native state too well. It is a great exchange filled with men of all nations who feel no attachments to each other from the ties of birth, education, and religion, and who from that circumstance are incapable of a *state* character. . . . Had it not been for what are called newcomers and strangers I could not have retained my standing in Philadelphia. With a few exceptions, they have been my most steady personal and professional friends. . . . There have been times when I have been ready to say of my native state what Dr. Swift said of Ireland, "I am not of this vile country." . . . But these times have been transient in their duration, and the hectic produced by them has soon passed away. . . .

Benjamin Rush[8]

The great Philadelphia Museum of Art is a monument to the civic leadership of Eli Kirk Price, an eighth-generation Philadelphian and a lawyer whose family represented the very core of the city's Quaker-turned-Episcopal gentry. Price's Quaker grandfather of the same name (see Table A–3) had been an extremely successful lawyer and the main force in originally putting together Fairmount Park; his great-grandfather had been a founder and the first principal of the famous Friends boarding school at Westtown, in Chester County (see Chapter 20). Eli Kirk Price acknowledged the difficulty of getting things done in Philadelphia and the lack of class cooperation in leadership when shortly before his death he said to a friend, "Every inch of this Park has been made a reason for unreasoning opposition at one time or another. Every stone in that Museum was placed there against someone's opposition. . . . It would be absurd for me to delay the work that still has to be done to placate the very people who will presently boast of the whole thing."[9]

Leaders live lonely lives in even the best of circumstances. What Rush, Price, and Wister, each in his own generation, were referring to was not only an unusual lack of drive toward leadership and accomplishment in their city but also a deeply ingrained class tradition that inhibited those who tried to do anything out of the ordinary. This attitude was almost exactly contrary to the tremendous Puritan emphasis on "calling" and the civic duties demanded of the "elect," which motivated men like Ticknor in Boston. To a Bostonian, being an aristocrat was not enough. As A. Lawrence Lowell once said of his brother, Guy, a successful architect: "What matters is not what he was but what he did."[10]

If George Ticknor provides a good example of the *doing* tradition of Puritanism, the *being* tradition of Quakerism is nicely illustrated in the Fisher family of Philadelphia. If Ticknor was concerned with the responsible use of wealth, Sidney George Fisher, a very proper, Quaker-turned-Episcopal Philadelphian, was interested not in doing his aristocratic duty but in being an aristocrat and enjoying the privileges thereof. After graduating from Dickinson College in 1827, he read law under Joseph R. Ingersoll and practiced at the Philadelphia bar for a brief period. Considering business, even a profession, beneath the dignity of a gentleman, he soon left the law to take up farming on an estate in Maryland that he had inherited from his mother. Visualizing himself as a scholar-farmer, Fisher wrote three books and many articles for the *North American Review*, some for Godkin's new *Nation*, and also for local newspapers. Unfortunately, his farming venture was not a financial success; Fisher ran through his inheritance and eventually was forced to live on the charity of his relatives. On October 3, 1857, he wrote in his diary: "I inherited the fortune and position for which others strive. What I had, because it was habitual, I did not value, and therefore instead of making exertions to increase it, I forgot that any exertion was necessary to maintain and keep it. I became self-indulgent, and my tastes and mental bias leading me to thought rather than action, thought instead of action became a habit."[11]

The Fishers had come to Philadelphia along with William Penn in 1682 and produced a long line of moneymaking Quaker merchants. What bothered Sidney Fisher was that his inheritance was not large enough. A first cousin, Joshua Francis Fisher, was far more fortunate financially. Yet he seems to have been pretty much of the same mold. After graduation from Harvard, he also read law under Joseph R. Ingersoll. "Having ample income," as his *DAB* biographer put it, "he never practiced his profession." But his position in Society was secure and respected. Whereas Sidney married an Ingersoll and produced only one child, Sydney George Fisher, Joshua Fisher married a Middleton of South Carolina, the sister of a Porcellian clubmate at Harvard, and had six children, who in turn married, within the heart of the city's upper class, Coxes, Cadwaladers, and Whartons. Joshua wrote numerous political essays and some long forgotten books. Perhaps his most lasting achievement was to found the Pennsylvania Institute for the Instruction of the Blind, on whose board he served for forty years.

Joshua Francis Fisher's *DAB* biography is brief and not very informative (ninety-seven lines); that of Sidney George Fisher, written in a careless style, damning him when not dismissing him with faint praise,* proved to be one of the three shortest in the sample (forty-two lines). But its author had not uncovered Sidney's intimate diary, kept between 1834 and his death in 1871, which today is far and away the best source for an understanding of the Proper Philadelphia mind. Excerpts from the diary were published in twenty-four issues of the *Pennsylvania Magazine of History and Biography.* "Nothing hitherto published in the *Magazine* attracted more comment," wrote Nicholas Biddle Wainwright in his introduction to the diary's publication in book form in 1967: "Readers were both repelled and fascinated by Fisher's candid exposition of his views."[12] Readers were probably repelled not only by Sidney's frank dissection of his own failure but also by his repeated comments on the essential mediocrity of the successful men of his class in Philadelphia, whose "money-mongering values" led even some of the better of them, like Philadelphia's most famous banker, Nicholas Biddle, to failure: "Tho he did not deserve to be called a *great* man," Sidney confided to his diary after Biddle's death in 1844,

---

*The Philadelphia "instinct of disparagement" is evident in many of the *DAB* biographies of Philadelphians. Apparently, scholars from outside the city had picked up the local habit. All the Boston biographies, as Owen Wister might have predicted, were positive when not downright laudatory, besides being accurate and complete.

yet he had more of the elements of greatness and the qualities allied to genius than any other prominent man in this city. . . . His life was active and fruitful, always seeking and achieving results. But money mongering, financiering, was not his true and congenial sphere. . . . As an author, a statesman, or even a lawyer, his talents would have found more congenial employment and his course, the less brilliant perhaps, would have led to better fortunes and a purer and more durable fame.[13]

Sidney Fisher knew that he and Biddle had been born into a class with little sense of history, wedded to momentary success rather than lasting accomplishment and fame. But he secretly admired Biddle's preference for a life of action rather than retirement to his stately estate on the Delaware, in the style of Proper Philadelphia. (Nicholas Biddle will be treated in more detail in Chapter 13.) In his judicious life of Biddle, Thomas Payne Govan, himself no Philadelphian, aptly expressed the real values of Proper Philadelphia in summing up the attitude of Biddle's heiress wife, Jane, toward her husband's career:

She had never wanted him to be a great man, distracted from his family by the affairs of the world, but had thought that he should follow the example of her brothers, who, having inherited enough money to have pleasant homes, fine horses, and all the pleasures of life, did nothing but manage their estates, entertain themselves and their friends, and travel.[14]

It is little wonder that Nathaniel Burt, the Cleveland Amory of Proper Philadelphia and a keen student of the Fisher diary, should have entitled one section of his book *The Perennial Philadelphians* "Born Retired." Burt concluded his discussion of the Biddles, who he reluctantly admitted were the city's foremost family, as follows: "It is probably just this distinction, mild as it is by comparison with the first families of other places, that tells against the Biddles in Philadelphia itself."[15]

These brief comments on the lives of George Ticknor and Sidney George Fisher are enough to suggest the contrasting attitudes toward leadership and accomplishment in Boston's and Philadelphia's upper classes. As the family is the main bearer of cultural traditions, especially at the upper-class level, let us now examine the subtle differences between the clan cultures of the two upper classes.

THE CLAN CULTURES OF BRAHMIN BOSTON AND PROPER PHILADELPHIA

The preeminent families of both Boston and Philadelphia traditionally refer to themselves as clans. In our increasingly atomized society, where even the nuclear family is being questioned, what they mean can be best understood if we view their familial values as not too different from those of the Italian-American family portrayed in *The Godfather*. The tremendous popularity of the two films based on Puzo's novel may suggest that the restless and divorcing members of the Protestant middle and upper classes in American have a nostalgic appreciation of the lost traditions of their ancestors. In *none* of the 334 biographies in the Boston and Philadelphia samples, incidentally, was there recorded a single divorce.

The clan is a historical as well as a biological unit. It is also the bearer of cultural and familial values. As the Puritan ethic was infinitely historical, whereas the Quaker ethic was definitely not, one would expect the clan idea to have more force in Boston than in Philadelphia. "Philadelphia," rightly noted Amory, "asks about a man's parents; Boston wants to know about his grandparents."[16] I should add that what counts in Philadelphia is largely the wealth of one's parents; in Boston the undoubted importance of wealth is balanced by pride in ancestral achievements. This is in accord with what we found statistically, that the Bostonians not only were men of greater distinction but also came from families with longer traditions of leadership. The fifty Boston families were of English stock with the exception of the Agassizes from Switzerland, the Wendells from Holland, the Forbeses from Scotland, and the Jacksons from Ireland. Though English stock predominated in Philadelphia, the Lloyds, Cadwaladers, and Robertses were originally from Wales; the Wistars and Peppers, from Germany; the Bories and Markoes, from France; the Duanes, Careys, and Meades, from Ireland; and the city's most famous modern banking family, the Drexels, was founded by an itinerant portrait painter from Austria. Almost all of the fifty Boston families were Puritan Congregationalists in the seventeenth and eighteenth centuries. The largest number of Philadelphia families were originally Quakers; some were Anglicans from the very beginning; and others, like the Ingersolls and Meigses, were originally Congregationalists from New England who became Presbyterians after settling in Philadelphia.* This difference can be explained partly by the fact that whereas nearly all the Boston families originated in Massachusetts (mostly in the seventeenth century), many of the Philadelphia families came from other colonies in the course of the eighteenth century. (The reasons for the contrast in settlement patterns will become clear in later chapters.)

Upper-class endogamy has been extremely strong in both Boston and Philadelphia from the outset. As we shall see, Lloyds, Logans, Norrises, Morrises, Pembertons, Fishers, Cadwaladers, and Biddles were all intermarried in eighteenth-century Philadelphia, and the pattern has continued down to the present. In Boston, the rate of interclan marriage was even higher, especially among the Essex County families who came to that city in the eighteenth century. Joseph Cabot, for instance, married Elizabeth Cabot and built a great house in Salem in 1748. From their eleven children descended many of the Cabots, Lees, Jacksons, Winthrops, Lodges, Lowells, and Holmeses of Boston. Bishop Lawrence's daughter Marian described the marrying habits of late nineteenth-century Brahmin Boston in her memoirs: "Harold Peabody's name kept coming up

---

*It should be emphasized that old families as a whole in Philadelphia are far more likely to have Quaker ancestors than is the case with our Fifty Family sample. Quakerism has tended to breed far more men like George Apley than like John Adams.

in my diary more and more frequently. . . . He and I had worked together at Sailors' Haven and on other projects, and we had come to know and admire each other very much."[17] She then quoted from her Christmas Day, 1905, entry.

> Grandpa Peabody had five children, Jack, Cotty, Frank, Martha and George. Jack, Frank and Martha all married Lawrences, and Cotty married his first cousin, Fanny Peabody. George was the only one who married out of the family, but his marriage did not last long. When the second generation began to marry, Marian married her first cousin, Jim Lawrence, and so we were the fifth such combination without any break, and what then was the use of fighting fate?[18]

The extreme clan consciousness of the Boston Brahmins is reflected in their institutions. Part of the reason for the excellence and completeness of the Bostonians' *DAB* biographies as compared to those of the Philadelphians, for instance, is that the first and best supported local historical and genealogical societies in America were founded in Boston. The Massachusetts Historical Society was established in 1791, over a quarter of a century earlier than the Pennsylvania Historical Society (1824). Furthermore, being a member or an officer of the Boston society carries far more social prestige than does membership in the Philadelphia society. Thus, James Winthrop was a founder, Robert C. Winthrop was president for thirty years, and the membership included a Winthrop every year from 1791 to 1940, the close of our period. The New England Historic Genealogical Society, founded in 1845, not only was the first in America but also is by far the most thorough in its research, according to no less an authority than British Royal Genealogist Anthony Richard Wagner, who wrote that "few problems of genealogy anywhere have had closer and more extensive study than those of the New England settlers' origins."[19] Surely, pride in family, clan, and class in Boston is very much in the Old Testament tradition of Calvinism, with its emphasis on the duties of God's elect, chosen to rule as ministers and magistrates over the whole community.

One learns a great deal about the values of any culture through its myths and folklore. The myth that "when a Biddle gets drunk he thinks he is a Cadwalader" is firmly rooted in the folklore of Proper Philadelphia. Similarly, in Boston, everybody knows that "the Lowells talk only to Cabots, and the Cabots talk only to God." Whereas the Biddle-Cadwalader tale suggests the convivial snobbery of a friendly and tolerant class, its Cabot-Lowell counterpart reflects the more serious (and humorless) hierarchical aspirations of a far more authoritarian class. Both myths, incidentally, place their more stolid (Cabot-Cadwalader) clans on a higher plane than the creative ones (Lowell-Biddle).

Just when the Puritan-Federalist bred authority of Boston's Brahmins was beginning to wane in 1878, Boston's best founded the notorious Watch and Ward Society. Though strongly backed by local Catholic potentates, the society has been dominated ever since its founding by Brahmin leaders, from the First Family preacher and Episcopal Bishop Phillips Brooks down to Bishop Lawrence and Endicott Peabody of Groton. As late as 1940, its patron saint and main source of financial support was Godfrey Lowell Cabot, the richest man in the city. What else would one expect from the patriarch of a clan whose members speak only to each other and to God? One cannot imagine a Biddle or a Cadwalader bothering about the purity of the reading habits of his fellow citizens.

PATTERNS OF HISTORICAL DEVELOPMENT
AND GENERATIONAL APPROPRIATENESS

Philosophers, it has often been observed, know very little about what is very important; scientists, a great deal about what is far less worth knowing. I doubt whether history will ever become a science. Its writing, as Justice Holmes once said of life, is more like painting a picture than doing a sum. Even though the reasons for the rise and fall of cultures and civilizations, in spite of men like Gibbon and Toynbee, have largely remained a mystery, perhaps some light will be shed on this fascinating problem in my attempt to explain why Boston has produced a far greater number of eminent men than has Philadelphia. Of equal interest is the very different historical development of the two cultures.

In Tables A-10 and A-11, the First Family leaders in each city are arranged according to decade of birth. The majority of leaders in Philadelphia were born in the eighteenth century; a majority of the Bostonians, in the nineteenth. The important question here is why Philadelphia went through its Golden Age during the second half century of its history, whereas Boston did not experience its greatest creative period until the age of Hawthorne and Emerson (fourteen men with a total of 4,994 lines in the *DAB* were born between 1800 and 1809), or more than two centuries after its founding. There is no final explanation for this very real difference in development. Perhaps a clue to it lies in the very different roles played by religious and class authority in the two cities. From its founding, as I have suggested, the Puritan culture of New England produced an extremely authoritative upper class that provided leadership in a whole homogeneous society for over two centuries. This class was composed first of ministers and magistrates and next of ministers, magistrates, and merchants. As the wealthy merchants came to the fore and authoritative Calvinism began to be replaced by Unitarianism in the early years of the nineteenth century, the Federalists, liberal in religion but firm believers in class authority in both society and politics, still dominated the state government (and Harvard College) until they were defeated by the Republicans in 1823.*

Over these centuries, then, class authority was the central cultural theme; members of the upper class were chosen by the people to lead them year after year in church and state and to provide models for the aspiring lower classes. Not only did this class possess the confidence born of the Calvinist theory of election, but Calvinism also produced a strong sense of anxiety and sin, which

---

*Williams and Bowdoin were founded at that time in order to combat the religious liberalism of Harvard and the Boston establishment. Harvard lost an annual grant of $10,000 from the state and was thereafter privately supported by the Boston ruling class.

drove generations of men like the Winthrops and the Mathers to take the lead in community building, education, and government. In Philadelphia, however, a series of atomized members of the elite, often auslanders like Franklin, tended to take the lead while all too many members of the upper class were satisifed to sit back and rest on their privileges, often in the name of preserving their perfectionist virtues.

This point has been made earlier and will be repeated again and again as my argument develops in later chapters. But what has class authority got to do with creativity? This is not an easy question to answer, especially in such an anti-authoritarian age as our own. As with understanding so much else in American history, the Adamses offer a clue.

An authoritative upper class must be composed of a group of consanguine families whose members take the lead over several generations: "One generation passeth away, and another generation cometh, that earth [we might substitute "class"] abideth forever," as Ecclesiastes put it. "To every thing there is a season . . . a time to break down, and a time to build up . . . a time to keep silence and a time to speak . . . a time for war, and a time for peace." John Adams, thoroughly steeped in the Old Testament and in the history of classical Greece and Rome, stated the theme of generational appropriateness in the building of both the Adams dynasty and the American nation better than anyone else.

> I must study politics and war that my sons may have liberty to study math and philosophy. My sons ought to study math and philosophy, geography, natural history and naval architecture, navigation, commerce and agriculture, in order to give their children a right to study painting, poetry, music, architecture, statuary, tapestry and porcelain.[20]

As a test case of the accuracy of John Adams's timetable it is interesting that his grandson Charles Francis Adams I lived through Boston's greatest creative age. Born the same year as Longfellow (1807), he was almost an exact contemporary of Emerson (1803), Hawthorne (1804), and the elder Holmes (1809).

But it is John Adams's great-grandson Charles Francis Adams II who provides the most useful insights into our problem, although he came to conclusions opposite to those that John Adams would have reached or that I offer here. In 1893, this fourth generation Adams gave four lectures to Professor Edward Channing's history class at Harvard, which he later published as a book entitled *Massachusetts, Its Historians and Its History: An Object Lesson*. The argument Adams presented to Channing's class centered around his disagreement with the conventional wisdom of Massachusetts historians of his day, who had said that the glacial age of theological intolerance had in the long run made possible the survival of an ordered community in New England (and, I should add, the creativity of their descendants). Briefly, Adams argued that

> the theologico-glacial period of Massachusetts may be considered as lasting from the meeting of the Cambridge Synod in September, 1637, to the agitation over the Writs of Assistance in February, 1761, culminating in what is known as "the Great Awakening" of 1740-45. . . . In Massachusetts, of writers or thinkers

whose names are still remembered, though their works have passed into oblivion, Cotton Mather and Jonathan Edwards can alone be named. They were indeed typical of the time,—strange products of a period at once provincial and glacial,—huge literary boulders deposited by the receding ice.[21]

Adams then criticized his opponents' interpretation of the positive function served by this glacial age.

Yet, strange to say, there is even now a generally accepted belief that, somehow or in some way, this degrading parody of religion, this burlesque of philosophy,— this system worse than that of Dotheboy's Hall, which, if in practice upon children today, would be indicted by any intelligent commission of lunacy,—the belief, I say, prevails that this system in its day subjected the people of Massachusetts to a most useful, though severe discipline, the good results of which their descendants enjoy, though they themselves have fallen away from the strict faith. Nor is this merely a popular belief; it silently pervades the pages of the historian and the moralist. It is needless to say that for any such belief no ground is disclosed by a closer historical research. . . . It is, indeed, one of the curious phenomena of man's mental make-up, this implicitly accepted belief that a religious practice or creed which has now become abhorrent, and is recognized as morbid, should have once produced most beneficent results; while, on the other hand, it is equally recognized that some Sangrado method of medical treatment, known to be bad now, was equally bad then. The simple fact is that the Calvinistic, orthodox tenets of the seventeenth and eighteenth centuries constituted nothing more nor less than an outrage on human nature productive in all probability of no beneficial results whatever.[22]

How modern Adams sounds. But of course he was more than a generation away from his Federalist ancestors, who were still guided by a secularized version of the Puritan values of class authority and even some of the intolerance that went with it. In other words, except in religion, the habits of mind and action of John Adams and even of his son John Quincy, were probably far closer to those of Mather and Edwards than they were to the Adamses of the fourth generation. For in between them came the creative and increasingly individualistic generation of Emerson and the first Charles Francis Adams.

This was the generation in which Tocqueville observed how the values of class and community were rapidly retreating before the rising tide of a mobile and leveling individualism and a possible new tyranny of manufacturers. It was a generation of increasing affluence, when immigration was ending the homogeneity of New England and creating the urban problems of poverty and crime, which continue to plague us. It was the age in which Wendell Phillips, of an old Puritan line, was challenging the ancient authority of slavery. And it was the time in the life of the mind of New England when Channing was preaching the optimistic doctrines of Unitarianism and when Emerson and Margaret Fuller were inventing a doctrine of Inner Light perfectibility, which one of their orthodox opponents labeled "transcendental"; it was the time of the *Dial* and Brook Farm, when cultivated ladies and gentlemen went out to Brookline in search of a new Sabine simplicity, dressed in blue linen smocks in the style of the French peasantry; it was the time when Hawthorne's brother-in-law, Horace Mann, was revolutionizing America's ideas about public education; and it was the period when all of them (except Hawthorne if he could avoid it) were forever talking, talking, talking at Elizabeth Peabody's bookshop on West Street. It was Peabody's soulmate and dear friend Emerson who set the new tone of the day: "The office of America is to liberate, to abolish kingcraft, priestcraft, caste, monopoly, to pull down the gallows, to burn up the bloody statute-book, to take in the immigrant, to open the doors of the sea and the fields of the earth."[23] It was indeed a wonderful time to break down, a time to speak out, and eventually a time to make a bloody civil war—and all of this in spite of the fact that when Tocqueville asked him whether the leveling principle might not eventually lead to a "tyranny of the majority," Channing replied: "I cannot believe that civil society is made to be guided by the always comparatively ignorant masses; I think we go too far."[24] It is perhaps the law of generational dialectics that those who inherit the habits of authority of their ancestors often sow the intellectual seeds of their destruction, which, in turn, grow up to be the conventional wisdom of their anti-authoritarian descendants.

What I am suggesting is that the most creative periods of history tend to come either right after or during the breakdown of long established systems of authority, when the individual is still submerged in the conventional values of church, class, or community. Thus, Machiavelli wrote at the turn of the fifteenth into the sixteenth century and Shakespeare almost exactly a century later, when both of them were watching their own worlds making the transition from the authority of the Christian synthesis to the discordant modern age of "mere oppugnosity." They both looked back with nostalgia to a past in which, as Shakespeare wrote, "degree . . . which is the ladder of all high designs" was still meaningful to men. Nor would Hawthorne have created his classic, *The Scarlet Letter*, without having a nostalgic empathy for the Salem of his authoritarian ancestors, one of whom presided as judge at the witchcraft trials. He surely showed a more penetrating view of his own relationship with Puritanism than did Adams.

> Doubtless, however, either of these stern and black-browed Puritans would have thought it quite a sufficient retribution for his sins, that, after so long a lapse of years, the old trunk of the family tree . . . should have borne, as its topmost bow, an idler like myself. No aim, that I have ever cherished, would they recognize as laudable; no success of mine—if my life, beyond its domestic scope, had ever been brightened by success—would they deem otherwise than worthless, if not positively disgraceful. 'What is he?' murmurs one gray shadow of my forefathers to the other. 'A writer of storybooks! What kind of a business in life,—what mode of glorifying God, or being serviceable to mankind in his day and generation,— may that be? Why the degenerate fellow might as well have been a fiddler!' . . . And yet, let them scorn me as they will, strong traits of their nature have intertwined themselves with mine.[25]

The intolerant Puritans of the glacial age were to haunt and stimulate the minds of their descendants for many generations after Hawthorne's. Thus, T. S. Eliot was always aware of how deeply he and Henry James were indebted to Hawthorne. He was also aware of his family roots in the glacial age, his first American ancestor, Andrew Eliott, having sat as a juror at the witch trials presided over by Judge Hawthorne. As an undergraduate, he voiced his views on the inspirational value of his Puritan roots, as well as on the importance of generational appropriateness in an article for the *Harvard Advocate*: "Those of us who can claim any New England ancestors may congratulate ourselves that we are their descendants, and at the same time rejoice that we are not their contemporaries."[26] And Victorian Boston's favorite divine, Phillips Brooks, spoke of his debt to his very great-great-greatgrandfather, John Cotton, in the style of Eliot rather than in that of his contemporary and cousin Charles Francis Adams II. "I thank him," Brooks said of Cotton, "I thank him, as a Church of England man, as a man loving the Episcopal Church with all my heart, I thank him for being a Puritan."[27] Brooks and Hawthorne and Eliot and the Massachusetts historians knew that there is a time for everything under the sun.

To argue with Adams's lectures at Harvard and the brilliant little book that resulted is much like the eternal debate over whether an authoritarian or a permissive childhood is more conducive to leadership and creativity. In this connection, it is interesting that the most prominent Philadelphian of his day, Benjamin Rush, was educated by a Scotch-Irish Calvinist clergyman, Samuel Finney, who, though courteous and kind himself, had his school of scholars, according to tradition, birched every Monday morning on general principles of discipline. (Finney later became president of the College of New Jersey, which in the eighteenth century was the preeminent school for leadership both in the colonies as a whole and in Philadelphia.) At any rate, a comparison of Boston's renaissance in the age of Hawthorne and Emerson with Philadelphia's in the age of Franklin should prove far more fruitful in the long run than any rational argument from either my own position or Adams's.

Before I turn to Franklin's Philadelphia, a brief look at how Adams explained the differences between Massachusetts and Rhode Island is in order. For Adams had to face the fact that the defenders of intolerance in Massachusetts had always pointed to Rhode Island as an example of how tolerance produces chaos. "So far as religious tolerance and intellectual activity were concerned," he wrote, "they had always before their eyes an object lesson of the most unfortunate character in the neighboring colony of Rhode Island,—an object lesson which was made to do active service with the Massachusetts theologians then, as it has with the Massachusetts historians since."[28]

> It does not need to be said that anything taken in excess acts as a poison. . . . The born agitator, the controversialist, the generally "otherwise-minded,"—every type of thinker, whether crude and half-crazy like Samuel Gorton, or only advanced like Roger Williams, there found refuge. Thus what was a good and most necessary element in the economy of nature and the process of human development, was in excess in Rhode Island; and the natural result followed,—a disordered community."[29]

But perhaps the Christian concept of sin means, among other things, that all men tend to pervert virtues into vices. If the vice of Massachusetts Bay was indeed fanatic intolerance, the vice of Pennsylvania, like Rhode Island, was excessive tolerance. As we shall see in Chapter 8, Pennsylvania, much like Rhode

Island, went through a period of amiable anarchy during the half century following its founding. At the same time, it was from the beginning a huge economic success. Especially after 1740, it was the most rapidly growing and affluent of all the colonies. In striking contrast to the more static and less affluent colony on Massachusetts Bay, the Quaker City inadvertently developed into a highly mobile and heterogeneous plutocratic democracy. Though the rich merchants surely reigned, they hardly ruled in the style of the authoritative Puritans, largely as a result of Quaker influence. But moneyed men have always been tolerant of others. Why assert one's authority when privileges and comfort can be purchased so easily?

Why, then, did Philadelphia go through its Golden Age almost a century before Boston and without any previous glacial age? The answer will have to await a more detailed study of this period in Chapter 10. Here I should like to make two points. In the first place, the flowering of New England was the product of an aristocratic social structure led by men with deep roots in the governing class of the society, going back to the glacial age; Philadelphia's Golden Age, on the other hand, was the product of a heterogeneous and democratic social structure whose leadership elites came largely from elsewhere and from all classes within the city. In the second place, the form of expression of these two ages was very different: in Boston it was predominant in creative literature and history; in Philadelphia it was in science, especially botany and medicine.

It must be remembered that eighteenth-century Philadelphia was the largest, richest, and most centrally located city in the colonies. With its well-known, almost mythical, reputation for tolerance and affluence, no wonder it made an ideal field for careerists of prodigious talent and ambition. Franklin, after all, was the foremost careerist in our history. Philadelphia's central location in the colonies, moreover, made it the ideal gathering place for the great generation that founded a nation there in the last quarter of the century. But it is important to stress that very few of the eminent men who walked the streets of the city between 1740 and Franklin's death in 1790 were natives of either Pennsylvania or Philadelphia. In short, Philadelphia's Golden Age was produced by an *elite*; the flowering of New England was led largely by Boston's *upper class*.

Perhaps added insight may be gained if one sees that eighteenth-century Philadelphia played more or less the same role in colonial America that New York City played in the two decades following World War II. Both were the wealthiest cities of their age; both acted as hosts to talented elites though neither produced a coherent leadership class; both were extremely stimulating cities where men and women, regardless of class, religion, or national origin, came together in a permissive atmosphere in which money rather than authority set the tone; and both were marked by tendencies toward social and political anarchy. If Philadelphia was the city that brought the Enlightenment to America, one wonders whether historians will one day write that New York in the postwar era was the city in American where the ideas of the Enlightenment finally went wild.

It has often been said that Philadelphia is the city of *firsts*, Boston of *bests*, and New York of *latests*. In this connection, it is indeed fitting that Philadelphia's renaissance should have come first, and in science rather than literature. For in science being first is of utmost importance; in literature, on the contrary, no one would think of ranking Philadelphia's Charles Brockden Brown, America's first novelist, above, or even in the same class with Hawthorne or Hemingway, who came much later. The forms of expression of the two cultures have been appropriate to their social structures in other ways, too. Science is classless, anti-authoritarian, ahistorical, and universalistic, whereas the great literature in America has been written largely by men and women with deep and particularistic roots in class, community, and region. This crucial difference has persisted down to our own day: thus, a large proportion of the college-bred authors of America's twentieth-century renaissance in literature were products of Harvard, Yale, or Princeton; a large proportion of our doctorates in science have been graduates of more plebeian institutions such as Clark University in Worcester, Massachusetts.*

In summary, if democratic societies tend to be universalistic and inventive, aristocracies are particularistic and creative. Franklin was inventive and Hawthorne creative. Franklin, the parvenu genius, was a man of all times and seasons; Hawthorne, a man of genteel poverty and fierce class pride, was the particularistic product of Salem and his ancestors. Whereas Franklin was a tremendous success in his lifetime, Hawthorne, a man of consummate accomplishment, largely awaited the judgment of posterity. Franklin has always been the mythical model of our democracy; Hawthorne, the inspiration for a very few.

It is revealing that in his talk to Channing's class at Harvard, Adams used Jonathan Edwards's contemporary Benjamin Franklin as the classic example of an American who represented the liberating spirit of empirical science as against the stultifying authority of Puritanism. For if ever there was a one-man city in American history, it was Franklin's adopted home of Philadelphia. As we shall see, he started everything, from the first fire company in the world to the first hospital in America. A giant of a genius, in both fact and myth, he was also the exception that illustrates the rule. Thus, the only classic work of literature to be produced in Philadelphia's Golden Age was Franklin's autobiography, the *first* and the greatest manual of careerist Babbittry ever written.

---

*The following leading writers in the interwar years went to Harvard: T. S. Eliot, Conrad Aiken, Heywood Broun, Stuart Chase, Malcolm Cowley, e. e. cummings, John Dos Passos, S. Foster Damon, John Gould Fletcher, Walter Lippmann, Samuel Eliot Morison, Charles Nordhoff, Wallace Stevens, and John Hall Wheelock. At the same time, in science Harvard had a "productivity index of 18.4 while Clark University's index was 55.6 or one of the top five in the nation," according to R. H. Knapp and H. B. Goodrich, *Origins of American Scientists* (Chicago: University of Chicago Press, 1952), p. 80.

PART II

PURITAN AND QUAKER PATTERNS OF CULTURE AND THEIR EUROPEAN ROOTS

Reformation England:
From Brawling Lord to Sober Judge

The new philosophy calls all in doubt;
'Tis all in pieces, all coherence gone;
All just supply and all relation.
Prince, subject, father, son, are things forgot,
For every man alone thinks he has got
To be a Phoenix, and that he can be
None of that kind of which he is but he.

John Donne

The core of the Rebellion . . . are the universities.

Thomas Hobbes

Walk worthy of the calling wherewith ye are called.

Ephesians 4:20

The origins of the contrasting cultures of Puritan Boston and Quaker Philadelphia can be traced back through the whole of the Judeo-Christian tradition: the ancient roots of Puritanism are to be found in the Ten Commandments, the Epistles of Paul to the Romans, and the ideals of Saint Dominic, who sought to educate the wavering *minds* of the elites of his day; the Quaker ethic owes more to the Sermon on the Mount, the apocalyptical writings of John on the lonely island of Patmos, and the ideals of Saint Francis of Assisi, whose life touched the *hearts* of the humble, then and now. In this chapter, however, I limit myself to identifying the sources of these two ethics in the Reformation, especially in England.

THE CONTINENTAL REFORMATION

Just as our own century of surprises and disillusionments began in a mood of Victorian complacency and confidence, set by white, Western, Protestant males who had dominated the world since 1588, so the sixteenth century

opened in a mood of Catholic complacency and confidence, created by a sacramental church that had stood at the core of Western civilization since the decline of imperial Rome. This book, then, is grounded in the Protestant era of
Western history, which might be conveniently thought of as embracing the
four centuries between October 1517, when Luther went to Wittenberg, and
October 1917, when Lenin went to the Finland Station.

Every Man a Monk. Luther's revolt against the authority of Rome began in the
spirit of reform. He had no intention of founding a new church but was concerned mainly with purifying his own in the direction of a more personal faith
based on the Bible and the Word rather than on the sacred authority of a
priestly hierarchy in sole control of the sacraments. This new emphasis on *faith
alone* challenged the Catholic idea of *good works*, which had been responsible
for the corrupt system of indulgences, the granting of forgiveness to sinners (often the rich) for their good works (donations to the church).

Luther's crucial departure from Catholic tradition was his reinterpretation
of the Mass, which he changed to the Lord's Supper. The Catholic Mass, according to Luther, was far too magical a rite of sacrifice performed by a priestly
caste. He saw the Mass as a mystical experience, a commemoration and a
thanksgiving to God wherein the Lord's presence depended on the faith of the
lay participants and not solely on the proper performance of the rite by the
priest, who could "put a wafer in the mouth but not engender faith in the
heart." Closely allied with this first reform of the Mass was Luther's insistence
that all participants in the Lord's Supper could drink the wine. This idea of the
"chalice for the laity," the reading of the Bible and the saying of the liturgy in
the native language, and the singing of hymns formed the cornerstone of the
Reformation.

Related to his reformation of the sacraments was Luther's challenge to the
dual morality of the Catholic church, which resulted from his concept of the
"calling." According to Luther, not only priests (especially monks) but all men,
regardless of occupation or calling, were engaged in God's work on earth.
Thus, the Catholic monastery was replaced by the Protestant congregation of
true believers. The invisible church (all Christians of all callings) replaced the
visible, hierarchical church of pope, bishop, priest, and monk. In emphasizing
faith alone, the Bible, and the calling, Luther opened the door to the democratic ideal of a priesthood of all believers, an ideal that the radical reformation
took far more literally than did Luther himself.

The Monk as Martyr: Anabaptism. "There are movements in the history of all
religions," wrote James Joll in his study of anarchism, "which reject all authority, whether temporal or spiritual, and claim complete liberty to act in accordance with the Inner Light."[1] Though Luther set out to regenerate and reform
the Roman church, he was, perhaps unfortunately, a bit of a mystic, who "had
all the ingenious enthusiasm of the anarchist."[2] At any rate, because of his enthusiasm, Luther paved the way, inadvertently and to his own horror, for the
Anabaptist movement, which replaced the authority of the sacraments and

even the Bible with the mystical and extremely democratic, yet anarchistic, concept of the "spirit," or Inner Light.

In general, the various Anabaptist sects sought to return to primitive Christianity, taking the Sermon on the Mount as their literal code. They carried perfectionism and the admonitions of 2 Corinthians to their extreme in pacificism, in the denouncing of all adornment, reveling, and drinking, and in the practice of egalitarian communism within segregated holy communities. The emphasis on egalitarianism meant that everyone, men and women alike, became a minister. This development was particularly upsetting to Luther, who felt that woman's place was definitely in the home. The Anabaptists' most important contribution to the radical reformation, however, was their sweeping denunciation of the "world" and all established authority. The world was hopeless and would remain so until the promised Second Coming. From this perfectionist and apocalyptic point of view, the only hope for real Christians was to withdraw into a ghetto of saints made up exclusively of converted beings who had seen the Inner Light and were marked by re-baptism.

If the higher classes in Germany, especially the princes and many of the newly rich such as the Fuggers, were attracted to Lutheranism, the members of the lower and disinherited classes were drawn to Anabaptism. In that extremely religious age, it was inevitable that Anabaptism should become involved in the peasant revolts that broke out all over Germany in 1524–1525, within a decade of Luther's nailing his theses on the church door at Wittenberg. The uprisings were bloody but brief. Lacking leadership, they were soon suppressed by the secular authorities at the cost of over 50,000 lives, including "batches of Lutheran ministers" hanged by Catholic princes, and a great deal of physical destruction (70 cloisters were demolished in Thuringia; 270 castles and 52 cloisters, in Franconia).

As the radical reformation spread down the Rhine, in 1534 the town of Münster was seized by a group of Anabaptists under the fanatical leadership of Jan Beuckels of Leiden. Unlike the majority of Anabaptists, who were peaceful, the Münsterites made the Old Testament their model and took the town by force. They immediately destroyed all records of debts and contracts in order to show their contempt for private property, burned books and manuscripts that represented un-Christian worldliness, and instituted polygamy and communism in goods. Eventually Beuckel's rule turned into an insane, megalomaniac terror. Catholics and Lutherans jointly raised an army to retake the town; Jan of Leiden was captured and tortured to death, and his followers were routed or killed on the spot.

The combination of polygamy and violence horrified the established community, and in 1536 Luther signed a memorandum recommending the death penalty even for peaceful Anabaptists. Because of his fear of violence and anarchy, moreover, he was forced by the logic of events to a kind of schizophrenic conclusion: in the secular "sphere of sin" force is necessary in the name of the laws of the prince; the church, however, should be involved solely with the inner life of freedom, where love operates in the name of faith and grace. Luther himself boasted that he had established better than anyone else the divine right of civil authority. And Lutheranism, from his day to our own, tends to leave secular, and even ecclesiastical, authority to the state and limits the church to the role of preaching to the faithful, who are taught the rightness of absolute political authority and their duty to suffer in silence, piously acquiescing to the prince's authority. Both bishops and clergy were to be appointed by the state, for the territorial principle allowed the prince to decide which religious confession was to rule; dissenters, including Anabaptists, were to go elsewhere in the interests of uniformity and peace.*

It was one of the tragedies of German history that the sects were banished in the sixteenth century. "Here we can discover one clue among others to the spiritual cleavage between Germany and the "West," wrote Roland Bainton. "In Germany in the sixteenth century Anabaptism and related movements were thoroughly suppressed and never again raised their heads, whereas in England in the seventeenth century the spiritual descendants of the left-wing gained a permanent foothold and did even more than the established Church to fashion the temper of England and America."[3] Though the German Reformed (Calvinist) Church played an important political role in early nineteenth-century Pennsylvania, the Lutherans tended to avoid political office; Mennonites and Amish withdrew from the world almost entirely.

The Monk as Magistrate: John Calvin. If Martin Luther, many-minded monk, was the all-encompassing and contradictory genius of the Reformation, surely John Calvin, his devoted follower in the second generation, was a single-minded general whose systematic theology disciplined and inspired the officers who led the march of Christian soldiers from the Second Rome in Geneva, across northern Europe to Britain, and thence to North America.

Whereas Luther finally despaired of governing the world, the nation, or even the small group by Christian principles, both the Anabaptists and the Calvinists were more optimistic, if in different ways: both believed in a minority of saints. The Anabaptists despaired of the world but had faith in their ability to lead a strict Christian life within small and segregated communities (witness the Amish in Pennsylvania); the Calvinists, however, were optimistic about the possibility of Christianizing the world through the disciplined leadership of the "elect," or spiritual aristocrats. Accordingly, the Lutheran attitude toward the world was one of *resigned participation*; the Anabaptist, one of *withdrawal*, and the Calvinist, one of *activist conquest*, by the sword if necessary. The logic of Lutheranism bred a race of pious bourgeois; of Anabaptism, a band of suffering martyrs; and of Calvinism, an elite of heroes. Whereas Lutheranism eventually became culture-bound (state churches in Germany and Scandinavia and ethnic denominations in America), both the Anabaptists and the Calvinists remained transcultural and international: the Anabaptist spirit

---

*In accepting Caesaro-papism and territorialism, Luther, in contrast to the left-wing reformers, who saw real Christians as monks everywhere, was forced to limit the ideals of the monastery to the home and private life. It was in this tradition that we find Bismarck living by New Testament ideals in the domestic sphere and realpolitik in the state.

sought the fringes and frontiers of cultural authority; the Calvinists fought to Christianize the centers of civilization.

John Calvin was converted from Catholicism in 1534, the year of the Münster uprising. Though Luther's personal life, in all its contradictory details, has been the subject of extensive study by theologians, psychiatrists, and playwrights, little is known about why or how Calvin was converted. At any rate, he was the son of a local notary in Moyan, France, and eventually obtained a master of arts degree from the University of Paris and a doctor of laws at Orleans. Though he practiced law, Calvin was always more interested in language and culture; in the spirit of the humanists, he was fascinated with history and antiquity in particular. He remained all his life, however, a rigorously logical theologian.

Calvin took the Christian teachings of Luther, produced a systematic theology, and shaped a church, as Ernst Troeltsch put it, "with the doctrinaire logic which is peculiar to men of the second generation, due to their sense of possessing a secure inheritance."[4]

Calvin's first edition of the *Institutes of the Christian Religion*, often referred to as the Protestant *Summa*, appeared in 1536. In accord with the Protestant tradition, Calvin's doctrine was biblical. Like Luther, he emphasized the Word but he stressed the need for a highly educated ministry to interpret the Bible. Here he stood firmly between Rome, on the right, with its monarchical doctrine of papal infallibility, and the Anabaptists, on the left, who were democratically inclined to let all believers interpret the Word themselves. Both Luther and Calvin were obsessed with God, but, whereas Luther emphasized personal faith and took as his text "Thy sins are forgiven," Calvin stressed the need for men to attempt to understand God's design and to follow his will: "If God is for us who can be against us?" History, for Calvin, was the theater of God's judgment. If the Anabaptist left was ahistorical and the Catholic right (eternal Rome) transhistorical, Calvinism was infinitely historical. Though God's design, Calvin taught, was determined and forever beyond man's understanding, some men (the elect) were predestined by God to carry out His design in history. Whereas Christians could come closer to God and obtain forgiveness for their sins, according to Luther, through grace and faith, and almost become one with God and even sinless, according to the mystical left-wing sects, Calvinism, logically more rigid than either, cruelly left natural man forever mired in sin, alienated from God, and anxious about his own election, yet driven, perhaps because of this very alienation and anxiety, to carry out God's predestined design.

Calvin argued that man's sinfulness condemned human institutions to imperfection. "We have no right," he wrote, "lightly to abandon a Church because it is not perfect." This position led him not to seeking sinless perfection outside institutional authority but rather to recognizing that *all* worldly institutions, including the church, continually need reform. And leadership in reform was the supreme task of the Calvinist elect.

Calvin accepted Luther's concept of the calling, but he possessed a far more intense sense of vocation. He considered the vocation of the magistrate to be the most honorable calling of the Christian layman, quite in contrast to Luther, who left the magistracy "to anyone who wanted to take it." Calvin knew that "men are of so perverse and crooked a nature, that everyone would scratch out his neighbor's eyes if there were no bridle to hold them in"[5] (a Hobbesian view). It naturally followed that government is "equally as necessary to mankind as bread and water, light and air, and far more excellent." Cognizant of man's sinfulness, Calvin also taught the inevitability of war; his theology and sermons, in fact, are full of military metaphors. Service as soldier, like service as magistrate, is the duty of the saints, for "God doth arm with sword and power whom he will have to be excellent in the world."[6] It was no wonder that the logic of Calvinism led to a holy commonwealth, or a theocracy.

The Genevan Theocracy. Luther was a German through and through and lived most of his life in the small university and cathedral town of Wittenberg. Lutheranism, moreover, developed within a medieval and agricultural setting and was, as it has continued to be, a more or less ethnic or national religion. Calvin, however, was a cosmopolitan refugee, and Calvinism developed in Switzerland, which, in the sixteenth century, was already an island of republican ideas in the midst of monarchical and feudal Europe. The fifteenth-century tales of William Tell have taught us that here was indeed the land of liberty.

Men through the ages have felt a sense of liberation on the high seas and in the mountains. Indeed, liberty was born in the mountainous peninsula of Greece. Yet liberty, like life in the mountains or on the seas, is a dangerous thing. And danger demands rigid discipline under a clear hierarchy of command. At the same time, danger demands leaders of proven merit and skill (vocation) along with obedient followers, in contrast to the lords and servants so often found on the fertile and tranquil plains. Lords provoke conflicting feelings of love and hate; leaders demand obedience and efficiency, and the Calvinist concept of authority rested on this type of relationship.

In many ways, Calvin took a quarterdeck view of leadership, whereas Luther borrowed his ideas from the pious peasant family. Accordingly, Luther replaced the monastery with the family as the ideal school for Christian character formation; Calvin's ideal, however, was the Christian magistrate—captain, as it were, of the ship of state. Calvin, like Hobbes, knew that men are deeply corrupted by sin, hating submission and always in danger of mutiny, and he rejected out of hand all pious, familial concepts of loving authority.

Much has been written, a good deal of it today biased by our temperocentric lack of sympathy for doctrinaire Calvinism, about the so-called authoritarian discipline of Calvin's rule in the city of Geneva during the 1550s. By our present standards, if not necessarily by those of medieval men, Geneva was indeed a rigidly controlled and highly disciplined city. But it was a critical time in history. Severe repression of Protestants was characteristic of Italy, France, and the Netherlands, and in England, of course, the Catholic Bloody Mary (1553–1558) was on the throne. Some 6,000 refugees streamed into Geneva, a city of only 13,000.

For a brief period, Geneva was a refuge for Calvinists from all over Europe, especially Huguenots from France, John Knox from Scotland, and the Marian exiles from Bloody Mary's England. It was indeed a school of leadership: "What manner of churches are these," wrote a sixteenth-century French Catholic, "which turn out captains?"[7]

Geneva's influence on the Puritan movement in England began with the Marian exiles. Some 800 left the country after Mary Tudor came to the throne in 1553, most of them settling in Frankfurt, Germany. The more ardent Puritans among the Frankfurt refugees, mostly ministers and divinity students, moved on to Geneva in 1555, in the same month in which Cranmer, Latimer, and Ridley were burnt at the stake in England. The English refugees were welcomed by Calvin and given the use of a church, which they shared with an already established group of Calvinist refugees from Italy. The caliber of the congregation is illustrated by its inclusion of such prominent Englishmen as James Pilkington, president of St. John's College, Cambridge, and later bishop of Durham, the bishop and dean of the Chichester cathedral, and two leading Fellows of Corpus Christi and Magdalen Colleges at Oxford. Almost a century later, John Milton called the Marian exiles in Geneva "the true Protestant divines of England, our fathers in the faith we hold."[8] In Geneva, the English exiles

> established a congregation and a discipline that set the standards of future Puritan ambition and they produced a translation of the Bible whose marginal notes carried Puritanism into countless English households. More than this, they addressed to their countrymen at home a series of extraordinary political tracts in which they elaborated a far more radical view of political activity than the Huguenots were to attain, and developed what was probably the first justification of revolution.[9]

Writers like Michael Walzer have fruitfully seen the Calvinists and the Puritans as the Bolsheviks of the Reformation. In contrast to Marxism, however, Calvinism taught the absolute sovereignty of God, not of the people. Revolution was never justified in the name of the people but only if called for by the establishment of magistrates.

> "The people" must be led by their social betters, the "many-headed monster" must take no independent political action, lest it indulge in Anabaptist "excesses" such as had thrown Lutheranism into the hands of the Princes. The Calvinist discipline arose after Munster had sent a thrill of horror through the respectable classes all over Europe.[10]

Calvin's Geneva, then, was a school for political leadership and magisterial Protestantism rather than, as Max Weber and others would have it, a school for acquisitive capitalism. It was a school for capable and successful men, driven by anxiety and doubt about their elect status but nevertheless convinced that as members of a veritable *noblesse de religion* their duty was to lead lesser men in forming a new Zion. This ethic, modified and even secularized over the years, prompted members of the English gentry to become revolutionaries and their gentlemanly heirs in America to take the lead down into the twentieth century. Elting Morison discussed this sense of class authority in the *DAB* biography of

Henry L. Stimson, who served in important federal posts under Presidents Theodore Roosevelt, Taft, Wilson, Coolidge, Hoover, Franklin Roosevelt, and Truman:

> On both sides of his family the lines ran back to the Massachusetts Bay colony of the early seventeenth century. . . . In that stock the sense of election postulated by John Calvin was qualified by the austerity of his vision of life and by his stern injunction that it was necessary not only to know but to do the will of God. . . . He had found out how to exercise power . . . using authority bounded and defined by legal systems, bureaucratic structures, and those ancestral sanctions that worked within him.[11]

REFORMATION ENGLAND

To understand the roots of American traditions, it is extremely important to bear in mind that from 1607 to 1776, more than a third of our history, we lived under British colonial rule; for well over half our history the population was predominantly British in origin. In spite of the modifying effects of a frontier environment, moreover, British cultural norms—in class and family, in religion, education, and law, and in government—dominated the colonial period and remained influential throughout the nineteenth century. At the upper-class level at least, the British ideal of the Christian gentleman held sway until the beginning of the First World War.* Finally, it was the turbulent era of Reformation England that spawned the Puritan Revolution† and the rise of Quakerism.

Henry VIII came to the throne in 1509, the year of Calvin's birth, and broke with Rome in 1534, the year of Calvin's conversion. Henry broke with Rome for political rather than theological reasons. In fact, he was hostile to the teachings of Luther, was awarded the title "Defender of the Faith" by the pope in 1521 for his *Defensis Septem Sacromentorum*, and at no time admitted that in creed he was anything but an orthodox Catholic. Henry's desire for a divorce was dictated by his need for a male heir. Nor was he theologically against the principles of monasticism; he sold the monasteries (many of them corrupt and decaying) to his friends and allies in order to raise revenue for the crown and to consolidate his political position. Indeed, Thomas Cromwell, Henry's brilliant but much maligned public servant, took charge of the dissolution of the monasteries as part of his attempt to rationalize, even bureaucratize, the state machine and spent much of the money received from their sale in strengthening

---

*It is no accident that in the film of John C. Marquand's *The Late George Apley*, the title role was played by an Englishman, Ronald Coleman.

†There is some confusion, or historical relativity, in my referring to the Puritan Revolution. Edward Hyde, earl of Clarendon, a contemporary and a participant, called his book on the era a *History of the Rebellion* (1702–1704). The great Victorian Samuel Rawson Gardiner called his many volumes the *History of the Great Civil War* but often referred to this period as the Puritan Revolution. Modern historians, some of them Marxists, usually speak of the English Revolution, the title of Christopher Hill's classic study. It seems natural to refer to the Puritan Revolution here, though I shall also refer to it as the Rebellion. (I refer to Edward Hyde as Clarendon.)

the working hierarchy of church and state, as well as in improving higher education.*

Like so many other institutions in English history, the church took the middle way, standing squarely between the traditions of Rome and the innovations of Wittenberg and Geneva and following the views of the gentle Erasmus rather than those of Luther or Calvin. At the two universities, to which Henry appealed for justification of his break with Rome, it was mostly those who belonged to the Erasmian and humanist groups who became leaders in the church hierarchy.

In doctrine and worship, the English church remained essentially Catholic throughout Henry's reign. It was during the brief reign of Edward VI that the Anglican church did away with confession and clerical celibacy; Latin gave way to the superb English prose of the Book of Common Prayer; the mystical doctrine of the real presence of Christ at the Mass was replaced by a more Zwinglian interpretation of Holy Communion as a spiritual commemoration of the Last Supper ("take and eat this in *remembrance* that Christ died for thee. . . ."); and, finally, in the Lutheran tradition, the wine and bread were given to the laity. In the meantime, the Bible, first translated into English during Henry's reign, was being read by more and more Englishmen.

It seems to be the nature of man that all political and religious movements eventually split into right, left, and center. At first the English Reformation divided into the moderate Anglican center, which stood for a traditional church hierarchy established by law and backed by the state; the right, composed largely of the Roman Catholic landed nobility; and the left, consisting of those who came to be called Puritans, originally a derogatory term applied to various types of extremists who all agreed on the need for freedom from a hierarchical establishment and for purging the church of all vestiges of Catholicism.

During the reign of Mary Tudor, right-wing Catholicism came back into power and many of the more ardent Puritans, as we have seen, exiled themselves on the Continent. After the death of Mary, most of the leading Marian exiles in Geneva returned to England, and Puritanism became a definite movement within the church. It was against all formalisms such as keeping holy days, making the sign of the cross, wearing elaborate vestments, and displaying stained glass windows; it stood for simplicity of worship, more rigid moral standards, and a more rational approach to religion centered on pulpit and preacher rather than altar and priest. Above all, truth was to be sought in the Bible, not in the pronouncements of a sacred hierarchy.

Queen Elizabeth, herself devoid of strong religious convictions, sought to solve the religious question on the basis of political expediency. Though the Thirty-nine Articles were more Calvinist than she would have liked, the Eliza-

---

*When Henry VIII used the spoils of the monasteries to found Trinity College and endow the first Regius professorships at Cambridge (1546), he sowed the seeds that were eventually to grow into the founding of Harvard College in the New World: the first head of Harvard (Nathaniel Eaton) and the second president (Charles Chauncy) were Trinity men, as were five of the first twelve overseers—Governor Winthrop, John Cotton, Hugh Peter, Thomas Weld, and John Humfrey.

bethan Settlement was an attempt to hold to the middle way. She was less interested in having everyone *think* alike than in their *acting* alike. Eternal salvation was left to God and the individual, but the public aspects of religion were relegated to the state. All of this pointed toward latitudinarianism in belief and uniformity in practice.

In the meantime, the Puritan movement gradually split into three groups: Presbyterians, Independents, and Separatists.* Both the Presbyterians and the Independents were content to remain within the established church; the Presbyterians hoped to reorganize the hierarchy along the lines of the Presbyterian Book of Discipline, whereas the Independents wanted the church to give more autonomy to local preachers and congregations. These two more conservative groups of Puritans were made up primarily of men of the kind who went into exile under Mary. Such men were rapidly coming to the fore in law, medicine, and science in the city of London, in the expanding universities, and in the counties as justices of the peace and members of Parliament. As Walzer put it, "The initial Puritan effort had been to turn gentlemen and magistrates into saints 'to convert great men,' so that 'hundreds would follow their example.' "[12] We are here mostly interested in the Independents, who, at first a minority compared to the Presbyterians, rapidly took precedence in the 1620s and led the way to Massachusetts Bay.

The Tudor monarchy was quite naturally marked by violence. After all, Henry VIII did away with wives, relatives, and trusted associates in the interest of the national (often his) will. Bloody Mary, essentially a mild and sincere Catholic, was nevertheless forced by reasons of state to burn some 300 Protestants at the stake, including such leaders as the Cambridge reformers Cranmer, Ridley, and Latimer. Elizabeth, a master politician of consensus who cared little for ideological or religious issues, was forced to less brutality than the rest of her family. (Though officially sanctioning it, she wept upon hearing of the beheading of her cousin Mary, Queen of Scots.) The politics of assassination, however, continued throughout her reign.

As late as the 1570s, for example, the earl of Oxford ventured forth from his castle with an armed following of client gentry, a retinue of personal servants, and a bodyguard of 100 "Tall Yeomen" dressed in distinctive livery. Thanks to the studied neutrality of the queen, he and many of his peers were allowed to commit murder after murder with complete impunity: "Both in the brutality of their tactics and in their impunity from the law," wrote Lawrence Stone, "the nearest parallels to the Earl of Oxford . . . in the London of Queen Elizabeth are Al Capone and Dion O'Banion, Bugs Moran and Johnny Torrio in the Chicago of the 1920's."[13]

---

*Though Elizabeth tolerated the Presbyterians and the Independents, she was largely successful in suppressing the Separatist movement by the end of her reign. One small group of them, however, remained intact at Scrooby Manor, in Nottinghamshire, eventually fleeing to Holland and thence to the New World, where they landed at Plymouth Rock in 1620. The ideal of Separatism eventually led to the left-wing sects that flourished during the Rebellion and the Protectorate, both political, such as the Levellers and Diggers, and religious, such as the Fifth Monarchy Men, Seekers, Baptists, and Quakers.

It is difficult for us to imagine the difference between the brawling Tudor nobility and the "quiet self-control" that Weber found in "the best type of English or American gentleman" in his day. For it would not be far from the truth to say that in terms of social character, the Tudor nobility had more in common with the brave Ulysses of Homer's heroic age than with the Eton-Oxford trained public servants of the nineteenth century. Among the earl of Oxford's peers, tempers were short, weapons to hand, impulsive and childish ferocity the norm, and, of course, loyalty above the law. In personal relations, direct action was the rule: "In 1578, Edward Windham was attacked on Fleet Street in broad daylight by twenty-five retainers of the 2nd Lord Rich, urged on by their master with bloodthirsty cries of 'Draw, villains, draw,' 'Cut off his legs,' and 'Kill him,' an assault that Windham met by firing a pistol at his Lordship and then fleeing into the French ambassador's house."[14] Such scenes were typical in that era of anarchy on the streets and in country lanes.

From Brawl and Duel to Law. The noble sport of brawling, along with the noble sport of war, declined after the turn of the seventeenth century as English society moved from the Tudors to the Stuarts. Technological factors were important in this transformation. Brawling declined as the deadly rapier and the pistol replaced the clumsy sword. Dueling, with its rigid code of rules, replaced the brawl and then itself died down under the Stuarts. James I made strenuous efforts to curb the duel, which seriously threatened the workings of his court. But it was the steadily increasing Puritan sentiment in England that partly explains why the duel never reached the heights that it did in France.* Both the duel and the assassination, to the rational Puritan mind, were impulsive and irrational ways of handling private disputes. Gradually, even among the leisured nobility, law replaced violence in the settling of private quarrels: "In the late sixteenth and early seventeenth centuries, more nobles and landed gentlemen acquired a smattering of legal education than at any time before or possibly since."[15] When a well-known diarist of the period came up to London, "he looked forward to three pleasures: good food and drink, the society of pretty women, and entertaining mornings in the law courts, watching the cases there."[16]

Throughout England the law was becoming more and more important. The legal profession, according to R. H. Tawney, increased by two-thirds between the decades of 1591–1600 and 1631–1640. The rise of the lawyers brought them wealth and social recognition. E. W. Ives observed that "between James I's accession and the calling of the Long Parliament, fourteen men presided over the courts of King's Bench and Common Pleas at Westminster. Of these chief justices, two were created earls and one a baron, the families of five more were later raised to the peerage, and another four established dynasties of landed gentry which endured into the nineteenth century."[17]

---

*Whereas dueling was almost unheard of in Puritan New England, it was surely a part of the Cavalier culture of the antebellum South. It was also not too unusual in Philadelphia and the middle colonies.

The rise of the lawyers was also related to the rise of the gentry. Those families who rose into this class, whether from the yeomanry of the country or from the class of merchants, tradesmen, or lawyers in the city, as well as those who rose above it into the nobility, like such Elizabethan families of achievement as the Cecils, Bacons, Russells, and Cavendishes, provided the dynamic leadership of the society that slowly emerged from the dying feudal age.

The dissolution of the monasteries played a vital part in bringing about this new society. For suddenly, over a decade or two, almost one-fifth of the land of England came on the market for investment and secular ownership. The land first passed into the hands of a narrow group of noble families, which meant the secularization of wealth and power. In the course of the seventeenth century, however, mismanagement and other factors caused the estates to be broken up and sold to rising country gentlemen, as well as to newly moneyed men from the city, most of them supporting the Puritan and parliamentary party as against the church and crown. These men, moreover, put the land to highly rational and profitable uses—investing in more capitalist forms of agriculture (enclosures), in the extracting industries, and in manufactures, especially the clothing industry. (The Marian exiles had brought back manufacturing and industrial techniques from abroad, and abbeys were converted into worsted mills, glass factories, and ironworks.)

Merchant, gentry, and lawyer were usually combined in one and the same person or family. It was, for instance, the grandfather of John Winthrop, governor of Massachusetts, who began the family's rise into the gentry class. As a successful clothier, Adam Winthrop founded the family fortune, got the freedom of the city of London, and finally obtained a grant of the manor of Groton, part of the dissolved monastery of Bury St. Edmonds in East Anglia. Adam's son was trained in the law and then became auditor of St. John's and Trinity colleges at Cambridge. John Winthrop was born at Groton and educated at Trinity College, as well as at the Inns of Court, after which he returned to Groton, where he became a justice of the peace at the age of eighteen. (In the seventeenth century the "J.P."—in the style of the Calvinist and Puritan ideal of the magistrate—became the symbol of the country gentleman's rule in England.)

This pattern of gentry-legal leadership is nicely illustrated by the career of Edward Coke, Elizabeth's attorney general, whose great rival at the Inns of Court was the more famous Francis Bacon. Whereas Bacon is now known for his rationalization of the new scientific philosophy, Coke was the brilliant legal mythmaker and architect of the British common law tradition. Like John Winthrop, Coke was born in East Anglia, near the city of Norwich, often called the "nursery of lawyers." And like Winthrop, he went away to Trinity and the Inner Temple. In the course of his highly successful legal and political careers, Coke made money and spent it wisely, unlike so many of his extravagant and noble contemporaries. As a mark of Coke's arrival at the top, he was knighted by James I, who opened the status-seeking seventeenth century by knighting some 900 men within four months of coming to the throne in 1603 (one of the greatest inflations in honors in British history.)

Universities and Alienated Intellectuals. After the abolition of the monasteries, the new landowners collected the tithes and patronized the clergy. The Puritan clergy would never have been such an influential group had it not been for such lay patronage. And it was these Puritan preachers, the alienated and polemical intellectuals of the Stuart period, who supplied the ideological propaganda for this age of change. For the pulpit was the major means of communication during the first half of the seventeenth century. It has been estimated that some 340,000 sermons were preached—in churches, at the Inns of Court, in Parliament, in meeting halls in London, at the court at Westminster, and in the universities—between 1600 and the opening of the Puritan Revolution in the 1640s.

Thomas Hobbes, obsessed with society's need for authority and order in an increasingly individualistic and revolutionary age, realized that the universities—which were training clergymen as well as an ever growing number of gentlemen—lay at the very core of the rebellion: "The universities," he wrote in *Leviathan*, "have been to this nation as the wooden horse was to the Trojans." Hobbes saw clearly that "the chief leaders were ambitious ministers and ambitious gentlemen; the ministers envying the authority of bishops, whom they thought less learned; and the gentlemen envying the privy council, whom they thought less wise than themselves. . . . Therefore I despair of any lasting peace among ourselves, till the universities shall bend . . . to the teaching of absolute obedience to the laws of the King and to his public edicts under the great seal of England."[18]

Hobbes was a critic of both his own Oxford and the far more Puritan Cambridge. Whereas Oxford, the older of the two universities, tended to be Catholic, medieval, Anglican, and Royalist, both Cambridge and many of the Inns of Court were more Elizabethan and eventually Puritan in character and in architecture. Elizabeth herself had been educated by Cambridge men and her bishops tended to come from the newer university. At Cambridge, though Trinity (1546) was the great college of the new age, Emmanuel, founded in 1584, and Sidney Sussex, in 1595, were also intellectual seedbeds of the Puritan Revolution in England that nurtured the establishment of Massachusetts Bay Colony and Harvard College. John Winthrop, as we noted, was a product of Trinity; John Harvard, of Emmanuel; and Oliver Cromwell, of Sidney Sussex.

The church was, on the whole, understaffed with poorly trained ministers when Elizabeth came to the throne. In 1564, for example, Cambridge had about 1,000 students, most of them from the poorer classes and preparing for orders. This number was increased to 3,000 by 1623, at which size the student body remained for some two centuries. At both universities, there was such an increase in the numbers preparing for the church, especially at the Puritan colleges, that a definite oversupply was created; about 100 more clergymen than were needed graduated from Oxford and Cambridge each year after 1600.

Many of the best educated, more capable, and politically oriented preachers, denied livings in local parishes, were forced to obtain lectureships. The widow who endowed Sidney Sussex College at Cambridge also endowed a lectureship at Westminster, and the total amount of charitable contributions to support lectureships in the four decades preceding the Rebellion far exceeded the sum given to supplement the stipends of parish clergy. These rootless lecturers, concentrated in London and the larger population centers, were the intellectual leaders of the Puritan movement.

Scholars and Gentlemen. At the same time that the Puritan saints were converting poor clerical scholars into polemical preachers, both Oxford and Cambridge, as well as the Inns of Court, were becoming veritable finishing schools for the sons of the gentry along with more and more of the younger sons of ambitious noble families. As the technical requirements for public service in the new nation-state demanded fewer leisurely and military virtues and more intellectual and organizing talents, new leaders such as Elizabeth's favorite courtier, William Cecil, chancellor of Cambridge from 1559 until his death in 1598, saw the need for producing an educated class of public servants. From Cecil's day on, the movement of the sons of the secular elite into the universities increased steadily; in the 1620s, for the first time, more sons of the gentry and the nobility than of the class of commoners were preparing for orders.

This was also the period in which certain select schools began to educate the sons of the nobility and the gentry in a common set of educational and cultural values. John Wilson, the first teacher at the Boston Church and later the most vehement opponent of Anne Hutchinson, was a product of Eton and King's College, Cambridge. Though early records are scarce, Stone noted that "we have a glimpse of Eton in the early 1630's showing two sons of the Earl of Peterborough, a son of the Earl of Dover, two sons of the Earl of Cork, four sons of the Earl of Southampton, and two sons of the Earl of Northampton sitting down to dinner at the second table with knights' sons. The picture is a familiar one: Eton has arrived."[19] The ideal of elite education had now become, for those who could afford it, a matter of private tutors or boarding school, Oxford or Cambridge, the Inns of Court, and, finally, the grand tour. In accord with this new pattern, it is important to stress that Oxford and Cambridge *did not* measure up to their continental counterparts in scholarship, research, or learning. For men like John Choke of Cambridge, former Marian exile, provost of Kings College, Regius Professor of Greek, tutor to Prince Edward, and brother-in-law and close friend of William Cecil, thought the production of an educated elite prepared to rule far more important than the production of scholars. And this tradition of class education was carried on by men like Jewett in nineteenth-century Oxford and at Harvard, at least through the regimes of Eliot and Lowell. The ideal of this educated vanguard was described by Morison.

> A new upper class was arising. Enriched by the woolens trade or overseas commerce, glutted by the spoils of the abbeys, families like the Cecils, Russells, Greshams, and Winthrops wished to educate their sons as gentlemen, and prepare them for active life. Oxford and Cambridge colleges were appropriate dwellings for such youths. They offered an opportunity, in luxurious surroundings and congenial company, to read the polite literature which Erasmus told them was necessary for a gentleman's education. It is true that the University did not admit the logic of the situation—Englishmen seldom do. All students were supposed to be clerics and behave as such.[20]

Puritanism and Science. Robert K. Merton, in his intensive study of the early members of the Royal Society, clearly established the affinity of Baconians and scientists with Puritanism. In the seventeenth century, Gresham College in London became the center of the scientific movement and the New Philosophy (four of the twelve founders of the Royal Society had been professors there). Despite pleas from his alma mater that the money might better be left to Cambridge, Gresham followed the example set by many merchants who endowed grammar schools and was careful to put control of his college in the hands not of clerics but of merchants like himself. Despite the merchants' formal control, it was Henry Briggs, an ardent Puritan and a professor of geometry, who built up the college and was of prime importance in the intellectual history of his age. Like Briggs, no leading scientist of the early seventeenth century—Gilbert, Napier, Harvey, and Bacon—held university posts.

Francis Bacon was the major proponent of the New Philosophy even though most of his voluminous writings were in the fields of religion, politics, and law. His *Novum Organum* (1620), the landmark book, urged substitution of the inductive methods of science for the deductive and authoritarian model stemming from Aristotle and Aquinas. Bacon's influence on this period is shown by the fact that his *Essays* went through seventeen editions before 1639 and a large proportion of his works were published during the two years preceding the outbreak of the Great Rebellion (1640–1641).

The New Philosophy had a strong leveling influence on the hierarchical Elizabethan and Stuart ages. The Copernican revolution "democratized the universe by shattering the hierarchical structure of the heavens; Harvey 'democratized' the human body by dethroning the heart."[21] As far as Bacon was concerned, "one researcher was as good as another, and better than any mere speculative scholar."[22] No wonder that Bacon's ideal was a career open to talents. And by the end of Elizabeth's reign Bacon was "one of the leading Commons Men . . . , on innumerable committees and a speaker always heard with attention."[23]

Parliament and Puritanism. The Puritan lawyer-gentry, spearheads of the emerging rational-legal age of achievement and mobility, found their political home in the House of Commons first in the Elizabethan period and much more notably under the Stuarts. During the course of the sixteenth century, Commons increased in size from 296 to 462 members, Elizabeth adding 32 boroughs and 64 members. The gentry contributed most of the new members. A father often sat from the shire while his son represented the local town. This suited the townsmen as it relieved them of the costs of maintaining a representative at Westminster, for the gentry usually were able to support themselves.

On the whole, the members of Parliament were rich and local in orientation. Some of the wealthiest men in England sat in Commons and it has been estimated that by 1628 their average income was three times as high as those sitting in the House of Lords. Local roots are suggested by the fact that in 1640–1641 the members included 122 sheriffs, at least 219, and probably more, justices of the peace, and over 250 members of local commissions. In accord with the spirit of the age, the proportion of university men sitting in Commons increased from 35 percent in 1593 to 57 percent by 1640.

The Crisis of Order and Authority. Clearly, seventeenth-century England was passing through a crisis of authority in which the new class of parliamentary and Puritan gentry was challenging the sacred authority of throne and altar. Perhaps when a "new philosophy calls all in doubt" and "all coherence" appears to be gone, as John Donne felt about his age, it is better to speak of a vacuum, rather than a decline, in authority; in historical perspective, laments over so-called declining authority turn out to be composed by advocates of new forms of authority who couch their rhetoric in terms of the need for more equality as against the evils of established authority at any given time.

Hobbes went to the heart of this problem in *Leviathan*, appropriately published in 1651 in the midst of the Great Rebellion. Many of his contemporaries viewed this work as a defense of absolute monarchy; others, especially the great historian of the Rebellion, Clarendon, as an iniquitous defense of the authoritarian ways of Oliver Cromwell. As Hobbes was loyal to his noble patrons, the Cavendishes, and as he presented his thesis first to King Charles, it is probable that he himself thought he was writing in support of the established authority of the day. Actually, Hobbes was an extreme atheist and, when read with care and historical hindsight, *Leviathan* definitely puts him in the camp of the New Philosophers. He recognized the decline of the sacred chain of being and the need for a new and secular chain of command; he saw that when passive faith in the sacred cross declines it must be replaced by the secular sword, which, of course has always been hidden behind the cross. The greatness and timelessness of Hobbe's book are that it laid bare the need for any and all de facto establishments, in the tradition of Machiavelli, to exercise power and force in the defense of order and authority against the ever present threat of anarchy, or a "war of every man against every man." With no faith in the sacred himself, Hobbes, as well as many materialists after him, saw life as a perpetual and restless desire for power.*

The Calling, Worldly Asceticism, and the Magistrate. The idea of the calling lies at the heart of the Puritan legitimation of authority. In contrast to the purposeful Puritan, "the normal medieval Catholic layman," wrote Weber, "lived ethically, so to speak, from hand to mouth."[24] His life had no rational plan or distant this-worldly goal but consisted largely of a series of spontaneous acts. Salvation, a matter of his following the traditional and magical rituals of his church, was

---

*It is in the work of Max Weber that we find an attempt to go further than Hobbes. Weber, like Hobbes, lived in a period of increasing disorder and what he called "the disenchantment of the world." Weber was also obsessed with the problem of order and authority. He believed that no secular institutions or systems of hierarchy and authority are ever self-justifying; rather, they always depend, in the long run, on some form of religious sanctification. Here Weber is going beyond Hobbes by admitting that whereas secular power is inevitably and ultimately backed by the sword, it must always be clothed, in an ordered society, by some form or other of sacred authority: men are willing to obey it because they believe it to be legitimate (or sacred).

not of this world but of the next. In other words, he had no vocation. In the Catholic double standard of morality, only monks had a definite calling.

Whereas the calling was central to continental Calvinism, it was even more crucial to English Puritanism, and its theological meaning was worked out far more systematically and emphasized by the leading English casuists. William Perkins, who wrote a lengthy treatise on vocations, was, according to Christopher Hill, "the first systematic theologian in England . . . the dominant influence in Puritan thought for forty years after his death in 1602."[25] Perkins's many books, translated into French, Dutch, Italian, and Spanish, were widely read in both Old and New England.

Like Hobbes and Weber, Perkins was obsessed with the problems of order and authority. In the Calvinist tradition, he saw order as imposed upon man by God; disorder and anarchy were the work of Satan. Perkins propounded an ordered and fixed society held together by functionally interdependent callings (anticipating Durkheim's *Division of Labor*). "God is the General," he wrote, using military analogies in the style of Calvin. "God is the General, appointing to every man his particular calling and as it were his standing: and in that calling he assigns unto him his particular office; in performance whereof he is to live and die."[26] Each calling requires reciprocal duties in the interests of society as a whole. "A vocation or calling," he continued, "is a certain kind of life, ordained and imposed on man by God, for the common good . . . For example, the life of a king is to spend his time in the governing of his subjects, and that is his calling; and the life of a subject is to live in obedience to the Magistrate. . . . A master of a family is to leade his life in the government of his family and that is his calling."[27] Every Christian must fulfill his calling by giving it the best of his ability; at the same time, because men have differing abilities as gifts from God, society must be hierarchically arranged. "Persons are distinguished by order," Perkins wrote, "whereby God hath appointed, that in every society one person should bee above or under another; not making all equal, as though the bodie should bee all head and nothing else."[28]

Though hierarchically organized on the basis of gifts and importance of function, all callings are of equal rank in the eyes of God. What Perkins, and the whole Puritan movement after him, sought was to replace the personal pride of birth and status with the professional's or craftsman's pride of doing one's best in one's particular calling. The good Christian society needs the best of kings, magistrates, and citizens. Perkins most emphasized the work ethic from Genesis: "In the swaete of thy browe shalt thou eate thy breade."

All good Christians must follow honorable callings; dishonorable callings, as well as idleness, are conducive to disorder and godlessness: "As for example, such as live by usury, by carding and dicing, by maintaining houses of gaming, by plaies and such like . . . are no callings or vocations, but avocations from God and his waies."[29] Perkins quite naturally condemned the idle members of the gentry or nobility who lived in "no proper calling" but spent "their time in eating, drinking, sleeping and sporting."[30] As with the leisure class at the top, so with the poor idlers at the bottom of society: "It is a foule disorder in any Commonwealth, that there should be suffered rogues, beggars, vagabonds; for such kind of persons commonly are of no civill societie or corporation, nor of any particular Church; and are rotten legges, and armes, that droppe from the body."[31] It is the function of the magistrate "to punish him for his idleness, and compel him to labour."[32] Both the idle rich and poor who "choose to live in their owne libertie, are in the kingdom of darkness, that is, Sinne and Satan."[33] Though idleness is indeed a sin, Perkins did see that God "admitteth lawful rec-reation . . . because it is a necessary means to refresh either bodie or minde, that wee the better doe the duties which pertaine unto us."[34] (One is reminded of the overworked American executive who plays golf on Sundays only to keep in shape for the rigors of the workweek ahead.)

Puritanism was indeed no radical or sentimental creed, but a new and de-manding system of order and authority. Nor was it a doctrine that either encouraged or even permitted the unregulated and individualistic pursuit of profit, which so many critics of Weber have accused him of attributing to the Protestant Ethic. Perkins was explicit on this point and emphasized an organic rather than an individualistic view of social structure.

> A vocation or calling is a certain kind of life, ordained and imposed on man by God . . . *for the common good*: that is, for the benefite and good estate of man-kinde. In man's body there be sundry parts and members, and every one hath his severall use and office, which is performeth not for it selfe, but for the good of the whole bodie, as the office of the eye, is to see, of the ear to heare, and the feete to goe. Now all societies of men, are bodies, a family is a bodie, and so is every particular Church a bodie, and the commonwealth also. . . . And that common saying, *Every man for himselfe, and God for us all*, is wicked, and is direct-ly against the end of every calling or honeste kind of life.[35]

For Perkins and his generation of English theologians, possibly even more than for Calvin, the office of magistrate was the highest secular calling. As Wal-zer wrote with great insight, "Magistracy was a far better description of the saints' true vocation than was either capitalist acquisition or bourgeois free-dom."[36] After all, this magisterial ideal drove the English gentry, with a new zeal after their conversion, first to seek local office and then to go to London to fulfill the duties of their calling as members of Parliament; likewise, the rising city merchant or lawyer, not allowed by this new ethic to remain satisfied with the mere accumulation of wealth, was led to purchase land, seek local office, and then come back to Parliament. The ideal of magistracy of course did not contradict but rather reinforced the more leisurely aristocratic ideal of noblesse oblige, a concept implying the duties associated with inherited advantages. One must bear in mind that Puritanism, from Perkins down through John Win-throp and Oliver Cromwell, was a conservative and rigidly hierarchical system that took even ascription for granted but, at the same time, placed far more em-phasis on the rational carrying out of the duties of office as against the sponta-neous fulfillment of the duties of birth alone, taught by the aristocratic ethic. John Winthrop was greatly influenced by Perkins, especially by his writings on the role of magistrate. And it was the Elizabethan Puritan ideals that Winthrop and the founders of New England brought to the New World, as Edmund S. Morgan has clearly seen:

Winthrop was not relying simply on his own notions of what a governor should be. A governor was a magistrate and sixteenth-century Puritan mentors like William Perkins had described the calling of a magistrate with some care. Throughout his tenure of office in Massachusetts Winthrop sought to practice the virtues described in Perkins' treatise on Christian equity. A magistrate was supposed to enforce the laws, but this did not mean an unbending application of the same punishment in every case. This much any fool could do. The calling of the magistrate demanded special talents to fit the punishment to the crime, to bend the law to the particular circumstance. Winthrop earned a good deal of criticism for his "leniency," but he was always ready to defend his practices as proper to his calling.

The social and political implications of the idea of the calling were conservative. It had been common in the Middle Ages to think of society as composed of different "estates" into which men were born and lived out their lives. . . . The idea of estate lingered on in Puritan times, helping a man to discern his calling; and the two conceptions easily merged in the often repeated Puritan warning that every man, for the good of society, must remain in the place to which God had called him. Winthrop could remind the emigrants to Massachusetts that God had so ordered the condition of mankind that "in all times some must be rich some poore, some highe and eminent in power and dignitie; others meane and in subjeccion," and he was properly shocked when a servant suggested to a master who was unable to pay him that they change places.[37]

Though the callings of the magistrate and the minister stood at the apex of the Puritan pyramid of authority, Perkins's generation of theologians was by no means against wealth per se. "Men are honoured for their riches," wrote Perkins* and then carefully qualified himself: "I meane not riches simple but the use of riches; namely as they are made instruments to uphold and maintain virtue."[38]

The Puritan emphasis on worldly asceticism and the right use of riches led to the tradition of private philanthropy that has been characteristic of both this country and England even down to our own day (witness the private endowing of schools and universities, from Oxford and Cambridge to Harvard and Yale, in contrast to government support of education on the Continent). W. K. Jordan, in his *Philanthropy in England, 1430–1660*, showed how this tradition was grounded in the ethic of the merchants and the Puritan gentry rather than in that of the peerage. For example, whereas the merchants and tradesmen contributed 71.65 percent and the gentry 15.46 percent of all funds donated in the period 1601–1640, the nobility contributed only 5.17 percent. Puritan philanthropy made possible the independent lecturers, but it also endowed and founded new schools and scholarships and went to correct the abuses of poverty.

Charity, in the Catholic and the aristocratic ethic, was a spontaneous, stopgap, and Christian response to the always visible and suffering poor in a world where poverty was accepted and even cherished. Philanthropy, on the other hand, was an infinitely Puritan and rational response to social conditions that, as Perkins saw, were dysfunctional to the best use of talent in promoting an efficient division of labor, or hierarchy of callings. In contrast to charity, the syste-

---

*This line often has been quoted out of context by those who accuse Calvinism of sanctifying pure acquisitiveness.

matic philanthropy of the Puritans lacked sentimentality; it transformed society, inadvertently bringing power and authority to the participants in the emerging world of careers open to talent.*

It was surely devotion to calling, the right use of riches, and systematic philanthropy—especially in the case of Harvard College and education in general—that informed the founders of Massachusetts Bay and their Brahmin descendants.

Exodus and Revolution. A good case can be made for the argument that revolutions are the products rather than the producers of social change. Just as Tocqueville saw that the seeds of the French Revolution were sown in the centralizing measures of Louis XIV, so the English Revolution of the 1640s and 1650s was a product of the social changes in Tudor and Stuart England that were reviewed in this chapter. Great social changes, unfortunately, are almost always accompanied by gradually accumulating reactionary sentiments, which eventually come to the fore in concrete events and personalities, often leading to violence and revolution. Thus, the immediate cause of both the English Revolution and the Puritan migration to Massachusetts Bay was the coming to power of Charles I in 1625. The last Parliament before the revolution of 1642 was dissolved by Charles I in 1629, and the next year a small band of Puritans set sail for the New World.

Soon afterward, Charles I appointed William Laud as Archbishop of Canterbury. A sincere and self-righteous High Church Anglo-Catholic, Laud was determined to oust the last vestiges of Calvinism from the church. He restored much of the ancient ritual, including the doctrine of the real presence at Mass, confession, and clerical celibacy, and attacked the Puritan party with puritanical zeal. And a flood tide of Englishmen departed for the shores of Massachusetts Bay in the decade preceding the outbreak of the Puritan Revolution.

---

*It should be noted that philanthropy and the idea of stewardship are far more characteristic of Puritanism than of Quakerism, which remained closer to the Catholic ideal of charity.

The Puritan Revolution and the Rise of Quakerism

> Calvin's creed was one fit for the boldest of the bourgeosie of his time. . . . While German Lutheranism became a willing tool in the hands of princes, Calvinism founded a republic in Holland, and active republican parties in England and above all in Scotland. In Calvinism the second great bourgeois upheaval found its doctrine ready, cut, and dried. This upheaval took place in England.
>
> *Friedrich Engels*

> Naturally not without some dependence on the Anabaptist movement, but more in response to a similar social and religious situation, Quakerism developed as the Anglo-Saxon parallel to Anabaptism.
>
> *H. Richard Niebuhr*

The 1630s in England were much like the Eisenhower years in America. Society went through a period of confident calm under the benevolent authority of Charles I. As Thomas Carew, a contemporary poet, wrote with smugness and pride:

> Tourneys, masques, theatres better become
> Our Halcyon days; what though German drums
> Bellow for freedom and revenge, the noise
> Concerns us not, nor should divert our joys.[1]

But the placid thirties were followed by the revolutionary forties and the anarchic fifties, when Englishmen, for the last time in their history, fought each other to the bloody and bitter end, abolishing bishops and lords, beheading their king, and eventually setting up a kind of military dictatorship in the face of increasing anarchy.*

---

*According to the Oxford dictionary, the term *anarchism* came into the English language in 1642, the year the English Revolution broke out; *antinomianism* was introduced in 1645. There are, ac-

It is probably safe to say that war broke out in 1642 not because the leaders on either side wanted it but rather because, as with our own involvement in Vietnam, they failed to see the collective and cumulative consequences of their individual actions. The vast majority of leaders of both parties believed in a monarchical form of government and an established church. When the members of the Long Parliament passed the Grand Remonstrance, a mild listing of the abuses of monarchical and episcopal authority, they made clear their belief in religious uniformity and authority.

> We do here declare that it is far from our purpose or desire to let loose the golden reins of discipline and government in the Church, to leave private persons of particular congregations to take up what form of divine service they please, for we hold it requisite that there should be throughout the whole realm a conformity to that order which the laws enjoin according to the Word of God.[2]

The parliamentary army, moreover, was raised "for the safety of the King's person, defense of both Houses of Parliament, the preservation of the true religion, the laws, liberty and peace of the kingdom." The commissions of its officers ran "in the name of King and Parliament."[3]

The Long Parliament was no revolutionary body. Its members were essentially a conservative cousinhood of knights, squires, and gentlemen from the counties, along with some city lawyers and wealthy merchants. When Cromwell first went to Parliament in 1628, he found nine cousins there; at the opening of the Long Parliament, he sat with eleven cousins; six more cousins and three other relatives joined him there later on. That the extremely mild Grand Remonstrance was passed by a slim majority of 11 votes out of 307 members present attests to the conservative and conciliatory mood as of December 1641. Unfortunately, Charles responded to Parliament's criticism by impeaching six members for treason (including John Hampden, the richest man in England and one of the most widely respected men of his day). This slender straw broke the camel's back, and war broke out. The parliamentary party eventually won a military victory, thanks to, among other things, the efficiency and skilled leadership of the New Model Army.

The New Model Army was indeed novel in English history. In the Puritan tradition of the calling, Cromwell had a great sense of professional pride. Rejecting the aristocratic ideal, he organized the New Model on the basis of merit rather than status. "The officers," wrote his more conservative contemporary Clarendon, "are of no better family than the common soldiers."[4] The New

---

cording to Webster, at least two meanings of the term *anarchy*: (1) a state of political disorder; and (2) a state of confusion or disorder. In the British, French, and Russian revolutions, the states were overthrown, creating political as well as societal disorder (1 and 2). The twentieth-century welfare state, however, is highly centralized and strong: thus, the anarchy of the 1960's in America was largely societal confusion and normlessness (2) rather than political anarchy (1). Anarchy, chaos, and lawlessness, according to Webster, are synonyms: anarchy implies absence or suspension of government; chaos, the utter negation of law and order; lawlessness, a prevalent or habitual disregard for law and order. I use the term *anarchy* here in the sense of chaos or lawlessness. In many ways, the theological term *antinomian* or the sociological term *anomie* might serve my purpose just as well.

Model thus opened careers to talent; it was also an ideological army, made up of volunteers, true believers in the righteousness of the holy crusade. All this was, of course, quite in contrast to the aristocratic ideal of warfare as a sport, with rules protecting priests, women and children, and fought for limited interests rather than ideological abstractions.

As was to be expected with this new ideological army, there soon developed, from colonel to common soldier, a belief in the right of self-expression, or a kind of participatory democracy. We often forget the revolutionary potential of all standing armies, of which the New Model was the first in English history. Down to 1640, for example, most Englishmen were extremely provincial. Even after years of Tudor and Stuart attempts at centralization, there was little sense of nationhood; one's *country* meant one's *county*, where everyone was bound together by local ties to family, lord and manor, vicar and village, all reinforcing the established customs of degree, priority, and place. Now, for the first time, large numbers of Englishmen were away from home and easily swayed by the opinions voiced so fervently in the all-male and atomized atmosphere of the ranks.

The men of the New Model were exposed to all kinds of new enthusiasms, which produced such secular counterparts of the Anabaptist sects as the Diggers and the Levellers. According to George Sabine, the great political scientist and biographer of the Digger leader Gerrard Winstanley, the heated discussions that took place around the army campfires marked the first appearance of public opinion as a factor in British politics. These debates, mirroring and reinforcing those of the revolutionary society as a whole, were part of the greatest outpouring of pamphlets in British history (a fine collection in the British Museum includes some 20,000 pamphlets, only part of the whole). In order to organize and regulate the expression of opinion, a council of the army was set up, representing the officers, and a council of agitators, representing the ranks.

The most famous of the army debates took place in the little village church at Putney in the autumn of 1647, after military victory in the Civil War had been won. Although the Leveller leader, John Lilburne, was imprisoned in the Tower at the time, the debate centered around his draft constitution, called Agreement of the People, which was concerned mainly with the franchise. For the first time in English history the possibility of universal male suffrage was taken seriously: in the famous words of Colonel Rainsborough (kin by marriage to John Winthrop of New England), "The poorest he that is in England has a life to live as the greatest he, and therefore . . . every man that is to live under a government ought first by his own consent to put himself under that government."[5] The Putney debate dragged on through October. Finally in November, Cromwell terminated the discussions and ordered the men back to their regiments, shooting one agitator on the spot for insubordination.

Events now moved steadily to the left, toward the logical conclusion of the revolution: execution of the king. During the next year (1648) the generals formed an alliance with the Levellers and proceeded to occupy London. In December, Colonel Pride forcefully expelled ninety-six conservative Presbyterians from Parliament. This left only some sixty more radical members, called the

Rump, who abolished the House of Lords and brought Charles before the High Court of Justice, which sent him to the scaffold on January 30, 1649.

Throughout recorded history, authority in England had been symbolized by the now abolished order of king, lords, and bishops. The regicide so shocked the people that, according to a contemporary witness, "Women miscarried, men fell into melancholy, some with consternation expired."[6] The great physician William Harvey told a bishop at the time that he met with "more diseases generated by the mind than from any other cause."[7] All indeed was in doubt, all coherence gone, and a host of seekers began to populate the melancholy land of England, very much in the style of the lonely and lost souls of our own day who once gathered at Woodstock and are now joining the Jesus cults.

Clarendon was horrified by the decline in traditional authority: "All relations were confounded by the several Sects in Religion, which discountenanced all Forms of Reverence and Respect. . . . Parents had no Manner of Authority over their Children, nor Children any Obedience or Submission to their Parents; but everyone did that which was good in their own Eyes."[8] Clarendon saw the extreme egalitarianism abroad in the land as a reversion to primitivism.

> In all well instituted governments, the heirs and descendants from worthy and eminent parents, if they do not degenerate from their virtue, have always been allowed a preference and kind of title to employments and offices of honour and trust. . . . Whatever is of Civility and good Manners, all that is Art and Beauty, or of real and solid Wealth in the World, is the . . . child of beloved Propriety; and they who would strangle this Issue, desire to demolish all Buildings, eradicate all Plantations, to make the Earth barren, and Mankind to live again in Tents, and nourish his Cattle where the grass grows. Nothing but the joy in Propriety reduc'd us from barbarity; and nothing but security in the same can preserve us from returning into it again.[9]

When formalism declines fanaticism comes to the fore, and the church is replaced by a host of sects. The Puritan interregnum saw the rise of Ethringtonians, Grindlestonians, Mugglestonians, Fifth Monarchy Men, Family of Love, Ranters, and a swarm of other seeking sectarians. It is always the ex-radicals who hate and hunt the newer radicals. Thus, the Reverend Thomas Edwards, who in 1628 had been dismissed from his post as university preacher at Cambridge for his violent attacks on the establishment of bishops, now turned around and attacked, in even more fanatical terms, the fanaticisms and heresies of the 199 sects he identified. Many of the new sectarians and seekers joined the Quaker movement, unquestionably the most interesting and important of them all.

Just as the hated Anabaptists rose to haunt the reformers and Lutherans during the fifteenth-century Reformation on the Continent, so the Quakers marked the extreme left wing of the English Reformation. "The Society of Friends," wrote Ernst Troeltsch, "represents the final expression in its purest form of the Anabaptist Movement."[10] After a century of reform, religious authority in England—once lodged in the pope and the priestly control of the seven sacraments, then in the Anglican bishops and the priestly control of two sacraments, and finally in local preachers interpreting the Bible—was suddenly transformed by the radically individualistic and subjective doctrine of the Inner Light. The hierarchical yet reforming ethic of the Puritans gave way to the radical egalitarianism of the Quakers: "When the Lord sent me into the world," George Fox said in one of the key passages of his journal, "He forbade me to put off my hat to any, high or low: and I was required to 'thee' and 'thou' all men and women, without any respect to rich or poor, great or small."[11] Whereas the Puritans were closer to Hobbes, the Quakers anticipated the tradition of Rousseau.

All revolts against the inevitable hypocrisies of established authority have called for a return to primitivism. Thus, many of the early founders of Quakerism went naked through marketplaces, and even into churches, as witness of their devotion to the "naked truth." As late as 1672, the only great Quaker theologian, Robert Barclay, went "naked as a sign through the chilly streets of Aberdeen."[12] Fox and other leaders of the Quaker movement preached the futility of "mere book knowledge," which tended to pervert the untainted prompting of the Inner Light. Winstanley, in his pamphlet "The New Law of Righteousness" (1649), wrote that "the Universities are the standing ponds of stinking waters."[13] Even Emmanuel College at Cambridge, once the seat of Puritan intellectualism, went through a period of extreme mysticism at this time. No wonder that at both Oxford and Cambridge stained glass windows were smashed and altar decorations destroyed in the name of Puritan and sectarian relevance.

Among a host of other parallels with the 1960s, there was, finally, the digging up and replanting of the common land on St. George's Hill in Surrey by the followers of Winstanley, a onetime religious mystic turned utopian communist. The Diggers, in appealing their arrest to the House of Commons, asked, much in the manner of their modern namesakes, "whether the common people shall have the quiet enjoyment of the Commons, or Waste Land, or whether they shall be under the will of the Lords of the Manor."[14] In that year of regicide, similar diggings took place in Buckinghamshire, Middlesex, Hertfordshire, and Berkshire—altogether in some thirty-four towns. The following lines, attributed to Winstanley, would have appealed to the Diggers of People's Park at Berkeley.

> The gentrye are all round, on each side they are found,
> Theire wisdom's so profound, to cheat us of our ground. . . .
> The clergy they come in, and say it is a sin
> That we should now begin, our freedom for to win.
>
> Stand up now, Diggers all.
> To conquer them by love. . . .
> To conquer them by love, as it does you behove,
> For he is King above; no power is like to love:
> Glory here, Diggers all.[15]

Durable civilizations are almost literally clothed in authority, and when the emperor's clothes are removed his only recourse is the exercise of *naked* power. The Diggers dug up St. George's Hill in April; in May mutinies broke out in the army that soon turned into a full-scale Leveller revolt. Parliament immediately declared mutiny in the army to be treason, and Cromwell led a lightning night attack on the rebels at Buford; three leaders were shot on the spot and a fourth was caught and shot three days later. Cromwell and Fairfax returned to Oxford, Royalist stronghold in Charles's last days, where they were feasted by the conservative city fathers. After Buford, the Puritan Revolution turned conservative.

As part of the reactionary trend, John Lilburne was brought to trial for sedition in October. If Cromwell was respected, admired, and feared, Lilburne was undoubtedly the most popular man in England at this time. When he was finally acquitted by a jury of his peers, the people shouted with joy. A jubilant mob followed him all the way from the Guild Hall to the Tower, where, in spite of his recent acquittal, and another in 1652, he was to remain until the end of his life. In the meantime, Lilburne lost all hope of secular solutions and became a Quaker.

THE QUAKER AWAKENING ON
THE NORTHERN FRONTIER

Whereas Puritanism was centered in the most sophisticated and prosperous parts of England—East Anglia, London, and even the clothing towns in the north like Leeds and Bradford—Quakerism took root in the lonely fens and dales of the north country, the most backward, least educated, most Royalist, Roman Catholic, and still feudal part of the nation. The Quaker awakening on the northern frontier of England was not unlike our own Great Awakening, which influenced Jonathan Edwards in western Massachusetts rather than his peers in Boston. Like so many religious revivals, from the time of Paul to the present, it was an appeal to the heart rather than the mind. In striking contrast to the highly educated and theologically sophisticated builders of both Calvinism and Puritanism, the founder of Quakerism, George Fox, was not unlike that "rough beast slouching towards Bethlehem," whom Yeats saw as the sole possible savior of our own seeking age of anarchy. Son of a humble weaver in a small Lancashire village and almost entirely self-educated, Fox was a charismatic mystic whom many have called the only religious genius of the English Reformation.

Fox's father was known by his neighbors as the "Righteous Christer" and his pious mother came "of the stock of martyrs"; little wonder that George was an extremely lonely, self-centered, and self-righteous youth. "When came to eleven years of age I knew pureness and righteousness," he said in his journal, which nowhere in its hundreds of rambling pages contains a single reference to his sense of personal sinfulness.[16] As a shoemaker and shepherd Fox had a great deal of time to meditate on divine things; he of course spent endless hours reading the Bible, in an age when the King James version was penetrating every corner of England and countless Englishmen were proclaiming themselves biblical exegetes.

A year after the outbreak of the Civil War, Fox, aged nineteen, left home to wander through the countryside, dressed in leather breeches, sleeping in haystacks, under hedges, and even, so legend has it, in the trunks of hollow trees, pursuing a new vision of life outside the establishment of hated "steeple-houses" and their hypocritical "professors." After four years of lonely seeking and five years of preaching to other seekers (and two imprisonments), he was inspired by the Lord to climb Pendle Hill, where, as he afterward wrote, he "saw the sea bordering upon Lancaster, and there, on the top, I was moved to sound the day of the Lord, and the Lord let me see in what places he had a great people to be gathered."[17] Quakers date the founding of their sect to Fox's vision on Pendle Hill, in that spring of 1652.

Although later generations of comfortable and so-called birthright Friends tended to withdraw from all worldly temptations, Fox and his small band of radical prophets were bent on convincing the whole world of their newly found truth. The first five years of the movement were spectacularly successful, with over 20,000 converts by 1657, the year some 4,000 Friends attended John Lilburne's funeral in far-off London. The fearless "publishers of truth," as the early Quaker missionaries were called, not only sought converts all over the British Isles but also proselytized on the Continent, in the Near East, and in the New World—within a decade of Fox's vision on Pendle Hill.

"Anyone who knows anything about history," Marx once wrote to a friend, "knows that great social changes are impossible without the feminine ferment."[18] This is as true today as it was in the seventeenth century. A voguish ditty of that day asserted:

> We will not be wives
> And tie up our lives
> To villainous slavery.[19]

And, indeed, women played a major role in the Quaker movement. In fact, Clarendon thought the Quakers were a female sect, as well he might have: Fox's first convert was Elizabeth Hooten; his most important early convert, later his wife and mother of the movement, was Margaret Fell, mistress of Swarthmore Hall, which became the movement's headquarters; the first Quaker publishers of truth in London, in the universities, and in Dublin were women; Mary Fisher, a Yorkshire domestic servant, was the first Quaker in America; and in England today more women than men are registered as Quaker ministers.

The Quakers of the first generation were a hardy, fanatical, and apocalyptical band of martyrs who were hated, hunted down, imprisoned, tortured, and hanged for their convictions. Puritan England was no permissive age. That the female "Friends of Truth" had a particular affinity for fanaticism and martyrdom is illustrated by the career of Elizabeth Hooten. A woman of good position, the mother of seven children, and forty-seven years old when she met Fox in 1646, Hooten took up the active ministry in 1650 and almost immediately went to prison, first at Derby, then at York Castle (sixteen months). After continuing her ministry in England, where she was imprisoned for six months in

1654 and three months in 1655, she set sail for America in 1657 but was soon shipped back by the Boston authorities. At the age of sixty-five Hooten returned to New England, where she suffered incredible hardships.

> At Cambridge she was tied to the whipping-post and lashed with ten stripes, with a three-stringed whip, with three knots at the end. At Watertown she had ten stripes more with willow rods. . . . And being thus beaten and torn, she was put on horseback, and carried many miles into the wilderness, and towards night they left her there among many wolves, bears and other wild beasts.[20]

Somehow she survived and escaped to Rhode Island. Hooten's last service to the cause was to accompany Fox to America. She died in Jamaica at the age of seventy-three.

Although Elizabeth Hooten, like Margaret Fell, was a married woman of established position, many of Fox's early followers were of a more simple sort. Mary Fisher was a single servant girl whose fanaticism led her on several almost unbelievable missions. During the two years after her conversion (1652), she was twice imprisoned in York Castle (for sixteen months the first time and then for another six); between imprisonments she undertook the hazardous mission of carrying the truth to Cambridge University, where she was "jeered and derided" by the students with "froth and levity." The mayor of the city ordered that she and her woman companion be stripped to the waist and "whipped at the market cross till the blood ran down their bodies."[21]

Unsuccessful at Cambridge, Mary Fisher and another Quaker, Ann Austin, about whom nothing is known beyond the fact that she was "stricken in years and the mother of five children," became the first "publishers of truth" in the New World. In 1655 they landed in Barbados, at that time the main port of entry into the colonies and at the height of its prosperity, having some 25,000 white inhabitants and 10,000 slaves. Fisher and Austin spent six months proselytizing. They were apparently successful, as Fisher wrote home: "Here is many convinced and many desire to know the way."[22] A wealthy sugar planter, Thomas Rous, and his son John (who later married Fox's stepdaughter Margaret Fell) were the first to join the movement. Barbados quickly became the New World nursery of Quakerism with as many as five meetinghouses. A number of leading Philadelphia family founders, as we shall see, came from there during the colonial period.

Apparently satisfied with their mission in Barbados, Mary Fisher and Ann Austin set out in July 1656 to spread their truth in the "bloody den" of Boston, where they were immediately thrown into prison, "deprived of all light, stripped stark naked, and searched for any tokens of witchcraft upon their bodies."[23] Five weeks later they were shipped back to Barbados, whence they returned to England.

Still on fire with the promptings of the Inner Light, Fisher, with a party of two other women and three men Friends, went off to convert the Jews in Jerusalem. Their mission was not very successful: two of the women were made prisoners of the Inquisition for four years, one of the men was hanged by the pope, and another was confined to a madhouse. Fisher herself, though never reaching Jerusalem, did arrange an interview with the young sultan of Turkey, who received her in a great and dignified ceremony.

Mary Fisher's missionary career typified the Quaker explosion set off in the 1650s in the north of England: the Friends were a simple, unworldly people, often "she-prophets" possessed of a mystical and powerful martyr complex, utterly and self-righteously convinced of their direct experience of the Lord's word, and prophetically sure that the whole world would eventually be won over to their truth. Their sense of inner oneness with the living Lord and their rejection of the outward restraints of sacrament or Bible interpreted by an educated priesthood frightened all authorities, Anglican and Puritan alike. The best Quaker historian of this period, Hugh Barbour, observed that

> the Quaker preacher and the Puritan pastor worked in opposite directions and never understood each other's purposes. . . . The Puritan leaders were men who had known life in its complexity. They knew the ambiguous nature of sin and grace in their own best actions and in the motives they least admired. They had discovered new levels of sin and evil in the moment of their seeming victory, when Cromwell and the forces of Parliament broke apart in the struggle to remake England. Inevitably, they regarded the Quakers as self-righteous and unrealistic. Both groups actually stemmed from the same traditions . . . but they were entirely different in mood and method. A great minister like Baxter felt man's unending need of God's love and forgiveness. Those who had really seen God, he said, would not speak of sinlessness, but would abhor themselves like Job. . . . When Baxter admitted his own imperfection, Naylor exulted. While Baxter daily prayed to receive God's Spirit, Friends insisted that they had it.[24]

A CRISIS IN LEADERSHIP: FROM MOVEMENT TO ORGANIZATION

Many of the opponents of early Quakerism in England, like the great Puritan preacher Richard Baxter, thought James Naylor was its leader. Actually, Fox and Naylor, his follower, were equally important charismatic leaders in the early days before Naylor was thoroughly discredited. Like Wesley as against Whitefield in the Methodist movement of a later day, Fox won out in the long run because of his genius for organization.

The year 1656 was a critical one for both the Quakers and the Cromwellian Protectorate. In the face of increasing anarchy, Cromwell finally had been forced to set up a military dictatorship in November 1655. Tolerance declined and the persecution of Quakers increased. In January, Fox was sent to prison outside Exeter, in southwestern England. "It was a nasty stinking place," he recorded in his journal,

> where the prisoners' excrements had not been carried out for scores of years, as it was said. It was all like mire, and in some places at the top of the shoes in water and piss. . . . The gaoler would not let us cleanse the place, nor let us have beds nor straw to lie on. . . . we were so bespattered with excrements that we could not touch ourselves nor one another, that our stink increased upon us. . . . In this manner we stood all night.[25]

By summer, Fox had been joined in the Exeter prison by twenty-six other Friends, including James Naylor, "the most brilliant of the Quaker preachers." Naylor, a Yorkshireman, was of good yeoman stock. When the war broke out in 1642, he joined the New Model Army as a foot soldier. He soon rose to the rank of quartermaster and became one of the most eloquent Independent preachers: "I was struck with more terror by the preaching of James Naylor," an officer later declared, "than I was by the battle of Dunbar."[26] Mustered out of the army in 1651, Naylor went back to farming. After hearing Fox preach in his local neighborhood, and having a vision while following his plow, he went off to Swarthmore Hall to join the movement. For several years he traveled with Fox in the north country, becoming the most prominent Quaker leader in London early in 1655.

In London, Naylor was idolized by the women in the movement.

> Quakerism had not yet emerged from the Ranter stage. Fox's discipline was as yet in the course of gradual formation. Naylor was a man of striking appearance. The arrangement of his hair and beard aided the fancy of those who saw in his countenance a resemblance to the common portraits of Christ. Foremost among his devoted followers was Martha, sister of Giles Calvert, the well-known publisher, and the wife of Thomas Simmonds, a printer.[27]

In the spring of 1656, Naylor and his followers were spreading the truth throughout the west of England, where they created such a stir that they were thrown into prison. On being released in the fall, Naylor led his followers into the city of Bristol in a manner, unfortunately for them, that reenacted Christ's entry into Jerusalem; the hysterical Martha Simmonds addressed Naylor as "the only Begotten Son of God . . . fairest of ten thousand . . . dear and precious Son of Zion whose mother is a virgin and whose birth is immortal . . . Thy Name shall be no more James Naylor, but Jesus."[28] As the little band of Quakers entered Bristol, chanting "Holy, Holy, Holy Lord God of Israel," the "whole city turned out and lined the streets" to watch the spectacle.[29] Naylor was apprehended by the local authorities and sent to London, where he was tried before Parliament.

There is always a tendency in times of arbitrary and shaky authority to blow minor incidents up into national scandals. The Naylor affair was given wide publicity and discredited the Quaker movement as a whole (though *none* of the Bristol Friends, roughly 1,000 in number, took part in the procession); the punishment meted out to Naylor was incredibly vindictive and unfair, far out of proportion to his so-called crime. Parliament spent three months in bitter debate over the affair before finally ordering that Naylor be "pilloried, whipped, branded, his tongue bored out," and sent to prison, where he remained until after Cromwell's death.[30]

Cromwell was disgusted by the Naylor incident and realized that an unchecked Parliament, even of saints, is as dangerous as an absolute monarchy: "There is a need for a check or balancing power," he told his officers, "for the case of James Naylor might happen to be your own case."[31]

While Naylor journeyed to Bristol, Fox, released after eight months in the Exeter prison, went immediately to Whitehall to visit Cromwell:

> It was one of the great moments of a great century, for here, face to face, were two of the most powerful personalities of the age. . . . The man who persisted in calling himself the "Son of God" was demanding nothing less than that the military ruler of all England should forthwith disavow all violence and all coercion, make Christ's law of love the supreme law of the land, and substitute the mild dictates of the Sermon on the Mount for the Instrument of Government by which he ruled. In a word, Fox would have had him make England a pilot project for the Kingdom of Heaven.[32]

Some histories of Quakerism have played down the embarrassing Naylor affair. But it had two important sociological consequences. First, the incident marked the change from a movement of fanatical prophets to an organized sect (Braithwaite, the leading English historian of Quakerism, called this transition a movement from "sect" to "church"). Fox may have been a fanatic but he was no fool. Thus, after the Naylor disgrace, he traveled all over the British Isles, to the point of exhaustion and even mental collapse, organizing a series of monthly and quarterly meetings; this strengthening of corporate responsibility as a protection against the radical individualism resulting from the doctrine of the Inner Light was absolutely necessary if Quakerism was to be saved from anarchy and eventual disintegration. Second, the Naylor affair discredited the movement in the eyes of growing numbers of Englishmen. Persecution increased during the remaining years of the Protectorate and especially during the Restoration: some 3,000 Quakers were sent to prison under Cromwell (20 died there) and over 15,000 during the Restoration (300 deaths). Almost every leader, from George Fox and Margaret Fell to Robert Barclay and William Penn, went to prison, usually more than once. No wonder that after 1656 the Quaker leadership looked outward from England, to the Continent and the New World. Before his death in 1690, Fox traveled on the Continent with four famous Quakers—Robert Barclay, William Penn, Isaac Penington, and George Keith—all important leaders, as we shall see, in the second generation; he also took a long trip through the American colonies, from Barbados north to New England, in the company of twelve faithful followers. By 1700, there were over 40,000 Friends in the American and Caribbean colonies (20,000 in Pennsylvania) and 50,000 at home in Britain.

THE QUAKER ELITE AND
THE FELLS OF SWARTHMORE HALL

From the beginning, Puritanism was a reform movement within the Church of England. Reform movements, usually led by, and appealing to, dissatisfied members of the establishment, tend to have a decentralized leadership. Revolutionary movements, however, are usually more centralized and elitist. This was the case with Puritanism as it disintegrated into a revolutionary movement under Cromwell, much to the sincere disappointment of Cromwell himself and many of his followers like John Lilburne and John Milton.

It is indeed one of the paradoxes of the human condition that all radical egalitarian movements, which by definition aim to get rid of all forms of authority, tend to be extremely elitist. George Fox's most devoted followers, called the "Valiant Sixty" by Quaker historians, formed a close-knit—and eventually rather inbred—elite from the beginning: Fox married the mistress of Swarthmore Hall, Margaret Fell, and all Fell's sons-in-law became Friends forming a small consanguine group of leaders.*

If the top leaders of radical movements generally come from the people, like George Fox, the continued success of such movements usually depends on a key group of what Marxists would call "renegades from the ruling class." Margaret Fell, wife of Judge Thomas Fell, lord of the manor of Ulverston and master of Swarthmore Hall, was surely a renegade from the ruling class in northern England. During the early and heroic stage of the Friends' movement, Swarthmore Hall served as the Quaker Kremlin, where strategy was planned, leaders like Fox and Naylor met, and epistles, or instructions, went out to all corners of the British Isles and to the New World. The most important thing about Swarthmore Hall was the fact that Judge Fell was among the leading Puritans in northern England: he was Cromwell's exact contemporary, born in 1599 and dying in 1658; he was bred to the law; in 1641 he was made justice of the peace for Lancastershire and after war broke out was sent to represent the county in the Long Parliament; like many other members of the Puritan gentry, Fell disapproved of the increasing centralization of power under Cromwell, as well as the increasing violence, and thus failed to be present in Parliament after 1647; in 1649, he was appointed vice-chancellor of the duchy of Lancaster and, two years later, judge of assizes for the Chester and north Wales circuit. A man of such secure position was of great help to the band of martyrs whom his wife so enthusiastically joined and eventually led. It is surely symbolic of the feminine appeal of Quakerism that although Margaret Fell became the mother of Quakerism and her seven daughters (and their husbands) all played major roles in the movement, neither Judge Fell nor his son ever became convinced. In fact, Thomas Fell, Jr., actively opposed both his mother and his sisters.

Margaret Fell was proud of the fact that she came of a stock of martyrs. Born Margaret Askew, she was, so legend has it, the great-granddaughter of Anne Askew, "who for her insistence on reading the Bible in Lincoln Cathedral and elsewhere was by Henry VIII's orders tortured and finally, in 1546, burnt at the stake in Smithfield."[33] Margaret certainly had the fanatical energy of her ancestor: she was imprisoned twice; traveled all over the British Isles propagating the truth; and wrote sixteen books (five addressed to the Jews), some twenty-seven

---

*One son-in-law, William Meade, wrote seven books, was co-defendant with William Penn in the famous London case establishing the independence of the English jury, and, later, in the typical style of the sect, led the Meadites against the Pennites in a Quaker internecine struggle. Another son-in-law, John Rous, was the first "convinced" Friend in Barbados; he eventually was martyred on the gallows in Boston. One of the serving maids at Swarthmore Hall, Ann Clayton, migrated to the New World, where she ultimately married two successive Quaker governors of Rhode Island.

epistles, mostly to Friends, and countless letters to persons in authority, including Charles II, the duke of York, the princess of Orange, and magistrates, mayors, and justices. Her position at the very heart of the movement was secured when she married Fox after her first husband's death. She was ten years older (fifty-five) than Fox (forty-five) at the time of their marriage, which was a spiritual and religious rather than, as they put it in those days, a carnal union. Fox wrote, "I had seen from the Lord a considerable time before, that I should take Margaret Fell to be my wife."[34] They of course were apart for most of their married life, publishing the truth throughout the world.

The pattern of leadership that emerged in the 1650s at Swarthmore Hall still characterizes the transatlantic Quaker community. The ideals of classless egalitarianism have not alleviated the need for an Anglo-American network of informal but nevertheless real leaders, then as now often closely related.

Puritan and Quaker Patterns of Culture: The Theology of Culture

In the beginning God gave every people a cup of clay, and from this cup they drank their lives.

> Digger Indian Proverb

The appeal to national character is generally a confession of ignorance. . . . To ascribe a unified national character to the Englishmen of the seventeenth century would be simply to falsify history. Cavaliers and Roundheads did not appeal to each other simply as two parties, but as radically distinct species of men, and whoever looks into the matter carefully must agree with them.

> Max Weber

Although class authority and its relation to the Puritan and Quaker positions on the hierarchy-equality continuum are the central concerns of this book, these strategic differences in value emphasis must be seen, as Ruth Benedict pointed out, as part of an interrelated whole, or value Gestalt. From the Quaker point of view, for instance, there is no need for an elite of magistrates and ministers, or any kind of church hierarchy, since God's authority is to be found through the promptings of the Inner Light. Nor would there be a need for government or war if all men followed the Sermon on the Mount; the Quakers, in accord with this perfectionist set of values, have on the whole tended to withdraw from both government responsibility and participation in war. The Puritans, however, held a very different set of values that included the conviction that sinful men need some sort of external authority such as the Ten Commandments and the Bible, as well as a set of leaders highly educated in interpreting the law or the Bible to provide strong government at home and a fighting force to protect society from external enemies (usually representing the so-called forces of evil).

Puritan Boston and Quaker Philadelphia are more alike in surface ways than any other two cities in America. Both are conservative and traditional and have been less touched by the acids of modernity than has New York, Chicago, or Los Angeles. Originally, moreover, Puritans and Quakers shared many values: both were anti-Episcopal and anti-clerical, opposed to both Canterbury and Rome; both were anti-monastic and disbelievers in the real presence at the altar; both were against ostentatious forms and rituals, elaborate vestments, stained glass windows, and idolatrous statuary—in short, both were anti-aesthetic; and, finally, both believed in worldly asceticism and hence made money and spent it unostentatiously (when they didn't save it). Yet in spite of their similarities and common antipathies, they fought each other in Old as well as New England.

Unfortunately, men are given to see only through a glass darkly and tend to fight over great truths in the name of great half-truths. Although the whole Christian truth includes both the Old and the New Testament, law and gospel, grace and works, and so forth, Christians have always disagreed on which should be emphasized in any given time and place. By and large, established churches will emphasize law and works, whereas dissenting members will stress grace and gospel. Accordingly, Puritans emphasized grace in England and defended works after settling in the New World; sectarians in Anglican England, they built their own church in Massachusetts. The Quakers, however, tried to remain true to their sectarian ideals in the New World; the history of Philadelphia Quakerism is replete with "disownments," heresies, and schisms.

We have seen how these two ethics were rooted in the history of Reformation Europe. I shall now attempt a more systematic analysis of their contents and trace their generation of very different cultural patterns in the two cities. As a guide to analysis, Table 6-1 summarizes the contents of these two ethics and their cultural consequences. In a very important sense, the ideal-typical contrasts in that table define the central concern of this book.

IDEAL-TYPES AS CONTINUA

Both historians and theologians have misunderstood Weber's use of ideal-types as tools of historical analysis. Though one speaks *as if* reality could be captured in either/or categories (Puritan/Quaker, law/gospel, grace/works), one must bear in mind that all abstract categories are nothing more than convenient and theoretically useful conceptualizations of extreme positions along a logical continuum (of course, some Puritans, at some times, emphasize grace more than works, just as some Quakers, especially solid Friends of second and third generation wealth, have emphasized works above grace). Ideal-types are definitely not descriptions of reality, which is always more complex and messy than our logical minds can apprehend. Let us not forget that what we conceptualize as a crowd is a collection of individual and unique souls in the eyes of God, who sees neither Puritan and Quaker, nor gentile and Jew, as we do. All historians abstract from reality (and that is what differentiates them from dull

Table 6-1
PURITAN AND QUAKER ETHICS AND
THEIR CULTURAL CONSEQUENCES

Puritan Ethic	Quaker Ethic
A Religious Patterns	

1. Old Testament
  a. Ten Commandments
  b. Law (head and reason)
  c. Sacred authority: Bible
  d. Danger: legalism and rationalism
	1. New Testament
	  a. Sermon on the Mount
	  b. Gospel (love and feeling)
	  c. Sacred authority: Inner Light
	  d. Danger: antinomian mysticism

2. God Transcendent
  a. Historical Jesus
  b. Servants of God (works)
  c. Glorify God in the world
  d. Duty and honor
    (anxiety-compulsion)
	2. God Immanent
	  a. Eternal Christ
	  b. Friends of God (grace)
	  c. Union with God (mysticism)
	  d. Conscience and honesty (peace of
	    mind)

3. Predestination and Election
  a. Educated clergy
  b. Learning and erudition
  c. Literature: sermon, history, and
    theology
  d. Danger: arrogance of elect
	3. God in Every Person
	  a. Charismatic laymen
	  b. Literacy and education
	  c. Literature: personal journal
	  d. Danger: plutocracy ("Weighty
	    Friends")

4. Particular Calling
  a. Professional pride
  b. Worldly asceticism (lay monk
    transforms the world)
  c. Institutional philanthropy
	4. General Calling
	  a. Anti-professional
	  b. Worldly asceticism (lay monk
	    withdraws from the world)
	  c. Spontaneous charity

5. Source of Evil: Sinful Man
  a. Optimistic about institutions,
    pessimistic about man
  b. War: crusade against evil enemy
	5. Source of Evil: The World
	  a. Optimistic about man,
	    pessimistic about institutions
	  b. War: perfectionist pacifism

B Cultural Consequences	

6. Hierarchical Communalism
  a. Church ideal (dominate
    community)
  b. Institution building (compromise)
  c. Intolerant-responsible
  d. Public servant ideal
    (ideal lawyer: judge)
  e. Ideal man: minister-magistrate
	6. Egalitarian Individualism
	  a. Sect ideal (withdraw to peers)
	  b. Anti-institutional (spontaneous
	    perfectionism)
	  c. Tolerant-irresponsible
	  d. Private citizen ideal
	    (ideal lawyer: advocate)
	  e. Ideal person: martyr-mystic

7. Aristocratic-Patrician
  a. Urban origin and values
  b. Representative republic
  c. Speaking aristocracy and silent
    democracy
  d. Level up (opportunitarian)
  e. Patriarchal
  f. Vices: arrogance, pride,
    chauvinism, provincialism
	7. Democratic-Plutocratic
	  a. Rural origin (suburban values)
	  b. Direct democracy
	  c. Speaking democracy and silent
	    plutocracy
	  d. Level down (egalitarian)
	  e. Sex equality (matriarchal)
	  f. Vices: smugness, snobbery,
	    self-satisfaction

Ethnocentrism	Xenophilia

antiquarians). Our method simply makes us more conscious of what we are doing.

The differences between the Puritan and Quaker ethics, then, are largely a matter of emphasis: either/or categories are nothing more than useful tools to guide us in asking relevant questions about the cultures of Boston and Philadelphia; they help highlight the theoretically relevant facts about crucial events in the histories of these cities. Their usefulness must be judged not at the beginning but at the end of our analysis.

PATTERNS OF AUTHORITY:
RELIGIOUS AND SECULAR

Though this is a sociological rather than a theological study of values, secular values, of social equality or hierarchy, for instance, are usually grounded in man's ultimate concern with religious values (or with the surrogate religious values found in the myriad secular myths and ideologies of our time). For both Puritans and Quakers in the seventeenth century, the authority of God was absolute; for both, the way men are, or should be, related to one another ultimately depended on how they were first related to their God. Godless men, both would have agreed, could hardly know, let alone love, one another.

Though their world was far more full of fear, cruelty, and material deprivation than our own, both the Puritans and the Quakers lived in a meaningful rather than an absurd world. Meaning derived from their sense of an absolute transcendental authority. I stress this point here because throughout the book I talk of Puritan *authority* as against the *anti-authority* of Quakerism. What is meant is that the Puritan and Quaker ethics differed over human, sociological, societal, institutional, or *existential* as against *transcendental* authority: whereas both the Puritans and the Quakers recognized the absolute authority of God, the Puritans, for theological reasons, assumed that *sinful man* needs an earthly and institutionalized hierarchical authority structure; the Quakers argued that *perfectible man* needs no such system but is capable of approaching God directly.

Sociologists are more interested in the unanticipated consequences of religious beliefs as they motivate secular men than in their effect on the men who held those convictions in a religious or sacred age. Although I agree with Hannah Arendt, who wrote in effect that a world without God will tend to be authorityless and ultimately absurd, I should go even further and suggest that a secular cultural pattern, originally grounded in the belief in the absolute authority of God but also, at the same time, postulating the need for the institutionalization of an existential class of experts to interpret this authority, will retain some semblance of human or secular authority long after the sacred or transcendental source has vanished. An egalitarian religious ethic such as the Quakers postulated, however, will be far more likely to be associated with a lack of authority, or extreme individualism, once the belief in the absolute authority of God has been lost. Thus, the Puritan faith in the need for institutional restraints and the Quaker mistrust of institutions have done political battle down through our history, beginning with the formation of the Federalist and Jeffersonian parties. The spiritual descendants of John Winthrop (and Hobbes) became Federalists; the spiritual heirs of William Penn (and Rousseau) became Jeffersonians. As Samuel Morison noted in comparing the political philosophy of John Adams with that of Thomas Jefferson:

> Jefferson thought that the safety of the Republic lay in removing restraints, and demolishing traditions; that if an institution was old it was probably bad. . . .
> Adams believed that the safety of the Republic depended on checks and balances against hasty decisions of mere numerical majorities, and that old institutions should sacredly be preserved until they were proven to be harmful.[1]

I shall now turn to a discussion of the religious capital originally accumulated by the Quakers and the Puritans, upon which their descendants in Philadelphia and Boston have been living for many secular generations. I should like first to show how both the Puritans and the Quakers tended to emphasize (and overemphasize) different aspects of the Christian value system built by the Roman church in the centuries between Augustine and Aquinas.

FROM MONASTERY TO MEETINGHOUSE

In the thirteenth and fourteenth centuries, Christendom meant one catholic, apostolic, and sacramental church centered in the West at Rome. The Roman ideal of the church as the mystical body of Christ was sociologically organized as a universal bureaucracy of priests, bishops, and monks headed by the pope. Ultimate worldly authority resided in this hierarchy of specialists who were in control of the sacraments and administered the canon law.

Martin Luther once said that the distinction between law and gospel "contains the sum of all Christian doctrine." It is in many ways unfortunate that the phrase "Judeo-Christian tradition" has recently come into vogue in America, especially among religious and secular liberals, largely as a spongy attempt to dispel prejudice and to counter anti-Semitism through homogenization. For it has always been the very essence of the driving and dynamic force of Christianity that it was built on a dialectical tension between the Old and the New Testament, between law and gospel, between Sinai and the cross. In striking contrast to Protestantism's endless exclusiveness and the consequent spawning of sects in every generation, the genius of Catholicism has been its ability to include, in each generation, both old and new truths, eventually absorbing the new into the old in a novel synthesis. This inclusiveness was made possible by an elitist and hierarchical ethic based on a double standard of morality. The spiritual elite, rather than breaking away in a sectarian schism, voluntarily joined a monastic order based on a perfectionist ideal.

Most orders were founded not by the official hierarchy but by a perfectionist layman or priest who, in the interest of some new truth, was usually branded a heretic. Thus, the order and the sect were commonly founded by members of discontented classes, often making a strong appeal to women (both the Franciscans and the Quakers received enthusiastic support from female servants). Unlike Protestantism, the Catholic church eventually absorbed and institutionalized the new truths and their propagators. Saint Benedict, the founder of monasticism, for instance, withdrew from the world sometime before the year 500, founded Monte Cassino in 529, and formulated a rigid set of rules that has served as a model for other rigorist movements down to the present day. In the dialectical tradition of thesis, antithesis, and synthesis—withdrawal and return—it is interesting that after 590, when Saint Gregory was elected pope, the Benedictine spirit came to permeate all Christendom. Later, in response to new problems arising out of the growth of town life in the thirteenth century, the Franciscan and Dominican orders were established. The Franciscans, emphasizing innocence and the great truths of the heart, went among the urban poor; the Dominicans, stressing rationalism and the great truths of the head, preached to the educated classes, urging them back to God. The Dominican ideal eventually was absorbed by the church through the dry and coldly rational scholasticism of Saint Thomas's *Summa*, and the Franciscan ideal has been coming to the fore in our day ever since Vatican II.

Thus, the great truths that led to the founding of Puritanism and its antithesis, Quakerism, had a long history in the one inclusive Catholic synthesis of the past, and perhaps of the future. Certainly, the Puritan and Thomistic values that have been at the heart of the American establishment for some three centuries are now faced with a new antithesis in a kind of New Testament or Franciscan perfectionism, symbolized in the antinomian 1960s by the younger generation's idealization of the doings of the Berrigan brothers and their many Quaker and crypto-Quaker cohorts.

Time is the great corrupter of all perfectionist ideals and enthusiasms. The double standard of morality within Catholicism allowed the orders to handle this problem through withdrawal from the world and adherence to the ideals of poverty, chastity, and obedience. What so many sectarian movements of the Reformation did was to abolish the monastic and elitist ideals of poverty and chastity while at the same time attempting to apply other perfectionist ideals—selectively—to all men, or at least to all their voluntary and "twice-born" followers. This was a major problem for both the Puritans and the Quakers, especially the latter, as we shall see.

TRANSCENDENCE AND IMMANENCE

In contrast to their predecessors and their contemporaries, who believed in the immanence of many gods, the ancient Hebrews gave to the world the idea of one transcendent God for all men. On the whole, the Catholic answers as to whether God is transcendent or immanent, whether men should be guided by law or gospel, the Ten Commandments or the Sermon on the Mount, the particular or the general calling, and all the other dichotomies that divided the right from the left wing of the Reformation, the Puritans from the Quakers, would have been *both, of course—but each in its proper place and proportion.* Whereas the Catholic God was transcendent in the tradition of the Old Testament, He was also immanent, according to the doctrine of the real presence at the Mass, as well as at other holy times and places, which were carefully controlled and ritualized by the church.

The Quaker doctrine of the Inner Light, which gave the early Friends their driving, if fleeting, force to convert the world, implied the danger of extreme individualism as well as the danger of blasphemy in thinking they really were sons of God, as the citizens of Bristol felt when James Naylor rode into the city on an ass in imitation of Christ. The immanence of God in every man and in all places has always been a problem to thoughtful Quakers. Even Fox saw the danger after the Naylor affair, when he rapidly proceeded to institute the modern Quaker tradition that God's presence is to be felt primarily when Quakers gather together in meetings, the empty space between the opposing rows of benches taking the place of the altar and cross in the Catholic Mass. At the same time, the Quakers, with their mystical relationship to the immanent deity, saw sin as derived largely from worldly contamination.

The transcendence of the authoritarian God of the Calvinists and Puritans allowed for no easy handling of sin. They needed an authoritarian class of ministers, backed by magistrates, to police the sinful. (In addition there was a great deal of gossiping and minding of other people's business in the towns of Puritan New England.)

Thus, the Catholic doctrine of limited transcendence and immanence lies between the Calvinist and Quaker alternatives, between Puritan anxiety, on the one hand, and Quaker peace of mind, on the other. The Catholic avoided both the extreme transcendental position of the Calvinists and Puritans (and the danger of emotionally sterile Deism) and the ubiquitous immanence (close to pantheism) of the Quaker position.

The average medieval layman took his imperfection and essential sinfulness for granted and led a more or less satisfying, sacramental religious life, confident of salvation in the hereafter. Sin was no real problem when the sacraments provided a regular cycle of mystical relationships with God. The medieval tendency toward mysticism and emotionalism, then, was closer to the religious values of the Quakers than to those of the Calvinists and Puritans. Calvin's suspicion of all feelings and emotions, along with his doctrine of transcendence, led to an ethic of systematic and ascetic action. And he modeled this ethic on the spiritual elitism of Western monasticism, "substituting for the spiritual aristocracy of monks, outside and above the world, the spiritual aristocracy of predestined saints of God, within the world."[2]

The English Quakers, born in the midst of the Puritan movement, absorbed the monastic ideal of an ordered and disciplined life. Nevertheless, after the first flame of missionary enthusiasm in Fox's generation had cooled, they had none of the single-minded and anxiety-ridden drive to transform the world, partly because of their mystical doctrine of the Inner Light, or their theory of God's immanence.

PARTICULAR AND GENERAL CALLING

Luther gave the idea of the calling to the Reformation. In Catholicism only the clergy, and especially the monks, had a strong sense of vocation. (In the female orders the first feminists were given a sense of vocation and executive responsibility, which they lost in the course of the Reformation, especially under patriarchal Puritanism.)

As I showed in Chapter 4, Calvin and later the Puritans developed the calling in its highest professional sense. The Puritans' seriousness toward vocational obligations gradually did away with the spontaneous enjoyment of life, which had marked the aristocratic amateurism of Merrie England. As Weber noted the Quakers remained traditionalists where calling was concerned, "Barclay looks upon the obligation of one's calling," he wrote of the only Quaker theologian, "not in Calvinistic or even Lutheran terms, but rather Thomistically."[3] As we shall see, the Quakers to this day mistrust professionalism. They are Quakers first and professionals and businessmen second, whereas the Puritan sought to please God through success and excellence in his chosen calling. The almost monastic devotion of the Puritans to their vocations, especially among the elite of leaders, derived from their emphasis on the calling, along with their belief in predestination and election.

DIVINE PROVIDENCE:
PREDESTINATION AND ELECTION

Someone once said that Goethe's *Faust* is the story of "salvation by aspiration." If so, the Calvinist-Puritan ethic was an infinitely Faustian faith. Max Weber called Calvinism

the faith over which the great political and cultural struggles of the sixteenth and seventeenth centuries were fought in the most highly developed countries, the Netherlands, England and France. . . . It served as a rallying-point to countless heroes of the Church militant, and in both the eighteenth and nineteenth centuries it caused schisms in the Church and formed the battle-cry of great awakenings.[4]

Others, too, have viewed Calvinism, and its key canons of predestination and election, as the great transforming ethic in the emergence of the modern world. In this connection, it is interesting that Calvin's spiritual ancestor in the church was Augustine, who watched his own Roman world disintegrating and came to very much the same conclusions about the role of the saving remnant, elected through God's grace. Both Calvin and Augustine, of course, went back to the Old Testament, which witnessed the transition from immanent, tribal polytheism to universal and transcendental monotheism.

Perhaps all great transforming ethics have been authoritarian and hierarchical. Indeed, in another great transforming age the Boston Brahmin Barrett

Wendell wrote of the materialistic philosophy that was rationalizing the authority of the leaders of the plutocratic revolution of his own Victorian era.

> Strangely enough, the conceptions which underlie the most popular scientific
> philosophy of our time have much in common with those which actuated Augus-
> tine and Calvin. Earthly life, the modern evolutionists hold, consists in a struggle
> for existence wherein only the fittest can survive; for every organism which per-
> sists, myriads must irretrievably perish. . . . [W]hat Augustine and Calvin saw, in
> the human affairs whence each alike inferred the systems of Heaven and Hell,
> was really what the modern evolutionists perceive in every aspect of Nature.
> Total depravity is only a theological name for that phase of life which in less
> imaginative times we name the struggle for existence; and likewise election is only
> a theological name for what our newer fashion calls the survival of the fittest.
> Old-world theology and modern science alike strive to explain facts which have
> been and shall be so long as humanity casts its shadow in the sunshine.[5]

Calvinism, then, was an aspiring and anxiety-producing ethic, especially as
far as the elect were concerned. They were constantly aware that no matter
how well they performed their duties, they might fall from grace at any time
and prove unworthy of salvation. That God should place such responsibilities
on any minority was a truly terrifying thought. "Though I may be sent to Hell
for it," Milton once wrote, "such a God will never command my respect." Both
the ancient Hebrews and the Puritans were cursed with the burden of being
chosen people—no wonder that Hebrew was the second language, and the Jewish prophets the favorite heroes, of the Massachusetts Bay settlers, led by a class
of magistrates and ministers who were determined that for the first time in history God's will was to be done on earth.

Both Judaism and Calvinism, like Marxism but in striking contrast to Quakerism, were infinitely historical creeds. The Old Testament, after all, is a rather
bloody historical record of God's people. The literature of Puritan New England was made up almost entirely of abstract theology, sermons, and history,
or history as sermon and vice versa. The Quakers, however, convinced of the
eternal Christ in every man, showed little interest in either the Old Testament
or the historical Jesus. Their principal literature was the personal journal, a
concrete rather than an abstract record of their search for God in their lives.
Peace with the Lord counted far more than proper performance in earthly callings.

Two of the most famous journals of colonial America were written by John
Winthrop and John Woolman. Winthrop was concerned mainly with whether
he was fulfilling God's will as magistrate, and his journal is an excellent and objective history of the first two decades of the Massachusetts Bay Colony. After
the opening pages, he refers to himself not as "I" but as "the governor." The
journal of the simple New Jersey tailor John Woolman, in contrast, is an intimate and subjective devotional classic, obsessed with how one becomes a good
person rather than a good magistrate or merchant. Much in the style of George
Fox, Woolman opens his journal with the characteristic statement "before I
was seven years old I began to be acquainted with the operations of Divine
Love."[6] Rather than government or leadership, Woolman's main worldly con-

cern was the plight of the downtrodden and the damned, the Indians, and the black slaves. A century before the Civil War, he traveled throughout the South protesting the evils of slavery, and he anticipated the modern faith in the symbolic boycotting of lettuce, grapes, and so forth by wearing undyed clothing because he believed that dyes were made by slave labor. "All who read Woolman," wrote Elton Trueblood in his history of Quakerism, "have a chance to realize that the best thing in the world is a really good person."[7] While Woolman and the Quakers were quietly concerned with the mysterious workings of divine love in the world, Winthop and the Puritans worried about divine authority and how best to carry out their duty to lead the damned.

QUAKER PERFECTIONISM

The Quaker emphasis on the general calling not only led them to place a low value on professionalism but also led to, and was a consequence of, their canon of perfectionism and their unanticipated withdrawal from the world. As leadership in the governing of men, especially in a democratic republic, inevitably means compromise, the Quaker elite was ultimately forced to withdraw from responsibility.

What the Catholics had required of an elite few voluntarily chosen in each generation, the Quakers set up as an ideal for all Friends, men and women, married and single, rich and poor, and, most important, the twice-born, or convinced, as well as the once-born, birthright members. Whereas each new generation of perfectionists in the Catholic elitist tradition took voluntary vows of poverty and chastity and thus produced no legitimate heirs, the Quakers sought perfection without these restrictions and thus were morally compromised by both the accumulation of wealth and its transmittal to the second and subsequent generations. The Catholics had long recognized the secularizing and corrupting influence of wealth and sexual desire, but their dual ethic imposed poverty and celibacy only on the leadership. The canon of celibacy was important sociologically as an inhibitor of ascribed status within the elite. Human nature being what it is, sectarian enthusiasm, as Troeltsch and Weber saw, is primarily a one-generational phenomenon. Accordingly, infant baptism has been anathema to sectarians everywhere (the Quakers did away with baptism entirely), for ascription was, and is, the archenemy of all enthusiasms. The essence of upper-class social organization, moreover, is the inheritance of wealth and high status. Yet Philadelphia Quakers who had accumulated wealth and ascribed privileges were prompted by their perfectionist ideals to abdicate social and political responsibility. Here, of course, we see a major cause of the differences between the early Puritan and Quaker upper classes and their secular descendants in Boston and Philadelphia down to the twentieth century.

War is an evil that the Catholic tradition deemed an inevitable aspect of sinful men's ways. The Roman church mitigated the evil, however, by the concept of a just war, and the double standard of morality allowed the perfectionist ideal of peace to guide the clerical elite, especially the members of the monastic orders, who were not required to bear arms. Rarely have modern Catholics viewed war, as the Calvinists and Puritans definitely did, as a moral crusade against evil. (They once did, of course, in the Crusades.) Catholics, like most Episcopalians, have been reluctant fighters. Thus, in our own Civil War, in many ways a duplication of the Cavalier-Puritan conflict in England, the Northern Episcopalians, in the Catholic tradition, were reluctant participants; the descendants of the Puritans, crusading idealists against evil; and the Quakers, perfectionists above the conflict.*

Just a word here about the ever present *possibility* of sin in all sexual relationships, if not in such relationships per se. Too little is known of Calvin's personal life to judge him on this question. Certainly Luther was not above temptation, but everyone familiar with George Fox's journal is struck with the fact that he appears to have had no sense whatever of his own temptations to sin. Indeed, all available evidence indicates that he probably went through a long and vigorous life without ever having had carnal knowledge of any woman, not even his wife, Margaret. (As Fox wanted it, the marriage was made in heaven.) Fox was quite different from his Puritan contemporary John Bunyan, whose *Pilgrim's Progress* is marked by a ubiquitous sense of sin. One gets the impression, in other words, that there is a mild sexlessness in the Quaker tradition, which is quite in contrast to the vicious suppression of sexuality in Puritan cultures.† *The Scarlet Letter*, I have always suspected, could not have been written in, or about, Philadelphia.

QUAKER TESTIMONIES AND PURITAN DOGMA

Whereas the heart of the Puritan value system, as I have emphasized, was the hierarchical doctrine of election and the closely allied concept of the calling, especially that of magistrate and minister, the bedrock of the Quaker value system was belief in equality. Equality to the Quakers meant equality of all men before God, not equality of economic conditions. Thus, the Friends rejected all earthly *authority*.

Quaker anti-authoritarianism grew directly out of the doctrines of perfectionism and the Inner Light and long antedated the testimony of pacifism or conscientious objection. Many Quakers, both officers and men, came out of Cromwell's army, and they withdrew or were dismissed mainly because of their antipathy to authority. As one colonel put it in a letter to General Monk: "My

---

*The Quakers' attitude toward war, like their attitude toward government, often has been morally ambiguous, especially among the rich and successful. How, for instance, can a wealthy and powerful man with a fine home and a family brought up in affluence be a perfectionist in refusing to defend the country in which he has made or inherited his money?

†Note, too, that the Quakers believed in and practiced sexual equality.

captain lieutenant is much confirmed in his principles of quaking, making all the soldiers his equals, according to the Leveller strain. . . . when I think of the Levelling design which had like to have torn the army to pieces, it makes me more bold to give my opinion that these things be curbed in time."[8] From the beginning, then, the Quakers were levelers of authority rather than levelers of wealth.

At this point it is important to emphasize that the anti-authoritarian ethic of the Quakers was loosely allied with their anti-intellectual antipathy to all theology—or abstract social theory. Theirs was a direct, empirical, and pragmatic approach to the natural man and his relationship to God. Whereas the Calvinists and the Puritans (like the Catholics before them and the Marxists since) produced a highly complex and intellectual body of dogmatic theology, the Quaker movement produced nothing of the kind. As a consequence, social control and social identity among the Quakers, guided by no intellectually binding dogma, had to rest on a series of petty symbols, or "testimonies," that were rigidly enforced within the community of Friends. In this connection, it is useful to go back to Tocqueville's analysis of American democracy. For he was the first to see how equality and individualism are two sides of the same coin; he then showed how both, far from producing a creative individuality, are likely to lead to a stultifying uniformity in manners as well as in ideas. *The authority of dogma, in other words, may in the long run prove to be more liberating than the anti-intellectual tyranny of public opinion and peer pressure, which has marked both the Quakers and Philadelphia Gentlemen throughout our history and characterizes American society today.* Let us now turn to the Quaker testimonies, which, in the absence of an authoritarian dogma, set them apart from their neighbors well into the nineteenth century.

THE TYRANNY OF PETTY TESTIMONIES

"Hat honor" was one of the weightiest customs of seventeenth-century England. At the trial of Charles I, for instance, the judges refused to uncover their heads and of course the king refused to recognize their standing by uncovering his. The refusal of hat honor was one of the most infuriating of the Quaker practices, and William Penn took perverse pride in wearing his hat at court, especially in the presence of his good friend and patron King James II.*

Penn also followed Quaker custom by referring to the king as "James" and by using the familiar "thee and thou" rather than the deferential "you." Other terms of respect likewise were rejected: thus, as "Mr." originally meant "Master," it was not used by the Friends. However, "Doctor" (medical) was retained, perhaps because George Fox once thought of becoming a physician or because it signified a helping rather than an authoritarian profession.

---

*Once when Penn wore his hat before Charles II, the monarch showed his sense of humor by remarking that it was not customary in such a situation for more than one person to remain covered and by taking off his own.

The Quakers proclaimed their egalitarianism by distinctive dress, too. James Naylor wore long, flowing hair in imitation of Christ. (The Puritan Round-heads, of course, started the efficient bourgeois custom of closely cropping hair to distinguish them from the haughty Cavaliers of the day.) And the Quaker uniform of simple gray homespun bespoke a leveling down in imitation of the humble.

The celebrated Quaker refusal to take oaths of any kind was another impor-tant and often frustrating testimony to equality. Whereas the honor of family, class, and country usually lies at the heart of hierarchical and aristocratic value systems, honesty is paramount in pluto-democracies and was one of the very highest values for the Quakers (indeed, their success in business depended on it). As the Quakers held that they were equally honest at all times and places, they categorically opposed oath taking.*

The egalitarian ideals of the Quakers were of critical importance as they af-fected leadership—or the lack thereof. As with all egalitarian movements, the Quakers saw the utility of education and literacy, but they thoroughly rejected the vanity that so often goes with erudition. (This view certainly accords with the tenets of American populism from our beginning down to the present: Americans worship education but suspect most learning and learned men.)

With no hierarchical class of clergy, the Friends developed the rather touch-ing ceremony of the "hand-fast marriage." The young couple marry themselves, as it were, and are witnessed by their friends and relatives, who sign a scroll tes-tifying to their union.

All days of the week and months of the year are equal and are named quan-titatively rather than qualitatively: First Month, Second Month; First Day, Second Day, etc. Antipathy to the vanity of quality and personality is likewise seen in the layout of Philadelphia: Penn allowed no Quaker names of note to adorn the streets but labeled them numerically in one direction and, in the Quaker pantheistic tradition, after trees in the other.

The Quakers held fast to their ideal of equality even unto death. All worldly civilizations have witnessed man's attempt to symbolize status after death with various sorts of monuments, from the ancient pyramids to the great and osten-tatious mausoleums in the graveyards of our Victorian ancestors.† In Quaker graveyards, however, all men and women are buried in graves with similarly unostentatious headstones.

---

*This line of reasoning is similar to the Quaker idea of the sacred. Since everything is equally sacred, the setting aside of sacred places or times is unnecessary. Thus, there were no meeting-houses at first, and even after they were established throughout England and America, they were not considered sacred. Indeed, in the city of Philadelphia today, there are no Quaker meeting-houses dating back to the seventeenth or eighteenth centuries: when neighborhood or real estate values change, meetinghouses are sold and the members move on.

†In our day, religion has been replaced by the worship of art, and the best people parade from gal-lery to gallery along 57th Street or Madison Avenue on Saturday, just as their ancestors once pa-raded down Park Avenue after attendance at church or synagogue. Status after death is now as-sured by such galleries as the Guggenheim and the Hirshhorn.

TOLERANCE, RESPONSIBILITY,
AND ETHNOCENTRISM

I should like to close this analysis by suggesting that one of the important consequences of the different emphases in the Puritan and Quaker value systems has been that, when transplanted to Boston and Philadelphia, they produced among the upper classes, and the rest of the citizens, too, an intolerant responsibility in the former city and a tolerant irresponsibility in the latter. Though corruption in municipal government is a universal phenomenon, when Lincoln Steffens found Philadelphia corrupt but content he pinpointed this anomaly. Steffens, as we shall see, also found Boston corrupt, but he found its citizens far less tolerant and far more active in trying to clean up the government. Of course, these differing attitudes have long histories in each city. From the beginning of the colonial period in Boston, immigrants other than English Puritans were not tolerated, but at the same time the upper class was determined to be a responsible ruling class. In Philadelphia, the Quaker leaders tolerated incompetent appointments of the chief executives without open revolt, if not without opposition, and acquiesced in Penn's importing large numbers of immigrants other than Quakers into the colony. And down through the city's history, the privileged upper class accepted misrule in city and state rather than take a responsible lead.

Just as corruption seems to be a universal phenomenon, so anthropologists have found ethnocentrism characteristic of all cultures. Now, Bostonians have always had more than their share of boosting ethnocentrism, and perhaps this is normal; what is curiously abnormal is the ethnophobia, or xenophilia, that has been characteristic of Philadelphia from the first. Whereas Bostonians are all too ready to see Boston as best in ways that it clearly is not, Philadelphians are equally ready to brand their city as worst in ways that it clearly is not. Bostonians are braggarts; Philadelphians, as Owen Wister put it, have a deep "instinct for self-disparagement."

These differences between Boston and Philadelphia will be evident (often between the lines) in much of the rest of this book. Here I should like to hazard a generalization that is surely counter to the conventional wisdom of our day at least. By and large, in a society that is led by an established and authoritative class there will be more self-respect and pride, among both the leaders and the led, than will be the case where a privileged class falls back on its wealth, leaving the reins of society to an egalitarian and democratic elite. This generalization seems to be in accord with the historical evidence in Boston and Philadelphia; it may also be true of our national history. At the time of the First World War, when a Protestant establishment was still in the saddle, atrocity stories about our enemies abounded; boosterism bloomed in the following decade. In the more recent past, when the Protestant establishment had become suspect and democratic elitism was firmly in the saddle, atrocity stories about Americans in Vietnam were the rule, and American boosterism was replaced by mistrust and a growing instinct for disparagement among more and more Americans, including both the privileged and the people. Thus, atrocities committed by the Russian secret service are now drowned out by endless stories of our own atrocity-minded CIA. Never has America been more tolerant and egalitarian—more like what Philadelphia has always been.

To paraphrase the Digger Indian proverb that opened this chapter, such were the two contrasting cups of clay that God gave to the people who settled around Massachusetts Bay and on the shores of the Delaware; from these cups they have always drunk, and still are drinking.

PART III

THE COLONIAL EXPERIENCE: COMPARATIVE HISTORY

The Founding of Massachusetts and Pennsylvania

By the Sword She Seeks Peace under Liberty
    Motto of the Commonwealth of Massachusetts

Virtue, Liberty, and Independence
    Motto of the Commonwealth of Pennsylvania

Institutions, to paraphrase Emerson, are but the lengthened shadows of their founders. Massachusetts and Pennsylvania differ because Massachusetts, and New England as a whole, was primarily the lengthened shadow of a founding class of Elizabethan Puritans, country gentlemen, city merchants, and Cambridge educated clergymen; Pennsylvania, more than any of the other proprietary colonies, was the lengthened shadow of a single charismatic leader, William Penn, a many-sided, even ambivalent, Restoration egghead or liberal courtier. Whereas Penn himself owned Pennsylvania lock, stock, and barrel, much in the style of a feudal baron, John Winthrop, chosen the first governor of Massachusetts, was only one of a class of leaders. Winthrop, the secular magistrate, and John Cotton, the "Pope of New England," firmly believed in the Elizabethan values of authority and hierarchy, order and degree, all held together by and depending on religious uniformity and the punishment of heretics. Penn founded Pennsylvania in the anti-authoritarian and tolerant tradition of the Quakers at a time when most Englishmen were sick and tired of religious intolerance; thus, the Acts of Toleration were passed in 1689, only a few years after the founding of Pennsylvania (1682). Whereas Winthrop was brought up in the Calvinist-Puritan tradition of magisterial responsibility (he became a justice of the peace at the age of eighteen), Penn was never elected to any responsible political office and, moreover, founded Pennsylvania in the spirit of tolerance after he himself had spent considerable time in jail. Winthrop grew up in the tradition of county-family authority; he lived most of his adult life in Boston, always serving as governor or assistant governor. Penn, like his father before him, lived most of his life amid the intrigues and power politics of the court, spending only four years in Pennsylvania on two visits there. Indeed, if Winthrop was a classic example of Thomas Jefferson's deeply rooted class of progenitors, Penn was the very essence of the rootless, though brilliant, cut-flower, at least as far as Pennsylvania was concerned.

The citizens of Massachusetts governed themselves from the very beginning; Pennsylvania, during the whole colonial period, was governed at the executive level by the appointed deputies of absentee owners, William Penn and his descendants. As we have seen, Massachusetts's leaders believed in an established church with religious uniformity enforced by the *authority* of a class of clergymen, on the one hand, and backed by the *power* of a class of magistrates, on the other. Pennsylvania, as every schoolchild knows, was ostensibly a holy experiment in religious tolerance and egalitarian democracy but was in fact "a seventeenth-century real estate development."[1] As Penn himself wrote in July 1681: "I cannot make money without special concessions. . . . Though I desire to extend religious freedom, yet I want some recompense for my trouble."[2] In short, whereas Massachusetts was founded by a class of men who were conservative but responsible, Pennsylvania was founded by one man who was surely liberal but quite irresponsible, in more ways than one, as we shall see.

Two main types of colony were founded by the English in North America—the chartered colony and the royal colony. Some chartered colonies were civil corporations, for example, Virginia and Massachusetts. Unlike the Virginia Company, however, the Massachusetts Bay Company was *not* governed from London; rather, its charter was carried overseas with the first settlers and the colony henceforth was an independent, self-governing commonwealth. Pennsylvania belonged to a second type of chartered colony, the proprietary colony, in essence a feudal land grant. It kept this status until the Revolution, except for a brief period of royal control (of the some £2.5 million paid by the British crown to *all* American Loyalists after the Revolution, Penn's descendants received by far the largest share, £500,000).

THE FOUNDING OF MASSACHUSETTS

William Laud, named bishop of London in 1625, sought both to disband the Puritan party and to restore High Church ritual.* Accordingly, "a group of Cambridge and East Anglia Puritans felt that the time had come to establish a new England overseas; and New England must include a new Emmanuel."[3]

---

*Charles I appointed Laud archbishop of Canterbury in 1633.

In March 1629, these East Anglian Puritans secured a royal charter from the king and formed the Massachusetts Bay Company, which was granted large powers of government within the territory covered by the charter. There next occurred a characteristic, if surprising, move by a group of the leading stockholders, who themselves expected to go to America. In late July, John Winthrop, Isaac Johnson (the earl of Lincoln's son-in-law), Thomas Dudley (the earl's steward), and several other lay leaders met at the earl's estate near Boston in Lincolnshire. Among the company were three ministers, John Cotton, Roger Williams, and Thomas Hooker. Here it was agreed that those stockholders who planned to go to the New World were secretly to buy up the shares of all those who planned to remain in England. Even though those who remained at home might be good Puritans and sympathetic to the ideals of the New Zion, so their thinking went, things might change. (This decision foreshadowed the New England way, which was not democracy, equality, or even freedom, but *self-government*.) These leaders were taking no chances with absentee control. As Cotton Mather later put it: "We came hither because we would have our posterity settled under the pure and full dispensations of the gospel, defended by *rulers which should be ourselves*."[4]

In August 1629, twelve shareholders met in secret at Cambridge and decided to emigrate, "provided that the government of the colony, together with the patent, be first transferred to us."[5] The general court of the company so voted a few days later and elected Winthrop governor of both the company and the colony. Word was spread among families and friends of the stockholders, and the following March, sixteen ships led by the *Arbella* sailed for the New World. John Cotton, one of the most learned and eloquent Puritan divines, preached the sermon for the departing fleet.

Aboard the *Arbella* were John Winthrop; the Lady Arbella Johnson, daughter of the earl of Lincoln, his steward, Thomas Dudley, and Lady Arbella's husband, Isaac Johnson, one of the wealthiest immigrants; Simon Bradstreet, later governor, and his wife, Anne, the first published poet in the New World; Sir Richard Saltonstall, wealthy nephew of the lord mayor of London and progenitor of a New England line that included Gurden Saltonstall, a colonial governor of Connecticut, and Leverett Saltonstall, a twentieth-century governor of Massachusetts; William Pynchon, founder of the town of Springfield; another founder of Springfield, Jehu Burr, the great-great-grandfather of Aaron Burr, president of Princeton, and builder of Nassau Hall; and John Phillips of Cambridge, who became minister at Watertown and whose descendants included Samuel and John Phillips, founders of the academies at Andover, Massachusetts, and Exeter, New Hampshire, and Wendell Phillips, the abolitionist.

By the end of 1630, some 900 immigrants had landed on the shores of Massachusetts Bay and settled at one of the seven original towns of the colony, five of them around Boston harbor. Conditions were severe and the colony barely managed to hold its own until 1633, when Laud became archbishop of Canterbury and the persecution of Puritans was intensified. The great migration began. By the outbreak of the Civil War, some 15,000 Englishmen had settled in Massachusetts Bay.

The Laudian reaction finally forced John Cotton to leave for the New World. Along with Cotton aboard the *Griffin* in 1633 came Thomas Hooker, founder of Hartford, and John Haynes, "a gentleman of great estate" from the county of Essex and later the leading and wealthiest parishioner of Hooker's congregation at New Town (now Cambridge). Haynes was governor of the Bay Colony before he left with Hooker for Hartford, where he was reelected governor of Connecticut every other year (succession was illegal) over an extended period of time. Also aboard were Edmund Quincy, the progenitor of one of Massachusetts's greatest families, which produced three mayors of Boston and a president of Harvard, among other leaders in New England down to our own time; William and Anne Hutchinson; and Thomas Leverett and his seventeen-year-old son John. John Leverett served as governor of the Bay Colony seven times; his grandson and namesake was one of the great presidents of Harvard (not a clergyman but a lawyer). Of Anne Hutchinson I shall write in Chapter 9, and of Thomas Hutchinson, her great-great-grandson, conservative and autocratic New Englander par excellence and the last royal governor of Massachusetts, in Chapter 10.

THE FOUNDING OF PENNSYLVANIA

England went through the greatest revolution in her history in the half century that separated the founding of Pennsylvania (1682) and the founding of Massachusetts (1630). Quakerism grew out of the turmoil of that period.

Though Quakerism was born among the disinherited seekers of northern England and made its appeal primarily to simple people, its headquarters in the early evangelical days was Swarthmore Hall, the stately home of the Fells. The Grange, home of Isaac and Mary Penington,* situated near the little village of Jordans, about twenty miles outside London in Buckinghamshire, became the headquarters of the educated vanguard of Quakerism in the second generation. Every movement of the people has had its few converts, like the Fells of Swarthmore Hall, from the educated classes. And Quakerism produced a small educated elite in the second generation.

> What is really surprising about the Quaker aristocrats is that they never sought power or authority for themselves. They never seemed to feel superior to the rude men from the north of England who, in spite of their lesser opportunities, were their major teachers. But they did something which the rude men were unable to do. They influenced governments; they thought systematically; they wrote brilliantly. Without these four men—Pennington, Ellwood, Penn and Barclay—it is doubtful if the Movement would have survived, or that the People Called Quakers would be generally known today.[6]

Isaac Penington (1616–1679) was the eldest son of Sir Isaac Penington, lord mayor of London at the outbreak of the Civil War, representative of the city of

---

*The English use "Penington" while Trueblood uses "Pennington." I follow the English.

London in the Long Parliament, one of the judges at the trial of Charles I, and stern member of the Puritan establishment. In 1654, the younger Penington married Mary Proud Sprigett, widow of another stern Puritan, Sir William Sprigett, and mother of Guliema, future wife of William Penn. In 1658, Isaac and Mary Penington publicly joined the movement, "apparently under the influence of Fox." Once Penington "had found a solid rock of conviction and was a Finder rather than a Seeker," his writings flowed; he became one of the few articulate spokesmen for the Friends.[7]

The only theologian ever produced by the Quaker movement was Robert Barclay, a Scotsman whose father, Colonel David Barclay, had served in the New Model Army and had sat in two of Cromwell's Parliaments. His mother, a Gordon, was related to the House of Stuart. Brought up a strict Calvinist, Barclay wrote his one major work, the *Apology*, published in Latin in 1676, when he was twenty-seven. He was, incidentally, the progenitor of two of the greatest Quaker families in England, the Barclays and the Gurneys of banking fame.

Thomas Ellwood, whose father was a staunch Puritan and a magistrate in Oxfordshire, was drawn into the movement through his friendship with the Peningtons. His greatest service to the Quaker cause was to edit Fox's crudely written journal, dictated by Fox over a period of years. The standard Ellwood edition, published in 1694, also contained a long preface, "The Rise and Progress of the People Called Quakers," by William Penn.

William Penn is by far the most famous Quaker who ever lived. Still, he remains an enigmatic and mythical figure: "A discerning biography of Penn is notably absent from studies of Quakerism and colonial Pennsylvania though several dozen stereotyped treatments exist."[8] Always living in the grand style, forever in debt, and assiduously cultivating friends at court, Penn was at the same time an anti-establishment egalitarian and a utopian dreamer who spent several years in jail for his Quaker principles (and for debt toward the end of his life). He was a poor judge of character and a loving but rather unsuccessful father. A pacifist, his best-known portrait shows him in a suit of armor.

Our psychological age would find Penn an excellent example of second generation revolt against the values of an extremely successful father. Born in humble circumstances, Admiral Sir William Penn rose to the highest levels of influence under Charles I, Cromwell, and Charles II. Clarendon and others saw treasonable behavior in his movement from high command under Cromwell to knighthood and court preferment under Charles II. Some disagreed with this estimate. At any rate, Admiral Sir William, of firm royalist convictions and possessor of vast estates in Ireland, looked forward to his son's pursuing a successful career in the family's now elevated style. Just after the Restoration, in 1660, he sent young William to Oxford, which expelled him a year later for organizing prayer meetings. "Bitter usage," said Penn, "I underwent when I returned to my father, whipping, beating and turning out of doors."[9]

Next the admiral sent his son to France "to finish his education among people of quality." Upon his return, young Penn briefly read law at Lincoln's Inn, then went to sea with the fleet for a short time, and eventually was put in charge of his father's Irish estates. In Ireland, Penn became interested in the

Quakers, was thrown into jail for attending a meeting, and was finally converted to the pariah faith. According to Pepys's diary the younger Penn was "a
Quaker again or some very melancholy thing."[10] The admiral

> was incensed at the course of events, telling his son that, if he would leave off his
> Quaker foolishness, he was fitted, by training, to be one of the King's ministers.
> The father even tried to be tolerant, saying that the son could "thee and thou"
> anyone he pleased, with the exception of the King, the Duke of York, and him-
> self. One of the first things the converted courtier did, of course, was to go to
> Court, in the summer of 1668, on behalf of persecuted and suffering Quakers.[11]

Indeed, Penn spent much time at court, when not preaching, defending his religious principles in law courts, or writing, especially during his several jail stays.

Penn's father died in 1670, leaving him a considerable fortune available immediately and a large claim on the crown for funds loaned by the admiral to
Charles II. As the position of the Quakers during the Restoration worsened,
Penn petitioned the king, in payment for the debt owed his father, for a grant
of land in the New World. The petition was approved in 1681 and the holy experiment was ready to be launched in Pennsylvania (which the king insisted on
naming after the late admiral).

The year the petition was granted, there were some 50,000 Quakers in England and Ireland, of whom roughly 20,000 had spent time in jail. The new colony was an excellent way out for many members of this persecuted minority.
The crown, as Penn put it in a letter to a friend, "was glad to be rid of us, at so
cheap a rate as a little parchment, to be practis'd in a desart, 3000 Miles off."[12]

Affairs at home delayed Penn's departure for the New World. Because he
was busy promoting the sale of land in the proposed colony, he appointed Captain William Markham, an Anglican first cousin and one of the "first purchasers" (5,000 acres), as deputy governor of the province. Markham set sail for
America in 1681, landing at Upland (now Chester) on the Delaware, in the
heart of New Sweden, a colony inhabited mainly by Dutchmen, Swedes, and
Finns, who had been living there for over half a century at peace with the Indians. Markham organized a provincial council and a judicial system and, along
with Thomas Holme, an Irish Quaker whom Penn had appointed surveyor
general, selected the site and laid out the plan for the city of Philadelphia.

In 1682 Penn came to America aboard the *Welcome*, first landing at New
Castle, in what is now Delaware, which had been given to Penn by his good
friend the duke of York. Most of his fellow passengers were undistinguished, ex-
cept William Bradford, Philadelphia's first printer, and Nicholas Waln and
Thomas Wynne, who became leaders in the early government of the province.
(Waln was the progenitor of a wealthy and prominent Quaker merchant family.)

Unlike Winthrop, who died in Massachusetts after nineteen years of continuous government service to his colony, Penn remained in Pennsylvania for
only twenty-two months. Though sole owner of the province in the style of a
feudal lord (he called his largest first purchasers "barons"), Penn spent little
time on the day-to-day problems of government. His most famous act was his
legendary treaty with the Indians under the Treaty Elm at Shackamaxon (Ken-

sington) late in 1682. As with so much else in Penn's life, and in the early history of the colony, no written records of this event exist. Even Penn's biographer in the *Dictionary of American Biography* admits that the "glorification of the Quaker peace policy by uncritical historians has been overdone."[13] At any rate, the half century of peace with the Indians enjoyed by previous settlers gave Penn some good feelings to build on, and he negotiated several purchases of land from the Indians. He also settled boundaries with Lord Baltimore to the south and the authorities in New York to the north and spent a good deal of time laying out his family estate, some twenty miles outside the city in Bucks County (named after his beloved home county in England). Pennsbury Manor, a 6,000-acre tract along the Delaware, suited Penn's lordly values and Quaker antipathies to city life and city values. Having spent perhaps the happiest period of his generally harassed life, Penn returned to England in August 1684, leaving his colony in ever increasing economic prosperity* and ever increasing political and social anarchy.

WHO CAME TO MASSACHUSETTS AND PENNSYLVANIA AND WHAT THEY FOUND THERE

Of utmost importance in understanding the difference between the social structures of Massachusetts and Pennsylvania from their founding to the present is the fact that, owing to the intolerance of the Puritan oligarchy, on the one hand, and the idealistic tolerance of Penn and the Quakers, on the other, Massachusetts was an extremely homogeneous community from the beginning whereas Pennsylvania has always been an ethnic and religious melting pot. Even though, according to James Truslow Adams, the vast majority of the population of Massachusetts in 1640, ten years after the founding of the colony, were not church members, the colony's government and social life were dominated by Puritan church leaders, lay and clerical. Pennsylvania, however, was from its inception rendered almost ungovernable as a result of continuous sectarian wrangling.

Massachusetts remained an ethnically and religiously homogeneous community with an established church from the 1630s to the 1830s. There was very little immigration after the great migration of the 1630s ended with the outbreak of the Civil War in England, and the original population grew largely by natural increase until the Irish came in the 1840s.

Not only was the population of Massachusetts predominantly English and deeply rooted in the New England soil for 200 years, but the largest and most influential group of immigrants were from the eastern and southeastern counties, where Puritanism was firmly established. These were the most prosperous and advanced counties in England outside London. In East Anglia, enclosures

---

*In 1683, sixty ships docked in Philadelphia, and the colony grew even faster than Massachusetts during its first decade.

had taken place earlier than in the rest of England; here had come artisans from Flanders and Huguenots from France; and agriculture had been supplemented by the thriving cloth industry, the clothing and Puritan capital, Norwich, being the second largest city in the nation at the time of the great migration. In addition to the Laudian reaction, a depression in the clothing industry drove many East Anglians to the New World. Samuel Eliot Morison was very proud of the East Anglian roots of his native Massachusetts.

> Here is our very homeland. In an afternoon's drive of seventy or eighty miles, we may visit Framlingham, Ipswich, Dedham, Braintree, Boxford, Groton, Sudbury, and Haverhill, and spend the night at Cambridge. Suffolk is the heart of East Anglia, the section of England which, according to Havelock Ellis' "Study of British Genius," has produced the greatest statesmen, scientists, ecclesiastics, scholars, and artists in English history, and which has always been distinguished for a profound love of liberty and independence. In East Anglia the Puritan movement bit deepest. From East Anglia came the heaviest contingent for the planting of Massachusetts Bay; and Massachusetts as colony and commonwealth, by every known test of eminence, has produced far more distinguished men and women in proportion to her population, than any other state of the Union.[14]

The Pennsylvania experience was altogether different.

> The simplest way to describe the populating of colonial Pennsylvania is to picture a stake driven into the ground at the waterfront of Philadelphia. A 25-mile radius from this peg would encompass the area of Pennsylvania settled mainly by English immigrants between 1680 and 1710. Extend the radius to the length of 75 miles, and the outer 50 miles of the circle would correspond roughly to the "Dutch" country from Northampton to York counties. Here, from 1710 to 1750, the German-speaking immigrants to colonial Pennsylvania made their homes. Again extend the radius to 150 miles, and in the outermost circumference, corresponding roughly to the arc of the Allegheny Mountains and valleys, the Scotch-Irish settled from 1717 to the Revolutionary War.[15]

By 1740, each of these major groups of immigrants—English, German, and Scotch-Irish—constituted about a third of the total population of 100,000. The English, Germans, and Scotch-Irish, numerically dominant, were "joined by a larger variety of other immigrants than could be found in any other American province."[16]

If the Massachusetts population came largely from the eastern counties of England, the Quaker settlers in Pennsylvania came from all over the British Isles. Though, as we have already seen, the Quaker movement first took root in northern England, it soon spread to Ireland and Wales. In fact, in Wales it appealed to the gentry far more frequently than to the educated classes in England; hence the leadership of Welsh Quakers, like the two Lloyds, in the early history of Philadelphia. Second in numbers to the English Quakers, the Welsh Quakers settled predominantly in Chester County, outside the city along what is now known as the "Main Line" (once called the "Welsh Barony"), in towns such as Bala, St. David's, Bryn Mawr, and Cynwyd. Small groups of Dutch and German Quakers settled in Germantown in the earliest days of the colony;

among their leaders was Francis Daniel Pastorious, one of the few highly educated immigrants to the colony.*

Though Quakers dominated the city of Philadelphia during the early years, by 1700 roughly 200 Anglicans were communicants at Christ Church; three congregations of English and Welsh Baptists had been organized; and immigrants from Barbados had established the first Presbyterian congregation in the city. The first Catholic church in Philadelphia was built in 1732, and by 1750 Pennsylvania had eleven Catholic congregations, next in number only to Maryland (fifteen). There were few Catholics in Massachusetts; nor, in spite of their Old Testament theology and use of Hebrew as a second language, did the Puritan oligarchy welcome Jews. However, Philadelphia had a Jewish congregation by 1745, and the first synagogue was erected in 1782.

The Germans came to Pennsylvania predominantly in two waves after 1700. Most of them were war refugees. First came the sectarians—Amish, Mennonites, Dunkers, and a few other perfectionist groups such as the Schwenkfelders and the Seventh-Day Baptists, who settled in Ephrata. These pious people have kept their ethnic identity, especially their anti-intellectual and anti-modern values, down to the twentieth century. The so-called church people followed—Lutherans, German Reformed, and Moravians. The Pennsylvania Dutch country, the richest farming land in America, is a remarkably homogeneous area even today. Indeed, for a long time the area was bilingual; the so-called Pennsylvania Dutch dialect is a mixture of English and German.

The third major group of immigrants to Pennsylvania were the Scotch-Irish, lowland Scots who had been living in northern Ireland for some generations. Almost all the Scotch-Irish were Presbyterians, and one might have expected them to go to Massachusetts, where their fellow Calvinists had settled. But, as one of their historians put it, they were "not welcomed there" (though New Hampshire eventually became the home of many). At any rate, they came to Pennsylvania in five great waves, from 1717 until the outbreak of the Revolution. By the middle of the eighteenth century Pennsylvania was known as the center of the Scotch-Irish in America, although these hardy, individualistic, and fighting Ulstermen eventually settled the frontier regions of our nation.

The Scotch-Irish came as individuals and families, not as congregations, as did both the New Englanders and the Germans in Pennsylvania. They soon set up their churches, however, and eventually their colleges. Unlike the Quakers and the Germans, especially the sectarians, they placed a very high value on education. We shall see how the descendants of these desperately poor immigrants rose to take the lead in the state—in law, education, and politics—just as they did in Virginia: ancestors of Jefferson, Patrick Henry, and Woodrow Wilson, among others, first came to America through Pennsylvania before going down the Shenandoah valley and thence out to the West after the Revolution. The values of the Germans and the Scotch-Irish have been nicely contrasted by Klein and Hoogenboom.

---

*This German group came to Pennsylvania as a result of the famous trip, in 1677, of four Quaker leaders—George Fox, William Penn, Robert Barclay, and George Keith—through Holland and Germany.

The first generation of Scotch-Irish settlers had little alternative but to farm for a living, but as a group they never achieved the reputation the Germans had of being careful husbandmen. In part, the land may have been to blame, and in part the remoteness of their settlements from the market. But also, the Scots seemed less devoted to farm work than the Germans, and unlike some of the German Plain Sects, did not view tilling the soil as the fulfillment of an ordinance of God. Impetuous, imaginative, ambitious for wealth and power, full of zest for a fight, impatient, and easily distracted, they viewed farming as a means to other ways of life rather than an end in itself.[17]

By the close of the colonial period, then, Pennsylvania was, ethnically and religiously, more like modern America than any other colony and diametrically opposite to the homogeneous and hierarchical society of Massachusetts. If the anti-authoritarian, tolerant, and egalitarian emphases of the Quakers brought forth the ethnic diversity in the beginning, this ethnic diversity in turn reinforced these values and generated the amiable anarchy that has always characterized the social and political structures of Philadelphia and Pennsylvania.

Not only were the populations of Massachusetts and Pennsylvania radically different, but so were their lands. New England was an isolated and homogeneous region, cut off from the rest of the colonies by the Hudson River to the west and Long Island Sound to the south. In natural resources, Massachusetts was relatively poverty-stricken. Three-fourths of its soil was made up of boulders and clay, on which land only subsistence farming was possible. An abundance of timber, countless natural harbors, and hundreds of miles of seacoast made the inhabitants, mostly small farmers in the beginning, eventually turn to shipbuilding and maritime occupations. From the outset Massachusetts men were disciplined by the unbountiful soil and the ever present dangers of seafaring life. The sea captains of Salem, Marblehead, Newburyport, Provincetown, and Boston soon saw the world as their marketplace as they went to sea during the eighteenth and early nineteenth centuries. Later, the region's many small rivers and lakes proved ideal generators of power, and the sons of New England sea captains took the lead in manufacturing, especially textiles.

Whereas Massachusetts was relatively poor in natural resources, Pennsylvania was blessed with the richest farmland in all the colonies. The farms were larger and the barns were far bigger than those of New England. (Some barns were fifteen times as big as the farmhouse.) However, there was no seacoast and Philadelphia looked to its hinterland rather than out to sea. Beneath the earth, Pennsylvania was rich in iron, and later discoveries of coal and oil made it the greatest heavy-industry state in the nation by the end of the nineteenth century. Finally, and most important, whereas New England was isolated by natural barriers, and divided up on a human scale, Pennsylvania was large, varied in landscape, and lacking in natural boundaries to set it off from the rest of the middle colonies. Moreover, a great chain of mountains, the Alleghenies, ran right down the middle of the state, creating two natural areas. Thus, Philadelphia had more in common with New York or Boston than with Pittsburgh, which looked westward to the Ohio and the Mississippi. Of tremendous psychological and symbolic, as well as practical, importance, was the fact that, whereas Boston still is the cultural, commercial, and political capital of the Bay State, the capital of Pennsylvania was moved to Lancaster after the Revolution and thence to Harrisburg after the War of 1812—the middle of nowhere, at least as far as most citizens of Philadelphia have always been concerned.

In a very real sense, then, the geography of Pennsylvania fostered egalitarian individualism. The geography of Massachusetts and New England encouraged hierarchical communalism.

TOWN AND COUNTY

The basic unit of settlement in Massachusetts was the town; in Pennsylvania it was the isolated family farm. From the original towns of Salem, Charlestown, Boston, Roxbury, Dorchester, and Watertown, the Puritans spread throughout New England in congregational and town units, symbolized in the minds of most schoolchildren by the picture of Thomas Hooker leading his flock through the forests and down the Connecticut valley.

> The Puritans moved into the wilds as a community, not as individuals. Civil authorities would not grant individuals the right to reside on farms outside the established towns until such time as they had a sufficient number of neighbors to found a new town, with a new church. . . . The voice of community was stronger in a frontier village because the village could not come into being unless it had a church and a preacher.[18]

The minister was far more than just a preacher of the Word; he was the town's main civilizer, educator, and historian.* Thus, in 1766, John Bernard could look back on his fifty-two years of leadership in Marblehead with some satisfaction.

> When I came, there was not as much as one proper carpenter, nor mason, nor tailor, nor butcher in the town, nor anything of a market worth naming; but they had their houses built by country workmen, and their clothes made out of town, and supplied themselves with beef and pork from Boston, which drained the town of its money. But now we abound in artificers, and some of the best, and our markets large, even a full supply. And what above all I would remark, there was not so much as one foreign trading vessel belonging to the town, nor for several years after I came to it; though no town had really greater advantage in their hands. The people contented themselves to be slaves that digged in mines, and left the merchants of Salem, Boston and Europe to carry away the gains; by which means the town was always in dismally poor circumstances, in-

---

*The position of the preacher in rural Pennsylvania was diametrically opposite of that of Marblehead's minister: "Throughout Pennsylvania the preachers do not have the power to punish anyone, or to force anyone to go to church. Nor can they give orders to each other, there being no consistory to impose discipline among them. Most preachers are engaged for the year, like cowherds in Germany; and when any one fails to please his congregation, he is given notice and must put up with it" (Gottlieb Mittelberger, *Journey to Pennsylvania*, ed. and trans. Oscar Handlin and John Clive [Cambridge: Harvard University Press, 1960], p. 47).

volved in debt to the merchants more than they were worth; nor could I find twenty families in it that, upon the best examination, could stand upon their own legs; and they were generally as rude, swearing, drunken, and fighting a crew, as they were poor. Whereas, not only are the public ways vastly mended, but the manners of the people greatly cultivated; and we have many gentlefolk and polite families, and the very fishermen scorn the rudeness of a former generation.[19]

In many ways the New England town was a transplanted English parish, with its church and commons, its clergyman, its "gentlefolk and polite families," and its unpaid elders and selectmen, along with common folk, mainly simple farmers or fishermen. It was above all an organic unit with strong communal bonds. Indeed, rather than a state, like Virginia or Pennsylvania, early Massachusetts (especially in the eighteenth century) was virtually a federated republic of largely autonomous towns.

The New England towns were small and extremely homogeneous units. By 1710, there were some 60,000 people in all of Massachusetts, spread out in roughly 200 or 300 towns, which meant fewer than 100 adult males in the average town. By 1765, when the final census of the provincial period was completed, a majority of towns had populations under 1,000; only fifteen towns were as large as 2,500. The biggest by far was Boston, with fewer than 15,000 souls. If political democracy works best among small, homogeneous groups, Massachusetts embodied the democratic ideal. By the end of the colonial period it was a cohesive series of homogeneous and segregated communities, democratic in political form, theocratic in religion, and hierarchical in secular social organization. These autonomous towns were spread across the state: Springfield had been settled by 1636; Northampton, by 1654; and, at the western end of the colony, Stockbridge, in 1739, and Pittsfield, by 1752. Just as Massachusetts was not a state in the manner of Pennsylvania or Virginia, so it really had no frontier, or frontiersmen like Daniel Boone, as Frederick Jackson Turner would have it; hence the much crueler treatment by the Indians, who played havoc with these tiny frontier settlements, isolated one from another in the early years.

Pennsylvania was settled largely by individuals rather than communities. Penn and his agents set up the city of Philadelphia and the two original counties of Bucks and Chester and sold the land to individuals or groups of investors. By the time Penn sailed for the New World, he had sold 875,000 acres of land, mostly to English Quakers. From the beginning in Pennsylvania, in contrast to Massachusetts, the franchise depended on property qualifications. Moreover the leadership in the new colony was almost entirely drawn from the wealthiest first purchasers of 5,000 or more acres of land.

Whereas the legislative and taxing unit in Massachusetts was the town, it was the county in Pennsylvania. In Massachusetts the counties came *after* the towns; in Pennsylvania the main towns were likely to be county seats. And whereas the commons and the church symbolize the nature of the New England social structure even today, Pennsylvania is a mosaic of rolling and rich farmland, isolated farmhouses, and gigantic barns; the towns seem to have just growed like Topsy; and even in the original counties, the Quaker meetinghouse is often hard to find and certainly plays no symbolic role as town center.

In striking contrast to the almost immediate settlement of isolated towns straight across Massachusetts, the frontier in Pennsylvania slowly moved west throughout the eighteenth and into the nineteenth centuries. The myth of the individualistic frontiersman centered on the character of Daniel Boone, who set out on his wanderings westward from Pennsylvania, where his Quaker ancestors from Exeter, in Devonshire, had settled.

Page Smith, in his interesting modification of the famous Turner thesis of the individualistic development of our western frontier, has shown the great importance of towns in the settlement of America. He conceptualizes the two major types of town settlement as the "colonized" (orderly and communal, as in Massachusetts) and the "cumulative" (haphazard and individualistic, as in Pennsylvania).[20] By and large, the "colonized" pattern marked the settlement of the Western Reserve and the Old Northwest by New Englanders (with the church as the symbolic center), while the "cumulative" towns tended to have been built by settlers from Pennsylvania and the other colonies to the south (with the county courthouse as the symbolic center).*

Little wonder that Tocqueville eulogized the New England town as both an ideal school for leadership and authority and an antidote to the extreme individualism that marked so much else in American society. (He also was the first to use the term *individualism* and to see its intimate relationship to egalitarianism.) Noting that "the gradual development of the principle of equality is a providential fact," Tocqueville added that "the New England town seems to have come directly from the hand of God."[21]

QUARTERDECK AND FARM

Though the pious Puritans of Massachusetts Bay were engaged primarily in farming and fur trading in the early years, it was not long before the restless and enterprising Yankees set out to sea to seek their fortunes. The ethics of command, authority, and liberty have been, from the days of the Athenian empire to the present, deeply rooted in the seafaring life. It is thus perhaps appropriate that Essex County, which includes the north shore of Boston, was the breeding ground of more of Boston's First Families than any other part of the state. For over two centuries, quarterdeck command was the dream of the more enterprising sons of Massachusetts farmers.

In contrast, although many of the great Quaker fortunes in Philadelphia were made in the triangular trade of the colonial period, Pennsylvania was not a maritime culture to anywhere near the same extent as was Massachusetts. The real hearts of the majority of Quakers and Pennsylvania Dutch lay in the

---

*See Appendix III for Boston Brahmin family members who founded towns across the nation.

rich farmlands of Bucks, Chester, Berks, and Lancaster counties and their rapidly developing market towns and county seats.*

Causation in history is a very slippery thing. One hardly ever finds a one-to-one relationship between cause and effect. Thus, I should not like to think that my main arguments add up to religious determinism. In fact, this chapter has had a lot to say about the important influences of geographical factors in history. Nevertheless, it is curious that the ideas and social organization of the Puritans were reinforced by the environment to which they came as also happened with the Quakers in Pennsylvania.

The Reverend Phillips Brooks, a favorite preacher among the Victorian gentry of both Boston's Beacon Hill and Philadephia's Rittenhouse Square, once summed up his feelings of the strange affinity between manners and geography.

> Philadelphia is a city where the Episcopal Church is thoroughly at home. Side by side with the gentler Puritanism of that sunnier clime, the Quakerism which quarrelled and protested, but always quarrelled and protested peacefully, the Church of England had lived and flourished in colonial days, and handed down a well-established life to the new Church which sprang out of her veins at the Revolution. It was the temperate zone of religious life with all its quiet richness. Free from antagonism, among a genial and social people . . . the Church in Philadelphia was to the Church in Boston much like what a broad Pennsylvania valley is to a rough New England hillside.[22]

Perhaps it would not be out of place (though hardly fashionable) to suggest that Providence may very well have played an important role in American history. Who would deny that the history of America might have been quite different had the East Anglian Puritans settled along the shores of the Delaware; the Quakers and the Germans, in rocky New England; or the Cavaliers in Massachusetts and the Puritans in Virginia? At the opening of the seventeenth century, above all, only the Deity knew that the English Quakers were to find the peaceful Lenni-Lenape Indians on the banks of the Delaware, while the Puritans were to face the warlike Pequots in New England.

---

*The difference between town-centered Massachusetts and county-centered Pennsylvania is reflected in the political organization of the two states in the twentieth century. Today in Massachusetts there are 312 unincorporated towns, 14 counties, and 39 cities; Pennsylvania has 67 counties, 1,554 townships, 955 boroughs, and 51 cities.

The Classic Ages of the Two Colonies

Few periods of history, with the exceptions of Greece and Rome, have been the subject of so many books and monographs dealing with nearly every phase of social, political, and intellectual life as has that of colonial Massachusetts.

George Lee Haskins

Sectarian histories of the Quaker migration have been numerous and indispensably important to an understanding of colonial Pennsylvania. But they have largely avoided any analytical inquiry into the agonizing struggle for political stability and maturity which absorbed the Quakers of Pennsylvania for almost half a century after Penn's charter was issued in 1681. . . . Penn himself has been subject to several dozen biographies and studies but still remains an enigmatic figure, hidden behind a veil of filiopietism.

Gary B. Nash

The first colonists to settle in Pennsylvania and Massachusetts Bay were drawn from many and various walks of life. As in all mass population movements, most of them came from the underprivileged and uneducated classes, presumably attracted by economic opportunity. If a large proportion of the British immigrants to North America in the seventeenth century belonged to the servant class, it was because servants formed the largest class in England at that time.

The great differences in social organization and government between the town theocracies of Massachusetts and the holy experiment in Philadelphia and its rural surroundings thus had little to do with the class origin, the native intelligence, or the moral worth of the majority of immigrants. I am therefore inclined to disagree with William Penn's comment that "there is hardly any frame of government in the world so ill designed by its first founders, that in good hands would not do well. . . . [G]overnments rather depend upon men, than men upon governments."[1] My thesis is that their ideals as to the governing of men (the "frame") in both church and state sharply distinguished the two colonies.

> The intellectual life of New England was determined by the top layers of society. . . . *Accepted* by the community, not *imposed* on it, I say; for men of education were the chosen leaders of the Puritan immigration. Deprived ministers or discontented country gentry gathered groups of neighbors, friends, and parishioners, emigrated on the same ship, and settled in the same place. They were the shepherds to whom the people looked for guidance and inspiration, on whose spoken word they hung, and whose written words they perused eagerly.[10]

Here is a classic case of class authority and deference democracy. Massachusetts was the seedbed of constitutional republicanism—the political theory upon which our Founding Fathers, men very much like the Bay Colony's leaders, later built this nation in Philadelphia, whose formative age was quite different from Boston's.

CLASS ANARCHY AND BOSS RULE IN QUAKER PENNSYLVANIA, 1682-1726

I have described Massachusetts's classic period rather briefly for two reasons: it was a clear-cut matter of class authority and deference democracy and it has been thoroughly covered by other writers. The continuity of class rule, however, did not preclude power struggles within the ruling group, especially the famous controversies over the heretical positions held by Roger Williams and Anne Hutchinson and their followers, which I examine in Chapter 9.

The chaotic classic period in Pennsylvania history is a far more complex, and far less well known, story. Pennsylvania, as we have seen, was the brainchild of the utopian Quaker aristocrat William Penn, an excellent salesman and publicist who sought settlers for his colony from all over the British Isles and the Continent. One of Penn's more admiring biographers, William I. Hull of Swarthmore College, described his recruitment efforts.

> The private motives of his prospective colonists to which Penn appealed—like the public reasons why they emigrated—were religious, political, and economic. To all these motives he appealed by voice and pen, in conversation, public addresses, letters and numerous pamphlets. The results of the appeal were of first-rate historical importance. It is true that they go far to justify the conclusion that he was, in modern mercantile parlance, a "super-salesman," whose high-powered salesmanship might well be envied by the most successful of "promoters" who have at their disposal all the devices of current advertising by means of newspapers and radio broadcasting.[11]

We have also seen what a heterogeneous and atomized lot were the ordinary colonists who responded to Penn's excellent salesmanship. Far more important, however, was his failure to attract a coherent class of leaders to the colony. (Indeed, it is hard to conceive of a class of men like John Winthrop or John Cotton submitting to Penn's arbitrary utopianism.) Having no religious theories of authority or leadership, Penn fell back on a property theory of government and counted on a small number of prosperous men for the purchase of nearly half the land and, what is more, counted on them for political leadership (see Table A–13 in Appendix I). Rather than a coherent class of men who knew what kind of society they wanted and set about getting it, these men constitute an ideal example of an atomized elite, neither self-selected nor elected by the people, but appointed by Penn for their plutocratic, rather than leadership, qualifications. In fact, the *only man* who seems to have possessed any outstanding qualities of leadership was Thomas Lloyd, a Welsh physician educated at Oxford and one of the few genuine patricians to be converted to Quakerism. From the time he came to the colony in 1683 to his death in 1694, Lloyd took the lead both in government and in the affairs of the Yearly Meeting of Friends. At first the leader of the Proprietary interests, Lloyd soon turned away from the arbitrary and irresponsible ways of Penn and his agents and became the leader of the popular, anti-proprietary Quaker party.

Lacking any authoritative class with which he might have identified, Lloyd was the first of a long line of bosses who, as we shall see in the cases of Benjamin Franklin, Boies Penrose, and others, dominated Pennsylvania politics for much of the state's history.

The Quaker attitude toward authority made them an almost impossible people to govern: "The Quarrelsome spirit was present constantly, and encompassed nearly everyone in the colony, even as fine a person as Thomas Lloyd," wrote Edwin B. Bronner. "There was a greater disrespect for law and order in Pennsylvania than might have been expected from a Quaker colony dedicated to a 'holy experiment.' "[12] Nevertheless, Thomas Lloyd did his best to bring some order out of the political chaos that was the inevitable result of Penn's utopian experiment.

> The Council failed to convene at regular intervals. . . . [T]hat there was no source of government which would be seen and respected by the colonists resulted in a spirit of anarchy. Penn recognized the spirit but could not explain it. The commonwealth had been created with the assurance that the people were the followers of Christ, that they had an inner discipline, that they could govern themselves personally or through the Friends business meeting. It was a disappointment to learn that outward evidence of government was necessary to enforce obedience to the laws.[13]

But it is so often the good people who foster the spirit of anarchy just because they have a naive view of collective human nature, as Gary B. Nash has suggested.

> In Pennsylvania, given their own government and free of persecution, Quakers might have been expected to sublimate their individualistic and anti-authoritarian tendencies and join hands in the work of building a reconstructed society. Certainly Penn expected no less. . . . Yet the Quakers in the New World seemed instinctively to act like Quakers in the Old, even though magistrates were of their own choice and the same religious persuasion. Penn's letters to the colony

in the 1680s are filled with dismay at a people so "governmentish," so "brutish," so susceptible to "scurvy quarrels that break out to the disgrace of the Province," so wont to question civil authority and eager to deny the legitimacy of proprietarial policies.[14]

Nash summed up the situation: "Utopian propaganda, frail institutions, the effects of the environment, and the anti-authoritarian instincts of the Quakers, all contributed to the breakdown of the sense of community in early Pennsylvania."[15] Nash also recognized that charismatic authority is probably the only answer to individualist anarchy: "Penn, who alone possessed the charisma to stabilize the Quaker community, if it could be unified at all, was absent for all but a few years during the first three decades of the colony's existence."[16]

By 1688, six years after the colony's founding, Penn had given "up his hopes that the Quakers could reform themselves internally and appointed a transplanted Massachusetts Puritan, Captain John Blackwell, as Deputy Governor . . . in order, as Penn put it, to suppress the 'animosities' in Pennsylvania, 'authoritatively' if no other method works."[17] Given the hysterically cruel treatment of Quakers by the Puritans of Massachusetts, this appointment was tactless at best, but perhaps Penn had no other choice in such a desperate situation. At any rate, even with his many years of experience in high government positions and in the army under Cromwell, Blackwell failed miserably as deputy governor. Thomas Lloyd took the lead in making it impossible for Blackwell to rule, a story that cannot be detailed here. More important is the fact that he was aided by his distant kinsman David Lloyd.

If Thomas Lloyd was a patrician boss, David Lloyd was, as Robert Proud (the first local historian of this period in Pennsylvania history) put it, a "quarrelsome demagogue."[18] Of an obscure and poor branch of the Lloyd family, David, with only a grammar school education, went to study law in the offices of a shrewd Welsh lawyer, Sir George Jeffreys, later one of the most controversial chief justices in English history. Lloyd came to the attention of Penn while he was working in the London office of Penn's lawyers, handling the deeds and warrants of the first purchasers. Penn appointed him attorney general and brought him to Pennsylvania in 1686. (Though not a Quaker, he was convinced soon after his arrival in the New World.)

Like his kinsman Thomas Lloyd, David came as a devoted agent of the proprietor and then almost immediately turned against him. If power politics is the inevitable result of the decline or absence of class authority, so shifting loyalties and personal feuding are characteristic of anarchical situations. Under the leadership of the two Lloyds the Quaker party finally forced Blackwell out of office.

The Blackwell incident was surely a portent of things to come in Pennsylvania. In a perceptive article on Blackwell's Philadelphia career, Nicholas Biddle Wainwright concluded that

> many a successor to Governor John Blackwell was in his own time to experience kindred difficulties. Many a governor may well have echoed Blackwell's complaint: "I have to do with a people whom neither God nor man can prevayle with for they dispise all Dominion and dignity that is not in themselves. . . . Alas! Alas! Poore Governor of Pennsylvania."[19]

Thomas Lloyd was back in control for a brief and chaotic period after Blackwell's return to Boston.

> For nearly three and one-half years, from the day Blackwell resigned until April, 1693, when Benjamin Fletcher arrived as royal governor, the people of Pennsylvania and Delaware ruled themselves. Penn could exert little control over the colonists, for he had been a friend and supporter of the recently deposed James II, and he was either in jail or in hiding from the crown during much of this time. The form of government changed several times, Delaware separated herself from Pennsylvania, and affairs were *so chaotic that there are almost no public records for the period.*[20]

After the death of Thomas Lloyd in 1694, David Lloyd became the boss of the anti-proprietary faction. He continued to lead this group and to serve as attorney general almost until his death in 1731.

Unlike Massachusetts, Pennsylvania saw its leadership change hands six times within the colony's first decade. Then, after the chaotic period following Blackwell's departure, King William took the colony away from Penn and placed it under the control of Governor Fletcher of New York. After the return of proprietary control in 1694, Penn and his heirs appointed a series of auslanders—all of them Puritans or Anglicans—to rule for the rest of the classic period. The one exception was Edward Shippen, president of council during 1703–1704. Though Shippen was a Philadelphia merchant and a founder of one of Pennsylvania's leading families, he was also an auslander, having only recently come from Boston, where he had been an extremely successful merchant. (An Anglican, he had become a Friend after marrying a Boston Quaker.)

Of the three lieutenant governors appointed after Shippen, "the first was dissolute; the second was deranged; and the third, dishonest."[21] (Running down leaders is a continuing custom in Philadelphia; few local Quakers have ever had much pride in the government of either their city or their state. But perhaps they have been right.) Nothing points to Penn's irresponsibility quite as much as his appointment of John Evans as the chief executive officer of the colony in 1704.

> Also contributing to the success of David Lloyd's anti-proprietary campaign was the ineptitude of Penn's deputy governors. John Evans, who held the office from 1704 to 1709, was only twenty-six years old when he reached the colony and was handicapped by an unstable personality. Though Penn could advertise him to the Board of Trade as liberally educated, well-travelled, sober, judicious, encumbered neither by debt nor aristocratic temperament, and a "known zealous member of the Church of England," the truth of the matter was that Evans had done nothing but play the gentleman since reaching adulthood, was utterly without experience in government, and had only his father's friendship with Penn to recommend him. That Penn would send such a stripling into the political jungles of Pennsylvania at a time when his colony lay politically paralyzed testified both to the proprietor's financial inability to employ a man with real qualifications and to the low regard which men of talent in England had for the job of governing the Pennsylvania Quakers.[22]

Understandably, things were so bad by 1708 that the government virtually ceased to function: "Evans gave up residency in Philadelphia, the courts lapsed for want of legislative backing, and the Council was reduced to a cypher."*

Whereas the merchant oligarchy of Boston came after the decline of the classic age of Puritan authority, the holy experiment in Pennsylvania, though failing to establish political and social authority, was an economic success from the very beginning. "There are few parallels in colonial history to the economic success of Pennsylvania in the first two decades," according to Nash.

> Only three years after settlement, its capital city was firmly established in the Barbados provisioning trade and had cut deep inroads into New York's control of the middle-Atlantic fur and tobacco markets. By 1700 Philadelphia was second in size only to Boston in the English colonies. Prosperity stemmed not only from the fertile soil of the Delaware River Valley and Penn's effectiveness in promoting immigration to his colony. . . . Equally important . . . was the immediate arrival of an experienced body of merchants, men long established in other seaports of the English world, men with sound credit and reputation, men whose close mercantile contacts throughout the world of English commerce gave the economy a headstart. Many were closely connected with a farflung circle of Quaker merchants, some of whom had invested liberally in Pennsylvania land. . . . Almost automatically, Pennsylvania merchants took their place in this intercolonial and intercontinental league of Quaker commerce.[23]

The Puritan magistrates and ministers who came to Massachusetts Bay sank deep roots in their new colony. Philadelphia, however, produced a cosmopolitan Quaker elite of merchants whose first New World roots were elsewhere and who, even after settling in Philadelphia, maintained their extracolonial loyalties. This difference reflects that between *sects* and *churches*: the sectarian is always rooted in his cosmopolitan in-group; the churchman is ideally rooted in his whole community or parish (a geographical rather than an ideological concept). Thus, by the end of the classic period, only a minority of the Philadelphia merchant oligarchy were original settlers or first purchasers. In his definitive study of this class Frederick B. Tolles† noted that

> from the outset there was in Philadelphia, as in the other colonial towns, a small nucleus of wealthy merchants who dominated the economic and social life of the community and played an important role in its religious and political life. One striking fact about the geographical provenance of these early Quaker merchants in Philadelphia is worth noting: most of them came not directly from England,

---

*I have carefully followed Bronner and Nash, both professional historians, who have no thesis of leadership such as mine. Bronner, himself a convinced Friend and curator of the Quaker Collection and professor of history at Haverford College, would hardly be expected to write with a bias against his adopted spiritual ancestors. Nash, professor of history at the University of California at Los Angeles, who takes a view of the contrasts between Pennsylvania and Massachusetts very different from mine, should provide an objective check on my own thesis: "If the Quaker system of beliefs could not prevent social and political disequilibrium in the early stages of settlement, Pennsylvania was *not significantly* different from Puritan New England" (Gary B. Nash *Quakers and Politics: Pennsylvania, 1681–1726* [Princeton: Princeton University Press, 1968], p. 342; italics added).

†Tolles was the leading Quaker historian of his generation before his tragic death at an early age. At the time of his death in the 1970s, he was curator of the Quaker Collection at Swarthmore.

but from the other American colonies, where for a period of years they had had an opportunity to exercise their talents in mercantile pursuits with somewhat less hindrance from persecuting authorities than in Great Britain. From Barbados came Samuel Carpenter, the richest man in early Philadelphia; from Jamaica, Samuel Richardson, reputed second only to Carpenter in the amount of his worldly goods. Isaac Norris and Jonathan Dickinson (1663–1722), great merchants and active figures in early Pennsylvania politics, also hailed from Jamaica. From Boston came Edward Shippen (1639–1712), who was reputed to be worth at least ten thousand pounds sterling, and who was known as the owner of the biggest house and the biggest coach in Philadelphia; from New York, Humphrey Morrey (d. 1716), and William Frampton (d. 1686), owner of one of the first wharves on the Delaware river front. William Fishbourne (d. 1742), Samuel Preston (1665–1743), and Richard Hill, all substantial traders, removed to Philadelphia from Maryland; and Anthony Morris (1654–1721), a wealthy brewer, mayor of Philadelphia, and provincial councillor, crossed from Burlington, New Jersey, when he saw that the commercial future lay on the other side of the Delaware.[24]

Tolles aptly summed up the cosmopolitan values of this pious sect.

> The world of the Quaker merchants may have been largely a Quaker world, but it was far from being parochial in the geographical sense. By virtue of their commercial, religious, personal, and family contacts, the Philadelphia Quakers were in close touch with the entire North Atlantic world from Nova Scotia to Curacao and from Hamburg to Lisbon. The intelligence which they received from their correspondents and from itinerant "public Friends" was chiefly concerned with prices current and the prosperity of Truth, but inevitably it broadened their view of the world, tending to overcome the provincialism so likely to be characteristic of a colonial people.[25]

As I remarked in Chapter 6, Lincoln Steffens found Philadelphia to be corrupt but contented. The very roots of this contentment, even in the face of extreme political corruption in both city and state, go back to Pennsylvania's classic period. The merchant elite cared little about law and order in government as long as they were allowed to seek their fortunes in a laissez-faire and private way. No wonder that a recent book on Philadelphia called it the "private city." Just as the great merchants were happily piling up wealth in the city and building beautiful country estates, so ordinary Friends in the counties were living orderly and quiet lives centered on the meetinghouse rather than the courthouse or city hall. As Howard Brinton, the leading Quaker thinker and historian of our day, noted, the Quakerism of Bucks and Chester counties was going through its Golden Age. No paragraph could shed more light on the Quaker (and Philadelphia) mind, of both the classic and the modern age, than Brinton's description of Quakerism in the first decades of the eighteenth century.

> But the most important product of the flowering of Quakerism in the New World was the unique Quaker culture. By culture is meant a clearly defined way of life with a spiritual basis. A true culture reflects every aspect of life. In the Quaker communities the meeting was the center, spiritually, intellectually and economically. It included a library and a school. Disputes of whatever nature were settled

in the business sessions of the meeting. The poor were looked after, moral delinquents dealt with, marriages approved and performed. There was little need for court or police force or officials of any kind except a few whose function was to transfer property and perform similar legal duties. Each group, centered in the meeting, was a well-ordered, highly integrated community of interdependent members. . . . This flowering of Quakerism was not characterized by any outburst of literary or artistic production. Its whole emphasis was on life itself in home, meeting and community. This life was an artistic creation as beautiful in its simplicity and proportion as was the architecture of its meeting houses. The "Flowering of New England" has been described in terms of its literature, but the flowering of Quakerism in the middle colonies can be described only in terms of life itself.[26]

In summary, to understand the essence of the differences between the classic ages of Boston and Philadelphia one must go back to the contrasting ideals of the church and the sect. The ideal of the church, and especially of the Calvinist in Geneva and the Puritan in Massachusetts, was one of established authority over the *whole* community, with an intimate relation (though functional differentiation of roles) between the minister and the magistrate. The life tenure of the educated minister, the election sermon, and the church at the head of the village green symbolized Massachusetts's communalism. Quite in contrast to the church ideal of the Puritans was the sectarian ideal of the Quakers, tolerant of, but not responsible for, the whole community. Indeed, the inconspicuous Quaker meetinghouse lacked the soaring steeple of the modern New England church, signifying watchfulness over the entire community's morals. No educated class of professional leaders was encouraged or even allowed in Pennsylvania; only the so-called weighty Friends, often the most affluent, embodied covert authority in the silent meeting of drably dressed men, women, and children. What mattered the morals of one's neighbors as long as the disciplined life within the meeting went on from generation to generation?

The ruling class of Boston and the privileged class of Philadelphia grew directly out of these opposed ideals. As Lawrence Gipson noted in his classic work on British colonialism: "No commonwealth has ever existed that has not been protected by those willing to preserve it with their lives. . . . The Quakers wanted to live in an orderly society that would protect them, their wealth, and also their right to refuse to protect themselves as well as others from public enemies."[27] The Philadelphia Quakers, and the Quaker-Episcopal upper class that eventually emerged in Philadelphia, preferred to live in an orderly and prosperous city and state, but they never thought it their duty to lead *others* toward the good life that they defined for themselves. Here, then, are the taproots of the intolerant and responsible values of the Beacon Hill Brahmin even today and of the tolerant irresponsibility of the modern Philadelphia Main Liner.

Heresy, Hierarchy, and Higher Education

*To every thing there is a season . . . a time to plant, and a
time to pluck up that which is planted . . . a time to break
down, and a time to build up.*

Ecclesiastes 3:1–3

As we have seen, the history of the Reformation revolved around the differing emphases placed, as Luther once put it, on the law or the gospel, on the Old or the New Testament, on works or grace, on the Word (the Bible) or the spirit (the Inner Light). Yet if "to every thing there is a season," then the law must be emphasized in some situations and the gospel in others. In the first decades of their classic ages, the settlers of both Massachusetts Bay and Philadelphia faced this dilemma. Massachusetts, in the famous antinomian controversy of 1637, took the side of law and authority and banished Anne Hutchinson and her more prominent followers. Philadelphia Quakers, in the lesser known Keithian controversy of 1692, took the opposite view and drove George Keith and his followers, called the Christian Quakers, into the Anglican establishment. An understanding of the origins and the resolutions of these two heresies will serve to highlight not only the classic ages of Massachusetts and Pennsylvania, discussed in the previous chapter, but also the character and social structure of Boston and Philadelphia down to this day.

THE ANTINOMIAN HERESY IN
MASSACHUSETTS BAY

Although the Bay Colony was dominated by an organic class of magistrates and ministers during the whole classic period, disputes of course arose among individual members of the ruling class. The task of forming a stable society in the wilderness was no easy one, and the leadership constantly confronted divisive issues. As in most viable societies, the divisions were *within the ruling class itself, not between the leaders and the led.*

The years 1635–1638 were particularly controversial: Roger Williams—an extreme individualist whose prose was thrilling, noble, and seditious—was allowed to leave Salem for Rhode Island; Thomas Hooker and John Haynes, finding Massachusetts too oligarchical and rigid, left to found Hartford, Connecticut; Theophilus Eaton and John Davenport, who regarded Massachusetts as too lax, settled New Haven; and William Pynchon and his followers left for Springfield. All these men were lay or clerical leaders within the original Puritan oligarchy.

The most important division within the Boston ruling class during the first decade resulted from the Hutchinson controversy. William Hutchinson, son of a well-to-do merchant, and his wife, Anne, had been married for twenty-two years and had had fourteen children before coming to Boston aboard the *Griffin* in 1634. They promptly became members of the Boston church, of which John Wilson was the minister and John Cotton the teacher. Wilson,

> . . . the product of a Windsor deanery, of Eton, and of King's, was an unusually cultivated man. . . . He had sacrificed one of the pleasantest posts at the University of Cambridge, renounced his certain opportunity of high ecclesiastical preferment, broken with his family, liquidated his property, and emigrated to New England, in order to live according to the way of truth; and he did not relish being called a false hireling and a priest of Baal. Nor did he like having half his congregation walk out when he began to preach, and a good part of the rest, well primed by Mrs. Hutchinson, remain to ask impudent and embarrassing questions after the close of the sermon.[1]

Needless to say, Wilson has never been a favorite of the Charles Francis Adams school of historians, who saw him as a leader of the glacial age, especially after his harsh treatment of such Quakers as Mary Dyer.

John Cotton, who had been Anne Hutchinson's mentor and idol at St. Botolph's in Boston, England, had once emphasized grace as opposed to the deadening Anglican stress on works alone; in Boston, Massachusetts, however, he established "an equipoise of grace and works so delicate that the weight of a hair might upset the balance."[2] Yet Anne Hutchinson, who had come to New England to be near her favorite preacher, was now a perfectionist, or a true and enthusiastic believer in grace alone, a mystical view not unlike the Quaker doctrine of the Inner Light. "I live," she was wont to say, "but not I but Jesus Christ lives in me."[3]

Immediately upon their arrival in Boston William and Anne Hutchinson took their places at the very heart of the establishment, settling on High Street right across from the John Winthrops. William, an unassuming gentleman of inherited means, whom John Winthrop referred to as "a man of very mild temper and weak parts, and wholly guided by his wife,"[4] was nevertheless a responsible member of his class, serving as deputy from Boston on the general court that proposed the founding of a college in 1636 and as one of the first benefactors of what was to become the famous Boston Latin School. Anne, "a woman of ready wit and bold spirit," according to John Winthrop, soon took on the role of prophetess.[5] Her enemies were the hypocrites who masqueraded as God's elect. At the height of her quickly gained popularity, some sixty or seventy men and women gathered twice a week at the Hutchinson house to listen to her message. (Her elite followers were not unlike the modern-day radical chic.) "Theoretically," wrote Emery Battis, "antinomianism was a rejection of power by placing the human will in the hands of God, to be manipulated by Him as He saw fit. Practically, however, it amounted to an assertion of unqualified personal power and autonomy."[6]

In 1636, the impulsive and popular Sir Harry Vane, succeeded John Haynes—who had gone off with Hooker to Hartford—as governor. Vane, who, as Winthrop put it, "went so far beyond the rest as to maintain a personal union with the Holy Ghost," naturally became an avid Hutchinsonian. As the year wore on the Hutchinsonians, under the charismatic leadership of Anne, attracted Governor Vane and most of Boston's best to their side. (At first even John Cotton was sympathetic.) They and their orthodox opponents, led by Winthrop, Thomas Dudley, and Hugh Peter, awaited the gubernatorial election in May 1637. The orthodox leaders cleverly had the court of elections moved to Newtown, hoping thereby to limit the attendance of Boston's new sectarians. On election day, Wilson preached to the multitude, and when the hands were counted Winthrop had won the governorship; Dudley was elected deputy-governor; Vane was not even made an assistant.*

A few days later, the first serious war against the Pequot Indians broke out; a quick victory ensued as "the Lord delivered up the heathen to the sword of his chosen people."[7] In August, the ministers and the fighting chaplains of the three Puritan colonies held the first church synod in New England. Finally, finding a formula with which even the ambivalent John Cotton could agree, they condemned some eighty "erroneous opinions." The voice of law and order and the covenant of works were now on the ascendancy.

The rulings of the synod now had to be enforced by the government, and the newly elected general court assembled at Newtown in November. First, the leaders of the Hutchinsonians—John Wheelwright, John Coggeshall, William Coddington, and William Aspinwall—were disfranchised; John Harvard and other recent immigrants were sworn in as freemen; and, finally, "toward the gloomy close of a November day," Anne Hutchinson was arraigned before the

---

*Vane left for England, never to return, in August 1637.

court on the charge of having "troubled the peace of the commonwealth and churches." Morison writes:

> It was on a small scale a state trial of the sort then common in England, where no legal safeguards were observed. . . . the result was a foregone conclusion. Yet the clever and witty woman conducted her case admirably. She admitted nothing and denied everything, John Cotton gallantly supporting her to the confusion of her over-eager colleagues. But just at the point when the ministers and magistrates were at their wits' ends what to do next, Anne's unruly member gave her away. She declared, even boasted, of her personal revelations from the Almighty; and that was to confess the worst. For in this the Puritan agreed with historical Christianity, that divine revelation closed with the Book of Revelation. Convicted out of her own mouth, Anne Hutchinson was sentenced to banishment from Massachusetts Bay "as being a woman not fit for our society."[8]

As Winthrop, the presiding official at the trial, put it to Hutchinson: "Your course is not to be suffered; . . . we see not that any should have authority to set up any other exercises besides what authority hath already set up."[9]

Governor Winthrop, no match for either John Cotton or Anne Hutchinson in analytical or theoretical ability, nevertheless possessed a sound practical instinct for which half-truth was needed in his day in Massachusetts. Thus, he felt, much as George Keith was later to feel in early Philadelphia, that in a new society in the wilderness, law and the need for community solidarity must take precedence over the autonomy of individual conscience. A fundamentally tolerant man, he knew, as he once put it, that "no truth is seasonable at all times." Or, as Oliver Wendell Holmes, Jr. observed almost three centuries later: "The character of every act depends on the circumstances in which it is done. The most stringent protection of free speech would not protect a man in falsely shouting fire in a theatre and causing a panic."[10]

At any rate, Anne Hutchinson, her husband, and many of her followers, left Massachusetts for Rhode Island, which even Charles Francis Adams reluctantly had to admit was the antinomian state par excellence.

THE KEITHIAN HERESY
IN PENNSYLVANIA

George Keith, a Scotsman with a master of arts degree from Aberdeen, was the best educated man in Philadelphia of the first decade. Born a Presbyterian, he became a convinced Friend in 1664, traveled on the Continent with Fox, Barclay, and Penn in 1677, and was supposed to have been a strong intellectual influence on Barclay, helping him with his *Apology*. Keith came to Philadelphia in 1689 and was appointed the first tutor of the Quaker school that became the William Penn Charter School. After the deaths of Barclay in 1690 and of Fox in 1691, the egotistical and combative Keith perhaps thought he should inherit the mantle of Quaker leadership. At any rate, just at the height of the anarchic Blackwell period, Keith led an attack on the sufficiency of the Inner Light as a guide to behavior and church organization.

Convinced by the tumultuous events of Blackwell's rule that Quakerism was failing in its new setting, Keith appeared before the Yearly Meeting of Friends—the gathering of all Quaker Monthly Meetings from West Jersey and Pennsylvania—to present a body of rules as a basis of church policy. Included were proposals for a confession of faith to be required of those seeking admission to the Society, for the election of elders and deacons within each meeting, and for the silencing of persons "raw and unseasoned" or unsure in their beliefs. In addition, Keith stressed the need to place more emphasis upon the Bible as a fountain of spiritual growth and less on hidden sources—the "light within" which Quakers taught was residual in every individual.[11]

These were radical proposals and, as might be expected, they were immediately rejected by the Yearly Meeting as "downright Popery." But Keith only broadened his attack, proposing greater order and discipline and less spontaneity in the Quaker meetings, going so far as to suggest that the profession of nonresistance rendered the Quakers unfit to perform their duties in private life and in government. Though Keith's arguments about the organizational weaknesses and theological thinness of the Quaker beliefs appealed to a handful of educated Friends (in 1692, Penn seemed to favor Keith), the vast majority of poorly educated Friends preferred the simple doctrine of the Inner Light.

Unfortunately, Keith was an unpleasant and tactless person, and the whole weight of the influence of Thomas Lloyd—in control of both the Quaker party and the Yearly Meeting—was turned against him. Yet, although he was disowned by the Yearly Meeting in 1692, he continued to attract followers. The climax came in 1693, at the largest meetinghouse in Philadelphia.

On a Saturday night, cloaked by darkness, partisans of Keith worked feverishly at one end of the meetinghouse to erect a gallery from which their leader might exhort the worshippers next morning. Keith's opponents had long controlled the permanent gallery at the opposite end of the room and denied the apostate entrance to it. The next day, as the Quakers filed into the meetinghouse for the weekly devotions, they found themselves caught in the crossfire of two groups of impassioned Friends. Accusations and counter-accusations filled the air as each side struggled to be heard. But the verbal exchange paled before the physical demonstrations that followed. Axes appeared from nowhere as each group sought to destroy the other's gallery. Posts, railings, stairs, seats—all went down before the angry blows of the two opposed camps.[12]

The Keithian controversy now became political as well as religious. And the so-called Christian Quakers were easily defeated by Thomas Lloyd's party. The anti-intellectual forces, and the theological position of the Inner Light as sufficient in itself, won out.

Keith returned to England, where he was read out of the London meeting and eventually ordained in the Anglican church. In 1702, he was sent to America by the Society for Propagating the Gospel in Foreign Parts in order to gather as many as possible into the Anglican church. In Philadelphia, Keith was welcomed by the remnants of the Keithians, who claimed that he brought 500 of them back into the true establishment. Thus, the seeds of Philadelphia's Quaker-turned-Episcopal upper class were planted.

CHARLES FRANCIS ADAMS II AND THE MASSACHUSETTS HISTORIANS FROM PALFREY TO MORISON

Charles Francis Adams's brief essay on the Massachusetts historians discussed in Chapter 3, argued against what he called the filiopietistic school of New England historians for their defense of John Winthrop's position in banishing the antinomians.

Among those filiopietistic defenders of intolerance, Palfrey wrote: "When two scores of years passed before the recurrence of any serious dissension in Massachusetts, the substantial wisdom of the course now pursued may be deemed to be vindicated by the event."[13] And Josiah Quincy asserted that "had our early ancestors adopted the course we at this day are apt to deem so easy and obvious, and placed their government on the basis of liberty for all sorts of consciences, it would have been, in that age, a certain introduction to anarchy. It cannot be questioned, that all the fond hopes they had cherished from emigration would have been lost. . . . The non-toleration which characterized our early ancestors, from whatever source it may have originated, had undoubtedly the effect they intended and wished."[14]

It is not my intention here to side with either the filiopietistic or the Adams school of historiography. Rather, it is to argue that the contents of the heresies, Anne Hutchinson's anti-intellectual antinomianism in Massachusetts and George Keith's intellectual anti-antinomianism in Pennsylvania, were of first importance. "The Puritan founders had their terrible faults," wrote Richard Hofstadter. "But the Puritan clergy came as close to being an intellectual ruling class—or, more properly, a class of intellectuals intimately associated with a ruling power—as America has ever had."[15] And the intellectual leadership in Massachusetts was schooled in the halls of Harvard College. If, as Samuel Eliot Morison has said, the suppression of Hutchinsonianism was "the price New England had to pay for a college," so the suppression of the Keithians in Philadelphia may well have contributed to the characteristic anti-intellectualism of that city.[16]

HERESY AND HARVARD

The founding of Harvard College has always been officially dated to 1636. In that year, the general court, under the leadership of Governor Vane, made the original proposal for establishing a "schoale or colledge" outside the village of Marblehead, near the farm of Hugh Peter. After a hectic year's delay, the orthodox victors over both the Indians and the heretics were ready to go ahead with their college. At the next meeting of the court following the Hutchinson trial, in November 1637, the assembled magistrates and deputies, after disfranchising a few more Hutchinsonians and rewarding some more Indian fighters, passed the following order: "The colledge is ordered to bee at Newetowne." After a recess of five days, the court committed the building of the college to six magistrates and six elders, the first board of overseers, and then ordered "that Newetowne shall henceforward be called Cambridge."

For more than three centuries, Harvard College has been intimately related to Boston's (and America's) ruling classes. From the beginning, not only its overseers but also its presidents and its faculty have been drawn from the city's upper class, at least until the time when President Eliot began to surround the college with professional and graduate schools, which drew their faculties increasingly from a national pool of specialists rather than gentlemen scholars. Just as Eton and Harrow, Oxford and Cambridge were the nurseries of statesmen (of the upper class) in England during Britain's imperial age, so Harvard, and particularly its law school, has been the nursery of New England's and America's leadership, far and away above any other educational institution in America. Harvard was the leading symbol of a class that believed deeply in education and intellect in general.

> When a small homogeneous group of men in a colonial legislature declares that education is of singular benefit to the commonwealth, and that it fits children for future service in church or state; and when they enforce these injunctions by suitable administrative regulations, pains, and penalties, it may be supposed without undue charity that they mean what they say, and that education was conceived of as a training for citizenship and service in a civilized state, rather than as a vehicle for sectarian propaganda, or "caste" dominance.[17]

Antinomianism, based on the mystical doctrine of "immediate revelation," or the Inner Light, has always been the enemy of education, intellect, and hierarchy. Why spend four years at college if learned ministers are inferior to prophets with the gift of immediate revelation? As someone in Anne Hutchinson's Boston put it:

> Come along with me. . . . I'll bring you to a Women that Preaches better Gospell than any of your black-coates that have been at the Ninneversity, a Women of another kinde of spirit, who hath had many Revelations. . . . I had rather hear such a one that speakes from the meere motion of the spirit, without any study at all, than any of your learned Scollers, although they may be fuller of Scripture.[18]

No wonder the Harvard man has been the main target of most anti-authoritarian and anti-intellectual attacks in our history, from the youthful Benjamin Franklin to Senator Joseph P. McCarthy in the 1950s and the New Left in the 1960s. The sixteen-year-old Franklin, under the pen name of Silence Dogood, showed his egalitarian resentment against upper-class Boston and Harvard when he wrote of the "extreme folly of those Parents, who, blind to their Children's Dulness . . . will send them to the Temple of Learning, where, for want of a suitable Genius, they learn little more than how to carry themselves handsomely, and enter a room genteely (which might as well be acquired at Dancing-School), and from whence they return . . . as great Blockheads as ever, only more proud and self-conceited."[19] And it was no accident that for Joseph McCarthy the archenemy of red-blooded America was none other than the Yale and Harvard bred Dean Acheson, a "pompous diplomat in striped pants, with a phony British accent." The so-called Harvard accent was of course the accent of upper-class Boston.

HERESY AND HIGHER LEARNING
IN PHILADELPHIA

In a recent biography of William Penn, Catherine Owens Peare described the intellectual climate in early Philadelphia as follows:

> New-born Philadelphia had many advantages that other New World cities had not had. She lured many merchants with both capital and experience. . . . When Robert Turner came, he brought seventeen servants. Philadelphia rapidly became a cultural center, because she attracted scholars as well and did not have to wait for them to torture their way up out of the primitive soil. Francis Pastorius, George Keith, Thomas Lloyd, and *many more* had fine classical educations. Since William Penn himself was a *tremendous scholar* he acted as a magnet for others.[20]

The facts of the situation in Philadelphia's classic period were quite the opposite. Whereas the city did attract experienced merchants from all over the New World, the complement of men of advanced education *was limited to* Pastorius, Keith, Lloyd, and one or two others at most. As late as 1713, James Logan, Penn's agent in Pennsylvania, warned a friend that the colony "was barren of 'men of Parts & Learning.' "[21] Penn, moreover, was *not* a "tremendous scholar," either in formal education or in accomplishments, but was rather a gifted and prolific polemicist in an age of religious controversy. An intellectual, yes; a scholar, no.

The point that must be stressed again and again is that Boston's upper class always has placed a high value on intellect and higher education, whereas Philadelphians have never placed a high value on either. The Philadelphia Quakers, like all too many other Americans, have valued education, especially its more practical aspects, while mistrusting learning. And down through the years, the city's Quaker-turned-Episcopal gentry have only halfheartedly supported the University of Pennsylvania, which throughout its long history has contributed surprisingly little to the nation's intellectual or political leadership. All this will be spelled out in more detail in later chapters. Here it is enough to note that Rufus Jones, the early twentieth century's leading Quaker historian and philosopher, felt that the suppression of George Keith's ideas might very well have put off the founding of Haverford College until late in the nineteenth century. Keith's journal

> shows also, perhaps more clearly than any other document, the dawn of those customs which soon crystallized into the conservatism of succeeding decades. The lack of educated leadership fed directly the tendencies to imitation of the virtues of the past. The fear of innovations and devotion to the orthodox literature of the first generation received a new impulse from the Keithian separation and the partisan spirit engendered, and the Society settled down to a century or more of doctrinal ease and quiet.[22]

Just as Massachusetts and Pennsylvania were founded on premises that were polar opposites, so the values of Anne Hutchinson were quite the opposite of those of George Keith. Rather, perhaps, they wanted to move their respective colonies in opposite directions: Keith toward the law and Hutchinson toward the gospel. And the subsequent histories of Boston and Philadelphia would surely been different if both had won out. At any rate, both intolerant Massachusetts and tolerant Pennsylvania got rid of their heretics.

POSTSCRIPT: ANNE HUTCHINSON
AND MARY DYER

It is not surprising that several of the Hutchinsonians, like William Coddington and Catherine Scott (a sister of Anne Hutchinson), became Quakers and early leaders in the colony of Rhode Island. Perhaps the most famous of the Hutchinsonians who became Quakers was Mary Dyer.

Mary and her husband, William, came to Boston about 1635. Well educated and of good family, the Dyers joined John Wilson's congregation and were among the first to attend the meetings of the Hutchinson clique. In 1637, the Dyers were disfranchised along with the other Hutchinsonians and migrated to Rhode Island, where William became one of the founders and leading citizens of Portsmouth.

Mary Dyer was Anne Hutchinson's best friend. Just as he had admired Anne, so John Winthrop found Mary to be a "very proper and fair woman." Shortly before the Hutchinson controversy came to a head, Mary gave birth prematurely, Anne and Goody Hawkins acting as midwives.

> It was for Anne and Goody Hawkins to see the hideous fruits of Mary's labors. A creature so horrible in its malformation as to bear only the slightest terrifying resemblance to mankind. Something such as only a nightmare in hell could conceive. It was most mercifully dead.[23]

After Anne Hutchinson departed for Rhode Island, word of Mary Dyer's miscarriage leaked out. It was, of course, seen as a sign of heavenly displeasure, as John Winthrop recorded, along with all the horrible details, in his journal.

William Dyer's ardor for grace alone and the promptings of the Inner Light quickly cooled after his arrival in Rhode Island. Mary, however, went back to England in 1650 and eventually became an ardent Friend. In the meantime, under the governorship of John Endicott, an ever increasing group of Quaker martyrs, from England and from many parts of the New World, were attracted to Boston. In October 1657 a new law was passed against the "cursed sect," imposing a fine of £ 100 on anyone bringing a Quaker into the colony. The law also provided that any Quaker returning from banishment should, if a man, have an ear cropped; for the second offense, another ear; and for the third, his tongue bored with a hot iron; an offending woman was to be severely whipped and on the third offense to have her tongue bored. Much to the embarrassment of Endicott and the other authorities, Quakers continued to come "as if they had been invited." Commissioned to "plant the truth" in Massachusetts "they could not do otherwise."

Passing through Boston on her return from England to Rhode Island in 1657, Mary Dyer was arrested and imprisoned but released upon her husband's entreaty. The next year she was banished from New Haven for preaching Quakerism. In September 1659, William Robinson, Marmaduke Stephenson, Mary Dyer, and an eleven-year-old girl, Patience Scott (Anne Hutchinson's niece), were apprehended in Boston and subsequently banished "on pain of death." As whippings, ear croppings, fines, and imprisonments had proved futile, the death penalty for Quakers easily passed in the House of Deputies in October 1658.

Mary Dyer, along with Robinson and Stephenson, soon returned to Boston, and all were condemned to be hanged on October 27 in spite of the efforts of John Winthrop, Jr., governor of Connecticut, who pleaded "as on his bare knees" for their release. Mary Dyer walked to the gallows between the two men, her arms and legs bound and her face covered with a handkerchief lent by her old pastor at the Boston church, the Reverend John Wilson. After the two men were hanged, she was suddenly reprieved. She stubbornly refused to accept the pardon but was finally set on horseback and carried away toward Rhode Island. She next went off to spread the truth on Long Island. But "the fire and hammer" were in her soul and she could not stay away from the "bloody town of her sad and heavy experience." Mary Dyer returned to Boston in May and was finally hanged on Boston Common on June 1, 1660.

As Mary Dyer's lifeless body swung from the gallows Humphrey Atherton of Boston pointed to it and said in jest, "She hangs there as a flag!"[24] Three hundred years later, as I have sought to understand the differences between Boston and Philadelphia in our own antinomian times, I have often thought of the symbolic importance of Atherton's gallows humor. And every time I walk by the statues of Anne Hutchinson and Mary Dyer, now facing the Commons in front of the State House on Beacon Hill, I am reminded of how differently the twig was bent in the formative periods of Boston and Philadelphia.

Provincial Boston and Cosmopolitan Philadelphia in the Age of Thomas Hutchinson and Benjamin Franklin

If you would not be forgotten as soon as you are dead and rotten, either write things worth reading or do things worth writing.

Benjamin Franklin

In the middle decades of the eighteenth century, the values of the French Enlightment—secular, rational, humane, democratic, egalitarian, and individualistic—were brought to America through the thriving city of Philadelphia. Cosmopolitan Philadelphia was a highly mobile society of laymen—merchants, scientists, doctors, reformers, artists, and craftsmen—drawn from all social classes and from many parts of the New and Old Worlds. In striking contrast, Boston remained a provincial and essentially Puritan town, ruled, despite bitter opposition, by appointees of the British crown.

BENJAMIN FRANKLIN AND THOMAS HUTCHINSON: PARVENU GENIUS AND ARISTOCRATIC AUTOCRAT

Benjamin Franklin was America's finest flower of the Enlightenment. Born in Boston, he found his natural homes in Philadelphia, London, and Paris. Bored by religious orthodoxy and horrified by Harvard snobs, he was in all respects the antithesis of his fellow townsman and contemporary Thomas Hutchinson, who by temperament, conviction, and breeding was molded in the honorable image of John Winthrop rather than in that of his own ancestor the heretic Anne Hutchinson. Although he was never quite accepted by Philadelphia's gentry, Franklin became the most beloved, the archetypical American of his age, respected in London and lionized in Paris. Thomas Hutchinson, however, by the time he accepted an honorary degree at Oxford as an exiled Tory, on July 4, 1776, was undoubtedly the most despised American of his generation.

Whereas Hutchinson, Harvard graduate, royal governor, and the most accomplished historian of his age, was of the essence of class authority in Boston, Franklin, classless and cosmopolitan auslander in Philadelphia, was the city's all-time first citizen. Hutchinson, humorless in the style of so many of Boston's best, saw the world as essentially tragic. Franklin found the human comedy endlessly entertaining. Only a moderately creative man, and full of inner tensions, Hutchinson needed a stable and hierarchical world in which to work; Franklin's genius, which included a profound inner serenity and security, thrived in the mobile, even anarchical world that finally witnessed the American and French revolutions.

In spite of their differences, the two men had once respected each other as they shared the leadership in planning a union of the colonies under British rule at the Albany Congress of 1754; the ultimate tragedy of their relationship was the fact that Franklin, in 1772, made public some confidential letters from Hutchinson to Thomas Whately, former secretary of the British Treasury under Grenville and a key figure in drafting the Stamp Act. Written in 1768–1769, the letters showed that Hutchinson had been secretly urging the British government to exert its authority over the colonies with more vigor. They expressed no views that Hutchinson had not already expressed publicly at the time. But, sent by Franklin in London to Boston, the letters were eventually serialized by the *Spy*, the *Boston Gazette*, the *Boston Evening-Post*, and the *Essex Gazette*, "with editorial comments likening the letters to 'footsteps stained with blood.' "[1] They were reprinted in every colony and Hutchinson was even burned in effigy in Philadelphia. Though lifted out of context in a period of paranoia, the Whately letters ruined Hutchinson and his family in America and sent them into lonely exile.

A look at the contrast between Franklin's Philadelphia and Hutchinson's Boston should shed additional light on my theme of class authority and leadership in the two colonial cities.

MASSACHUSETTS: CLASS AUTHORITY IN
THE ROYAL COLONY, 1689–1776

During the half century or so before 1686, when Sir Edmund Andros, "in Scarlet Coat, Laced," became the first royal governor of the province of Massachusetts Bay, the Boston ruling class, as we have seen, "did what it had a mind to do." Though now somewhat limited by the authority of the British crown, the same pattern of class rule prevailed during the rest of the colonial period. In the years between the downfall of the hated Andros in 1689 and the outbreak of the Revolution in 1776, fifteen men were appointed chief executive of the colony by the crown. Six of them—Simon Bradstreet, Joseph Dudley, William Stoughton, William Dummer, Jonathan Belcher, and Thomas Hutchinson—held the office for over half the time. All six belonged to the same local class of ruling families as had the governors who served under the first charter, and all of them exhibited the same habit of authority and will to power that had marked their ancestors in the first generation.

Simon Bradstreet, the last of the first generation, was the very essence of the Puritan ideal of class authority and leadership. He came to America with Winthrop and served in public office for sixty-two years, including forty-nine years as an assistant and two terms as governor. After graduating from Puritan Emmanuel College at Cambridge, he married Anne Dudley, the first poet of New England. Bradstreet was a typical, long-lived progenitor: his wife, daughter of Thomas Dudley, the second governor, produced eight children. Among her famous descendants are Richard Henry Dana, Wendell Phillips, and the two Oliver Wendell Holmeses.

The Dudleys were part of Boston's governing class for almost a century—from 1634, when Thomas was first elected governor, to 1715, when his son, Joseph, retired from public life. Although his integrity was impeccable, Thomas Dudley was "dogmatic, austere, prejudiced, and unlovable. Like many others of his class, he was no friend of popular government and a strong believer in autocracy."[2] Joseph likewise was "ambitious, self-seeking, cold and ungrateful to his friends."[3]

William Stoughton, close political friend of Joseph Dudley, was fired in the same stern Puritan mold. He had served as chief justice in the Salem witchcraft trials and had never yielded to feelings of compassion even after others had become more enlightened: "Cold, proud, and obstinate in nature, he was still one of the most respected citizens of the colony."[4] His father, Reverend Israel Stoughton, who had come to Massachusetts with the Winthrop fleet in 1630, was one of the founders of the town of Dorchester and one of the largest landowners in the Bay Colony. In an election sermon at Dorchester in 1669, William anticipated the Social Darwinists by several hundred years when he thus justified his own ruling class: "God sifted a whole nation that he might send Choice Grain into the Wilderness."[5]

Though not quite of the same choice grain as the Bradstreets, Dudleys, and Stoughtons, William Dummer and Jonathan Belcher were nevertheless well-connected members of New England's ruling class. Governor Dummer was Joseph Dudley's son-in-law, and Governor Belcher was related through marriage to the Olivers of Rhode Island and Massachusetts and the Partridges, a leading New Hampshire family. Belcher, after being dismissed from the combined governorships of Massachusetts and New Hampshire in 1741, allegedly for taking a bribe, returned to London, where in 1746 he secured a royal appointment as governor of New Jersey; his greatest contribution to our history was the active part he played in founding the College of New Jersey and building Nassau Hall. Belcher was surely in the Puritan tradition of the Dudleys and William Stoughton in exercising the authority of his class. As James Truslow Adams wrote, he was "aggressive where he had the power," and "no one could fawn lower to secure advantage to himself and his family."[6]

In their classic age under the first charter, as we have seen, the Boston Puritans, were in the habit of governing themselves. And the town meeting was the classic instrument. Under the royal charter, there was a continuing battle between those who wanted to preserve the town meeting traditions of self-government and the conservative supporters of the royal prerogative. Elisha Cooke (1637–1715), the most popular Boston politician of his age, was the recognized leader of the party that opposed both clerical dominance and royal prerogative.

After graduating from Harvard, Cooke married the daughter of Governor Leverett, which immediately gave him an impeccable social standing. For a time he practiced medicine but eventually went into politics. He took a leading part in the overthrow of Andros and became a member of the Council of Safety after the Revolution. The Cooke home on School Street was the central meeting place of the opposition party throughout the rule of Governor Dudley (1702–1715). Every year the popular Cooke was elected to the general court; every year his enemy Dudley refused to seat him. Finally, a few months before Cooke's death at the age of seventy-eight, Governor Dudley allowed him to take his seat. At his death Cooke was one of the wealthiest men in Boston.

Elisha Cooke, Jr. (1678–1737), carried on in the family tradition of liberal opposition. Because of his high social standing, young Elisha was placed first in his class when he entered Harvard in 1697.* He further consolidated his position through marriage to the great-granddaughter of Governor Winslow of Plymouth colony. Like his father, he became a physician before going into politics. Chosen a member of council in 1717, Cooke spent the rest of his life leading the opposition to royal rule. Governor Belcher referred to Cooke as his "inveterate enemy" who had "a fixt enmity to all Kingly Governments." The death of Cooke and the departure of Belcher from the governorship marked the end of one of the most turbulent political periods in the history of the Bay Colony. Cooke and his father had inherited the independent traditions of the old colony, kept them alive, and passed them on to the revolutionary generation of Samuel Adams, John Adams, and James Otis.

Our Anglo-American system of two-party democracy has depended largely on leaders who have come from similar upper-class backgrounds but at the same time have been divided in their political convictions and party affiliations. Thus, the Cookes, the Dudleys, and Belchers were all members of the same social class that had had authority in the Bay Colony since the days of John Win-

---

*In the seventeenth and eighteenth centuries, each student in a Harvard class was listed, not alphabetically or academically, but according to his family's social position. The subtleties of the very accurate system are indicated in the case of the "brace of Adamses." Thus, Samuel of Boston was ranked sixth in his class (out of twenty-three); John of Braintree was ranked fifteenth (out of twenty-four).

throp; their disputes were not unlike the Whig and Tory divisions within the British ruling class at that time and afterward; nor were they unlike the divisions between the Jeffersonian Republicans and the Adams Federalists at our nation's founding or between the upper-class followers of Franklin D. Roosevelt of Harvard and the followers of Robert A. Taft of Yale in our New Deal days. To put it another way, the traditional authority of any ruling class in the long run depends on its producing leaders of more than one party or set of political convictions. This point has always been hard for Marxists to understand because they come out of the continental tradition, where there is a much closer fit between class and party; economic determinists, moreover, cannot quite understand how millionaires like Roosevelt and Taft, or Kennedy and Rockefeller, could possibly have differing political convictions. But then, they are ideologists, and it is just when parties become too class-bound that they often become ideological and former political *opponents* become class *enemies*. This is exactly what happened to the New England Federalists in the years leading up to the Hartford Convention (and why John Quincy Adams eventually shunned his peers and became a Democratic-Republican) and to the Massachusetts Tories under the governorship of Thomas Hutchinson.

GOVERNOR HUTCHINSON:
LAST DEFENDER OF ROYAL AUTHORITY

With his wealth, abilities, and family traditions it was natural that Thomas Hutchinson should devote himself to public life. His great-great-grandfather William had been a responsible figure in Boston and a leading citizen of Portsmouth, Rhode Island, after going there with his famous wife, Anne. Hutchinson's grandfather had been a member of council and a judge of common pleas; his father had been on the council for two decades (1719–1739). Countering the ministerial-magisterial traditions of Boston's early ruling class, however, the Hutchinsons for 150 years had been merchants, "counting not a single minister, lawyer, teacher, or clergyman in their line."[7]

A Harvard graduate, Thomas entered politics at the age of twenty-six and was thereafter never out of it. He was a representative in the Massachusetts House from 1737 to 1749 and a councillor for the succeeding seventeen years, eventually reaching the pinnacle of authority and power as lieutenant governor, chief justice, and royal governor. It was largely Thomas Hutchinson's single-minded advancement of members of his closely knit family that enraged his political opponents. In the 1770s, the governorship, the lieutenant governorship, and the chief justiceship of Massachusetts were held by three of his brothers and a brother-in-law; none but a Hutchinson or an Oliver had been lieutenant governor of Massachusetts after 1758 or chief justice after 1760. At this point, where there was too close a fit between class and party, Hutchinson's political opponents started to become his political enemies; violence erupted and eventually led to the Boston Massacre, the Tea Party, and the outbreak of war at Lexington and Concord.

The trouble began when the Stamp Act was passed by Parliament in 1764. Though Hutchinson disapproved of the act he nevertheless supported Parliament's right to tax the colonies; this position and the fact that his brother-in-law Andrew Oliver was appointed stamp distributor enraged such rising opposition leaders as Samuel Adams. In the summer of 1764, the splendid Hutchinson mansion on Garden Court Street was attacked by mobs, looted, and burned to the ground. Hutchinson barely escaped with his life. Nothing like this had ever happened in Boston history, and news of the violence spread throughout the colonies.

Though Hutchinson increased his power and was eventually appointed royal governor, his authority rapidly declined in the course of the 1770s. Publication of the Whately letters in 1772 dealt him a mortal wound; his role in the Boston Tea Party in 1773 marked the end of his American career; and he left for England the next year.

In the winter of 1776, as Washington's army was besieging the British at Boston, Thomas Hutchinson's good friend the Reverend Henry Caner of Anglican King's Chapel left the country, taking the church's valuable silver and the parish records with him. The occupants of thirty of the church's seventy-three pews, all sharing Caner's sentiments, also departed, most of them for good, and many others of Hutchinson's stylish party soon followed suit. Symbolically, the Mather dynasty in Massachusetts also came to an end: the Reverend Samuel Mather, son of Cotton and brother-in-law of Thomas Hutchinson, died in 1785; of Samuel's three sons, Increase was lost at sea, Thomas died in 1782, and his namesake joined the Loyalist exodus, never to return.*

The end of the Hutchinson and Mather dynasties marked the end of an era in the history of Boston's upper class. But the authoritative traditions of leadership were carried on in the revolutionary generation. Young John Adams, the first of his family to come to Boston when he entered Harvard in 1751, had opposed the dynastic rule of Thomas Hutchinson for fifteen years before the governor's downfall. Yet he himself was the founder of the greatest political dynasty in our nation's history. When a Boston town meeting, at the beginning of the end of Thomas Hutchinson in 1772, voted to appoint a Committee of Correspondence, the twenty-two original members included, along with John Adams's radical cousin Samuel, James Otis, Josiah Quincy, Joseph Warren, and Robert Pierpont, all of them progenitors of leading upper-class families in Boston and elsewhere in the United States.

THE FRANKLIN BROTHERS DEPART FOR
THE LIBERAL AND LEVELING COLONIES
OF RHODE ISLAND AND PENNSYLVANIA

In any society, religious and class authority does not necessarily preclude the growth of radical criticism. In fact, such authority may encourage it, as Bos-

---

*See Appendix III for Mather leadership outside Massachusetts.

ton's radical role in the Revolution, in contrast to Philadelphia's cautious vacillation, suggests.

A brief period of radical and witty criticism of authority began in provincial Boston in the hot summer of 1721, when James Franklin founded the *New England Courant*. Franklin was encouraged by a small clique of friends including a colorful and radical Scotsman named William Douglas, who had studied medicine in Edinburgh, Leiden, and Paris and was the only man with a medical degree in the city. James himself had only recently returned from London, where he had steeped himself in the theological, literary, and political discussions of the day (mostly aired in the *London Courant*). And he had seen how powerful a gazette could be in the hands of the dissatisfied.

The favorite targets of the editors of the *New England Courant* included haughty Harvard College, the outmoded Puritan virtues, and all forms of establishment hypocrisy and pomposity. In one of the early issues, William Douglas, knowing nothing of bacteriology but with most of the city's medical men on his side, launched a bitter attack on Cotton Mather's support of the use of inoculations against smallpox. (The city at the time was suffering an epidemic of the disease.) James Franklin's younger brother, Benjamin, also agreed with the merry Scottish doctor.*

Though neither he nor anyone else knew it at the time, young Benjamin Franklin had the best mind in Boston. Fiercely ambitious from an early age, he spent every spare moment reading, not to pass the time but to instruct himself in how both to do good and to succeed in the world. Among his favorite books was Cotton Mather's *Essays to Do Good*. Franklin first appeared in print at the age of sixteen, in his brother's gazette, using the pen name of Silence Dogood. The Mrs. Dogood series, infinitely popular with readers, was most revealing of the young man's mind. But the establishment did not take kindly to the wit of the brothers Franklin, and James was eventually forbidden by the general court to publish the *Courant* or any other such gazette. From then on it was issued under the name of Benjamin Franklin. James, however, became more and more jealous of his younger brother and drew up a secret contract keeping Benjamin in an apprenticeship position. Unable to bear the ambiguity of this situation, Benjamin slipped away from Boston in October 1723.

> I was sensible that, if I attempted to go openly, means would be used to prevent me. My friend Collins, therefore, undertook to manage a little for me. He agreed with the captain of a New York sloop for my passage, under the notion of my being a young acquaintance of his that had got a naughty girl with child, whose friends would compel me to marry her, and therefore I could not appear or come away publicly. So I sold some of my books to raise a little money, was taken on board privately, and, as we had a fair wind, in three days I found myself in New York.[8]

Here were the methods of a born politician. In the meantime, brother James got married and took himself off to the more congenial, antinomian state of

---

*Franklin later changed his mind about the value of vaccination.

Rhode Island, where he set up a press and edited a newspaper for many happy years in the thriving and free commercial town of Newport.

In his last winter in Boston, Benjamin wrote a revealing article in the *Courant* attacking hereditary privilege and authority. Those who suffered through the deference-debunking 1960s in this country, when it seemed as if everyone was referred to as Johnny or Joe, will find a comforting sense of historical perspective in the following paragraph taken from this charming article.

> Honour, Friend, properly ascends and not descends, yet the Hat when the Head is uncover'd descends and therefore there can be no Honour in it. Besides Honour was from the Beginning but Hats are an invention of a late Time and consequently true Honour standeth not therein. In old Time it was no disrespect for Men and Women to be call'd by their own Names; Adam was never called Master Adam, we never read of Noah Squire, Lot Knight and Baronet, nor the Right Honourable Abraham, Viscount Messoppotamia, Baron of Canaan. No, no, they were plain men, honest country graziers, that took care of their families and their flocks. Moses was a great prophet and Aaron a priest of the Lord; but we never read of the Reverend Moses nor the Right Reverend Father in God, Aaron, by Divine Providence Lord Archbishop of Israel. . . . It was no incivility then to mention their naked names as they were expressed.[9]

Nothing written by George Fox or William Penn equals this anti-authoritarian appeal, and Boston's young egalitarian was bound to feel more at home in Quaker Philadelphia.

PHILADELPHIA'S GOLDEN AGE OF BENJAMIN FRANKLIN

Eighteenth-century Boston, as we have noted, had a fairly stable population compared to that of the rapidly growing city of Philadelphia. Having no immigration from abroad to speak of, suffering severe smallpox epidemics in 1721 and 1730 (which took some 2,000 lives) and depressions during the 1720s and 1740s, Boston reached its peak population of 16,000 in 1730 and remained about the same size throughout the rest of the colonial period. Philadelphia, however, grew rapidly, in spite of several smallpox epidemics, throughout the same period, increasing in population by more than 200 per cent between 1740 and 1776, when it was the second largest city in the British empire, surpassed only by London.

As Philadelphia's population increased steadily, its wealth increased geometrically. Chief Justice William Allen, contemporary of Thomas Hutchinson (both died in England in 1780), was the most influential man in Pennsylvania for thirty years before the Revolution. At the same time, he probably had more liquid wealth than any other American of his generation, besides owning thousands of acres of land in both Pennsylvania and New Jersey. Though Allen started out with some inherited wealth, Philadelphia was far more likely than Boston to have men of conspicuously new wealth. Young Benjamin Franklin instinctively knew where the best way to wealth was to be sought.

After leaving Boston, Franklin first landed in New York. Having no letters of introduction, he nevertheless soon made the acquaintance of William Bradford, the small town's only printer (as yet there was no newspaper). Bradford, a good Quaker who had come to Philadelphia along with Penn, was driven out of the city during the Keithian controversy and eventually, like many of the Keithians, joined the Anglican church. His family had become firmly established in New York, where he served on the vestry of Trinity Church. Having no position for Franklin in New York, Bradford sent the young printer to Philadelphia, where his son needed an apprentice.

Franklin, on foot, reached Philadelphia on a Sunday morning. Seeing many "clean-dressed people" all walking in the same direction, he followed them into a Quaker meetinghouse on Market Street, where, in the silence, he soon fell asleep. "This was, therefore," he wrote in his autobiography, "the first house I was in, or slept in, in Philadelphia."[10]

Franklin had been a compulsive and lonely reader in studious Boston. He mentions in the autobiography only one boy and no girls from his youth in that city. In Philadelphia, however, he writes chiefly of his friends: he knew everybody and also brought some of his countless friends from other colonies and abroad to the city—and he knew more people of consequence in London and Paris than any other American of his generation. But like other men of gregarious genius Franklin was close to very few, if any, of his circle. Similarly, in his youth "he went to women hungrily, secretly, and briefly"[11] and married Deborah Read, a woman of little education who never understood him, in order to break the habit.* But Franklin, much like William Penn, was away from home for a large part of his married life; in fact, Debbie died when he was in London and was buried at Christ Church before he ever got word of it.

Franklin was the greatest joiner and founder of associations in American history; yet, he liked to serve behind the scenes or as secretary or treasurer rather than as president (except in his old age). A fox rather than a lion, Franklin was neither by birth nor by natural presence a man of authority but rather one of great manipulative ability. He eventually attained the status of universal sage.

PHILADELPHIA LEADERSHIP IN THE AGE OF FRANKLIN: A HETEROGENEOUS ELITE

Every creative period in history has been led by a small minority of talented and ambitious men, one among them seeming to symbolize the age and give direction to all the rest. Some measure of how important Franklin's leadership was to Philadelphia's Golden Age is indicated by the following list of his accomplishments. Though it is not possible here to discuss his many accomplishments in any detail, I look at a few of them in this chapter as I examine what

---

*Debbie, the daughter of Franklin's first Philadelphia landlady, had been previously married to a man who had simply vanished, so she and Franklin lived as husband and wife in common law.

kind of social system he worked in. Surely a key test of the nature of a social system is the kind of leaders it produces from within and attracts from abroad. Table A–14 in Appendix I lists a representative group of the city's leaders. Franklin was a consummate politician and he worked with, sometimes for and sometimes against, all these men. Observing Franklin's agility in moving from one faction to another and always ending up leading the winning side, a Quaker friend once asked him, "How is it that thee always manages to be with the majority?"

Table 10-1
THE FOUNDING OF PHILADELPHIA INSTITUTIONS
IN THE AGE OF FRANKLIN

1727   Franklin founds the Junto, a "society meeting weekly for their mutual improvement in useful knowledge"

1730   Franklin founds the *Pennsylvania Gazette*; marries Deborah Read; and joins the first Masonic lodge in America (and writes its by-laws in 1732)

1731   Franklin, along with fellow Junto members, founds the first circulating library in America

1733   Franklin launches *Poor Richard's Almanac*, most popular publication in the colonies (circulation 10,000 a year by 1740)

1736   Franklin founds the Union Fire Company, the world's first; becomes clerk of the assembly; and is on his way to becoming leader of the popular party

1740   Interdenominational group including Franklin founds a charity school (the University of Pennsylvania uses this as its founding date, hence antedating Princeton)

1741   America's first two magazines are founded: Andrew Bradford's *American* magazine and Franklin's *General Magazine*

1743   Franklin founds the American Philosophical Society, which soon dies out because "idle gentlemen take no pains"

1747   Franklin founds a private association that raises an army of 10,000 volunteers to defend the Quaker City

1748   Franklin retires from business at the age of forty-two, his fortune secure

1749   Franklin becomes Grand Master of the Pennsylvania Masons

1751   Franklin is instrumental in founding the first hospital in America, the Pennsylvania Hospital; his *Experiments and Observations on Electricity* is published in London and Franklin becomes world famous; he founds the Academy, which becomes the College of Philadelphia

1752   Franklin founds the first American fire insurance company, the Philadelphia Contributionship for the Insurance of Houses from Loss by Fire

1754   Franklin takes the lead, along with Thomas Hutchinson, in attempting to unite the colonies at the Albany Congress

1755   Franklin is made president of the board of trustees of the College of Philadelphia; he becomes postmaster general of the colonies

1756   Franklin brings the Reverend William Smith to Philadelphia as first provost of the College; Quakers resign from the Pennsylvania Assembly

1757 Franklin is sent to England by the Assembly to negotiate a royal charter for Pennsylvania in place of the hated proprietorship of the Penns; he remains in England, except for two years, until 1775

1764 On a brief visit home, Franklin defends the city against the march on the city of armed frontiersmen, the so-called Paxton Boys

1769 Franklin, in absentia, is elected first president of the reorganized American Philosophical Society

1774 First Continental Congress meets in Philadelphia; Franklin attends the next year

1775 Quakers found the first abolition society in America: the Pennsylvania Society for Promoting the Abolition of Slavery, the Relief of Negroes Unlawfully held in Bondage, and for Improving the Conditions of the African Race; Franklin becomes its first president

1776 Franklin signs the Declaration of Independence

1787 The United States of America is founded in Philadelphia; Franklin, grandfather of the convention, signs the Constitution

1790 Franklin dies soon after hearing that the Constitution has been ratified

The men listed in Table A–14 were a very different breed from the authoritarian Mathers, Stoughtons, Belchers, and Hutchinsons of Boston. Whereas the Boston leaders tended to be natives of Massachusetts of English stock and members of the Congregational church, over half of the Philadelphia group, an ethnic and religious mix, were born outside Pennsylvania.

I shall briefly review the roles played by the twenty men besides Franklin listed in Table A–14. James Logan and Isaac Norris I led the proprietary interests in the colony while Penn was alive. After Penn's death the Pemberton brothers and Isaac Norris II were leaders of the Quaker party; the Hamiltons and William Allen were leaders of the Anglican centered proprietary faction (Penn's descendants left the sect and joined the church). In Philadelphia, physicians filled the authority roles usually occupied by ministers in Massachusetts: thus, John Kearsley, Thomas Bond, and Thomas Cadwalader were doctors prominent in society as a whole; all three were allied with the Anglican faction within the upper class (though Bond never joined the church). William Smith and Francis Alison, two talented auslanders, served as provost and vice-provost of the newly chartered College of Philadelphia. The Reverend Richard Peters, probably the most learned man in the colony in his generation, served as rector of the combined congregations of Christ Church and St. Peter's; he was also an organizer of the Library Company, the Pennsylvania Hospital, and the College of Philadelphia (president of the board of trustees). Members of the younger, revolutionary generation, Dr. John Morgan and Dr. William Shippen, Jr., were instrumental in founding the medical school at the College. John Bartram, Thomas Godfrey, and David Rittenhouse, all self-educated natural geniuses, were artisan-scientists. Anthony Benezet was the city's leading Quaker humanitarian. He and John Woolman of New Jersey, the earliest American leaders in the anti-slavery movement, persuaded the Philadelphia Yearly Meeting in 1776 to disown all Friends who still owned slaves.

POLITICS AND CLASS STRUCTURE

Winston Churchill once said that in any organization or society the number one position is infinitely more important than the second, third, or fourth positions. The captain, as anyone who has been to sea knows, *is* the ship. The first and most important difference between Boston and Philadelphia throughout the colonial period was the fact that in Massachusetts Bay the chief executive officer during the entire period of the first charter and for over half the period under the crown was a member of the city's ruling class of extended families. In Pennsylvania, however, the Penns chose a series of auslanders to rule their colony throughout the whole colonial period. Of the chief executive officers of Pennsylvania during the period under discussion in this chapter, only James Logan and James Hamilton, both holding office for brief periods, were members of the local upper class. William Penn, apparently having no trust in his fellow Friends as far as government was concerned, appointed Puritans or Anglicans, but *no Quakers*, as his deputy governors from outside. His heirs, who abandoned the sect and joined the Anglican church, also seemed to have little faith in their father's co-religionists.

In this connection it is important to emphasize that the popular assemblies of *both* Massachusetts as a royal colony and proprietary Pennsylvania opposed executive authority. There was, however, a crucial difference between the two colonies: the citizens of Massachusetts wanted to govern themselves without the authority of the royal prerogative; the opposition party in Pennsylvania preferred the authority of the crown to the hated domination of the Penns. Nothing is recorded about their wanting to govern themselves under their own charter, as the Puritans had done for the first half century after settlement.

From the very beginning, then, Philadelphians were accustomed to being ruled by others, whereas Bostonians were in the habit of ruling themselves. No wonder so many commentators on the history of colonial Pennsylvania found the Quaker ethic of tolerance to be largely one of indifference. As one eighteenth-century citizen of Philadelphia commented: "To govern is absolutely repugnant to the avowed principles of Quakerism, to be governed absolutely repugnant to the avowed principles of Presbyterianism." Thus, the anti-authoritarian Quaker ethic, plus their experience in Pennsylvania, led even the wealthier Friends to develop a tradition of dissent in their own colony. As Isaac Norris I put it in a letter to Penn:

> We say our principles are not destructive or repugnant to civil government and will admit freedom of conscience for all, yet it appears to me according to the best scheme I can form from the opinion of many Friends, that to be concerned in government and to hold [maintain] ourselves, we must either be independent or entirely by ourselves . . . or be as thou used to express it, "Dissenters in our own country."[12]

Throughout the colonial period in Pennsylvania, the basic problem of authority revolved around the question of whether the representatives of the proprietors or the Assembly should rule. Although the dates given are only approximations, the political history of the colony can be divided into three periods.

1. From the colony's founding until the 1730s the Quaker party, dominated by the two Lloyds and rural Friends, was in opposition to the proprietors, whose interests were defended by James Logan, Isaac Norris I, and Israel Pemberton I. The last two were founders of Quaker clans that remained socially if not politically prominent in Philadelphia well into the twentieth century.

2. From the 1730s until the coming of the French and Indian War to Pennsylvania in 1756, the Quaker party was dominated by the Pembertons and the Norrises of the second generation and the auslander Benjamin Franklin. James Logan, who came to the colony with William Penn in 1699, led the proprietary faction until his retirement from politics in 1739, after which the Allen and Hamilton families took the lead.

3. After 1756, when prominent Quakers like Israel Pemberton II withdrew from politics because of their pacifist principles, the Quaker party was led first by Isaac Norris II and later by Franklin and, while Franklin was abroad, by Joseph Galloway, a wealthy auslander from Maryland. The Allens and the Hamiltons, intermarried with each other and with the Penns, remained leaders of the proprietary interests. Throughout this period the Quakers and their spokesman, Benjamin Franklin, who represented them in London, negotiated to have the colony taken over by the crown.

A look at the political leaders, especially in the second and third periods outlined here, and the class structure of Philadelphia that they represented is very important to understanding the history of the city down to the twentieth century. Perhaps the most significant development occurred in the eighteenth century, as a miscellaneous *elite* of Quaker merchants gradually evolved into a solid and consanguine Quaker *upper class*, which included the Whartons, Shippens, Morrises, Cadwaladers, Fishers, and Biddles and was led by members of the Logan, Shippen, Norris, and Pemberton clans. By the middle of the century, according to William S. Hanna,

> the Yearly Meeting was directed and closely controlled by heads of the leading Quaker families, who usually resided in Philadelphia. Heading the oligarchy in the 1750's were two commanders [both second generation Philadelphians]: Israel Pemberton, scion of the great Pemberton clan and, as Clerk of the Yearly Meeting, the high inquisitor of the faith and guardian of unity; and Isaac Norris, a member of an equally illustrious family, who managed the political interests of the Society as Speaker of the Assembly.[13]

In the first half of the eighteenth century, James Logan was Philadelphia's most distinguished citizen. His career provides an excellent illustration of the Quaker ambivalence toward authority and government. Logan's father, who held a master of arts from Edinburgh, was a clergyman in the established church of Scotland until his conversion to Quakerism in 1671; his mother was of a noble family connected with the lairds of Dundas. Young James was thoroughly grounded in Greek, Latin, and Hebrew by his father, who eventually became a schoolmaster in the Quaker stronghold of Bristol. In 1695, after his first wife's death, William Penn married Hannah Callowhill, the daughter of a wealthy Bristol merchant, and it was at Bristol that he met young Logan. Penn was immediately attracted to Logan and brought him to Pennsylvania as his private secretary on his second visit in 1699. One of the more interesting insights into the Quaker mind comes from the following anecdote, related in Franklin's autobiography. It seems that the ship carrying Penn and Logan to the New World was attacked by pirates; Logan took a spirited part in the defense of the ship; Penn, the devout pacifist, retired below decks. On being reproved by Penn for resorting to arms, Logan retorted: "I being thy servant, why did thee not order me to come down?"[14]

Penn appointed Logan his legal agent in the colony. As secretary of the council, mayor of Philadelphia, chief justice, and acting governor, Logan not only served his colony but remained throughout his career a loyal defender of proprietary authority. Though he thoroughly disagreed with them, he was always tolerant and tactful in his dealings with "stiff" Quakers. In 1741, for instance, he addressed a conciliatory letter to the Yearly Meeting that admitted the unlawfulness of all wars according to strict Christian standards but then went on to say that, as all governments are founded on force, there are times when citizens must be drilled and armed to defend themselves. On the whole, then, Logan was a Quaker leader of the highest caliber, but he was neither active in the Yearly Meetings nor entirely sympathetic toward their rigid values, as were the Lloyds, Norrises, and Pembertons.

After James Logan withdrew from politics at the end of the 1730s, William Allen took his place and, along with the Hamiltons, led the proprietary party until the eve of the Revolution. The party was now composed largely of Anglicans and Presbyterians; their opponents were mostly Quakers and plain-sect Germans. In other words, rather than a division between rich city as against less wealthy country Friends, the split was along religious lines. The proprietors were Anglicans, supported by the Scotch-Irish, who hated the Quakers because of their pacifism and consequent attitudes toward the Indians, whom the Scotch-Irish, not the Quakers, were facing on the frontier. The plain-sect Germans took little interest in politics but were content to support their fellow sectarians, at least until many of them also suffered from the Quaker irresponsibility toward Indian raids.

Benjamin Franklin became a major figure in Pennsylvania politics after becoming clerk of the Assembly in 1736. Although he had befriended William Allen and James Logan soon after settling in Philadelphia, and had been helped along by both of them early in his career, Franklin eventually joined the opposition party. He had an ability to get along with both the Quakers and the Germans and soon became the best politician in the city, much in the style of David Lloyd. Needless to say, the Penns learned to despise Franklin. When he was elected president of the American Philosophical Society in 1769, for example, Governor John Penn declared, "I shall never be a patron of a Society which has for its President such a _____ as Franklin."[15]

Franklin shared the leadership of the opposition party with Isaac Norris II. (Toward the middle of the century, in fact, the party came to be called the Norris party.) The first Isaac Norris was born in London and came to Philadelphia from Jamaica. He was extremely successful and wealthy as a merchant, and his marriage to a daughter of Thomas Lloyd brought him into the Quaker establishment. Next to Logan, the elder Isaac Norris was the chief representative of Penn's interests in the colony and was named an executor in his will. Norris, a large landowner (the present industrial suburb of Norristown was built on his property), built himself a mansion of great opulence, Fair Hill, where he collected a fine library.

The younger Isaac Norris, grandson of Thomas Lloyd and son-in-law of James Logan, was born to political leadership in the heart of the Quaker upper class. After attending a Friends school, he rounded out his education with a trip to England and the grand tour. Norris subsequently served in the Assembly from 1734 to 1764—as speaker from 1750 to 1764—when he resigned either because of failing health or because of the influence of his son-in-law John Dickinson, by then a leader of the proprietary party. Norris left the library at Fair Hill to Dickinson, who in turn left it to Dickinson College. Although many have said that "his militant pacifism was the pride of Quaker historians," Norris nevertheless remained in the Assembly after 1756, when his good friends James and Israel Pemberton and other Quakers resigned because of their pacifist principles.

The Pembertons were the leading Quaker family in eighteenth-century Philadelphia and one of the most interesting clans in the city's history. The family founder in America, Phileas Pemberton (1649–1702), had come with William Penn and settled on a 300-acre estate in Bucks County, near Pennsbury manor. He was the first citizen of Bucks County, which he represented in the Assembly. His son Israel came to Philadelphia, made a fortune, married James Logan's sister-in-law, and, as befit his affluent position, became clerk of the Yearly Meeting. He also spent nineteen years in the Assembly.

Israel Pemberton had three sons, Israel, James, and John, all leading Quakers in their generation. Israel and James were successful and wealthy merchants; John lived on his inheritance and spent most of his life as a traveling minister for the Society of Friends. (He died while on a mission to Holland and Germany.) Israel Pemberton, known as "King of the Quakers," took an active part in the affairs of his meeting and in a host of other Friendly concerns. Most of his time and money were spent in founding and supporting the Friendly Association for Regaining and Preserving Peace with the Indians by Pacific Measures; friend and foe alike called him "King Wampum." Though Israel Pemberton's heart was in the meeting rather than in political leadership, he served intermittently in the Assembly until his resignation in 1756, after which he refused to vote for many years.

From our point of view, James was the most interesting of the first Israel Pemberton's three sons largely because his letters and papers shed the most light on the Quaker attitudes toward authority, war, and government responsibility. Whereas Israel II was a man of courage and initiative, always full of aggressive plans and projects, he seldom settled down to official life. James was the useful man, the politician, the officeholder, and the letter writer. He was an active leader in the affairs of both the Society of Friends and the Assembly until his resignation in 1756. For thirty years he was clerk of the Yearly Meeting, which was the highest position of authority and the court of last appeal in the Quaker system. James Pemberton was a good friend to and, except on the war issue, an admirer of Franklin. When he founded the Pennsylvania Abolition Society, he persuaded Franklin to take the presidency.

WAR AND THE PHILADELPHIA QUAKERS

The Achilles' heel of politically active Quakers like James and Israel Pemberton was their perfectionist attitude toward war and the defense of the colony. In 1744, when King George's war with France broke out, the Quaker dominated Assembly voted £4,000 for beef, pork, flour, wheat, and "other grains," which Franklin suggested to the governor could be interpreted to mean grains of gunpowder. Later, in 1747, Franklin attempted to solve the defense problem by founding a private association that recruited 10,000 volunteers to defend the city. The money was raised by the religiously questionable means of a lottery—to which many plain Friends contributed unofficially. But the real crisis came when the French and Indian War broke out in 1754. In that year, the Penns appointed Robert Hunter Morris as governor. Morris, whose father had been governor of New Jersey, was an even more authoritative, opinionated man than his friend Governor Jonathan Belcher. He never understood the Quakers and stayed in Philadelphia only two years, spent primarily in wrangling over the defense issue with the Quaker dominated Assembly.

Braddock's defeat set off a wave of Indian massacres on the frontier. Petitions for help poured into the executive office, and Morris finally called the Assembly into session in early November 1755. For three weeks the leadership "continued to act out its traditional ritual, abusing the Proprietary leaders and rejecting all defence measures."[16] Late in the month, an enraged mob of Germans from the frontier entered the Assembly hall, demanding the passage of a defense bill. Such a bill was passed on November 25, 1755; although it "devoted most of its verbiage to exempting conscientious objectors from military service, it did create a militia, and it did appropriate £60,000 for defence."[17]

The bill was not very effective as a military measure but it had vital symbolic importance in the history of authority and leadership in Pennsylvania. First, it split the Quakers into the Pemberton "Old Party," whose members largely withdrew from the Assembly, and the Norris "War Quakers," now led by Franklin and Isaac Norris II, who chose power over rigid principle. Second, the behavior of the Quakers in this crisis marked the beginning of an alliance between the Germans and the Scotch-Irish that continued well into the next century. Consequently, as we shall see in later chapters, Philadelphia lost its political, and also its cultural, hegemony over the rest of the state, which it has never regained (see Chapter 18).

The Quaker historian Isaac Sharpless wrote in his *Political Leaders of Provincial Pennsylvania*:

> In the spring of 1755 the Quarterly Meeting of Philadelphia largely under Pemberton influence sent to London a paper explaining the circumstances of Quaker ascendency in the legislature. They told how the Friends had been elected without exertion on their part often against their wishes, and that this applied to counties where they were in a minority as well as others; that for sixteen years they had been kept in power by voters who did not share their pacific principles . . . . It was the last defense of active Quaker participation in politics and in the main unanswerable.[18]

The London Friends, though well on their way to wealth, were still a pretty isolated and rigid sect; it must be remembered that this was long before the rise of Quaker leadership in English reform politics in the great generation of John Bright, Elizabeth Fry, and her brother Joseph John Gurney. At any rate, the London Friends advised their Philadelphia co-religionists to remain true to their perfectionist principles rather than continue in the leadership of their colony and city.

> When the crisis came in 1756 the London Friends advised abstention. . . . James Pemberton and six other Friends gave up their places in the Assembly. This was the beginning of the break. The meetings acting on the advice used their efforts to have others withdraw and four more yielded and resigned. In the fall a number refused reelection. James Pemberton probably held the key to the situation.[19]

The cosmopolitan loyalties* of the Philadelphia Quaker leaders led Thomas Jefferson, after the Revolution, to call them

> a religious sect . . . acting with one mind, and that directed by the mother society in England. Dispersed as the Jews, they still form, as those do, one nation, foreign to the land they live in. They are Protestant Jesuits, implicitly devoted to the will of their superior, and forgetting their duties to their country in the execution of the policies of their order.[20]

The events of 1756 set a pattern of withdrawal and dissent within a group of the most opulent and respected families in the city's upper class. Isaac Sharpless has described how this period affected the revolutionary postures of Massachusetts and Pennsylvania.

> Each was approaching the same goal by a different method, the Puritan by a process which was sure to culminate in avowed resistance, the Quaker by legal methods, by appeal and argument, by a refusal to obey oppressive laws, and a willingness to take the consequences of disobedience. Had they been able to control the province at the outbreak of the Revolutionary War a test of the efficacy of their policy might have been made, but the action of 1756 put them out of power, as they probably did not appreciate, forever.[21]

---

*Although the cosmopolitan loyalties of the Quakers did cause them to abdicate the responsibilities of power in government, these very same loyalties, as we shall see, played an important role in Philadelphia's leadership in colonial science and medicine.

As far as the continuity of authority and leadership in Philadelphia was concerned, this outcome was tragic enough; it was aggravated in the revolutionary period.

After the French and Indian War, the auslander Joseph Galloway was elected to the Assembly and eventually rose to the leadership of the Quaker party. When Isaac Norris finally withdrew from the Assembly in 1764, Galloway was elected annually to the speakership from 1766 to 1775. The Galloways were a Maryland family of great wealth and owned land in both Maryland and Pennsylvania. After coming to Philadelphia, Galloway married well and rose to eminence at the bar. Though close to the Quakers, he was never of them. Along with his ally Franklin, Galloway proved to be one of the more articulate colonial statesmen in the years leading up to the Revolution; both Franklin in London and Galloway in Philadelphia did their best to persuade the crown to take the colony out of the hands of the Penns. Unlike the agile Franklin, however, Galloway eventually sided with the British and became a leading Loyalist spokesman in the colonies and then in England, where he died in exile.

THE DEVELOPMENT OF
AN ANGLICAN UPPER CLASS

In the course of the eighteenth century, the merchant elite of Philadelphia gradually evolved into an upper class composed of two wealthy wings, one Anglican and fashionable, the other Quaker and plain. As we have seen, the Keithian schism led to large-scale Quaker defections to the Anglican communion, and Christ Church was finally built in 1727. The Anglican communion was also increased in size by the events of 1756, and a second Anglican congregation was formed at St. Peter's, built in 1758. Indeed, there had been a steady loss of wealthy Friends to the Anglicans throughout the century: "Because they were long in command of the political order," wrote Hanna of the second half of the century, "the Quakers tended to grow conservative and rigid. . . . As they faced an ever-expanding non-Quaker population, the Quakers turned in on themselves, ceased proselytizing, and guarded their own behind walls of orthodoxy and conformity."[22] Economic success was also a major problem, according to Hanna.

> Increasing wealth weakened the faith's foundation of plain living and simple virtue. Some of the prosperous Friends shed the external forms of dress and address, or kept these but lost the inner light. This loss was grave, for it made the Quaker susceptible to outside political and social contagion. A small but growing number gave up altogether and surrendered to the Anglican form of worship, finding in the Church of England pomp and prestige without troubled consciences. Though few in number, these apostates were often among the richest and most highly placed Friends, and their defection set an alarming example.[23]

William Penn's son Thomas became the principal proprietor of the colony in 1746. Up to that time, the Penns had actually lost money on their colonial venture. It was Thomas Penn, "in whose perception the pound sign dominates,"[24] who gradually recouped the family fortunes. He spent nine years in the colony, 1732-1741, all the while striving to straighten out the family's interests there. After returning to England, he wrote the Quakers in Pennsylvania that he "did not hold their opinions concerning defence," adding: "I no longer continue the little distinctions of dress."[25] And, upon marrying Lady Juliana, daughter of the first earl of Pomfret, in 1751, he considered himself a member of the Church of England.

Thomas Penn, undoubtedly the ablest of the Penn line, nevertheless had a very difficult time governing the colony. In the first place, "men of the first rank," according to Hanna," did not seek the Governorship, because the pay was not large and difficulties with the Assembly had given it a bad reputation in England."[26] In the second, the Anglican supporters of Penn did not make up a purposeful or unified ruling class: they formed "a collection of independent interests directed by some great man or aristocratic cliques desiring power. The Proprietary Party in Pennsylvania was led by a number of highly independent gentlemen."[27]

In the half century before the Revolution, these "highly independent gentlemen" were mostly Allens and Hamiltons. Their power was consolidated by the marriage of Lieutenant Governor John Penn, Thomas Penn's nephew, to a daughter of Chief Justice William Allen and granddaughter of Andrew Hamilton. Indeed, the Hamiltons at one time or another held most of the important offices in the city and the colony, but unlike the Hutchinsons in Massachusetts, they had no deep roots in Pennsylvania.

Andrew Hamilton, the family founder, was the most obscure and one of the most brilliant auslanders to come to eighteenth-century Philadelphia.* His original name and birthplace are lost to history. In the last part of the seventeenth century, so hearsay had it, he came to Virginia, where he ran a school and managed an estate. After he married the wealthy widow of the estate's owner, he took the name of Hamilton. He eventually moved north and bought a 6,000-acre estate in Maryland. Visiting England in 1713, Hamilton was admitted to Gray's Inn, and two weeks later was called "per favor" to the bar. Coming next to Philadelphia, he soon became the Penn family's favorite lawyer and made a fortune. Hamilton's main claim to fame, however, rests on his defense of John Peter Zenger in New York. His victory in this landmark case of freedom of the press won him fame all over the colonies and in England. Hamilton also designed the most sacred shrine in America, the Pennsylvania State House, now Independence Hall. Andrew Hamilton's son James carried on the family tradition of leadership, serving as chief executive officer of the colony three different times (1748-1754, 1759-1763, and in 1771). His brother-in-law, William Allen, was at the same time the political leader of the proprietary inter-

---

*No relationship has been established between Andrew Hamilton, auslander deputy governor of Pennsylvania in 1701 (see Chapter 9), and the Philadelphia lawyer Andrew Hamilton. What little is known, moreover, of the early life of *either* of the two Andrew Hamiltons is only another example of the lack of scholarly zeal in Philadelphia.

ests and the richest and most powerful man in the city for many years. (Even though Allen was a Presbyterian, his family and social ties were rooted in the fashionable Anglican community.)

The Hamiltons and the Allens were not only leaders in government and civic affairs in Pennsylvania; they were also leaders in the Anglican centered social life of the fashionable wing of Philadelphia's upper class. Thus, when the Philadelphia Dancing Assembly was founded in 1748, James Hamilton and William Allen were among the original subscribers. And when the First Troop, Philadelphia City Cavalry, was organized in 1774, William Allen's son Andrew was first lieutenant (he resigned when war broke out and followed his father into exile). Until well into this century membership in the City Troop and annual invitations to Dancing Assembly balls were major marks of acceptance into the inner circles of Proper Philadelphia. Needless to say, good Quakers have avoided both institutions down through the years.

Philadelphia, then, approached the Revolution in an ambivalent political mood: neither the proprietary interests nor those who wanted the colony placed under the authority of the crown were in sympathy with the revolutionary movement. Even Franklin, who was in London during the critical decade of 1765–1775 attempting to persuade the crown to take over the Colony, did not doubt the right of Parliament to levy the Stamp Act. But he gradually came to see the inevitability of independence and sailed for America in the spring of 1775, just in time to take part in the debates and sign the Declaration. In the confused situation in Philadelphia at the time, a loose coalition of those in sympathy with the cause of independence finally came together under the leadership of an auslander Scotch-Irish Presbyterian named Charles Thomson, whom John Adams called the "Sam Adams of Philadelphia."

If Philadelphians were confused politically, they nevertheless took the lead in colonial medicine and science, which we shall come to in a moment.

THE FOUNDING OF THE
COLLEGE OF PHILADELPHIA

By mid-century, Philadelphians began to be aware of the need for higher education in the colony. As one would expect, Franklin took the lead. In an unsigned article in the *Pennsylvania Gazette* of August 24, 1749, he wrote that since

> a number of our inhabitants are both able and willing to give their sons a good education . . . free from the extraordinary expense and hazard in sending them abroad for that purpose; and since a proportion of men of learning is useful in every country, and those who of late years come to settle among us, are chiefly foreigners, unacquainted with our language, laws and customs; it is thought a proposal for establishing an ACADEMY in this province, will not now be deemed unreasonable.

Franklin had not approved of the classical emphasis of the Boston Latin School and preferred a more practical curriculum for Philadelphia in which the teaching of English and science would be more important than that of Latin and Greek. The leading Anglicans and Presbyterians, however, were impressed with the prestige of the classics. The Academy, founded in 1751, began with a compromise, having both a Latin and an English department.

In accord with Franklin's ideas on education, the Academy was in theory a secular institution; nevertheless, three-quarters of its original board of twenty-four trustees were Anglicans, including several vestrymen of Christ Church. Two Quakers—James Logan and Samuel Rhoads (designer of the Pennsylvania Hospital)—consented to sit on the original board. The Quaker community as a whole, however, contributed neither labor nor funds and actually was hostile to the whole idea, expecially after the Academy became the College of Philadelphia in 1755 and granted its first degree two years later. The first class to graduate from the College included Francis Hopkinson, later a signer of the Declaration of Independence, and his future brother-in-law, John Morgan, who, after earning a medical degree at Edinburgh, returned to found the medical school at the College.

Two remarkable scholars, William Smith and Francis Alison, dominated the early days of the Academy and College. Both were auslanders, Smith from Scotland and Alison from Ireland. The Reverend William Smith, after graduating from Aberdeen, came to America and was ordained in the Anglican communion in New York in 1753. While a tutor for a New York family he published a pamphlet on his ideas of a college in the New World and sent a copy to Franklin. Much impressed with the young man's proposals, Franklin brought him to the Academy in 1754. The Reverend Francis Alison, educated at the University of Glasgow, came to Maryland in 1735, where he became a tutor in the household of Samuel, father of John Dickinson. He eventually opened a grammar school in New London, Pennsylvania, under the Presbyterian synod of Philadelphia. It was one of the best schools in the colony and eventually became the University of Delaware. When he was called to the ministry at the First Presbyterian Church in Philadelphia, Alison became active in the movement to found the Academy.

William Smith was made provost and Francis Alison vice-provost after the school was chartered in 1756 under "The Trustees of the College, Academy and Charitable School of Philadelphia."* Smith and Alison were both classicists, and the aristocratic ideal of a classical education won out at the College in the long run.

From its founding, the College was plagued by religious factionalism. The trustees and Smith were Anglican; Alison, a Presbyterian, was the leader of the faculty. Richard Peters, now president of the College's board of trustees and rector of Christ Church, and Smith finally succeeded in swinging the College over to the Church of England by 1762. The move was more political and social than religious, but it nevertheless drained off many sons of local Presbyte-

---

*After George Whitefield visited the city during the Great Awakening, an interdenominational group of Philadelphians founded a charity school, in 1740. The "New Building" which housed the school, also called "Whitefield's Chapel," was taken over by the Academy and College, and hence the University of Pennsylvania dates its founding as 1740, six years ahead of nearby Princeton (1746).

rian families to Princeton. This development, along with Quaker opposition to the College, kept the school small and weak throughout the colonial period. Whereas Harvard graduated sixty-three students in 1771, for example, the College of Philadelphia granted about seven degrees a year (none in 1758 and 1764) between 1757 and the outbreak of the Revolution. I shall have more to say about the University of Pennsylvania and Harvard in Chapter 14, but their founding a century or more apart—Harvard by the united efforts of the whole community, and Pennsylvania in an atmosphere of sectarian controversy—set a tone of strong local support for one and relative local neglect for the other, which has lasted to the present day.

PHILADELPHIA TAKES THE
LEAD IN MEDICINE

The differential development of medicine in Boston and Philadelphia will be treated in Chapter 17. Here it is enough to show how Philadelphia pushed far ahead of Boston in the colonial period. Most physicians of that day in both cities were trained in the apprenticeship system. In Philadelphia, the office of Dr. John Kearsley was known as the "first college in the province," and he trained such leading physicians as the two Bond brothers, Thomas and Phineas, Thomas Cadwalader, John Redman, and William Shippen. But where Philadelphia excelled was in sending far more young men abroad to study medicine at London, Edinburgh, Paris, and Leiden. Of the seventeen physicians practicing in Philadelphia in the years between 1740 and the outbreak of the Revolution, all but three had some training abroad. Most of them took advantage of the Quaker network centering on Dr. Fothergill in London.

Dr. John Fothergill (1712–1780) was a prominent figure in the Anglo-American Quaker community. After taking his degree at Edinburgh in 1735, he soon rose to the top of the medical profession in England. Moreover, Fothergill had a multitude of Quakerly concerns: he worked tirelessly with John Howard in prison reform; he anticipated the anti-slavery movement and introduced John Woolman to England; he was instrumental in founding Ackworth, a famous Quaker school upon which the Westtown School in Philadelphia was modeled; he was a leading light in the Royal Society and, along with Peter Collinson, was the center of the transatlantic natural history circle; and he wrote the introduction to and helped promote Franklin's book on electricity. Fothergill and Franklin, as Dr. Thomas Bond once put it, were indeed the foster fathers of Americans abroad, especially Philadelphians who came there to study medicine. It was Fothergill who introduced young John Morgan of Philadelphia to European medicine and to membership in the Royal Society (he not only sponsored Morgan but also lent him the money to pay his fees in the society). Finally, Fothergill supervised the European education of his Rhode Island nephew, Benjamin Waterhouse, one of the founders of the Harvard Medical School.

While abroad, John Morgan was thinking about the need for medical education in America. Upon his return, he presented his proposals for a medical school to the trustees of the College on May 3, 1765; two weeks later, at commencement, he deliverd his "Discourse upon the Institution of Medical Schools in America," one of the classics of American medical literature. The school opened the next fall, and unlike the College, with its feuding leadership, the medical school thrived from the outset and remained the leading medical school in America until the early twentieth century. The five original lecturers—Morgan, William Shippen, Jr., Thomas Bond, Adam Kuhn, and Benjamin Rush—were in many ways the founders of American medicine. (All were educated in Europe—Bond in Paris and the other four at Edinburgh.) These five physicians were perhaps, next to Franklin, the most distinguished men in the whole history of Philadelphia, as well as very interesting examples of the city's social heterogeneity at the close of the colonial period: Shippen, Bond, and Rush were of English stock, Morgan was Welsh, and Kuhn was German; Bond and Morgan were disowned Quakers, Shippen and Rush were Presbyterians, and Kuhn was affiliated with the German Reformed Church.

His training abroad had filled Dr. Thomas Bond with enthusiasm for the English hospital movement, and with Franklin's help he founded the Pennsylvania Hospital in 1751.* The Friends took the lead at the hospital from the very beginning. Israel Pemberton, Isaac Norris, and George Emlen were major contributors, and eight of the original twelve managers were Friends, as was Samuel Rhoads, the designer of the first building. Indeed, the hospital became a sort of rallying point for the Quakers, as was the College of Philadelphia for the Anglicans.

Quakers have always played a major role in promoting the humane treatment of the mentally ill. Many of the heroic first generation in England had been driven to the verge of insanity while in prison. In 1669, George Fox advised his followers to provide "a house for them that be distempered." Thomas Bond had visited the hospital at Bethlehem, where he was horrified to see patients being baited and ridiculed. When the Pennsylvania Hospital was opened, therefore, it became the first hospital in the world to foster humane treatment of the insane. Later, the Friends of Philadelphia founded the nation's first private hospital for the insane, the Frankford Asylum (1813). When the Pennsylvania Hospital opened its Institute for the Insane in 1841, Thomas Story Kirkbride, of the staff of the Frankford Asylum and kin of the Pembertons, was appointed director, a post he held for forty-three years. Finally, it is important to note that the first American book on mental illness was written by the Philadelphia humanitarian, prison and political reformer, author, and professor in the medical school, Benjamin Rush. His pioneer work, *Mental Inquiries and Observations upon the Diseases of the Mind*, was published in 1812.

---

*Thomas Bond was, next to Franklin, the city's outstanding founder of institutions in the late colonial period. An auslander like Franklin, he was born to a wealthy and prominent Maryland family, his mother being a Chew. A lapsed Quaker himself, he married a Roberts, from one of the oldest Welsh Quaker clans in Philadelphia. The Bonds were not named as one of the city's First Families in Chapter 3 because Thomas's descendants included no one distinguished enough to be listed in the *DAB*. The Bonds, however, were leaders in the privileged social circles of Philadelphia and Baltimore throughout the nineteenth century.

SELF-IMPROVEMENT AND SCIENCE

Eighteenth-century Philadelphia, as we have seen, was an open society with little of Boston's intellectual and religious deference to authority. "The poorest labourer upon the shores of the *Delaware*," wrote Jacob Duche, assistant to Richard Peters at Christ Church and St. Peter's, "thinks himself entitled to deliver his sentiments in matters of religion or politics with as much freedom as the gentleman or scholar. Indeed, there is less distinction among the citizens of Philadelphia, than among those of any civilized city in the world."[28] And Gottlieb Mittelberger, a visitor to the Pennsylvania German back country in the 1750s, was horrified at the egalitarian manners he found there.

> I myself would rather be the humblest cowherd at home than a preacher in Pennsylvania. Such outrageous coarseness and rudeness result from the excessive freedom in that country, and from the blind zeal of the many sects. Liberty in Pennsylvania does more harm than good to many people, both in soul and body. They have a saying there: Pennsylvania is heaven for farmers, paradise for artisans, and hell for officials and preachers.[29]

The anti-authoritarian ideals of equality and democracy came to America through the hospitable port of Philadelphia. And the spirit of capitalism, the cult of self-improvement, and the pursuit of science were of the very essence of American democracy. All of them were products of the middle-class mind so brilliantly exemplified in Benjamin Franklin. To Max Weber he was the essence of the spirit of capitalism; to the sophisticates of the French Enlightenment, the essence of the natural man of simplicity and equality; and to the members of the British Royal Society, the father of American science. Like John Adams, Franklin also had a keen sense of generational appropriateness. Thus, he wrote in 1743 of his aspirations for Philadelphia and all the colonies: "The first drudgery of settling new colonies which confines the attention of people to mere necessities is now pretty well over; and there are many in every province in circumstances that set them at ease, and afford the leisure to cultivate the finer arts and improve the common stock of knowledge."[30]

It has often been noted that the open and relatively democratic society of rapidly expanding wealth and population made eighteenth-century Philadelphia so receptive to the new science. But there were other important factors, too. Both Franklin, who spent half of his adult life abroad, and the cosmopolitan character of Quakerism exposed Philadelphians to the dynamic intellectual circles of Europe. Likewise, the Penns were of course transatlantic and cosmopolitan rather than provincial. (William Penn, a friend of Sir William Petty and other leaders of the Royal Society, became a Fellow just before founding his colony in 1682.) Finally, the Quaker ethic was egalitarian and experimental as against the hierarchical and deductive nature of Calvinism. All these factors combined to make Philadelphia the center of colonial science, or, rather, the center of the transatlantic natural history circle, which tended to dominate eighteenth-century science in both the colonies and in Europe.*

---

*Carolus Linnaeus's *Systema Naturae* was the epoch-making book of the century and the Comte de Buffon's *Histoire Naturelle* received more attention than the literary classics of Voltaire and Rous-

One might have expected Boston rather than Philadelphia to take the lead in eighteenth-century science. When the century opened, Boston was the cultural and educational leader of the colonies. Increase Mather had attempted to found a philosophical society as early as 1683. John Winthrop II had been made a Fellow of the Royal Society in 1663, soon after its founding, and a clear majority of the colonial Fellows were New Englanders, as the following listing shows*:

Name	Born	Died	Elected Fellow	Colony
John Winthrop	1606	1676	1663	Connecticut
William Byrd	1764	1744	1696	Virginia
Cotton Mather	1663	1728	1713?	Massachusetts
William Brattle	1662	1717	1714	Massachusetts
John Leverett	1662	1724	1714	Massachusetts
Paul Dudley	1675	1751	1721	Massachusetts
Thomas Robie	1689	1729	1725	Massachusetts
Zabdiel Boylston	1679	1766	1726	Massachusetts
John Winthrop	1681	1747	1734	Connecticut
John Mitchell	?	1768	1743	Virginia
Benjamin Franklin	1706	1790	1756	Pennsylvania
John Morgan	1735	1789	1765	Pennsylvania
John Tennent	?	c.1770	1765	Virginia
John Winthrop	1714	1779	1766	Massachusetts
Alexander Garden	1730?	1791	1773	South Carolina
Benjamin Thompson (Count Rumford)	1753	1814	1779	Massachusetts
James Bowdoin	1726	1790	1788	Massachusetts
David Rittenhouse	1732	1796	1795	Pennsylvania

Thomas Brattle had made some astronomical observations that Newton included in his *Principia Mathematica*. In the smallpox epidemic of 1721, Cotton Mather and Zabdiel Boylston made the first test in the Western world of the theory of inoculation, which Richard H. Shryock considered to be the "chief American contribution to medicine prior to the mid-nineteenth century."[31] New Englanders had contributed most of the articles from the colonies in the *Philosophical Transactions* of the Royal Society, some of them of first rank. And John Winthrop IV was the leading Newtonian physicist, astronomer, and mathematician of his generation in the colonies.

But the scientific achievements of Boston and Cambridge were made by a small minority of clergymen and laymen who had accepted the new science of the seventeenth century. Most of the erudite clergymen felt that the study of nature was "not sufficient for salvation or saving faith."[32] Thomas Brattle and

---

seau. Thomas Jefferson's only book, *Notes on Virginia*, was inspired by the French Enlightenment and, as Boorstin put it, "was an omnium-gatherum of information about minerals, plants, animals, institutions, and men" (Daniel J. Boorstin, *The Americans: The Colonial Experience* [New York: Random House, 1958], p. 166).

*From Samuel Eliot Morison, *The Puritan Pronaos*. New York: New York University Press, 1935, p. 275.

the governor's son Paul Dudley, himself an accomplished naturalist, complained that very few of their neighbors were interested in experimental science. Of the greatest importance in this connection was the provincialism of eighteenth-century Boston. New Englanders and Harvard had been part of the transatlantic Puritan culture in the Cromwellian period. After the Restoration, however, Oxford and Cambridge became Anglican and closed to dissenters. Bostonians were not to go abroad again intellectually until young George Ticknor and Edward Everett set sail in 1815 to bring back European, and especially German, learning to Harvard. Bostonians in this interim period remained at home, except for those who went abroad for political reasons. John Winthrop IV spent his whole life in Boston and Cambridge, and Thomas Hutchinson first saw England when he went there in exile. Eighteenth-century Boston, then, had a small and provincial scientific elite, the members of which were at least equal to those in Philadelphia, but it had no democratic and transatlantic scientific community of the sort that Benjamin Franklin was so ideally suited to lead in Philadelphia.

Soon after Franklin came from Boston to Philadelphia in 1723, he went abroad, where he was educated in the more sophisticated ways of the city of London. Upon his return, he founded his famous Junto, a group made up of young artisans and mechanics and other ambitious members of the city's rising middle class. Thomas Godfrey was perhaps the most interesting of the founding members of the Junto. A glazier by trade, he had taught himself mathematics and Latin in order to gain access to the literature of the astronomical sciences. One day he turned up at James Logan's estate to repair some windows. After finishing the job, he asked Logan whether he might borrow his copy of the *Principia* (the first copy owned by an American). Logan was delighted with the young man of "excellent natural genius"[33] and encouraged him to borrow books whenever it pleased him. And it pleased him often.

James Logan represented one eighteenth-century ideal, the aristocracy of intellect, the very antithesis of the ideal of democracy, which was so soon to become dominant in America. Although he was a great public servant, he took greater pride in his role as aristocratic sponsor of the intellectual and scientific life of his city. Having made a large fortune in land speculations and in trading with the Indians, he built a fine family seat at Stenton on an estate of some 500 acres on the city side of Germantown. Here he collected the finest scientific library in the colonies and devoted himself to the study of natural history, especially botany. Logan's scientific experiments in his gardens at Stenton led him into correspondence with the London Quaker merchant and botanist Peter Collinson and with the great Linnaeus of Sweden (who named the *Loganiancae* in his honor). Above all, he was of vital importance in encouraging young men like Franklin, Godfrey, and especially John Bartram, America's first botanist.

James Logan also helped Franklin, Godfrey, Thomas Cadwalader, and other Junto friends in founding the first circulating library in America and prevailed on Collinson to purchase books for them in London. The library "soon held the finest collection of scientific books in the country," wrote Brooke Hindle. "It became a good nucleus for the formation of a scientific community because it served not only the members of the Library Company, but also the general public, particularly the city artisans who made much use of the reading privileges freely extended to all."[34] The library was also a bit of a museum or scientific society, its rooms containing natural history specimens as well as pumps, globes, telescopes, and electric machinery. Indeed, it was the democratic counterpart of elitist Harvard.

After Logan's death, his library became the foundation of the Loganian Library. The Junto and Loganian libraries were then combined in 1792 to form the Library Company of Philadelphia, which today has one of the nation's finest private collections of colonial material.

Historians of Quakerism have always stressed the kinship between the Quaker ethic and the spirit of science. When in his journal George Fox described his first revelation of the Inner Light he ended with the words "This I know *experimentally*."[35] The Quaker appeal to direct experience rather than to religious authority or tradition, or even the words of the Bible, was closely akin to the spirit of empirical science, or the New Philosophy, which became so popular in England at the time Fox had his vision on Pendle Hill. The spirit of science was also in a way much in accord with Quaker anti-intellectualism: the *thing*, as Fox and Penn stressed (and Emerson later noted about Quakerism), is far more important than the *word*. "Languages are not to be despised or neglected," wrote William Penn, "but things are still to be preferred."[36] Robert K. Merton showed the affinity between Puritanism and the rise of science in seventeenth-century England by carefully analyzing the religious affiliations of the early members of the Royal Society. This affinity may have been even more pronounced in the case of the Quakers: between 1663 and 1915, for instance, fifty-eight Friends were elected Fellows of the Society, a far larger number in proportion to the small size of the Society of Friends than any other religious group contributed. Finally, of course, the Quaker antipathy to higher education was no handicap in the pioneering days of science and medicine.

The Quaker influence on science in Philadelphia was a strong one, as we have seen in the case of James Logan. At the same time, the nature of this influence nicely illustrates the Quaker ambivalence, if not downright hostility, toward leadership in all spheres of society: the leaders in the development of science in the city either tended to be disowned Quakers or, as in the case of James Logan, were looked on with suspicion by the orthodox. Thus, the colonial counterpart of the British Royal Society, the American Philosophical Society, was founded in 1743 by Franklin, along with Dr. Thomas Bond, who had been disowned the previous year, and John Bartram, a good Quaker who was eventually disowned after the French and Indian War. (Both Bond and Bartram continued to go to meeting with the Friendly members of their families.) This society soon lapsed for lack of interest but the events leading up to its refounding in 1769 are highly revealing of the nature of Philadelphia leadership from the eighteenth century to the present day.

When America's first learned society, the American Philosophical Society, was reestablished in January 1769, it incorporated two societies that had been devoted to the advancement of science. One association went back to 1750, when some friends founded a group that met in secret for several years. In 1766, this informal group was reorganized into the American Society for the Promotion and Propagating of Useful Knowledge, popularly referred to as the American Society. The original nine members of this new society were mostly Quakers and included John Bartram's two sons, Isaac and Moses, both druggists, and Owen Biddle, clockmaker. The three leaders of the reorganization were Charles Thomson, a Presbyterian importer, Edmond Physick, an Anglican civil servant, and Isaac Paschall, a Quaker ironmonger. Yet this religiously heterogeneous group, according to Hindle, was "more strongly under the Quaker influence than might at first appear."

> The driving force was supplied by Charles Thomson, who, although raised as a Presbyterian, had a peculiar affinity for Quaker friends and a marked respect for the Quaker faith. Before turning his hand to business, he had taught in the Friends' school and when married for a second time on the eve of the Revolution, he chose a Quaker wife. Ultimately, he left the Presbyterian church to take up a position, "attached to no system nor particular tenets of any sect or party." He spent many years at the end of his life translating the Bible. Thomson had so many relationships with the Quakers and so many of their characteristics that he has even been mistaken for one.
>
> Edmond Physick was a Proprietary officer who belonged to the political faction which bitterly opposed the aims and aspirations of the Quaker party. Yet even he demonstrated an unusual closeness to the Quaker group in his personal associations and in his decision to send his son to the Friends' school.
>
> Isaac Paschall was a Quaker, as were the remaining six members who constituted the "young Junto" in 1766, but they were Quakers of a very special stamp. Before the Revolution was over, four of these seven men had either been disowned or had voluntarily left the Society of Friends. Three of them took an active part in the conflict and became leaders in the Free Quaker movement. None of the seven was ready to follow the Quaker leaders into the unhappy wartime exile at Winchester, Virginia. These were worldly Quakers, but even when they came to the point of breaking with the Society, they retained the bulk of their Quaker heritage.[37]

The implications of Hindle's perceptive description of Quaker influences on the formation of this society are highly relevant to the central thesis of this book. It should become abundantly clear in the next chapter, when more is said about the career of Charles Thomson, that he exhibited all the strengths and weaknesses of the Quaker attitude toward leadership and of Philadelphia's upper-class mind. It is important, too, that Edmond Physick's son Philip, often called the "Father of American Surgery," was sent to a Quaker school and married into the Emlen family,* a large and prolific clan that has stood at the heart of Philadelphia Quakerism for 200 years. Finally—and this point cannot be overemphasized—women, especially in their roles as wives, mothers, and schoolteachers, at least in eighteenth- and nineteenth-century America, were

---

*George Emlen was one of the major subscribers to the Pennsylvania Hospital. Today, what remains of the Emlen estate in the heart of Germantown's black ghetto is referred to by insiders as the "Quaker Kremlin," for it is the home of the Quaker director of the local branch of the American Civil Liberties Union and of various officials of the American Friends Service Committee.

the principal bearers of cultural and religious traditions. And this was even more true of matriarchal Quakerism than of patriarchal Puritanism. Thus, it is significant that Charles Thomson and many other non-Quaker leaders in eighteenth-century Philadelphia had Quaker wives; moreover, the wives of countless disowned Friends like John Bartram and Thomas Bond remained faithful followers of the rules of the Yearly Meeting. It is no accident that Westtown School, the Groton of Philadelphia Quakerism for almost two centuries, has always had, as we shall see, more females than males among its staff and student body (Chapter 14).

While the American Society was making plans for its future, another group of Philadelphians under the leadership of Thomas Bond was resurrecting the American Philosophical Society. Even though Bond wanted to avoid partisan feelings, this group soon took on a definite proprietary-Anglican-Presbyterian complexion. In addition to a handful of physicians, several college teachers, and the self-taught astronomer David Rittenhouse, all of whom had scientific interests, proprietary party leaders like William Allen, James Hamilton, and Benjamin Chew, as well as merchants like Thomas Willing, soon joined the group. Like almost everything else in colonial Philadelphia, even science was now divided along party and religious lines.

The differences between the two societies are very revealing. The American Society began as a liberal Quaker group that wanted to advance science in the interest of the country's development; the Philosophical Society wanted to advance pure science along the same lines as the Royal Society. Both societies had local and corresponding members. "The caliber of corresponding members," according to Hindle, "was higher than that of domestic members in either society, more of the best scientists being associated with the Philosophical Society."[38] As might be expected from its Quaker emphasis, the American Society stressed natural history, agriculture, and invention; the Philosophical Society, however, paid little attention to natural history and stressed basic science, astronomy receiving most attention largely because Provost William Smith of the College of Philadelphia had discovered and promoted David Rittenhouse to membership in the society.

David Rittenhouse was the only man in colonial America who could be compared with John Winthrop IV in mathematics, physics, and astronomy. Though Rittenhouse was of solid Quaker stock and his two successive wives were Friends, he never joined the Society. As was typical of the Pennsylvania Quaker community, however, he had little or no formal education and was largely a self-taught prodigy. Perhaps his most famous accomplishment was the ingenious construction of an orrery or mechanical planetarium, which was the best concrete representation of Newton's mechanistic world in the colonies. Though Rittenhouse was eventually awarded an honorary master of arts by the College of Philadelphia, where he later was a professor, it is indicative of the Philadelphia mind that he sold the orrery to the College of New Jersey, whose Scotch-Calvinist president, John Witherspoon, visited Rittenhouse one day and bought it on the spot for £300.*

---

*The University of Pennsylvania now has a copy in its library.

After considerable political maneuvering and compromise, the two societies joined to form the new American Philosophical Society. Franklin, even though he was abroad, was elected president. To Europeans, of course, the society was known as Franklin's society.

Franklin had brought international fame to Philadelphia through his experiments in electricity. It was a Quaker merchant in London, Peter Collinson, who introduced Franklin to the world. In 1751 he published a collection of Franklin's letters describing his experiments. Dr. John Fothergill wrote the preface to Franklin's *Experiments and Observations on Electricity*. Hindle wrote:

> Franklin's book was the most important scientific contribution made by an American in the colonial period. In it, his ability to construct hypotheses that were often brilliant and to check them with adequate experiments was made clear for the first time. His most important accomplishments were in the realm of *pure theory* where he was able to show how his single fluid concept fitted the observed conditions more satisfactorily than the two-fluid theory then widely accepted under the stimulus of Charles Dufay's writings. Franklin also suggested the terminology that became so widely useful, calling one charge negative and the other positive. . . . At many points, notably when confronted with an example of induction, Franklin showed the ability to grasp the essential nature of the phenomenon and *fit it into his conceptual scheme.*
>
> The response that met Franklin's work was overwhelming. His book passed through five English and three French editions, and was translated into German and Italian as well. In England, the Royal Society awarded him its Copley Medal and admitted him to fellowship without requiring him to request the election, sign the register, or pay the usual fees—a rare honor. In France, the King directed his own Thanks and Compliments in an express Manner to Mr. *Franklin of Pennsylvania*, while the Académie des Sciences elected him one of its eight *associés étrangers*. In America, Harvard, Yale and William and Mary granted him honorary degrees. Franklin became a world celebrity.[39]

Franklin's real contribution to electrical theory was overshadowed by the tremendous popularity of the famous kite experiment, which led to the invention of the lightning rod. Here was a veritable magician who had tamed lightning in an age when it was held in superstitious dread. The great Immanuel Kant likened him to a new Prometheus who had stolen fire from heaven. Franklin's popularity and charm, moreover, were enhanced by his living in an age that worshipped the virtues of a simple society and distrusted scholastic learning: "The Philadelphia Prometheus with his kite was also an American Adam in his electrical garden."[40]

Nevertheless, this American Adam was a universal genius who belonged to the world rather than to the city he made so famous. Far more typical of the Quaker and Philadelphia mind was the fact gathering botanist John Bartram, who, like Franklin, was introduced to the scientific community by Peter Collinson.

In the years following Linnaeus's publication of his famous book in 1735, Collinson became the central figure in the transatlantic natural history circle. His London office served as a clearinghouse for specimens and communications from Linnaeus in Sweden, Dillenius at Oxford, Gronovius at Leiden, and Americans like John Bartram and James Logan in Philadelphia. Collinson was an amateur naturalist and spoke for a whole generation of gentlemen gardeners. As is true of most Quakers, his own faith in science was empirical and utilitarian rather than theoretical and humanistic. He once protested that the Linnaeun system of classification was "too much perplex'd."[41]

John Bartram was introduced to the Collinson circle through a young member of Franklin's Junto, Joseph Breintnall. A "down right plain Country Man" and a "Quaker too Into the Bargain," Bartram was an original in the style of David Rittenhouse.[42] Primarily a noble nurseryman, seedsman, and farmer, he traveled throughout the American colonies, much like an itinerant Quaker minister, compulsively collecting botanical specimens rather than converting souls to the Inner Light. Though Bartram's knowledge of the principles of botany was limited and he never learned Latin, Linnaeus called him "the greatest natural botanist in the world"[43] and helped secure him a membership in the Royal Society of Science at Stockholm in 1769. He was never elected to the British Royal Society but was pensioned by the king. Bartram is remembered today as the first American botanist,* but even his friend Collinson had to admit that he ranked behind three of his far more sophisticated contemporaries, John Clayton and Dr. John Mitchell of Virginia and Dr. Cadwalader Colden of New York.

Of third generation Quaker stock and, like Rittenhouse, married twice to Quaker women, Bartram was read out of meeting, perhaps because of his Deism and his attitudes toward the Indians, among other things. "Unless we bang the Indians stoutly," he once said, "and make them fear us, they will never love us, nor keep peace long with us."[44] (As a nice example of generational reaction, Bartram's son William remained a Friend all his life and was a great advocate of the red man and disseminator of the concept of the noble savage. His *Travels through North and South Carolina, Georgia, East and West Florida, the Cherokee Country, the Extensive Territories of Muscogulges or Creek Confederacy, and the Country of the Chactaws* made him famous, was translated into Dutch, French, and German, and had a great influence on Wordsworth, Coleridge, Chateaubriand, and the whole Romantic school of literature.)

THE QUAKER AND PURITAN ETHICS AND THE SPIRIT OF SCIENCE

In the eighteenth century, the sciences were divided into *natural history*, or the study of zoology, botany, mineralogy, and so forth (studied, according to Webster, "in a more or less unsystematic way"), and *natural philosophy*, or the systematic analysis of the laws of astronomy, physics, and chemistry (especially mechanics). Natural philosophy required a thorough training in mathematics and therefore was incomprehensible to most laymen; natural history did not require mathematics and therefore was open to all who were curious. Natural philosophy, in short, was elitist.

---

*Bartram's botanical garden, the first in America, passed on to his sons, John and William.

In the Puritan seventeenth century, the great scientists like Boyle and Newton, following in the tradition of Copernicus and Galileo, were seeking the laws of nature; the Enlightened eighteenth century, however, tended to concentrate on the collection of endless facts about the world of nature.

The Quakers were indeed leaders in eighteenth-century science, as their disproportionate representation in the Royal Society indicates, but their interest was in natural history, specifically botany. Interest in botany had a long Quaker tradition: William Penn, for instance, once described George Fox as a "divine and a naturalist" who was largely "ignorant of useless and sophisticated science."[45] To most Quakers theory was as useless as theology. Fact collecting better fitted the Quaker preference for things over words and was infinitely amateur, democratic, and egalitarian. Thus, Philadelphians, largely through their ties with London Friends,* took the lead in the colonies in the transatlantic natural history circle. But, as we have seen, they did not write the better books on this subject.

In contrast to the Philadelphians, Bostonians took the lead in natural philosophy. Their finest flower in the field of science was John Winthrop IV. At the age of twenty-three he was given the Hollis professorship in natural philosophy at Harvard. "He became a great teacher and a creative scientist—one of the few to appear in natural philosophy in the colonial period," noted Brooke Hindle.

> As his first recorded scientific writing was on sunspots, so astronomy continued to be the field in which he most delighted although he wrote on earthquakes, weather, and mathematics as well. He published occasional lectures and pamphlets and eleven of his papers were printed in the *Philosophical Transactions.* His writings were distinguished by their clarity and sweep as well as their occasional flashes of brilliant insight. Alone among the teachers, Winthrop was elected to the Royal Society. He was twice offered and twice he refused the presidency of Harvard and he was suggested for the provostship of the College of Philadelphia.

According to Ezra Stiles, Winthrop "had not his equal in Europe."

There was a long tradition in natural philosophy at Harvard before Winthrop's day. Theories are always more threatening than facts. Thus, all over Europe, the teaching of the theories of Copernicus was suppressed well into the seventeenth century (it was unsafe at Paris to praise or defend Copernicus as late as 1686). The clerical leaders at Harvard were far more tolerant of the New Philosophy. Although their first president, Henry Dunster, taught his students the physics of Dante's day, the Copernican theories were taught there, according to Samuel Eliot Morison, as early as 1659. John Winthrop II, educated abroad and avidly interested in science, gave Harvard the first telescope in the colonies in 1672; four years later Thomas Brattle made his observations, which attained a certain immortality through being recorded in Newton's *Principia.* Several generations of Harvard students under the older Winthrop's guidance

---

*Dr. John Fothergill, for example, had a private collection of some 3,400 exotic plants from all over the world.

obtained at least a nodding acquaintance with pneumatics, hydrostatics, mechanics, statics, optics, astronomy, geography, natural history, navigation, and surveying. But they were of the New England elite.

Things are atomizing and meaningless; unity and meaning come only through *words*. The differing emphases in science in Philadelphia and Boston clearly reflected their differing theories of society. Whereas the Goddess of Miscellany, as Daniel Boorstin put it, reigned in Quaker Philadelphia, the Puritan God of Theology was more receptive to scientific theory in Boston. "To say," Boorstin cautioned,

> that a society can or ought to be "unified" by some total philosophic system—whether a *Summa Theologica*, a Calvin's *Institutes*, or a Marx's *Capital*—is to commit oneself to an aristocratic concept of knowledge: let the elite know the theories and the values of the society; they will know and preserve for all the rest.[47]

This is of course exactly what the class of Massachusetts ministers and magistrates had a mind to do from the very beginning and what the citizens of atomized and democratic Philadelphia have always avoided. And so, more and more, have the people of all America. For if our democracy worships science, it also, at the same time, worships facts (things) and mistrusts theory (words). In this sense, colonial Philadelphia stood at the source of the mainstream in America. Bostonians, with their elitist, theological-theoretical, and organic view of both society and science, stood, and still stand, apart. Needless to say, our contemporary theory-spinning guru Buckminster Fuller grew up in the Boston suburb of Milton and not along Philadelphia's Main Line.

PART IV

THE AGE OF TRANSITION

The Great Generation:
Founders of the New Nation

The Revolution of the United States was the result of a mature and reflecting preference for freedom. . . . It contracted no alliance with the turbulent passions of anarchy, but its course was marked, on the contrary, by a love of order and law.

Alexis de Tocqueville

If the Patrons and Friends of Liberty succeed in the present and glorious Struggle, the Quakers and their Posterity will enjoy all the Advantages derived from it, equally with those who procured them, without contributing a single Penny, and with safety to their Persons. But if the Friends of Liberty fail, the Quakers will risk no Forfeitures, but be entitled by their Behavior to Protection and Countenance from the British Ministry, and will probably be promoted to Office.

Philadelphia Committee of Safety, 1775

Cavaliers and Puritans fought each other bitterly in the 1640s and then joined together as Whigs and Tories in the peaceful Glorious Revolution, which brought William and Mary to the throne in 1688. Their political heirs in Virginia and Massachusetts, often referring to the "real Whig" spirit of the Glorious Revolution, came to Philadelphia in the fall of 1774 to take the lead in the first Continental Congress. The congress, actually a convention of patriots, was called at the instigation of the Massachusetts House of Representatives. The meetings, as befitted their unofficial status, were held in Carpenters' Hall rather than in Pennsylvania's State House. After about seven weeks the congress adjourned, agreeing to meet again the next spring.

From the fall of 1774 until 1800, when John and Abigail Adams left the city for the new capital in Washington, the leading members of America's great generation walked the streets of Philadelphia, along with many visitors from abroad, including Thomas Paine. Paine, whose anti-hierarchical ideals some have traced to his Quaker father, came to the city in the fall of 1774 with letters of introduction from Franklin, whom he had known in London. And the critical year of 1776 opened with Paine's publication of "Common Sense" (the title

was suggested by Benjamin Rush) on January 9. John Adams, who had no use
for Paine's optimistic philosophy of progress and the perfectibility of man, later
observed (1806): "I know not whether any man in the world has had more influence on its inhabitants or affairs for the last thirty years than Thomas
Paine."[1] Paine's "Common Sense," a diatribe against monarchy in general and
the tyranny of George III in particular, urged immediate independence. It was
read by more Americans than any other eighteenth-century pamphlet.

War broke out at Lexington and Concord in April 1775. The Second Continental Congress met in May (at Philadelphia's Independence Hall) and elected
Washington commander-in-chief of the Continental Army. The Battle of Bunker Hill took place just before Washington arrived in Boston to assume command.

The following June, Richard Henry Lee, on behalf of the Virginia delegation
to the Second Continental Congress, introduced a resolution urging independence. John Adams seconded the motion and he and Lee led its supporters.
John Dickinson of Pennsylvania led those who still hoped for conciliation.
When the final vote was taken on July 2, the motion was passed, nine colonies
in favor and four against. Jefferson was chosen to write the formal declaration.

The differences between the men who represented Massachusetts and Pennsylvania at the Second Congress and their behavior there were very characteristic of the social and political structures of the two colonies. Massachusetts
sent four men, John Hancock, Samuel and John Adams, and Elbridge Gerry.
Hancock was elected President, Samuel Adams was the skillful and dedicated
worker behind the scenes, and John Adams took the lead in debate from the
very beginning: Jefferson called him "our Colossus on the floor," and Richard
Stockton of New Jersey called him "the Atlas of American independence." All
four delegates voted for the Lee motion and signed the Declaration of Independence.

Pennsylvania had more signers of the Declaration than any other colony,
which was largely the result of "geography and historical circumstances rather
than revolutionary ardor."[2] Actually of the nine Pennsylvania signers, only
four voted on the Lee motion of July 2. The members of Congress on that day
from Pennsylvania were Benjamin Franklin, James Wilson, John Morton, Robert Morris (all signers), John Dickinson, Thomas Willing, Charles Humphreys,
Edward Biddle, and Andrew Allen. Edward Biddle and Andrew Allen were absent on the day of the vote: Biddle was on his deathbed and Allen became
"frightened and held back"[3] and eventually fled with the Loyalists to England.
Only five took their seats at the meeting; Franklin, Wilson and Morton voted
in favor of the Lee motion and Willing and Humphreys opposed it. Morris and
Dickinson, in the hall when the voting took place, abstained, Morris being opposed and Dickinson paralyzed by "timidity and hair-splitting irresolution."[4]
Franklin, Morton, Wilson, and Morris (always ready to bend to accomplished
facts) signed the final Declaration, but Dickinson did not. In the meantime, as
we shall see, Pennsylvanians, led by the radical Whigs, were making their state
constitution and on July 20 sent five new delegates to the congress: George

Taylor, James Smith, and George Ross, from the upstate towns of Easton, York and Lancaster, respectively, and George Clymer and Benjamin Rush from Philadelphia. These five men, in addition to the original four, were the nine signers from Pennsylvania.

The Massachusetts delegates were members of a unified class, and all were from the eastern part of the state: of the Adamses, the radical Samuel and the conservative John had been closely associated throughout the critical decade leading up to the Declaration; Hancock, the richest man in Massachusetts, and John Adams had been raised together from the cradle in Braintree; and Gerry was one of the wealthier citizens of Marblehead. All were natives of Massachusetts and Harvard graduates.

The heterogeneous elite that signed the Declaration for Pennsylvania was made up of a very different breed of man. Only three were born in the state: George Clymer, a successful Philadelphia merchant, Benjamin Rush, a radical young physician, and John Morton, a Chester County farmer of Swedish stock. Of the three giants, Franklin was a native of Boston, Wilson of Scotland, and Morris of Liverpool, England. Of the three signers from upstate, Ross was a native of Delaware and Smith of northern Ireland; Taylor "seems to have been born in Ireland."[5] Of the nine, only two had advanced degrees, Rush from the College of New Jersey and Wilson from St. Andrew's in Scotland.

No wonder only a bare majority of the Pennsylvania delegation voted for independence on July 2, for the year 1776 found Pennsylvania in a state of social and political confusion. When the news of Lexington and Concord reached Philadelphia in April 1775, Pennsylvania was the only colony that had never had compulsory military service. As the radical Whigs led the colony in preparing for war and organizing a militia, the Society of Friends was put in a difficult position: beginning in July, several hundred patriotic Friends were read out of meeting, including Thomas Mifflin, first governor of the state. In October, the Society presented a formal address to the Assembly protesting the financial assessment on pacifists in place of militia service. The members of the Committee of Safety were enraged and even the Quaker bred Thomas Paine, in the third edition of "Common Sense," argued strongly against the Friends' passivity toward the tyranny of George III. "Call not coldness of soul, religion; nor put the *Bigot* in place of the *Christian*," he wrote of their position and then added: "The principles of Quakerism have a direct tendency to make a man the quiet and inoffensive subject of any, and every government which is set over him."[6]

Nevertheless, both the Quaker and proprietary wings of the Assembly and Governor John Penn now drew together in a defensive position. But they gradually lost control of events entirely, and on June 13, while the congress was debating Lee's resolution, the Assembly made its last quorum. Five days later, a provincial conference made up of those in favor of independence and led by radical Whigs, many of them Presbyterians from both the city and the Scotch-Irish frontier, came together at Carpenters' Hall. Their main objectives were to declare Pennsylvania's support for independence and to organize a constitutional convention.

THE CONSTITUTIONS OF
MASSACHUSETTS AND PENNSYLVANIA

The pattern of upper-class political and social hegemony in colonial Massachusetts and the far less stable authority structure in colonial Pennsylvania clearly influenced the constitutional histories of the two states after the colonies declared their independence from the British empire. Whereas the first Pennsylvania constitution, put through in September 1776, was by far the most democratic in all the original thirteen states, the Massachusetts constitution, one of the last to be written and ratified (October 1780), was a conservative but more flexible instrument, much like the federal Constitution, for which it served as an important model. The differences in timing and tone of the two constitutions reflected the contrasting class relations of the two states in the revolutionary period, which were briefly as follows.

The Declaration of Independence was first proclaimed to the public at a joyful celebration in Philadelphia on July 8, and the Pennsylvania constitutional convention, originally planned for that date, finally met on July 15. Led by radicals like the immigrant Scotch-Irishman George Bryan, using Franklin as an establishment figurehead, and advised and prodded by the two auslander radicals Sam Adams and Tom Paine, Pennsylvanians wrote a constitution that included a unicameral legislature (Franklin's idea) and an impotent "group executive" called the supreme executive council, which was to choose a president of Pennsylvania mainly to serve as a figurehead on state occasions. This anti-authoritarian document, highly reminiscent of the group decisionmaking principles of leadership in the Quaker meeting, was not very different from William Penn's frame of government, which had been in force since 1701.

> The Assembly, still unicameral, retained the central position of power. The substitution of the Supreme Executive Council for the earlier appointed governor brought this function within control of the electorate; but it remained subordinate to the Assembly as the executive had been during the colonial era. The big change wrought by the 1776 constitution came not in the structure of government, but in the people who assumed the management of government. In place of the propertied men, the freeman Associators now had exclusive control of the ballot box, and they voted a new hierarchy of public servants into office, few of them experienced in administrative, legislative, or judicial work. This constituted the basic revolution in Pennsylvania.[7]

Because of the confusion in the city at the time of the adoption of the state constitution, Philadelphia failed to elect anyone to the new Assembly until February 1777, when it finally chose Thomas Wharton, a lapsed Quaker and an ardent patriot. In March both the Assembly and the executive council elected Wharton the first president of Pennsylvania. His loyalty to the radical government was demonstrated when, by order of Assembly and council, he sent twenty of the most prominent Quakers in the city, including his own cousin, into forced exile in Virginia. The "Virginia exiles"—including Israel and James Pemberton, Edward Penington, Thomas Wharton, Elijah Brown (father of Charles Brockton Brown, America's first novelist), Henry Drinker, Miers Fisher (great-uncle of Sidney George Fisher), and Thomas Gilpin—have always held a prominent place in the history of Philadelphia Quakerism.

The demand for a state constitution in Massachusetts came from the extreme western frontier county of Berkshire and was led by a fighting parson, Thomas Allen, who had fired the first shot at the Battle of Bennington. The constitutional convention gathered in 1777–1778 and wrote a liberal document not unlike Pennsylvania's. It included a unicameral legislature, the head of which was to be governor; thus, it lacked separation of powers. It also lacked a bill of rights. The first state constitution in the new nation to be submitted to popular vote, it was turned down by an overwhelming majority, thanks largely to a pamphlet called the "Essex Result," written by Theophilus Parsons of Newburyport after a heated meeting of Essex County Federalists at Treadwell's Tavern in Ipswich. Parsons was a great friend and admirer of John Adams (John Quincy Adams studied law under Parsons), and both were strong believers in Montesquieu's doctrine of the separation of powers.

A second convention opened on September 1, 1779, at the First Church, on Harvard Square in Cambridge. The most distinguished men in the Massachusetts establishment, except for those in military service or in other government posts, came to Cambridge—among them, James Bowdoin, Samuel Adams, John Hancock, Samuel Otis, and John Lowell of Boston; John Adams of Braintree; Increase Sumner of Roxbury; John Pickering and Henry Higginson of Salem; Theophilus Parsons of Newburyport; George Cabot of Beverly; Levi Lincoln of Worcester; Caleb Strong of Northampton; James Sullivan of Groton; and Nathaniel Gorman of Charlestown.

Soon after the convention was called to order a subcommittee composed of James Bowdoin, Samuel Adams, and John Adams was charged with drafting the constitution. This group entrusted the entire task to John Adams, perhaps the leading constitutional thinker of his or any other day in America. Thoroughly familiar with the theory of mixed forms (monarchy, aristocracy, and democracy) and the need for balancing them in any society, Adams also believed in balancing reason with experience. Not only had he studied the famous republican theorists from Polybius through Harrington and Montesquieu, but he also was to perform a thorough autopsy of some fifty historical constitutions, mainly in antiquity.

The final Massachusetts constitution followed pretty much in the style of the "Essex Result" pamphlet. It called for a strong executive and a bicameral legislature, one body to represent the property of the state and the other the people at large. Above all, there was to be a clear separation of executive and legislative powers. The conservative aspects of the constitution included a property base for the Senate and the virtual establishment of Congregationalism as the state religion. Yet, the constitution also provided for a bill of rights to protect the people from their rulers, and, in the tradition of their ancestors in Winthrop's day, annual elections of the governor by an electorate that included 95 percent of the adult male residents. There was no limit set on the consecutive reelection of governors. In other words, the Massachusetts establishment kept its *leaders responsive to the people's will but allowed capable men to hold office as long as they did a good job in the opinion of the voters.*

THE AMERICAN REVOLUTION: POLITICAL REBELLION IN MASSACHUSETTS AND SOCIAL REVOLUTION IN PENNSYLVANIA

In 1909, Carl Becker came to the conclusion that the political arguments leading up to the Revolution in New York could be summed up in the twin questions of "home rule" and "who should rule at home."[8] Ever since, American historians have argued whether or not Becker's aphorism was an accurate description of the American Revolution as a whole. I contend that the political question of home rule dominated the history of revolutionary Massachusetts whereas the societal question of who should rule at home was the major issue in Pennsylvania. In a most thorough study of revolutionary Pennsylvania, Richard Alan Ryerson came to the same conclusion.

> The Revolution in Pennsylvania was a revolution. . . . By late 1776 the Commonwealth of Pennsylvania was perhaps the most vital participatory democracy in the world. Whatever may have been political reality in Massachusetts or Virginia before or after Independence, the Revolution had transformed Pennsylvania from insular, docile freemen bowing to their cultural betters . . . into cosmopolitan, contentious citizens eager for national glory and the main chance, and loyal to aggressive young leaders who would secure these prizes for them. . . . And as at no other time in Pennsylvania before or since, institutions were suddenly destroyed, traditions overturned, received authority subverted and then rejected, and established elites sent on the road to extinction to be replaced by others.[9]

Although I agree with Ryerson's excellent analysis of revolutionary Pennsylvania, I disagree with his implication that the Pennsylvania situation characterized the Revolution as a whole: "The American Revolution," he writes in the last paragraph of his book, "mobilized tens of thousands of ordinary men in hundreds of communities, large and small, to change both the political and social order."[10]

Whereas class revolution and resentful democracy marked the writing of the first constitution of Pennsylvania, continuity of class authority and deference democracy prevailed in Massachusetts throughout the revolutionary period. As an index of class revolution in Pennsylvania, for instance, not a single member of the executive council had held office in the last colonial government, which included Allens, Chews, Cadwaladers, Logans, Penns, Peterses, and Shippens—all prominent Philadelphians in the last half of the eighteenth century. Of the councillors who ruled Massachusetts from the time of Hutchinson's departure in 1774 until the calling of the first state constitutional convention, James Bowdoin, president of council, and seven other members—Caleb

Cushing, Benjamin Greenlief, John Hancock, James Otis, Sr., James Pitts, Walter Spooner, and John Winthrop IV—had all served as councillors under Hutchinson's royal government.

That John Winthrop IV was a member of both the royal and the revolutionary council was a symbol of continuous class authority since the colony's founding in 1630. That James Otis, Sr., was sitting on the council when he died in 1778, just as the first constitutional convention was called, was a reminder both of class continuity and of the bitter political struggles *within* the ruling class that finally led to the ousting of Hutchinson and the outbreak of the war at Lexington and Concord.

The Otis and Hutchinson families had been leaders in the royal colony for several generations: Thomas Hutchinson's father and grandfather had been members of council and when James Otis's father died in 1727 he had been a member of council for nineteen years. The Hutchinson-Otis family feud began in 1760, when Thomas Hutchinson was chosen chief justice by the royal governor, Francis Bernard, over James Otis, then speaker of the House and acknowledged leader of the bar. Otis's son James, partly because of this injustice done to his father, became the leader of the revolutionary and anti-Royalist party in Massachusetts, which he dominated until he began to drink too heavily and was finally declared non compos mentis in 1771. His younger brother and legal guardian, Samuel A. Otis, however, sat at the convention that wrote the Massachusetts constitution in 1779–1780.*

Perhaps the best example of the continuity of class authority in the founding of the state of Massachusetts is the career of James Bowdoin. A man of great inherited wealth (including large landholdings in Maine), Bowdoin had sat on the royal council for all but one year from 1757 to 1774, when Hutchinson departed. All this time, though a conservative, he kept in close touch with James Otis, Jr., Sam Adams, John Hancock, and other young radicals. As head of the provincial council during the revolutionary years, Bowdoin was naturally chosen president of the constitutional convention of 1779–1780, as well as chairman of the subcommittee charged with drafting the instrument. He ended his long career of public service as second governor of Massachusetts and has since been considered, much like John Winthrop in the founding years, as "the great governor" in the long interval between the departure of General Gage from Boston and the inauguration of John A. Andrew during the Civil War.

All institutions reflect the nature of both their founding and their founders. Of all the constitutions written by the thirteen original states, only that of Massachusetts remains in force today. In contrast, the Pennsylvania constitution proved unworkable almost immediately. Soon after meeting to ratify the federal Constitution, Pennsylvanians drew up a new constitution, this time written by the leaders of the more conservative establishment. The first governor of the state, Thomas Mifflin, took office in 1790. The new constitution included a

---

*When Senator Harrison Gray Otis (Samuel's son) died in 1848, his family had been leaders in Massachusetts for well over a century.

bicameral legislature and a strong executive, with considerable appointive powers, to be elected for a three-year term. The traditional fear of leadership in the
state was reflected in a three-term limit on governors. As we shall see in Chapter 18, Pennsylvanians drew up new constitutions three more times, in 1838,
1873, and 1967.

THE GRAND CONVENTION

In the hot summer of 1787, the most important political event in our nation's history took place in Philadelphia when fifty-five men from twelve states
(antinomian Rhode Island sent no delegates) came to the city to write the Constitution of the United States. With understandable exaggeration, Jefferson,
our minister in Paris, wrote his friend John Adams, minister in London, that
they were virtually a "group of Demi-Gods." The tone of the gathering was set
by Washington soon after his arrival in Philadelphia: "If to please the people we
offer what we ourselves disapprove, how can we afterwards defend our work?
Let us raise a standard to which the wise and the honest can repair; the event is
in the hands of God."[11]

More than any other group of leaders in our nation's history, these fifty-five
individuals provide a classic example of leadership by men of long established
class authority. Two of them, Washington and Franklin, were of world renown, a dozen or so were national figures, the rest were more or less established
local leaders. Three of the framers had attended the Stamp Act Congress,
seven the First Continental Congress, eight had signed the Declaration of Independence, thirty had served in the Revolutionary Army (fifteen hardened vet-
erans), forty-two had served in Congress under the Articles of Confederation,
and all save two or three had held public office in their colony or state (twenty
helped write their state's constitution).

They were an unusually wealthy and educated group for that day. Forty of
the fifty-five held government securities or were bankers or moneylenders; fifteen were slave owners. Though only some dozen were practicing lawyers, a
majority had been trained in the law. Twenty-nine were college educated—nine
at Princeton, five each at Yale and William and Mary, three at Harvard, two
each at the College of Philadelphia, King's College (Columbia), and Oxford,
and one, James Wilson, at St. Andrew's and Aberdeen.

Most of the men who came to Philadelphia that summer were determined to
mold a united nation out of thirteen independent sovereignties. Thus, the
framers were a self-selected group of privileged men who immediately developed
an esprit de corps and trust among recognized equals. More radical local leaders
like R. H. Lee and Patrick Henry of Virginia, Willie Jones of North Carolina,
the Bryans, father and son, of Pennsylvania, and George Clinton of New York
were jealous of their local power and would have no part in such a deliberation.
In many ways the gathering was a happy meeting of old friends and comrades:
Washington could look around the room at half a dozen men who had voted
him into command back in 1775, a dozen who had been with him at Trenton,

Valley Forge, or Yorktown, and another dozen who had supported him in Congress or fished with him on the Potomac.

In an attempt to understand the durability of the legend of the Founding Fathers, Stanley Elkins and Eric McKittrick thoughtfully emphasized the common upper-class background of the framers and their decision to meet in absolute secrecy.

> Being relieved from all outside pressures meant that the only way a man could expect to make a real difference in the convention's deliberations was to reach, through main persuasion, other men of considerable ability and experience. Participants and audience were therefore one, and this in itself imposed standards of debate which were quite exacting. In such a setting the best minds in the convention were accorded an authority which they would not have had in political debates aimed at an indiscriminate public. . . . Indeed, this was in all likelihood the key mechanism . . . in explaining not only the genius of the main compromises but also the general fitness of the document as a whole. That is, a group of two or more intelligent men who are subject to no cross-pressures and whose principal commitment is to the success of an idea, are perfectly capable—as in our scientific communities of today—of performing what appear to be prodigies of intellect.[12]

Washington took the secrecy rule so seriously that he broke a long habit and recorded nothing in his diary during the convention.* And he presided over the gathering with consummate grace, born of both his personal and his class charisma. The continuity of political authority of the framers was attested to in the new government, which included Washington as president and a Congress made up of eleven framers in the Senate and eight in the House.

Although this is a study of Massachusetts and Pennsylvania, I have emphasized the setting and the backgrounds of the framers as a whole for two reasons. First, they indicate that the class characteristics of the delegates and the secrecy of the deliberations raised the political level of debate above the individual abilities and experiences of the delegates, which of course were considerable. Second, and perhaps more important to my thesis, they suggest how and why the political history of Massachusetts, led by an established class in a deference democracy, has been so very different from that of Pennsylvania, led largely by ever changing political elites in a defiant democracy with no continuing traditions of class authority. As we have seen, the Massachusetts constitution was written by the same class of men who framed our federal Constitution; the Pennsylvania constitution clearly was not.

THE FRAMERS FROM MASSACHUSETTS
AND PENNSYLVANIA

The largest delegation of framers consisted of the eight Pennsylvanians, all from the host city of Philadelphia. Massachusetts sent four men: Rufus King

---

*The convention met in secret sessions for sixteen weeks; Madison's notes were not made public until 1840.

from Newburyport, Elbridge Gerry from Marblehead, Nathaniel Gorham from Charlestown, and Caleb Strong from the western town of Northampton.* The most obvious thing about the Massachusetts delegation was the absence of the state's more famous men: John Adams was in London; Samuel Adams was growing old in Boston, but his parochial point of view was represented by his friend Gerry; Hancock was governor; William Cushing was chief justice of the state; and Henry Knox was in New York serving as secretary of war.

At the time of the convention, Massachusetts was marked by vigorous factional politics and under the leadership of James Bowdoin had just put down Shays' Rebellion. Pennsylvania had developed two well-organized political parties: the Radicals, a loudly democratic and anti-nationalist coalition of farmers and tradesmen devoted to defending the state constitution, and the Republicans, a coalition of lawyers and merchants who wanted to destroy the constitution. The former had no interest in the grand convention; the latter advocated a stronger national government. Fortunately, the Republicans were in power (and would write a new state constitution in 1790) and chose a distinguished group of seven men of their own persuasion—and then added the nationalist democrat Franklin just before the convention opened. The Pennsylvania delegation included Franklin, James Wilson, Robert Morris, and George Clymer, all of whom had signed the Declaration; Thomas Mifflin, a wealthy and hospitable merchant (retired), war hero, and first governor under the new state constitution; Jared Ingersoll, a native of Connecticut who had spent the war years at the Inns of Court in London and was one of Philadelphia's more successful lawyers; Thomas Fitzsimons, a native of Ireland and one of the two Catholics among the framers, who had come to the city, married into the wealthy Meade family, and become a successful merchant himself; and Gouverneur Morris, a giant of a man and scion of the manor of Morrisania (his mother had been a staunch Tory during the Revolution and a half brother a general in the British army), who had moved to Philadelphia to practice law after having failed to win reelection to the New York legislature.

On the whole the Philadelphians were the richer group; the Massachusetts men, the better educated. Mifflin and Robert Morris were extremely rich, although Gerry was one of the wealthiest men of Massachusetts (he also held more government securities than any other man at the convention). Gorham of Massachusetss and Wilson and Fitzsimons of Pennsylvania were well on their way to becoming rich (all three died in debt); Franklin, Clymer, and Gouverneur Morris were well-to-do; Strong and King, as well as Ingersoll, were comfortable. Whereas three (Strong, King, and Gerry) of the four Massachusetts delegates were graduates of Harvard, only half the Pennsylvanians had gone to college: Ingersoll to Yale, Mifflin to the College of Philadelphia, Gouverneur Morris to King's College (Columbia), and Wilson to St. Andrew's.

Although ranking the fifty-five framers according to the importance of their roles in the convention is a risky business, I shall follow Clinton Rossiter,[13]

---

*All the Massachusetts delegates were natives of the state; six of the eight Pennsylvanians (Franklin, Wilson, Robert Morris, Fitzsimons, Gouverneur Morris, and Ingersoll) were auslanders.

who classified them as principals (four), influentials (eleven), very useful (seven), usefuls (eight), visibles (ten), ciphers (seven), inexplicable disappointments (two), and dropouts (six). Of the eight Pennsylvanians, according to Rossiter, James Wilson and Gouverneur Morris were principals (along with James Madison and Washington); Franklin was one of the influentials; George Clymer was a visible; Mifflin, Ingersoll, and Fitzsimons were ciphers; and Robert Morris (along with Hamilton) proved to be an inexplicable disappointment. Three of the Massachusetts contingent were ranked by Rossiter among the influentials; Strong was a visible.

Gouverneur Morris, at thrity-five one of the youngest delegates, was the main surprise of the convention, speaking more times than anyone else.* He also, according to himself and Madison, wrote the principal draft of the Constitution. James Wilson was, next to Madison, the leading constitutional thinker of the group. Gerry, the wealthy but radical friend of Sam Adams, was one of the more vocal framers. King of Massachusetts was the most devoted committee member, whereas Ingersoll of Pennsylvania served on no committees and spoke hardly at all; nor did his colleagues Mifflin, Fitzsimons, and Robert Morris. Franklin, of course, was the grandfather of the convention and an aging national monument: he proposed the opening prayers, helped to produce the Great Compromise, opposed property qualifications for voters, and made a famous speech on the last day.

> I confess that there are several parts of this constitution which I do not approve. . . . The older I grow the more apt I am to doubt my own judgment, and to pay more respect to the judgment of others. . . . Though many private persons think almost as highly of their own infallibility as of that of their sect, few express it so naturally as a certain French lady, who in a dispute with her sister said "I don't know how it happens, Sister, but I meet with nobody but myself, that's always in the right—*Il n'y a que moi qui a toujours raison.*"[14]

TWO PHILADELPHIA GENTLEMEN OF
MISSED OPPORTUNITIES

This chapter argues that the continuity of class cohesion and authority was responsible for the high level of political debate in the great generation that made a revolution and produced the Constitution of the United States. No two members of this generation better illustrate the confusion of class authority in Pennsylvania than John Dickinson, whom Taylor called the "Penman of the Revolution" and John Adams a "piddling genius of overgrown fortune,"[15] and Charles Thomson, known as the "Sam Adams of Philadelphia."[16] Both men were of first rank in ability; both played vital roles in the political and civic life of their city, colony, state, and nation; both were participants in the making of

---

*Washington addressed the convention only once, at the very end, urging passage of a motion to represent better the people in the House.

the Declaration and the Constitution; but both have been relatively neglected by historians (neither has a full-length modern biography—whereas the facts of Dickinson's life are well known, Thomson's life has remained obscure, partly because he deliberately destroyed all his papers). Finally, both failed to follow through at critical times in their careers. Unfortunately, Dickinson too often has been cited in history for his refusal to sign the Declaration, even though he was one of the only two men in the congress to take up arms in the Revolution; he also held high offices afterward in Pennsylvania and in the new state of Delaware, which he represented at the Constitutional Convention. Like Dickinson, Thomson was a leader in all the colonial controversies with England, but he is best known as the "perpetual secretary" of the congress from 1774 until after the Constitution was ratified in 1789. He knew everybody in that great generation and was chosen to notify Washington personally of his election to the presidency; yet, "to his great mortification, he was given no part in the inaugural ceremonies nor any position in the new government"[17] (I have been unable to find any adequate explanation as to why this was so).* At any rate, Thomson withdrew from public life entirely and retired to the country estate at Harriton that his wealthy Quaker wife had inherited. Although Thomson was in the best position to write the first definitive history of the nation's founding, he burned all his records and spent the last twenty years of his life translating the Septuagint testament.

Dickinson and Thomson missed their opportunities largely because of their own moral and psychological characteristics, but they also lacked the support of a leadership class in Philadelphia, at least as compared to the Adamses and others in Boston. Moreover, although neither man was a practicing Quaker, both were immersed in the local Quaker milieu, which opposed the War of Independence and took no part in the making of the Constitution.

John Dickinson was the scion of a long established and wealthy Quaker family from Maryland's eastern shore. His father gave up his Quakerism and moved to the lower counties of Pennsylvania primarily because his daughter had been read out of meeting for marrying a non-Quaker. Dickinson's mother, Mary Cadwalader, was a good Quaker member of one of Philadelphia's First Families. After studying law at the Middle Temple in London, young Dickinson returned to Philadelphia, where he became a great success at the bar, and married the daughter of the Quaker leader Isaac Norris II. Dickinson inherited the Norris country estate and its famous library, along with a considerable fortune.

In the style of John Adams and Jefferson, Dickinson was a lover of books, widely read in history, political thought, and law. After 1760, he gave up the active practice of law to devote himself to politics. His *Letters from a Farmer in Pennsylvania to the Inhabitants of the British Colonies* (1768) made him famous throughout the colonies as well as in England; from then on he was a leading Whig participant in the debates leading up to the Revolution. The following

---

*Unaccountably, although Thomson signed the original Declaration, attesting to the signature of John Hancock, his name does not appear on the embossed parchment that has come down to us.

passage from John Adams's autobiography sheds some light on why Dickinson chose not to sign the Declaration at the last moment.

> Mr. Charles Thompson [sic] . . . told me, that the Quakers had intimidated Mr. Dickinson's Mother, and his Wife, who were continually distressing him with their remonstrances. His mother said to him: "Johnny you will be hanged, your Estate will be forfeited and confiscated, you will leave your Excellent Wife a Widow and your charming Children Orphans, Beggers and infamous."[18]

Vernon Louis Parrington, however, believed that Dickinson's fear of the future was largely the product of his legalistic mind and he compared Dickinson with men like Jefferson and John Adams.

> The lawyers of the middle and southern colonies were better trained than those of New England. Many were from the Inns of Court. . . . If, on the other hand, the revolutionary leaders of New England—and Virginians like Jefferson and Patrick Henry—were poorer lawyers they were better political scientists, for their legal training had been too casual and too scanty to contract their minds to statutes and precedents. Jefferson and John Adams were alike in this respect; their interests were speculative rather than legal; and they wrote more convincingly when defending the principles of Locke than in expounding Coke. But Dickinson remained always the lawyer. . . . This scrupulous legalism he carried to such lengths that when the new constitution for Pennsylvania was adopted he refused to take office because he doubted the legality of the convention that framed it.[19]

As we have already seen in the case of colonial science, Dickinson's legalism was very much in the tradition of Quakerism's emphasis on things (facts) and mistrust of theory. In Chapter 17 we shall see that his legalism was also characteristic of the Philadelphia bench and bar in contrast to Boston's.

Philadelphia's Silver Age and Boston's Federalist Family Founders

> *The love of the people exactly resembles an honorable pas-*
> *sion for a woman. In both cases, those whom in the days of*
> *courtship, extolled them as angels, never failed, in the time*
> *of attained power, to treat them as brutes; while those who*
> *truly loved them would not hesitate to remonstrate gently,*
> *even at the hazard of their displeasures, and to point out*
> *where their true happiness sat, where it always sits—en-*
> *throned between truth and virtue.*
>
> Josiah Quincy

In the year 1800 Philadelphia, with a population of 70,000, was the first city in America: New York was growing rapidly (its population rose from 33,000 to 60,000 between 1790 and 1800); Boston, however, was a more or less static provincial town of 25,000. Philadelphia was not only the temporary capital of the new nation but also its publishing, artistic, literary, and social center. As Henry Adams put it, Boston was our Bristol, New York our Liverpool, and Philadelphia our London.

Philadelphia's silver decade began with the death of Benjamin Franklin, at the age of eighty-four, in 1790. On April 21, some 20,000 people, nearly half the city, lined the route of Franklin's funeral procession from the State House to the Christ Church burying ground. The procession was led by the clergy of the city, and the coffin was carried by six pallbearers: General Thomas Mifflin, president of Pennsylvania; Thomas McKean, chief justice; Samuel Powell, mayor of Philadelphia; Thomas Willing, president of the Bank of North America; David Rittenhouse, professor of astronomy at the College of Philadelphia; and William Bingham, the richest man in America, member of the Pennsylvania Assembly, and soon to be appointed United States senator from the state. There followed the family and close friends, members of the state Assembly, judges of the State Supreme Court, gentlemen of the bar, printers with their journeymen and apprentices, and member of the Philosophical Society and a host of other associations that Franklin had founded. Doctor Rush sent a lock of Franklin's hair to the marquis de Lafayette, and when the news reached revolutionary France, the National Assembly heard a eulogy on the "sage of two worlds" by Mirabeau and sent a letter of sympathy to its sister Republic.

PHILADELPHIA AS HOST OF
FEDERALIST AMERICA

Between Franklin's death and November 1800, when John and Abigail Adams moved into the new White House, Philadelphians, with their genius for charm and hospitality, were hosts to an elite of men and women from all over the nation, as well as from Europe, who came to the city seeking not only their fortunes but also place and power in the new government. Like postwar periods in every age, the decade began in a mood of affluent ostentation: Hamilton's financial programs had been a success, and Philadelphia's exports were running close to $7 million a year, one-fourth of the nation's total.

In this gay and hospitable city, Anne Willing Bingham was the nation's most brilliant and charming hostess and, when the government moved to Philadelphia, she became queen of the "Republican court." "She attracted to her drawing room," wrote her cousin Joshua Francis Fisher, "all that was distinguished and accomplished in the country."[1] Anne Bingham had been well prepared for her role as leader of the Republican court when her wealthy husband took her abroad on a grand tour in 1783; she was presented to the court of Louis XVI and spent several years at the center of fashionable society in London and Bath. "There was nothing of the democrat and nothing of the Puritan about Mrs. Bingham," wrote her *DAB* biographer. "Her vocabulary and taste in anecdote are reported to have been those of her contemporary the Duchess of Devonshire, and the extravagance of her entertainments surprised, and, in the case of Brissot de Warville at least, shocked European visitors."[2] No wonder Brissot, leader of the Girondists, whose ideological ideal of America centered on the stereotype of *le bon Quakeur*, was horrified at "the pomp which ought for ever to have been a stranger to Philadelphia,"[3] as he wrote after returning home (in Quaker garb) to hasten the Revolution.

If Brissot was outraged, Bostonians were reluctantly impressed. Harrison Gray Otis, who along with John Hancock was a leader in what un-Puritan and extravagant society there was in postwar Boston, was both shocked and pleased at the gay ways of Anne Bingham and Philadelphia Society as a whole. "Mrs. Bingham has certainly given laws to the ladies here, in fashion and elegance," wrote Abigail Adams after Mrs. Washington's Christmas reception in 1791.[4] Even John Adams, sitting next to his hostess at a dinner at the Binghams', was surprised to be able to carry on "something of a political conversation with her" in which she had "more ideas on the subject and a correcter judgment" than he would have suspected in such a beautiful woman.[5] It was indeed generally agreed that, although people were originally attracted to Anne

Bingham because of her beauty and her husband's wealth, it was "certainly her intelligence, sagacious wit, and flair for analysis which made them listen to her."[6] It must be remembered that "Anne was given a careful education characteristic of the Philadelphia of that day, where the advanced and liberal theories of the Quakers on the education of young women had taken root."[7]

Twenty-one years of age in 1791, when the government moved from New York to Philadelphia, Anne Bingham was born and raised at the very center of the Quaker City's Anglican upper class. Her father, Thomas Willing, along with his partner, Robert Morris, was a major financier of the Revolution; her mother, Ann McCall, was a member of one of the city's most fashionable and affluent families, having more (four) founders of the city's exclusive Dancing Assembly (1748) than any other. Her grandfather Charles Willing, son of a prosperous and influential merchant in Bristol, England, was the family founder in America. Two years after his arrival in Philadelphia, in 1728, he married Anne Shippen, the granddaughter of Edward Shippen, president of council in 1703 and 1704 under the proprietorship and owner of the biggest house and biggest coach of his day in Philadelphia.

Both the Willings and the Shippens were leaders of Philadelphia's Anglican upper class during the revolutionary and federal periods. Edward Shippen (1728–1806) and Thomas Willing (1731–1821), both great-grandsons of Edward Shippen, were mildly Loyalist during the Revolution. Thanks to the tolerant ways of Philadelphia (in striking contrast to Boston) both men remained leaders of Society throughout. Thomas Willing, president of the provincial congress in 1774, delegate to the Continental Congress, and member of the Pennsylvania Committee of Public Safety, came under something of a cloud when he refused to vote for the Declaration of Independence and then remained in Philadelphia during the British occupation. Although Chief Justice Benjamin Chew, John Penn, and the elder Jared Ingersoll were arrested and placed on parole by the executive council, Willing was apparently left alone. Undoubtedly, his work in financing and supporting Washington's armies secured his position.

Edward Shippen kept more aloof from politics than did Willing and limited his career to the bar and bench. Trained at the Middle Temple in London and in the office of Tench Francis,* dean of the Philadelphia bar, Shippen was a member of the Pennsylvania Supreme Court from 1791 until shortly before his death in 1806 and chief justice after 1799. Shippen's reputation survived both his own mild Toryism and the treasonous behavior of his son-in-law, Benedict Arnold. (After his marriage to Peggy Shippen, Arnold purchased a magnificent country seat on the banks of the Schuylkill, Mount Pleasant, and the couple became social leaders in the city during the occupation. Benedict Arnold's later treasonous acts may be explained in part by his having gotten heavily into debt trying to keep up with Philadelphia Society during the British occupation.)

Toryism was a matter of personal conviction rather than of class affiliation alone. Thus, another great-grandson of Edward Shippen, William Shippen, a Princeton graduate trained in medicine in Edinburgh, was active in the Revolu-

---

*Edward Shippen married Francis's daughter.

tion as chief physician and director general of hospitals in the Continental Army. (Perhaps his ardent patriotism was related to the fact that his wife was the sister of Francis Lightfoot Lee and Richard Henry Lee of Virginia.) After the war, William Shippen helped found the College of Physicians of Philadelphia, and in 1791, when the University of Pennsylvania was established, he was appointed professor of anatomy, surgery, and midwifery.

William Bingham was born into one of the more rapidly rising families in the city. His great-great-grandfather had come from London and settled in Burlington, New Jersey, before Penn's arrival in Pennsylvania. His father, William, a saddler in Philadelphia, had made an excellent marriage to the daughter of John Stemper, a prosperous English merchant who had settled in the city, becoming one of its wealthiest citizens, member of the common council, and mayor. William joined with his father-in-law in building a fortune out of the rum trade in the West Indies. By the time of his son's birth, he was a member of the common council, a vestryman at fashionable St. Peter's (Anglican) Church, and a charter member of the city's exclusive Dancing Assembly.

William Bingham and Anne Willing were married in October 1780, during a very gloomy period of the Revolution (the following New Year's Day, 1,300 men of the Pennsylvania division revolted at Morristown, New Jersey, killing one of their officers and wounding several others). Christ Church was thronged with relatives of the bride and bridegroom: Willings, Benezets, Powells, Stempers, Hares, Harrisons, Francises, Coxes, McCalls, Shippens, and Byrds. A member of the Loyalist Rawle family described the match thus:

> Speaking of handsome women brings Nancy Willing to my mind. She might set for the Queen of Beauty, and is lately married to Bingham, who returned from the West Indies with an immense fortune. They have set out in highest style; nobody here will be able to make the figure they do; equipage, house, cloathes, are all the newest taste—and yet some people wonder at the match.[8]

The Shippen-Willing-Bingham clan and their associates in business and finance were representative of Philadelphia's Episcopal upper class in its Silver Age—especially during the city's years as host to the national government. But the giants of the city's splendid age at the end of the eighteenth century, as Jefferson noted, were cut-flowers. For example, Thomas Willing, after his resignation from the Bank of North America in 1807, became the veritable patriarch of the city, but no member of his family rose to prominence after him, even though his descendants retained their fashionable position in Society. Robert Morris, Willing's brilliant junior partner before the Revolution, went bankrupt in the panic of 1797* and spent several years in the Walnut Street jail. James Wilson, perhaps the most brilliant cut-flower of them all, also was jailed for debt, in Burlington, New Jersey, and in Edenton, Carolina, where he died of fever in 1798. William Bingham likewise failed to found a Philadelphia dynasty, but as we shall see, he was the progenitor of a prominent English family.

---

*William Bingham was one of the few wealthy Philadelphians easily to survive the panic of 1797.

The Constitution gave Thomas Jefferson no right to spend $15 million to double the size of the country, but, as Hamilton advised, the right to act in the public interest was surely an implied power. And William Bingham helped finance the Louisiana Purchase. In brief, the secretary of the treasury, Albert Gallatin, was able to raise $3,750,000 at home in cash; the Bingham, Baring, and Hope combine agreed to take $11,250,000 in United States government bonds, at 6 percent, redeemable in fifteen years. "Technically," wrote Bingham's biographer, "the Barings, the Hopes, and William Bingham bought the Louisiana Territory from France and resold it to the United States. Gallatin estimated their profit at $3,000,000."[9]

In 1801, the year of his beloved wife's death and just before his own departure from America forever, Bingham somewhat reluctantly accepted the appointment of James Logan's grandson George to fill his seat in the Senate of the United States. For George Logan, strict Quaker (the first and last of his breed to sit in the Senate), pacifist, and devoted follower of Thomas Jefferson, had always been an opponent of the opulent Bingham and the dancing ways of his wife. Three years earlier, Logan had attempted, as self-appointed emissary to Paris, to end the half war with France. Because of his action Congress passed the so-called Logan Act, which forbade private citizens to undertake diplomatic negotiations without official sanction. (Though the act is still the law of the land, George Logan's spiritual descendants seem to have followed in his footsteps, negotiating with Hanoi without official reprimand during our own antinomian 1960s.)

William Bingham and George Logan were the last upper-class Philadelphians to serve full terms in the Senate of the United States until Boies Penrose was sent there at the end of the century. At this point it is important to note that the contribution of leaders of any distinction, by the Lloyd, Logan, Shippen, Willing, Bingham, Mifflin, Chew, Dickinson, Markoe, and White families in my First Family sample, came to an end soon after the federal period. Nevertheless, William Bingham's daughter Ann married Alexander Baring and produced five sons and four daughters; thus, the Philadelphia cut-flower was ancestor to one of England's most distinguished families. Baring inherited the leadership of the family firm from his father in 1810 and built the most powerful banking house in England (he was made first Baron Ashburton in 1835). In 1842 Sir Robert Peel sent Baring to settle the border dispute between Maine and Canada—the result was the Webster-Ashburton Treaty.*

To sum up, Philadelphia's cut-flowers made a brilliant but nevertheless brief display of opulence, and even the rooted plants had limited seasons of leadership. This is not to say that Philadelphia's upper-class families, especially the Willings, Chews, Markoes, Shippens, and Whites, failed to produce charming descendants who were leaders in Society—managers of the Assembly balls,

---

*Alexander and Ann Baring kept the Bingham country estate, Lansdowne, on the banks of the Schuylkill, until it was burned down by playful boys on July 4, 1854. The land later was sold to some Philadelphians who gave it to the city as a part of the developing Fairmount Park. The Bingham mansion in the city was the scene in November 1805 of the most opulent auction the nation had seen up to that time. People thronged to the house to bid and buy.

wardens of fashionable Episcopal churches, captains of the City Troop, and presidents or dozing members of the Philadelphia Club. But after the federal government moved to Washington, and after the state government moved to Lancaster and then to Harrisburg, Proper Philadelphians, like their Quaker ancestors in the 1750s, turned inward, with very few exceptions, to enjoy their privileges in the most delightful upper-class Society in America.

ESSEX COUNTY FEDERALISM AND
FIRST FAMILY FOUNDERS

Along the eastern seaboard of North America, soft and sandy beaches stretch south from Boston harbor, around Cape Cod, to Florida. The stern and rocky coast of New England begins north of Boston, extending around Cape Ann to Maine. This north shore in Essex County, Massachusetts, like East Anglia in England, was the nursery of the strictest Puritanism, as well as the birthplace of the founders of such leading Boston First Families as the Cabots, Lowells, Peabodys, Lees, Higginsons, and Jacksons—a fiercely proud, enterprising, and clannish race. Their ships set out to sea from Marblehead, Salem, Beverly, Gloucester, and Newburyport in the early family founding days and prepared the way financially for the building of the great cotton mills along the little Merrimack, at towns like Haverhill, Lawrence, and Lowell.

George Cabot, the sage of the Essex County Federalists, was born in Salem, where his grandfather had settled in 1700. His father, Joseph Cabot, married Eliza Higginson, became a wealthy merchant, and founded the First Family of Boston. George Cabot was sent to Harvard, where he was ranked seventeenth in a class of forty-two, but he dropped out after taking part in the Harvard rebellion of 1766. In the Salem and Boston style, he married Elizabeth Higginson, his double first cousin, made a fortune in privateering during the Revolution, and was chosen United States senator from Massachusetts in 1791. Weary of politics, Cabot retired from the Senate in 1796. His very indolence became a virtue and he was soon looked upon as the Federalist sage of Park Street, where the Cabots moved in 1803. He hated the French Revolution and considered Jefferson an anarchist. But in politics he was a moderate when compared with some of his friends who attended the Hartford Convention in 1814, which elected him president. "His cool wisdom," wrote Samuel Eliot Morison, "seconded the cautious leadership of H. G. Otis, in preventing radical action."[10]

If George Cabot and Timothy Pickering were the elder statesmen of the Essex County Federalists, young John Lowell was their main publicist. He was known as "The Rebel," not because he was against the federal establishment in Boston but because he was radically against those men of rising power who were bound to destroy it. Henry Adams referred to him as "the literary representative" of Timothy Pickering.[11] Unlike George Cabot and Harrison Gray Otis, John Lowell was against the Hartford Convention because it was not radical enough for his tastes. Like George Cabot, Lowell retired early (from a lucrative law practice); he devoted himself to publicizing the Federalist position and carrying out his Proper Boston duties as an overseer of Harvard, a founder of the Massachusetts General Hospital, and an early and influential member of the Athenaeum and the Massachusetts Historical Society.

The fourth John Lowell descended from the first American Lowell, Percival Lowle, who came to Newbury in 1639. His father, also named John, the "Old Judge," was the family founder. Born in Newburyport, he graduated from Harvard in 1760 and was elected to the Harvard Corporation in 1784. The third John Lowell moved to Boston during the Revolution, served in the Continental Congress in 1782 and 1783, and was appointed chief judge of the First Circuit under the new organization of the United States courts. The Old Judge married three times and produced a dozen Boston Lowell descendants who were eminent enough to be included in the *Dictionary of American Biography.* The clannishness of upper-class Boston is clearly revealed by a listing of his three wives and his distinguished descendants and their wives. First he married Sarah Higginson, who produced John, "the Rebel" (m. Amory)—the grandfather of Judge John Lowell (m. Emerson) and the great-grandfather of Percival Lowell, astronomer and builder of the Mars Hill Observatory at Flagstaff, Arizona (m. Keith)—Abbot Lawrence, Harvard president (m. Lowell), and Amy, the poet. The Old Judge next married Susan Cabot, who was the mother of Francis Cabot, founder of the family textile fortune (m. Jackson), grandmother of John, who founded the Lowell Institute (m. Amory), and great-grandmother of Edward Jackson II, historian, whose *Eve of the French Revolution* is much like Tocqueville's *Ancien Regime* (m. Goodrich); Guy Lowell, an architect (m. Sargent), was his son. The judge's third wife was Rebecca Tyng, the grandmother of both Robert Traill Spence,* Episcopal clergyman and headmaster of St. Mark's School (m. Daune), and James Russell, one of the most famous men of letters in his day, on both sides of the Atlantic, and the first editor of the *Atlantic Monthly.*

While Cabots, Lowells, and other Essex County family founders were taking the lead in Federalist Boston and Massachusetts, the two most eminent members of the Adams family, of the south shore at Braintree, were taking the lead at the highest levels of national government. John Adams, the most judicious and penetrating conservative political philosopher in our history, was nevertheless not quite at home with the Essex County men, just as his descendants were never really at home on Boston's State Street. Lacking the Essex County faith in an organic social order led by the members of the best families, Adams was, as they would say today in sociology, a conservative "conflict theorist" who believed in a balanced constitution, ever ready to redress and restrain the excesses of both democracy and aristocracy. Always respected and admired, the Adamses were never popular with any one group, and John Adams lost out after one term in the White House to the increasingly popular Jeffersonian Republicans. In that year, 1801, John Quincy Adams, according to David Hackett Fisher, was the most notable of the young Federalists: "The contrast between

---

*Robert Lowell, one of America's leading twentieth-century poets, was of this line.

John Quincy Adams and the young Federalists in Congress is in many ways sharp and extreme. They were extroverts; he was shy and withdrawn. They were shallow men, bored by appeals to political fundamentals; he meditated and wrote profoundly upon all manner of subjects."[12] Also unlike many of his peers, Adams was consumed by political ambition and suffered miserably from presidential fever. Just as his father had spent a term in the White House during the Jeffersonian era, so John Quincy went there in 1825, when federalism was dying in Massachusetts and the Jacksonian era was dawning in the nation. (No other Harvard man went to the White House until Theodore Roosevelt, and no Massachusetts man until Calvin Coolidge.)

In the history of this Republic, class authority probably reached its peak in Federalist Massachusetts. No wonder it was a great family founding era. Boston federalism was a secularized version of the Puritan ethic and came at a time, as we shall see, when liberal and rational Unitarianism was becoming the Boston religion. Almost all the Essex County Federalists counted one or more Puritan ministers or sea captains among their ancestors. The pulpit and the quarter-deck were the sacred and secular symbols of authority in the family, in society, and in politics. These Federalists of Massachusetts looked upon Jefferson as an atheistic and mutinous first mate and despised his sympathy for the French Revolution: they were francophobes and anglophiles almost to a man. They modeled themselves not only on the Puritan ideal of authority but also on the old Roman ideal of *gravitas*: self-interest, yes; self-indulgence, no. Accordingly, they looked down on the lavish living and the popularity mongering of John Hancock. They *stood*, rather than *ran*, for office; they listened to their own consciences, not to the voice of the people. As one young Federalist, fearing the consequences of his party's rigidity, put it in a letter to Robert Treat Paine in 1810: "Let us have men who can relax their principles of morality as occasion may require and adapt themselves to circumstances."[13] In an important sense, men like George Cabot were collectivists rather than individualists, believing in family and class as organic communities and in society as the family writ large.

In essence, then, the Puritan-Federalist ethic implied what might be called a deference democracy, in the style of Walter Bagehot's view of England. Many writers on our colonial period, especially Robert E. Brown in *Middle-Class Democracy and the Revolution in Massachusetts, 1691–1780*, have found Massachusetts to be the most democratic of the colonies. It was, *politically*. But its vigorous political democracy thrived in a *society* marked by deference and hierarchy; the best people, in wealth and family reputation, were elected to office time after time in town after town for over 200 years. And it was this deference democracy, in striking contrast to the defiant democracy of Pennsylvania, that took the lead in the Revolution. This point should not be hard to understand for, as a matter of fact, from the days of the two Massachusetts Adamses and the great Virginia dynasty from Washington to Monroe, all the way down to Taft, the two Roosevelts, and Woodrow Wilson, one finds deference democracy to have been the rule rather than the exception at the level of presidential leadership in this country. Moreover, Andrew Jackson, who attended the only Latin school in town and at the age of fourteen read the Declaration of Independence to his illiterate fellow townsmen, was indeed a frontier aristocrat by the time he entered the White House. By the time Lincoln went there, he had married an Episcopalian banker's daughter and was one of the leading railroad and corporation lawyers in Illinois. Woodrow Wilson always called himself a Federalist in private, which he surely was at the deepest level of his being (and a Puritan preacher, too).

But there has always been more than a little hypocrisy in our American political traditions. After the decline of federalism, overt elitism was replaced by a more covert variety. Whereas the Puritan Federalists preached what they practiced, and lost, the majority of our greatest statesmen since have been successful in preaching what they practiced (and told themselves they believed in) only when they simply had to in order to get elected or stay in office.* Perhaps Morison best summed up the mind of Boston federalism in the last lines of his *DAB* biography of Josiah Quincy.

> Josiah Quincy was a fine example of a cultured and aristocratic public servant, with the faults and virtues of his class, and a pungency and impetuosity all his own. These individual qualities unsuited him for party politics; but in a position of responsibility and quasi-autocratic power, like the Boston mayorality and the Harvard presidency, he was really great.[14]

The year 1823 is a convenient date to mark the passing away of Massachusetts federalism as a political creed. Governor John Brooks, a staunch Federalist, refused to stand for reelection, and the Jeffersonian Republicans came into power. At the same time, the town of Boston, which had grown by 250 percent between 1790 and 1820 (18,000 to 43,000), became a city in 1822, with John Phillips, Federalist, as the first mayor; he died in 1823, however, and Josiah Quincy, an indefatigable and autocratic reformer, became the first of three in the Quincy line to hold the office.

As we learned only too well in the 1960s, college students are always sensitive to rapid changes in the larger society. Thus, at Harvard, the "great rebellion," in which John Quincy Adams's son was expelled along with many others of his class, took place in that transition year of 1823. That the students were in revolt against the authority of the Federalist establishment is indicated by the following observations from a sympathetic faculty member of the time.

> Our college is under the absolute direction of the Essex Junto, at the head of which stands Chief Justice Parsons, . . . a man as cunning as Lucifer and about half as good. This man is at the head of the Corporation. . . . He is not only the soul of that body, but . . . the evil councillor, the Ahithophel of the high federal party.[15]

Perhaps partly because of the rebellion, Josiah Quincy was chosen president of Harvard in 1829, the year John Quincy Adams was defeated by Andrew Jack-

---

*One of the reasons Henry Cabot Lodge disliked Woodrow Wilson was that Wilson was an anglophile and Burkian conservative throughout his academic career and then did an about-face as governor of New Jersey and presidential candidate.

son. Quincy was one of the great autocratic presidents of Harvard and adhered to his Federalist principles until his death during the Civil War. (The last autocratic Brahmin to be president of Harvard, A. Lawrence Lowell, was likewise cast in the anglophile-Federalist mold.)

Although the Puritan-Federalist ethic died out as an official political creed in the 1820s, the families founded when this ethic was their guiding light contributed to their city, state, and nation for many generations. The golden dome of the most famous state house in America, built by Charles Bulfinch atop Boston's Beacon Hill in 1800, still stands as a symbol of class authority in the city. And when the Irish finally took over city politics in Boston in the last part of the nineteenth century, both governors and United States senators continued to be chosen more or less according to the principles of deference democracy.

The Federalist ethic was the dominant class creed not only of Essex County and Boston; it was also the creed of the "gentry of the interior" or the "mansion people," in town after town across the whole state of Massachusetts. The Strongs of Northhampton were Puritan Federalists of the deepest dye. Farther west, at Stockbridge, Theodore Sedgwick (1746–1813), who followed Caleb Strong to the U.S. Senate, was the political boss of Hampshire County and a staunch Federalist of national repute throughout his life. Like John Lowell and George Cabot of Boston, Sedgwick was a Federalist First Family founder, and the prolific Sedgwicks are to this day *the* first clan in Stockbridge, though they also are at home in literary Boston, where they are thoroughly intermarried with Russells, Cabots, Channings, and Peabodys.

During their city's Silver Age, of course, many members of Philadelphia's merchant, banking, and legal aristocracy were Federalists. But federalism was not, to anywhere near the same extent as in Boston and Massachusetts, *the* upper-class creed in Philadelphia (and certainly not in the rest of the state). The Federalist upper-class was more or less isolated from the rest of society, and the increasingly rare Proper Philadelphians who retained a taste for public office were forced to become Jeffersonians and then Jacksonians as the center of political power in the state moved west after the turn of the century. Thus, Thomas McKean, of Scotch-Irish and Calvinist ancestry, was a leading Federalist in Delaware and in Philadelphia and a strong supporter of the federal Constitution in the Pennsylvania convention of 1787–1790. Cold, proud, and vain, he was personally of very much the same domineering mold as Theodore Sedgwick and Josiah Quincy. After 1792, however, the Federalist foreign policy and McKean's friendship with France and aversion to England, in addition to his itch for public office, forced him into the Republican party, which elected him to the governorship in 1799. He remained a Jeffersonian, if in the definitely conservative wing of the Republican party in the state, for the rest of his life.*

---

*The intricate threads of family continuity in ideas and values are always of interest to those with an organic view of history. Thus, it is noteworthy that two of the descendants of the autocratic Philadelphia Calvinist Thomas McKean, both of the class of 1913 at Harvard, live on the north shore of Boston; one, with the historically revealing name of Quincy Adams Shaw McKean, married Katherine Winthrop, who kept her family name at the top of the heap as a ranking tennis player, along with Sarah Palfrey, before World War II.

As we have seen, the Philadelphia Ingersolls were leaders in the city for many generations. Charles Jared Ingersoll was ambitious for public office, which was surely in accord with his New England and Puritan heritage but unusual for his class in Philadelphia. Although his grandfather Jared had been a famous Connecticut Loyalist, his father a leading Federalist, and he himself a federal man in the beginning, Ingersoll, like Thomas McKean before him (their descendants today are kin), eventually became a staunch francophile and Jeffersonian and then a Jacksonian Democrat. He served in the U.S. Congress between 1813 and 1815 and again from 1841 to 1849.

Ingersoll's sensitivity to the mood of Pennsylvania politics is nicely revealed in a letter to Rufus King in 1805 and in a statement he made while in Congress in 1814. He wrote to King:

> You are building a house, I hear—pray heaven the Jacobins mayn't burn or demolish it. . . . But I believe your property is safe in New York—for your democracy's at least an aristocracy, whereas ours is literally a mobocracy, and I fear nothing will bring us back to level but a theocracy or a convulsion.[16]

In 1814, now a Jeffersonian congressman, he said:

> According to my persuasion, majority bespeaks popularity, and popularity involves right. I have great faith in the instinct of the people. I prefer those instincts to the reasoning faculties of honorable gentlemen. With their impulse to sustain me forward, I proceed with confidence that justice and sound policy are on my side.[17]

Josiah Quincy of course would never have sanctioned Ingersoll's newly acquired values, but then he was president of Harvard in Boston while Ingersoll was serving Jacksonian Pennsylvania in Washington. Perhaps the best indication of the differences between Federalist and Republican (Democratic) values, differences that have echoed throughout our history, appears in Morison's brief description of the reaction of the Harvard board of overseers to the so-called Bread and Butter Rebellion of 1805, when the students walked out in protest against bad food.

> The college authorities, as in 1766, suspended half the College, and demanded unconditional surrender; the students were too spirited to submit. A committee of the Overseers, led by Lieutenant-Governor Levi Lincoln (A.B. 1772), a Republican, reported in favor of reforming commons, and pardoning the offenders. This led to a prolonged debate in the Overseers on strict party lines, the Federalists insisting on upholding authority, and the Republicans on students' rights. The Lincoln report was rejected by the narrow margin of twenty-nine votes to twenty-six.[18]

The Federalist party died out after the first three decades of our Republic. That it did so was perhaps inevitable; that it was a good thing for our nation is a moot point. At any rate, the period witnessed the founding of many of Boston's First Families; in the days of John Adams and John Quincy Adams, George Cabot, John Lowell, and Josiah Quincy, as well as Caleb Strong and

Theodore Sedgwick, class authority and deference democracy were hegemonic values in Massachusetts, as they had been since the colony's founding—and as they continued to be, in culture and education if less so in politics (but far more so than in Pennsylvania), well into the twentieth century. In contrast, class authority and deference democracy were rarely since the beginning, and almost never after 1800, hegemonic values in the colony and commonwealth of Pennsylvania. Finally, the Boston upper class went on to produce great men and build great institutions in the nineteenth century, whereas upper-class Philadelphia's most creative days were surely over.

PART V

THE NATIONAL EXPERIENCE: COMPARATIVE INSTITUTIONS

Wealth: The Fertilizer of Family Trees

God helps them who help themselves.

Benjamin Franklin

The accumulation of wealth is not the loftiest end of human effort.

Charles Francis Adams, Jr.

All social systems are grounded in the division of labor and the production and distribution of wealth. And all advanced civilizations must be involved with distributing the surplus wealth each generation creates. By and large, in middle-class market societies, such as the United States has been throughout most of our history, control of surplus wealth rests with the upper classes. Any upper-class way of life, then, is based on inherited wealth.

In this chapter, I shall discuss four main issues: (1) how and when did the family founders acquire their wealth; (2) how successful have their heirs been in keeping (or enlarging) their inheritances; (3) how does an upper class, in each generation, assimilate new men of wealth and their families into an upper-class style of life; and (4) how do upper-class values serve to motivate men of privilege to contribute to the enrichment of the cultural and political life of the society as a whole? The fourth, and surely the most important point, will be analyzed in more detail in the following five chapters, which compare the roles of Boston Brahmins and Philadelphia Gentlemen in building educational institutions (Chapter 14); in literature and the life of the mind (Chapter 15); in art and architecture (Chapter 16); in law, medicine, and the church (Chapter 17); and last, but perhaps of greatest importance, in government (Chapter 18).

Egalitarian and individualistic societies of great social and economic mobility tend to be hundred-yard-dash cultures; hierarchical and communal cultures are more likely to emulate the style of the long-distance runner. Similarly, democracies foster the making of fabulous fortunes; aristocracies, the preservation of more modest ones. As we have seen in the case of family continuity of leadership, Bostonians tend to be long-distance runners whereas hundred-yard-dash cut-flowers are more characteristic of Philadelphia. And so it has been with wealth and the preservation thereof. Perhaps there is no better way of introducing this point than to take a look at what happened to the small legacies left by Benjamin Franklin to both of his beloved cities.

In a codicil to his will, written in 1789 and put into effect in 1791, the year following his death, Franklin bequeathed £1,000, or $4,444, each to the citizenries of the town of Boston and the city of Philadelphia. The money was "to be let out upon interest at 5 per cent per annum to young married artificers, under the age of 25."[1] Fascinated by the uses of money, Franklin carefully estimated that at the end of 100 years, the value of these two legacies would amount to £131,000 (about $582,000) each and £4,061,000, or about $18 million, by the time of their final liquidation in 1991.

The story of how this money was used in the two cities is too long and complicated to tell here.[2] It is perhaps enough to say that as of July 1891, at the end of the first century, the Franklin Fund endowment in Philadelphia amounted to about $90,000, less than one-fourth of the Boston fund of $391,000. As of 1962, Philadelphia's fund totaled $315,000, or less than one-fifth of Boston's total of $1,750,000. In that year the trustees of Boston's fund decided to begin helping medical students. The first loans were made to interns and medical students, at interest rates of 2 percent during their training and of 5 percent during the repayment period. By 1972, some $2.5 million had been lent to 1,300 student and intern borrowers. In contrast to the still independent Franklin Foundation in Boston, the Philadelphia fund is now merged into the investment portfolio of the Board of City Trusts, which manages some 100 other public bequests including the enormous Girard estate. I do not know exactly how this money is being used, but I imagine that it is increasing in value just as slowly as in the past.

It is no wonder that the trustees of the Franklin Foundation in Boston have done so much better a job in augmenting and using this endowment than their peers in Philadelphia; for, although trust funds lie at the core of family continuity at the top in both cities, Boston trustees in the George Apley mold have long been nationally famous managers of other people's money. "Through its interpretation of their so-called 'spendthrift' trusts," wrote Cleveland Amory, "Boston's First Family fortunes have long been tied up beyond the reach of any power save possibly, as one financial writer put it, the Communist International."[3]

Today, though hundred-yard-dash speculators flock to Wall Street, the long-distance runners entrust their fortunes to the money managers of Boston. "Handling other people's money," wrote the Boston Globe's man on Wall Street, Robert Lenzner, in 1972, is a major industry in Boston. More than $81 billion of other people's money is managed by Boston financiers. Consider: Boston is the birthplace of the mutual fund, the tool of people's capitalism. Approximately 35 percent of the mutual fund industry's $58 billion is harbored here. More college endowment money is handled here than in any other city: The budgets of Harvard, Yale, MIT, Brown and many others rely on the expertise of a handful of money men in this city. Law firms and private trustees alone manage an estimated $4 billion in wealth.[4]

A. Lawrence Lowell once expressed concern that nobody in his family was still engaged in moneymaking. He need not have. For, according to Lenzner, scions of the "early Colonial families" are now doing well as money managers: "Names like Paul Cabot, Richard Saltonstall, George Putnam, John P. Chase, Augustus Loring, John Lowell, and Nick Thorndike still grace the chief executive offices of the city's leading financial institutions." Boston's values have nowhere been better expressed than when a member of the firm of Thorndike, Doran, Paine & Lewis, the counseling arm of Wellington Management Company, told the *Globe*: "Divorced from Wall Street and the herd, we are thought to have an independent point of view. People think 'here's a group that can sit back and reflect.' "[5]

Moneymaking and civic responsibility still mark the breed. Thus, John Lowell (Harvard, class of 1942) for more than a quarter century has worked for the Boston Safe Deposit and Trust Company, of which his father was once chairman. In 1972, John Lowell was trustee or director of forty-one institutions (including the Franklin Foundation) all over the land. The breadth and diversity of his financial, religious, cultural, and educational responsibilities are indicated in the *Directory of Directors in the City of Boston and Vicinity, 66th Edition*.

LOWELL, JOHN, One Boston Place, Director, Boston Safe Deposit and Trust Company.
Bailey and Rhodes, Los Angeles, Director
Bangor Theological Seminary, Trustee
Boston College, Director and Member of Executive Committee
Boston Episcopal Society, Trustee
Boston Hospital for Women, Trustee and Member of Executive Committee
Committee for the Central Business District, Inc., Treasurer
Consolidated Investment Trust, Trustee and Member of Executive Committee
Franklin Foundation, Vice-President
Franklin Institute of Boston, Trustee
Greater Boston Charitable Trust, Board of Managers
International Grenfel Association, Director and Assistant Treasurer
Johnson Securities Company, Director
Johnston & Co. (Douglas T.), Inc., Director
Massachusetts Capital Development Fund, Inc., Director
Massachusetts Company, Director
Massachusetts General Life Insurance Company, Director and Member of Finance Committee
Massachusetts Income Development Fund, Inc., Director
Massachusetts Investors Growth Fund, Director
Massachusetts Investors Trust, Trustee
Museum of Science, Member of the Corporation
Nahant (Town of), Moderator

New England Committee for Project Hope, Chairman
New England Grenfel Association, Director and Treasurer
Noble and Greenough School, Trustee
Northeastern University, Trustee
Perkins School for the Blind, Trustee
Pierce Company, Inc., Director
Provident Institution for Savings in the Town of Boston, Trustee and Member of
   Board of Investment
South End Community Development, Inc., Vice-President
Douglas A. Thom Clinic, Member of the Corporation
Thompson Academy, Member of Advisory Board
Trustees of Donations to the Protestant Episcopal Church, Trustee
Trustees of the Sears and Other Funds, Treasurer
United Community Services, Member of the Corporation
United South End Settlements, Member of the Corporation
WGBH Educational Foundation, Treasurer
Wheelock College, Chairman of Board of Trustees
World Affairs Council, Director
Yale–New Haven Educational Corporation, Director

As might be expected, no contemporary Philadelphians, regardless of class background, possess John Lowell's energy and sense of duty toward the community.

Further insight into the contrasting money mores of Boston and Philadelphia is supplied by articles on local millionaires published in *Philadelphia* magazine and in its Boston counterpart called *Boston*. Measuring someone's wealth is a tricky business at best, but *Philadelphia* listed the ten richest Philadelphians in descending order as follows:

John T. Dorrance, Jr.	Chairman, Campbell Soup
John C. Haas	Vice-President, Rohm & Haas
F. Otto Haas	Chairman, Rohm & Haas
Walter Annenberg	Publisher; former U.S. ambassador to Great Britain
Henry S. McNeil	Built McNeil Laboratories; now largest single stockholder in Johnson & Johnson, outside Johnson Foundation
Fitz Eugene Dixon, Jr.	Sportsman heir of P. A. B. Widener and William L. Elkins, traction magnates
John F. Connelly	Runs Crown Cork & Seal and Connelly Containers
Lessing Rosenwald	Sears Roebuck heir, retired
Walter C. Pew	Sun Oil
Ella Widener Wetherill	Sportswoman and socialite[6]

The *Boston* article listed nine millionaires, in most cases making no estimate of their total fortunes or listing them in any order of wealth.

Edward Kennedy	U.S. senator
Sidney Rabb	Builder of Stop & Shop chain
Edwin Land	Founder of Polaroid

Maurice Gordon	Real estate
Serge Semenke	Banker and money man
Charles Francis Adams	Raytheon Company
Louis W. Cabot	Cabot Corporation
George Peabody Gardner, Jr.	Paine, Webber, Jackson & Curtis
Kenneth H. Olson	Founder, Digital Equipment Corporation[7]

There were very interesting differences between the two groups.

First, the Philadelphians were richer: whereas Dorrance, the two Haas brothers, Annenberg, and McNeil each had personal fortunes of over $200 million, only one Bostonian, Edwin Land, likely reached this level. (Of course, the Dorrance, Rosenwald, and Pew families are among the richest in the land.)

Second, the Philadelphia group included far more persons of inherited wealth (nine out of ten) than did the Boston list (five out of nine). John F. Connelly was the only genuinely self-made man in the Philadelphia group; he was born in a poor but proud Irish neighborhood and had to drop out of school in the eighth grade in order to support his widowed mother. Henry S. McNeil inherited the family pharmaceutical business but built his large fortune mainly himself. Similarly, Walter Annenberg inherited a fortune from his rather notorious father, but multiplied it many times over through his own enterprising ability. Of the Boston group, Maurice Gordon seems to have been the only entirely self-made man. Serge Semenke's parents were refugees from the Russian Revolution but were able to provide him with a college education; yet, he was largely a self-made banker as far as Boston was concerned. Land and Olson built their own extremely successful companies, though both were of educated backgrounds. Although he inherited a successful family business, Sidney Rabb built Stop & Shop and his own great fortune himself. Charles Francis Adams, whose family had been more engaged in making history than in making money, nevertheless inherited a small fortune; still, he largely built his own while for the most part living on his salary from Raytheon.

Third, the Bostonians were a better educated group than the Philadelphians. Of the ten Philadelphians, only five graduated from college—Dorrance from Princeton, the Haas brothers from Amherst, Pew from MIT, and McNeil from Yale; although Land left Harvard after his freshman year to pursue his own intellectual interests, six of the Bostonians graduated from Harvard and one from MIT. None of the Philadelphians graduated from the University of Pennsylvania; although Annenberg went to the Wharton School of Finance and Commerce he did not take a degree.

Finally, the tone of Philadelphia and Boston is suggested by comparing the richest men from both cities. John T. Dorrance, Jr. inherited a great fortune from his father (some $20,000 a month at the age of eleven). Edwin Land built his own fortune.

This rundown suggests that Boston is a far more enterprising city than Philadelphia; it is also a city in which inherited wealth lasts longer. Thus, none of the heirs in the Philadelphia group came from the sample of fifty First Families. Dorrance, the Haas brother, Annenberg, Rosenwald, and McNeil were all men of second generation wealth. Walter C. Pew was the grandson of his family founder, Joseph Newton Pew. Fitz Eugene Dixon, Jr., was the grandson of two of Philadelphia's most fabulous traction kings at the turn of the century, P. A. B. Widener and William Lukens Elkins. Ella Widener Wetherill, the youngest of the Philadelphia group and probably the wealthiest woman in the city, was a great-granddaughter of P. A. B. Widener.

The men of inherited wealth in Boston were a very different breed from their Philadelphia peers. The Kennedys were Boston's first Irish Brahmins and are the most famous First Family in America today. It is significant that Senator Kennedy was the only multimillionaire in the two samples to attain national elective office, although Walter Annenberg, like the senator's father, was ambassador to the Court of St. James. Of most significance here, however, is the fact that three Boston men—a third of the sample—were from families of eight or nine generations of wealth and civic pride. The Adamses are, of course, America's all-time First Family. Money came into the family initially when Charles Francis Adams I married the daughter of one of the last merchant princes, Peter Chardon Brooks. The Cabots, Proper Boston's biggest clan, have been better known for marrying and making money than for producing statesmen or intellectuals: they began their way to real wealth in 1812, when Samuel Cabot married the daughter of Boston's greatest merchant prince, Thomas Handasyd Perkins. Yet Louis W. Cabot, chairman of the Cabot Corporation, founded by his grandfather Godfrey Lowell Cabot, had a brilliant record at Harvard, magna cum laude at the college and cum laude at the business school. Peabodys and Gardners have intermarried down through the years. The inherited wealth of George Peabody Gardner, Jr., president and director of Paine, Webber, Jackson & Curtis, derives from an ancestor, Lowell Gardner, one of the last East Indian merchants, who left some $5 million when he died in 1884. (The family also invested in the Calumet and Hecla mines which we shall discuss below.)

To repeat, if upper-class Philadelphia is richer (there is no exact way of knowing) than upper-class Boston, there is more continuity in family fortunes in the latter city. Even more important, the wealth of upper-class Philadelphia has been augmented in every generation by new men who single-mindedly built up huge fortunes but rarely produced descendants of distinction. In Boston, however, new men of wealth have been more likely to produce families of accomplishment, such as Cabots, Lowells, Peabodys, Phillipses, Lawrences, and Forbeses. An understanding of upper-class wealth in Philadelphia, then, must include such men as I have listed in Table A–15.* Although these individuals made far larger fortunes than all but a few of the money-makers in the Philadelphia First Families sample, they were largely auslanders and cut-flowers. Of the thirty men listed, for instance, only six—William Bingham, E. T. Stotesbury, Peter A. B. Widener, E. J. Berwind, Charles Lennig, and Joseph Harrison, Jr.— were native Philadelphians; only David Jayne and Widener had descendants with those surnames in the *DAB*. Although fifteen surnames—Clark, Elkins,

---

*All tables cited in this chapter are presented in Appendix I.

Widener, Wood, Rosengarten, Lennig, Scott, Wanamaker, Cassatt, Converse, Baird, Berwind, Dolan, and Pew—are prominent in contemporary *Social Registers* in the city, only Enoch W. Clark and Edward Bok had heirs of contemporary distinction: Joseph Sill Clark, reforming mayor and U.S. senator after World War II, and Derek Bok, present president of Harvard.

FIRST FAMILY MONEY-MAKERS IN BOSTON AND PHILADELPHIA

The men in the First Families samples who were primarily money-makers are listed in Table A-16. Note that a higher proportion of the Philadelphia sample was engaged in moneymaking (40 of 146, or 27 percent of the Philadelphians, as against 31 of 187, or 17 percent of the Bostonians). The thirty-one Boston money-makers, moreover, formed a much more cohesive group than the forty Philadelphians. They came from only sixteen families, all but one—the Ameses of North Easton, who have always stood somewhat apart—interrelated through business and marriage. The histories of their fortunes (in shipping, in textiles and a few other manufacturing enterprises, in banking and land speculation, and in railroads) thus reveal a clear-cut pattern of continuous economic growth. The Philadelphia group of money-makers was larger and far less coherent: the forty Philadelphians came from twenty-five families, or exactly half of the Philadelphia First Families sample. Except in the early years, moreover, when Shippens, Norrises, Pembertons, Biddles, and Cadwaladers typically intermarried, there was less endogamy (especially cousin marriages) than in Boston, at least among the families that produced *DAB* subjects.

This finding leads to another vital difference between the samples: the *DAB* biographies of the Bostonians, by and large, were complete and to the point; those of the Philadelphians, especially the money-makers, were far less complete and often obscure on important points. Most of the very brief biographies of the seventeenth- and eighteenth-century Quaker merchants, for example, said no more about the subject's business career than that he was a "prosperous merchant" before going on to tell of his religious interests in, or disaffection from, the Society of Friends and of the offices he may have held in local government. The biography of Francis Rawle (some 600 words) is typical: it tells us that Rawle and his father were imprisoned in the notorious Exeter jail in Devonshire (where, as we have seen, Fox and Naylor spent some time); that they came to Pennsylvania after receiving a grant of 2,500 acres from Penn; that Rawle was a leader in the antiproprietary party and held a few minor offices in the city's government; and that he was a merchant (but nothing is said about where, how, or with whom he traded). In the biography, the phrases "it is said" and "it is believed to be" are each used once, and "probably" is used several times. Thus, at the end of the biography, its author writes, "Rawle is said to have been the first person in America to write on political economy." He then lists only two pamphlets, one entitled "Ways and Means for the Inhabitants of the Delaware to Become Rich" (1725).[8] Perhaps there were no records available to Rawle's *DAB* biographer—a lack, as we noted earlier, quite in contrast to Massachusetts's wealth of genealogical and historical material.

Moreover, there is very little secondary literature available on Philadelphia merchants in the style, say, of Samuel Eliot Morison's *Maritime History of Massachusetts* or Bernard Bailyn's *New England Merchants in the Seventeenth Century*. The exception for Philadelphia is Frederick B. Tolles's very fine *Meeting House and Counting House: The Quaker Merchants of Colonial Philadelphia, 1682–1763*. But Tolles's book is a group portrait and he had very little to say in detail about any one merchant in our sample.

At any rate, there *are* very clear, if sometimes suble, differences between the organic and familial moneymaking patterns of the Boston sample and the more atomistic patterns of Philadelphia. Let us now turn to the record to uncover these contrasts.

MERCHANT CAPITALISTS

As we have seen, the founders of Massachusetts Bay Colony were men of means who stuck to their callings as ministers and magistrates, even though some of them surely augmented their incomes through trade and land speculation. Philadelphia, however, was dominated from the very beginning by a merchant oligarchy composed of men who sat quietly in their meetings and only occasionally took part in government in an avocational, rather than professional, way. The Shippens, Norrises, and Pembertons were merchants first and magistrates second—by necessity; John Winthrop was almost always thought of as the governor, as he referred to himself in his journal.

Always in debt and hounded by creditors in the years after he founded Pennsylvania, William Penn was naturally preoccupied with the returns on his investments there. He attracted "Men of Universal Spirits, that have an eye to the Good of Prosperity" to lead his colony and advertised all over Europe for people of "Laborious Handicrafts" to do the dirty work and develop the rich farmlands of Bucks, Chester, and Lancaster counties.

> It is no mere coincidence that Franklin, whom modern sociologists have regarded as the arch-exemplar of the capitalist spirit, received his early business training and developed his economic philosophy in Quaker Philadelphia. The pattern of Franklin's life in Philadelphia—his rise from journeyman printer to wealthy and respected bourgeois—was a familiar one in the Quaker town, where from its founding people of "Laborious Handicrafts" had been rising by dint of industry and thrift into the ranks of the respectable and the well-to-do. Franklin was the model of those "Men of Universal Spirits" whom Penn considered indispensable to colonial society, but it should be remembered that Franklin was preceded and surrounded by a group of Quaker merchants who had risen by the same route and who lacked only Franklin's brilliant versatility and talent for self-advertisement.[9]

That Philadelphia was dominated from the outset by a merchant oligarchy whereas the Boston theocracy was dominated by magistrates and ministers is clearly suggested in Table A–16: thus, although Boston is the older city, no money-makers there, but five from Philadelphia, were born in the seventeenth century; moreover, twenty-one of the Philadelphians, as against only two Bostonians, were born before 1750. This is not to say that the Boston clans did not have many merchants at the roots of their family trees,* but they were less important than the professional men who graced their family founding days. Thus, the Lowells were leaders in Newburyport for several generations before their first real money-maker, Francis Cabot Lowell, was born (1775); his father, Judge John Lowell, moreover, also was included in the *DAB*, as was his half brother John, a lawyer and a Federalist publicist who made money, too.

In Philadelphia, a mercantile and bourgeois city from its founding days, the twenty-one money-makers who were born before 1750 (and consequently played their roles in the city from its founding through its Golden and Silver ages in the second half of the century) were all merchants save Anthony Morris, brewer, Caspar Wistar, glass manufacturer, and Samuel Wetherill, manufacturing chemist; all but Abraham Markoe and Richard Bache, who attended Anglican Christ Church soon after coming to the city, and George Meade, a staunch Catholic, were Quakers.

Unlike the great merchants of Salem and Boston, who sailed the seven seas, these Quaker merchants of Philadelphia confined themselves largely to the Atlantic triangular trade, sailing their cargoes to the West Indies, to Lisbon and London or Bristol, and back to Philadelphia. They were following the routes of the traveling ministry of Friends who founded Quaker colonies all along the western rim of the Atlantic in the first, heroic generation. Although these men did not found conspicuously large fortunes, they were extemely successful progenitors of First Families in the city: seventeen of them from eleven Quaker families—Biddle, Cadwalader, Mifflin, Morris, Norris, Pemberton, Rawle, Shippen, Wetherill, Wharton, and Wistar—had descendants listed in the 1940 *Social Register*.

Something should be said here about the Cadwaladers and the Biddles, the city's two most prominent Quaker-turned-Episcopal families, especially as neither family, with the exception of the banker Nicholas Biddle, had members prominent enough to be treated in the chapters that follow. The Cadwaladers were the more representative of Proper Philadelphia in that they seem to have combined little distinguished accomplishment and national obscurity with great local social prestige. The Biddles, in contrast, have stood somewhat apart in the city because of their bent for accomplishment and flair for publicity, which have brought them a certain degree of national prestige. Nathaniel Burt, who had to admit reluctantly that they were actually the city's First Family, said: "It is probably just this very distinction, mild as it is by comparison with

---

*The lack of Boston First Family money-makers reflects to some degree the Loyalist emigration of such prominent merchant families as the Hutchinsons.

the first families of other places, that tells against the Biddles in Philadelphia itself. . . . From a true Philadelphia point of view, it is perhaps not really good form for the Biddles to have been as greatly distinguished as they have been."[10]

Three members of these two families, almost exact contemporaries, were eighteenth-century merchants listed in the *DAB*: Clement Biddle (1740–1814), John Cadwalader (1742–1786), and Lambert Cadwalader (1743–1823). The first Cadwalader, John, came to Philadelphia's Welsh barony (modern-day Main Line) from Pembroke in Wales. John and Lambert Cadwalader were the sons of Dr. Thomas Cadwalader, a civic leader in Franklin's Philadelphia. Their mother was an heiress, so they got off to a good start in life. They themselves seem to have been successful merchants, trading under the firm of John & Lambert Cadwalader. What fame the brothers attained rested on their both raising and training aristocratic companies that fought in the Revolution. John appears to have been the more distinguished of the two brothers (Lambert's *DAB* biography of thirty-seven lines was the shortest in the sample). Captain of the so-called Silk-Stocking Company, John was made a brigadier general in the Pennsylvania militia in 1777. He was a strong supporter of his friend George Washington, whom he resembled in dignity and bearing, in the famous Conway cabal, but in the Philadelphia "declining tradition," he twice refused Washington's offer of a permanent commission in the regular army.

General John's son Thomas was the agent for the Penn family's vast American estates. He married Clement Biddle's daughter, Mary, and their two sons, John and George, were the foremost nineteenth-century Cadwaladers. His accomplishments make Judge John Cadwalader the most distinguished of the family line (107 lines in the *DAB*). His brother, George, however, was a dashing fellow who "made and spent fortunes, his house was the grandest in town, his carriages the most elegant, his trotter Ned Forrest the fastest in the world."[11] He was a leader in the First City Troop, a general in the Mexican War, and the first head of the Philadelphia Club (organized in 1834). Yet Sidney Fisher had little use for him. After dining with George Cadwalader on March 13, 1857, Fisher wrote in his diary: "He is a fine animal, with great energy & a practical ability which have made him successful in all his pursuits of sportsman, man of pleasure, soldier & man of business. He is immensely rich. He is also coarse, ignorant & profligate, keeping a mistress now openly at his place in Maryland."[12]

The Biddles are unquestionably the most famous Philadelphia family: when Edward VIII was Prince of Wales, he is said to have remarked after a visit to Philadelphia, "I met a very large and interesting family named Scrapple, and discovered a rather delicious native food they call biddle."[13]

William Biddle, the first of his family in America, was a Quaker shoemaker who served several terms in English jails as a testimony to his faith in the Inner Light. In 1681, he settled in New Jersey, across the Delaware from Philadelphia, where Biddles still reside today (some still Quakers). Two restless grandsons, William III and John, established their families in Philadelphia in the 1730s. John—the founder of a line of "solid Biddles"—prospered in a modest way as an importer; William III—progenitor of the "romantic Biddles"—was an inveterate plunger and went bankrupt, leaving a well-connected wife and nine children when he died.

It was in the revolutionary generation that the Biddles "did well," as the Quakers put it. John had two sons, both officers in the Revolutionary War: Owen, watchmaker, astronomer, and member of the American Philosophical Society, came back into the Society of Friends after the war and was one of the main founders of the Westtown School; Clement, the first of the line in the *DAB*, was Washington's aide-de-camp and close personal friend. Clement did well in his father's shipping and importing firm. When his first wife died soon after their marriage, he wed a Rhode Island Quakeress, Rebekah Cornell, whose father was lieutenant governor and chief justice of that state. They had thirteen children, eight of whom lived to maturity. Two of his sons, Thomas and Clement, Jr., were locally prominent bankers. Clement's nine married children all had large families and thus established the so-called solid Biddle line, involving themselves in law and finance, belonging to the Philadelphia Club, being managers of the Assembly balls, and marrying everybody worth marrying. Algernon of this line (the seventh generation in America) married the great-granddaughter of John Randolph of Virginia, first U.S. attorney general, and produced four sons who graduated from Groton and Harvard in Franklin Roosevelt's generation. Two of them, Francis and George, were the most distinguished twentieth-century Biddles. Francis, like his Randolph ancestor, was U.S. attorney general, under Roosevelt, as well as a judge at the Nuremberg trials; George, a painter and writer, proposed the WPA art project to his Groton friend Roosevelt and helped supervise its development and direction. Both Francis and George eventually exiled themselves from their native city, following careers in Washington and New York. Their two brothers, of less distinction, remained in Philadelphia: Moncure was an investment banker and bibliophile; Sidney was a psychiatrist—a rather shocking (and "Jewish") profession to most of his generation of Proper Philadelphians.

The so-called romantic Biddles descended from William III, who went bankrupt. His son Nicholas, armed with letters of introduction from Thomas Willing, went to England, where he joined the British navy as a midshipman in 1772. The next year, he accompanied a naval expedition to the North Pole that was organized by the Royal Geographical Society. He and his friend Horatio Nelson had taken cuts in rank to participate in this great adventure. After the voyage, Nicholas Biddle returned to America and was eventually put in command of the brig *Andrea Doria*, part of the naval force of the united colonies. This strikingly handsome and romantic hero died unmarried at the age of twenty-seven, when his ship, the *Randolph*, was blown up in a sea battle in 1778.

Nicholas Biddle's brother Charles was also a naval officer; though he was shipwrecked several times and spent part of the war as a British prisoner, he survived to produce seven sons, two of whom were included in the *DAB*. James Biddle (1783–1848), a naval officer, was imprisoned as a young man in the expeditions against Tripoli; he had several commands during the War of 1812 and was sent up the Columbia River to take possession of the Oregon Territory in 1817; his final accomplishment, in 1846, was to negotiate the first treaty between the United States and China. James's most famous brother, the banker Nicholas, is discussed subsequently.

The first moneymakers in the Boston sample were John Phillips (1719–1795) and his two nephews, William (1750–1825) and Samuel Phillips (1752–1802). John made his fortune in real estate speculation and moneylending at high interest. Samuel made a fortune manufacturing gunpowder and supplying the Revolutionary Army; he also served on the bench and in government but is best remembered as the founder of the first endowed academy in New England, the Phillips Academy, at Andover. Samuel was a friend of George Washington, who visited him at Andover in 1789 and who sent one nephew and eight grand-nephews to Phillips Academy. Soon after the founding of Andover Academy, Samuel's uncle John founded a similar school at Exeter, New Hampshire. And thus began a Boston tradition that combined moneymaking with public service and educational philanthropy. William Phillips, nephew of John and cousin of Samuel, was one of the leading philanthropists and the leading commercial banker in his generation in Boston. A staunch Federalist, he was also elected, along with Governor Strong, for eleven successive terms as lieutenant governor of the state. His political career came to an end in 1823, after a term in the Massachusetts Senate. William Phillips was president of the board at Andover Academy, the sixth in his family to hold this position, and contributed liberally to the school all his life. When he died, he left money to both the Andover Academy and the Andover Theological Seminary, in addition to several other institutions largely having to do with the church.

Perhaps the most romantic family fortunes in Boston were made by men who built ships and sent them out to sea, as Morison showed us in his beautiful book on *The Maritime History of Massachusetts*: "The American Revolution in eastern Massachusetts was financed and in part led by wealthy merchants like John Hancock, Josiah Quincy, James Bowdoin, Richard Derby, and Elbridge Gerry."[14] And it was men like these, many of whom came to Boston from Salem, whose wealth watered the First Family trees.

Salem, in 1790 the sixth largest town in the United States and the first in per capita wealth, was Boston's greatest rival in the contest for Oriental wealth. It was also the most Puritan city in Federalist New England. Stephen Higginson was of the sixth generation of his family in Salem. The first two generations were Cambridge graduates and clergymen harried out of England by Bishop Laud's reactionary reforms. The next four generations produced sea captains and merchants. Stephen, whose father had married a Cabot, was a very successful merchant and a staunch Federalist, like his cousin and friend George Cabot (the so-called Federalist sage of Boston); he also was a member of the Continental Congress and took an active part in the military expedition to put down Shays' Rebellion in Hampshire County.

Whereas Boston dominated the Oriental trade that sailed west around the Horn, up along the northwest coast, thence to Canton, and back to Boston,

Salem merchants usually sailed east, around the Cape of Good Hope, to various ports in the East Indies. The Derby wharf, stretching out into Salem harbor from the foot of Derby Street, was the center of the seafaring life in the town. Elias Hasket Derby ("King Derby," as he was called) was the town's leading East India merchant of his day. He left $1.5 million to his son when he died in 1799.*

The ethics of the quarterdeck were, as we have noted, important in molding the New England character. "The sea was no wet-nurse to democracy," wrote Morison. "Authority and privilege are her twin foster-children. Instant and unquestioning obedience to the master is the rule of the sea; and your typical sea-captain would make it the rule of the land if he could."[15] And the social structure of Elias Derby's Salem did pretty much mirror the authoritarian mores of the sea. But the men who manned the ships of Salem were no seagoing proletariat; there was endless opportunity to rise from the deck to command and even ownership. A small Salem brigantine, for instance, once sailed with thirteen men aboard, all of whom eventually became masters of their own vessels. Indeed, many a Boston First Family fortune began with young men who first went to sea on Elias Derby's ships. One of the more famous was the *Astrea*, which set sail for China in 1789, carrying young Thomas Handasyd Perkins, who was to become Boston's foremost merchant prince.

Thomas Handasyd Perkins's contemporary and friend Peter Chardon Brooks, son of the Reverend Edward Brooks (Harvard, class of 1757), set himself up as an insurance broker in the Bunch of Grapes Tavern soon after his father's death in 1781 which left the family almost destitute. By underwriting vessels and making judicious investments in the East Indian trade, Brooks was so successful that he retired in 1803, at the age of thirty-six, with a comfortable fortune. He was perhaps helped on his way to wealth by his marriage to the daughter of wealthy Nathaniel Gorham, one of the four Massachuetts delegates to the Constitutional Convention in Philadelphia. Brooks, who had thirteen children with Nancy Gorham, put his wealth to good use in various philanthropies and in promoting the political ambitions of two sons-in-law, Edward Everett and Charles Francis Adams.†

Joseph Peabody of Salem founded one of America's greatest families. A successful privateer during the Revolution, Peabody was the town's leading merchant in the 1830s. And he and his fellow Salem merchants often banked their money with his cousin George Peabody, an Essex County lad who made a fortune in Baltimore before setting up his famous banking house in London. A bachelor, George Peabody left most of his wealth—more than $8 million—to museums and other institutions that now bear his name; his partner and suc-

---

*Although the Derbys were not included in the First Families sample, a Hasket Derby was listed in the 1940 Boston *Social Register*.

†Nancy Gorham's sister married John Phillips and was the grandmother of the Reverend Phillips Brooks. Peter Chardon Brooks's brother, Cotton Brown Brooks, was the great preacher's other grandfather.

cessor in London, Junius Spencer Morgan, left a son, J. P. Morgan, who was, among other things, a member of the first board of trustees at Endicott Peabody's school at Groton.

When Joseph Peabody died in 1844, Salem's great days were over. Two years previously, Nathaniel Hawthorne had married Sophia Peabody and in 1851 published *The House of Seven Gables*, which nicely reflects Salem's decline into shabby gentility.

TEXTILE MANUFACTURING

In both England and this country, the textile industry was closely associated with the industrial revolution. But whereas Brahmin Boston was intimately involved in the rise of the textile industry in New England, Proper Philadelphia, with the exception of Tench Cove, seems to have played no major role in textile manufacturing, even though our foremost contemporary business historian, Thomas Cochran, noted that by 1900 "Pennsylvania would become the leading textile state."[16] Leadership in the Philadelphia textile industry, then, came largely from new men, often auslanders and cut-flowers, who were not First Family progenitors.

Soon after moving to Boston in 1816, Daniel Webster became the champion of the local shipping interests. He was first elected to Congress as a Federalist advocate of free trade, but he soon developed close associations with the Lawrences, Lowells, and other mill owners. By the time Webster was elected to the Senate in 1827, he was an aggressive champion of protectionism, and the leading Whig in Massachusetts.

Within the Boston sample of fifty families, Henry Lee (1782–1867), a contemporary of Daniel Webster, had been an articulate and thoughtful champion of federalism and free trade, as well as a leading East India merchant. A year after Webster was sent to the Senate, Lee lost his congressional seat from Boston to Nathan Appleton, a family founder who built a fortune in textiles. This marked the end of federalism and the rise of the manufacturing Whigs to power in the 1830s.

Such pioneers in the Boston area textile industry, as Francis Cabot Lowell, Patrick Tracy Jackson, Charles S. Storrow, and the Appleton and Lawrence brothers made major contributions to Brahmin Boston's wealth and later accomplishments in the arts and the professions.

The Lowells first became really rich in textiles. Francis Cabot Lowell graduated from Harvard in 1793 and became a successful merchant in partnership with his uncle William Cabot. Though he resigned in 1810, when ill health required him to take a rest abroad, he used the occasion to make a close study of textile machinery in Lancashire. Upon Lowell's return to America in 1812, he interested his brother-in-law Patrick Tracy Jackson, who had accumulated some money in the East India trade, in building a mill on the Charles River at

Waltham. Lowell, with the aid of a mechanical genius named Paul Moody, was the brains behind the Boston Manufacturing Company at Waltham, believed to be the first mill in the world to combine all the operations of converting raw cotton into finished cloth. Only a few years after the mill's founding, Lowell died, at the age of forty-two. His money went into the founding of Proper Boston's famous Lowell Institute, which has supported adult education down through the years and was one of the original sponsors of Boston's educational television station, WGBH.

Patrick Tracy Jackson carried on after his partner's death and founded the Merrimac Manufacturing Company in what is now the city of Lowell. Thus, the Manchester of America came into being. Jackson soon found that canal and turnpike transportation was becoming inadequate and he directed the building of the Boston & Lowell Railroad. The technical know-how for this venture was supplied by a young engineer named Charles Storer Storrow, who graduated first in his class from Harvard and then took a degree in Paris at the Ecole Nationale des Ponts et Chaussées.

Charles Storrow was descended from a British prisoner-of-war, Captain Thomas Storrow, who married into Boston Society in 1777. His mother married an Appleton and Storrow consolidated his social position by marrying into the Jackson family; his wife, Lydia Cabot Jackson, was Patrick Tracy Jackson's niece.

William, Amos, and Abbott Lawrence came from one of the leading farming families in Groton, Massachusetts. Their father, Samuel, fought at Bunker Hill, rising to the rank of major during the war, and then settled down in Groton as a farmer for the rest of his life.* The brothers moved to Boston and made money in the importing business. They soon became associated with the Lowell mills, also acting as their sales agents. Eventually, in 1845, Abbott Lawrence took the lead in founding the city of Lawrence, where the family textile mills soon began to rival those at Lowell, which had been built much earlier. Charles Storrow helped the Lawrences in building both their mills and their town, becoming the first mayor when Lawrence, Massachusetts, was incorporated as a city in 1853.

The Lawrences were benefactors of many Massachusetts institutions, including the Lawrence Scientific School at Harvard. Amos Abbott Lawrence, Amos Lawrence's son, led Proper Boston's best back into the Anglican communion after the Civil War. His son William became a bishop, founder of a dynasty of bishops, and a veritable Boston institution.

Nathan Appleton and his brother, Samuel, moved to Boston from their native New Hampshire and became very successful shopkeepers. In 1813 they invested $5,000 in the new Lowell mill at Waltham; two years later their firm became sales agents for the Lowells. They both made fortunes and built themselves mansions on Beacon Street. Nathan had five children: one son, Thomas

---

*The Lawrences were always strong supporters of Groton Academy (which became Lawrence Academy in 1846, after being handsomely endowed by William and Amos.)

Gold Appleton, was an occasional essayist, member of the Saturday Club, and one of the best talkers and dinner companions in Boston Society. A grandson was also listed in the *DAB*, presumably for his work as founder and supporter of the Society for the Preservation of New England Antiquities. Nathan's wealth, through his daughter, helped one of America's most popular poets, Henry Wadsworth Longfellow, live in the grand style on Brattle Street in Cambridge. Samuel Appleton, who was childless, left a large fortune to the American Academy of Arts and Sciences, the Boston Athenaeum, the Massachusetts Historical Society, and Dartmouth, Amherst, and Harvard.

Whereas Francis Cabot Lowell and Patrick Tracy Jackson did not establish their first mill until after the War of 1812, as early as 1775 Tench Coxe, nationalist, economist, publicist, and friend of Alexander Hamilton, was busily engaged in promoting cotton manufacturing in Philadelphia. Under his leadership, the United Company of Philadelphia for Promoting Manufactures was founded in that year, with Dr. Benjamin Rush as president. This is said to have been the first joint stock company for the manufacture of cotton in America. The industry grew slowly in Philadelphia until 1810, when a young Quaker named Alfred Jenks, who had studied under Samuel Slater in Providence, Rhode Island, established the first regular factory of cotton machinery. By the Civil War, Philadelphia was a thriving textile center. No members of the fifty First Families sample, however, seem to have been industry leaders. Chief among the latter group were John B. Elison, who in 1823 established what became John B. Elison & Sons; Samuel Riddle, who founded the Glen Riddle Mills in 1842; and John Bromley, who built one of the great textile fortunes in the city. Two English brothers founded the J. and J. Dobson Company in 1855, and Thomas Dolan founded Thomas Dolan & Company, in 1861, which became the Keystone Knitting Mills, the largest in the nation in its day.

Although they did not take the lead themselves, a great deal of textile wealth filtered into Philadelphia Society. Jenks, Bromley, Riddle, Dobson, and Dolan surnames, moreover, were prominent in the city's twentieth-century *Social Registers*. But they were not names associated with education, the arts, or the professions; nor were they First Family names in any sense of the term. Leadership in the Philadelphia textile industry was indeed atomized as compared to its Boston counterpart.

THE PHILADELPHIA-WILMINGTON AREA: CHEMICAL CAPITAL OF THE NATION

Solid First Family wealth in Boston came from textiles; Philadelphia First Families such as the Wetherills and the Harrisons made their money in the chemical industry.

Samuel Wetherill (1736–1816) came of a long line of leading Quakers who had originally settled in Burlington, New Jersey, in the seventeenth century. He himself was a Quaker minister until the Revolution, when he took the oath of allegiance to the colony and organized a Quaker troop. After the war, he and his son and namesake founded the family firm, Samuel Wetherill & Son, which, enlarged and consolidated with other ventures by his able and inventive descendants, was very much in business in 1940.

Another early manufacturing chemist was John Harrison (1773–1833). His father had come to Philadelphia from England just before the Revolution; his mother was a prominent minister in the Society of Friends. After apprenticing to a druggist and spending some time abroad studying chemistry under Joseph Priestley, he founded John Harrison & Sons, which was one of the major chemical firms in the city by the time of his death. His son George Leib Harrison founded the Franklin Sugar Refining Company during the Civil War and made one of the biggest fortunes in his generation. In turn, his son Charles C. Harrison (1844–1929), brought even more wealth into the family when he sold out to the so-called sugar trust at the end of the nineteenth century (the du Ponts bought out the family chemical firm), after which he devoted his time to various civic causes, including the running of the University of Pennsylvania (Chapter 14).

At about the time of the War of 1812, many other chemical firms were founded in the Philadelphia-Wilmington area, which had become the chemical manufacturing capital of the nation by the Civil War. Eleuthère Irenée du Pont, son of the famous French physiocrat Pierre Samuel du Pont de Nemours, left extremely comfortable circumstances in France to come to America at the invitation of Thomas Jefferson. In 1802, he settled in a little log house on the Brandywine River and converted an old mill on the property into a gunpowder factory, which finally reached a secure financial position during the War of 1812. Although the du Ponts, like the Boston Ameses, have kept to themselves in their barony on the Brandywine, some of the profits of the E. I. du Pont de Nemours & Company have flowed, through marriage, into several other Philadelphia families. At the same time, four prominent Philadelphia chemical fortunes were founded after the War of 1812: John T. Lewis & Brothers in 1819, George D. Rosengarten & Sons in 1823, Powers & Weightman in 1825, and Nicholas Lennig & Company in 1829. The Lewis firm eventually merged with the Pennsylvania Salt Manufacturing Company, founded by George T. Lewis, grandson of the founder of the family firm (today the firm is the Pennwalt Company). The Rosengartens merged with Weightman to form Powers, Weightman & Rosengarten. The firm then merged, in 1927, with Merck & Company, which was led through the depression by George Rosengarten's capable descendants. The Lennig family firm was managed by descendants until the 1920s, when it was bought up by Rohm & Hass, one of the city's leading chemical companies today. Of all these family founding chemical firms, none of their leaders or their descendants, except William Weightman,* was included in the *DAB*. All their wealth, however, flowed into large family lines.

---

*Though Weightman was one of the two or three richest men in Philadelphia when he died in 1904, he left no family of the name and thus was excluded from the Philadelphia sample.

IRON AND STEEL,
MACHINERY AND RAILROADING

"Whether generally realized or not," wrote Cochran, "Pennsylvania's greatest effects on the nation as a whole have been in business and industry. . . . The lathe and the roller, rather than the jenny and the loom, are more surely the precursors of mechanized industry. It was the machine shops of Chester, Philadelphia, and Wilmington (Delaware) that insured rapid industrialization in the United States."[17]

Samuel Vaughan Merrick (1801–1870) and Joseph Wharton (1826–1909) were the two leading industrialists in the Philadelphia First Family sample. Merrick was born of a prominent family in Hollowell, Maine, and came to Philadelphia at an early age to work for John Vaughan, his uncle, a prosperous local merchant. He soon deserted his uncle's countinghouse and founded his own machine manufacturing firm, the Southwark Foundry, which eventually became a leader in the nation. And he played a major role in the industrial development of the city as a whole, founding the Franklin Institute "for the promotion of mechanical arts" in 1823. Merrick's status in the local business community was attested to by his election to the presidency of the Pennsylvania Railroad at its founding in 1846. Though Merrick was the only member of his family to be included in the DAB, his descendants have been active in education, both at the University of Pennsylvania and in New England, where John Vaughan Merrick was vice-rector of St. Paul's School before becoming headmaster of St. George's School in Newport, Rhode Island, in 1928.

After the Civil War, Joseph Wharton built up one of Proper Philadelphia's greatest fortunes, in zinc, white lead, nickel, and iron and steel manufacture. Wharton was one of the founders of the Bethlehem Steel Corporation. Although most of his fashionable descendants became Episcopalians, Wharton remained a Hicksite Friend all his life; he was one of the prominent founders of Swarthmore College and the founder of the Wharton School at the University of Pennsylvania.

In the early decades of the nineteenth century Philadelphia began to lose its financial and business leadership of the nation: first, in 1825 the Erie Canal opened up the West to New York City merchants; second, financial supremacy was lost to New York with the failure of Biddle's bank in the 1830s; third, the Baltimore and Ohio Railroad began to build its line to the West in the 1840s. Facing up to this disastrous situation, a group of Philadelphia capitalists, aided by the state, established the Pennsylvania Railroad in 1846 in order to provide Philadelphians with a means of transportation to Pittsburgh and the West. For almost a century the railroad never failed to pay a dividend and remained Proper Philadelphia's proudest accomplishment. Though its board was dominated by Philadelphia's best for most of this period, a majority of its presidents came from outside the inner circles of Society; Samuel Vaughan Merrick and George Brooke Roberts (1833–1897) were the only two presidents to be drawn from the First Family sample.

Roberts came of a long line of Welsh Quakers who purchased land outside Philadelphia in the seventeenth century and were successful farmers, maltsters, and ironmongers for several generations. As president of the railroad, Roberts showed all the conservative caution of his Quaker ancestors,* although he diverged from them in religion, becoming a leading layman in the Episcopal church. He gave the land, helped to plan, and was the first rector's warden of St. Asaph's Episcopal Church in Bala Cynwyd.† And Roberts's descendants subscribed to the best Quaker-turned-Episcopal traditions in the city, going off to St. Paul's School and Princeton University, belonging to the best clubs, and attending the Assembly balls. (They also had a nose for marrying money: Roberts had a granddaughter and a great-granddaughter who married Rockefellers.)

The only other railroad man in the Philadelphia sample, Richard Peters (1810–1889), was also of old Philadelphia stock (Anglican rather than Quaker). His grandfather Richard Peters (1744–1828) was the nephew of the Reverend Richard Peters (1704–1776), an agent of the Penns in the colony and rector of the combined parishes of Christ Church and St. Peter's. Although the Reverend Richard Peters was a loyalist who died in England, his nephew was a leading patriot in the city and major exposer of the peculations of Benedict Arnold. He was also the proprietor of one of Philadelphia's handsomest estates—and a historic site today—Belmont, located on the banks of the Schuylkill, not far downriver from the Roberts plantation. Richard Peters of the fourth generation became a railroad man at the urging of J. Edgar Thomson, president of the Pennsylvania Railroad during the Civil War. Peters, however, left Philadelphia and eventually made a large fortune railroading in Georgia. He was also a planter and a financier, as well as a leading Episcopalian layman in Atlanta, which he helped to rebuild after Sherman's devastating march.

By the First World War, the Pennsylvania Railroad was a large and relatively conservative corporation with the solid prestige of General Motors in a later day, and it was run by executives rather than buccaneering entrepreneurs like E. H. Harriman, Jay Gould, or Jim Fiske. The Boston railroad men in the sample, the Forbeses, the Ameses, and Charles Francis Adams, Jr., were more in the entrepreneurial tradition. Just as their merchant ancestors had sought wealth in the East rather than in the tried and true triangular trade, so they went out to the West to seek their railroad fortunes.

Charles Francis Adams, Jr., was the major moneymaker in the Adams line. Whereas his favorite brother, John Quincy, was a perennial loser in politics, and Henry and Brooks stood aloof from it all, including the money game, Charles Francis did extremely well at what he and his brothers despised. "I have seen much of life and affairs," he wrote after losing out to Jay Gould at the Union Pacific, "and taken my full share in the great game."[18] Adams lived at

---

*In striking contrast to Roberts, the most enterprising and imaginative presidents of the railroad were two outsiders, Thomas A. Scott (1823–1861) and Alexander J. Cassatt (1839–1906).

†St. Asaph's, Bala, is almost an exact copy of the beautiful cathedral at St. Asaph's in Wales.

least five lives—as a soldier in the Civil War, as a railroad reformer, as an urban land developer in the West, as president of the Union Pacific, and as historian and educator. Refusing high staff positions to remain with his black regiment, Adams fought in two of the Civil War's greatest battles, Antietam and Gettysburg, which he vividly described in his letters home. After a year's rest abroad in 1865–1866, he came back to become a railroad reformer; his famous *Chapters of Erie* illustrates his great contempt for Wall Street—with which he was nevertheless involved for a large part of his career. Despairing of reform, however, Adams determined to make his own fortune and set out to become the Vincent Astor of the West.

The linchpin of Adams's fortune was his investment in the development of Kansas City, especially in the stockyards there, which were part of the Armour empire. Adams also realized a 400 percent return on his farmland investments in what became Kansas City, Kansas. He next moved west, to Denver, to San Antonio and Houston, to Portland and Seattle and, finally, to mining towns like Helena, Spokane Falls, and Lewiston, Idaho. Adams's land speculations eventually led him to railroads and the presidency of the Union Pacific in 1884. His railroad career there ended in 1890, when the Gould crowd pushed him out. He never quite got over this failure: "In railroads," he wrote, "I was the typical college man—my success would have been the success of my class, my failure is now regarded as the failure of my class. . . . my class is discredited through me, and that hurts."[19] His ancestors had been defeated before him and they never took it lightly. But Charles Francis Adams, Jr., was among the giants of his line and certainly no simple money-maker or simple historian either. He was a man of all seasons living in one of the most spiritually dismal seasons for his class and family.

Frederick Lothrop Ames, Adams's close friend and sometime business associate, was a great Gilded Age capitalist. He was one of the largest owners of Boston real estate and a director of some seventy-five railroads. Ames owned $5 million worth of stocks and bonds in the Union Pacific while Adams was its president. Oliver Ames, his father, and Oakes Ames, his uncle, had been major promoters and builders of the Union Pacific before the Civil War; Oakes was later disgraced for his part in the Crédit Mobilier scandal (the best opinion is that his actions were highly improper but did not amount to bribery).

The younger Oliver Ames, brother of Frederick Lothrop Ames, was also a great capitalist, a dominant figure in the family business, Oliver Ames & Sons, president of the Union Pacific, and three times governor of Massachusetts. He once bought at auction some stock in the central Kansas branch of the Union Pacific for twenty-five cents a share, later selling it at $250 per share to Jay Gould, thereby adding $1 million to his already sizable estate.

Although two generations of the Ames family made fortunes in railroading, the family began on its way to wealth when the first Oliver Ames (1779–1863) incorporated his shovel business (worth $200,000) in the name of Oliver Ames & Sons, in 1844. He also built the family factory town at North Easton, Massachusetts. The first Oliver's father, Captain John Ames, had fought in the Revolution, at the same time making crude guns and shovels in his blacksmith's shop in Braintree. The Ames shovel business boomed with the opening of the West, especially after gold was discovered in California. In some places, the shovels served as legal tender.

The members of the Ames family were generous benefactors of many institutions, including Harvard University and especially its Arnold Arboretum. The arboretum was of special interest to Frederick Lothrop Ames and his nephew Oakes Ames (1874–1950), a botanist on the Harvard faculty for over forty years and a world renowned expert on orchards.

The Ameses never belonged to Proper Boston's inner circle of First Families like the Lowells, Cabots, and Peabodys. After all, they had their own feudallike barony at North Easton: their shovel factory was there and their paternalism included the donation of the first Catholic church, the town library, the high school, parks, and the well-known railroad station built by H. H. Richardson. Instead of moving to Beacon or Park Street in Boston or to the fashionable North Shore suburbs, the Ameses remained at North Easton, where their mansions were close to the source of their wealth. Perhaps this close-knit community demanded exogamy; at any rate, the Ameses were not in the habit of marrying cousins in the style of the Lowells and the Cabots.

The Forbeses have long been one of the leading moneymaking families of Proper Boston. Their family founder in America, John (died in 1783), was a Scotsman and graduate of King's College in Aberdeen who set off to become the veritable Benjamin Franklin of East Florida. He was the first Anglican clergyman to be licensed there, built the church at St. Augustine, and acted for a time as chief justice. The Forbeses came to Boston by way of John's marriage to Dorothy Murray of Milton, where Forbeses have lived ever since.

Among John's grandsons were Robert Bennett Forbes and John Murray Forbes. With the help of their uncle Thomas Handasyd Perkins, these brothers became successful China merchants. At age thirteen, Robert Bennett Forbes sailed before the mast to China on one of his uncle's ships. He obtained his first command at twenty and eventually owned a large fleet, including several steamers. He spent many years in China, where he made a fortune. John Murray Forbes was a veritable giant of an entrepreneur who made three fortunes— in the China trade, in railroading in the West, and in early investments in the tinkerings of a young Scotsman named Alexander Graham Bell. Like his older brother, he went to sea in his teens, later representing his uncle's counting-house in Canton. After seven years in the Orient, Forbes (at twenty-four) returned to Milton with a fortune. He married Sarah Hathaway, of a large New Bedford Quaker clan, whose English relatives were a help to him when he was sent on a secret mission to England by Lincoln during the Civil War. After marriage, he led a group of investors in purchasing the unfinished Michigan Central Railroad for $2 million. He completed the Michigan Central line into Chicago and put lines in operation between Chicago and the Mississippi and thence into Iowa, which became the Chicago, Burlington & Quincy system. He also built the Hannibal & St. Joseph Railroad into Missouri. During and after the Civil War, Forbes devoted much time to public service, behind the scenes rather than in office. For some years, he was a member of the executive committee of the Republican party (in the gentlemanly tradition, however, he was a Mugwump and voted for Cleveland in 1884).

Alexander Graham Bell, who brought wealth to the Forbeses and many other Boston families, started out in life as a devoted humanitarian. His father, Alexander Melville Bell, the inventor of visible speech, first came to Boston to give a lecture at the Lowell Institute in 1868. The next year, one of his listeners started a day school for the deaf in Boston, to which Alexander Graham Bell was brought from London as a teacher in 1871. Outside of teaching hours, he tinkered with his ideas for a telephone. The historic first telephone patent was issued to Bell on his twenty-ninth birthday in 1876. The announcement and demonstration of the telephone was made by Bell in an address to the American Academy of Arts and Sciences that spring. The Bell Telephone Company was formed in 1877. Bell's friend William Hathaway Forbes, son of John Murray Forbes and husband of Emerson's daughter, eventually became president of the company.*

PHILADELPHIA MINING AND EXTRACTING FORTUNES

As we have seen, Pennsylvania has always been far richer in natural resources than has Massachusetts, especially in coal and oil. Northeastern Pennsylvania contained the largest anthracite coal deposit in the world. Profits from the black gold of Lehigh, Carbon, Wyoming, and Luzerne counties built many mansions around Rittenhouse Square in the Victorian era and many stately homes on the Main Line since. The story of all the Proper Philadelphia coal barons cannot be related here; it is enough to show how the Coxe family mined one of the largest fortunes of them all, at Drifton, Pennsylvania, in the valley of the Lehigh River.

Tench Coxe laid the foundations of the family coal fortune. Between 1790 and 1820, he acquired large holdings of land in Luzerne, Carbon, and Schuylkill counties, later the heart of the hard coal region of Pennsylvania. Coxe had ten children by his second wife. His sixth child, Charles Sidney Coxe, was a lawyer and civic leader of some local distinction, judge of the district court, and president of the board of directors of the Eastern State Penitentiary at its founding. Charles made it the chief business of his life to hold intact the lands inherited from his father. The land was unproductive for many years, taxes were high, squatters and timber thieves abounded, and title disputes led to endless litigation. Judge Coxe, however, knew every inch of his land and every angle of the law and trained his five sons to carry on after him. His third son, Eckley Brinton Coxe (1839–1895), was educated as a mining engineer at the

---

*In the most prolonged and important litigation in the history of American patent law, the United States Supreme Court upheld all Bell's claims, declaring that he was the discoverer of the only way speech could be transmitted electrically. James Jackson Storrow, Charles Storer Storrow's son, a legal genius with a strong mechanical bent, played a major role in all these successful cases.

University of Pennsylvania and also abroad, during the Civil War. He returned to America, founded Coxe Brothers and Company during the last year of the war, and devoted the rest of his life to the coal industry. By 1886 the Coxe firm controlled roughly 35,000 acres of coal-rich land. Eckley Coxe held some seventy patents, built a technical school for miners' sons near his home in Drifton, founded the American Institute of Mining Engineers (president, 1878–1879), and became state senator from Luzerne and Lackawanna counties in 1880.

From the early days, most of the railroads in Pennsylvania were closely associated with coal mining. In 1872, the Pennsylvania Railroad, primarily a national and diversified carrier, purchased 28,000 acres of hard coal lands at a cost of about $5 million. By 1907, three-fourths of the total anthracite output was being mined by railroad companies. The Coxe firm was one of the last to sell out to the railroads.

Eckley Coxe and his wife, Sophie, known as the "angel of the hard coal fields" because of her philanthropic devotion to the miners' welfare, spent their lives in Drifton, the family company town in the heart of the coal region. But most of the Coxe family, none of whom has since attained national distinction, moved to Philadelphia, where they were leaders in Society—captains of the City Troop, managers of the Assembly balls, and presidents of the Philadelphia Club. This was especially true after 1906, when the family firm sold out its mining rights (not the land) to the Lehigh Valley Railroad for the sum of $19 million. Money brought the fashionable Coxes much pleasure and social prestige but hardly the pride in accomplishment that marked their Quaker-turned-Episcopal ancestors.

Although oil had been discovered in Pennsylvania as early as 1775, the petroleum age really began in 1859, when the first successful oil well was drilled in Titusville, Pennsylvania. As late as 1900, 60 percent of the nation's oil was being produced in the state.

The production and refining of oil was a widly competitive and chaotic business in 1868, when John D. Rockefeller, a Cleveland merchant, entered the field; within two years, largely through secret rebates from railroads, he had gained control of the largest refineries in the world. In Pennsylvania, Rockefeller worked closely with Tom Scott of the Pennsylvania Railroad, forming the notorious South Improvement Company (the brainchild of Scott's lawyers) in 1872 in order to systematize control of rebates and railroad traffic. Though Scott and many other Philadelphia capitalists such as the Wideners, Elkinses, and Houstons made fortunes in oil, by 1878, ten years after entering the field, Rockefeller (at the age of thirty-eight) controlled 97 percent of all refining.

The greatest Pennsylvania fortune in oil was built by the Pew family. Joseph Newton Pew, a schoolteacher in Mercer County, where he was born, moved to Titusville and in 1874 married Mary Anderson, whose family had been pioneers in the oil business. In 1880, Pew founded the Sun Oil Company and moved to Philadelphia, where he built a large estate on the Main Line. Staunch Calvinists and teetotalers, the Pews remained aloof from Society until the third generation, when Sun Oil money enriched through marriage several old family clans, including the Morrises.

The last two Philadelphia First Family money-makers (in Table A–16) the Penrose brothers, made fabulous mining fortunes in the West. I shall have more to say of R. A. F. and Spencer Penrose when discussing their brother Boies, the notorious Pennsylvania political boss.

Although Massachusetts contained no coal and oil, Boston First Families benefited from mining ventures elsewhere, as Amory noted in his discussion of Alexander Agassiz's career.

> He became interested in some copper mines purchased by his brother-in-law, Quincy Adams Shaw, in Northern Michigan. Searching for geological specimens on the shores of Lake Linden, he came upon a prospector who showed him a nugget of copper he had found. Agassiz thanked the man, asked him where he found the nugget, and near where the man told him to search he discovered a likely looking vein of copper ore. Filing claim to the property, Agassiz hustled back to Boston, told his sisters, Pauline Shaw and Ida Higginson, the good news; then, all together, they founded on a distinctly social basis—not only Shaws, Higginsons and Russells [Alexander's wife's family], but also among Cabots, Paines, Grays, Gardners, Bowditches, Coolidges, etc.—a fabulous revival of Boston First Family wealth. . . . For half a century, from 1871 through the 1920's, the magic words Calumet and Hecla were Beacon Hill passkeys. . . . Henry Lee Higginson realized in dividends alone some four hundred per cent on his original investment.[20]

BANKERS: THE GENTLEMANLY IDEAL IN AMERICA

Philadelphia was the cradle of American finance from the nation's founding until the demise of the Second Bank of the United States in 1836. Robert Morris and Thomas Willing were the major financiers of the Revolution. Unfortunately, as we have seen, Morris was jailed for debt in 1798. Willing was made president of the private Bank of North America at its founding in 1781 and then served as first president of the quasi-public First Bank of the United States from 1791 to 1797. Willing, the ideal Philadelphia Gentleman of his day, left no heirs of any distinction, even though Willings lived at the center of fashionable Philadelphia for many generations after him.

Congress failed to recharter the First Bank just before the War of 1812; Vice-President De Witt Clinton cast the deciding vote in a tied Senate, suggesting New York's jealousy of Philadelphia's financial supremacy, which eventually led to the defeat of Nicholas Biddle and the demise of the Second Bank. Stephen Girard (1750–1831) bought the First Bank building on Third Street, where he opened the private Girard Bank. Girard, who made a large fortune, was the first systematic philanthropist in American history, but he founded no Proper Philadelphia family line.*

---

*Robert Morris and Stephen Girard, both auslanders, were also cut-flowers in Philadelphia. Unlike Girard, however, Morris was indeed a progenitor of a distinguished family, but not in Philadelphia: a daughter married a brother of Chief Justice John Marshall of Virginia; a son, Thomas Morris, was sent to Congress from New York; two other sons also went to Congress, Isaac Newton Morris, from Illinois, and Jonathan David Morris, from Ohio.

The Bank of North America was about to open a branch in Boston when some local leaders, determined to retain financial affairs in their own hands, established the Massachusetts Bank in 1784 (a few months before the Bank of New York opened for business). From the outset, William Phillips (1750–1827) was the brains behind the Massachusetts Bank, even though he had James Bowdoin (a figurehead) appointed its first president. His careful and conservative policies set a precedent that has guided Boston banking over the years. Both Phillips's son and grandson followed him in the leadership at the bank, and according to the business historian N. S. B. Grass, the Massachusetts Bank "might well have been called Phillips' Bank."[21]

The social and financial rectitude of commercial banking in Boston and Philadelphia down through the years is attested to by the fact that the Bank of North America and the Massachusetts Bank did business into the twentieth century, when both merged with local banks that are still doing business today.

Philadelphia's Famous Banker: Nicholas Biddle. In many ways Nicholas Biddle (1786–1844) was the exception that nevertheless illustrated the Proper Philadelphia rule of deprecating anything but monetary achievement. Biddle was a scholar, litterateur, statesman, lawyer, architect, agricultural specialist, and farmer, as well as a charming and witty leader in Society. As Sidney Fisher wrote in his diary, had Biddle been born to a class with more intellectual values, such as Boston's, he might have achieved lasting fame as a man of letters. At any rate, he was not, and he went along with Philadelphia's money mores to become its most famous banker.

Historians in the Progressive tradition have not as a rule treated Biddle kindly. But he was not simply an enemy of the people or anti-Jacksonian. Pennsylvania was the Jacksonian state, and Biddle was a francophile and Jeffersonian Republican who voted for Jackson when he ran in 1824. In fact, his choice of a banking career was strongly influenced by his early friendship with James Monroe. Biddle was first called to public service in his early twenties as an under secretary to Monroe when he was minister to France and then Britain. With Monroe in Paris, Biddle worked with William Bingham and the Barings in negotiating the Louisiana Purchase. He became a lifelong friend of Monroe and his family. Later, as president, Monroe persuaded Biddle to leave the law and literature to become a director of the Second Bank of the United States. He immediately devoted himself to the study of banking and was soon both president and guiding force of the bank. Biddle's closest associate was Thomas Cadwalader. They made an excellent combination: in the tradition of the two families, Biddle was brilliant, impetuous, and daring; Cadwalader was his equal in intelligence but more cautious and conservative.

There is no need here to go into the details of Biddle's stormy career at the bank. It should be said, however, that he anticipated, as did Alexander Hamilton before him, the need for a central banking system in this country (a need not met until the New Deal). But Jackson was against all banks. Biddle was also attacked by the money interests in New York, which, after the opening of the Erie Canal in 1825, had become the de facto commercial capital of the nation. New Yorkers like De Witt Clinton and Martin Van Buren resented the traditional financial hegemony of Philadelphia. At any rate, Jackson refused to re-charter the bank. Chaos ensued in the banking system, with its pet banks in each state, which brought on inflation and the panic of 1837—and the failure of the Bank of the United States of Pennsylvania (which carried on after Jackson declined to recharter the Second Bank), too.

Although Biddle had retired before the crash, he was blamed for the bank's failure. Court action followed, but Biddle was never brought to trial. He retired, nevertheless, in virtual disgrace, and many of his old friends and associates, even those he had started on their way to wealth, turned against him. In 1844, he died in seclusion. The New York editor and staunch Jacksonian William Cullen Bryant reported that Biddle had died "at his country seat, where he had passed the last of his days in elegant retirement, which, if justice had taken place, would have been spent in the penitentiary."[22] But animosities were forgotten in Philadelphia, where dignitaries of all political persuasions attended Biddle's funeral at St. Peter's Episcopal Church.

Biddle was the first and last great man produced by the inner circles of Bid-dle-Cadwalader Philadelphia. "Once capital of the United States and of Pennsylvania, largest, richest, most luxurious of American cities, center of fashion and intellect," wrote Burt,

> Philadelphia had lost everything but Biddle and the Bank. When the Bank broke, when Biddle closed the classic doors of *Andalusia* against the world, Philadelphia closed its doors against the nation as a whole. The nation had rejected the leadership of Old Philadelphia; very well, Old Philadelphia rejected the nation. Like Biddle, Old Philadelphia retired into itself. Henceforth let vulgar Washington take over politics and vulgar New York take over finance. Philadelphia gentlemen would at least remain Philadelphian and gentlemen.[23]

In spite of Philadelphia's withdrawal into self, the romantic Biddle line remained in the public eye down into the twentieth century, largely, however, outside Philadelphia. Nicholas Biddle had a grandson, Edward, who brought real wealth into the family by marrying a Drexel banking heiress. Then two of Edward's grandchildren, Cordelia Biddle and Anthony Drexel Biddle, married heirs to the Duke tobacco fortune.* Both were eventually divorced, beginning a family tradition that flourished in the next generation, especially in the New York-Long Island line. Anthony Drexel Biddle, an extremely handsome sportsman, spent many years of public service under Franklin Roosevelt—as ambassador to Poland, as ambassador to governments-in-exile in London during World War II, and, finally, under President Kennedy, as ambassador to Spain.

---

*The Cadwaladers made no such showy marriages as the Biddles; nor did they play important roles on the national scene. Most of them, however, married well and went to, and supported, the University of Pennsylvania. An outstanding exception was Richard M. Cadwalader (Princeton, class of 1900), who married a Roebling heiress from Trenton, New Jersey. Her family founder, John Augustus Roebling (1806–1869), came from Germany and made a fortune in steel, wire rope, and bridge building (among his more famous constructions were the Brooklyn Bridge and the first suspension bridge over Niagara Falls).

Cordelia Biddle's older son, Angier Biddle Duke, followed his uncle's pattern, becoming chief of protocol under Kennedy and envoy to San Salvador and ambassador to Spain under President Johnson.

The Investment Banker: Gentlemanly Ideal in the Age of Enterprise. Roughly between the failure of Biddle's bank and the New Deal, investment bankers came to stand at the apex of upper-class authority and social prestige in America. Between the Civil War and the First World War, they orchestrated the financial growth of America into the most powerful industrial nation in the world. No wonder they set the tone in the more polite drawing rooms, the select men's clubs, and the fashionable Episcopal churches along the eastern seaboard. J. P. Morgan, for instance, was on the original board of Groton, was senior warden at St. George's Church on Stuyvesant Square, and was the leading lay figure at every general convention of the Protestant Episcopal church in America. (Just before the panic of 1907, he hired two special railroad cars to take him and his guests, including three American bishops and the bishop of London, to the convention held in Richmond, Virginia, that year.)

Nowhere have the Puritan roots of upper-class authority in America been more clearly shown than in Fritz Redlich's *Molding of American Banking*.

> In American financial capitalism, the organization of the large-scale sector of the national economy under the guidance and to the advantage of the investment banker, was the work of no more than half-a-dozen firms and hardly twice as many men. Outstanding among the former were: J. P. Morgan and Company, the First National and the National City Banks of New York, Kuhn, Loeb and Company, and to a smaller extent the two Boston houses, Lee, Higginson and Company and Kidder, Peabody and Company. The leaders of these firms, with the single exception of the German Jew, Jacob Schiff, were the descendants of New England Puritans, although some of them had not themselves grown up as Puritans. These men were first of all: J. P. Morgan, descendant of Connecticut [and Massachusetts] pioneers, although himself educated in England and Germany; James Stillman, Texas-born Yankee; and George F. Baker who grew up on a Massachusetts farm in a strictly Puritan atmosphere. (The Yankee, Levi P. Morton, was in the beginning very close to this set of men, but fell behind because of his political ambitions.) . . . The Bostonians, Robert Winsor, Gardiner M. Lane, and James J. Storrow, about twenty years younger than Morgan and Baker, no longer belonged to the pioneers of finance capitalism, and yet came early enough to play a part in its creation.[24]

The Puritan influence in investment banking was also evident in the case of such lesser New York leaders as Robert Winthrop (1833–1892), who married the daughter of Moses Taylor and multiplied his family's fortune many times over as an investment banker (Robert Winthrop & Co.), and James Handasyd Perkins (1876–1940), who carried on James Stillman's tradition as chairman of the National City Bank during the depression. Although both Winthrop and Perkins were from the Boston fifty families sample, two leaders of investment banking in Philadelphia, Enoch W. Clark (1802–1856) and Jay Cooke (1821–1905), were new men whose ancestors were deeply rooted in the Puritan culture of New England.

The Boston bankers Lane, Storrow, and Winsor built the two firms of Lee, Higginson and Kidder, Peabody into national leaders between the panic of 1907 and the First World War.* Lee, Higginson and Company was founded as a brokerage house in 1848; in the last two decades of the nineteenth century, the senior partners were George Cabot Lee and Henry Lee Higginson, both sons of the company's founders. Their business was largely local and derived from personal and family relations with leaders of such corporations as the Merrimac Manufacturing Company, the Massachusetts Cotton Mills, the Hecla Copper Mining Company, and the American Telephone and Telegraph Company. Gardiner Martin Lane, son of a Harvard professor and protégé of Charles Francis Adams, Jr., and James Jackson Storrow, son of James Jackson Storrow, the Bell Telephone patent lawyer, and grandson of Charles S. Storrow, the engineer for the Lowell and Lawrence mills, were the major partners at Lee, Higginson in its days of national prominence. At the same time, Robert Winsor ran Kidder, Peabody, and he had closer ties to the Morgan people than anybody else in New England. Kidder, Peabody, founded in 1865, grew out of John E. Thayer and Brother, founded in 1838 (the Thayer family might well have been included in the Boston sample). Kidder, Peabody is still doing business today, headquartered in New York but with branch offices in both Boston and Philadelphia. This organic web of Brahmin banking families in Boston and New York surely represented class authority of national and even international scope in the nineteenth and twentieth centuries.

After Nicholas Biddle retired to his estate, wildcat finance took over and led to the panic of 1837. In that year, Francis M. Drexel (1792–1863), a charming, Austrian born portrait painter who had dabbled in finance all over the world, founded a brokerage firm in Philadelphia.

A. J. Drexel (1826–1893) went to work for his father at the age of thirteen and devoted the rest of his life to building up one of the nation's greatest investment banking establishments. Although Drexel & Company soon had branch offices in London and Paris, the firm's New York connections were unsatisfactory. One day in the spring of 1871, Anthony J. Drexel asked young J. P. Morgan down to Philadelphia for dinner and proposed that the New Yorker join Drexel & Company as a partner. Drexel, Morgan & Company opened for business in 1871, and the Drexel people in Philadelphia have since been closely allied with the Morgan people in New York.

Anthony J. Drexel, concerned primarily with business, still found time for cultural and civic interests. His major contribution to the city was to found and generously to endow the Drexel Institute of Technology, which opened in 1892. Drexel was interested in educating poor boys for careers in business and engineering. From the beginning, the Drexel Institute had low tuition fees, a liberal scholarship program, night classes, and work-study programs. In accord with Drexel's wishes, moreover, the college was open to all, regardless of race, creed, or ethnic background.

---

*Between 1907 and 1912, according to Redlich, each firm handled corporate issues amounting to over $1 billion.

After A. J. Drexel's death in 1893, Drexel, Morgan & Company became J. P. Morgan and Company in New York and Drexel and Company in Philadelphia; nevertheless, as I noted previously, the two firms continued to act together, the senior partner in Philadelphia also being a Morgan partner in New York. No Drexel descendants have carried on in the firm's leadership. Between 1894 and the Second World War, the senior partners at Drexel were George C. Thomas (1839–1909), Edward T. Stotesbury (1849–1938), and Thomas S. Gates (1873–1948), none of them born into the inner circles of Proper Philadelphia. After the war, Edward Hopkinson, Jr., became the dominating partner at Drexel. The great-great-great-grandson of Thomas Hopkinson, a founder of the American Philosophical Society, and the great-great-grandson of Francis Hopkinson, signer of the Declaration of Independence, Hopkinson was the last of his family line to play a major role in the city's leadership. He was also the last upper-class leader of the Philadelphia establishment, which then centered on the Drexel firm, the Pennsylvania Railroad, and the University of Pennsylvania. It is indeed symbolic that these three once sacred Philadelphia institutions, founded by the talented auslanders Ben Franklin, Samuel Vaughan Merrick, and Francis Drexel, are now being run by men and women from outside the city altogether.*

BOSTON AND PHILADELPHIA MONEY AT THE CLOSE OF THE GILDED AGE

Following the Civil War, as America gradually became the foremost industrial nation in the world, many men of enterprise, often called robber barons, built up fabulous family fortunes that have influenced our history down to the present day. Many reformers in that age of great vulgarity and conspicuous consumption felt that there should be a check on the increasing concentration of wealth in fewer and fewer hands. Among others, the editors of Joseph Pulitzer's New York World were fervent crusaders for graduated income and inheritance taxes. In 1902, the World published a list of 4,000 millionaires as a twelve-page supplement to the World Almanac of that year. The list was carefully compiled, and the integrity of the editors was not questioned. An inspection

---

*Since Hopkinson's day, the city has been run by an increasingly atomized elite rather than a traditional establishment: the Drexel firm, for example, has recently been merged with Burnham & Company of New York (the name persists, perhaps for historical reasons, in the style of Drexel, Burnham & Company); in the 1960's, the Penn-Central Railroad (after the merging of the Pennsylvania with the New York Central) went bankrupt in Proper Philadelphia's Watergate-like scandal; at the same time, the University of Pennsylvania was experiencing the greatest renaissance in its history; but it is now (1976) being led, not by Proper Philadelphians as in the past, but by a nationally representative board of trustees, which includes chairman Donald T. Regan, of Merrill Lynch & Company, in New York, I. W. Burnham II, of New York, Harold Zellerbach of San Francisco, and Marietta Tree of New York, granddaughter of Endicott Peabody of Groton. The chairman of the executive board, Thomas S. Gates II, a New York Morgan partner, is one of the few remaining Proper Philadelphians on the board.

of the Massachusetts and Pennsylvania millionaires (see Table A–17) provides some useful and revealing information as to the differences between these groups—differences that are in accord with what one would expect from my analysis of the history of the upper classes of Boston and Philadelphia so far.

In the first place, even though Pennsylvania was more populous and is far larger and much richer in natural resources than Massachusetts, there were more millionaires in the latter state (417 versus 317). There is reason to believe, however, that extremely large fortunes are more characteristic of Pennsylvania than of Massachusetts. In Ferdinand Lundberg's notorious *America's 60 Families*, based on 1924 income tax returns, for instance, there were nine families that got their start in Pennsylvania (more than in any other one state) as against only one from Massachusetts.* James J. Storrow of Lee, Higginson ranked fifty-seventh, with an estimated fortune of $34,500,000. Lundberg ranked the Pennsylvanians as follows:

5th	Mellon	$450,000,000
13th	Guggenheim	190,000,000
15th	Curtis-Bok	174,000,000
17th	Berwind	150,000,000
19th	Widener	118,500,000
25th	Pitcairn	99,600,000
29th	Phipps	89,100,000
38th	Drexel	21,000,000
60th	S. S. Kresge	30,000,000[25]

In the second place, citizens of Massachusetts had three times the opportunity of Pennsylvanians to become millionaires (15, as against five, per 100,000 population).† As social and political power in Massachusetts is far more concentrated in Boston than is the case in Pennsylvania and Philadelphia, it is not surprising that 74 percent of the state's millionaires were located in Boston, as against 60 percent of Pennsylvania's 317 millionaires located in Philadelphia.

Millionaire status in both Boston and Massachusetts, then, seemed to be more widely and democratically distributed than in Philadelphia and Pennsylvania. How does this finding square with my thesis that since the nation's founding, and all through the colonial period, too, Massachusetts has been ruled by a more continuous class authority than Pennsylvania? Does this suggest that class authority is more compatible with a wide distribution of wealth than is a more democratic social structure? I think it does. Moreover, this generalization runs parallel to my argument that political (representative) democracy was more vigorous where leaders consistently were drawn from an upper

---

*For some reason Lundberg ranked Storrow and Kresge lower on the scale than, say, the Drexels because they paid taxes as individuals rather than as families—a small point but confusing. Note also that Lundberg ranked the du Ponts ninth on his list, with a fortune of $238,500,000. Though these barons on the Brandywine lived in a different state, they were listed in the Philadelphia *Social Register* in 1940 and are intermarried with several Philadelphia families.

†The citizens of Boston had four times the opportunity of Philadelphians to become millionaires (56 as against 14 per 100,000 population).

class (as in colonial Massachusetts).* Let us now turn to an analysis of the relationship between class and wealth in the two cities.

The smaller Boston upper class had more millionaires (157) than the larger class in Philadelphia (115). But, at the same time, a higher proportion of all the millionaires in Philadelphia (184) were members of its upper class (63 percent) than was the case in Boston (not quite 50 percent). This suggests, among other things, that where wealth is more widely distributed in an upper class, it is also more widely distributed in the social structure as a whole. A qualitative analysis of the millionaires in each upper class reveals more subtle patterns.

Whereas forty-eight, or 40 percent, of the Boston upper-class millionaires were drawn from the sample of fifty First Families, only thirty, or 25 percent, of the upper-class millionaires in Philadelphia came from this group. Thus, twenty-seven, or over half, of the fifty Boston families had members who were millionaires in 1902, as against only fourteen, or less than a third, of those in the Philadelphia sample. Thus, there was far less historical continuity in Philadelphia than in Boston. An inspection of the family names in the two cities quickly reveals this to be even more the case than the quantitative evidence suggests. Of the ninety-five millionaire families in upper-class Boston, for instance, at least twenty—Amory, Codman, Crocker, Cushing, Dana, Dexter, Gardner, Gray, Grew, Hemenway, Hunnewell, Loring, Russell, Minot, Sargent, Sears, Shaw, Thayer, Weld, Wigglesworth, and Wolcott—were old families, any one of which might easily have been included in my sample. From the eighty millionaire Philadelphia families, however, it would be hard to find substitutions (fourteen of these were among the fifty First Families), in many cases because none, or in a few cases only one, of their members was listed in the DAB. The Lewises, for instance, a very old and originally a Quaker family, built a great fortune in chemicals but had no members in the DAB. Similarly, of the Coates, Griscom, Moore, Parrish, Scull, Wood, Strawbridge, and other families with old Quaker roots, only Clement Griscom, a millionaire shipping magnate, was listed both in the World Almanac and in the DAB.

The main difference between the two classes was the fact that Philadelphia, of necessity rather than choice, was more receptive to families whose founders made fabulous fortunes in the second half of the nineteenth century. Old Bostonian families, in other words, expanded their own fortunes; Proper Philadelphians on the whole did not and consequently had to assimilate more new men. Though there is both newer and older wealth in Boston, in the late nineteenth and the early twentieth century in Philadelphia a large group of new

---

*In America as a whole, since the 1902 World survey of millionaires, there has been a steady effort to equalize income and inherited wealth; yet, study after study has shown that distribution is as unequal as ever. This trend of course is in accord with Tocqueville's view that increasing social democracy means increasing political centralization. And so it is with wealth. Surely in the years since the Second World War, the relentless atomization of society has gone along with an ever increasing concentration and control of both wealth and political power in the central government. In 1902, Wall Street (and State Street and Walnut Street, too) symbolized both societal and class authority, which is now more and more subservient to government decisions in Washington.

men and their families not only were breaking into Society but also were very much needed (their wealth, that is) by families of older but declining wealth. Hence, the arrogance and aloofness of Brahmin Boston as against the snobbery of Proper Philadelphia. There are always insecure snobs at all levels of every kind of society, but arrogant aloofness tends to be an aristocratic vice; snobbery is characteristic of more democratic plutocracies.

THE PHILADELPHIA AND SOMERSET CLUBS: ASSIMILATING ASSOCIATIONS

"What I like about the Order of the Garter," Lord Melbourne, Queen Victoria's proto-Prime Minister, is reputed once to have observed, "is that there is no damned merit in it."[26] Members of both the Somerset and Philadelphia Clubs would find this a fitting way of introducing the spirit of each club. Although congeniality rather than achievement is the manifest criterion for membership, the latent function of these clubs is to assimilate new men or their descendants into their ranks—they measure how achievement (especially moneymaking) is gradually turned into congeniality over the generations.

The Philadelphia Club, founded in 1834, is the oldest city men's club in America. That its presidents during the first century of its history included three Cadwaladers, one Biddle, two Markoes, a Borie, Richard Vaux, a Meade, a Coxe, and Owen Wister (the club's centenary historian) attests to its central place in the history of Proper Philadelphia. That three Cadwaladers were presidents is surely the best index of their premier First Family status in the city.

The younger Somerset Club was founded in Boston in 1846. Though it stands for much the same kind of patrician congeniality as the Philadelphia Club, there is a subtle difference between them and their roles in upper-class society. Of the twenty-seven presidents of each of the two clubs in the first century of their history, for example, eleven of the Philadelphians were from the First Families sample; only three from the Boston sample—a Warren, a Coolidge, and a Palfrey—were presidents of the Somerset, whose presidents included two Searses, two Wolcotts, and a Fay, Russell, Loring, Thayer, and Sturgis (all from families that might have been included in the Boston list). That no Adams, Lowell, Cabot, or Winthrop was chosen, or chose, to fill this position would be inconceivable to a Philadelphian: whereas Somerset Club membership (and leadership) is of great importance to many Bostonians, it is not *all*-important as is Philadelphia Club membership.* In other words, where achievement is emphasized and recognized, acceptance and congeniality are

---

*Of course, many Proper Bostonians of the Apley mold take Somerset membership very, very seriously. Thus, one Brahmin was in the habit of enrolling his younger kin at birth; when one of them wanted to wait a few years after college before joining, he agreed to pay his dues until the young man was ready to do so himself, saying, "Young man, some day you may do something. Whatever you do some member of the Somerset Club will disapprove of it" (Cleveland Amory, *The Proper Bostonians* [New York: Dutton, 1947], p. 358).

virtues, but where achievement has a far lower status, as in Philadelphia, acceptance and congeniality (or popularity) become sacrosanct.

As I have said before, only a very small proportion of the men and women in any upper class are driven to distinguished achievement. Thus, less than 10 percent of the members of the Philadelphia and Somerset clubs were included in the first twenty volumes of the *DAB* (both clubs are about the same size, limiting membership to 500). The eighty-three members of the Somerset Club who were included, however, had 11,775 lines written about them (average 142); the fifty members of the Philadelphia Club who were included had only 5,521 lines (average 110) written about them. Although merit is not a criterion for membership in either club, the Somerset members down through the years have had more of an itch for fame than their peers in the Philadelphia Club.*

The assimilation process at the Philadelphia Club is nicely illustrated by a look at eighteen of the money-makers listed in Table A–16: William Weightman, George D. Rosengarten, Enoch W. Clark, Jay Cooke, William L. Elkins, P. A. B. Widener, Henry Disston, Frederick W. Taylor, Alan Wood, John Wanamaker, Thomas A. Scott, Alexander J. Cassatt, Matthew Baird, John H. Converse, Henry H. Houston, Edward J. Berwind, Thomas Dolan, and Edward T. Stotesbury. All these individuals made fabulous fortunes; all had descendants of the name included in the 1902 *World Almanac* list of millionaires, as well as in the 1940 Philadelphia *Social Register*. Of these eighteen new men only three were taken into the Philadelphia Club—Scott in 1868, Berwind in 1874, and Cassatt in 1875; eight others had descendants of the name who became members (mostly in the twentieth century). Such, then, was the process of converting cash into gentlemanly congeniality at the Philadelphia Club.

Scott, Berwind, and Cassatt are interesting examples of the assimilating process and the club's values. Cassatt, a charming and imaginative man, the scion of an old Pittsburgh family, was taken in almost automatically at the age of thirty-six (birthright Philadelphia Gentlemen are usually accepted in their twenties). That Scott, the son of a small town tavern keeper upstate, and Berwind, son of a humble German immigrant, were taken into the club in their forties had to do with their personalities and not with their social origins (a point often forgotten by today's ubiquitous sociological determinists). Both of course were very big Philadelphians in terms of wealth and power. But Scott was also an extremely handsome and cultivated man whose descendants have been among the most polished and cultured members of Philadelphia Society (Groton and Harvard rather than St. Paul's and Princeton). Berwind, with the bearing of a Prussian general and the polishing of an Annapolis education, was a domineering and socially charming host. Though he belonged to the Philadelphia Club, Berwind was not a Philadelphian by temperament and spent

---

*As might be expected, the Somerset membership was far more rooted in the soil of Massachusetts than was the case with the Philadelphia Club. Of the eighty-three Somerset members in the *DAB*, for instance, 70 percent were born in Massachusetts, 28 percent in other states, and 2 percent abroad. Of the fifty Philadelphia Club members, only 54 percent were native Pennsylvanians, 40 percent came from other states, and 6 percent were born abroad.

most of his later life in the gay and ostentatious society of New York and New-port. His far less distinguished brothers remained in the city but neither they nor their descendants have belonged to the club (Berwind died childless).

OTHER STATUS ASCRIBING
ASSOCIATIONS

There are associations besides the Somerset and Philadelphia Clubs that place people and families within the upper classes of Boston and Philadelphia. The Athenaeum, the Massachusetts Historical Society, and the Tavern Club have a special appeal to Bostonians of bookish and historical interests. But Boston's vice may be intellectual snobbery. At any rate, solid, old family status may be better measured by leadership at the Athenaeum and the Historical Society than at the fashionable Somerset Club: only three members of the fifty family sample, for instance, were presidents of the Somerset Club, whereas the officers and trustees of the Athenaeum between its founding in 1807 and 1900 included men from twenty-eight families in the sample: Bowditch (five), Lyman (five), Cabot (four), Lowell (four), Lawrence (four), Adams (three), Appleton (three), Perkins (three), Coolidge (three), Eliot (two), Holmes (two), Jackson (two), Quincy (two), and one each from the Emerson, Otis, Everett, Ticknor, Brooks, Phillips, Bigelow, Ware, Parkman, Lodge, Shattuck, Winthrop, Wendell, Longfellow, and Putnam families.

As might be expected, members of the Adams and Winthrop families valued their membership in the Historical Society above all others. James Winthrop was one of the society's founders in 1791. Robert C. Winthrop, a Proper Boston institution in the second half of the nineteenth century, was president of the society for three decades. And between its founding and 1940, except for a year or two in the early part of the twentieth century, there have always been Winthrops on its active rolls. Among the many Adams members of the society was Charles Francis Adams, Jr., who was elected to membership in 1874 and served as president from 1895 until his death in 1915.

Intellectual snobbery carries far less weight in Philadelphia than in Boston. Although Philadelphia has two private libraries—the Athenaeum and the Library Company—with socially circumspect boards, these groups have nowhere near the social prestige that comparable bodies have in Boston. The major status conferring institutions besides the Philadelphia Club are the First City Troop, two exclusive dining clubs, the Fish House and the Rabbit, and the Assembly balls, held annually since the eighteenth century. Although exclusive First Family dancing assemblies have been held from time to time in Boston, they have hardly been comparable to the Philadelphia Assembly. That the First City Troop is of such social importance in the Quaker City (there is nothing comparable in Boston) is undoubtedly because it was founded during the Revolution, when so many members of now fashionable families were read out of meeting for participating in the war; they joined the Troop as an index of their patriotic convictions; and over the generations, convictions have a way of dissolving into conventions.

Long before the newly rich millionaires were knocking on the doors of Society, Proper Philadelphia faced the problem of assimilating lapsed Quaker families into the Philadelphia Club and Dancing Assembly circle, which was largely Episcopalian. The Pembertons, the First Family of eighteenth-century Quakerism, for instance, began attending the Assembly in the early years of the nineteenth century and eventually became Episcopalians. The first of the line from Israel Pemberton to join the Philadelphia Club was a namesake who was accepted in 1853.* This Proper Philadelphia need for continually assimilating new families of old, but Quaker, roots (and all the embarrassing ritual of arranging proposals, and seconding, and so forth) has led to a subtle brand of old family social climbing, a phenomenon hard to understand outside Philadelphia.

PHILADELPHIA CULTURAL
INSTITUTIONS, ASSEMBLY VALUES,
AND THE WIDENERS

In all societies, new men take on the values of the class to which they aspire. Although many old family Philadelphians would hate to admit it, great insight into their own values can be gained from a look at how, in the early decades of the twentieth century, they treated the descendants of Peter A. B. Widener, who piled up the city's largest post–Civil War fortune. If Proper Philadelphians then took the Assembly and what it stood for too seriously, unfortunately (but understandably) some of the Widener heirs did, too.

Peter A. B. Widener's rise to great wealth is a classic example of the political and business mores of American civilization in the Gilded Age. No wonder Theodore Dreiser based his Copperwood novels on the rise and fall of a young Philadelphia Quaker, Charles Tyson Yerkes, who was Widener's sometime business associate in the traction game. Though the Yerkeses were English Quakers who came to Philadelphia in Penn's time, the first Widener in the city, Johann Christoph, arrived from Rotterdam in 1752.

The Widener family remained undistinguished until Peter A. B., a butcher, realized a $50,000 net profit from a contract to supply meat to all the Union troops stationed in the Philadelphia area during the Civil War. The cornerstone of Widener's real fortune, however, was his appointment in 1873 by the local boss of Matthew Quay's notorious Pennsylvania Republican machine to fill an unexpired term as city treasurer. His predecessor had been convicted of

---

*The Roberts family followed the same path somewhat later. President Roberts of the Pennsylvania Railroad was from one of the oldest Quaker families in the city. Although he was a leading Episcopalian layman, he did not join the Philadelphia Club. His sons, however, were sent to Princeton, where they joined the best club (Ivy), and then came back to Philadelphia, where they moved and married within the best families, lunching at the Philadelphia Club and dancing at the Assembly balls.

fraud and sent to the Eastern State Penitentiary; Charles T. Yerkes, a rising young banker at the time, was sent to the county jail for his part in the affair. From this convenient office in the city government, Widener began buying up horsecar companies throughout the city. After the introduction of electric streetcars to Philadelphia in 1887, he became one of the leading traction magnates of his day. Along with his son George D. Widener, his close friend William L. Elkins in Philadelphia, Thomas Fortune Ryan and William C. Whitney in New York, and Charles T. Yerkes, now in Chicago, Widener acquired control of 527 miles of streetcar tracks in several cities—200 in Philadelphia, 49 in New York, 229 in Chicago, 35 in Baltimore, and 14 in Pittsburgh. Widener branched out into other fields of enterprise: he made large investments in the Reading Railroad Company, the Baltimore & Ohio Railroad, Standard Oil, the United Gas Improvement Company, and the Pennsylvania Land Title and Trust Company, besides being an original organizer of the United States Steel Company, the International Mercantile Marine Company, and the American Tobacco Company.

Peter A. B. Widener had three sons. The first, Harry, died of typhoid fever at the age of fifteen. His second son and close business associate, George, went down on the *Titanic*, along with *his* son Harry, a Harvard graduate and an ardent bibliophile who was returning with his parents from London where he had gone to purchase a rare edition of Bacon's essays. George's wife, daughter of William L. Elkins, donated the Harry Elkins Widener Memorial Library to Harvard University in memory of Peter A.B.'s favorite grandson.* George D. Widener had another son, his namesake, and a daughter, Eleanor. The younger George D., Jr. (the first Widener to be taken into the Philadelphia Club) died childless and left a large sum of money to the second-rate Pennsylvania Military College, now Widener College. Eleanor Widener married Fitz Eugene Dixon, whose son and namesake was discussed in the early part of this chapter. Peter A. B. Widener's third son, Joseph E. Widener, spent his youth in his father's enormous Victorian mansion on North Broad Street (William L. Elkins lived next door), an unfashionable neighborhood settled by newly rich contractors and traction magnates. Joseph E. Widener's values were quite typical of many aesthetically sensitive Americans of second generation wealth. Unlike his father and his older brother George, both of whom loved business and cared little for fashionable society, Joseph was all too aware of living on the wrong side of the tracks (to Rittenhouse Square Society "nobody" lived north of Market Street). He was, for example, never quite at ease at the ritual Saturday night poker games that so satisfied his brother and father and their old friends and poker partners William L. Elkins and John G. Johnson. But he avidly participated in the long postgame discussions of art and art collecting, the major avocational passions of both his father and John G. Johnson.

---

*Mrs. Widener had originally planned to give Harvard only her son's collection of some 3,000 rare books, but A. Lawrence Lowell, in his autocratic and persuasive style, convinced her of the desirability of housing the collection in a suitable library, much needed by Harvard at the time. (The Widener library was built by the Widener family architect, Horace Trumbauer.)

The Widener family moved to Lynnewood Hall, completed in 1900 on a 300-acre tract of land in Elkins Park, a fashionable suburb north of Philadelphia.* The Georgian mansion, a tribute to both the energy of the father and the taste of his son Joseph, was designed by Trumbauer, with its formal French gardens laid out by Jacques Greber, redesigner of the outskirts of Paris. Lynnewood Hall, housing some 500 paintings, soon became a rendezvous for art lovers from all over the world. As far as Joseph was concerned, it was also on the right side of the tracks.

Joseph E. Widener was educated at private schools, attended Harvard, and studied architecture for a brief period at the University of Pennsylvania. He showed little interest in business, practiced no profession, and devoted himself to his twin passions, horses and art. Best known to the general public as a leading turfman, builder of Hialeah Park in Florida, and major owner of Belmont Park after the death of August Belmont, he bred and raced many famous horses and maintained elaborate stables in France and at Elmendorf in Kentucky. Of far more historical importance, however, was Widener's interest in art, especially his determination to put together a collection of only the best works of the most famous artists. After his father's death in 1915, he gradually cut the family collection from 410 to 100 paintings, housed in what was in 1940 "the finest private art gallery in the world."

In 1894, Widener, tall and distinguished looking and a man of recognized taste, married a beautiful young widow, Eleanor Holmes Pancoast, of an old and fashionable Philadelphia family. Yet he was never quite accepted by the Philadelphia Club–Assembly circle, although he was often asked to serve on cultural and civic committees, including the boards of the University of Pennsylvania and the Art Commission. (Widener created quite a stir and aroused not a little opposition when, in 1936, he purchased for the Philadelphia Art Museum one of the finest pictures in its present collection, "The Bathers," by Cézanne.)

In his will, Peter A. B. Widener had stipulated that his art collection should be given either to Philadelphia ($10 million was set aside to build a gallery for the city if this alternative were decided upon by Joseph) or to New York or to Washington. Throughout the twenties and thirties, there was much local speculation as to whether this treasure would remain in the city or go elsewhere. Though the leaders of Society who then controlled the cultural institutions of

---

*The sociology of architecture and neighborhood change is a fascinating subject. Elkins Park, built by Elkins and Widener, and the whole Jenkintown-Ogontz area was, before the First War, the home of multimillionaires like Jay Cooke, John Wanamaker, and the Harrisons, Wideners, and Elkinses. As many commuted more or less regularly to Wall Street, the Jenkintown station on the Reading Railroad, the most direct line to downtown New York, was an important attraction. But large palaces, like too much money too quickly made, are far less stable than, say, the Houston-Woodward development of Chestnut Hill. Thus, after World War II, Elkins Park became the major upper middle-class Jewish neighborhood in the city. Incidentally, *Alverthorpe*, built by Joshua Francis Fisher (see our DAB sample) in 1850-51, where Sidney Fisher often visited, and thought it to be "the finest establishment we have here in Philadelphia," is now in the possession of a Sears, Roebuck heir, Lessing Rosenwald (see above), whose priceless print collection has, for various reasons, not been kept in Philadelphia but is part of the National Gallery in Washington.

the city, including the Art Museum, were not always able to distinguish between a person's taste and his lineage, the trustees of the museum, and especially their president, Sturgis Ingersoll, were saddened when, on October 18, 1940, the *Bulletin* proclaimed: "The Widener Collection Goes to Washington: Philadelphia Cut Off without a Painting." In 1948, John Walker, chief curator of the National Gallery, wrote in the catalogue for the Widener exhibition that the donation of the collection "by Mr. Joseph E. Widener in memory of his father will remain one of the greatest events in the history of American museums." Today the Mellon and Widener collections, along with the Dale and Kress collections, form the heart of the National Gallery in Washington. There is perhaps no better example of the lack of local pride in both Philadelphia and Pennsylvania than the fact that the Mellon, Widener, and Rosenwald collections have gone outside the state.

Joseph E. Widener had two children, Peter A. B. Widener II and Josephine ("Fifi") Widener. In the same year that it was announced that the Widener collection was to go to Washington, Peter A. B. Widener II published his autobiography, a rare thing for a Philadelphian to do. He summed up the theme of his book thus: "I want," he wrote, "to set myself up as a horrible example of what an empty existence it is to be a son of great wealth sheltered from reality and surrounded by a sea of snobbery."[27] Lacking the purposeful stability of a calling or profession, he was all too susceptible to the shallow mores of Society. The following paragraphs from Widener's autobiography, which express the reactions of an alienated young man of privilege without purpose, provide some insight into why so much Philadelphia wealth has not gone into the support of Proper Philadelphia's favorite institutions.

> Up until some time after the World War Philadelphia society was the most high hat in America. It was an orchidaceous growth on democracy. Newport, New York, and Palm Beach Four Hundreds—and even the elect of Boston—were an ordinary lot compared with Philadelphians. The City of Brotherly Love, shrine of American liberty, was dedicated to the principles of snobbery more than any other American city.
>
> Back in the 'nineties Philadelphia society raised its eyebrows when Mother married Father. She had committed an unpardonable faux pas. She had married across the tracks!
>
> As Ella Pancoast, daughter of one of the oldest families of Philadelphia, Mother had always attended the Assembly, which is one of the outstanding social events of America. It is one of the oldest social functions in the United States, dating back to Revolutionary days, to the time when Broad Street was an Indian trail connecting York and Philadelphia. Guests invited from other cities consider themselves lucky. And Philadelphians who are on the Assembly list consider themselves the cream of American society. But when Mother married Father she changed her social ranking from cream to skim milk in the eyes of the Assembly crowd. As Mrs. Joseph E. Widener, she was never again invited to the Assembly Ball. . . .
>
> Grandfather was a self-made man. . . . Now he was rich, fabulously wealthy, and society called him and his sons *nouveau riche*.
>
> Grandfather didn't care. His eldest son, George, didn't care. Mother didn't care. But Father cared. It rankled for a long time, the slight to him and the Wide-

ner name. Later when Father had entertained and been entertained by princes and the nobility of Europe and by society leaders in other American cities, Philadelphia opened its doors. . . .

In 1919 Fifi made her debut at a tea attended by most of Philadelphia society. Later when invitations for the Assembly were out, Fifi was one of the many debutantes to be overlooked that season. About that time Father was asked to serve on one more of the many civic committees to which he had always contributed generously in time and money. The project was backed by some of the Assembly crowd.

"I have the good taste to be asked to join this project," Father said, "but still my daughter is not considered eligible for the Assembly. I refuse."

Within a very short time an invitation arrived bidding Fifi to the Assembly. She was asked, of all things, as an "out-of-town" guest! Our home by then, as it is now, was just across the city line in Montgomery County. The Assembly Committee was indulging in a bit of face-saving, but it didn't fool us. I was not at all for Fifi's accepting. If she couldn't be asked as a Philadelphian, I heatedly championed her staying at home.

Father, however, was delighted. So was Fifi. And so Fifi went, and it was up to me to escort her.

I went, but I was hot under the collar. I was mad clean through because it seemed to me the invitation to Fifi had contained a back-handed flip at Mother. It's the custom for a debutante to be chaperoned at the Assembly by her mother. . . . . But Mother had not been asked.[28]

In our day of ever more atomized democracy, it is hard to understand how the Assembly crowd and the Wideners took the structure of Society so seriously. Without doubt, the Widener Library is at Harvard, the great Widener art collection is in Washington, Widener College is in the Philadelphia suburbs, and Fitz Eugene Dixon, Jr. lends his support to Temple rather than to the University of Pennsylvania partly because of the way Proper Philadelphia behaved toward the Wideners in the incident described by Peter A. B. Widener II.*

---

*During the 1960s the Assembly prohibition against divorce was abolished and the size of the ball doubled. But perhaps the Philadelphia problem has not yet been solved. Thus, Ambassador Walter Annenberg, sponsored by an aide in London, the polished descendant of Thomas Scott of the Pennsylvania Railroad, was turned down for membership in the Philadelphia Club, even though he has been a generous benefactor of both the Episcopal Academy (where many members and their sons have been educated) and the University of Pennsylvania. Many have seen Annenberg's case as a matter of anti-Semitism, but it is perhaps better understood as part of an old Philadelphia syndrome of short-sighted snobbery.

Education and Leadership

Go the rich and tell them of the substantial glory of literary patronage! Tell them of the Maecenases of former days! Tell them that the spirit of commerce has always been propitious to the arts and sciences! Show them the glories of the Medici of Florence; the republican renown of Holland, once studded with splendid universities, and fruitful of great men, fostered by the rich merchants of their cities. . . . And if this will not touch them, read the roll of the former benefactors of our university [Harvard]; of the Hollises and Hancocks. These were merchants; and men too, whom posterity will never cease to honour; men, whom all the great and good spirits that have issued from this seat of learning will go and congratulate in heaven, as their benefactors!

Joseph Buckminster

Much reading is an oppression of the mind, and extinguishes the natural candle, which is the reason for so many senseless scholars in the world.

William Penn

The Lord opened up to me that being bred at Oxford or Cambridge was not enough to fit and qualify men to be ministers of Christ.

George Fox

The most important consequences of the ethics of the Puritans of Massachusetts Bay and the Quakers who came to Pennsylvania were their diametrically opposed ideas about education in general and higher education in particular. "Harvard College," wrote Samuel Eliot Morison, "was the acme of a series of cultural efforts in the 1630s and 1640s, made by the ruling class of New England and supported by the people at large. Common schools, compulsory education laws, grammar schools such as Boston Latin, and the Cambridge printing press, belong to the same category."[1] According to Richard Hofstadter, "the Puritan clergy came as close to being an intellectual ruling class—or, more properly, a class of intellectuals intimately associated with a ruling power—as America has ever had."[2]

For over half a century after its founding, Quaker Pennsylvania had no college, no common schools, no compulsory education laws, and no common grammar school. "The first three quarters of the eighteenth century," wrote James Pyle Wickersham, "are almost a perfect blank so far as anything was done by the public authorities to provide an education for the people. Indeed, the last Charter of Privileges granted by Penn himself, in 1701, which continued in force until the adoption of the Constitution of 1776, contains no section or clause relating to education."[3] The Quakers of course established their own elementary schools soon after coming to Pennsylvania. Most of them were limited to a "guarded" and utilitarian education. The affluent Anglican families educated their children at home under private tutors or sent them to Quaker schools. The handful of university men in the early years of the colony had been educated in Europe. In the 1740s Franklin decided to do something about the lack of formal educational institutions in the city. In his widely circulated *Proposals Relating to the Education of Youth in Pensilvania*, he wrote that "it has long been regretted as a Misfortune to the Youth of this Province, that we have no Academy, in which they might receive the Accomplishments of a regular Education."[4] Years later, looking back on this period in his autobiography, he summed up the essence of the values of Quaker Philadelphia as follows: "There were two things that I regretted, there being no provision for defense nor for a compleat education for youth."[5]

Within a decade of their landing and settling in a few towns around the shores of Massachusetts Bay, the Puritan colony, with over 100 graduates of Oxford and Cambridge, was surely the best educated community the world has ever known, before or since. "In its inception," wrote Moses Coit Tyler in his history of American colonial literature, "New England was not an agricultural community, nor a manufacturing community, nor a trading community: it was a thinking community; an arena and mart for ideas; its characteristic organ being not the hand, nor the heart or the pocket, but the brain."[6]

The ministers and magistrates who founded Massachusetts Bay Colony were bearers of an ancient intellectual and educational tradition. John Calvin was the best educated and most coldly intellectual of all the great Reformation leaders. As we have seen, Cambridge was the nursery of both English and New England Puritanism. In Max Weber's terms, the English Revolution witnessed the rising importance of the "certificate of education" as the mark of the gentleman. And it was the Old Testament and elitist values of the founders of Massachusetts that led them to see the need for an educated class of gentlemen as a major means of insuring social control in times of stability, social reform in times of needed change, and revolution from the top in times of crisis.

If our intellectual traditions came to America through the port of Boston, our equally strong anti-intellectual traditions came through the port of Philadelphia. This latter tradition, perhaps more typically American than the former, had its roots in the antinomian and Anabaptist movements of the continental Reformation and was then transplanted or reborn in the course of the

English Revolution. Hofstadter described the birth of the ideas that came to America through the port of Philadelphia.

> As the English religious reformers became convinced that the Reformation had gone far enough to meet the social and spiritual needs of their followers, successive waves of Millenarians, Anabaptists, Seekers, Ranters, Quakers assailed the established order and its clergy, preached a religion of the poor, argued for intuition and inspiration as against learning and doctrine, elevated lay preachers to leadership, and rejected the professional clergy as "null and void and without authority." At the time of the Puritan revolution, the preachers of the New Model Army were unsparing in their anti-professional and anti-intellectual broadsides against the clergy, the university teachers, and the lawyers. . . . the left-wing chaplains, in the line of the Levellers and Diggers, followed Gerrard Winstanley's example in calling the universities "standing ponds of stinking waters," in pointing out that a liberal education did nothing to make men less sinful, and in stirring the egalitarian passions of the poor.[7]

If the heirs of the left-wing sects of the Reformation have continued to stir the "egalitarian passions of the poor," the Congregational and Presbyterian heirs of rational and hierarchical Calvinism in America surely stirred the passions of the successful to use their privileges to take the lead in many areas of American life, and especially in the founding of institutions of higher learning. Of the nine colleges established before the Revolution, for example, the heirs of Calvinism founded five: the Congregationalists founded Harvard, Yale, and Dartmouth; the Presbyterians, Princeton; and the Dutch Reformed, Rutgers. Of the other colonial colleges, Anglicans founded William and Mary and Columbia; and the Baptists, Brown.* The University of Pennsylvania, partly because of Franklin's secular and scientific convictions but predominantly because of sectarian rivalries in the colony, was founded as the first secular institution of higher learning in the colonies. Nevertheless, the College of Philadelphia was in fact dominated by Anglican members of the proprietary party from its beginning.

HIGHER EDUCATION IN EARLY MASSACHUSETTS AND PENNSYLVANIA

In contrast to Massachusetts, where four still surviving colleges were founded before the Civil War—Harvard (1636), Williams (1793), Amherst (1825), and Tufts (1852)—Pennsylvania was always plagued by sectarian rivalry and lack of broad public support for higher education. Of the thirty-one colleges founded

---

*Of the 207 institutions of higher learning in America founded before the Civil War, all save 27 (founded by state and municipal governments) were founded by religious groups. Of these 180 religiously founded institutions 65, or about a third, were founded by the heirs of Calvinism: Presbyterian, 49; Congregational, 21; German Reformed, 4; and Dutch Reformed, 1. One must remember that Congregationalists on the frontier outside New England tended to become Presbyterians, that is, bureaucratically rather than class dominated. In settlement after settlement Presbyterian ministers founded academies, many of which grew into colleges, in order "to prepare the men who should feed the flock of God," as the Congregationalist-Presbyterian founders of Western Reserve University once put it. No wonder that by 1851, "two-thirds of the colleges in the land were directly or indirectly under the control of the Presbyterian Church" (Donald G. Tewksbury, *The Founding of American Colleges and Universities before the Civil War* [New York: Archon, 1965], p. 92).

in Pennsylvania before the Civil War, only sixteen survived, most of them having severe financial difficulties throughout their early histories. Naturally, the Presbyterians led all other religious groups in the state. Of the sixteen surviving colleges, the heirs of Calvinism founded nine—the Presbyterians founded Dickinson (1783), Washington and Jefferson (1802), Allegheny (1817), University of Pittsburgh (1819), Lafayette (1826), Geneva (1850), Waynesburg (1850), and Westminister (1852); the German Reformed Church founded Franklin and Marshall (1787); the Lutherans founded Gettysburg (1832) and Irving Female College (1857); the Baptists founded Bucknell (1846); the Catholics founded Jesuit St. Joseph's (1852) in Philadelphia and the Augustinian College of Villanova (1848) on the Main Line; finally, Orthodox Friends, in reaction to the Hicksite separation of 1827, founded Haverford College (1856). In the education of American leadership, none of these Pennsylvania colleges, save Quaker Haverford, has reached the first-rate status of Amherst or Williams, nor have they educated many sons of the American upper class from Pennsylvania or elsewhere.*

The three major upper-class institutions in America have been Harvard, Yale, and Princeton. From the beginning of the nation, graduates of these schools have dominated positions of leadership. Thus, the signers of the Declaration of Independence were graduates of the following institutions:

Harvard	Yale
John Adams (1755)	Lyman Hall (1747)
Samuel Adams (1740)	Philip Livingston (1737)
William Ellery (1747)	Lewis Morris (1746)
Elbridge Gerry (1762)	Oliver Wolcott (1747)
John Hancock (1754)	
William Hooper (1760)	Princeton
Robert Treat Paine (1749)	Benjamin Rush (1760)
William Williams (1751)	Richard Stockton (1748)

William and Mary	Pennsylvania
Carter Braxton	Francis Hopkinson (1757)
Thomas Jefferson (1762)	William Paca (1759)
Benjamin Harrison (1745)	
George Wythe	

---

*Sack showed how 274 institutions (87 failed) had been founded in the state since its beginning. In the concluding pages of his exhaustive book, he emphasized the utilitarian and technological aspects of higher education in Pennsylvania after 1850.

A phenomenon of higher education in Pennsylvania has been its relative lack of leaders of national stature. . . . Considering the large number of institutions, living and dead, which Pennsylvania has nurtured, there have been few whose leadership has extended much beyond the boundaries of the State. Three, however, gained a secure place in our national educational history. Benjamin Franklin is virtually without peer as an educational architect. William Smith, the first provost of the College, Academy and Charitable School of Philadelphia, with his College of Mirania and his curriculum of 1756, profoundly affected the course of colleges in the United States. Further, colleges for women everywhere owe an incalculable debt to Martha Carey Thomas of Bryn Mawr (Saul Sack, *History of Higher Education in Pennsylvania* [Harrisburg: Pennsylvania Historical and Museum Commission, 1963], p. 741).

Incidentally, none of these three leaders was a native of Pennsylvania.

Although Harvard men predominated in the founding of the nation in 1776, Princetonians predominated at the Constitutional Convention. James Madison of Princeton took the intellectual lead, along with Hamilton of Columbia, in writing the *Federalist Papers*. Of the fifty-five delegates, nine were from Princeton, five each from Yale and William and Mary, three from Harvard, and two each from Columbia and the University of Pennsylvania.

Of presidents of the United States, five—two Adamses, two Roosevelts, and John F. Kennedy—graduated from Harvard; Taft was from Yale; and Madison and Wilson were from Princeton (Rutherford B. Hayes got a bachelor of laws from Harvard, and Gerald Ford a law degree from Yale).* Of the forty-four secretaries of state between 1789 and 1962, exactly half were graduates of Harvard (eleven), Princeton (six), or Yale (five). No president or secretary of state graduated from the University of Pennsylvania.

PRINCETON AND THE EXPANSION OF NEW ENGLAND

"The expansion of New England," wrote Thomas Jefferson Wertenbaker, "is one of the major movements of American history."[8] The first exodus from Massachusetts Bay, as we have seen, was a response to the orthodox rigidity of the Puritan saints. And upon the banishment of the Hutchinsonians, Harvard College was founded to protect against any further liberalizing tendencies among the people. From then on, however, the various exoduses from the Puritan colonies, especially to the West, were the result not of orthodoxy but of increasing liberalism at home. Davenport and his followers founded New Haven on an even more rigid Calvinism than was practiced in Boston. Yale, established after the Mathers lost out to the more liberal and secular forces at Harvard, began as a stronghold of orthodoxy. In the meantime, after the liberalizing halfway covenant in Connecticut, the more orthodox Calvinists in New Haven went west and founded Newark, New Jersey, in order to maintain their purity. In northern New Jersey, Newark, Elizabeth, and many smaller towns throughout Essex, Union, and Morris counties emulated New England architecture and religious and political organization. Indeed, for eighty years after the founding of Newark and Elizabeth, only Harvard and Yale graduates were acceptable there as ministers.

Two of these ministers, Jonathan Dickinson, of Elizabeth, and Aaron Burr, of Newark, became the first two presidents of Princeton after its founding in 1746. Dickinson was born in Massachusetts and taken by his parents to Connecticut, where he graduated from Yale in 1706. His first calling was to the Congregationalist church at Elizabeth. He eventually led his congregation to join the Philadelphia presbytery in 1717. In the great schism in the presbytery of Philadelphia he and Gilbert Tennent led the "New Side" forces, which

---

*The only president from the state of Pennsylvania was Buchanan, a graduate of Presbyterian Dickinson College; Coolidge, Garfield, and Pierce graduated from Amherst, Williams, and Bowdoin respectively, all Congregationalist offshoots of Harvard.

joined the presbytery, or synod, of New York in 1745, with Dickinson as moderator. The "Old Side" leaders remained in Philadelphia.

"It may be doubted," wrote John E. Pomfret, "whether, with the exception of the elder Edwards, Calvinism ever found an abler and more efficient champion of Calvinism in this country than Dickinson."[9] And he soon saw the need for an institution of higher education in the middle colonies. In 1746 Dickinson and other leaders of the New Side synod of New York and New Brunswick obtained a charter for the College of New Jersey. The original board of trustees—six members from Yale and one from Harvard—elected five more—four graduates of Tennent's Log College and one from Yale. The college opened in 1747, classes being held in Dickinson's parsonage at Elizabeth. Six months later Dickinson died and classes moved to the parsonage of Aaron Burr in Newark.

Burr's great-grandfather Jehu Burr had come to Massachusetts with the Winthrop fleet and then gone out with William Pynchon to settle the wilderness town of Springfield. In the second generation, the Burrs moved to Fairfield, Connecticut, where Aaron Burr was born and raised. After graduating from Yale with high honors, he was called to Newark, where he took an active part in local religious revivals, married the daughter of Jonathan Edwards, and ran a school.

Burr was the first organizer of the College of New Jersey, drawing up its entrance requirements, its curriculum, and its code of rules for internal government. He also helped his close friend, ally, and fellow New Englander Governor Jonathan Belcher in building Nassau Hall on newly acquired land in Princeton. Burr and Belcher died within a year of the college's move to Princeton, and Jonathan Edwards was called to the presidency. He died shortly after taking office, and the Reverend James Finley, a Scotch-Irish immigrant with a divinity degree from Glasgow, was called to the presidency in 1761, where he remained until his death in 1766.

The College of New Jersey, in the Calvinist tradition of its founders, was the first cosmopolitan school for leadership in North America, educating young men from the southern and middle colonies as well as from New England. Many of its early graduates were educational leaders throughout the colonies: Tapping Reeve (1763) founded his famous law school in Litchfield, Connecticut; John Ewing (1754) became the first provost of the newly reorganized University of Pennsylvania; among the founders or first presidents of other colleges were James Manning (1762) of Brown, Jonathan Edwards, Jr. (1765), of Union College, Samuel Kirkland (1765) of Hamilton College, Joseph Alexander (1760) of North Carolina, and Benjamin Rush (1760) of Dickinson College. Princetonians also took the lead in politics and government: George Washington appointed Oliver Ellsworth (1766) chief justice, and William Patterson (1763) associate justice, of the U.S. Supreme Court; his first two attorneys general were William Bradford (1774) and Charles Lee (1775).*

The greatest president of the College of New Jersey was John Witherspoon, direct descendant of John Knox, doctor of divinity from Edinburgh, and con-

---

*Princeton, moreover, produced five senators from Pennsylvania as against only two from the University of Pennsylvania.

servative leader in the Scottish General Assembly, who was called to the presidency from Paisley, Scotland, in 1768. The only divine to sign the Declaration of Independence, Witherspoon educated the greatest leadership generation in Princeton history. Of the 230 men graduating under his presidency, for example, James Madison became president, twelve sat in the Continental Congress and six in the Constitutional Convention, twelve were members of Congress, three were justices of the Supreme Court, three were attorneys general, two were foreign ministers, one was secretary of state, and one (Aaron Burr) was vice-president.

I have discussed the founding of Princeton in detail, first, in order to show how the three principal upper-class institutions of higher learning in America, from colonial times to the present, were spiritual heirs of the values of the 130 Puritan graduates of Oxford and Cambridge who came to Massachusetts Bay between 1630 and 1646; and, second, to demonstrate that though Princeton has educated many leading Philadelphians down through the years, Philadelphians had little to do with its founding. It was the Presbyterian brainchild of New England Congregationalists and Scottish Calvinists. Princeton, moreover, has drawn Philadelphians away from their native city throughout its history, first for religious reasons and later for reasons of fashion and social prestige. Of the men in the Philadelphia sample, for instance, William Shippen, Nicholas Biddle, Benjamin Rush, George Mifflin Dallas, Charles Jared Ingersoll, George Boker, and the members of the leading legal family of Sergeants (descendants of Jonathan Dickinson) went to Princeton for religious reasons.

Princeton became the most fashionable Proper Philadelphia college after the First World War. Of the families listed in the 1940 Philadelphia *Social Register*, 442 individuals graduated from college during the 1920s and 1930s, of these, 10 percent went to Harvard, 13 percent to Yale, and 34 percent to Princeton (57 percent in all), as against only 22 percent who went to the University of Pennsylvania. These figures reflect the lack of local pride in Philadelphia, which I shall try to explain by comparing the history of Harvard with that of the University of Pennsylvania.

HARVARD AND PENN: BOSTON ETHNOCENTRISM AND PHILADELPHIA XENOPHILIA

Hierarchical and deference democracies tend to exhibit a certain amount of pride in their own institutions; in contrast, leveling and defiant democracies seem to suffer from a curious lack of faith in themselves and tend to look abroad for examples of excellence.* This rule has characterized Philadelphians for most of their history, as Owen Wister's previously quoted remark about his

---

*Throughout most of our history, educated Americans have suffered from anglophilia; and perhaps the popularity of Ho Chi Minh or Chairman Mao's *Little Red Book* among so many talented members of our younger generation in the levelling 1960s, to say nothing of the Russophilia which infected both British and American intellectuals during the 1930s, were also examples of this general rule.

native city's curious instinct for self-disparagement so sadly reveals. Cheering *against* the home team is a time-honored tradition in Philadelphia. Even today, when the university is in the midst of the greatest renaissance in its history, Penn* students and faculty have a propensity for running themselves down—a tendency in striking contrast to Boston's chauvinistic view of itself as the hub of the universe, which is matched by the arrogant self-confidence exhibited by the students and faculty at Harvard.

Harvard was founded in 1636 and graduated its first class of nine bachelors of art in 1642, the year of the outbreak of the English Revolution. Penn dates its origin to the founding of a charitable school in 1740, but the College of Philadelphia graduated its first class of nine bachelors of arts in 1757, three-quarters of a century after the colony's founding.

From its beginning, Harvard has had the support not only of the Boston ruling class but also of the whole city and state. Penn, however, has never been supported to anywhere near the same extent by either the city's upper class or the rest of the people in the city and state. Other characteristic differences also reflect their distinct founding ideals and, more important, the contrasting values of the two cities in which these institutions are located. Thus, Harvard was named after an obscure graduate of Emmanuel College, Cambridge; Penn has for over a century thought of renaming itself after its famous patron saint, Benjamin Franklin, but has never done so. Moreover, Harvard has always been located on the same campus in Cambridge. Penn did not build its own campus until it moved to its present site in West Philadelphia in the 1870s. It built its first College Hall in 1872 and its first dormitories at the very end of the nineteenth century, not housing a majority of its students on campus until well after the Second World War. Harvard students have lived in the Yard from the beginning. Its first president, Henry Dunster, made sure that the Harvard degree was recognized by Oxford and Cambridge and even modeled the school after the colleges there: the campus was designed for a communal life for all students, rich and poor alike; from the beginning "it was the intention of the college laws," wrote Morison, "to confine Harvard students to the College and the Yard twenty-four hours a day."[10] They were allowed to go home only a few days a term. Penn, more in the continental tradition, was a commuter college for most of its history, the sons of the rich going home to study in their fathers' ample libraries and the poor doing the best they could in simple surroundigs.† (Harvard's first library building, Gore Hall, was built in 1838, largely from a be-

---

*I use "Penn" here for several reasons. First, it is less cumbersome than "University of Pennsylvania." Second, it points up a persistent identity problem suffered by Philadelphia's local university: "Oh, you went to Penn State," is the auslander's usual reaction to an alumnus. Officials of the university have long been aware of this problem and have often thought of renaming the school Franklin University or, as I should prefer, Penn University.

†People used to speak of the haughty Harvard man with the accent, the earnest Eli, the proper Princetonian, and the Bryn Mawr Woman in the Hepburn style, but nobody ever characterized the typical Penn man, perhaps because the student body lacked the collegiality that comes of a shared campus life. This sort of stereotyping has been done away with on elite campuses today, where particularistic values have been replaced by more universalistic and uniform (SAT score) values.

quest of $100,000 from Christopher Gore, governor of Massachusetts and United States senator. Penn's first library building was designed by Frank Furness and completed in 1891.)

In many ways the most important difference between Penn and Harvard has been in their leadership structure. From 1636 to 1940, Harvard was run by a unified ruling class of Bostonians—Puritans and clergymen at first, later, State Street Brahmins. At the same time, it has always had presidents, usually Harvard bred, with considerable power in theory and practice, especially men like Dunster, Leverett, Kirkland, Quincy, and its two great builders, Eliot and Lowell, who ruled for sixty-four years between them. That the board trusted presidential leadership is best illustrated in the case of Charles W. Eliot: though many were hesitant about his appointment in the first place, and few approved of his utilitarian philosophy of strengthening professional and graduate schools at the expense of the college (or of his replacing the classical curriculum with the utilitarian and cafeterialike elective system), they knew a good man when they saw one and let him have his way. The overseers stood by Eliot even though, as Morison put it, "If at any time before 1886, perhaps before 1890, his policies had been referred to a plebiscite of Harvard alumni, they would surely have been reversed."[11]

The leadership at Penn has been very different. In the beginning, though founded as religiously neutral, the school was dominated by wealthy Anglicans. In the political revolution that shook the city in 1776, the Anglican trustees of the college were ousted (in 1779) and the University of Pennsylvania formed by the revolutionary forces led by Presbyterians. In many ways the trustees during the brief period of Presbyterian control of the university (between 1779 and 1789, when the old conservative forces came back into power) were most like the upper-class leaders at Harvard in that this board was truly representative of the ruling, rather than the fashionable, class of the city and state.*

PRESIDENTS AT HARVARD, PROVOSTS AT PENN

John Ewing, first provost during the Presbyterian interlude, resigned in 1802 because of ill health, and a new board of trustees took over. From that day to 1940, the board has been made up of "the pick of the representative men of the old families of Philadelphia."[12] These men represented money, fashion, and family but were hardly a ruling class in either the city or the state. Not only were the trustees drawn from a narrow social circle but they, or the various

---

*The new board included Joseph Reed, president of the executive council of Pennsylvania, William Moore, vice-president of the state, Timothy Matlack, secretary, John Bayard, speaker of the Assembly, John Dickinson, attorney general, and Chief Justice Thomas McKean. The board also included a representative group of clergymen: John Ewing, also provost, was a Presbyterian divine and a graduate of Princeton; Bishop William White was an Episcopalian; a Dr. Kunze and a Dr. Weiberg represented the two factions among the Lutherans; and a Father Farmer represented the Catholics.

committees among them, ran the university and controlled every detail of administration and policy.

That Penn is the only institution of higher learning in America to have had a provost rather than a president at its head throughout most of its long history surely symbolizes the ancient mistrust of leadership in the city. From its founding, with the exception of William Smith and possibly Dr. William Pepper and Charles C. Harrison at the turn of the nineteenth century, the provosts at Penn were limited in taking any initiative by the stultifying committee system of the trustees. The provosts were not members of the board, nor were they allowed to sit in on its deliberations. And whereas Harvard's presidents were graduates of the college and, after Kirkland, secular educators trusted and encouraged by the overseers to take the lead, the provosts at Penn—mainly clergymen rather than educators—were chosen largely from outside the city and were educated elsewhere.

Typical of Penn's nineteenth-century leadership was the Reverend John Ludlow, a graduate of Union College. The only thing the historian of Penn, Edward Potts Cheyney, had to say of Ludlow, who held office longer than any other provost in the nineteenth century, was that "in spite of the twenty years of his provostship he left little personal impress on the University."[13] A critic during Ludlow's tenure wrote of the "absence of any pride in the institution or any interest shown by the public" and then went on to point out that only one donation—of $5,000—had been made to it in the preceding eighty years. Lack of local pride in higher education in the city was also felt by the Reverend Daniel R. Goodwin, a native of Maine and graduate of Bowdoin, who was Provost at Penn during the Civil War. When a young and enthusiastic professor made some suggestions about changes which might make the University more influential in the city, Provost Goodwin observed that "only about one hundred young men in Philadelphia wanted a college education, and that this number was not likely to increase very much even with an increase in population, and that any modification of the present system to meet the demands of public opinion was unlikely to be agreed to by the University authorities."[13]

BOARD NEPOTISM AT HARVARD
AND AT PENN

Cheyney attributed the extreme conservatism of Penn's leadership to the selection of trustees from a closed circle of upper-class Philadelphians. But I suggest that the values of this group, not its social origins, kept the university small and provincial. It is here that comparative history is useful, for nepotism was far more characteristic of Harvard's administrators, though that school produced so many of the nation's leaders. When Eliot became president in 1869, he observed that the overseers were drawn from the same families that had ruled the college for over a century. His own family dynasty at Harvard was outlined by Morison as shown in Figure 14–1. The Lowell dynasty at Harvard

Figure 14–1   The Eliot Dynasty

Andrew Eliot, 1683–1749; cordwainer of Beverly,
subsequently merchant of Boston

Andrew Eliot, 1718–78;
A.B. 1737, Fellow 1765–78,
Secretary Board of
Overseers 1758–78

Samuel Eliot, 1713–45;
Boston bookseller

Andrew Eliot, 1743–1805;
A.B. 1762, Librarian,
Tutor, and Fellow 1763–74,
minister of Fairfield.

Joba Eliot,
1754–1813;
A.B. 1772,
Fellow 1804–13

Samuel Eliot, 1739–1820;
merchant, founder of Eliot
Professorship of Greek

William Havard Eliot,
1795–1831; A.B. 1815

Samuel Atkins Eliot,
1798–1862; A.B. 1817.
Treasurer
1842–53

Catharine,
m. Andrews
Norton, A.B.
1804, Tutor,
Librarian,
and Dexter
Professor
1811–30

Anna, m. Geo.
Ticknor, A.B.
1814, Smith
Professor
1817–35

Samuel Eliot, 1821–98;
A.B. 1839, Overseer
1866–72, President
of Trinity College,
Hartford

Charles William Eliot,
1834–1926; A.B. 1853,
Tutor and Asst. Prof.
1854–63, President
1869–1909, Overseer
1868–69, 1910–16

Charles Eliot Norton,
1827–1908; A.B. 1846,
Lecturer and
Professor 1874–98,
Overseer 1899–1908

Source: Samuel Eliot Morison, *Three Centuries of Harvard, 1636–1936* (Cambridge: Harvard University Press, 1963), p. 225.

was even longer than that of the Eliots. When A. Lawrence Lowell resigned from the presidency in 1933, his family had been connected with the college for over two centuries, as Figure 14-2 shows.

Nepotism combined with the very high value placed on achievement and leadership proved to be good for Harvard, where membership in the board of overseers has brought the highest social prestige within the city's upper class for over 300 years. Indeed, *all the families* in the Boston sample have been connected with Harvard in one way or another—as students, faculty members, overseers, or presidents. At Penn, students, teachers, and administrators generally have not been intimately related either to Philadelphia's upper class or to the city and state leadership as a whole.

Figure 14–2   The Lowell Dynasty

Rev. John Lowell, A.B. 1721

Judge John Lowell, 1743–1802; A.B. 1760, LL.D. 1792
Fellow 1784–1802

John Lowell, 1769–1840
A.B. 1786, LL.D. 1814
Fellow 1810–1822
Overseer 1823–1827

Francis Cabot Lowell
1775–1817; A.B. 1793

Rev. Charles Lowell
1782–1861; A.B.
1800, S.T.D. 1823
Overseer 1806–51
Fellow 1818

John Amory Lowell
1798–1881; A.B. 1815
LL.D. 1851, Fellow
1837–1877

John Lowell
1799–1836
Class of 1817
Founder of the
Lowell Institute

Francis Cabot Lowell
1803–1874; A.B. 1821

James Russell Lowell
1819–1891; A.B.
1838; LL.D. 1884
Professor 1855–86,
Overseer 1887–91

Judge John Lowell
1824–1897; A.B.
1843, Overseer
1875–1886

Augustus Lowell
1830–1900
A.B. 1850

George Gardner Lowell
1830–1885; A.B. 1850

Abbott Lawrence Lowell
b. 1856; A.B. 1877
LL.D. 1880, LL.D. 1934
Lecturer and Professor
1897–1909. President
1909–1933

Judge Francis Cabot Lowell
1855–1911; A.B. 1876
Overseer 1886–1895
Fellow 1895–1911

Source: Samuel Eliot Morison, *Three Centuries of Harvard, 1636–1936* (Cambridge: Harvard University Press, 1963), p. 159.

THE COLLEGE AT HARVARD, PROFESSIONAL EDUCATION AT PENN

A significant difference between Penn and Harvard lies in their attitudes toward the importance of an undergraduate education in the classics and the liberal arts. The college, even during Eliot's efforts to emphasize the graduate schools, has always been the heart of Harvard. At Penn, undergraduate education was more or less neglected until after the Second World War. In the early days the medical school overshadowed the college and in later years, as we shall see, the liberal arts gradually took second place to the more practical subjects such as engineering and business education. The differences began early: Franklin had looked down on the Harvard snobs in his youth and preferred that the College of Philadelphia be "utilitarian rather than cultural," as Cheyney put it. "It should include mathematics, geography, history, logic, and natural and moral philosophy. It should be an education for citizenship, and should lead to mercantile and civic success and usefulness."[14] Here Franklin was following the utilitarian educational values of early Quakerism. Even though the Anglican trustees and William Smith preferred Latin and the classics, and won out temporarily, Franklin had his way in the long run, especially after the founding of the Wharton School by a prominent Philadelphia Quaker.

The weak position of the college at Penn can be seen in the year 1836, when the *Albany Register* published a list of the number of bachelor of arts degrees granted by leading northern colleges: Yale, eighty-one; Union, seventy-one; Princeton, sixty-six; Dartmouth, forty-four; Harvard, thirty-nine;* Amherst, thirty-eight; Middlebury, thirty-two; Williams, twenty-nine; New York University, twenty-six; Brown, twenty-two; Bowdoin, twenty-two, Rutgers, twenty-one; Columbia, twenty. Penn, which granted only seventeen bachelor of arts degrees that year, was not included in the *Register's* list. The subservient position of the college at the time is illustrated by the fact that in 1836 the medical school graduated 124 physicians, by far the largest number in the nation.† In the spring of 1836, Philadelphia's great Horace Binney, a graduate of Harvard, and two of his fellow trustees resigned from the board in protest over the emphasis on the medical school at the expense of the college.

PHILADELPHIANS GO TO COLLEGE ELSEWHERE

Cheyney suggested Penn's weak position in Philadelphia when he casually noted that in 1854, when there were only eighty students enrolled in the college, forty-two Philadelphians were attending colleges elsewhere, fourteen of them Princeton. Nevertheless, throughout the nineteenth century, a majority of the sons of Proper Philadelphia families did go to Penn if they went to college at all. Without dormitories, however, Penn was unable to draw many students from outside the city. One is led to the conclusion that the fashionable families from which the trustees and the wealthy students were drawn were inadvertently fostering a so-called guarded education for their sons in the traditional Quaker style. This was brought out in a Philadelphian's answer to an editorial in the *Nation*, in December 1885, that outlined the deplorable state of civic and political affairs in Philadelphia, a provincial city "drivelling in village swaddling

---

*Harvard granted only thirty-nine bachelor of arts degrees in 1836 because of the large number of student expulsions in 1834, when there was a major rebellion after the autocratic President Josiah Quincy called the local police to quell rioting within the Yard.

†Harvard graduated only twenty men from the medical school in 1836, among them Oliver Wendell Holmes.

clothes."[15] The writer of the letter to the *Nation* was no birthright detractor like Sidney Fisher but a relatively new resident of Philadelphia who loved the mild charm of his adopted city and its people. He nevertheless saw the connection between the backward and provincial city and the backward and provincial local university.

> Philadelphia's regeneration will come . . . if the principle of protection should cease to be applied to the University itself. The institution has no dormitories. . . . It being the case that no provision is made for students from a distance, few such come, and the great majority of undergraduates is composed of those who live in Philadelphia. . . . Some years ago the trustees had a large legacy offered them if they would build dormitories. After consideration, they declined it, as it would involve a change in their whole policy. The aim of this policy is to train boys up in the way they should go, meaning by that, so they will regard Philadelphia doctrines, ideas, atmosphere, and surroundings as final. The result is, that the institution is an advanced kind of high school, where the scholars go and recite their lessons, are marked, and then go home again.[16]

Harvard, too, was an intensely local and parochial institution throughout its early history. By 1810, however, 11 percent of the entering class came from outside New England, 18 percent by 1816, and 27 percent by 1820. That Harvard was becoming a national school at the upper-class level, moreover, is indicated in Morison's history of the college: "In the Porcellian Club for the classes of 1822–1826, one finds a Carroll, a Calvert and a Bonaparte from Maryland; a Taloe from Washington; a Carter, a Marshall, and a Taliaferro from Virginia; an Elliott, a Yates, and two Minigaults from Charleston; a Cheves, a Fisher, and a Willing from Philadelphia; Larz Anderson from Louisville; and representatives of Savannah, St. Augustine, Mobile, New Orleans, Havana, Natchez, New York, Hartford, Vermont, Salem, and Boston."[17] While these young bloods gave a certain national tone to Harvard, the majority of their classmates were still from New England families of middling income.

When Penn moved to West Philadelphia in the 1870s, Charles J. Stillé, Philadelphia lawyer and Yale graduate, was provost. He was surely the best man to hold the office since John Ewing resigned in 1802. Stillé took office with high hopes for improving the university but finally resigned in despair because of the high-handedness of the trustees, who treated the faculty as mere servants with no clear authority over the students. At the end of his long and bitter letter of resignation, he wrote: "We shall never succeed until we find a man whom we shall recognize as an organizer, a leader, whom we shall trust, because we know he has been specially trained, and that he will give all his energy and capacity to this work in which he is engaged."[18]

Stillé was succeeded by Penn's two great builders, Dr. William Pepper* and Charles C. Harrison.

---

*In 1881, the year Pepper took command, the college graduated a class that began with 97 freshmen, of whom 48 did not take degrees, 18 were awarded bachelor of science degrees, and only 31 took bachelor of arts degrees (that year 117 medical degrees were awarded). Of the 198 members of the Harvard class of 1881, 161 men, including Philadelphians Boies Penrose (magna cum laude) and his brother Charles Bingham Penrose (summa cum laude), received bachelor of arts degrees from the college (31 medical degrees were awarded). That only half the entering freshmen at Penn took degrees has been a persistent pattern in Philadelphia, especially among the sons of the upper classes.

BUILDERS OF THE MODERN UNIVERSITIES AT HARVARD AND PENN: PRESIDENTS ELIOT AND LOWELL AND PROVOSTS PEPPER AND HARRISON

The Olympian Age at Harvard spanned the sixty-four years between 1869 and 1933 when Charles W. Eliot (1869–1909) and A. Lawrence Lowell (1910–1933) held the presidency. The two great builders of the modern university at Penn were provots William Pepper (1881–1894) and Charles C. Harrison (1895–1910).

Brahmins both, Eliot and Lowell nevertheless held very different views about higher education in America. Whereas Eliot concentrated his efforts on building the graduate and professional schools, somewhat at the expense of the College, which he atomized with his famous elective system, Eliot paid more attention to the College and will be remember as the greatest builder in Harvard's history. While Eliot admired the German university system and was an optimistic utilitarian in the Franklin mold (he had won the Franklin Medal at Boston Latin), Lowell was an ardent Anglophile and saw the need to restore a sense of collegiality at the rapidly expanding College. In the years of Eliot's reign, there began to develop two Harvards at the College, partly due to lack of dormitory space for all undergraduates. While the less affluent lived in the less expensive and college-run dormitories, or commuted, the wealthy, who also were now coming increasingly from private schools, were housed in more luxurious dormitories built by private money and private contractors, or later, in boarding houses that came to be called the "Gold Coast." Eliot saw this but did not do anything about it. Lowell, far more of an elitist and authoritarian than Eliot, was nevertheless a strong believer in an aristocracy of intellect rather than of money. Admiring the collegial nature of Oxford and Cambridge, and also the tutorial and honors systems there, he proceeded to modify Eliot's system by creating concentrations, and above all, by building a system of dormitories and tutors assigned to student residents. It was hard going until, as a crowning symbol of his whole philosophy, he accepted in ten seconds the offer of Edward S. Harkness (Yale, 1897) to endow a House Plan at Harvard in 1928.

At roughly the same time as Eliot was running Harvard, two Philadelphia Gentlemen took over the provostship at Penn. As the only two provosts to be drawn from our Fifty Family sample, they were able to exert their inherited class authority in the provost's office. They were also both wealthy men, in a city where the latent respect for money is even stronger than the manifest respect for family. They had both graduated from Penn in the class of 1862, along with John Cadwalader, a long-time trustee. Pepper came to the office at the prime of his active life (age thirty-eight), spent mostly in the medical school, where he continued to serve after assuming the duties of provost. He built some twenty new buildings, including a medical school and a hospital side by side, which was unique in America. He added thirteen new departments including the Wharton School, doubled the student body, and left the University with five million dollars' worth of property (a million and a half when he took office). He also built the Furness Library. He wore himself out at the job, resigned because of ill health, and died at the age of fifty-five. Harrison continued his work and, if anything, was even more of a money-raiser. He built thirteen new buildings to house the thirteen departments founded by Pepper. In many ways most important of all, he built the first dormitories, and Houston Hall, the first student union in America. He founded the graduate school and endowed it himself with a large number of Harrison Fellowships, which are still bringing talented students to the school from all over the nation and abroad.

Penn's great building era came to an end when Harrison resigned in 1910. In that year Harvard graduated perhaps the most distinguished class in its history, which included T. S. Eliot, Walter Lippmann, and John Reed. Harvard awarded 440 A.B.'s and 72 M.D.'s that year. In striking contrast to Harvard's continuing emphasis on the liberal arts, Penn's utilitarian emphasis was now stronger than ever. Of the 697 students who entered with the class of 1910, 407 failed to take degrees; of the 290 who did, 255 were given B.S. degrees in engineering, science, and in business (Wharton); only 35 were awarded A.B.'s from the still small college (only four more than the 31 who got A.B.'s in 1881; the medical school graduated a class of 135). This same utilitarian emphasis at Penn continued down to 1940, when the majority of undergraduates took B.S. degrees in Economics from the Wharton School.

WHARTON AND THE HARVARD
BUSINESS SCHOOL

When Provost Pepper, in his inaugural address in 1881, announced that Joseph Wharton, one of the most successful manufacturers in the city and a birthright and loyal Friend, had donated $100,000 to the university in order to found the Wharton School of Finance and Commerce, he firmly pressed the utilitarian stamp on undergraduate education at Penn, which it has not as yet fully cast off. At first Wharton was a department within the college, but gradually it became a self-directing and separately financed school.* By 1910, Wharton was granting more degrees than the college and engineering school combined, and its popularity increased steadily. Its graduates, moreover, are proud to call themselves Wharton men (no one confuses them with alumni of Penn State) and, as measured by alumni giving, they have always been far more loyal to their alma mater than have their counterparts to the college.

In contrast to Wharton, primarily an undergraduate school until well after World War II, the Harvard Graduate School of Business has never been allowed to contaminate undergraduates. Thus, John P. Marquand's George Apley always kept eyes right† when driving along the Charles from Boston to

---

*Although Quakers have long been conspicuous by their absence from the faculty at Penn, several deans of Wharton have been Friends.

†Whereas Wharton is located in the heart of the Penn campus, the Harvard Business School was placed on the opposite bank of the Charles River from College Yard.

Cambridge, in order to avoid seeing this "most damnable example of material-ism, . . . the new School of Business Administration."[18] This monument to ma-terialism, however, was not given to Harvard by anyone of Apley's breed but by George F. Baker of New York. "Though widely different," Apley wrote to his son in the 1920s,

> it is as great a threat to idealism as Prohibition itself. I have, of course, not been to see it and when I motor by it I look the other way; but I hear that there is a tablet upon one of the buildings which greatly amuses me. If I am not mistaken it speaks of business as the "newest of the arts and the oldest of the professions." If this is so, it is wrong on both counts. Certainly there is one profession which is older.[19]

The Boston Apleys, with generations of graduates from Harvard College, had no faith in the utilitarian values of Philadelphians like Joseph Wharton.

FACULTY ORIGINS: BRAHMINS AT HARVARD, OUTSIDERS AT PENN

Whereas members of the Harvard College faculty have always enjoyed con-siderable prestige in Boston, this has never been true of the Penn faculty (except that of the medical school) in Philadelphia. Of the fifty Boston First Families a large proportion have had members who belonged to the faculty of Harvard College: John Winthrop IV, in science; George Ticknor, in Spanish literature; Edward Everett, first Eliot Professor in Greek Literature and later university president; Charles W. Eliot, in chemistry; A. Lawrence Lowell, who founded the department of government; Henry Adams, Henry Cabot Lodge, and Ed-ward Jackson Lowell, in history; Francis Greenwood Peabody, in Christian ethics, who gave the first course at Harvard in sociology; Percival Lowell, founder of the Harvard Observatory at Flagstaff, Arizona, and Edward Charles Pickering, in astronomy; Theodore Lyman, in zoology; Henry Wadsworth Longfellow, James Russell Lowell, and Barrett Wendell, in literature; Charles Eliot Norton, who founded art history at Harvard; Frederick Ward Putnam, first George Peabody Professor of Anthropology and one of the founders of his science in America; Charles Pickering Bowditch, in archeology; Oakes Ames, in botany; and Jean Louis Rodolphe Agassiz,* in science.

Faculty members at Penn have always had an entirely different relationship with Philadelphia Society. Of the city's fifty First Families, for instance, only two men—Robert Hare and Thomas Harrison Montgomery—spent a major part of their careers at the college. Montgomery taught zoology until his death at the age of thirty-nine. Hare, who spent thirty years teaching in the college, was an eminent chemist with a wide European reputation. "His lectures were

---

*Agassiz's second wife, Elizabeth Cabot Cary Agassiz, founded an institute for educating women at Harvard under Eliot. This school eventually became Radcliffe College, of which Elizabeth Agassiz was the first president.

celebrated," wrote Sidney Fisher in his diary,* "less however for the ability of the lectures than for the brilliant and extraordinary experiments by which they were illustrated."[20]

A few other individuals in the Philadelphia sample taught briefly in the college. Alexander Dallas Bache taught science for a short while before going on to other things. This distinguished descendant of Benjamin Franklin, however, had very little respect for Proper Philadelphia's negative attitude toward academics and intellectuals in general. In a letter to a friend, written in 1854, he referred with discouragement to the "Trustees of the Old Philad. stamp" who had little sympathy for Trustee Alonzo Potter's attempt to found a graduate school at the university (Potter, who had recently been elected bishop of New York, eventually resigned from the board). Bache, in his own mind and in the tradition of his famous ancestor, did not consider himself of the "Old Philad. stamp" or, as some wit put it, a part of "Philadelphia's unburied dead." Another descendant of Franklin included in the sample was William Duane, a physicist who made important contributions in the field of radioactivity and X rays. But Duane, valedictorian of his class at Penn in 1892, went on to graduate study at Harvard, where he spent the rest of his scientific career.

One solidly rooted Philadelphia family of some distinction was closely related to the faculty at Penn. Thus, in 1834 Henry Hope Reed, a graduate of the class of 1825, was appointed by Provost Delancey as professor of rhetoric and belles lettres, a position, according to Cheyney, "to which he gave great distinction for twenty years." Reed's father had been a member of the board, and his grandfather Joseph Reed had led the Presbyterian reformers as president of the board of the newly formed University of Pennsylvania in 1779. Joseph Reed was a revolutionary statesman and soldier whose grandfather had come to New Jersey in 1671 from northern Ireland. His father, a Philadelphia merchant of substantial wealth, sent Joseph to the Academy of Philadelphia and then to the College of New Jersey. Although of Presbyterian roots, Henry Hope Reed was a staunch Episcopalian and anglophile. He spent almost every summer in England and was the foremost student (even worshiper) of Wordsworth in America. Reed, a prolific writer, was the star of the Penn faculty: "He was one of the few University teachers whose public lectures in Philadelphia drew large and interested audiences."[21]

Henry Hope Reed's brother William Bradford Reed also taught at the university. A lawyer, member of the Pennsylvania Assembly, and district attorney of Philadelphia, William Reed taught the first course in history ever given at Penn. He resigned in 1856, and no courses in history were taught at Penn for thirty years thereafter.

Although three Reeds—Joseph, Henry Hope, and William Bradford—were listed in the DAB, I did not include the family in the Philadelphia sample for two reasons. First, perhaps because of their wit and intellectualism, they were

---

*As Sidney Fisher's diary contains the best insights into the Proper Philadelphia mind in the nineteenth century, it is indicative that this reference to Professor Hare is the only time the University of Pennsylvania is ever mentioned in its more than 500 published pages.

never of the Philadelphia Club–type inner circle. Second, their brains were eventually lost to the city. Henry Hope Reed drowned at sea. William, who became a staunch Democrat in reaction to the mindless Know-Nothing movement in Philadelphia, was ostracized for his bitter opposition to Lincoln and the Union cause. After the war, he moved to New York, where he wrote for the *World*. Today, another Henry Hope Reed, a graduate of Philadelphia's favorite boarding school, St. Paul's, and of Harvard, is a prominent architectural historian and preserver of landmarks in New York City.

FINANCIAL SUPPORT:
HARVARD AND PENN

Perhaps the final test of the educational values of any community is how well its institutions of higher learning are supported financially by their alumni and friends. Whereas Bostonians contributed to their college from earliest days until it became far and away the best endowed undergraduate institution in the nation, Philadelphians left their college in almost total financial neglect throughout most of the nineteenth century. When Penn moved to West Philadelphia in the 1870s, its college still had no endowment whatsoever. At the same time, the medical school was moderately well supported; it was, moreover, almost independent financially, responsible to the authority of the board of trustees but related only tenuously to the non-authority of the provost.

One useful measure of the support of liberal education, and the self-respect and independence of faculty members, is the number of endowed professorships in an institution. Beginning with the Hollis professorship of divinity and the Hollis professorship of mathematics and natural philosophy, founded by Thomas Hollis of London in 1721 and 1727, Harvard has steadily built up its endowed professorships. By the time of the First World War, thirteen of Boston's fifty families—Perkins, Phillips, Parkman, Eliot, Jackson, Shattuck, Peabody, Paine, Lee, Higginson, Lawrence, and Frothingham—had endowed seventeen chairs at Harvard. No chairs had been endowed at Penn by members of the Philadelphia sample except the Pepper professorship of public health (1890) and the Rush professorship of biochemistry (1910), both in the medical school.

According to the report of the U.S. commissioner of education in 1872, the year Penn began building College Hall, Harvard College had thirteen endowed professorships, the largest number in the nation. At the same time, Penn, located in the cultural center of the state, had none, although the twenty-five other colleges in Pennsylvania had a total of twenty-six endowed professorships. Little Allegheny College, on the western frontier of the state, had the most (six).*

---

*But Allegheny had a good New England heritage; its first and longtime president was Timothy Alden of Exeter Academy and Harvard, and the first benefactor of its library was his good friend and overseer of the new college James Winthrop, a founder of the Massachusetts Historical Society. Incidentally, whereas the twenty-six colleges reporting from Pennsylvania had twenty-six endowed chairs among them, the four Massachusetts colleges—Harvard, Tufts, Amherst, and Williams—had thirty-eight. Little Bowdoin, in Maine, had twelve.

The first chairs at Penn were given not by educated alumni or members of the fifty family sample but by two self-educated and very distinguished Philadelphians, John Welsh and Thomas A. Scott. Welsh was an extremely successful merchant who founded his fortune in the West Indian sugar trade, then went into railroading. He was a devoted civic leader, a main force in building up Fairmount Park, and the financial director of the Centennial Exhibition of 1876. In 1877, Welsh gave the first chair at Penn, the John Welsh Centennial professorship of history and English literature. Scott, one of the greatest presidents of the Pennsylvania Railroad, had a great respect for education. He spent many years on Penn's board and contributed financially to the school in a variety of ways, among them by establishing the Thomas A. Scott professorship of mathematics in 1881.* Two years later, one of the Seybert family, kin of Provost Pepper, endowed the Adam Seybert professorship of moral and intellectual philosophy. One other chair, in astronomy and astrophysics, was given to the college in the nineteenth century; in the twentieth century, several other chairs were given to Penn in the sciences, but the next chair in the humanities awaited the close of the First World War—the Henry Charles Lea professorship in medieval history was donated in 1928. By 1940, Penn still had very few chairs in the college, and the university as a whole had the lowest endowment per student in the Ivy League.†

The reasons Philadelphia has neglected Penn, morally, socially, and financially, are many. The all-pervasive anti-intellectualism of the city from its founding days has of course been important. But the major factor has been the combination of anti-intellectualism and social snobbery that has always marked the city's Quaker-turned-Episcopal gentry. Provosts Pepper and Harrison were fairly successful with the members of the class to which they belonged, but even they had their problems.

> semi-mythical and semi-humorous stories went the rounds of the panic of well-to-do persons on seeing Mr. Harrison approach, realizing that before their interview was over their names would be duly signed in his famous "little black book" promising a contribution to some University purpose. A variation is the story of a good Philadelphia Quaker, a Trustee, who was asked to contribute $10,000 to a certain project. He took the matter under advisement, then sent $5,000 with the explanation that he knew he would grudge giving the larger sum but could give $5,000 cheerfully, and "the Lord loveth a cheerful giver."[22]

Most Proper Philadelphians, in the cheerful tradition of the Quaker trustee, have neither given away nor preserved and multiplied their fortunes with anywhere near the same pride as their peers in Boston. In contrast, following the tradition of his class and family, A. Lawrence Lowell donated more money to Harvard than was ever given to Penn by all the members of Philadelphia's fifty First Families of his generation combined. Whereas Lowell gave Harvard some $2 million, most of it anonymously, the largest single gift ever received by Penn

---

*The Scotts are now a Harvard family.

†As of 1936, Harvard University had an endowment of over $130 million, the first in the nation. Penn ranked thirty-fourth, with an endowment of some $19 million, just a bit above Oberlin College in Ohio, which ranked thirty-fifth.

in the first two centuries of its history, according to Cheyney, was "the Duhr-ing bequest of more than $900,000, received in 1913,"[23] part of this fund being used to enlarge the college library. Professor Louis A. Duhring, a parsimonious bachelor with a passion for investing in gold stocks, had spent his life on the faculty of the medical school, where he was a pioneer in dermatology. Though a member of the Philadelphia Club, he liked to say that he was *of* Society in Philadelphia but not *in* it.

NEW MILLIONAIRES AND PENN AND HARVARD

New moneymakers and their families have come to the fore in every genera-tion and they have aspired to give their offspring the best available education— identified by many as Harvard, where their money soon followed. This was especially true of New York at the turn of the nineteenth century, when mil-lionaires of old New England roots like the Morgans, as well as a host of newly moneyed men from all over the nation, settled there in order to be near Wall Street.

It has often been said that money breeds money, and certainly the fact that old Boston money has always gone to support Harvard helped attract new money from Boston, Philadelphia, and especially New York in the early and af-fluent years of the twentieth century. But if money attracts money, excellence does, too, and the high academic standards and creative teaching at Harvard were vital factors in building Harvard in those crucial years.

Charles Eliot Norton, son of Professor Andrews Norton, nephew of George Ticknor, and first cousin of President Eliot, was born in 1827 at the very heart of Brahmin Harvard. Norton wrote for the first issue of the *Atlantic Monthly* and with Frederick Law Olmsted (first holder of the Charles Eliot professorship of landscape architecture) was one of the founders of the *Nation*. He was the first art history professor at Harvard, from 1874 to 1899, and emeritus professor until his death in 1908. According to Martin Green, Norton was "teacher, edi-tor, emender, critic, guide, philosopher, and friend to a whole complex of New England literary life, including its protégés in the rest of America, and its sym-pathizers in Britain, for half a century and more."[24] He knew everyone in the cultural world of his day, from Isabella Stewart Gardner to Edith Wharton to Ticknor to Emerson. He knew and guided Longfellow, Holmes, and Howells, all the Adamses and Jameses of Henry Adams's generation, Godkin and Olm-sted, and his students Irving Babbitt, Santayana, and Berenson. He was a friend of Leslie Stephen, Dickens, Mill, and Carlyle in England and a close friend of Ruskin, whose literary executor he became. In many ways, Norton was the "last great statesman of cultural responsibility"[25] in America. Like Henry Adams, Norton was an intellectual aristocrat in a plutocratic age who despised, and despaired at, the anti-intellectualism of our materialistic democ-racy. Perhaps just because he put high cultural values and intellectual excel-lence before all else in life, Norton attracted to Harvard the scions of plutocracy who wanted more out of life than Wall Street had to offer. Among his many devoted students were two members of New York's leading investment banking families, James Loeb, founder of the Loeb Classical Library, and Paul J. Sachs, associate director of the Fogg Museum. Loeb established the Charles Eliot Norton fellowship in Greek studies in 1901 and made many gifts to the Fogg Museum. Sachs, after a brief career in the family banking house, returned to Harvard to become professor of fine arts. And this same Norton tradition of excellence has continued to attract money to Harvard. When a professor at Penn died several years ago, for instance, he left Harvard an estate valued in the millions, largely because he had once admired a professor there above all other men and began his scholarly career as his assistant.

The point is that Harvard has always had faculty members like Charles Eliot Norton or his friend James Russell Lowell, cultivated men of letters who influenced the whole culture of their age. In contrast, Penn faculty members have been oriented largely toward science and engineering (and business) rather than the humanities, and even those in the humanities have been vocational rather than intellectual—narrow scholars and specialists recognized in their chosen discipline but rarely influential in the broad culture of their times.* Even today, when the university has one of the highest paid faculties in the nation, its teachers are hardly known outside their own fields. In the years since World War II, during which Penn has experienced its great renaissance, for example, it is a rare member of the faculty who has written either for such widely read cultural publications as *Commentary*, *Harper's*, the *Atlantic*, *Encounter*, or the *New York Review of Books* or for such general intellectual quarterlies as *Foreign Affairs* or the *American Scholar*.

Unfortunately, the lack of loyalty to and pride in their local university so characteristic of old Philadelphia families was further compounded by their treatment of the many newly rich millionaires who made their fortunes in the city between the Civil War and World War I.† Of the Philadelphia millionaires listed in Table A-15, for example, no members of the Baird, Disston, Elkins, Widener, Dolan, Wanamaker, Berwind, Cooke, Cassatt, or Converse families have ever made major gifts to the university. As we have seen, Thomas A. Scott was always a generous supporter of the university, and the Houston family donated the money for Houston Hall. The Weightman family contributed to the building of the university's first gymnasium, Weightman Hall, completed in 1904 (according to Cheyney, it took the university ten years to raise the whole

---

*It may be broadly true that just as theorizing influences the wider intellectual world in any age, fact gathering limits a scholar's influence to his own discipline. Insight into the fact-gathering mind of Philadelphia as against the analytical or theorizing mind of Boston is nicely revealed in the careers of Louis Agassiz (1807–1873) and Joseph Leidy (1823–1891), both leaders in natural science. When Agassiz died, his post at Harvard was offered to Leidy, who preferred to remain at Penn. Whereas Agassiz was forever coming up with hypotheses and theories (often wrong), Leidy, true to local tradition, was "almost wholly devoid of all ambition but that of the collection of facts. He was not given to theory, and disliked controversy on any subject." He was once quoted as saying, "I am too busy to theorize" (*DAB*, Vol. xi, p. 152a).

†In Chapter 13 we saw how Philadelphia lost a library, an art collection, and a school through snubbing the Wideners.

sum of $500,000–600,000 to complete this project). A new gymnasium, completed in 1927, was named in honor of Sidney Emlen Hutchinson, Edward T. Stotesbury's fashionable son-in-law. Stotesbury himself, though the dominant partner at Drexel, bankers for Penn and the Pennsylvania Railroad, made no major gift to the university. The two Proper Philadelphia presidents of the Pennsylvania Railroad, A. J. Cassatt and George B. Roberts, never made any large contributions to Penn either.*

Provosts Pepper and Harrison knew only too well how much the snobbish provincialism of Philadelphia's Rittenhouse Square gentry cost the university. In 1894, at the elaborate funeral service for Philadelphia's greatest Victorian banker, Anthony J. Drexel, founder of the Drexel Institute of Technology, Pepper must have pondered this point. "It is very disturbing," he wrote at the time; "a few years ago what great hopes all of us had; now, of course, whatever is done must and should be altogether for the Drexel Institute."[26]

Benjamin Franklin over two centuries ago referred his fellow Philadelphians to the *Letters of Pliny the Consul* when proposing the founding of an academy in his adopted city. In one letter, the younger Pliny addressed Cornelius Tacitus on the advantages of being educated in one's native city: "Your sons should receive their education here, rather than anywhere else," he wrote. "They will, by this means, receive their education where they receive their birth, and be accustomed, from infancy, to inhabit and affect their native soil."[27]

While the Puritans of Franklin's native city surely followed the advice of Pliny the younger and cultivated their native soil with a great college and university, the Quaker-turned-Episcopal gentry of Philadelphia have usually preferred to follow fashion elsewhere, taking no great pride in cultivating either their native soil or their local university.

SECONDARY EDUCATION:
MASSACHUSETTS AND PENNSYLVANIA

It is difficult for a college or university to rise above the general climate of educational opinion in its community. The contrasts between Harvard and Penn, after all, have been but a reflection of the different historical development of public education in Massachusetts and Pennsylvania as a whole, and especially of the Boston Latin School and Philadelphia's Central High School.

Whereas from the outset every community in Massachusetts was required to set up schools for its youth, Pennsylvania relied on sectarian and religious schooling for the first century and a half of its history. The three oldest schools in Pennsylvania today, are private: the William Penn Charter School, dating from 1689 and founded by Quakers; the Protestant Episcopal Academy, founded in 1760 by Bishop White; and the Germantown Academy, founded by Germans in 1785.

---

*As we have seen, Roberts's sons followed fashion and went to Princeton. One of Cassatt's sons did start out at Penn but, like Joseph Clark, transferred to Harvard, where he took a degree in the college in 1895.

In Pennsylvania, the first laws requiring local communities to set up public schools came in the third decade of the nineteenth century, after a long and bitter political struggle led by Governor George Wolf. Wolf, whose father had come to Pennsylvania from Germany in 1751, was born on the German frontier of the state in 1777. He attended a local classical school in his youth, worked on his father's farm, and taught at a local academy before finally being admitted to the bar at Easton, where he built up a lucrative law practice. Wolf was of the German Reformed faith and deeply interested in education. When elected governor of Pennsylvania in 1829, he made the cause of free public education for rich and poor alike one of the central goals of his administration. Wolf was defeated for a third term in 1835 on the issue of "no school tax, no free schools." He was opposed mainly by the followers of other faiths, especially the Lutherans, who had their own system of parochial schools. The most enduring achievement of Wolf's six years in the state house, however, was the passage in 1834 of the first public school act in Pennsylvania history. The next year, the act was almost repealed because of citizen reaction to school taxes. It was saved by a famous speech in the Pennsylvania House of Representatives by a cantankerous Gettysburg lawyer and legislator named Thaddeus Stevens.* Nevertheless, after Governor Wolf's defeat in 1835, the next administration changed the law to allow each community to vote every three years on whether or not it desired to retain its free school system. This privilege was done away with in 1848 and free schools were required of all communities.

Just as Massachusetts led the nation in establishing the principle of community schools, so it also led the nation in passing the first compulsory school attendance law in America in 1852; Pennsylvania did not pass such a law until 1895, the twenty-eighth state to do so and the last eastern seaboard state above the Mason-Dixon line.†

Boston Latin School. Boston Latin School was founded in 1635, a year before Harvard. This oldest of secondary schools in America has educated more distinguished men than any other school (and most colleges) in the nation. One hundred forty-six alumni of the school were listed in the first twenty volumes of the *DAB*, as against 136 from Andover and 90 from Exeter, its closest competitors. Among its distinguished seventeenth-century alumni were Governor Leverett and his grandson John Leverett, president of Harvard; Governor William Stoughton; Cotton Mather; and Jonathan Belcher, governor of Massachusetts and New Jersey and a founder of Princeton. Among the more famous students in the eighteenth century were Thomas Hutchinson, Benjamin Franklin, Sam-

---

*In the Pennsylvania auslander tradition of leadership, Stevens was born on a Vermont farm and graduated from Dartmouth. True to his Calvinist and New England heritage, Stevens began his political career as an "implacable and undeviating Federalist and violent opponent of Andrew Jackson" (*DAB*, Vol. xvii, p. 621b).

†The last midwestern state to pass such a law was Indiana (1897). Indiana, virtually founded by Quakers, has a larger Quaker population today than does Pennsylvania. Earlham College, in Richmond, Indiana, incidentally, has more Quaker students than Haverford and Swarthmore combined.

uel Adams, Governor James Bowdoin, Thomas Treat Paine, and John Hancock, signer of the Declaration of Independence; Josiah Quincy, defender, along with John Adams, of the British soldiers involved in the Boston Massacre; Henry Knox, the revolutionary general; Winthrop Sargent, governor of the Mississippi and Northwest territories; Christopher Gore, Charles Bulfinch, Charles Jackson, and John Collins Warren. When Wendell Phillips entered the Latin School in 1822, his schoolmates included Charles Francis Adams, Charles Sumner, Robert Winthrop, and John Motley; among other students at the school in the nineteenth century were Thomas Bulfinch, mythology anthologist, Governor Edward Everett, Ralph Waldo Emerson, Samuel Gridley Howe, Henry Ward Beecher, Edward Everett Hale, Charles William Eliot, Phillips Brooks, Henry Lee Higginson, Charles Francis Adams, Jr., David S. Muzzey, popular historian, John F. Fitzgerald, grandfather of President Kennedy, Bernard Berenson and George Santayana. The more famous men who went to the Latin School in the twentieth century included Joseph Kennedy, the family founder; Roy E. Larson, publisher of *Time*, *Life*, and *Fortune*; and the conductors Arthur Fiedler and Leonard Bernstein.

For over 300 years, the Latin School was the major preparatory school for Harvard College. As late as 1951, 102 of its graduates entered the freshman class at Harvard, far more than came from any one of the New England boarding schools.

With a touching pride in the Latin School's anti-egalitarian values, Philip Marson, teacher of English at the school between 1926 and 1957, explained how

> unconsciously the original settlers of Massachusetts Bay—far removed from equalitarian philosophy as they were—laid the groundwork for the greatest democratic experiment in human history. By founding the Boston Latin School in 1635, only five years after landing, they were certain that they were beginning to condition generations of Puritan conformists. Instead, by equipping their sons with the tools of communication, they began breeding debators and demagogues, radicals and revolutionaries, idealists and iconoclasts. Little did they know that they were fomenting a revolution which would separate them from the mother country and change the course of political history throughout the world.[28]

Down through the years, according to Marson, "the Boston Latin School . . . has remained as conservative and unbending as its Puritan founders would have wished it to be."[29] Charles W. Eliot was horrified that the rigid classical education he received at the school had not changed since the school's founding, nor had its strict discipline. "When I was a boy in the best public school in Boston," he later wrote, "the control used was physical force, the application of torture—that was the long and short of it."[30] Although young Eliot disapproved of the narrow curriculum and the ancient belief in the effectiveness of flagellation, he thoroughly approved of the Latin School's great emphasis on public speaking, debating, and formal oration, which bred young men like Charles Sumner, Wendell Phillips, and Edward Everett in the classic traditions of Cicero and Demosthenes. Eliot himself was one of the best declaimers in his class. Perhaps it was a reaction to the authoritarian ways of the Latin School, which assumed the chaos of unformed human nature, that led Eliot to institute his liberal reforms at Harvard. But the Latin School made no concessions to the optimistic liberalism of its famous alumnus; it spurned the elective system and held on to its classical curriculum into the twentieth century, long after its students had ceased to be the sons of the Protestant descendants of its Puritan founders.

In the second half of the nineteenth century, Boston's old stock Protestants began to send their sons to private schools. Thus, A. Lawrence Lowell attended Mr. Nobel's private school on Beacon Hill (later Noble and Greenough School, located in Dedham since 1922). In the course of the twentieth century, the Boston Latin School gradually became a melting pot of ethnic minorities. As early as 1908, a survey of family names at the school revealed thirty-four Sullivans, twenty-eight Cohens, thirteen Murphys, eleven Levines, ten Donovans, but not a single Jones. Two of its more famous alumni, George Santayana and Bernard Berenson, were symbols of the change in ethnic composition but definitely not in the intellectual standards of the school.

The composition of the faculty also began to change in this century. The first Irish-American headmaster took office in the 1920s—he was a Harvard man, however. His three Irish successors were graduates of Boston College. By 1958, according to Marson, "the roster of the faculty, which included ninety-one names, was distributed as follows: Irish, 60; Jews, 14; Italians, 4; Armenians, 2; and one each of Belgian, Swedish, Scotch, Lithuanian, French, and Greek ancestry. Only one representative of the original Anglo-Saxons was left."[31]

Yet the Puritan Ethic still informed the intellectual values of the Latin School. Marson proudly noted that during his thirty-one years of teaching at the school "approximately 7750 boys were able to survive the rigorous demands of the curriculum: six years of English, five or six years of Latin, three or four of French, two or three of either Greek or German, four of history, five or six of mathematics, and three to five years of science."[32] He was sorry to observe, however, that more than twice as many boys failed to complete the course as succeeded: of the some 750 qualified youngsters entering the school each year, only about 250 graduated.

Born and reared among the Dorchester Irish, Marson was a proud defender of the Puritan tradition of democratic elitism. When so many of the pampered scions of old Puritan families, in Boston and Harvard and elsewhere, were avidly opposing the elitist values of the Latin School, he stood up for its ancient traditions. At the end of the egalitarian 1960s, when anti-elitism was fashionable, Marson closed his book on the history of the Latin School with the following sentence: "It is to prevent the tragic dissipation of our finest minds—potentially our saints and saviors—that society must supply free schools of the quality of Boston Latin School. . . . Only then can we fulfill the promise of freedom and democracy."[33]

Philadelphia's Central High. Soon after the Pennsylvania Assembly passed the state's first education act in the administration of Governor Wolf, the Central High School of Philadelphia came into being, two centuries after the founding of the Boston Latin School. The first president of the school was Alexander Dallas Bache, great-grandson of Boston Latin School's most famous alumnus, Benjamin Franklin. Bache, a graduate of the United States Military Academy and sometime professor at Penn, took office in 1839 and thoroughly organized the school in his three-year presidency. In contrast to the classical emphasis at Boston Latin, Bache laid the foundations for a continuing emphasis on science at Central High.

From its beginning down to the present, Central has been proud of its democratic elitist traditions. Whereas the index to the first twenty volumes of the *DAB* listed only fourteen graduates of the Protestant Episcopal Academy, five from the Germantown Academy, and none from the William Penn Charter School, it named forty-five graduates of the younger Central High School.* (The paucity of graduates from the city's three oldest private schools listed in the *DAB* index presumably reflects to some extent the incompleteness of so many of the biographies of Pennsylvanians, which I noted elsewhere.) Considering its much later start, Central compares favorably with the Boston Latin School in terms of distinguished alumni. Clearly, native talent in Philadelphia is equal to that in Boston, but the upper-class values of the two cities have made them quite different.

Robert Ellis Thompson, president of Central between 1894 and 1920, the longest tenure in the school's history and the most influential, did not share the values of Penn's old family trustees. After twenty-four years as a professor at his alma mater, Penn, where he was the most stimulating teacher on the faculty and a citywide celebrity, he was dismissed by the trustees, in a style unusual at the university before or since, "without reason given, and in spite of general protest from his colleagues in the Faculty, and from the Alumni of the University."[34]

Thompson was born near Belfast and brought to Philadelphia at the age of thirteen. He was a student at Central and graduated from the university, where he taught until his fiftieth year—professor of social science, first dean of the Wharton School, and John Welsh Centennial Professor of History and English Literature. He preached in many pulpits in Philadelphia and elsewhere, lectured at Harvard, Yale, Princeton, Williams, Cornell, Amherst, and Bryn Mawr, and was an editor and author of wide renown. Thompson never lost his Irish brogue: as a historian of Central put it, "He was an Ulsterman by geography, a Presbyterian by inheritance, a polymath by native intellectual power, and the son of the 'auld sod' in every word he spoke."[35]

Pat Thompson, as the boys affectionately called him, ruled with an iron hand. He was not only a great leader at Central but a force in the whole city.

---

*A Central graduate correctly showed that the *DAB* actually included seventy alumni of his alma mater.

And the school went through great changes under his leadership of almost three decades. Students and faculty held him in awe. Finally, it is important to note that Pat Thompson, like Ben Franklin before him, was an auslander and, as far as Philadelphia's genteel gentry was concerned, an outsider.

Although neither Central nor any other Philadelphia institution ever produced the great line of statesmen such as were educated at the Boston Latin School, it did produce a higher proportion of leaders of real distinction than any other Philadelphia institution, including Penn. Its alumni included Thomas Eakins, the painter; Dr. Albert Barnes, multimillionaire Philadelphia eccentric, whose art gallery is one of the most famous in America (and most idiosyncratically run); P. A. B. Widener, Thomas Dolan, and Charles T. Yerkes, traction kings; John G. Johnson, lawyer; Ellis Gimbel; Simon Guggenheim; Samuel S. Fels; Louis Kahn, architect; and Samuel Dash, of Watergate fame.

Like Boston Latin, Central has maintained high standards down through the years: of the 109,606 matriculants at the school between 1838 and 1966, for instance, only 27,993 took degrees. Boys are accepted from all parts of the city on the basis of academic potential, regardless of neighborhood or racial background. Blacks have been at the school from its beginning and throughout the twentieth century, in increasingly large numbers. As in Boston, however, the selective and elitist values of Central came under increasing attack during the 1960s. Nevertheless, through pressure exerted by loyal and proud alumni, standards have been preserved.*

Both Boston Latin and Central High have followed the very best traditions of opportunitarian democracy, and both are now threatened by the various egalitarian fads of our homogenizing age. They differ, however, in that whereas Boston Latin was intimately associated with the authoritarian and elitist values of Boston's ruling class for well over 200 years and still embraces these values, Central High has never subscribed to the Quaker-Episcopal mores of Philadelphia's privileged class. The very existence of Central High in Philadelphia, in other words, may give us all hope that even in the most egalitarian climates of opinion, where mediocrity is sure to rule, there will nevertheless remain those few who continue to believe in excellence and take pride in large accomplishment.

Groton and St. Paul's: Boston and Philadelphia First Family Surrogates. The Boston Latin School and Philadelphia's Central High School have been engaged in educating boys in the best traditions of Thomas Jefferson's ideal of a natural aristocracy. Groton and St. Paul's schools, however, have been educational models for what John Adams, in the course of his long correspondence with his friend Jefferson, came to call an artificial aristocracy. Although both schools were founded by members of the Boston sample of First Families, an intricate

---

*The school is now faced by the egalitarian ideology of the women's movement and is being sued by a female applicant. Alumni resistance to coeducation is strong (the young woman lost her case).

historical network of men and ideas led to St. Paul's becoming the ideal Proper Philadelphia school, whereas Groton grew out of and reflected the ideals of Brahmin Boston.

In the town of Boston, from its founding days to the end of the Federalist period, the Latin School served the purpose of educating the town's natural aristocrats and sending them on to Harvard College. In the 1820s, the decline of the Federalist ideal of an organic community was symbolized by the formation of the city of Boston (1822), the great rebellion at Harvard and the taking over of the state house by Jeffersonian Republicans (1823), and the defeat of President John Quincy Adams by the forces of Jacksonian Democracy (1829).

Urbanization has always been seen as an enemy of the Jeffersonian ideals of democracy. But it was also an important factor in the rise of Jacksonian Democracy, the decline of federalism, and the introduction of social forces in America that led to the creation of an artificial aristocracy. Earlier I noted that the population of Boston increased by 250 percent between the first U.S. census in 1790 and 1820. Responding to the growing heterogeneity (and supposed unhealthiness) of city life, upper-class families in Boston and elsewhere began to see the need for educating their sons in the fresh and wholesome air of the countryside. Accordingly, Joseph Green Cogswell and George Bancroft founded the Round Hill School, near Northampton, Massachusetts, in 1823, and the New England boarding school idea was born.

In 1817, Cogswell had gone abroad with Edward Everett and George Ticknor, and Bancroft followed them overseas the next year: Ticknor and Everett brought back the German university ideal to Harvard; Cogswell and Bancroft founded Round Hill School on the model of the German gymnasium. If Cogswell and Bancroft were what Jefferson and Adams would have called natural aristocrats, they consciously attracted to their new school the sons of the nation's urban, artificial aristocracy. As one of the alumni later put it, the "prospectus drew, like a magnet, boys from Maine to Georgia, sons of parents the most cultivated and wealthy the country could then boast."[36]

The purpose of the school was to take boys away from the contaminations and distractions of urban life and mold them in the Federalist ideal of the gentleman and scholar. "Round Hill," according to James McLachlan "was forging a common national subculture among the sons of many rich urban Americans."[37] In the decade of the school's existence (it closed for financial reasons), some 300 of the sons of the fortunate went there, about 40 percent from New England, 30 percent from the South, and 18 percent from the middle states.

George Cheyne Shattuck (1783–1854), a Boston philanthropist, was the first of a long line of prominent Shattuck physicians that continues to the present day. After graduation from Harvard, he went to Philadelphia and took a medical degree from the University of Pennsylvania in 1807. He returned to become one of Boston's leading physicians and most prominent citizens. He had six children, only one of whom survived, the oldest son, George Cheyne Shattuck, Jr. Understandably, Dr. Shattuck was obsessed with his son's health and sent him away from Boston at an early age to the healthy country air at the Round Hill School. The younger Shattuck later became a prominent Boston physician and dean of the Harvard Medical School. He married the daughter of a respected Episcopalian family in Baltimore and eventually joined the Episcopal church himself. With the zeal of a convert, Shattuck became very active in the Church of the Advent, the center of High Anglicanism and the Oxford movement in Boston. (One Easter Sunday he put a check for $20,000 in the collection plate.) He supported an infinite variety of church causes and counted more Episcopal clergymen among his friends than any other layman in America. Perhaps Shattuck's most lasting achievement was to found St. Paul's School on his country estate on the Merrimac River, outside Concord, New Hampshire, in 1855. He founded the school on Cogswell's formula for Round Hill: "Physical and moral culture can best be carried on where boys live with, and are constantly under the supervision of, teachers; and in the country."[38] But whereas Round Hill was guided by the Federalist ideal of the gentleman scholar, St. Paul's was guided by the Episcopalian ideal of the Christian gentleman.* This orientation naturally appealed to Dr. Shattuck but had far more to do with the saintly young autocrat he chose for headmaster, Henry Augustus Coit, who dominated the school for forty years after its founding.

After Cogswell closed Round Hill School, he advised parents to send their sons to another boarding school, St. Paul's College, in Flushing, Long Island. The school was founded and run by the Reverend William Augustus Muhlenberg, an evangelical High Churchman who believed in educating young boys to be Christian gentlemen. Muhlenberg belonged to one of Pennsylvania's most famous clerical and political families. Although born a Lutheran, he was brought up an Episcopalian and after attending the University of Pennsylvania, studied for the Episcopal ministry under Bishop White, first Bishop of Pennsylvania.

Life at Muhlenberg's school centered on the chapel, the ritual of High Anglicanism, and a classical curriculum. Henry Coit entered the school in 1845 and considered Muhlenberg to be the single most important influence on his life. Many of the rituals at St. Paul's College on Long Island were followed at St. Paul's in Concord.

The Coits were an old New England family of no particular historical distinction, the first of the line having come to Salem from Wales in 1636. For many generations, they were solid Connecticut Congregationalists, until Henry Coit's father was converted to Episcopalianism while attending the Princeton Theological Seminary (Presbyterian). He sent his son to Muhlenberg's school from his Episcopal parsonage in Plattsburg, New York. After St. Paul's, young Henry Coit, like Muhlenberg, attended the University of Pennsylvania but left because of ill health. He was eventually ordained an Episcopalian priest in Philadelphia and, just before taking up his duties as headmaster of St. Paul's, married Mary Bowman Wheeler, of a wealthy and prolific Episcopalian clan in Philadelphia.

---

*Of the 108 different family names of boys from New England, New York, and Pennsylvania at Round Hill, 75 of the same family names, roughly 70 percent, appeared on the alumni lists of St. Paul's for 1856–1914.

Henry Coit's first class in Concord consisted of three boys—two Shattucks, who eventually became prominent Boston physicians and philanthropists like their father, and a Bigelow of the famous Boston medical family. By the end of the century, there were more than 300 boys at the school. Although many boys in the early years came from Boston, because of Dr. Shattuck's wide acquaintanceship there, Henry Coit did not approve of Unitarian Harvard. Although both he and Eliot were autocrats, Coit was a firm conservative whereas Eliot, in Coit's mind at least, was dangerously liberal. Gradually, fewer and fewer Bostonians, always loyal to Harvard, sent their sons to St. Paul's; by 1894–1895, there were only six boys from Boston at the school. At the same time, as St. Paul's was undoubtedly the most fashionable school in Victorian America, Philadelphians increasingly sent their sons there. Both Sidney George Fisher and his close friend Dr. Owen Wister sent their sons there in the 1870s, and members of the Cadwalader, Biddle, Morris, Rush, Chew, White, McKean, Borie, Ingersoll, Lippincott, Roberts, Merrick, Mitchell, and Drexel families have gone to St. Paul's since.

While Bostonians were turning away from St. Paul's, they were looking approvingly toward young Endicott Peabody's new school, which he founded at Groton, Massachusetts, in 1884. When Peabody retired from Groton after fifty-six years as headmaster, his school had produced one of the greatest presidents in the nation's history, and he himself was the most famous headmaster in the English-speaking world, a fitting tribute to his ancestral roots in Salem Puritanism and his family's affinity to Harvard Unitarianism.

Endicott Peabody was a descendant of the authoritarian magistrate John Endicott and the moneymaking merchant Joseph Peabody. The Peabodys came to Salem in 1635 and by the end of the colonial period had already begun to make a name for themselves in history as clergymen, judges, lawyers, intellectuals, and soldiers. As we have seen, it was Joseph Peabody, of Essex Street in Salem, who founded the family fortune, first as a privateer during the Revolution and then as one of the leading China merchants in New England.

If Joseph Peabody of Salem first brought real wealth into the family, it was George Peabody of Danvers (now Peabody), Massachusetts, who became the most famous and the richest of the Peabody line. Of a poor branch of the family, he left school early and slowly made his way to wealth as a New England merchant, eventually peddling his wares through Pennsylvania, Maryland, and Virginia and ending up as the leading merchant-financier in Baltimore. After successfully floating a large loan in London for the city of Baltimore, George Peabody became an interntional banker in 1837, when he founded his firm in London (where he knew everyone from the governor of the Bank of England and the brothers Baring to Wellington and Queen Victoria). Unmarried, he rarely spent more than $3,000 a year on himself while earning over $300,000 annually. When Peabody retired in 1857, he was well on his way to being the first systematic Anglo-American philanthropist, having established and endowed a wide variety of cultural and educational institutions both in this country and in England.

In 1854, Peabody had hired a young Yankee merchant from Hartford, Junius Spencer Morgan, with the intention of leaving his firm's management to Morgan when he retired. At George Peabody's funeral in 1869, Junius Morgan asked Samuel Endicott Peabody to join him as a partner in London. The Peabody influence was carried into the twentieth century by Samuel Endicott's son Endicott, who was sent to Cheltenham School and Trinity College, Cambridge, where he absorbed the best British traditions of class authority and leadership, traditions he later brought to his school at Groton.

Upon returning to America, Peabody entered his grandfather's investment banking firm, Lee, Higginson & Company. Unsatisfied with this easy way to success, he went to Phillips Brooks for advice about the possibility of his entering the Episcopal ministry. While in England he had come under the spell of "muscular Christianity" and the Christian socialism of Charles Kingsley. With Brooks's sympathetic encouragement, Endicott Peabody overcame the opposition of his staunchly Unitarian family and left business to enter the Episcopal Theological School in Cambridge, Massachusetts. The school was closely allied to Harvard because of its Low Church values and its emphasis on "uplift," as represented in the Social Gospel movement then being led, as Henry May wrote, by "the Episcopal Church—the Church of wealth, culture, and aristocratic lineage."[39]

Before completing his course at the divinity school, Peabody spent seven months as a missionary at Tombstone, in the Arizona Territory. Coming back to Cambridge, he studied hard, taught Sunday school, and worked, in the Kingsley tradition, in a Boston city mission, at the same time courting his beautiful first cousin Fanny Peabody, who was to be Groton's first lady for over half a century. In the meantime, Henry Coit offered Peabody a job as a master at St. Paul's, but he wanted a school of his own. This became a real possibility when kinsmen of his, the Lawrence brothers of Groton, bought a ninety-acre farm and gave it to the as yet unfounded school in memory of their sister Gertrude, wife of Peabody's brother John.

Peabody easily raised enough money from his relatives and friends to open the school in 1884. The grounds were laid out by Frederick Law Olmsted, and the first building was designed by the architectural firm of Peabody and Stearns. The original board of trustees—Phillips Brooks and William Lawrence, both of whom later became bishops of Massachusetts; Peabody's father, Samuel Endicott Peabody, and his prominent business associate J. Pierpont Morgan; and James Lawrence, relative by marriage, was a nice blend of clerical and old stock financial authority. For his faculty, Peabody chose two classmates from the divinity school: the Reverend Sherrard Billings and Peabody's cousin William Amory Gardner, a wealthy and eccentric sportsman who had been reared by the rich and eccentric Isabella Stewart Gardner, his aunt. In the typical Brahmin tradition, Groton began and remained an extremely familial institution.

That Peabody and his two masters, both of whom remained at the school for years and stamped their idiosyncratic ways upon its boys, were far from professional educators was of no account in a school that was to become famous for breeding Christian gentlemen with a broad sense of civic responsibility and an itch for public office and leadership. The ethos of the new school combined ancient Salem Puritanism and North Shore federalism with current Boston Brahminism and Victorian Anglophilia. Peabody's English experience, especially his admiration of Charles Kingsley, naturally led him to sympathize with the American Social Gospel movement, in many ways the religious counterpart of the Progressive movement, which brought the American gentleman back into politics and urban reform. Its values were embodied in men like Theodore Roosevelt, who sent his sons to Groton. No wonder Charles Francis Adams, Jr., who had himself gone to the Boston Latin School, sent his twin sons, Henry and John, to his friend's school at Groton. Of the fifty families in the Boston sample, Adamses, Ameses, Bigelows, Bowditches, Cabots, Coolidges, Forbeses, Frothinghams, Higginsons, Lawrences, Motleys, Peabodys, Prescotts, Saltonstalls, and Winthrops have sent their sons to Groton.

The character of American upper-class institutions has usually been more the product of interpersonal networks than of ideological affinities. More than most institutions, Groton and St. Paul's were surely the lengthened shadows of their founding headmasters, and whereas Endicott Peabody was almost a perfect personification of the Puritan-Episcopal values of Brahmin Boston, Henry Coit's values were far more in accord with the Quaker-Episcopalianism of Proper Philadelphia. I have shown how the Peabodys were deeply rooted in both New England and international banking in London and New York. At the same time, both Dr. Shattuck and Henry Coit, particularly through their wives, had connections in the middle states and especially in Philadelphia. By the end of the nineteenth century, then, Groton was primarily a Brahmin Boston school, which also drew boys from New York families, often of New England origins, and of both old and new wealth. At St. Paul's, "the New England influence was negligible, if not nil," according to Owen Wister.[40]

Henry Coit and Endicott Peabody were, of course, far more than just products of their different heritages. Both were charismatic educators who made lasting impressions on the boys at their schools. Both were handsome and imposing persons. Coit was tall and spare, a shy autocrat with a genius for understanding boys. Behind his cold exterior there lurked a keen sense of humor, which, when it occasionally came to the surface, he quickly apologized for. Peabody was a big and rugged extrovert, without the tragic sense of life that surely informed Coit's deep sense of humor. Whereas Coit was a High Churchman and withdrawn, Peabody was a Low Churchman with a mission to educate the sons of Christian gentlemen to go out and reform the world. Coit cultivated the inner life; Peabody was an evangelist with utter confidence in the mission of upper-class Victorians to Christianize America and the world. Whereas Peabody's roots were in Cambridge Whiggery, Coit's were in Oxford Toryism; Peabody was molded in the image of Cromwell, whereas Coit would have had far more sympathy with Archbishop Laud.

Groton by and large chose its boys from old rich families in Boston and New York (many of them friends of the Peabodys). St. Paul's was more likely to attract the sons and grandsons of the newly rich millionaires of the Gilded Age. Groton always remained about a third the size of St. Paul's and its boys were almost an extended family, dominated by the patriarchal authority of Peabody for over half a century. (He officiated at many old boy marriages, including that of Franklin Roosevelt.) In this intimate and inbred class atmosphere, Peabody endlessly preached the duties of inherited privilege. As the most famous of his old boys recalled:

> More than forty years ago you said, in a sermon in the old Chapel, something about not losing boyhood ideals in later life. Those were Groton ideals—taught by you—I try not to forget—and your words are still with me and with hundreds of others of "us boys."
> My love to you and to Mrs. Peabody.
>
> Affectionately yours,
> Franklin D. Roosevelt[41]

Peabody, as his biographer wrote of his ancestor John Endicott, "was not a scholar himself, but a man of duty."[42] And he was, like Endicott, an authoritarian who was not afraid to inculcate a sense of the duties of class authority in his overprivileged students like Franklin Roosevelt, Averell Harriman, Dean Acheson, Francis Biddle, and Douglas Dillon.

Several years ago, Arthur M. Schlesinger, Jr., caught the difference between class schools like Groton and St. Paul's* and elite schools like Exeter and Andover.

> Exeter turns out many splendid businessmen, who work hard for good local government and the Community Fund. It turns out many scholars and teachers and writers. It turns out scientists and engineers. But it turns out remarkably few political leaders. Compared to Groton, a much smaller school, compared even to Choate, Exeter's contribution to the public leadership of America in the 20th century has been negligible. I repeat: I don't know why this should be. Perhaps the Exeter ethos is inclined to accept social values as they are because Exeter has been a school to train middle-class boys to do well in society as it is; while the best of the church schools have attempted to train upper-class boys to meet their responsibilities in society and have in consequence been more concerned with instilling (however fitfully and imperfectly) a sense of social duty.[43]

Westtown School in Chester County. Groton and St. Paul's are relatively new schools compared to Westtown in Chester County, outside Philadelphia. The fashionable New England boarding school goes back to the founding of Round Hill School in 1823. Philadelphia Quakerism has a far older boarding school tradition, which dates to the founding of the Westtown School in 1799. Quakers after all have always wanted to guard their children from dangers of secular city life.

---

*Although it goes beyond our story, it is relevant to the theory of this book that whereas Harvard College as well as Groton and St. Paul's were class institutions until the Second World War, they are now, especially since the 1960s, increasingly anomic and elitist. One wonders whether the students and the nation will benefit from this change.

Philadelphia Friends, as we have seen, were part of a transatlantic Quaker culture throughout the eighteenth century, especially in science and medicine. John Fothergill in London was the hub of this community. A prominent figure in science and medicine, Dr. Fothergill was one of the educational leaders of the London Yearly Meeting when it founded the Ackworth School in Yorkshire in 1779. After the Revolution many Philadelphia Friends again went abroad, some of them becoming interested in Ackworth through Dr. Fothergill. In 1794, the Philadelphia Yearly Meeting appointed a committee of forty-five men to explore the possibilities of a Quaker boarding school; led by Owen Biddle, the committee included many men whose descendants were part of Philadelphia's upper class in the nineteenth and twentieth centuries.

The school opened in 1799, on beautiful farmland property in Chester County, where it has remained to this day. From its beginning, Westtown School has been coeducational (with more girls than boys in the twentieth century).

Proper Philadelphians, especially before they became Episcopalians, and the unfashionable branches of their families to this day are surely more rooted in Westtown than St. Paul's, the fashionable favorite. Thus, of the fifty families in the Philadelphia sample, no fewer than twenty have had ancestors and relatives at Westtown: Barton, Biddle (32), Coxe, Dickinson, Fisher, Hare, Lippincott (over 100), Lloyd, Logan, Wetherill, Mifflin, Morris, Norris, Pemberton, Price, Roberts (over 100), Rush, Vaux, and Wistar.* As we have seen, Owen Biddle was a founder of Westtown and many Biddles have studied there since, but Biddles have also gone to Groton, beginning with Francis and his three brothers, who went there in the Roosevelt era. Biddles also went to St. Paul's, as did Cadwaladers, Fishers, Lippincotts, Morrises, Robertses, Rushes, and Wisters (mostly in the 1920s and 1930s).

I shall have more to say about Westtown in later chapters. Here it is of interest to take a look at how graduates of this school, Groton, and St. Paul's have contributed to twentieth-century leadership in America. Thus, Groton (Puritan Boston roots) was about twice as likely as St. Paul's (more rooted in Quaker-Episcopal Philadelphia) and five times as likely as Westtown (pure Quaker roots) to have its alumni from the period 1890–1940 included in *Who's Who* in the years up to 1970. Table A–19 (see Appendix I) is therefore a nice index of the leadership values of Philadelphia and Boston.

---

*Whereas sixteen Cadwalladers went to Westtown, no Cadwaladers with one *l* did; there were over fifty Wistars, but no Wisters with an *e*.

Boston and Philadelphia and the American Mind

Here we have a homogeneous people, living close to the soil, intensely religious, unconscious, unexpressed in art and letters, with a strong sense of home and fatherland. One of its towns becomes a "culture-city," for Boston, with Cambridge and Concord considered as suburbs, answers to this name, which Spengler accords to Florence, Bruges and Weimar, as no other town has ever answered in either of the Americas. There is a springtime feeling in the air, a joyous sense of awakening, a free creativeness . . . and—at first a little timid, cold and shy—the mind begins to shape into myths and stories the dreams of the pre-urban countryside. There is a moment of equipoise, a widespread flowering of the imagination; . . . the culture-city dominates the country, but only as its accepted vent and mouthpiece. Then gradually the mind, detached from the soil, grows more and more self-conscious. . . . The Hawthornes yield to the Henry Jameses . . . Boston surrenders to New York—which stands for cosmopolitan deracination.

Van Wyck Brooks

Here there is no literature or appreciation of it or literary men or appreciation of them. The whole tone of public opinion is opposed to intellectual culture of any kind, which is discouraged & any manifestation of it rebuked by the narrow jealousy of ignorance. "So you think yourself wiser than me & that you can instruct us," are the questions indignantly tho impliedly asked by the look and manner of the friends and acquaintances of anyone here who ventures to do anything so boldly out of the common track as to write a book.

Sidney George Fisher

"An aristocracy in the days of its strength," wrote Tocqueville, "does not merely conduct affairs; it still directs opinions, gives tone to the writers and authority to ideas. In the eighteenth century the French nobility had entirely lost this part of its supremacy."[1] What Tocqueville was saying was that the French nobility in the eighteenth century had increasingly become a privileged caste rather than, as in England, a true aristocracy of authority and leadership. Ideas were divorced from class authority, and the French Revolution and the rise of charismatic leadership in the person of Napoleon were the result. In the realm of ideas, it is appropriate that Puritan Boston, extremely anglophilic in the Federalist period, should have followed in the British traditions of aristocracy, whereas Quaker Philadelphia, a francophilic and Enlightenment city, should have followed the caste traditions of the ancien régime.

No other city in America and very few in Western history as a whole have equaled Boston between the ages of Cotton Mather and Henry Adams in dominating the ideas and values of a developing nation. Even after the agonizing death of Puritan piety in Cotton Mather's generation, a secular puritanism, as H. L. Mencken saw and ridiculed, still dominated American values down to the flapper and ballyhoo years of the 1920s. Until our own time, in fact, the history of ideas in America has been based largely on evidence drawn from the culture of New England and Boston. Indeed, before the rise of the academic and professional historian in the generation following Henry Adams's, American history was the product primarily of Boston's leisured class of gentlemen historians like Prescott, Palfrey, Parkman, Motley, and the Adams brothers. New England hegemony in America is nicely suggested by the history of the term *Yankee*: originally referring to the envied, and often hated, New Englander, it was applied to the whole North during the Civil War and then to all the Americans who fought on the western front in the First World War. At the war's end, and after Henry Adams's death in 1918, Henry Cabot Lodge prepared *The Education of Henry Adams* for publication and general circulation. When Adams privately released *The Education* in 1906, he liked to think it marked and explained the end of the rule of both his family and his class in America; as he looked back on his youth in the 1840s and 1850s, the height of Boston's hegemony over the American mind, he was convinced that those halcyon days were far closer to the year one than they were to the twentieth century, which had passed him by.

In contrast to Boston, Philadelphia produced, in Tocqueville's terms, a privileged caste that has never given tone to the ideas of either the state of Pennsylvania or the nation. Frederick Jackson Turner's anti-intellectual and deterministic interpretation of the influence of the frontier on the American mind might well have been based on evidence from the history of Pennsylvania: it was from Pennsylvania that atomized families in Conestoga wagons set off westward throughout the eighteenth and nineteenth centuries; the Pennsylvanian Daniel Boone, traveling down the Shenandoah valley into Virginia and thence out to the Kentucky frontier, was surely an excellent mythical model for Turner's thesis.* In the same individualistic vein as the Turner thesis, Philadel-

---

*The corporate and cooperative town settlements of the Western Reserve and the Northwest, which other historians have described as a modification of the Turner thesis, were largely New England phenomena.

phia's Benjamin Franklin, in his autobiography, modified the Calvinist ideal of devotion to a calling in a fixed status hierarchy to produce a later American ideal of individual moneymaking and mobility as a sign of secular salvation according to the gospel of success. Another Philadelphian, Cyrus H. K. Curtis, a century after Franklin's death, bought the *Saturday Evening Post* and hired George Horace Lorimer to build it into the most successful publishing venture of the first four decades of the twentieth century (the era of the Protestant Ethic and middle-class business hegemony); the *Post*—every cover page of which announced that it was "Founded A.D. 1728 by Benj. Franklin"—was built on Lorimer's conservative and middle-class faith in success and self-reliance.

This is no place to go into the history of the American mind; in order to place the minds of Boston and Philadelphia within a national context, however, I have supplied a brief list of selected authors, along with their dates of birth and the publication dates of some of their major works (Table A–20).* In many ways, the table speaks for itself and illustrates the hegemony of Boston and New England in the development of the American mind.† It also suggests two patterns of ideas: the *rights* tradition of egalitarian individualism and the *duties* tradition of hierarchical communalism.

The history of ideas in America was greatly influenced from the days of the Mathers down to the death of Henry Ward Beecher in 1887 by the authority of the oral culture of the pulpit. One must remember that a man like Emerson was probably more generally known for his secular lectures at lyceums and elsewhere than for his writings. And similarly for the abolitionist Wendell Phillips, whose annual income from lecturing was between $10,000 and $15,000—and he gave his abolitionist lectures free.

The supreme leadership culture of Boston, as I have emphasized time and again, was rooted in the pulpit culture of rigid Calvinism, which was always on the defensive and became less and less important in molding the American mind of the twentieth century. But it is noteworthy that Lyman Beecher's daughter, Harriet Beecher Stowe, was deeply affected by her father's stern Calvinism. And regardless of its literary merits, her *Uncle Tom's Cabin* was surely one of the most influential books in all American history. Her brother, Henry Ward Beecher, whose theological liberalism had little in common with their father's conservatism, was the last of the great preachers in America; in spite of the scandals and disgrace toward the end of his life, when he died in 1887, some 40,000 people came to view his body as it lay in Plymouth Church in Brooklyn. Ironically, the very values that made Boston and New England great in the first place were losers in the course of our history. For these values were based on a

---

*All tables cited in this chapter are presented in Appendix I.

†As the history of the Boston mind has been written about so thoroughly by Van Wyck Brooks and others, I shall have more to say later on of the Philadelphia mind. Others have explored success, as historians very often do, so I shall take as my task the exploration of failure, which is quite as interesting and important a problem. In this connection, I have often thought of Winston Churchill's comment that if he ever had to spend six months on a desert island, he would rather have as a companion an unsuccessful dentist than a successful statesman: the single-mindedness of the successful, Churchill thought, is all too often a predictable bore.

profoundly *pessimistic* view of human nature, which in turn demanded a stern status system of hierarchical communalism, and an emphasis on duties rather than rights, to keep men on the straight and narrow path. The classic reflections of this view of man in American literature are Hawthorne's *Scarlet Letter* and Melville's *Moby Dick*. When Melville finished his greatest book, which he dedicated to his friend Hawthorne, they were neighbors in western Massachusetts, and both were poor but fiercely proud of their aristocratic and Calvinist ancestry.

Whereas the ideas of his indirect mentor Cotton Mather and of his contemporary Jonathan Edwards were ultimate losers, Benjamin Franklin's philosophy was surely the grand winner in the battle for control of the American mind. It was natural that Franklin should find his home in Quaker Philadelphia, the city of egalitarian individualism, where all had the right to choose their own gods and their own ways to wealth without interference from pulpit or class authority. Franklin's autobiography, Paine's "Common Sense" and "Rights of Man," as well as Joel Barlow's *Advice to the Privileged Orders* shared a belief in anti-authoritarian individualism. This tradition was carried on by two contemporary Harvard bred Bostonians, Horatio Alger, Jr., and Charles W. Eliot: Alger has become a household word among America's business class of once rugged individualists and Eliot's elective system has plagued our antinomian college curricula down to the present day.

The optimistic and individualistic tradition of thought in America reached its apogee in Emerson and Whitman, as well as in Emerson's younger, cantankerously individualistic Concord neighbor Thoreau. Transcendentalism, the *Dial*, and Thoreau's two years at Walden Pond marked a turning point in the American mind in the direction of an anti-institutional individualism that emphasized individual *rights* almost to the exclusion of communal *duties*. In the epilogue I note the affinities between Emerson, Whitman, and Thoreau on the one hand, and Quakerism, on the other, as well as their links with the enthusiasms of the 1960s. Note here that Emerson's Concord was, as it were, America's first intellectual community, but Pfaff's restaurant in New York, which opened in 1854 and where Whitman became a prominent charismatic figure, was America's first bohemia, signifying the gradual divorce of our intellectuals from community or class authority. As Thomas Bailey Aldrich put it in a letter to Bayard Taylor in 1866·

> The people of Boston are full-blooded *readers*, appreciative, trained. The humble man of letters has a position here which he doesn't have in New York. To be known as an able writer is to have the choicest society opened to you. . . . In New York—he's a Bohemian! outside of his personal friends he has no standing."[2]

If Emerson and, more so, Walt Whitman celebrated the infinite possibilities of the new human nature characteristic of rootless and self-reliant democratic man in America, Mark Twain, especially in his misanthropic later years, had some doubts about the consequences of such a radical transformation of human nature. His doubts were exaggerated in the mind of Henry Adams, who became the prophet of doom and disillusionment as he watched the degradation of the democratic dogma in the Gilded Age and the years leading up to the First World War. I should imagine that Henry Adams will have increasing appeal in our day, partly as a reaction to the antinomian and anti-authoritarian tenor of the 1960s, an orientation Henry's brother Charles Francis found so attractive in Anne Hutchinson and her followers.

At the moment, however, it seems that the antinomian ideals that were brought to America through the port of Philadelphia have won the field. And this is spite of the historical experience of Philadelphia, where the rare men of ideas led lonely lives and, like Sidney George Fisher, were mostly losers. In a moment, we shall take a look at some literary losers in Philadelphia whose class situation was so very different from that of their peers in Brahmin Boston.

BOSTON AND PHILADELPHIA FIRST
FAMILIES AND THE LIFE OF THE MIND

The influence on the life of the mind in America of such giants as the Mathers, the Adamses, the Lowells, the Holmeses, and the James brothers, to say nothing of Emerson and Hawthorne, is well documented in our history. But these exceptional men were only outstanding examples of the larger class of Boston Brahmins. No group of fifty families in our history has produced so many men of ideas as the Boston First Family sample: the eighty-three Bostonians listed in Table A–21 had 21,676 lines written about them in the *DAB*, as against the 5,494 lines written about the forty Philadelphians. This quantitative evidence is only part of the story, for many other members of the Boston sample also wrote—for example, William Lawrence and Phillips Brooks, whom I did not include because they were primarily men of the cloth rather than the pen. In contrast, almost no Philadelphian not listed in Table A–21 wrote a word. No Philadelphian, moreover, equaled Cotton Mather in prolificacy; his 400 titles exceeded the output of all the Philadelphians combined, and no Philadelphian matched the twenty-volume output of the almost blind Brahmin historian William H. Prescott. With the exception of Charles Henry Carey, his kinsman Henry Charles Lea, and S. Weir Mitchell, in fact, no Philadelphia Gentleman produced more than a handful of books.

Boston Brahmins, then, were a reading and writing people; Proper Philadelphians were neither to anywhere near the same degree: according to Frank Luther Mott's exhaustive *History of American Magazines*, the average annual circulation of periodicals per inhabitant in 1850 was 404 in Boston, 157 in New York, 147 in Baltimore, and 125 in Philadelphia. Although the differences between Boston and Philadelphia are far less in today's homogenized world than in the 1850s, Boston is still more of a reading city. Although no comparable figures were available for the two cities, the periodical-reading habits of the states of Massachusetts and Pennsylvania in 1967 are compared in Table A–22: the citizens of Massachusetts were more than twice as likely to read elite periodicals and somewhat more likely to read mass circulation magazines.

In the nineteenth century, Boston was the home of elite journalism; Philadelphia was the home of the first mass magazines in America. The *North American Review*, from its founding in 1815 by members of the Anthology Club
(which also founded the Athenaeum) to its movement to New York in 1878,
published the most serious thinking in America, comparable to the *Edinburgh
Review* in Britain. And it was the house organ of both Harvard and Boston's
ruling class. Its editors, for instance, included the two Everett brothers, Edward
and Alexander Hill, John G. Palfrey, James Russell Lowell, Charles Eliot Norton, Henry Adams, and Henry Cabot Lodge, all from the Boston First Family
sample. Its leading contributor was Edward Everett, and even Philadelphia's
Sidney Fisher contributed from time to time.

Whereas the *North American Review* was primarily a scholarly journal, the
organ of Boston's literary establishment par excellence was the *Atlantic Monthly*,
founded in 1857. Its first editor was James Russell Lowell and its first issue included contributions from Emerson, Holmes, Longfellow, Whittier, Harriet
Beecher Stowe, John Lothrop Motley, and Lowell himself. Barrett Wendell, in
his *Literary History of America* (1901), devoted a whole chapter to a discussion of
the *Atlantic*, and he listed among its leading contributors Edward Everett,
Rufus Choate, George Ticknor, William Prescott, John Motley, Francis Parkman, Wendell Phillips, and Emerson, all of whom belonged to the Boston sample of families.

The famous Saturday Club came into being at about the same time as the
Atlantic; though Barrett Wendell in 1901 felt it was "too private for detailed
mention," he went on to say that the writers of the *Atlantic* "were more con-
cerned as to what the Saturday Club might think of their productions than
they ever deigned to be about the public."[3] Both the *Atlantic* and the Saturday
Club were launched and lunched into being at the Parker House, where the
Saturday Club gathered once a month, when Emerson came into Boston from
Concord. Its members were no literary bohemians but solid members of the
Boston Brahmin establishment, as indicated by the handwritten list of guests at
a Parker House lunch on May 31, 1873 (Figure 15-1). The names included surely show that here was a class of men—poets, philosophers, judges, senators, editors, doctors, businessmen; and the president of Harvard—who formed a
broadly responsible society, or, as Tocqueville would say, a true aristocracy of
ideas and action. By 1873, the flowering of New England literature was over,
but no history of the American mind would be complete without taking into
account the men and women who published *Representative Men, The Scarlet
Letter, Moby Dick, Uncle Tom's Cabin, Walden*, and other key works during the
1850s.

It is indicative of Boston chauvinism that Barrett Wendell in his literary history of America did not mention the *Port Folio*, which flourished in Philadelphia at the beginning of the nineteenth century. After a wandering literary career in New England, Joseph Dennie decided to try his luck in Philadelphia,
then the literary capital of America, along with his Harvard classmate and
good friend Thomas Boylston Adams. They boarded with a "Quaker family of

Figure 15–1   Diagram of a Saturday Club Dinner, in the Handwriting of John S. Dwight.

Source: M.A. DeWolfe Howe, Boston: *The Place and the People* (New York: Macmillan, 1903), p. 245.

repute" while Adams practiced law and Dennie founded the *Port Folio*. Dennie, a conservative and a Federalist in a Jeffersonian city, wrote under the pen name of Oliver Oldschool. *Port Folio* was the first quality literary periodical in the new nation. Two things about the *Port Folio* are relevant to my theory of leadership: first, the publication was started and edited not by a Philadelphia Gentleman but by a Boston and Harvard auslander; second, though many Philadelphia

Gentlemen were occasional contributors to *Port Folio* and members of Dennie's circle at the Tuesday Club—for example, Nicholas Biddle, Charles Jared Ingersoll, Thomas Sergeant, Thomas I. Wharton, Horace Binney, Richard Rush, Joseph Hopkinson, and Thomas Cadwalader, all from the fifty family sample—they were gentlemen first, lawyers second, and literati on the side. Nevertheless, the *Port Folio* was a first-rate journal in its day, and its very existence in Philadelphia showed what the city might have continued to do had the members of its educated classes been inclined to write and to take the lead in things of the mind. But they were not, and the *Port Folio* passed into history soon after Dennie's death in 1812.

After the *Port Folio* died, the *North American Review* and the *Atlantic Monthly* took its place at the head of serious journalism in America. At the same time, Philadelphia became the center of middle-class and business journalism, often led by outsiders and auslanders like Joseph Dennie rather than by members of the city's upper class.

The first successful mass circulation magazine in the young nation was founded by George R. Graham, a local cabinetmaker who studied law in the office of Charles Jared Ingersoll while working at his trade. Graham never practiced law but instead bought the *Gentleman's Magazine* and founded *Graham's Magazine* in 1825. One of the first magazines to use illustrations, *Graham's* aimed to be amusing rather than profound: Graham's code was to (1) use business techniques, (2) combine moneymaking with literature, (3) get exclusive rights to writers and pay them well, and (4) reflect what the public wanted. His methods foreshadowed those of Louis A. Godey and Cyrus H. Curtis. Edgar Allen Poe, during his brief editorship in the 1840s, tried to raise the literary level of *Graham's* but without much success. Nevertheless, its contributors included many of the literary lights of the day, such as Poe, Cooper, Longfellow, and James Russell Lowell (who wrote under the pen name H. Perceval); and among its editors were Robert T. Conrad, Philadelphia lawyer and mayor, as well as Bayard Taylor and Charles Godfrey Leland. Leland was the last editor before the magazine's demise in 1858. He brought the circulation up to 17,000, high for that day, but seemed to have no respect for *Graham's* quality: "I filled it recklessly," he later wrote in his memoirs, "with all or any kind of literary matter as best I could."[4]

The most successful magazine in mid-nineteenth-century America was *Godey's Lady's Book*, founded in 1830 by Louis A. Godey, an auslander from New York. Providing "unalloyed pleasure to the female mind," *Godey's* never admitted anything to its pages that was not "as pure as the driven snow."[5] By the Civil War, it had attained the unprecedented circulation of 150,000 (the *North American Review* had a circulation of some 3,000 at the time). Godey had little literary ability but he had the business acumen to buy out the Boston *Ladies' Magazine* in 1837. Sarah Hale, a widow of old Yankee stock who had gone to work for the magazine in order to support her five children, edited *Godey's* during its most successful years (she resigned in 1877, two years before her death). A great editor who knew and guided the female mind of her day,

Hale had an absolute faith in those of her sex who she believed were "God's appointed agents for morality in the world who should accomplish their mission through moral influence rather than by direct influence in public affairs."[6]

Cyrus Hermann Kotzschmar Curtis,* a native of Portland, Maine, published his first paper, *Young America*, at the age of thirteen. He came to Philadelphia from Boston in 1876 and established the *Ladies Home Journal* in 1883. By 1893, circulation had passed the million mark, and it reached 2,567,265 by the time of his death in 1933. In 1897 he bought the *Saturday Evening Post* for $1,000 and built it into the most popular magazine of its time (2.7 million circulation by 1933).

Curtis, according to his *DAB* biographer, "never made any pretense of being an editor"[7] but built his success on the editorial abilities of Edward W. Bok, an immigrant of distinguished Dutch ancestry, who ran the *Ladies Home Journal*, and George Horace Lorimer, whom Curtis brought from Boston to head the *Post*. In the tradition of Franklin, Lorimer was a pioneer in the writing of business fiction and the success ethic; his *Letters from a Self-Made Merchant to his Son*, first serialized in the *Post*, was published in several countries and sold well for some forty years. Edward Bok also wrote a series of books in the Horatio Alger tradition, including *The Americanization of Edward Bok: The Autobiography of a Dutch Boy Fifty Years After*, an immediate best seller, which won the Pulitzer Prize in 1921. The Curtis publications were built on the glorification of the small businessman, the middle class, and the Protestant Ethic of self-reliance and self-improvement. Curtis himself, though many times a millionaire, always prided himself on remaining middle-class to the core and extremely conservative.

The Curtis-Bok family is surely one of Philadelphia's more distinguished twentieth-century clans. (Edward Bok married Curtis's only child.) Both Curtis and his son-in-law were great philanthropists and contributed to the cultural and civic life of Philadelphia in many areas: Curtis gave generously to the Philadelphia Orchestra for years, and the Curtis Institute of Music is one of the truly first-rate institutions in the city today; Bok founded the Bok Award (now the Philadelphia Award) to be given to the outstanding Philadelphian each year.† Neither the family founders nor their descendants, however, seem to have been interested in, or accepted by, the inner core of Proper Philadelphia Society. The "figure on the carpet," as Henry James would have expected, thus repeated itself in their case. In the third generation, Curtis Bok—judge, witty essayist, novelist, yachtsman, and crusader against capital punishment—had little time for Philadelphia Society and in fact became a convinced Friend during World War II; appropriately enough, his son, Derek Bok, is now the president of Harvard.

---

*Curtis was of pure Yankee stock. The name Kotzschmar derived from his family's love of music: his parents had patronized an immigrant German organist by that name and named their son after him.

†Though Curtis and Bok money has gone to many educational institutions (including Temple University) no important contribution was ever made to the University of Pennsylvania.

THE LIFE OF THE MIND IN PHILADELPHIA

As we have seen, Joseph Dennie came to Philadelphia and founded the *Port Folio* when the city was the literary capital of the nation. After the federal government left for the wilderness city on the Potomac, however, the cosmopolitan atmosphere was gradually replaced by Quaker drabness and middle-class complacency.

Matthew Carey, the young nation's leading publisher, was a major figure in the city's most stimulating days. Between 1787 and 1792 he published the *American Museum*, the best magazine of its time, with contributions from men like Thomas Paine, Benjamin Rush, and Philip Freneau. Carey was also the patron of Parson Weems, who often referred to himself as "Mother Carey's Chicken" as he traveled for years over the dusty roads of the South collecting anecdotes about George Washington. Under Carey's sponsorship, this Livy of the common people and mythmaker supreme published his magnum opus, *The Life and Memorable Actions of George Washington*, which went through some seventy editions after its first publication in Philadelphia in 1800.

Carey, an Irish Catholic born in Dublin, was a typical Philadelphia auslander leader in the heady days when Talleyrand, Chateaubriand, Lafayette, Volney, Priestley, and other distinguished men from abroad, as well as our founding fathers, walked the city's streets. Carey's ardent republicanism soon alienated the British authorities in Dublin; he escaped to France, where he worked for a time in Franklin's printing shop at Passy before coming to Philadelphia. Arriving almost penniless, he was helped on his way to wealth by a loan of $500 from Lafayette, whom he had known in France. He eventually made a fortune in publishing and founded the Carey-Lea clan, one of the few really distinguished intellectual families in the city's history.

Along with Tench Coxe, Carey was a founder of the Philadelphia Society for the Promotion of National Industry. As the society's major publicist, he was instrumental in founding the first school of economic thought in America. In this connection, it is interesting that of the eighty-three authors in the Boston sample (see Table A–21) none wrote on economics, and it is indeed appropriate that Philadelphia was the home of our first school of economic theory: thus, Matthew's son, Charles Henry Carey, was the leader of "the only group that can be said to constitute an American school of political economy."[8] Carey was an intense nationalist in economic theory and led the opposition to the pessimistic classical school, as well as to the socialist school that rose in opposition to Ricardo's council of despair. Not only was he a prolific writer and original thinker, but Carey's home in Philadelphia was for many years a gathering place for his followers and other distinguished visitors to the city. The "Carey Vespers," as these gatherings were affectionately called, "formed almost the only American counterpart to the salons of the French Physiocrats."[9] Carey had many disciples both here and abroad, among them Stephen Colwell, Condy Raquet, E. Pershine Smith, Henry C. Baird, William Elder, Robert Ellis Thompson, and Simon N. Patten. (Thompson and Patten were early leaders of the Wharton School—Thompson its first dean and, after his forced resignation in 1892, the great builder of Central High School.)

Matthew Carey's daughter, Frances Anne, married Isaac Lea, of old Philadelphia Quaker stock. Lea himself, however, was disowned for enlisting for service in the War of 1812. A chemist and a prolific writer, Lea was one of the foremost scientists of his day, as indicated by his election to the presidency of the American Association for the Advancement of Science (1860) and the vice-presidency of the American Philosophical Society.

Isaac Lea's son, Henry Charles Lea, was Philadelphia's major post–Civil War civic leader in the style of Boston's Mugwumps and Progressives. His *History of the Inquisition of the Middle Ages* (1888) is a classic—praised by Lord Bryce and the Catholic Lord Acton and still indispensable today. He was the only Proper Philadelphian ever to be elected president of the American Historical Association and was honored both here and especially abroad. Like his father before him, he was president of the Wistar Association until his death. (The association held so-called Wistar parties, the Philadelphia forerunner and counterpart to Boston's Saturday Club.) Lea spent a large part of his life managing the family publishing firm, which gradually became one of the most respected and lucrative medical publishing houses in the nation.* He was also a very successful dealer in urban real estate; insight into the Philadelphia mind is gained from a local newspaper headline announcing Lea's death: "Well-Known Real Estate Operator Passes Away."

Except for Charles Henry Carey, who was influential in the history of American economics, Proper Philadelphians have made almost no serious contributions to the history of the American mind. James Russell Lowell once wrote: "As long as I have anything to do with the *Atlantic* it shall be expressly not for the mob of well-dressed gentlemen who read with ease."[10] Lowell was speaking with the voice of class authority and was referring to the shallow values of the popular journalism of his day in Philadelphia. He was speaking also from a Boston tradition, which men like Henry Charles Lea and Sidney Fisher envied.

> It is difficult to struggle against a moral & intellectual atmosphere, the whole tendency & training of the society in which one lives, sympathy, encouragement, friendly recognition, & companionship are necessary to sustain any but the highest genius in arduous or even light labors of the mind. We are all more or less influenced by the people around us. I sometimes think that I might have done something had I lived among people of real culture, who loved letters, philosophy, & art—at least did not despise them or feel towards them the indifference of ignorance.[11]

Sidney Fisher was articulating the feelings of the very few Proper Philadelphians who ever tried to live the creative life or do anything out of the money-

---

*Under the leadership of Charles Henry Carey, the family firm was the largest and richest publisher of fiction in the nation: Scott, Dickens, Cooper, and Irving were Carey authors and glad of it. Today the firm goes under the name of Lea & Febiger, a successful publisher of medical books. Just as the Carey-Lea family was the exception to anti-intellectual Philadelphia, so in the twentieth century their descendants went to Groton rather than to Philadelphia's favorite, St. Pauls.

making mainstream. The city has of course produced its share of natural geniuses, but Philadelphia's manners and mores have often hindered and have
never fostered the growth of their talents. Further insight into the Philadelphia
mind can be gained through a look at the lives of two lonely birthright Friends,
Charles Brockden Brown, America's first novelist, and Bayard Taylor, "Poet
Laureate of the Gilded Age," as one of his biographers called him; George
Boker, a Proper Philadelphian who hid his considerable literary gifts and was
admired locally as the leading club-man of the Civil War era; S. Weir Mitchell,
Victorian patrician and physician, extremely popular writer, and leader of the
city's only literary circle since *Port Folio* days; and Owen Wister, Mitchell's kinsman, whose book *The Virginian*, a minor classic, was the prototype of the cowboy novel and film.

It is appropriate that Philadelphia, the city of firsts, should have produced
America's first novelist, Charles Brockden Brown. Brown's earliest American
ancestor had come with Penn, and his father was exiled to Virginia during the
Revolution with other Quakers. Educated at the Quaker school of Robert
Proud, the first historian of Pennsylvania, Brown read widely and absorbed all
the romantic and revolutionary ideas of his time—the perfectibility of man, the
rights of women, the abolition of slavery, and educational reform; he knew
Diderot's *Encyclopedia*, as well as the works of Thomas Paine, Mary Wollstonecraft, and especially William Godwin, whose *Political Justice* and *Caleb Williams*
influenced him greatly. A lonely dreamer as a boy, Brown was always taking
long, solitary walks along the rugged banks of the Wissahickon, where he was
fascinated by the mystical followers of Jacob Boehme who had settled there to
await the Second Coming, expected in the year 1700. The Wieland mansion,
the center of Brown's most famous novel, was situated on a rugged crag above
this mysteriously romantic stream.

After a brief apprenticeship in the law, Brown moved to New York, where
he published six novels in rapid succession, *Wieland* in 1798 and the last in
1801. He then returned to Philadelphia, where he tried, not very successfully,
to support his family as a merchant and as a part-time literary hack until his
death at the early age of thirty-nine. He never wrote another novel. "Romance
had been only a chapter in Brown's life, and it belonged primarily to New
York," wrote Carl Van Doren; "the later Philadelphia chapter was plain
prose."[12] Brown's Gothic novels had some influence both here and abroad,
where they were translated into French and German. Poe, Hawthorne, and
even Henry James owed him some debt, as did Shelley, Keats, and Scott; his
work anticipated Mary Wollstonecraft Shelley's *Frankenstein*.

Though neither Brown himself nor his critics seem to have noted it, the
theme of his most successful novel, *Wieland*, seems to be related to the Quaker
ethic of the Inner Light. Its central character is a Philadelphia Gentleman who,
in the midst of an ideally happy family life, hears a mysterious voice that orders
him to put to death his superhumanly perfect wife and children. Brown shows
how he carries out these horrifying deeds, at the command of the voice of God,
with great and compelling power. The end of the story, however, is hopelessly
weak as Brown reveals that the supposed voice of God was really only that of a

malevolent ventriloquist. Was Brown perhaps pointing out the dangers of the Quaker belief in the Inner Light? Who knows?

If the natural genius of Charles Brockden Brown isolated him, in his brief creative days, from prosaic, Quaker Philadelphia, so Bayard Taylor, born with an insatiable will to power and success, was also alienated from his birthright in Kennett Square, a stronghold of Hicksite Quakerism. Taylor came of a long line of English Friends who had settled in the Brandywine valley in Penn's time. Although his grandfather had been read out of meeting for marrying a Swiss Mennonite, Taylor was brought up in the strict Quaker way of his English ancestors. And all his life he betrayed a humorless bitterness toward the intellectually stultifying, if unusually beautiful, Quaker country south of Philadelphia (known as Wyeth country today) where he was born and raised.

Taylor moved to New York at an early age and befriended Horace Greeley, who encouraged him to go abroad with a promise to print his travel articles in the *Tribune*. Taylor sailed for Europe at the age of nineteen and within two decades was one of the most celebrated professional literary men of his time. By 1863, at the age of thirty-eight, he had written six volumes of verse, some 500 newspaper and magazine articles, and countless personal letters to his host of friends around the world, and had become one of the most popular lecturers in the land. He was the Marco Polo of the age, his nine travel books and numerous travel articles describing his wanderings all over Europe, Egypt, Abyssinia, Syria, Palestine, Turkey, India, and China; Taylor also went with the Perry squadron to Japan and covered the California gold rush. The recipient of many honors, he valued most an invitation to read the annual Phi Beta Kappa poem at Harvard in 1850; acceptance by the Boston Brahmins was considered by Taylor the highlight of his very successful career.

Tired of his peripatetic success, Taylor finally came home and spent all his savings in building a large mansion, Cedarcroft, where he tried to settle down in the land of his birth. In 1863, he published his first novel; he wrote several others, including the *Story of Kennett*, the most successful. Though his novels sold well and were accurate portraits of the local Quakers, they had no lasting literary merit. Taylor was in many ways too bitter about his native country and lacked the talent to see either his contemporaries or his ancestors with any deep understanding; perhaps he betrayed a sad estimate of himself when a character in one of his novels remarked, "I have touched neither the depths nor the heights: I have only looked down into the one and up toward the other, in lesser vibrations on either side of the noteless middle line which most men travel from birth to death."[13] At any rate, Cedarcroft finally drove him into debt, and he was forced to go abroad to recoup his fortunes. Taylor died in Germany in 1878, not long after he had been honored with the ministry to Bismarck's government. He was widely mourned in Germany and lay in state at New York's City Hall before being brought back to the Brandywine valley, where he now lies buried in the Hicksite cemetery, largely forgotten.

"Men are free," D. H. Lawrence once wrote, "when they are in a living homeland, not when they are straying and breaking away. Men are free when they are obeying some deep, inward voice of religious belief. Obeying from within. Men are free when they belong to a living, organic, believing community, active in fulfilling some unfulfilled, perhaps unrealized purpose."[14]

Following Lawrence, I should imagine that great works of literature must inevitably be grounded in an author's metaphysical, rather than purely psychological or sociological, sense of the human condition. There has been no creative literature of the first rank by, or about, Philadelphia Quakers.* Perhaps this lack is partly the result of the metaphysical shallowness of antinomian enthusiasm or simple perfectionism. Thus, Charles Brockden Brown, after a burst of Gothic fantasy in New York, came home to an unsatisfying life in mercantile Philadelphia; Bayard Taylor, wandering the world in search of himself, always remained a second-rate success: "The brilliance of his life for years blinded men to the mediocrity of his actual achievement."[15]

If Taylor, as one of his biographers put it, was "a martyr to the American way of life" in his avid pursuit of success, his good friend George Boker was surely a martyr to the snobbish and anti-intellectual values of fashionable Philadelphia. Whereas Taylor was a professional writer all his life, always playing the poet, Boker hid his considerable poetic gifts and passion to create behind his surface life as a prominent club-man and Society leader. His longing for literary recognition was shared with only a few intimates and was best revealed in his letters to Taylor. Born of old Quaker and Mennonite stock, Boker was a millionaire of inherited wealth and eventually joined the Episcopal church, as befitted his position in Proper Philadelphia. At Princeton, he was a bon vivant and founder of the *Nassau Literary Monthly*. A romantic and poetic dramatist, Boker took a friend's advice to "get out of your age as far as you can." His most successful play, *Francesca da Rimini*, was based on a medieval theme. First produced on Broadway in 1855, it was a critical but not a popular success. It was widely recognized as one of the major American plays of the nineteenth century only when, toward the end of Boker's life, it was produced by Lawrence Barrett, with Otis Skinner in a leading role. After the disappointing reception of *Francesca da Rimini* Boker turned to the task of clearing his family name. His father, president of the Girard Bank, had been blamed for its failure and sued by several men whose fortunes he had helped to make.

George Boker was one of the first Proper Philadelphians to support the Union cause; a patrician, Boker, unlike many of his peers, immediately saw Lincoln as "Lord of himself, an inborn gentleman."[16] Boker and men like Henry Charles Lea took the lead in founding the Union League, which raised money and supported several regiments. Boker, in fact, was shot at on Chestnut Street for taking this unpopular position. After the war, the courts cleared his father's name and he then went on to serve as minister to both Turkey and Russia. He

---

*In my judgment, the best book on Philadelphia Quakers is Theodore Dreiser's posthumously published novel *The Bulwark*; it has the emotional power and tragic sense almost totally lacking in Taylor's *Story of Kennett* or S. Weir Mitchell's extremely popular but now forgotten *Hugh Wynne*. It is also of interest that Dreiser's *Financier* is one of the most powerful novels ever written about American business and businessmen. The protagonist, as I noted earlier, was modeled on Charles T. Yerkes, a Philadelphian of old Quaker roots who broke away from his faith in search of the pleasures of power and eventually was faced with the emptiness of success.

ended his days with all kinds of local honors, including election to the presiden-
cies of the Union League and the Philadelphia Club. "The one thing which
Philadelphia would not do," wrote his biographer, "was to perceive that he was
a poet."[17]

As Taylor had been in 1850, so Boker was honored by Harvard with an invitation to deliver the 1865 Phi Beta Kappa poem. His feelings were shown in a
letter to Taylor at the time.

> The Boston people were good to me during my entire visit. They kept me half
> crazy and whole drunk all the time. I am not used to what we call "ovations,"
> great or small. . . . I am used to being despised and trampled on at home; why
> should I not bury my head in the dirt, and accept my fate?[18]

After Boker's death in 1890, an anonymous contributor to the *Atlantic
Monthly* wrote of him with great praise and affection, perceptively estimating
his position in Proper Philadelphia.

> Most of his companions and local society were inclined to scoff at his ambition or
> inspiration, his idealism. They believed that a young man well provided with
> wealth and station, who definitely proposed to set out as a poet and make poetry
> his chief aim in life, was throwing a sort of discredit on the class to which he be-
> longed.[19]

Boker wrote over 300 sonnets, which made him, along with Longfellow, one
of the major practitioners of this art in America. His published sonnets brought
him recognition among the discerning few, but none of his contemporaries
knew of 229 of them, which were discovered and published for the first time by
Sculley Bradley in 1925. Apparently, the great bulk of these sonnets were written to his mistress between 1857 and 1867, when he was going through the trying period of supporting the war and defending his family's name. At the same
time, the passion that lay behind Boker's facile and fashionable façade was revealed in the 107 poems written during 1859–1860, which expressed his bitterness toward his father's detractors. (These works were collected and published
in 1882 in Boker's *Book of the Dead*.) "If I had not been able to give vent to my
feelings in these poems," he wrote to Taylor, "I should have gone mad."[20]

As Sidney Fisher wondered about himself, who knows what Boker might
have done had he lived and written in Salem, Cambridge, or Concord, Massachusetts? At any rate, I like to think of him in terms of the last paragraph in the
Atlantic eulogy quoted earlier.

> Early portraits of Boker show an extraordinary resemblance to Nathaniel Haw-
> thorne in his prime; and I fancy there was a likeness between them, not only in
> their outward appearance, but also in their shyness and reserve. Hawthorne hid
> himself behind the veil of seclusion. Boker sought shelter behind the variegated
> tapestry of society, where he remained to the last a poet, a man of ideas.[21]

Whereas George Boker was a lonely artist of considerable accomplishment
without public recognition, S. Weir Mitchell was a medical, literary, and social

success. In his younger years, he made lasting contributions to medicine and when he turned to the writing of fiction in his sixties he averaged some $10,000 a year in royalties. Mitchell's achievements were widely recognized both in this country and abroad, where he collected many honorary degrees.* And he was generally acknowledged as Philadelphia's first citizen as no one before him had been since the death of Franklin. Like Franklin, to whom he was increasingly compared in later life, Mitchell eventually became the indispensable man when any cultural project was proposed. He once predicted that his epitaph would read: "Committeed to the grave." But unlike Franklin, Mitchell lived at the heart of Philadelphia Society, especially after he married Mary Cadwalader (a sensible and successful rather than romantic alliance) at the age of forty-six. In 1875, the year he married, Mitchell was taken on the board of trustees at Penn, where he served for more than a quarter of a century as chairman of the medical and many other committees. This important mark of social acceptance in Proper Philadelphia was especially valued by Mitchell because he had once been turned down for a professorship in the medical school in spite of strong recommendations by Agassiz and Holmes of Boston and William A. Hammond, surgeon general of the United States Army. Agassiz was appalled, and Hammond wrote Mitchell: "I am disgusted with everything and can only say that it is an honor to be rejected by such a set of apes."[22]

Mitchell had no Philadelphia Quaker roots. His grandfather, a Scottish physician, had come to Virginia in the eighteenth century. His father, John Kearsley Mitchell, after studying at Edinburgh, settled in Philadelphia, where he took a medical degree at the University of Pennsylvania in 1819. A prominent physician with a large practice, the elder Mitchell was a poet of sorts as well as a musician. Weir Mitchell, the third of eleven children, took his medical degree at the Jefferson Medical College, where his father was a professor. He then spent a year in Paris studying under the famous Claude Bernard. Back in Philadelphia Mitchell practiced medicine, got married, and had two sons, John Kearsley Mitchell, who became a physician, and Langdon Mitchell, a playwright. During the Civil War, after paying $400 for a substitute recruit, he threw himself wholeheartedly into treating the wounded at a local army hospital.

The official record of Mitchell's war work amazed European medical men because of its wealth of statistics and careful experiments. Among his many scientific papers, *Gunshot Wounds and Other Injuries of Nerves* (1864) is still the authority on what has come to be called shell shock. His war work led him to pioneer in neurology; Mitchell published 34 articles in this area between 1870 and 1878, a total of 119 during his lifetime, in addition to 42 articles in related fields. Moreover, his book on "Mitchell's rest cure" was influential here and abroad

---

*"Perhaps the one he valued most," wrote a biographer, "was a LL.D. from Harvard, presented at the University's two hundred and fiftieth anniversary in 1886. As he had told Holmes a decade before, 'I like praise from Boston. . . . Indeed, I am un-American enough to think that a degree from Harvard would nowadays be worth more than one from Oxford. . . .' Next to the M.D., he most often used the Harvard degree after his name on title pages" (Ernest Earnest, *S. Weir Mitchell: Novelist and Physician* [Philadelphia: University of Pennsylvania Press, 1950], p. 121).

and was carefully read by the young Sigmund Freud. Mitchell anticipated Freud in his studies of hysteria in women, but he never developed any theoretical system such as Freud's theory of transference though he carefully recorded his observations on his women patients, who often improved if and when they "fell in love" with him.[23]

Weir Mitchell's father had been a friend of Oliver Wendell Holmes, who took an interest in the younger Mitchells' writing career. As literary doctors, Holmes and Weir Mitchell often have been compared. But whereas Mitchell was a patient and empirical medical investigator, Holmes was a brilliant dilettante who once said of himself that "it is my nature to snatch at all fruits of knowledge and take a good bite out of the sunny side—after that let in the pigs."[24] In literature, Holmes's *Autocrat at the Breakfast Table*, a partly autobiographical record of a great talker, has lived down to our own time; Mitchell's very similar autobiographical books—*Characteristics* and *Dr. North and His Friends*—although revealing more subtle psychological insight, lack Holmes's vitality and are unknown to modern readers.

During 1889, the year he turned sixty, Mitchell published five medical articles, a volume of verse, and a novel. And he went on to become one of the most popular writers of his time. His *Hugh Wynne, Free Quaker* (1896), the story of a Philadelphia Quaker who took part in the Revolution, as Mitchell's wife's ancestors had done, was an immediate best seller and it continued to sell well until Mitchell's death at the start of World War I. (The book was praised by Thomas Bailey Aldrich of the *Atlantic*, who called it and *The Scarlet Letter* the two best works of fiction written by Americans up to that time.) Mitchell wrote even better, though never as popular, books in his seventies.

Weir Mitchell, essentially a lonely man, nevertheless had a real talent for friendship. He knew everyone of importance in his time, including Andrew Carnegie, Walt Whitman,* Holmes, Agassiz, Lowell, Aldrich, Bancroft, and Presidents Roosevelt and Taft.

Mitchell was also a lifelong friend of his cousin Henry Charles Lea. But whereas Lea was the city's leading patrician political reformer, Mitchell was more typical of Proper Philadelphia in that he seemed to take no interest whatever in the social and political issues of his day (Lea was a cerebral Unitarian; Mitchell was a fashionable, Philadelphia Club Episcopalian). Lea was greatly indebted to Mitchell, whose medical advice and treatment restored him to health after six years of mental collapse and near blindness had delayed his

---

*Mitchell was Whitman's doctor and respected him as a poet but hardly accepted him as a social equal. When he read Horace Traubel's *Walt Whitman in Camden* (1906), he was annoyed at the poet's damning him with faint praise: "He is my friend—has proved it in divers ways," Whitman told Traubel. "He is not quite as easy going as our crowd—has a social position to maintain. . . . I can't say that he's a world author—he don't hit me for that size—but he's a world doctor for me." Mitchell recorded the following revealing remarks on Whitman's comments in his diary: "He thought lightly of me and J.K.M. [Mitchell's son] but says no word of the fifteen dollars a month I paid for more than two years to keep him alive nor of the care I gave declining fees—nor of a hundred dollars I gave him to buy a pony or wagon. . . . I thought him self-pleased as a god and with no good opinion of any but those who flattered or admired a poetic tramp" ("Mixed Americana," *New Yorker*, August 5, 1950, p. 58).

writing a book on the Inquisition. He planned to dedicate this work to Mitchell as a token of his gratitude but finally wrote his friend saying that he felt so much doubt about its reception among scholars he did not want to connect Mitchell's name with what might prove to be a failure. (Aldrich of the *Atlantic* had recently rejected an article on torture taken from its pages because it was "too horrible.") On his part, Mitchell praised the scholarship in Lea's classic *History of the Inquisition* but knew that it would not qualify its author for a statue in Fairmount Park. Mitchell had a keen eye for success; Lea longed for lasting fame.

By the time of his death in 1914, Mitchell had conquered both Proper Philadelphia and the literary world of his day, besides being a medical man of international repute. But somehow he has suffered from what he once called "the immortality of a decade." Today he is remembered neither by Philadelphians nor by historians or critics of American literature. "What then keeps Mitchell from being first rate?" asked his most perceptive biographer, Ernest Earnest, in *S. Weir Mitchell: Novelist and Physician.* "Part of the answer is Philadelphia," Earnest continued.

> Mitchell never threw off its reticences, its social mores, its emphasis on class and family. He could support Walt Whitman, but he could never forget that Walt was not a gentleman. He was a friend of Carnegie's and he put Xerxes Crofter, the malefactor of great wealth, into his books, yet he has no conception of the America of *The Pit* and *The Octopus.* His people are the absentee owners of coal lands, the Philadelphia aristocracy of bankers and lawyers for inherited estates. . . . His social order is paternalistic; it revolves around the dinner tables of the wealthy. Even the American Revolution becomes an affair of Philadelphia drawing rooms. . . . He never wrote anything which might offend a Philadelphian. . . . It was this same tendency to conform to the mores of a highly conservative community which perhaps kept him from entertaining more daring theories of psychiatry. . . . Mitchell was a great man in his era; he did not transcend it."[25]

Earnest was surely right about Mitchell, but he did not go far enough. In perhaps the most exhaustive study of American literature, the *Literary History of the United States* (1969), edited by Robert E. Spiller, Willard Thorpe, Thomas H. Johnson, Henry Seidel Canby, and Richard M. Ludwig, a whole chapter is devoted to "The New England Triumvirate: Longfellow, Holmes, Lowell," but not a single line to Mitchell.* One may wonder whether Longfellow, Holmes, and Lowell were not just as limited by the genteel mores of their class in Boston as Mitchell was in Philadelphia. Yet they occupy permanent places in the history of American literature. And they hold them at least partly because they belonged to a proud class whose members have dominated the American mind for a large part of our history. In contrast, Mitchell's class in Philadelphia, devoid of real pride in accomplishment, as Sidney Fisher felt, made no effort to write about and boost those men and women of talent in the city who did at-

---

*One cannot accuse this volume of New England chauvinism, at least as far as its editors are concerned. The senior editor, Robert E. Spiller, the son of a native physician of distinction, has spent his life at Swarthmore and the University of Pennsylvania, where he founded the American studies program. He is a proud, but perhaps not chauvinistic enough, Philadelphian.

tempt to express themselves. When, for example, Earnest's book on Mitchell was published in 1950, a reviewer in the *New Yorker* suggested the reasons why Mitchell is almost unknown today.*

"S. Weir Mitchell: Novelist and Physician," by Ernest Earnest . . . is the first full-length study of this remarkable man since 1929. Mr. Earnest has produced a book that is undistinguished but not unintelligent. The earlier biography apparently included more personal documents. The new one is on a small scale, and it gives a certain impression of a job done merely in passing. It does not really take us into the late-nineteenth-century American world and the special Philadelphia milieu in which Mitchell flourished. There is a story here that has still not been told, a chapter of intellectual history that has not been adequately written. The Philadelphia of the Mitchells and the Wisters, of Horace Howard Furness, of Thomas Eakins and Mary Cassatt, of the days when Walt Whitman used to visit the parents of Logan Pearsall Smith, has not yet had much attention from the historians of literature, but it must have been at least as alive as the Boston of the same period.[26]

Owen Wister, S. Weir Mitchell's younger kinsman and friend, could have written a fascinating history of Philadelphia's literary and artistic circles in the age of Cassatt, Eakins, Whitman, Furness, and Mitchell. A man of many gifts, Wister was as interested in historical and cultural theories of literature as he was in the writing of fiction. He was, moreover, born and bred at the very heart of intellectual Philadelphia: Sidney Fisher was an intimate friend of both his mother and his father and Sidney's only son, Sydney George Fisher, a historian, was Wister's schoolmate at St. Paul's; John Kearsley Mitchell, Weir Mitchell's son, was Wister's closest Philadelphia friend; and it was Mitchell who advised Wister to take a rest out west in order to cure a nervous condition, a rest that launched Wister on his writing career. Finally, Wister was the grandson of the most fascinating and creative woman who ever lived in Philadelphia, the actress Fanny Kemble Butler.

But Wister would not, or could not, write of his native city; he was unable to complete a projected novel about Proper Philadelphia that he planned to call *Monopolis*. For he never really felt at home or, like George Boker, appreciated in Philadelphia. Thus, he wrote from Yellowstone Park in 1891 that he looked forward to a winter in the East "with unmixed dislike. . . . There are few people I care to see and care to see me, but Philadelphia is not a place I should choose for my friends or myself if I could help it."[27] When one of his Western stories was published, Philadelphia friends said either "I haven't read your story" or "It isn't as good as Bret Harte." "New York and Boston friends," Wister noted in contrast, "made no comparisons in the very welcome letters which they wrote." And Roosevelt wrote, "Bully for you."[28]

---

*This is not the only Philadelpia story that has never been adequately told. How many Philadelphians know that Ezra Pound grew up just off Old York Road, not far from the Wisters' Butler Place; that he roomed with William Carlos Williams at Penn; that among his small group of friends in Philadelphia were Marianne Moore and Hilda Doolittle (both "H.D"'s father and grandfather were members of the Penn faculty at one time or another)? For a delightful introduction to this story see Emily Mitchell Wallace, "Penn's Poet Friends," *Pennsylvania Gazette*, February 1973, pp. 33–36.

Though Wister felt most at home in the East at Boston and Cambridge, he finally found himself and his vocation among the ordinary cowpunchers and the refugee gentlemen from Harvard who formed the heart of the Wyoming Stock Growers Association, which gathered to drink, play tennis, and talk shop at the Cheyenne Club in the 1880s. Wister was a brilliant listener; he faithfully recorded the lingo of the West in his journals during his dozen visits there between his enforced rest in 1885 and publication of *The Virginian* in 1902.

Owen Wister came of a long line of Philadelphia Quakers on his father's side; Sally Wister was the famous chatty diarist of eighteenth-century Philadelphia, and Dr. Caspar Wistar, of another branch of the family, was the founder of Philadelphia's Wistar parties, which Weir Mitchell so enjoyed. Owen's father was a stolid family doctor in Quaker Germantown, as well as a typical anti-intellectual Proper Philadelphian. Dr. Wister's hardly compatible wife, Sarah Butler Wister, was the grand lady of the neighborhood, who "swept into the opera and symphony concerts in black velvet and black lace, and carved at the table while wearing white kid gloves"[29] and whose friends and correspondents included Henry James, Mendelssohn, Thackeray, and Browning. She wrote unsigned articles for the *Atlantic* and reviewed James's first novel *Roderick Hudson*, for the *North American Review*. Her mother, Fanny Kemble, once wrote of Sarah as follows: "S--- was as fond of her baby as I think she could be of any creature too nearly resembling a mere animal to excite her intellectual interest, which is pretty much the only interest in infants or adults that she seems to me to have."[30] In her memoirs, Fanny Kemble never referred to any tender relationship between Sarah and either her husband or her only son. Owen, perhaps fortunately, spent two years of his early youth abroad before going away to St. Paul's in New Hampshire and then to Harvard. At Harvard he majored in music, joined a select group of some twenty students in the Porcellian Club, took an active part in the Hasty Pudding shows, wrote for the *Advocate* and the *Lampoon*, and graduated summa cum laude. Wister made many friends in both Cambridge and Boston, especially Theodore Roosevelt and Henry Lee Higginson, a frustrated musician and supporter of the Boston Symphony.

Much against his father's will, Wister went abroad after Harvard and enrolled in the Paris Conservatory of Music. The highlight of Wister's year abroad was to play one of his own compositions for his grandmother's good friend Franz Liszt, who wrote Fanny Kemble that her grandson possessed "*un talent prononcé.*" Back in America, Wister got a job in a Boston bank at the recommendation of Henry Lee Higginson. He hated the work and finally decided to go to the Harvard Law School because, as he wrote his father, "American respectability accepted lawyers, no matter how bad, which I was likely to be, and rejected composers, even if they were good, which I might possibly be."[31] After law school, he returned to Philadelphia, where he worked in the Rawle office before being sent out west by Mitchell for a rest cure.

Owen Wister, through his mother and his grandmother, was brought up on the language of Shakespeare and Walter Scott's romantic ideals of chivalry. His favorite music was Wagner's. Although he was unable to find, or write about, any romantic heroes in Proper Philadelphia's drawing rooms, he finally created them in a genteel schoolteacher from Vermont and a gentleman cowboy out on the Western range. Like his friends Henry James and Henry Adams, Wister was romantically obsessed with the power of the virgin, but whereas James sent Daisy Miller east to find herself in the Old World, Wister's heroine, Molly Wood, of a prominent family in Bennington, went west, where she easily tamed a whole community of rowdy and rootless cowpunchers.

In many ways Owen Wister was a gentleman of the old school in the best nostalgic sense. An incurable romantic, he detested the "unmanly" money values of his age, which he found all too characteristic of the Philadelphia Gentleman. In the introduction to *The Virginian*, he wrote: "The cow-puncher's ungoverned hours did not unman him. If he gave his word, he kept it; Wall Street would have found him behind the times. Nor did he talk lewdly to women; Newport would have thought him old-fashioned."[32] And Wister had a keen historical sense, born of nostalgia: the cowboy, he told readers of *The Virginian*, "will never come again. He rides in his historic yesterday." Yet in the first line of the book, Wister predicted ("between ourselves") that his cowboy was "going to live a long while," as indeed he has done, largely through Wister's myth-making.[33]

Dedicated to Theodore Roosevelt, the gentleman cowboy in the White House, *The Virginian* was an instant best-seller when it appeared in 1902. Made into a play it ran successfully on the road for a decade, after a minor success on Broadway; it was made into four popular movies and a very popular television series after World War II. By Wister's death in 1938, *The Virginian* had sold more than 1.5 million copies in several languages, and it is still available in paperback editions. Thus, Wister became one of the famous Americans of his day.

As we have seen, Wister's literary heritage was closely allied to Boston and Massachusetts, especially in the person of his grandmother. Fanny Kemble was born into one of the famous families of the British stage. When she was brought to America by her actor father to recoup the family's fortunes with her wildly popular readings from Shakespeare, she was pursued around the country by Pierce Butler, an auslander Proper Philadelphian whose grandfather, an aristocratic Charlestonian, had represented South Carolina at the Constitutional Convention. Butler finally won the hand of the fabulous Fanny, and they settled down at Butler Place just north of Germantown. The Butlers were miserably unhappy in a marriage that finally ended in divorce: Butler, a wealthy slave owner, fitted perfectly into Philadelphia Society; Fanny, an intellectual snob surrounded by social snobs, was a misfit from the first. Her closest American friend, for instance, was Catherine Sedgwick of Stockbridge, where Fanny Kemble spent many of her happiest days in America; her intimate friend and informal marriage counselor was Charles Sumner; and her lawyer in the infamous divorce was Proper Boston's favorite, Rufus Choate. And she spent endless hours talking about the evils of slavery with her dear friend, the Unitarian saint, William Ellery Channing.* Her most faithful Philadelphia defender was a fellow Channingite, the Reverend William Furness, a transplanted Bostonian.

Fanny Kemble's grandson had a natural affinity for Boston and Cambridge from his days at Harvard to his death in 1938; his most sympathetic older friend was Henry Lee Higginson; along with his earlier mentor, William Dean Howells, Wister was one of the founders of the Tavern Club in 1884; Henry James, close friend of both Wister's mother and grandmother, was his literary model and close friend for many years. Wister maintained a lifelong relationship with Harvard, reading the Phi Beta Kappa poem there in 1897 and serving on the board of overseers for several terms. He was also the only Philadelphian in the fifty families sample to belong to Boston's Somerset Club. Finally, and most important, he married Mary Channing Wister, his second cousin, whose mother was a Boston Eustis and kin to the Channings. It was an extremely successful marriage. Wister was very proud of his wife's public service, especially her long leadership of the board of education: "[Her work] was a step rather conspicuously outside of established convention—the things that 'a lady could do,'" wrote Wister. "When Roosevelt discovered what sort of person she was who had been willing to have me as a husband, I think that his good opinion of me increased considerably."[34]

Very much in the Philadelphia style, Wister had a real talent for friendship; in his last book, *Roosevelt: The Story of a Friendship*, he described a visit with his wife to the White House in 1903.

> It filled me with a certain pride to reflect that I was the fourth generation of my family that had stayed there. My great-great aunt, Miss Isabel Mease, went there when Dolly Madison presided over it; my grandfather Pierce Butler when General Pierce was President; my mother during the same administration; and now here we are, the guests of Colonel and Mrs. Roosevelt. None of us had ever been invited for political reasons, but merely because of personal friendship; which seemed a better sort of welcome.[35]

Friendship rather than devotion to calling is an ancient Proper Philadelphia tradition. Thus, Wister, in spite of great talent, was far less devoted to the craft of fiction than was his dear friend Henry James. After the great success of *The Virginian*, he wrote a popular novel on Charleston society, *Lady Baltimore*, which came out in 1907, and then spent most of the remaining years of his life as a popular club-man. In a tribute to Wister at the American Academy of Arts and Letters, his Harvard classmate and friend Henry Dwight Sedgwick called

---

*Fanny Kemble spent the winter of 1838–1839 at her husband's plantation in Georgia, where she kept an intimate journal and wrote many letters to Channing and her other Massachusetts friends. That her husband refused to allow her to publish any of her observations, or to have anything more to do with the Sedgwicks, was an important factor in their divorce. When she finally published her unique observations on the "peculiar institution" in *The Journal of a Residence on a Georgia Plantation, 1838–39*, in England in 1863, it was too late to affect the war, but Kemble's "pen of burning gold" had produced a book that was the rage on both sides of the Atlantic.

him a "highly civilized gentleman of the eighteenth-century English type . . . and a delightful friend."[36]

The Virginian has a far more secure place in the cultural history of America than in the history of American literature and its reputation has far outlived the fame of its author.* As was George Boker before him, Wister was honored locally as a Philadelphia club-man but hardly boosted as the city's only gentleman novelist of national renown in his day. No full-length biography has yet appeared. His devoted daughter, Fanny Kemble Wister Stokes, brought his name before the public after World War II, when she published his Western journals, first in the Atlantic Monthly and then as a book (1958). In her introduction to Owen Wister Out West: His Journals and Letters, Fanny Stokes inadvertently revealed how Philadelphians tend to neglect the reputations of their more creative kinsmen. According to Stokes, in 1951, a Mr. Rush, director of the library at the University of Wyoming, wrote her about plans for celebrating the fiftieth anniversary of the publication of The Virginian and asked for any papers the family might have available for the Wister Room there. Wister, according to his daughter, had "never talked about the West to his family" and "because we had always been told that my father destroyed his manuscripts as soon as they were typed (and we had never seen a manuscript of his), we assumed there were none. I replied to Mr. Rush that there was little we could add to the Wister Room."[37] At about the same time, a neighbor and friend, who was also a niece of Henry James, asked her whether she had any letters to Wister from James. To make a long story short, Stokes and her brothers for the first time looked through their father's papers and found some forty letters from James and a series of letters written by Wister to his mother between 1870 and 1908. In the meantime Rush wrote again asking the whereabouts of Wister's Western journals (mentioned in his book on Roosevelt). "It seemed hopeless to try to find them," wrote Stokes,

> but I determined to look. . . . My younger brother said he would start with my father's desk, which had been in the second floor library that adjoined Owen Wister's bedroom and that was his study during his life at Butler Place. The very first drawer my brother opened contained the Western Journals. The fifteen journals had been in the drawer for sixty-five years. The cover of each is inscribed with my father's signature and a date and the names of the places he visited.[38]

The journals are now in the Wister Room of the University of Wyoming library; the bulk of Wister's paper are in the Library of Congress; and some correspondence is in the Houghton Library in Cambridge.

Among Owen Wister's schoolmates at St. Paul's in the 1870s were Weir Mitchell's two sons, John Kearsley and Langdon, as well as Sidney Fisher's only son, Sydney. Soon after graduating from Harvard, Wister wrote a novel with

---

*In informal polls of my colleagues at the University of Pennsylvania, I found that most of them knew of The Virginia but far fewer had heard of Owen Wister; hardly anyone knew that he was a Philadelphia Gentleman.

Langdon Mitchell that was never published because William Dean Howells thought it contained "too much knowledge of good and evil. . . . A whole fig tree couldn't cover one of the women characters in it."[39] Langdon was a bit of a rebel from Proper Philadelphia. He was expelled from St. Paul's for mischievously locking up Dr. Coit in a room and he dropped out of Harvard to follow a writing career. He married a British actress and attained considerable success as a playwright, spending most of his life in New York and Santa Fe, New Mexico, all the while, according to his *DAB* biographer and friend, Arthur Hobson Quinn, remaining a Proper Philadelphian "in all his instincts."[40]

Whereas Henry Charles Lea was a distinguished medievalist, Sydney George Fisher was the only American historian in my Philadelphia sample. Following his father's values, however, he was not a professional. On Sydney's fourth birthday, his father wrote in his diary that he could not

> bear to think that he will ever engage in business or even a profession. The snares, temptations and perils of either are dreadful to imagine when the character of a child is at stake. All money-making pursuits, even the *learned* professions as they are called, *bread studies*, as Carlyle calls them, are moreover narrowing to the mind. . . . I would make him a farmer . . . an educated one, with the tools and accomplishments of a gentleman.[41]

After the deaths of both his parents, within ten months of each other, Sydney went away to St. Paul's in the fall of 1872, where he did rather poorly, before going on to Trinity College in Hartford. All his life he was a devoted churchman and alumnus of Trinity, serving on the board of trustees from 1897 until his death. At first he wrote on constitutional history (he was, like his father, a member of the bar but rarely practiced) and then concentrated on the colonial history of Pennsylvania. A Proper Philadelphian of ancient Quaker roots and strong Episcopalian convictions, Sydney Fisher knew in his bones, as it were, the history and social character of his native city and state. In the last chapter of his very readable book, *The Making of Pennsylvania: An Analysis of the Elements of the Population and the Formative Influences That Created One of the Greatest of American States*, published in 1896, he summed up the history of the state.

> This brief summary . . . reveals the origin and cause of that strong feeling of jealousy for Philadelphia which has always been shown by the rest of the State. The city has been regarded by the country not as a metropolis to be proud of, but as a distinct community to be disliked and suspected, a condition of things which has often seemed strange and inexplicable to those not familiar with the history of the State. A State so constituted necessarily lacks the civic pride and united action which have given commonwealths of inferior situation and resources, like Massachusetts, such an ascendancy in the Union. . . .
>
> Our State once contained the metropolis of the country; the most important events in the Revolution and in the framing of the Constitution happened within our borders; and these, with our own conflicts, were of the sort that bring into prominence strong characters and high intellect. There has been no lack of good ability among our people. Bright and able men have appeared at all times, and from pretty much all the cliques into which we are dissipated. But almost every

one of them has been neglected and forgotten, or his reputation deliberately attacked or ruined. It is really extraordinary the vindictiveness with which the Pennsylvanians have assailed any one of their own people who has shown striking or supreme ability.[42]

Fisher then documented the Pennsylvania instinct for disparagement, especially in "neglecting their dead." Thus, although biographies of William Penn had been written by Englishmen, Frenchmen, and men of several other states of the the Union, Fisher's own book, *The True William Penn*, was the first to be written by a native Pennsylvanian, as was his book *The True Benjamin Franklin* (there were then some fifty biographies of Franklin by citizens from all over the world). Fisher also noted that neither Robert Morris nor John Dickinson was included in Spark's "American Biographies" and that they were completely neglected in Philadelphia (William Graham Sumner of Yale wrote the first biography of Robert Morris; no complete biography has yet been done of Dickinson). Finally, Fisher observed:

Massachusetts sets the highest example in this respect. Not even a minor character is allowed to die without being followed within two or three years by biographies so keenly written that every salient point is driven home into the minds of the whole nation. The man's personality is continued while everything is fresh. His picture is drawn for the future before the color has left his face. The encouragement and hero-worship which developed him to greatness in life preserve him, with Egyptian fidelity, in death.[43]

Sydney George Fisher, bachelor, died alone but for the servants at the Corinthian Yacht Club, where he had made his home for many years. In 1932, his *Making of Pennsylvania* was reissued by J. B. Lippincott; George Wharton Pepper's warm introduction called it "an indispensable introduction to the history of Pennsylvania which no Philadelphian can afford to neglect."[44] Few today have read this book or heard of either its author or his father.

Art and Architecture

*The arts always travelled westward, and there is no doubt of
their flourishing hereafter on our side of the Atlantic, as the
number of wealthy inhabitants shall increase, who may be
able and willing to reward them; since, from several in-
stances, it appears that our people are not deficient in genius.*

Benjamin Franklin

*I am an enthusiast on the subject of the arts. But it is an
enthusiasm of which I am not ashamed, as its object is to improve the taste of my countrymen, to increase their reputation, to reconcile to them the respect of the world, and produce them its praise.*

Thomas Jefferson

*I cannot help suspecting that the more elegance, the less vir-
tue, in all times and countries. . . . Is it possible to enlist the
fine arts on the side of truth, of virtue or piety, or even of
honor? . . . From the dawn of history, they have been prosti-
tuted to the service of superstition and despotism.*

John Adams

Whereas Boston and Harvard have been the self-appointed guardians of the
spoken and written word in America, more modest Philadelphians have taken
to heart the ancient Chinese proverb that "one picture is worth more than ten
thousand words." Inarticulate Philadelphia has been best interpreted in three
iconographically significant paintings by Benjamin West (1728-1820), Edward
Hicks (1780-1849), and Thomas Eakins (1844-1916). West's *William Penn's
Treaty with the Indians* (1772) mythologized the founding of Pennsylvania; this
painting of a treaty concluded under an elm at Shackamaxon, which event
probably never took place, now hangs as one of our national icons in Independence Hall. Edward Hicks, simple Quaker preacher in Bucks County, turned
from sign painting to become one of the leading American primitives; he spent
the last thirty years of his life painting "peaceable kingdoms," some sixty of
which have survived. Taking their text from Isaiah 11:6—"And the wolf shall

dwell with the lamb, and the leopard shall lie down with the kid . . . and a little child shall lead them"—many of Hicks's peaceable kingdoms show, in the foreground, how peace will come to the warring jungles of men and animals and, in the distance, Penn's apocryphal treaty making under the elm. If West and Hicks perpetrated utopian myths, Thomas Eakins was a stark naturalist: his *Gross Clinic** is surely the finest example of realism in American art; completed in 1873, it was too disturbing to be included in the Centennial Exhibition of 1876.

As I noted in Chapter 15, writers of literature and history often seem to be closely allied to the educated or upper classes. In contrast, practitioners of the visual and auditory arts seem to be far less class conditioned. In fact, the talent for drawing, painting, sculpting, or especially music making seems to be more God-given or culture-free than the talent for any other occupation or pursuit. Benjamin West, a simple Quaker boy born into the anti-aesthetic culture of rural Chester County, outside Philadelphia, was nevertheless recognized by the age of twelve as a professional painter by his neighbors and made a name for himself in Philadelphia by the age of twenty; he then went abroad to become one of the famous painters of his era in London, figuring among the thirty-six charter members of the Royal Academy (1768) and, after the death of his friend Sir Joshua Reynolds, its second president, a post he held for twenty-six years. West's talent and phenomenal career surely transcended his native or class origins.

Though talent in the arts is democratically spread throughout the social structure, patronage of the *fine* arts, until very recent times at least, usually has fallen to the upper classes.† West's patrons, for example, were fashionable members of the upper classes of both Philadelphia and London. Thus, he was helped on his way to fame by Provost William Smith of the College of Philadelphia, as well as by two of the city's leading art patrons, John Morgan and William Allen. In London, even though "he spoke with a curious uncouth accent and wrote illiterately,"[1] West soon became the darling of the aristocracy and a favorite of King George III; at his death, his body lay in state at the Royal Academy and he was buried with great honors, alongside Sir Joshua Reynolds, in St. Paul's Cathedral.

As the first settlers of both Massachusetts and Pennsylvania were engaged primarily in clearing the wilderness and building shelters, there was little time for the cultivation of either the fine arts or the learned professions. As in any

---

*Samuel Gross was, after Benjamin Rush, the supreme representative of Philadelphia's medical tradition, which was rooted in transatlantic Quakerism.

†Philadelphia provides three excellent examples of this rule in the Johnson, Widener, and Barnes art collections; but true to auslander and outsider leadership in the city, the three founders of these collections were self-made men and graduates of Central High School. Only John G. Johnson was accepted into the inner circle of Philadelphia Society, and his collection is now an important part of the Philadelphia Museum of Art. The Widener collection, for reasons discussed earlier, was donated to the National Gallery of Art. The Barnes collection, the finest private collection of Cézanne and Matisse ever assembled, is housed on the former Barnes estate along the Main Line (it took lawsuits to open it up to the public, especially to WASP Main Liners) in a handsome museum built by Paul Cret in 1925.

primitive situation, however, the manual and folk arts played an important role from the start. Only when wealth and leisure had been cultivated for some generations within a few privileged families did the fine arts and the learned professions come into their own. At first, of course, artists and professional men were either brought from abroad or educated there; this was especially so in early Massachusetts, whose original population included trained Oxford and Cambridge ministers, and in Philadelphia, where foreign-trained physicians played key roles in the early Quaker culture.

PAINTING, SCULPTURE, AND PORTRAITURE

Although the American upper classes have patronized artists, they have not encouraged their children to take up the arts as a serious career. The Boston and Philadelphia fifty family samples included only two sculptors and two portrait painters. Of the Philadelphians, William Rush, kin of Benjamin, has a permanent place in art history as the first American sculptor; Howard Roberts was of no great stature; and Adolphe Borie, a very talented portrait painter, had only a local Philadelphia reputation. Ernest Wadsworth Longfellow, the sole artist in the Boston sample, probably would not have been included in the *DAB* but for his famous family name. This dearth of upper-class artists is a reflection of class mores rather than of genes; surely John Adams would have felt that his peers and their descendants had more important things to do in the building of the new nation.

John Singer Sargent, the leading class portrait painter of his generation in both England and America, is the exception who illustrates the general rule. Although the Sargent family, with ancient roots in Gloucester, Massachusetts, has played a major role in the creative, business, and political history of Boston from the eighteenth century to the present, I did not include it in the Boston sample for several reasons:* in the first place I wanted to emphasize that its most prominent member, John Singer Sargent, was a deviant case; in the second place, he was born to an expatriate Philadelphia family in Italy, and today Sargents are listed in the *Social Registers* of both Philadelphia and Boston; final-

---

*The Sargents, however, were surely one of the most distinguished Brahmin families, with ten members in the *DAB*. See Table A-3 in Appendix for explanation of this listing.

10 Sargents (1793–1925—132— SR—WW-1) 1177

Winthrop (1753–1820) 75H	Soldier-Magistrate
Henry (1770–1845) 95 NC	Artist
Lucius Manlius (1786–1867) 89H	Author
Henry Winthrop (1810–1882) 60H	Horticulturist
John Osborne (1811–1891) 87H	Author-Journalist
Epes (1813–1880) 127 NC	Poet-Journalist
Fitzwilliam (1820–1889) 62 Jeff.	M.D.
Winthrop (1825–1870) 52 UP	Author-Historian
Charles Sprague (1841–1927) 89H	Arboriculturalist
John Singer (1856–1925) 441 NC	Artist

ly, and of great symbolic significance, Sargent—even though he considered Boston his American home and his murals in the Boston Public Library his masterwork—was the supreme class portrait painter in an era when the local gentry in Boston and Philadelphia, along with those of other cities, were merging into a transnational upper class. In fact, Sargent was the fashionable favorite of an Anglo-American upper class that took shape in the last years of the nineteenth century.

The first professional artists in both Boston and Philadelphia (see Table A-23 in Appendix I) were born abroad, John Smibert in Scotland, Peter Pelham in England, and Gustavus Hesselius, a cousin of Emanuel Swedenborg,* in Sweden. Smibert, who settled in Boston in 1730, did many portraits of Society luminaries, including Peter Oliver and some ten other members of his family, as well as Hancocks, Quincys, Sewells, Tyngs, and Wendells. Father of a large family, he also ran an art emporium, selling prints, ancient busts, copies of old masters, and so forth, to supplement his commissions. A jack-of-all-trades, Smibert designed Faneuil Hall, build in 1742 from funds provided by Peter Faneuil, whose portrait Smibert painted. Many of Smibert's portraits have been lost or misplaced, but almost all of Hesselius's paintings of Philadelphians have eluded historians. John Hesselius, his son, settled in Maryland, where he painted portraits of many of the prerevolutionary gentry including the Calverts and Samuel Chew, whose descendants became Proper Philadelphians.

Benjamin West was of course the founding father of American painting. Though an expatriate in London for the last fifty-six years of his life, West taught most of the more talented colonial artists of his day. He brought Copley to London and, among others, taught Charles Willson Peale, his son Rembrandt Peale, and Thomas Sully, Gilbert Stuart, John Trumbull, Washington Allston, and Henry Sargent.

John Singleton Copley, son of a humble Boston tobacconist, married the daughter of a wealthy Tory merchant and owned a large tract of land on Beacon Hill (including the present site of the Somerset Club). His mother married a second time to the artist Peter Pelham, a contemporary and a friend of Smibert. Copley thus was brought up in a painting environment. He was a member of Trinity Church and most of his clients were leaders of the Tory establishment, Anglican communicants either at Trinity or at the older King's Chapel. Fortunately, before Copley sailed for England with the Tory exodus in 1774, he had painted the portraits of some 275 leading Americans of his day, including John Adams, Abigail Adams, and their friends James Warren and Mercy Otis Warren, the first historian of the Revolution; that Copley painted these patriots as well as a host of Tories, including Thomas Hutchinson and Andrew Oliver (and nine other Olivers), indicates that the Revolution, as I noted earlier, was an intraclass rather than a class conflict. Thus, Copley's portraits

---

*Pennsylvania, the land of sectarians, today contains the major Swedenborgian community in the world, at Bryn Athyn, a suburb of Philadelphia. Its main patrons and supporters are members of the Pitcairn family, plate-glass millionaires. Needless to say, schisms have set brother against brother within the sect and within the Pitcairn family.

reflect the makeup of upper-class Boston in the eighteenth century; his subjects included Jonathan Belcher, Francis Bernard, James Bowdoin, Nicholas Boylston, George Cabot, Richard Dana, Judith Bulfinch, William Brattle, Mrs. John Forbes, General Thomas Gage, several members of the Gore, Gray, and Hancock families, Joseph Jackson, John Lowell, Josiah Quincy, Paul Revere, Richard Saltonstall, John Winthrop IV and his wife, and Epes Sargent (money-making merchant and family founder, not in the *DAB*), along with six other members of his family. In Philadelphia, Copley also painted several members of the gentry, including General and Mrs. Thomas Mifflin. But whereas Copley was the fashionable portrait painter of Tory Boston, he was not, as was Benjamin West, much of a success in England, where he died and was buried in the Hutchinson tomb in the outskirts of London.

This nation was founded in the great age of Georgian art and architecture. Copley was an exact contemporary of George III. Not since the Flemish artist and student of Rubens, Van Dyck, had come to Puritan England in 1632 to be the court painter of Charles I had England produced so distinguished a group of painters as Reynolds, Romney, and Gainsborough, whose portraits romanticized the Georgian gentry of their day. No wonder Copley's simple realism, so appropriate in Boston, was out of step with fashionable England.

If Copley was the portraitist of Tory Boston, Gilbert Stuart was the master painter of the heroes of the Republic. Born in Rhode Island, he eventually attended a small school for poor boys at Trinity Church, Newport, where his classmate Benjamin Waterhouse (later a professor at the newly founded Harvard Medical School) wrote of Stuart's early talent for drawing. In 1775, at the age of twenty, Stuart, with almost no money, sailed for England, determined to become a famous painter. He studied with Benjamin West for five years and went on to become one of the leading artists in London. His prices soon were equal to any, except those of Reynolds and Gainsborough. Stuart suddenly left London, however, for Ireland, where he was also highly successful but where he ran into debt. He set sail for New York in 1792, planning to recoup his fortune by painting the fathers of the new nation. And he "made the leaders of the American Revolution more vivid to posterity than any comparable group in history," wrote a biographer: "George Washington and his generals, Adams, Jefferson, Madison, and Monroe, their wives, Cabinet members, and friends have a unique historical vitality, overshadowing the Royal Governors who preceded them and the pale figures who later filled their places, precisely because they were preserved as complex human beings in Gilbert Stuart's portraits."[2] Stuart was an extreme naturalist who left no room for romantic flattery in his paintings: "I copy the works of God," he once said, "and leave clothes to tailors and mantua-makers."[3] Toward the end of his life, Washington sat for Stuart in Philadelphia; the so-called Vaughan and Athenaeum portraits now hang in the National Gallery and in the Boston Museum of Fine Arts. After 1805, Stuart settled in Boston, where he remained the rest of his life. He was of course a success there and soon "had all the beauty and talent of Boston under his pencil."[4] But he was, above all, the master painter of the founders of the nation. Of the

fifty First Families in Boston and Philadelphia, the following had one or more
members painted by Stuart:

Boston		Philadelphia
Adams	Motley	Binney
Ames	Otis	Chew
Appleton	Paine	Dallas
Bowditch	Parkman	Hopkinson
Brooks	Peabody	Logan
Coolidge	Perkins	McKean
Eliot	Phillips	Meade
Everett	Pickering	Mifflin
Gardner	Prescott	Montgomery
Gray	Quincy	Morris
Higginson	Shattuck	Rawle
Jackson	Warren	Willing
Lee	Winthrop	
Lowell		

In the half century between the Declaration of Independence and 1825, Philadelphia was the creative center of American art. If Harvard College has considered itself the guardian of the mind and word in America for some three centuries now, the Pennsylvania Academy of the Fine Arts, founded in 1805, was
the original center of the visual arts in this country and is today our oldest and
one of our more distinguished art schools. The major force in founding the
academy was Charles Willson Peale, the Benjamin Franklin of Philadelphia art.
An auslander like Franklin, Peale possessed a very similar versatility and optimistic middle-class mind. He was born in Maryland, where his father, a London bon vivant and Cambridge man, had fled to avoid imprisonment after being convicted of embezzlement. Apprenticed at an early age to a local saddler,
young Peale soon excelled in his trade until, after brief instructions from John
Hesselius, he took up the fine art of miniature painting. An active agitator during the Stamp Act crisis in Maryland, Peale subsequently moved to New England, the center of political activity. He painted miniatures in Newburyport
and Boston, where he met Copley, and then set sail for London, where he studied under West and met Franklin, who became his devoted friend.

Peale first came to Franklin's city of Philadelphia in 1776. A prominent
leader among the radical Whigs, he fought through the battles of Trenton and
Princeton; at Valley Forge he painted miniatures of Washington and of some
forty officers. After the war, he served a brief period in the radical Pennsylvania
Assembly but then gave up politics in disgust.

In 1794, Peale opened the first museum in America, a combined art gallery
and museum of natural history. Peale's museum was a wonder of the new nation, Jeremy Belknap finding it easily worth a 400-mile trip to see. Peale's close
friend Thomas Jefferson wanted to make it a federal institution, along with his
projected university in Virginia, but the Constitution prohibited this action.
Out of this museum, first housed in the Philosophical Society and then in Inde-

pendence Hall, grew the Academy of the Fine Arts, founded by Peale and a group of Philadelphia merchants and lawyers. Today the Pennsylvania Academy is housed in one of the nation's architectural landmarks, designed by Frank Furness and George Hewitt.

Peale painted Washington sixteen times from life, beginning in 1772, when he went to Mount Vernon to paint the vigorous, young militia captain. Though Peale was never in the same class with Copley or Stuart as an artist, he was a far greater and more versatile man. Washington had little use for the aggressive Stuart and sat for him only twice; yet he was very fond of the charming Peale, his comrade in arms and friend for many years.

Peale—saddler, soldier, politician, painter, naturalist, museum founder, and dentist—was an eighteenth-century gentleman jack-of-all-trades; he founded not only the nation's first museum and first art academy but also a dynasty of artists. Married three times, he produced seventeen children, eleven of whom lived to maturity. Peale named his first group of children not from the Bible but from a popular history of art and then named his last two sons Linnaeus and Benjamin Franklin as witness to his avid interest in science and natural history. In Philadelphia, only the Rushes had more lines written about them than the Peales in the *DAB*.

Charles Willson Peale (1741–1827)	Artist-Naturalist
James Peale (1791–1878)	Artist
Raphael Peale (1774–1825)	Artist
Rembrandt Peale (1778–1860)	Artist
Anne Claypool Peale (1791–1878)	Artist
Titian Ramsay Peale (1799–1885)	Artist
Sarah Miriam Peale (1800–1885)	Artist

The Pennsylvania Academy of the Fine Arts was the leading American art school throughout the nineteenth century. From the beginning it made use of its European connections to build the finest art collection in America. Benjamin West, teacher of three generations of American artists in London, was its first honorary member, and Nicholas Biddle, as a nineteen-year-old member of the American legation in Paris, was commissioned to collect plaster casts and antique statuary for the academy. The first exhibition of over 400 paintings, almost half by Americans, was held at the academy in 1811. The art school opened the next year, with Thomas Sully, a pupil of West's in London, as a member of the committee on instruction.

Born in Lincolnshire, England, Sully emigrated to Charleston, South Carolina, in 1792. With a letter of introduction from Washington Irving to Rebecca Gratz, he came to Philadelphia in 1808, where, except for two periods of study under West in London, he remained for the rest of his life. (Rebecca Gratz, famous beauty and model for Sir Walter Scott's Rebecca, was a member of the city's leading Sephardic Jewish family; five men in her family were members of the Philadelphia Club in the days before blanket anti-Semitism set in, Hyman Gratz serving as the club's president between 1845 and 1847.)

After the deaths of Peale (1827) and Stuart (1828), Thomas Sully became America's major portrait painter. For over half a century, he painted the portraits of most of Philadelphia's prominent citizens, including twenty-nine members of the Biddle family, twenty-three Wetherills, fourteen Rushes, twelve Fishers, ten Dallases, ten Ingersolls, seven Gratzes, six Cadwaladers, five Whartons, and five Hopkinsons, as well as various members of the Peters, Logan, Shippen, McKean, Coxe, Carey, Bache, White, Harrison, Duane, Rawle, Hare, Sergeant, Meigs, Meade, and Furness families. In all, he painted the portraits of members of well over half of the fifty families in the Philadelphia sample. He also did some dozen portraits of Fanny Kemble, as well as one of her actor father and of several other members of the family in England. In Boston, Sully painted John Quincy Adams, George Ticknor, William Tudor, Jared Sparks, David Sears, and Thomas Handasyd Perkins, whose famous Sully portrait now hangs in the Athenaeum. Sully's transatlantic reputation was secured when he painted young Queen Victoria's portrait in 1837.

Art and aesthetics were of course alien to both the Puritan and the Quaker ethic. Copley's clients were mainly Anglican, and it was largely vanity and his sense of posterity that persuaded the moralistic John Adams to sit for him. Philadelphia Quakers limited themselves to black silhouettes, which still adorn the drawing room walls of the best Philadelphia Quaker-turned-Episcopal families in the city today. The Sully portraits were done mostly for families that had become affluent and deserted Quakerism for Assembly balls, the Philadelphia Club, and the fashionable Episcopal churches.

Bookish Boston had no native tradition of art to compare with Philadelphia's. The Athenaeum, hub of Boston intellectualism, was founded in 1807, two years after the Pennsylvania Academy of the Fine Arts. Until the Museum of Fine Arts opened the doors of its newly completed Copley Square building to the public in 1876, it was the center of what art existed in Boston. The Athenaeum held its first art exhibition in 1827; it had no art school. In fact, there was no art school of any consequence in the city until the museum opened a school in 1877. Before that time, most artists in Boston were trained elsewhere. Henry Sargent, who started out in Thomas Handasyd Perkins's countinghouse, took up painting only when John Trumbull encouraged him to go abroad to study with Benjamin West. His one painting of note, *The Dinner Party*, now hangs in the Boston Museum of Fine Arts. Though Winslow Homer was born in Cambridge, Massachusetts, he studied at the National Academy of Design in New York after a brief apprenticeship to a French engraver in Boston. Homer's interest in the sea surely derived from his New England heritage, but he spent most of his time in New York and at Prout's Neck in Maine rather than in Boston. Ernest Wadsworth Longfellow, inheriting a fortune from his mother, studied in Paris. His paintings generally were cold and unsympathetic, but he did play an active role in fostering the arts in Boston. Longfellow left his private art collection and $200,000 to the Boston Museum of Art.

As we have seen, Philadelphia's longtime art tradition centered on the Academy of the Fine Arts throughout the nineteenth century and into the twentieth. John Hicks, nephew of Edward Hicks, studied there and went on to become a portrait painter of some popular success. His sitters included Henry Ward Beecher, Harriet Beecher Stowe, Edwin Booth, and Abraham Lincoln, as well as Oliver Wendell Holmes and Henry Wadsworth Longfellow of Boston and General George Gordon Meade and Bayard Taylor of Philadelphia. Just before the Civil War, two of the greatest American painters, Thomas Eakins and Mary Cassatt, studied at the academy.

Mary Cassatt, a very Proper Philadelphian by adoption, was born in Pittsburgh of a prominent family of French Huguenot stock. Educated abroad in her youth and fluent in French, Cassatt spent a brief period at the academy before going back to Paris, where she became a distinguished member of the impressionist school. She was hardly appreciated in Philadelphia, even by her family. When she visited the city after having made a name for herself abroad, for instance, a newspaper reflected local values when it announced that "Miss Mary Cassatt, sister of Mr. Cassatt, president of the Pennsylvania Railroad, returned from Europe yesterday. She has been studying painting in Paris, and owns the smallest Pekinese dog in the world."[5]

Unlike Mary Cassatt, Thomas Eakins was born and died in the same house in Philadelphia. Upon graduation from Central High School, he entered the Academy of the Fine Arts. After the Civil War, Eakins spent three years at the Ecole Nationale des Beaux-Arts in Paris, where he worked so hard that his health broke down. During a rest in Spain he became fascinated with the work of Goya and Velásquez, whose realism remained an influence on Eakins for the rest of his life. Returning to Philadelphia, he had his first one-man show at the Union League, which was holding a series of art shows while Frank Furness's new building for the academy was being built. For the next three years, Eakins worked on his portrait of Dr. Samuel Gross, which represents the height of his creative powers.

Eakins was a man of broad education who spoke five languages. He immediately recognized Whitman's genius and, unlike Weir Mitchell, became a close friend. His portrait of Whitman was the poet's favorite. Eakins dominated the art school at the academy, where he served as dean until 1886, when he was virtually forced to resign because of his insistence on the use of nude models as a necessary part of his philosophy of scientific realism in art. Conservative members of the board like John G. Johnson were especially offended by the appearance of nude male models in classes that included women students.

Thomas Eakins introduced a heroic vision of science and technology into American art. He insisted that his students make a careful study of anatomy and he himself spent some time at the Jefferson Medical College studying anatomy. Scientists and professors were his favorite subjects. His famous *Gross Clinic* was, in his own mind, not a genre painting but a portrait of Gross in a vocational setting. Eakins had no time for conventional leisure-class portraits, the trivial, or the merely sensually charming in art. Actually, in his laborious attention to fact and detail, Eakins was very much in the Philadelphia scientific tradition of Franklin, Rittenhouse, and Bartram. He was also in the Quaker tradition of the tyranny of facts and things. His work is a painstaking record of

Philadelphia life, of its men and women both at work and at play, in the operating rooms at Jefferson or Penn, sailing on the Delaware, or sculling on the Schuylkill.

Cecilia Beaux, born in Philadelphia of a French father, was a well-connected Philadelphian who was brought up in the cultured home of her Quaker uncle William Biddle. Although she was a great admirer of Thomas Eakins and spent many hours at the academy studying his and other paintings there, she was forbidden by her uncle to attend the school because of the "rabble of untidy art students" who attended the life classes. Nudes were not for ladies. With nowhere near the power of Eakins or Cassatt, Cecilia Beaux was an extremely successful painter who was recognized both here and abroad and was far more popular with the Philadelphia establishment than either. Like her contemporary and acquaintance John Singer Sargent, she had the ability to please and to flatter.*

Eakins's student and successor on the faculty at the academy, Thomas Anshutz (1851–1912), carried on the tradition of scientific realism. Anshutz, "the maker of painters," taught a series of students who later became successful, among them William Glackens (1870–1938), John Sloan (1871–1951), and John Marin (1872–1953), all painters, and the sculptor Alexander Stirling Calder (1870–1945).

Most of Eakins's and Anshutz's students migrated to New York, which became the mecca of American art in the twentieth century. Marin, who painted seascapes but was far more abstract than Winslow Homer, was a major modernist figure in New York in the twenties. William Glackens and John Sloan, classmates at Central High School, also went to New York, where they became leaders of the Ashcan school of American realism. Glackens was the principal organizer of the 1913 Armory show, a landmark in American art history. The show not only struck a blow at the painting establishment's intolerance of the new realism in America; it was also the first full representation in this country of Cézanne, Gauguin, Van Gogh, and others of the French school. The shock of the exhibit was Marcel Duchamp's *Nude Descending a Staircase.*

A younger student of Anshutz, Arthur B. Carles (1882–1952), was also an organizer of the Armory show. A cantankerous Philadelphian like Eakins and also a faculty member of the academy, Carles was hardly known outside Philadelphia in his lifetime but has gradually become recognized as one of America's major twentieth-century painters.†

In the years between the two world wars, the convivial Carles belonged to a small, informal circle of restless and creative Philadelphians that included Leopold Stokowski, flamboyant conductor of the Philadelphia Orchestra, George Howe, fascinating talker and famous architect, and such members of the sam-

---

*Cecilia Beaux's sister married a Drinker and was the mother of Catherine Drinker Bowen, popular historian, who wrote delightfully about her Aunt Cecilia.

†One of Carles's best private students, Jane Piper, is a prominent painter in the city today. She is also on the faculty of the Philadelphia College of Art, which grew out of the School of Industrial Art, founded by Charles Godfrey Leland, author and polymath, who was a childhood friend and Princeton classmate of George Boker, whom we discussed in the previous chapter.

ple of Proper Philadelphia families as Sturgis Ingersoll, Adolphe Borie, and George and Francis Biddle.* George Biddle, who eventually settled in the fashionable, radical New York suburb of Croton-on-Hudson, was an important American artist, especially during the socially concerned years of the Depression. Franklin Roosevelt's contemporary at Groton, he had the president's confidence in helping to found the Federal Art Project under the Works Progress Administration. During the Depression the WPA supported many young artists, such as Willem de Kooning, who were instrumental in New York's replacing Paris as the center of modern Western art after the war. Thus, displaced Philadelphians took the lead in staging the Armory show in 1913 and in creating the WPA art project during the New Deal.

Philadelphia has a tradition in sculpture unequaled in any other city in America. William Rush was the nation's first sculptor, and three generations of Calders have adorned the city and become famous throughout the world. Alexander Stirling Calder, as we have seen, studied at the Academy of the Fine Arts at the same time as Marin, Glackens, and Sloan and he, too, was a strong supporter of the Armory show. His most famous work in Philadelphia is the Swan Fountain at Logan Circle on the Benjamin Franklin Parkway. Among his many other works around the city are a statue of Dr. Samuel Gross at Jefferson Hospital and the Henry Charles Lea Memorial in Laurel Hill Cemetery, the Proper Philadelphia resting place (comparable to Brahmin Boston's Mount Auburn in Cambridge).

Alexander Stirling Calder was one of six sons of Alexander Milne Calder, a Scottish stonecutter who settled in Philadelphia, where he spent twenty years adorning City Hall with a myriad of statues and symbols, including the thirty-seven-foot-tall figure of William Penn that still tops the tower as a symbol of the Quaker origins of the now secular city.† The mobile sculptures of Alexander Stirling Calder II (1898–1976) made the Calder name world famous in the third generation. Unlike his father, "Sandy" Calder roamed the world and died in New York City. Today, his grandfather's statue of William Penn looks westward along the Benjamin Franklin Parkway to his father's Swan Fountain at Logan Circle and thence to the end of the parkway, where the Greek revival Art Museum stands atop the leveled hill of Fairmount, much in the style of the Athenian Acropolis. In the great hall of the museum hangs a large Calder mobile called *Ghost*. Thus, Calder art decorates both ends and the middle of perhaps the most beautiful parkway entrance to any city in America.

---

*Francis Biddle, who deserted Philadelphia for Washington when he became U.S. attorney general under Roosevelt, found these gatherings an oasis: "If it had not been for these casual and informal gatherings life in Philadelphia for Katherine and me would have been emptier, with the formal dinner parties where the same faces appeared and reappeared each year, each season a little older, the cautious well-bred talk, the amiable and routine minds, not so much disillusioned as devoid of curiosity and of any passion" (Francis Biddle, *A Casual Past* [New York: Doubleday, 1961], p. 387).

†There is an unwritten law in the city that no skyscraper can be higher than the Penn statue. Before World War II, the statue dominated the city's skyline. As an example of the monotony of equality, however, the building boom since the war has resulted in a dull and flattened skyline with a whole series of buildings exactly level with each other and hiding Penn from many angles of view.

In addition to Philadelphia's urban art tradition, a great tradition of art grew up in the neighboring, and heavily Quaker, counties of Bucks and Chester, centering at New Hope, on the Delaware to the north, and along the Brandywine valley, at Chadds Ford, to the south. Today, largely because of the worldwide fame of Andrew Wyeth, Chadds Ford is the more famous of the two. Here Howard Pyle (1853-1911), author and illustrator of romantic books for children, and descendant of a long line of original Quaker settlers in the area, founded a school for illustrators at the close of the nineteenth century. His most famous student, N. C. Wyeth (1882-1945), of an old Yankee family from Cambridge, Massachusetts, founded a dynasty of artists: of his five children, Henrietta, Carolyn, and Andrew became painters, Nathaniel an inventor, and Ann a musician and composer; Jamie, Andrew's son, is well on his way to fame as a painter. N. C. Wyeth stimulated the visual senses of a whole generation of children with his vivid illustrations for such classics as Robert Louis Stevenson's *Treasure Island*, *Kidnapped*, and *David Balfour*; Charles Kingsley's *Westward Ho!*; and James Fenimore Cooper's *Last of the Mohicans* and *Deerslayer*. Andrew Wyeth is surely America's most popular contemporary artist, and in 1976 he was inducted into the French Académie des Beaux-Arts, the only American to be so honored besides John Singer Sargent.

John Singer Sargent (1856-1925) was a cosmopolitan by birth and breeding as well as in style. In this as in almost every other respect, he was the antithesis of Thomas Eakins, the provincial Philadelphian. Whereas Eakins, in his portraits, fearlessly penetrated the depths of character, Sargent was a master psychologist of class. Whereas Eakins shunned the establishment, Sargent was the most successful Anglo-American class painter in our history. Whereas Eakins was very similar to his friend Walt Whitman, Sargent was more like Henry James, his dear friend and confidant. Yet Sargent admired Eakins, and both were greatly influenced by Velásquez.

Sargent's grandfather Winthrop Sargent moved to Philadelphia when the family firm, sustained by five generations of successful merchants in Gloucester and Boston, went bankrupt in the 1830s. The painter's father, FitzWilliam Sargent, after earning a medical degree from the University of Pennsylvania (1843), practiced medicine and surgery in the city and published one book on surgery. In 1850, he married Mary Newbold Singer, daughter of a prosperous Philadelphia merchant. (A musician and watercolorist of some talent, Mary Singer was proud that her mother had been painted by Sully.) When her father died, the income from Mary Singer's small inheritance was more than her husband was making from his practice of medicine, and she decided that they should live abroad. Dr. Sargent resigned from the staff of the Wills Eye Hospital and they sailed for Italy, where their son was born in 1856. FitzWilliam Sargent became an amateur student of U.S. naval affairs and saw his son as a future admiral; his wishes were thwarted, however, when young Sargent showed an early bent for drawing, a talent encouraged by his mother, who was his first instructor. Traveling with his family all over Europe, Sargent's pencil was never idle. When the family settled in Paris in 1874, he entered the Ecole Nationale des Beaux-Arts and also began to study with Carolus Duran, a fashionable artist. Sargent soon surpassed his master, though he always gave him credit for starting him on his career. The family paid a brief visit to the United States in 1876. Returning to Europe, Sargent painted in Spain, Morocco, Italy, and Paris before finally settling in London in 1885, the scene of his greatest triumphs. He returned to America in 1887 to do some portraits, including his famous one of Isabella Stewart Gardner; he also had his first one-man exhibition at the St. Botolph Club in Boston, which served as his American headquarters during many subsequent visits. Sargent was by now the most popular portraitist of the Victorian age on both sides of the Atlantic.

Queen Victoria's death and the formation of the United States Steel Company, both in 1901, marked the height of the Anglo-American industrial and political hegemony of the world, the culmination of a long process that began with the rise of Puritanism in Elizabethan and Stuart England. John Singer Sargent was the supreme interpreter in oil of the values of the ruling classes in that supremely confident age. Demand for his portraits was so high that it was not a question of who wanted them but of whom he wished to paint. Yet he seems to have painted everybody who was anybody: lords and ladies, dukes and duchesses, millionaires like the Astors, Sassoons, Wertheimers, and Vickerses in England; Vanderbilts, Wideners, and Rockefellers in America; Henry Cabot Lodge, Henry Lee Higginson, and Isabella Stewart Gardner in Boston; A. J. Cassatt, president of the Pennsylvania Railroad, S. Weir Mitchell, and Mrs. Joseph E. Widener in Philadelphia; college presidents—Charles W. Eliot and A. Lawrence Lowell of Harvard and M. Carey Thomas of Bryn Mawr; George Peabody, international banker and philanthropist, and Endicott Peabody of Groton; and Presidents Theodore Roosevelt and Woodrow Wilson. No wonder Rodin called Sargent "the Van Dyck of our times!"[6]

Unlike his friend Henry James, the foremost novelist of their transatlantic world, who finally became a British citizen, Sargent although he died in England and was buried at Westminster Abbey remained a devoted American. Even though he caught the spirit of a very different age, he remained rooted in the America of Copley and Stuart. Just as Bostonians never went so far in succumbing to the temptations of ostentatious plutocracy as did New Yorkers or Londoners or even Philadelphians, so Sargent never really respected the age whose leaders he nevertheless depicted; perhaps that was why he had such a great psychological understanding of its beautiful people. As he told J. William White of Philadelphia: "I HATE DOING POUGHTRAITS,"[7] an emphasis and spelling he used to indicate his distaste for the affectations of fashionable London ladies.

In 1910, as the body of Edward VII lay in state at Windsor, Sargent was summoned to do for the king what he would not do in life, draw him. He did his duty but about the same time vowed to give up portraiture as a career (he did a few more portraits, however, including ones of Woodrow Wilson and John D. Rockefeller, both in 1917). "It seemed strangely fitting," wrote a Sargent biographer, that the death of the King should coincide so well with the end of Sargent's career as a portraitist, for it meant that the Edwardian era and the Sargent era had come to a close together. . . . The period ended, and its chief recorder, the man who stood to it as Van Dyck had stood to the Cavalier era of Charles I and Holbein to the reign of Henry VIII, brought his work to a close at the same time. A page in history turned.[8]

And for those who read between the lines, that page marked the beginning of the end of class authority in America, the main subject of this book.

It is symbolically fitting, too, that Sargent was the great exception to the rule that those who have led the visual arts in both England and America have had plebeian origins. Sargent was deeply rooted in the history of Brahmin Boston. That his life work was not in literature or history but in painting related partly to the dominance of his Proper Philadelphia mother. He combined, then, the Puritan drive to excel with the visual talent so characteristic of the silent tradition of Philadelphia Quakerism. Though lionized in his time, he was almost unable to say two words on his feet before an audience, even at a dinner of friends and peers. And though Sargent refused a knighthood under Edward VII and the presidency of the Royal Academy, he did accept honorary degrees from Oxford and Cambridge, as well as from Harvard, Yale, and Penn.

MUSIC IN BOSTON AND PHILADELPHIA

To an even greater extent than in the visual arts, the mores of the American upper class have discouraged professional careers in music. We have already seen how Owen Wister gave up his first love, music, for a conventional career in the law. Stephen Foster, perhaps the nation's most beloved popular composer, failed to live up to the mercantile values of his Pittsburgh family and eventually died in poverty in Bellevue Hospital in New York City. Of the members of the First Family samples, only Francis Hopkinson* of Philadelphia has a permanent place in the history of American music: his "My Days Have Been So Wondrous Free" is considered to be the first secular song to have been composed by a native American. But Hopkinson, along with Jefferson and Franklin, usually has been classified by musical historians as one of our three "gentlemen amateurs."

Neither the Puritans nor the Quakers took much stock in secular music; but whereas the Quakers were against all forms of music (pianos were prohibited in Quaker schools well into the twentieth century), the early Puritans were avid psalm singers, the *Bay Song Book* (1640) being one of the first books published in the English colonies. Yet Philadelphia Quakers were tolerant of the musical interests of their neighbors, especially the singing sectarians from Germany like the Dunkers, who founded the Ephrata Cloister outside Philadelphia in the

---

*His son, Joseph Hopkinson, wrote "Hail, Columbia," which was our informal national anthem until Admiral Dewey preferred "The Star-Spangled Banner."

1720s, and the Moravians, who founded a great musical tradition at Bethlehem (1741) that is carried on in the annual Bach Festivals of the present day. In Philadelphia itself, the Germania Orchestra, founded in 1856, was the city's leading orchestra for the rest of the nineteenth century.

Just as the Pennsylvania Academy of the Fine Arts symbolizes Philadelphia's long tradition of leadership in painting and sculpture, so the Academy of Music symbolizes the city's supreme cultural achievement as the home of the Philadelphia Orchestra. The Academy of Music, an acoustical and aesthetic masterpiece, opened in 1857 and is today the oldest auditorium in the nation still in use in its original form for its original purpose; it has been the home of the Philadelphia Orchestra ever since its first concert there in 1900.

Just as Franklin made Philadelphia world famous in the eighteenth century, so the two Philadelphians of world renown in the twentieth century were Marian Anderson and Leopold Stokowski.* Brought to the city from Cincinnati in 1912, Stokowski built the Philadelphia Orchestra into the finest in the world by the time of his retirement in 1936. Although the Boston Symphony has been equally great under Koussevitzky and the New York Philharmonic under Toscanini and Bernstein, neither orchestra has matched the continued excellence of the Philadelphia Orchestra from 1912 to the present under only two conductors—Stokowski and Ormandy.

"In no other country in the world," according to John H. Mueller "has the symphony orchestra won the priority of status accorded to it in the United States."[9] Even in Germany, its ancestral home, the symphony assumed second rank to the opera. From the beginning, American symphony orchestras have been staffed and led by European artists, mostly Germans and Eastern Europeans; but their high status here has derived largely from Society patronage and financial backing, especially in Boston and Philadelphia. In general, the older families of more seasoned wealth have tended to support the symphony; the newly affluent and socially ascending have tended to patronize the opera.

At the same time that newly rich New Yorkers were making plans to build the Metropolitan Opera House (completed in 1883), Henry Lee Higginson announced his "resolve to hire an orchestra of sixty men and a conductor, paying them all by the year";[10] in the interest of excellence, he estimated an annual deficit of some $50,000, which he planned to meet himself. Higginson continued to make up the deficit of the Boston Symphony until 1918, when he announced that the burden must henceforth be borne by others, as has been done ever since by a group led largely by First Family women.

The Philadelphia Orchestra was organized in 1900 by a fashionable and wealthy board of directors that chose Alexander Van Rensselaer as its president, a post he held until his death in 1933 at the age of eighty-two. An adopted Philadelphian and a Drexel in-law, "Mr. Van," as he was affectionate-

---

*Marian Anderson was not the only South Philadelphian to sing her way to fame. Mario Lanza, Eddie Fisher, Fabian, Frankie Avalon, Bobby Rydell, and Jimmy Darren, all South Philly natives, have been leaders in a worldwide pop culture far more extensive than anything known in Franklin's day.

ly known at the orchestra, was a boardsman and sportsman in the best style; his mansion on Rittenhouse Square was one of the city's social centers. Whereas Higginson of Boston had studied in Vienna and was a frustrated musician all his life, Van Rensselaer had never heard a note of symphony music when he was chosen president of the orchestra. At any rate, it was not Mr. Van but an exhibitionist and genius, Leopold Stokowski ("Stokie"), a semi-Pole with an accent who actually was a native Englishman and Oxford man, who built the Philadelphia Orchestra into the world's finest. Financially, the orchestra was made, as it were, by an "anonymous donor" who in 1916 offered to meet the annual deficit himself if the board would agree to raise a $1 million endowment by 1920; the board, and especially the women's committee, headed by Frances Wister, Owen Wister's sister-in-law, raised twice that amount. At its twentieth anniversary the orchestra was both the most talked about and the most financially secure in the nation. The anonymous donor turned out to be Edward Bok, whose son carried on after him as a major supporter of the orchestra.

Both the Boston Symphony and the Philadelphia Orchestra have always stood for Society and Culture, especially among Proper Women in both cities. Every Friday afternoon in season, year after year, Boston women, after an uplift lecture and a simple lunch at the Chilton Club, arrive at their hereditary seats at Symphony Hall; rarely early, they are *never* late. At the same time on Fridays, year in and year out, slightly more stylishly dressed Philadelphia ladies, after a delicious lunch at the Acorn Club, walk three blocks down Locust Street and take their customary seats at the Academy of Music; some are always late and some always leave early to catch the Paoli or Chestnut Hill locals. Gentlemen in both cities, along with music lovers of every description, attend symphony at other times during the week.

Philadelphians never boast or boost, but they have even more pride in their orchestra than in their art museums. The composer-critic Virgil Thomson once compared the orchestras in the two cities; their style had more to do with their locales than with their conductors, so he felt, and he contrasted "Boston, the intellectually elegant and urbane" with "Philadelphia, where everything, even intellectual achievement and moral pride, turns into luxury, into a sort of sensuous awareness of social differences."[11]

ARCHITECTURE AND CLASS STRUCTURE

Architecture is a visible record of the changing nature of class aspirations and class authority in any civilization, and Boston and Philadelphia are two of our richest cities as far as the history of American architecture is concerned. Their architecture—and especially their architects, who are our main concern here—nicely reflects the different styles of leadership in the two cities: thus, King's Chapel in Boston and Christ Church in Philadelphia symbolize the nature of class authority in the eighteenth century; the State House and the Athenaeum across the street similarly symbolize Brahmin authority in government and literature in pre–Civil War Boston, whereas Independence Hall and the great Greek revival Second Bank of the United States in Philadelphia remind us today that the city was once the center of political and financial power in the young nation; and, finally, the aspirations of Back Bay Boston in the Victorian period are recorded architecturally in Trinity Church and the Boston Public Library, on Copley Square, just as Philadelphia's aspirations in art and music are beautifully symbolized in the Pennsylvania Academy of the Fine Arts on North Broad Street and the acoustical miracle of the Academy of Music on South Broad Street.

Colonial architecture in both Boston and Philadelphia was largely the work of amateur architects, either gentlemen of broad culture and leisure or master craftsmen and builders. In Boston, Peter Harrison, a builder well grounded in the Palladian manuals and designer of the Redwood Library and the Sephardic synagogue in Newport, built King's Chapel in 1749; the artistic jack-of-all-crafts John Smibert designed Faneuil Hall in 1740. In Philadelphia, a far more sophisticated city than Boston in the eighteenth century, two cultured amateurs, Andrew Hamilton and Dr. John Kearsley, designed the great architectural landmarks of Christ Church in 1727 and Independence Hall in the 1730s; two master craftsmen, Samuel Rhoads and Robert Smith, built the Pennsylvania Hospital in 1755 and Carpenters' Hall in 1770 (Smith also did Nassau Hall at Princeton). Eighteenth-century Philadelphia, in the Anglican-Quaker style of escape, had the greatest collection of country houses north of Virginia, from William Penn's manor, Pennsbury, in Bucks County (1692) to James Logan's Stenton (1728), Andrew Hamilton's Woodlands (1742), Benjamin Chew's Cliveden (1763), and the most perfect Georgian mansion of them all, Mount Pleasant (1761), where Benedict Arnold and his bride, Peggy Shippen, lived during the Revolution. In contrast to Philadelphians, Bostonians remained in town; even though Governors Shirley, Hutchinson, and Hancock built country places of some distinction, the most splendid mansion of them all, Gore Hall, which Bulfinch designed for Governor Gore, was not built until 1805.

The architectural profession in America is a product of the nineteenth century. Table A–24 (see Appendix I) lists the professional architects in Boston and Philadelphia who were included in the *DAB*. Benjamin Latrobe, a native Englishman, is considered the first professional architect in America; Charles Bulfinch, after losing his fortune in the speculative building of a Boston replica (Franklin Place) of Georgian Bath, became the first native American to be classified as a professional architect.

The important thing to notice about the architects listed in Table A–24 is that whereas half of the fourteen Boston architects came from the First Family sample, none of Philadelphia's architectural leaders did (with the exception of Frank Furness, who was not in the *DAB*). Both the Boston and Philadelphia upper classes have produced many architects but apparently none of the Philadelphians has attained preeminence in the profession. From the Philadelphia sample, the Meigs, Borie, Pepper, Lippincott, Montgomery, and Willing families have all produced good local architects: Charles L. Borie, Jr., and his firm, along with Horace Trumbauer, designed the Art Museum and Arthur Ingersoll Meigs, together with his brilliant partner, George Howe, built many Norman style mansions for wealthy Philadelphians in the period between the two world wars. But the point is that whereas Brahmin Bostonians have been national leaders in American architecture from Bulfinch onward, the foremost architects in Philadelphia have tended to be either auslanders or outsiders as far as the city's upper class is concerned.

As I noted previously, painters, sculptors, and musicians have usually been drawn, throughout history, from all levels of the class structure; however, architects, like literary men and historians, have been far more likely to come from the privileged classes, and they have usually been organizers and patrons if not dictators of the other plastic arts, such as Charles McKim, who commissioned his friend John Singer Sargent to do the murals in the Boston Public Library. Thus, whereas talented sons of privilege have been discouraged from following precarious careers in music and arts, their parents have promoted their interest in architecture. Richard Morris Hunt, for instance, had a mother, a sister, and a brother, William Morris Hunt, who were painters; he, however, was encouraged by his mother and older brother to put his early talent for drawing to work in architecture. Similarly, Stanford White, who from childhood showed a genuine talent for drawing and watercolor, was turned toward architecture rather than painting by his father's friend John La Farge, and through another of his father's friends, Frederick Law Olmsted, he was apprenticed to the office of H. H. Richardson, where he was its most talented draftsman for a dozen years. And Proper Philadelphia's only architectural genius, Frank Furness, first listed himself in a city directory as an artist; all his life he was an inveterate caricaturist, which some have said influenced his architectural style. In both Boston and Philadelphia, then, the leading architects have been primarily privileged men of artistic talent, along with a few talented craftsmen of more humble origins; Boston has produced more of the former and Philadelphia of the latter.

The great periods in the history of American architecture, as Wayne Andrews has so clearly shown in *Architecture, Ambition, and Americans*, have tended to reflect the class aspirations rather than the individual taste of the architect's clients. So it was with Virginia's landed gentry, like William Byrd of Westover (Jefferson was an exception to the rule), as well as with such newly rich tycoons as the Wideners and Stotesburys of Philadelphia. Not until the increasing individualism and decline of class standards in the twentieth century could such an extreme individualist as Frank Lloyd Wright design houses with their natural setting and the personal characteristics of the client (or himself) in mind. Until Wright's generation, then, most American architecture reflected class formality rather than individualism, especially in the classic periods of increasing affluence such as eighteenth-century Virginia, Bulfinch's Boston and McIntire's Salem, or Newport and New York in the Gilded Age.

Upper-class leadership in Boston architecture contrasted sharply with the heterogeneous and democratic elitism of Philadelphia architecture. Although all save Richardson in the Boston group were native New Englanders and predominantly Bostonians, in Philadelphia, Latrobe, Haviland, McArthur, and Cret were born abroad, whereas Walter was the grandson and Le Brun the son of immigrants. Seven of the Boston architects were Brahmins, as was Richardson by adoption, but only three of the Philadelphia group—Furness, Stewardson, and Cope—were from the upper-class families. Finally, though a majority of the Boston architects graduated from Harvard, only one Philadelphian, Stewardson, who spent two years at Harvard, attended an American university.

Brahmin leadership in Boston architecture was established by Charles Bulfinch; no other architect in American history, with the possible exception of Jefferson in Virginia, has set his stamp on the architecture of a whole region as did Bulfinch in New England, especially in Massachusetts and Boston. Even as late as the 1920s and 1930s at Harvard, the firm of Coolidge, Shepley, Bulfinch, and Abbott was designing the Harkness houses in the English neo-Renaissance style of the eighteenth-century Bulfinch.

Charles Bulfinch was of the fourth generation of a Boston family that had prospered from the time of its first American ancestor; both his father and his grandfather were physicians. His mother, Susan Apthorp, was the daughter of one of Boston's richest merchants; her father not only gave most of the money for the construction of King's Chapel but also had his friend Peter Harrison come from Newport to design the building. After attending the Boston Latin School, Bulfinch graduated from Harvard (1778) and later was awarded a master of arts (1784). Subsequently, on a two-year tour of England and the Continent, he explored Paris with his friend Thomas Jefferson and then toured southern France and northern Italy, staying for an extended time in Florence and Rome. Upon his return to Boston, his first commission was for the State House on Beacon Hill; finally completed in 1800, it was one of the finest public buildings in America, and to the Boston mind it remains, as Oliver Wendell Holmes once said, "the hub of the universe." Many public buildings followed, including prisons, courthouses, town halls, state houses, and banks throughout New England. Bulfinch also built University Hall at Harvard and directed the completion of the Capitol of the United States. But Bulfinch was more than an architect; as a Boston selectman for many years, he turned the neglected Common into a park and surrounded it on three sides with fine residences on Park Row (1803–1804), Colonnade Row, on Tremont Street (1809–1811), and on Beacon Street. He also built three mansions (all still standing) for Harrison Gray Otis. In the style of William Bingham of Philadelphia, Otis was Boston's preeminent gentleman, and Bulfinch modeled the Otis house on Cambridge Street on the Bingham mansion in Philadelphia and Manchester House in London. Bulfinch, then, made his version of the Adam style the dominant one in republican Massachusetts; his earliest and most gifted follower was a self-trained carpenter, Samuel McIntire, who built the famous mansions on Chestnut Street in Salem. Alexander Parris, another gifted carpenter, worked with Bulfinch on the Massachusetts General Hospital and then carried the Adam style to Portland, Maine, where he built several distinguished houses.*

---

*Richard Upjohn (1802–1878), an Englishman, worked with Parris when he first came to America and then went to New York, where he was a founder and first president of the American Institute of Architects (1857–1876).

Alexander Parris's most important buildings in Boston were the Sears house on Beacon Street, now remodeled as the Somerset Club, and St. Paul's Church, across the Common on Tremont Street. He did St. Paul's with Solomon Willard (nephew of President Willard of Harvard), whose most famous work is the Bunker Hill monument in Charlestown.

If the State House is the hub of the universe, the grand, Italianate Athenaeum is the hub of the Boston mind. Edward Clark Cabot was a gentleman farmer when he won the competition for the design of the Athenaeum (1845). Cabot is important in the history of Boston architecture less for his architecture (except for the Athenaeum) than for the fact that as president of the Boston Society of Architects he was the beloved leader of the local architectural community for some thirty years.

Arthur D. Gilman, a native of Newburyport, eventually left Boston for New York; his importance in Boston rests on his design of the Arlington Street Unitarian Church (1861) and the Boston City Hall (1862).

William R. Ware and Henry Van Brunt, both graduates of Harvard, had a major impact on Boston architecture as well as on the nation as a whole. Before Ware retired from the firm to devote his time to architectural education, they designed the First Church in Boston, Memorial and Weld halls at Harvard, and the Episcopal Theological School on Brattle Street. Commissioned by his friend Charles Francis Adams, president of the Union Pacific, Van Brunt built many railroad stations throughout the West. He played a key role in the Columbian Exposition in 1893, held in Chicago, and served as president of the American Institute of Architects (1899). William R. Ware, who first apprenticed in the office of Edward Clark Cabot and then in the atelier of Richard Morris Hunt in New York, was the father of American architectural education, founding schools at the Massachusetts Institute of Technology (1865) and at Columbia (1881).

The first professional architects in Philadelphia were of far more humble origins on the whole than were their Boston peers. And none of them set his architectural stamp on either Philadelphia or Pennsylvania as did Bulfinch on Massachusetts. Latrobe, of French Huguenot ancestry, spent only a brief period in Philadelphia before Jefferson brought him to Washington to design the Capitol. His major works in Philadelphia were the First Bank of Pennsylvania and the waterworks at Center Square, both designed in the Greek revival style and both now torn down.

William Strickland, whose father was a carpenter for Latrobe, was the city's first native-born architect of prominence. His most famous architectural monument in the city is the Second Bank of the United States (Biddle's bank), a commission he won in a competition with his mentor, Latrobe. Strickland did many other buildings in the Greek revival style, including the Friends Lunatic Asylum, the United States Naval Asylum, and the Philadelphia Exchange. Strickland was far more than a local architect for he designed distinguished buildings all over the new nation.

John Haviland, a well-connected Englishman, emigrated to Philadelphia, where he conducted a school in architectural drawing. Among his many buildings in the city, by far the most important was Eastern State Penitentiary. Built in accordance with the Quaker theory of solitary confinement, this was the first radial prison in the world; Tocqueville and Beaumont visited it, and through their book on American penitentiaries Eastern State became a model for similar institutions throughout Europe (though not in this country). Haviland also designed the Western Penitentiary at Pittsburgh, as well as county jails and state penitentiaries in other parts of the country, including the now infamous Tombs in New York City. The handsome Greek revival front building of the Philadelphia College of Art was also done by Haviland; the back building was designed by Frank Furness as the Deaf and Dumb Asylum.

Thomas U. Walter, whose grandfather had come to Philadelphia from Germany as a so-called redemptioner, learned his profession from William Strickland and others at the Franklin Institute while working as a bricklayer for his father. His first major commission was for the Philadelphia County prison, called Moyamensing; his second and most important was for Girard College, which was commissioned by his patron, Nicholas Biddle. Girard College both marked the climax and sounded the death knell of Greek revival architecture in America. Walter also designed Nicholas Biddle's country place, Andalusia, a Greek revival masterpiece overlooking the Delaware River to the north of the city. Andalusia is surely the most distinctive example of domestic architecture north of Virginia still lived in by the same family. Like Strickland, Walter was an architect of national stature, adding the wings and the dome of the United States Capitol and becoming the second president of the American Institute of Architects (1876).

Napoleon Le Brun showed an early aptitude in art and was sent by his parents to study under Thomas U. Walter. His most distinguished building in Philadelphia, the Academy of Music, was completed just before the Civil War. Le Brun moved to New York after the war, where he practiced for many years.

John McArthur, Jr., born in Scotland, also studied with Walter while apprenticed to his uncle as a carpenter. McArthur's greatest achievement was to design City Hall (1869), which was not completed until 1890, eleven years after his death. A gigantic architectural monument (one of the two largest public buildings in the nation when built), it has in this century been viewed as a symbol of political corruption in the city.

The years between 1876 and the First World War marked the most creative period in Philadelphia history since the days of Benjamin Franklin: the Centennial Exposition, held in Fairmount Park, brought both the park and the city worldwide attention; the city had the nation's finest art school at the Pennsylvania Academy of the Fine Arts, where Thomas Eakins was dean; William Pepper was Penn's greatest provost; John G. Johnson was the nation's leading corporate lawyer; Weir Mitchell was one of the most popular novelists of his day; and Frank Furness was at the height of his creative powers, completing the new Academy of the Fine Arts and several of the original buildings of the Philadelphia Zoological Gardens, the first zoo in the nation, just as the Centennial was opening.

Henry Hobson Richardson and Frank Furness. The differences between Boston and Philadelphia architects are probably best understood in the contrasting careers of two almost exact contemporaries, Henry Hobson Richardson, an adopted Bostonian, and Philadelphia's Frank Furness, son of a Boston schoolmate of Emerson, whose family was one of the most creative in Philadelphia's second creative age. Furness's new building for the Pennsylvania Academy of the Fine Arts was completed in 1876; Richardson established a national reputation with his completion of Boston's Trinity Church the following year.

Richardson was the great-grandson of Joseph Priestley, the founder of Philadelphia's first Unitarian congregation, of which Frank Furness's father was pastor. Born on the Priestley plantation outside New Orleans, Richardson was turned down by West Point because of a speech defect and went instead to Harvard, where he was taken into the best Brahmin circles after joining the Porcellian Club as an undergraduate.

Graduating in 1859, he studied in Paris and then settled in New York, where he practiced for seven years. Richardson's first building was a church in Springfield, Massachusetts, a commission he owed to the influence of one of his Harvard and Porcellian classmates. Because most of his work was in New England and upstate New York, Richardson moved to Brookline, a suburb of Boston (in 1874, while working on Trinity Church), his home for the rest of his short life.

Richardson was a gregarious and Gargantuan man who constantly entertained all the best people of his day in his ever expanding home and office: the "best of people and music" he wrote Henry Adams describing an elegant Sunday afternoon party in 1884. Clients, friends, associates, and students were all part of one large social circle. Richardson worked closely with Frederick Law Olmsted, a neighbor, as well as with artist friends like William Morris Hunt, Augustus Saint-Gaudens, and John La Farge. His neighbor and landlord, Ned Hooper, was on the university's building committee when Richardson was commissioned to design two buildings at Harvard. Austin Hall, of the law school, and Sever, in the Yard. He did many residences for his friends not only in New England (Oakes Ames and Robert Treat Paine) but also in Washington (Henry Adams and John Hay), Chicago (John Jacob Glessner), and St. Louis (Henry S. Potter, son of Bishop Potter of Philadelphia, whom I discuss in Chapter 17). Richardson, through the influence of his friend Frederick Lothrop Ames, designed the library and the railway station at North Easton; William E. Dorsheimer, a Harvard classmate, had Richardson build his own house in Buffalo and helped him obtain commissions for the Buffalo State Hospital, as well as for the State House and City Hall at Albany; he also did work for the Boston and Albany Railroad through his neighbor Charles Sprague Sargent, a director, and Vice-President James A. Rumrill, a classmate and Porcellian clubmate from Harvard.

Henry Hobson Richardson was the first of three native geniuses, along with Frank Lloyd Wright and Louis Sullivan (a native of Boston), who molded modern American architecture. He was given the opportunity to exercise his talent on a national scale partly because of his relationships with members of the Boston-Harvard upper class who still had a broad national influence in his day.

Both Henry Hobson Richardson and Frank Furness were romantics at heart; both had architecture in their bones and were never theorists like Olmsted, Wright, or Sullivan. But Richardson was gregarious and forward-looking; Furness was a spare and sharp-tongued curmudgeon who fled from his critics and the crowd to his country estate. Whereas Richardson loved fashionable and Brahmin Brookline, Furness and all his clan settled in the Wallingford-Media area, a bohemian suburb far to the south of the fashionable Main Line and Chestnut Hill. Finally, though Richardson was a recognized success from the beginning, Furness is only now coming back into vogue.*

Frank Furness grew up in a cultivated home that was Unitarian and abolitionist, intellectual and artistic. His Boston born father, the Reverend William Henry Furness, far more than a clerical leader, was a draftsman of some talent as well as a popular lecturer on many cultural subjects and controversial issues of his day. In 1870, he delivered the major address at the fourth convention of the American Institute of Architects; his speech was a plea for "new orders of architecture" in which "liberty was a vital principle"—especially liberty from what he called "the Quaker style, marble steps and wooden shutters" in his own city of Philadelphia.[12] The Reverend Furness impressed the audience with his architectural knowledge; in fact, his wide interests embraced the fine and practical arts, literature, religion, scholarship, and civil rights. And his four children exhibited his passion for the arts and literature. The oldest, William Henry, Jr., had started on a promising art career when he died at an early age. Annis Lee, who married Dr. Caspar Wistar, shared her father's interest in German literature and became a translator. Horace went to Harvard and devoted his life to the study of Shakespeare. Frank, the youngest, did not go to college, nor did he ever travel abroad; instead, he was apprenticed in his teens to John Fraser, designer of the Union League, an architectural landmark in Philadelphia today. He then went to New York to study with Richard Morris Hunt, whose atelier was a strong influence on post–Civil War architecture in America. Frank's young peers at the Hunt atelier included William R. Ware, Henry Van Brunt, Charles Gambrill (Richardson's early partner), and George Post.

Furness returned to Philadelphia to become the leading architect of his day (locally if not nationally). His masterpiece is now considered to be the Pennsylvania Academy of the Fine Arts. Furness's position in upper-class Philadelphia was attested to by his many commissions for both the Pennsylvania and the Reading Railroads. Furness did several churches besides his father's First Unitarian and designed many Proper Philadelphia residences along the Main Line, as well as the Bryn Mawr Hotel (now the Baldwin School) and the Merion Cricket Club; he also designed Penn's first library. Unlike Richardson, Furness

---

*Richardson was written about in his lifetime, as well as in a major monograph by Mariana Griswold Van Rensselaer published soon after his death. Furness is currently being resurrected by the Philadelphia school of romantic brutalists and was the subject of a 1973 monograph by James F. O'Gorman of Boston, the leading contemporary authority on Richardson.

built many banks and commercial fronts throughout the city. But although Furness was patronized by many Proper Philadelphians, they never quite recognized his genius (as Owen Wister might have predicted) and most of his center city buildings have been torn down.

Richardson and Furness differed perhaps most crucially that whereas Richardson trained a host of younger architects who later became famous, Furness trained none of more than local distinction except for Louis Sullivan and George Howe, who both worked briefly in his office.*

Among the architects who began their careers in the Richardson office were Charles F. McKim and Stanford White, who later formed one of the most famous partnerships in the history of American architecture; Herbert Langford Warren, for twenty years head of architectural studies at Harvard; Welles Bosworth, architect of MIT's Cambridge campus; John Galen Howard, head of architectural studies at the University of California at Berkeley; and Charles A. Coolidge and George Shepley, who established Richardson's successor firm. The history of the Richardson firm, today the oldest in the nation, surely confirms the continuity of family accomplishment so typical of Brahmin Boston: George Shepley, a well-connected native of St. Louis, was Richardson's son-in-law whose sister married Charles Allerton Coolidge; moreover, the Shepley and Richardson partners after 1952 were both Richardson's grandsons.

Charles A. Coolidge was the dynamic leader of the firm for over half a century (until his death in 1936). In personal style, if not in architectural genius, he was cut from the same gregarious mold as Richardson; he knew everybody of worth in his day and was a personal friend of both Charles Eliot and A. Lawrence Lowell of Harvard, where he was an overseer from 1922 to 1935, president of the alumni association (1930), and recipient of its first honorary doctor of arts degree (1906). In the pursuit of fame and fortune, Coolidge moved to Chicago at the time of the Exposition of 1893 when the city went through its greatest period of architectural expansion. To soften the jealousy of local architects he formed a Chicago partnership under the name of Coolidge & Hodgdon. He personally supervised the planning and building of the University of Chicago, the Art Institute, and the Chicago Public Library, among many other buildings. Coolidge, in fact, led the firm in becoming the greatest campus architects in American history: it planned (in consultation with Olmsted) and built

---

*Furness's office was near the Jayne Building, in many ways the forerunner of the skyscraper, when Sullivan worked for the firm. Although the building was tragically torn down after World War II, it is said to have been a great influence on Sullivan's work. At any rate, Sullivan made Furness famous in his book *The Autobiography of an Idea*, written in the 1920s. He described Furness as "a dog-man" who "made buildings out of his head" and was an "extraordinary" draftsman; "he affected the English fashion . . . wore loud plaids, and a scowl, and from his face depended fan-like a marvelous red beard. . . . his face was gnarled and homely as an English bulldog's. . . . He had Louis hypnotized when he drew and swore at the same time." Sullivan came into the Furness office after seeing one of his houses on South Broad Street, which he later wrote was "something fresh and fair . . . , a human note, as though someone were talking." It is of interest that only recently, along with the local revival of reverence for Furness, has the building referred to by Sullivan been discovered by two young architectural historians, George Thomas and Hyman Myers. Its front had been completely remodeled to conform to the taste of its second owner, John G. Johnson.

the original campus at Stanford (1891), as well as new campuses for the University of Oklahoma at Norman (1911), Southern Methodist at Dallas (1911), and the University of Nebraska at Lincoln (1920). The firm also was closely allied with the development of modern medical education, designing the original buildings (Founders, Flexner, and Theobold Smith Halls) at the Rockefeller Institute of Medical Research (1905–1931), as well as medical schools and hospitals for Harvard, Western Reserve, Vanderbilt, and other institutions.

The firm also designed countless buildings in Boston including the Ames and Samuel buildings, the Boston Safe Deposit & Trust Company, the John Hancock Insurance Building, and the Old Colony Trust. Perhaps of most importance, from Richardson's day on, the partners were, according to a historian of the firm, "without question the Harvard Architects."[13] They made the key decision in the 1890s not to follow the popular college Gothic style of the day but to keep Harvard, with a few exceptions such as their own design of Langdell Hall for the law school, in the original brick tradition.

Coolidge was the first American architect to see the need for a large partnership in organizing work on the national scale demanded after 1890. Frank Furness, however, was content with a small firm with no more than a local reputation. Two of his draftsmen, Henry Fleinfelder and George Casey, joined together and spent most of their time repairing and remodeling original Furness buildings; his more fashionable apprentices formed the firm of Willing, Sims, and Talbot, which built many charming residences in Chestnut Hill but lacked a national reputation.

Other Principal Boston and Philadelphia Architects The career of Robert Swain Peabody is illustrative of my argument in this book. Son of the Reverend Ephraim Peabody of King's Chapel, his mother was a Salem Derby and he married a Putnam. After graduating from Harvard and spending three years studying in London and Paris, Peabody went on to achieve a national reputation, being elected president of the American Institute of Architects in 1900. If the Richardson firm was preeminent in college and university architecture, Peabody was a great school architect; he designed the original building for his kinsman Endicott Peabody's Groton School and built for some thirty other schools including Lawrenceville, Exeter, Andover, and Middlesex. His nationwide practice in residential architecture included many "cottages" rather than palaces, at such fashionable Victorian resorts as Newport and Lenox; in the Philadelphia area he designed homes along the Main Line and in Chestnut Hill for members of the Drexel, Biddle, Roberts, and Houston families, as well as the Van Rensselaer mansion on Rittenhouse Square. Peabody's buildings at Harvard include Matthews Hall, the Hemenway Gymnasium, and the Peter Bent Brigham Hospital for the medical school.

Charles Eliot, son of Harvard's president, had a very brief career in landscape architecture before his untimely death at the age of thirty-eight; much of his work was done in partnership with Frederick Law Olmsted. In fact, he and Olmsted were largely responsible for defining and establishing the field in America. In 1892, Eliot succeeded in securing legislation establishing the Boston Metropolitan Park Commission. The next year he joined the Olmsted firm, where he masterminded the Boston metropolitan park and transportation systems. In 1900, when the landscape architecture department was founded in Harvard, he was memorialized with the Charles Eliot professorship, the Charles Eliot traveling fellowship, and the Charles Eliot collection of books.

The Eliot family, as President Eliot would have deemed desirable in our democracy, was still playing a leadership role in America on the eve of the Second World War. Thus, Charles W. Eliot II, his grandson and nephew of Charles Eliot, took a master's degree in landscape architecture at Harvard in 1923 and then went on to play a vital role in the New Deal as executive officer of the National Planning Board, Public Works Administration (1933–1934), National Resources Board (1934–1935), and the National Resources Commission (1935–1940).

Ralph Adams Cram was an architect, a broad social critic in the style of William Morris, and a propagandist who urged a return to the hierarchical traditions of our Gothic past. His multitude of books included *The Gothic Quest*, published in 1907, and *The End of Democracy*, published in 1937. Son of a poor but highly intellectual Unitarian minister, Cram hated the Reformation and longed, like Henry Adams, for the certainties of the Catholic synthesis but eventually joined the High Church, or Anglo-Catholic, wing of the Episcopal church. His work on the rebuilding of West Point (1903) gave him a bold site on the Hudson for exploiting his Gothic dreams, as did the most challenging work of his career, the Cathedral of St. John the Divine, on Morningside Heights, in New York. Perhaps Cram's most congenial commission was from his friend John Nicholas Brown to design a chapel for St. George's School at Newport. Cram was a consulting architect and builder for many other schools and colleges, including Princeton (where he did the imposing chapel), Rice University in Houston, Wheaton, Williams, Sweet Briar, Bryn Mawr, and Wellesley colleges, and Phillips Exeter Academy. He was awarded honorary degrees by Princeton, Yale, Notre Dame, and Williams.

Guy Lowell, brother of A. Lawrence Lowell, studied architecture at MIT and in Paris after graduating from Harvard. He did Emerson Hall and the president's house at Harvard and was the leading spirit in architecture at Phillips Andover Academy. Lowell's most notable single work was the design that won the open competition for the county courthouse in New York City.

The Philadelphia architectural partnership that most closely resembled the Coolidge firm in Boston was Cope & Stewardson. John Stewardson was born in Philadelphia but attended the Adams Academy in Quincy, Massachusetts, and Harvard before going to Paris to study at the Ecole Nationale des Beaux-Arts. In Philadelphia he entered the office of T. P. Chandler, a Proper Bostonian who founded the architecture department at the University of Pennsylvania. Walter Cope also worked in this office. Cope was the great-grandson of Thomas Pym Cope (1768–1854), one of the most successful Quaker merchants of his day. Educated at the Germantown Friends School, Cope served his apprenticeship in the office of a leading Quaker architect, Addison Hutton, before entering the Chandler firm.

Cope & Stewardson, like the Coolidge firm in Boston, earned a national reputation as designers of campus buildings. Their earliest important commission was Radnor Hall at Bryn Mawr College, where they did many other buildings. Eventually made the official architects of the University of Pennsylvania, they designed the dormitories in the style of St. John's College, Cambridge; they also did several other buildings on the campus including the handsome Georgian law school and the museum (in association with Frank Miles Day and Wilson Eyre), an eclectic masterpiece. At Princeton they began an epoch-making building, Blair Hall, in 1896 and later did Stafford Little Hall and the fashionable Ivy Club on Prospect Street. Perhaps Cope & Stewardson's finest campus planning work was done at Washington University in St. Louis. They of course designed many residences in the Philadelphia suburbs, including a Norman style mansion for the Cassatt family.

The architectural careers and contrasting styles of Frank Furness and Horace Trumbauer nicely illustrate the schizophrenic divisions within Philadelphia's upper class during the late nineteenth and the early twentieth century. Whereas Furness designed for the old stock rich, Trumbauer was the architect for parvenu millionaires not only in Philadelphia but also in New York and Newport, too. Furness was a romantic and an original; Trumbauer was a romantic eclectic who derived his main inspiration from the architectural vocabulary of the French Renaissance.

Horace Trumbauer, a salesman's son, was born in Philadelphia. At sixteen he went to work as a messenger in the architectural office of George Hewitt, one-time partner of Frank Furness and designer of the Bellevue-Stratford Hotel. Trumbauer soon took his turn at the drafting boards and eventually went out on his own. His first commission was the castellated residence Gray Towers (now Beaver College), which he designed for the sugar trust magnate William Welsh Harrison. Harrison introduced him to Peter A. B. Widener and Trumbauer's fabulously successful career was launched. In 1898, he designed the Widener palace, Lynnewood Hall, and the nearby Elkins mansion, both in what is now Elkins Park. He next did exquisite town and country houses for a Widener in-law, Dr. Alexander Hamilton Rice, in New York City and in Newport. Then followed a series of townhouses for such newly rich businessmen as Perry Belmont, George J. Gould, James B. Duke, and James Speyer; he also did the showrooms for Duveen Brothers and the delicate Wildenstein Gallery. For James B. Duke, Trumbauer laid out and built the entire campus of Duke University, the women's college in the Georgian style and the men's college in the Gothic tradition.

Although Trumbauer built for the newly rich up and down the eastern seaboard, he was also active in Philadelphia, where he designed several hotels, a huge addition to the Union League, the Widener Building, the Art Museum, the Free Library, and one of his most ambitious private palaces, Whitemarsh Hall, built for Edward T. Stotesbury with Versailles-like gardens laid out by the French architect Jacques Gréber.

Success and wealth nevertheless brought Trumbauer little lasting satisfaction or relief from his overwhelming shyness and sense of inferiority at his lack

of formal education.* He never consented to an interview. After completion of
the Harry Elkins Widener Library, at Harvard, he had literally to be dragged
to Cambridge and dressed in his academic gown by Mrs. Widener for the graduation ceremonies in June 1915, when Harvard awarded him his only honorary
degree, a master of arts. He drank more and more heavily to bear his burden of
inferiority and died, a childless widower, of cirrhosis of the liver in 1938.

Dean William D. Laird brought the Frenchman Paul Cret to the Penn architectural school in 1903; by the time of Cret's retirement in 1937 he had done
many prominent buildings, bridges, and battle monuments in this country and
abroad. He also was the chief critic at Penn when the school became the best in
the nation; in the year of Cret's retirement from Penn, Dean Hudnut brought
Walter Gropius to Harvard, which then became the leader in the nation.†

Penn went downhill until 1951, when President Harold Stassen brought G.
Holmes Perkins, Norton Professor and chairman of the department of regional
planning at Harvard, to Penn as dean and chairman of architecture in the graduate school of fine arts. Perkins, a Yankee autocrat of sorts, built the school into the nation's finest, especially after he brought Louis Kahn to Penn as chief
critic in 1955. In the meantime Gropius had retired from Harvard, and for almost two decades, with far less money available for scholarships than many
other schools, Penn's school of architecture under Perkins's dynamic leadership
and Kahn's fame as critic and teacher attracted the best students in the nation,
as well as a distinguished faculty.‡

Philadelphia is today one of the main architectural centers in America.
George Howe (1886–1955), a native of Massachusetts and graduate of Groton
and Harvard but brought up in Philadelphia by his widowed mother, who encouraged his early interest in drawing and led him into architecture, was one of
the nation's foremost twentieth-century architects; his Philadelphia Saving
Fund Building is a masterwork. And his protégé, Louis Kahn (1901–1974), of
immigrant parents but raised in Philadelphia and a graduate of Central High
School and Penn, won worldwide acclaim as an architect and teacher. The
Philadelphia school of architects and architectural historians has been engaged
for some time in showing America that the city is a veritable gold mine of architectural history. No city in America, for instance, has a collection of eigh-

---

*It is mysterious how this shy and insecure man made such an impression on his wealthy clients.
After success came, he did very little of his own designing. One of Trumbauer's leading designers
and draftsmen was Julien Francis Abele, son of a Philadelphia physician. Abele got his degree in architecture from Penn in 1902; he was introduced to Trumbauer, who sent him at his own expense
to the Ecole Nationale des Beaux-Arts in Paris, where he studied for three years and won a *diplôme
d'architecture* in 1905. Abele was probably the first black to graduate from Penn's architectural
school and the Ecole Nationale des Beaux-Arts and to be elected a member of the American Institute of Architects.

†I use "Penn" to refer to the University of Pennsylvania.

‡Among the faculty members under Perkins, Robert Geddes became dean of architecture at
Princeton; Romaldo Giurgola, chairman at Columbia; Lee Copeland, chairman at the University
of Washington, Seattle; David Crane, dean at Rice University; Martin Myerson and William L. C.
Wheaton, successive deans at Berkeley; Thomas R. Vreeland, chairman at UCLA; Gerald A. P.
Carrother, dean at York University, in Canada; and Robert Venturi, a leading contemporary ar-
chitectural theorist, Davenport Professor in the Yale School of Architecture.

teenth-century architecture like Philadelphia's Society Hill. A veritable slum by the end of World War II, this area was restored and rebuilt by local architects and their patrons, led by city planner Edmund Bacon and the National Park Service under the direction of Charles Peterson. No other street in America quite compares with Broad Street, in the newer and Victorian part of the city uptown, where Furness's Academy of the Fine Arts looks southward to McArthur's City Hall, McKim Mead and White's Girard Trust,* Hewitt's Bellevue-Stratford, Fraser's Union League, Le Brun's Academy of Music, and the Philadelphia College of Art, with Haviland's Greek revival front backed by Furness's school for the Deaf and Dumb.

Boston may very well have produced more famous architects on the national scene down through the years, but Philadelphia architecture today is by all odds the most exquisite and richly varied in the nation. As the boosters outnumber the disparagers in the city, as indeed they eventually will, its true worth in architecture will become conventional wisdom.

---

*When the Greek revival Girard Trust Building was commissioned in 1906, Effingham B. Morris, the last of the Morris line to play a leadership role in the city, was president; he wanted none of Furness's romanticism and McKim Meade & White, in association with Allan Evens, once Furness's partner, got the commission. After hearing of Morris's views on his work, Furness sat down and drew a conventional banker's dream of what a bank should be. Somehow this original sketch of the present building was purloined in a gentlemanly way and used by the final architects. Furness was furious; he sued and won.

The Learned Professions:
Law, Medicine, and the Church

If I were asked where I place the American aristocracy, I should reply without hesitation that it is not among the rich, who are united by no common tie, but that it occupies the judicial bench and the bar.

Alexis de Tocqueville

Medicine is seen at its best in men whose faculties have had the highest and harmonious culture . . . Morgan, Shippen, Redman, Rush, Coxe, the elder Wood, the elder Pepper, and the elder Mitchell of Philadelphia—Brahmins all, in the language of the greatest Brahmin among them, Oliver Wendell Holmes—these and men like unto them have been the leaven which has raised our profession above the dead level of a business.

William Osler

As late as 1891, American theological schools possessed a total endowment of $18,000,000; whereas medical schools could boast of only $500,000.

Richard H. Shryock

From the days of our nation's founding, law and medicine have been the principal gentlemanly professions in America. In Massachusetts, of course, ministers held the highest positions of societal authority for almost three centuries after the founding of the Bay Colony. And although clerical authority in America has gradually declined throughout the twentieth century, in Boston Endicott Peabody of Groton and Bishop William Lawrence were important authority figures in the establishment right down to the eve of the Second World War. Philadelphia, however, never had an authoritative clerical tradition. Yet, William White, a founder of the Episcopal church in America and first bishop of the diocese of Pennsylvania, played an authoritative role in the city for almost half a century; even the Quakers respected his authority, as witness their choosing him to lead their pet reforming institution, the Philadelphia Prison Society.

At any rate, forty-four, or 88 percent, of the Boston fifty First Families and thirty-six, or 72 percent, of the Philadelphia families, had one or more members who trained for the law, medicine, or the church (see Table A–25).* In each city, moreover, there tended to be medical or legal families. In Boston, the Adamses (six),† Lowells (six), Winthrops (three), Quincys (three), Paines (three), Grays (three), Hoars (three), and Pickerings (two) inclined toward the bar, though many did not remain in active practice; the Boston medical families included the Shattucks (four), Warrens (four), Cabots (three), Bigelows (three), Bowditches (two), Putnams (two), and Jacksons (one). In Philadelphia, the legal families included the Ingersolls (four), Rawles (three), Sergeants (three), Fishers (three), Hopkinsons (two), McKeans (two), Dallases (two), Penroses (two), Prices (two), Biddles (one), and Binneys (one);‡ the city's leading medical families included the Peppers (three), Bartons (three), Meigses (three), Mitchells (two), Norrises (two), Rushes (two), and Wistar-Wisters (one). As might be expected, Brahmin Boston has produced a solid core of clerical families, whereas Philadelphia has produced only one, the Hares (two). The Boston clerical families include the Mathers (four), Wares (four), Higginsons (three), Peabodys (three), Frothinghams (three), Emersons (two), Nortons (two), Everetts (two), Brookses (two), and Lawrences (one).

BOSTON AND PHILADELPHIA
GENTLEMEN OF THE BENCH AND BAR

In Jacksonian America, Tocqueville saw lawyers as a useful conservative and aristocratic force in an otherwise restless and egalitarian society. Actually, they have been both an innovative and a conserving force throughout our history: lawyers took the lead in revolutionary Boston as well as in the founding of our nation in Philadelphia; in the history of the U.S. Senate, men trained in the law held 55 percent of the seats in 1789, 95 percent in 1845, 77 percent in 1895, and 70 percent in 1945. In this leadership tradition, it is appropriate that more members of the First Families in both cities were trained in the law than in any other profession.

As Blackstone taught, in America a knowledge of the law has long been seen as an essential part of a liberal and polite education, and the term *Esquire* traditionally has been used for both gentlemen and lawyers.** It is of sociological

---

*All tables cited in this Chapter are presented in Appendix I.

†The number after each family name indicates how many lawyers or doctors from each family were included in the *DAB*.

‡Although Nicholas Biddle, the famous banker, was the only Biddle lawyer included in the *DAB*, more than twenty Biddles were members of the Philadelphia bar during the nineteenth century. Francis and other Biddles were prominent members of the twentieth-century bar. Horace Binney was followed at the bar by Horace, Jr., and Horace III, though neither was of much distinction.

**This practice is giving way in the law, and in keeping with the egalitarian tone of our times, it was abandoned in official mailings to alumni of St. Paul's School in the 1960s.

significance that the professional ethics of both law and medicine have their historical roots in the code of the gentleman; moreover, just as the code of the gentleman is widely dismissed as elitist in America today, so both doctors and lawyers seem to be guided increasingly by pecuniary rather than professional values.*

Although training in the law has been held in high regard by upper-class Americans, it has been used in very different ways in Boston and Philadelphia. By and large, Bostonians have been more likely to see legal training as preparation for leadership in general rather than as preparation for simply a career at the bar. Not only were Philadelphians more likely to train for the law (56 percent of the Philadelphia, as against only 44 percent of the Boston, families had one or more members trained in the law) but they were also more likely to spend a major part of their careers at the bar. Thus, the two leading legal families in Philadelphia, the Ingersolls and the Rawles, have had members who spent a major part of their careers at the bar for six generations now. Of the forty-five Proper Bostonians who qualified for the bar, only Rufus Choate and James Jackson Storrow spent their lives in practice. In the Calvinist tradition, the Proper Bostonians admitted to the bar sought societal and magisterial authority in the broadest sense.

As my central theme is the problem of authority in Boston and Philadelphia, it is useful, where the law is concerned, to differentiate between the major functions of the bench and bar: members of the bar are engaged primarily in defending private and partial interests; members of the bench are engaged in upholding the authority of the total community. Accordingly, the Ingersolls and the Rawles were mostly advocates, but there were three Judge John Lowells in Boston's history; John G. Johnson was Philadelphia's greatest advocate, whereas Oliver Wendell Holmes, Jr., probably had one of the greatest judicial minds in our nation's history.

It is indeed appropriate that the term *Philadelphia lawyer* stands for advocacy rather than authority. The term goes back to 1735, when Andrew Hamilton, at the age of eighty, defended John Peter Zenger in the first case of freedom of the press in America. The case was given wide publicity at the time both here and in England, and ever since the term Philadelphia lawyer has meant excellence

---

*Sidney Fisher noted that professional values were losing out to pecuniary ones in his own day, as the entry in his diary for September 15, 1869, shows: "Bet . . . went to town & brought out the news that Harry Meigs had made up his mind to give up the law & to study divinity. . . . No wonder . . . the learning necessary for practice is a dry mass of details of no interest and the practice itself has become little better than a mere trade under the degrading influence of democracy. It by no means follows that a successful lawyer is a gentleman, that he is a man of honor, or that he has received a liberal education, and indeed those who are now most successful in *making money*, the great object of all, are notoriously deficient in these qualities, which were once regarded as requisites. The bar & bench, too, have fallen very far below the dignified & respectable position it held when I knew it thirty years ago. I saw & knew the last of the old set who gave it so much influence & reputation—Rawle, Binney, Sergeant, Chauncey, the two Ingersolls, Scott, etc.—all of them gentlemen by culture, birth, and manners, all of them distinguished for learning & ability, Binney & Sergeant pre-eminent for eloquence & power, all of them, too, with scarcely an exception, worthy of all confidence & respect for integrity, professional honor, and moral worth. . . . All is now changed—culture, elegance, refinement, courtesy, eloquence, wit, scholarship have vanished."

at the bar. Unfortunately, outside Philadelphia, where Hamilton is a patron saint of the local bar, the term has often meant shrewdness but also sharp and devious practices, somewhat analogous to the term *sea lawyer*.

Horace Binney and the Philadelphia Declining Tradition. The nineteenth-century idol of the Philadelphia bar before the Civil War was surely Horace Binney. Proper Philadelphians are most proud of his defeat in 1844 of Daniel Webster, the darling of Boston's State Street, in a locally famous case involving the will of Stephen Girard. Even Boston's Justice Story, who wrote the Supreme Court decision, had to admit that Binney's argument was far more brilliant than Webster's. But Webster went on to a famous career in government while Binney remained all his life a local figure and distinguished Philadelphia lawyer. Actually, the Girard case marked Binney's last appearance as an active advocate in court, though he served in an advisory capacity for many years. Except for one brief term in Congress before resigning because of his preference for "associating only with gentlemen," Binney refused to serve in public office, either in politics or on the bench. The following summary of Binney's career by Nathaniel Burt illustrates the private nature of the Proper Philadelphia mind.

> Horace Binney, perhaps the Representative Philadelphian of the nineteenth century, came to the bar in 1800, at the age of twenty, and for seventy-five more years dominated the city, though he actually withdrew from active practice when he was only fifty. Binney declined, as any good Philadelphian should, an appointment to the United States Supreme Court and then, in 1869 after the death of Taney, the Chief Justiceship of the same. His tenure of the Chancellorship (head of the Philadelphia Bar) was brief, only two years, from 1852 to 1854. Yet despite, or even because of this seeming avoidance of responsibilities, he remained till he died in 1875 unquestionably Philadelphia's leading citizen, giving advice, active on boards, writing eulogies of his less durable friends, honored and beloved by all. "It would be difficult to mention a death that caused a sensation more widespread than his," said his eulogist, the Honorable William Strong of the United States Supreme Court.[1]

Horace Binney was the prototypical example of Philadelphia's tradition of declining, which as we have seen, was followed by John G. Johnson.* Though both men were eventually taken into Proper Philadelphia Society, attending the Assembly balls and dining at the Philadelphia Club, neither was of old Philadelphia origins: Johnson was a self-made man of humble birth, whereas Binney, though born in Philadelphia, was taken to Massachusetts when his widowed mother married a Boston physician, and was educated at Harvard. Many of Binney's personal traits—a natural gift for leadership, a chilly rectitude, and even his longevity (he was the oldest living Harvard alumnus in his day)—were more in the Boston than in the Philadelphia mold. Sidney Fisher summed up Binney in his customary style.

---

*Philadelphians have been both ready decliners and reluctant volunteers. Thus, one might have predicted that Joseph Welch, of the Boston bar, would be a leading factor in the defeat of Joseph McCarthy in the 1950s and St. Clair, Cox, and Richardson, all of the Boston bar, major actors in the Watergate affair of the 1970s. Perhaps it is also in character that Sam Dash, a graduate of Central High, was a principal technical and fact-gathering figure in the Watergate affair.

Mr. Binney is a self-made man. His family tho respectable was obscure. He was introduced into society by Joshua Fisher's mother. He inherited, however, an independent fortune, was from early youth a student and a scholar. . . . Binney is respected and admired but not loved. He is not genial but hard & cold, exact & severe. He rarely unbends and always bears himself as a superior, talks as tho he were instructing and listens with indulgence rather than sympathy. . . . He is a great lawyer and, except in a democracy, would have been a great statesman.[2]

Judicial Appointment and Tenure in Massachusetts and Pennsylvania. By and large, the appointment of judges to sit during good behavior, as Tocqueville saw, is in accord with the aristocratic principle of government, whereas the election of judges for stated terms of office is more in accord with the principles of democracy. As might be expected, the former has been characteristic of Massachusetts; the latter, of Pennsylvania.

Horace Binney remained a staunch Federalist in spirit all his life; his heroes were Alexander Hamilton and John Marshall, who applied Hamiltonian principles on the bench when he presided as chief justice of the Supreme Court between 1801 and 1835. The Federalists, Binney once said, led "the only honest party we have ever had."

Binney, as Sidney Fisher suggested, might well have been a famous statesman or great jurist had he remained in Massachusetts to practice law after graduating from Harvard.* For, as we saw in an earlier chapter, the Massachusetts constitution was made by members of the upper class, who were primarily Federalists, and the appointment of judges to serve during good behavior has been a legal cornerstone of that constitution from the days of John Adams and Theophilus Parsons down to the present. But Binney lived through the radical democratization of the Pennsylvania judicial system during the first half of the nineteenth century. The Jeffersonian Republican and then the Jacksonian Democratic leaders of the state in his day mistrusted lawyers in general and the independence of the judiciary in particular. In this atmosphere the Pennsylvania constitution of 1838 abolished lifetime judicial appointments, instead prescribing tenures of fifteen, ten, and five years. Then, in 1851, the judiciary was made directly responsible to the people when state judgeships at all levels were made elective.

Proper Philadelphia lawyers, almost to a man, fought these attacks on the independence of the judiciary. The Ingersolls, Sergeants, Rawles, and especially Horace Binney took the lead in this losing battle. Binney saw that the integrity of the bench depends on an independent judiciary. In his nostalgic book on *The Leaders of the Old Bar of Philadelphia* (1859), for instance, he wrote: "We must confess that a system is perilous, which holds out to the best Judge, if he displeases a powerful party, nothing better than the Poorhouse."[3] He also noted that the integrity of the bar rests on an authoritative and independent bench.

A good Bar cannot exist long in connection with a favor-seeking Bench,—a Bench on the lookout for favors from the people or from anyone. Such a Bench is not an independent body, whatever some of the Judges may be personally. . . .

---

*Binney's earliest American ancestors settled in Hull, Massachusetts, in the seventeenth century.

The Bench therefore as now constituted, is not raised sufficiently above the Bar, to command it by the power of its political constitution. The Bar is constitutionally the higher body of the two, the more permanent, the more independent, and, popularity being the motive power, the more controlling body, though only for its personal and several ends. This is the fatal derangement that the present judicial tenure makes between the two corps. The subordinate becomes the paramount. The private and personal will control the public; not by reason, not by virtue, not always openly, but by influence.[4]

Philadelphia Gentlemen of the Bar; Boston Brahmins on the Bench. Binney's perceptive analysis of judicial tenure in Pennsylvania suggests why the Philadelphia bar has tended to be dominated by gentlemen whereas the state bench, especially after 1851, has tended to draw mediocre men from the hinterland. Between 1827 and 1900, for instance, the ten chancellors of the Philadelphia bar— William Rawle, Peter S. Duponceau, John Sergeant, Horace Binney, Joseph R. Ingersoll, William Meredith, Peter McCall, George Washington Biddle, Richard C. McMurtrie, Joseph B. Townsend, George Tucker Bispham, and Samuel Dickson, in that order—were all not only distinguished leaders of the bar but also, except for the French auslander Duponceau, Philadelphia Gentlemen. The leadership of the judiciary at the highest level of authority, the Supreme Court of Pennsylvania, however, tended to attract mediocre men after the tenure rules were changed.

A comparison of the judges of the Supreme Court of Pennsylvania with their peers on the Supreme Judicial Court of Massachusetts is infinitely revealing. Of the ten chief justices of the Supreme Judicial Court under the royal charter of Massachusetts, six were included in the *DAB.* Of these six, all graduated from Harvard; four were natives of Boston or Salem and two were born in England. In contrast, of the eighteen chief justices of colonial Pennsylvania, only seven were distinguished enough to be included in the *DAB;* of these seven, none was a college graduate, though four had studied in London at the Inns of Court; none was a native of Pennsylvania (one was a native of Wales, two of England, two of Ireland, and one each of New Jersey and Maryland). Table A–26 lists the chief justices of Massachusetts and Pennsylvania who assumed office from the nation's founding to 1940. The sixteen justices from Massachusetts were a far better educated and more distinguished group. All save one were college educated, eleven of them at Harvard. A majority (thirteen) of the Pennsylvania men did not go to college, two were graduates of the University of Pennsylvania, two of the Western University of Pennsylvania (now the University of Pittsburgh), one of Harvard, and the other five of various small colleges around the state. Whereas six of the sixteen justices of Massachusetts obtained law degrees (five from Harvard and one from Boston University), only three of the Pennsylvania men did so (one each from Penn, Dickinson, and the University of Virginia). Three of the Massachusetts men went on to the Supreme Court of the United States, but none of the Pennsylvania men did. Finally, Boston dominated the Massachusetts bench, whereas Philadelphia characteristically did not exercise hegemony in Pennsylvania. Thus, two-thirds of the Massachusetts justices came from the Boston area (Boston proper and the leadership county of

Essex); only one-third of the Pennsylvania justices were natives of Philadelphia or the neighboring counties of Chester and Bucks.

Horace Binney foresaw the mediocre character of the Pennsylvania bench after 1851 and blamed it on the democratic elective process. But he also recognized the role played therein by his fellow Philadelphians' lack of chauvinism. In his book on the Philadelphia bar, he anticipated later critics like Owen Wister and Mark Sullivan. Philadelphia, he wrote,

> is wanting in civic personality, or what is perhaps a better phrase for the thought, a family unity or identity. She does not take, and she never has taken, satisfaction in habitually honoring her distinguished men as *her* men, as men of her *own* family. It is the City that is referred to, as distinguished, perhaps, from the rest of the State. She has never done it in the face of the world, as Charleston has done it, as Richmond has done it, as Baltimore has done it, as New York has done it, or at least, did it in former times, and as Boston did it, has done it, and will do it forever. She is more indifferent to her sons than she is to strangers; and this perhaps may be the reason why other parts of the State so much more readily advance their own men to public office and distinction.[5]

Binney also suggested the Quaker origin of this self-deprecating civic attitude:* "The fact has often been stated for sixty years past, but it is not easy to explain, nor will I attempt to account for it with any confidence. Perhaps it grows out of her Quaker origin. It is certainly in harmony with it, to put nothing more striking than a drab-colored dress upon the men who have done the best for her."[6]

Binney's dismal prediction about an elected judiciary is borne out by the fact that the most distinguished chief justices of Pennsylvania—McKean, Shippen, Tilghman, and Gibson—all held office before 1851. McKean and Shippen were eminent members of the city's aristocracy; Tilghman, who belonged to a prominent Maryland family, had come to Philadelphia to study law in the office of Benjamin Chew, last colonial chief justice, and had married into the great Allen family.† But undoubtedly the most distinguished chief justice of Pennsylvania was John Bannister Gibson, a giant of a man in stature and accomplishments, who came from the Scotch-Irish capital of the state, Carlisle.

Gibson was appointed to the Pennsylvania Supreme Court in 1816 and elevated to the chief justiceship in 1827, a position he retained until 1851, when the entire court was retired because of a constitutional amendment that year. In Gibson's case it is important to stress that he was an intellectual and an artist by inclination and temperament. Perhaps one decisive difference between men attracted to the bench rather than to the bar was that the former saw law as an intellectual challenge, above all, as a matter of principle and not simply of precedent. It will be remembered in this connection that Parrington compared

---

*This paragraph, written in 1859 of Philadelphia, certainly reminds one of the drabness of the ethnophobic 1960s in America as a whole, and both states of affairs, according to the major thesis of this book, were the result of egalitarian individualism.

†The family has populated the ranks of Philadelphia Gentlemen ever since. In the 1930s, there was a Benjamin Chew Tilghman from Philadelphia at St. Paul's School, along with Cadwaladers, Ingersolls, Chews, and other Proper Philadelphians. Tilghman married a Boston Forbes and spent his career as a publisher in that city.

John Dickinson and the precedent seeking Philadelphia lawyers with the more analytical and principle seeking Bostonians like John Adams. Certainly, the Boston bench, from John Adams (who was appointed first chief justice of Massachusetts but did not serve) to Oliver Wendell Holmes, seemed to be more involved with principles than with precedents alone. And Gibson's *DAB* biographer placed him in this intellectual tradition when he wrote that Gibson "avoided where possible any survey of precedents, seeking to found his decisions upon principles."[7] Naturally, Gibson was more a student of Coke, the Whig, than of Blackstone, the Tory, favorite of most Proper Philadelphia lawyers. The same thing might have been said of Holmes. And, like Holmes, Gibson was widely read in English literature (he was "a profound student of Shakespeare"); he also read in the original the classics of French and Italian literature.* A universalist in the style of Jefferson, he was a skilled mechanic, an expert piano tuner, a competent dentist; he also had more than an amateur acquaintance with both medicine and the fine arts. Gibson's favorite leisure time pursuit was music, especially playing the violin (which he did by the hour in his early and not entirely happy days at the bar). Again like Holmes, Gibson was bored with practicing at the bar but loved the bench. In short, of all the chief justices of the Supreme Court of Pennsylvania, John Bannister Gibson, the Scotch-Irish Calvinist, was most like the Massachusetts giants of the bench.†

Even though Proper Philadelphia legal reputations were made primarily at the bar, something should be said of the members of the Hopkinson, Hare, Cadwalader, and Sergeant families who did serve on the bench. No member of the legal Ingersoll family ever sat on the bench, although John Adams offered Jared Ingersoll a position in the federal judiciary, which he declined for financial reasons.

Francis and Joseph Hopkinson, father and son, played versatile if not exactly leading roles in the nation's founding. Both were lawyers who served as judges on the U.S. district court of eastern Pennsylvania, Francis being appointed by Washington and Joseph by John Adams; both have secure places in the nation's history, Francis as a signer of the Declaration of Independence and Joseph as the author of "Hail, Columbia." Francis was the first graduate of Penn, and the family served the university and the city down to the 1950s, when Francis Hopkinson, also a lawyer, was the city's foremost citizen, senior local Morgan partner, and trustee of the university.

John Cadwalader, surely the most distinguished of his clan, was also appointed to the U.S. district court of eastern Pennsylvania and served with distinction from 1858 until his death in 1879.

---

*Unlike Holmes, however, Gibson, in the typical Pennsylvania vein, hated to write and wrote nothing to speak of outside his judicial decisions, which were brilliantly brief.

†Naturally, Gibson was not in sympathy with the attacks on judicial independence in Pennsylvania in 1838 and again in 1851. And he was always frank, according to Wister, "in expressing his low value of popular judgment." Once when a colleague on the bench, referring to the new amendment of 1851, remarked that "the people will probably get tired of the new system and return to the old," Gibson replied, "No, the people are like the grave—what they get they never give up" (Owen Wister, "The Supreme Court of Pennsylvania," *The Green Bag*, undated, p. 80). Judges in Pennsylvania face the electorate to this day.

The Hares were the only clerical family produced by Proper Philadelphia, but John Innis Clark Hare, son-in-law of Horace Binney and good friend of Sidney Fisher, followed the law. In 1851, he was elected to the district court of Philadelphia, where he served for twenty-five years. "Though political conditions kept him in a subordinate court," wrote his *DAB* biographer, "he was one of the half-dozen greatest judges that Pennsylvania has produced."[8]

Like the Ingersolls, the Sergeants were one of the foremost legal families in the city; also like the Ingersolls, the family originated in New England; but unlike the Ingersolls, the first Philadelphia Sergeant was a radical patriot and revolutionary leader. Jonathan Dickinson Sergeant, the first of his family in the city, was descended from Jonathan Sergeant, who came to New Haven in 1644; his maternal grandfather was the Reverend Jonathan Dickinson, first president of the College of New Jersey. Like so many Princeton graduates, Jonathan Dickinson Sergeant fell in with the Sons of Liberty and played a prominent role in the Stamp Act controversy. He was part of the radical Bryan wing in the making of the first Pennsylvania constitution and was appointed attorney general of the state in 1777. He died while fighting the yellow fever epidemic in 1793. "Nothing but the yellow fever which removed . . . Jonathan Dickinson from this world," wrote John Adams, "could have saved the United States from a fatal revolution of Government."[9]

Jonathan Dickinson Sergeant's two sons, John and Thomas, were leading members of the city's nineteenth-century bar. John Sergeant, a close associate of Horace Binney, inherited a great deal of New England's intellectuality and passion to lead; he was a member of Joseph Dennie's circle at the *Port Folio* and served several terms in Congress; yet he was also a victim of the city's declining tradition. "His stature can be measured," wrote his *DAB* biographer, "by the offices that he declined; these included a seat on the bench of the United States Supreme Court, a cabinet post under Harrison, and the embassy to England under Tyler."[10] Whereas John Sergeant was a great advocate and avoided the bench, his younger brother, Thomas, was appointed to the Supreme Court of Pennsylvania in 1834. "Like his brother," wrote Thomas's *DAB* biographer, "he strongly opposed the amendment in the constitutional convention of 1837–38 proposing popular election of judges, and so bitter was his resentment at its inclusion in the state constitution that he resigned his judgeship, October 1, 1846, largely on that account."[11] As has so often been the case in Philadelphia, the Sergeants left no descendants of distinction in the city.*

Upper-class Boston, as we have seen, had far more influence in the higher judiciary of the commonwealth than was the case with Philadelphia; but this

---

*Sidney Fisher was a great admirer of John Sergeant but wrote of his son's funeral: "*July 28, 1856.* at 4 went to the funeral of Jno. Sergeant, who died a few days ago. He led a dreadful life, drank to horrible excess, died indeed of delirium tremens. For some years he had lived with a mistress, openly, as if she was his wife. He was, however, a manly goodhearted fellow, a gentleman in his manners & of considerable talent. A sad end for his father's son. Walked to the church with Mr. Binney by his own invitation. John's mistress was in the church, a handsome woman." It is my impression that successful men's sons have a harder time in democratic and individualistic societies than they do in more hierarchical and aristocratic ones. (Nicholas B. Wainwright, ed., *A Philadelphia Perspective: The Diary of Sidney George Fisher Covering the Years 1834–1871* [Philadelphia: Historical Society of Pennsylvania, 1967], p. 259.)

group also has taken the lead at the bar. Since the founding of the Boston Bar Association in 1876, for instance, Yankees have dominated its presidency, which has included Hoars, Lowells, Shattucks, Grays, Warrens, and Cabots from the First Family sample. (Interestingly, ethnic influence in the local bars of both cities came to the fore at about the same time: at the Boston bar, the first Irish-Catholic president served in 1941–1942, the first Jew in 1946–1947; the first Irish-Catholic chancellor in Philadelphia took office in 1937, the first Jew in 1952.)

Joseph Choate, favorite First Family lawyer, and Charles Jackson Storrow, patent lawyer for the Bell Telephone System, were the only Bostonians in the sample who spent their lives at the bar; other, less distinguished members of Boston's First Families also have had lifelong careers as partners in the city's leading law firms. Today, for instance, Ropes, Gray, founded by John Codman Ropes and John Chipman Gray soon after the Civil War, is the largest firm in Boston; other First Family firms include Hauserman Davidson & Shattuck and the Rufus Choate firm, Choate Hall & Stewart. In Philadelphia, though Rawle & Henderson is an old, nineteenth-century firm, such prominent First Family firms as Drinker Biddle & Reath, Pepper Hamilton & Scheetz, and Ballard Spahr Andrews & Ingersoll are mainly twentieth-century creations.

Gentlemanly traditions at the bar, in other words, have characterized both cities down to the present day; as a hard-boiled newspaperman from Chicago once said to me after working on a Philadelphia paper for several years: "I used to think of lawyers as merely mouthpieces but they really do seem to be barristers here in Philly."

The Massachusetts Bench and the Founding of American Law and Legal Education. Just as Bostonians have been distinguished justices within both Massachusetts and the nation, so they have dominated legal education in this country. It was natural that New England Puritanism should have set the stage for the development of American law. "The pulpit, not the altar," wrote Daniel Boorstin, "was the focus of the Congregational church, for Puritans adored the word. Their theology, like much of the rest of their thinking, was legalistic; its 'federal' theology depended on 'covenant,' a legal concept. Colonial New Englanders strove ingeniously to live by the laws of God and the Laws of England."[12] Even though the Harvard Corporation passed from the control of clergymen to that of lawyers in 1816, the Calvinist-Federalist ideas of law and authority lasted at least until the Lowell regime in the twentieth century.

When William Blackstone, of All Souls, gave the first of his Vinerian lectures in law at Oxford in 1753, academic legal education began in the Anglo-American world; his lectures, published as *Commentaries on the Laws of England* (1765–1769), were even more important in the American colonies than in England. The founding fathers fed on Blackstone, whose theory of natural law was a vital source of the Declaration of Independence. James Kent, a New Yorker of old Connecticut clergyman stock, became the American Blackstone when he published his *Commentaries on American Law* (1826–1830). If Kent proved that American law existed, it was Associate Justice Joseph Story of the U.S. Supreme Court whose books (revisions of his Harvard lectures) made it work and have remained the basis of legal education all over America down to the twentieth century.

Joseph Story's works insured the dominance of the common law in the United States, but it was three prolific chief justices of the Supreme Judicial Court of Massachusetts, according to Boorstin, who "established the independence, the adaptive vigor, and the traditionalism of American law." Theophilus Parsons, known in his day as the "Giant of the Law," published nine volumes of his opinions on the bench—the first judicial monument of the American common law. Parsons's work was carried on by his successor, Chief Justice Isaac Parker, who was also first Royall Professor of Law at Harvard. Finally, Lemuel Shaw, who served as chief justice longer than any other man in the history of the Massachusetts court, was the American giant of railroad and commercial law, leaving a record of 2,200 opinions; few judges, according to Boorstin, "have shaped a great legal system so decisively and so enduringly."[13] Perhaps Felix Frankfurter was thinking of Shaw's importance in railroad law when he told his Harvard classes that James Watt, inventor of the steam engine, had had the greatest influence on American law. In the twentieth century, Oliver Wendell Holmes, Jr., a key member of a small Boston discussion group that included Charles Sanders Peirce and William James, elevated Shaw's common law approach to the philosophy of legal pragmatism (which Dean Roscoe Pound of the Harvard Law School later elaborated in his system of sociological jurisprudence).

The American law school was a New England invention, and the Harvard Law School became a nationalizing influence on American leadership somewhat comparable to Eton and Harrow and Oxford and Cambridge in England. Although Judge George Wyeth held the first American professorship of law, at William and Mary College in Virginia (where he taught John Marshall for a brief period), the earliest American law school was founded by Tapping Reeve, a Princeton graduate, at Litchfield, Connecticut, in 1784. During the school's life (1784–1833) it drew students from every state in the young nation, its graduates including sixteen U.S. senators, fifty U.S. congressmen, forty justices of higher state courts (eight chief justices), two justices of the U.S. Supreme Court, ten governors, and five federal cabinet members. Also among its graduates were the founders of new law schools in Northampton and Dedham, Massachusetts; in Cincinnati, Ohio; in Augusta, Georgia; and in Albany, New York.

Throughout our history, the intellectual leaders of the American bench, from Joseph Story to Oliver Wendell Holmes, have been educators of the highest authority not only of lawyers but also of legislators and the general public—and of presidents, too, as the two Roosevelts learned to their sorrow, each in his own day and way.* It was thus appropriate that when Nathan Dane—whose eight-volume *General Abridgement and Digest of American Law* was the

---

*The Court, for instance, educated Theodore in the *Northern Securities* case and Franklin in the case of the N.R.A.

first of its kind—offered the incoming president of Harvard, Josiah Quincy, a gift of $15,000 to found a new chair of law, he insisted that Associate Justice Joseph Story of the Supreme Court fill this position. A successful lawyer from Salem, Story had been appointed to the Court by Madison in 1811, at the age of thirty-two, the youngest justice in the history of the Court. John Marshall approved of the appointment, and Story, whom Jackson once called "the most dangerous man in America," carried the Federalist ideals of authority into an increasingly democratic age. Though the Court salary was less than half his income at the bar, Story was honored by the appointment, especially valuing the lifetime tenure, which would afford him a chance "to pursue, what of all things I admire, juridical studies."[14] Story also accepted the Dane Chair at Harvard and commuted between Cambridge and Washington for the rest of his life.* He built up the law school from 18 students to almost 150 when he died in 1845.

The Harvard Law School, the first in America to be affiliated with a university, was actually founded in 1816. In that year, four of the seven Fellows of the Harvard Corporation were lawyers: John Lowell, wealthy Federalist propagandist, John Phillips, later first mayor of Boston, Senator Christopher Gore, once governor, and Judge John Davis. An expatriate Loyalist, Isaac Royall, had left a legacy to Harvard at his death in England in 1781 in order to endow either a professor of laws or of physic and anatomy. The Fellows chose the former, and John Lowell was urged to accept the Royall professorship; he declined but suggested his Harvard classmate Isaac Parker, chief justice of the Supreme Judicial Court, who became the first Royall Professor in 1816. Harvard awarded its first bachelor of laws degree in 1820 and has since produced more than its share of preeminent lawyers. Of the ninety-five men who sat on the Supreme Court of the United States between 1789 and 1963, for instance, fifty-three had graduated from law school,† eleven from Harvard, seven from Yale, five from Columbia, three from Michigan, two each from the University of Virginia, Cincinnati, and Union (including the Albany Law School), and one each from twenty-one other law schools, including the University of Pennsylvania.

Legal Education at Penn and Harvard. In the colonial period Philadelphia lawyers were probably better trained than those of New England. Of the 115 Americans who studied at the London Inns of Court between 1760 and the close of the Revolution, for instance, 47 were from South Carolina, 21 from Virginia, 16 from Maryland, 11 from Pennsylvania, and 5 from New York. Only one or two New Englanders studied there. Whereas John Dickinson, Thomas McKean, Jared Ingersoll, William Rawle, Peter Markoe, and Benjamin Chew, from the Philadelphia First Families, went there during this period, no member of the Boston sample did so.

---

*In Story's day, the Supreme Court rarely sat for more than a few weeks during the year. Most of the justices commuted, many of them living in the same boardinghouse in Washington, where John Marshall's consummate charm converted them to his point of view.

†Most judges before the end of the nineteenth century were products of the apprenticeship system: Joseph Story, for example, studied in the office of Chief Justice Samuel Sewell of Massachusetts.

Philadelphia was in many ways the center of the nation's bench and bar in the early national period. According to Gary B. Nash,

> The great prominence of Philadelphia lawyers, dating to the adroitness and profundity of Andrew Hamilton in defending Peter Zenger in 1735, continued throughout the eighteenth and nineteenth centuries, making Philadelphia the cynosure of the legal profession in the early national period. The city's position as the nation's center of commerce and banking until about 1835 encouraged a large and mature legal body. In Philadelphia law was in the air. In City Hall sat the United States Supreme Court at the end of the eighteenth century, as well as the United States Circuit and District Courts. In the nearby State House the Pennsylvania Supreme Court convened. Nowhere in the country could be found such an outstanding body of men expert in commercial, criminal, and maritime law. A British traveller of wealth and education epitomized the prevalent view: "I have never met a body of men," he remarked in 1833, "more distinguished by acuteness and extensive professional information than the members of the Philadelphia bar."[15]

Perhaps it was the very success of the Philadelphia bar that delayed the development of formal education in the law at the University of Pennsylvania. The leading members of the bar, in fact, had a stake in perpetuating an apprenticeship system that allowed them to choose their young clerks and thus maintain control over the bar's membership. These apprentices, or law clerks, paid fees to their patrons, did routine work around the offices, including endless copying of legal forms, accompanied their patrons to court, ate at their tables, absorbed their philosophies, and not infrequently married their daughters. Their legal education depended on the whims of their sponsors rather than on any formal curriculum. No wonder that the first concerted effort to found a law department at Penn (1832) was opposed by the city's foremost lawyers, including Chews, Binneys, Hopkinsons, Cadwaladers, Sergeants, Ingersolls, Rawles, and Biddles.

But, as I have suggested, the bench rather than the bar has sponsored the educational and intellectual aspects of the law.* Just as Joseph Story was the first real builder of the Harvard Law School, so in Philadelphia George Sharswood, president judge of the city's common pleas court at the time and later chief justice of Pennsylvania, founded the law department at Penn (1850). The university awarded its first bachelor of laws degree in 1852 (Yale awarded its first law degree in 1843; Harvard, as noted in 1820). Penn's law department remained small and local for the remaining years of the century: its lecturers were part-time volunteers from the Philadelphia bar, and classes were held in various office buildings downtown; most students were commuters, an average of fifteen taking degrees each year.

---

*Abortive attempts to found a law school at Penn were made in 1790 and 1817. In 1790, Justice James Wilson of the Supreme Court opened a series of lectures at the college in the presence of Washington and his cabinet, the Houses of Congress, the executive and legislative departments of the governments of the state of Pennsylvania and the city of Philadelphia, judges of the courts, members of the bar, Mrs. Washington, Mrs. Hamilton, and many others. The lectures, with such an auspicious beginning, nevertheless were discontinued after the first year. Then, in 1817, Charles Willing Hare, brother of Judge John Innis Clark Hare, gave a series of law lectures at Penn the year before his death.

The modern Penn Law School was built by William Draper Lewis, lecturer in the law department as well as in the Wharton School, who was appointed the first full-time dean in 1896. Disregarding dire warnings from colleagues that teaching law was a hobby rather than a profession, he took the job at the age of twenty-nine because, as he later recalled, he was "perhaps the only lawyer then living who would take it and agree to give his whole time to it." By 1900, Lewis had built the present law school on the West Philadelphia campus, which now is named in his honor.

Of ancient Quaker ancestry and a graduate of Haverford College, Lewis was a Proper, Philadelphia Club Philadelphian.* But he hardly followed the conventional wisdom of his class: an unqualified admirer (and biographer) of Theodore Roosevelt, he saw the New Deal as a continuation of the Progressive tradition and even went so far as publicly to defend Franklin Roosevelt's packing of the Supreme Court. Lewis brought a distinguished group of auslanders to the law school faculty, including Edwin R. Keedy, a Maryland native with a Harvard law degree, and William E. Mikell, a South Carolinian and graduate of the University of Virginia Law School, both of whom subsequently served as dean. Under Lewis's leadership the law school prospered, awarding seventy-eight degrees in 1914. After the First World War, he left Penn and became the presiding genius of the American Law Institute, which he helped to found and keep in Philadelphia.†

Between the two world wars, the law school drew its students largely from Pennsylvania, New Jersey, and metropolitan New York; most were commuters, among them, especially during the Depression, many Proper Philadelphians who, after graduating from Harvard, Yale, or Princeton, attended the law school before taking their birthright places in the best law firms in the city. (These firms, much larger today, now recruit on a national scale.)

In 1952, President Gaylord Harnwell brought Jefferson Fordham, a distinguished Southern gentleman with law degrees from the University of North Carolina and Yale, from the faculty of the University of Virginia to Penn. As dean, Fordham transformed a first-rate school into a national institution; he completely renovated the original building and raised funds for two residence halls (the first at the law school), named in honor of Justice Owen Roberts, his predecessor as dean, and Senator George Wharton Pepper, part-time lecturer for many years.

Harvard's law school, in contrast to Penn's, was housed on the Cambridge campus from the very beginning. President Quincy persuaded Nathan Dane to endow a building, and Dane Hall was completed in the 1830s under Story's leadership. The modern law school was built under the presidency of Charles W. Eliot, who in 1870 appointed a relatively unknown New York lawyer named Christopher Columbus Langdell as dean. While an undergraduate at Harvard, Eliot had met and been tremendously impressed with Langdell, then a law student.

---

*Lewis married Caroline Mary Cope, a member of one of the city's Quaker First Families.

†I am much indebted to my Penn colleague George Lee Haskins, Proper Bostonian and Biddle Professor of Law, who pointed out William Draper Lewis's important role in building the law school.

Under Langdell's leadership, Austin Hall, designed by H. H. Richardson, was built in 1882, and Hastings Hall, a dormitory and student center, was completed in 1890. (Langdell Hall was completed in 1906 during Eliot's presidency.) Langdell, above all, brought a famous faculty to Harvard. His recruits included James Barr Ames, John Chipman Gray, James Bradley Thayer, and Roscoe Pound. (Pound, one of the great legal minds of the twentieth century, later became dean.)

By the 1920s, Harvard was educating over 1,000 law students a year, drawn from all over the nation; by the 1960s, its student body was truly international. In the academic year 1965–1966, for instance, the 1,683 students came from 362 institutions of higher learning both here and abroad: 34 from Oxford, 15 from Cambridge, 18 from London University, 16 from the University of Paris, and one or more students from schools in Australia, New Zealand, Japan, Taiwan, China, South Africa, Iran, Germany, Sweden, Belgium, Italy, India, Brazil, Canada, Norway, Ireland, Cuba, the Philippines, Puerto Rico, and the U.S.S.R.

Massachusetts and Pennsylvania Justices on the Supreme Court of the United States. Though power in America centers in the Congress and the White House, it has always been balanced and finally checked by the authority of the Supreme Court. John Marshall, chief justice from his appointment by John Adams in 1801 until his death at the age of eighty in 1835, firmly established the Federalist principles of judicial review and of the Supreme Court as the final authoritative interpreter of the Constitution, in spite of determined opposition from the Jeffersonian Republicans and the Jacksonian Democrats, who held political power during most of his tenure. His firm ally on the bench was Joseph Story, who often supplied scholarly support for Marshall's brilliant intuitive grasp of legal principles.

Table A–27 lists the five Massachusetts men and the six Pennsylvanians who sat on the Supreme Court of the United States from the nation's founding to 1940. There was far more continuity of distinguished service on the Court among the Massachusetts justices; all save Benjamin Curtis, who resigned because of his fundamental disagreement with Chief Justice Taney's method of handling and conclusions in the *Dred Scott* case,* served for more than two decades. Holmes and Story served longer than any other two men in the Court's history; they were also, according to the length of their biographies in the *DAB*, among the 100 most distinguished men in American history; both were educators in the broadest sense and major architects of American law.

All five Massachusetts justices embodied upper-class Boston's dominance of the leadership of the state. Though only Horace Gray and Holmes were members of the Boston First Family sample, Benjamin Curtis was kin to George Ticknor, who helped support him at Harvard; moreover, both the Cushings and the Storys were as distinguished as many families in the Boston sample. None of the Philadelphia First Families sent any members to the Supreme Court though several were offered and declined the honor; only Justice Owen

---

*Dred Scott was represented by George Ticknor Curtis, Justice Curtis's brother.

Roberts was a native of Philadelphia and a graduate of the University of Pennsylvania, but Roberts was of achieved upper-class status and no kin to the Robertses of my sample. James Wilson was one of the more distinguished founders of the nation but, unlike Story and Holmes, who had deep roots in Massachusetts, he was both an auslander and a cut-flower,* as have been so many of the outstanding leaders of his adopted city and state; Wilson served only nine years on the Court before his tragic death in 1798. Of the other four justices, Henry Baldwin and William Strong were auslanders; Robert C. Grier and George Shiras came from the western part of the state. Finally, whereas all the Massachusetts justices were Harvard graduates, Wilson was educated in Scotland; Baldwin, Shiras, and Strong at Yale; and Grier at Dickinson.

William Cushing provides an excellent example of the continuity of class leadership and authority in Massachusetts. Both his father and his paternal grandfather served on the governor's council and on the Supreme Judicial Court of the royal province. His maternal grandfather, Josiah Cotton, was a member of the general court and the grandson of Cotton Mather. William himself graduated from Harvard and studied law under the famous provincial lawyer Jeremiah Gridley of Boston. He then moved to what is now Maine and was often associated with John Adams before the superior court at Falmouth. He next followed his father on the superior court of the province. In 1776, however, Cushing led his hometown of Scituate to come out in favor of independence. He took a leading role in forming the government of the new nation and state, as first chief justice of Massachusetts, as a member of the convention that framed the state constitution in 1779, as vice-president of the state convention that ratified the federal Constitution in 1788, and, finally, as the first associate justice appointed by Washington to the Supreme Court. When Cushing died without issue, he marked the end of a long line of Puritans with a passion for authority and leadership; he is reported to have been the last American judge to wear the full-bottomed English judicial wig. "He was a man," wrote a contemporary, "whose deportment surpassed all the ideas of personal dignity I had ever formed."

Benjamin R. Curtis also had the Puritan passion to lead the righteous side in the public questions of his day (even though he was born a Unitarian and eventually became an Episcopalian). As we have seen, Curtis resigned from the Court because he disapproved of Taney's presentation of Dred Scott's rights; he spent the rest of his active life at the bar, arguing fifty cases before the U.S. Supreme Court and eighty before the Supreme Judicial Court of Massachusetts. His last act of public service in the cause of right, as leading counsel for President Johnson in the impeachment trial of 1868,† set a precedent at the

---

*James Wilson's son, Bird Wilson, was included in the *DAB*. He was ordained an Episcopal clergyman but left Philadelphia for New York, where he became professor at and dean of the General Theological Seminary.

†Curtis's *DAB* biographer noted that "his speech opening the President's defense was his greatest forensic effort, displaying the dignity, coolness, and clarity which marked his style, and was admitted by his opponent Butler to have so thoroughly presented Johnson's case that nothing more was added throughout the trial" (*DAB*, Vol. IV, p. 635*a*).

Boston bar that was followed a century later when Joseph Welch defeated the forces of evil in the McCarthy affair of the 1950s.

Whereas the five Boston Brahmins represent an excellent example of class authority, the six Pennsylvanians on the Supreme Court exemplify democratic elitism; they had in common only their preeminence at the Pennsylvania bar in their respective generations and, excluding Owen Roberts, they shared a Calvinist background in a state founded by Quakers and, in Philadelphia, at least, dominated in its early years by Episcopalians. Robert Grier, whose father and grandfather were Presbyterian clergymen, embodied the Scotch-Irish traditions of leadership, both in his ancestry and in his attendance at Dickinson College in the Scotch-Irish capital of the state, Carlisle. But the two men of most interest to my thesis were William Strong and Henry Baldwin, both, like Franklin before them, auslander New Englanders.

William Strong belonged to the Strong clan which settled in Northampton, Massachusetts, in the seventeenth century and produced one of the great governors of that state. A Yale graduate, Strong taught school in various Connecticut towns before coming to Philadelphia, where he was admitted to the bar in 1832. Almost immediately he moved to Reading, Pennsylvania, where the principal language was German. Strong mastered the German language and rose to be one of the city's leading citizens, being elected first to Congress and later to the Pennsylvania Supreme Court for a fifteen-year term. He then came back to Philadelphia, where he built up a large practice before going to the U.S. Supreme Court. Next to James Wilson, Strong was probably the most distinguished representative on the Court from his adopted state. Strong was also for many years the most prominent layman of the Presbyterian church, president of the American Sunday School Union (1883–1895) and vice-president of the American Bible Society (1873–1895). His roots were certainly not deep in Pennsylvania and, after retiring from the Court, he taught law at Georgetown University, where he died.

Henry Baldwin, a native of New Haven and a graduate of Yale,* came to Philadelphia and studied law in the office of Alexander J. Dallas. Baldwin subsequently moved to Pittsburgh and became a leader of the bar, as well as a political force in the western part of the state. He was an avid student, slept little, read most of the night, and built one of the finest private libraries in the city. Although he was an ardent admirer of the Federalist John Marshall, he strongly supported Andrew Jackson in 1828 and was rewarded with an appointment to the Supreme Court in 1830, filling the seat left vacant at the death of Bush-

---

*Baldwin was the son of Michael Baldwin, a self-taught blacksmith of wide learning and great ambition who moved to New Haven because of his desire to obtain an education for his children. Henry was the child of his father's second wife (a Wolcott). Abraham Baldwin, Henry's older half brother, managed to graduate from Yale with high honors, after which he taught theology at his alma mater before going south to Georgia. In his adopted state, Abraham practiced at the bar, became the state's foremost citizen, and founded the University of Georgia; he also served as congressman, senator, and delegate to the Constitutional Convention. As father of the University of Georgia, he hired his Yale classmate Josiah Meigs as first president. Meigs was the father of Charles de Lucena Meigs, founder of one of Philadelphia's medical families. Abraham Baldwin, after his father's death, financed the education of his half siblings, including Henry Baldwin.

rod Washington. In the debate within the state for the Supreme Court nomination, Baldwin had the support of the bench and bar of western Pennsylvania, John Bannister Gibson of the Calhoun forces, and Horace Binney of the Philadelphia bar. Binney suggested why Baldwin won the seat: "My friend Baldwin got it, and I saw his letter to my friend Chauncey, in which he did me the honour to say that I deserved it, but that he *wanted* it more."[16]

Binney's remark also reveals why class authority has always been relatively strong in Massachusetts and relatively absent in Pennsylvania. The Quaker-Episcopal gentry of Philadelphia have really never wanted the responsibilities of power and authority, and if the members of a privileged class decline to serve their communities over a long enough period of time, eventually even those who want authority will be unable to obtain it because the political and legal community is accustomed to an upper class without leadership traditions. Binney was right in seeing that few gentlemen of integrity would want to expose themselves to the electorate in order to obtain and remain in judicial office; what he did not see was that where class authority is strong, as in Massachusetts, the people tend to trust their men in authority as signified by the Massachusetts principle of judicial appointment and tenure for life during good behavior. Class authority, then, is a two-way street: where members of a class assume authority over a long period of time, the people will assume their right to authority, too, and political and judicial mores will in turn reflect upper-class values and gentlemen will be appointed *and* elected to high office.*

THE MEDICAL PROFESSION IN PHILADELPHIA AND BOSTON

Because the law lies at the core of any authority system, I have gone into considerable detail in pointing out differences in upper-class influences on the legal profession in the two cities. In these differences are to be found the major reasons for the hegemony of upper-class authority in Boston and the relative lack of it in Philadelphia. Although the physician's role is far less relevant to class authority than that of the judge or the lawyer, the history of medical practice and education in the two cities is equally revealing of the differences in class leadership between Boston and Philadelphia.

---

*Gentlemen of authority inspired by the values of service and excellence are likely to recognize new men of ability outside their own ranks. Thus, it is no accident that two of the most distinguished Americans to sit on the Supreme Court of the United States, Louis Brandeis and Felix Frankfurter, both of them auslanders, outsiders, and Jews, made Boston and Cambridge their home for a major part of their careers. "For me," Brandeis once said, "the world's center was Cambridge" (*DAB*, Supp. III, p. 94a). Frankfurter spent a quarter of a century on the faculty of the Harvard Law School before succeeding to Brandeis's seat on the Supreme Court in 1939. Although both men felt at home in, and were welcomed by, intolerant Boston, they surely would have felt alienated, if not bored, in tolerant Philadelphia. There was never anyone in that city like Justice Holmes, the arrogant aristocrat who knew good men when he saw them, immediately took to both Brandeis and Frankfurter, and in turn was admired by them to the point of idolatry. And Horace Gray, a Brahmin authoritarian if there ever was one, found his law clerk Brandeis to be "the most ingenious and most original lawyer I ever met" (*DAB*, Supp. III, p. 94a).

Both Philadelphia and Boston have long traditions of leadership in the American medical profession. Whereas, as we have seen, there is really no comparison between the Harvard and Penn law schools in their impact on the development of American law and legal education, the medical schools of the two universities have been equally important in the history of medicine, if eventually in different ways. The nation's first medical school, first hospital, and first mental institution were founded in Philadelphia; from the outset, the Philadelphia area has been the center of the chemical and drug industries in America; the first American school of pharmacy, the Philadelphia College of Pharmacy, was established in 1821 and supported through the years by Philadelphia's patent medicine millionaires. As late as 1847, when the American Medical Association was founded in Philadelphia to bring order out of the chaos of standards then regulating the profession, all the officers either were practicing in the city or were graduates of the Penn Medical School; eight of the first ten presidents of the AMA trained at Penn. Yet Harvard ultimately forged ahead of Penn, at least in research and intellectual distinction, especially after Abraham Flexner's *Medical Education in the United States and Canada* was published in 1910.

The practice of medicine in America has been an ideal means of social mobility, first into the higher socioeconomic brackets and finally into Society; patients of fashionable physicians have always been available to open the right doors. But the science of medicine has not necessarily been advanced by those with either the best bedside manners or the best social connections; rather, it has been advanced by doctors who have spent their days and years in the halls of the great city hospitals and in the laboratories and classrooms of the great medical schools. The hospitals and medical schools of Philadelphia and Boston have made both cities centers of medical progress since the nation's founding. The Pennsylvania Hospital, founded by Philadelphia Quakers in 1751, was the first in America; the first medical school was founded by Presbyterians and Episcopalians at the College of Philadelphia in 1765. In Boston, the Harvard Medical School was founded in 1782, and the Massachusetts General Hospital, planned in 1811, opened its doors in 1821 (before completing his design for the hospital, Bulfinch went to Philadelphia to have a look at the Pennsylvania Hospital). Down through the years, upper-class families in both cities have provided the major financial support, as well as the staff leadership, in these four medical institutions.

Medical Families and Medical Schools. Patrician physicians from Boston and Philadelphia have played prominent roles in the development of American medicine. Although Boston Brahmins and Philadelphia Gentlemen have been more likely to be trained in the law than in medicine (see Table A-25), each city has produced its share of fashionable and famous medical families: twenty-eight physicians from sixteen of the Boston families and twenty-three physicians from fourteen of the Philadelphia families (see Table A-28). Whereas the medical traditions of Quaker Philadelphia are older and more distinguished than those of Puritan Boston, the Warren and Shattuck families of Boston have had a far longer history of continued medical leadership than either the Rushes or the Peppers, Philadelphia's most renowned medical families. A look at the history of the medical profession in the two cities will emphasize and contrast the leadership roles of Boston and Philadelphia First Family physicians.

Philadelphia physicians, largely because of the transatlantic Quaker network, were far more likely to be trained at Edinburgh or London in the eighteenth century. And the medical school at the College of Philadelphia was founded by John Morgan, along with William Shippen, Benjamin Rush, and Adam Kuhn, all educated abroad. Likewise, Benjamin Smith Barton, Caspar Wistar, and John Redman Coxe, all professors in the early years of the medical school, were trained abroad.

None of these early leaders in Philadelphia medicine produced descendants of distinction in this field. John Morgan had no heirs, and although Rush, Shippen, Kuhn, Barton, Wistar, and Coxe left families of social prominence (and wealth) in the city, no one in this group was important in medicine, even though some were prominent local physicians down into the twentieth century. Adam Kuhn, Caspar Wistar, William Shippen, and John Redman Coxe had no medical heirs included in the *DAB*, and even the Bartons and Rushes included in the *DAB* were hardly distinguished physicians: James Rush and John Rhea Barton, for instance, married sisters who were daughters of the city's most prominent Quaker merchant, Jacob Ridgway. James Rush spent most of his adult years as an eccentric recluse and surely would not have been included in the *DAB* except for his distinguished ancestry and extreme wealth; John Rhea Barton—who published just two medical papers before retiring at the age of forty-six, over thirty years before his death—is remembered in the history of Philadelphia medicine chiefly because of the John Rhea Barton Chair in Surgery, endowed by his wealthy widow.*

This is no place to go into the technical details of the theory and practice of medicine in Boston and Philadelphia. A few details, however, are crucial to my thesis. To begin with, Benjamin Rush, a great systematizer and grand theorist in the style of Karl Marx in economics, was undoubtedly the most famous American physician of his time. Following the ideas of his great teacher at Edinburgh, William Cullen, he saw all diseases as caused by tension and spasms in the extreme arteries and prescribed the single remedy of bloodletting to relieve the tension. Rush, like so many other leaders in the early development of a science, was intellectually blinded as a result of carrying one theory to its logical extreme. He was so impressed by his own theory, in fact, that he once claimed that "the doctrine of one disease had done for medicine what a belief in one God had achieved in religion."[17] At any rate, Philadelphia medicine, under the shadow of Rush and Edinburgh, led the nation well into the nineteenth century. But grand theory, as Robert K. Merton has pointed out about the history of

---

*If the Barton Chair is important in the history of the Penn Medical School, it is interesting (and a reminder of the Widener Library syndrome in Philadelphia) that the Hamilton Kuhn professorship of biological chemistry at Harvard was endowed in 1909 in honor of a wealthy and socially prominent Philadlphia descendant of Adam Kuhn.

sociology, was eventually replaced by more modest theories of the middle range based on careful clinical observation and statistical controls. The leaders of the Harvard Medical School, who had not had the benefit of Edinburgh training, as had their Philadelphia peers, were more receptive to the Parisian tradition of medical empiricism advocated by Pierre Louis (1787–1872), the founder of medical statistics.

When the Harvard Medical School opened in Cambridge, John Warren and Benjamin Waterhouse were its first two professors. John Warren was not only the major founder of the Harvard Medical School but also the founder of Boston's First Family in medicine. Waterhouse, thanks to his Quaker uncle in London, was trained in Edinburgh, London, and Leiden and lectured in the didactic tradition of Benjamin Rush. He was forced out of the medical school when he opposed its move from Cambridge to Boston, a move sponsored by Warren, his son John Collins Warren, and James Jackson, who wanted to leave Cambridge in order to benefit from clinical observations of the large number of cases in Boston's hospitals. John Collins Warren, trained in Paris, succeeded his father as professor of anatomy and surgery, a post he held until 1847, when he was succeeded by Oliver Wendell Holmes, also trained in Paris. James Jackson, who succeeded Benjamin Waterhouse as professor at the medical school, was the major founder of the Massachusetts General Hospital. He was also the founder of medical dynasties: Jacksons of a collateral line are still practicing medicine in Boston today; James Jackson's daughters, moreover, were mothers of two prominent medical families. Elizabeth Cabot Jackson married Dr. Charles G. Putnam and was the mother of Charles Pickering Putnam, president of the American Pediatric Society (1898) and a reformer and beloved Boston civic leader, and James Jackson Putnam, a famous neurologist, trained in Leipzig, Vienna, and London, who was instrumental in bringing Freud's ideas to America; another of Jackson's daughters, Harriet, married George Richards Minot and produced a Brahmin medical family of the first rank;* their son, James Jackson Minot, was a prominent Boston physician, and his son, George Richards Minot (1885–1950), was a leading professor at the Harvard Medical School in its greatest days and a winner of the Nobel Prize.

James Jackson Putnam worked closely with Henry Pickering Bowditch, grandson of Nathaniel Bowditch and great-grandson of Timothy Pickering, who was a veritable giant in the history of American medicine. Trained at Harvard and at Paris under Claude Bernard, Bowditch studied in Leipzig under Carl Ludwig, the greatest teacher of physiologists who ever lived. He returned to the Harvard Medical School, where he opened the first physiological laboratory in the United States, training among others George Richards Minot, James Jackson Putnam, William James, G. Stanley Hall, and John W. Warren. He was also a pioneer in anthropometry and a founder of the American Physiological Association. As dean of the Harvard Medical School in a critical period (1883–1893), Putnam introduced the four-year curriculum.

---

*The Minots were not included in the Boston First Families sample, but easily might have been.

From its founding and throughout the nineteenth century, then, the Harvard Medical School was led by members of the Warren, Jackson, Bowditch, and Putnam families, the first generation being apprenticed to local physicians and the second going abroad after Harvard for the best training available in their day. To this distinguished group must be added the Shattuck and Bigelow families, whose members were educated in Philadelphia in the first generation and in Paris in the second.

George Cheyne Shattuck was the son of Benjamin Shattuck, who was of the fifth generation of the family in America, a graduate of Harvard College, and one of the most respected physicians in Massachusetts. After graduating from Dartmouth and studying briefly at Harvard, George Shattuck went to Philadelphia, where he took a degree at the Penn Medical School in 1807. His letters home are a revealing record of the Yankee mind; devoted to his calling, he avoided the charming social life of Philadelphia and spent most of his little leisure time attending local churches (and a synagogue). He returned to Boston, where he married an extemely wealthy heiress and built up one of the largest fashionable practices in the city. Shattuck was also president of the Massachusetts Medical Society and the American Statistical Association; his gifts to Harvard included the Shattuck professorship of pathological anatomy in the medical school. Of his six children, all died in infancy except his son and namesake.

A graduate of Harvard College and Medical School, George Cheyne Shattuck II went to Paris, where he fell under the spell of Pierre Louis. After his return, he, along with James Jackson and Oliver Wendell Holmes, founded the Boston Society of Medical Observation. Shattuck followed Jacob Bigelow as professor of clinical medicine at Harvard and acted as dean for a brief period. A leading layman in the Episcopal church, he served on the board of the Episcopal Theological Seminary and founded the Church of the Advent in Boston and St. Paul's School on the family estate in Concord, New Hampshire. Two of his sons became physicians. One, Frederick Cheever Shattuck, was James Jackson Professor of Clinical Medicine at Harvard. (His son, George Cheever Shattuck, the fifth in a direct line of Shattuck physicians, was a professor at the Harvard Medical School in the great days of John Edsall.)

The first effective attack on Benjamin Rush's grand theory of medicine was voiced by Jacob Bigelow in his paper "On Self-limited Disease" read at Boston in 1835. Years later, in a lecture before the American Academy of Arts and Sciences in 1879, Oliver Wendell Holmes said that Bigelow's paper "exerted more influence upon medical practice in America than any work that had been published in this country."[18]

Jacob Bigelow, the son of a poor country parson in Waltham, Massachusetts, possessed the traditional Puritan passion to excel in his chosen calling. After graduation from Harvard College at the age of sixteen, he and his friend and classmate Walter Channing (brother of the Unitarian divine William Ellery Channing) followed George Shattuck to Philadelphia, where they took their degrees in medicine at Penn in 1810. If Harvard was not the center of medical education in his day, Bigelow, his local pride notwithstanding, was determined to go to the source of excellence: "It was exceptional to the lead which

Massachusetts has generally taken in the interest of academic and professional opportunities that any of its youth should have needed to go to another state of the Union for medical instruction which he could not find here."[19] Bigelow was far less impressed with the grand theories and charismatic and didactic teaching of Benjamin Rush than he was with the more pedestrian teaching of Benjamin Smith Barton, the famous botanist and professor of materia medica. Bigelow returned to Boston and Harvard, where he followed James Jackson as professor materia medica, a post he held until his retirement in 1855. He was the founder of a dynasty of physicians who are still practicing in Boston today. Bigelow's son, Henry Jacob Bigelow, trained by Pierre Louis in Paris after Harvard, was the dominant figure in New England surgery for some forty years and was said to be the equal of Dr. Samuel Gross of Philadelphia.

Samuel David Gross (1805–1884) was the most distinguished American surgeon of his time. As we have seen, his portrait by Eakins is a fine example of nineteenth-century realism in art, as well as the best known medical painting in America; he is also the only American physician to have had a statue erected in his honor in the nation's capital. Gross was, however, neither a Proper Philadelphian nor a professor at the Penn Medical School.

Gross was born on a farm near Easton, in the heart of the Pennsylvania Dutch country, where his great-grandparents had come as refugees from the German Palatine. An obsessive and largely self-taught botanist from childhood, Gross came to Philadelphia, where he took his medical degree from the Jefferson Medical College in 1828. After working closely with Dr. George Mc-Clellan, founder of Jefferson, he held professorships in medical schools in Cincinnati, Louisville, and New York City before returning to Jefferson as professor of surgery in 1856. Gross remained at Jefferson for the rest of his life, his teaching and scientific writings bringing him world renown. He wrote many important scientific articles and invented several surgical instruments; his first great book, *Elements of Pathological Anatomy*, after several rejections, was published in Boston in 1839; twenty years later, he published a two-volume textbook, *A System of Surgery: Pathological, Diagnostic, Therapeutic, and Operative*, considered the greatest surgical treatise of his time and one of the greatest ever written. Gross received honorary degrees from Edinburgh, Oxford, and Cambridge but valued most the doctor of laws awarded him by the University of Pennsylvania on his deathbed. Gross was far more than simply a famous surgeon: his autobiography, charmingly philosophical and written in a beautifully cultivated style, is the most distinguished ever written by a Philadelphian (except, of course, that of Benjamin Franklin).

That Gross, the preeminent American physician of his era, never taught at Penn is a good example of the antinomian and sectarian spirit of Philadelphia medicine, which has always been in such striking contrast to the upper-class hegemony over medical practice and education in Boston, centered throughout the years at Harvard. In this connection, a word should be said of two other leaders of Philadelphia medicine in the nineteenth century, George McClellan (1796–1847) and Nathaniel Chapman (1780–1853), auslanders from Connecticut and Virginia.

Dr. Nathaniel Chapman, a native Virginian of Scottish ancestry, came to Philadelphia to study privately under Benjamin Rush. He graduated with honors from the Penn Medical School in 1801 and then trained in Edinburgh, where he was a social lion. Back in Philadelphia, Chapman married the daughter of Colonel Clement Biddle and built up one of the largest and most fashionable practices in the city. He was, however, scientifically eminent as well as socially prominent; he served the Penn Medical School as professor of materia medica and then as professor of the theory and practice of medicine; he was elected the first president of the American Medical Association and was also president of the American Philosophical Society. Finally, and symbolic of the class differences betweeen Philadelphia and Boston, whereas the Brahmin John Collins Warren founded the *New England Journal of Medicine* in 1812, the most distinguished medical journal in America today, it was the charming auslander from Virginia, Nathaniel Chapman, who founded (1820) and edited the *Journal of Medical and Physical Sciences*, which is published today as the *American Journal of Medical Sciences*. Chapman, as befitted a Virginia gentleman, was quickly assimilated into Philadelphia Society; both his son and his grandson (also a physician) married well and were Proper Philadelphia Club Philadelphians.

A contentious Connecticut Yankee rather than a Virginia gentleman, George McClellan, a Yale College graduate, took his medical degree at Penn in 1819. His stormy medical career included the founding of Jefferson Medical School, which graduated its first doctor in 1826. Though not a Philadelphia First Family, the McClellans were surely an American first family of considerable accomplishments: George McClellan's son, George Brinton McClellan, graduated second in his class at West Point and went on to become Lincoln's choice to head the Union Army, Democratic opponent of Lincoln in the presidential campaign of 1864, and governor of New Jersey; his son, Dr. George McClellan, was professor of anatomy at the Pennsylvania Academy of the Fine Arts in the days of Eakins.*

The Jefferson Medical School (now part of Thomas Jefferson University) has always held a position of second rank behind Penn in Philadelphia. The leaders at Penn did their best to oppose its formation in the beginning and to do away with or absorb the school later on. But it has remained and has had some great men on its staff including, in addition to Samuel Gross, two auslander founders of Philadelphia First Families, Charles de Lucena Meigs and John Kearsley Mitchell.

The Meigses were a prominent American family with deep roots in Connecticut and Yale. Charles de Lucena Meigs, whose father was president of the Uni-

---

*The McClellans were a fighting clan in the tradition of their Scottish ancestors. Dr. George McClellan's grandfather rose to become a Brigadier-General in the Revolution. General George Brinton McClellan's younger brother, Arthur, was one of his aides-de-camp; his first cousin, Henry Brainard McClellan, was chief of staff to the Confederate generals Stuart and Hampton, and wrote a biography of Stuart. George Brinton McClellan (1865-1940), son of Lincoln's General, served as a Lieutenant-Colonel in the U.S. Army in the First World War and was a successful publicist and author.

versity of Georgia, came to Philadelphia, graduated in medicine from Penn, and spent most of his medical career as a professor of obstetrics and diseases of women at Jefferson. John Forsyth Meigs, his son, married the daughter of Charles Jared Ingersoll and became a Proper Philadelphia physician, as did Arthur Vincent Meigs, Charles's grandson. Though both men were resident physicians at the prestigious Pennsylvania Hospital, neither served on the staff of the Penn Medical School.

John Kearsley Mitchell, the son of a Scottish physician who settled in Virginia in the eighteenth century, went to Scotland after his father's early death and took his undergraduate degree at Edinburgh. Returning to Virginia, he studied medicine there before coming to Philadelphia to study with Nathaniel Chapman at Penn, where he received his medical degree in 1819. Mitchell ended his career as professor of the theory and practice of medicine at Jefferson. He was a prolific writer of poetry and literature as well as a medical author. His son, Weir Mitchell, as we have seen, was Philadelphia's First citizen in the later years of his long life. Weir Mitchell's son John Kearsley was the last of the line to practice medicine, though his descendants have been wealthy (through marriage) and fashionable Proper Philadelphians.

Samuel Gross, George McClellan, and Nathaniel Chapman, surely three of the most important figures in the history of Philadelphia medicine in the years between Benjamin Rush and the second William Pepper, were excellent examples of the Proper Philadelphia syndrome that so often allows auslanders and outsiders to lead those more to the manor born. This was not true, however, of the Proper Philadelphia Peppers, at least in medicine.

The Peppers were Proper Philadelphia's only real medical dynasty; they virtually ran the Penn Medical School between the Civil War and World War II. William Pepper I taught the theory and practice of medicine at Penn from 1860 until his death in 1864. William Pepper II was in many ways the greatest provost of the University of Pennsylvania since William Smith, its founder. In 1862, he entered the Penn Medical School, which then consisted of his father, Joseph Leidy, and Richard A. F. Penrose (father of Boies), and took his degree in 1864. After his appointment to the faculty in 1868, Pepper went abroad to study methods in medical education and institutional administration, incidentally laying the foundations of a distinguished career in education. At Penn, he was an energetic committee member, prodding conservative and wealthy Philadelphians, as well as members of the state legislature, to support the university. His efforts resulted in the opening of the first hospital in America intimately associated with a medical school, the University Hospital. Pepper continued in a leadership position at the medical school even after becoming provost in 1880. In medicine he published several hundred papers, founded and endowed the William Pepper Laboratory of Clinical Medicine, and established or presided over a number of medical societies; his best known book, *A Practical Treatise on the Diseases of Children*, went through many editions (the fourth in collaboration with John Forsyth Meigs). In many ways Pepper was an innovator in both medical and general education in the style of Charles W. Eliot of Harvard. Unfortunately, after his retirement and early death in 1898, the Penn Medical School experienced a long period of reaction that coincided with Harvard's golden age in medical education.

Many historians date the advent of modern medical education to the founding of the medical school at Johns Hopkins in 1893, under the leadership of Dean William Henry Welch, a native of Connecticut and graduate of Yale. Welch was one of the great men of modern American medicine, both a founder of Johns Hopkins and first chairman of the board of scientific directors at the Rockefeller Institute of Medical Research, a post he held until his death in 1934. Welch and the Rockefeller Institute were very important influences on the differential development of the medical schools at Harvard and Penn in the twentieth century.

Charles W. Eliot, who listed the medical school as a first priority in his plans to reform postgraduate education at Harvard, laid the foundations for the school's becoming the foremost in the nation, if not in the world, during the administration of A. Lawrence Lowell. The new medical school building, designed by Charles A. Coolidge, opened in 1906; the Peter Bent Brigham Hospital, closely affiliated with the school, in 1912. Funds for these projects were obtained primarily from the Morgans, Huntingtons, and Rockefellers, largely through the efforts of the second John Collins Warren, great-grandson of the school's founder, and Henry Pickering Bowditch.

Penn lost its position of medical leadership partly because three members of the faculty left in this critical period of the birth of modern medicine: first, Welch brought the great Sir William Osler from Penn to Johns Hopkins; second, and perhaps more decisive, Simon Flexner (a protégé of Welch) left Penn in 1903 and went on to become the driving force at the Rockefeller Institute for many years; and David Edsall, who left in 1910, went on to build the modern Harvard Medical School. While Hopkins and Harvard (supported by the Rockefeller interests) took the lead in the modern emphasis on original research and pure science, in the style of Pierre Louis of Paris, the Penn Medical School continued its traditional emphasis on teaching rather than on advancing knowledge. Flexner and Edsall left Penn both because of their intellectual commitment to pure science and because of the growing nepotism at the Penn Medical School in the Pepper era.*

Simon Flexner was born into a Jewish merchant family in Louisville, Kentucky. He and his brothers were eminent in American intellectual life in the twentieth century. His brother Abraham, author of the Flexner Report on medical education for the Carnegie Corporation, was the first director of the Institute for Advanced Study at Princeton. Another brother was a lawyer and

---

*The year Flexner left, Charles Harrison Frazier, nephew of Provost Harrison, became dean of the medical school; Allen J. Smith, brother of Edgar Fahs Smith, who succeeded Harrison as provost, filled Flexner's post on the faculty. After Edsall left, Alfred Stengel succeeded him in the chair of medicine and later became the first vice-president of medical affairs at the university. At the same time, William Pepper III, Stengel's father-in-law, became dean of the medical school, a post he held for thirty-three years until his retirement in 1945. His brother, Oliver Hazard Perry Pepper, was also a professor of medicine at Penn.

leading Zionist. Through marriage to the sister of M. Carey Thomas, president of Bryn Mawr, Simon Flexner became part of the broader intellectual world of his time. After earning a degree from a local college of pharmacy in Louisville, he went to Baltimore, where as Welch's assistant at Hopkins he was duly infected with the zeal for research. Flexner published some 200 papers between 1890 and 1909 and was the sole editor of the *Journal of Experimental Medicine* (founded by Welch) from 1904 to 1923. He came to Penn in 1899 and left in 1903, largely because of the anti-intellectual and nepotistic atmosphere there: in a letter to Welch at the time of his decision to leave Penn he wrote that "there is a small group of men to whom I have not been welcome—those men you know—and their attitude is about the same as it was when I first came. . . . What is, however, important with reference to the future is . . . to what extent I will participate in the research movement."[20]

A Princeton graduate, David Linn Edsall (1869–1945) took his medical degree at Penn, where he attracted the notice of William Pepper, who took him into the Pepper Laboratory. Edsall was an extremely popular professor and had attained a national reputation by 1897. He gradually rose to become the top professor at the medical school, being awarded the chair in medicine in 1910; however, he found little sympathy for his interest in research and left Penn that very year. One of the immediate causes of his leaving was the fact that Alfred Stengel, director of the Pepper Laboratory, refused to give Edsall adequate space for research.

The situation at the Penn Medical School when Edsall left was described by the school's historian, George W. Corner.

> The University's medical teachers had always been superb clinicians—masters of diagnosis and treatment and polished expositors. Their aim was perfection in practice and teaching rather than advancement of knowledge through experimental science. Now, however, the advance of bacteriology, biochemistry and experimental pathology was bringing into their field young men with new aims. The enthusiasm for research shown by these newcomers (of whom David Edsall was the leader, in Philadelphia) their laboratory work, their diagnostic tests, their burgeoning publications, gave to men trained only in the older arts of medicine a disquieting sense that their own experience and methods might be judged inadequate for the new era in medical teaching.[21]

Both Harvard and the University of Pennsylvania, as we have seen, were led by an inbred group. But the Boston Brahmins, especially leaders like Charles W. Eliot and A. Lawrence Lowell, had great respect for intellectual excellence and were determined to keep Harvard at the head of all intellectual developments; and they knew and respected new men of eminence when they saw them. Thus, Edsall was hired as Jackson Professor of Clinical Medicine when Frederick Cheever Shattuck retired from the position in 1912.

Edsall moved to Harvard for a variety of reasons in addition to the better opportunities for research there. For one, his wife, a graduate of Radcliffe, whom he married when she was a young teacher at a Philadelphia private school, came of a solid Boston family. But mainly he admired the loyalty and team spirit at Harvard, a spirit he had not found at Penn, where in-fighting was the rule: "There is no other institution in America," Edsall once wrote, "where social conditions and traditions arouse so general and warm a spirit of universal loyalty as that which exists at Harvard." "I do not like the general spirit of this community," he wrote of Philadelphia, "and whatever I might be able to do here myself I should feel that my boys would be better off growing up in the midst of a finer spirit toward public things."[22] (His son, John Edsall, was on the faculty of the Harvard Medical School in its great days under Edsall.)

The loyal spirit at Harvard was illustrated in the case of Professor Richard C. Cabot, who had long expected to be appointed Jackson Professor when Shattuck retired. "Yes, I have always expected to succeed Shattuck, my whole life has been planned with that in view," Cabot told Dr. Edwin A. Lock when he learned of the plan to bring Edsall to Harvard. "I have done all the post-graduate teaching with this aim," Cabot continued. "That however is of no importance whatsoever. Edsall is a better man than I am and if you can tell me that there is any chance of getting him here to Boston I will do anything and everything in my power to help get him and if he comes I shall be only too happy to serve under him."[23] Richard Cabot was a bit of a saint whose career reached far beyond medicine: he taught at both the medical school and Harvard College, where he was appointed to the chair of social ethics in 1920; he pioneered the development of social work in America and was president of the National Conference of Social Work in 1931; and, along with his colleague Lawrence J. Henderson, he played an important role in the department of social relations, which was then taking the lead in the development of American sociology. Richard Cabot's younger brother, Hugh Cabot, was also a medical reformer of wide influence, especially in the Middle West, where he taught in Michigan and Minnesota.*

David Edsall became dean of the Harvard Medical School in 1918. Several years later, through Rockefeller funds, he founded and became dean of a separate school of public health. At both schools he build up large endowments and brilliant faculties. Always close to the Rockefeller medical people, he became a trustee of the Rockefeller Foundation in 1927. The ultimate measure of Edsall's success is the great faculty he brought to Harvard, which in 1933–1934 included Walter Cannon, Lawrence J. Henderson, John Edsall, Cecil Drinker (brother of Philadelphia's Catherine Drinker Bowen), Hans Zinsser, John F. Enders (Nobel Prize winner and the most distinguished graduate of St. Paul's School in his generation), and George Richards Minot (Nobel Prize winner), as well as George C. Shattuck, Tracy J. Putnam, John Warren, and Francis Peabody (all from families in the Boston sample).

Whereas Penn remained a school that transmitted received wisdom from the past, Harvard became the center of science and intellectual curiosity. Philadelphia produced more physicians and practitioners; Harvard, more deans and professors of medical schools and more specialists in advancing knowledge. The

---

*The brothers belonged to the second generation of Cabots in medical education; Arthur Tracy Cabot taught in the medical school at Harvard in the 1880s and 1890s.

quantitative evidence is revealing: in a study by the editors of the *Dictionary of American Medical Biography* in 1928, of 1,957 eminent physicians from colonial times to 1927, the Penn Medical School took the lead with 381 graduates; Harvard had 188; the New York College of Physicians and Surgeons, 171; and Jefferson Medical College, 129; none of the 315 other medical schools in the nation produced as many as 100 physicians each. Philadelphia has surely spawned more physicians of eminence than any other city in the nation by far.[24] Another study of the distribution of medical alumni in 1950 is revealing of the different values in Boston and Philadelphia.[25] As of that year, for instance, Jefferson had the largest number of living graduates (5,742), Penn was second (5,642), and Harvard was fourth (4,987). The distribution of the graduates of these three schools in the various branches of the profession was as follows:

	General Practice %	Part-time Specialty %	Full-time Specialty %	Full-time Medical Faculty %
Jefferson	33.7	13.0	31.3	0.6
Pennsylvania	26.0	11.0	38.7	1.6
Harvard	18.1	7.3	44.6	2.9

As these figures suggest, quantitative leadership was characteristic of democratic Philadelphia; qualitative leadership, of Boston.

THE CHURCH IN BOSTON
AND PHILADELPHIA

Contrary to the old saw about prostitution, the priesthood is certainly the oldest of the professions from which all others have come: that Abiel Holmes was a Puritan divine, his son, Oliver Wendell, a physician, and his grandson, Wendell, a judge was very much in accord with the natural course of history. In the long run, it was the early institutionalization of clerical authority in Massachusetts and the lack of it in Pennsylvania that distinguished the leadership styles of Boston and Philadelphia in our secular age. Though pious Puritanism died out in Boston, as did Quakerism as a major force in Philadelphia, both cast their shadows on the values of the upper classes in the two cities. Just as the Puritan ministers, with tenure for life, exercised total community authority in the towns of early Massachusetts, so the members of the fifty families in my Boston sample, whether trained in law, medicine, or the church, were driven by the Calvinist concept of stewardship and the secular ideal of noblesse oblige to assume positions of leadership and authority in their local communities as well as in their state and nation. And just as the Phildelphia Quakers traditionally guarded their personal and in-group integrity and let the total community go its own way, so Proper Philadelphians have tended carefully to maintain their class position intact while feeling very little need to exercise authority in Philadelphia, Pennsylvania, or the nation.

As might be expected, more than three times as many members of the Boston sample as of the Philadelphia group were trained in the ministry (Table A-25; see also Table A-29). Ten of the Boston First Families could be classified as clerical families, but there was only one such family in Philadelphia. At least fourteen of the Boston families, moreover, had *family founders* who were ministers: Mather, Higginson, Lowell, Norton, Forbes, Emerson, Longfellow, Ware, Frothingham, Everett, Phillips, Brooks, Holmes, and Palfrey. Although the Lowells, for example, were primarily a legal and literary family, the first Judge John's father, the Reverend John Lowell (1704-1767) of Newbury, was the first of the line to graduate from Harvard and the real family founder; when he added the motto *Occasionem cognosce* to the Lowell arms he set the tone not only of his own family's values but also of those of a whole class of Boston Brahmins. In contrast, only Richard Peters, William White, and the Unitarian William Henry Furness (of Boston)* were founders of First Families in Philadelphia. Finally, although almost all of Boston's fifty families had a clergyman ancestor (even the secular Adamses had the "Bishop of Bloody Point"), there were fewer than a dozen clergymen among Philadelphia's fifty families.†

Class authority is a communal and cooperative phenomenon. In the discussion of medicine, for instance, it was readily apparent that whereas class leadership characterized medicine in Boston and at Harvard, medical leadership in Philadelphia was far more individualistic and competitive. As my theory of leadership argues, these contrasting values had their historical roots not only in Boston's clerical tradition and Philadelphia's lack thereof but also in the very different ways in which Boston Brahmins and Proper Philadelphians gave up their original Puritanism and Quakerism. Thus, Bostonians moved from Trinitarian to Unitarian Congregationalism in a communal and congregational way, while Philadelphians deserted the Quaker faith of their fathers on an individualistic basis.

The mark of change in the Boston religion came when the first Henry Ware (1744-1845) was elected Hollis Professor of Divinity at Harvard in 1805. Ware was the liberal candidate and his victory in a heated contest set the stamp of Unitarianism on Harvard (twice when the college was without a president, 1810 and 1828, he served as its chief executive officer). Ware's contemporary, the Reverend Abiel Holmes, became a victim of the same Trinitarian-Unitarian controversy when he was ousted from his pulpit at the First Church in Cam-

---

*Needless to say, cerebral Unitarianism never really appealed to the Proper Philadelphia mind, although, as we have seen, Henry Charles Lea, the city's leading scholar and political reformer in his day, was one of Dr. Furness's parishioners. It is, moreover, perhaps natural that Senator Joseph Clark, reforming mayor of the city in the 1950s and undoubtedly the most distinguished Philadelphian alive today, has retained his ancestral affiliations with Unitarianism. Both the Clark (originally from New England) and the Sill family were among Dr. Furness's parishioners. And Unitarian Joe Clark of Chestnut Hill is a very different breed from his Episcopalian and Main Line cousins who have made no great name for themselves (except as Rockefeller wives).

†Two of America's greatest preacher-poets in the secular twentieth century, Thomas Stearns Eliot and Robert T. S. Lowell, were grandsons of Brahmins trained at the Harvard Divinity School. As T. S. Eliot once put it: "We know too much, and are convinced of too little. Our literature is a substitute for religion, and so is our religion."

bridge in 1829, after thirty-seven years of serving his parishioners. But the true saint of the new Boston religion was William Ellery Channing. A son of anti-nomian Rhode Island, Channing came to Harvard, graduated in 1798, and was ordained and installed as minister of the Federal Street Church in Boston in 1803, where he remained the rest of his life. His sermon at the ordination of Jared Sparks in Baltimore in 1819, like Ware's winning of the Hollis professor-ship, was a landmark in the history of Boston Unitarianism. Channing re-placed the Calvinist view of man's depravity with a new sense of his dignity, and he continued to preach from a position precisely opposite to that of ortho-dox Calvinism, basing his texts on the goodness of God, the perfectibility of man, and the freedom of the will, with its consequent responsibility for action. He founded the Unitarian Association in 1825; the Massachusetts Peace Socie-ty was organized in his study; and his sermon on war, delivered in 1838, was al-most Tolstoyan in its anti-militarism. By the time of Channing's death in 1842, optimistic and rational Unitarianism was the orthodox religion of Proper Bos-ton. The movement from intolerant Calvinism to tolerant Unitarianism also witnessed the disestablishment of religion in Massachusetts in 1833.

In striking contrast to communal Boston, where whole congregations changed from Trinitarian to Unitarian Congregationalism in the course of the first three decades of the nineteenth century, Proper Philadelphians, from the days of William Penn's children onward, moved to the Anglican and then the Episcopal communion on an individual basis—when their Quaker birthright became an impediment to their desire to take the lead in community affairs, when they felt the need to fight for their country, when they married out of meeting, or when they wanted to make a more open display of their wealth by leading a more fashionable style of life. Attendance at the Assembly balls usual-ly marked the entrance of an ancient Quaker family into Society.

Fashionable society in Philadelphia was predominantly Anglican at the time of the Revolution, when the ranks of the church were swelled by ex-Quaker families whose members felt the need to take up arms. At the same time as the Constitution was being written, the Episcopal church in the United States of America was founded at Christ Church. The diocese of Pennsylvania was formed in 1787 with the Reverend William White as its first bishop, a position he held until his death in 1836 at the age of eighty-nine.*

Though Philadelphia has always been a wealthy center of American Episco-palianism, no Proper Philadelphian since White has served as bishop of the dio-cese of Pennsylvania. In fact, the only other Proper Philadelphian to become a bishop was William Hobart Hare (son of the Reverend George Emlen Hare and grandson of Bishop John Henry Hobart of New York), who spent his tenure ministering (in the Quaker style) to the Sioux Indians of South Dakota. In their churches as elsewhere, then, fashionable Philadelphians have been content to follow the lead of auslanders. Thus, seven of the twelve bishops of the local diocese have been New Englanders. The greatest leader of the local church after

---

*White was a giant of a leader in Philadelphia. Born in the city and graduated from the College of Philadelphia, he was the first of his family to be born in the colonies and had no Quaker ancestors.

William White, for example, was the Right Reverend Alonzo Potter, bishop between 1845 and his death in 1865. Potter was a community leader in the style of William White: he revived the Protestant Episcopal Academy, founded the Episcopal Hospital and the Philadelphia Divinity School, and was a prominent trustee of the University of Pennsylvania (where he declined the provostship).*

Not only were Philadelphia's bishops primarily auslanders, but so were most of the city's more fashionable preachers. The greatest of them all was the Reverend Phillips Brooks of Holy Trinity on Rittenhouse Square.† Brooks was preceded at Holy Trinity by another popular preacher, Alexander Hamilton Vinton, who came to Philadelphia from St. Paul's Church in Boston, where he had made a strong impression on his young parishioner Phillips Brooks. Both Vinton and Brooks went back to their native New England as rectors of Emmanuel and Trinity churches in Boston.

Anglicanism in Massachusetts was discredited in the revolutionary period, when so many of Dr. Caner's congregation joined the Tory exodus. Actually, Dr. Caner's King's Chapel, the seat of colonial Anglicanism, became the first Unitarian church in Boston. It changed in a communal way when James Freeman, its leader, was denied Episcopal ordination; he quietly and informally renamed the ancient church Stone Chapel and became the first Unitarian minister in America.

In many ways, Emerson's 1838 address at the Harvard Divinity School introduced *individualism* to the Boston theological mind. And the gradual movement of many Brahmin families back to the Trinitarian and ritualistic religion of the Episcopal communion occurred on a far more individualistic basis than the earlier move to Unitarian Congregationalism. The religious history of the Lawrence family is instructive here. When the three Lawrence brothers, Amos, Abbott, and William, founded the family fortune in textiles, they left the Puritan faith of their ancestors and became Unitarians; then Amos Adams Lawrence, Amos's son, was confirmed at Dr. Vinton's St. Paul's Church in Boston in 1842 and founded a Boston Episcopalian dynasty. Amos Adams Lawrence's son William, a young admirer and friend of Phillips Brooks, shared his father's interest in the church; after a catholic training at the Andover Seminary (Congregational), the Philadelphia Divinity School, and the Episcopal Theological School in Cambridge, he followed his first call to a church in Lawrence, Massachusetts, and eventually became bishop of Massachusetts, upon the death of Bishop Phillips Brooks in 1893, a post he held for thirty-four years. Bishop Law-

---

*A New York native of New England ancestry, Potter was the son-in-law of Eliphalet Nott, the builder of Union College. All eight of Bishop Potter's sons followed careers in New York rather than Philadelphia: Eliphalet Nott Potter became president of Union College; Henry Codman Potter was bishop of New York and a particular favorite of J. Pierpont Morgan, the church's leading layman; four sons—Clarkson, Howard, Robert, and Frank—became lawyers; and two, Edward and William, became architects.

†At one time both Phillips Brooks and Samuel S. Drury, rector of St. Paul's School in Concord, were elected bishops of the diocese of Pennsylvania; both declined the honor. For a more thorough discussion of Rittenhouse Square Episcopalianism in the post–Civil War period see E. Digby Baltzell, *Philadelphia Gentlemen: The Making of a National Upper Class* (New York: Free Press, 1959), chap. 10.

rence was far more than a local bishop and paragon of authority in Boston; he was veritably a national institution—board member of Groton for fifty-six years, chairman of the board at St. Mark's School, and an overseer and president of the alumni association at Harvard (where he obtained, in 1924, a gift of $5 million from the New York banker George F. Baker to found the Harvard Business School). Both his sons entered the church, William Appleton becoming bishop of western Massachusetts and Frederick Cunningham suffragan bishop of Massachusetts; Charles Lewis Slattery, Lawrence's son-in-law, succeeded him as bishop of Massachusetts.

Whereas Brahmin Bostonians moved into the Episcopal church in an individualistic way, they were unlike their Philadelphia peers in that they also took the lead in their new church. There have been no Philadelphians since Bishop White who have had the clerical stature of Phillips Brooks, William Lawrence, or Endicott Peabody, nor such laymen leaders as Amos Adams Lawrence* or George Shattuck, founder of St. Paul's School.

The Episcopal church thrived in Boston and elsewhere as the American upper classes became more and more affluent in the decades following the Civil War. Women have always come to the fore in ages of affluence; it was inevitable that ritualistic Episcopalianism should have had more appeal to Boston women than rationalistic Unitarianism, a point that Cleveland Amory has made:

> Many a First Family woman turned with joy to the more definite ritual of this Episcopalianism, which included kneeling for prayer—Unitarians bend and make "slight obeisance" but do not kneel—and belief in the divinity of Christ.† Sometimes she brought her husband along with her; sometimes First Families were split on the question. When the handsome young bachelor Phillips Brooks came to Boston in 1869 from Philadelphia, it was the Boston women who soon made a social as well as an ecclesiastical lion out of him. With ringing rhetoric from his Trinity Church pulpit Brooks soon had even such staunch Unitarian feminists as the daughters of James Russell Lowell and Dr. Oliver Wendell Holmes proudly referring to him as "our bishop"; since Brooks had been a Unitarian, his success was singularly important in placing Episcopalianism on a par with Unitarianism in the fight for the No. 1 religion of Boston's best.[26]

Unlike Philadelphia, where upper-class members have long been monolithically Episcopalian, by no means all of Boston's best have left the Unitarian fold; no Episcopalian was Harvard's Charles W. Eliot, whose reforms were made in the best Unitarian tradition; his mother once said to an Episcopalian friend, "Eliza, do you *kneel* down in church and call yourself a miserable sinner? Neither I nor any member of my family will ever do *that!*"[27] And Lees, Higgin-

---

*Amos Adams Lawrence was a national force in the years leading up to the Civil War; he sent money to John Brown and played a major role in the crucial border state of Kansas, among other things founding a college in Lawrence, which eventually became the University of Kansas; he also founded a little college in Appleton, Wisconsin, which later sent out Senator Joseph McCarthy on his national rampage and from which, at the same time, Nathan Pusey was called to the presidency of Harvard.

†Quakers do not kneel, nor do most of them believe in the historic Christ on the cross.

sons, Cabots, Saltonstalls, and many other families have remained Unitarians. Amory described a fashionable suburban Unitarian church thus:

> Chestnut Hill's church is a social match for any church in America of any denomination. So exclusively aristocratic in tone is its congregation that the church's annual meeting is always a "formal" affair, with all women present in evening dress and all men in tuxedos. Only one member of the church is recognized as underprivileged even by Chestnut Hill standards but there is no question of any embarrassment from this angle. Probably the only church in which no collection plate is ever passed, the First Church handles its finances by a First Family finance committee which decides on a proportional annual assessment for each family in the parish.[28]

Although a solid core of Boston Brahmins has continued to be Unitarian, Proper Philadelphians in the twentieth century have divorced themselves from their Quaker roots almost entirely. How they live in a very different world from that of their Quaker kin will become clearer in Chapter 20.

The Governing of Men:
Deference and Defiant Democracy

The English aristocrats were haughtier by nature than the French and even less disposed to demean themselves by hob-nobbing with persons of lower rank; nevertheless . . . no sac-rifice was too great if it insured their power.

The French nobility, after having lost its ancient political rights, had ceased more than any other country of feudal Europe to govern and guide the nation. . . . It not only pre-served, but considerably enlarged its pecuniary . . . advan-tages.

Alexis de Tocqueville

Meddle not with government; never speak of it, let others say and do as they please; . . . I have said little to you about dis-tributing justice, or being just in power or government, for I should desire you should never be concerned therein.

William Penn

If you do not rise to the head not only of your profession but of your country, it will be owing to your own laziness, sloven-liness, and obstinacy.

John Adams

In our Anglo-American tradition of democracy, money and education have been major means to power and privilege, which in turn are justified only when they lead to social and political authority.

The history of Massachusetts from colonial days through the close of the Federalist period in the 1820s was largely the story of vigorous political democ-racy led and balanced by more or less hierarchical social structures in which the rich, the wellborn, and the best were chosen by the people to rule. Through the colonial period, the Calvinist (Puritan) ethic was the principal ideology of au-thority. Even the most radical political leader in Massachusetts, Sam Adams, was deeply rooted in the conservative ethic of pious Puritanism and in the Ro-man virtue of *gravitas*. And Essex County federalism was surely a secularized version of this same Calvinist and elitist ethic. Although the personnel changed from the days of Winthrop through the Hutchinson era and down to the rule of the Adamses, class authority informed by elitist Puritanism remained supreme. As John Adams wrote in his *Defence of the Constitution,* "Go into every village in New England, and you will find that the office of justice of the peace, and even the place of representative, which has ever depended only on the freest election of the people, have generally descended from generation to generation, in three or four families at most."[1] The history of Penn's colony on the banks of the Delaware was very different. In Pennsylvania, the chief executive officers, chosen by absentee owners, were mostly non-Quakers and often non-Pennsylvanians. William Penn, like most utopians, planned an earthly paradise *for* his co-religionists but hardly trusted them to rule themselves; as far as politics was concerned, moreover, all too many Quakers, like their Quaker-turned-Episcopal descendants, were content to let the other fellow take care of government. In short, Massachusetts was an experiment in political democracy set within a hierarchical social structure, essentially a clerical theocracy; Pennsylvania very soon became a tolerant, secular, plutocratic society plagued by sectarian politics. Although there was never a Puritan party in Massachusetts, there was a fiercely partisan Quaker party in colonial Pennsylvania, where class and party lines usually followed religious affiliations: the Quakers generally opposed the Quaker proprietors (who soon became Anglican); the Anglicans were loyal to the proprietors, many of them finally supporting the crown and empire; and it was the radical Presbyterians (Calvinists), both in Philadelphia and on the Scotch-Irish frontier, who led the reluctant colony into the Revolution.

I attempt in this chapter to show how the political patterns developed in Massachusetts and Pennsylvania from their founding days through the Revolution have carried down through two centuries of our national experience—how the habit of authority led many members of Boston's upper class to participate vigorously in governing their city and state as well as the nation, whereas the habit of comfortable privilege that marked the Philadelphia gentry almost from the beginning caused them to avoid political responsibility. As Benjamin Rush, the most distinguished patriot in the sample of Philadelphia First Families, wrote in his autobiography:

> To my sons, I bequeath a father's experience, and I entreat them to take no public or active part in the disputes of their country beyond a vote at an election. If no scruples of conscience forbid them to bear arms, I would recommend to them rather to be soldiers than politicians, should they ever be so unfortunate as to live in a country distracted by a civil war. In battle men kill, without hating each other; in political contests men hate without killing, but in that hatred they commit murder every hour of their lives.[2]

AMERICAN POLITICAL DYNASTIES

Although the Constitution explicitly states that "no title of nobility shall be granted in the United States," our democracy has not been without its aristocratic families who have taken the lead in political life over several generations.

In an extremely revealing book, Stephen Hess analyzed the political contributions of sixteen dynasties in American politics: the Adamses, Lodges, and Kennedys of Massachusetts; the Lees, Harrisons, Breckenridges, and Tuckers of Virginia; the Livingstons and Roosevelts of New York; the Frelinghuysens and Stocktons of New Jersey; the Washburns of Maine; the Longs of Louisiana; the Tafts of Cincinnati; the Bayards of New York and Delaware; and the Mühlenbergs of Pennsylvania. According to Hess, these families, including their collateral relatives, have contributed no fewer than "eight presidents, three vice-presidents, thirty senators, twelve governors, fifty-six members of the House of Representatives or Continental Congress, and nine cabinet officers."[3]

There are no Philadelphia First Families in Hess's sample. Moreover, the only Pennsylvania family of continuing national distinction came not from the economic and cultural capital of the state but from the counties of Montgomery, Lancaster, and Berks, the heart of the Pennsylvania Dutch frontier.

Henry Melchior Mühlenberg, the first of his family in America, was a graduate of the University of Göttingen and of Halle, the great center of German Pietism. He came to America in 1742 at the age of thirty not because of hunger and religious persecution, as was the case for the vast majority of his fellow German immigrants, but because his church fathers had sent him. Within a decade of his arrival, he had founded the Lutheran church in America, married the daughter of Conrad Weiser, the famous Indian agent, and produced seven children, including three sons—John Peter Gabriel, Frederick Augustus Conrad, and Gotthilf Henry Ernest—all of whom were educated at Halle and became Lutheran clergymen. Three of his daughters married clergymen, and one son-in-law, John Andrew Schultze, turned from the church to politics and became governor of Pennsylvania (1823–1829).

In the history of Pennsylvania, the Mühlenbergs were far more distinguished than any of the fifty First Families of Philadelphia. Seven members of the family—the family founder, his three sons, one grandson, and two great-grandsons—had a total of 934 lines written about them in the *DAB* (the seven Whartons, the leading Philadelphia family, had only 655 lines). The Mühlenbergs took the lead in the church, in education, and in war and politics. In the fourth generation, William Augustus Mühlenberg founded St. Paul's College in Flushing, Long Island, from which Henry Coit got the educational ideas he put into practice at St. Paul's in Concord. Finally, the Mühlenbergs were closely allied (four times intermarried) with the Heisters, another political family in the state. (Joseph Heister was governor from 1820 to 1823.)

In spite of their great accomplishments, there was a provincial quality to the Mühlenbergs that is typical of Pennsylvania culture.

> The power base of the Muhlenbergs was narrow, generally the tri-counties of Berks, Lancaster, and Montgomery, so that they rarely rose above the House of Representatives. But quantitatively their record was remarkable. Only three families have sent more members to Congress. Taken together with the Heisters—who represented the economic wealth of the Pennsylvania Germans, while the Muhlenbergs represented the intellectual—their achievement was unsurpassed: twenty-seven national election victories, sixty-five years in Congress.[4]

Yet the Mühlenberg-Heister clan was rarely in the mainstream of national political life. Indeed, the Mühlenbergs' greatest accomplishments were in education and the church.*

BOSTON BRAHMIN AND PROPER PHILADELPHIA MAYORS BEFORE THE CIVIL WAR

In *The Private City: Philadelphia in Three Periods of Growth*, Sam Bass Warner, Jr., attributed urban political corruption in America to what he called privatism: "The goal of a city is to be a community of private money-makers."[5] Most students of urban politics, from Lincoln Steffens to Edward Banfield, would probably agree that privatism is a useful concept for understanding the growth of urban corruption after the Civil War and into the twentieth century. The particular value of Warner's study of Philadelphia, however, is that he traced this tradition of privatism in the city to prerevolutionary times.

> Like the Puritans of Massachusetts and Connecticut, the Quakers of Pennsylvania had proved unable to sustain the primacy of religion against the solvents of cheap land and private opportunity. . . . Already by the time of the Revolution, privatism had become the American tradition. Psychologically, privatism meant that the individual should see his first loyalty as his immediate family, and that a community should be a union of such money-making, accumulating families; politically, privatism meant that the community should keep the peace among individual money-makers, and, if possible, help to create an open and thriving setting where each citizen would have some opportunity to prosper.[6]

Warner used the career of Jay Cooke, a leading Philadelphia financier during and after the Civil War, as an excellent example of privatism: "No deep knowledge of, or concern for, the general welfare of his city informed Cooke's business, politics, or philanthropy. The problems of Philadelphia were irrelevant to all the major concerns of his daily life."[7] And, according to Warner, Cooke was typical of his generation of Philadelphia businessmen.

> The failure of Jay Cooke's generation and later generations of Philadelphia businessmen to take responsibility for the consequences of the scale and organization of their business has turned their personal benevolence to ashes. Jay Cooke was an honest, open-hearted man. He did not abandon his youthful promise to use his wealth to "display his social and generous spirit." His philanthropy, however, was at best peripheral to the needs of the city. . . . He gave some of his wealth to Kenyon, Princeton, and Dartmouth, donated large sums to local charities, was an active supporter of the Y.M.C.A. and the American Sunday School Union, and joined the Academy of Natural Sciences and the Historical Society of Pennsylvania. All in their way were worthy causes, of some help to a few people, but

---

*It is of historical interest that although no member of the Philadelphia sample is today on the liberal arts faculty of the University of Pennsylvania, a Mühlenberg teaches in Penn's school of fine arts.

considering Jay Cooke's intelligence, the sum of his benevolence exerted a pitifully small leverage upon the problems of his city.[8]

As I have stressed in countless ways, privatism indeed has been typical of Philadelphia from the very beginning; it has not characterized Boston to anywhere near the same extent. Though Cooke had his Boston counterparts, the differences between the two cities were nevertheless considerable. During Cooke's lifetime (1821-1902), for instance, three members of the Brahmin Quincy family served as mayors of Boston: the first Josiah Quincy, an active and autocratic reformer, was the newly formed city's second mayor (1823-1828) and, later, president of Harvard; the second Josiah Quincy was mayor between 1846 and 1848; and the last Josiah Quincy was mayor between 1896 and 1899, by which time the Irish were well on their way to political rule in Boston. Moreover, whereas Cooke was an auslander Philadelphian (of New England stock), the Quincys were deeply rooted in the soil of Massachusetts for over two centuries.

Jay Cooke never met any Proper Philadelphians quite like the last Josiah Quincy, who graduated from Harvard (1880) at the height of the Mugwump era. He won the Lee Prize in his freshman and sophomore years, the Boylston Prize in his junior year, and the Bowdoin Prize as a senior. He was a member of Phi Beta Kappa, president of the *Crimson*, and class speaker at commencement. Quincy was anything but the genial gentleman so prized in polite Philadelphia Society. A bachelor until late in life, he had a host of admirers but few friends. Scion of a rock-ribbed Republican class, he spent his life in political reform as a member of the Democratic party. Quincy believed in the extension of the powers of government and in the rights of organized labor and as mayor employed many of the newly risen class of professional urban reformers, among them the settlement worker Robert A. Woods, the social worker Alice N. Lincoln, and the founder of the playground movement, Joseph Lee (of the Boston sample). Quincy traveled extensively in Europe seeking new ideas on urban government. When the British Fabians Sidney and Beatrice Webb visited America in 1898, they were most impressed with Quincy: "Quite the hero from the pages of a novel,"[9] wrote Beatrice Webb in her diary. As Geoffrey Blodgett, in *The Gentle Reformers: Massachusetts Democrats in the Cleveland Era*, summed up his chapter on Quincy's mayorality: "He made Boston's city government for a brief time the cutting edge of urban reform in America."[10]

In Boston, Brahmin leadership in the mayor's office was typical down to the Civil War. When the governor approved the creation of the city of Boston in 1822, the citizens continued the town meeting tradition of deference democracy by electing John Phillips (father of Wendell Phillips) as its first mayor. Of the sixteen mayors elected between 1822 and the outbreak of the Civil War, moreover, six—the two Josiah Quincys, John Phillips (1822-1823), Harrison Gray Otis (1829-1831), Theodore Lyman (1834-1835), and Samuel Eliot (1837-1839), the father of Charles W. Eliot—were members of the First Family sample. Three others—Jonathan Chapman (1840-1842), Martin Brimmer (1843-1844), and John P. Bigelow (1849-1851)—also belonged to the city's upper class. These nine upper-class Bostonians, all of them graduates of Harvard College, held the mayoralty for twenty-four of the thirty-eight prewar years. Two other mayors were college graduates, whereas only five were self-made men who had not gone to college.

In contrast to the Bostonians, the Philadelphia mayors were a more heterogeneous and less educated group. Of the fifteen mayors who held office in the thirty-eight years before the Civil War, only six, or 40 percent, were college graduates (in Boston the figure was eleven of sixteen, or 70 percent). At the same time that John Phillips was mayor of Boston, for instance, Robert Wharton, Proper Philadelphia's most popular sportsman, with a "decided distaste for learning,"[11] was serving his fifteenth term in the mayor's office. Besides Wharton, only two other mayors, Richard Vaux (1858–1859) and George M. Dallas (1828), were members of the First Family sample. Of the six college graduates who served as mayor of Philadelphia, only one was a Penn alumnus. John Swift, of an impeccably Proper Philadelphia family, graduated from the college in 1808 and served longer than any other mayor during this period (1832–1837, 1839–1841, and 1845–1849). Of the five other college men, four (including Dallas) graduated from Princeton and one from Yale. John M. Scott, a native New Yorker and a Princeton graduate, was the first popularly elected mayor in the city's history. (The first mayors were appointed by the proprietor; subsequent mayors were elected by the city council.) Peter McCall, a Princetonian and a member of a very fashionable Philadelphia Anglican family, served as mayor for one year (1844). Joel Jones, a Yale graduate, was born in Connecticut of an old Puritan family, practiced law in Philadelphia, and served one term as mayor (1849–1850). Finally, Alexander Henry, a Princeton graduate, was elected mayor in 1858 and served through the war years until 1866, when he refused to stand again. Henry was a Proper Philadelphia civic leader of distinction—a trustee of the university, bank director, and member of the board of the Centennial Exposition.

BOSTON BRAHMINS AND PROPER
PHILADELPHIANS IN CONGRESS
BEFORE THE CIVIL WAR

After John Quincy Adams left the presidency in 1829, his fellow citizens of Massachusetts sent him to Congress for eight consecutive terms, from 1831 until his death in action on the floor of the House in 1848. In this Puritan tradition of class authority and public service, fourteen members of the Boston sample of fifty families served a total of thirty-nine terms in the U.S. House of Representatives before the Civil War—Fisher Ames (1789–1797), Harrison Gray Otis (1799–1801), Josiah Quincy (1805–1813), John Quincy Adams (1831–1848), Nathan Appleton (1831–1833, 1841–1843), Rufus Choate (1831–1834), Abbott Lawrence (1835–1837, 1839–1840), Leverett Saltonstall (1837–1843), Robert C. Winthrop (1839–1851), John G. Palfrey (1847–1849), Samuel A. Eliot (1849–1851), William Appleton (1851–1855, 1861–1863), Edward Everett (1853–1855), and Charles Francis Adams (1859–1861).

Proper Philadelphians were much less likely than their Boston peers to serve the nation in the House of Representatives. Thus, only seven members of the First Family sample—Charles Jared Ingersoll (1813–1815, 1841–1843, 1845–1847, 1847–1849), Joseph Hopkinson (1815–1819), John Sergeant (1815–1823, 1827–1829, 1837–1841), Horace Binney (1833–1835), Joseph R. Ingersoll (1835–1837, 1841–1843, 1845–1849), John Cadwalader (1855–1857), and Charles J. Biddle (1861–1863)—served a total of twenty terms in the House before the close of the Civil War.*

Not only were the Proper Philadelphians only half as likely to serve in Congress as were their Massachusetts counterparts, but they were also far less likely to have sustained political careers in the House or in other offices of government. No one from the Philadelphia group attained the position of Speaker of the House, as did Robert Winthrop of Boston; none went on to the U.S. Senate, as did Otis, Adams, Choate, Winthrop, and Everett of Boston; and none served in the mayor's office, whereas Quincy was the second mayor of Boston and Saltonstall became the first mayor of Salem in 1836.

The Boston Brahmins and Philadelphia Gentlemen in politics before the Civil War were different in another respect: they were, by and large, class deviants in Philadelphia and representatives of class authority in Boston. During this period, both the Boston and Philadelphia upper classes were predominantly Federalists first and then Whigs. But whereas the Boston Brahmins in politics were almost to a man members of the Federalist and Whig parties, all the Philadelphia Gentlemen who went into politics were either Jeffersonian Republicans or Democrats, with the exception of Joseph Hopkinson, who went to Congress as a Federalist, and Horace Binney, who was sent there by the Whigs. Again, Sidney Fisher probably best expressed the passive and private values of most Proper Philadelphians of his day when he wrote of George Mifflin Dallas after his death in 1865: "Mr. Dallas I knew very well from the time I was admitted to the bar, & was a frequent visitor at his house. He was very gracious & kind in his manners, had the air and breeding of a gentleman, was handsome, a tall well-made figure, pleasing countenance, white hair, was worthy & amiable in all private relations, but he was a Democrat and a demagogue."[13]

After the Civil War, few gentlemen from either city served their communities in the House of Representatives. Industrialization, mass immigration, and rapid urban growth made political corruption a widespread problem in American cities, including Boston and Philadelphia, as the muckrakers showed.

GILDED AGE POLITICS IN BOSTON AND PHILADELPHIA

In city after city during the Gilded Age, privatism increased among the "decent people" who left the problems of urban government to others while they devoted their lives to making money out of the great trusts and corporations that were rapidly transforming America into the foremost industrial nation on

---

*All of these men were college graduates—Cadwalader and Hopkinson from Penn, the two Ingersolls, Sergeant, and Biddle from Princeton, and Binney from Harvard.

earth. As might be expected, no member of the First Family samples, with the outstanding exception of Josiah Quincy, served in the mayor's office of either city between Appomattox and Pearl Harbor. The influence of class authority on the politics of Boston and Philadelphia during this long period, however, was quite different.

Whereas class authority and deference democracy held sway in Boston for most of the last three decades of the nineteenth century, until Yankee political leadership was defeated forever by the rise to power of a series of capable and ambitious Irish-Catholic politicians, class authority had little real influence in Philadelphia, which was ruled more or less by an urban and Republican political machine from the 1870s until the 1950s. The differences in the governing of the two cities are illustrated by the educational qualifications of the men who served in the mayor's office. Of the eighteen mayors of Boston between the Civil War and the end of Quincy's rule in 1899, eight were college graduates. five from Harvard and one each from Dartmouth, Brown, and Bowdoin. If Brahmins were no longer attracted to the mayor's office, at least a college education, especially at Harvard, was still important. In Philadelphia, however, of the ten mayors who held office between the Civil War and 1900, none was a college graduate. Two, however, were outstanding civic leaders of achieved upper-class status, Morton McMichael (1866–1869) and Edwin Henry Fitler (1887–1891).

McMichael was a founder and fourth president of the Union League; Fitler was its sixth president. It is relevant to my theory of Philadelphia privatism that although most of the more prominent Pennsylvania Republicans in both politics and business have belonged to the league down through the years, and although it was founded by idealistic and partisan supporters of Abraham Lincoln, since the 1870s the club has had a firm official policy of avoiding participation in either city or state politics except in a quiet and advisory way.

Both McMichael and Fitler were Victorian family founders in Philadelphia (and hence not a part of the First Family sample). Though both were eminent members of the Union League, Fitler was not taken into the Philadelphia Club until his forties; McMichael's son and namesake was so honored in 1892, more than a decade after the death of his distinguished father.

In the twentieth century, upper-class Bostonians and Philadelphians—that is, those who were concerned with politics—faced quite different problems in the governing of their cities. The first Irish-Catholic mayor of Boston, Hugh O'Brien (1885–1888), was an immigrant. He was an exception to the Yankee rule, but after 1900 only two mayors, Andrew J. Peters (1918–1921) and Malcolm E. Nichols (1926–1929), were of old Yankee stock. Peters, a graduate of St. Paul's and Harvard, was a Democrat who had the misfortune to be in the mayor's office during the notorious police strike of 1919.* Nichols, also a Harvard man, was the last Republican mayor in the city's history. The rest of the mayors were mainly Irish-Catholics.

---

*Peters was the only St. Paul's alumnus to be mayor of a major American city until John V. Lindsay was elected mayor of New York in the 1960s.

Philadelphia has never had an Irish-Catholic voting bloc, and the first Irish-Catholic mayor did not take office until the 1960s. Unlike any other major city in America, Philadelphia had a political machine that was solidly Protestant and Republican during the first five decades of the twentieth century. But the city's Protestant bosses were largely an uneducated lot. Only two of Philadelphia's mayors between 1866 and 1940 were college graduates; most were self-made men of little distinction. (During this same period in Boston, there were ten Harvard graduates in the mayor's office.)

The ancient traditions of native leadership in Boston and auslander leadership in Philadelphia are nicely illustrated by the mayors of the two cities. All save two (both born in Maine) of the Boston Protestant mayors were natives of the city (the Irish-Catholic mayors were either native born sons of immigrants or immigrants themselves); of the ten Protestant mayors of Philadelphia in the twentieth century, however, seven—two born in Europe, one each in Ohio, Massachusetts, and New Jersey, and two upstate—were born outside the city.

CLASS AUTHORITY AND POLITICAL REFORM IN BOSTON AND PHILADELPHIA

"An aristocracy," Louis Napoleon once said, "requires no chief, but the very nature of democracy is to personify itself in an individual . . . to obviate the want of fixedness and sequence."[14] And, as Louis Napoleon and his contemporary Tocqueville warned in the case of France, the absence of class authority inevitably leads to the rule of charismatic men on horseback, with their legions of personal followers. One way of looking at the political leadership of urban America in the twentieth century is to see it as a dialectical contest between the reforming forces of class authority, on the one hand, and personal loyalties to the boss of a political machine, on the other. As yet, at least, the little Caesars in American politics have been confined to the urban and state levels and have never won out on the national scene (though Roosevelt surely feared this development during the Depression in the case of Huey Long). If Louis Napoleon or Tocqueville were useful guides to the future, we should expect boss rule to be more characteristic of Philadelphia than of Boston.

Any student of urban politics in twentieth-century America should probably begin with the writings of Lincoln Steffens. In approaching the work of Steffens, however, it is useful to be aware that he tended to see *all leadership* as more or less a matter of *exploitation*; there are no good or bad men but only good or bad social or political situations; by and large, good men are on the bad side, and bad men on the good side. Steffens preferred the honest realism of men like Martin Lomasny of Boston and Israel Durham of Philadelphia to the genteel hypocrisy of even the gentleman reformers in the two cities, to say nothing of gentleman money-makers. And he had no faith in the good people who "believed that bad people caused the evil which good people, if elected to power, would cure."[15]

Steffens raked the muck in Philadelphia in 1903; that of Boston, in 1909. In *The Shame of the Cities*, he began his article on "Philadelphia: Corrupt and Contented" by noting that

> our American cities, no matter how bad their conditions may be, all point with scorn to Philadelphia as worse—"the worse-governed city in the country." St. Louis, Minneapolis, Pittsburgh submit with some patience to the jibes of any other community; the most friendly suggestion from Philadelphia is rejected with contempt. The Philadelphians are "supine," "asleep"; hopelessly ring-ruled, they are "complacent." "Politically benighted," Philadelphia is supposed to have no light to throw upon the state of things that is almost universal.[16]

"This is not fair," Steffens continued,

> Philadelphia is, indeed corrupt; but it is not without significance. . . . with 47 percent of its population native-born of native-born parents, it is the most American of our greater cities. It is "good," too, and intelligent. . . . Philadelphia has long enjoyed great and widely distributed prosperity; it is the city of homes . . . and the people give one a sense of more leisure and repose than any community I have ever dwelt in. Philadelphia is surer that it has a "real aristocracy" than any other place in the world, but its aristocrats, with few exceptions, are in the ring, with it, or of no political use. Philadelphia is simply the most corrupt and the most contented. . . . At least you must admit that our machine is the best you have ever seen.[17]

What horrified Steffens was not necessarily the fact of machine rule. That was normal for his day in American cities. But Philadelphia was unique in that its machine had truly disfranchised its citizens: "The enduring strength of the typical American political machine is that it is a natural growth—a sucker, but deeply rooted in the people. The New Yorkers vote for Tammany Hall. The Philadelphians do not vote; they are disfranchised."[18] Steffens then cited the case of "Rudolph Blankenberg, a persistent fighter for the right and the use of the right to vote (and, by the way, an immigrant), [who] sent out just before one election a registered letter to each voter on the rolls of a certain selected division. Sixty-three per cent were returned marked 'not at,' 'removed,' 'deceased,' etc."[19] (Blankenberg found similar corruption in other divisions.)*

At the time that Steffens was visiting Philadelphia, the Republican machine had put a very respectable man, John Weaver, into the mayor's office (1903–1907). Senator Matthew Quay, a specialist in the proper use of the reform image in strategic situations, backed Weaver, through his Philadelphia henchmen, against the reformers' choice, Peter Rothermell, an audacious district attorney who had previously had the guts to bring Quay to trial on

---

*In discussing the extreme apathy that marked the voters of all classes in Philadelphia, Steffens related the following example of the political ring's humor: "The gang voted for fun all the names of the signers of the sacred Constitution of the United States, of the new charter and the membership lists of the swell clubs" (Lincoln Steffens, *The Autobiography of Lincoln Steffens* [New York: Harcourt, 1931], p. 410).

charges of corruption. At any rate, good Philadelphians placed great faith in Mayor Weaver's promises to reform the voting system in the city. Steffens nevertheless closed his article on Philadelphia on a pessimistic note.

> Think of a city putting its whole faith in one man, in the *hope* that John Weaver, an Englishman by birth, will *give* them good government! And why should he do that? Why should he serve the people and not the ring? The ring can make or break him; the people of Philadelphia can neither reward or punish him. For even if he restores them their ballots and proves himself a good mayor, he cannot succeed himself; the good charter forbids more than one term."[20]

Steffens proved right about the ability of Mayor Weaver to save Philadelphia. But eventually, Mayor Rudolph Blankenberg (1911–1915) did lead the most successful reform administration in Philadelphia in the years between the Civil War and World War II.

Blankenberg, a clergyman's son, was born in Germany. After a good education under private tutors and at the local gymnasium, he decided to go into business rather than the ministry. Having laid the foundations of a successful business career in Germany, he came to Philadelphia at the close of the Civil War (largely because of his concern for social justice, reinforced by his reading of *Uncle Tom's Cabin*). He almost immediately joined the Society of Friends, married the daughter of an old Quaker family, and began his way to business success as the European buyer for a local textile firm. In 1875, he established R. Blankenberg & Company, which he sold in 1905 at a great profit.

In the Quaker style, Blankenberg combined business success with an abiding concern for the downtrodden. But, unlike most birthright Quakers, he was also an active political reformer. As a member of the reform Committee of 100, founded by Henry Charles Lea in 1880, he worked hard for the election of another convinced Friend, Samuel G. King, the last Democratic mayor (1881–1884) of the city until the Clark and Dilworth political renaissance after World War II.

Blankenberg also worked hard for the election of his friend the merchant John Wanamaker, who lost a race for the U.S. Senate in 1897 to Boies Penrose. Finally, in 1911, Blankenberg led a successful campaign for mayor, on an independent ticket, against Penrose's regular Republican choice, George H. Earle, Jr. (father of Pennsylvania's first Democratic governor in this century). Blankenberg, with the help of professional urbanologists like Morris L. Cooke, ran a very efficient and honest administration, but, as might have been expected, the independents gradually drifted back to the Republican party. The machine, now dominated by the fabulous Vare brothers, South Philadelphia pig farmers and garbage collectors whose pious mother was of old New England Puritan stock, took over once more. Even "Old Dutch Cleanser," as Blankenberg was affectionately called, had very little lasting impact on boss-ridden Philadelphia, which Steffens called "a defeated city" in his autobiography (1931).

When Steffens went to Boston in 1909, the Irish were already well on their way to taking over political power in the city, even though a Republican,

George A. Hibbard, was in the mayor's office. John F. Fitzgerald had been mayor in 1906–1907 and was to be elected again in 1910, defeating James Jackson Storrow, "a patrician Protestant of enormous wealth and chilling rectitude."[21] Boston Irishmen like Fitzgerald, contrary to much conventional and superficial opinion, were legitimate political leaders in both Congress and the mayor's office and not citywide bosses in the behind-the-scenes style of Tweed in New York or of Israel Durham and the Vare brothers in Philadelphia.

In Steffens's view, municipal political corruption is inevitable. He nevertheless found Boston to be quite different from Philadelphia. "The first impression I got," he wrote in his autobiography, "was that Boston was worse than Philadelphia. But . . . there was no one boss of Boston, as there was in most cities."[22]

The most important thing about Boston from our point of view is that the city still being led by members of its upper class: "The political boss," Steffens wrote,

> had passed out in Boston; the business bosses have dispensed with him, and they have found that they can manage the corruption of politics themselves much better. There was less scandal in Boston, fewer exposures, and those that were started were kept within bounds as in old England, where likewise there were no bosses, where likewise gentlemen attended to all politics. This made Boston look better than Philadelphia; this made it harder to muckrake.[23]

Steffens did indeed have a very hard time raking the muck in class dominated Boston. In fact, he was never able to complete the book he proposed to call *Boston, A Promise*, even though he stayed longer in Boston than in any of the other cities he studied.

Though he recognized the inevitable corruption of the business gentlemen on Beacon Hill ("legitimate grafters" he called them), Steffens still had hope for the city: "What interests me in Boston is that practically everyone wants to see things made right. I have doubts about mere good will, but it ought to be tried somewhere. If it will succeed anywhere, it will here."[24]

GENTLEMEN REFORMERS IN
BOSTON AND PHILADELPHIA

In the course of the plutocratic revolution that overtook America after the Civil War, many men of long established wealth were led to revolt or reform, if not to withdraw altogether. As representatives of their class, the four Adams brothers, in the fourth generation, struggled against the money mood of their times. While John Quincy became a perennial loser as a Democratic statesman in a solidly Republican state, the other three brothers took up their pens to attack the evils of plutocracy. Charles Francis came back after serving in the war and anticipated the muckrakers with his exposure of railroad frauds in *Chapters of Erie*; Henry published the novel *Democracy* in 1880, which, through the eyes of a beautiful and brilliant widow from Philadelphia, lays bare the corruptions of Grant Republicanism.* And Brooks, in *The Law of Civilization and Decay,* published in 1896, saw the final decline of civilization as due to the triumph of the moneyed-type.

While the Adamses were attacking the evils of plutocracy on the national scene, upper-class businessmen and professionals were becoming aware of extensive corruption and neglect in America's rapidly growing cities. In both Boston and Philadelphia, the cause of reform became fashionable among the "best people."

The Reform Club of Philadelphia was founded under the leadership of the patrician reformer and historian Henry Charles Lea. "A group of men was called together by Lea at his home," wrote Edward Sculley Bradley, Lea's biographer, "to organize a private club which would meet in every way the best standards, both in appointments and selection of members, but should be composed entirely of men who had the cause of political reform at heart and were willing to take independent action to secure it."[25] The founders chartered an old mansion on Chestnut Street for a clubhouse, which boasted "well-equipped club-rooms, restaurant, library, wine-rooms, and a ball room."[26] In a footnote, Bradley noted that "the purposes of the Reform Club were chiefly social."[27] Indeed, its membership roll of 991 names in May 1875 reads like a *Social Register;* most of the families in the First Family sample had members in the club, including seven Biddles and one Cadwalader. As the club was originally formed to insure the maintenance of a high tariff, dangerous Democrats were not likely to join (Richard Vaux was not a member, nor were any Ingersolls).

Whereas Proper Philadelphians took reform rather casually, Boston Brahmins joined in a veritable orgy of reform activity in the last two decades of the nineteenth century. The Massachusetts Reform Club, whose some 200 members gathered at the Parker House rather than waste money on an ornate clubhouse as in Philadelphia, was founded in 1882. On a Friday in June 1884, the club met to consider its position on the Republican candidacy of James G. Blaine. Young Richard Dana recorded in his private journal: "All was excitement, and everybody was on fire. Not a man in the room wished to support Blaine."[28]

"The Reform Club was only the most renowned of Mugwump haunts," wrote Blodgett.

> In the 1880s it was said that no two Bostonians could have an idea in common without forming a club around it. The city was overrun with clubs—not only St. Botolph's, the Somerset, the Algonquin, and other sanctuaries of the powerful and well-born—but a club to match every political notion and persuasion. Republicans had the Massachusetts Club, Democrats the Bay State Club. Young Republicans and young Democrats had separate clubs. Nationalists, philanthropists, protectionists, free traders, civil service reformers, and Butlerites all had

---

*Mrs. Lightfoot Lee was modeled on Elizabeth Cameron, Adams's closest confidante in his Washington circle and the wife of J. Donald Cameron, son of Simon Cameron, Pennsylvania political boss par excellence. Madelaine Lee's senator friend, Silas P. Ratcliffe was perhaps unwittingly modeled on James G. Blaine, the plumed knight of Republicanism.

their particular clubs. Forty years later one of the Mugwumps recalled that "every Saturday afternoon Parker's and Young's Hotel were filled with clubs, dining and talking heavily, smoking and drinking to excess, in order to save the Republic." ("Now they are playing golf instead," he added.)[29]

Most of Boston's foremost businessmen of solid social position and solid Republican credentials were in the Mugwump camp in 1884. From the First Family sample, John Murray Forbes, the most powerful Boston capitalist of the day, Robert Treat Paine, the philanthropist, and the investment bankers Henry Lee, Henry Lee Higginson, and Charles Cabot Jackson were all leaders in the Mugwump movement on State Street and Beacon Hill. Most of the important Boston Mugwumps were Harvard men, and of course President Eliot, William James, Barrett Wendell, and Charles Eliot Norton were active supporters in Cambridge. Norton, whose friend Godkin, as editor of the *Nation* and the *New York Evening Post*, championed the cause of Cleveland against Blaine on the national scene, was the intellectual leader of Boston Mugwumpery. As Blodgett put it, Mugwumpery in Boston gave men of established family an opportunity to "break loose from their role as passive heirs. . . . It effected a stewardship of quality . . . and a focus for their elitist instincts."[30]

Most of the Mugwumps went back into the Republican party after 1884, but some of them remained Democrats. Josiah Quincy, for instance, came of age in the Mugwump movement and then, as a Democrat, became a leader of his party in Massachusetts and a great reforming mayor, as we have seen, in the last years of the century. Another Bostonian of old Yankee stock, Nathan Matthews, began his political career in the Mugwump movement in 1884. Like Quincy, he remained a Democrat and founded the Young Men's Democratic Club in 1888. In the meantime, in 1885, Hugh O'Brien, an Irish Catholic, was elected mayor for the first of four terms, supported and praised by members of the Reform Club. The city charter was amended in 1885, centralizing leadership in the mayor rather than the council, and Matthews, who became mayor in 1891, was the first to use this new power to its fullest extent, and on the side of reform.

At the same time that Boston got its new charter, Philadelphia was also passing through a reform period that culminated in the Bullitt bill,* which gave the mayor some power while in office but no sustained power because he was prohibited from running for reelection. The movement did not come from the type of men who belonged to Philadelphia's Reform Club of the 1870s but was spearheaded by the Committee of 100, formed in 1880. This committee led the reformers in ousting the Republican ring and in electing as mayor Samuel G. King, a convinced Quaker of impeccable integrity, who had been the lonely Democrat on the city council since 1860. At the same time, the Democrat Pattison captured the governorship and the Bullitt bill became law.

Unlike the Reform Club, the Committee of 100 included not a single member of the Philadelphia First Family sample except Henry Charles Lea. Though

---

*The writing and passing of the bill were largely the work of two patrician Philadelphia lawyers, John C. Bullitt, an auslander from Louisville, Kentucky, and William C. Bullitt, his son.

suffering from ill health, Lea agreed to serve on its executive board and took a very active part in King's campaign. Indeed, Henry Charles Lea was Philadelphia's leading Mugwump. And whereas he was in constant and sympathetic correspondence with Charles Eliot Norton, the sage of Shady Hill, he had few spiritual kin among Proper Philadelphians. Blankenberg, a member of the Committee of 100, supported Blaine, as did another prominent reformer, Judge Samuel W. Pennypacker who explained: "In this campaign I prepared a paper giving reasons why the Independents should support the nomination of Blaine, and we succeeded in having it signed by most of the men of *representative character* . . . but excluding . . . Lea."[31] Pennypacker also noted with pride that "had the same sentiment prevailed and the same activity been displayed in New York, Blaine would have been elected."[32] But perhaps it was just as well that the gentlemanly sentiment in both New York (J. P. Morgan was a Mugwump) and Boston was very different from that in Pennypacker's city and state. At any rate, reform fell apart in Philadelphia in 1884: Mayor King failed to be re-elected and the Republicans came back into power until after World War II (even the Blankenberg reformers were independent Republicans).

PHILADELPHIA: URBAN PROGRESSIVISM AND THE HOFSTADTER THESIS

Lincoln Steffens saw urban reform as an uprising of the public, demanding good government in opposition to the political machine and its allies, or business interests. Since the Second World War, however, historians have tended to see the Progressive movement more as a conflict within the business ruling classes than simply as a matter of the people against the vested interests.

Richard Hofstadter was perhaps the most famous of these revisionist historians. In his influential book *The Age of Reform*, he saw the Progressives of Roosevelt's generation as the spiritual sons of the Mugwumps. In the best known chapter in this book, called "The Status Revolution and the Progressive Leaders," he showed that the Mugwumps were members of the established gentry who resented the new plutocrats coming to power in city after city during the Gilded Age.

> The newly rich, the grandiosely or corruptly rich, the masters of the great corporations, were bypassing the men of the mugwump type—the old gentry, the merchants of long standing, the small manufacturers, the established professional men, the civic leaders of an earlier era. In a score of cities and hundreds of towns, particularly in the East but also in the nation at large, the old-family, college-educated class that had deep ancestral roots in local communities and often owned family businesses, that had traditions of political leadership, belonged to the patriotic societies and the best clubs, staffed the governing boards of philanthropic and cultural institutions, and led the movement for civic betterment, were being overshadowed and edged aside in the making of basic economic and political decisions. In their personal careers, as in their community activities, they found themselves checked, hampered, and overridden by agents of the new corporations, the corrupters of legislators, the buyers of franchises, and allies of

the political bosses. In this uneven struggle they found themselves limited by their own scruples, their regard for reputation, their social standing itself. To be sure, the America they knew did not lack opportunities, but it did seem to lack opportunities of the highest sort for men of the highest standards. In a strictly economic sense these men were not growing poorer as a class, but their wealth and power were being dwarfed by comparison with the new eminences of wealth and power. They were less important and they knew it.[33]

In light of the political histories of Massachusetts and Pennsylvania, it was quite natural that Hofstadter's theory of the status revolution should apply preeminently to Boston, and also New York, but hardly at all to Philadelphia. No wonder there was no Mugwump movement to speak of in the Quaker City, where the upper class had never had much of a "tradition of political leadership" in either the state or the nation. Whereas Boston Brahmins resented their loss of power and authority, Proper Philadelphians, "members of patriotic societies and the best clubs," really had nothing to lose, at least politically. But they, too, responded to the rise of the new plutocracy, in their traditionally snobbish and private way, by excluding men of new wealth and their families (like the Wideners) from membership in such cherished institutions as the Philadelphia Club and from the Assembly balls. At the same time, the passionate patrician reformer Henry Charles Lea must have been a very lonely gentleman as he sat in the stately library of his Walnut Street mansion, pondering the evils of both the Spanish Inquisition and machine politics in Philadelphia and Pennsylvania. (But then Lea was a Unitarian and not a member of the Philadelphia Club.)

Just as Proper Philadelphians did not become Mugwumps to anywhere near the same extent as their Boston peers, so the Progressive movement largely passed them by, even though they tended to support the vigorous patrician Theodore Roosevelt when he ran for the presidency in 1904. A most useful study of Philadelphia progressivism was made in 1967 by Bonnie R. Fox, then a graduate student at Columbia University. In "The Philadelphia Progressives: A Test of the Hofstadter-Hays Thesis," she analyzed the membership of the Committee of Seventy which in 1911 took the lead in supporting Rudolph Blankenberg for mayor. Fox asked whether Philadelphia had "a progressive movement which corresponded to the reform administrations that existed in other cities or states and eventually reached the national level" and replied, "The answer must be negative, unless we are to conclude that progressivism everywhere was mainly an efficiency movement."[34] In other words, the reform movement under Blankenberg was, according to Fox, not a product of what Hofstadter called a status revolution. Rather, it illustrated a theory put forward by Samuel P. Hays after a detailed study of the 745 members of the two main reform organizations in Pittsburgh that rescued that city from its machine in 1910–1911. Hays's theory, developed in "The Politics of Reform in Municipal Government in the Progressive Era," modified Hofstadter's thesis by showing that the Pittsburgh reformers were likely to be upper-class businessmen interested mostly in replacing the wasteful methods of machine politics with the more scientific and efficient methods of business. Civic virtue and efficiency, so Hays argued, "would be best achieved if the business community controlled the city government."[35]

Following Hays and using the method of collective biographical analysis, Fox found the members of Philadelphia's Committee of Seventy to be largely upper-class business and professional men: "These Philadelphia reformers had ancestral roots in the community, were college-educated, and were established business and professional men, who owned family businesses. They were members of the best clubs and staffed the boards of philanthropic and cultural institutions. These factors emphasize their patrician background."[36] Fox went on to show that these men were not resentful of rising immigrants or new plutocrats. Rather, they were themselves extremely successful men and leaders of the community. And they were interested in efficiency: after all, Morris Cooke, Blankenberg's right-hand man after he got into office, was a student of Frederick W. Taylor, the famous efficiency engineer.

Fox's analysis of the Philadelphia Progressives is excellent and revealing but fails to note the lack of First Family representation in this movement. Just as the Committee of 100 during the Mugwump era included none save Henry Charles Lea from the sample of fifty families, so the Committee of Seventy in 1911 included none at all. Of the seventy members of the committee, moreover, only a handful were from *Social Register* families, of that time or later, and none belonged to the Philadelphia Club.* They were, in short, concerned, upper middle-class, Protestant businessmen, lawyers, and doctors who were rising in the world. As far as the strictly inner circle of Proper Philadelphia was concerned, it was outsiders on the make who supported the auslander Rudolph Blankenberg in 1911. But so it has always been in the Quaker City, since at least the days of Benjamin Franklin. The Progressive movement in Philadelphia, then, did not represent upper-class authority; nor was it a status revolution. It provides an example, moreover, of how so much of the first-rate interpretive history of this nation has been written in terms of New England rather than of Pennsylvania.

GOVERNORS OF MASSACHUSETTS
AND PENNSYLVANIA

The differing attitudes toward governmental authority in Massachusetts and Pennsylvania are all too clearly symbolized in the location and architecture of their capitols. Whereas the Massachusetts State House is located in the very heart of the historical, financial, cultural, and social center of the state, the Pennsylvania State House, which was moved from what is now Independence Hall to Lancaster in 1799 and to the frontier village of Harrisburg during the War of 1812, is surrounded by a cultural and social desert. What small town charm Harrisburg once had is today symbolized by a series of decaying old mansions left vacant (as is the more recently built, and extravagantly costly,

---

*The best clubs referred to by Fox were not the best in the Proper Philadelphia sense.

pseudo-Williamsburg executive mansion) because of the continuing floods of the neglected Susquehanna River. People have always been aware of the symbolic value of architecture: Beacon Hill symbolizes historical continuity, civic pride, and class authority; Harrisburg symbolizes neither continuity nor pride and certainly not class authority, especially as far as Philadelphians are concerned.

As we have seen, the Massachusetts constitution, written in 1780 by the Beacon Hill Brahmins of that day, remains in force today. A conservative but flexible document, like our federal Constitution, it has of course been amended many times: in the 1820s, the religious test for office was done away with, and the establishment of Congregationalism abolished a decade later. At the time of the First World War, because of the expense involved in elections, gubernatorial terms were extended from one to two years.

In contrast, the first Pennsylvania constitution, written by radicals in 1776, proved inadequate almost immediately and was replaced in 1790 by a more conservative document. But Pennsylvanians continued to mistrust executive authority and leadership: in 1838, a new constitution was written that limited the governor to two terms rather than three and cut down his appointive powers considerably. Executive authority was further weakened in 1873, when a new constitution increased the governor's term to four years but allowed no consecutive second term in office; all Pennsylvania governors were to be lame ducks upon taking office from 1873 to 1967, when a new constitution was written, allowing the governor to serve two consecutive terms.

Massachusetts governors, with one- and then two-year terms—as compared to the three- and four-year terms of Pennsylvania governors—have nevertheless been far more likely to be reelected. Of the fifty-eight elected governors of Massachusetts between 1780 and 1965, forty-four were elected to office more than once: Governors John Hancock and Caleb Strong eleven times each; Levi Lincoln, Jr. nine times (1825–1834); and Leverett Saltonstall, three times (1939–1945). In contrast, Pennsylvanians removed the governor from immediate voter control by increasing his term of office; at the same time, however, the constitution limited his power, first by restricting reelection and then by abolishing it. Of the sixteen governors between 1790 and 1873, a period during which governors were allowed to succeed themselves, none was reelected more than once and eight, or half, served only one term in office. After 1873 only two governors, Robert E. Pattison, Democratic reformer in the Mugwump era, and Gifford Pinchot, Progressive Republican reformer, held office twice, but not in succession.

Whereas Boston Brahmins usually have been eager to serve their state on Beacon Hill, Proper Philadelphians have taken almost no part in governing Pennsylvania. After the first governor of Pennsylvania, Thomas Mifflin, left office in 1799, no native Philadelphian held the office until 1907, when Edwin S. Stuart became governor. After the second governor, Thomas McKean, stepped down in 1808, no more members of the First Family sample ever became governor; the only upper-class Philadelphian to serve in the office was George H. Earle III, maverick scion of a wealthy Main Line family and the first Democratic governor in the twentieth century (1935). In the whole history of Pennsylvania, then, only three native Philadelphians—Mifflin, Stuart, and Earle—and only three members of the city's upper class—Mifflin, McKean, and Earle—served in the governor's office.

Not only have Philadelphia Gentlemen shown little interest in becoming governor, but they have also looked down on those who did. In this sense as in others, Sidney Fisher was typical of his class. In the years between 1834 and 1871, when he kept his diary, ten men held the governorship of Pennsylvania, only two of whom, Joseph Ritner (1835–1839) and Andrew G. Curtin (1861–1867), are mentioned in its pages, and he looked down on both. On December 29, 1837, after "a feed" at the home of Daniel W. Coxe (brother of Tench Coxe), Fisher recorded his observations on some of his fellow guests— politicians then attending the constitutional convention in the city.

> They were, as might be expected, rather a coarse looking set of men. The crack orator of the convention & the legislature, Mr. Steevens [Thaddeus Stevens], a man of undoubted talent, and our stout governor Ritner were there. . . . Steevens . . . has a good face, and a fine, massy head, indicative of much intellectual power, tho he wants refinement of manner & I suspect, cultivation of mind. Ritner is a bluff, good-humored, honest looking, fat, dutchman, without the slightest approach to the appearance or manner of a gentleman. This however is not to be expected in a Governor of Penna.; it is more than we dare hope for that he is a sensible, honest, well-meaning man.[37]

In striking contrast to Proper Philadelphia's record, no fewer than sixteen upper-class Bostonians have served in the governor's office. Six were members of the fifty families in the Boston sample—Samuel Adams (1793–1797), John Brooks (1816–1823), Edward Everett (1836–1840), Oliver Ames (1887–1890), Leverett Saltonstall (1939–1945), and Endicott Peabody (1963–1965). The ten other upper-class Boston governors were John Hancock (1780–1785, 1787–1793), James Bowdoin (1785–1787), Increase Sumner (1797–1799), Christopher Gore (1809–1810), William Eustis (1823–1825), William Eustis Russell (1891–1894), Roger Wolcott (1896–1900), Curtis Guild, Jr. (1906–1909), Eben S. Draper (1909–1911), Robert Bradford (1947–1949), and Christian Herter (1953–1957). Moreover, all of this group except Brooks and Ames graduated from Harvard College.*

In addition to the sixteen governors from upper-class Boston, Massachusetts governors have come from leading families of other cities and towns of the state. Caleb Strong and Levi Lincoln, Jr., members of mansion families in Northampton and Worcester, respectively, were two of the most popular governors in Massachusetts history.

Pennsylvania governors, as we have seen, have tended to be self-made men and military heroes. The contrast between the political leadership in the two states is nicely illustrated in the cases of two post–Civil War governors, William

---

*Of the three upper-class governors from Philadelphia, only Thomas Mifflin graduated from Penn. McKean did not go to college. Earle went to Harvard but did not take a degree.

Claflin, elected governor of Massachusetts in 1869, and John White Geary, elected in Pennsylvania in 1867.

William Claflin embodied the Massachusetts tradition of inherited wealth in public service. His father, Lee Claflin, was an extremely successful boot and shoe manufacturer in Milford, Worcester County. A staunch Methodist, he was one of three financial founders of Boston University. Young William Claflin was educated at a private academy and sent to Brown University, which he left before graduating in order to enter the family business. Claflin served the commonwealth as governor and was also elected to the Senate and House of the state, as well as to the U.S. House of Representatives. Moreover, sharing the typical interest of his class in education, Claflin for many years sat on the boards of Boston University, Wellesley and Mount Holyoke colleges, and Claflin University (named after Lee Claflin), a school for blacks in Orangeburg, South Carolina.

The colorful and charismatic career of John White Geary was far different from Claflin's. Born in a small town in the far western frontier county of Westmoreland, Geary was forced to leave little Jefferson College after his father died heavily in debt. His career for the next few years was varied: he taught school, clerked in a store, studied law and engineering, gained admittance to the bar, and was sent off to Kentucky on a surveying expedition. At sixteen he had joined the local militia and at twenty-nine he went off to fight in the Mexican War, participating in the assault on Mexico City under General Winfield Scott. After the war President Polk appointed Geary postmaster of San Francisco. He became the city's first mayor and played an important role in bringing California into the Union as a free state. Geary finally returned to his Westmoreland County farm because of his wife's ill health. He declined Polk's offer of the governorship of Utah but when Kansas fell into anarchy he accepted an appointment as governor of that territory. Through wise military means he brought order to Kansas before again returning to Pennsylvania. When the Civil War broke out, Geary was made colonel of the Pennsylvania Twenty-eighth Division (which later won fame in the Battle of the Bulge); he fought through the whole war, was wounded twice, and saw his son killed. He came back home a military hero and was promoted for the governorship by the Cameron machine. In his two terms, Geary pursued his own opinionated and autocratic way and fought many battles with the legislature, vetoing 390 of the 9,242 bills passed during his tenure. He died in 1873, soon after retiring from the governorship.*

Claflin and Geary illustrate my theory of authority: where class authority is weak, charismatic leaders such as Geary come to the fore. With the exception of the notorious Ben Butler, military charisma has not characterized the political leadership of militant Massachusetts as it so very often has the milder and more passive state of Pennsylvania. Thus, in addition to Geary (handpicked by

---

*A descendant and namesake, and a graduate of Harvard, was president of the Philadelphia Club at its hundredth anniversary in 1934.

the Pennsylvania political boss Simon Cameron because of his military record), Governors Hartrant (1873-1879), Beaver (1887-1891), and Hastings (1895-1899) were all boss picked Civil War heroes and were always referred to as "General" (as was Cameron himself even though his only military service was with the local militia).

In all, there were fifty-eight governors of Massachusetts between 1790 and the close of Endicott Peabody's rule in 1965; in Pennsylvania, thirty-eight governors were elected to office between 1790 and the end of William Scranton's term in 1967. Let us now take a look at the collective characteristics of the governors of the two states.

In the first place, Philadelphia's lack of political hegemony in the state is shown by the fact that only four governors, or less than 8 percent, were born in the city or its suburbs, in contrast to twenty-six, or 44 percent, of the governors of Massachusetts who were born in the Boston area.

As an indication of class origins, it is interesting that the Massachusetts governors were a far better educated group—forty-two, or 72 percent, were college graduates, as against sixteen, or 43 percent, of the Pennsylvanians. After Thomas Mifflin, for example, there was not another college graduate in the executive mansion until James Pollack, a Scotch-Irish Pennsylvanian and a graduate of Princeton, was sent there in 1855. Just as Proper Philadelphians took very little interest in governing their state, so their major cultural institutions, especially the University of Pennsylvania, had very little influence on the state's leadership. Thus, whereas twenty-one, or 30 percent, of the Massachusetts governors were graduates of Harvard (all bachelors of arts), only two governors in the whole history of Pennsylvania took undergraduate degrees at Penn. After Thomas Mifflin (bachelor of arts, 1775), no Penn graduate was governor until George Leader (bachelor of science in education, 1935) was elected in 1955.

Another contrast between the governors of the two states is that thirty-three, or 57 percent, of the Massachusetts governors went on to hold national offices during their careers as against only twelve, or 33 percent, of the Pennsylvanians. Of the Massachusetts men, Calvin Coolidge reached the presidency and Elbridge Gerry the vice-presidency; seven governors—Eustis, Everett, Boutwell, Long, Tobin, Herter, and Volpe—held cabinet posts; and eight—Strong, Davis, Everett, Boutwell, Washburn, Crane, Walsh, and Saltonstall—went on to the U.S. Senate. The governorship of Pennsylvania has proved to be a political graveyard. As Philip S. Klein noted in 1940:

> From 1790 to the present day no Pennsylvania Governor has ever entered the national cabinet, much less become President or Vice-President of the United States. Only two of them, William Findley and William Bigler, found their way into the United States Senate. The majority were not heard from again.
>
> It was possibly because of this fatal touch of the governorship that Pennsylvania failed to produce any Websters, Clays, Calhouns, Van Burens or Bentons. The state certainly was lacking in dynamic political leadership. The passage of a century has brought all too few changes. Pennsylvania politics is still a game—a game without rules—which is after all, perhaps democracy in its most natural state.[38]

ETHNICITY, RELIGION, AND LEADERSHIP
IN MASSACHUSETTS AND PENNSYLVANIA

The intolerant Puritan colony on Massachusetts Bay was an ethnically and religiously homogeneous community throughout its history, as was the state of Massachusetts until the coming of the Irish in the 1830s and 1840s. Penn's colony on the Delaware was a sectarian and multicultural society from almost the very beginning. At the time of our first census in 1790, Pennsylvania was the most ethnically heterogeneous state in the new nation. This ethnic and religious contrast between Massachusetts and Pennsylvania of course contributed to the differences in leadership.

As might be expected, almost all the governors of Massachusetts between 1780 and 1935 were of English Puritan stock. And although the two major exceptions, James Sullivan (1807–1808) and David Ignatius Walsh (1914–1915), were sons of poor Irish immigrants, they were very much in the traditional Massachusetts mold of class authority and high standards of leadership (see Chapter 19).

The defiant democracy of Pennsylvania, by contrast was led predominantly by the sons of Scotch-Irish immigrants, all of them heirs to the traditions of Scottish Presbyterianism, brought from John Calvin's Geneva by John Knox. Knox's zeal for education transformed the sheep-herding and sheep-stealing lowland Scots into the best educated people of eighteenth-century Europe. These lowlanders settled northern Ireland at the time of the Stuarts and then came in large numbers to Pennsylvania in the eighteenth century. Every Scotch-Irish community soon had its educated minister who ran a church and also a school. Of all the religious groups in the colonies, only the Puritans of New England exerted more influence than the Scotch-Irish Presbyterians in the founding of schools and colleges in America.

Like the New England Puritans, the Scotch-Irish Presbyterians of Pennsylvania emphasized education as a preparation for a calling to leadership in church and state. The only natives of Pennsylvania to achieve first rank in American history, James G. Blaine and James Buchanan, were sons of the Scotch-Irish frontier. Of the thirty-eight governors of Pennsylvania between 1790 and 1967, no fewer than sixteen were of Scotch-Irish descent, ten were of German ancestry (German Reformed Churchmen and Lutherans rather than sectarians), and the rest were of English or mixed ancestry. Even in the period 1800–1850, when seven of the ten German governors held office, the Scotch-Irish dominated politics, as well as the bench and the bar of the state.

> During the period [1817–1832] all the governors but one were Pennsylvania Germans, and all but one came from east of the Susquehanna River. The exception was William Findley of Franklin County, a Scotch-Irishman. The Scotch-Irish seemed a great deal more willing to support a German candidate than the Germans a Scotch-Irishman. This, perhaps, was because the Scotch-Irish politicians had a more realistic conception of the governor's office than their German neighbors. The latter, for centuries accustomed to think in terms of feudal relationships and one-man sovereignty, felt that they had gained all when they placed in

the governor's chair one of their compatriots. The Scotch-Irish, not so impressed by the titular authority of the chief magistrate, obtained more substantial political power by exacting from the German governors, as a price for their continued electoral support, most of the important appointive posts. About fifty percent of the state cabinet officers and a much higher proportion of the judges during the period were Scotch-Irishmen who were commissioned by German governors.[39]

The class hegemony of Brahmin Boston in Massachusetts contrasted sharply with the minority and ethnic politics of Pennsylvania. Thus, Massachusetts was a stronghold of federalism until the governorship of John Brooks, who failed to run for reelection in 1823. Although Proper Philadelphians on the whole were Federalists, much like their peers in Boston, the influence of federalism (the party of class authority) was very weak in both the city and the state. Pittsburgh, the Scotch-Irish Presbyterian capital of Pennsylvania even today, was the last stronghold of federalism in the state.

> Scotch-Irish drive and the roughness and readiness of the frontier were the dominating elements. But with all its energy and impatience Pittsburgh was politically more conservative than other parts of the West. It had for many years been a Federalist stronghold; as late as 1816 it voted for the Federalist presidential electors and in 1817 and 1820 supported the Federalist candidate for governor. One of its strongest newspapers, the *Pittsburgh Gazette*, was dubbed the "lone outpost of Federalism in the West." The causes for this need not concern us here save to note that reaction against the violence of the Whiskey Rebellion and the controlling influence of a few powerful families were of major importance.[40]

I question Klein's apparent assumption that "energy and impatience" (in spite of his own example of Pittsburgh) are incompatible with "conservative" political values. It may be just the other way around. Federalist Boston in its family and nation founding days, for instance, probably would have had more in common, in terms of religious piety and political conservatism, with the conservative and driving citizens of Houston or Dallas today than with the liberal establishment centered at Harvard during the 1960s and early 1970s. The conservative energy and drive of the "few powerful families" of Pittsburgh, moreover, has always contrasted with the liberal and mild style of Proper Philadelphia. As a matter of fact, Philadelphia's mildness and humility has often covered up resentment toward democracy itself within the establishment. Today, for instance, Philadelphia, as far as industrial and manufacturing firms are concerned, is largely an absentee owned city whereas Pittsburgh surely is not. And the Pittsburgh renaissance after World War II was led by the Scotch-Irish Mellons and the business establishment, in cooperation with the energetic Scotch- Irish and Catholic mayor David Lawrence, later the first Catholic governor of Pennsylvania. It is surely appropriate that Philadelphia's postwar renaissance was inspired and guided by auslander Richardson Dilworth, scion of an old Pittsburgh steel family and Philadelphia's greatest citizen since the auslander Benjamin Franklin.

In the years before the Civil War, the vast majority of upper-class members in all America supported first the Federalist and then the Whig Party. In Massachusetts, where class hegemony was the rule, either Federalists or Whigs held the governorship for all but a dozen years in the period 1800–1860.* During the same sixty years in Pennsylvania, where class authority was lacking and defiant democracy was the rule, no Federalist served as governor; Jeffersonian Republicans and Jacksonian Democrats were in power except for five years of Whig domination (1848–1853). Whereas Boston Brahmins had either their own men or men of their own party in the governor's office most of the time, Philadelphia Gentlemen, none of whom held the governorship in this period, developed the habit of voting for losers and, like Sidney Fisher, took it for granted that governors of Pennsylvania would not be gentlemen.

ETHNICITY AND RELIGION AS FACTORS IN CLASS AUTHORITY

It may very well be a sociological law that class authority and deference democracy tend to characterize homogeneous societies; charismatic authority and defiant democracy, heterogeneous ones. If this is so, it is not the contrasting ethics of elitist Calvinism as against egalitarian Quakerism that made the difference between Massachusetts and Pennsylvania but rather their contrasting ethnic and religious makeups. Nevertheless, ideas and social structures are intricately interacting forces in history. Thus, the ethnic and religious homogeneity of Massachusetts in its founding days reflected the ideas of the Puritan gentlemen and clergy who settled the Bay Colony in order to rule themselves in church and state, just as the religious and ethnic heterogeneity of Pennsylvania represented the ideas of one charismatic and utopian leader who wished to establish a refuge in the New World for his persecuted co-religionists. At the same time and perhaps inadvertently, Penn set the stamp of heterogeneity on his colony forever because of his desire to attract as many colonists as possible in order to maximize the economic returns on his colonial investment. To put it another way, egalitarian ideals and ethnic heterogeneity are mutually reinforcing factors in history that tend to produce materialistic plutocracies, as we Americans should surely understand in our day; authoritarian and deference values militate against the growth of pure plutocracies. Money has always talked in all societies, but aristocratic societies also exhibit deference to class manners and culture; plutocracies are subservient to moneyed elements alone.

Another way of looking at the difference between Massachusetts and Pennsylvania is to see that the problem of authority in the latter state has *always* been somewhat similar to the problem of authority in America as a whole in the Gilded Age of plutocratic enterprise. Just as William Penn urged settlers to come to Pennsylvania from all over Europe, largely for economic reasons, so

---

*This figure does not include the eleven years when Levi Lincoln, Jr., was governor. Though he was a Jeffersonian by tradition, his tenure was an era of good feeling for both Jeffersonians and Federalists.

the leaders of the Republican business establishment in the Gilded Age encouraged immigration from Europe and Asia, largely in order to have a cheap supply of labor to build their railroads and factories and work their mines. It was not the conservative business interests that wanted to restrict immigration in those heady times but the reformers, Progressives, and liberal intellectuals (often drawn from the privileged classes of inherited rather than newly acquired wealth), who sympathized with the exploited masses in the slums of urban industrial centers and mining towns from Pennsylvania to Colorado.

The history of Pennsylvania differed from our national history in the age of enterprise after the Civil War in one very important respect: class authority with some sense of responsibility toward the whole community never asserted itself either in Philadelphia or in the rest of the state as it did on the national scene, for instance, in the case of the Progressive movement, led by men like Theodore Roosevelt. The one outstanding exception to this rule was Gifford Pinchot, Roosevelt's friend, fellow conservationist, and ardent Progressive, who dominated Pennsylvania politics during the 1920s and early 1930s, serving as governor from 1923 to 1927 and then again from 1931 to 1935. In the Franklin auslander tradition of distinguished leadership in Pennsylvania, Pinchot was a native of Connecticut and a descendant of Huguenots and Calvinists.

Pinchot managed to give Pennsylvanians a Progressive administration in the generally reactionary 1920s. According to Klein and Hoogenboom:

> His administration (1923–1927) was probably the most outstanding up to that time in Pennsylvania history. Pinchot's achievements stemmed not only from reorganizing the state's government, improving election laws, and settling an anthracite strike, but also from his ability as an administrator. . . . Pinchot developed great esprit de corps among his staff, and it filtered down through the civil service. Not content with generalities, Pinchot, as he left office, condemned the Vare-Mitten machine in Philadelphia (the Mittens controlled Philadelphia Rapid Transit) and the Mellon machine in Pittsburgh; he also rebuked the "great moneyed interests" that ran Pennsylvania. Though it is sometimes questioned whether individual administrators can affect a bureaucracy, Pinchot's style made a difference. "Pinchot is no longer governor," remarked a dairyman to a local health officer. "It isn't necessary to be so strict now."[41]

Pinchot provides an excellent example of the patrician in politics, a rare phenomenon in Pennsylvania. A Calvinist moralist (an ardent supporter of Prohibition) of independent means,* he was a forceful leader who owed nothing to bosses and machines. Mrs. Pinchot, whom he met and married at the age of forty-nine during his unsuccessful campaign for the Senate (1914), was an avid champion of working women and campaigner for women's suffrage. The Pinchots took the obligations of their advantages in life seriously. "My own money," Pinchot remarked in 1914, "came from unearned increment on land in New York held by my grandfather, who willed the money, not the land, to me.

---

*He and his wife contributed $112,000 of the $118,000 collected for his gubernatorial campaign.

Having got my wages in advance in that way, I am now trying to work them out."[42]

In spite of his wealth and patrician ancestry, the crusading Pinchot was never quite liked by Proper Philadelphians or particularly welcome in their drawing rooms. How very different the political history of Pennsylvania might have been had Philadelphia Gentlemen down through the years really believed in Pinchot's aristocratic values, to which of course they have always given lip service. Owen Wister, who knew Pinchot not from the drawing rooms of Philadelphia but as a fellow member of President Roosevelt's inner circle of friends in Washington, once wrote: "If such miracles could be, I would set up at Yale an image of Gifford Pinchot for all boys dowered with the gift of wealth to touch and be inspired to serve their country discerningly for the sheer love of serving."[43]

With Pinchot in mind, I should like to make one final refutation of the Proper Philadelphia excuse that gentlemen had no chance to take the lead in governing their state because of its ethnic and religious diversity. Although this excuse may have been true at one time (which I doubt), it certainly has no validity in the twentieth century. By the turn of the century, Massachusetts was far more of a melting pot than Pennsylvania. In 1900 the foreign born population of Massachusetts was 56 percent of the whole, whereas Pennsylvania had only 34 percent foreign born; Boston and Philadelphia had populations that were 65 percent and 53 percent foreign born, respectively. Massachusetts had six upper-class Boston governors—Curtis Guild, Jr., Ebin S. Draper, Leverett Saltonstall, Robert Bradford, Christian Herter, and Endicott Peabody—between 1900 and 1965; George H. Earle III was the only upper-class Philadelphian (and the first since 1800) to be elected governor in this period. In the rough and tumble of ethnic politics in twentieth-century Massachusetts, in other words, class authority was far from dead. Thus, Republican Leverett Saltonstall beat the Boston Irish idol, James M. Curley, for the governorship in 1939 (Curley was the only important Massachusetts Democrat to lose in that New Deal year) and then went on to two more terms as governor. In Irish dominated Boston, class authority still held sway at the state and senatorial levels. When Saltonstall was running against Foster Furcolo for the U.S. Senate in 1954, poll workers in the South End were not above advising their people, with a wink and dig in the ribs, "When you go in there, you may as well vote for old Salty."[44]

The Proper Philadelphia excuse hardly holds much water, furthermore, if one considers national politics in the ethnic twentieth century, when the White House has been occupied by such men as the two Roosevelts from Harvard, Taft from Yale, and Woodrow Wilson from Princeton. It was Franklin Roosevelt and his Brahmin associates who had the greatest appeal among ethnic minority voters, surely in part because of their aristocratic sense of responsibility to the whole American community, as against the Republican adherence to the same plutocratic values that brought them such political success in the Gilded Age and the Roaring Twenties.

GOVERNOR SAMUEL W. PENNYPACKER
AND THE PENNSYLVANIA MIND

During the Victorian era, Samuel W. Pennypacker was one of the more distinguished cultural and civic leaders of his adopted city of Philadelphia. If the best insight into the mind of the Philadelphia Gentleman is to be found in the pages of Sidney Fisher's diary, so Pennypacker's rambling autobiography is equally revealing of the Pennsylvania mind from an almost diametrically opposite point of view. Whereas Fisher took pride in his social position at the heart of genteel Philadelphia, Pennypacker was equally proud of his ancestral roots in the Pennsylvania Dutch country and even of his residence north of Market Street, far across the tracks from Fisher's fashionable world. When Pennypacker was elected president of the Historical Society of Pennsylvania in 1900, he recorded that "the event marked an innovation in the conduct of the Society. Up to my time the president had always been selected from among the families long identified with the life of the city and had always dwelt south of Market Street."[45] As governor of Pennsylvania (1903-1907) he was largely responsible for obtaining state funds with which to build the handsome fireproof building on Locust Street that still houses the society. Naive but successful, Pennypacker was a rare booster of his adopted city and native state, never losing an opportunity to place *his* Pennsylvania in a more favorable light than *his enemy state* of Massachusetts. His history textbook, *Pennsylvania the Keystone*, ponders "whether the 'Scarlet Letter' of Hawthorne or the 'Story of Kennett' by Taylor [Bayard Taylor was a childhood friend] holds the higher rank among American novels."[46] Although Pennypacker possessed an impressive collection of Frankliniana, he quite naturally had little use for the grasping auslander from Boston, who, so Pennypacker wrote,

> published solely for gain . . . remained with the Quakers so long as they retained power and left them when they lost it . . . secured the favors of women without marriage . . . claimed to have founded the University of Pennsylvania, because he wrote a pamphlet, although he endeavored to prevent Dr. William Smith, the provost and real founder, from getting money in England for its support . . . claimed to have founded the American Philosophical Society, although the minutes show that he never read a paper before it and while president even failed to attend the meetings.[47]

Pennypacker was convinced that the sectarian religious heritage of Pennsylvania was far more pure than that of the Puritans who founded Massachusetts. "Of the Reformers," he wrote, "Luther was a charcoal burner; Calvin a peasant; and among them all the only man of long lineage and high culture was Caspar Schwenkfeld von Ossing, a nobleman of Silesia. He taught a system of sweet and pure theology which, carried through the Mennonites of Holland to England, led to the origin of the Quakers."[48] Pennypacker explained that "Pennsylvania in achievement was above any other state" because of "the law of nature" and the "scientifically proved" fact that "the crossing of allied stocks leads to the increase of vital activities."[49]

Pennypacker also took great pride in his family's role in the Civil War.* As a young man he had fought in the front lines at Gettysburg, and in an article on "The War of the Rebellion" he wrote that his family had

> sent into the war two generals, an adjutant-general, four colonels, a lieutenant-colonel, two surgeons, two assistant surgeons, an adjutant, nine captains, seven lieutenants and one hundred and sixteen sergeants, corporals and privates, including the most youthful of American generals—in all one hundred and forty-five men, and, so far as has been ascertained, an unequalled contribution to the great struggle."[50]

He was pleased that Theodore Roosevelt often referred to this example of family patriotism. Pennypacker was also careful to point out how Pennsylvania played the most important role of all the Northern states, including Massachusetts, in the winning of the war. "Pennsylvania," he wrote, "furnished two of the five commanders of that magnificent force, the Army of the Potomac, upon which, after awarding due credit to other organizations, we must concede the burden of overwhelming the rebellion was cast—McClellan, who gave it form, and Meade, under whom it won its greatest victory and its final success."[51]

Pennsylvania, according to Pennypacker, was a leader not only in military affairs but also in education and learning. Thus, he wrote that William Penn attracted to his colony "more men of learning than other colonies whose promoters were simply seeking for profit, or were bent upon enforcement of illiberal policies."[52] After all, the tolerant sectarians of Pennsylvania, so he put it, "were people of great intellectual activity."[53]

Pennypacker's lifelong interest in history, literature, and education was finally rewarded by his election to the socially exclusive board of trustees of the University of Pennsylvania in 1886. Perhaps his antiquarian research was a critical factor in his election: "Before I became a trustee, the University always traced its origin to a pamphlet written by Franklin in 1749, but I succeeded in proving that it really began with a charity school for which a building was erected in 1740, thus adding nine years to its life at the other end and making it antedate Princeton."[54] Though not a man of either extremely large means or eminent social position, Pennypacker was proud of bringing money to the university: "When I became Governor, by an act of May 15, 1903, an appropriation of one hundred thousand dollars was made for the maintenance of the University, thus setting a precedent which has been followed since."[55] He admired both William Pepper and Charles Harrison, the "real founders" of the modern University of Pennsylvania, which, as Pennypacker put it, "has taken again its former place in the foremost rank of American universities" under their provostships.[56]

---

*Matthew S. Quay, his kinsman, won the Congressional Medal of Honor, as did a Quaker cousin, Galusha Pennypacker. After reading of the life and writings of the Pennsylvania chauvinist Pennypacker, one sees more clearly than ever why military charisma, rather than class authority, was the major factor in Pennsylvania politics.

Pennypacker, as both judge and governor was a simple, direct, and impeccably honest public servant. His incorruptible administration at Harrisburg was, he freely admitted, partly the result of his possession of adequate inherited means. In his autobiography he carefully related the many ways he saved the taxpayers money by simple living in the executive mansion.

But Pennypacker betrayed a certain naiveté in politics. He was put into the governorship by his notorious kinsman Matthew Quay and he accepted boss Quay's "suggestions" on all the top appointments in his administration except for Hampton Carson, an old friend at the Historical Society, whom he insisted upon naming attorney general. On the whole, Proper Philadelphians were pleased with Pennypacker's election. And probably more of them served in Harrisburg during his administration than in any other, before or since. "Carson, Wharton and Montgomery, who came with myself," Pennypacker wrote in his autobiography, "and Dr. Samuel G. Dixon, president of the Academy of Natural Sciences, and John C. Groome, captain of the First City Troop, whom I drew along later, were referred to as the influx of gentlemen into the political life of the state."[57]*

Nevertheless, Henry Charles Lea was far from approving of Pennypacker's administration ("more of the same," he put it at the time), and his lack of enthusiasm was certainly understandable: like "most of the men of representative character" in Philadelphia, Pennypacker had been a strong supporter of Blaine in the presidential election of 1884, when Lea and all the genteel Mugwumps of Boston had deserted their beloved Republican party and voted for Cleveland. "Blaine," according to Pennypacker, "was the most astute and sagacious statesman of his period."[58] Pennypacker had also refused to follow "the radicalism of Lea" when he formed the Committee of 100 in 1880, and he never had much use for the Reform Club, established under Lea's leadership in 1872. And of course he was against the Anti-Quay League, with Lea as a vice-president. (The league's campaign to defeat bossism in Pennsylvania included opposition to Quay and Pennypacker in the gubernatorial election of 1902.)

There is no better example of corruption in Pennsylvania politics than the scandal surrounding the building of the new state capitol during Pennypacker's administration. The old capitol had burned down in 1897, and Pennypacker laid the cornerstone for a new capitol in 1904. On the completion of the Vic-

---

*Pennypacker, however, was not an unquestioning admirer of the Philadelphia Gentleman, as the following evaluation of John Cadwalader, Jr., whom he appointed to a minor office in 1906, suggests.

Cadwalader I appointed against the earnest protest of the leaders of both the Republican and Democratic parties, because he was a gentleman who I knew would be fair, though narrow, and beyond influence, and partly because of my great regard for his father. I have found as a general thing that nice people have little sense of gratitude. They are apt to feel that they confer a favor by accepting what is given them. . . . Some year later, over another matter, Cadwalader wrote a paper for the *Public Ledger* assailing my personal motives. . . . It was unmanly and disingenuous. He made a capable and useful official (Samuel W. Pennypacker, *The Autobiography of a Pennsylvanian* [Philadelphia: Winston, 1918], p. 431).

torian pile in 1906, at a cost of $4 million, the governor called it "the most beautiful and most inexpensive state capitol in the country" (the modernizing of Bulfinch's capitol on Beacon Hill, Pennypacker pointed out in a message to the legislature, had cost $6,980,531.55).[59] Unfortunately for the governor, soon after he and thousands of other proud citizens had finished celebrating the dedication of this building, Democrat William H. Berry, a local Methodist minister who had been elected state treasurer in 1905,

> discovered and announced that the capitol had actually cost closer to $13,000,000 thanks to its decoration and furnishings. After Berry heard that fifteen men had performed the impossible feat of laying $90,000 worth of parquet flooring in two weeks, he became suspicious and sought independent estimates for decorations in his office. His ceiling, estimated at $550, actually cost $5,500, and oak wainscoting worth $1,800 had cost $15,500. Furthermore, contractor John H. Sanderson of Philadelphia had sold the state chairs and chandeliers by the foot or pound. For example, he had offered to supply a chandelier for $193.50 but had billed it at $4.85-per-pound rate for odds and ends, making the actual cost $2,500. The state, Berry estimated, had paid $5 million more for its capitol than it should have paid. Sure of Pennypacker's own honesty, the public blamed him only for lack of judgment.[60]

If Governor Pennypacker was lacking in judgment with regard to the capitol's construction, it would seem, in light of the almost unanimous findings of historians of both Pennsylvanian and national politics in the Gilded Age, that he was guilty of a more curious, and nearly incomprehensible, lack of judgment with regard to Senator Matthew Quay.

> Mr. Quay is a plain, simple, modest and kindly man, with a taste for books and literature, with no propensity for the acquisition of riches, and with a genius for the organization and control of men in masses, such as, *like the gift of Shakespeare*, comes but once in a century. . . . his fame is assured as a statesman who deserves well of his country, and in whose achievements *even Massachusetts may properly take pride*."[61]

Thus wrote Pennypacker on the final page of a very slim and embarrassing book entitled *Pennsylvania and Massachusetts: A Historical Parallel*, which he published privately in Philadelphia in 1901. The book originally had been written to refute an article called "The Ills of Pennsylvania," signed by "A Pennsylvanian" and published in the *Atlantic Monthly* of October 1901. Pennypacker's reply, apparently written in haste, catalogued the mythical achievements of past Pennsylvanians to counter the *Atlantic* article's closely reasoned discussion of the causes of the widely recognized ills of Pennsylvania bossism.

In spite of Pennypacker's naive if not downright inaccurate views of Pennsylvania history and his ostrichlike attitudes toward his notorious cousin, the governor's lifelong defense of his native ground is touching. Proud of his achievements in office, he lived out his final days in his beloved Pennsylvania Dutch country, dying at Pennypacker's Mills in 1916.

UNITED STATES SENATORS: CLASS AUTHORITY IN MASSACHUSETTS AND BOSS RULE IN PHILADELPHIA

According to the political theory of mixed forms, which dominated the thinking of our founding fathers, the Senate was to represent the property interests and the social forces of aristocracy in the new nation, just as the House was to represent the people and the social forces of democracy. From the nation's founding to the present, no other state, including aristocratic Virginia, has sent a more cohesive class of distinguished gentlemen to the Senate than has Massachusetts. Pennsylvania, however, has probably sent a less distinguished group of senators to the nation's capital than has any of the other thirteen original states; by and large, even those Pennsylvania senators of great natural talents, as we shall see, have been forced to use up their energies in eternal jockeying for power at home rather than in taking the lead in making our laws. Though all students of American political history have heard of Daniel Webster, the only Pennsylvania senator they may have heard of is David Wilmot, author of the controversial proviso that would have prohibited slavery in any territory acquired as a result of the Mexican War (the proviso was defeated in Congress). Wilmot, a Free Soil Democrat and friend of Lincoln, was one of the founders of the national Republican party and the first Republican senator from Pennsylvania. As has been so often the case with distinguished Pennsylvanians, Wilmot came of an old Puritan family from Connecticut that had migrated to northeastern Pennsylvania during the late eighteenth century.

The Senate of the United States has often been called the most distinguished club in America, which indeed it has been and still is. But during the entire first century of the Philadelphia Club's history (1834–1934), no member ever sat in the Senate or inhabited the governor's mansion in Harrisburg. When Senator Logan refused to stand for reelection in 1807, he became the last senator to be *elected* from Philadelphia until Boies Penrose went to Washington in 1897. In fact, Logan, George Mifflin Dallas (appointed 1831–1833), Penrose, and George Wharton Pepper (appointed in 1922 upon the death of Penrose and defeated for reelection), were the only members of the First Family sample to represent their state in the Senate.

Proper Philadelphia's indifference toward Pennsylvania's senators is nicely revealed, as usual, in the diary of Sidney Fisher. For instance, he recorded talks with Webster, Clay, and Calhoun, as well as with President Jackson. He also knew several members of such senatorial families as the Otises, Sumners, and Silsbees of Massachusetts; the Bayards of Delaware; and the Wadsworths of New York. Yet, he never mentions having met a single senator from Pennsylvania besides Dallas. Like his views on governors quoted earlier, his rare comments on Pennsylvania senators are anything but complimentary, as his remarks on the two major politicians of his day in Pennsylvania show. Thus, Fisher described James Buchanan (like himself a graduate of Dickinson College) as a man of "incompetency & entire want of principle" and Simon Cameron as a "vindictive, unscrupulous and able man."[62]

The senators from Massachusetts have been a very different breed of men. Though Irish Catholics took over the mayor's office in the early years of the twentieth century and the governorship after 1930, the voters of Massachusetts have continued to the present day (with the outstanding exceptions of David I. Walsh and the Kennedy brothers) to choose Yankee gentlemen from Boston, as well as from the mansion families in other towns and cities throughout the state, to represent them in the Senate. Deference democracy has been the rule in Massachusetts, especially where its senators have been concerned. Whereas, for example, only four gentlemen from the Philadelphia First Family sample, two elected and two appointed, sat in the U.S. Senate, ten Massachusetts senators belong to the Boston sample: George Cabot (1791–1797), Timothy Pickering (1803–1811), John Quincy Adams (1803–1808), Harrison Gray Otis (1817–1823), Rufus Choate (1841–1845), Robert C. Winthrop (1850–1851), Charles Sumner (1851–1874), Edward Everett (1852–1854), Henry Cabot Lodge (1893–1924), Henry Cabot Lodge, Jr. (1937–1944), and Leverett Saltonstall (1945–1967).*

That the Brahmin tradition of the educated gentleman in politics influenced the senatorial history of Massachusetts is clearly illustrated in Table A–30 (see Appendix I). Not only were a large majority of the senators college graduates, but the predominance of Harvard men set a tone of class authority and cohesion on the leadership of the state as a whole. Moreover, several of the non–college graduates among the senators were also connected with Harvard as overseers after they made their way to the top. The Yale men belonged to the same class tradition, coming from leading Connecticut River families in the towns of the western counties.

In Pennsylvania, the majority of senators, were not college graduates, and those who did go to college attended a heterogeneous group of small institutions with no common class traditions. For example, William Bingham graduated from the College of Philadelphia in 1768; the next Penn graduate to be sent to the Senate from Pennsylvania was George Wharton Pepper, who took office in 1922. Though five Princetonians served as senators from Pennsylvania, this group was linked only in that they belonged to Scotch-Irish Calvinist families from the western and northern parts of the state.

THE NATION FOUNDING ERA: CLASS AUTHORITY IN MASSACHUSETTS AND POLITICAL CHAOS IN PENNSYLVANIA

Class authority in Massachusetts was at its height during the Federalist period. Of the seventeen senators who served Massachusetts between the nation's founding and the close of Harrison Gray Otis's career in 1827, all save one were

---

*The defeat of Robert Winthrop (Speaker of the House before being appointed to fill the senatorial vacancy caused by Webster's death) in the election of 1851 by Charles Sumner marked the end of over two centuries of the Winthrop family's public service to Massachusetts. But Senator Sumner carried on the same Brahmin tradition and became the most powerful senator in Washington during and right after the Civil War. And Henry Cabot Lodge and Leverett Saltonstall served their state in the Senate for over fifty years between them.

both college graduates and Federalists; eleven went to Harvard. The majority of these sixteen educated gentlemen either stood (rather than ran) for office or served when called; that so many served short terms was an indication that they took an active role in civic and political life, filling a wide variety of other important positions of leadership. They were, in short, public servants of authority and distinction rather than careerist politicians. Indeed, during this formative period, Massachusetts might be said to have represented class rather than party politics, even though the Massachusetts Federalists were fiercely partisan party men on the national scene. The one Massachusetts senator who was neither a college graduate nor a Federalist, Joseph B. Varnum, was no party hack but a statesman and national leader of some note. A self-taught farmer of humble origins, Varnum served with distinction in the Revolution. He went to Congress for eight consecutive terms, eventually becoming Speaker of the House, and in 1811 was chosen to succeed Timothy Pickering in the Senate, where he became president pro tempore and acting vice-president of the United States in 1813. Thus, even this exception as to background, education, and party illustrates the Massachusetts rule of leadership.

During this same formative period in Pennsylvania, the class and political situation was just the opposite from that in Massachusetts: of the fourteen Pennsylvanians elected to the Senate only two were college graduates, Bingham from the College of Philadelphia and Mühlenberg from the University of Halle in Germany. Moreover, the majority of the Pennsylvania senators were self-made men from the frontier counties. Though some of them had great natural ability, they lacked authoritative class traditions and proved to be mediocre senators—the result of sectionalism, provincialism, and, especially, extreme individualism.

Tocqueville saw with great insight that egalitarianism and individualism are two sides of the same coin and that both are products of excessive democracy. No wonder Klein found Pennsylvania politics to be suffering from

> the dominant spirit of the age—individualism . . . too much opportunity, too much equality, too much democracy, which expressed themselves in overweening ambition, an obstinate unwillingness to compromise, a contempt for all who consented to do so, and a steady refusal to take half a loaf so long as there was the remotest prospect of having the whole one.[63]

Klein also realized that the roots of excessive democracy in early nineteenth-century Pennsylvania lay largely in its lack of a ruling class.

> The aristocracy of birth or wealth which in other states was actively interested in public life, was in Pennsylvania growing more and more self-contained, politically passive and unwilling to assume the responsibility of governing. Unlike the planter aristocracy of the South, Pennsylvania's "high-toned" set was city bred and preoccupied with commerce and finance. . . . the officers of government and the officers of party . . . were drawn from the middle class—from the ranks of professional men of average means, or from the farm. Among these men there was nothing of the sort of unity or singleness of purpose which is so often found among the very rich. Dominating the professional group was personal ambition. Dominating the farming group was sectionalism.[64]

Though Pennsylvanians were Andrew Jackson's most consistent supporters in the Union, the state received very little patronage from Washington. Nothing better illustrates how anarchic individualism led to Pennsylvania's political impotence in Washington than Klein's description of Pennsylvania politics in 1832.

> The situation was almost incredible. Jackson opposed internal improvements, opposed the Second Bank of the United States, refused to uphold the protective tariff, and allied himself with Van Buren. Pennsylvania voters desired internal improvements, favored the bank, insisted upon the protective system, and hated Van Buren. Yet these same voters, without blinking an eye, were ready to drop Jackson ballots into the box one minute, and the next to elect local representatives to the State Assembly and to Congress who were directly pledged to pursue a course in opposition to the presidential program.[65]

No wonder Pennsylvania senators had such mediocre records in Washington; they would have had to be giants indeed to rise above the anarchy at home.

In 1838, Sidney Fisher, always alert to both democratic anarchy and Pennsylvania mediocrity, colorfully described a riot in the State House in Harrisburg.

> A band of ruffians, trained bullies, heroes of the cockpit and the grogshop, were *hired* by the opposition party and sent to Harrisburg to intimidate & control the legislature. They rushed into the House with yells for blood, and dispersed both it and the Senate. The life of the speaker was threatened, and he would have been killed had he not, meanly enough, made his escape. They succeeded in overturning the government and producing a state of complete anarchy, and prostration of law and authority. Nothing but the arrival of troops prevented a scene of bloodshed and violence, & restored order. Such is the natural working of democracy.[66]

The Speaker of the Pennsylvania Senate referred to by Fisher was an acquaintance from Philadelphia, Charles Bingham Penrose. He and Thaddeus Stevens saved their lives in this "Buckshot War" by jumping out a back window of the State House. Speaker Penrose was, by the way, Simon Cameron's liaison man in Philadelphia for several years, and he was also the grandfather of Boies Penrose. Thus, both Simon Cameron, through political experience, and Boies Penrose, through his knowledge of family history, were well prepared to rescue Pennsylvania from the impotence of classless chaos by creating and assuming the leadership of the Republican machine that took control of Pennsylvania politics just before the Civil War.

DEFIANT DEMOCRACY AND
THE TYRANNY OF BOSSISM

After the Civil War, and especially after the new state constitution of 1873, when governors were limited to one term in office, a neanderthal Republican political machine, led successively by Senators Cameron, Quay, and Penrose, dominated the state of Pennsylvania and eventually Philadelphia. Even Lincoln Steffens was shocked at the power of the state machine in Philadelphia, in spite of the reforms introduced by the Bullitt bill: "The old city boss knocked out by Quay and the new charter, the Senator appointed Israel W. Durham, a ward politician, to be boss of Phiadelphia. This was new to me; no State boss could have named the boss of any city I had seen. . . . There is something to study in all this."[67]

A great deal has been written about boss rule in Pennsylvania. But perhaps Erwin Stanley Bradley, biographer of Simon Cameron (elected to the Senate in 1845), the founder of the Pennsylvania senatorial machine, showed the greatest insight into the inevitability of bossism in a state so chaotic politically. Bradley presented a detailed discussion of Cameron's pre-1845 somersaulting political career and went on to describe the state's political situation.

> It was in such a witches' brew of chaotic state politics that highly controversial state and national problems of the time had to be discussed. An adroit manipulator could hardly have asked for a more favorable political medium in which to operate. Here was furnished the opportunity for a skilled political craftsman to shape a hierarchy founded not on the shifting, ephemeral issues of the day, but rather on a personal loyalty not likely to suffer from such vicissitudes. . . .
>
> Simon Cameron was slow in arriving at the momentous decision to build a political machine ostensibly Democratic in substance but whose members swore liege loyalty to him. To act in such a capacity Cameron must no longer deal with Buchanan in a manner a lieutenant deals with his chieftain, but rather like one equal antagonist pitted against the other, struggling for recognition as the state Democracy's generalissimo.[68]

It is important at this point to differentiate clearly between political offices, on the one hand, and such societal forces for social cohesion and continuity of leadership as the class or the boss, on the other. Such political offices as mayor, governor, or senator, for example, are constitutionally defined and limited in authority by the state. Rotation of office and the democratic and periodic election of officers are the very essence of political democracy. Yet, in a democracy of limited terms in office and constantly changing personnel, political stability or "fixedness and place" must come from society, either traditionally in the form of class leadership or, when class leadership is lacking, in the natural growth of the political machine, based on "liege loyalty" to one man who is able and willing to take the responsibility over the long run, usually behind the scenes, where various forms of bribery may well be called for from time to time. Representative democracy was quite successful in nineteenth-century England, and to a degree in this country, too, largely because the motion and commotion of political democracy were balanced by the stability of an upper class that continually contributed enough men to the highest political positions in the state. This is the message of Tocqueville's brilliant analysis of the failure of a privileged caste in France as against the success of the ruling aristocracy in Great Britain. It is the essence of the difference between class authority in Massachusetts and the lack of it in Pennsylvania. The atomization of society, fostered by the fanatic forces of egalitarian individualism, is the greatest threat to political freedom in our time. And it was this atomized individualism that produced the Cameron-Quay-Penrose political machine in Pennsylvania.

Simon Cameron, of German and Scottish ancestry, was born on a farm in Lancaster County in 1799. Family reverses and misfortunes obliged him to go to work at an early age. Eventually he built up an ample fortune, first in newspaper work and then in iron and steel, banking, and railroading. All the while, he kept in close touch with state and national politics. He was an important force both in Jackson's nomination and reelection in 1832 and in sending his good friend James Buchanan to the Senate. When Buchanan resigned his Senate seat to enter Polk's cabinet in 1845, Cameron—backed by a coalition of Whigs, native Americans, and protectionist Democrats—defeated Buchanan's handpicked successor. After Buchanan became president, Cameron opposed his former friend, in typical Pennsylvania style, with implacable zeal. In the meantime, his power in the state steadily increased until, at the Republican convention of 1860, he became the Pennsylvania delegation's choice for the presidential nomination. Cameron finally swung his votes to Lincoln, who in return appointed him secretary of war. An excellent and autocratic executive, Cameron nevertheless dispensed civil and governmental offices, as well as army contracts, in so notorious a fashion that Lincoln sent him off in 1862 as minister to Russia in order to get rid of him. After the war, in 1867, Cameron went back to the Senate and reigned supreme in Pennsylvania for the rest of his active career. In 1905, one of Cameron's longtime political enemies in Pennsylvania wrote:

> There is not an important complete chapter of political history in the State that can be written with the omission of his defeats and triumphs, and even after his death until the present time no important chapter of political history can be fully written without recognizing his successors and assigns in politics as leading or controlling factors.[69]

Simon Cameron made sure that his son was in a position to carry forward the political dynasty. J. Donald Cameron graduated from Princeton and inherited one of the larger Pennsylvania fortunes of his day through his first wife, Mary McCormick. After her death, he married Elizabeth Sherman, niece of the Civil War hero William Tecumseh Sherman. The Camerons belonged to the famous Adams circle in Washington, which included Henry Cabot Lodge, Theodore Roosevelt, Owen Wister, and John Hay.

In 1877, Simon Cameron had his son appointed secretary of war in the cabinet of President Grant, his close political ally. When President Hayes refused to keep Donald Cameron on in the office, the subservient Pennsylvania legislature was easily persuaded to appoint him to fill the two remaining years of his father's Senate term. Donald Cameron was then returned to the Senate in 1879, 1885, and 1891. In twenty years in that office, according to his *DAB* biographer, "he made politics, not statesmanship his principal public business."[70] After taking over his father's position,

> Don also took over the active management of the state political machine which his father had built up and with the aid of lieutenants like Matthew Quay ran it

skillfully and defiantly as long as he remained in public life. . . . A more striking
example of entrenched political power could hardly be found in America.*[71]

A Civil War hero honored with the Congressional Medal of Honor, Matthew Stanley Quay took over the political machine after Donald Cameron's retirement. He spent his whole life in Pennsylvania politics. The son of a Presbyterian minister of Scotch-Irish descent, Quay was born in Chester County but
built up his political career in Beaver County, just outside Pittsburgh. Often
called the "Napoleon of politics," Quay was not above making millions out of
his chosen profession. He was once refused a seat in the U.S. Senate by resolution and, in his fifteen years there, did not hold a major committee chairmanship. He was such a successful political boss, especially behind the scenes, however, that Quayism became part of the language of American politics during
the Gilded Age.

Upon Quay's death in 1904, his longtime ally Boies Penrose, who had been
handpicked by J. Donald Cameron to succeed him in the Senate in 1897, became the undisputed boss of Pennsylvania and remained so until his death in
1921. Penrose, of impeccably patrician lineage in Philadelphia, was in many
ways Quay's ideal of what a senator from Pennsylvania should be. Although
alike in their love of power and mistrust of mere statesmanship, Quay, the self-
made Scotch-Irish Presbyterian, and Penrose, the Proper Philadelphia Quaker-
turned-Episcopalian, were very different in other ways. Though Quay spoke
several languages and had one of the finest private libraries in the state, Penrose
despised the trappings of culture and played the role of the hard-boiled and
hard-drinking politician all his life. Above all, Penrose, a multimillionaire by
inheritance (his father owned most of the beachfront in Atlantic City before it
became a famous resort), had no respect for men like Quay, who made money
out of politics: "Take it from me, Mr. Quay," he once warned, "this petty
thievery won't pay. You almost went to the pen over a measly hundred thousand . . . look at all the things these corporations can do; all the millions they
can uncover, with a little encouragement from the legislature."[72]

Although he assiduously cultivated the backing of the great corporate
wealth of Pennsylvania, Penrose was interested in "power not pelf," as he once
put it. When asked why he seemed to take no interest in the nation's problems,
he replied:

What's the use? I propose to stay senator. I want power. It is the only thing I
crave. I have it. There are about twenty-thousand to twenty-five thousand Republican workers who can carry divisions and bring out the vote. I must know all
these men. They must know me. If I do not meet them and never see them, I

---

*No wonder Henry Adams, who deeply resented the declining authority of his class in the Gilded
Age, should have felt that his friend Don Cameron belonged to the class of American politicians
who had done most to block his intended path in life: "and to Adams the Cameron type had keen
interest, ever since it shipwrecked his career in the person of President Grant. Perhaps it owed life
to Scotch blood; perhaps to the blood of Adam and Eve, the primitive strain of man. . . . The Pennsylvania mind, as minds go, was not complex; it reasoned little and never talked; but in practical
matters it was the steadiest of all American types; perhaps the most efficient; certainly the safest"
(Henry Adams, *The Education of Henry Adams*, Boston: Houghton Mifflin, 1918, p. 333).

must know where they are, what they want, and how and when. My hand must always be on the job. I can never take it off; if I do, I am gone. The interests of the state? Of course, I look after those. But the job is managing and knowing the twenty-thousand men who run the election divisions. As for great measures and issues, such as you talk about, no senator of a state this size, *run as it is*, has the time to take them up. I am always glad to hear suggestions. Come to me, write to me. I shall always be glad to hear you, but staying senator is my job.[73]

Senator Boies Penrose instinctively knew, as had the two Camerons and Matthew Quay before him, that getting and keeping political power were far more important than leadership in a state with no traditions of class authority. They all understood the inner workings of natural democracy and were totally cynical about the virtues of either the average voter or the average petty politician. And these four Pennsylvania senators dominated the politics of their state for some seventy-five years.

HENRY CABOT LODGE, BRAHMIN STATESMAN FROM MASSACHUSETTS, AND BOIES PENROSE, PATRICIAN POLITICAL BOSS OF PENNSYLVANIA

There is perhaps no better way of contrasting the styles of political leadership in Massachusetts and Pennsylvania than by examining the characters and careers of Senator Henry Cabot Lodge of Brahmin Boston and Senator Boies Penrose of Proper Philadelphia. They were almost exact contemporaries in the United States Senate, where they served longer than any of their predecessors from their respective states: Lodge sat in the Senate from 1893 until his death in 1924, at the age of seventy-four; Penrose, from 1897 until his death in 1921, at the age of sixty-one.

Both men were members of the Boston and Philadelphia First Family samples. Both graduated from Harvard, Lodge, in the middle of his class, in 1871; Penrose, magna cum laude in 1881.* Both were conservatives, though Lodge was an intimate friend and political supporter of Theodore Roosevelt, whereas Penrose considered Roosevelt a "cock-eyed little runt" and a "conceited ass" since their Harvard days together;[74] both supported Roosevelt for the vice-presidency under McKinley, Lodge because he felt it would help Roosevelt's political career, Penrose because he felt the office would surely bury "the cowboy" in political obscurity; both were consummate politicians and partisan Republi-

---

*Penrose graduated second in his class; his brother Charles Bingham Penrose graduated first in the same class, summa cum laude, and became a leading Philadelphia physician. Another brother, R. A. F. Penrose, graduated summa cum laude in 1884 and then took a doctorate in chemistry, before going on to make many, many millions in mining (he left a substantial legacy to the American Philosophical Society). The youngest Penrose brother also went to Harvard, with the class of 1886, but took no degree; he too, made millions, lived opulently, and built the resort town of Colorado Springs, Colorado.

cans, neither achieving preeminence in American history; finally, both disliked Woodrow Wilson, Lodge because he thought him intellectually dishonest, Penrose because he hated all sniveling reformers and sanctimonious statesmen of the Wilson stamp.*

The great differences between Lodge and Penrose are suggested by the contrast in their habits and personal appearances. Lodge was a spare and wiry Yankee whose disciplined life kept him trim well into his seventies. He was always carefully groomed and dressed. He seemed tall because he stood so straight and possessed an unusually high forehead, topped by a shock of curly hair. Though his portrait by Sargent reflects his class style, he should, according to Owen Wister, have been done by Copley, who had a way of revealing character. Lodge was all Boston of the old school. In striking contrast, Penrose was a giant with gargantuan appetites and total disregard for his personal appearance. He weighed close to 200 pounds while at Harvard and close to 300 when he died. His eating and drinking habits are legendary: his favorite breakfast consisted of "one dozen fried eggs, one huge slice of ham, a half-inch thick, a dozen hard rolls, and a quart of black coffee."[75]

Whereas Lodge was an extremely idealistic American patriot, Penrose was a born cynic about everything; whereas Lodge spent his life trying to serve his nation as a statesman in Washington, Penrose was first and last a political boss who cared nothing for statesmanship; whereas Lodge modeled his life on the ideal of the gentleman scholar in politics, Penrose, perhaps an even more naturally gifted intellect, flouted gentlemanly and scholarly pretensions and modeled himself on the local Caesars of American politics; whereas Lodge began his career as a historian at Harvard and as an editor of the *North American Review* and wrote many books and articles in his lifetime, Penrose wrote one first-rate monograph in his younger, reforming days, *Philadelphia, 1681–1887: A History of Municipal Development*, and then turned away from both reform and intellectual production forever in favor of the cynical pursuit of power; finally, whereas Lodge left us some delightful memoirs of his formative years, Penrose determined to cover his tracks for posterity, writing nothing and saying as little as possible about his personal life.†

What most set Lodge and Penrose apart was that Lodge grew up in, and was a representative member of, an authoritative class in Massachusetts, whereas Penrose grew up the privileged son of Proper Philadelphia but was forced to desert his origins in order to seek power in a state without any traditions of class authority. One of Penrose's biographers noted that he had the usual patrician's disdain for plebeians; this is only half true—Penrose had no respect for patricians either.

---

*Penrose's comments on the reformer Pinchot are illustrative. "Pinchot is as important," Penrose said, "as any cheap sideshow outside the fence of a county fair. He's as important as the tattooed man or the cigarette fiend" (John Lukacs, "Big Grizzly," *American Heritage*, October 1978, p. 79).

†Bishop Lawrence, in the usual Boston style, wrote a personal memoir of Lodge, his college classmate and lifelong friend, and at least one definitive biography has since been written, by John A. Garraty. There exist only two hastily written, badly documented, and shallowly damning biographies of Penrose.

Lodge and Penrose grew up in very different worlds. Lodge spent his boyhood in the shadow of the Massachusetts State House, at 31 Beacon Street. His father, an extremely wealthy clippership merchant, entertained, with grace and elegance, all the most interesting men of his day in Boston, including Senator Charles Sumner; John Lothrop Motley and Francis Parkman, historians; men of letters like Longfellow, the elder Holmes, and James Russell Lowell; Dr. Samuel Gridley Howe, abolitionist, champion of the people, and ardent philhellene; and Professor Louis Agassiz. Lodge observed his father's friends carefully and was especially close to his boyhood hero, the lonely Sumner, as well as to Longfellow, the Lodges' neighbor at Nahant.*

Lodge's father died when he was twelve, and he was thereafter raised, and spoiled, by his devoted Cabot mother; her grandfather Senator George Cabot became Lodge's first political hero after his beloved Sumner. (Later Lodge wrote the standard biography of his Federalist ancestor and followed it with biographies of two other Federalist heroes of his, Alexander Hamilton and George Washington.)

Educated at a private school under two admired masters, Thomas Russell Sullivan and Epes Sargent Dixwell, Lodge went on to Harvard, where he was not much concerned or impressed with his courses, except for Henry Adams's history seminar. He loved the theater, fancied himself a good actor, and took an active part in the Hasty Pudding shows. And along with his good friends in later years—Roosevelt, Wendell Holmes, and Owen Wister—he was a member of Porcellian.

A decade after Lodge graduated, Boies Penrose and his brother Charles Bingham were sent to Harvard by their Boston mother. They were carefully chaperoned by an aunt, who took a house in Cambridge near the Yard in order to protect her nephews from contamination by their social inferiors. Boies Penrose was a class behind Theodore Roosevelt and a class ahead of his fellow townsman Owen Wister; yet there is no evidence that he knew either of them well or that he had any real friends while at college or afterward. "It was his dictum," wrote a biographer, "that friends were only maudlin sentimentalists and used their friendships as a cloak under which to ask favors. Most friends were stupid anyway."[76] Penrose majored in political economy, and his thesis on Martin Van Buren, wizardly machine politician from New York, was pronounced "masterly."

Boies Penrose was born and lived all his life in Philadelphia. His family was extremely proud of their Biddle and Penrose ancestors, the first of whom, William Biddle and Bartholomew Penrose, were Quakers who came over with William Penn. Penrose liked to boast that he could trace his ancestry "back to the first Adam, and I wouldn't be surprised if I didn't inherit some of his original sin."[77] There is no record of his family life or of his knowing or idolizing any

---

*Nahant, founded as a resort by Thomas Handasyd Perkins, was the summer place for Boston's best during the nineteenth century. Its residents included Senators Daniel Webster, Robert C. Winthrop, and Henry Cabot Lodge. For a fascinating discussion of Nahanters, see Joseph E. Garland, *Boston's North Shore* (Boston: Little, Brown, 1978).

members of the older generation of Proper Philadelphians. Apparently, the family was not a very warm or hospitable one, his father devoting himself to medicine and his mother to social activities. Both his parents were buried at entirely private family ceremonies. At his mother's death, Penrose wrote to her best friend, who was in Europe at the time: "You might be interested to know that our mother was buried yesterday."[78] Not another word.

The day after his graduation from Harvard, Cabot Lodge married a cousin, Anna Cabot Mills Davis, his constant companion and critic throughout their ideal marriage. He was a patriarch and was extremely proud of his record as the first father and first grandfather in his Harvard class. Everybody from Blaine to Henry Adams loved Nannie Lodge, and none appreciated this charming, intelligent, blue-eyed beauty more than her devoted husband.

Boies Penrose remained a bachelor all his life,* resorting to prostitutes whenever his appetites so demanded. When he left Harvard, his main ambition was to become mayor of Philadelphia. He had the Republican nomination in his pocket in 1895 but was forced to withdraw when the opposition got hold of a photograph showing him coming out of a house of prostitution at three in the morning.

Cabot and Nannie Lodge spent two years abroad on their honeymoon. Cabot was an ardent lover of culture and history and did his best to see everything. After returning home, he got a job through Henry Adams at Harvard and set out on an intellectual career, combining teaching under Adams with editing the *North American Review*. He obtained, on the way, the first doctorate in political science ever given at Harvard. All the while, he and Nannie continued the hospitable tradition of his parents in entertaining Boston's best at their table, including Justices Horace Gray and Wendell Holmes, George and Rockwood Hoar, Henry Lee, Henry Lee Higginson, and the aging Robert C. Winthrop. Lodge also made sure he stood for all the best things in Boston: he was a member of the Somerset Club from the age of twenty-two until his death, president of the Massachusetts Historical Society after Charles Francis Adams, and a trustee of the Athenaeum. Above all, he was an overseer at Harvard and president of the alumni association, in which position he was called on to give the main address, of "wondrous beauty, lore and charm," according to Bishop Lawrence, at the dedication of the Widener Library.

Boies Penrose, as I have noted, apparently had no friends either at Harvard or in later life. Nor did he seem to have any loyalties to institutions. Whereas Lodge maintained a lifelong relationship with Harvard (which honored him with a doctor of laws in 1904, as did Williams, Clark, Amherst, and Yale), there is no record that Penrose had any dealings with his alma mater after he graduated. His life was all politics, and his associates were political allies and cronies rather than friends. Although two of his brothers, and some nine Penroses in

---

*Soon after college, his mother talked him into a six months' trip abroad in order to promote a romantic relationship with the beautiful daughter of one of her friends. Penrose met the young lady but was uninterested and after two weeks persuaded his mother to let him return home alone. He never went abroad again, nor did his mother try subsequently to lure him into matrimony.

all, have belonged to the Philadelphia Club, he had neither the time nor the friends there to make it worth his while to join (he probably was never asked). Penrose entertained when he had to, in the lonely Gatsby style, at lavish parties held in hotels. He always maintained a large staff of servants at his Spruce Street house but preferred to take his meals at the Union League (he liked the impersonal service). A large part of Penrose's life was lived in hotels, especially at the Willard in Washington.

When the Lodges went to Washington, they took a house there, where they entertained in exquisite style, both for political associates and for their intimate and old friends. Lodge's close friendship with Roosevelt is one of the most touching in American political history. He was a mainstay of Roosevelt's little circle of White House regulars, which included Justice Holmes, Owen Wister, Winthrop Chanler, Elihu Root, Henry Adams, and eventually the young, handsome, and extremely rich idealist Gifford Pinchot. The Lodges were also, as we have seen, among Henry Adams's intimate friends in Washington. Nannie, next to Elizabeth Cameron, being one of Henry's favorite women.

Roosevelt, Lodge, and Pinchot are excellent examples of men who were proud of their class and inherited traditions; all three, of Calvinist origins, attempted to take the lead in exerting class authority in the rough and tumble of American politics. In many ways, of course, they were exceptions: "I have known few men of wealth who use their wealth to full advantage," Roosevelt once wrote. "I have known plenty of men who are only able to do their work because they have inherited means. This is absolutely true of both Cabot and myself, for instance. Cabot is quite a rich man, but I am not; but each of us has been able to do what he has actually done because his father left him in such shape that he did not have to earn a living."[79]

Like any man who spends a long time in public life, Cabot Lodge was admired by some and hated by others. All who knew anything of his long career in the Senate would have agreed, however, that Lodge did everything in his power to raise the level of debate on the issues of his age. "His great contribution in the Senate," Elihu Root once told Bishop Lawrence, "was his background of history and culture. He was the educator of the Senate away from bombast or pretense towards reality and forceful expression. He had great influence in this way. Senators heard him, felt the force and unconsciously or consciously changed their form of expression. He was the only man in public life of the time who in his speech had style."[80] Bishop Lawrence closed his brief biography of his lifelong friend with an excerpt from a speech Lodge made at Symphony Hall in Boston in 1910. It was in many ways the most important speech of Lodge's life; the political tide in the state was running against him; his friends had engaged the hall, which was packed that night, and many more people thronged the streets outside. Alone on the stage, without any support and without an introduction, Lodge told the story of his political life in simple words and won the applause of the multitude.

> My public record is all public; I have no secrets, nothing to conceal. Whatever my shortcomings, I have cherished with reverence the dignity and the traditions of the great office which I hold. My first allegiance as an American is to the great

Nation founded, built up, preserved by heroic sacrifices and untold treasure. I was born and bred in Massachusetts. I love every inch of the old State, from the rock of Essex and the glittering sands of the Cape to the fair valley of the Connecticut and the wooded Berkshire Hills. Here my people have lived before me since the days of the Massachusetts Bay Company. Here they lie at rest in the graveyards of Essex, on Boston Common, beneath the shadows of Park Street Church. Here I have lived all my life. Here my dead are buried. To her service I have given my all: no man can give more. Others may easily serve her better than I in those days yet to be; but of this I am sure: that no man can ever serve her with greater love or deeper loyalty.[81]

Senator Boies Penrose would never have given such a speech in Philadelphia's Academy of Music, and had he heard Lodge that night in Boston, he undoubtedly would have sneered at his fellow senator's sentimentality. Penrose, who all his life exuded a sense of presence and dignity in spite of his careless ways, had a strange and fascinating psychological affinity for the political demands of his time in Pennsylvania. Perhaps the most incredible thing about Penrose is the fact that he anticipated his whole political career in Pennsylvania in his thesis on "Martin Van Buren as a Politician," written as a senior at Harvard. The following excerpt sums up the thesis of this chapter.

Martin Van Buren was the first and the greatest of American politicians. . . . He marks the transition in American politics from statesmen like Adams and Webster to the great political bosses and managers of today. . . . Adams was the last statesman of the old school who was to occupy the White House, Van Buren was the first politician president. . . . When management is all that is essential have we a right to be disappointed if Van Buren is not Webster?[82]

Penrose surely knew that the opponents of class authority and the advocates of pure democracy have no right to expect anything more than Quayism if not outright Caesarism.

In reviewing the lives of Cabot and Nannie Lodge of Massachusetts and Boies Penrose of Pennsylvania in some detail, I have attempted to show the difference between the organic assertion of class authority, deeply rooted in the traditions of one community, on the one hand, and the lonely exercise of pure power in a community without any organic traditions of class leadership, on the other. Class authority, like all other forms of authority, is a mysterious blend of sentiment and myth, of love and loyalty, and the graceful charm of quiet leadership. It is, above all, a product of faith bred of ancient traditions and a long continuing organic relationship between the leaders and the led. Born to privilege in a class without any traditions of authority in the state or nation, Penrose broke with his heritage and set out alone in the pursuit of pure power. As we should know today in our post-Watergate age, whereas authority is a product and producer of love and trust, the pursuit of power is a breeder of cynicism in both the lonely leaders and the lonely led.

Henry Cabot Lodge and Boies Penrose died and were buried in the style in which they had lived. Bishop Lawrence, by then a veritable Boston institution, presided over the funerals of Nannie in 1915 and of Cabot in 1924, both held in the church they had attended for half a century, a host of Boston's best in attendance. Boies Penrose died in 1921 in Washington; two doctors and two nurses were with him in his hotel room as he breathed his last. His body was brought back to the house on Spruce Street where he was born. "At the dawn of a raw January day," wrote a biographer,

> the bare casket bearing all that remained of the nation's greatest political boss was carried out of the Spruce Street home where he was born and shoved into a waiting hearse to be whisked away to Laurel Hill Cemetery. Four automobiles accompanied the close relatives of the dead man. That was all. No flowers, no minister of religion to add a work of condolence, no statesmen, no friends, not even the mayor of the great city which he had called home, nor lowly politicians, were present at the funeral. The five cars rumbled briskly through the deserted streets and through the cemetery gates, which were promptly snapped shut by a half-dozen hired detectives to keep out the curious, and the journey of Boies Penrose came to an end.[83]

A CONTEMPORARY'S VIEW OF PENNSYLVANIA IN THE GILDED AGE

Few have understood the tenacity of the traditional political patterns of Massachusetts and Pennsylvania better than the anonymous author of the *Atlantic Monthly* article that so enraged Judge Pennypacker of Philadelphia when it appeared in 1901. The author proved to be the journalist Mark Sullivan (Harvard, class of 1900), who was writing for the conservative *Boston Transcript* in order to earn his way through Harvard Law School. Sullivan had been born and raised by immigrant Irish parents on a farm in the heart of Quaker country, in Chester County, Pennsylvania. As he grew up, Sullivan had nothing but admiration for his Quaker neighbors.* Yet he was to lay the blame for political corruption and citizen apathy in Pennsylvania on the same factors that are central to my theory of leadership: the lack of authority and leadership in Pennsylvania, according to Sullivan, was rooted in Quaker passivity combined with the materialism preached by Benjamin Franklin.

In the *Atlantic* article, Sullivan first dismissed the usual reasons advanced to explain the notorious corruption in Pennsylvania politics after the Civil War, among them the doings of the "hoards of ignorant foreigners" in the state.

> You may go over the whole list of bosses and sub-bosses in the state and find hardly ever a "Mac," or an "O," or a "berg," or a "stein," or a "ski." It is the sons

---

*The Sullivans were poor farmers. *Uncle Tom's Cabin* was the only novel, almost the only book in the house. Sullivan devoured the novel; as a Catholic among Quakers, he eagerly read the occasional issues of the *Boston Pilot* that he came across. He determined to be a journalist and eventually saved some money and became part owner of a weekly newspaper in Phoenixville, Pennsylvania. At his boardinghouse in Phoenixville, he met, for the first time, young college graduates and engineers. One day he met Hope Cox, fiancée of one of the engineers, whose father was dean of the Cincinnati Law School, onetime governor of Ohio, and a member of Grant's cabinet. "Hope Cox," Sullivan later wrote in his autobiography, "impressed that boy editor as much, and in much the same way, as if an archangel had been introduced to him." Cox persuaded Sullivan to go to Harvard and gave him letters of introduction to her friends on the faculty.

of the revolution, descendants of the first inhabitants, that are responsible for Pennsylvania's condition. Now why? Why is Massachusetts, with her native-born in a numerical minority, the best governed commonwealth in the Union, while Pennsylvania, with her native-born in a large majority, wallows in corruption?[84]

After citing many examples of blatant buying and selling of votes that he himself had witnessed in his Pennsylvania days, Sullivan summed up the reasons for this tragic (if often amusing) situation. The following paragraphs highlight much of the argument in this book.

Franklin is preeminently the apostle of "brownstone-front respectability." All Poor Richard's maxims are but variations of one exhortation, "Young man, put money in the purse. . . . "

Pennsylvania is a state of large corporations. . . . The president of the Pennsylvania Railroad gets $50,000 a year; the governor of the state, $10,000. . . . Is it any wonder that the best young men take to the corporation, and devote their every energy to promotion therein, leaving politics to the less capable, the less intelligent, the less moral?

Besides, in Pennsylvania, the young men of wealth and good birth look with disfavor on politics. No less a Philadelphian than Mr. Owen Wister, who was born in a position to know whereof he speaks, tells this story: The descendant of an old Philadelphia family had written some verses, and showed them to a fellow clubman. "Excellent," said his friend. "I shall publish them," said the author. The other was horrified. "The verses are all very well," he said, when pressed for a reason, "but—publish a book—is that the sort of thing one does, don't you know?" Now, politics, like publishing books, is not "the sort of things one does, don't you know," in Philadelphia. Had Senator Lodge and the late Governor Wolcott been born in Philadelphia, they might have attained fame as golf champions or cotillion leaders, but never as writers, college professors, or politicians, except at the sacrifice of social position.

There is an historic reason. The Quakers were—and are—a good people. This cannot be too much emphasized. Membership in the Society of Friends is as strong an evidence as can be given that a man possesses every personal virtue. For the conditions that beset Pennsylvania the present generation of Quakers are in no sense responsible. They are now too few to sway the state one way or another. But if the early Quakers had had the spirit of the Puritan fathers, Pennsylvania might have been held steadier to the moorings of civic decency. It is unnecessary to draw any comparison between the personal virtues of the Puritans and the Quakers. That question was thrashed out at length on the Boston Common some years ago, and was decided, in the manner of the time, to the satisfaction of the Puritans, at least, by a gallows rope with a Quaker at the end of it.

It is one of the anomalies of history that when the Puritan hanged the Quaker, both were happy—the one to hang a man for his belief, the other to die for his belief. This brings out strongly the distinction between them. The Puritans were a church militant. The Puritans went to church with a Bible in one hand and in the other a musket for hostile Indians. The Quaker settled his difficulties with the Indians by reading tracts to them. When the Quaker came to the Puritan commonwealth to spread a doctrine which the Puritan didn't like, the Puritan beat him and drove him out; and when the Quaker came meekly back to turn the other cheek, the Puritan hanged him. The point is this: the Puritan insisted in governing his commonwealth in his own way. He founded his commonwealth to carry out a certain set of ideas, and he never let his eye wander from that purpose. What the Puritan resolved upon was to be done: he would have no objector, be he Roger Williams, Anne Hutchinson, or Quaker. The Puritan formed the dominating habit, and to this day Puritan ideas dominate the essentially non-Puritan population of Massachusetts.

Among the Quakers, on the other hand, meekness was the cardinal virtue. Their creed forbids them to bear arms. It does not, in so many words, forbid them to take part in politics, but certainly the rough and tumble of actual party contest is hostile to the ideal which the Quaker seeks to follow. The early Quakers, instead of strangling doctrines not in agreement with their own, instead of casting out the apostles of strange creeds, welcomed them, tolerated them. They soon came to the point where they were tolerating intolerance. Put in a minority by the unrestricted immigration of less worthy people, and lacking the strenuous, dominating spirit of the Puritans, the early Quakers soon let the control of the colony pass into the hands of the less desirable elements; and there it has always remained.[85]

The differing leadership traditions of Massachusetts and Pennsylvania have of course carried down far beyond the days of Henry Cabot Lodge and Boies Penrose. Lodge, a typical and proud New England progenitor, produced two grandsons of some political distinction, Governor John Davis Lodge of Connecticut and Senator Henry Cabot Lodge, Jr., of Massachusetts. The latter was surely one of the most prominent Republicans in Washington during the Eisenhower and Nixon years. Penrose, in contrast, was a typical Pennsylvania cutflower. George Wharton Pepper, a very Proper Philadelphian, was appointed to fill Penrose's unexpired Senate term but was not reelected. Senator Pepper was for many years the unofficial dean of the Philadelphia bar, as well as of the alumni and trustees of the University of Pennsylvania and the Episcopal diocese of Pennsylvania. He was a man of exceptional talent and great capacity for work, a gifted speaker with an excellent memory for facts, appropriate anecdotes, and apt verses; his moral standing was attested to by his almost daily attendance at early communion, in a wheelchair for the last several years of his long and happy life. Pepper gave the major address at the annual convention of the Episcopal church in 1907, celebrating 200 years of English Christianity in America, and was still practicing law after World War II. Yet this highly gifted Philadelphia Gentleman, who had all the natural prerequisites for the attainment of absolutely first rank in the political history of his time, betrayed the passive political attitudes of his Quaker-turned-Episcopal heritage in the following lines from his autobiography, *Philadelphia Lawyer*: "The simple fact is that never in my life have I felt the itch for public office, impossible as it may be to make people believe this."[86] It would indeed be very hard to believe had Pepper been born and bred anywhere else but in Proper Philadelphia.

PART VI

TWO TEST CASES

Catholics in Two Cultures

*[Joseph Kennedy, Jr.] had his heart set on a political career.
He often sat in my study and submitted with that smile that
was pure magic to relentless teasing about his determination
to be nothing less than President of the United States.*

Harold Laski

*If you endorse my son as the Democratic party's candidate
for mayor of this city I will go on television and I will tell the
city that it should not have my son for mayor and I will tell
the city why. And I have better access to that than you do.
And I will financially support his opponent!*

Mrs. John B. Kelly

"I am inclined to believe," wrote Tocqueville in *Democracy in America*, "that our posterity will tend more and more to a division into two parts, some relinquishing Christianity entirely and others returning to the Church of Rome."[1] At its founding our nation was overwhelmingly Protestant; there were about 25,000 Roman Catholics, of whom 16,000 lived in Maryland, 7,000 in Pennsylvania, 1,500 in New York, and the rest in the other ten states; there were fewer than 100 in Massachusetts. By the Second World War, somewhat less than half the U.S. population was church affiliated (about 65 million): of these, 97 percent belonged to 52 church bodies of 50,000 or more members and the other 3 percent belonged to some 200 small denominations or sects.[2] The atomization of Protestantism is just what Tocqueville would have predicted of our egalitarian and individualistic democracy; he also was partially correct in his prediction about Catholicism in that by far the largest body of church affiliated Christians (some 24 million) were the Roman Catholics. By the 1960 election, when our first Catholic president was sent to the White House, 60 percent of the population of Rhode Island, 50 percent of Massachusetts, 49 percent of Connecticut, 32 percent of New York, 30 percent of Pennsylvania, and 20 percent of Maryland was Roman Catholic. At the same time, a large majority of the church affiliated citizens of Massachusetts, and well over one-third of those in Pennsylvania, were members of the Catholic church.

The Roman conquest of America began with the coming of Catholic refugees from famine-stricken Ireland, which migration peaked in the 1840s. To this day the American Roman Catholic hierarchy is dominated by their descendants. As a test of the validity of the thesis of this book, let us examine whether Irish Catholics in Boston and Philadelphia have tended to take on the values of their host cities. If the thesis has any predictive value, the Boston Irish should have developed far more of a drive toward total community leadership and authority than their Philadelphia peers.

John B. Kelly, whom Franklin Roosevelt once called the handsomest man he had ever met, was certainly the most representative Irishman of his generation in Philadelphia.[3] Whereas Alfred E. Smith became governor of New York and almost went to the White House, and James Michael Curley was many times mayor of Boston and a one-term governor of Massachusetts, Kelly, primarily an athlete, sportsman, and money-maker, was a longtime member of the Republican party who ran for mayor as a Democrat in the 1930s and was defeated. My analysis of class authority and leadership in Boston and Philadelphia would predict that the Puritanical Irish Catholicism of Boston would produce the first Catholic president of the United States, whereas the milder and Quaker-like Catholicism of Philadelphia would produce, in the same generation, the beautiful and charming international socialite Princess Grace of Monaco, John B. Kelly's daughter.

THE FOUNDING OF CATHOLICISM
IN BOSTON AND PHILADELPHIA

Maryland was the only British colony in North America founded by Roman Catholics. The Calverts, however, lost control of the colony in 1691, when the Anglican church was established and the capital moved from the Catholic stronghold of St. Mary's City to the Protestant center at Annapolis. Nevertheless, to this day Catholic families are more prevalent in the upper class of Maryland than of any of the other original colonies. The Fenwicks of St. Mary's County, many of whom are still Proper Baltimorians, supplied the first bishop of Cincinnati, Edward Dominic Fenwick (1768–1832), and the second bishop of Boston, Benedict Joseph Fenwick (1782–1846).

The Carrolls of Maryland were unquestionably the preeminent family of American Catholicism. Charles Carroll (1737–1832) of Carrollton Manor was born at Annapolis, where he was educated at a small Jesuit school before being sent to Paris for further study. As one of the colony's first citizens, he attended the Continental Congress, signed the Declaration of Independence, and served as senator from Maryland in the first U.S. Congress. When religious freedom was made the law of the land under the Constitution, the first Roman Catholic bishop in the nation was John Carroll (1735–1815), Charles's cousin and schoolmate. Bishop John Carroll of Baltimore had jurisdiction over all Catholics in the original thirteen states. In 1808, the dioceses of Boston and Philadelphia were established, the former including all of New England and the latter including all of Pennsylvania and Delaware, as well as southern New Jersey. At the same time, John Carroll became archbishop of Baltimore.*

Although Catholics were excluded from early Massachusetts, they were accepted—but not welcomed—from the very beginning in Pennsylvania. The first Catholic church in Philadelphia, St. Joseph's, was built on an inconspicuous spot on Willing's Alley by Jesuits in 1732. Even before that, members of the Willcox family, among the first Catholics to come to the city and still prominent today, celebrated mass at their homestead outside the city. There, at Ivy Mills, they established the second paper mill in the state (David Rittenhouse built the first), supplying paper for Franklin's *Gazette* and eventually becoming the leading manufacturers of paper money for the United States government (as well as for Germany, Japan, Greece, and many South American countries) throughout most of the nineteenth century.

St. Joseph's had grown from 50 to 378 permanent parishioners by 1757, when a plot of land was purchased on South Fourth Street for the second Catholic church, St. Mary's, completed in 1763. A third church, Holy Trinity (the first German Catholic parish in America), was completed in 1789. Thomas Willcox, George Meade, and Thomas FitzSimmons headed the foremost Catholic lay families in the city; these successful merchants were parishioners at St. Mary's, the most prominent Catholic church in America at the nation's founding.†

Philadelphia Catholics played a significant role in the city at the time of the nation's founding: Thomas FitzSimmons, for example, was one of the two Catholic signers of the Constitution (Daniel Carroll of Maryland was the other). Born in Ireland, FitzSimmons settled in Philadelphia and married into the socially and financially prominent Meade family, fought in the battles of Trenton and Princeton, served in both the Continental Congress and the Pennsylvania Assembly, and became a trustee of the University of Pennsylvania and a director and president of the Bank of North America. Another parishioner of St. Mary's, Captain John Barry, was a founder of the United States Navy.

In eighteenth-century Boston there was no Catholic church. Anti-Catholicism in the city was ritualized in the annual observance of Pope's Day, a custom discontinued only when George Washington deprecated its bigoted purpose. The first native Bostonian to become a priest was John Thayer (1758–1815). A onetime Congregational minister and a graduate of Yale, Thayer entered the church in Paris, where he was lionized by ecclesiastics as the first converted American divine. Returning to Boston, he was mocked as "John Turncote." He died at Limerick, in Ireland. Thayer left his mark on Boston through a legacy

---

*The four dioceses first detached from the mother see of Baltimore were Boston, Philadelphia, New York, and Louisville-Bardstown (in Kentucky).

†The Continental Congress attended services there on at least two occasions: a Te Deum was chanted to celebrate the third anniversary of the Declaration of Independence; and George Washington attended services there both as a delegate to the Continental Congress in 1774 and as a delegate to the Constitutional Convention in 1787.

that eventually was used to found the Ursuline convent at Charlestown, burned by a nativist mob in 1834 (see below).

The first Catholic church in Boston, Holy Cross, was built in 1803 by two French priests, Francis Anthony Matignon and Jean Lefebvre de Cheverus, both refugees from the French Revolution. The church, designed by Charles Bulfinch, served as Boston's first cathedral after Cheverus became bishop of Boston in 1808. Father Cheverus was a beloved man and many Protestants, including John Adams, contributed to the building fund for the Church of the Holy Cross.

As might be expected, there were no Catholic families in the Boston First Family sample. In Philadelphia the Willcoxes are the only upper-class family to have remained Catholic from the eighteenth century to the present. Two families in the Philadelphia sample, the Meades and the Drexels, were originally Catholic.

The Meades have been one of the more distinguished families in Philadelphia, five of them having been included in the *DAB*. The family founder, George Meade, was born in the city in 1741; his father, probably born in Ireland, had come there from Barbadoes. George Meade, a staunch Catholic, was one of the main benefactors of St. Mary's and a founder of both the Society of the Friendly Sons of St. Patrick (1771) and the Hibernian Society (1792), two of the oldest Catholic brotherhoods in America. George Meade's son, Richard Worsam Meade, became a merchant like his father; the other three Meades in the First Family sample were military men. The most famous was George Gordon Meade, commander of the Union forces at the Battle of Gettysburg. General Meade was one of the more distinguished Proper Philadelphians of his day; as park commissioner from 1866 until his death, he was instrumental in laying out Fairmount Park. In 1855, Meade was baptized an Episcopalian at St. Mark's Church, just off Rittenhouse Square; his funeral service was held there in 1872, all of Philadelphia's best in attendance, along with such dignitaries as President U.S. Grant. And General Meade's descendants are Proper Protestants in the city today.

Although considered by some as latecomers to Philadelphia Society, the Drexels have been one of the more stylish, cultivated, and wealthy families in twentieth-century Philadephia. The family founder, Francis Martin Drexel, a Catholic born in a small Austrian town, spent his early life as a portrait painter, traveling all over Europe before coming to the New World, where he continued to paint portraits in both North and South America. (His works were exhibited on several occasions at the Pennsylvania Academy of the Fine Arts.) While sojourning among the rich, Drexel kept his eyes open and developed a keen knowledge of the mysteries of money. After Biddle's bank failed and brought on the panic of 1837, Drexel settled in Philadelphia. He opened a brokerage house on South Third Street and married the daughter of a prominent German Catholic family. Drexel died during the Civil War, and his son Anthony took over the family firm. Another son, Joseph William Drexel, handled the Drexel interests in Paris and New York. As befit Anthony J. Drexel's prominent position in Philadelphia banking he was eventually baptized an Episcopalian. He built and endowed an Episcopal church near the Drexel compound in West Philadelphia (now on the Penn campus), and his funeral was celebrated by the highest clerical dignitaries of the Episcopal church in his day.*

EARLY BISHOPS OF BOSTON
AND PHILADELPHIA

When the dioceses of Boston and Philadelphia were founded, the latter city had a solid Catholic community with a core of wealthy and respected lay leaders like the Meades and the Willcoxes and four churches (St. Augustine's, north of Market Street, the largest church in the diocese, was completed in 1801; its main lay benefactors included President Washington, Stephen Girard, and Commodore John Barry). At the same time, Father Cheverus in Boston had only a small flock of parishioners at the Church of the Holy Cross. Various differences in the leadership of the two dioceses demonstrate how the Catholics of Boston followed in the Puritan pattern discussed in previous chapters whereas the Philadelphia church hierarchy reflected the authority patterns of the Quaker City.

As Table A-31† shows, there was a greater continuity of Catholic leadership in Boston than in Philadelphia: there have been only six bishops and archbishops in the former diocese between its founding and Cardinal Cushing's death in 1970, as against eleven in Philadelphia during the same period. (This contrasting pattern also marked Episcopalian and political leadership in the two states.)

There were also important differences in the kind of men chosen to lead each diocese. In Boston, for instance, all save Cheverus were native Americans;

---

*The oldest of the three Drexel brothers, Francis Anthony (not in the *DAB*), remained a Catholic and was widely admired in the whole Philadelphia community for his philanthropic works. His last surviving daughter, moreover, was one of the greatest figures in the history of the American Catholic church. Katherine Drexel, while leading an extremely luxurious life, made the decision to desert her world of ease and fashion in favor of a life in the church. Mother Katherine founded the Sisters of the Blessed Sacrament and devoted herself to helping the most downtrodden and despised Americans, the Indian and the black. She founded an endless number of missions and schools for them all over the United States, including Xavier University near New Orleans. The beneficiary of a $14 million trust fund established by her father, she nevertheless lived in a simple room, sleeping on an iron bed and often getting down on her knees to scrub the floor. Just before Katherine Drexel died at the age of ninety-seven, she was officially recognized by Pope Pius XII in a eulogy that began:

To Our Beloved Daughter in Christ
Katherine Drexel
Foundress
of the Sisters of the Most Blessed Sacrament
Pope Pius XII
Beloved Daughter of Christ
Health and Apostolic Blessing

Mother Katherine, who may well be canonized a saint some day, surely chose a vocation which was very much in accord with one of the main concerns of her Quaker neighbors in Philadelphia.

†All tables cited in this chapter are presented in Appendix I.

likewise, all save Cheverus and Fenwick were the sons of Irish immigrants and were born within the borders of the present diocese of Boston.* In striking contrast but very much in accord with the Philadelphia tradition of auslander leadership, the top positions in the local Catholic hierarchy have always been held by men who were not natives of the city. The first four bishops, Egan (Ireland), Conwell (Ireland), Kenrick (Ireland), and Neumann (Bohemia) were born abroad, as were Archbishops Ryan (Ireland) and Prendergast (Ireland) in a later day. Archbishop Wood provides a partial exception to the tradition of auslander leadership. Born a Protestant of English parents in Philadelphia, he was educated largely in England and in Cincinnati, where he eventually converted to Catholicism. He was an auslander in the sense that he was brought to Philadelphia from Cincinnati. Like other Philadelphians, then, Catholics in the city have not been driven to seek positions of leadership, even of their own diocese.†

The Boston Catholic hierarchy was, especially in its founding days, led by men who were more willing and able to exercise authority than were their Philadelphia peers. The early years of the diocese of Philadelphia were marked by a continuing confusion of authority, centered in the problem of trusteeism. Trusteeism, a difficulty faced by Catholicism in general in early American history, revolved around the issue of who was in control of the financial affairs of a parish, the hierarchy or the parishioners. According to Catholic teaching, authority in both religious and financial affairs is lodged in the hierarchy. However, in the Protestant tradition, in the early days American churches (as well as the land on which they were built) often were held in the name of the lay trustees. The diocese of Philadelphia, well into the term of its fifth bishop, James F. Wood, was plagued by trusteeism. In fact, Bishop John Carroll came to the city in 1797, before the diocese was formed, to excommunicate two priests who were leading the parishioners of Holy Trinity against clerical authority. The problem became especially acute under the weak leadership of the first two bishops, Michael Egan and Henry Conwell.

Egan was appointed one of the pastors of St. Mary's in 1803. After he was named the first bishop of the diocese and St. Mary's was designated the cathedral church, his disputes with the trustees, always acute, intensified. The trustees claimed exclusive rights to pew rents and refused to use them for the bishop's support. So devastating were these quarrels that when Bishop Egan died in office at the age of fifty-three, the archbishop of Baltimore at the time wrote to Rome that "religion had been almost overthrown in Philadelphia."[3] Back in

---

*The original dioceses of Boston and Philadelphia gradually were divided. Thus, today they are both metropolitan sees ruling over their respective provinces. The province of Boston includes the archdiocese of Boston (the city and its surrounding towns and cities), as well as the dioceses of Maine, New Hampshire, and Vermont, and the Massachusetts dioceses of Worcester, Springfield, and Fall River. The province of Philadelphia includes the metropolitan area, or the Philadelphia archdiocese, as well as the dioceses of Erie, Pittsburgh, Greensburg, Johnstown, Altoona, Harrisburg, Allentown, and Scranton.

†If they were, they went elsewhere. Thus, John Joseph Hughes (1797–1864), a native of Ireland raised in Pennsylvania, was for a time the priest at St. Mary's in Philadelphia; yet he went on to become a great and combative bishop of the diocese of New York.

1808, when John Carrol was asked about Egan's qualifications as bishop of Philadelphia, he replied: "He is truly learned, remarkable for his humility, but deficient, perhaps, in firmness and without great experience in the direction of affairs."[4] Perhaps a people get the kind of leadership they deserve. In any case, Egan's successor was no improvement, and it was five years before he was even appointed.

Three priests who later held high office in the church turned down appointments to head the diocese before Henry Conwell, vicar general of Armagh, Ireland, was appointed bishop in 1819. Conwell, aged seventy-three when he came to Philadelphia, immediately was opposed by William Hogan, a priest from Albany who had been brought into the diocese without proper credentials in the first place and who preached a sermon against Conwell in the bishop's presence within two weeks of his taking office. The so-called Hogan schism, the most celebrated case of trusteeism in the annals of the American Catholic church, was a complicated and messy affair. Though Hogan was banished from the diocese in disgrace in 1824, Conwell continued to feud with the parishioners of St. Mary's and finally was forced to sign a pact giving the trustees the right to veto his appointments of their pastors. The pact was rejected by the Congregation of Propaganda, and Conwell was called to Rome to explain his case. The Holy See named Francis Patrick Kenrick coadjutor with the right of succession. Unfortunately for the problem of authority in the diocese, however, Conwell, who still retained the title of bishop, unexpectedly returned to Philadelphia and gave many anxious moments to Kenrick and the Holy See until his death in 1842 at the age of ninety-four.[5]

Trusteeism also disrupted Philadelphia Catholicism under Kenrick's rule. In 1831, when he was still coadjutor, he was forced to close the cathedral church of St. Mary's as well as its cemetery. But the major problem of authority came during his reign as bishop with the anti-Catholic riots of 1844. Just as Hoganism symbolized the problem of trusteeism in American Catholicism as a whole, so the Philadelphia riots of 1844 were the most violent in the history of America's Catholic community. Churches were burned, many people were wounded or killed, and the governor was forced to send in troops and declare martial law in the city. The convent of the Sisters of Charity of the Blessed Virgin Mary, in the heavily Irish borough of Kensington, was burned to the ground, as was St. Augustine's Church, along with its invaluable library and its monastery. Some forty houses were burned and among the churches threatened was St. John's, the wealthiest center city parish, which was saved only when the First City Troop was called in. Altogether, 1844 was a very sorry year in the history of the City of Brotherly Love,* and the riots were a major factor leading to the con-

---

*Although Philadelphia publicly mourned its dead and openly deplored its period of carnage, many among even the more substantial citizens were secretly exultant. Quaker merchants, who spoke indignantly of the outrage in public, returned to their shops to express the sincere belief that 'the Papists deserve all this and much more,' and, 'It were well if every Popish church in the world were levelled to the ground.' . . . A city investigating committee laid the blame for the riots entirely on the Irish who had broken up a peaceful procession of American citizens" (Ray Allen Billington, *The Protestant Crusade, 1800–1860* [New York: Macmillan, 1938], p. 230).

solidation of fiercely independent boroughs and townships like Kensington into Philadelphia in 1854. Perhaps the most insight into Philadelphia's traditional lack of leadership is provided by the fact that Bishop Kenrick, although he was surely an honorable and learned man of great compassion, left the city for three days at the height of the rioting to stay with the Willcoxes on their estate at Ivy Mills, some twenty miles outside Philadelphia.

In 1852 Kenrick became archbishop of Baltimore and a pious immigrant from Bohemia, John Nepomucene Neumann, was made bishop of Philadelphia, much against his will. The German Catholics in the diocese were delighted by this appointment but many others thought Neumann a disastrous choice, especially the aggressive bishop of Pittsburgh, who wrote to Rome that Neumann "is very timid, not so well versed in the language as to be able to address the people effectively . . . and when he returns from a visitation of his diocese, is accustomed to say that he feels like a man, as it were, being led to the gallows."[6] The new bishop surely exemplified the Philadelphia tradition of antipathy toward the exercise of authority. Even Archbishop Kenrick was obliged to inform Rome that his appointee was incompetent and that "affairs at Philadelphia" had become "more sad and involved."[7] Neumann was so incapable of exercising authority and so incompetent in financial affairs that in 1856 James Wood, an expert in finance, was appointed by Rome as coadjutor of Philadelphia with the right of succession. Wood was in much the same position as Kenrick had been in under Bishop Conwell. But Neumann was less obstructive than Conwell and was glad to have Wood take over, especially in the matter of finance and in the completion of the Cathedral of Saints Peter and Paul, designed by Napoleon LeBrun. Though Neumann was a misfit as bishop, he was a saintly man in a Quakerly way and was canonized in 1977.

As a Catholic convert of pure British and Protestant stock, James Wood, the city's first archbishop (1875), was quite naturally a very popular leader in Victorian Philadelphia, perhaps partly because he was so very much in the Philadelphia style. Thus, the local antiquarians J. Thomas Scharf and Thompson Westcott noted that "the prudence which guided him in the ecclesiastical sphere was seen in his reserved and reticent attitude on many public questions, upon which there is a strong temptation for men in his position to pronounce. Content with being a good citizen, he carefully abstained from politics and forbade their presence or discussion in the church."[8] This passive style of Catholic leadership in Philadelphia, both clerical and secular, continued for many decades after Archbishop Wood. Thus, almost a century later, James Reichley found John B. Kelly, the leading Catholic layman in the city, to be "a widely admired figure, and a devoted defender of the powers-that-be, who seemed to represent well the peculiar combination of acceptance into and submission to existing society that has been the lot of Irishmen in the Quaker City."[9]

Bishops Egan, Conwell, Kenrick, and Neumann of Philadelphia were a breed of men very different from Bishops Fenwick and Fitzpatrick, who led Boston Catholicism in the pre–Civil War period. Bishop Fenwick, a Maryland aristocrat whose great-grandfather had come to America along with Leonard Calvert, was the real organizer of the diocese of Boston. Educated as a Jesuit, he came to Boston after serving in New York, where he was mainly responsible for building that city's first cathedral, St. Patrick's, and in Washington, where he had been procurator general of the Society of Jesus and president of Georgetown College. Fenwick had all the leadership qualities of a man of both class and bureaucratic authority. Fortunately, he also possessed an independent income, for during his early years in Boston there were far too few Catholics to support him.

When Fenwick took over the diocese from Cheverus, Boston had only three priests, eight churches besides the cathedral church, Holy Cross, and 7,000 Catholics. At his death in 1846 he had authority over 39 priests, 48 churches, and some 70,000 Catholics, among them 2,000 converts. He also founded the Jesuit College of the Holy Cross in Worcester (1843) and the most influential Catholic newspaper in America (first called the *Jesuit* and then the *Pilot* after 1836). Fenwick of course faced the same problem of trusteeism from within and anti-Catholicism from without that his Philadelphia counterparts faced. Nevertheless, partly because of the long tradition of ministerial authority within the Congregational church but mainly because of Fenwick's firm leadership, trusteeism never got out of control as had Hoganism in Philadelphia. The bishops of Boston, according to the *New Catholic Encyclopedia*, kept matters in hand throughout New England in contrast to other parts of the country. The most serious case of trusteeism occurred at St. Mary's Church in Boston's North End in 1842; after Fenwick dealt with both the members of the parish and the two insubordinate Irish priests in a series of conferences at St. Mary's, he called the first synod of the diocese. Several statutes were adopted, of special importance being the decree that firmly stated that "the titles of all churches in the Diocese must be vested in the Bishop in trust for the congregation; and that any priest who encouraged the attempts of lay trustees or others to interfere in the designation or rejection of pastors or impede the exercise of episcopal authority should incur the penalty of suspension."[10]

Although trusteeism was controlled by the bishops of Boston, they were not able to prevent anti-Catholic demonstrations. Thus, the Ursuline convent, in neighboring Charlestown, was burned down in the summer of 1834. The burning of the Charlestown convent was part of a bitter struggle in Boston between the liberal and fundamentalist branches of local Protestantism at the time. The rigid Congregationalism of the public schools had persuaded many of the best Brahmin families in Boston, mostly Unitarians, to educate their daughters at the convent. Quite naturally the fundamentalists saw an evil conspiracy between the Unitarians and the papists. The most prominent of the fundamentalists was Lyman Beecher, then pastor of the Park Street Church. Beecher preached violent anti-Catholic sermons in three churches on Sunday, August 10, and the next night the convent was burned to the ground. As the lower-class mob seems to have planned the burning well in advance, there was probably no causal connection between the Boston sermons (many other clergymen ranted against popery on that Sunday) and the fire in Charlestown, except that both were part of the anti-Catholicism of the time. Fortunately, just before the convent was set on fire the nuns and their pupils were evacuated and no lives were lost. The next day, Irish mobs roamed the streets of Boston, and Mayor Lyman and Bishop Fenwick worked diligently to prevent further violence.

Bishop Fitzpatrick was fired in very much the same mold as the aristocratic Fenwick although he was born in Boston of immigrant Irish parents. Fitzpatrick was educated at the Boston Latin School, where he was a close friend of George Cabot, Henry Cabot Lodge's uncle. (The bishop often visited the Lodge family at Nahant and sometimes said mass in the local church at which Cabot Lodge's father was warden and treasurer.) Fitzpatrick was a widely respected community leader whose main task was to assimilate the hordes of Irish immigrants who came to Boston in the pre–Civil War years. There is no better reward for total community leadership in Boston than an honorary degree from Harvard. And Harvard not only made Fitzpatrick an honorary member of the class of 1861 but also granted him an honorary doctorate in sacred theology, the first such degree ever given to a Catholic.*

CATHOLIC EDUCATION IN BOSTON AND PHILADELPHIA

That Bishop Fitzpatrick attended the Boston Latin School rather than a parochial school points to another important difference between the Catholic traditions in the two cities. The church hierarchy in Philadelphia has built up perhaps the most effective parochial school system in the nation. This development in Catholicism parallels the long tradition among Quakers and Episcopalians in the city, who preferred to support their own private schools rather than work for compulsory public education. In Boston, Catholic boys attend public schools as a way to achieve leadership in the larger community. Bishop Fitzpatrick surely built up the parochial system but not with quite the same zeal as his contemporary Bishop Neumann in Philadelphia. It is no accident that Mayor John Francis Fitzgerald and his son-in-law Joseph Kennedy both went to the Boston Latin School and that whereas Joseph Kennedy's daughters attended Catholic schools their brothers were educated at the best Protestant private schools. These differing attitudes of Catholics in the two cities as regards education, a contrast that dates to the days of Fitzpatrick and Neumann, are nicely reflected in Table A–32. As might be expected, the proportion of Catholics educated in Catholic schools in Philadelphia was almost three times as great at the primary level, and four times as great at the secondary level, as was the case in Boston.

---

*Harvard's recognition of Fitzpatrick marked the beginning of a tradition of Catholic participation in the leadership of the city as a whole, a pattern not found in Philadelphia. Harvard offered honorary degrees to Bishop Williams on two occasions, though he was too humble to accept, and gave one to Archbishop O'Connell in 1937. It has never occurred to the trustees at the University of Pennsylvania to honor a Catholic prelate in the same way, even today, when Cardinal John Joseph Krol is widely recognized as the first prelate of the American church; and this is the case even though the University is heavily dependent financially on the state legislature, which now is almost half Catholic (47 percent at last count).

Catholic higher education in the two cities has followed very much the same pattern as primary and secondary education. The Boston archdiocese today has Boston College, founded for men in the nineteenth century by the Jesuits, and Merrimack College, founded for men by the Augustinians in 1947. There are also two women's colleges, Emmanuel and Regis, founded after the First World War (two other Catholic women's colleges were founded in Boston after World War II but have since closed). In Philadelphia, there are three men's colleges founded in the nineteenth century: Villanova (Augustinian), La Salle (Christian Brothers), and St. Joseph's (Jesuit). There are eight women's colleges: Rosemont, Immaculata, and Chestnut Hill, founded in the 1920s, and Gwynned-Mercy, Cabrini, Holy Family, Our Lady of Angels, and the Ukrainian Manor Junior College, all founded after World War II. (Philadelphia Catholics, in contrast to their Boston counterparts, seem to prefer that their daughters be educated in religiously guarded institutions of higher learning.)

Perhaps the most useful way of understanding the leadership ethics of the Catholics in the two cities is to compare the Jesuit colleges in each city, Boston College and St. Joseph's. Whereas Boston College seems to have modeled itself on Harvard, striving in modern times to become a nationally superior Catholic university, St. Joseph's has been content to remain a small undergraduate college, more in the style of nearby Haverford College.

Boston College was chartered as an institution of higher learning by the state of Massachusetts in 1863 and had twenty-two students when it opened its doors in downtown Boston the next year. It grew slowly but steadily to 500 students in 1905. The modern history of the college began in 1907, when Thomas Ignatius Gasson was made president. Gasson, born into an aristocratic English family, converted to Catholicism after coming to America. He joined the Jesuits in Maryland. In 1911, Gasson moved Boston College to its present site, on the former Lawrence estate in Chestnut Hill. By the third decade of the twentieth century, Boston College was one of the largest and finest Catholic institutions of higher education in the nation.

St. Joseph's went through a far more irregular period of growth and decline during the nineteenth century. Founded in 1851, it was actually a citywide prep school attached to St. Joseph's parish on Willing's Alley during its early years; for two decades after the Civil War the school suffered from lack of funds and was mainly a local parish school. After the first major donations in the history of St. Joseph's were made—$35,000 from Francis Anthony Drexel in 1885 and $37,000 in 1886—the school was revived at a new uptown site with seventy-seven students in 1889; at that time it was recognized by the Jesuit authorities as a true institution of higher learning. By the turn of the century St. Joseph's had somewhat fewer than 200 students compared to 500 at Boston College. Under the leadership of Father Albert G. Brown,* the college moved to its present site, just inside City Line on the lower Main Line. In 1940, St. Joseph's had an

---

*Although Father Gasson was a widely recognized Catholic educator in his day and was included in the *DAB*, there seem to be no published biographical data on Father Brown.

enrollment of 519 students compared to 2,895 at Boston College. Whereas St. Joseph's had a local reputation and lacked distinction, Boston College had obtained a position of first rank among American Catholic institutions.

St. Joseph's had a difficult time during the Second World War, dropping down to eighty-one students by 1945. Since the war, both institutions have done well: by 1960, there were 1,212 students at St. Joseph's as against 7,416 at Boston College. Although both colleges drew most of their students from their local areas, Boston College was far more of a national institution, with students from forty-six states and thirty-two foreign countries; St. Joseph's had students from fifteen states and fourteen foreign countries. Finally, just as Harvard has educated a national and international elite over the years and at the same time has contributed leaders within the state of Massachusetts, so Boston College has been concerned with producing city and state leaders. (Cardinals O'Connell and Cushing were educated at Boston College, for instance; no comparable prelates in Philadelphia have as yet been graduated from St. Joseph's, Villanova, or La Salle.)

Perhaps the value placed on higher education in the two cities is most objectively revealed in the comparative statistics shown in Table A–33.

If endowment size is a quantitative measure of the value placed on education and the intellect in any community, it is significant that the comparative endowments of Boston College and St. Joseph's are not too dissimilar from the comparative endowments of Harvard and the University of Pennsylvania. Thus, whereas the Boston College endowment suggests that Boston's Catholic community made about seven times the effort to raise money as did Catholics in Philadelphia, so Harvard, according to the *World Almanac* of 1967, had an endowment of over $1 billion, about ten times that of the University of Pennsylvania (close to $95 million), which, under President Harnwell, had just completed the largest capital campaign in its history.

INTELLECTUAL CLIMATES OF BOSTON AND PHILADELPHIA CATHOLICISM

Boston College and St. Joseph's were founded and grew up in very different intellectual climates. The intellectual traditions of Boston Catholics as a whole were far more vigorous and influential than those of Philadelphia's Catholic community. The *Pilot*, Bishop Fenwick's brainchild, was the main intellectual force in American Catholicism during the second half of the nineteenth and in the early twentieth century. No Philadelphia Catholic had the intellectual drive of Boston's John Boyle O'Reilly. Born in Ireland, he joined the Fenian movement as a young soldier in the British army and was eventually court-martialed, thrown into prison, and from there sent out on a prison ship to Australia. O'Reilly soon escaped and sailed to America on a whaling ship, landing in Philadelphia in 1869, where he immediately took out citizenship papers. As "there was no field for his ambition in Philadelphia," according to his biographer, he went to Boston, where he took a job on the *Pilot*, then the most influential publication among the Irish in America.[11] O'Reilly became part owner of the *Pilot* and the most famous Catholic editor in the nation. But he was also an intellectual leader with a host of friends among Bostonians of all faiths; a measure of his stature in the city was his being asked to give the main oration at the funeral of Edward Everett. O'Reilly died at too young an age to have reached his full potential as a poet, but Boston paid tribute to him with a memorial on the Fenway and a statue in the Boston Public Library; in Washington, there is a statue of him on the campus of the Catholic University. John Boyle O'Reilly surely followed in the intellectual tradition set by the Puritan and Brahmin Bostonians who preceded him.

In our mobile and status-striving society, Protestant denominational affiliation is closely correlated with socioeconomic position. When affluent and educated Protestants convert to Roman Catholicism, however, intellectual or theological convictions are probably more important than status considerations. If this is indeed the case, one would expect upper-class Bostonians to have been more likely to have converted to Catholicism than their Philadelphia counterparts. Thus it is appropriate that, whereas the article on the Philadelphia diocese in the *New Catholic Encyclopedia* does not mention conversions, the comparable article on Boston not only cites the figure of 2,000 conversions during Bishop Fenwick's time alone but also discusses several of the more prominent converts of that day in some detail.

It may be a law of intellectual history that in times of crisis attitudes will follow a bimodal rather than a normal curve; that is, more men will be found at the extremes of the liberal-conservative spectrum than in the middle. Such a crisis period in the life of the mind of Boston marked the dozen years between the burning of the Ursuline Convent in 1834 and the death of Bishop Fenwick in 1846. In the year the convent was burned, for instance, the Transcendental Club, which included Emerson, Alcott, Orestes Brownson, Theodore Parker, Margaret Fuller, and Elizabeth Peabody, was planning its future, which was to include the founding of the *Dial* (1840) and the Brook Farm experiment (1841–1847). In the meantime, Brownson, who had many friends at Brook Farm, among them his oldest son and George Ripley, was moving in the opposite direction, toward Catholicism. An antinomian seeker if there ever was one, Brownson had tried many churches in his career as a Protestant minister and an influential journalist, but he never felt quite at home until he settled in the bosom of the Catholic church in 1844. He did his best to take his good friend Henry Thoreau into the Church with him, but Thoreau went to Walden Pond instead.

Often compared to John Newman in England, who converted in 1845, Brownson was undoubtedly American Catholicism's most distinguished convert in his day or any day since. Between 1838, when he established the *Boston Quarterly Review*, and his death in 1876, he was one of the most influential editors in America, first in Boston and then in New York after his conversion.

Brownson's celebrated conversion encouraged others to join the Catholic church, including several participants in the Brook Farm experiment: Isaac Thomas Hecker, William J. Davis, George Leach, Sophia Ripley, and his son,

Orestes, Jr.. Father Hecker founded the Paulists, and many other distinguished converts, whose fascinating stories cannot be told here, played leading roles in the American Catholic church. It is enough to note that Hawthorne's daughter, Rose, and Longfellow's niece Marian both entered the Church.*

The aggressive, intellectual, and proselytizing style of Boston's Irish Catholicism contrasted sharply with the guarded separatism of Philadelphia Catholicism. As one might expect, the Boston Irish have been far more active politically than their counterparts in Philadelphia. In other words, there is a direct causal connection between the lives of Bishop Fenwick, Orestes Brownson, and John Boyle O'Reilly and the facts that the Boston Irish elected their first mayor in 1884 and sent the first Irish Catholic to the White House in 1960; at the same time, the style of leadership provided by Bishops Kenrick, Neumann, and Wood in Philadelphia is causally related to the facts that the city has had no organized Catholic vote to speak of and, unlike any other major city in America, was ruled by a Protestant and Republican machine for over half a century preceding Pearl Harbor. (The Quaker City elected its first Irish-Catholic mayor in the 1960s.)

CATHOLIC POLITICAL TRADITIONS IN MASSACHUSETTS AND PENNSYLVANIA

Conventional wisdom has had it that Brahmin Boston has always been horrified by the shady Irish politicians who have run *their* city throughout most of the twentieth century. Though this may have been true of the gentlemanly rentiers at the Somerset Club, it was surely not true of most of the politically responsible Brahmins in the days when the Irish were first coming to power. Most of the Boston Mugwumps, for instance, were astonished by the essential soundness and moderation displayed by the two immigrant politicians, Hugh O'Brien and Patrick Collins, who first brought the Irish to power in the city. Collins, who worked his way up from poverty to graduate from the Harvard Law School and join the Suffolk County bar, was the first Irish Catholic in the city to be sent to the United States Congress (1880); he also served as mayor of Boston (1902–1905). O'Brien was elected mayor in 1884 and served until 1888. Both men were part of the Democratic reform movement in the city, which included the Yankee mayors Nathan Matthews and Josiah Quincy. As we have seen, Irish Catholics have more or less dominated the mayor's office in Boston ever since, some in the style of John Francis Fitzgerald, who cooperated with the Yankees, and others in the manner of James Michael Curley (1922–1926, 1930–1934), who fought them tooth and nail. Mayor Kevin White is surely in the Collins, O'Brien, and Fitzgerald tradition.

---

*Rose Hawthorne married an Englishman and both converted in 1891. Rose carried on the rich literary tradition of her family and then, after her husband's death, became a religious; as Mother Alphonsa, she founded the Servants of Relief for Incurable Cancer, eventually established in Hawthorne, New York.

Whereas Philadelphia has been tolerant of Catholics from the very beginning (as long as they kept to themselves, which they did), it was the last of the older cities in America to elect a Catholic to the mayor's office. The first Irish-Catholic mayor in Philadelphia's history, James H. J. Tate, was elected in 1964, after the great reform movement under Joseph S. Clark and Richardson Dilworth had lost its steam. Though of little intellectual or educational stature, Tate was a solid and honest public servant with a thorough knowledge of city government. He was, moreover, nothing like his political enemy and charismatic successor, Frank Rizzo, an Italian Catholic whose sometimes bizarre behavior brought him a national reputation and a majority of the city's votes.

When John F. Kennedy was in the White House, John W. McCormack became the first Roman Catholic Speaker of the U.S. House of Representatives. Born among the deserving poor of South Boston, McCormack went to work at age thirteen after his father died. He became a member of the bar at twenty-one, having studied and worked in a local law office. McCormack won a seat in the state legislature and later went to Washington, where he spent thirty-three years in the House before becoming Speaker. Thomas P. O'Neill, a native of Cambridge and a graduate of Boston College, followed McCormack in the Speaker's chair.* There have been no Speakers from Pennsylvania in the twentieth century, Catholic or Protestant.

In spite of the Roman Catholic conquest of Boston, the Brahmins and Protestants have pretty much retained control of the offices of governor and senator, until recent times at least. Though Governor James Sullivan was the son of Irish (and presumably Catholic) immigrants in the early nineteenth century, he was not a practicing Catholic. Thus, David Ignatius Walsh, of Worcester, Massachusetts, was the first Irish Catholic to serve both as governor (1914–1915) and as senator (1919–1925, 1926–1947) from the state. The son of poor immigrant parents, Walsh, through the help of his siblings and his mother, who worked in a textile mill, was able to go to Holy Cross and Boston University Law School. Though a Catholic, Walsh served his state very much in the style of his Puritan and Yankee predecessors. According to his *DAB* biographer, although "identified with elements that were destructive of the Massachusetts status quo, he took pains to avoid unnecessarily offending the old-stock establishment. He remained aloof from the maneuverings of the Irish Democratic bosses—Curley, Fitzgerald, Lomasney, and the rest—who squabbled in Boston. Consequently, Walsh appeared to be 'different' from that breed—more dignified—an asset when this son of immigrants sought to win votes among Republican and Democratic Yankees."[12] Walsh appealed to voters of all faiths and backgrounds: "Most significant of all was the unparalleled support accorded him by minority ethnic groups other than the Irish: the Italians, Jews, Poles, French Canadians, Portuguese, and Negroes, who together controlled much of the Commonwealth's population."[13] He was one of the six sen-

---

*There have been fourteen Speakers of the House in the twentieth century, four of them, including McCormack and O'Neill, from Massachusetts.

ators to vote against the Johnson Immigration Act of 1924. In 1926, Walsh was sent back to the Senate to fill the vacancy caused by the death of Henry Cabot Lodge; he died soon after being soundly beaten for reelection in 1946 by young Henry Cabot Lodge.

When John F. Kennedy defeated Lodge in 1953, he became the second Irish-Catholic senator to serve his state in Washington. His brother Edward, elected in 1963, now represents Massachusetts in the Senate. In 1935, James Michael Curley became the second Irish-Catholic governor of Massachusetts, and many Catholics have followed him in the office since. The original Puritan tradition of Massachusetts, in other words, is continuing to motivate leaders both locally and nationally, regardless of their religious background.

In striking contrast to Massachusetts, Pennsylvania has had only two Catholics in the highest offices in the state. David Lawrence, a Catholic Scotch-Irishman from Pittsburgh, served one term as governor after World War II. The only Catholic ever sent to the Senate from Pennsylvania was Francis John Myers, who failed to be reelected after one term (1945–1951). (Myers was a graduate of St. Joseph's and the Temple Law School.)

Whereas Philadelphia Catholics have been largely content to cultivate their own garden, Catholic Bostonians have been busy cultivating voters of all faiths in their city, their state, and their nation. During the 1930s, for example, it used to be said that the best real estate in Philadelphia was owned by Cardinal Dougherty and Albert M. Greenfield (a local real estate tycoon). In a very different vein, it was once said of Cardinal Cushing that he was "the most pervasive social force in Boston." And he was surely the most famous Catholic prelate in America on that frigid January day in 1961 when he watched his friend's inauguration and heard him say, "Ask not what your country can do for you; ask rather what you can do for your country"—a pretty sound summary of the values inherent in the old New England Way.[14]

Philadelphia Orthodox Quakerism: A Deviant Case Suggests a Rule

The Revolutionary War left the Philadelphia Yearly Meeting more moral internally, more devoted to moral reforms, more conservative of ancient traditions, custom and doctrine, more separate from the world, more introversive in spirit, than it found it. . . . Had the active public spirited Friends, who went off with the revolutionary movement, remained to mold their generation, a type more outward, more progressive, more intellectual would have resulted. . . . As a result of the narrowing and uniting processes combined Friends are what they are. What they would have been with a wider outlook upon life and looser standards of conduct, we can only conjecture. But he who understands Philadelphia Quakerism of a century past must read it in the light of the Revolution—a revolution not less in Quaker development than in American history.

Rufus Jones

It is impossible to have an adequate understanding of modern Quakerism without considerable attention to the remarkable family which lived in Earlham Hall in East Anglia at the beginning of the nineteenth century. One of these, Joseph John Gurney, became the most influential Quaker of the nineteenth century, while his sister Elizabeth, who married Joseph Fry, became the most famous of all Quaker heroines. . . . Apart from Joseph John's American visit, American Quakerism would today be utterly different and in many parts, might not even exist.

D. Elton Trueblood

In preceding chapters I have tried to show that Bostonians, whether Puritans, Unitarians, Episcopalians, Catholics, Jews, agnostics, or atheists, have continued to be influenced by the hierarchical communalism of Puritanism just as their counterparts in Philadelphia are still infected by the egalitarian individualism of the Quaker founders of the holy experiment on the Delaware. In this concluding chapter, I should like to speculate on what might have been in Philadelphia by taking a look at a small group of Orthodox and Gurneyite Quaker families (an exception that illustrates a rule) who went through a renaissance in leadership and creativity in the city from about the time of the Civil War down to 1955, when Hicksite and Orthodox Friends came together in one United Philadelphia Yearly Meeting for the first time since the tragic separation in 1827 (see Figure 20–1).

THE HICKSITE SEPARATION OF 1827

Philadelphia Friends had two traumatic experiences in the eighteenth century: the Indian wars of the 1750s and the Revolution. We have seen how many of their leaders were read out of meeting during these crises. After the Revolution, Philadelphia Friends withdrew from the "World" more than ever and went through a stultifying period of quietism, rigidly living by the Book of Discipline and led by an increasingly conservative group of wealthy Quakers. In the steadily expanding and prosperous city, moreover, more and more men and women were disowned for marrying out of meeting, often with their Episcopalian peers. As Rufus Jones wrote in *The Later Periods of Quakerism:* "It was unfortunately often difficult for a distinguished person to remain a Friend during the dull, arid, and contentious period of early nineteenth century Quakerism."[1] It was during this time, for instance, that the Pembertons, the leading eighteenth-century Quaker family in the city, began to go on to the Assembly balls and attend fashionable Episcopal churches.

Schisms have characterized most sectarian movements, as well as all too many Protestant denominations. And the most important and tragic schism in the history of Quakerism occurred in Philadelphia when Elias Hicks visited the city between 1819 and 1827. Hicks, a birthright Friend, had been a charismatic preacher for over fifty years when he came to preach in Philadelphia.* The Hickses were a prominent family on Long Island and in New York City; during the Revolution, when young Elias visited Philadelphia, he was strengthened in his faith by the example set by Henry Drinker and the Pembertons, who were exiled to Virginia for abiding by their perfectionist faith.

Seeds of trouble were first sown in Philadelphia Quakerism in 1819, when Hicks, then in his seventies, visited the old Pine Street Meetinghouse. Preaching to standing room only, Hicks upset the leading elders, including Jonathan Evans, Joseph Whitall, and especially Samuel Bettle, Clerk of the Yearly Meeting; most of the rank and file enthusiastically approved. Hicks came back to the

---

*Walt Whitman had been extremely impressed in his youth with Hicks's charismatic style and later wrote of his impressions: "A pleading tender, nearly agonizing conviction, and magnetic stream of natural eloquence, before which all minds and natures, all emotions, high or low, gentle or simple, yielded entirely; without exception—not argumentative or intellectual, but so penetrating—so different from anything in books" (Rufus M. Jones, *The Later Periods of Quakerism* [New York: Macmillan, 1921], Vol. I, p. 441).

Figure 20-1   American Quakerism after the Hicksite Separation

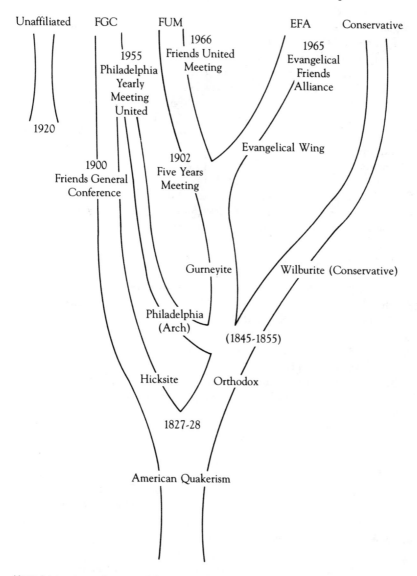

NOTE: It is important to bear in mind that the Philadelphia Gurneyites discussed in this book *did not separate* from Arch Street Yearly Meeting, and hence should properly be thought of as Orthodox-Gurneyites in the nineteenth century and just plain Orthodox Friends in the Twentieth.

Source: Edwin B. Brenner, ed., *American Quakers Today* (Philadelphia: Friends World Committee, 1966), p.31.

city in the 1820s and finally provoked the separation at the Yearly Meeting in April 1827.

Elias Hicks preached the absolute authority of the Inner Light as opposed to the authority of Scripture; he also downgraded the historic Jesus and the idea of the vicarious atonement. In every way, he was a radical egalitarian;* all days, for instance, were holy days for him, and he attacked Thanksgiving as a "clerical plot." "He taught," wrote Bliss Forbush, "that the Spirit would lead men into all truth, and that revelation was a continuous process. He stood against all external authorities which would curb new revelations of truth, whether in the form of creed, sacred Scripture, or hierarchy. He was a true liberal."[2] Perhaps Jones was closer to the truth when he saw Hicks as a prophet of the past in setting up the infallibility of the Inner Light to the exclusion of all other external aids to spiritual progress. As Hicks wrote in his journal: "I was led in my communication to-day, to show the unreasonableness of some people, in looking to, and depending on, being made Christians, by the ministrations of men, and information derived from books and writings; when, alas, the ministration of angels would be entirely sufficient for that purpose."[3] Hicks's dogmatism about the dangers of dogmatic creeds, hierarchies, and all intellectual approaches to the truth had a great and divisive appeal to many Quakers (just as that of his spiritual ancestor Anne Hutchinson had once had in Boston). But the leaders of Philadelphia Quakerism, like those of John Winthrop's generation in Boston, saw this brand of antinomian absolutism as a threat to their authority.

When Philadelphia Quakerism split into the irreconcilable branches of Hicksite and Orthodox Friends, most of the leaders sided with the Orthodox branch, whereas two-thirds of the Yearly Meeting eventually joined the Hicksites. By and large, the urban and more wealthy Friends remained Orthodox; the rural and poorer Friends became Hicksites. At the same time, the Hicksites who were well-to-do at the separation, as well as those who became rich later, were more likely to join fashionable Philadelphia in the Episcopal church. Two of the wealthiest Philadelphians at the time were the Quaker merchants Thomas Pym Cope and Jacob Ridgway. Cope, close friend and rival of Stephen Girard, stayed with the Orthodox Friends and, as we shall see, left a family whose members are still playing important roles in the Quaker community. Ridgway, however, became a Hicksite, and his descendants are now part of fashionable Philadelphia. Of even more significance is the history of the Price family, whose members were fourth generation Quakers when Phillip and Rachel Price became the first heads of the newly founded Westtown School in 1799. Their son, Eli K. Price, who built up a great real estate fortune in his sixty years as one of the leading lawyers in the city, became a Hicksite. His grandson and namesake was the foremost civic and cultural leader in early twentieth-

---

*Hicks, as befit his egalitarian views, was an ardent abolitionist. And the anti-slavery movement in Philadelphia was more likely to be supported by Hicksite than Orthodox Friends. Perhaps the most famous Philadelphia abolitionist was Lucretia Coffin Mott, who was strongly influenced by Hicks. An auslander Philadelphian, as was her fellow abolitionist and friend Dr. William Furness, Mott attended the organization of the American Anti-Slavery Society, held in Philadelphia in 1833, and immediately afterward formed the Philadelphia Female Anti-Slavery Society (she was president during most of its existence). At the anti-slavery convention in London in 1840, Mott was one of the leading figures, even though she was not recognized as an official delegate because of her sex. This led her to take an active part in the women's movement: she was one of the chief organizers of the first women's rights convention at Seneca Falls, New York, in 1848. Finally, it should be noted that Hicksite women were very influential in founding the "Female Medical College of Pennsylvania, for the purpose of instructing females in the Science and Art of Medicine," in Philadelphia in 1850—the first of its kind in the nation if not in the world.

century Philadelphia, but Eli K. Price II was a fashionable Walnut Street and Philadelphia Club Episcopalian. The Biddles followed pretty much the same path as the Prices. Although Owen Biddle was one of the founders of West-town School, later Biddles tended to become Hicksites if they remained Friends and leaders of Proper Philadelphia when they left the Society.*

Philadelphia Friends remained antagonistic for more than a century after the separation. From 1827 until 1954, the Orthodox Yearly Meeting was held at the old meetinghouse at Fourth and Arch streets in the colonial part of the city; the Hicksites met at Sixth and Green until 1856 and afterward at Fifteenth and Race Streets. Each branch of the Society also had its own journal: the Orthodox Quakers founded the *Friend* in 1827 and the Hicksites founded the *Friends' Intelligencer* in 1838. Moreover, a whole series of institutions marked off the Orthodox families from those of the "other branch," as insiders called the Hicksites, with a certain amount of condescension. Thus, Westtown School remained Orthodox and the George School, at Newtown, in Bucks County, was founded in 1893 to educate Hicksite boys and girls. Both Haverford and Bryn Mawr colleges were founded and run by Orthodox Friends; coeducational Swarthmore was founded by Hicksites. The Orthodox branch had two secondary day schools, Friends Select in center city and the Germantown Friends School, and the Hicksites had their own Friends Central School, first in the city and now on the Main Line.

There were also Quaker neighborhoods, not on the Main Line but in the southern and unfashionable part of the countryside along the Baltimore Pike, where the suburb of Swarthmore was Hicksite and nearby Media was Orthodox; Lansdowne was Orthodox and Upper Darby was Hicksite. Germantown was a strongly Quaker suburb containing both Orthodox and Hicksite families. (Even summer resorts in the mountains were segregated.)

To fashionable Philadelphians, of course, all Quakers were one and peculiarly alike. Thus, Senator George Wharton Pepper wrote in his autobiography of a trip to Europe in 1887. His fellow passengers aboard ship included "some interesting Philadelphia Quakers: Robert Pearsall Smith, his young and attractive unmarried daughter and several friends of hers. . . . That I had never heard of these fellow-townsmen of mine was due to the fact that within the limits of Philadelphia we had lived in different worlds. The Quaker community, with its center in Germantown, was effectively set off from the social group into which I was born as if between us there had been a Chinese wall."[4] George Pepper soon found out that the Smiths were a prosperous and aristocratic family as well as important religious leaders on both sides of the Atlantic. He also observed in the Smiths the usual circumspection and the habit of probing the social credentials of strangers so characteristic of his own world: "When we struck up an acquaintance with the young people of his party," Senator Pepper wrote,

Mr. Smith was careful to interview us and to subject us to a rather severe examination respecting our social qualifications. I was somewhat puzzled, in Mr.

---

*I am indebted to Margaret Bacon of the American Friends Service Committee for pointing out that there are Biddles, Ridgways, and Prices playing active roles in Yearly Meetings today.

Smith's case, by the combination of evangelistic ardor and an attitude not far removed from snobbishness. I was to find confirmation fifty years later for my boyhood suspicion that worldliness may penetrate even a Chinese wall, when I read
the reminiscences of Mr. Smith's son Logan Pearsall Smith, entitled *Unforgotten
Years*. In this interesting, if rather cynical, volume one reads of the social contacts between Philadelphia Quakers and prominent English members of their Society.[5]

Smith's *Unforgotten Years* also reveals an unsuspected snobbery and divisive-
ness within the Germantown Quaker community.

> Both my father's and my mother's families were adherents of the orthodox or
> conservative party, and Hicksite Quakers were to my boyish apprehensions
> nothing less than children of the Devil. . . . I remember climbing the wall that
> surrounded one of the Hicksite meetinghouses, and gazing in on those precincts
> with all the horror of one who gazes into Hell. . . . This theological horror was ac-
> companied, among the orthodox at least, by an immense sense of social superior-
> ity: ours were the high places, we felt, in this world as well as in the next. This
> feeling that the Hicksites were outcasts and untouchables and social pariahs,
> though it had no foundation in fact, for they were as well off and as well-de-
> scended as we were, and probably a more enlightened and cultivated set of peo-
> ple—this sense of social superiority is the main religious feeling which I still
> retain; and even now, when, as sometimes happens, I meet in London Philadel-
> phians with a taint in their veins of Hicksite blood, I seem to know them at once,
> as by a kind of instinct, by a subtly mingled sense of theological and social
> repugnance, which I find it extremely difficult to overcome.[6]

We shall return to the Smith family later. Here it is enough to indicate the
feelings of the Orthodox toward the Hicksite Quakers, which lasted for so long
in Philadelphia. The separation spread elsewhere; but whereas there were
Hicksite and Orthodox divisions in New York and Maryland, the New England Yearly Meeting remained Orthodox and had no time for the anti-intellectual Hicksites; Indiana, which has gradually become more of a center of
Quakerism (quantitatively) than Pennsylvania, also remained with the Orthodox wing. British Friends sympathized with the Orthodox, and the London
Yearly Meeting went so far as to refuse to recognize the American Hicksites.

THE SECOND SEPARATION (1845): GURNEYITES AND WILBURITES

"The twenty years from 1835 to 1855 were the darkest and saddest in the history of Quakerism."[7] In Philadelphia, for instance, the Radnor meeting, once
an Orthodox stronghold on the Main Line, disowned no fewer than 360 members between 1825 and 1850. About half of them became Hicksites but the rest
were lost to the faith forever.

English Friends were also going through a critical period, especially in re-
thinking their theological position. Just as Swarthmore Hall had been the
Quaker headquarters in the founding days and the Grange, the home of the

Peningtons, had been the focus of the Quaker aristocracy in the late seventeenth and the early eighteenth century, so Earlham Hall, outside Norwich, the capital of East Anglia, became the main gathering place for the Quaker elite in the early nineteenth century.

Joseph John Gurney was one of eleven children born at Earlham Hall. His father was a wealthy banker.* His mother, Catherine Bell, was the great-granddaughter of the Quaker theologian Robert Barclay. The children of the privileged Gurney family grew up in a home full of fun and games, the girls always dressed in bright colors; naturally, they were branded "gay Quakers" by visiting dignitaries of the faith. Eventually, four Gurney children, including Elizabeth Fry and Joseph John, became Quaker leaders; two joined the Church of England.

Joseph John Gurney, next to Robert Barclay the leading theologian in the history of Quakerism, was brought up as a typical upper-class Englishman of his day. After eight years in boarding school, he studied three years at Oxford (as a nonconformist he was unable to register offically for a degree) under the tutorship of a sound Anglican scholar. Returning to Earlham Hall he entered the family banking business in Norwich. Most of Gurney's friends were Anglicans, including ministers and the local bishop, and many were leaders in the British evangelical movement of the day. It was natural that he gradually drifted toward the Church of England; at the same time, he had a basic sympathy for the faith of his ancestors, which was finally tested in a crisis that he described in his journal.

> I was engaged to a dinner party at the house of one of our first county gentlemen. Three weeks before the time was I engaged, and three weeks was my young mind in agitation from the apprehension, of which I could not dispossess myself, that I must enter his drawing-room with my hat on. From this sacrifice, strange and unaccountable as it may appear, I could not escape. In Friend's attire, and with my hat on, I entered the drawing-room at the dreaded moment, shook hands with the mistress of the house, went back into the hall, deposited my hat, spent a rather comfortable evening, and returned home in some degree of peace. I had afterwards the same thing to do at the Bishop's; the result was, that I found myself the decided Quaker, was perfectly understood to have assumed that character, and to dinner parties, except in the family circle, was asked no more. . . .
>
> The wearing of the hat in the house is not my practice. I have no wish to repeat what then happened. . . . I also think that there is a danger in the Society of laying too great a stress upon trifles.[8]

(Gurney's sister Elizabeth Fry also abandoned the "flirtatious and worldly ways" of her youth, as she once put it in her journal, in favor of life as a prison reformer by donning the drab dress and bonnet of her Friendly ancestors.)

Many leaders of English Quakerism in Joseph John Gurney's generation were dissatisfied with the anti-intellectual doctrine of the Inner Light as the theological center of their faith. With his Oxford background and his host of

---

*W. S. Gilbert, in *Trial by Jury*, noted the notorious wealth of the Gurneys: "At length I became as rich as the Gurneys."

friends among the Anglican evangelicals, Gurney naturally came to center his faith on the doctrine of atonement. Although he never entirely deserted Barclay's theology of the Inner Light, as some of his contemporaries did, he stressed, exactly contrary to George Fox, the evangelical doctrine of the depravity of ruined man—what Gurney called "the fall and moral ruin of our species." Questioning the infallibility of the Inner Light, he emphasized scriptural truths and read the Bible every day of his life. He was a leader, along with Anglican evangelicals, of the British and Foreign Bible Society. He strongly supported the need for improving education among Friends and the development of an educated ministry. And this very handsome, polished, and extremely wealthy Friend became the foremost Quaker minister in England, his numerous theological works widely read on both sides of the Atlantic by Christians of many denominations. Finally, to place Gurney in historical perspective as regards Philadelphia Quakerism, he surely would have sided with George Keith in the heresy that marked the founding years of Pennsylvania. "Theologically," wrote Jones, "Gurney stood in line with the Puritan opponents of Quakerism rather than with Fox and Barclay and Penington. They were mystics; he was non-mystical, even anti-mystical. They were profoundly against the central positions of Augustine and Calvin; he was very near of kin to both these pillar evangelicals."[9]

Gurney spent three years (1837–1840) preaching in the United States and the West Indies. Large crowds gathered almost everywhere he went, and he was especially well received in New England and the Middle West. Some 3,000 persons crammed into the meetinghouse in Richmond, Indiana; his success in this frontier community led to the founding of a boarding school there in 1847, the year of Gurney's death, which later became Earlham College, partly through gifts from English Friends. Gurney was also a great success in North Carolina, where another boarding school was founded at the time of his visit (1837). This school became Guilford College in 1888 (with gifts from Gurney's widow).

Gurney was the acknowledged champion of evangelical Quakerism in both England and America. In the meantime, a stout defender of the faith of Fox and Hicks appeared: John Wilbur, of Hopkinton, Rhode Island. Though Wilbur was strongly supported by his own monthly meeting, the leaders of the New England Yearly Meeting were ardent Gurneyites. In a long and complicated struggle, the elders of Wilbur's local quarterly meeting were persuaded to disown him in 1843, and New England remained Gurneyite.

It was a different story in Philadelphia, where the extremely conservative leaders of the Orthodox branch were strongly anti-Gurney and more in sympathy with the anti-intellectual Wilburites.* This was so even though on Gurney's first visit to the city some 2,000 Friends turned out to hear him at the Arch Street Meetinghouse, "the largest assembly of Friends that has been

---

*Though Gurney had far more success in New England than in Philadelphia, he took as his third wife Elizabeth Paul Kirkbride, a spirited Quaker whose brother, Dr. Thomas Story Kirkbride (included in the DAB), was for over forty years superintendent of the Pennsylvania Hospital for the Insane. After Gurney's death in 1847, his widow came back to Philadelphia, where she reigned as a sort of Quaker queen, especially among the Gurneyites at the Twelfth Street meeting.

known there since the Hicksite separation."[10] As Elton Trueblood put it, Gurney suffered from "the envy of those who thought him too handsome, too eloquent, too rich, and too successful."[11]

Although the Arch Street meeting sided with Wilbur,

> there was a strong, resolute, and very intelligent minority in Philadelphia, extremely loyal to Joseph John Gurney who had awakened and kindled them. These Friends believed that the future of Quakerism was with the Gurney movement, not with the Wilburite tendency. They were forward-looking, and they were eager to ally themselves with those forces in the Society which would in the long run bring enlargement and expansion. It was the group of this kind and attitude who were the educational leaders of their body. They were the makers and managers of Haverford College, and they were also the creators of a very important literary journal for the exposition of the truth, *Friends' Review*, begun at this crisis.[12]

Gurney almost caused another schism in Philadelphia, but gradually the pillars of Arch Street Orthodoxy agreed to disagree with their uptown neighbors of Twelfth Street. Thus, the second separation, as Jones called the Wilburite-Gurneyite alignment, was not as decisive as the Hicksite separation. Gurneyites and Wilburites, in Philadelphia at least, remained Orthodox Friends. Indeed, a large number of the leading Twelfth Street families had joined the Orthodox (Wilburite) Germantown meeting by the time of the founding of the American Friends Service Committee during the First World War.

It should be noted that the followers of Gurney in Indiana and North Carolina went even further toward the evangelical position than did Gurneyite Friends in Philadelphia or New England. Thus, Indiana Quakers, and those in the West generally, tended to have programmed meetings, which meant paid ministers who led the singing of hymns and the reading of the Bible. As a result of this movement toward a more hierarchical structure, Quakerism grew far more rapidly in the West than in the East in the century after Gurney's visit (see Table A–34 in Appendix I). And Indiana, not Pennsylvania, is now the most Quaker state in the nation.*

LEADING PHILADELPHIA FAMILIES OF GURNEYITE ORTHODOX QUAKERISM

Table A–35 (Appendix I) is designed to provide a systematic base for an analysis of the Quaker renaissance in Philadelphia. Except for the auslander Browns and Joneses and the Cadburys, all of these families had deep roots in colonial Quakerism—in Philadelphia and in New Jersey, especially the Burling-

---

*Quakers responded to the slavery issue by moving in large numbers from North Carolina to Indiana in the decades before the Civil War. It is of interest that the meeting on the campus of Earlham College today is unstructured and similar to the Haverford meeting in Philadelphia; at the same time, the main meeting in Richmond is "programmed" and far closer to other Protestant denominations in structure.

ton and Salem areas. (The Cadburys, wealthy chocolate manufacturers in Birmingham, were among the first families of English Quakerism. The American branch of the Cadburys came to Philadelphia in the early nineteenth century.) One measure of rootedness in the Philadelphia Quaker community, as Table A-35 shows, was attendance at Westtown School.* All the families but the Browns and the Joneses met this test. The most prolific of them—Cope, Evans, Garrett, Rhoads, Sharpless, Taylor, and Wood—each had more than 100 graduates of the school, a record unmatched by any family at such newer and fashionable Episcopalian schools as Groton or St. Paul's. Eighteen, or 72 percent, of these families, moreover, had one or more members on the staff at Westtown. The most prolific Westtown family, the Sharplesses, supplied three superintendants of the school (as well as Isaac Sharpless, the greatest president of Haverford).

The two auslander families included in Table A-35 also played an indispensable part in the Gurneyite renaissance; the Browns from Providence, Rhode Island, and the Joneses from China, Maine. T. Wistar Brown, a founder and a director for over forty years of the Provident Life and Trust Company, was, quietly and unobtrusively, the greatest benefactor Haverford College ever had (he was a manager for an unmatched sixty-three years). His father, Moses Brown, of the great shipping and textile family in Providence, had settled in Philadelphia and married a Wistar. The first Moses Brown (1738–1836), a founder, along with his brothers, of Rhode Island's First Family, was a convinced Friend who freed his slaves and helped start the Rhode Island Abolition Society. This first Moses Brown also played a major role in founding modern Brown University and the Moses Brown Academy, a Quaker boarding school in its early days.

The Jones family gave Philadelphia two of its greatest educators, Richard Mott Jones, the first headmaster (1875–1917) of the reorganized William Penn Charter School, and Rufus M. Jones, who taught at Haverford for over fifty years and was the major spark of the Gurneyite renaissance in the city. Rufus Jones eventually became the most famous Friend in America; the London Yearly Meeting invited him to give the first of the Swarthmore Lectures in 1908 (he returned for a second lecture in 1920, the only person ever invited to do so). Jones, who attended both the Moses Brown School and Haverford, studied abroad before coming to the college as an instructor in 1892. (He later obtained a master of arts degree at Harvard, where he studied under James, Royce, and Santayana.)

As the goading editor of the new *American Friend*, by far the most intellectual and lively of the Quaker journals, Jones revitalized conservative Philadelphia Quakerism, as well as Friendly communities throughout the nation. Through his close friendship with the English Quaker leader John Wilhelm Rowntree, Jones dominated the transatlantic Quakerism that was so important to Gurneyite Philadelphians in his day. At the same time, his independent

---

*Westtown remained with the Orthodox Wilburites and became increasingly conservative and rural in orientation during the nineteenth century.

Yankee spirit made him feel somewhat of an outsider in his adopted city of fam-
ily-proud Friends, of whom it has been said: "To appoint a committee" was
their most decisive action.[13] For many years Jones kept his birthright membership in the meeting of China, Maine, rather than transfer it to Philadelphia.
His position in Philadelphia, as well as in England, was finally consolidated,
however, when he married Elizabeth Bartram Cadbury, Henry J. Cadbury's
older sister, at the Twelfth Street Meetinghouse in 1902.*

TWELFTH STREET MEETING, PENN
CHARTER SCHOOL, HAVERFORD AND
BRYN MAWR COLLEGES, AND
PROVIDENT LIFE AND TRUST

After the second separation, the followers of Joseph John Gurney tended to
congregate at the Twelfth Street Meetinghouse, built in 1812, a year after the
completion of the Arch Street headquarters of Orthodox Friends. Between
1875 and 1911 members of twenty-two of the families in Table A–35 belonged
to the Twelfth Street meeting, as did the Browns and Joneses of New England.
Today, a goodly proportion of their descendants attend the Haverford meeting, adjacent to Haverford College, if they have not become Episcopalians.

Next door, on the old Pennock homestead, the Penn Charter School was reorganized into what is now one of the leading boys' day schools in the city.
(Penn Charter moved to a new campus in Germantown in 1925.) Unlike the
Germantown Friends School and others like it in the city, which are attached
to various monthly meetings, Penn Charter, as reorganized in 1875, has been
run by a self-perpetuating board of overseers, most of them originally Gurneyite members of the Twelfth Street meeting. Rather than a strictly Friends
school, in other words, it is more like its rivals in the Interacademic League,
such as the Protestant Episcopal Academy on the Main Line, the old Germantown Academy, and the Chestnut Hill Academy. (Until recently, and unlike
the coeducational Friends schools, all of these schools were for boys only.)

Penn Charter's overseers chose a young New England schoolteacher, Richard Mott Jones, as their first headmaster. And every year for many years, Jones
went to New England to recruit his faculty. Down through the years, the

---

*At the time of his marriage, Jones was forced to make one of the most important decisions of his
life. His wife's uncle, head of the Cadbury chocolate firm, had given his house, Woodbrooke, as a
center for Quaker education, and Rowntree wanted Jones as the first principal. Among others, M.
Carey Thomas urged him to accept the offer. He refused after long deliberation, in spite of the fact
that he "felt," as he wrote Rowntree at the time, "in spirit more deeply identified with English
Quakerism than with any other branch of organized Christianity in the world." Haverford's reaction to the possibility of losing its star young faculty member was a far cry from the bribing mores of
modern academia, as is indicated in Elizabeth Gray Vining's delightful biography: "After the decision was made, but not before, T. Wistar Brown, in consultation with Isaac Sharpless, arranged for
Rufus Jones' salary to be increased to $5000 and the following year he was raised to full professor
rank" (Elizabath Gray Vining, *Friend of Life: The Biography of Rufus M. Jones* [Philadelphia: Lippincott, 1958], p. 98).

school has sent its best students to Harvard and other New England colleges, as well as to Princeton, rather than to the University of Pennsylvania. David Riesman, Henry Ford II Professor of Sociology at Harvard College, is certainly the most distinguished living alumnus of the school.

Following the death of Richard Mott Jones in 1917, Richard Mott Gummere, a graduate of Haverford School, Haverford College, and with a doctorate from Harvard, became the school's second headmaster. He remained until 1934, when he took on the duties of director of the admissions committee at Harvard. He was followed by Richard Knowles, with Harvard undergraduate and graduate degrees—a typical Yankee schoolmaster if there ever was one. Knowles led the school until the Second World War, when John F. Gummere* took over the post.

Over the years, Penn Charter gradually became a more and more secular school, Quaker in tradition rather than in fact. By 1941, for instance, only three members of the faculty and staff belonged to the Society of Friends. In accord with the general movement of many groups in America to recapture their ethnic and religious roots, however, an effort was made to make the school more Quaker in feeling, and by the early 1970s there were nineteen Quakers on the staff.

Just as the Boston Puritans founded Harvard right after the Hutchinson controversy, so, and for very much the same reasons, a group of Orthodox Friends opened a boarding school for boys in Haverford soon after the Hicksite separation. The separation might have been avoided, they reasoned, as had John Winthrop's generation in Boston before them, if their young men had been better educated. Although Haverford remained a school in name until 1856, Rufus Jones wrote that "in intellectual quality of work and in breadth of culture it was from the first an institution of college grade."[14]

The pride and joy of Gurneyite Friends in Philadelphia was surely their college at Haverford. All save two of the families in Table A–35, for example, have had one or more members on the board of managers down through the years. James Whitall, a graduate of the college, served on the board for thirty-nine years (1857–1896), where he was a benefactor in the manner of T. Wistar Brown; John M. Whitall, his son, served from 1907 to 1926. Two brothers from the wealthy and prominent Garrett family also served in the Brown-Whitall style: Phillip C. Garrett was a manager between 1862 and 1905; John Biddle Garrett, Philadelphia railroad and banking leader (president of the Girard Trust Company), served for forty-one years (1872–1914). Over the years, the managers of Haverford College surely have been an inbred group of Gurneyite Friends, devoted to intellectual excellence in the style of the equally inbred overseers at Harvard. Many of the faculty and staff of the college also have been

---

*The Gummeres, whose first American ancestor was a French Huguenot who settled in Germantown in 1719, have been perhaps the leading Quaker family of educators in the nation's history. The first of four members of the family to be included in the DAB was John Gummere, who after graduating from Westtown opened a Quaker boarding school in Burlington, New Jersey, in 1814. In 1862 his son, Samuel James Gummere, became the second president of Haverford College.

drawn from these families, including three presidents—Samuel James Gummere, Isaac Sharpless, and William Wistar Comfort—and a dean—William E. Cadbury, Jr.

Isaac Sharpless, the great builder of Haverford College, joined the faculty in 1875, served as president between 1887 and 1917, and finally, after his retirement from the presidency, became dean of the T. Wistar Brown Graduate School. Sharpless was born on a farm in Chester County that his family had owned since coming to America in the 1690s. After attending Westtown, he went on to Harvard, graduated in 1873, and married Lydia Cope three years later. In the Friendly tradition, Sharpless was determined to keep Haverford a small liberal arts college: his motto, so contrary to the American ideal, was "better but not bigger," and he became the most respected small college president of his day.

Haverford's American educational model, in intellectual excellence if not in size, has always been Harvard College. (Many of its faculty and managers have taken degrees at Harvard.) Yet, as might be expected of Gurneyite Friends, Haverford has also been rather British in tone and tradition: the game of cricket was always an important pastime on the campus, and the handsome new library has a Cricket Room filled with memorabilia.

Haverford, finally, is far more like Harvard than the University of Pennsylvania in that its presidents have been alumni and members of a group with well-established traditions (Gurneyite Friends). Four of them—Samuel James Gummere, Isaac Sharpless, William Wistar Comfort, and Hugh Borton—were drawn from the extended family network listed in Table A–35. (Only Harrison and Pepper of the fifty Proper Philadelphia families served the University of Pennsylvania as provost or president.)* The Gurneyite leadership pattern at Haverford, moreover, has differed from the Hicksite pattern at Swarthmore, where all the presidents in the twentieth century have been both auslanders and outsiders and only one of them, Joseph Swain, a birthright Friend (though John W. Nason married a Friend and became a convinced member of the Society).†

Bryn Mawr College, like Haverford, was founded and led by Gurneyite Friends in its early years. It was, however, far less of a Quaker college (even though its founder stipulated in his will that the board be composed entirely of Orthodox Friends), especially under its greatest president, M. Carey Thomas. Though a birthright Friend, Thomas was far more of a secular intellectual and

---

*The greatest builder in Penn's history was Gaylord Harnwell, who led the university in the 1950s and 1960s. Harnwell was a graduate of Haverford as was Jonathan Rhoads, whom he chose as provost. Dr. Rhoads, John Rhea Barton Professor of Surgery at Penn, was on the boards of Haverford, Bryn Mawr, and the Provident Mutual, president of the American Philosophical Society, and generally acknowledged to be the city's first citizen when he received the Philadelphia Award in 1977. Harnwell received the award in 1964.

†Haverford's Quaker Collection is rivaled in America only by the one at Swarthmore College. Swarthmore's collection excels in materials on slavery and black Americans, reflecting the concern of Hicksites like Lucretia Mott with the abolition movement. Haverford has a more complete collection of Indian materials. See Appendix IV for a discussion of Swarthmore College.

a feminist; she considered herself a professional philologist and linguist who also happened to be a Quaker.* She had graduated from Cornell with a Phi Beta Kappa in 1877 and, because no women were eligible for doctorates in her day in America, had gone abroad and obtained a doctorate summa cum laude at the University of Zurich.

Bryn Mawr was founded and endowed by an Orthodox Friend, Joseph Wright Taylor, whose parents had been respectively matron and physician at the Friends' Asylum in Frankford. Taylor, a manager at Haverford for many years, wanted a similar education for Orthodox daughters. In close association with his fellow managers at Haverford—James E. Rhoads and two Baltimore Friends, James Carey Thomas and the wealthy banker Francis T. King—Taylor bought the land, closely supervised the Quaker architect Addison Hutton in the construction of Bryn Mawr's first building (Taylor Hall), and left the college close to $1 million in his will. He also chose a board of Gurneyite Friends, including Francis T. King, president, James Carey Thomas, James Whitall, David Scull, Jr.,† Francis R. Cope, James E. Rhoads, John B. Garrett, treasurer, and his brother, Phillip C. Garrett (president after King's death). The board first met in Philadelphia after Taylor's death in 1880, and the college opened in 1884, with James E. Rhoads as president and M. Carey Thomas as dean. (The only member of the original faculty without a doctorate was Woodrow Wilson, who taught history, economics, and politics while completing his doctorate at Johns Hopkins.) Thomas succeeded Rhoads as president in 1894 and remained in charge until her retirement in 1922, all the while building up the first and finest graduate school for women in America.

Twelfth Street Friends were leaders in Philadelphia's business community, in manufacturing, banking, and insurance. Just as they had founded Haverford, and Bryn Mawr to educate their children, so they founded the Provident Life and Trust Company in 1865 to insure the lives of their fellow Quakers in America. The Provident was modeled on the Friends' Provident Institution of Bradford, Yorkshire, which began by insuring the lives of birthright Friends only. The original board was composed of Orthodox Friends, including T. Wistar Brown, Richard Cadbury, Joshua H. Morris, Richard Wood, and John B. Garrett from the families in Table A-35. The board elected Samuel R. Shipley, a Quaker, as its first president. Shipley, a graduate of Westtown, remained as president for forty years; he was of course a member of the Twelfth Street meet-

---

*M. Carey Thomas, born of an old Quaker family in Baltimore, was well connected in the Philadelphia Gurneyite community. One grandfather, Richard Henry Thomas, had been on the Haverford board before the Civil War. Her father, Dr. James Carey Thomas, Haverford graduate (1851) and board member (1860–1897), married Mary Whitall, sister of Hannah Whitall Smith, Logan Pearsall Smith's mother (it was from her mother and her Aunt Hannah that President Thomas got her feminist values).

†David Scull, Jr., member of the board of managers at Haverford for over forty years and a great benefactor there, as his father had been before him, was the strictest and most conforming Friend on the original board at Bryn Mawr and served for the longest period, mainly as chairman of the building and grounds committee. He worked closely with Addison Hutton on Taylor Hall and then with Walter Cope (and John Stewardson) on Radnor and Denbiegh Halls.

ing, as were most of the original board members. The Provident prospered from the outset, and at its hundredth anniversary its insurance branch,* Provident Mutual, was one of the major life insurance companies in the nation.

The business life of these Gurneyite Friends was by no means limited to leadership at the Provident. Many of them, like the Garretts and the Scattergoods, were wealthy and influential leaders of diverse business enterprises. Charles J. Rhoads, son of a founder and first president of Bryn Mawr College, provides an excellent example of Gurneyite leadership. After graduation from Haverford in 1893, where he was an athlete, scholar (Phi Beta Kappa), and president of his class, he went to work at the Girard Trust and rose to a vice-presidency before resigning to become governor of the Federal Reserve Bank of Philadelphia. Rhoads served in France with the Red Cross during the war and was subsequently elected president of the Central Penn National Bank. He later joined the investment banking firm of Brown Brothers & Company, where he remained for the rest of his career. Rhoads was a director or board member of almost everything worthwhile in the city, including the Girard Trust, the Provident Life and Trust, and the Pennsylvania Hospital; but his heart lay in his work on the boards of Haverford, Bryn Mawr, and Penn Charter. Though he was an active Friend whose social life was deeply rooted in the Haverford–Bryn Mawr Quaker community, Rhoads's position in the city made it inevitable that he belong to the Philadelphia Club and list his family in the *Social Register*, a need felt by many other well-to-do Gurneyites who by and large led lives apart from Society. Thus, almost all the families in Table A–35 were represented in the Philadelphia *Social Register*, although a good proportion of the family members who were so listed had left the Quaker community by 1970, some remaining nominal Friends if not becoming nominal Episcopalians.

Whereas many members of these twenty-seven Quaker families were successful businessmen, very few were lawyers; there has been no first-rate large Quaker law firm in the city to compare, for example, with the Provident. However, these families certainly have had more than their share of eminent physicians, which is to be expected from the spiritual (and actual) descendants of Caspar Wistar, who succeeded Benjamin Rush as professor of chemistry in the Penn Medical School. Jonathan Rhoads is the most eminent surgeon in the city today. And Joseph Wright Taylor, founder of Bryn Mawr, was a graduate of the Penn Medical School, as was Bryn Mawr's first president, James E. Rhoads.† The Woods, who served every institution listed in Table A–35, were the city's first Quaker medical dynasty in the style of the fashionable Peppers of

---

*The banking offspring of the original Provident is now the Provident National Bank, led during the 1960s by William G. Foulke, a Philadelphia Club Episcopalian from one of the oldest Quaker clans in the city (twenty-four graduates of Westtown).

†Like the Rhoads family, the Copes continue to be leaders in medicine and education. The 1976–1977 edition of *Who's Who in America* listed two members of the family: Oliver Cope, born in Germantown in 1902 (son of Walter Cope, the architect) and educated at Harvard, was a professor of surgery in the Harvard Medical School; Harold Cary Cope, born at Westtown in 1918 and a graduate of Cornell, was president of Friends University, Wichita, Kansas. (He had also served on the faculty of Earlham College and as a director of the American Friends Service Committee.)

Philadelphia or the Shattucks of Boston. Their family tree includes no fewer than eighteen prominent physicians in the city, going back to George Bacon Wood (1797–1879), who was professor of materia medica and chemistry at Penn (he left $50,000 to the department of auxiliary medicine, which he founded and supported himself for many years). His nephew Horatio Charles Wood (1841–1920), a graduate of Westtown, also served on the faculty of the Penn Medical School. These Orthodox Gurneyite Woods were no egalitarians, as is suggested by a remark once made by the imperious Dr. George to his nephew: "Horatio, I would have thee know that I never have and never will demean myself to ride in a streetcar; when I ride, I ride in my carriage."[15] Dr. Horatio's son and grandson (Horatios both) followed him in the profession and as professors of medicine at Penn. (Indeed, the Wood medical dynasty at the university was even longer than that of the Peppers.)

THE AMERICAN FRIENDS
SERVICE COMMITTEE

Today the American Friends Service Committee is the most famous Quaker institution in the world. It was founded in 1917 at the Twelfth Street Meetinghouse (where its headquarters remained until the building was torn down). Among the members of the board in that founding year were Alfred Garrett Scattergood, Charles J. Rhoads, Stanley R. Yarnall, Henry W. Comfort, L. Hollingsworth Wood, Rufus Jones, Harold Evans, and Henry J. Cadbury, all members of the Gurneyite families listed in Table A–35. Two leaders of the AFSC in its earliest years, J. Henry Scattergood and Morris Leeds, were abroad at the time working with the Red Cross. The AFSC has done good works all over the world, especially in France, Poland, Germany, and Russia during and after World War I, in Spain during its Civil War, and in World War II throughout Europe. Rufus Jones was its first chairman, serving continuously until 1928 and again from 1934 to 1944. In 1929, Rufus Jones was made honorary chairman of the board, and Henry J. Cadbury took over the active chairmanship. At the same time, Clarence Pickett, a graduate of both Penn College (Quaker), Iowa, and the Hartford Theological Seminary and a student at the Harvard Divinity School, was brought to Philadelphia from Earlham College, where he was professor of biblical religion, to serve the AFSC as executive secretary. In 1939, Rufus Jones and Clarence Pickett were joint recipients of the Philadelphia Award.

In 1947 the varied work of the AFSC was recognized as basically a service for peace when, along with the Friends Service Council in London, with which it had worked from the beginning, it was awarded the Nobel Peace Prize. Although, as Emerson might have said, the AFSC was surely the lengthened shadow of Rufus Jones, the board thought that its active chairman, Henry Cadbury, should go to Oslo to receive the award officially. After dutifully rearranging his teaching schedule at Harvard, where he was Hollis Professor of Divinity, he did so (borrowing white tie and tails for the occasion). In his speech, the chairman of the Nobel Committee emphasized that the award was actually for all Quakers whose contribution to peace was far greater than their mere refusal to take part in war. "It is the silent help from the nameless to the nameless," he said, "which is their contribution to the promotion of brotherhood among nations."[16] In New York City on the same evening, Rufus Jones gave a speech at a dinner honoring the award; the guests included Nobel laureates and other dignitaries.

A year later, Jones died in his sleep at home in Haverford. Funeral services were held at the Haverford Meetinghouse and Jones was buried in the corner of the little graveyard, close by his friends and colleagues John Wilhelm Rowntree and Isaac Sharpless. When Henry J. Cadbury died at the age of ninety-one, in 1974, it was a symbol of the end of the Gurneyite renaissance in Philadelphia. For Cadbury was born at the very heart of the Gurneyite community; raised in the Twelfth Street meeting and educated next door at Penn Charter, he went on to earn a bachelor of arts at Haverford and a doctorate at Harvard. From the Haverford faculty, Cadbury was called to the Harvard Divinity School, where for many years he was the only Quaker teacher.* An eminent biblical scholar, he also wrote prolifically on the history of Quakerism.† Like Boston Brahmins and unlike fashionable Philadelphians, both Rufus Jones and Henry Cadbury were intellectuals and professors who were also leaders in their whole community.

THE LESSON OF PHILADELPHIA'S GURNEYITE RENAISSANCE

This analysis of Philadelphia Quakerism's deviant case is an important test of my argument in this book. It suggests the continuing heuristic value of Max Weber's thesis as to the relationships between ideas and action, especially as he developed this thesis in *The Protestant Ethic and the Spirit of Capitalism*. For just as the leaders of modern capitalism (broadened to include leaders in general in such works as Michael Walzer's *Revolution of the Saints*) once had an affinity for the ethic of Calvinism, as had the original leaders of Massachusetts Bay, so this small and deviant group of Philadelphia Friends had an affinity for the teachings of Joseph John Gurney, who liberated Quakerism from the anti-intellec-

---

*In 1918, when war hysteria was at its worst in America, young Henry Cadbury was dismissed from the Haverford faculty. According to Ray H. Abrams, Cadbury was dismissed after he wrote a letter to the *Philadelphia Public Ledger* "protesting as a Christian and an American against the orgy of hate indulged in by the press and people upon the receipt of peace overtures from the enemy" (Ray H. Abrams, *Preachers Present Arms* [Philadelphia: Round Table Press, 1933], p. 230).

†Frederick B. Tolles, Howard M. Jenkins Professor of Quaker History and Research and director of the Friends Historical Library at Swarthmore at the time of his death, was a leading American historian of his generation. A Yankee from Maine, with ancestral roots in Puritanism, Tolles was a convinced Friend. It is said that his conversion began when he met Henry Cadbury in the Harvard Yard.

tual and egalitarian absolutism of the Inner Light and moved the faith more in the direction of hierarchical and intellectual Calvinism. The members of our small group of Gurneyite families in turn proceeded to found and build three first-rate educational institutions in the city, the William Penn Charter School (as reorganized in 1875) and Haverford and Bryn Mawr Colleges. They also founded the most famous privately supported international welfare and peace program in the modern world.

But religious beliefs do more than motivate individual behavior; they also influence, if sometimes indirectly, the nature of social structures. And the Philadelphia Gurneyite families, a tacit ruling class within the city's Quaker population, had far more in common with their Boston Brahmin peers than they did with their privileged and fashionable Quaker-turned-Episcopal peers in Philadelphia. The Gurneyites were an inbred group with common religious roots in seventeenth-century Quakerism. In this sense they were like the fifty Boston First Families, which were homogeneously Congregational—Trinitarian Puritans for two centuries before becoming Unitarians, a conversion effected by congregations rather than individuals. (They became Episcopalians to a significant degree only in the generation of the Adams brothers, when, as Henry, Charles Francis, and Brooks saw so clearly their golden days were surely waning.)

At this point it should be emphasized once again that it was not so much either the Quaker or the Anglican religious values per se that were responsible for the lack of any ruling passion in Philadelphia's upper class. Rather, the perfectionist values and resulting social structure of Quakerism were such that the Quaker community was unable to retain many of its spirited and enterprising members. Their becoming stylish Anglicans on an individual basis in turn led to a snobbish concern for status rather than a larger concern for leadership and sustained accomplishment.

The law of extremes may be important here. Thus, the drabness of eighteenth-century Quakerism may have inadvertently produced the plushness and charm of Proper Philadelphia Episcopalianism. The Anglican church moreover, had no established roots in colonial Philadelphia; it was, rather, the church of partisans in the Quaker-Anglican-Presbyterian struggle for power that marked Philadelphia almost from its founding days until the eve of the Revolution. Hence, the importance of the Gurneyite renaissance in the city was its allowing, and motivating, a small group of rooted Friends to take the lead in creative excellence.

Here again I must emphasize the insights of Tocqueville, who saw that the ethics of *equality* and *individualism* are actually two sides of the same coin: when equality motivates the lonely crowd, individualism inhibits its lonely leaders. Both are destructive of community roots and especially of the development of any kind of traditional, or class, authority. Antinomian absolutism in religion is dangerous to social order and continuity of leadership precisely because it slowly but steadily erodes established authority and inevitably leads to anarchy at all levels of society. And amiable anarchy has always marked the lifestyle of mild Philadelphia in general and of the mild and polished Philadelphia Gentleman in particular. I should imagine that anyone who has lived among Proper Philadelphians for any length of time would have observed their lack of the kind of seriousness and deep concern exhibited by Proper Bostonians, as well as by Gurneyite Friends in Philadelphia. At the Philadelphia Club, for example, one rarely meets a professor or college president, to say nothing of such inveterate scribblers as the Holmeses or the Adamses, or Rufus Jones and Henry Cadbury.

All in all, the Gurneyite families were like their Boston counterparts, and unlike their Proper Philadelphia neighbors, in three critical ways. First, they were firmly rooted in the religion of their ancestors. Second, they were extremely successful in business, but money was not an end in itself; rather, wealth was a means for building a set of excellent institutions, which the Gurneyites themselves led. Third, they produced intellectual leaders like Rufus Jones and Henry Cadbury, as well as Howard Brinton, whose *Friends for 300 Years* is one of the classics in Quaker history and philosophy. Finally, the Smiths, more than any other upper-class family in Philadelphia (Quaker or Episcopal) played an important role in twentieth-century, Anglo-American intellectual and artistic circles. Hannah Whitall Smith, very unlike her fashionable friends, wrote wildly popular inspirational books. Her son Logan Pearsall Smith was far and away Philadelphia's closest counterpart to Boston's Henry Adams: his *Unforgotten Years* is in so many ways similar in tone to *The Education of Henry Adams*; both men looked disdainfully down on their fellow countrymen and their vulgar materialism; Henry had an expatriate mind, while Logan expatriated himself in both mind and body (he lived and died in England); both of Logan's sisters spent a good part of their lives abroad, one married to Bertrand Russell and the other as the wife of Bernard Berenson.

The Philadelphia Gurneyites were different from the Brahmin Bostonians, however, in one important respect. None of them ever served their city, their state, or their nation in any major elective office. They were provincial and parochial leaders rather than people of broad community or class authority in the style of the Adamses, Lodges, or Saltonstalls of Boston. Nevertheless, many of them were allies of Henry Charles Lea in the Mugwump and Progressive movements in Philadelphia.

In conclusion, these well-off Gurneyites in Philadelphia certainly took *oblige* far more seriously than *noblesse*. Perhaps Roland Bainton of the Yale Divinity School, a birthright Congregationalist and a convinced Friend, caught the Gurneyite spirit of leadership best in a cartoon he drew of Henry Cadbury while listening to him give a talk on his trip to Oslo: the cartoon was entitled "Nobel Oblige."

How different Philadelphia's history might have been if its Quaker founders had subscribed to the teachings of George Keith or Joseph John Gurney rather than to the antinomian George Fox or Elias Hicks. How different Boston's history might have been had the antinomian ideas of Anne Hutchinson and Mary Dyer won out over the authoritarianism of John Winthrop and John Endicott.

Epilogue

I ponder all these things, and how men fight and lose the battle, and the thing they fought for comes in spite of their defeat, and when it comes turns out to be not what they meant, and other men have to fight for what they meant under another name.

William Morris

At the close of this analysis of the histories of Puritan Boston and Quaker Philadelphia, it is perhaps appropriate to suggest that although America as a whole has been Puritan and Calvinist throughout most of its history (Ernst Troeltsch, in 1911, wrote that "Calvinism . . . may be described as 'Americanism' "),[1] it has now moved—especially since the 1960s—far closer to the ideals of Quakerism. And it was the prophet of Concord, Ralph Waldo Emerson, who sowed the seeds of the antinomian individualism of our day.

The product of seven generations of Congregationalist ministers and the pastor of Boston's Second Church in the 1820s, Emerson finally decided that he could no longer "administer the Lord's Supper as a divinely appointed, sacred ordinance of religion."[2] His parishioners disagreed, and he was faced with the problem of resigning. Frederick B. Tolles has shown that Emerson was aided in his decision to resign through his study of Quakerism. Though Tolles's detailed analysis of Emerson and Quakerism cannot be covered here, it should be noted that when Emerson went up to the White Mountains for a few weeks to make up his mind about resigning, he took along Sewel's *History of the Quakers* and Tuke's *Memoirs of the Life of Fox*. In his resignation sermon in 1832, he carefully observed that it was "now two hundred years since the Society of

453

Quakers denied the authority of the rite altogether."³ Emerson not only informed himself about Quakerism, but he also became friends with several prominent Quakers, whom he often mentioned in his journals. He referred to George Fox and William Penn many times, always favorably. The closeness of Emerson's ideas to those of Quakerism was aptly summed up by Tolles.

> The doctrines of self-reliance and the Inner Light are, as Emerson himself was aware, only two figures of speech to express the same basic concept of individualism; the reliance upon self is, in the end, reliance upon God as the Over-Soul made manifest in individual consciences. Emerson's "spiritual religion" is entirely at one with Quakerism in this respect. Religion for him, as for George Fox and Mary Rotch [his close Quaker friend from New Bedford], was an intuitive and personal experience, completely divorced from traditional forms and authority.⁴

If Emerson was the philosopher of mystical and pantheistic individualism, Walt Whitman was surely its major poet. Whitman drew his strength from Emerson and the Quaker preacher Elias Hicks. His parents, belonging to no organized religion, were nevertheless believers in New Testament Christianity as modified by the Deism of Tom Paine (Whitman's father had known Paine in Brooklyn) and in the preaching of their Quaker neighbor Hicks. As a boy Whitman had been taken to hear Hicks preach, and many have noted the similarities between the distinctive rhythms of *Leaves of Grass* and Hicks's chanting style of preaching. Although Whitman always admired Hicks and the Quakers, he repeatedly denied his debt to Emerson, largely because of his obsession with self-reliance and originality. Scholars, however, have unearthed many examples of Whitman's debt to the sage of Concord. In fact, in later life Whitman admitted to a friend that in 1854 "I was simmering, simmering, and Emerson brought me to a boil."⁵ And he told Horace Traubel, "I look in all men for the heroic quality I find in Emerson. . . . Emerson was a far-reaching force: a star of the first, the very first magnitude maybe."⁶ And Emerson's famous letter of 1855 welcomed the first edition of *Leaves of Grass* as "the most extraordinary piece of wit and wisdom that an American has yet contributed."⁷

At any rate, all virtues and all great ideas when carried to their logical conclusions become absurd. Anyone reading or rereading Emerson and Whitman in the course of the 1960s in America would have seen the sources of the ideas that dominated the anti-establishmentarian and egalitarian minds of the academic community (both faculty and students) at the time.* And where can one find a better definition of our present obsession with antinomian narcissism than in the following lines in Whitman's *Leaves of Grass*:

> Divine am I inside and out, and I make holy whatever
>   I touch or am touched from;
> The scent of these arm-pits is aroma finer than prayer,
> This head is more than churches or bibles or creeds.

---

*In this climate of opinion, no wonder Henry David Thoreau, Emerson's Concord neighbor, became a hero.

In so many ways, the 1640s and 1650s in England were very much like the 1960s and 1970s in our own land. Alan Simpson, in a brilliant essay on *Puritanism in Old and New England*, noted that "the origins of English Puritanism are to be found among the Protestant reformers of the mid-sixteenth century; it takes shape in the reign of Elizabeth; produces thrust after thrust of energy in the seventeenth century, until the final thrust throws up the Quakers; and then ebbs away."[8] Perhaps some future intellectual historian will write of our own age: "The origins of Western liberalism are to be found among the utilitarian reformers of the mid-nineteenth century; it takes shape in the Victorian age; produces thrust after thrust in America during the Progressive, New Freedom, New Deal, and New Frontier years of the twentieth century, until the final thrust throws up the New Left and a host of other antinomian movements; and then, like English Puritanism in another day, ebbs away."

For more than a century, Puritans in England and liberals in America were successful in backing more or less orderly and evolutionary change. Then suddenly and in times of apparent victory, reform turned upon itself and died in periods of radicalism and anarchy. Among other things there was a generation problem. Thus, John Winthrop was born in the Armada year of 1588; William Penn was born in 1644, the year of the great Puritan victory at Marston Moor. Winthrop was born the same year as Hobbes, whereas Penn was a friend of Locke. To put it another way, Winthrop and Penn were born as far apart in time and societal values as were Franklin Roosevelt and the generation of the 1960s.

There is a haunting similarity between the pattern of anarchy that followed the execution of England's king in January 1649 and the assassination of President Kennedy in November 1963. Once again, the established church has disintegrated and a host of self-righteous seekers are loose upon the land. In this climate of opinion, it is understandable that the ideas and ideals of Quakerism are now more popular in America, especially among intellectuals and academics, than at any other time in our history. Since the close of the Second World War, for example, there has been both a reversal of the downward trend in numbers and a very real renaissance within the Society, as symbolized by the award of the Nobel Peace Prize to the American Friends Service Committee. The Quaker ranks have been swelled by all sorts of refugees from the institutional churches and synagogues. In a study of the American Friends Service Committee by a *New Yorker* writer, for example, it was interesting to see that the leaders of the many projects discussed in the book were convinced rather than birthright Friends.[9]

Most of the Quaker meetings founded since the war have been formed, often by academics, in and around college or university communities. In the 1960s, for instance, the largest meeting in Massachusetts was located in Cambridge, right off fashionable Brattle Street. And the chairmen of several departments in the humanities and the social sciences at Harvard were convinced Friends and members of the Cambridge meeting, as were three faculty members of the divinity school.

To understand the problem of authority and leadership in America today, then, one must study the history of Philadelphia and Pennsylvania. It is not an altogether encouraging story. At the same time, there is hope of a change to come. Thus, at the height of our antinomian era, in 1970, Robert Penn Warren made an acceptance speech after being awarded the National Medal for Literature that ended reassuringly.

> Hawthorne and Emerson met on the wood paths of Concord, and passed on, Emerson with his head full of bright futurities and relevancies, Hawthorne with his head full of the irrelevant past. As Henry James was to say of them: "Emerson, as a sort of spiritual sun-worshiper, could have attached but a moderate value to Hawthorne's cat-like faculty of seeing in the dark."
>
> We revere Emerson, the prophet whose prophesies came true. But having once come true, those prophesies began to come untrue. More and more Emerson recedes grandly into history, as the future he predicted becomes a past. And what the cat's eye of Hawthorne saw gave him the future—and relevance. He died more than a century ago, but we find in his work a complex, tangled, and revolutionary vision of the soul, which we recognize as our own.
>
> Emerson spoke nobly about relevance. Hawthorne was relevant.[10]

Tocqueville pondered the meaning of America in the age of Emerson and Hawthorne and, with a cat's eye for the future, warned of the dangers of democratic despotism. Quite unlike Emerson, he saw that both anarchy and despotism proceeded from the same cause: "namely, that *general apathy* which is the consequence of individualism."[11] His French contemporaries were quick to see that Tocqueville had studied democracy in America in order to understand the future of his beloved France. Similarly, I have studied Puritan Boston and Quaker Philadelphia with an eye to an understanding of the future of our beloved, but now troubled, America. There is thus no more relevant way to close this book than by quoting the last sentence of *Democracy in America*:

> The nations of our time cannot prevent the conditions of men from becoming equal, but it depends upon themselves whether the principle of equality is to lead them to freedom or servitude, to knowledge or barbarism, to prosperity or wretchedness.[12]

The Boston and Philadelphia
First Family Leadership

The tables in Appendix I constitute, as it were, the quantitative backbone of the narrative analysis of the leadership style of Boston and Philadelphia in the preceding pages.

Although most readers will have referred to these tables from time to time while reading the text, the tables may also be read together as a systematic summary of the quantitative evidence supporting the arguments of this book.

Table A-1
FOUR HUNDRED NOTABLE AMERICANS
BY OCCUPATION AND PLACE OF BIRTH

Occupation	Place of Birth				
	Massachusetts	Pennsylvania	Virginia	Other States and Foreign	Total Elite
Presidents	3	1	9	22	35
Jurists and Lawyers	4	0	1	22	27
Statesmen	8	1	7	40	56
Military Men	0	2	7	17	26
Total Power and Authority	15 (24)[1] (10)	4 (21) (3)	24 (75) (17)	101 (36) (70)	144 (36) (100)
Belles Lettres	7	1	1	24	33
History and Social Philosophy	7	0	0	10	17
Art	4	1	0	11	16
Theater	1	1	0	8	10
Journalism	2	0	0	7	9
Music	1	1	0	6	8
Total Arts and Letters	22 (34) (24)	4 (21) (4)	1 (3) (1)	66 (23) (71)	93 (23) (100)
Architecture	2	0	0	4	6
Religion	3	0	0	13	16
Education	5	1	0	12	18
Medicine	1	2	1	9	13
Total Professional	11 (17) (21)	3 (16) (5)	1 (3) (2)	38 (13) (72)	53 (13) (100)
Businessmen	2	2	1	14	19
Social Reformers and Labor Leaders	7	2	1	15	25
Pioneers and Explorers	0	2	3	5	10
Scientists	3	1	1	22	27
Inventors	4	1	0	24	29
Total Innovation and Change	16 (25) (15)	8 (42) (7)	6 (19) (5)	80 (28) (73)	110 (28) (100)
Total All Occupations	64 (100) (16)	19 (100) (5)	32 (100) (8)	285(100) (71)	400(100) (100)

Source: Richard B. Morris, ed., *Encyclopedia of American History*, rev. ed. (New York: Harper, 1965), pp. 661–808.

NOTE: Of the nineteen natives of Pennsylvania, the following made their careers almost entirely outside the state: James G. Blaine; George B. McClellan; George C. Marshall; Louisa May Alcott; Edwin Forrest; Stephen Foster; William H. McGuffey; Henry George; Terrence Powderly; Daniel Boone; Robert Peary; Henry Rowland; and Robert Fulton. Only three, Benjamin Rush, Nicholas Biddle, and Thomas Eakins, made their careers in Philadelphia.

[1]Figures within parentheses are percentages.

Table A-2
SUBJECTS IN THE *DAB* BY BIRTHPLACE AND STATE
IN WHICH COLLEGE EDUCATION WAS RECEIVED

	Birthplace			College Graduates by State	
New York	1,876	(14)[1]		543	(12)
Massachusetts	1,868	(14)		979	(21)
Pennsylvania	1,255	(9)		325	(7)
Connecticut	784	(6)		615	(14)
Virginia	726	(5)		146	(3)
Ohio	475	(3)		145	(3)
Total	6,985	(51)		2,753	(60)
		West Point	329		
		Naval Academy	84		
				413	(9)
		Educated Elsewhere in			
Natives of		United States		1,445	(31)
Other States	3,874	(29)	Total Educated		
Born Abroad	2,775	(20)	in United		
Total Subjects	13,634	(100)	States	4,611	(100)

Source: B. W. Kunkel, "Eminent Graduates of American Colleges," *Association of American Colleges Bulletin*, Vol. xxx (December 1944), pp. 578–594.

NOTE: 65 percent of the 10,859 native Americans were born in New York, Massachusetts, Pennsylvania, Connecticut, Virginia, or Ohio.

[1]Figures within parentheses are percentages.

Table A-3

FIFTY FIRST FAMILIES OF BOSTON AND PHILADELPHIA ELITE MEMBERS INCLUDED IN THE DICTIONARY OF AMERICAN BIOGRAPHY

Boston

Name	Occupation
8 Adams (1762–1927—165—SR—WW-1) 4935*	
Samuel (1722–1803) 685 H	Patriot-Gov.
John (1735–1826) 1056 H	President
Abigail (1744–1818) 53 NC	First Lady
John Quincy (1767–1848) 1033 H	President
Charles Francis (1807–1886) 866 H	Diplomat
Charles Francis, Jr. (1835–1915) 439 H	Bus.-Hist.
Henry (1838–1918) 718 H	Historian
Brooks (1848–1927) 85 H	Historian
3 Agassiz (1847–1910—63—SR) 1258	
Jean Louis Rodolphe (1807–1873) 886 Zur	Scientist
Elizabeth Cabot Cary (1822–1907) 64 NC	Pres. Radcliffe
Alexander (1835–1910) 308 H	Calumet
9 Ames (1748–1950—202—SR—WW-4) 1242	
Nathaniel (1708–1764) 80 NC	Astronomer
Fisher (1758–1808) 281 H	Statesman
Oliver (1779–1863) 46 NC	Manufacturer
Oakes (1804–1874) 248 NC	Capitalist-R.R.
Oliver (1807–1877) 108 NC	Mfg.-R.R.
Oliver (1831–1895) 147 NC	Cap.-Governor
Frederick Lothrop (1835–1893) 29 H	Philanthropist
Winthrop (1870–1937) 138 H	Theatre
Oakes (1874–1950) 165 H	Botanist

Philadelphia

Name	Occupation
4 Bache (1777–1867—90—SR) 341	
Richard (1737–1811) 42 NC	Merchant
Benjamin Franklin (1769–1798) 112 UP	Journalist
Franklin (1792–1864) 83 UP	M.D.-Professor
Alexander Dallas (1806–1867) 104 USMA	Scientist
4 Barton (1806–1869—63—SR) 312	
Benjamin Smith (1766–1815) 89 UP	M.D.-Botanist
William D. Crillon (1786–1856) 190 Pr.	M.D.-Botanist
John Rhea (1794–1871) 46 NC	Surgeon
Thomas Pennant (1803–1869) 68 NC	Bibliophile
4 Biddle (1780–1844—64—SR—WW-6) 500	
Clement (1740–1814) 54 NC	Merch.-Soldier
Nicholas (1750–1778) 151 NC	Naval Hero
James (1783–1848) 106 UP	Naval Hero
Nicholas (1786–1844) 189 Pr	Banker-Author
1 Binney (1820–1875—55) 202	
Horace (1780–1875) 202 H	Lawyer
1 Boker (1863–1890—27) 323	
George Henry (1823–1890) 323 Pr	Author
2 Borie (1849–1934—85—SR—WW-1) 126	
Adolph Edward (1809–1880) 62 UP	Merch.-Diplomat
Adolphe (1877–1934) 64 NC	Artist

5 Appleton (1795–1927—152—SR—WW–1) 446
  Nathaniel Walker (1755–1795) 52 H — Physician
  Samuel (1766–1853) 67 NC — Textiles
  Nathan (1779–1861) 164 NC — Text.-Pol.
  Thomas Gold (1812–1884) 66 H — Essayist-Talker
  William Sumner (1874–1947) 97 H — Preservationist

3 Bigelow (1826–1926—100—SR—WW–2) 302
  Jacob (1786–1879) 125 H — M.D.-Botanist
  Henry Jacob (1818–1890) 112 H — Surgeon
  William Sturgis (1850–1926) 65 H — M.D.-Orientalist

4 Bowditch (1813–1921—108—SR) 655
  Nathaniel (1773–1838) 175 NC — Astronomer
  Henry Ingersoll (1808–1892) 145 H — M.D.-Reformer
  Henry Pickering (1840–1911) 263 H — Physician
  Charles Pickering (1842–1921) 72 H — Archaeologist

4 Brooks (1792–1938—146—SR) 794
  John (1752–1825) 134 H — Governor
  Peter Chardon (1767–1849) 52 NC — Merchant
  Phillips (1835–1893) 487 H — Clergy-Bishop
  John Graham (1846–1938) 121 H — Clergy-Reformer

2 Bulfinch (1803–1867—164) 228
  Charles (1763–1844) 167 H — Architect
  Thomas (1796–1867) 61 H — Author

5 Cabot (1792–1945—153—SR—WW–9) 798
  George (1752–1823) 202 H — Senator

4 Cadwalader (1747–1879—132—SR) 317
  Thomas (1707–1779) 107 NC — Physician
  John (1742–1786) 66 NC — General
  Lambert (1743–1823) 37 UP — General
  John (1805–1879) 107 UP — Jurist

2 Carey (1800–1879—79) 346
  Matthew (1760–1839) 141 NC — Publisher
  Charles Henry (1793–1879) 205 NC — Economist

1 Chew (1762–1810—48—SR—WW–1) 65
  Benjamin (1722–1810) 65 NC — Jurist

6 Coxe (1713–1895—182—SR) 554
  Daniel (1673–1739) 98 NC — Landowner
  Tench (1755–1824) 126 UP — Economist
  William (1762–1831) 79 NC — Palmologist
  John Redman (1773–1864) 72 UP — Physician
  Richard Smith (1792–1865) 77 Pr — Law
  Eckley B. (1839–1895) 102 NC — Mining

2 Dallas (1799–1864—65—SR) 354
  Alexander James (1759–1817) 194 NC — Law-Gov.
  George Mifflin (1792–1864) 160 Pr — Gov.-Dip.

2 Dickinson (1772–1809—37—SR—WW–1) 271
  John (1732–1808) 176 NC — Statesman
  Philemon (1739–1809) 95 UP — Soldier-Pol.

3 Drexel (1832–1893—61—SR—WW–1) 237
  Francis M. (1792–1863) 71 NC — Banker

*See interpretive note on page 469.

Table A-3 Continues

Table A-3 Continued

Boston		Philadelphia	
		Anthony J. (1826–1893) 94 NC	Banker
		Joseph W. (1833–1888) 72 NC	Banker
Edward Clark (1818–1901) 77 NC	Architect		
Arthur Tracy (1852–1912) 74 H	Surgeon		
Richard Clark (1868–1939) 216 H	M.D.-Reformer		
Hugh (1872–1945) 229 H	M.D.-Reformer		
		3 Duane (1800–1935–135—SR) 361	
		William (1760–1835) 110 NC	Journalist
1 Choate (1839–1859–20—SR—WW–2) 410		William John (1780–1865) 125 NC	Lawyer-Girard
Rufus (1799–1859) 410 Dart	Lawyer	William (1872–1935) 126 UP	Physics-Harvard
3 Coolidge (1871–1936–65—SR—WW–2) 363		3 Fisher (1847–1927–80—SR) 250	
Thomas Jefferson (1831–1920) 71 H	Merch.-R.R.	Joshua Francis (1807–1873) 97 H	Essayist
Charles Allerton (1858–1936) 158 H	Architect	Sidney George (1809–1871) 42 Dick	Diarist
Archibald Cary (1866–1928) 134 H	Librarian	Sydney George (1856–1927) 111 Trinity	Historian
4 Eliot (1838–1926–88—SR—WW–5) 1119		3 Furness (1842–1930–88—SR) 247	
Samuel Atkins (1798–1862) 109 H	Mayor	William Henry (1802–1896) 67 H	Clergyman
Samuel (1821–1898) 71 H	Pres. Trinity Col.	Horace Howard (1833–1912) 118 H	Scholar
Charles William (1834–1926) 838 H	Pres. Harvard	Horace Howard (1865–1930) 62 H	Scholar
Charles (1859–1897) 101 H	Lands. Arch.		
5 Emerson (1809–1930–121—SR—WW–4) 1301		4 Hare (1821–1909–88—SR—WW–1) 363	
William (1769–1811) 69 H	Clergyman	Robert (1781–1858) 85 NC	Chemist
Mary Moody (1774–1863) 78 NC	Genealogist	George Emlen (1808–1892) 79 Union	Clergyman
George Barrell (1797–1881) 108 H	Naturalist	John Innis Clark (1816–1905) 98 UP	Jurist
Ralph Waldo (1803–1882) 988 H	Clergy-Author	William Hobart (1838–1909) 101 UP	Bishop
Edward Waldo (1844–1930) 58 H	M.D.-Author		
2 Endicott (1629–1900–271—SR—WW–2) 294		2 Harrison (1813–1929–116—SR) 156	
John (1589–1665) 183 NC	Governor	John (1773–1833) 63 NC	Mfg.-Chemist
William Crowninshield (1826–1900) 111 H	Jurist	Charles C. (1844–1929) 93 UP	Provost

3 Everett (1830–1900—70—SR) 562
  Alexander Hill (1790–1847) 91 H — Editor-Diplomat
  Edward (1794–1865) 371 H — Statesman
  Charles Carroll (1829–1900) 100 Bow — Clergy-Dean

4 Forbes (1780–1898—118—SR—WW–3) 350
  John (1740–1783) 58 Aberdeen — Clergy-Gov.
  John Murray (1771–1831) 72 H — Law-Diplomat
  Robert Bennett (1804–1889) 111 NC — China Merchant
  John Murray (1813–1898) 109 NC — Merch.-R.R.

3 Frothingham (1833–1926—93—SR—WW–1) 260
  Nathaniel Langdon (1793–1870) 68 H — Clergyman
  Octavius Brooks (1822–1895) 80 H — Clergy-Author
  Paul Revere (1864–1926) 112 H — Clergy-Author

4 Gray (1790–1915—125—SR—WW–1) 448
  William (1750–1825) 110 NC — Merch.-Lt. Gov.
  Francis Calley (1790–1856) 60 H — Philanthropist
  Horace (1828–1902) 146 H — Jurist
  John Chipman (1829–1915) 132 H — Law-Education

5 Higginson (1626–1919—293—SR—WW–1) 643
  Francis (1586–1630) 69 Camb — Rev. Salem
  John (1616–1708) 113 NC — Rev. Salem
  Stephen (1743–1828) 67 NC — Merchant
  Thomas Wentworth (1823–1911) 227 H — Clergy-Reformer
  Henry Lee (1834–1919) 144 H — Banker

4 Hoar (1670–1904—234—SR) 437
  Leonard (1630–1675) 87 H — Pres. Harvard

2 Hopkinson (1777–1842—65—SR—WW–1) 324
  Francis (1737–1791) 220 UP — Law-Literature
  Joseph (1770–1842) 104 UP — Jurist

4 Ingersol! (1762–1893—131—SR—WW–2) 415
  Jared (1722–1781) 121 Y — Law-Loyalist
  Jared (1749–1822) 80 Y — Lawyer
  Charles Jared (1782–1862) 170 Pr — Law-Gov.
  Edward (1817–1893) 44 UP — Lawyer

3 Lea (1832–1909—77—SR) 464
  Isaac (1792–1886) 104 NC — Science
  Matthew Carey (1823–1897) 69 NC — Chemist
  Henry Charles (1825–1909) 291 NC — Historian

1 Lippincott (1853–1886—33—SR—WW–1) 88
  Joshua B. (1813–1886) 88 NC — Publisher

2 Lloyd (1680–1731—51) 214
  Thomas (1640–1694) 73 Ox — M.D.-Pol.
  David (1656–1731) 141 NC — Law-Pol.

3 Logan (1714–1839—125—SR) 353
  James (1674–1751) 171 NC — Statesman
  George (1753–1821) 123 NC — M.D.-Senator
  Debby (1761–1839) 59 NC — Diarist

2 Markoe (1767–1806—39—SR) 158
  Abraham (1727–1806) 73 NC — Merchant
  Peter (1752–1792) 85 NC — Poet

3 McKean (1774–1865—91—SR) 404
  Thomas (1734–1817) 275 NC — Gov.-Jurist

Table A-3 Continues

Table A-3 Continued

Boston

Name	Occupation
Samuel (1778-1856) 98 H	Congressman
Ebenezer R. (1816-1895) 108 H	Jurist-Cong.
George F. (1826-1904) 144 H	Senator
3 Holmes (1803-1935—132—SR—WW-1) 1937	
Abiel (1763-1837) 87 Y	Clergyman
Oliver Wendell (1809-1894) 726 H	M.D.-Author
Oliver Wendell, Jr. (1841-1935) 1124 H	Jurist
3 Jackson (1815-1867—52—SR—WW-1) 319	
Charles (1775-1855) 89 H	Jurist
James (1777-1867) 108 H	Physician
Patrick Tracy (1780-1847) 122 NC	Textiles
5 Lawrence (1823-1941—118—SR—WW-3) 725	
William (1783-1848) 56 NC	Textiles
Amos (1786-1852) 123 NC	Textiles
Abbott (1792-1855) 210 NC	Mfg.-Statesman
Amos Adams (1814-1886) 136 H	Churchman
William (1850-1937) 167 H	Bishop
2 Lee (1822-1947—115—SR—WW-3) 251	
Henry (1782-1867) 84 NC	Merchant
Joseph (1862-1937) 167 H	Social Worker
3 Lodge (1890-1942—52—SR—WW-2) 549	
Henry Cabot (1850-1924) 352 H	Senator
George Cabot (1873-1909) 96 H	Poet
John Ellerton (1876-1942) 101 H	Museum Dir.

Philadelphia

Name	Occupation
Joseph Borden (1764-1826) 74 UP	Jurist
William Wister (1800-1865) 55 NC	Naval Officer
5 Meade (1781-1897—116—SR) 556	
George (1741-1808) 58 NC	Merchant
Richard Worsam (1778-1828) 85 NC	Merchant
Richard Worsam (1807-1870) 67 NC	Naval Officer
George Gordon (1815-1872) 250 USMA	General
Richard Worsam (1837-1897) 96 USNA	Naval Officer
5 Meigs (1832-1929—97—SR—WW-1) 513	
Charles de Lucena (1792-1869) 112 Ga	M.D.-Author
Montgomery C. (1816-1892) 125 USMA	General
John Forsyth (1818-1882) 84 UP	Physician
Arthur Vincent (1850-1912) 93 UP	Physician
William Montgomery (1852-1929) 99 UP	Law-History
1 Merrick (1841-1870—29—SR—WW-2) 74	
Samuel Vaughan (1801-1870) 74 NC	Pres. Pa. R.R.
1 Mifflin (1784-1800—16—SR) 217	
Thomas (1744-1800) 217 UP	1st Gov. Pa.
3 Mitchell (1833-1935—102—SR) 515	
John Kearsley (1793-1858) 65 UP	Physician
Silas Weir (1829-1914) 349 UP	M.D.-Author
Langdon E. (1862-1935) 101 H	Poet

3 Longfellow (1847-1921—74) 689
- Henry Wadsworth (1807-1882) 501 Bow — Poet
- Samuel (1819-1892) 104 H — Clergyman
- Ernest Wadsworth (1845-1921) 84 NC — Artist

12 Lowell (1783-1943—160—SR—WW-1) 2419
- John (1743-1802) 81 H — Jurist
- John (1769-1840) 80 H — Author-Law
- Francis Cabot (1775-1817) 87 H — Textiles
- John (1799-1836) 68 H — Lowell Inst.
- Robert T.S. (1816-1891) 84 H — Clergy-Educator
- James Russell (1819-1891) 683 H — Author
- John (1824-1897) 102 H — Judge
- Edward Jackson (1845-1894) 77 H — Historian
- Percival (1855-1916) 154 H — Astronomer
- Abbott Lawrence (1856-1943) 625 H — Pres. Harvard
- Guy (1870-1927) 110 H — Architect
- Amy (1874-1925) 268 NC — Poet

2 Lyman (1832-1897—65—SR—WW-1) 184
- Theodore (1792-1849) 110 H — Mayor-Philan.
- Theodore (1833-1897) 74 H — Zoologist

4 Mather (1636-1785—149—SR—WW-4) 947
- Richard (1596-1669) 117 Ox — Clergy-Author
- Increase (1639-1723) 384 H — Pres. Harvard
- Cotton (1662-1726) 369 H — Clergy-Author
- Samuel (1706-1785) 77 H — Clergyman

1 Motley (1854-1877—23—SR) 482
- John Lothrop (1814-1877) 482 H — Historian

2 Montgomery (1906-1949—43—SR—WW-1) 299
- James Allen (1866-1949) 224 UP — Clergy-Scholar
- Thomas Harrison (1873-1912) 75 UP — Zoologist

4 Morris (1694-1884—190—SR—WW-1) 201
- Anthony (1654-1721) 64 NC — Brewer-Mayor
- Cadwalader (1741-1795) 40 NC — Merchant
- Anthony (1766-1860) 44 UP — Merch.-Law
- Caspar (1805-1884) 53 UP — Physician

4 Norris (1711-1901—190—SR—WW-2) 333
- Isaac (1671-1735) 74 NC — Merch.-Mayor
- Isaac (1701-1766) 75 NC — Party Boss
- George Washington (1808-1875) 73 UP — Surgeon
- William Fisher (1839-1901) 111 UP — Physician

4 Pemberton (1755-1881—126—SR—WW-1) 334
- Israel (1715-1770) 78 NC — Merchant
- James (1723-1809) 77 NC — Merchant
- John (1727-1795) 78 NC — Quaker
- John Clifford (1814-1881) 101 USMA — General

4 Penrose (1838-1938—100—SR—WW-1) 379
- Charles Bingham (1798-1857) 63 NC — Lawyer
- Boies (1860-1921) 114 H — Political Boss
- R.A.F. (1863-1931) 88 H — Geologist
- Spencer (1865-1938) 114 H — Mining-Promoter

4 Pepper (1848-1947—99—SR—WW-3) 533
- George Sechel (1808-1890) 72 NC — Philanthropist
- William (1810-1864) 58 Pr — M.D.-Professor

Table A-3 Continues

Table A-3 Continued

Boston		Philadelphia	
		William (1843–1898) 287 UP	Provost-M.D.
		William (1874–1947) 116 UP	M.D.-Dean
3 Norton (1646-1908—262) 500			
John (1606-1663) 124 Camb	Clergyman		
Andrews (1786-1853) 98 H	Clergyman		
Charles Eliot (1827-1908) 278 H	Author-Educ.		
		3 Peters (1744-1899—155—SR) 337	
		Richard (1704-1776) 92 Ox	Clergyman
2 Otis (1765-1848—83—SR—WW—1) 639		Richard (1744-1828) 135 UP	Jurist
James (1725-1783) 478 H	Patriot	Richard (1810-1889) 110 NC	R.R. Engineer
Harrison Gray (1765-1848) 161 H	Statesman		
		2 Price (1837-1933—96—SR) 184	
4 Paine (1771-1916—145—SR—WW—2) 436		Eli Kirk (1797-1884) 101 NC	Lawyer
Robert Treat (1731-1814) 155 H	Statesman	Eli Kirk (1860-1933) 83 UP	Lawyer
Robert Treat (1773-1811) 99 NC	Poet		
Charles Jackson (1833-1916) 77 H	Capitalist	4 Rawle (1702-1930—228—SR) 302	
Robert Treat (1835-1910) 105 H	Philanthropist	Francis (1662-1727) 67 NC	Merchant
		William (1759-1836) 107 NC	Law-Loyalist
1 Parkman (1863-1893—30—SR—WW—2) 356		William Henry (1823-1889) 71 UP	Law
Francis (1823-1893) 356 H	Historian	Francis (1846-1930) 57 H	Law-Pres. ABA
2 Palfrey (1836-1906—70—SR) 139		2 Roberts (1873-1900—27—SR—WW—1) 118	
John Gorham (1796-1881) 76 H	Historian	George Brooke (1833-1897) 66 RPI	Pres. Pa. R.R.
John Carver (1833-1906) 63 H	Engineer	Howard (1843-1900) 52 NC	Sculptor
7 Peabody (1797-1944—147—SR—WW—4) 826		4 Rush (1785-1869—84—SR—WW—1) 843	
Joseph (1757-1844) 92 NC	Privateer	Benjamin (1745-1813) 347 Pr	M.D.-Patriot
Elizabeth Palmer (1804-1894) 105 NC	Author-Educ.	William (1756-1833) 117 NC	Sculptor
Andrew Preston (1811-1893) 110 H	Professor	Richard (1780-1859) 287 Pr	Law-Diplomat
Robert Swain (1845-1917) 104 H	Architect	James (1786-1869) 92 Pr	Physician
Francis Greenwood (1847-1936) 149 H	Professor		

466

Endicott (1857–1944) 152 Camb	Headmaster
Josephine Preston (1874–1922) 114 NC	Poet
3 Perkins (1804–1940—136—SR—WW-4) 327	
Thomas Handasyd (1764–1854) 116 NC	Merchant
Thomas Nelson (1870–1937) 121 H	Law-Gov.
James Handasyd (1876–1940) 90 H	Banker
5 Phillips (1633–1884—251—SR—WW-1) 445	
George (1593–1644) 73 Camb	Minister
John (1719–1795) 59 H	Founder Exeter
William (1750–1827) 66 NC	Merch.-Philan.
Samuel (1752–1802) 91 H	Founder Andover
Wendell (1811–1884) 156 H	Abolitionist
4 Pickering (1785–1919—134—SR—WW-2) 612	
Timothy (1745–1829) 303 H	Statesman
John (1777–1846) 110 H	Law-Philologist
Charles (1805–1878) 64 H	Med.-Naturalist
Edward Charles (1846–1919) 135 H	Astronomer
3 Prescott (1766–1859—92—SR) 534	
William (1726–1795) 69 NC	Patriot
Oliver (1731–1804) 71 H	M.D.-Patriot
William Hickling (1796–1859) 394 H	Historian
3 Putnam (1879–1918—39—SR—WW-2) 308	
Frederick Ward (1839–1915) 156 H	Anthropologist
Charles Pickering (1844–1915) 64 H	Physician
James Jackson (1846–1918) 88 H	Neurologist

3 Sergeant (1786-1860—74) 334	
Jonathan Dickinson (1746–1793) 104 Pr	Law-Patriot
John (1779–1852) 141 Pr	Lawyer
Thomas (1782–1860) 89 Pr	Jurist-Author
3 Shippen (1679-1808—129—SR) 267	
Edward (1639–1712) 75 NC	Council-Mayor
Edward (1728–1806) 87 NC	Jurist
William (1736–1808) 105 Pr	Physician
2 Vaux (1826-1895—69—SR) 173	
Roberts (1786–1836) 93 NC	Reformer
Richard (1816–1895) 80 NC	Reformer
2 Wetherill (1776-1890—114—SR) 134	
Samuel (1736–1816) 72 NC	Quaker-Preacher
Samuel (1821–1890) 62 UP	Mfg.-Inventor
1 White (1788-1836—48—SR) 138	
William (1748–1836) 138 UP	Bishop
7 Wharton (1772-1928—156—SR) 655	
Samuel (1732–1800) 74 NC	Merchant
Thomas (1735–1778) 114 NC	Merch.-Pol.
Robert (1757–1834) 87 NC	Merch.-Mayor
Thomas I. (1791–1856) 76 UP	Lawyer-Author
Francis (1820–1889) 124 Y	Law-Clergy
Joseph (1826–1909) 100 NC	Mfg.-Philan.
Anne H. (1845–1928) 80 NC	Author

Table A–3 Continues

Table A-3 Continued

Boston		Philadelphia	
		1 Willing (1771–1821—50—SR) 133	
		Thomas (1731–1821) 133 NC	Banker
		4 Wistar-Wister (1736–1938—202—SR—WW–1) 434	
		Caspar Wistar (1696–1752) 83 NC	Manufacturer
		Caspar Wistar (1761–1818) 113 UP	Physician
		Sarah (Sally) Wister (1761–1804) 68 NC	Diarist
		Owen Wister (1860–1938) 170 H	Author
4 Quincy (1784–1910—126—SR) 634			
Josiah (1744–1775) 164 H	Lawyer-Patriot		
Josiah (1772–1804) 324 H	Pres. Harvard		
Edmond (1808–1877) 79 H	Author-Reformer		
Josiah Phillips (1829–1910) 67 H	Author		
2 Saltonstall (1650–1724—74—SR—WW–1) 166			
Richard (1610–1694) 66 Camb	Magistrate		
Gurdon (1666–1724) 100 H	Governor		
4 Shattuck (1823–1929—106—SR—WW–1) 310			
George Cheyne (1783–1854) 82 Dart	M.D.-Philan.		
George Cheyne (1813–1893) 88 H	M.D.-Churchman		
George Brune (1844–1923) 68 H	Physician		
Frederick Cheever (1847–1929) 72 H	Physician		
2 Storrow (1849–1904—55—SR) 184			
Charles Storer (1809–1904) 83 H	Engineer		
James Jackson (1847–1897) 101 H	Lawyer		
2 Ticknor (1831–1864–33—SR) 389			
George (1791–1871) 311 D	Educator		
William Davis (1810–1864) 78 NC	Publisher		
6 Ware (1804–1915—111—SR—WW–1) 587			
Henry (1764–1845) 116 H	Hollis Prof. Div.		
Henry (1794–1843) 104 H	Clergy-Prof.		
John (1795–1864) 98 H	M.D.-Editor		
William (1797–1852) 64 H	Clergy-Author		

John Fothergill Waterhouse (1818–1881) 76 H	Clergyman
William Robert (1832–1915) 129 H	Architect

4 Warren (1781–1927—146—SR—WW-3) 402

Joseph (1741–1775) 115 H	M.D.-General
John (1753–1815) 112 H	Surgeon
John Collins (1778–1856) 108 H	Surgeon
John Collins (1842–1927) 67 H	Surgeon

1 Wendell (1895–1921—26—SR) 147

Barrett (1855–1921) 147 H	Man of Letters

7 Winthrop (1628–1894—266—SR—WW-3) 1133

John (1588–1649) 380 Camb	Governor
John (1605–1676) 213 Trinity (Dublin)	Governor
Fitz-John (1638–1707) 91 NC	Governor
John (1714–1779) 149 H	Scientist
James (1752–1821) 64 H	Librarian
Robert C. (1809–1894) 84 H	Senator
Theodore (1828–1861) 152 Y	Author

NOTE: These elite members were listed in the original twenty volumes of the *DAB*, as well as in the three supplementary volumes, the last of which was published in 1973 and included individuals who died between 1941 and 1945.

Each family surname is listed first: 8 Adams (1762–1927—165—SR—WW-1) 4935. This means that 8 Adamses were included in the *DAB*; 1762 is the date when the first member of the family was 40 years of age and presumably at the height of his powers (i.e. Samuel Adams, born in 1722, was 40 in 1762); 1927 is the date of the death of the last Adams included in the *DAB*; 165 refers to the length of family leadership, or 165 years between Samuel at age 40 and Brooks' death in 1927; SR means that one or more Adamses were listed in the 1940 *Social Register*; likewise WW-1 means that one Adams was listed in the 1940 *Who's Who in America*; and finally, 4935 means that the eight Adamses had 4,935 lines written about them in the *DAB*.

Below the family surname, each individual is listed with dates of birth and death, as well as the lines in the *DAB*, college (NC means no college), and main occupation.

Colleges are abbreviated as follows: Ox (Oxford), Camb (Cambridge), H (Harvard), Y (Yale), Pr (Princeton), UP (University of Pennsylvania), USMA (West Point), USNA (Naval Academy), Dart (Dartmouth), Zur (Zurich, Switzerland), Bow (Bowdoin), Dick (Dickinson), Tr (Trinity College, Hartford), Ga (University of Georgia).

Table A-4
BOSTON AND PHILADELPHIA FIRST FAMILIES:
NUMBER OF MEMBERS IN THE *DAB* PER FAMILY

Members in *DAB*	Boston Families		Philadelphia Families	
1	4	(8)[1]	8	(16)
2	9	(18)	13	(26)
3	13	(26)	11	(22)
4	12	(24)	14	(28)
5 or more	12	(24)	4	(8)
Total	50	(100)	50	(100)

[1]Figures within parentheses are percentages.

Table A-5
BOSTON AND PHILADELPHIA FIRST FAMILIES:
YEARS OF *DAB* LEADERSHIP

Years of Leadership	Boston		Philadelphia	
200+	7	(14)[1]	2	(4)
100–199	22	(44)	14	(28)
< 100	21	(42)	34	(68)
Total	50	(100)	50	(100)

NOTE:
Boston Families
   200+:   Winthrop, Endicott, Higginson, Norton, Phillips, Ames, Hoar

   100–199: Mather, Adams, Quincy, Peabody, Pickering, Paine, Cabot, Lowell, Lee, Perkins, Warren, Shattuck, Bowditch, Bigelow, Gray, Forbes, Emerson, Ware, Brooks, Lawrence, Appleton, Holmes

Philadelphia Families
   200+:   Wistar-Wister, Rawle

   100–199: Logan, Norris, Shippen, Pemberton, Peters, Wharton, Wetherill, Morris, Coxe, Cadwalader, Ingersoll, Duane, Penrose, Pepper.

[1]Figures within parentheses are percentages.

Table A-6
BOSTON AND PHILADELPHIA FIRST FAMILIES:
NUMBER OF LINES IN THE *DAB*

Lines in *DAB*	Boston		Philadelphia	
1000+	7	(14)[1]	0	
500–999	16	(32)	8	(16)
< 500	27	(54)	42	(84)
Total	50	(100)	50	(100)

NOTE:

Boston Families

1,000+: Adams, 4,935; Lowell, 2,419; Holmes, 1,973; Emerson, 1,301; Ames, 1,242; Winthrop, 1,133; Eliot, 1,119

500–999: Mather, 947; Peabody, 826; Cabot, 798; Brooks, 794; Lawrence, 725; Longfellow, 689; Bowditch, 655; Higginson, 643; Otis, 639; Quincy, 634; Pickering, 612; Ware, 587; Everett, 562; Lodge, 549; Prescott, 534; Norton, 500

Philadelphia Families

500–999: Rush, 843; Wharton, 655; Meade, 556, Coxe, 554; Pepper, 533; Mitchell, 515; Meigs, 513; Biddle, 500.

[1]Figures within parentheses are percentages.

Table A-7
BOSTON AND PHILADELPHIA FIRST FAMILIES
ELITE MEMBERS BY NUMBER OF LINES IN THE *DAB*

Lines in *DAB*	Boston		Philadelphia	
1000+	3	(2)[1]	0	
500–999	10	(5)	0	
400–499	5	(3)	0	
300–399	10	(5)	3	(2)
200–299	12	(6)	10	(7)
100–199	70	(36)	50	(34)
50–99	76	(41)	76	(52)
< 50	2	(1)	7	(5)
Total	188	(100)	146	(100)

NOTE:

Boston Elite with 300+ Lines

Oliver Wendell Holmes, Jr., 1,124; John Adams, 1,056; John Quincy Adams, 1,033; Ralph Waldo Emerson, 988; Jean Louis Rodolphe Agassiz, 886; Charles Francis Adams I, 866; Charles William Eliot, 838; Oliver Wendell Holmes, 726; Henry Adams, 718; Samuel Adams, 685; James Russell Lowell, 683; Abbott Lawrence Lowell, 625; Henry Wadsworth Longfellow, 501; Phillips Brooks, 487; John Lothrop Motley, 482; James Otis, 478; Charles Francis Adams II, 439; Rufus Choate, 410; William Hickling Prescott, 394; Increase Mather, 384; John Winthrop, 380; Edward Everett, 371; Cotton Mather, 369; Francis Parkman, 356; Henry Cabot Lodge, 352; Josiah Quincy II, 324; George Ticknor, 311, Timothy Pickering, 303

Philadelphia Elite with 300+ Lines

Silas Weir Mitchell, 349; Benjamin Rush, 347; George Henry Boker, 323

[1]Figures within parentheses are percentages.

Table A–8
BOSTON AND PHILADELPHIA FIRST FAMILIES:
EDUCATION OF ELITE MEMBERS

Boston			Philadelphia		
Harvard	136	(72)[1]	University of Pennsylvania	39	(27)
Bowdoin-Yale-Dartmouth[2]	7	(4)	Harvard-Yale-Princeton[4]	28	(19)
Cambridge	6	(3)	Other American[5]	10	(7)
Other European[3]	4	(2)	Oxford	2	(1)
No College	35	(19)	No College	67	(46)
	188	(100)		146	(100)

NOTE: Eighty-one percent of Bostonians graduated from college and 54% of Philadelphians. Of the Bostonians who went to college in the United States, 95% went to Harvard and 100% to Harvard, Yale, Dartmouth, or Bowdoin, all in New England.

[1]Figures within parentheses are percentages.

[2]Bowdoin, one; Yale, two; Dartmouth, three.

[3]Oxford, Trinity (Dublin), Zurich, Aberdeen.

[4]Princeton, fifteen; Harvard, ten; Yale, three.

[5]West Point, four; one each to the Naval Academy, Dickinson, Trinity, Georgia, Union, and Rensselaer Polytechnic Institute.

Table A–9
PHILADELPHIA FIRST FAMILIES:
EDUCATION OF ELITE MEMBERS BY
NUMBER OF LINES IN THE DAB

Lines in DAB	Harvard-Yale-Princeton		University of Pennsylvania		No College	
200+	4	(14)[1]	5	(13)	3	(4)
100–199	14	(50)	11	(28)	18	(27)
50–99	10	(36)	21	(54)	44	(66)
< 50	0		2	(5)	2	(3)
Total	28	(100)	39	(100)	67	(100)

NOTE: Attendance at Harvard, Yale, or Princeton in eighteenth- and nineteenth-century Philadelphia was broadly correlated with New England or Calvinist family origins; attendance at the University of Pennsylvania, with Anglican; and lack of college attendance, with Quaker origins.

[1]Figures within parentheses are percentages.

Table A-10
BOSTON AND PHILADELPHIA FIRST FAMILIES:
ELITE MEMBERS BY YEAR OF BIRTH
AND NUMBER OF LINES IN THE *DAB*

Boston				Philadelphia			
Year of Birth	Name		Lines in *DAB*	Year of Birth	Name		Lines in *DAB*
1586	Francis Higginson		69				
1588	John Winthrop		380				
1589	John Endicott		183				
1593	George Phillips		73				
1596	Richard Mather		117				
1605	John Winthrop II		213	1639	Edward Shippen		75
1606	John Norton		124	1640	Thomas Lloyd		73
1610	Richard Saltonstall		66	1654	Anthony Morris		74
1616	John Higginson		113	1656	David Lloyd		141
1630	Leonard Hoar		87	1662	Francis Rawle		67
1638	Fitz-John Winthrop		91	1671	Isaac Norris		74
1639	Increase Mather		384	1673	Daniel Coxe		98
1662	Cotton Mather		369	1674	James Logan		171
1666	Gurdon Saltonstall		100	1696	Caspar Wistar		83
	Totals, 1586–1699	14	2,369			9	856
				1701	Isaac Norris II		75
1706	Samuel Mather		77	1704	Richard Peters		92
1708	Nathaniel Ames		80	1707	Thomas Cadwalader		107
	Totals, 1700–1709	2	157			3	274
1714	John Winthrop III		149				
1719	John Phillips		59				
	Totals, 1710–1719	2	208	1715	Israel Pemberton	1	78
				1722	Benjamin Chew		65
				1722	Jared Ingersoll		121
				1723	James Pemberton		77
1722	Samuel Adams		685	1727	Abraham Markoe		73
1725	James Otis		478	1727	John Pemberton		78
1726	William Prescott		69	1728	Edward Shippen II		87
	Totals, 1720–1729	3	1,232			6	501
				1731	Thomas Willing		133
				1732	Samuel Wharton		74
				1732	John Dickinson		176
				1734	Thomas McKean		275
				1735	Thomas Wharton		114
				1736	Samuel Wetherill		72
				1736	William Shippen		105
1731	Oliver Prescott		71	1736	Francis Hopkinson		220
1731	Robert Treat Paine		155	1737	Richard Bache		42
1735	John Adams		1,056	1739	Philemon Dickinson		95
	Totals, 1730–1739	3	1,282			10	1,306

Table A-10 Continues

Table A-10 Continued

Boston			Philadelphia		
Year of Birth	Name	Lines in *DAB*	Year of Birth	Name	Lines in *DAB*
			1740	Clement Biddle	54
			1741	Cadwalader Morris	40
			1741	George Meade	58
			1742	John Cadwalader	66
1740	John Forbes	58	1743	Lambert Cadwalader	37
1741	Joseph Warren	115	1744	Thomas Mifflin	217
1743	John Lowell	81	1744	Richard Peters	135
1743	Stephen Higginson	67	1745	Benjamin Rush	347
1744	Abigail Adams	53	1746	Jonathan Dickinson Sergeant	104
1744	Josiah Quincy	164	1748	William White	138
1745	Timothy Pickering	303	1749	Jared Ingersoll	80
	Totals, 1740–1749 7	841		11	1,276
1750	William Gray	110			
1750	William Phillips	66			
1752	Samuel Phillips	91	1750	Nicholas Biddle	151
1752	George Cabot	202	1752	Peter Markoe	85
1752	James Winthrop	64	1753	George Logan	123
1752	John Brooks	134	1755	Tench Coxe	126
1753	John Warren	112	1756	William Rush	117
1755	Nathaniel Walker Appleton	52	1757	Robert Wharton	87
1757	Joseph Peabody	92	1759	Alexander James Dallas	194
1758	Fisher Ames	281	1759	William Rawle	107
	Totals, 1750–1759 10	1,204		8	990
1763	Abiel Holmes	87	1760	Matthew Carey	141
1763	Charles Bulfinch	167	1760	William Duane	110
1764	Thomas Handasyd Perkins	116	1761	Caspar Wistar	113
1764	Henry Ware	116	1761	Debby Logan	59
1765	Harrison Gray Otis	161	1761	Sally Wister	68
1766	Samuel Appleton	67	1762	William Coxe	79
1767	Peter Chardon Brooks	52	1764	Joseph Borden McKean	74
1767	John Quincy Adams	1,033	1766	Benjamin Smith Barton	89
1769	John Lowell	80	1766	Anthony Morris	44
1769	William Emerson	69	1769	Benjamin Franklin Bache	112
	Totals, 1760–1769 10	1,948		10	889
1771	John Murray Forbes	72			
1772	Josiah Quincy II	324			
1773	Nathaniel Bowditch	175			
1773	Robert Treat Paine	99			
1774	Mary Moody Emerson	78			
1775	Charles Jackson	89			
1775	Francis Cabot Lowell	87			
1777	John Pickering	110			
1777	James Jackson	108	1770	Joseph Hopkinson	104
1778	Samuel Hoar	98	1773	John Harrison	63

Continues

Table A-10 Continued

Boston			Philadelphia		
Year of Birth	Name	Lines in *DAB*	Year of Birth	Name	Lines in *DAB*
1778	John Collins Warren	108	1773	John Redman Coxe	72
1779	Oliver Ames	46	1778	Richard Worsam Meade	85
1779	Nathan Appleton	164	1779	John Sergeant	141
	Totals, 1770–1779 13	1,558		5	465
			1780	Horace Binney	202
			1780	William John Duane	125
			1780	Richard Rush	287
			1781	Robert Hare	85
1780	Patrick Tracy Jackson	122	1782	Thomas Sergeant	89
1782	Henry Lee	84	1782	Charles Jared Ingersoll	170
1783	William Lawrence	56	1783	James Biddle	106
1783	George Cheyne Shattuck	82	1786	James Rush	92
1786	Amos Lawrence	123	1786	William D. Crillon Barton	190
1786	Andrews Norton	98	1786	Roberts Vaux	93
1786	Jacob Bigelow	125	1786	Nicholas Biddle	189
	Totals, 1780–1789 7	690		11	1,628
1790	Francis Calley Gray	60			
1790	Alexander Hill Everett	91			
1791	George Ticknor	311			
1792	Theodore Lyman	110			
1792	Abbott Lawrence	210			
1793	Nathaniel Langdon Frothingham	68	1791	Thomas I. Wharton	76
1794	Henry Ware	104	1792	Franklin Bache	83
1794	Edward Everett	371	1792	Charles de Lucena Meigs	112
1795	John Ware	98	1792	Francis M. Drexel	71
1796	John Gorham Palfrey	76	1792	George Mifflin Dallas	160
1796	Thomas Bulfinch	61	1792	Richard Smith Coxe	77
1796	William Hickling Prescott	394	1792	Isaac Lea	104
1797	George Barrell Emerson	108	1793	John Kearsley Mitchell	65
1797	William Ware	64	1793	Charles Henry Carey	205
1798	Samuel Atkins Eliot	109	1794	John Rhea Barton	46
1799	Rufus Choate	410	1797	Eli Kirk Price	101
1799	John Lowell	68	1798	Charles Bingham Penrose	63
	Totals, 1790–1799 17	2,713		12	1,163
1803	Ralph Waldo Emerson	988			
1804	Elizabeth Palmer Peabody	105	1800	William Wister McKean	55
1804	Oakes Ames	248	1801	Samuel Vaughan Merrick	74
1804	Robert Bennett Forbes	111	1802	William Henry Furness	67
1805	Charles Pickering	64	1803	Thomas Pennant Barton	68
1807	Charles Francis Adams	866	1805	John Cadwalader	107
1807	Jean Louis Rodolphe Agassiz	886	1805	Caspar Morris	53
1807	Henry Wadsworth Long- fellow	501	1806	Alexander Dallas Bache	104
			1807	Richard Worsam Meade II	67
1807	Oliver Ames	108	1807	Joshua Francis Fisher	97

Continues

Table A-10 Continued

Boston			Philadelphia		
Year of Birth	Name	Lines in *DAB*	Year of Birth	Name	Lines in *DAB*
1808	Edmond Quincy	79	1808	George Washington Norris	73
1808	Henry Ingersoll Bowditch	145	1808	George Emlen Hare	79
1809	Robert C. Winthrop	84	1808	George Sechel Pepper	72
1809	Oliver Wendell Holmes	726	1809	Adolph Edward Borie	62
1809	Charles Storer Storrow	83	1809	Sidney George Fisher	42
	Totals, 1800–1809 14	4,994		14	1,020
1810	William Davis Ticknor	78			
1811	Wendell Phillips	156			
1811	Andrew Preston Peabody	110			
1812	Thomas Gold Appleton	66			
1813	George Cheyne Shattuck	88			
1813	John Murray Forbes	109	1810	Richard Peters	110
1814	Amos Adams Lawrence	136	1810	William Pepper I	58
1814	John Lothrop Motley	482	1813	Joshua B. Lippincott	88
1816	Ebenezer Rockwood Hoar	108	1814	John Clifford Pemberton	101
1816	Robert Traill Spence Lowell	84	1815	George Gordon Meade	250
1818	Henry Jacob Bigelow	112	1816	Montgomery Cunningham	
1818	Edward Clark Cabot	77		Meigs	125
1818	John Fothergill Waterhouse		1816	Richard Vaux	80
	Ware	76	1816	John Innis Clark Hare	98
1819	Samuel Longfellow	104	1817	Edward Ingersoll	44
1819	James Russell Lowell	683	1818	John Forsyth Meigs	84
	Totals, 1810–1819 15	2,469		10	1,038
1821	Samuel Eliot	71			
1822	Elizabeth Cabot Cary Agassiz	64			
1822	Octavius Brooks Frothingham	80			
1823	Thomas Wentworth				
	Higginson	227			
1823	Francis Parkman	356			
1824	John Lowell	102			
1826	George F. Hoar	144	1820	Francis Wharton	124
1826	William Crowninshield		1821	Samuel Wetherill II	62
	Endicott	111	1823	George Boker	323
1827	Charles Eliot Norton	278	1823	William Henry Rawle	71
1828	Theodore Winthrop	152	1823	Matthew Carey Lea	69
1828	Horace Gray	146	1825	Henry Charles Lea	291
1829	Josiah Phillips Quincy	67	1826	Anthony J. Drexel	94
1829	Charles Carroll Everett	100	1826	Joseph Wharton	100
1829	John Chipman Gray	132	1829	Silas Weir Mitchell	349
	Totals, 1820–1829 14	2,030		9	1,483
1831	Oliver Ames	147			
1831	Thomas Jefferson Coolidge	71			
1832	William Robert Ware	129			
1833	John Carver Palfrey	63	1833	Joseph W. Drexel	72
1833	Theodore Lyman	74	1833	George Brooke Roberts	66

Table A-10 Continued

Boston			Philadelphia		
Year of Birth	Name	Lines in DAB	Year of Birth	Name	Lines in DAB
1833	Charles Jackson Paine	77			
1834	Henry Lee Higginson	144			
1834	Charles William Eliot	838			
1835	Charles Francis Adams II	439			
1835	Robert Treat Paine	105			
1835	Frederick Lothrop Ames	29	1833	Horace Howard Furness	118
1835	Phillips Brooks	487	1837	Richard Worsam Meade	96
1835	Alexander Agassiz	308	1838	William Hobart Hare	101
1838	Henry Adams	718	1839	Eckley Brinton Coxe	102
1839	Frederick Ward Putnam	156	1839	William Fisher Norris	111
	Totals, 1830–1839 15	3,785		7	666
1840	Henry Pickering Bowditch	263			
1841	Oliver Wendell Holmes, Jr.	1,124			
1842	Charles Pickering Bowditch	72			
1842	John Collins Warren	67			
1844	George Brune Shattuck	68			
1844	Charles Pickering Putnam	64			
1844	Edward Waldo Emerson	58			
1845	Ernest Wadsworth Longfellow	84			
1845	Edward Jackson Lowell	77			
1845	Robert Swain Peabody	104			
1846	James Jackson Putnam	88			
1846	Edward Charles Pickering	135			
1846	John Graham Brooks	121	·1843	Howard Roberts	52
1847	Frederick Cheever Shattuck	72	1843	William Pepper II	287
1847	James Jackson Storrow	101	1844	Charles C. Harrison	93
1847	Francis Greenwood Peabody	149	1845	Anne H. Wharton	80
1848	Brooks Adams	85	1846	Francis Rawle	57
	Totals, 1840–1849 17	2,732		5	569
1850	William Sturgis Bigelow	65			
1850	William Lawrence	167			
1850	Henry Cabot Lodge	352			
1852	Arthur Tracy Cabot	74			
1855	Barrett Wendell	147			
1855	Percival Lowell	154			
1856	Abbott Lawrence Lowell	625			
1857	Endicott Peabody	152	1850	Arthur Vincent Meigs	93
1858	Charles Allerton Coolidge	158	1852	William Montgomery Meigs	99
1859	Charles Eliot	101	1856	Sydney George Fisher	111
	Totals, 1850–1859 10	1,995		3	303
			1860	Owen Wister	170
			1860	Boies Penrose	114
1862	Joseph Lee	167	1860	Eli Kirk Price	83
1864	Paul Revere Frothingham	112	1862	Langdon E. Mitchell	101

Table A-10 Continued

Boston			Philadelphia		
Year of Birth	Name	Lines in *DAB*	Year of Birth	Name	Lines in *DAB*
			1863	R. A. F. Penrose	88
			1865	Spencer Penrose	114
1866	Archibald Cary Coolidge	134	1865	Horace Howard Furness	62
1868	Richard Clark Cabot	216	1866	James Allen Montgomery	224
	Totals, 1860–1869 4	629		8	956
1870	Thomas Nelson Perkins	121			
1870	Winthrop Ames	138			
1870	Guy Lowell	110			
1872	Hugh Cabot	229			
1873	George Cabot Lodge	96			
1874	Oakes Ames	165			
1874	William Sumner Appleton	97	1872	William Duane	126
1874	Josephine Preston Peabody	114	1873	Thomas Harrison	
1874	Amy Lowell	268		Montgomery	75
1876	John Ellerton Lodge	101	1874	William Pepper III	116
1876	James Handasyd Perkins	90	1877	Adolphe Borie	64
	Totals, 1870–1879 11	1,529		4	381

Table A-11

BOSTON AND PHILADELPHIA FIRST FAMILIES: MEMBERS IN THE *DAB* BY DECADE OF BIRTH AND NUMBER OF LINES

Decade of Birth	Boston Families		Philadelphia Families	
	Members in *DAB*	Lines in *DAB*	Members in *DAB*	Lines in *DAB*
1500–1699	14 (8)[1]	2,369 (7)	9 (6)	856 (5)
1700–1709	2	157	3	274
1710–1719	2	208	1	78
1720–1729	3	1,232	6	501
1730–1739	3	1,282	10	1,306
1740–1749	7	841	11	1,276
1750–1759	10	1,204	8	990
1760–1769	10	1,948	10	889
1770–1779	13	1,558	5	465
1780–1789	7	690	11	1,628
1790–1799	17	2,713	12	1,163
Total 1700–1799	74 (40)	11,833 (35)	77 (53)	8,570 (54)

Table A-11 Continued

BOSTON AND PHILADELPHIA FIRST FAMILIES: MEMBERS IN THE *DAB* BY DECADE OF BIRTH AND NUMBER OF LINES

Decade of Birth	Boston Families		Philadelphia Families	
	Members in *DAB*	Lines in *DAB*	Members in *DAB*	Lines in *DAB*
1800–1809	14	4,994	14	1,020
1810–1819	15	2,469	10	1,038
1820–1829	14	2,030	9	1,483
1830–1839	15	3,785	7	666
1840–1849	17	2,732	5	569
1850–1859	10	1,995	3	303
1860–1869	4	629	8	956
1870–1879	11	1,529	4	381
Total 1800–1879	100 (52)	20,163 (58)	60 (41)	6,416 (41)
Total	188 (100)	34,365 (100)	146 (100)	15,842 (100)

[1]Figures within parentheses are percentages

Table A-12

AUTHORITY IN MASSACHUSETTS DURING THE CLASSIC AGE, 1630–1686

Magistrates		Ministers
John Wintrhop	1629–34	John Cotton (Cambridge)
Thomas Dudley	1634–35	Richard Mather (Oxford)
John Haynes	1635–36	Thomas Hooker (Cambridge)
Henry Vane	1636–37	Roger Williams (Cambridge)
John Winthrop	1637–40	Henry Dunster (Cambridge)
Thomas Dudley	1640–41	Thomas Shepard (Cambridge)
Richard Bellingham	1641–42	Nathaniel Ward (Cambridge)
John Winthrop	1642–44	John Wilson (Cambridge)
John Endicott	1644–45	Hugh Peter (Cambridge)
Thomas Dudley	1645–46	John Eliot (Cambridge)
John Winthrop	1646–49	Thomas Welde (Cambridge)
John Endicott	1649–50	Charles Chauncy (Cambridge)
Thomas Dudley	1650–51	Leonard Hoar (Harvard-Cambridge)
John Endicott	1651–54	
Richard Bellingham	1654–55	Increase Mather (Harvard)
John Endicott	1655–65	
Richard Bellingham	1665–72	
John Leverett	1672–79	
Simon Bradstreet	1679–86	

NOTE: Under the original Massachusetts charter, governors were chosen annually. Ministers enjoyed lifetime tenures.

Table A-13
INITIAL APPOINTMENTS TO PROVINCIAL AND
PROPRIETARY OFFICES IN PENNSYLVANIA

Office	Appointee	Acres Purchased	Religion	Occupation in England
Deputy Governor	William Markham	5,000	Anglican	Gentleman
Assistant Deputy Governor	Silas Crispin[1]	5,000	Quaker	Gentleman
	Thomas Holme	5,000	Quaker	Gentleman
Commissioners for Settling the Colony	Silas Crispin	5,000	Quaker	Gentleman
	William Haige	500	Quaker	Merchant
	Nathaniel Allen	2,000	Quaker	Cooper
	John Bezar	1,000	Quaker	Maltster
Keeper of the Seal	Thomas Rudyard[2]	5,000	Quaker	Lawyer
	Thomas Lloyd	5,000	Quaker	Gentleman
Master of the Rolls	Thomas Rudyard	5,000	Quaker	Lawyer
	Thomas Lloyd	5,000	Quaker	Gentleman
Surveyor General	Thomas Holme	5,000	Quaker	Gentleman
Receiver General	Christopher Taylor	5,000	Quaker	Schoolteacher
Receiver General for the Lower Counties	Thomas Holme	5,000	Quaker	Gentleman
Register General	Christopher Taylor	5,000	Quaker	Schoolteacher
Provincial Secretary and Clerk of Provincial Council	Richard Ingelo[3]	500	Quaker	(?)
	Nicholas More	10,000	Anglican	Gentleman
Provincial Treasurer	Robert Turner	6,000	Quaker	Merchant
Chief Justice of Provincial Court	Silas Crispin	5,000	Quaker	Gentleman
	Nicholas More	10,000	Anglican	Gentleman
Provincial Judges	William Welch	(?)	Quaker	Merchant
	William Wood	2,500	Quaker	Merchant
	Robert Turner	6,000	Quaker	Merchant
	John Eckley	1,250	Quaker	Yoeman
Attorney General	John White	1,000	Quaker	(?)
Commissioners of Propriety	James Claypool	10,000	Quaker	Merchant
	Robert Turner	6,000	Quaker	Merchant
	Thomas Lloyd	5,000	Quaker	Gentleman
	Samuel Carpenter	5,000	Quaker	Merchant
Proprietary Secretary	Philip Lehman	1,000	Quaker	Gentleman
Proprietary Steward	James Harrison	5,000	Quaker	Shopkeeper

Source: Gary B. Nash, *Quakers and Politics: Pennsylvania, 1681–1726* (Princeton: Princeton University Press, 1968), pp. 26–27.

[1]Died en route to Pennsylvania.

[2]Relinquished appointments to assume lieutenant governorship of East New Jersey.

[3]Served only five months.

Table A-14
REPRESENTATIVE LEADERS IN FRANKLIN'S PHILADELPHIA

	Dates	Birthplace	Religion
Benjamin Franklin	1706–1790	Boston	Christ Church Deist[1]
Quaker Political Leaders			
James Logan	1674–1751	Ireland	Quaker
James Pemberton	1723–1809	Pennsylvania	Quaker
Israel Pemberton II	1715–1779	Pennsylvania	Quaker
Isaac Norris I	1671–1735	England	Quaker
Isaac Norris II	1701–1776	Pennsylvania	Quaker
Leaders of the Anglican Proprietary Party			
Andrew Hamilton	? –1741	Unknown[2]	Unknown
James Hamilton	1710–1783	Virginia[3]	Anglican
William Allen	1704–1780	Pennsylvania	Presbyterian
Physician–Civic Leaders			
Dr. John Kearsley	1684–1772	England	Anglican
Dr. Thomas Cadwalader[4]	1707–1779	Pennsylvania	Quaker-Anglican
Dr. Thomas Bond	1712–1784	Maryland	Disowned Quaker
Dr. John Morgan	1735–1789	Pennsylvania	Quaker-Anglican
Dr. William Shippen, Jr.	1736–1808	Pennsylvania	Presbyterian of Quaker roots
Educators at the Academy and College			
Rev. Francis Alison	1705–1779	Ireland	Presbyterian
Rev. William Smith	1727–1803	Scotland	Anglican
Rector of Christ Church and St. Peter's			
Rev. Richard Peters	1704–1776	England	Anglican
Artisan-Scientists			
John Bartram	1699–1777	Pennsylvania	Quaker-Deist[5]
Thomas Godfrey	1704–1749	Pennsylvania	Unknown[6]
David Rittenhouse	1732–1795	Pennsylvania	Quaker stock
Quaker Humanitarian			
Anthony Benezet	1713–1748	England	Quaker[7]

[1]Though a Deist, Ben Franklin had a family pew at Christ Church and was buried in the Christ Church graveyard.

[2]Nobody seems to know where or when Andrew Hamilton was born or even his original name.

[3]Presumably, Andrew Hamilton was in Virginia when James, his son, was born; nobody knows for sure.

[4]Dr. Thomas Cadwalader was undoubtedly the most distinguished and versatile member of this First Family.

[5]John Bartram, of old Quaker stock, was read out of meeting and took a great interest in Deism thereafter.

[6]Thomas Godfrey was probably of Bucks County Quaker stock, but nobody knows for sure. The Godfreys wrote hardly a word.

[7]Born to French Huguenots, Anthony Benezet was convinced at the age of thirteen in London, where his family had gone after the revocation of the Edict of Nantes.

Table A-15
PHILADELPHIA MONEYMAKERS
OUTSIDE FIFTY FIRST FAMILIES

Name	Occupation or Source of Wealth
Robert Morris (1734–1806	Financier of the Revolution
Stephen Girard (1750–1831)	Merchant banker, philanthropist
William Bingham (1752–1804)	Merchant banker, land
Enoch W. Clark (1802–1856)	Investment banker
Jay Cooke (1821–1905)	Investment banker
E. T. Stotesbury (1849–1938)	Investment banker
William L. Elkins (1832–1903)	Traction magnate
Peter A. B. Widener (1834–1915)	Traction magnate
Henry Disston (1820–1878)	Saws
Frederick W. Taylor (1856–1915)	Originator of scientific management
Alan Wood (1800–1881)	Steel
William Weightman (1810–1874)	Chemicals
George D. Rosengarten (1801–1881)	Chemicals (Merck & Company today)
Charles Lennig (1809–1891)	Chemicals (Rohm & Haas today)
David Jayne (1798–1886)	Patent medicines
S. S. White (1822–1879)	S. S. White Dental Manufacturing Company
John Wanamaker (1838–1922)	Merchant prince
Thomas A. Scott (1823–1881)	President, Pennsylvania Railroad
Alexander J. Cassatt (1839–1906)	President, Pennsylvania Railroad
Matthias Baldwin (1795–1866)	Baldwin Locomotive Works
Matthew Baird (1817–1877)	President, Baldwin Locomotive Works
John H. Converse (1840–1910)	President, Baldwin Locomotive Works
Joseph Harrison, Jr. (1810–1874)	Locomotives
Henry Howard Houston (1820–1895)	Railroads, gold, oil, land
E. J. Berwind (1848–1936)	Coal
Joseph Newton Pew (1848–1912)	Sun Oil founder
Thomas Dolan (1834–1914)	Textiles, traction
Cyrus H. K. Curtis (1850–1933)	Curtis Publishing
Edward Bok (1863–1930)	*Ladies Home Journal*
George Horace Lorimer (1867–1937)	*Saturday Evening Post*

NOTE: All save Enoch Clark, E. T. Stotesbury, Alan Wood, George Rosengarten, Charles Lennig, David Jayne, and Joseph Pew were included in the *DAB*. Robert Morris, S. S. White, and Joseph Harrison, Jr., were not related to families with those surnames in the First Family sample.

Table A-16
BOSTON AND PHILADELPHIA
FIRST FAMILY MONEYMAKERS

Boston		Philadelphia	
Year of Birth	Name	Year of Birth	Name
1719	John Phillips	1639	Edward Shippen
1743	Stephen Higginson	1654	Anthony Morris
1750	William Phillips	1662	Francis Rawle
1752	Samuel Phillips	1671	Isaac Norris
1752	George Cabot	1696	Caspar Wistar
1757	Joseph Peabody	1701	Isaac Norris II
1764	Thomas Handasyd Perkins	1715	Israel Pemberton
1766	Peter Chardon Brooks	1723	James Pemberton
1766	Samuel Appleton	1727	Abraham Markoe
1779	Nathan Appleton	1731	Thomas Willing
1775	Francis Cabot Lowell	1732	Samuel Wharton
1780	Patrick Tracy Jackson	1757	Robert Wharton
1782	Henry Lee	1735	Thomas Wharton
1783	William Lawrence	1736	Samuel Wetherill
1786	Amos Lawrence	1737	Richard Bache
1792	Abbott Lawrence	1740	Clement Biddle
1809	Charles Storer Storrow	1741	Cadwalader Morris
1779	Oliver Ames	1741	George Meade
1804	Oakes Ames	1742	John Cadwalader
1807	Oliver Ames	1743	Lambert Cadwalader
1831	Oliver Ames	1744	Thomas Mifflin
1835	Frederick Lothrop Ames	1755	Tench Coxe
1804	Robert Bennett Forbes	1766	Anthony Morris
1813	John Murray Forbes	1773	John Harrison
1831	Thomas Jefferson Coolidge	1778	Richard Worsam Meade
1834	Henry Lee Higginson	1786	Nicholas Biddle
1835	Alexander Agassiz	1792	Francis M. Drexel
1835	Charles Francis Adams, Jr.	1801	Samuel Vaughan Merrick
1833	Charles Jackson Paine	1808	George Sechel Pepper
1835	Robert Treat Paine	1809	Adolph Edward Borie
1837	James Jackson Storrow	1810	Richard Peters
		1821	Samuel Wetherill II
		1826	Anthony J. Drexel
		1833	Joseph W. Drexel
		1826	Joseph Wharton
		1833	George Brooke Roberts
		1839	Eckley B. Coxe
		1844	Charles C. Harrison
		1863	R. A. F. Penrose
		1865	Spencer Penrose

Table A-17
BOSTON AND PHILADELPHIA UPPER-CLASS FAMILIES WITH MEMBERS IN THE 1902 *WORLD ALMANAC* LISTING OF AMERICAN MILLIONAIRES

First Families in 1940 *Social Register*		Other Families in 1940 *Social Register*			
Boston	Philadelphia	Boston		Philadelphia	
Adams	Biddle	Aldrich	Hunniwell	Adamson	Levis
Agassiz	Coxe	Allen	Inches	Allen	Lewis
Ames	Drexel	Amory	James	Antelo	McFadden
Appleton	Fisher	Anderson	Kidder	Baird	Martin
Bigelow	Harrison	Andrews	Kimball	Baker	Milne
Brooks	Lea	Bliss	King	Barney	Moore
Bowditch	Lippincott	Bradley	Knowles	Benson	Norris
Cabot	McKean	Bremer	Little	Berwind	Parrish
Coolidge	Morris	Brigham	Loring	Bromley	Paul
Endicott	Price	Brown	Lothrop	Brown	Philler
Forbes	Roberts	Carter	Mason	Caner	Potts
Frothingham	Wharton	Cheney	Means	Cassatt	Rogers
Higginson	Willing	Claflin	Minot	Clark	Rosengarten
Lawrence	Wistar	Clark	Moseley	Clothier	Scott
Lee		Codman	Parker	Coates	Sellers
Lodge		Crocker	Pierce	Coleman	Smith
Lowell		Cushing	Proctor	Converse	Scull
Lyman		Dana	Pratt	Cooke	Stotesbury
Motley		Dexter	Richards	Disston	Strawbridge
Paine		Draper	Richardson	Dolan	Thomas
Parkman		Faxon	Rotch	Earle	Thompson
Peabody		Fay	Russell	Elkins	Tower
Perkins		Fitch	Sargent	Farnum	Tyler
Phillips		Fiske	Sears	Fell	Van Rensselaer
Pickering		Frost	Shaw	Fitler	Wanamaker
Putnam		Gardner	Stone	Forderer	Weightman
Winthrop		Gray	Thayer	Frazier	Widener
		Grew	Thomas	Garrett	Wood
		Hemenway	Warren	Griscom	Welsh
		Hill	Weld	Griswald	Wright
		Hollingsworth	Welch	Harris	
		Hooper	Wigglesworth	Houston	
		Hovey	White	Jayne	
		Howe	Wolcott	Johnson	
				Knight	

NOTE: The Warren (Boston) and Norris (Philadelphia) millionaires were not from the Warren and Norris families in my samples.

Source: Sidney Ratner, ed., *New Light on the History of Great American Fortunes* (New York: 1953), pp. 95–106.

Table A-18
WORLD ALMANAC MILLIONAIRES IN 1902
IN BOSTON AND PHILADELPHIA

	Boston		Philadelphia	
	Number of Families	Number of Millionaires	Number of Families	Number of Millionaires
First Family Sample	27	48	14	30
Other Families in 1940				
Social Register	68	109	66	85
Total Upper-Class				
Millionaires		157 (50)[1]		115 (63)
Other Millionaires		160 (50)		69 (37)
Total Millionaires		317 (100)		184 (100)
City Population in 1900[2]	560,892		1,293,697	
Proportion of Millionaires				
per 100,000	56		14	

	Massachusetts	Pennsylvania
Total Millionaires in State	417	317
State Population in 1900	2,805,346	6,302,115
Proportion of Millionaires per 100,000	15	5

NOTE: As a sidelight on what happened during the nineteenth century to the greatest leadership state at the nation's founding, it is of interest that the *World Almanac* in 1902 listed only sixteen millionaires from Virginia, among them six from Richmond and five from Norfolk.

[1]Figures within parentheses are percentages

[2]These city population figures are not quite comparable, as Boston does not include, for example, Cambridge or Milton-Chestnut Hill; Philadelphia does include West Philadelphia and Chestnut Hill. They are indicative for our purposes, however.

Table A-19
STUDENTS AT GROTON, ST. PAUL'S, AND WESTTOWN,
1890-1940

	Groton	St. Paul's	Westtown
Number of Students	1,458	5,040	981[1]
Number in *Who's Who*	215	361	33
Percentage in *Who's Who*	(15)	(7)	(3)

Source: Groton School, "Address Book" (1968); St. Paul's School, "Alumni Directory" (1975); "Westtown through the Years; Catalog, 1799-1945" (1945); *Who's Who in America*, 32d ed. (1971-1972); *Who Was Who in America*, Vol. V (1969-1973), with an index to all *Who Was Who* volumes.

[1]As Westtown is coeducational, I included only male graduates (in this same period there were 1,244 girls at Westtown).

Table A–20
THE AMERICAN MIND, 1630–1906

The Nation	Boston	Philadelphia
Jonathan Edwards 1703	Cotton Mather 1662	Benjamin Franklin 1706
Hartford Wits	Thomas Hutchinson 1711	Thomas Paine 1737
John Trumbull 1750	George Ticknor 1791	Francis Hopkinson 1737
Timothy Dwight 1752	Edward Everett 1794	1776 "Common Sense"
Joel Barlow 1754	William Hickling Prescott 1796	1794 *The Autobiography of Benjamin*
Washington Irving 1783	John Gorham Palfrey 1796	*Franklin*
James Fenimore Cooper 1789	George Bancroft 1800	Matthew Carey 1760
1800 *Life of Washington* (Mason Locke	Ralph Waldo Emerson 1803	Charles Brockden Brown 1771
Weems)	Nathaniel Hawthorne 1804	*Port Folio* 1801–1812
1819 *The Sketch-Book* (Washington	Henry Wadsworth Longfellow 1807	Joseph Dennie 1768
Irving)	John Greenleaf Whittier 1807	Charles Jared Ingersoll 1782
1826 *The Last of the Mohicans* (James	Oliver Wendell Holmes 1809	Nicholas Biddle 1786
Fenimore Cooper)	Henry David Thoreau 1817	Charles Henry Carey 1793
Edgar Allen Poe 1809	James Russell Lowell 1819	Sidney George Fisher 1809
Harriet Beecher Stowe 1811	John Lothrop Motley 1814	George Henry Boker 1823
Walt Whitman 1819	Francis Parkman 1823	Charles Godfrey Leland 1824
Herman Melville 1819	Emerson leaves the pulpit 1832	Bayard Taylor 1825
Mark Twain 1835	Emerson to Concord 1834	Henry Charles Lea 1825
Henry James 1843	*Dial* 1840–1844	S. Weir Mitchell 1829
New York bohemia	Brook Farm 1841–1847	*Graham's* 1825–1858 (Edgar Allen Poe,
Pfaff's restaurant 1854	Thoreau to Walden Pond 1845–1847	ed., 1841–1842)
1845 "The Raven" (Edgar Allen Poe)	*North American Review* 1815–1878 (to	*Godey's Ladies' Book* 1830 (Sarah
1850 *Representative Men* (Ralph Waldo	New York)	Hale, ed.)
Emerson)	*Atlantic* 1857	Sydney George Fisher 1856
The Scarlet Letter (Nathaniel	Horatio Alger 1834	Owen Wister 1860
Hawthorne)	Charles William Eliot 1834	Langdon Mitchell 1862

1851 *The House of the Seven Gables* (Nathaniel Hawthorne)
Moby Dick (Herman Melville)
Uncle Tom's Cabin (Harriet Beecher Stowe)
1852 *Pierre* (Herman Melville)
1854 *Walden* (Henry David Thoreau)
1855 *Leaves of Grass* (Walt Whitman)
"Hiawatha" (Henry Wadsworth Longfellow)
1856 "Barefoot Boy" (John Greenleaf Whittier)
Nation 1865
Edith Wharton 1862
1867 *Ragged Dick* (Horatio Alger)
1869 *The Innocents Abroad* (Mark Twain)
1873 *The Gilded Age* (Mark Twain)
1876 *Tom Sawyer* (Mark Twain)
1905 *The House of Mirth* (Edith Wharton)

Charles Francis Adams, Jr. 1835
William Dean Howells 1837
Henry Adams 1838
Oliver Wendell Holmes, Jr. 1841
William James 1842
Henry James 1843
1881 *Common Law* (Oliver Wendell Holmes, Jr.)
Washington Square (Henry James)
1886 *The Bostonians* (Henry James)
1890 *Principles of Psychology* (William James)
A Hazard of New Fortunes (William Dean Howells)
1906 *The Education of Henry Adams*
1907 *Pragmatism* (William James)

Cyrus H. K. Curtis 1850
Ladies Home Journal 1883
Edward W. Bok 1863
Saturday Evening Post 1897
George Horace Lorimer 1867
Logan Pearsall Smith 1865
1902 *The Virginian* (Owen Wister)

Table A-21
BOSTON AND PHILADELPHIA FIRST FAMILY AUTHORS

Boston

Date of Birth	Lines in DAB	Author	Area of Activity
Historians			
1588	380	John Winthrop	Journal
1662	369	Cotton Mather	History, theology, medicine (400 books)
1728	94	Mercy Otis Warren	First history of American Revolution
1735	1056	John Adams	History, government
1763	87	Abiel Holmes	Annals of America, biographies
1767	1033	John Quincy Adams	Memoirs (12 vols.)
1796	394	William Hickling Prescott	Spain, Spanish America (20 vols.)
1796	76	John Gorham Palfrey	Theology, history of New England, biographies
1807	866	Charles Francis Adams	Family papers, history, politics
1809	84	Robert C. Winthrop	Essays in American history
1814	482	John Lothrop Motley	Netherlands (works, 17 vols.)
1823	356	Francis Parkman	*Oregon Trail* (works, 20 vols.)
1829	67	Josiah Phillips Quincy	Poetry, fiction, American history
1835	439	Charles Francis Adams, Jr.	*Chapters of Erie*, etc.
1838	718	Henry Adams	*Education*, etc.
1841	1124	Oliver Wendell Holmes, Jr.	*Common Law*
1845	77	Edward Jackson Lowell	French Revolution
1848	85	Brooks Adams	*Law of Civilization and Decay*
1850	352	Henry Cabot Lodge	Colonial history, biographies
Literature			
1773	99	Robert Treat Paine	Poet
1796	61	Thomas Bulfinch	*The Age of Fable*
1797	64	William Ware	Religion, fiction, poetry, history
1803	988	Ralph Waldo Emerson	Philosophy, literature
1807	501	Henry Wadsworth Longfellow	Poetry
1809	726	Oliver Wendell Holmes	Literature, medicine
1819	683	James Russell Lowell	Letters, fiction, essays, Bigelow Papers
1828	152	Theodore Winthrop	Fiction, essays
1873	96	George Cabot Lodge	Poetry
1874	114	Josephine Preston Peabody	Poetry
1874	268	Amy Lowell	Poetry
Editors, Essayists, and Pamphleteers			
1722	685	Samuel Adams	Revolutionary promoter (works, 4 vols.)
1725	478	James Otis	Revolutionary promoter
1744	164	Josiah Quincy	Revolutionary promoter
1769	80	John Lowell	Federalist promoter
1769	69	William Emerson	*Monthly Anthology*; Anthology Club

Table A-21 Continued

Boston

Date of Birth	Lines in DAB	Author	Area of Activity
1808	79	Edmond Quincy	Ed., *Abolitionist*; fiction, biographies
1804	105	Elizabeth Palmer Peabody	Educational essays, history
1811	156	Wendell Phillips	Abolition, literary essays
1812	66	Thomas Gold Appleton	Conversationalist, essayist
1823	227	Thomas Wentworth Higginson	Women's suffrage, slavery, biographies
1844	58	Edward Waldo Emerson	Family papers, biographies

Publisher

1810	78	William Davis Ticknor	Publisher of Hawthorne

Scholars and Educators

1630	87	Leonard Hoar	Pres., Harvard
1639	384	Increase Mather	Pres., Harvard
1714	149	John Winthrop IV	Scientist
1752	64	James Winthrop	Librarian, historian
1764	116	Henry Ware	Hollis Prof. Divinity, Harvard
1772	324	Josiah Quincy	Pres., Harvard
1773	175	Nathaniel Bowditch	Classic book on navigation
1777	110	John Pickering	Philologist
1786	98	Andrews Norton	Prof., Harvard Divinity School
1790	91	Alexander Hill Everett	Pres., Jefferson College, Kentucky; NAR
1791	311	George Ticknor	Prof. German, Harvard
1794	371	Edward Everett	Pres., Harvard
1794	104	Henry Ware	Prof., Harvard Divinity School; editor
1795	98	John Ware	Prof., Harvard Medical School
1797	108	George Barrell Emerson	Educator, especially of women
1799	68	John Lowell	Founder, Lowell Institute
1805	64	Charles Pickering	Naturalist
1807	886	Jean Louis Rodolphe Agassiz	Naturalist
1811	110	Andrew Preston Peabody	Acting pres., prof. divinity, Harvard; NAR
1816	84	Robert T. S. Lowell	Headmaster, Saint Mark's School
1821	71	Samuel Eliot	Pres., Trinity College, Hartford
1822	64	Elizabeth Cabot Cary Agassiz	First pres. Radcliffe
1827	278	Charles Eliot Norton	Prof., Harvard; ed., *Atlantic*; NAR; a founder of *Nation*
1829	100	Charles Carroll Eliot	Dean, Harvard Divinity School
1829	132	John Chipman Gray	Prof. law, Harvard; founder, *American Law Review*
1832	129	William Robert Ware	Founder architectural education in United States, at MIT and Columbia
1833	74	Theodore Lyman	Prof. zoology, Harvard

Table A-21 Continued

Boston

Date of Birth	Lines in DAB	Author	Area of Activity
1834	838	Charles William Eliot	Pres., Harvard
1839	56	Frederick Ward Putnam	Founder academic anthropology at Harvard
1842	72	Charles Pickering Bowditch	Prof. archeology, Harvard
1846	135	Edward Charles Pickering	Prof. astronomy, Harvard; founder, pres., American Astronomical Society
1846	88	James Jackson Putnam	Prof. neurology, Harvard Medical School
1847	149	Francis Greenwood Peabody	Prof. sociology, Harvard
1850	65	William Sturgis Bigelow	Orientalist
1855	154	Percival Lowell	Founder, Harvard Observatory, Flagstaff, Arizona
1855	147	Barrett Wendell	Prof., Harvard
1856	625	Abbott Lawrence Lowell	Pres., Harvard
1857	152	Endicott Peabody	Founder, Groton School
1866	134	Archibald Cary Coolidge	Librarian, Widener Library, Harvard
1874	165	Oakes Ames	Prof. botany, Harvard; builder, Arnold Arboretum
1876	101	John Ellerton Lodge	Orientalist; museum director, D.C.

Philadelphia

Literature

Date of Birth	Lines in DAB	Author	Area of Activity
1737	220	Francis Hopkinson	Poet, musician, satirist
1752	85	Peter Markoe	Poet
1761	68	Sarah Wister	Diarist
1782	170	Charles Jared Ingersoll	Dennie circle *Port Folio*
1782	89	Thomas Sergeant	Dennie circle *Port Folio*
1786	189	Nicholas Biddle	Dennie circle *Port Folio*
1791	76	Thomas I. Wharton	Dennie circle *Port Folio*
1809	42	Sidney George Fisher	Diarist, essayist
1823	323	George Henry Boker	Poet, playwright
1829	349	Silas Weir Mitchell	Novelist
1845	80	Anne H. Wharton	Manners, travel
1860	170	Owen Wister	Novelist, essayist
1862	101	Langdon E. Mitchell	Poet, playwright

Publishers

Date of Birth	Lines in DAB	Author	Area of Activity
1760	141	Matthew Carey	*American Museum*; economist
1760	110	William Duane	*Aurora*
1769	112	Benjamin Franklin Bache	*Aurora*
1813	88	Joshua B. Lippincott	Gazetteers, dictionaries, medicine

Economists

Date of Birth	Lines in DAB	Author	Area of Activity
1662	67	Francis Rawle	First essay of economics
1755	126	Tench Coxe	Promoter of manufactures
1793	205	Charles Henry Carey	Protectionist

Table A-21 Continued

Philadelphia

Date of Birth	Lines in DAB	Author	Area of Activity
Historians			
1761	59	Debby Logan	Edited family papers
1807	97	Joshua Francis Fisher	Political essays
1825	291	Henry Charles Lea	History of the Inquisition
1852	99	William Montgomery Meigs	Biographies
1856	111	Sydney George Fisher	Pennsylvania history
Scholars and Educators			
1745	347	Benjamin Rush	Medicine, general literature
1781	85	Robert Hare	Prof. chemistry, Penn
1792	112	Charles de Lucena Meigs	Prof. obstetrics, Jefferson
1792	104	Isaac Lea	Malacologist; pres., AAAS
1806	104	Alexander Dallas Bache	Scientist, U. of P., Central
1808	79	George Emlen Hare	Episcopal Academy, Philadelphia Divinity School
1833	118	Horace Howard Furness	Shakespeare scholar
1843	287	William Pepper	Provost, Penn
1844	93	Charles C. Harrison	Provost, Penn
1863	88	R. A. F. Penrose	Founder, first pres., Soc. Ec. Geol.
1865	62	Horace Howard Furness	Shakespeare scholar
1866	224	James Allen Montgomery	Prof., Philadelphia Divinity School
1872	126	William Duane	Prof. physics, Harvard
1873	75	Thomas Harrison Montgomery	Prof. zoology, Penn
1874	116	William Pepper	Dean, Penn Medical School

Table A-22
PERIODICAL CIRCULATION FOR 1967 IN
MASSACHUSETTS AND PENNSYLVANIA

| | Massachusetts | | Pennsylvania | |
Periodical	Circulation Per 10,000[1]		Circulation Per 10,000	
Harper's	8,867	17	11,739	10
Atlantic	14,000	27	14,000	12
New Republic	6,863	13	6,431	6
National Review	2,481	4	3,640	3
Commentary	340	0.65	317	0.28
Total Elite Periodicals	32,551	61	36,127	31
Time	172,042	334	218,616	193
Life	265,120	514	496,828	439
Saturday Evening Post	207,846	404	398,601	352
Total Mass Periodicals	645,008	1,252	1,114,045	984

Source: Circulation figures supplied me by the circulation managers of each periodical; figures varied as to paid subscriptions or paid circulation; in either case, they were comparable for the two states.

[1]In 1960 the population of Massachusetts was 5,158,678; that of Pennsylvania, 11,319,396.

Table A-23
PHILADELPHIA AND BOSTON ARTISTS

Boston	Philadelphia
John Smibert (1688–1751)	Gustavus Hesselius (1682–1755)
Peter Pelham (1695–1751)	Benjamin West (1728–1820)
John Singleton Copley (1738–1815)	Charles Willson Peale (1741–1827)
Henry Sargent (1781–1828)	Thomas Sully (1783–1872)
	Edward Hicks (1780–1849)
	John Hicks (1823–1890)
	William Rush (1756–1833)
	Howard Roberts (1843–1900)
Winslow Homer (1836–1910)	Thomas Eakins (1844–1916)
	Mary Cassatt (1845–1926)
Ernest Wadsworth Longfellow (1845–1921)	Cecilia Beaux (1855–1942)
	William Glackens (1870–1938)
	John Sloan (1871–1951)
	Alexander Stirling Calder (1870–1945)
	Adolphe Borie (1877–1934)
	Arthur B. Carles (1882–1952)
John Singer Sargent (1856–1925)	

NOTE: Painters and sculptors of upper-class origins are italicized. This list of Philadelphia and Boston artists includes only enough men and women to show the differing traditions of the two cities and the superiority of Philadelphia.

Table A–24
BOSTON AND PHILADELPHIA
ARCHITECTS IN THE *DAB*

Boston	Philadelphia
Charles Bulfinch (1763–1844)	Benjamin H. Latrobe (1764–1820)
Alexander Parris (1780–1852)	William Strickland (1788–1854)
Solomon Willard (1783–1861)	John Haviland (1792–1854)
Edward Clark Cabot (1818–1901)	Thomas U. Walter (1804–1887)
Arthur D. Gilman (1821–1882)	Napoleon LeBrun (1821–1901)
William R. Ware (1832–1915)	John McArthur, Jr. (1823–1890)
Henry Van Brunt (1832–1903)	
Charles A. Cummings (1833–1905)	
H. H. Richardson (1838–1886)	*Frank Furness* (1839–1912)
Robert Swain Peabody (1845–1917)	
Charles A. Coolidge (1858–1936)	John Stewardson (1858–1896)
Charles Eliot (1859–1897)	Walter Cope (1860–1902)
Ralph Adams Cram (1863–1942)	Horace Trumbauer (1868–1938)
Guy Lowell (1870–1927)	Paul Cret (1876–1945)

NOTE: First Family architects are italicized. Frank Furness was the only architect *not* included in the *DAB*, even though his work probably will have a more lasting effect on American history than that of his father, his brother, and his nephew, all of whom were included.

George Thomas, a leading architectural historian in Philadelphia, thinks that Furness and other excellent Philadelphia architects failed to receive national recognition partly because the first modern professional journal, the *American Architect and Building News*, was founded (1876) in Boston and published there until it moved to New York in 1913.

Table A–25
BOSTON AND PHILADELPHIA FIRST FAMILY MEMBERS
TRAINED IN THE LEARNED PROFESSIONS

Professions	Boston		Philadelphia	
Law	45	(24)[1]	43	(29)
Medicine	28	(15)	23	(16)
Clergy	32	(17)	7	(5)
Total professionals in *DAB*	105	(56)	73	(50)
Total family members in *DAB*	188	(100)	146	(100)
Families with one or more professionals	44	(88)	36	(72)

[1]Figures within parentheses are percentages.

Table A-26
JUDICIAL AUTHORITY IN MASSACHUSETTS
AND PENNSYLVANIA

Chief Justices of Massachusetts	Chief Justices of Pennsylvania
William Cushing (1777–1789) d, SC	Thomas McKean (1791–1799) d
Nathaniel P. Sargent (1790–1791)	Edward Shippen (1799–1806) d
Francis Dana (1791–1806) d	William Tilghman (1806–1827) d
Theophilus Parsons (1806–1813) d	John B. Gibson (1827–1851) d
Samuel Sewell (1814–1814)	Jeremiah S. Black (1851–1854) d
Isaac Parker (1814–1830) d	Ellis Lewis (1854–1857) d
Lemuel Shaw (1830–1860) d	Walter H. Lowrie (1857–1863)
George Tyler Bigelow (1860–1868)	George W. Woodward (1863–1867)
Reuben A. Chapman (1868–1873)	James Thompson (1867–1872)
Horace Gray (1873–1882) d, SC	John Meredith Read (1872–1873) d
Marcus Morton (1882–1890) d	Daniel Agnew (1873–1879)
Walbridge Abner Field (1890–1899) d	George Sharswood (1879–1883) d
Oliver Wendell Holmes, Jr. (1899–1902) d, SC	Ulysses Mercur (1883–1887) d
Marcus P. Knowlton (1902–1911) d	Isaac G. Gordon (1887–1889)
Arthur P. Rugg (1911–1938) d	Edward M. Paxson (1889–1893)
Fred Tarbell Field (1938–1947) d	James P. Sterrett (1893–1900)
	Henry Green (1900–1900)
	J. Brewster McCollum (1900–1903)
	James T. Mitchell (1903–1910) d
	D. Newlin Fell (1910–1915)
	J. Hay Brown (1915–1921)
	Robert von Moschzisker (1921–1930) d
	Robert S. Frazer (1930–1936)
	John W. Kephart (1936–1940)

NOTE: d means the chief justice was listed in the *DAB*. SC means he went on to the U.S. Supreme Court. Massachusetts produced sixteen justices; Pennsylvania, twenty-four.

Table A-27
U.S. SUPREME COURT JUSTICES FROM
MASSACHUSETTS AND PENNSYLVANIA

Justices from Massachusetts	Tenure	Years in Office	Lines in DAB
William Cushing	1789–1810	21	177
Joseph Story	1811–1845	34	370
Benjamin Curtis	1851–1857	6	234
Horace Gray	1882–1902	20	146
Oliver Wendell Holmes	1902–1932	30	1,124
Total		112	2,049
Justices from Pennsylvania			
James Wilson	1789–1798	9	473
Henry Baldwin	1830–1844	14	112
Robert C. Grier	1846–1870	24	124
William Strong	1870–1880	10	165
George Shiras	1892–1903	11	
Owen J. Roberts	1930–1945	15	
Total		83	874

NOTE: George Shiras was among a handful of Supreme Court justices not included in the DAB. Owen Roberts, who died in 1955, was not included because the last supplementary volume covered persons who died before 1950.

Table A-28
BOSTON AND PHILADELPHIA FIRST FAMILY PHYSICIANS

Boston	Philadelphia
Warren	Rush
Joseph (1741–1775)	Benjamin (1745–1813)
John (1753–1815)	James (1786–1869)
John Collins (1778–1856)	Barton
John Collins (1842–1927)	Benjamin Smith (1766–1815)
Shattuck	William D. Crillon (1786–1856)
George Cheyne (1783–1854)	John Rhea (1794–1871)
George Cheyne (1813–1893)	Meigs
George Brune (1844–1923)	Charles de Lucena (1792–1869)
Frederick Cheever (1847–1929)	John Forsyth (1818–1882)
Bigelow	Arthur Vincent (1850–1912)
Jacob (1786–1879)	Mitchell
Henry Jacob (1818–1890)	John Kearsley (1793–1858)
William Sturgis (1850–1926)	Silas Weir (1829–1914)
Bowditch	Norris
Henry Ingersoll (1808–1892)	George Washington (1808–1875)
Henry Pickering (1840–1911)	William Fisher (1839–1901)
Putnam	Pepper
Charles Pickering (1844–1915)	William (1810–1864)
James Jackson (1846–1918)	William (1843–1898)
Cabot	William (1874–1947)
Arthur Tracy (1852–1912)	Thomas Lloyd (1640–1694)
Richard Clark (1868–1939)	Thomas Cadwalader (1707–1779)
Hugh (1872–1945)	William Shippen (1736–1808)
Leonard Hoar (1630–1675)	George Logan (1753–1821)
Nathaniel Ames (1708–1764)	Caspar Wistar (1761–1818)
Oliver Prescott (1731–1804)	John Redman Coxe (1773–1864)
John Brooks (1752–1825)	Franklin Bache (1792–1864)
Nathan Walker Appleton (1755–1795)	Caspar Morris (1805–1884)
James Jackson (1777–1867)	
John Ware (1795–1864)	
Charles Pickering (1805–1878)	
Oliver Wendell Holmes (1809–1894)	
Edward Waldo Emerson (1844–1930)	

NOTE: Boston had twenty-eight physicians from sixteen families; Philadelphia, twenty-three from fourteen families.

Table A-29
BOSTON AND PHILADELPHIA FIRST FAMILY CLERGYMEN

Boston	Philadelphia
Mather	Hare
Richard (1596–1669)	George Emlen (1808–1892)
Increase (1639–1723)	William Hobart (1838–1909)
Cotton (1662–1726)	Richard Peters (1704–1776)
Samuel (1706–1785)	William White (1748–1836)
Ware	William Henry Furness (1802–1896)
Henry (1764–1845)	Francis Wharton (1820–1889)
Henry (1794–1843)	James Allen Montgomery (1866–1949)
William (1797–1852)	
John Fothergill Waterhouse	
(1818–1881)	
Higginson	
Francis (1586–1630)	
John (1616–1708)	
Thomas Wentworth (1823–1911)	
Peabody	
Andrew Preston (1811–1893)	
Francis Greenwood (1847–1936)	
Endicott (1857–1944)	
Frothingham	
Nathaniel Langdon (1793–1870)	
Octavius Brooks (1822–1895)	
Paul Revere (1864–1926)	
Emerson	
William (1769–1811)	
Ralph Waldo (1803–1882)	
Norton	
John (1606–1663)	
Andrews (1786–1853)	
Everett	
Edward (1794–1865)	
Charles Carroll (1829–1900)	
Brooks	
Phillips (1835–1893)	
John Graham (1846–1938)	
George Phillips (1593–1644)	
Gurdon Saltonstall (1666–1724)	
John Forbes (1740–1783)	
Abiel Homes (1763–1837)	
John Gorham Palfrey (1796–1881)	
Robert T. S. Lowell (1816–1891)	
Samuel Longfellow (1819–1892)	
William Lawrence (1850–1937)	

Table A-30
EDUCATION OF U.S. SENATORS FROM MASSACHUSETTS
AND PENNSYLVANIA 1790-1960

Massachusetts			Pennsylvania		
Harvard	20		Princeton	5	
Yale	6		Washington and Jefferson	3	
Dartmouth	2		University of Pennsylvania	2	
Other Colleges	8[1]		Dickinson	2	
			Franklin and Marshall	2	
			Harvard	2	
			Other Colleges	6[2]	
College Graduates	36	(84)[3]	College Graduates	22	(44)
Non-Graduates	7[4]	(16)	Non-Graduates	26	(54)
Total Senators	43	(100)	Total Senators	48	(100)

[1]One each from Amherst, Williams, Middlebury, Princeton, Brown, the Naval Academy, Holy Cross, and Bryant-Stratton Commercial School.

[2]One each from Swarthmore, Waynesboro, St. Joseph's, Randolph Macon, Mount Union, and the University of Halle, in Germany.

[3]Figures within parentheses are percentages.

[4]George Cabot withdrew from Harvard before the authorities would have expelled him for his role in the student rebellion of 1766.

Table A-31
CATHOLIC BISHOPS AND ARCHBISHOPS OF BOSTON AND PHILADELPHIA, 1808 TO THE PRESENT

Boston	Philadelphia
Jean Lefebvre de Cheverus 1808–1825	Michael Egan 1808–1814
Benedict Joseph Fenwick 1825–1846	Henry Conwell 1819–1842
John Bernard Fitzpatrick 1846–1866	Francis Patrick Kenrick 1842–1851
John J. Williams 1866–1907 (Archbishop 1875)	John Nepomucene Neumann 1852–1860
William H. O'Connell 1907–1944 (Cardinal 1911)	James F. Wood 1860–1883 (Archbishop 1875)
Richard James Cushing 1944–1970 (Cardinal 1958)	Patrick J. Ryan 1884–1909
	Edmund F. Prendergast 1911–1918
	Dennis Dougherty 1918–1951 (Cardinal 1921)
	John F. O'Hara 1951–1961 (Cardinal 1958)
	John Joseph Krol 1961– (Cardinal 1967)

Table A-32
ARCHDIOCESES OF BOSTON AND PHILADELPHIA: EDUCATION STATISTICS FOR 1963

	Boston	Philadelphia
Geographical Area (square miles)	2,465	2,182
Total Population	3,335,895	3,591,523
Catholic Population	1,733,620	1,263,625
Percentage Catholics	52	35
Parochial and Private Elementary Schools		
Number of Schools	241	301
Number of Pupils	118,000	212,035
Diocesan, Parochial, and Private Secondary Schools		
Number of Schools	100	50
Number of Pupils	25,000	54,436
Percentage of Catholic Population in Catholic Schools		
Elementary	(7)	(18)
Secondary	(1)	(4)
Institutions of Higher Learning	14	11

Source: New Catholic Encyclopedia.

Table A-33
BOSTON COLLEGE AND ST. JOSEPH'S COLLEGE
COMPARATIVE CHARACTERISTICS, 1962-1963

	Boston	St. Joseph's
Endowment	$5,319,095	$747,623
Plant Value	41,171,820	3,407,457
Library Volumes	690,744	86,300
Current Periodicals	3,961	1,156

Source: William F. Kelley, *The Jesuit Order and Higher Education in the United States, 1789–1966* (Milwaukee: Wisconsin Jesuit Press, 1966).

Table A-34
NUMBER OF QUAKER MEETINGHOUSES
IN SELECTED STATES, 1850 AND 1950

| | Number of Meetinghouses | |
| |------|------|
State	1950	1850
Pennsylvania	72	149
New York	55	133
Ohio	57	94
Indiana	152	89
New Jersey	26	52
Massachusetts	8	39
North Carolina	76	31
California	26	0

Source: Edwin Scott Gaustad, *Historical Atlas of Religion in America* (New York: Harper, 1962), pp. 168–169.

Table A–35
Leading Philadelphia Gurneyite Families

Family	Westtown Students	Westtown faculty and staff	Twelfth Street meeting	Penn Charter students	Penn Charter overseers and headmasters	Haverford students	Haverford managers, faculty, presidents	American Friends Service Committee board	Provident Life & Trust board	Social Register	DAB
Baily	53	X	X	X	O	X	M	X		X	
Bettle	10		X	X	O	X	M			X	
Brinton	65	X	X			X	F	X		X	
Cadbury	21	X	X	X	O	X	MF	F	F		
Comfort	63	X		X		X	MP	F			
Cope	178	X	X	X	O	X	M	X		X	X
Evans	247	X	X	X		X	M	F		X	
Garrett	103	X	X		O	X	M		F	X	X
Gummere	16	X	X	X	2H	X	MFP			X	X
Hutton	30		X			X		X			
Kirkbride	37		X	X		X				X	X
Leeds	37	X				X	M	F			
Morris	70		X	X	O	X	M	X		X	X
Rhoads	148	X	X	X	O	X	M	F	X	X	X
Roberts	183	X	X	X		X	M			X	X
Scull	15		X	X		X	M			X	
Scattergood	93	X	X		O	X	M	F	X	X	X
Sharpless	249	X	X			X	MP		X	X	X
Strawbridge	5		X			X	M			X	
Taylor	222	X	X	X		X	M	X	X	X	X
Vaux	2		X	X		X	M			X	X
Whitall	29	X	X	X	O	X	M			X	X
Wistar	60		X	X		X	M			X	X
Wood	128	X	X	X	O	X	M	F	F	X	X
Yarnall	70	X	X	X		X	M	F		X	
Brown			X		O	X	M		F	X	X
Jones			X		H	X	F	F			X

NOTE: X means that at least one member of the family was a participant. O means that at least one member was an overseer at Penn Charter School; H stands for headmaster. M means that at least one member was a manager at Haverford College; F stands for faculty member and P for president. The founding board members of the AFSC and the Provident are also noted by an F.

Genius, Fame, and Family:
Heredity or Environment?

Any study of stratification and leadership must face the issue of whether heredity or environment is more important in causing the differences between groups, classes, or races of men. The dichotomy is probably a false issue, however, as the characteristics of individuals are always a product of heredity *in* an environment. Nevertheless, the debate has persisted with strong arguments on both sides. In the nineteenth century, Francis Galton, Darwin's nephew, was the leading advocate of the hereditarian point of view, which dominated the values of the Anglo-Saxon Victorian world. The American sociologist Charles Horton Cooley was an equally capable advocate of the environmental point of view. Briefly, Galton argued that fame is a sufficient test of genius; genius as a rule achieves fame; and the number of illustrious men a race produces is therefore a valid criterion of the native, or hereditary, ability of that race. Cooley countered Galton's view concisely.

> Every race probably turns out a number of greatly endowed men many times larger than the number that attains fame. By greatly endowed I mean with natural abilities equal to those that have made men famous in other times and places. The question which, if any, of these geniuses are to achieve fame is determined by historical and social conditions, and these vary so much that the production

of great men cannot justifiably be used as a criterion of the ability of races except under rare and peculiar circumstances.[1]

Cooley answered Galton's hereditarian views with brilliant arguments from history that I cannot outline in detail here. He showed how the Greeks, without any radical changes in genetic makeup, suddenly produced a host of famous men in the age of Pericles. Similarly, in Renaissance Italy, the same native stock produced no famous artists in the twelfth century, seven in the thirteenth, seven in the fourteenth and thirty-eight in the fifteenth, including Leonardo, Titian, Michelangelo, and Raphael. Likewise, in the century beginning in 1550 when London was a town of some 150,000 souls, England produced a group of famous men, including Shakespeare, Raleigh, Bacon, Milton, Hobbes, and Newton (as well as John Winthrop and William Penn). Finally, he showed how America's first literary renaissance occurred within a generation of the nation's founding, quoting John B. McMaster.

> Irving was not a year old when peace was declared. Cooper was born the same year Washington went into office. Halleck one year later. Prescott, in the year Washington came out of office. The Constitution was five years old when Bryant was born. The first year of the present century witnessed the birth of Bancroft, and, before another decade had come and gone, Emerson was born, and Willis, and Longfellow, and Whittier, and Holmes, and Hawthorne, and Poe. . . . Scarcely a twelvemonth went by unmarked by the birth of a man since renowned in the domain of letters—1783, 1789, 1790, 1791, 1794, 1795, 1796, 1800, 1803, 1806, 1807, 1808, 1809, 1811, 1814, such is the almost unbroken succession.[2]

Surely, Cooley argued, historical and social conditions, not sudden genetic changes, produced these four creative ages in Western history.

My theory of social causation is far closer to Cooley's than to Galton's. In fact, I tend to lean even further toward the psychological and subjective in arguing that religious values largely governed the social and historical differences between Boston and Philadelphia. And the analysis of *DAB* biographies clearly shows that the production of famous men in the two cities was as discrepant as that between twelfth- and fifteenth-century Italy. It is hard to believe that the native endowments of the Boston sample were so superior to those of the Philadelphians as to cause such extremes in achievement. There is, nevertheless, a possibility that the Bostonians were hereditarily superior. But how can this superiority be measured?

Perhaps most of us, regardless of our views on social causation, would admit that life span has more to do with heredity than with either environment or religious values. In order to test this hypothesis, I took the average life span of 142 Philadelphia men (of the total sample of 146: three were women, and one man was killed in the Revolution) and compared it with that of 179 Bostonians (six of the sample of 188 were women, one man was killed in the Revolution, and two in the Civil War). The Boston men lived, on the average, about two years longer: 71.988 years versus 70.007. This is certainly not a great difference. However, if we take the thirteen Bostonians whose *DAB* biographies ran to more than 500 lines and compare them with the thirteen leading Philadelphians, whose biographies ran to more than 200 lines (none over 350), the difference in life span is striking:

BOSTON AND PHILADELPHIA FIRST FAMILIES:
Eminent Elite Members by Number of Lines in the *DAB* and Life Span

Boston	Lines in *DAB*	Life Span	Philadelphia	Lines in *DAB*	Life Span
O. W. Holmes, Jr.	1,124	94	Horace Binney	202	95
C. W. Eliot	838	92	H. C. Carey	205	86
John Adams	1,056	91	S. W. Mitchell	349	85
A. L. Lowell	625	87	H. C. Lea	291	84
O. W. Holmes	726	85	Thomas McKean	275	83
J. Q. Adams	1,033	81	J. A. Montgomery	224	83
Samuel Adams	685	81	Richard Rush	287	79
Henry Adams	718	80	Benjamin Rush	347	68
Charles F. Adams	866	79	George Boker	323	67
R. W. Emerson	988	79	G. G. Meade	250	57
H. W. Longfellow	501	75	Thomas Mifflin	212	56
J. R. Lowell	683	72	William Pepper	287	55
J. L. R. Agassiz	886	66	F. Hopkinson	220	54
Total Lines	10,729			3,472	
Average Life Span		81.69			73.23

There does, then, seem to be a positive relationship between fame and longevity. In terms of life span, the Boston males were slightly superior to the Philadelphians and the truly eminent men were clearly superior. Nevertheless, I think it may legitimately be argued, especially in the case of the thirteen eminent Bostonians, that life span may have a lot to do with one's desire to live; hence, perhaps the more one accomplishes in life, the greater one's will to live. George Ticknor, for instance, died in 1871 at the age of eighty; Sidney Fisher died the same year at sixty-two. Assuming hereditary equality, Ticknor's life of positive accomplishment and Fisher's pronounced tendency toward disparagement might very well have contributed to their differences in life span. Perhaps Nicholas Biddle, the Philadelphia banker who died in financial disgrace at the age of fifty-eight, might have lived to a ripe old age had he chosen the career of statesman or author. The longevity of the thirteen eminent Bostonians, in other words, may have resulted at least partly from their living in a stimulating environment of accomplishment. All this may seem to be a rather slim argument, but let us look further.

It is important to make the point that the family, and not the class or the race, is the hereditary unit in society. Admittedly, the men in the Boston and Philadelphia samples came from two small, much intermarried, and thus fairly homogeneous genetic groups of families. But let us look at the family variations within these two samples:

BOSTON AND PHILADELPHIA FIRST FAMILIES WITH FIVE OR MORE MEMBERS IN THE *DAB*:
Average Male Life Span

Boston	Members in *DAB*	Life Span	Philadelphia	Members in *DAB*	Life Span
Peabody	5	83.4	Meigs	5	71.2
Adams	7	81.6	Coxe	6	70.66
Higginson	5	78.8	Wharton	6	67.5
Cabot	5	71.6	Meade	5	59.4
Lawrence	5	71.4	Cadwalader	4	67.5[1]
Appleton	5	70.8	Biddle	3	65.6
Winthrop	6	70.0			
Ware	6	66.7			
Phillips	5	65.4			
Ames	9	66.1			
Lowell	11	62.1			
Emerson	5	58.2			

[1]The Biddle and Cadwalader families were included here so they may be compared with the Cabots and the Lowells.

This table lists the twelve Boston and four Philadelphia families with five or more members in the *DAB*, arranged according to average life span. Again, the Boston group was superior. It is also of interest that the Meigs family, of New England roots, was the most long-lived of the Philadelphia group, while Horace Binney, of New England stock, was the longest lived of the eminent Philadelphians.

Within the Boston group of families, the Peabodys and Adamses were long-lived whereas the Lowells and Emersons were not. However, the more eminent Emersons and Lowells—Ralph Waldo Emerson, Abbot Lawrence, and James Russell Lowell—were all long-lived. Was it success and the zest for life or hereditary superiority that distinguished them from the other members of their own families?

No final answer is possible here. At the very least one needs a wider sample; one might, for example, take all the members of the 100 Boston and Philadelphia families and see whether those in the *DAB* were longer lived than their siblings. A test case of this hypothesis may be made of the Adamses, by all odds both Boston's and America's First Family.

Included in the *DAB* were the following ten descendants of the original Henry Adams of Braintree (in addition to the 7 Boston and Braintree Adamses).

John (1772–1863), principal of Andover Academy, where he taught Josiah Quincy and Oliver Wendell Holmes, among others. . . . His son William (1807–1880) was a Presbyterian clergyman, one of the founders of Union Theological Seminary (1836) and later president (1874). He was often rated the leading Presbyterian clergyman of his time. Alvin (1804–1877), of Watertown, Massachusetts, founded the Adams Express Company, capitalized at $100,000 in 1854 and a competitor of Wells Fargo and American Express. Charles Baker (1814–1853), Andover, Yale, and a graduate of Amherst (head of his class, which had Henry

Ward Beecher at the foot), spent his life as professor of history and astronomy at Amherst. Dudley W. (1831–1897), horticulturist, one of the founders of the National Grange of the Patrons of Husbandry (1873). Hannah (1755–1831), historian, antiquarian, and compiler of dictionaries. Herbert Baxter (1850–1901), head of his class at Amherst (1872), Ph.D. Heidelberg (1876), and then professor at the newly opened Johns Hopkins University; founded Johns Hopkins Studies in Historical and Political Science and the American Historical Association (1884); an organizer and teacher of great energy, rather than a scholar. Jasper (1793–1841), first president of Hobart College (1826). John Coleman (1849–1922), Universalist clergyman and author. William Taylor (1822–1897), author.*

These kin of the Boston Adamses were surely an intellectually distinguished group although less eminent than their Boston relations. Accordingly, one would expect them to be shorter lived, and the average life span of the nine males in the group was 65.4 years (compared to 81.6 of the 7 Boston Adamses).

That there is no simple answer to the parts played by heredity and environment in character formation is clearly illustrated by the history of the Boston Adams family. Great hereditary gifts they had in abundance. At the same time, of all American families, none took so seriously the Puritan emphasis on magisterial calling. Only the Adamses have as yet produced a father and son who both filled the highest magisterial position in the nation. The Boston family founder, John, who suffered from anxiety, self-doubt, and fear of failure, was forever driven on by the spur of fame and an inner sense of his own destiny. He and his wife, Abigail, a "disciple of Wollstonecraft," according to her husband, instilled in their family a magisterial myth that made no allowances for what their eldest son, John Quincy, once called the "intermediate stations" in life. As their grandson Charles Francis, who could hardly bear "the constant references in connection with himself to the first two Adamses," put it: "If it were not that I was under the perpetual stimulus of family pride, I would never have mixed in politics."[3] And he himself perpetuated the heavy hand of family pressure on the fourth generation: "In plain language, I do not like my own father," wrote Charles Francis II; "he had a stern not generous, kindly or sympathetic nature," he continued, "self-contained, introspective, Puritanic in the English, and virtuous in the Roman, sense. . . . It never occurred to him that he might have been wrong or pursued an unfriendly course to his children, though he at times even late in life, inflicted on me frightful mortifications."[4] Understandably, this Adams in the fourth generation, as we have seen, repudiated the filiopietistic school of Massachusetts historians.

In a perceptive article on "The Youth of John Quincy Adams," David F. Musto showed how the Adams family myth caused a temporary nervous collapse in young John Quincy Adams.[5] Educated at home for the first twelve years of his life, largely by his mother, he was instructed along the lines of most boys of his time and class but also, as his mother phrased it, to be her own "hero and statesman." After six lonely years abroad, during which time his associations were mostly with famous elders, he returned to Harvard, where he had his first sustained peer relationships. Although Adams made a few close

---

*All these names, and the brief facts, are to be found in the *DAB*.

friends, he seemed aloof and self-contained to most of his classmates. In careful character sketches of each of his fifty classmates, he mentioned twice as many negative as positive characteristics. In his relations with women he was quick to note any deviations from "proper" female passivity, and he chose a wife with characteristics the very opposite from his mother's.

Though John Quincy Adams would have preferred a life of letters, family pressure sent him to study law in the office of Theophilus Parsons of Newburyport. In the course of his legal apprenticeship, Adams suffered a nervous collapse that forced him to drop his studies and undergo a complete rest, first at the home of his Aunt Elizabeth Shaw in Haverhill and then at the family place in Braintree, where he got to know his father.

Though Adams was able in the long run to thrive under the pressure of the family myth, his two brothers were not: Charles died in disgrace at the age of thirty and Thomas Boylston, "an often melancholy and irresponsible man," died at sixty; both were alcoholics. Moreover, "The burden of the myth upon the eldest of John Quincy Adams' sons," wrote Musto,

> had tragic consequences in 1829. Like his father, John Quincy had been defeated in reelection. Also in accordance with his father's judgment and example, John Quincy was not expected to return to Braintree to live in respectable retirement. His eldest son, George Washington Adams, then twenty-seven, started south to help his parents move to Massachusetts, but on the way to Washington, after giving evidence of psychotic, paranoid delusions, committed suicide. The prospect of the myth's burden was intolerable. The next eldest, John Adams II, simply chose not to enter politics and managed an unsuccessful grist mill along Rock Creek in Washington, D.C. He died at the age of thirty-one.[6]

The Adams myth, born of the Puritan ethic and intensified by the family's fascination with classical Rome, was a spur to fame for the strong, and failure for the weak, all within the same family. No wonder Henry Adams found the doctrine of natural selection appealing. But I believe it is the myths men live by, rather than either their genes or their social milieus, that determine individual fame or failure.

Cooley opened his article on fame and genius by arguing that

> genius is that aptitude for greatness that is born in a man; fame is the recognition by men that greatness has been achieved. Between the two lie nurture and training, schools, the influence of friends and books, opportunities, and, in short, the whole working of organized society upon the individual. One is biological, the other is social; to produce genius is the function of race, to allot fame is the function of history.[7]

Though I do not dismiss the possibility of hereditary superiority in Boston's upper class as against that of Philadelphia, I think that the disparity in the production of famous men between the two cities can be explained largely by their very different histories.

Brahmin Relatives as Leaders and Founders of Towns across the Nation

Although the Mather pulpit dynasty died out in Boston at the time of the Revolution, the family has continued to play leadership roles in other communities down to the present day. Richard Mather had four sons who were clergymen, and twenty-eight of his direct descendants in the male line and fifty-two in the female line held pulpits at various towns in Connecticut, New York, Ohio, Michigan, Wisconsin, and Minnesota in the nineteenth century. The Reverend Charles Backus Storrs, direct descendant in the fifth generation, was the first president of Western Reserve College in Cleveland. The Mathers from Connecticut, moreover, were original stockholders in the Connecticut Land Company, which settled the Western Reserve on the south shore of Lake Erie.

In addition to the four Boston generations included in my sample, there were six other Mathers listed in the *DAB* who were descendants of Richard Mather. Three of them were instrumental in building the city of Cleveland: Samuel Livingston Mather (1817–1890) and his son, Samuel Mather (1851–1931), and their kinsman, Samuel Holmes Mather (1813–1894).

Samuel Livingston Mather (1817–1890) was the grandson of Samuel Mather, an original stockholder in the Connecticut Land Company. Upon graduation from Wesleyan College in his hometown of Middletown, Connecticut, he went to Cleveland to supervise the family's interests there. Although he first became a member of the local bar, the discovery of iron ore along Lake Superior determined his career. As president of the Cleveland Iron Mining Company and director of numerous other companies, Mather had more to do with the building of Cleveland's industrial leadership than any other man.

Samuel Mather carried on the family interests in business and, in the New England tradition, also took the lead in local civic, religious, and cultural affairs. For forty-five years he was a trustee and vice-president of Western Reserve College and a generous benefactor of Episcopalian Kenyon College. His main passion was the church: he was senior warden of Trinity Cathedral and a member of the National Council of the Episcopal Church. In the Mather tradition, "his vigorous, dominating personality impressed all who were associated with him."[1] His son, Samuel Livingston Mather II, was listed in *Who's Who* in 1940 and is still carrying on the family traditions in Cleveland.

Samuel Holmes Mather, kin and contemporary of Samuel Livingston Mather moved to Cleveland after graduating from Dartmouth. He founded the Cleveland Society for Savings, "a benevolent institution, without capital, managed by trustees without salary, in the interest of depositors only, to whom profits were paid, for whose benefit they are accumulated and reserved."[2] Under Mather's direction the society became a powerful conservative force in the local banking community; by the time of his death, one-sixth of the citizens of Cleveland had accounts there. Samuel Holmes Mather's main avocation (like that of his Episcopalian kinsman) was the church; he was prominent as a benefactor and an elder of the Second Presbyterian Church.

Three other Mathers played important enough roles in our nation to be listed in the *DAB*: Stephen Tyng Mather (1867–1930), a conservationist of national reputation, was the first director of the National Park Service, established in 1916. Fred Mather (1833–1900) was a leading pisciculturist, writer on outdoor life and conservation, and member of the United States Fish Commission at its founding in 1872. He did a great deal in preserving the Adirondacks (where Emerson and Saturday Club friends were frequent hikers and campers). Finally, William Williams Mather (1804–1859) was a geologist who ended his active career as professor and acting president of Ohio University at Athens.

The point to be made and stressed here is that the Winthrops and the Mathers were not only the founders of a tradition of class authority in Boston that was carried down throughout our national period by such families as the Adamses, Lowells, and Cabots; they were also leaders outside Boston in all areas of national life (church, education, business, and government) for three centuries, a record unsurpassed by any other families in American history.

Other Boston First Families followed in their footsteps in spreading the Puritan tradition of authority and community building throughout the nation. One is struck with the number of members of the Boston sample of families who were listed in the *DAB* from elsewhere. Thus, a grandfather of T. S. Eliot, William Greenleaf Eliot (1811–1887), was the Benjamin Franklin of early St. Louis. As president of the school board, he "permanently established the financial foundations of the public school system of St. Louis."[3] He founded Washington University and a host of other cultural and charitable institutions. His children and grandchildren not only carried on his traditions in St. Louis but also went west and became leaders in the building of Portland, Oregon.

The Putnams, like the Eliots, also became community builders outside their home state. James Osborne Putnam (1818–1903), lawyer and diplomat, was the Benjamin Franklin of his beloved Buffalo, New York, where he founded the Historical Society, the Fine Arts Academy, and a host of other institutions, including the University of Buffalo in 1846. He was a University trustee for thirty-two years and unpaid chancellor for the last seven years of his life. Another New York Putnam, Gideon (1763–1812), was the founder of Saratoga Springs. A third pioneer, Rufus Putnam (1738–1824), was appointed surveyor general of the United States and a judge of the Northwest Territory by George Washington; he was one of the founders of Marietta, Ohio.

Colonel Thomas Handasyd Perkins, acknowledged king of the merchant princes of his day in Boston, not only founded his own family but also launched a good many of other First Family founders in the city: Cabots, Lodges, Forbeses, Appletons, Coolidges, Parkmans, and others not in my sample, according to Cleveland Amory, "all owe something of their fortunes to the great 'Long Tom' as he was first called in Salem."[4] Some of his descendants went west and others east to Wall Street to seek their fortunes. One nephew, James Handasyd Perkins (1810–1849), was a cultural leader in Cincinnati. Admitted to the bar in 1834, he was repulsed by the practice of law, which offended his ethical standards; he became minister at large for the Cincinnati Congregational Society, a Unitarian body. He was founder and first president of the Historical Society of Ohio (1844) and the Historical and Philosophical Society (1849). Another James Handasyd Perkins (1876–1940) was chairman of the board of the National City Bank and a director of numerous banks, insurance companies, and industrial corporations during the depression.

The bare quantitative evidence of my *DAB* sample only begins to indicate the tremendous achievements of the members of the fifty Boston First Families both in creating a powerful class authority in Boston and in carrying their inherited ideals of authority and community building to towns all over the West and to the centers of national power on Wall Street and, with the Adamses, on Pennsylvania Avenue.

A Brief History of Swarthmore College

Swarthmore College (the first coeducational college on the east coast) was founded by Hicksite Friends as a preparatory school and college in 1869.[1] The pattern of leadership at Swarthmore is relevant to my thesis in that discipline and authority were major problems in the early years, as well as in the late 1960s and early 1970s. The first president of the college, a distinguished Philadelphia Hicksite, was forced to resign after two years because of his inability to maintain discipline. He was replaced by Edward Hicks Magill, the first builder of the college, who had been hired as principal of the preparatory school in 1869. When Magill came to Swarthmore he had already spent twenty years as an educator in New England, at the Providence High School and the Boston Latin School. Born on a farm in Bucks County (kin of the primitive painter Edward Hicks), he attended Westtown before earnings degrees at Yale and Brown. Magill remained as president until his retirement in 1889; by this time, the preparatory department enrolled only one-third of the students and was done away with three years later. Between 1889 and 1902, of the four men elected to the presidency, only three served, each for a more or less brief period. The board finally decided to go outside Pennsylvania for leadership and chose an Indiana Friend, Joseph Swain, then president of Indiana University. Swain agreed to come to Swarthmore only after obtaining from the managers and the faculty a firm agreement as to his ultimate authority. And he authoritatively built up a predominantly Quaker college of fun, fraternities, and football, emphasizing engineering and science rather than the humanities (thought more appropriate to guarded education). In 1916, Swarthmore beat both Penn and Columbia in football, which pleased Isaac H. Clothier, Hicksite partner in the department store Strawbridge & Clothier and Swarthmore board member—the Clothier Memorial Tower dominates the modern campus. Swain increased the school's endowment from $400,000 in 1902 to $3 million at his retirement in 1920, leaving Swarthmore with the third largest endowment per student, after Haverford and Bryn Mawr, in the state of Pennsylvania. At the last commencement under Swain, A. Mitchell Palmer and Drew Pearson held center stage; both these distinguished Swarthmorians later became paranoid crusaders on the side of righteousness, if from different points on the political compass.

Another gentleman from Indiana, Frank Aydelotte, was the real builder of modern Swarthmore. He was no Quaker but a staunch Presbyterian and an anglophile elitist with degrees from Indiana, Harvard, and Oxford. The predominantly anti-intellectual managers got far more than they had bargained for. A Rhodes Scholar himself and secretary of the Rhodes scholarship committee in the United States for thirty-five years, Aydelotte was determined to place the Oxford stamp of intellectual elitism, as he understood it, on American education. He introduced the famous honors program at Swarthmore, deemphasized sports, fraternities, sororities (abolished in 1934), and the powerful men's secret society, Book and Key (modeled on Yale's Skull and Bones). He also brought highly motivated and intellectual students, regardless of background or religion, to the college (by his retirement, less than one-fourth of the undergraduates were Quakers). Though backed by a majority of his faculty, Aydelotte retired in 1940, somewhat tired of alumni criticism, to become the second director of the Institute for Advanced Study at Princeton.

Aydelotte was followed in the presidency by two other Rhodes Scholars. John W. Nason was a native of Minnesota and a graduate of Carleton, Harvard, and Oxford. He was followed, in 1952, by Courtney Smith, a native Iowan and a Harvard man, who in January 1969 had a fatal heart attack while negotiating with dissident student leaders.

By the 1960s Swarthmore had become a highly intellectual but lonely and anomic campus. In his policy of intellectual elitism, Aydelotte had unwittingly atomized the student body, a process described by Everett Lee Hunt in *The Revolt of the College Intellectual*.[2] The book was not widely read, yet it is a brilliant and perceptive predictor of the anomie and student unrest that marked elite campuses all over America in the 1960s. Hunt, who had spent his career at Swarthmore and was dean of men for many years, takes the reader step by unsensational step through the Aydelotte reform years and shows their atomizing consequences. What Aydelotte, though not Hunt, failed to see was that his elitism at Swarthmore was individualistic and antinomian whereas that of Oxford was intellectual within a context of strong class cohesion. In light of Hunt's book, it should be noted that two of Aydelotte's students at Swarthmore, Clark Kerr and James A. Perkins, were presidents of the University of California at Berkeley, and Cornell, respectively, when campus unrest began in 1963. Both were eventually forced to resign because of their inability to maintain authority on their campuses.

Law and Science

It would be fair to say that lawyers as a profession traditionally have been in-volved with the problems of order and authority, whereas scientists have been seeking universal truths, which in the long run tend to be corrosive of any par-ticularistic authorities. We might accordingly expect the sons of the privileged to be attracted to the law; the sons of the deprived, to science. In *Origins of American Scientists*, R. H. Knapp and H.B. Goodrich developed a productivity index based on the proportion of male graduates (1924–1934) of various institu-tions of higher learning in America who were later listed in *American Men of Science*. Harvard College, then educating a high proportion of sons of privilege, had a productivity index of 18.4; two small colleges for less privileged sons of Massachusetts, Massachusetts State (now the University of Massachusetts) and Clark University, had productivity indexes of 55.6 and 39.0, respectively.[1]

The Harvard Law School has been the leading producer of America's legal elite for several generations, and a large proportion of its students have been drawn from Harvard College and a few other select institutions such as Yale and Princeton. As we are interested here primarily in the values of Puritanism and Quakerism, let us take a look at the contrasting attitudes toward law and science at three Quaker colleges, Swarthmore, Haverford, and Earlham, as against Williams, Amherst, and Bowdoin, three small colleges founded in the early nineteenth century in a conservative reaction to Harvard's liberal Unitarianism. If we assume that attendance at the Harvard Law School reflects hierarchical–authoritarian values and a high productivity index of scientists more egalitarian–universalistic values, the following figures for 1924–1934 are revealing:

College	Harvard Law School Graduates	Productivity Index of American Scientists
Williams	420	9
Amherst	272	22
Bowdoin	174	15
Swarthmore	43	30
Haverford	41	40
Earlham	13	58

Source: The law figures were obtained from the Harvard Law School catalogues for the years 1924–1934 by my former student Jeffrey Jacobs.

Knapp and Goodrich tried to explain why Williams and Haverford, both colleges with high endowments per student and with rather privileged WASP student bodies, had such different productivity indexes. Needless to say, they were not much interested in the religious origins of the two colleges. I suggest that Haverford was an anomaly largely because of its Quaker roots, whereas Williams was an anomaly both because of its religious roots and because of its president, Harry Augustus Garfield, who ruled the college with an iron hand, in the style of Eliot, Lowell, Henry Coit, and Endicott Peabody, between 1908 and 1934.

President James A. Garfield, whose first ancestor in America came to Massachusetts with the Winthrop fleet, grew up in relative poverty on the Western Reserve frontier but finally saved enough money to attend Williams College. He sent his son, Harry, to St. Paul's School and then to Williams College. After Williams, Harry taught Latin and Roman history at St. Paul's, went to the Columbia Law School and All Souls College, Oxford, and read law in London at the Inns of Court. After taking a chair in political science at Princeton at his friend Woodrow Wilson's urging, he went to Williams as president in 1908. And he surely brought to Williams the British values of class authority and responsibility, which he shared with A. Lawrence Lowell and Woodrow Wilson. Garfield sent his Williams students to law school to prepare them for a tradition, to paraphrase Wilson of Princeton, of "Williams in service of the Nation."[2]

By and large, Earlham remains very much a Quaker college. Swarthmore and Haverford in the 1960's had a small proportion of Quaker students and suffered from more than the average amount of antinomianism. In the years between 1924 and 1934, however, they were still essentially Quaker both in students and in values, with a large majority of students from upper middle-class and WASP families.

Notes

CHAPTER 1. A Problem Defined

1. Alexis de Tocqueville, *Democracy in America* (New York: Knopf, 1945), Vol. II, pp. 247–248 (italics added).
2. Walter Lippmann, *A Preface to Morals* (New York: Macmillan, 1929), pp. 66–67.
3. John W. Gardner, *Excellence: Can We Be Equal and Excellent, Too?* (New York: Harper, 1961), pp. 13–14.
4. John W. Gardner, "The Antileadership Vaccine," *Princeton Alumni Weekly*, Vol. LXVI, No. 29 (1966), p. 27.
5. Charles S. Syndor, *American Revolutionaries in the Making* (New York: Free Press, 1952), p. 112.
6. Perry Miller, *Orthodoxy in Massachusetts, 1630–1650* (Boston: Beacon, 1959), pp. xi–xii.
7. H. Richard Niebuhr, *The Kingdom of God in America* (Hamden: Shoe String, 1956), p. 43.
8. Samuel Eliot Morison, *The Intellectual Life of Colonial New England* (Ithaca: Cornell University Press, Great Seal Books, 1956), pp. 5–6.

517

9. Henry Adams, *The United States in 1800* (Ithaca: Cornell University Press, Great Seal Books, 1961), p. 54.
10. Ibid., p. 83.
11. Ibid., pp. 82–83; italics added.
12. Gardner, "Antileadership Vaccine," pp. 27–28.
13. Tocqueville, p. 133.
14. Catherine Drinker Bowen, *Yankee from Olympus: Justice Holmes and His Family* (Boston: Little, Brown, 1944), p. 417.
15. Barnie F. Winkelman, *John G. Johnson: Lawyer and Art Collector, 1841–1917* (Philadelphia: University of Pennsylvania Press, 1942), p. 285.
16. *New York Times*, April 15, 1917.
17. Winkelman, p. 74.
18. Ibid., p. 187.
19. *Who Was Who in America, 1897–1942* (Chicago: Marquis, 1942), p. 582a.
20. Bowen, p. 285.
21. Ibid., p. 361.
22. Ibid., p. 370.
23. Ibid., p. 219.
24. Ibid., p. 253.
25. *Dictionary of American Biography*, 20 vols. (New York: Scribner's, 1927–1972), Supp. I, p. 426a; hereafter cited *DAB*.
26. Winkelman, p. 283.

CHAPTER 2. Privileged and Ruling Classes

1. E. Digby Baltzell, *Philadelphia Gentlemen: The Making of a National Upper Class* (New York: Free Press, 1958), p. 5.
2. E. Digby Baltzell, *The Protestant Establishment: Aristocracy and Caste in America* (New York: Vintage, 1966), pp. 380–381.
3. Włodzimierz Wesołowski, "Some Notes on the Functional Theory of Stratification," in Reinhard Bendix and Seymour Martin Lipset, eds., *Class, Status, and Power* (New York: Free Press, 1966), pp. 68–69; italics added.
4. Hans Gerth and C. Wright Mills, eds., *From Max Weber: Essays in Sociology* (New York: Oxford University Press, 1946), pp. 84–86.
5. Ibid., p. 93; italics added.
6. George W. Pierson, *Yale College, 1921–1937* (New Haven: Yale University Press, 1955), p. 596.
7. Alexis de Tocqueville, *The Old Régime and the French Revolution*, trans. Stuart Gilbert (New York: Doubleday, Anchor Books, 1955), p. xiii.
8. Reinhold Niebuhr, *The Self and the Dramas of History* (New York: Scribner's, 1955), p. 184.
9. Scott Greer, "Metropolitan Anomie and the Crisis in Leadership," in E. Digby Baltzell, ed., *The Search for Community in Modern America* (New York: Harper & Row, 1968), p. 158.

10. Daniel Boorstin, *The Americans: The Colonial Experience* (New York: Random House, 1958), p. 244.
11. Ibid., p. 245.
12. Ralph Linton, *The Study of Man* (New York: Appleton-Century, 1936), p. 111.
13. Zoltán Haraszti, *John Adams and the Prophets of Progress* (Cambridge: Harvard University Press, 1952), p. 230.
14. Ibid.

CHAPTER 3. Boston Brahmins and Philadelphia Gentlemen

1. Cleveland Amory, *The Proper Bostonians* (New York: Dutton, 1947), p. 166.
2. *DAB*, Vol. XX, p. xvii.
3. Martin Green, *The Problem of Boston: Some Readings in Cultural History* (New York: Norton, 1966), p. 82.
4. Ibid., p. 90.
5. Ibid., p. 41.
6. *DAB*, Vol. XIX, p. 528a.
7. Owen Wister, Introduction to Thomas Wharton, *Bobo and Other Fancies* (New York: Harper, 1897), p. xiv.
8. John A. Schutz and Douglas Adair, ed., *The Spur of Fame: Dialogues of John Adams and Benjamin Rush, 1805-1813* (San Marino: Huntington Library, 1966), p. 237.
9. *DAB*, Suppl. I, p. 609a.
10. Amory, p. 63.
11. Nicholas B. Wainwright, ed., *A Philadelphia Perspective: The Diary of Sidney George Fisher Covering the Years 1834-1871* (Philadelphia: Historical Society of Pennsylvania, 1967), pp. 280-281.
12. Ibid., p. iii.
13. Ibid., p. 158.
14. Thomas Payne Govan, *Nicholas Biddle: Nationalist and Public Banker, 1786-1844* (Chicago: University of Chicago Press, 1959), p. 410.
15. Nathaniel Burt, *The Perennial Philadelphians* (Boston: Little, Brown, 1963), p. 58.
16. Amory, p. 12.
17. Marian Lawrence Peabody, *To Be Young Was Very Heaven* (Boston: Houghton Mifflin, 1967), p. 361.
18. Ibid.
19. Anthony Richard Wagner, *English Genealogy* (New York: Oxford University Press, 1972), p. 282.
20. James Truslow Adams, *The Adams Family* (New York: Blue Ribbon, 1930), p. 67.
21. Charles Francis Adams II, *Massachusetts, Its Historians, and Its History: An Object Lesson* (Freeport: Books for Libraries, 1971), pp. 64-65.
22. Ibid., pp. 83-84.

23. Frederick Ives Carpenter, *Emerson Handbook* (New York: Hendricks House, 1953), p. 159.
24. George W. Pierson, *Tocqueville and Beaumont in America* (New York: Oxford University Press, 1938), p. 423.
25. Nathaniel Hawthorne, *The Scarlet Letter*, in Norman H. Pearson, ed., *The Complete Novels and Selected Tales of Nathaniel Hawthorne* (New York: Modern Library, 1937), p. 89.
26. T. S. Eliot, "Gentlemen and Seamen [May 1909]," in Donald Hall, ed., *The Harvard Advocate Anthology* (Freeport: Books for Libraries, 1970), p. 109.
27. M. A. DeWolfe Howe, *Boston: The Place and the People* (New York: Macmillan, 1903), p. 7.
28. Charles Francis Adams II, p. 61.
29. Ibid., pp. 61–62.

CHAPTER 4. Reformation England

1. James Joll, *The Anarchists* (New York: Grosset & Dunlap), p. 18.
2. R. H. Tawney, *Religion and the Rise of Capitalism* (New York: Harcourt, 1926), p. 90.
3. Roland H. Bainton, *Studies in the Reformation* (Boston: Beacon, 1966), p. 129.
4. Ernst Troeltsch, *The Social Teaching of the Christian Churches* (New York: Harper, Harper Torchbooks, 1960), Vol. II, p. 581.
5. Michael Walzer, *The Revolution of the Saints: A Study in the Origins of Radical Politics* (Cambridge: Harvard University Press, 1965), p. 33.
6. Ibid., p. 35.
7. Ibid., p. 87.
8. Ibid., p. 113.
9. Ibid., p. 96.
10. Christopher Hill, *Society and Puritanism in Pre-Revolutionary England* (London: Secker & Warburg, 1964), p. 240.
11. *DAB*, Suppl. IV, p. 784a.
12. Walzer, p. 264.
13. Lawrence Stone, *The Crisis of the Aristocracy, 1558–1641* (New York: Oxford University Press, 1967), p. 113.
14. Ibid., p. 109.
15. Ibid., p. 312.
16. E. W. Ives, ed., *The English Revolution, 1600–1660* (New York: Barnes & Noble, 1968), p. 112.
17. Ibid., p. 116.
18. Stone, p. 310.
19. Samuel Eliot Morison, *The Founding of Harvard College* (Cambridge: Harvard University Press, 1935), p. 54.
20. Mark H. Curtis, "The Alienated Intellectuals of Early Stuart England," in

Trevor Aston, ed., *Crisis in Europe, 1560–1660* (New York: Basic Books, 1965), p. 295.

21. Christopher Hill, *Intellectual Origins of the English Revolution* (Oxford: Clarendon, 1965), p. 112.
22. Ibid.
23. A. L. Rowse, *The England of Elizabeth* (New York: Macmillan, 1951), p. 307.
24. Max Weber, *The Protestant Ethic and the Spirit of Capitalism* (New York: Scribner's, 1958), p. 116.
25. Christopher Hill, *Puritanism and Revolution: Studies in Interpretation of the English Revolution of the 17th Century* (London: Secker & Warburg, 1965), pp. 215–216.
26. Edmund S. Morgan, ed., *Puritan Political Ideas, 1558–1794* (Indianapolis: Bobbs-Merrill, 1965), p. 37.
27. Ibid., p. 36.
28. Ibid., p. 51.
29. Ibid., p. 37.
30. David Little, *Religion, Order, and Law* (New York: Harper & Row, Harper Torchbooks, 1969), p. 119.
31. Ibid., p. 121.
32. Ibid., p. 126.
33. Ibid., p. 109.
34. Ibid., p. 111.
35. Morgan, p. 39; italics added.
36. Walzer, p. 307.
37. Morgan, p. xvii.
38. Little, p. 119.

CHAPTER 5. The Puritan Revolution and the Rise of Quakerism

1. C. V. Wedgewood, *The King's Peace, 1637–1641* (New York: Macmillan, 1955), p. 21.
2. E. W. Ives, ed., *The English Revolution, 1600–1660* (New York: Barnes & Noble, 1968), p. 93.
3. Charles Blitzer, ed., *The Commonwealth of England: Documents of the English Civil Wars; The Commonwealth and Protectorate, 1641–1660* (New York: Putnam, Capricorn Books, 1963), pp. 21–22.
4. Christopher Hill, *Puritanism and Revolution: Studies in Interpretation of the English Revolution of the 17th Century* (London: Secker & Warburg, 1965), p. 206.
5. Christopher Hill, *The Century of Revolution, 1603–1714* (New York: Norton, 1961), p. 131.
6. Christopher Hill, *Intellectual Origins of the English Revolution* (Oxford: Clarendon, 1965), p. 5.
7. Ibid., p. 9.

8. Hill, *Puritanism and Revolution*, pp. 209–210.

9. Ibid., p. 211.

10. Ernst Troeltsch, *The Social Teaching of the Christian Churches* (New York: Harper, Harper Torchbooks, 1960), Vol. II, p. 781.

11. Hugh Barbour, *The Quakers in Puritan England* (New Haven: Yale University Press, 1964), p. 39.

12. Ibid., p. 234.

13. George Sabine, ed., *The Works of Gerrard Winstanley, with an Appendix of Documents Relating to the Digger Movement* (Ithaca: Cornell University Press, 1941), p. 238.

14. Ibid., p. 273.

15. Ibid., pp. 663–664.

16. William C. Braithwaite, *The Beginnings of Quakerism*, rev. Henry J. Cadbury (Cambridge: At the University Press, 1961), p. 29.

17. Ibid., p. 79.

18. George Seldes, *The Great Quotations* (New York: Lyle Stuart, 1960), p. 475.

19. Keith Thomas, "Women and the Civil War Sects," in Trevor Aston, ed., *Crisis in Europe 1560–1660* (New York: Basic Books, 1965), p. 328.

20. Mabel R. Brailsford, *Quaker Women, 1650–1690* (London: Duckworth, 1915), p. 34.

21. Ibid., p. 100.

22. Ibid., p. 108.

23. Ibid., p. 111.

24. Barbour, pp. 134–135.

25. John Sykes, *The Quakers* (Philadelphia: Lippincott, 1959), pp. 147–148.

26. Braithwaite, p. 61.

27. *DAB*, Vol. XIV, p. 131*a*.

28. Sykes, p. 111.

29. Ibid.

30. Ibid.

31. Braithwaite, p. 266.

32. Frederick B. Tolles, *Quakers and the Atlantic Culture* (New York: Macmillan, 1960), p. 38.

33. Isabel Ross, *Margaret Fell: Mother of Quakerism* (London: Longmans, Green, 1949), p. 5.

34. Ibid., p. 214.

CHAPTER 6. Puritan and Quaker Patterns
of Culture

1. Samuel Eliot Morison, *By Land and by Sea* (New York: Knopf, 1954), p. 227.

2. Max Weber, *The Protestant Ethic and the Spirit of Capitalism* (New York: Scribner's, 1958), p. 121.

3. Ibid., p. 150.

4. Ibid., p. 99.

5. Barrett Wendell, *A Literary History of America* (New York: Scribner's, 1900), pp. 16–17.

6. D. Elton Trueblood, *The People Called Quakers* (New York: Harper & Row, 1966), p. 153.

7. Ibid., p. 167.

8. Werner Stark, *The Sociology of Religion: A Study of Christendom*, Vol. II: *Sectarian Religion* (New York: Fordham University Press, 1967), p. 148.

CHAPTER 7. The Founding of Massachusetts
and Pennsylvania

1. Hannah Benner Roach, "The Planting of Philadelphia: A Seventeenth-Century Real Estate Development," *Pennsylvania Magazine*, Vol. XCII, Nos. 1, 2 (1968), pp. 3–47, 143–194.

2. Ibid., No. 1, p. 9.

3. Samuel Eliot Morison, *The Founding of Harvard College* (Cambridge: Harvard Univerity Press, 1935), p. 107.

4. Thomas Jefferson Wertenbaker, *The Puritan Oligarchy* (New York: Grosset & Dunlap, 1947), p. 32.

5. Ibid., p. 31.

6. D. Elton Trueblood, *The People Called Quakers* (New York: Harper & Row, 1966), p. 62.

7. Ibid., p. 46.

8. Gary B. Nash, *Quakers and Politics: Pennsylvania, 1681–1726* (Princeton: Princeton University Press, 1968), p. 6.

9. Trueblood, p. 50.

10. Ibid., p. 51.

11. Ibid.

12. Nash, p. 9.

13. *DAB*, Vol. XIV, p. 535*b*.

14. Samuel Eliot Morison, *Builders of the Bay Colony* (Boston: Houghton Mifflin, 1958), pp. 52–53.

15. Philip S. Klein and Ari Hoogenboom, *A History of Pennsylvania* (New York: McGraw-Hill, 1973), p. 37.

16. Ibid.

17. Ibid., p. 42.

18. Larzer Ziff, *Puritanism in America: New Culture in a New World* (New York: Viking, 1973), p. 113.

19. Ibid., p. 288.

20. Page Smith, *As a City upon a Hill: The Town in American History* (New York: Knopf, 1966), chap. 2.

21. Alexis de Tocqueville, *Democracy in America* (New York: Knopf, 1945), Vol. I, pp. 6, 60.

22. Alexander V. G. Allen, *Life and Letters of Phillips Brooks* (New York: Dutton, 1901), Vol. II, p. 113.

CHAPTER 8. The Classic Ages of the
Two Colonies

1. Gary B. Nash, *Quakers and Politics: Pennsylvania, 1681–1726* (Princeton: Princeton University Press, 1968), p. 46.
2. George Lee Haskins, *Law and Authority in Early Massachusetts: A Study in Tradition and Design* (New York: Macmillan, 1960), p. 86.
3. Ibid., p. 255.
4. Walter Muir Whitehill, *Boston in the Age of John Fitzgerald Kennedy* (Norman: University of Oklahoma Press, 1966), p. 7.
5. Samuel Eliot Morison, *Builders of the Bay Colony* (Boston: Houghton Mifflin, 1958), p. 95.
6. Edmund S. Morgan, ed., *Puritan Political Ideas, 1558–1794* (Indianapolis: Bobbs-Merrill, 1965), p. 76.
7. James Truslow Adams, *The Founding of New England* (Boston: Little, Brown, 1949), p. 143.
8. *DAB*, Vol. V, pp. 484–485.
9. Ibid. (emphasis in original).
10. Samuel Eliot Morison, *The Intellectual Life of Colonial New England* (Ithaca: Cornell University Press, Great Seal Books, 1963), p. 18.
11. William I. Hull, *William Penn: A Topical Biography* (New York: Oxford University Press, 1937), pp. 221–222.
12. Edwin B. Bronner, *William Penn's "Holy Experiment": The Founding of Pennsylvania, 1681–1701* (Philadelphia: Temple University Publications, 1962), p. 252.
13. Ibid., p. 91.
14. Nash, p. 174.
15. Ibid., p. 175.
16. Ibid., p. 275.
17. Ibid., pp. 114, 116.
18. *DAB*, Vol. XI, p. 329b.
19. Nicholas B. Wainwright, "Governor John Blackwell," *Pennsylvania Magazine of History and Biography*, Vol. LXXIV, No. 0 (1950), pp. 471–472.
20. Bronner, p. 134; italics added.
21. Howard M. Jenkins, ed., *Pennsylvania Colonial and Federal* (Philadelphia: Pennsylvania Historical Publishing Association, 1903), Vol. I, p. 348.
22. Nash, pp. 256–257.
23. Ibid., pp. 56–57.
24. Frederick B. Tolles, *Meeting House and Counting House: The Quaker Merchants of Colonial Philadelphia, 1682–1763* (Chapel Hill: University of North Carolina Press, 1948), pp. 43–44.
25. Ibid., p. 91.
26. Howard Brinton, *Friends for 300 Years* (Wallingford: Pendle Hill Publications, 1964), p. 184.
27. Lawrence Henry Gipson, *The Great War for the Empire: The Years of Defeat, 1754–1757* (New York: Knopf, 1946), p. 67.

CHAPTER 9. Heresy, Hierarchy, and Higher Education

1. Samuel Eliot Morison, *The Founding of Harvard College* (Cambridge: Harvard University Press, 1935), p. 173.
2. Emery Battis, *Saints and Sectaries: Anne Hutchinson and the Antinomian Controversy in the Massachusetts Bay Colony* (Chapel Hill: University of North Carolina Press, 1962), p. 38.
3. Ibid., p. 39.
4. Ibid., p. 12.
5. Ibid., p. 5.
6. Ibid., p. 56.
7. Morison, p. 177.
8. Ibid., p. 178.
9. Battis, p. 194.
10. *Schenck v. United States*, 249 U.S. 47 (1919).
11. Gary B. Nash, *Quakers and Politics: Pennsylvania, 1681–1726* (Princeton: Princeton University Press, 1968), p. 146.
12. Ibid., pp. 152–153.
13. Charles Francis Adams II, *Massachusetts, Its Historians, and Its History: An Object Lesson* (Freeport: Books for Libraries, 1971), p. 48.
14. Ibid., pp. 45–46.
15. Richard Hofstadter, *Anti-Intellectualism in American Life* (New York: Knopf, 1963), p. 59.
16. Morison, p. 179.
17. Samuel Eliot Morison, *The Intellectual Life of Colonial New England* (Ithaca: Cornell University Press, Great Seal Books, 1963), p. 67.
18. Morison, *Founding of Harvard College*, p. 176.
19. Carl Van Doren, *Benjamin Franklin* (Garden City: Garden City Publishing, 1941), p. 23.
20. Catherine Owens Peare, *William Penn* (Ann Arbor: University of Michigan Press, 1966), pp. 265–266; italics added.
21. Nash, p. 286.
22. Rufus M. Jones, *The Quakers in the American Colonies* (New York: Norton, 1966), p. 457.
23. Battis, p. 178.
24. Jones, p. 89.

CHAPTER 10. Provincial Boston and Cosmopolitan Philadelphia

1. Bernard Bailyn, *The Ordeal of Thomas Hutchinson* (Cambridge: Harvard University Press, 1974), p. 243.
2. *DAB*, Vol. V, pp. 484–485.
3. Ibid., p. 483a.
4. Ibid., Vol. XVIII, p. 114a.

5. Samuel Eliot Morison, *Builders of the Bay Colony* (Boston: Houghton Mifflin, 1958), p. 382.

6. *DAB*, Vol. II, p. 144*b*.

7. Bailyn, p. 10.

8. Carl Van Doren, *Benjamin Franklin* (Garden City: Garden City Publishing, 1941), pp. 32–33.

9. Ibid., pp. 31–32.

10. Ibid., p. 40.

11. Ibid., p. 91.

12. Isaac Sharpless, *Political Leaders of Provincial Pennsylvania* (New York: Macmillan, 1919), p. 132.

13. William S. Hanna, *Benjamin Franklin and Pennsylvania Politics* (Stanford: Stanford University Press, 1964), p. 10.

14. *DAB*, Vol. XI, p. 361*a*.

15. Carl Bridenbaugh and Jessica Bridenbaugh, *Rebels and Gentlemen: Philadelphia in the Age of Franklin* (New York: Reynal & Hitchcock, 1942), p. 339.

16. Philip S. Klein and Ari Hoogenboom, *A History of Pennsylvania* (New York: McGraw-Hill, 1973), p. 63.

17. Ibid., p. 64.

18. Sharpless, p. 217.

19. Ibid.

20. Daniel Boorstin, *The Americans: The Colonial Experience* (New York: Random House, 1958), pp. 64–65.

21. Sharpless, pp. 216–217.

22. Hanna, p. 11.

23. Ibid., p. 12.

24. James H. Hutson, *Pennsylvania Politics, 1746–1770: The Movement for Royal Government and Its Consequences* (Princeton: Princeton University Press, 1972), p. 11.

25. *DAB*, Vol. XIV, p. 432*b*.

26. Hanna, pp. 19–20.

27. Ibid., p. 18.

28. Bridenbaugh and Bridenbaugh, p. 99.

29. Gottlieb Mittelberger, *Journey to Pennsylvania*, ed. and trans. Oscar Handlin and John Clive (Cambridge: Harvard University Press, 1960), pp. 47–48.

30. Van Doren, p. 139.

31. Richard H. Shryock, *Medicine in America: Historical Essays* (Baltimore: Johns Hopkins Press, 1966), p. 8.

32. Brooke Hindle, *The Pursuit of Science in Revolutionary America, 1735–1789* (Chapel Hill: University of North Carolina Press, 1956), p. 4.

33. Bridenbaugh and Bridenbaugh, p. 307.

34. Hindle, p. 65.

35. Frederick B. Tolles, *Quakers and the Atlantic Culture* (New York: Macmillan, 1960), p. 65.

36. Brooke Hindle, "The Quaker Background and Science in Colonial Philadelphia," *Isis*, 46 (1955), p. 243.

37. Ibid., pp. 244–245.
38. Hindle, *Pursuit of Science in Revolutionary America*, p. 132.
39. Ibid., pp. 132, italics added.
40. Van Doren, p. 173.
41. Hindle, *Pursuit of Science in Revolutionary America*, p. 19.
42. Ibid., p. 20.
43. Bridenbaugh and Bridenbaugh, p. 317.
44. Ibid.
45. Tolles, p. 69.
46. Hindle, *Pursuit of Science in Revolutionary America*, pp. 88, 89.
47. Boorstin, p. 168.

CHAPTER 11. The Great Generation

1. Eric Foner, *Tom Paine and Revolutionary America* (New York: Oxford University Press, 1976), p. xii.
2. Dumas Malone et al., *The Story of the Declaration of Independence* (New York: Oxford University Press, 1954), p. 160.
3. J. Thomas Scharf and Thompson Westcott, *History of Philadelphia, 1609–1884* (Philadelphia: Everts, 1884), Vol. I, p. 318.
4. Ibid.
5. Malone, p. 174.
6. Thomas Paine, "Common Sense," in Sidney Hook, ed., *The Essential Thomas Paine* (New York: New American Library, 1969), pp. 68, 70.
7. Philip S. Klein and Ari Hoogenboom, *A History of Pennsylvania* (New York: McGraw-Hill, 1973), p. 83.
8. Carl Becker, *The History of Political Parties in the Province of New York, 1760–1776* (Madison: University of Wisconsin Press, 1909).
9. Richard Alan Ryerson, *The Revolution Is Now Begun: The Radical Committees of Philadelphia, 1765–1776* (Philadelphia: University of Pennsylvania Press, 1978), p. 5.
10. Ibid., p. 256.
11. Fred Taylor Wilson, *Our Constitution and Its Makers* (New York: Revell, 1937), p. 224.
12. Stanley Elkins and Eric McKittrick, "The Founding Fathers," *Political Science Quarterly*, Vol. LXXVI, No. 2, p. 213.
13. The data for the statistics compiled in this paragraph and the following one are from Clinton Rossiter, *1787: The Grand Convention* (New York: Macmillan, 1966).
14. Ibid., p. 235.
15. Moses Coit Tyler, *The Literary History of the American Revolution, 1763–1783* (New York: Barnes & Noble, 1941), pp. 24, 34.
16. Charles Francis Adams, ed., *The Works of John Adams*, 10 vols. (Boston: 1856), Vol. II, p. 358.
17. *DAB*, Vol. XVIII, p. 482a.

18. Lyman Butterfield, ed., *John Adams Diary, 1771-1781* (Cambridge: Harvard University Press, 1961), Vol. III, p. 316.

19. Vernon Louis Parrington, *Main Currents in American Thought, 1620-1800* (New York: Harcourt, 1930), Vol. I, p. 222.

CHAPTER 12. Philadelphia's Silver Age and Boston's Federalist Family Founders

1. Robert C. Alberts, *The Golden Voyage: The Life and Times of William Bingham, 1752-1804* (Boston: Houghton Mifflin, 1969), p. 213.

2. *DAB*, Vol. II, p. 273b.

3. Ibid.

4. Alberts, p. 212.

5. Ibid., p. 214.

6. *DAB*, Vol. II, p. 273b.

7. Alberts, p. 94.

8. Ibid., pp. 96-97.

9. Ibid., p. 423.

10. *DAB*, Vol. III, p. 396a.

11. Ibid., p. 465b.

12. David Hackett Fischer, *The Revolution of American Conservatism* (New York: Harper, 1965), p. 43.

13. Ibid., p. 29.

14. *DAB*, Vol. XV, p. 311b.

15. Ibid., Vol. XIV, p. 272b.

16. Fischer, pp. 349-350.

17. Ibid., p. 350.

18. Samuel Eliot Morison, *Three Centuries of Harvard, 1636-1936* (Cambridge: Harvard University Press, 1963), pp. 211-212.

CHAPTER 13. Wealth: The Fertilizer of Family Trees

1. "Poor Sidney," *Philadelphia*, May 1972, p. 67.

2. Ibid.; Carl Van Doren, *Benjamin Franklin* (Garden City: Garden City Publishing, 1941), pp. 762 ff.

3. Cleveland Amory, *The Proper Bostonians* (New York: Dutton, 1947), pp. 32-33.

4. Robert Lenzer, "Boston's Money Managers," *Boston Globe*, 1972 (supplement).

5. Ibid., p. 2.

6. Dan Rottenberg and Madelyn Appelbaum, "The Ten Wealthiest Philadelphians," *Philadelphia*, March 1974, pp. 100-107.

7. Russell Adams, "Do You Sincerely Want to Be a Millionaire?" *Boston*, November 1972, pp. 42–45, 90–99.

8. *DAB*, Vol. XV, pp. 399b–400a.

9. Frederick B. Tolles, *Meeting House and Counting House: The Quaker Merchants of Colonial Philadelphia, 1682–1763* (Chapel Hill: University of North Carolina Press, 1948), p. 46.

10. Nathaniel Burt, *The Perennial Philadelphians* (Boston: Little, Brown, 1963), p. 58.

11. Ibid., p. 60.

12. Nicholas B. Wainwright, ed., *A Philadelphia Perspective: The Diary of Sidney George Fisher Covering the Years 1834–1871* (Philadelphia: Historical Society of Pennsylvania, 1967), p. 270.

13. Burt, pp. 43–44.

14. Samuel Eliot Morison, *The Maritime History of Massachusetts, 1783–1860* (Boston: Houghton Mifflin, 1961), p. 28.

15. Ibid., p. 24.

16. Thomas C. Cochran, *Pennsylvania: A Bicentennial History* (New York: Norton, 1978), p. 138.

17. Ibid., p. 4.

18. Edward Chase Kirkland, *Charles Francis Adams, Jr., 1835–1915: The Patrician at Bay* (Cambridge: Harvard University Press, 1965), p. 129.

19. Ibid., p. 127.

20. Amory, pp. 184–185.

21. N. S. B. Grass and Henrietta M. Larson, *Casebook in American Business History* (New York: Appleton-Century, 1939), p. 162.

22. Thomas Payne Govan, *Nicholas Biddle: Nationalist and Public Banker, 1786–1844* (Chicago: University of Chicago Press, 1959), p. 412.

23. Burt, p. 52.

24. Fritz Redlich, *The Molding of American Banking* (New York: Johnson Reprint, 1968), p. 381.

25. Ferdinand Lundberg, *America's 60 Families* (New York: Vanguard, 1937), pp. 26–27.

26. Hugh Whitney and Walter Muir Whitehill, *The Somerset Club, 1851–1951* (Boston: Privately printed, 1951), p. 7.

27. Peter A. B. Widener II, *Without Drums* (New York: Putnam, 1940), p. 8.

28. Ibid., pp. 9–11.

CHAPTER 14. Education and Leadership

1. Samuel Eliot Morison, *Three Centuries of Harvard, 1636–1936* (Cambridge: Harvard University Press, 1963), p. 4.

2. Richard Hofstadter, *Anti-Intellectualism in American Life* (New York: Knopf, 1963), p. 59.

3. J. P. Wickersham, *A History of Education in Pennsylvania* (New York: Arno, 1969), p. 52.

4. Benjamin Franklin, *Proposals Relating to the Education of Youth in Pensilvania*, facsimile ed. (Philadelphia: University of Pennsylvania Press, 1931), p. 3.
5. William Pepper, Introduction to ibid., p. viii.
6. Moses Coit Tyler, *A History of American Literature, 1607–1765* (Ithaca: Cornell University Press, 1949), pp. 85–87.
7. Hofstadter, pp. 57–58.
8. Thomas Jefferson Wertenbaker, *The Founding of American Civilization: The Middle Colonies* (New York: Scribner's, 1938), p. 119.
9. *DAB*, Vol. V, p. 302*a*.
10. Morison, p. 28.
11. Ibid., p. 358.
12. Edward Potts Cheyney, *History of the University of Pennsylvania, 1740–1940* (Philadelphia: University of Pennsylvania Press, 1940); p. 131.
13. Ibid., p. 29.
14. *Nation*, November 26, 1885, p. 440.
15. Letter by "B.J.," *Nation*, December 10, 1885, pp. 485–486.
16. Morison, p. 199.
17. Cheyney, p. 287.
18. John P. Marquand, *The Late George Apley* (New York: Modern Library, 1940), p. 330.
19. Ibid.
20. Nicholas B. Wainwright, ed., *A Philadelphia Perspective: The Diary of Sidney George Fisher Covering the Years 1834–1871* (Philadelphia: Historical Society of Pennsylvania, 1967), p. 302.
21. Cheyney, p. 243.
22. Ibid., p. 375.
23. Ibid., p. 377.
24. Martin Green, *The Problem of Boston: Some Readings in Cultural History* (New York: Norton, 1966), p. 123.
25. Ibid., p. 134.
26. Francis Newton Thorpe, *William Pepper* (Philadelphia: Lippincott, 1904), p. 464.
27. Quoted in E. Digby Baltzell, *Philadelphia Gentlemen: The Making of a National Upper Class* (New York: Free Press, 1958), p. 334.
28. Philip Marson, *Breeder of Democracy* (Cambridge: Schenkman, 1970), p. v.
29. Ibid., p. 139.
30. Ibid., p. 123.
31. Ibid., p. 148.
32. Ibid., p. 172.
33. Ibid., p. 179.
34. William H. Cornog, *School of the Republic, 1893–1943: A Half Century of the Central High School of Philadelphia* (Philadelphia: Rittenhouse Press, 1952), p. 57.
35. Ibid., p. 60.

36. James McLachlan, *American Boarding Schools: An Historical Study* (New York: Scribner's, 1970), p. 90.

37. Ibid., p. 95.

38. Ibid., p. 142.

39. Henry May, *Protestant Churches in Industrial America* (New York: Harper, 1949), p. 186.

40. Owen Wister, "Dr. Coit of St. Paul's," *Atlantic Monthly*, December 1928, p. 765.

41. Frank D. Ashburn, *Peabody of Groton* (New York: Coward-McCann, 1944), p. 347.

42. Ibid., p. 4.

43. Arthur M. Schlesinger, Jr., "Exeter, 1931–1933: In the Eye of the Hurricane," in Henry Darcy Curwen, ed., *Exeter Remembered* (Exeter: Phillips Exeter Academy, 1965), p. 108.

CHAPTER 15. Boston and Philadelphia and the American Mind

1. Alexis de Tocqueville, *The Old Regime and the French Revolution*, trans. Stuart Gilbert (New York: Doubleday, 1955), p. 142.

2. Richmond Croom Beatty, *Bayard Taylor: Laureate of the Gilded Age* (Norman: University of Oklahoma Press, 1936), p. 105.

3. Barrett Wendell, *A Literary History of America* (New York: Scribner's, 1901), p. 377.

4. Frank Luther Mott, *A History of American Magazines* (Cambridge: Harvard University Press, 1957), Vol. I, p. 554.

5. Ibid., pp. 580–582.

6. *DAB*, Vol. VIII, p. 112*b*.

7. Ibid., Vol. I, p. 213*a*.

8. Ibid., Vol. III, p. 489*a*.

9. Ibid.

10. Horace E. Scudder, *James Russell Lowell* (Boston: Houghton Mifflin, 1901), p. 423.

11. Nicholas B. Wainwright, ed., *A Philadelphia Perspective: The Diary of Sidney George Fisher Covering the Years 1834–1871* (Philadelphia: Historical Society of Pennsylvania, 1967), p. 528.

12. *DAB*, Vol. III, p. 109*b*.

13. Beatty, p. 242.

14. D. H. Lawrence, *Studies in Classic American Literature* (New York: Doubleday, 1953), pp. 16–17.

15. *DAB*, Vol. XVIII, p. 316*a*.

16. Ibid., Vol. II, p. 417*a*.

17. Edward Sculley Bradley, *George Henry Boker: Poet and Patriot* (New York: AMS, 1927), p. 326.

18. Ibid., p. 229.

19. *Atlantic Monthly*, March 1890, p. 428.

20. Bradley, p. 186.

21. *Atlantic Monthly*, March 1890, p. 430.

22. Ernest Earnest, *S. Weir Mitchell: Novelist and Physician* (Philadelphia: University of Pennsylvania Press, 1950), p. 59.

23. Ibid., p. 230.

24. Ibid., p. 60.

25. Ibid., p. 237.

26. "Mixed Americana," *New Yorker*, August 5, 1950, p. 57.

27. Fanny Kemble Wister, ed., *Owen Wister Out West: His Journals and Letters* (Chicago: University of Chicago Press, 1958), p. 130.

28. Owen Wister, *Roosevelt: The Story of a Friendship, 1880–1919* (New York: Macmillan, 1930), pp. 30–33.

29. Fanny Kemble Wister, p. 4.

30. Ibid., p. 5.

31. G. Edward White, *The Eastern Establishment and the Western Experience: The West of Frederic Remington, Theodore Roosevelt, and Owen Wister* (New Haven: Yale University Press, 1968), p. 70.

32. Owen Wister, *The Virginian: A Horseman of the Plains* (New York: Macmillan, 1929), pp. x–xi.

33. Ibid., p. x.

34. Owen Wister, *Roosevelt*, p. 58.

35. Ibid., pp. 106–107.

36. Henry Dwight Sedgwick, *Commemorative Tribute to Owen Wister* (New York: American Academy of Arts and Letters, 1939), pp. 119–120.

37. Fanny Kemble Wister, p. 24.

38. Ibid., pp. 25–26.

39. Ibid., p. 11.

40. *DAB*, Supp. I, p. 558a.

41. D. G. Brinton Thompson, "Sydney George Fisher: Son of the Diarist," *Pennsylvania Magazine of History and Biography*, April 1967, p. 191. Sidney's hopes for his son were not included in the published diary, edited by Wainwright.

42. Sydney George Fisher, *The Making of Pennsylvania* (Philadelphia: Lippincott, 1932), pp. 357–359.

43. Ibid., p. 367.

44. Ibid., Introduction (pages not numbered).

CHAPTER 16. Art and Architecture

1. *DAB*, Vol. XX, p. 8b.

2. Charles Merrill Mount, *Gilbert Stuart* (New York: Norton, 1964), p. 11.

3. *DAB*, Vol. XVIII, p. 168a.

4. Ibid., p. 167*a*.
5. Nathaniel Burt, *The Perennial Philadelphians* (Boston: Little, Brown, 1963), p. 333.
6. Charles Merrill Mount, *John Singer Sargent* (New York: Norton, 1955), p. 232.
7. Ibid., p. 299.
8. Ibid., pp. 310–311.
9. John H. Mueller, *The American Symphony Orchestra* (Bloomington: Indiana University Press, 1951), p. 23.
10. Ibid., p. 78.
11. Burt, p. 474.
12. James F. O'Gorman, *The Architecture of Frank Furness* (Philadelphia: Philadelphia Museum of Art, 1973), p. 15.
13. J. D. Forbes, "Shepley, Bulfinch, Richardson & Abbott, Architects: An Introduction," *Journal of the Society of Architectural Historians*, Vol. XVII, No. 3, p. 26.

CHAPTER 17. The Learned Professions

1. Nathaniel Burt, *The Perennial Philadelphians* (Boston: Little, Brown, 1963), pp. 125–126.
2. Nicholas B. Wainwright, ed., *A Philadelphia Perspective: The Diary of Sidney George Fisher Covering the Years 1834–1871* (Philadelphia: Historical Society of Pennsylvania, 1967), pp. 303–304.
3. Horace Binney, *The Leaders of the Old Bar of Philadelphia* (Philadelphia: Sherman, 1859), p. 115.
4. Ibid., pp. 117–118.
5. Ibid., pp. 111–112.
6. Ibid., p. 112.
7. *DAB*, Vol. VII, p. 255*b*.
8. Ibid., Vol. VIII, p. 262*b*.
9. Ibid., Vol. XVI, p. 590.
10. Ibid., p. 589*a*.
11. Ibid., p. 591*a*.
12. Daniel Boorstin, *The Americans: The National Experience* (New York: Random House, 1965), p. 35.
13. Ibid., p. 40.
14. *DAB*, Vol. XVIII, p. 105*a*.
15. Gary B. Nash, "The Philadelphia Bench and Bar, 1800–1861," *Comparative Studies in Society and History*, January 1965, p. 205.
16. *DAB*, Vol. I, p. 534*a* (italics added).
17. Richard H. Shryock, *Medicine and Society in America, 1660–1860* (Ithaca: Cornell University Press, Great Seal Books, 1962), p. 70.
18. *DAB*, Vol. II, p. 258*a*.

19. Leonard K. Eaton, "Medicine in Philadelphia and Boston, 1805–1830," *Pennsylvania Magazine of History and Biography*, Vol. LXXV, No. 1 (1951), p. 66.

20. George W. Corner, *Two Centuries of Medicine: A History of the School of Medicine, University of Pennsylvania* (Philadelphia: Lippincott, 1965), pp. 205–206.

21. Ibid., p. 232.

22. Joseph C. Aub and Ruth K. Hapgood, *Pioneer in Modern Medicine: David Linn Edsall of Harvard* (Cambridge: Harvard Medical Alumni Association, 1970), pp. 60, 64.

23. Ibid., p. 63.

24. Data from Howard A. Kelly and Walter L. Burrage, *Dictionary of American Medical Biography* (New York: Appleton-Century, 1928); summary table in George W. Pierson, *The Education of American Leaders: Comparative Contributions of U.S. Colleges and Universities* (New York: Praeger, 1969), p. 55.

25. Data in Frank G. Dickinson, *Distribution of Medical School Alumni in the United States as of April 1950*, Bulletin 101, American Medical Association, 1956; summary table in Pierson, p. 63.

26. Cleveland Amory, *The Proper Bostonians* (New York: Dutton, 1947), p. 105.

27. Ibid.

28. Ibid., p. 106.

CHAPTER 18. The Governing of Men

1. Garry Wills, *Inventing America: Jefferson's Declaration of Independence* (New York: Doubleday, 1978), p. 35.

2. George W. Corner, ed., *The Autobiography of Benjamin Rush* (Princeton: American Philosophical Society, 1948), p. 162.

3. Stephen Hess, *America's Political Dynasties* (New York: Doubleday, 1966), p. 3.

4. Ibid., p. 164.

5. Sam Bass Warner, Jr., *The Private City: Philadelphia in Three Periods of Growth* (Philadelphia:University of Pennsylvania Press, 1968), p. x.

6. Ibid., p. 3.

7. Ibid., p. 84.

8. Ibid., pp. 85–86.

9. Geoffrey Blodgett, *The Gentle Reformers: Massachusetts Democrats in the Cleveland Era* (Cambridge: Harvard University Press, 1966), p. 255.

10. Ibid., p. 243.

11. *DAB*, Vol. XX, p. 31*b*.

12. *DAB*, Vol. IX, p. 467*a*.

13. Nicholas B. Wainwright, *A Philadelphia Perspective: The Diary of Sidney George Fisher Covering the Years 1834–1871* (Philadelphia: Historical Society of Pennsylvania, 1967), p. 490.

14. J. L. Talmon, *Political Messianism* (New York: Praeger, 1960), p. 490.

15. Lincoln Steffens, *The Autobiography of Lincoln Steffens* (New York: Harcourt, 1931), p. 604.
16. Lincoln Steffens, *The Shame of the Cities* (New York: Hill and Wang, 1957), p. 134.
17. Ibid., pp. 134–136.
18. Ibid., p. 138.
19. Ibid., p. 139.
20. Steffens, *Autobiography*, p. 410.
21. Justin Kaplan, *Lincoln Steffens* (New York: Simon & Schuster, 1974), p. 172.
22. Steffens, *Autobiography*, pp. 605–606.
23. Ibid., p. 606.
24. Kaplan, p. 168.
25. Edward Sculley Bradley, *Henry Charles Lea* (Philadelphia: University of Pennsylvania Press, 1931), p. 189.
26. Ibid.
27. Ibid., p. 158.
28. Blodgett, p. 1.
29. Ibid., p. 29.
30. Ibid., pp. 20–21.
31. Samuel Whitaker Pennypacker, *The Autobiography of a Pennsylvanian* (Philadelphia: Winston, 1918), p. 187; italics added.
32. Ibid., pp. 187–188.
33. Richard Hofstadter, *The Age of Reform: From Bryan to F.D.R.* (New York: Random House, Vintage Books, 1960), p. 137.
34. Bonnie R. Fox, "The Philadelphia Progressives: A Test of the Hofstadter-Hays Theses," *Pennsylvania History*, Vol. XXXIV (1967), p. 394.
35. Samuel P. Hays, "The Politics of Reform in Municipal Government in the Progressive Era," *Pacific Northwest Quarterly*, Vol. LV (October 1964), p. 160.
36. Fox, pp. 385–386.
37. Wainwright, p. 39.
38. Philip S. Klein, *Pennsylvania Politics, 1817–1832: A Game without Rules* (Philadelphia: Historical Society of Pennsylvania, 1940), p. 368.
39. Ibid., p. 26.
40. Ibid., p. 11.
41. Philip S. Klein and Ari Hoogenboom, *A History of Pennsylvania* (New York: McGraw-Hill, 1973), p. 404.
42. Ibid., p. 398.
43. Owen Wister, *Roosevelt: The Story of a Friendship, 1880–1919* (New York: Macmillan, 1930), p. 174.
44. William V. Shannon, *The American Irish* (New York: Macmillan, 1963), p. 228.
45. Pennypacker, p. 155.
46. Samuel Whitaker Pennypacker, *Pennsylvania the Keystone* (Philadelphia: Sower, 1914), p. 188.

47. Pennypacker, *Autobiography*, pp. 161–162.
48. Ibid., p. 163.
49. Ibid., p. 16.
50. Samuel Whitaker Pennypacker, *Pennsylvania in American History* (Philadelphia: Campbell, 1910), p. 375.
51. Ibid., pp. 374–375.
52. Ibid., p. 434.
53. Ibid., p. 436.
54. Pennypacker, *Autobiography*, p. 152.
55. Ibid., p. 152.
56. Ibid., p. 153.
57. Ibid., p. 284.
58. Ibid., p. 180.
59. Ibid., p. 524.
60. Klein and Hoogenboom, p. 381.
61. Samuel Whitaker Pennypacker, *Pennsylvania and Massachusetts: A Historical Parallel* (Philadelphia: Campbell, 1901), pp. 26–27; italics added.
62. Wainwright, pp. 308, 415.
63. Klein, p. 362.
64. Ibid., p. 365.
65. Ibid., p. 324.
66. Wainwright, p. 69.
67. Steffens, *Autobiography*, p. 409.
68. Erwin Stanley Bradley, *Simon Cameron: Lincoln's Secretary of War* (Philadelphia: University of Pennsylvania Press, 1966), p. 77.
69. *DAB*, Vol. III, p. 438a.
70. Ibid., p. 436a.
71. Ibid., p. 435b.
72. Robert Douglas Bowden, *Boies Penrose: Symbol of an Era* (New York: Greenberg, 1937), p. 69.
73. Talcott Williams, "After Penrose, What?", *Century*, Vol. CV (1922), p. 52; italics added.
74. Bowden, p. 5.
75. Klein and Hoogenboom, p. 372.
76. Bowden, p. 11.
77. Ibid., p. 6.
78. Ibid., p. 7.
79. Elting Morison, ed., *The Letters of Theodore Roosevelt* (Cambridge: Harvard University Press, 1951), p. 108.
80. William Lawrence, *Henry Cabot Lodge: A Biographical Sketch* (Boston: Houghton Mifflin, 1925), pp. 127–128.
81. Ibid., pp. 199–200.
82. John Lukacs, "Big Grizzly," *American Heritage*, October 1978, p. 74.
83. Bowden, pp. 264–265.
84. [Mark Sullivan], "The Ills of Pennsylvania," *Atlantic Monthly*, October 1901, p. 559.

85. Ibid., pp. 564–566.

86. George Wharton Pepper, *Philadelphia Lawyer: An Autobiography* (Philadelphia: Lippincott, 1944), p. 137.

CHAPTER 19. Catholics in Two Cultures

1. Alexis de Tocqueville, *Democracy in America* (New York: Knopf, 1945), Vol. II, p. 31.

2. Edwin Scott Gaustad, *Historical Atlas of Religion in America* (New York: Harper, 1962), Appendix A.

3. *DAB*, Vol. VI, p. 50*b*.

4. Ibid., p. 51*a*.

5. *New Catholic Encyclopedia*, prepared by an editorial staff at the Catholic University of America (New York: McGraw-Hill, 1967), Vol. XI, p. 263*a*.

6. James F. Connelly, ed., *The History of the Archdiocese of Philadelphia* (Philadelphia: Archdiocese of Philadelphia, 1976), pp. 238–239.

7. Ibid., p. 240.

8. J. Thomas Scharf and Thompson Westcott, *History of Philadelphia, 1609–1884* (Philadelphia: Everts, 1884), Vol. II, p. 1,386.

9. James Reichley, *The Art of Government: Reform and Organization Politics in Philadelphia*, A Report to the Fund for the Republic (Philadelphia: *Philadelphia* reprint, ca. 1959), p. 23.

10. Robert H. Lord, John E. Sexton, and Edward T. Harrington, *History of the Archdiocese of Boston* (New York: Sheed & Ward, 1944), Vol. II, p. 307.

11. *DAB*, Vol. XIV, p. 53*b*.

12. Ibid., Suppl. IV, p. 858*b*.

13. Ibid., p. 859*a*.

14. As I noted in Chapter 14, President Kennedy surely recalled his first year at Choate: the headmaster always told the new boys to remember that "it is not what Choate can do for you but what you can do for Choate."

CHAPTER 20. Philadelphia Orthodox Quakerism

1. Rufus M. Jones, *The Later Periods of Quakerism* (New York: Macmillan, 1921), Vol. II, p. 770.

2. Bliss Forbush, *Elias Hicks: Quaker Liberal* (New York: Columbia University Press, 1956), p. 176.

3. Jones, Vol. I, p. 450.

4. George Wharton Pepper, *Philadelphia Lawyer, An Autobiography* (Philadelphia: Lippincott, 1944), p. 43.

5. Ibid., p. 44.

6. Logan Pearsall Smith, *Unforgotten Years* (Boston: Little, Brown, 1939), pp. 30–32.

7. Jones, Vol. I, p. 488.
8. Ibid., pp. 497–498.
9. Ibid., p. 529.
10. Ibid., p. 519.
11. D. Elton Trueblood, *The People Called Quakers* (New York: Harper & Row, 1966), p. 182.
12. Jones, Vol. I, pp. 532–533.
13. Elizabeth Gray Vining, *Friend of Life: The Biography of Rufus M. Jones* (Philadelphia: Lippincott, 1958), p. 79.
14. Rufus M. Jones, *Haverford College: A History and an Interpretation* (New York: Macmillan, 1933), p. 34.
15. *DAB*, Vol. XX, p. 459a.
16. Vining, p. 306.

EPILOGUE

1. Ernst Troeltsch, *The Social Teaching of the Christian Churches* (New York: Harper, Harper Torchbooks, 1960), Vol. II, p. 577.
2. Frederick B. Tolles, "Emerson and Quakerism," *American Literature: A Journal of Literary History, Criticism, and Bibliography*, Vol. X, p. 149.
3. Ibid., p. 151.
4. Ibid., pp. 164–165.
5. Frederick Ives Carpenter, *Emerson Handbook* (New York: Hendricks House, 1953), p. 227.
6. Ibid., p. 229.
7. Ibid., p. 227.
8. Alan Simpson, *Puritanism in Old and New England* (Chicago: University of Chicago Press, 1964), p. 103.
9. Gerald Jonas, *On Doing Good: A Quaker Experiment* (New York: Scribner's, 1971).
10. Reprinted in *New York Review of Books*, January 7, 1971.
11. Alexis de Tocqueville, *Democracy in America* (New York: Knopf, 1945), Vol. II, p. 388; italics in original.
12. Ibid., p. 352.

APPENDIX II

1. Charles H. Cooley, "Genius, Fame, and the Comparison of Races," *Annals of the American Academy of Political and Social Science*, May 1897, pp. 318–319.
2. Ibid., p. 354.
3. Edward Chase Kirkland, *Charles Francis Adams, Jr., 1835–1915: The Patrician at Bay* (Cambridge: Harvard University Press, 1965), p. 2.
4. Ibid., pp. 5–6.

5. David F. Musto, "The Youth of John Quincy Adams," *Proceedings of the American Philosophical Society*, August 1969.
6. Ibid., p. 281.
7. Cooley, p. 317.

APPENDIX III

1. *DAB*, Vol. XII, p. 397*b*.
2. Ibid., pp. 397*b*–398*a*.
3. Ibid., Vol. V, pp. 82–83.
4. Cleveland Amory, *The Proper Bostonians* (New York: Dutton, 1947), pp. 49–50.

APPENDIX IV

1. Burton R. Clark *The Distinctive College: Antioch, Reed and Swarthmore* (Chicago: Aldine, 1970), p. 207. For this history of Swarthmore I have drawn on Clark, as well as on Francis Blanchard, *Frank Aydelotte of Swarthmore* (Middletown: Wesleyan University Press, 1970).
2. Everett L. Hunt, *The Revolt of the College Intellectual* (New York: Human Relations Aids, 1963).

APPENDIX V

1. R. H. Knapp and H. B. Goodrich, *Origins of American Scientists* (Chicago: University of Chicago Press, 1952).
2. See the *DAB* biographies of James A. Garfield (Vol. VII, pp. 145–150) and Harry Augustus Garfield (Suppl. III, pp. 292–294).

Bibliography

Because this book is a study in comparative history, I have taken the view of the great British sociologist T. H. Marshall, who wrote that one "must inevitably rely extensively on secondary authorities . . . because life is too short to do anything else when using the comparative method." The purpose of this note is to indicate which sources I have found most useful. It by no means includes everything that has gone into the writing of this book but is, rather, a selective list that will allow the reader to explore further certain ideas and topics covered here.

The central theme of this book is grounded in the works of Alexis de Tocqueville and Max Weber, especially Tocqueville's *Democracy in America* (New York: Knopf, 1945), Vol. II, and *The Old Régime and the French Revolution*, trans. Stuart Gilbert (New York: Doubleday, Anchor Books, 1955); and Weber's *Protestant Ethic and the Spirit of Capitalism* (New York: Scribner's, 1958), and two of his essays—"Politics as a Vocation" and "Class, Status, and Party"—both of which are included in Hans Gerth and C. Wright Mills, eds., *From Max Weber: Essays in Sociology* (New York: Oxford University Press, 1946).

I am most indebted to Seymour Martin Lipset, among modern authors, especially for his *First New Nation: The United States in Historical and Comparative*

Perspective (New York: Basic Books, 1963) and *Revolution and Counter-Revolution* (New York: Doubleday, Anchor Books, 1963). My perspective on American history draws heavily on various works by Daniel Boorstin, particularly his insightful book *The Americans: The Colonial Experience* (New York: Random House, 1958). Finally, my understanding of American history, and of the differences between Boston and Philadelphia as well, has been shaped by the ideas and lives of John Adams and Thomas Jefferson: anyone will be enriched by reading Lester J. Cappon, ed., *The Adams-Jefferson Letters* (Chapel Hill: University of North Carolina Press, 1959), and Merrill D. Peterson, *Adams and Jefferson: A Revolutionary Dialogue* (New York: Oxford University Press, 1976).

Indispensable to an understanding of the sociology of the Christian religion are Ernst Troeltsch, *The Social Teaching of the Christian Churches*, 2 vols. (New York: Harper, Harper Torchbooks, 1960), and Werner Stark, *The Sociology of Religion: A Study of Christendom*, 4 vols. (New York: Fordham University Press, 1966–1970). My view of the Reformation was vitally enriched by H. Richard Niebuhr's little book *Christ and Culture* (New York: Harper, 1951) and his two interpretations of American Protestantism: *The Social Sources of Denominationalism* (New York: Holt, 1929) and *The Kingdom of God in America* (Hamden: Shoe String, 1956). The classic study of Quakerism is Howard Brinton, *Friends for 300 Years* Wallingford: Pendle Hill Publications, 1964); it is a brilliant and beautiful book.

I have also found the following books, arranged by subject matter, to be of value:

RELIGION

Margaret H. Bacon, *The Quiet Rebels: The Story of the Quakers in America* (New York: Basic Books, 1969).

Roland H. Bainton, *The Reformation of the Sixteenth Century* (Boston: Beacon, 1952).

_____, *Christian Unity and Religion in New England* (Boston: Beacon, 1964).

_____, *Studies in the Reformation* (Boston: Beacon, 1966).

William C. Braithwaite, *The Beginnings of Quakerism*, rev. Henry J. Cadbury (Cambridge: At the University Press, 1961).

_____, *The Second Period of Quakerism* (Cambridge: At the University Press, 1961).

A. Neave Brayshaw, *The Quakers* (London: George Allen & Unwin, 1921).

A. G. Dickens, *The English Reformation* (New York: Schocken, 1964).

Edwin Scott Gaustad, *Historical Atlas of Religion in America* (New York: Harper, 1962).

William Haller, *The Rise of Puritanism* (New York: Harper, Harper Torchbooks, 1957).

Van A. Harvey, *A Handbook of Theological Terms* (New York: Macmillan, 1964).

Rufus M. Jones, *The Later Periods of Quakerism*, 2 vols. (New York: Macmillan, 1921).

_____, *The Story of George Fox* (Philadelphia: Society of Friends, 1943).

_____, *The Quakers in the American Colonies* (New York: Norton, 1966).

M. M. Knappen, *Tudor Puritanism* (Chicago: University of Chicago Press, 1939).

Ronald A. Knox, *Enthusiasm: A Chapter in the History of Religion with Special Reference to the XVII and XVIII Centuries* (New York: Oxford University Press, 1950).

Harold Loukes, *The Quaker Contribution* (New York: Macmillan, 1965).

John T. McNeill, *The History and Character of Calvinism* (New York: Oxford University Press, 1954).

Perry Miller, *Orthodoxy in Massachusetts, 1630–1650* (Boston: Beacon, 1959).

_____, *Errand into the Wilderness* (New York: Harper, Harper Torchbooks, 1964).

Perry Miller and Thomas H. Johnson, *The Puritans*, 2 vols. (New York: Harper, Harper Torchbooks, 1963).

Edmund S. Morgan, *The Puritan Dilemma: The Story of John Winthrop* (Boston: Little, Brown, 1958).

_____, ed., *Puritan Political Ideas, 1558–1794* (Indianapolis: Bobbs-Merrill, 1965).

William A. Mueller, *Church and State in Luther and Calvin* (New York: Doubleday, Anchor Books, 1965).

Alan Simpson, *Puritanism in Old and New England* (Chicago: University of Chicago Press, 1964).

Willard L. Sperry, *Religion in America* (Boston: Beacon, 1963).

William Warren Sweet, *The Story of Religion in America* (New York: Harper, 1930).

_____, *Religion in Colonial America* (New York: Scribner's, 1942).

John Sykes, *The Quakers* (Philadelphia: Lippincott, 1959).

R. H. Tawney, *Religion and the Rise of Capitalism* (New York: Harcourt, 1926).

D. Elton Trueblood, *The People Called Quakers* (New York: Harper & Row, 1966).

Larzer Ziff, *Puritanism in America: New Culture in a New World* (New York: Viking, 1973).

BOSTON, MASSACHUSETTS, AND PHILADELPHIA, PENNSYLVANIA

James Truslow Adams, *The Adams Family* (New York: Blue Ribbon, 1930).

Cleveland Amory, *The Proper Bostonians* (New York: Dutton, 1947).

E. Digby Baltzell, *Philadelphia Gentlemen: The Making of a National Upper Class* (New York: Free Press, 1958).

Nathaniel Burt, *The Perennial Philadelphians* (Boston: Little, Brown, 1963).

Mary Caroline Crawford, *Famous Families of Massachusetts*, 2 vols. (Boston: Little, Brown, 1930).

Thomas C. Cochran, *Pennsylvania: A Bicentennial History* (New York: Norton, 1978).

Sydney George Fisher, *The Making of Pennsylvania* (Philadelphia: Lippincott, 1932).

Joseph E. Garland, *Boston's North Shore* (Boston: Little, Brown, 1978).

Martin Green, *The Problem of Boston: Some Readings in Cultural History* (New York: Norton, 1966).

Ferris Greenslet, *The Lowells and Their Seven Worlds* (Boston: Houghton Mifflin, 1946).

Albert Bushnell Hart, ed., *The Commonwealth History of Massachusetts*, 5 vols. (New York: States History Company, 1927–1930).

Helen Howe, *The Gentle Americans: Biography of a Breed* (New York: Harpers, 1965).

M. A. DeWolfe Howe, *Boston: The Place and the People* (New York: Macmillan, 1903).

Edwin P. Hoyt, *The Peabody Influence* (New York: Dodd, Mead, 1968).

R. Sturgis Ingersoll, *Recollections of a Philadelphian at Eighty* (Philadelphia: Privately printed, 1971).

Philip S. Klein and Ari Hoogenboom, *A History of Pennsylvania* (New York: McGraw-Hill, 1973).

David Loth, *Pencoyd and the Roberts Family* (New York: Privately printed).

John P. Marquand, *The Late George Apley* (New York: Modern Library, 1940).

Lawrence Shaw Mayo, *The Winthrop Family in America* (Boston: Massachusetts Historical Society, 1948).

J. Thomas Scharf and Thompson Westcott, *History of Philadelphia, 1609–1884*, 3 vols. (Philadelphia: Everts, 1884).

John A. Schutz and Douglas Adair, eds., *The Spur of Fame: Dialogues of John Adams and Benjamin Rush, 1805–1813* (San Marino: Huntington Library, 1966).

Nicholas B. Wainwright, ed., *A Philadelphia Perspective: The Diary of Sidney George Fisher Covering the Years 1834–1871* (Philadelphia: Historical Society of Pennsylvania, 1967).

Walter Muir Whitehill, *Boston in the Age of John Fitzgerald Kennedy* (Norman: University of Oklahoma Press, 1966).

ENGLISH REFORMATION AND THE PURITAN REVOLUTION

Maurice Ashley, *Oliver Cromwell and the Puritan Revolution* (New York: Collier, 1958).

Trevor Aston, ed., *Crisis in Europe, 1560–1660* (New York: Basic Books, 1965).

Hugh Barbour, *The Quakers in Puritan England* (New Haven: Yale University Press, 1964).

Mabel Richmond Brailsford, *A Quaker from Cromwell's Army: James Naylor* (New York: Macmillan, 1927).

Carl Bridenbaugh, *Vexed and Troubled Englishmen, 1590–1642* (New York: Oxford University Press, 1968).

G. R. Elton, *The Tudor Revolution in Government* (Cambridge: At the University Press, 1953).

J. H. Hexter, *Reappraisals in History: New Views on History and Society in Early Modern Europe* (New York: Harper, Harper Torchbooks, 1961).

———, *On Historians: Reappraisals of Some of the Makers of Modern History* (Cambridge: Harvard University Press, 1979).

Christopher Hill, *The English Revolution of 1640* (London: Lawrence & Wishart, 1940).

———, *Society and Puritanism in Pre-Revolutionary England* (London: Secker & Warburg, 1964).

———, *Intellectual Origins of the English Revolution* (Oxford: Clarendon, 1965).

———, *Puritanism and Revolution: Studies in Interpretation of the English Revolution of the 17th Century* (London: Secker & Warburg, 1965).

———, *The World Turned Upside Down* (New York: Viking, 1972).

———, *Change and Continuity in Seventeenth-Century England* (London: Weidenfeld & Nicolson, 1974).

G. Huehns, ed., *Clarendon: Selections from* The History of the Rebellion and Civil Wars *and* The Life by Himself (New York: Oxford University Press, 1953).

E. W. Ives, ed., *The English Revolution, 1600–1660* (New York: Barnes & Noble, 1968).

David Little, *Religion, Order, and Law* (New York: Harper & Row, Harper Torchbooks, 1969).

Robert K. Merton, *Science, Technology, and Society in Seventeenth-Century England* (New York: Harper, Harper Torchbooks, 1970).

Wallace Notestein, *The English People on the Eve of Colonization, 1603–1630* (New York: Harper, Harper Torchbooks, 1962).

Isabel Ross, *Margaret Fell: Mother of Quakerism* (London: Longmans, Green, 1949).

A. L. Rowse, *The England of Elizabeth* (New York: Macmillan, 1951).

———, *The Expansion of Elizabethan England* (New York: Harper, Harper Torchbooks, 1965).

Leo F. Solt, *Saints in Arms: Puritanism and Democracy in Cromwell's Army* (New York: Oxford University Press, 1959).

Lawrence Stone, *The Crisis of the Aristocracy, 1558–1641* (New York: Oxford University Press, 1967).

———, ed., *Social Change and Revolution in England, 1540–1640* (London: Longmans, Green, 1965).

Ernest E. Taylor, *The Valiant Sixty* (London: Bannisdale, 1951).

H. R. Trevor-Roper, *Historical Essays* (New York: Macmillan, 1957).

———, *Archbishop Laud, 1573–1645*, 2d ed. (New York: Macmillan, 1963).

————, *Religion, the Reformation, and Social Change* (New York: Macmillan, 1967).

Michael Walzer, *The Revolution of the Saints: A Study in the Origins of Radical Politics* (Cambridge: Harvard University Press, 1965).

COLONIAL MASSACHUSETTS
AND PENNSYLVANIA

Charles Francis Adams II, *Massachusetts, Its Historians and Its History: An Object Lesson* (Freeport: Books for Libraries, 1971).

James Truslow Adams, *The Founding of New England* (Boston: Little, Brown, 1949).

Bernard Bailyn, *New England Merchants in the Seventeenth Century* (New York: Harper, Harper Torchbooks, 1964).

————, *The Ordeal of Thomas Hutchinson* (Cambridge: Harvard University Press, 1974).

Emery Battis, *Saints and Sectaries: Anne Hutchinson and the Antinomian Controversy in the Massachusetts Bay Colony* (Chapel Hill: University of North Carolina Press, 1962).

Carl Bridenbaugh, *Cities in the Wilderness: The First Century of Urban Life in America, 1625–1742* (New York: Ronald, 1938).

————, *Cities in Revolt: Urban Life in America, 1743–1776* (New York: Knopf, 1955).

Carl and Jessica Bridenbaugh, *Rebels and Gentlemen: Philadelphia in the Age of Franklin* (New York: Reynal & Hitchcock, 1942).

Edwin B. Bronner, *William Penn's "Holy Experiment": The Founding of Pennsylvania, 1681–1701* (Philadelphia: Temple University Publications, 1962).

Bonamy Dobrée, *William Penn: Quaker and Pioneer* (Boston: Houghton Mifflin, 1932).

Mary Maples Dunn, *William Penn: Politics and Conscience* (Princeton: Princeton University Press, 1967).

Richard S. Dunn, *Puritans and Yankees: The Winthrop Dynasty of New England, 1630–1717* (New York: Norton, 1971).

Carl Van Doren, *Benjamin Franklin* (Garden City: Garden City Publishing, 1941).

Brooke Hindle, *The Pursuit of Science in Revolutionary America, 1735–1789* (Chapel Hill: University of North Carolina Press, 1956).

Edmund S. Morgan, ed., *The Founding of Massachusetts: Historians and Sources* (Indianapolis: Bobbs-Merrill, 1964).

Gary B. Nash, *Quakers and Politics: Pennsylvania, 1681–1726* (Princeton: Princeton University Press, 1968).

Thomas Jefferson Wertenbaker, *The Puritan Oligarchy* (New York: Grosset & Dunlap, 1947).

Samuel Eliot Morison, *Builders of the Bay Colony* (Boston: Houghton Mifflin, 1958).

_____, *The Founding of Harvard College* (Cambridge: Harvard University Press, 1935).

_____, *The Intellectual Life of Colonial New England* (Ithaca: Cornell University Press, Great Seal Books, 1963).

Catherine Owens Peare, *William Penn* (Ann Arbor: University of Michigan Press, 1966).

George Lee Haskins, *Law and Authority in Early Massachusetts: A Study in Tradition and Design* (New York: Macmillan, 1960).

William I. Hull, *William Penn: A Topical Biography* (New York: Oxford University Press, 1937).

Howard M. Jenkins, ed., *Pennsylvania Colonial and Federal*, 2 vols. (Philadelphia: Pennsylvania Historical Publishing Association, 1903).

Frederick B. Tolles, *Meeting House and Counting House: The Quaker Merchants of Colonial Philadelphia, 1682-1763* (Chapel Hill: University of North Carolina Press, 1948).

_____, *Quakers and the Atlantic Culture* (New York: Macmillan, 1960).

William S. Hanna, *Benjamin Franklin and Pennsylvania Politics* (Stanford: Stanford University Press, 1964).

James H. Hutson, *Pennsylvania Politics, 1746-1770: The Movement for Royal Government and Its Consequences* (Princeton: Princeton University Press, 1972).

Gottlieb Mittelberger, *Journey to Pennsylvania*, ed. and trans. Oscar Handlin and John Clive (Cambridge: Harvard University Press, 1960).

Isaac Sharpless, *Political Leaders of Provincial Pennsylvania* (New York: Macmillan, 1919).

John W. Jordan, ed., *Colonial Families of Philadelphia*, 2 vols. (New York: Lewis, 1911).

Thomas Jefferson Wertenbaker, *The Founding of American Civilization: The Middle Colonies* (New York: Scribner's, 1938).

Michael Zuckerman, *Peaceable Kingdoms: New England Towns in the Eighteenth Century* (New York: Knopf, 1970).

THE AGE OF TRANSITION

Robert C. Alberts, *The Golden Voyage: The Life and Times of William Bingham, 1752-1804* (Boston: Houghton Mifflin, 1969).

Bernard Bailyn, *The Ideological Origins of the American Revolution* (Cambridge: Harvard University Press, 1967).

Carl Becker, *The History of Political Parties in the Province of New York, 1760-1776* (Madison: University of Wisconsin Press, 1909).

Robert E. Brown, *Middle-Class Democracy and the Revolution in Massachusetts, 1691-1780* (Ithaca: Cornell University Press, 1955).

Robert L. Brunhouse, *The Counter-Revolution in Pennsylvania, 1776-1790* (Harrisburg: Pennsylvania Historical Commission, 1942).

H. Trevor Colbourn, *The Lamp of Experience: Whig History and the Intellectual Origins of the American Revolution* (New York: Norton, 1974).

Elisha P. Douglas, *Rebels and Democrats* (Chicago: Quadrangle, 1965).

David Hackett Fischer, *The Revolution of American Conservatism* (New York: Harper, 1965).

Eric Foner, *Tom Paine and Revolutionary America* (New York: Oxford University Press, 1976).

Zoltán Haraszti, *John Adams and the Prophets of Progress* (Cambridge: Harvard University Press, 1952).

David Hawke, *In the Midst of a Revolution* (Philadelphia: University of Pennsylvania Press, 1961).

Sidney Hook, ed., *The Essential Thomas Paine* (New York: New American Library, 1969).

David L. Jacobson, *John Dickinson and the Revolution in Pennsylvania, 1764–1776* (Berkeley: University of California Press, 1965).

J. Franklin Jameson, *The American Revolution Considered as a Social Movement* (Princeton: Princeton University Press, 1967).

Charles H. Lincoln, *The Revolutionary Movement in Pennsylvania, 1760–1776* (Philadelphia: University of Pennsylvania, 1901).

Dumas Malone et al., *The Story of the Declaration of Independence* (New York: Oxford University Press, 1954).

James Kirby Martin, *Men in Rebellion: Higher Governmental Leaders and the Coming of the American Revolution* (New York: Free Press, 1973).

Clinton Rossiter, *1787: The Grand Convention* (New York: Macmillan, 1966).

Richard Alan Ryerson, *The Revolution Is Now Begun: The Radical Committees of Philadelphia, 1765–1776* (Philadelphia: University of Pennsylvania Press, 1978).

Moses Coit Tyler, *The Literary History of the American Revolution, 1763–1783* (New York: Barnes & Noble, 1941).

Fred Taylor Wilson, *Our Constitution and Its Makers* (New York: Revell, 1937).

MONEYMAKING

Charles Francis Adams II, *An Autobiography, 1835–1915* (Boston: Houghton Mifflin, 1916).

Thomas Payne Govan, *Nicholas Biddle: Nationalist and Public Banker, 1786–1844* (Chicago: University of Chicago Press, 1959).

N. S. B. Gras and Henrietta M. Larson, *Casebook in American Business History* (New York: Appleton-Century, 1939).

Bray Hammond, *Banks and Politics in America from the Revolution to the Civil War* (Princeton: Princeton University Press, 1957).

Matthew Josephson, *The Robber Barons: The Great American Capitalists, 1861–1901* (New York: Harcourt, 1934).

Edward Chase Kirkland, *Charles Francis Adams, Jr., 1835–1915: The Patrician at Bay* (Cambridge: Harvard University Press, 1965).

Ferdinand Lundberg, *America's 60 Families* (New York: Vanguard, 1937).

Samuel Eliot Morison, *The Maritime History of Massachusetts, 1783–1860* (Boston: Houghton Mifflin, 1961).

The *Philadelphia Club, 1834–1934* (Philadelphia: Privately printed, 1934).

Fritz Redlich, *The Molding of American Banking* (New York: Johnson Reprint, 1968).

Frederick B. Tolles, *Meeting House and Counting House: The Quaker Merchants of Colonial Philadelphia, 1682–1763* (Chapel Hill: University of North Carolina Press, 1948).

Hugh Whitney and Walter Muir Whitehill, *The Somerset Club, 1851–1951* (Boston: Privately printed 1951).

Peter A. B. Widener II, *Without Drums* (New York: Putnam, 1940).

EDUCATION

Frank D. Ashburn, *Peabody of Groton* (New York: Coward-McCann, 1944).

Edward Potts Cheyney, *History of the University of Pennsylvania, 1740–1940* (Philadelphia: University of Pennsylvania Press, 1940).

William H. Cornog, *School of the Republic, 1893–1943: A Half Century of the Central High School of Philadelphia* (Philadelphia: Rittenhouse Press, 1952).

Franklin Spencer Edmonds, *History of the Central High School of Philadelphia* (Philadelphia: Lippincott, 1902).

Benjamin Franklin, *Proposals Relating to the Education of Youth in Pensilvania,* facsimile ed. (Philadelphia: University of Pennsylvania Press, 1931).

Helen G. Hole, *Westtown through the Years, 1799–1942* (Westtown: Westtown Alumni Association, 1942).

Seymour Martin Lipset and David Riesman, *Education and Politics at Harvard* (New York: McGraw-Hill, 1975).

James McLachlan, *American Boarding Schools: An Historical Study* (New York: Scribner's, 1970).

Philip Marson, *Breeder of Democracy* (Cambridge: Schenkman, 1970).

Samuel Eliot Morison, *The Founding of Harvard College* (Cambridge: Harvard University Press, 1935).

_____, *Three Centuries of Harvard, 1636–1936* (Cambridge: Harvard University Press, 1963).

Arthur Stanwood Pier, *St. Paul's School, 1855–1934* (New York: Scribner's, 1934).

George W. Pierson, *The Education of American Leaders: Comparative Contributions of U.S. Colleges and Universities* (New York: Praeger, 1969).

Saul Sack, *History of Higher Education in Pennsylvania,* 2 vols. (Harrisburg: Pennsylvania Historical and Museum Commission, 1963).

Donald G. Tewksbury, *The Founding of American Colleges and Universities before the Civil War* (New York: Doubleday, Anchor Books, 1965).

Francis Newton Thorpe, *William Pepper* (Philadelphia: Lippincott, 1904).

A. W. Wallace, *The Muhlenbergs of Pennsylvania* (Philadelphia: University of Pennsylvania Press, 1950).

J. P. Wickersham, *A History of Education in Pennsylvania* (New York: Arno, 1969).

BOSTON AND PHILADELPHIA
AND THE AMERICAN MIND

Richmond Croom Beatty, *Bayard Taylor: Laureate of the Gilded Age* (Norman: University of Oklahoma Press, 1936).

Edward Sculley Bradley, *George Henry Boker: Poet and Patriot* (New York: AMS, 1927).

Van Wyck Brooks, *The Flowering of New England, 1815-1865* (New York: Dutton, 1936).

_____, *New England Indian Summer, 1865-1915* (New York: Dutton, 1940).

_____, *The Time of Melville and Whitman* (New York: Dutton, 1947).

_____, *The Confident Years, 1885-1915* (New York: Dutton, 1952).

Ernest Earnest, *S. Weir Mitchell: Novelist and Physician* (Philadelphia: University of Pennsylvania Press, 1950).

Richard Hofstadter, *Anti-Intellectualism in American Life* (New York: Knopf, 1963).

D. H. Lawrence, *Studies in Classic American Literature* (New York: Doubleday, 1953).

Frank Luther Mott, *A History of American Magazines*, 4 vols. (Cambridge: Harvard University Press, 1957).

Vernon Louis Parrington, *Main Currents in American Thought*, 2 vols. (New York: Harcourt, 1930).

Ben Merchant Vorpahl, *My Dear Wister: The Frederic Remington–Owen Wister Letters* (Palo Alto: American West Publishing, 1972).

Barrett Wendell, *A Literary History of America* (New York: Scribner's, 1901).

G. Edward White, *The Eastern Establishment and the Western Experience: The West of Frederic Remington, Theodore Roosevelt, and Owen Wister* (New Haven: Yale University Press, 1968).

Fanny Kemble Wister, ed., *Owen Wister Out West: His Journals and Letters* (Chicago: University of Chicago Press, 1958).

Owen Wister, *The Virginian: A Horseman of the Plains* (New York: Macmillan, 1902).

_____, *Roosevelt: The Story of a Friendship, 1880-1919* (New York: Macmillan, 1930).

ART AND ARCHITECTURE

Wayne Andrews, *Architecture, Ambition, and Americans*, rev. ed. (New York: Free Press, 1978).

Bainbridge Bunting, *Houses of Boston's Back Bay* (Cambridge: Harvard University Press, 1967).

Nancy Hale, *Mary Cassatt* (New York: Doubleday, 1975).

Gordon Hendricks, *The Life and Works of Thomas Eakins* (New York: Grossman, 1974).

Henry Russell Hitchcock, *The Architecture of H. H. Richardson and His Times* (New York: Museum of Modern Art, 1936).

M. A. DeWolfe Howe, *The Boston Symphony Orchestra* (Boston: Houghton Mifflin, 1931).

Herbert Kupperberg, *Those Fabulous Philadelphians: The Life and Times of a Great Orchestra* (New York: Scribner's, 1969).

James T. Maher, *The Twilight of Splendor: Chronicles of the Age of American Palaces* (Boston: Little, Brown, 1975).

George C. Mason, *The Life and Works of Gilbert Stuart* (New York: Scribner's, 1879).

Charles Merrill Mount, *John Singer Sargent* (New York: Norton, 1955).

John H. Mueller, *The American Symphony Orchestra* (Bloomington: Indiana University Press, 1951).

Lewis Mumford, ed., *Roots of Contemporary American Architecture* (New York: Dover, 1972).

James F. O'Gorman, *The Architecture of Frank Furness* (Philadelphia: Philadelphia Museum of Art, 1973).

————, *H. H. Richardson and His Office: A Centennial of His Move to Boston, 1874* (Boston: Harvard College Library, Department of Printing, 1974).

George Roberts and Mary Roberts, *Triumph on Fairmount: Fiske Kimball and the Philadelphia Museum of Art* (Philadelphia: Lippincott, 1959).

Charles Coleman Sellers, *Charles Wilson Peale*, 2 vols. (Philadelphia: American Philosophical Society, 1947).

Robert A. M. Stern, *George Howe: Toward a Modern American Architecture* (New Haven: Yale University Press, 1975).

Edward Teitelman and Richard W. Longstreth, *Architecture in Philadelphia: A Guide* (Cambridge: M.I.T. Press, 1974).

Helen Howe West, *George Howe, Architect, 1886–1955* (Philadelphia: Nunn, 1973).

Marcus Whiffen, *American Architecture since 1780: A Guide to the Styles* (Cambridge: M.I.T. Press, 1969).

Walter Muir Whitehill, *Boston: A Topographical History* (Cambridge: Harvard University Press, 1959).

————, *Museum of Fine Arts Boston: A Centennial History*, 2 vols. (Cambridge: Harvard University Press, 1970).

Richard Saul Wurman and John Andrew Gallory, *Man-Made Philadelphia: A Guide to Its Physical and Cultural Environment* (Cambridge: M.I.T. Press, 1972).

THE LEARNED PROFESSIONS

James Thayer Addison, *The Episcopal Church in the United States, 1789–1931* (New York: Scribner's, 1951).

Alexander V. G. Allen, *Life and Letters of Phillips Brooks* (New York: Dutton, 1901).

Joseph C. Aub and Ruth K. Hapgood, *Pioneer in Modern Medicine: David Linn Edsall of Harvard* (Boston: Harvard Medical Alumni Association, 1970).

Horace Binney, *The Leaders of the Old Bar of Philadelphia* (Philadelphia: Sherman, 1859).

Daniel Boorstin, *The Americans: The National Experience* (New York: Random House, 1965).

Anton-Hermann Chroust, *The Rise of the Legal Profession in America*, 2 vols. (Norman: University of Oklahoma Press, 1965).

George W. Corner, ed., *The Autobiography of Benjamin Rush* (Princeton: American Philosophical Society, 1948).

_____, *Two Centuries of Medicine: A History of the School of Medicine, University of Pennsylvania* (Philadelphia: Lippincott, 1965).

Simon Flexner and James Thomas Flexner, *William Henry Welch and the Heroic Age of American Medicine* (New York: Viking, 1941).

William Lawrence, *Memories of a Happy Life* (Boston: Houghton Mifflin, 1926).

George Wharton Pepper, *Philadelphia Lawyer: An Autobiography* (Philadlephia: Lippincott, 1944).

Richard H. Shryock, *Medicine and Society in America, 1660–1860* (Ithaca: Cornell University Press, Great Seal Books, 1962).

_____, *Medicine in America: Historical Essays* (Baltimore: Johns Hopkins Press, 1966).

Arthur E. Sutherland, *The Law at Harvard: A History of Ideas and Men, 1817–1967* (Cambridge: Harvard University Press, 1967).

Barnie F. Winkelman, *John G. Johnson: Lawyer and Art Collector, 1841–1917* (Philadelphia: University of Pennsylvania Press, 1942).

GOVERNING OF MEN

Geoffrey Blodgett, *The Gentle Reformers: Massachusetts Democrats in the Cleveland Era* (Cambridge: Harvard University Press, 1966).

Robert Douglas Bowden, *Boies Penrose: Symbol of an Era* (New York: Greenberg, 1937).

Edward Sculley Bradley, *Henry Charles Lea* (Philadelphia: University of Pennsylvania Press, 1931).

Erwin Stanley Bradley, *Simon Cameron: Lincoln's Secretary of War* (Philadelphia: University of Pennsylvania Press, 1966).

Walter Davenport, *Power and Glory: A Life of Boies Penrose* (New York: AMS, 1969).

John A. Garraty, *Henry Cabot Lodge* (New York: Knopf, 1968).

Stephen Hess, *America's Political Dynasties* (New York: Doubleday, 1966).

Richard Hofstadter, *The Age of Reform: From Bryan to F.D.R.* (New York: Random House, Vintage Books, 1960).

Justin Kaplan, *Lincoln Steffens* (New York: Simon & Schuster, 1974).

Philip S. Klein, *Pennsylvania Politics, 1817–1832: A Game without Rules* (Philadelphia: Historical Society of Pennsylvania, 1940).

William Lawrence, *Henry Cabot Lodge: A Biographical Sketch* (Boston: Houghton Mifflin, 1925).

Arthur Mann, *Yankee Reformers in the Urban Age* (Cambridge: Harvard University Press, 1954).

Samuel Whitaker Pennypacker, *Pennsylvania and Massachusetts: A Historical Parallel* (Philadelphia: Campbell, 1901).

_____, *Pennsylvania in American History* (Philadelphia: Campbell, 1910).

_____, *The Autobiography of a Pennsylvanian* (Philadelphia: Winston, 1918).

Lincoln Steffens, *The Autobiography of Lincoln Steffens* (New York: Harcourt, 1931).

_____, *The Shame of the Cities* (New York: Hill and Wang, 1957).

Mark Sullivan, *The Education of an American* (New York: Doubleday, 1938).

Sam Bass Warner, Jr., *The Private City: Philadelphia in Three Periods of Growth* (Philadelphia: University of Pennsylvania Press, 1968).

Conrad Weiler, *Philadelphia: Neighborhood, Authority, and the Urban Crisis* (New York: Praeger, 1974).

CATHOLICS IN TWO CULTURES

Ray Allen Billington, *The Protestant Crusade, 1800–1860: A Study of the Origins of American Nativism* (New York: Macmillan, 1938).

Dennis Clark, *The Irish in Philadelphia: Ten Generations of Urban Experience* (Philadelphia: Temple University Press, 1973).

James F. Connelly, ed., *The History of the Archdiocese of Philadelphia* (Philadelphia: Archdiocese of Philadelphia, 1976).

Consuela Marie Duffy, *Katherine Drexel: A Biography* (Cornwells Heights: Sisters of the Blessed Sacrament, 1966).

Oscar Handlin, *Boston's Immigrants: A Study in Acculturation*, rev. and enl. ed. (Cambridge: Harvard University Press, 1959).

J. Joseph Huthmacker, *Massachusetts People and Politics, 1919–1933* (New York: Athenaeum, 1969).

Arthur H. Lewis, *Those Philadelphia Kellys: With a Touch of Grace* (New York: Morrow, 1977).

Robert H. Lord, John E. Sexton, and Edward T. Harrington, *History of the Archdiocese of Boston*, 3 vols. (New York: Sheed & Ward, 1944).

James Reichley, *The Art of Government: Reform and Organization Politics in Philadelphia*. A Report to the Fund for the Republic (Philadelphia: Philadelphia reprint, ca. 1959).

James Jeffrey Roche, *The Life of John Boyle O'Reilly* (New York: Cassell, 1891).

Arthur M. Schlesinger, Jr., *A Pilgrim's Progress: Orestes A. Brownson* (Boston: Little, Brown, 1966).

William V. Shannon, *The American Irish* (New York: Macmillan, 1963).

ORTHODOX FRIENDS

Philip S. Benjamin, *The Philadelphia Quakers in the Industrial Age, 1865–1920* (Philadelphia: Temple University Press, 1976).

Anna Brinton, ed., *Then and Now: Quaker Essays by Friends of Henry Joel Cadbury* (Philadelphia: University of Pennsylvania Press, 1960).

Howard H. Brinton, ed., *Children of Light: In Honor of Rufus M. Jones* (New York: Macmillan, 1938).

Edwin B. Bronner, ed., *American Quakers Today* (Philadelphia: Friends World Committee, 1966).

Robert W. Doherty, *The Hicksite Separation: A Sociological Analysis of Religious Schism in Early Nineteenth-Century America* (New Brunswick: Rutgers University Press, 1967).

Bliss Forbush, *Elias Hicks: Quaker Liberal* (New York: Columbia University Press, 1956).

John F. Gummere, *Old Penn Charter* (Philadelphia: William Penn Charter School, 1973).

Gerald Jonas, *On Doing Good: A Quaker Experiment* (New York: Scribner's, 1971).

Rufus M. Jones, *Haverford College: A History and an Interpretation* (New York: Macmillan, 1933).

Cornelia Meigs, *What Makes a College: A History of Bryn Mawr* (New York: Macmillan, 1956).

Logan Pearsall Smith, *Unforgotten Years* (Boston: Little, Brown, 1939).

David E. Swift, *Joseph John Gurney: Banker, Reformer, and Quaker* (Middletown: Wesleyan University Press, 1962).

Elizabeth Gray Vining, *Friend of Life: The Biography of Rufus M. Jones* (Philadelphia: Lippincott, 1958).

INDEX

Index

Library Company of Philadelphia, 169, 240
Life and Memorable Actions of George Washington, The (Weems), 290
Lightning rod, Franklin's invention of, 172
Lilburne, John, 81, 84, 85
Lincoln, Abraham, 34, 36, 294, 404
Lincoln, Alice N., 373
Lincoln, Levi, 183, 202
Lincoln, Levi, Jr., 386, 387
Linnaeus, Carolus, 166n, 168, 172, 173
Linton, Ralph, 26
Lippmann, Walter, 3
Liszt, Franz, 300
Literary History of America (Wendell), 286
Literary History of the United States (Spiller et al., eds.), 298
Literature, Boston's flowering and, 54, 55
Lloyd, David, 128, 129
Lloyd, Thomas, 127–29, 137
Lloyd family, 39
Lodge, Anna (Nannie), 409-11
Lodge, Henry Cabot, 200n, 262, 282, 286, 400
  Bishop William Lawrence and, 409–11
  Boies Penrose compared to, 406–12
Lodge, Henry Cabot, Jr., 400, 414
Lodge family, 240, 426
Loeb, James, 267
Logan, George, 196, 399
Logan, James, 140, 153–56, 163, 169, 322
  science and, 168
Logan Act, 196
Loganian Library, 169
London Quarterly Review, 12
London Spectator, 13
Longfellow, Ernest Wadsworth, 308, 313
Longfellow, Henry Wadsworth, 222, 262, 288
Longfellow family, 240
Lord's Supper, 60
Lorimer, George Horace, 283, 289
Louis, Pierre, 355–57
Louisiana Purchase, 196
Lowell, Abbott Lawrence, 23, 44, 201, 209, 242n, 257, 260, 262, 265, 271
Lowell, Augustus, 257
Lowell, Rev. Charles, 257
Lowell, Edward Jackson, 262
Lowell, Francis Cabot (1775–1817), 220–21, 257
Lowell, Francis Cabot (1803–1874), 257
Lowell, Francis Cabot (1855–1911), 257
Lowell, George Gardner, 257

Lowell, Guy, 331
Lowell, James Russell, 36, 257, 262, 286, 288, 291
Lowell, Rev. John (1704–1767), 257, 364
Lowell, John (1743–1802), 183, 198, 257
Lowell, John (1769–1840), 197–98, 257
Lowell, John (1799–1836), 257
Lowell, John (1824–1897), 257
Lowell, John (financier), 209-10
Lowell, John Amory, 257
Lowell, Percival, 198, 262
Lowell, Rebecca Tyng, 198
Lowell, Robert, 39n
Lowell, Sarah Higginson, 198
Lowell, Susan Cabot, 198
Lowell family, 48, 198, 215, 240, 336, 364
  Harvard and, 255–57
  in textile industry, 220–21
Lowell Institute, 221
Lowle, Percival, 198, 262
Ludlow, Rev. John, 255
Ludwig, Carl, 355
Lundberg, Ferdinand, 236
Luther, Martin, 60–64, 96, 102
  secular authority and, 61–62
Lutheranism, 61, 64
  civil authority and, 62
Lutherans, 249
Lyman, Theodore, 262, 373
Lyman family, 240
Lynd, Helen M., 32
Lynd, Robert S., 32
Lynnewood Hall, 243

McArthur, John, Jr., 326
McCall, Peter, 374
McCarthy, Joseph, 139–40
McClellan, George, 357, 358
McClellan, George (son of George Brinton), 358
McClellan, George Brinton, 358
McCormack, John W., 431
McIntire, Samuel, 324
McKean, Thomas, 192, 201, 341
McKean family, 336
McKim, Charles F., 323, 329
McKim, Mead & White, 334n
McKinley, William, 11
McKittrick, Eric, 187
McLachlan, James, 274
McMichael, Morton, 376
McNeil, Henry S., 210, 211
Madison, James, 36, 189
Magazines, 285–90
Magistracy (magistrates):
  Calvin's view of, 63–64

X-MEN: MESSIAH COMPLEX

X-MEN: MESSIAH COMPLEX. Contains material originally published in magazine form as X-MEN: MESSIAH COMPLEX, UNCANNY X-MEN #492-494, X-MEN #205-207, NEW X-MEN #44-46 and X-FACTOR #25-27. Eighth printing 2018. ISBN 978-0-7851-2320-0. Published by MARVEL WORLDWIDE, INC., a subsidiary of MARVEL ENTERTAINMENT, LLC. OFFICE OF PUBLICATION: 135 West 50th Street, New York, NY 10020.

X-MEN: MESSIAH COMPLEX ONE-SHOT

Writer: **ED BRUBAKER**
Penciler: **MARC SILVESTRI**
Inkers: **JOE WEEMS** with **MARCO GALLI**
Background Assists: **SHELDON MITCHELL**
Colorist: **FRANK D'ARMATA**
Letterer: **CHRIS ELIOPOULOS**

UNCANNY X-MEN #492-494

Writer: **ED BRUBAKER**
Penciler: **BILLY TAN**
Inkers: **DANNY MIKI**
with **ALLAN MARTINEZ**
Colorist: **FRANK D'ARMATA**
Letterer: **JOE CARAMAGNA**

X-FACTOR #25-27

Writer: **PETER DAVID**
Penciler: **SCOT EATON**
Inkers: **JOHN DELL**
with **ANDREW HENNESSY**
& **DAVE MEIKIS**
Colorists: **FRANK D'ARMATA**
with **BRIAN REBER**
Letterer: **CORY PETIT**

NEW X-MEN #44-46

Writers: **CRAIG KYLE** & **CHRIS YOST**
Penciler: **HUMBERTO RAMOS**
Inkers: **CARLOS CUEVAS**
with **DAVE MEIKIS**
Colorist: **STUDIO F'S EDGAR DELGADO**
Letterer: **DAVE SHARPE**

X-MEN #205-207

Writer: **MIKE CAREY**
Penciler: **CHRIS BACHALO**
Inkers: **TIM TOWNSEND**
with **JON SIBAL**,
VICTOR OLAZABA & **AL VEY**
Colorists: **BRIAN REBER**
with **EDGAR DELGADO**
Letterers: **CORY PETIT**
with **JOE CARAMAGNA**

Cover Artists: **DAVID FINCH**
with **DANNY MIKI**,
JASON KEITH, DAVE MCCAIG,
MORRY HOLLOWELL
& **FRANK D'ARMATA**

Assistant Editor: **WILL PANZO**
Editor: **NICK LOWE**
Executive Editor: **AXEL ALONSO**

Special Thanks to
ANDY SCHMIDT,
C.B. CEBULSKI,
DANIEL KETCHUM
and **AUBREY SITTERSON**

X-Men created by **STAN LEE & JACK KIRBY**

Collection Editor: **CORY LEVINE**
Assistant Editor: **CAITLIN O'CONNELL**
Associate Managing Editor: **KATERI WOODY**
Editor, Special Projects: **MARK D. BEAZLEY**
Senior Editor, Special Projects:
JENNIFER GRÜNWALD
VP Production & Special Projects:
JEFF YOUNGQUIST
SVP Print, Sales & Marketing:
DAVID GABRIEL
Book Design: **RODOLFO MURAGUCHI**

Editor in Chief: **C.B. CEBULSKI**
Chief Creative Officer: **JOE QUESADA**
President: **DAN BUCKLEY**
Executive Producer: **ALAN FINE**

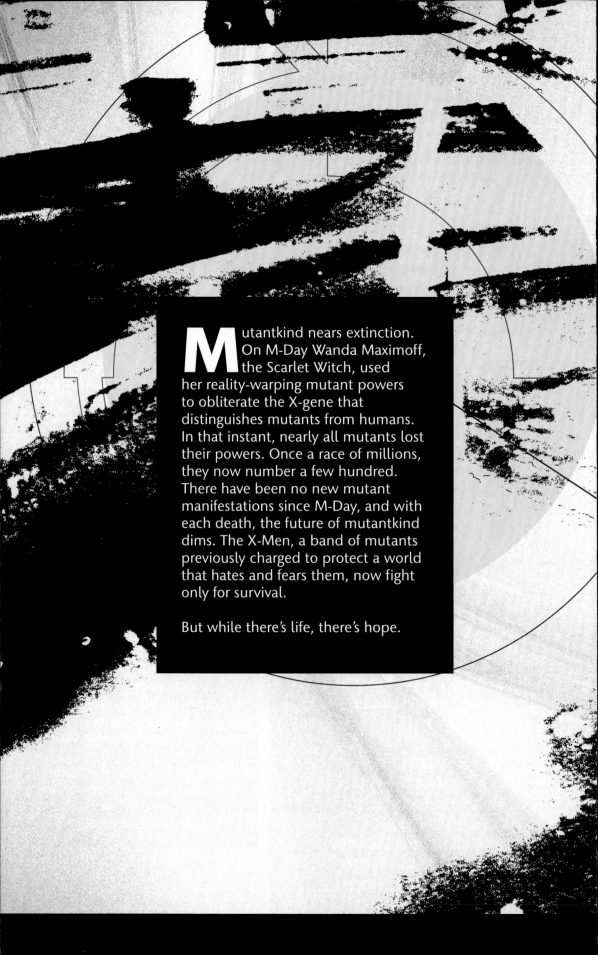

Mutantkind nears extinction. On M-Day Wanda Maximoff, the Scarlet Witch, used her reality-warping mutant powers to obliterate the X-gene that distinguishes mutants from humans. In that instant, nearly all mutants lost their powers. Once a race of millions, they now number a few hundred. There have been no new mutant manifestations since M-Day, and with each death, the future of mutantkind dims. The X-Men, a band of mutants previously charged to protect a world that hates and fears them, now fight only for survival.

But while there's life, there's hope.

THE BLACKBIRD-- CROSSING INTO ALASKA, MOVING AT TOP SPEED.

THE X-MEN.

CYCLOPS.

EMMA FROST.

YOU PICKING UP ANYTHING? WE SHOULD BE CLOSE BY NOW.

NOTHING... WHICH IS A *BIT* TROUBLING.

NIGHTCRAWLER.

WHAT DO YOU MEAN?

WOLVERINE.

IT'S A WHOLE TOWN FULLA PEOPLE, AN' EMMA AIN'T HEARIN' *ANY* OF THEIR THOUGHTS...

ANGEL.

IT'S A TRAP.

CHARLES!

--THE HELL?

UHNN!

MS. FROST? WHAT'S THE MATTER?

ARE WE BEING ATTACKED? AWESOME!

CHARLES...?

I'M ALRIGHT... I JUST...I'M ALRIGHT...

WHAT *WAS* THAT? THE ENTIRE *SYSTEM'S* BEEN FRIED...

THAT...

...MAY JUST HAVE BEEN THE REBIRTH OF *HOPE.*

Uh... PROFESSOR?

FIX IT, HENRY. WE NEED *CEREBRA* UP AND RUNNING...SOON AS POSSIBLE...

I'LL GET THE *AUXILIARY POWER* STARTED...

...AND THEN I'LL BE *RIGHT BACK* TO ASSIST.

SCOTT, EMMA... ASSEMBLE A FIELD TEAM AND MEET ME AT THE *HANGAR*-- NOW.

BAMF

BAMF

BAMF

BAMF

BAMF

BAMF

BAMF

BAMF

WHAT ELSE *CAN* WE THINK, EMMA? WE'RE LOOKING FOR THE *FIRST* NEW MUTANT SINCE *M-DAY* AND WE FIND A DISASTER INSTEAD.

IF OUR NEW MUTANT DID THIS, SCOTT, IT *MUST* HAVE BEEN AN *ACCIDENT.*

A REACTION TO THE *ONSET* OF MUTATION.

WHAT IF BLOWING UP THE TOWN *WAS* HIS MUTATION?

I NEARLY *KILLED* PEOPLE WHEN *MY* ABILITIES APPEARED...AND I'M *FAR* FROM THE FIRST TO HAVE THAT PROBLEM.

THEY KILLED... BABIES...

THOSE SONS OF BITCHES KILLED *BABIES* IN CASE ONE WAS A MUTANT...

BAMF

DON'T TOUCH ANYTHING.

I NEED TO...

...GET THE...

DAMN IT.

NOTHING?

NAH. TOO DAMN MUCH SMOKE AND *CHEMICALS* IN THE AIR...CAN'T ISOLATE ANYTHING.

...SO WE DON'T HAVE *TIME* FOR TURF WARS.

SCOTT.

PROFESSOR.

WHY DIDN'T YOU *INFORM* ME YOU'D SENT OUT A TEAM?

HANK AND I HAVE BEEN TRYING TO GET CEREBRA BACK ONLINE, BUT THAT DOESN'T MEAN--

SINCE WHEN DO I NEED *YOUR* PERMISSION TO LEAD THE X-MEN?

IN CASE YOU'VE FORGOTTEN, PROFESSOR, THE *FIRST* NEW MUTANT TO APPEAR SINCE *M-DAY* IS PROBABLY IN THE HANDS OF ONE OF OUR *WORST NIGHTMARES.*

SO I'M NOT GOING TO *DEBATE* EVERY PLAN OF ACTION WITH *YOU.*

ESPECIALLY IN LIGHT OF YOUR *TRACK RECORD* LATELY.

SCOTT... THAT'S NOT FAIR.

ISN'T IT? AREN'T YOU THE MAN WHO LEFT MY BROTHER IN OUTER SPACE LAST MONTH?

THE MAN WHO LIED ABOUT THE *DANGER ROOM*, AND *KRAKOA*? WHO *STOOD BY* WHILE MY FATHER WAS *KILLED*?

THAT'S *NOT* HOW IT HAPPENED, AND YOU *KNOW* IT.

AND I'M *ALSO* THE MAN WHO *TRAINED* ALL OF YOU, AND WHO KNOWS *MORE* ABOUT NEW MUTANTS THAN ANYONE ON THIS PLANET.

EXCEPT MAYBE *SINISTER*, RIGHT?

DAMN IT. LET ME *HELP*, SCOTT.

HELP BY LETTING ME DO WHAT YOU TRAINED ME TO DO...TO *LEAD*.

AND HELP BY GETTING *CEREBRA* WORKING AGAIN AS QUICKLY AS YOU CAN.

JAMIE, RICTOR... I APOLOGIZE FOR THE WAY EMMA GOT YOU HERE, BUT AS SHE TOLD YOU...THIS IS IMPORTANT.

MORE IMPORTANT THAN THE PROBLEMS BETWEEN OUR TEAMS.

WHAT IS *GOING ON*, SUMMERS? I HAVEN'T SEEN YOU THIS TENSE SINCE *PROTEUS* TRIED TO EAT YOUR GIRLFRIEND...

EVERYTHING'S CHANGED.

YOU BROUGHT *LAYLA MILLER?* THAT WASN'T PART OF THE REQUEST.

I KNOW, MS. FROST...AND THAT'S *WHY* I TAGGED ALONG.

JAMIE'S GOING TO NEED ME *WITH* HIM FOR WHAT COMES NEXT.

AND WHAT'S *THAT?* WHAT'S COMING NEXT?

STUFF I *DON'T* KNOW, ACTUALLY.

BUT I KNOW I NEED TO *BE* THERE. AND I KNOW--

THAT EVERYTHING *HAS* CHANGED.

IT'S TRUE. THERE'S A NEW *MUTANT* IN THE WORLD.

AND YOU'RE ALL GOING TO HELP US SAVE IT.

SOMETHING YOU'RE NOT GOING TO **WANT** TO DO...

I'M LIKING THE SOUND OF **THIS** ALREADY...

HE WANTS YOU TO **INFILTRATE** THE PURIFIERS.

HEY--I CAN TALK FOR MYSELF.

SORRY. BUT YOU'RE RIGHT. IT MAKES **SENSE.** THE PURIFIERS' PUBLIC PERSONA MEANS A FRONTAL ASSAULT WOULD BE A NIGHTMARE.

BUT RICTOR'S NOT A **MUTANT** ANYMORE, SO HE COULD MAYBE SNEAK IN.

YOU WANT TO PUT ME **UNDERCOVER** WITH THOSE SICK, TWISTED **MUTANT-HATERS?**

THE PEOPLE WHO PROBABLY KILLED EVERY **CHILD** IN THAT TOWN?

YES, IS THAT GOING TO BE A PROBLEM?

WHAT'S JAMIE'S **JOB,** THEN?

GOING TO THE SAVAGE LAND TO HAVE LUNCH WITH **SAURON?**

DO YOU WANNA TELL HIM, LAYLA?

WE'RE GOING TO SEE FORGE...

WHO'S FORGE?

--JUST THOUGHT ENOUGH TIME HAD PASSED... THAT I'D PROVEN... I DON'T KNOW, SOMETHING...

THIS GETS STRANGER AND STRANGER...

I AGREE.

NO, I'M SORRY, I MEAN THIS BLASTER THE PURIFIERS WERE CARRYING...I THOUGHT IT WOULD BE MORE FUTURE-TECH THEY SALVAGED FROM NIMROD...

WHICH, I'M ASSUMING, IS HOW THEY KNEW ABOUT THE CHILD'S BIRTH BEFORE CEREBRA DID.

BUT THIS WEAPON ... IT'S NOT FUTURISTIC IN DESIGN AT ALL. IN FACT, IT LOOKS KIND OF FAMILIAR.

WHICH, AS I SAID...IS STRANGE... I NEED TO LOOK THROUGH MY PURIFIER FILES AGAIN.

I'M SURE SCOTT WILL GET TO THE BOTTOM OF IT.

HE WILL, CHARLES...YOU TRAINED HIM WELL. TAKE PRIDE IN THAT, AND LET HIM LEAD...

I DON'T KNOW WHAT ELSE TO TELL YOU.

I'M GOING TO GO CHECK THE REROUTING...

NOOOOOOO!

EASY, I GOT YOU.

BAMF

AND I... HAVE THIS ONE.

HUTT--

KRAK

I CAN DO THIS ALL NIGHT, YOU RUSSIAN FREAK!

THEN IT IS GOING TO BE A LONG NIGHT...

LOOK OUT PETE!

UK--

KA-WHAMM

NOW LOOK AT *THAT.* YA HURT YER OWN GUY... *PATHETIC.*

AND FOR WHAT, TO PROTECT A GUY LIKE *EXODUS?*

A GUY WHO YA DIDN'T WANNA *FOLLOW* IN THE FIRST PLACE?

ALL RIGHT... ALL RIGHT... FINE...

...WHAT DO YOU WANT TO KNOW?

LATER...

LOGAN JUST REPORTED IN.

LOOKS LIKE THEY GOT A *LEAD* ON TRACKING EXODUS...AND *HOPEFULLY* THE MARAUDERS HE JOINED UP WITH.

GOOD.

YOU SHOULD TAKE SOME TIME TO SPEAK WITH THE *STUDENTS*, IF YOU CAN. THEY'RE COMPLAINING ABOUT SITTING THIS OUT...

THIS MEANS *A LOT* TO THEM, A NEW MUTANT BIRTH...

IT MEANS THEY MIGHT NOT BE THE *LAST* GENERATION.

I'LL TALK TO THEM SOON.

I HAVE TO FINISH A FIELD REPORT FOR FORGE, AND THEN HANK NEEDS TO SHOW ME SOMETHING...

I LIKE IT WHEN YOU'RE LIKE THIS...ALL IN CHARGE. IT SUITS YOU.

I DON'T KNOW ABOUT THAT.

I STILL FEEL LIKE THERE'S SOMETHING *BIG* I'M MISSING HERE...

SOMEWHERE IN CANADA.

"...SOME WILD CARD WE HAVEN'T EVEN CONSIDERED."

PREDATOR X MOVES AT A SPEED FUELED BY HUNGER.

THE TWO DEAD MUTANTS IN ALASKA LAST NIGHT GAVE HIM THE ENERGY TO MOVE ON...

...BUT THEY WOULD BE A MORSEL COMPARED TO THE OTHER ONE--THE NEW ONE--THAT HE FEELS OUT THERE SOMEWHERE...

...IN THE DISTANCE.

EEYARRRHHHH!!!

SPASH

WOLFSBANE GET IN!

UNHHH...

IT'S WOUNDED! FINISH IT OFF!

UNFFFF!

DON'T LET IT GET AWAY, BOYS.

IS THAT WHAT I THINK IT IS?

SURE WAS, MY FRIEND. A MUTANT.

FREAKIN' THINGS ARE RUINING THE CITY FOR THE REST OF US. YOU'RE ONE OF STRYKER'S BUNCH, RIGHT? BEEN LOOKING FOR YOU FELLAS.

YEAH? WHAT'S YOUR NAME, PAL?

JOAQUIN. JOAQUIN MURRIETA. FRIENDS CALL ME JAKE.

OKAY. WE LOST THEM.

CYCLOPS? RICTOR'S IN. THEY TOTALLY BOUGHT IT.

ACH. STUPID FAKE BLOOD. I'LL *NEVER* GET THESE STAINS OUT.

AND THE SQUIBS STING LIKE A SON OF A--

DO YOU *COPY*, CYCLOPS?

LOUD AND CLEAR, SIRYN. HOW'S WOLFSBANE?

COMPLAINING THAT THE SQUIBS HURT.

BULLETS WOULD HAVE HURT MORE.

YO. SCOTT.

CAN WE TALK?

AH, MADROX. YOU'RE HERE. GOOD.

AND WHO IS THIS?

I'M LAYLA MILLER.

SHE KNOWS STUFF.

YOU NOTICE I HAVEN'T HAD TO SAY THAT IN A WHILE? EVERYBODY ELSE KEEPS SAYING IT FOR ME. ISN'T THAT FUNNY?

HILARIOUS. YOU WANT TO STEP ASIDE, FORGE? LET US IN OUT OF THE--

--RAIN?

FZZT

IS THIS AMONG THE "STUFF" THAT SHE JUST KNOWS?

YOU HAD NO SHADOW. HALF THE STUFF I KNOW JUST COMES FROM PAYING ATTENTION.

THAT DAUNTING-LOOKING DEVICE IN THE CORNER IS A COFFEEMAKER. POUR YOURSELF SOME IF YOU'RE SO INCLINED.

HOW MUCH DID SCOTT TELL YOU?

NOT A TON. MOSTLY THAT YOU HAD A LITTLE GADGET DESIGNED FOR GATHERING INFORMATION.

YES, WELL...THIS IS IT.

WHAT IS IT?

TIME MACHINE.

WELL, ACTUALLY, TO BE MORE ACCURATE, A SORT OF GPS FOR TIME AND SPACE. I CALL IT A CHRONAL TRACER. NEXT ONE'LL BE MORE COMPACT, BUT IT WORKS.

I'VE GOT AN IDEA. MAKE IT A DELOREAN.

FUNNY. HERE'S THE THING: TIME BRANCHES OFF INTO INFINITE DIRECTIONS. BUT AFTER M-DAY, ALL BRANCHES INVOLVING MUTANTS... WELL...

FLATLINED, FOR LACK OF A BETTER WORD.

I SEARCHED COUNTLESS FUTURES FOR SIGNS OF MUTANTS.

CAME UP WITH SQUAT.

BUT SINCE THE BIRTH OF THE MISSING CHILD, TWO BRANCHES HAVE SPIKED.

IT BEARS INVESTIGATION.

AND THAT'S WHERE I COME IN, WHAT WITH ME BEING AN INVESTIGATOR AND ALL.

HEY, VOGHT. LONG TIME NO SEE.

WOLVERINE!

WANTED TO GET IN QUICK, AND LETTIN' MYSELF GET RUN OVER SEEMED THE FASTEST WAY.

NOW, NURSE VOGHT, LET'S YOU AND ME--

WHAT THE--?!?

FWOOSH

YO, ELF. SHE'S RUNNING. MISTED HERSELF INTO THE VENT.

WE'RE ON IT.

EXCELLENT. LET'S GET THIS ROLLING.

FIRST VOLUNTEER ON THE PLATFORM, PLEASE.

IGNITION IN THREE...TWO... ONE...

'TIS A FAR, FAR BETTER THING I DO NOW, THAN I HAVE EVER--

LAUNCH!

OH, THANK GOD HE'S GONE.

NEXT.

IGNITION IN THREE...TWO... ONE--

LAYLA!!!

REVERSE IT! REVERSE IT RIGHT NOW!

I CAN'T! BOTH OF THEM ARE ONE-WAY TRIPS!

ONE WAY?! HOW THE HELL IS MY DUPE SUPPOSED TO GET BACK?

THEY'RE NOT. WHEN EACH OF THEM VANISHED, A MESSAGE WAS PSIONICALLY TRANSFERRED INTO THEIR BRAIN CELLS. ONCE THEY ARRIVE, THEY'LL JUST KNOW...

KNOW WHAT?!?

THAT AS SOON AS THEY'VE GATHERED THE INTEL, THEY SHOULD KILL THEMSELVES. THEN THE KNOWLEDGE WILL BE TRANSFERRED DIRECTLY TO YOUR MIND, WITHIN SECONDS.

THE DOMINION RANGE, ANTARCTICA.

SOMETHING'S GONE WRONG.

RELAX. ELF KNOWS WHAT HE'S DOING.

BAMF!

KURT! WELL?

JA... ...THEY'RE HERE.

NICE CHURCH.

THAT'S A LOT OF TITHING, I'M GUESSING.

FATHER MATTHEW SUMMONED THE SHEPHERDS OF THE EAST TO THE CATHEDRAL IN WASHINGTON.

SOON ALL OF OUR BROTHERS FROM THE EASTERN CHURCHES WILL BE AMONG US. WE MUST BE PREPARED FOR THEIR ARRIVAL.

HOW MANY CHURCHES ARE WE TALKING ABOUT HERE?

I JUST NEVER GUESSED THERE'D BE SO MANY.

AND, YOU KNOW...WITH SO MANY GUNS.

HUNDREDS...BUT THAT'S JUST IN THE EAST. THIS IS HAPPENING ALL ACROSS THE WORLD, BROTHER.

ALL MY LIFE, I'D PRAYED THAT ONE DAY I'D FIND PEOPLE JUST LIKE ME.

AT THIS TIME OF NIGHT, ALL *GOOD* LITTLE CHILDREN ARE TUCKED UP SAFE IN THEIR *BEDS.*

SO IT FOLLOWS THAT *THESE* CHILDREN ARE NOT GOOD AT ALL.

REAVERS--

--BE *SEVERE* WITH THEM.

KEEP AWAY FROM JULIEN KELLER.

I'M *WARNING* YOU.

NARRHHHRR!

SIHAL NOVARUM CHIN--

ZZZZZHHHHH

CRUNCH

CRASH

DRGGEG

SPLASH

AAAHRRR!

SC-SCOTT! THE **STUDENTS**-- OH GOD!

EMMA, WHAT IS IT? WHAT'S **HAPPENED**?

THEY-- THEY WENT TO FIGHT THE **PURIFIERS**.

THEY BARELY GOT AWAY ALIVE. THAT WAS **PIXIE'S** SCREAM INSIDE MY HEAD.

RICTOR'S WITH THEM. THE PURIFIERS **DON'T** HAVE THE BABY.

WHERE ARE THEY **NOW**?

SPREAD OUT BETWEEN HERE AND **WASHINGTON**. IT WAS A BLIND TELEPORT, AND IT ALMOST KILLED THEM.

I'LL BRING THEM IN.

THANK YOU BOBBY, BUT THAT'S NOT THE **WORST** OF IT. I WAS--DISTRACTED. I LOST **CONTACT** WITH THE ASSAULT TEAM FOR A MOMENT.

AND NOW I CAN'T GET IT **BACK**.

"SINISTER IS LOCKING ME **OUT**."

ELF--

REST *EASY,* LOGAN. I'LL GET YOU OUT OF *HERE.*

NO! *LISTEN* TO ME!

MARAUDERS-- GHH!--DON'T HAVE-- THE *BABY!*

SHE'S WITH--

BLAAM

AAAA!

BAMF

YOU *IMBECILE!* YOU MISSED YOUR SHOT.

HE GOT *AWAY!*

DON'T WORRY. WITH 9MM FLUTED *HOLLOWPOINT--*

"--GETTING *AWAY*
DOESN'T MAKE ALL
THAT MUCH OF A
DIFFERENCE."

BAMF

GAAAAAH!

L-LOGAN!
I
C-CAN'T--

EMMA--
COME *IN!*

COME IN
IF--YOU CAN
HEAR *ME.*

I'M HEARING
YOU, LOGAN. WHERE
ARE YOU, AND HOW
DID YOU DO?

DID YOU
RETRIEVE THE
BABY?

NEGATIVE. THE
MARAUDERS DON'T
HAVE THE BABY. ONE
OF *OUR* SIDE HAS
HER.

AN X-MAN
TOOK HER FROM
COOPERSTOWN.

HEY, LEX. I'M FEELING A LITTLE *QUEASY* HERE. ANY CHANCE I COULD CLOCK OFF *EARLY*?

NEGATIVE, SLAYTON. ROSTER'S SHORT ALREADY.

USE YOUR COCKPIT DIAGNOSTICS. IF YOU'RE SICK, THE TECH WILL KNOW.

WOW. THANKS FOR THE OVERFLOWING *COMPASSION,* MAN.

OKAY, FINE. I'LL JUST--

H-HEY!

WHAT'S--?

LEX! LEX, SOMETHING *CRAZY'S* HAPPENING!

HELP ME!

LEX, CAN YOU *HEAR* ME?

OH GOD! GOD, PLEASE DON'T *RRRZZZZZZZ*

IT'S WHAT *GAMBIT* TOLD LOGAN. AND LOGAN *BELIEVES* IT.

THAT MAKES NO *SENSE!*

BUT—HE WOULD HAVE *CONTACTED* US!

WOULD HE? ONLY IF HE SHARED OUR *AGENDA*, SCOTT. AND IF HE DID, WOULDN'T HE HAVE BEEN IN *TOUCH* ALREADY?

TO TELL US HE WAS STILL *ALIVE?*

TELL *STORM* TO PULL OUT. NOW!

I CAN'T *REACH* STORM. BUT WOLVERINE SAYS HE AND NIGHTCRAWLER ARE—

KREEE!!

"...THAT CHANGES EVERYTHING."

WAAAHHHHH!

BWAA--AAA!

COME ON, KID... SHUT UP FOR A MINUTE...

...KEEP SCREAMIN' LIKE THAT... YOU'RE GONNA ATTRACT PREDATORS.

KROOOM

HEY! ANY TIME *ONE OF YOU* WANTS TO *JUMP* IN HERE!

HANG ON, WARPATH!

DUST, YOU *UP* FOR THIS? WE NEED TO KNOW WHAT'S GOING ON *INSIDE* THIS THING.

I BELIEVE SO, CYCLOPS... SIR...

JAMES... WE CAN'T KEEP UP AT THIS...

I KNOW... BUT... MAYBE WE DON'T HAVE TO.

GET BEHIND ME-- NOW.

"HAVE YOU LOST YOUR MIND?

"DID YOU EVEN *CONSIDER* THE CONSEQUENCES OF WHAT YOU'VE DONE?"

DISPATCHING OUR BEST TRACKERS, OUR MOST FORMIDABLE FIGHTERS? IT NEEDED TO BE DONE. WE'RE AT THE MUTANT EQUIVALENT OF DEFCON 1...

AND YOU PANICKED, HONESTLY, SCOTT...I'M DISAPPOINTED. I...WELL, I THOUGHT I'D TAUGHT YOU BETTER.

PEOPLE... GIVE US SOME SPACE, PLEASE?

I'M SORRY, SCOTT. WHATEVER CONCERNS I HAVE...I SHOULDN'T HAVE EXPRESSED THEM IN FRONT OF THE OTHERS. I ONLY DID IT BECAUSE--

BECAUSE IT SEEMED LIKE A GOOD IDEA AT THE TIME.

BUT SCOTT, YOU'VE GOT TO ADMIT--SENDING KILLERS AFTER YOUR OWN SON?

CHARLES, YOU TRAINED ME TO BE LEADER OF THE X-MEN.

DIDN'T IT EVER OCCUR TO YOU THAT, FOR ME TO TAKE THE REINS...

YOU'D HAVE TO STOP DRIVING?

INTELLECTUALLY... YES. BUT NOW...

THAT'S WHAT I THOUGHT.

SCOTT, DON'T YOU SEE? THESE ARE SPECIAL CIRCUMSTANCES.

THEY'RE ALWAYS SPECIAL CIRCUMSTANCES, CHARLES.

I WANT TO KNOW EVERYTHING YOU KNOW ABOUT THAT MUTANT CONCENTRATION CAMP OVER THERE.

UNHHHH!!!

GO TO HELL, MUTIE.

I'M LOOKING AT HELL RIGHT OVER THERE! AND YOU'RE ONE OF THE DEMONS WHO--

UNFFFFF!

JAMIE!

WE WANT TO FIND OUT AS MUCH AS WE CAN ABOUT THAT PLACE.

IF YOU BEAT HIM TO DEATH, WE'LL NEED A OUIJA BOARD TO LEARN ANYTHING.

I KNOW YOU'RE RIGHT, LAYLA. YOU USUALLY ARE. IT'S JUST...

IT'S UNBELIEVABLE. BACK IN OUR OWN TIME, MUTANTS ARE A DYING BREED...

BUT IF WE MANAGE TO SURVIVE ALL THAT... THEN THIS IS WHAT WE HAVE TO LOOK FORWARD TO?

ALBERTA, CANADA; NOW.

COORDINATES, EMMA.

THREE DEGREES LEFT OF *ARC*, TWO THOUSAND METERS.

BUT THERE'S NO NEED TO *HURRY*, SCOTT.

THE BATTLE'S OVER, AND *CABLE'S* GONE.

WE'RE TOO *LATE*.

"NOW--

"--DO YOU WANT THE *BAD* NEWS?"

YOU'LL MAKE A GOOD *SOLDIER* SOME DAY, KID. YOU'VE GOT THE RIGHT PRIORITIES.

DOESN'T MATTER WHERE YOU ARE, A SQUARE *MEAL* COMES FIRST.

BUT MAN SHALL NOT LIVE BY *BREAD* ALONE. WE ALSO NEED A LITTLE SOMETHING CALLED A CHRONAL *SLIPPAGE* REGULATOR.

ONLY *ONE* PLACE I KNOW OF WHERE WE CAN GET IT.

AND HERE COMES OUR *RIDE.* RIGHT ON TIME.

SCREEE

THIS IS YOUR NEW *HOME*, GENE-JOKE. COME ON, TAKE A LITTLE *LOOK*.

YOU'RE GONNA *LIKE* IT HERE. IT'S KIND OF LIKE A *BEACH RESORT*.

ONLY, Y'KNOW, WITH LESS SAND. AND MORE *BARBED WIRE*.

HE LOOKS A BIT *ROUGH*.

SO YOU THINK WE SHOULD DRAG 'IM OVER TO *DOC KEEVER*?

SO?

HEY, LET THE *MUTIES* TAKE CARE O' THEIR *OWN*.

MY *BREAK* STARTS IN FIVE.

YOU OUGHTA BE THANKIN' US.

AAAHHH!

STAND CLEAR, SUNFIRE...

...THIS HAS GONE ON LONG ENOUGH.

KABOOM

...NO...

WE SHOULD KILL HIM.

NO...THE X-MEN WILL BE HERE SOON...

DEALING WITH THIS TRAITOR MIGHT SLOW THEM DOWN A BIT.

HOW'S THE CHILD?

PERFECT... CABLE KEPT IT SAFE.

BUT YOU ARE CORRECT, MY LINK TO OUR *MUTANT TRACKER* TELLS ME THAT THE X-MEN'S ARRIVAL IS IMMINENT. WE SHOULD DEPART NOW.

IS THERE SOME PROBLEM, GAMBIT?

NO, JUST...

...WONDERIN' WHAT *CHANGED* FOR *HIM*, THAT HE'D TURN ON 'EM.

WONDERIN' WHAT THE HELL HE WAS THINKIN'...

HEY, I'M TRYING TO FIND MY FRIEND...YOUNG GIRL, TALKS A LOT...

UH... HELLO?

JUST IGNORE HIM.

WHAT'S YOUR PROBLEM?

BETTER LEARN TO X THAT *ATTITUDE* NEWBO...AN' LEAVE ME THE FRICK ALONE.

MY GOD... THIS *FUTURE* SUCKS.

--GOT THE CUCKOOS' *DISTRESS CALL* AND I RUSHED TO DALLAS IN MY SHIP...

BUT WHEN I GOT HERE, CABLE HAD ALREADY TAKEN FORGE OUT AND WAS PILLAGING HIS EQUIPMENT ROOM.

HE AND I FOUGHT... I SHOT HIM A FEW TIMES. SHOULD'VE *HAD* HIM.

DON'T BEAT YOURSELF UP, LUCAS...JUST TELL US WHAT HAPPENED.

JUST AS I WAS ABOUT TO GRAB THE KID, THE MARAUDERS 'PORTED IN...

...AND IT ALL WENT TO *HELL*, SCOTT. I DON'T KNOW HOW ELSE TO PUT IT.

BY THE TIME I *CAME TO* AND DRAGGED MYSELF OUT OF THE RUBBLE, THEY WERE ALL GONE...

...EVEN *CABLE*, THOUGH I DOUBT THEY TOOK HIM WITH THEM.

YEAH, NOT TOO LIKELY... THEIR FOCUS HAS BEEN THE *BABY* ALL ALONG.

YEAH... SO LET'S MOVE.

AN' JAMES, IT AIN'T YER SAY WHO'S ON MY SQUAD.

HEPZIBAH'S GOT SKILLS AN' LIKE SLIM SAID... WE NEED EVERYONE WHO CAN FIGHT RIGHT NOW.

THE XAVIER INSTITUTE.

NO, MISS FROST... IT'S NOT THAT...

WE INTERFACE PERFECTLY WITH CEREBRA NOW.

BUT THE BABY IS FLICKERING IN AND OUT.

IT'S ALMOST AS IF SHE'S JAMMING HER SIGNAL.

THAT'S NOT POSSIBLE... SOMEONE ELSE MUST BE DOING THAT.

A BABY BLOCKING OUT CEREBRA?

PRODIGY JUST SAID PRACTICALLY THAT SAME THING, MISS FROST.

AND HE'S THE SMARTEST BOY IN THE ROOM. SMART LIKE A GIRL, ALMOST.

BUT EVEN HE DOESN'T KNOW WHAT TO DO NOW.

SO NOW YOU'VE GOT WHAT YOU NEED TO FIX YOURSELF... SO YOU CAN GET OUT OF HERE...

BUT YOU'RE SCREWED ANYWAY.

NICE WORK, IDIOT.

SO I GUESS THIS IS IT...CAN'T DO THIS ON YOUR OWN ANYMORE.

THE STAKES ARE TOO HIGH.

TIME FOR PLAN B.

AH, JAMIE... LOOK WHAT THIS HAS COME TO. YOU UNCONSCIOUS...LAYLA MISSING...

ALL FOR WHAT? A VAGUE CHANCE THAT MAYBE YOU'LL TURN UP SOMETHING USEFUL?

LORD, THE WHOLE WORLD'S GONE MAD.

CALIBAN DEAD... AND THAT POOR DEVIL, PEEPERS, RIPPED APART BY WHO-KNOWS-WHAT.

IS THIS SENSE OF... OF HOPELESSNESS PERVADING EVERYTHING... IS THIS WHAT THE END TIMES ARE LIKE?

IT'S JUST NOT FAIR.

GOD? EXCUSE ME...IT'S, UHM, THERESA CASSIDY. ALTHOUGH I GUESS YOU'D BE KNOWING THAT.

YOU'RE, UH... YOU'RE PUTTING US THROUGH A LOT DOWN HERE. I KNOW THEY SAY YOU DON'T GIVE PEOPLE MORE THAN THEY CAN HANDLE.

BUT HONESTLY, YOU'RE REALLY PUSHING THAT AXIOM TO THE LIMIT HERE.

ANYWAY...

WITH EVERYTHING THAT'S GOING ON... WE COULD, Y'KNOW... USE ONE IN THE "WIN" COLUMN.

SO ON THAT BASIS, I'D REALLY APPRECIATE HAVING JAMIE SNAP OUT OF THIS. CALL IT...I DON'T KNOW...A GOOD FAITH GESTURE?

I KNOW, I KNOW, I KNOW....IT'S SELFISH. I JUST...

WE NEED HIM BACK.

I NEED HIM BACK.

FOR STARTERS, YOU'RE SUPPOSED TO BE *DEAD*.

THEN WE DISCOVER THAT YOU'VE SOMEHOW COME BACK TO LIFE-- WITHOUT CONTACTING US, I MIGHT ADD--AND *KIDNAPPED* THE FIRST NEW MUTANT SINCE M-DAY.

AND IF THAT WEREN'T ENOUGH, THE PILOTS OF THE GIANT ROBOTS *GUARDING* THE MANSION SUDDENLY INFECTED WITH NANO-SENTINELS-- WHICH *YOU* WERE RECENTLY IN CONTACT WITH-- OBLITERATING OUR HOME AND KILLING SEVERAL OF OUR COMPATRIOTS.

SO YOU'LL HAVE TO EXCUSE US A LITTLE DOUBT.

CHARLES. LISTEN TO ME. WE DON'T HAVE TIME FOR THIS. THE ONLY THING THAT IS IMPORTANT IS THE SURVIVAL OF THAT *BABY*.

THE *ONLY* THING.

I HAVE SEEN THE FUTURE, CHARLES. IT'S DARKER THAN YOU CAN IMAGINE. IT NEARLY KILLED ME.

BUT *WITHOUT* THAT BABY...?

IT'S OVER, NATHAN.

GIVE ME THE BABY.

SCOTT--

SHE'S THE FUTURE. THE ONE WHO SAVES US. AND IF SHE STAYS HERE-- SHE'LL DIE.

YOU DON'T KNOW THAT.

YES I DO.

FOR GOD'S SAKE, LOOK AROUND YOU!

EVERYBODY HAS A PLAN. AN AGENDA. EVERYBODY WANTS TO STAKE A CLAIM, OR TO TAKE HER OUT OF THE EQUATION.

SHE WON'T LAST A DAY HERE, WHATEVER YOU DO OR DON'T DO.

IF YOU WERE GOING TO PULL THAT TRIGGER, YOU'D HAVE DONE IT BY NOW.

SCOTT-- DAD--PLEASE. PLEASE DON'T MAKE ME--

CABLE.

DO AS SCOTT SAYS. GIVE HIM THE BABY.

WAIT. WHAT *HAPPENED* TO ME?

WHERE *AM* I?

IT WAS *DESTINY.* MY BELOVED IRENE.

STRAIN 88, THE HECATOMB, SHE *SAW* IT ALL. AND WHAT IT WOULD *TAKE* TO SAVE YOU.

A TERRIBLE *PRICE,* BUT IT WORKED. IT WAS ALL *WORTHWHILE.*

THAT WAS WHAT HER DIARIES WERE FOR. TO *MAKE* THIS HAPPEN.

WHAT PRICE?

TO *MOVE* EVERYONE-- SINISTER, THE X-MEN, THE MARAUDERS--INTO THE RIGHT *PLACES* SO I COULD DO THIS.

WHAT PRICE, MYSTIQUE?

THE *BABY.* I HAD TO USE--

YOU *KILLED* A *CHILD?*

NO, IT--IT *SURVIVED* YOUR TOUCH, SOMEHOW. IT'S *ALIVE.*

AND THAT'S WHAT? A--A HAPPY ENDING?

THUKK

OH GOD, RAVEN, WE CAN'T *DO* THIS ANY MORE.

EVEN WHEN YOU TRY TO *HELP* ME, PEOPLE GET CAUGHT IN BETWEEN US, AND--THEY GET HURT. THEY GET *KILLED.*

THIS HAS TO BE THE LAST *TIME,* MOTHER.

DID THEY RUN OUT OF *FULL-SIZED* X-MEN?

THEY'RE SENDING IN THE *KINDERGARTEN* CLASS NOW?

WELL, I HOPE YOU REMEMBERED TO BRING YOUR *LUNCH MONEY*, KIDDO.

THOK

AND YOUR WARM, WOOLLY *MITTENS.* AND YOUR BEST--

SKOWW

GUUUH!

--SOUL-DAGGER?

YEAH. I BROUGHT THAT.

MESSIAH COMPLEX ONE-SHOT TOP COW EXCLUSIVE VARIANT
BY MARC SILVESTRI, JOE WEEMS & FRANK D'ARMATA

NEW X-MEN #44 VARIANT BY J. SCOTT CAMPBELL, BRIAN HABERLIN & EDGAR DELGADO

X-MEN #205 VARIANT BY J. SCOTT CAMPBELL, BRIAN HABERLIN & EDGAR DELGADO

UNCANNY X-MEN #493 VARIANT BY JIM CHEUNG, JOHN DELL & JUSTIN PONSOR

X-FACTOR #26 VARIANT BY MARC SILVESTRI, JOE WEEMS & STEVE FIRCHOW

X-MEN #206 VARIANT BY SIMONE BIANCHI, ANDREA SILVESTRI & SIMONE PERUZZI

X-FACTOR #27 VARIANT BY JIM CHEUNG, JOHN DELL & JUSTIN PONSOR

X-MEN #207 VARIANT BY JIM CHEUNG, JOHN DELL & JUSTIN PONSOR

X-MEN DATA FILES>>>
ACCESSING>>>

SECURITY LEVEL:
CLASSIFIED

USER: CYCLOPS
PASSWORD: ****

LOG ENTRY/BEGIN.

TAN • D'ARMATA

When we first met, Professor Xavier told me his dream. He saw a world where mutants and humans lived together without fear or hate. Where mutants could discover their potential and use their gifts to serve all mankind.

And on M-Day, when most mutants lost their powers, when we became an endangered species...that vision became just that. A dream.

The X-Men have always defended both mutants and humans, so that humans could see that, just like them, there were good mutants as well as bad.

But now, I can't honestly say it made a difference. Reacting to threats instead of being proactive may have brought about the end of both the X-Men and all of mutantkind.

Whereas the X-Men are on the front lines, X-Factor takes a more investigative approach. Jamie Madrox annoys me. But he and his team are valuable.

And with our enemies always seemingly one step ahead, X-Factor's methods may be mutantkind's only hope.

Sinister and his Marauders are the worst mutantkind has to offer. Architect of one of the first massacres of mutantkind, Sinister cares nothing for his people. Only his agenda.

That agenda is a mystery to us now. But for whatever endgame he's planning, Sinister is gathering an ARMY. Marauders, Acolytes, and even former allies are now under his control.

But if Sinister wants a war, I'm prepared to give him one.

The Professor told us that humans fear what they don't understand, and that fear leads to hate.

The Purifiers are the most extreme example of this. Grossly justifying their hate with religion, the Purifiers were assembled by the Reverend William Stryker. And while he's dead now, his army marches on.

They are responsible for the deaths of forty-five of my students. And they'll never stop. The X-Men don't kill...but the Purifiers will have to be dealt with, and soon.

This is the length some will go in order to destroy us. A creature made to hunt mutants based on their DNA. It feeds off us, has to KILL MUTANTS to survive.

The New X-Men nearly died fighting three of these things.

One escaped. How many mutants will pay for that with their lives?

LAND • LEISTEN • PONSOR

CHARACTER SKETCHES
by Billy Tan and David Finch

COVER SKETCH GALLERY

Goals

To be a mutant today is to be part of an endangered species. There is no cycle of life and death anymore. Only death. Every time you put one of your kind into a hole in the ground, you are one step closer to extinction. We're going to hammer this point home from now until November, when we kick off our event. This will be the backdrop in all the monthly titles. In addition, we are going to run a series of short stories, entitled "Endangered Species" that will take a broad look at the predicament. If there ever were a time for mutants to (a) reassess whatever drives them, whether faith or science, (b) form alliances that they'd have never previously considered, or (c) _____, it's now. Tomorrow is coming too soon. And there won't be too many more of those.

X-MEN: THE MESSIAH COMPLEX

The Event is divided into three acts told across four titles (UNCANNY X-MEN, X-MEN, NEW X-MEN and X-FACTOR) over three months (Nov' 07-Dec. '07-Jan. '08).

ACT ONE:

This act will set the stage of the conflict, bring the players onstage and define the "camps" they all fit in. There will be four camps:

1 Good Mutants: X-Men who want to find the baby to keep it safe. This includes pretty much everyone you'd expect, with one mutant [Cyclops] playing General. Their goal: SAVE the baby.

2 Bad Mutants: Bad guys who want to find the baby to control it. This includes the Marauders. Their goal: CONTROL the baby.

3 Mutant Haters: Bad guys who want that baby dead. Plain and simple. Their goal: KILL the baby. This includes the Purifiers and one mystery character from another camp.

4 Wild Card Faction: As you'll see there is an individual within one of the camps that has his/her own, more personal agenda.

5 Our "T-Rex": Predator X. A mutant creature who feeds off mutant DNA, already established in NEW X-MEN. Its goal: EAT the baby, or any mutant that gets in its way.

Chapter One (Uncanny X-Men #492)

• Cerebra blips, and blows up. Gets everyone's immediate attention. Evidence of a mutant manifestation?

• The X-Men send a team to the location of the blip (*we're thinking somewhere in Alaska*) and discover a hospital that, from all appearances, was recently under siege. More curiously, they discover two things that prompt big questions: (1) Dead Purifiers and dead Marauders (Prompting the question — What the hell went down here?)
(2) Three babies were born that night. Two of them were killed; the third is missing. (Prompting several questions: Was this a mutant "birth" and not a teenage manifestation of mutant powers? Who's got the baby?)

• End with epilogue showing Predator X.

Chapter Two (X-Factor #25)

• A power struggle: Professor X, of course, tries to take control of the Good Guys camp, but Scott Summers elbows him aside. They exchange terse words that underscore that Scott thinks Xavier's had his shot. His time is over.

• Archangel returns to the X-Mansion for the first time in months and notices that Rogue is gone. It is explained that she was kidnapped by the Marauders. The mention of the Maruaders fills him with rage. "I thought we took care of those bastards."

• Having won the power struggle, Cyclops acts like a general. He immediately forms team, dispatching the A-TEAM (Wolverine, Colossus, Storm, Nightcrawler, and Angel [?]) to find the Marauders, who he believes has the baby.

• Meanwhile, the subplot involving X-Factor kicks in.

Discovering a major time-stream diversion at a distinct point in the future, a concerned Forge requests that X-Factor go into the future to investigate. They do just that. [is this the whole team? Or just a Jamie-dupe and Layla? My vote is for the whole team.] All except Wolfsbane (she got a call from Cyclops and wants to stay and help the X-Men.) When they arrive in the future, they notice there are no X-Men.

Chapter Three (New X-Men #44)

• Cyclops orders the New X-Men to remain at the mansion with him and the remaining X-Men. This doesn't please them, of course. They want some action.

• Predator X feasts on another mutant and grows stronger.

• Professor X goes to the New X-Men and to tries to convince them to join with him. They reject him. They're sick of old men telling them what to do.

• The New X-Men decide to strike out on their own. Feeling responsible for the Purifiers since their last encounter, they set out to find them.

• Hot on the trail of the Marauders, the A-Team begins to realize how the Marauders ranks have swelled. They've got a lot of juice now. And the guy at the top appears to be none other than Mr. Sinister (*who'll have been reintroduced into X-Men by then.*)

• On their time-travel mission, X-Factor delves further into the future and finds that mutants are hated and hunted.

• The New X-Men find the Purifiers — and learn that they *don't* have the baby.

• A big fight ensues and the New X-Men defeat most of the Purifiers. At a key moment in the fight, Hellion is suddenly stabbed from behind. When he crumples to the ground, the New X-Men are shocked to see that the Purifiers have a new member. Lady Deathstrike has joined her fellow mutant-haters and is heading up a team of cybernetically enhanced Purifiers. It's on.

Chapter Four (X-Men #206)

• The New X-Men don't fare well against Lady Deathstrike and her Purifier Kill-Squad. Realizing that they're overmatched, they retreat/escape to fight another day.

• The A-Team faces off with the Marauders. They begin a fight, looking for the baby, but also looking for Rogue [*who was lost to the Marauders in X-Men #203*]. Gambit, who has been with the Marauders, assures them that he has Rogue and they can forget about getting to her. The A-Team finally discover that the Marauders *don't* have the baby. The Marauders are equally surprised. They thought the X-Men had the baby. Why? Well, *because an X-Man took it!*

• Cut to a windswept hill. A caped figure, walking purposefully. The camera pulls around to show him. It's

Cable, and he's got the baby strapped to his chest.

• Through Emma's telepathic rapport, the A-Team reiterates to Emma and the X-Men (Cyclops, Beast and Bishop among them) that Cable has the baby and seconds later they see something terrible through the window — The Sentinels suddenly turn toward the X-Mansion and begin to attack.

ACT TWO:
This act takes the status quo from Act One and turns it on its head.

Chapter Five (Uncanny X-Men #493)
• The Sentinels attack the X-Mansion. The X-Men (minus the A-Team) fight them.
• New X-Men return, shaken and bloody, and help fight.
• Cyclops orders the A-Team to return right away or there might not be a mansion for them to return to.
• The Mansion is destroyed (Dan?), and the X-Men defeat the Sentinels, but not without casualties. Emma is in a coma, a few others are down for the count. Beast discovers the problem: The Sentinel pilots were infected with the Nano-Sentinels that Cassandra Nova created. Who was one of the last people known to have the Nano-Sentinels (from X-Men #192)? Cable.
• Cut back to Cable. We learn that he is hurt and most of his tech damaged. Also, the baby needs changing.
• The A-Team arrives back at the mansion. Wolverine finds Cyclops in his destroyed bedroom. In Cyclops' hand is a necklace with an odd-looking pendant. We don't know what it is, but he grasps it tightly in his hand. Cyclops looks at the situation they're in. Their home is destroyed, his lover and many of his friends are terribly injured, and the hope for mutantkind is in the hands of an incredibly powerful mutant who just betrayed them. Times have become desperate. And you know what desperate times call for. Cyclops tells Wolverine to gather the "War Pack."
• Professor X learns what Cyclops has done and is furious. He has gone too far. The conflict leads to Professor backhanding Scott, the red glasses hitting the ground. Xavier: "Come on, Scott. The ends justify the means. Open your eyes." Scott: "Take a look around, Charles. You open **your** eyes."
• What is this War Pack? Wolverine, War Path, X-23, Wolfsbane (and possibly Hepzibah and Caliban). Their orders? Track down Cable and get the baby, no matter what the cost.

Chapter Six (X-FACTOR #26)
• War Pack is hot on the trail of Cable. Lots of interesting character stuff: X-23 interacts with Wolverine; they get to know one another better. Wolfsbane worries about her friends from X-Factor...
• On the time-travel mission, X-Factor continue their investigation. They discover that all the mutants are being held in concentration camps. Not much is known about the concentration camps, but they discover one thing: The person who caused the camps to exist is a *mutant*.
• Predator X feasts on another mutant and grows in strength.
• Cable is on the move. His day is ruined when he is caught by Lady Deathstrike and the Purifier Kill-Squad. They want the mutie-baby dead.
• And on the time-travel mission, X-Factor is caught and sent to a concentration camp.

Chapter Seven (NEW X-MEN #45)
• The Purifier Kill-Squad attacks Cable, who tries to fend them off and keep the baby safe. But it isn't going well until...
• ...the Warpack arrive. Elite trackers that they are, they

found him. It's a three-way showdown: Warpack vs. Purifers vs. Cable.
• On the time-travel mission, X-Factor arrive at a concentration camp in Brooklyn. It is not a happy place, but they have yet to see a single mutant.
• War Pack vs. Purifier Kill-Squad. When Lady Deathstrike steps up to Wolverine, he steps aside. She's all yours, he tells X-23, cuing up a savage battle between X-23 and Lady Deathstrike.
• Predator X feasts on another mutant, building strength.
• The rest of the X-Men are gathering to join the Warpack on the hunt.
• The War Pack defeats the Purifier Kill-Squad. X-23 stabs Lady Deathstrike with both hands and leaves her gutted and dying, just like LD left Hellion. Fight over, they turn...
• ...and discover that Cable and the baby are long gone.

Chapter Eight (X-MEN #206)
• On the time-travel mission, X-Factor is processed in the concentration camp. They are given clothes and their heads are shaved. We don't see what happens next.
• Predator X feasts on another mutant. Continues to build in strength and size.
• More time with Scott and the Warpack, advancing that subplot.
• Cable finally arrives at his destination: Forge's lab. We get clarification on his goal — the time machine. But what he finds doesn't please him.
• On the time-travel mission, X-Factor's processing is finished. They are put with the rest of the inmates who, like X-Factor, now have the letter "M" tattooed over their right eye.
• Cable finds Forge bleeding on the ground and the time machine destroyed! From out of the shadows steps a familiar face. Bishop. Cable's expression shows he knows what's up. Bishop shoots him.

ACT THREE:
This act will be end game, climax and dénouement.

Chapter Nine (UNCANNY #494)
• Cable is down. Shot. The baby has spilled to the floor. Bishop walks toward it. He looks down at the baby, raises the gun. So small. One bullet is all it will take. His finger presses the trigger. And then he hesitates —
• — and that's all it takes. BAM! The Marauders swoop in, knock out Bishop (Gambit, who is with the Marauders, does this) and take the baby. They are content to just wound Bishop. Why don't they kill him? They're amused by one X-Man turning on another.
• Meanwhile, the X-Factor have a big problem: With the time-machine destroyed, they are stranded in the future!
• War Pack shows up and finds only Bishop, on the ground, bloody and despondent. Cable is gone. *What the hell happened here?* they ask Bishop.
• Bishop dupes them, tells them that he came to save the baby from Cable, and that the Marauders now have the baby. War Pack calls for the X-Men to come help the wounded Forge. [If we do this — reasoning to be revealed later — we need to figure out why the X-Men back home aren't curious about Bishop's presence.]
• The War Pack, with Bishop in tow, go after the Marauders and the baby. (In subsequent scenes, we'll seed the notion that X-23 senses something's fishy about Bishop's story.)
• When we come back to Cable, he's in deep trouble. He lost the baby! Sure Bishop didn't get his chance to kill the baby, but still, things have gone down the crapper. Time for Plan B. He needs help. Who does he ask? An old friend. Professor Charles Xavier.

Chapter Ten (X-FACTOR #27)

• Elixir (the healer from New X-Men), Beast and some of the X-Men attend to the wounded Forge (*who, you'll remember, was shot by Bishop*). At first, Forge doesn't remember anything; seeing the damaged time machine, he suddenly freaks, realizing that X-Factor is stranded in the future. A lot of the time-travel equipment is missing (*an important point because this plays into the story later*), but he and Beast begin working on fixing the time machine.

• In the future, X-Factor is in the concentration camp. They meet a young Lucas Bishop.

• The Marauders present their leader, Mr. Sinister, with the baby. He retires to a private room with Gambit. And then Mr. Sinister's appearance begins to change. He morphs into Mystique. Behind her, in the corner of the room, we see the corpse of the real Mr. Sinister. She looks at Gambit. "It's time for the next step."

• Most of the New X-Men are back at what remains of the mansion. One looks out the window and sees the graveyard in the yard. Much of it is dug up. They see Predator X. He's feasting on the dead bodies in the graveyard (hey, mutant DNA is mutant DNA. Doesn't matter if you're alive or dead). It attacks them.

• Forge and Beast bring X-Factor (minus Layla?) back to the present. They reveal that Bishop is the traitor.

• End with High Noon — all players converge — Marauders, War Pack, X-Men.

Chapter Eleven (NEW X-MEN #46)

• Mystique (in Sinister's form) orders the Marauders to keep the X-Men back — she needs time.

• When out of sight, Mystique and Gambit go down into a dungeon where Rogue is being held (*She's been their captive since #204. We'll seed her early in the story, so she doesn't come from out of nowhere.*). Mystique believes (*through the Destiny Diaries, already established*) that contact with the baby will heal the recent awful damage to her daughter. She's shared her theory with Gambit, which will explain his continued membership with the Marauders. What Mystique *doesn't* tell Gambit is that the process will likely *kill* the baby. That's why she couldn't tell Sinister of her real motives. It would have been contrary to his plan to use the baby's genetics. They place the baby on Rogue's skin.

• Cable and Prof X arrive at the High Noon Showdown. The immediately fan out to find the baby.

• Meanwhile, Mystique and Gambit have begun the rite that Mystique hopes will save her daughter. Gambit immediately sees that the baby isn't going to make it. He takes out Mystique and, even though it might mean that his love might not be healed, pulls the baby away from her, saving its life.

• At that same moment, Professor X arrives. Gambit hands him the baby. Professor X asks him what's next? Gambit says he's going to stay with Rogue, where he belongs.

• The X-Men vs. Marauders fight rages on.

• Meanwhile, miles away at the institute, Predator X closes in on the remaining New X-Men. Looks like they're goners. Unless...Pixie gets an idea. Maybe if she teleports them all to the vicinity of the only person she knows has killed a Predator X — X-23? BAM! She does just that —

• — and they all land in the middle of the fight. *Including Predator X!*

• Professor X gives the baby to Cable and tells him to go to the future. Before Cable can do anything, however, Bishop gets in his way. Cable tries to hightail it the other direction, only to find his escape route blocked by Predator X. Crap.

Chapter Twelve (X-MEN #207)

• Trapped between a gun-wielding Bishop and the slavering

beast known as Predator X, Cable does the only thing he can do. He plays them off against one another. Not sure exactly how he'll do this, but he'll pull a Yojimbo on them and Predator X will eat Bishop's arm.

• Cyclops tasks the War Pack to stop Predator X (they do just that) and turns his attention to Cable and Prof X, who now have the baby.

• Cyclops demands the baby. Cable refuses. Says the baby has to go with him — it's the only way to save the future. Cyclops says that he's sick of all the B.S., step away from the baby or I'll fry you where you stand. It's a tense standoff. What's it gonna be...?

• Professor X reaches out and takes the baby from Cable. Turns to Cyclops. The choice is yours, Scott, he tells his former student, and hands him the baby.

• Scott looks down at the baby nestled in his arms. Pulls back the covers to see its face. The baby looks up at him, then reaches out with one little hand and pulls out the necklace that we saw earlier. Fondles it. Scott's eyes widen. Could it be? He looks at Professor X. "It's your choice, Scott," Xavier says again.

• In that moment, some part of Scott — one not ruled by science and facts and empirical evidence — realizes who this baby really is, realizes why Cable has to go. Scott hands the baby back to Cable. "Go. Now!" he says. And just like that, Cable — and the baby — are gone [*Note: Cable engages his time travel device (he fixed it with the machinery from Forge's workshop).*]

• Uh-oh! Seeing Cable escape, an enraged, one-armed Bishop steps forward and shoots Professor X at point-blank range to the head. A split-second later, Cyclops takes down Bishop with an eye-blast.

• The X-Men finally defeat the Marauders. War Pack kills Predator X.

• Rogue emerges from the dungeon, healed by the baby, Gambit by her side. She is absolutely pissed that Mystique would sacrifice a baby's life for her, especially the first mutant birth.

• Epilogue #1: A shadowy figure disappears with the body of Professor X.

• Epilogue #2: Bishop is in custody.

• Epilogue #3: Cut to the remains of the mansion graveyard. Mysterious egg-shaped metal objects sit on the grass. Could they be Predator X-babies?

• Epilogue #4: Cable and the baby in another time and place.

Major Status-Quo Changes:

• Cyclops is the alpha-dog of the X-Men. End of story. He proved his vision and skill and emerged from the shadow of Xavier.

• Professor X is away from the X-Men for good. The #1 option is that he will lead the Acolytes (who used to follow Magneto).

• Cable is jumping the timestream with the baby. The leading adversary for this is Bishop, jumping around after him.

• The War Pack will continue on, either replacing one of the teams on one of the X-books or getting a book of their own.

• The relationship between Rogue and Mystique is changed. Rogue and Mystique's relationship is done. She pushed Rogue too far, and Rogue will state once and for all that she is done with Mystique.

• The relationship between Rogue and Gambit is something that can take another step, too. He's back in his nebulous "is-he-good-or-bad" area that made him cool in the first place. She is healed and unsure and they've been through a lot. This is ripe with possibilities.

• X-Force is up in the air, as well. Bishop was a thought for this. Mystique is another possibility.